THE COMPLETE SERIES

BLACK CREEK

R.A. SMYTH

REBELS & REJECTS

BLACK CREEK SERIES BOOK ONE

R.A. SMYTH

Eight years ago

"P-p-please," the pathetic sack of shit at my feet pleads. "I told you everything I k-know."

I tilt my head as I stare down at him impassively, noting every shake and tremble of his body as I press the muzzle of my gun against the center of his forehead. Why do they always beg? They know who I am, who I represent. They know we don't offer mercy. Who would want to die groveling on their fucking knees? When my time comes, I wanna go out staring death straight in the face, giving it a final *fuck you*.

Bang. There's minimal kickback from the revolver as the loud sound ricochets off the stone walls, echoing around the dark alley. The bullet makes a perfect circle in the front of the scumbag's forehead, and I watch as he crumples into a heap on the ground, feeling absolutely nothing—no remorse, no guilt. Not even happiness or satisfaction at a job well done. There's something fundamentally wrong with me. My father knows it too. Apparently, the fact that I'm incapable of feeling emotions is a good thing. It's why I'll be the most ruthless leader the Antonellis have ever had. Because it means I can make the hard decisions, do what needs to be done—like kill this sorry fucker who thought he could spy on us—and still sleep like a baby tonight.

Staring down at the sorry sack of shit, I take in the pool of blood around his head that's growing progressively larger and his saggy, sallow skin that looks yellow in the dim light from the flickering street lamp down the block. Something sparks within me. It's small, and it disappears before I can place it. Hunger maybe? It definitely has a heady feel to it.

"Hey!" a voice barks from behind me. The deep bellow is followed by the sounds of a scuffle that draws my attention away from the corpse at my feet, and turning around, I find Lor wrestling to contain a scrawny little street urchin in his arms. The kid is writhing and kicking out as he grunts and groans with exertion, attempting to escape the bands of steel wrapped around his waist. He's so busy fighting against Lor that he is oblivious to the real threat observing him closely—me.

Whoever the fuck this kid is, he's just seen me commit a crime. Not that I'm worried he'll go to the police. *Ha, that's a laugh.* Every police officer in this city is in someone's pocket. If it's not ours, it's The Feral Beasts or one of the other smaller gangs running around in this rat-infested city. Regardless of whose pocket they're in, none of them would dare pull any of us in.

No, what I can't have is this bag of bones running off and telling The Feral Beasts that I've just taken out one of their moles. They'll find out in a few days when they don't hear from him, only it will be too late. By then, we will have fished out the other fuckers they've planted within our organization.

"Let me go!" the little thing snarls out, surprising me. It's not just the angry tone and defiant boldness that catches me off guard, but the high pitch of the voice.

He's not a he, but a *she*—a girl.

I cast my eyes over her squirming frame once again, but it's impossible to see any curves or tits in those baggy clothes that hang off her scrawny frame. By the looks of things, she's too fucking skinny to have any anyway.

"Why would he do that?" I bark out in a deep, menacing growl that thunders through the narrow alley. She instantly freezes in Lor's arms, her head snapping up to meet my steely gaze as I slowly close the distance between us. My heavy boots boom with every step I take until I loom over her, casting her in shadow.

She peers up at me with wide, fearful eyes as I silently take her in. There's nothing special about her. Coated in dirt and grime, with her dark hair like a bird's nest, filled with knots and split ends, she looks like some sort of feral animal; a wildcat—similar to every other street urchin... except for those eyes. Even in the poor lighting, those endless pools of blue hold me captive. They're a brilliant cerulean, like how I imagine the Caribbean Sea looks. Not that I've ever seen it in real life, but I've caught a glimpse of it on TV. It's one of those scenes you can't tear your eyes from. You're convinced you can see right to the seabed at the bottom, read all of the secrets hidden in its dark depths, but it's a lie. While it draws you in, making you think you can see more than you can; in reality, it holds all of its mysteries close, unwilling to give any of them up.

The girl's eyebrows draw together, and her chin lifts in defiance, probably thinking my silence is a scare tactic and not that she just rendered me mute. I shake off the weird feeling she's evoked and give a slight jerk of my head, silently telling Lor to let the girl go. Before she can scamper away, I grab ahold of her arm with my free hand. My gun is still clasped in my other, and I bring it up to aim at her head, watching as the fight instantly drains out of her and she goes stock-still in my grip. Her eyes widen, making her look like a deer caught in headlights, but unlike the sorry sack of shit behind me, she doesn't collapse to her knees at the realization she's about to die. Instead, she surprises me by setting her jaw into a hard line and pushing back her shoulders. Straightening her spine, she stares brazenly back at me. *Hell, she's got bigger balls than most of the men who find themselves on the wrong end of my revolver.*

However, despite her bravado, I can see the terror in her eyes. It's the same fear everyone seems to experience when they realize their time is up. Seeing it doesn't bother me, though. If anything, it just makes me more curious about human nature. I don't understand the notion of fear. It seems pointless. Yet, looking into her captivating eyes as she blinks rapidly—as if hoping she can just blink the scene in front of her away—for the first time in my life, it makes me pause. I don't want to have to kill her. *What the fuck is happening to me?* It must be because she's a kid. I've never killed anyone so young before. That's gotta be it.

We both continue to stare at one another, and I recognize the flicker of warmth that ignites in my chest. I've felt it only a handful of times in my life and it always seems to extinguish before I can place it. But not today. Instead, it sits there in my chest, simmering at a low heat, like the dying embers of a fire. It's still too small for me to identify, but it's present all the same.

What is this? Who is she? Questions arise to the forefront of my mind as my gaze bores into hers, hungrily seeking answers. She returns my stare unbidden, and I have no idea what she sees when she looks into my soulless eyes. Can she glimpse the monster I am? Or am I nothing more than a cold, hard, unreadable shell?

The whole time, she spears me with her incensed glare. Fearful but defiant 'til the very end. It's impressive.

Keeping the barrel pointed at her forehead, I lift my thumb and pull back on the hammer, cocking the gun. She startles at the sound of the loud click before hardening her features again, refusing to let me peer any deeper into her psyche. I press my finger against the trigger, knowing what I need to do. It's easy. Merely the flexing of a finger, and yet...

A lifetime seems to pass in a single moment as her life hangs in the balance, while I find myself struggling for the first time in my life with knowing what needs to be done. Her death was written in the stars as soon as Lor caught her. And yet something I can't quite put my finger on is urging me to go against the rules of the Family, rules that are ingrained into the very fabric of my being.

Time ticks on, one long second after another, as my finger repeatedly tenses against the trigger before hesitation hits, and I relax it again.

She needs to die.

But...

She's a witness.

Still...

Without giving the action any conscious thought, I ease my finger off the trigger and drop my arm down to my side, ignoring the flash of confusion that darkens her irises. Using my tight grip on her arm, I yank her into me so I can hiss in her ear, "If you mention this to anyone, I'll fucking gut you," before flinging her backward, away from me. The distance between us allows me to take a much-needed breath that thankfully douses the confusing heat in my chest.

She stumbles before quickly righting herself, gaping at me in astonishment, most likely unable to comprehend how she's still alive; how she's about to walk away with her life. Trust me, it's something I'm still struggling to understand.

"Get the fuck out of here before I change my mind," I bark when she makes no move to run. "Don't show your face here again!"

Without a second's hesitation, she sprints for the end of the alleyway and ducks out of sight. In her absence, I can feel the heavy weight of Lor's gaze on me, and when I finally look away from the spot where the baffling girl disappeared, I find him watching me with a mixture of surprise and confusion.

"Boss?" he questions. I don't fucking blame him. For the first time in my life, I just showed someone mercy, and a witness, no less. One of our cardinal rules is that witnesses can't be allowed to live. Witnesses who walk, talk. It's as simple as that. Only the dead can keep secrets.

"Follow her," I order. "Make sure she doesn't talk to anyone."

His gaze lingers on me for a second longer before he nods, following after the kid who has somehow managed to fuck with my head. I stand and watch the darkness swallow him up as he disappears down the alley, still trying to wrap my head around what just happened. I've never disobeyed an order. Never put our Family at risk by letting someone who I know needs to die, live. Whatever that girl did to me, it's a weakness I can't afford. A shortcoming I can't let my father know about.

Pretending like my interaction with the street urchin never occurred, I turn on my heel and stride out of the alley toward my awaiting car and climb in. On the outside, I'm the epitome of calm and control. No one else would be aware of the inner turmoil currently whipping up a storm within me. Whatever that spark of warmth was that that girl ignited, as much as I want to pretend I never felt its electrifying heat, there's a more prominent part of me that wants to feel its soft caress again. And I have no idea what the fuck that means.

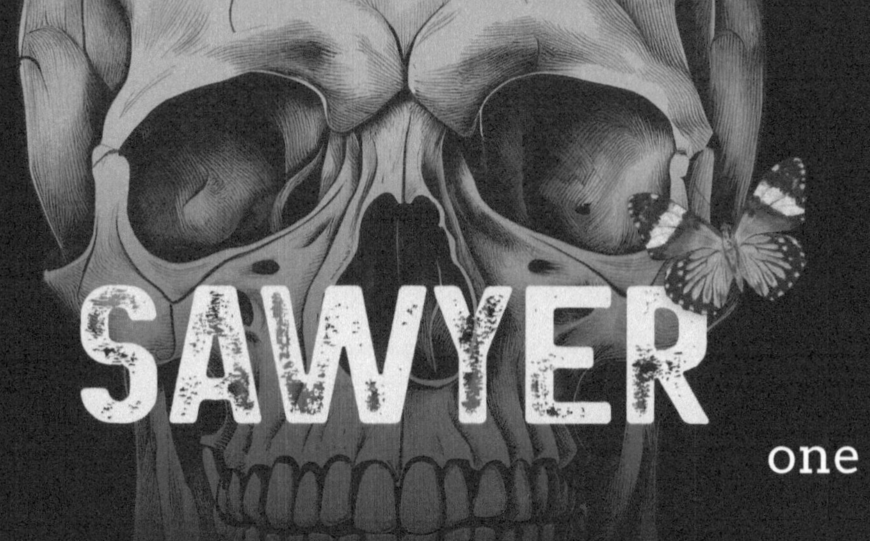

one

With a final shove and a grunt, the package rolls over the side of the dock, splashing into the black ocean below. It bobs on the surface for a moment before the water drags it under, welcoming the tarp-wrapped shitstain into her murky depths where he can forever rot amongst the fishes and algae.

So long, motherfucker. May you forever burn in hell.

Turning my back on the water, I pull the burner phone out of my pocket and fire off a quick text to confirm the job is done. While I wait for a response, I pull up my contacts, find the number I'm looking for, and call it.

Arnie answers on the first ring. "Yup?"

"Got a delivery for you down by the docks."

"A good one?"

I smirk. "I think you'll be pretty happy. Brand new Camaro."

He lets out an appreciative whistle. "Alright, kid. I'll get someone down to pick her up now. It's late, get yourself home."

As I'm hanging up the phone, I receive an alert that payment for tonight's job has been received. Finished here, I pull out a Henley and black leather jacket out of my duffel bag, pulling the top on over my bralette and slipping into the jacket before slinging the bag over my back. I lift my helmet off the seat and push it on over my head as I lift a leg to straddle Raven, my black Ducati Streetfighter. She was payment for making sure Arnie's daughter's abusive boyfriend didn't keep coming around to harass her... that, and thanks for the regular work I send his way. Arnie is a balding, brick wall of a man in his mid-fifties. Covered in tattoos and with a RAP sheet the length of his arm, he's not someone you wanna mess with, although what he doesn't let most people see is that he's a fucking softie underneath his hard exterior. He runs the chop shop in Black Creek, so he's someone most people want to keep on their good side, and *man*, does he get some of the sweetest rides. Sometimes, on nights like tonight, I get to send him an expensive car that he can make some decent money from, even though his ware-house is full of cars that are already worth a fucking fortune. I have no idea how he accrued so many, but hey, who was I to complain, especially when he told me to pick any ride I wanted. I'm telling you, it was a hard choice. Most of the cars he had were models I would never be able to afford, but when I saw this beauty hiding at the back of his shop, I knew I had to have her.

Starting the ignition, I rev the engine, loving the deep rumble and resounding roar as I peel out of the docks onto the street. People stop to stare as I pass by, but no one can see who I am with my full-face helmet and black-tinted visor on. I prefer it that way, to be a faceless person in the crowd. It's the only way to survive in Black Creek. If anyone knows your name here, it's because they have some sort of beef with you.

I ride through the derelict city, and even though it's late, the streets here are never quiet. There are always homeless people trying to carve out a safe corner for themselves, gang members patrolling their territory, and hookers shaking their tits in the hopes of earning themselves enough to buy a solid meal the next day. It never used to be so bad. Black Creek has always been home to vagrants and outlaws, but there was some sort of order before—when The Feral Beasts ruled the town. Sure, they instilled fear in the hearts of residents, and the streets ran red with just as much blood as they do now, but there was order to the chaos. Now, it's just complete and utter mayhem.

Broadly speaking, you could divide the city into three main territories based on who they belong to. The Antonellis own the docks, Grim Bastards have laid claim to most of the East District, and the Reaper Rejects are quickly accruing land in the Downtown area. The problem is, any part of the city that isn't owned by one of these three has been snatched up by small, disorganized street gangs, evidently breaking the city up into a multitude of different pieces. It's impossible to keep track of who owns what, and each gang is just as dimwitted as the last. Boys with guns and absolutely zero common sense. Idiots who will shoot first and ask questions later, and then think they're big shit because they strut around with a gun that's bigger than their dicks. It's just asking for trouble, and with each passing day, tensions rise. Rival gangs are at each other's throats, and all of them are dissatisfied with the tiny bit of land they occupy.

It's hitting two a.m. when I slow down, pulling into a small garage hidden behind an abandoned building. I'm a block away from my apartment, but I don't dare park Raven on the street—she'd be stripped and sold for parts before sunrise. I also don't need people questioning how I came about owning her. She's all pretty and new looking, with her shiny black fairing—not something that just anyone in Black Creek can afford. Don't get me wrong, there's the odd, brand spanking new Benz or SUV that's obviously stolen, but for the most part, gangsters drive around in souped-up Buicks or Lincolns, with their arms hanging out the window, thinking they look like hot shit. The point is, everyone knows it's only gang members who can get their hands on that sort of thing. And anyone who knows me knows I have absolutely zero fucking affiliations with any gangs. They bring nothing but trouble and heartache to the everyday residents of Black Creek, those who are just trying to carve out some sort of existence for themselves.

Anyone who had the means or opportunity to leave Black Creek left years ago, back when I was barely more than a baby. It was apparent back then—as soon as The Feral Beasts started making a name for themselves—that things were only going to go from bad to worse. Whoever is left has stayed because they crave the life of being an outlaw, with all its bloodshed and violence, or because they couldn't leave. They didn't have the money, they couldn't risk the livelihood they had here, or some other reason kept them trapped. I, unfortunately, fall into category B—I can't leave. I grew up here. I work my fucking ass off to make a living here for myself. I don't even know what the fuck I'd do if I moved to another town. My skill set is not exactly transferable nor is it one that can be applied to most legal occupations. So, I guess, for now, I'm stuck here. And on days like today, when I rid the city of one more piece of trash, I'm okay with that. Ask me again tomorrow, though. I'll most likely have a different answer.

Turning off the engine, I remove my helmet and shake out my waist-length, copper-colored hair, and climb off the bike. Patting the seat in farewell, my chunky-heeled boots tap against the concrete floor as I walk out of the garage, closing and securing the door behind me.

Once I'm sure that she's safely tucked away for the night, I make the short walk to my apartment at a brisk pace, keeping my senses on high alert. You can never let your guard down in Black Creek, especially not at this time of night. No matter who you are, no one is safe in this town.

I've just rounded the corner onto my street when I hear a gunshot go off, but it sounds like it's several blocks away, so it's nothing to worry about. I pick up my pace nonetheless and quickly reach my dilapidated apartment building that is covered in graffiti and looks like it's one minor earth-rumbling tremor away from collapsing. Heading inside, I stride past the elevator that has been out of service since I moved in here five years ago, and hike up the dimly lit stairwell to the top floor, hurrying past bland, paint-peeling doorways until I reach number twenty-three. My apartment.

Sticking my key in the lock, I have to jiggle it before the mechanism gives and the door opens into a gloomy interior. The only light is the faint glow of the TV, bathing the small apartment in an array of colors as images flicker across the screen, which has been left on. I scowl. *Seriously? Every night. How difficult is it to turn the TV off after yourself?*

My apartment is tiny—barely enough space for two people to co-exist. A narrow kitchen with chipped cabinet doors and a linoleum floor that, no matter what I do, always bubbles up, has a view into the living room through a window cut in the separating wall. The living room isn't much bigger. It just about fits a television set, a side table, and a small sofa wedged under a grimy window that constantly lets cold air in during the winter. Off the living room are two bedrooms and a small bathroom, containing the main reason why I chose *this* apartment over the other shitholes I looked at... the tub. It's nothing special or fancy, but it's a tub all the same, and I am all for soaking in a hot bubble bath after a long day like today.

I drop the duffle bag on the floor and kick my boots off by the door, hanging my leather jacket on the wall hook before I cross the shaggy, discolored carpet. I flick on the kitchen light as I pass by, snatching the remote off the sofa to turn off the TV, bathing the room in silence. Pausing, I take a second to listen for any movement coming from the bedroom. When all I hear is the noise of the always-bustling city coming up from the street, the sound of our neighbors arguing through the thin walls, and the always present hum of our old refrigerator, I move to the bathroom.

Turning the rusty taps, I run the water for the bath and light a few candles. Adding a lavender-scented bath bomb—one of the few extravagances I allow myself—I let it disperse while I head back into the kitchen. I open the fridge and grab a bottle of white wine from the door, fetch a glass from the cupboard, and pour myself a large serving. Alcohol and Black Creek go hand in hand. We're all borderline alcoholics at best. I'm not sure if it's a poverty thing, a despair thing, or a need-to-forget thing for most people. For me, it's a *you successfully dealt with shitheads all day and didn't drag their brains out through their nostrils, so you deserve a glass of wine* thing.

I sip on the drink, the tension slowly dropping from my shoulders as the cold, dry, fruity flavor slides down my throat, taking with it the last of today's problems as I let out a long, low, "ahhh," before carrying the glass with me back to the bathroom. I ignore the blackened grout lines that never seem to stay clean for long and the chipped tiles along the wall as I set it on the cheap, plastic bath caddy before stripping out of my leather pants, black Henley, and bralette.

When the water is piping hot, and bubbles are threatening to overflow the side of the tub, I step into it and lower myself into the warmth with a sigh. Tilting my head back, I close my eyes, inhaling the soft lavender scent and allowing it to calm me.

My thoughts drift to the asshole back on the dock. He'd been way too fucking easy to lure there, but then again I'd been watching him for a while, and I knew precisely what to say and do to get him all alone.

The fucker had been beating on his wife for the last ten years of their marriage. I guess the wife finally had enough. A quick phone call and explanation of my price, and that shithead was all mine to do with as I pleased.

I've spent the last week stalking him, and tonight, I made a point of bumping into him at a club on the outskirts of town. Most people avoid Black Creek like the plague, but you get plenty of middle and upper-class men—and women—who come here for the thrill; who think it'll be fun to hang with the ruffians for a night. Our whores are dirtier than the high-class prostitutes, and there are plenty of bored middle-aged house-wives who find some excitement in fucking a thug covered in tats.

It wasn't difficult to coax him into taking a drive with me. Dressed in skin-tight leather pants that hug my ample curves and enhance my ass, along with a bralette that draws men's eyes to my D cups, it was practically a sure thing. Add in a hushed whisper about how I wanted to choke on his cock, and he was almost coming in his pants as he escorted me out of the club.

I directed him to the docks, where I'd left my bike earlier. It was a piece of cake, distracting him with my tits and pussy as I ground against his dick until I could slip my gun out of my clutch and bash him over the head with it—I couldn't very well blow his brains out all over the gorgeous leather interior and ruin a perfectly good car for Arnie.

The hardest part was dragging his heavy ass out of the car and over to the edge of the dock where I'd stashed my duffel bag, equipped with everything I needed to wipe the sorry sack of shit off the face of the earth for good. But once I'd finally managed it, getting him all wrapped up and into the water was a cinch. I didn't even give him the courtesy of killing him first. The dark, sadistic part of me hopes the cold water startled him to consciousness, just in time for him to drown.

A sick sense of achievement warms me at that thought. It would be nothing less than he deserves. I'll never understand a man's need to inflict violence on the very people they claim to love and should instinctively feel the need to protect. Does it honestly make them feel more manly to beat on people smaller and weaker than them? It's the same pattern I've witnessed every day of my life. I grew up with it, and I've watched women and children around me be subjected to it, so there has to be some reasoning behind it. Just not one I'll ever understand.

My thoughts move on to my to-do list for tomorrow. I have my regular meeting with Enzo and then work tomorrow night because, in this town, a girl needs to have multiple sources of income in order to get by.

The water is lukewarm by the time I drag myself out of it, wrapping a towel around me as I pull the plug before heading to my bedroom—which is really more of a box room. Suddenly feeling exhausted, I throw on some sleep shorts and an oversized t-shirt and climb under the covers. I fall asleep to the satisfying thought that tonight there is one less abusive shitstain on the planet.

———

STRANDS OF MY STILL-DAMP HAIR WHIP AROUND MY FACE AS I JOG ACROSS the street. My electric cut out this morning, so I couldn't blow dry my hair, which also meant the coffee machine wouldn't work, and to top it all off, I forgot to set my alarm. So I'm running late, and all-in-all, I'm in a crabby mood by the time I arrive at G&T that afternoon for my monthly meeting with Enzo.

Beyond the paycheck, I never look forward to these meetings. They're awkward and extremely uncomfortable. I always feel like I'm under a microscope with my every action and inaction being analyzed and cataloged for future examination. Something about Enzo just doesn't sit right with me. Besides, I do not enjoy spending my free time in dingy bars with drunken assholes. I get enough of that at work.

The rickety door of the bar squeaks on its hinges as I pull it open and step into the dark interior. I'm immediately assaulted by the smell of stale cigarette smoke, sweat, and beer. It's midday, but every seat at the bar is occupied with patrons talking in hushed whispers, staring absently into their drinks, or watching this afternoon's entertainment —an aged stripper dancing on the small stage at the side of the room.

I glance around the small, stuffy space, faintly aware of some song from the nineties playing from the ancient jukebox as I locate Enzo through the haze of smoke, sitting at a table for two at the back of the room. I make sure my resting bitch face is in place before striding towards him while ignoring the way the soles of my boots stick to the floor with every step.

"Where's my money?" I demand once I've reached the table. The legs of the barstool scrape against the wooden floor as I pull it back, sliding onto the hard seat and fixing Enzo with a stony-faced expression.

"What, no *hello, how ya doing?*" Enzo asks, one side of his lip hooking up in a small grin that I think is supposed to be friendly, yet it doesn't quite hit the mark. He's a strange guy and probably not much older than me. He's attractive with his dirty blond hair and striking green eyes, but there's something about him I can't quite put my finger on. I don't know if it's his too clean appearance, the lack of desperation in his eyes, or the fact that he doesn't leer at me the way everyone else does. I'm not big-headed. However in a town where everyone is stick and bones, my wide hips, round ass, and big tits definitely make a splash, regardless of how much I try to hide them. I gave up even trying a long time ago and learned to embrace my femininity, using it for my own gain. Whatever it is about him, though, he just stands out from everyone else in the bar, and everyone in Black Creek, for that matter. But he's never made a wrong move toward me, and he does pay me handsomely for the tidbits of information I slide his way. "At least let me get you a drink."

"No, thanks," I reply bluntly. He's always trying to get me to stay and have a drink with him, but this is nothing more than business to me, and it will remain that way.

He ignores me as he waves over a waitress, ordering two glasses of whiskey before focusing his apple-green eyes on me. Getting down to business, I pull an envelope out of the inner pocket of my leather jacket and hold it out for him to take.

He gives me one of his placating smiles, not making any move to take it from me. "How have you been?"

I sigh, dropping the envelope on the sticky bar table in front of him. It's the same song and dance every time. Has been for the last seven years. I first met Enzo when I tried to steal his wallet. I was pretty damn good at it, so I've got no idea how he even knew I'd done it. I barely made it two steps before he grabbed me by the back of my shirt and threw me against a wall.

He looked absolutely furious, but after a second, some of the anger bled out of his expression, and he offered me an opportunity to earn the money instead. All I had to do was tell him anything I knew about a small street gang making moves on the old, abandoned docks at the time. I think they called themselves the Mad Dogz. Something stupid like that. They're long gone now—no surprise there. Anyway, I didn't know much. I'd overheard one of their members discussing their plans outside a bar down the road from the shelter I was staying at one night, and I relayed the information to Enzo. He seemed satisfied with what I knew and asked if I wanted the opportunity to earn more money. My shoulders slumped when he offered me that, assuming he was after a quick fuck or a blow job. It wasn't the first time I'd been offered money for such an exchange. Nor would it have been the first time I'd accepted, but he shocked me when he told me I just had to keep my ear to the ground, and there'd be more money if I could tell him anything useful.

Since then, we have been meeting once a month, and I hand over any information I have. He no longer bothers to go through what's in the envelope. He just hands over a wad of cash, asks a fuckton of personal questions, and goes on his merry way. I have no clue what he uses the information for—whether it's for his own gain or sells it—nor do I give a shit. His money made it possible for me to get off the streets. It helped me survive when I had no other prospects and before I was old enough to get a job at one of the strip clubs—apparently, there is a very gray moral line even in Black Creek. The point is, the money he gave me every month prevented me from having to resort to less than savory actions just to get by, and for a fifteen-year-old girl, that meant everything.

"Fine," I snap in answer to his question. I learned a long time ago it's just easier to give him something small about my life.

He nods his head at my response. "Good. You're being smart?"

"Always."

"And no one's giving you any trouble?"

I smirk. "Why? You gonna handle them for me if they are?"

He frowns, and something that makes him look ten times more deadly than half the thugs walking the street with their big-ass guns, flashes across his eyes before he blinks and it's gone.

Ignoring whatever that was, I shake my head. "No, they aren't. And even if they were, I can deal with them myself."

Living on the streets for most of your childhood makes you scrappy in a fight, and after I watched a girl no older than myself kill a man with a single punch to his throat, I sought her out and made a deal for her to teach me a few things. The moves she showed me... were insane, and I get the impression what she did teach me had only been a very small part of her repertoire. Although we had built a tentative relationship, she was always reluctant to talk about how she became so proficient in the art of killing. Unfortunately, she rarely comes around to Black Creek now. Still, our shared pain—and the fact that we were both young females trying to survive in a male-dominated world—bonded us in a way that will last a lifetime.

The waitress returns with our drinks, and while I make no move to take mine, Enzo lifts it right out of her hands, frowning at the glass before lifting it to his lips. He stifles a grimace as the liquid burns its way down his throat. Just another red flag that—if I ever had the inclination to open up to him—he can't be trusted. No one, and I mean *no one* in Black Creek, would screw up their nose at the taste of cheap whiskey. We grow up on the shit. We can down it like water, yet the bitter taste seemingly doesn't appeal to this guy's more refined palate.

Feeling annoyed and frustrated now, I snap out, "Money," repeating the word with more force.

"You know, a man could get his feelings hurt. Is my company really that bad?"

I purse my lips, trying to keep my cool as I let out a long, suffering exhale. The last thing I want to do is piss him off. While I have other, more lucrative means of income now, his money means I don't have to get on my knees for some asshole if I don't want to.

"I'm sorry," I grit out with a tight smile. "I just have a lot to do today."

He nods, downing the rest of his whiskey with an unimpressed frown. It's the same expression every time. You'd think he'd stop ordering the damn drink if he truly didn't like it. It's as if he's trying too hard to fit in, to appear like one of us. When you put all of his minor abnormal behaviors together, he stands out worse than a polar bear in the desert. Even though I file all of the weird mannerisms away for future analysis, I don't let myself dwell on who he really is for long. I don't give a shit, and it's better not to ask; not to get involved. If I know jack shit, then I don't have to worry about some gangster showing up at my door in the middle of the night, waving a gun in my face, and demanding answers.

So instead of overthinking it all, I let it go and hold out my hand in a silent gesture for him to give me my payment. Fucking finally, he slaps the bills into my palm, but when I go to tug them out of his grip, he tightens his hold around the pile of notes until I look up at him in confusion.

"Same time and place next month?"

"Isn't it always?"

He grins brightly, finally letting go and getting to his feet. "Looking forward to it."

With that, he turns and strides out of the pub. I don't relax until the squeaky door swings shut behind him. If push came to shove, I'm not sure if he'd be an ally or a foe. If he's not from Black Creek, who knows what sort of people he has backing him or how much money lines their pockets. I just hope I never have to find out.

two

Standing in the doorframe with my arms crossed, I watch my men hard at work as they rip off wallpaper, tear out kitchen cabinets, and drag worn mattresses along with rotten furniture from the bedrooms of the long-abandoned apartment complex I've claimed as home to the Reaper Rejects. Our numbers have grown considerably in the last few months, and it was past time I found a base of operations for all of us. Not to mention, many of these men deserve a place to call home, somewhere they can rest their heads at night and feel protected. Given the harrowing past of many of my newest—and youngest—members, I want them, more than anything, to know they are safe here. That their lives are theirs, and they are free to come and go as they please. I might need every able body for my war, but these men are more than just soldiers to me. They are my responsibility and under my protection, but more than anything, they are my family.

Pride and hope swell in my chest as I watch them all hard at work, turning this shell of a building into a home for us all. It will take some time, but I know we will get there. And, in the meantime, I plan on continuing to take over the southern part of the city. With every passing day, more and more people recognize our name, and with every block we claim as ours, they'll come to realize we are an indomitable force not to be messed with.

It's all just killing time as I wait to go after my actual target. The source of everything that has gone wrong in my life. The cause of all my pain and suffering. The Antonellis—the Italian Famiglia who hover like a dark cloud over this city for as long as anyone can remember. Always present, always watching, yet rarely ever seen.

Anger burns through my body as I think of them. Vengeance sears a path through my veins, increasing the pounding of my heart so it pulses in my ears, and my vision blurs as the scene before me is replaced with the image of a girl with a rueful grin and long, black, untameable hair. *Evie.* My sole reason for existing; the purpose behind everything I do.

I'm getting closer, Evie. I'm almost there. One day soon, revenge will be mine. Their blood will run beneath my boots, and they will rue the day they took you from me. From us. Your death will not be in vain.

This promise has been my driving force since that fateful day. The one I recite over and over in my head. I was only a boy when they stole my sister from me, but the horrors of that day molded me into the man I am now. I'm no longer the helpless kid who hid when bullets started flying, unable to help my sister as she screamed and cried for me. I may be too late to save her from her fate, but I refuse to let her death pass without consequence. What the Antonellis did to my family, they have done to countless others; to anyone who gets in their way. Of course, I've managed to recruit many of the aggrieved family members—brothers, fathers, sons—to my cause, and one day, we will rise up against them.

Unfortunately, though, going after the Antonellis isn't as easy as storming some street gangs' territory and gunning them down. The Antonellis have resources, money, and men on their side, all of which makes them an enemy no sane man should try to conquer. *Thankfully, no one has ever claimed I was right in the head.*

If I want to go up against them and win, I need to play it smart, and that starts with building a secure home for us. One that will protect us from any backlash from the many unorganized gangs that run rampant in this city, or the Grim Bastards. I need to ensure we have adequate resources and a reliable income. I can't hope to face the Antonellis on equal footing; however, I need to give us the best possible chance at success.

"Things are coming along well," Oliver says, coming to stand beside me. "Most of the bedrooms have been gutted and are ready to be painted and furnished, and security cameras have been installed all along the perimeter. Once everyone has suitable accommodations, I'll get them to start on the lobby."

"Good." I eye the insubstantial fencing along the sidewalk, still tempted to build a thick, cement wall in its place. Except, many here have spent their entire lives imprisoned behind concrete walls, and I refuse to make them feel trapped ever again. So instead, I've built a new, ten-foot-tall iron fence, topped with electrified barbed wire, and ensured every inch of the property is under surveillance. We've set up a room filled with monitors which will be manned twenty-four seven. I've also hooked up an alarm system to all of our phones, so we'll be notified no matter where we are, if someone dares to breach our property line.

All in all, I'm confident in our defense mechanisms, although I'm hopeful we won't need them. I don't think many of the lesser gangs would dare darken our doorway, and while the Grim Bastards are an ever-growing thorn in my side, I don't think they will start a war with us any time soon either. The main reason I'm so intent on establishing such a high level of security is in case the Antonellis catch wind of our plan, and inevitably make a counterattack.

Oliver claps me on the shoulder, giving it a quick squeeze. Looking in his direction, I find him scanning our surroundings, taking in the men hard at work, and the gradual coming together of the apartment complex before he turns to meet my eye. There is the same determined resolve in his eyes that he no doubt sees in mine. Oliver is my closest ally, the one person who I trust whole-heartedly. We're together in this fight, unified in our hunger for justice, and it feels good to have him at my side in this. To see the same war waging in his eyes and the shadows darkening his features. He craves this vengeance just as fiercely as I do. We were all friends once—before everything fell apart. Before our lives were destroyed. Before Evie was taken.

"Evie would be proud of all you've achieved," he says in a soft voice before quickly glancing away, hiding his pain from me. Not that he needs to. It's an all-consuming ache I'm far too familiar with.

I give him a sharp nod, unable to respond to his statement with words. Would Evie be proud? I'm not so sure. She never believed in an eye for an eye. She was always asking me to take the high road. Evie was my moral compass, my guiding star when I was lost. I always felt like she was an angel, filled with an ethereal purity that shone so bright it should protect her from the violence of men. Of course, I know now that's total bullshit.

I swallow roughly, clearing my voice before tilting my head toward the interior of the apartment complex. "Come on. We need to discuss our next moves."

I hear the light scuff of his boots against the hardwood floor behind me as we make our way toward my office, stepping inside. The room isn't much bigger than my old office, in what used to be my mother's house—mine, now that she's gone. As a gang, we've vastly outgrown the small terrace house, but I still own it. I'm not sure I'll ever be able to bring myself to part with it. Although, I have to admit, it's like a weight off my chest no longer living under the same roof I shared with my sister. I swear her ghost haunts the place, taunting me, whispering in my ear, and pursuing me into my dreams.

I hear the door close behind Oliver as he follows me into the room, and I skirt around the desk, sitting down behind it as he collapses into a seat on the opposite side.

"We have firm control over Joker territory, and I've sent men to help rebuild and aid the residents in whatever way they need," Oliver begins, getting straight down to business. I simply nod my head, already expecting as much. The Unfazed Jokers owned the part of town we're currently residing in. We had easily destroyed them and took control several months ago. So far, we've had minimal resistance, but we always have to remain alert.

"The fighting pit has proven to be very popular." A grin flashes across Oliver's face, similar to my own.

"Excellent." I'd been hoping the fights would be lucrative and provide us with another viable source of income.

He grabs a file off my desk, holding it out to me. "Marcus showed me last month's figures this morning. We doubled the previous month's income, and have already out-earned last month."

My grin widens at the news as I take the file and flick through it. "Fantastic. We'll have to scout locations for an expansion soon." Oliver gives a nod of agreement, and I know the task is in capable hands.

Having updated me, he leans back in his chair, the smile slipping off his face as it's replaced with a more intense expression. "How are things coming along on your end?"

While Oliver has been getting the apartment block up to scratch for my men and ensuring no one thwarts our rule, I've been busy looking into our sworn enemies, learning everything I can about them—not that I've been able to learn a whole hell of a lot. The Antonellis have more people in their organization than we could ever hope to obtain, and they're immensely more organized. Still, ultimately, my beef is with one man in particular—the head of the Antonelli family. The Don himself. The man who made the final call when it came to kidnapping my sister and destroying my family. His entire empire needs to come crumbling down, though his death will be at *my* hands.

My lips flatten as I release a long sigh. "Not so well," I admit, running a hand through my thick coal-black hair in frustration. I've employed some men to spy on the Antonellis, but unfortunately, it hasn't been an easy task. The Antonelli family is well protected. The Don has an extensive security team who escort him every time he's in the city, making it impossible for any of my men to get close to him, even to gather information. The men I've planted—a croupier in their casino and a bouncer at one of their sex clubs—are at the bottom of the food chain within the organization, meaning they have to gain the trust of the caporegime and prove their loyalty to the Antonellis before they can work their way up, which is a time-consuming process.

"We're going to be waiting a while until they are in a position to undermine them or provide us with the intel we need to make any drastic moves."

Oliver pinches his lips as he mulls over what I'm saying. "I don't see that we have much choice for now. At least we have eyes and ears inside their operation. Let's see what they come back with while we get ourselves established here, then we can go from there."

With a reluctant nod of agreement, I reach down to open the bottom drawer of my desk and pull out two tumblers and a bottle of the whiskey I know Oliver likes. I have to admit, he's got me hooked on this expensive shit ever since he came back from Crescentwood. You'd think prison would have knocked that refined taste out of him, but evidently not. Pouring the amber liquid into the glasses, I hold one out to him. He takes it from my outstretched hand, and we both knock the drink back, swallowing our frustrations as the alcohol burns a path down our throats.

HOURS LATER, MY HEAD IS JUST THIS SIDE OF FUZZY AS I SAG AGAINST A couch in the half-completed bar, where a party rages around me. The surrounding noise and alcohol coursing through my system are enough to quiet the incessant voice in the back of my head telling me to move faster, fight harder, be better, and every time the voice starts up again, I just down another glass of whiskey.

I refocus my gaze on the skinny blonde grinding her ass against my dick as she moves to the music. *Fuck, yes.* This is exactly the stress reliever I needed. My head falls back against the sofa, my eyes drifting shut as she moves to crouch between my legs, her nimble hands making quick work of my belt, and I groan as she sucks me into her mouth.

In a blissed-out daze, I tilt my head to the side, watching as another girl rubs herself all over Oliver. He's staring at his phone with a ridiculous amount of intensity, making a very clear point of ignoring the girl without downright telling her to fuck off.

"Dude." The word isn't much more than a grunt as the blonde sucks me deeper into her mouth. "Chill the fuck out. Let her blow you. You'll feel so much better for it."

He lifts his head to scowl at me before casting a quick glance at the girl between my legs. His scowl shifts to a frown before he focuses back on his phone.

Whatever, his loss. Shaking my head, I look away from him, choosing to watch the hottie as she sucks and slurps at my dick like it's her favorite flavor of ice cream. If Oliver wants to walk around with all that tension, then so be it. Personally, I prefer to offload it whenever I can.

Later that night, I'm lying in my bed with my arm bent, my hand behind my head as I stare up at the ceiling. My buzz from earlier has worn off, and the sniping voices have returned, preventing me from getting a restful night's sleep.

I run my hand down the front of my face, groaning. With every passing day, I'm getting increasingly agitated as next to no progress is made. It's become impossible for me to think about anything other than my goal. It's become an obsession, one that haunts me and refuses to let me have one single moment to myself. Fighting, drinking, and fucking no longer hold the same appeal they once did. No matter how hard I try to drown out the thoughts, guilt gnaws on my insides, mixed with anger, and the memory of deep green eyes that assault me as I slip into the past.

"CAIN! CAIN!" THE SOUND OF MY SISTER'S SCREAMS REACHES ME IN THE silence between rounds of gunfire. The fear in her voice has me looking out from where I'm hiding in a ditch underneath the side of the house as she is hoisted into some asshole's arms.

Another round of gunshots go off, and wooden fragments spray down around me as the bullets imbed themselves somewhere in the boards above my hiding place. I look around our small yard frantically searching for help. But no one is around. Everyone disappeared as soon as the sound of the first gun going off echoed around our usually quiet street. I can't even see any signs of Beck or Oliver, but they must be hiding nearby. The four of us were hanging out on the front porch steps when we heard the squeal of tires that preceded whatever's happening right now.

My sister emits another terrified scream, and I whip my head back to look at her. She's writhing and squirming in the asshole's arms, but he doesn't let her go as he drags her toward the pavement and the cars abandoned in the middle of the street. Digging my toes into the dirt beneath me, I wriggle out from beneath the house to go to her aid. The other men, all of whom are dressed sharply in black suits that seem in complete contrast to the devastation they are leaving in their wake, have lowered their automatic rifles to their sides and turned to follow the man carrying my sister back to the car.

The second I'm free, I jump to my feet and rush toward her. She sees me and struggles more frantically to get free, clawing the man's arm and screaming bloody murder. Tears stream down her face as she kicks and twists in his hold, but if anything, he only grips her tighter as she thrashes against him. None of them pay her any attention, but one of them must spot me running their way out of the corner of his eye as he turns to face me, lifting his gun. I don't even register the significance of the action, or maybe I just don't care. I'd happily die if it saved my sister from these monsters.

I barely spare the man pointing the gun at me any attention, my focus too intent on my sister as I push myself faster across the dried grass in an attempt to reach her. Her glassy eyes, sheening with tears, widen as the scene unfolds, and she freezes in the man's arms as his comrade's gun comes level with my chest. I hear the pow-pow-pow of bullets firing rapidly within seconds after someone tackles me from behind, taking me to the ground and knocking the air out of my lungs. Whoever it is probably just saved my life, except I can't find it in me to even look at them—never mind, thank them—as my sister is thrown into the back of one of the cars.

Shaking off whoever it is, I push to my feet once again as the car door is slammed shut, blocking my view of her tear-stained face as her screams for help are cut off. Before I can even reach the sidewalk, the car speeds off down the street. I can't do anything aside from watch as it disappears around a corner, and my heart crumbles to dust in my chest. The other cars parked in the street take off, and in slow motion, still not able to comprehend the reality of what is happening, I turn my stunned gaze to the last one as the man who just tried to kill me climbs into the front passenger seat. He turns at the last second, and I see the details I missed earlier—the tattoos on his fingers and the row of X's running like a line of tears down one cheek. His neatly trimmed russet-brown hair is styled back, and the corner of his lip hooks up in a malicious grin when he catches me watching him.

"Payment for your daddy's sins, kid. Next time tell him not to fuck with the Antonellis."

The car door closes behind him, and I watch helplessly as the car speeds down the road and out of sight. The street appears abnormally quiet in the aftermath of the chaos, and I'm not sure how long I stand there for, watching the spot where the cars disappeared as if the one carrying my sister might turn around and come back, deliver her back to me safe and sound.

I'm faintly aware of two people moving to stand beside me, their shoulders brushing against mine. My best friends. I can feel their devastation as potently as my own, but I can't tear my eyes away from the end of the street. All the while I stand there, I can feel that newly vacated space in my chest where my heart once resided, filling with something dark and menacing. It floods into my bloodstream and whispers sweet promises of revenge in my ears until the only reason my heart still beats; my lungs still expand; my legs still hold me upright, is to save Evie and gut the motherfucking assholes who took her.

A snort of disgust rips from between my lips as I shake off memories of that day. What a foolish, naive child I was then, making promises I could never keep. I could make my sister all the promises in the world, but I had no means by which to follow through with them.

I'm eleven years too late, and Evie is long gone by now, but revenge still beats a rhythm in my chest. It's ingrained in my every move, every action, every thought. It's the sole reason for my continued existence.

I might be too late to save you, Evie, but I will not let your kidnappers go unpunished.

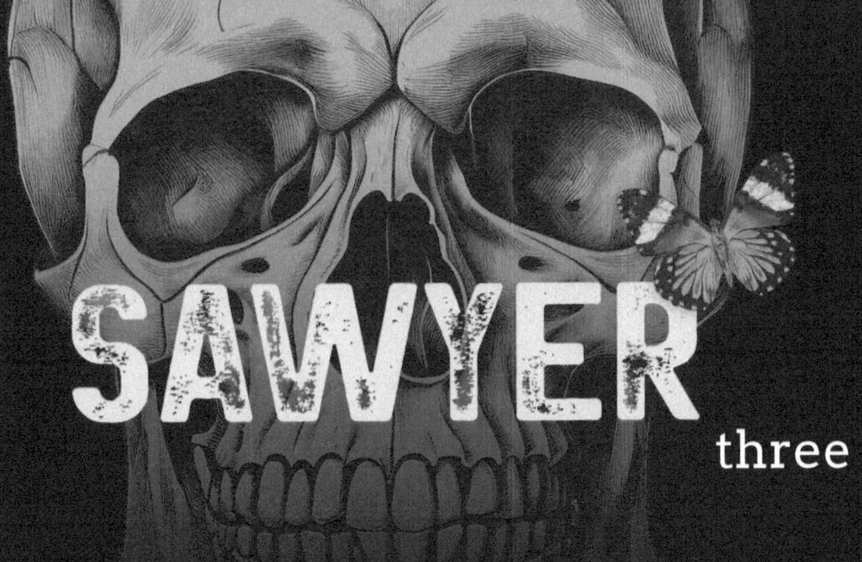

three

"Evening, Kenny."

"Red." The bouncer by the staff entrance nods his head, opening the door for me to enter. The pounding of the club's music—*Closer* by Nine Inch Nails—thuds through the walls as I make my way along the narrow hallway, passing the manager's office and staff toilets before reaching the changing rooms.

"Hey, girl!" Bee greets as I walk in.

"Hey, Bee." I smile as I pass by her, not really paying attention as she pushes her tits into a bikini that barely has enough material to cover her nipples before plonking my bag down at my own dressing table and lifting up the outfit that's been laid out for me —a black g-string with matching lace suspenders and thigh-high stockings, a bra that doesn't appear to have much more material than Bee's does, and a pair of clear-colored platform heels.

"You're up in five, Red," a gruff voice barks through the door while I'm in the process of changing, belonging to Drew, the floor manager here at Strip Tease.

Sighing, I quickly slather my face in excessive makeup and my body in glitter, then stuff my bag in a locker and head out of the dressing room, ready to put on a show for the horny-ass men of this town.

I slip through the staff entrance door into the front area of the club as the dancer before me on the main stage finishes up. The club is dimly lit, with spotlights directed at the three stages, where different dancers are performing. I can just make out enough outlines of men in the audience to know we have a full house tonight.

The tables around the stages are all occupied, and most of the booths are full, too, by the looks of things. Scantily clad waitresses skirt around tables and crowds of people on their way to deliver drinks, and I can just about make out a few men receiving lap dances or being escorted to private stalls for some more *intimate* attention.

The song comes to an end, and the dancer—a relatively new girl I haven't had the chance to get to know yet—steps down from the stage, giving me a soft smile before she moves toward the bar, ready to work the floor.

I run my hands over my outfit, flattening the lace strap of my g-string before I climb the steps onto the stage. The music switches, the fast-paced beat of *I Get Off* by Halestorm starting up as I wrap my hand around the pole. The overhead spotlight flashes down on me, blinding my view of the rest of the darkened room as I shift my weight and swing my body around the pole in time to the music. I've been perfecting these moves for over five years now. I can work the pole like a goddamn pro. It helps that I've got an ass that men seem to enjoy digging their fingers into and hips they can picture themselves grabbing ahold of. Not to mention my long auburn-colored hair that they all want to wrap around their fists and tug on.

The next thirty minutes pass in a blur of swaying hips, shaking my tits, and grinding my ass, so when the last song in my set comes to an end, Drew meets me at the side of the stage.

"You're on the floor the rest of the night."

Nodding, I stride past him to the bar. Drew's all business. He keeps it professional, never allowing his eyes to stray or linger where they shouldn't. The same can't be said for some of the other staff here.

"Damn, Sugar, you're looking hot tonight," Mike, one of the bartenders, greets as he pours a shot of something—vodka, maybe—into a glass and slides it across the counter to a customer. Mike is in his mid-twenties, probably only a year or two older than me, and he's an absolute flirt. The thing is, he knows he's hot shit. The other girls here drool all over him, only boosting his ego further, and I've seen more than a few of them leave with him at the end of a shift. But he's a one-time-only kinda guy, and I'm sure a couple of the girls have been left with broken hearts after spending the night with him.

I'm all for a good time, and I've no doubt he would have some pretty decent bedroom skills, but I don't mix business with pleasure. And honestly, overinflated egos aren't really my thing. Sure, I like a guy with confidence, but Mike is just too much. That cocky, flirty personality just doesn't do it for me, even if his good looks are on point—and with his muscular biceps, high cheekbones, and the dark dusting on his chin, his looks are *definitely* on point.

Giving him a flirtatious wink, which has become our usual banter—I think by now he's figured out I'm not interested in him, not that that stops him from trying—I grab a tray already loaded with drinks and move to distribute them around the lively room.

Without the bright lights blinding my view, I scan my eyes over tonight's crowd—which seems to consist of the usual mixture of rowdy drunkards—as I sashay around the room, dropping off drinks and taking orders while ignoring the occasional hand brushing along the side of my breast or over my ass.

The largest throng of people are gathered around the stages, wanting an up-close and personal view of the dancers. Still, plenty of others are sitting at the small circular tables, with some of the wealthier out-of-towners occupying the velvet booths that line the walls. You can tell they don't live in Black Creek. It's obvious—from their crisp white shirts, fitted black pants, and polished shoes to their expensive haircuts and the way they cast their eyes over the rowdy Black Creekians with a look of casual disgust. They think they're so much better than us, yet here they are, in our town, in our club, with their hard-ons and sleazy leers, so how much better can they actually be?

As much as most of us want to escape the daily grind, violence, and bloodshed that occurs here, the appeal of it also draws men like them to our chaotic neck of the woods. Men with money who come to Black Creek to revel in debauchery and bathe in sin. This city is a far cry from their daily lives. It's a place they can come to escape their boring marriages, relieve the stress of their busy workday, and avoid whatever other nonsense privileged, rich people have to endure.

For the most part, customers who live in Black Creek are pretty easy to handle. They're mostly here for the stage show and maybe a lap dance, but if they do want *extras*, they're usually pretty good when I say no. However, men with money... they're not so easy to turn down—hence why we have bouncers on the doors and security dotted along the perimeter of the room.

As I work my way across the floor, my gaze swivels to the biggest threat in the room. A crowd even more relentless than the wealthy assholes in their cushy booths. Satan's Advocates.

Satan's Advocates is the street gang that currently occupies this part of the city. They usually stop by a couple of nights a week to cause havoc and remind us all of their dominion over this area. They're easy to spot, all of them wearing their Satan's insignia like a badge of honor, either sewn onto their leather jackets or tattooed onto their skin. The atmosphere in the room changes the instant they walk in, and one by one, people get up and move away from their large group, not wanting to inadvertently gain their attention or incur their wrath. Those who are brave enough to remain nearby frequently flick their gaze in their direction, watching them warily and ready to make a run for it if shit hits the fan.

"Hey, baby, give us a lap dance," one of them calls out as I pass by.

Plastering a fake, coy expression on my face, I turn to look at him. "Sure thing, handsome. Let me just offload this round of drinks, and I'll be over, yeah?"

I hate this part of my job, especially when it's with an arrogant, self-entitled shitstain like this idiot appears to be, but it's a job requirement if you're working the floor, and even if it wasn't, I can't say no to a Satan. None of us can.

He gives me a cocky smirk, biting on his lower lip as his gaze roams over every inch of my exposed skin. I'm more than used to it, so I don't feel any of the revulsion or sudden need to cover up that most people would probably experience. It's just part of the job, and I've been doing it for long enough. The nervousness that comes with strutting around half-naked and on display for everyone to see quickly dissipates in this line of work. Within a month, I learned to walk with my head held high, confidence brimming with every step. Not only does it help with the tips, but I quickly realized I have nothing to be ashamed of. So I use my body to make money? Everyone in this fucking town does that. Men use their bodies to intimidate other gangsters, to threaten and coerce whoever they need to. Just because they do it with their clothes on, that somehow makes it better?

"Yeah, okay," he pouts. "But I might need more than just a lap dance if you keep me waiting too long."

I smile tightly at him, ducking my head and moving on through the crowd to disperse the last of my drinks. Being up on stage is one thing. It's actually something I enjoy. With the bright lights beaming down on the stage, it's next to impossible to pick anyone out of the crowd. It makes it easy to pretend no one is watching, and I can just fall into the music and escape into my own world. Lap dances, not so much. It's impossible to forget what you are to the men in this room when they're trying to shove their face in your tits and grab a handful of your ass.

The great thing about Strip Tease is that *extras* are at the discretion of the girls. If we don't want to partake, then that's fine. I personally choose not to. I've made a point of ensuring I earn enough money from various sources to no longer have to. I wasn't always so fortunate, though I have come a long way from the teenage girl struggling to survive from one day to the next.

The only challenge comes when it's a Satan's Advocate asking for that *extra*. The club pays its protection tithe, but we can't afford to have them pull that protection, or worse, decide to get rid of us altogether just because we piss them off. It sounds crazy, but businesses have been destroyed over less. The gangs here run our lives. We live and breathe on their say so. Last week, the pawnshop on 8th and Hudson was set on fire because the owner fucked some girl the leader of the Black Spiders had apparently claimed. The Spiders didn't even own that territory, but they got their hands on it, and next thing, a Molotov cocktail was being thrown through the shop owner's front window—with the owner still inside.

Too many hard-working men and women, just trying to get by, rely on Strip Tease. As such, we all do whatever we can to keep the Satan's Advocates happy, and you can bet your ass we will do exactly the same with whatever gang takes control after them. That's just the way it is now. The Satan's seized control of our little part of Black Creek when The Feral Beasts collapsed, and the whole city was suddenly up for grabs. At first, they weren't too bad. They mainly kept to themselves and were too busy making sure they held onto the five-block radius they'd seized control over to hassle us too much. However, as time has gone on, they've gotten cocky, showing their true colors and demanding anything they want from us.

Dropping off the last of my drinks, I return the tray to the bar and make my way over to the rowdy table of Satan's Advocates. The guy jumps to his feet as I approach, once again taking the time to skim his eyes over my body.

"Don't you want a lap dance?" I question, eyeing the table of burly men, many of whom are watching me with eager eyes. They're all rough-looking, with scruffy beards and stained teeth. It's very evident hygiene doesn't factor in all that high on their daily routines.

The man smirks. "I was thinking we'd go somewhere more private."

I nod my head, painting on a seductive smile while smothering my groan. "Of course, follow me."

"Baby, I'd follow you anywhere when you sway your hips like that."

It's the same sort of shit every guy says, and it evokes zero response from me as I lead him toward a line of private booths at the side of the room, intended for precisely this purpose. A couple of back rooms have been repurposed solely to accommodate *extras,* but I deliberately don't take him there, hoping I can still get by with just a private dance.

He's grinning like a fucking idiot as he plunks himself into the chair. I take the time to look over his scrawny frame. He's young and arrogant looking, with a short, wiry, dark-haired beard that looks like it hasn't fully grown in some places.

I pull across the heavy purple curtain, blocking people's views of the booth and giving us some privacy before turning back to face him. The stall is darker now, making it harder to read his expression, although his wide eyes and the way he rubs his hand over his crotch are telling enough.

"Money." I hold out my hand for the fee, and he happily slaps the small pile of one-dollar bills into my palm. I tuck them into the tiny strip of fabric covering my tits, and as a new song starts up—*Addicted* by Saving Abel—I step between his spread thighs and sway my hips. Leaning in, I stroke my hands down the front of his top before thrusting my chest out, practically shoving my tits in his face.

He groans and squeezes his dick. I spin, mentally counting down the seconds as I jut my ass out. When he smacks his hand against my skin, grabbing hold of my ass, I spin round and glower at him. "No touching."

"Oh, come on, baby. I'll pay you extra."

"No."

The muscle in the back of his jaw works as he grinds his teeth, anger flashing across his face. I mentally chastise myself, working to soften my naturally brash personality as I move to straddle him, grinding down on his erection.

The anger quickly melts off his face as he takes my continued performance to mean free rein to touch what he wants, sliding his palms up my thighs and groping my tits in a painfully firm grip. I keep my mouth shut, biting the skin along my inner cheek as I hold back each snarky retort I want to spew out. When the song finally comes to an end, I move to get off his lap, but his hands clamp tightly on my upper thighs, holding me in place as his finger trails along the strap of my g-string.

"Come on, baby. It was just getting good." I try again to get off him, but then he digs his fingers into my skin, no doubt marking it, and that flash of anger from before re-emerges. "You got me all worked up. You can't just leave me hanging."

I have to swallow back the reminder that *he's* the one that asked for a fucking lap dance. He starts using his grip on my legs to pull me in against him, so the bulge in his jeans bumps against my scantily clad pussy, and all I can think about is wiping the arrogant as fuck look off his face. The one that says he *knows* he's going to get his way and he *knows* I can't stop him.

Except, I definitely could. He might think he's the most dangerous one in the room, but in reality, it's me. I've killed many men like him—self-centered assholes who don't give a shit about anything or anyone but themselves. But I can't. That would only get all of us in deep shit. This type of behavior from a Satan isn't unusual. It's just something I have to grin and bear, so taking a steadying breath, I do just that. I have to work really hard to fix a tantalizing smile onto my lips and trail my fingers down the front of his shirt instead of wrapping them around his neck like I want to.

"That'll be another fifteen." I grind my pussy against his hard cock, distracting him so he can't begin to haggle with me. If I'm going to have to give the asshole a blow job, the least he can do is fucking pay me.

"Fine," he grits out, hissing between his teeth as I grind down on him again.

Now that negotiations are done, he slaps a few more bills into my hand, and I don't waste any time getting it over with. I quickly lower myself to the ground between his legs as he unzips his pants and pulls himself out, giving his dick a few tugs before eyeing me up expectantly. I give him a pretty mediocre blow job, refusing to do anything but the bare minimum to get him off. As he swells in my mouth, his hand slams down on the back of my head, forcing me further down on him as he comes down my throat. *Fucking asshole.* I curse him out in my head while keeping my face impassive as I release him with a pop and get to my feet.

He tucks himself away with a smile on his face, and I open the curtains in a silent indication for him to get the fuck out. With one final squeeze of my ass, he murmurs, "I'll be back for more real soon, baby," as he steps out and moves to rejoin his buddies.

With a roll of my eyes, I readjust my bra and g-string before getting back to work. The rest of my shift goes by without incident. Thankfully, the Satan's left not long after, and the regulars are usually pretty easy to handle.

It's the early hours of the morning when I finally leave the club, showered and dressed in black jeans and my kickass black, chunky-heeled boots. I'm walking back to the apartment when my phone goes off in my pocket. Checking the caller ID, I immediately know what this is about and that I won't be getting any sleep for a while yet.

"Yeah?" I say into the receiver, bringing it to my ear.

"She's back."

I sigh. *Yup, exactly what I thought.*

"What shape is she in?"

"A black eye. I'd guess a few broken ribs too. She's got the kid with her." The woman hesitates before blurting out, "She's got bruises on her, too."

Goddammit. I told her this would happen. I fucking knew it would. It's the same fucking pattern every time with these assholes.

"I'll be right there."

Hanging up the phone, I stuff it in my pocket and pick up my pace. At the next block, rather than heading in the direction of my apartment building, I turn the opposite way down the street toward the *New Beginnings Women's Shelter.*

The shelter is in a repurposed community hall, and the place is quiet when I push open the door. Beatrice, a gray-haired woman in her sixties with balls of steel—making her tougher than any man I've ever met—is sitting behind the check-in desk. She looks up as I walk in, giving me a sad smile. Beatrice and I go way back. I've spent more than my fair share of nights here, under her watchful eye. She's good people, and even most of the men in this town know not to mess with her. She's got herself a reputation, although I guess that's what happens when you bludgeon your deadbeat husband and cut off his cheating dick. At least, those are the rumors. No one knows for certain since his body was never found.

"Where is she?"

She jerks her head toward the back of the building. "I put her in one of our private rooms. Last door on the right."

With a nod, I move to head down the hall, but as I'm walking past the counter, she leans across it and hisses in a low voice, "Don't let her go back to him. If she can't make the decision for herself, then make it for her."

I press my lips together, glancing at her out of the corner of my eye, before walking on and passing the doorway to a large, cafeteria-style dining hall that, during the day, is normally filled with residents and volunteers. However, at this late hour, it's dimly lit, with only a few women sitting around, nursing hot drinks or consoling one another.

Moving on, I pass another, smaller hall which has been set up as a communal sleeping area, with bunk beds filling up the room. No doubt every one of them is already occupied with women and children in need of a safe space for the night. Unfortunately, come morning, many of them will go back home to their abusive, cheating, scumbag partners, with apologies pouring from their lips, only to end up right back here in a week or month.

Every single one of their worthless partners should be shoved off the side of the dock and left to drown. It's the only fitting fate for any asshole who uses his larger size and greater strength to beat on someone weaker than them. I just don't have the time or resources to do it all myself. Getting rid of them all would be a full-time job, and most of these women can't afford to retain my services—which is why I have to be so selective with the cases I take on.

As I pass by several more communal sleeping rooms, I can hear the faint sounds of women whispering, children crying, and the crinkle of plastic sleeping mats as someone rolls over in their bed. It brings back memories of my own time living in shelters like this. I was only a child, and thankfully, many of the volunteers took pity on me, but it still wasn't an easy life. I had to fend for myself, scavenge my own food and clothing, and move from shelter to shelter when I'd stayed for as long as I could.

I preferred staying in a women's shelter since being with just women and children was generally safer. I had a few incidents in homeless shelters, instances where men would try to corner me or sneak into my bed at night, which resulted in me sleeping with a stolen kitchen knife under my pillow and learning never to let myself be alone in a room with someone of the opposite sex. It's one thing for men to proposition a thirteen-year-old girl, but to try and just take what doesn't belong to them—that's a whole different level of fucked up.

I push thoughts of the past aside as I reach the last door at the end of the corridor, where Beatrice said she'd put Sheryl, and knock on the door.

A weak sob comes in response. "Y-yeah?"

Opening the door, I slip into the room and take in the pitiful state of my oldest—and only—friend as she sits on the bottom bunk, sobbing. Her eyes widen as I close the door behind me, and she awkwardly gets to her feet, coming to hug me.

"Sheryl," I sigh into her embrace, careful not to hold her too tightly. Beatrice said she thought she had broken ribs, and based on the way she's favoring her right side and wincing with every deep inhale, I'd say she's right.

I pull back, running my gaze over her face. She's skinny—far too skinny—and her right eye is already swollen shut and turning a horrific shade of black. Her one good eye is red and puffy, glistening with fresh tears, and blood is crusted around her nose. There's another red smear on her chin where blood has trickled from her split lip.

Once I've taken in all I can bear to look at of her face, I glance behind her to where there's a small lump sleeping in the top bunk.

"How's Grace?"

Sheryl's shoulders drop, and a fresh set of tears build in her eyes before she dabs them away, "H-he hurt her." She chokes on a sob, burying her face in her hands as I rub soothing circles along her back and usher her over to the bed. Once I've got her settled, I rifle through the duffle bag she most likely hastily packed before escaping, digging out some baby wipes and tucking my hand under her chin. I gently lift her face, dabbing around her nose and chin to clean her up.

This isn't the first time Sheryl has turned up here with Grace. Hell, it isn't even the third time this month. Sheryl and I grew up together. Black Creek is filled with street kids, but Sheryl was one of the first people I met when I first joined them. See, I wasn't always homeless, though I barely remember that time of my life, and the only memories I do have are coated in violence and drenched in blood. Not ones I care to think about most days. When I was first trying to figure out this new life I'd been upended into, she showed me the ropes. She was the one who pointed out the best homeless shelters and taught me how to survive from one day to the next. I owe her my life.

As we grew older, our lives took very different paths. Sheryl fell into gang life, enticed by the adrenaline rush of booze, drugs, and partying. When we were fifteen, she started hanging around with the Crystal Takers—I'm sure you can guess how they made their money. They were nothing more than drug users who thought they should be more. Back then, Python—the leader of the Satan's—was a runner for them, but he took a special interest in Sheryl and didn't waste any time claiming her as his and knocking her up. And at first, I think things were going okay for them, but Python had bigger ambitions than simply working for some drug-taking idiot, and when The Feral Beasts left, he saw the opportunity to form his own little ruthless gang. Over the last couple of years, the power—or maybe it was the drugs—has gone to his head and he's begun to unravel.

Sheryl was seven months pregnant with baby number two when she first showed up at the shelter down the road from me, so beaten and bloody I was worried she wouldn't make it through the night.

Thankfully, she did, but the baby didn't. That was nearly two years ago, and I still remember the unadulterated fury that pumped through me when I saw her. I wanted to murder Python there and then, but she begged and pleaded for me to leave it alone. Ever since then, she shows up here every few months with Grace clinging to her, covered in new bruises and injuries—although never as bad as that first time. She always stays a few nights, allowing the worst of the injuries to heal while she rests before going back to him, even when I've pleaded with her to let me deal with him.

"What happened?" I ask her softly.

She ducks her head, lowering her gaze. I sit and wait patiently as she fidgets, gathering her thoughts and building her courage.

"He... " The emotion is thick in her voice, and she trails off, gathering herself before continuing, "Sometimes he makes me... perform for the others, and... d-do things."

Her hands are shaking, and her eyes remain glued to her lap as she struggles to get the words out. I'm already close to blowing a fuse, picturing the asshole's death, and I'm pretty sure I haven't even heard the worst of it yet.

"Usually, I put Grace to bed before any of them get too drunk or rowdy, but she's been having trouble sleeping recently. S-she's been wetting the bed." She shakes her head, her chin wobbling. "She got up when I was... " Unable to put words to whatever he was making her do—based on what she has said already, I think I can work it out— she trails off as fresh tears stream down her face, and she sniffs, wiping at her nose. "I tried to explain to him I just needed to sort her out, but he'd had too much snow. There was no reasoning with him." She shakes her head again. "He's never hit me like that in front of her. And when she started crying, he screamed at her and shoved her backward. She... she crashed into the table behind her."

She falls apart then, her voice breaking as she buries her face in her hands. Her shoulders quake as she cries, and I rub soothing circles along her back. We stay like that for a long time until she cries herself out, sagging against me as I wrap an arm around her shoulders.

As her sobs quieten, a hush falls over the room until she whispers in a small voice, "I've found bruises on her recently. Along her arms. When I asked her about it, she said she tripped."

I sigh, pushing past my anger so I can provide the comfort Sheryl needs right now. But hearing that determines one thing for me—Python must die. Whether or not Sheryl agrees or wants me to act, I *have* to. It's no longer acceptable for me to just sit back and take her word for it, hoping she will come to her senses and leave him on her own. Sometimes we need someone to give us a push in life, to overcome the things we are afraid to face, and that's exactly what I'm going to do for Sheryl.

"You know this can't continue, right?"

She nods but doesn't lift her head to look at me.

"It's not a safe environment for her," I push. "If he's already hurting her, just think about what he might do in the future."

She nods again. "I know. I know. But I'm scared."

I squeeze her shoulder and nudge her, so she looks up at me. Her eyes are wet and clouded with fear. "Let me take care of it." My words are pleading, yet there's an insistence behind them that I'm hoping she will heed. Even though I'm expecting her to tell me to leave it, the way she hesitates, gnawing on her bottom lip as she mulls over the idea, gives me hope. I mean, I'm killing him either way, but I'd feel a hell of a lot better about it if Sheryl was on board.

I push harder. "You can't take her back there, Sheryl. She deserves better. Do you want her to end up trapped in this town, just like us?"

She frowns, and it takes a long moment before she responds, "O-okay... do whatever it is you do."

Sheryl doesn't know much about the late-night activities I get up to when I'm not at the club, nevertheless I've offered to permanently remove Python from her life enough times that she knows I'm not just saying it for the sake of it. The first time I brought it up, she laughed me off, but when I mentioned it again, I knew she could see how serious I was. I wasn't half as experienced back then as I am now, but I'd have done it for Sheryl. For Grace.

I run my eyes over her face, giving her a chance to change her mind. I can see the resolve in her eyes, though. Tonight—him hurting Grace—has crossed a line for her. She might finally be starting to accept the toxic relationship she's in.

We don't say much else as I pull her down onto the bed and lie down beside her. It takes a while, but eventually I hear her soft snores. As I lie there, I stare up at the bottom of the top bunk, where Grace is sleeping soundly, and mull over various plans. It won't be the easiest job I've had—getting to Python—but it's definitely doable. Being the leader of a gang, he will have a certain level of protection around him at all times, despite that I'm hopeful their arrogance is a weakness I can use to my advantage.

Regardless of the obstacles in my way, my blood hums at the challenge and the knowledge that one more scumbag will soon meet his fate. I live for this. It gives me a sense of purpose and allows me to sleep easier at night. It's not enough for me to just struggle from one day to the next, doing a job I hate and abandoning any principles I might otherwise have if I had a choice in this life. At least, this way, I'm contributing something to this fucked-up world.

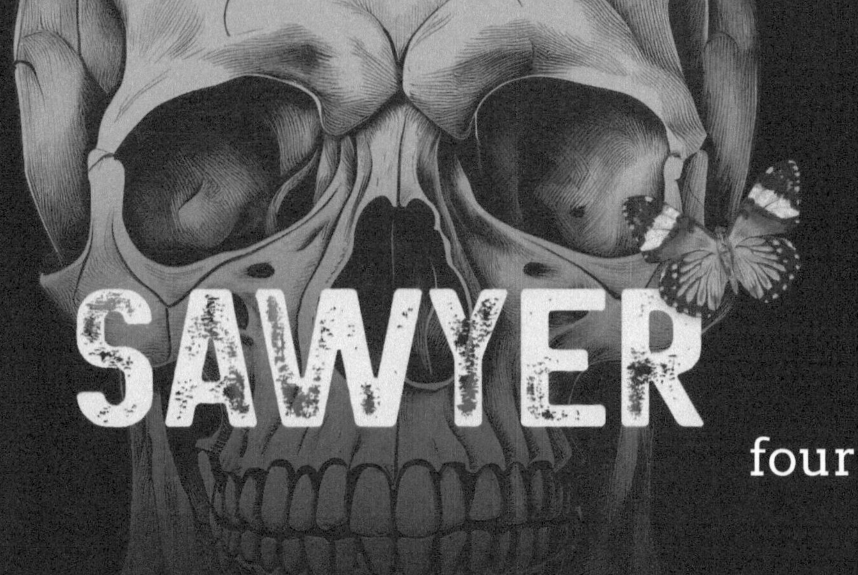

four

My thighs burn, and my body is stiff from crouching for so long. I'm hidden in the shadows of an empty lot across the way from the dilapidated house that the Satan's have claimed as their main base. They seem to have taken over most of the street, but the place I'm watching is Python's, and it's where they currently have a rager of a party underway. I've spent the last couple of days watching them from afar, learning their movements. I already knew the basic things about them —that they drink too much and do too many drugs, that they usually spend their days harassing citizens, and that they like to hang out at Toxic on a Friday night, but I don't know anything about *them*.

In order to figure out the best way of getting to Python, I need to learn what security measures they have, pinpoint their weaknesses, and identify my window of opportunity where I'm least likely to be seen or caught. So far, it appears the Satan's are more concerned with getting high than with delegating anyone to the task of security. Even as I watch their house now, people are coming and going freely like it's any other house party. It seems ridiculous to me, but it works in my favor.

Leaning down, I unzip my duffle bag and shimmy out of my black skinny jeans, switching them out for a short skirt that matches the skin-tight crop top I'm wearing. I shrug out of my leather jacket and stuff it along with my pants into the bag before lifting out a blonde wig. Ensuring my unique, red strands are carefully hidden beneath it, I get to my feet and slip through a hole in the chain-link fence onto the sidewalk.

With slow, unhurried steps and an exaggerated sway of my hips, I cross the street and step into the house. Nobody tries to stop me or ask any questions. I have to restrain my eye roll at how fucking easy it is. I knew the Satan's maintaining their place of power for this long had gone to their heads, but this is fucking ridiculous. They're just asking for someone to strut in here and gun them all down. *Hmm, tempting.*

As I cross the threshold, I'm immediately bombarded by the deafening boom of horrendous rap music and suffocated by the stench of sweat, alcohol, and utter hopelessness. I'm in a narrow entryway, with stairs in front of me leading to the floor above

The room on my right is lit by flashing neon lights, and I can barely see through the dense crowd of drunk and high dancers. Ignoring them for now, I turn left into a brightly lit, old-fashioned kitchen, the countertops overflowing with bottles of beer and spirits.

There are plenty of people in here too, snorting cocaine off the small, linoleum-topped table, fucking in the corner, and getting wasted on cheap alcohol. I ignore them all as I do a sweep of the room, grabbing a beer and twisting off the cap on my way past. There are a couple of Satan's in here, unfortunately not the one I'm looking for. Taking in their glazed-over eyes and the red tinge around their noses as they watch me walk by, I'm guessing they won't remember even seeing me in the morning. *Good.*

Moving back into the hall, I glance up the stairs, taking a long tug of my beer before climbing them to a small landing with four doors leading off it. I put my ear to the first door, hearing the distinct sounds of people fucking before I move on to the next room. There aren't any sounds coming from behind it, but it's locked when I turn the doorknob.

Out of the final two doors, one is a grimy bathroom, with black grout in the sink, the toilet seat up, and what I'm pretty sure is piss covering the floor. Scowling in disgust, I toss my now empty beer bottle into the room, not giving a shit that it breaks, and tiny fragments of glass spread out all over the floor. I close the door and move on to the final room, hearing the sound of more sex coming from behind the door.

Now that I've got a general layout of the house, I head down the stairs and into the only room that's left, where the rest of the Satan's must be hanging out. It takes a second for my eyes to adjust to the darkness, but as I push my way through the packed crowd of dancers, I spot them spread out on chairs and couches along the back wall, ignoring the rest of the room while they put on their own show of fucking and snorting drugs. There in the middle, with a girl sucking him off, is Python, with his greasy hair slicked back and an overgrown beard that desperately needs a comb run through it. He's a large, burly man with a bit of a beer belly and a snake tattoo that winds around his neck. I think *he* thinks it makes him look intimidating. *I* think it just makes him look like a fucking idiot.

I have to force my face not to contort at the sight of him as I dance to the shitty music they have pumping through the stereo in an attempt to blend in with the crowd. He clearly doesn't give a shit about where Sheryl is or if she's okay. Not that I expected him to, but seeing him here, partying like it's any other night while he lets some random skank give him a blow job, just drives the reality home for me. Is this the life Sheryl and Grace have been living? Where the fuck do they even sleep? There's no way Grace could be in this house when there's a party raging like this.

All of it only serves to heat the blood in my veins, although I'm sure the shitty beer is helping with that too. I've had to rebuff several guys by the time I notice Python shove the girl away and tuck himself back in his pants. I watch as his eyes scan the room, and I give him a coy look when his gaze meets mine.

A cocky smirk lifts one side of his lips, and as I trail my fingers down the side of my neck and between the valley of my breasts, his eyes drop to follow. His smirk deepens, clearly pleased with what he sees. *Good.* I feel a warm presence at my back, and rather than moving away from whichever new asshole is trying his luck, I lean into him. Knowing Python will hate my dismissal of him, I look away instead of focusing on the guy behind me, not really seeing him as I mentally count down the seconds.

Five. Four. Three. Two...

"Get the fuck out of here."

Right on time.

Python's deep, possessive growl resonates from behind me, and without having to be told twice, the guy whose hands are on my hips flinches and scurries away through the crowd, and Python's hands replace his as he steps in front of me. I look up at him through my eyelashes, noticing his gaze glued to my chest. *Charming.*

"You must be new around here. I'd definitely remember an ass like that."

Oh, how you make me swoon with your romantic words.

Playing my part, I bite down on my lower lip and give him a lascivious look.

"Come join me and my guys."

Fuck, that is not what I want to happen.

I run my hand up the front of his leather jacket and press my body flat against his. This close, I can make out his pupils, dilated with a combination of lust and drugs as I grind my hips against his.

"Don't you want to dance first?" I purr.

With an arrogant smirk, he spins me and grabs hold of my hips, yanking them back against his pelvis as he attempts to grind his dick between my asscheeks.

His hands are everywhere—clasping my thighs, brushing my stomach, squeezing my tits. Thank god my back is to him, 'cause I don't think I could hide the hatred flaring in my eyes.

Once a new song starts up, he leans in, his beard scratching the side of my face as he grunts in my ear, "Alright, you've had your song. Maybe you should show me your thanks by getting on your knees."

It takes me a second to unclench my teeth and be sure I'm not going to chew him out for that sickening statement. As soon as I turn my head to look up at him, ready to take this somewhere more private so I can get on with what I came here to do, one of his fellow Satan's steps up to us.

His eyes dart from mine to Python's before he speaks up, "Python, gotta problem."

Anger sparks in Python's eyes, and he grits out, "fine" before spearing me with a look. "Don't move. I'll be back."

Fuck.

I'd been planning on luring him up to the bedroom without any of his men getting a good look at me. Sure, they're probably drunk and high, but I can't take the risk that one of them will remember me in the morning. The last thing I need is these assholes searching all over town for me. I can't risk making my move tonight... which means I'll just have to come back.

With tonight's plan officially ruined and with zero desire to hang around so I can suck that shitstain's dick, I push my way through the crowd and out of the house, quickly ducking across the street and into the abandoned lot where I left my duffel bag earlier. Frustration courses through me as I hastily remove the wig and change back into my pants and leather jacket. Once I'm ready, I swing the bag onto my back and get the fuck out of there.

By the time I make it back to my apartment building, the sun is starting to rise, the faint gray light of dawn only drawing unwanted attention to the grubby state of my street and the run-down, filthy building I call home.

I'm exhausted, frustration giving way to tiredness, as I step into the dark entranceway, barely even noticing the flicker of the lightbulb or the smell of damp and mildew in the stairwell as I climb to the top floor. There are the typical, varying sounds of people getting up and starting their day as I pass by apartments, but I'm so used to the constant hum of life in the building that it's nothing more than background noise.

Reaching my apartment, my eyes feel gritty as I unlock and open the door, dropping my bag and kicking off my boots before I pad into the kitchen.

"Morning." I yawn as I greet Luc, who is sitting at the small two-person table, looking annoyingly fresh as he munches on his cereal.

"You look like shit."

I toss a glower at my asshat of a brother as I grab my own bowl and sit down opposite him, but there's zero heat behind it. "Yeah, well, so would you if you had the night I had," I grumble, helping myself to the box of cereal and filling my bowl. I top it off with some milk before digging my spoon in and turning to lean against the counter. I watch him over the lip of my bowl. We both have our mother's red hair—although his is slightly darker—and blue eyes—some sort of deep Irish heritage thing I think—but that's where the similarities stop. His nose is broader, his skin darker and cheeks more defined, and even though he's only fifteen, he's already a good head taller than me. "How's school?" I ask around a mouthful of food.

"It's good."

I roll my eyes. Getting information out of him recently is like drawing blood from a stone. I guess that's just part of living with a teenager. I should probably just be grateful he doesn't leave the toilet seat up and his dirty clothes scattered all over the living room, although I do make a point of not going into his bedroom, so god only knows what state that's in.

"How's work?" he counters with a knowing look.

"It's good," I snark, throwing his own words back at him. It's not like I'm about to tell him anything more than that, and he damn well knows it. I don't talk about the club with him, and I sure as shit don't include him in my extracurriculars.

He chuckles under his breath, but I notice his gaze lingers on me for a moment before he finishes off his bowl and gets to his feet. He sets it in the sink and then reaches down to grab his school bag. Slinging it onto his back, he pauses before leaving the kitchen, and turns to look at me.

"You know, if you need me to help out, I can."

I'm shaking my head before he's even finished speaking. "No," I insist, lifting my head to meet his eyes. "I have it covered. Let me worry about money, and you just focus on school, okay?"

"I'm fifteen," he says with a frown, as if being fifteen somehow means he should be pulling his weight. He might be taller than me now, but he's still just a kid. Life has forced him to grow up faster than he should have; I'm not about to rob him of any more of his childhood.

"Yeah, and until you're eighteen, your job is to go to school." His school is a joke. I'm fairly certain even some of his teachers never graduated high school, never mind obtaining teaching qualifications, but it's the principle of the matter.

I pin him with a *don't argue with me* look, to which he rolls his eyes. It's not the first time we've had this argument, and I'm sure it won't be the last.

"Okay," he agrees on a sigh. "I'm off. I'll see ya later."

"Have fun," I call out just before the door slams shut behind him.

Luc is the reason I've fought so hard for what we have. He was only five when we ended up on the streets, and trying to look after him while keeping us both safe was the hardest thing I've ever had to do. His young age granted us nights in shelters I wouldn't have gotten otherwise, but I had to do things I'm not proud of so that we could get by. I couldn't bear seeing him go hungry any longer or continuing to run around in clothes several sizes too small with shoes that needed the toes cut out just so they fit him. These were all the reasons and justifications I needed to get through every back alley blow job, pick-pocketing people, and stealing food.

So, when Enzo first approached me with the offer of money for information, of course , I jumped at the chance. I was still too young to get a job anywhere, forcing me to take any cash-in-hand jobs I could find—which are few and far between and usually of the unsavory kind. Money in exchange for information was a lot easier and less degrading than some of the other things I'd had to resort to doing. It made a big difference until I was able to get a job in a strip club—one of the few places where you can actually earn enough to get off the streets and create a semi-stable home for yourself.

I get up on that stage every night and shake my ass so Luc can have a roof over his head, food in his belly, clothes on his back. So he can have the things he needs for school and the comic books he loves. So his life can be a little bit more normal than mine ever was.

It's to ensure he has a better life than I have—a brighter future than I can ever hope for. That's why I get up every morning and do what I do. It's why I don't piss off the Satan's or try to find a lesser-paying job that would let me keep my clothes on. Wanting him to live in a better world than the one we currently exist in is why I don't think twice when I'm draining the life out of some scumbag and pawning off their things. Luc is the reason for my existence, for every decision I make on a daily basis. He's the only thing in this world that matters to me. I'd die for him. I'd kill for him.

Finishing off the last of my cereal, I dump my bowl in the sink with Luc's before going for a shower. It's Friday, and I have just enough time to squeeze in a few hours of sleep before needing to be at work. I'm on the day shift today, which means I have tonight off. The Satan's go to Toxic on Friday nights, and while I'm not sure if I can approach Python there, I'm going to stalk him everywhere until the perfect window of opportunity presents itself again. I can't let him slip through my fingers next time, and if tonight isn't the night, then it's only a matter of another day or two until I get my opening. From what I can tell, the Satan's throw parties most nights. No matter what, Python will be nothing more than a decaying corpse by the end of the weekend.

I SPEND THE AFTERNOON TRYING OUT A FEW NEW DANCE ROUTINES IN between serving customers. The day shifts are entirely different from the evening ones. Strip Tease is much quieter and the patrons more subdued, allowing us to practice new dance moves and show any new girls the ropes.

Once my shift is over, I change in the dressing room into a short red skirt, my thigh-high leather, heeled boots, and a black crop top, ready to hit Toxic and hopefully kill an abusive shithead. There's no better way to spend a Friday night, am I right?

Toxic is a large club housed in one of the warehouses down by the old, deserted docks. It's a popular spot on the weekends. Regardless of how broke the citizens of Black Creek are, they can usually still scrounge enough pennies together to get drunk on the weekend and pretend their problems don't exist for a little while.

The heavy bass of the music vibrates through the street as I step up to the door, paying the entrance fee before I pass by the bouncers and into the club. Multi-colored strobe lights illuminate the dimly lit, ample, open space, and I notice that there is already quite a crowd on the dance floor, and the bar is packed. I do a loop of the room, spotting the Satan's in the cordoned-off VIP section before moving to the bar and ordering a shot of tequila.

Downing it, I blend seamlessly into the crowd as I move onto the dance floor, swaying my hips and shaking my shoulders in time to the music until I find the perfect spot where I can hide among the other dancers while also keeping an eye on the Satan's, and more importantly, Python. The man himself is lounging in the middle of his crew of idiots, looking like the king of his kingdom as he surveys the room.

I watch for a while as he and his buddies do lines of cocaine, harass waitresses, and drink their weight in hard liquor. In the crowded venue, I notice Python is never left alone. At least one of his little followers is always with him, and he never comes out from behind the separated VIP area, meaning it's going to be next to impossible for me to get to him tonight.

I'm not one to easily give up, though, and I continue my pretense of dancing as the night wears on. As the hours pass by, the club only gets busier, and eventually, I have to accept that I won't get to relish in spilling Python's blood tonight. My thumbs stroke longingly over the hilt of the short blades hidden in the lip of my thigh-high boots. *Soon,* I promise them.

With a final glance in Python's direction, I sigh and turn away. There's no point continuing to stand here and watch him berate women and snort cocaine all night. Frustrated, I move over to the bar, figuring I may as well let my hair down and have a couple of drinks while I'm here. It is a Friday night, after all. If I'm not working, I may as well enjoy my night off. And nothing says *let's have fun* like another shot of tequila.

five

After being gone for over three years, it's weird being back here. Everything's the same, yet entirely different. How can a place change so much? Or maybe it's me that's changed? The last time I was here, I was a member of The Feral Beasts, the most feared and ruthless gang that ran the streets. After I left and everything went sideways, I started seeing myself in a new light. Being away from Black Creek gave me some much-needed perspective. It enabled me to re-evaluate the man I want to be and gain some further clarity for what I want out of life.

I was barely sixteen when I joined The Feral Beasts. Nothing but an angry, confused, lost kid who thought joining a group of violent thugs would provide me with the structure and aggressive outlet that I needed. And it did... initially, but over time, I came to see it for what it was—a bunch of lowlifes who cared about nothing but them-selves. There was no line they wouldn't cross, and as they became more and more barbaric, I knew I had to get out. So when I saw my chance, I took it... even if it did result in me ending up locked up for two years. I haven't once regretted it.

I'd never planned on coming back to Black Creek. After the shit that went down in Crescentwood, I was done with gang life. Prison also gave me plenty of time to figure out what I wanted, and you know what I came up with? Nothing. Not a single damn thing. The truth is, I have no fucking clue what I want in this world. I just know I want to be a part of something bigger than myself. The anger and vengeance that was coursing through my veins the day I patched into the Beasts are still there, sitting like a lead weight on my chest, dragging me down. So when I got Cain's letter informing me of his plan for revenge, I knew I had to be involved. It's what I'd been trying—and failing miserably—to do when I joined the Beasts. However, this time, I'm not a sad, lost, lonely sixteen-year-old boy. This war is as much mine as it is Cain's, and I can feel it in my gut that this is what I'm supposed to do—even if it kills me. For Cain and Evie, but also for myself. I need closure. I need to come to terms with what happened that day and finally put it behind me so I can move on with my life.

I've been back in Black Creek for a month now, and it's amazing how quickly I've fallen into the swing of things. Most of Cain's crew is relatively new. He gave me the whole rundown when I first arrived, and I was shocked to hear how he'd ended up recruiting some of them. Rescuing them from a facility that trains children to be killers? It sounded like insanity to me, yet you only have to watch some of the kids he's taken in —some of whom are barely eighteen—in the ring. They're lethal machines, able to obliterate their opponent within seconds.

Cain dubbed me his second in command when I returned, and I've been kept busy ensuring we have a firm control over the parts of downtown Black Creek that are ours, sorting out the new premises we recently moved into and starting up a fighting pit in the shell of an empty swimming pool in a long-abandoned gym across the road from us. It's been a huge success, with plenty of men—and even some women—coming to compete. Not to mention the outlet it has provided for the kids Cain rescued. They've quickly gained a name for themselves as being unbeatable in the ring, and people come from all over the city, and further afield, to fight against them, thinking they can win the title of victor—and the nice sum of cash we offer the winner. In fact, it has become such a popular attraction that we're now looking to expand and set up another one, ideally in larger premises where we could fit in a bigger crowd—which is why I'm here tonight.

Glancing around the large warehouse, I can't help but think how perfect this place would be. The vast open space lends itself nicely to what we have in mind, and there is more than enough space for a fighting ring, plus a large audience and even a bar. The fact that it's outside territory we already own is just an added bonus. We're not necessarily looking to take control of all of the downtown area. Still, it will undoubtedly make us appear as more formidable of an opponent if we occupy a majority of the city. Besides, we're playing the long game with the Antonellis, so we may as well keep ourselves busy by taking control of what we can of Black Creek until we're in a position to go after our real targets.

I'd been scouting out possible venues when I first came across this club. Looking at it from the outside, I had a gut feeling it would be perfect for our needs, but I needed to suss out the current gang in charge of this part of town before we could even make any moves to claim the land and the club for ourselves. So I've spent the last two days stalking them and finding out what I could. Once I'd confirmed they could easily be removed, I headed here, wanting to get the lay of the land inside the building before taking my proposition to Cain.

I lift my gaze to the large mirror hanging on the wall along the back of the bar. It gives me a perfect view of the VIP section on the far side of the room, where the current controllers of this part of the city reside, lording it up as they get trashed and put on a pornographic show for the rest of the club. The Satan's Advocates are a relatively minor, disorganized street gang who own a sliver of land by the old docks—where this warehouse is located. The ports have been out of service for years now, ever since the Antonellis took charge of the Tideside Docks on the opposite side of the river and declared that all goods coming into the city had to go through them.

I don't know much about the Satan's, but watching them the last couple of days has me confident that they pose no threat to the Rejects. Our guys will easily destroy them. A thrill of excitement rushes through me at the thought of confronting a rival gang and taking another step toward achieving our ultimate goal.

The bartender sets a glass of whiskey in front of me, the clunk of the glass against the wood drawing me out of my thoughts as he moves on down the bar. Lifting the drink to my lips, I take a sip, grimacing at the taste. Damn, you'd think more than two years of no alcohol would mean I'm not picky about what I drink, but this cheap swill tastes like shit in comparison to the fancy stuff floating around Crescentwood.

I down half the glass because, regardless of how crappy it tastes, it's still alcohol, and it's exactly what I need tonight. Observing the Satan's yesterday and today, and seeing the dilapidated state of their territory has not been fun. Just from what little I've noticed, I can tell that they are the typical, power-deluded, small-dicked assholes who try to claim every other street corner in Black Creek. They use their guns and a *because I can* attitude to terrorize the people here, forcing them to do whatever they want.

From what I can tell, they have every business in this part of town paying them a protection tithe—a pretty common thing in any part of the city—nevertheless what these people really need is protection from the Satan's. Only yesterday, I watched as one of them shot up a butcher's shop before dragging the owner's daughter out of there. I followed him back to their clubhouse—which had been just several run-down houses on a derelict street—where he proceeded to shove alcohol and drugs down her throat before fucking her and moving on to the next thing that caught his eye. I made sure I got the girl home in one piece, but I nearly blew my cover just to go in and rescue her. That shit is not fucking okay. I wanted to slaughter every single one of those assholes there and then. But we need to do this the right way, with the full force of the club, so we can make a statement to anyone who might think to rise up against us and properly claim Satan's Advocates territory as our own.

With my drink in hand, I turn in my stool to peruse the room. For the most part, the club is full of regular everyday men and women who are just trying to have a bit of fun on the weekend. A loud roar of laughter draws my attention to the VIP area, where several booths are overflowing with raucous Satan's members. I've been casually keeping an eye on them since they walked in. From what I can tell, their lewd behavior is just more of the same as it was last night. Drugs and girls, just in a different location.

I noticed the change in the atmosphere, though, as soon as they walked in. Tension bled into the air, and most people have been keeping a safe distance from them ever since; never getting too close and frequently casting fearful glimpses out of the corner of their eyes. Not that I can blame them. The second they arrived, they picked out several scantily clad women and all but dragged them to their table, demanding they dance and put on a show for them.

I don't let my gaze linger on the group for too long, not looking to draw any unwanted attention. Nor do I have any desire to watch the show they are forcing the girls to put on. Downing my drink, I turn back to the bar, lifting the glass when I catch the bartender's eye in a silent gesture for a second one. A few moments later, another glass of cheap whiskey is set in front of me. With a nod of thanks, I slap a few dollar bills onto the counter and take a sip, letting the whiskey warm me up from the inside as I turn to face the room again. I'm not expecting to find anything different, however I do need to remain vigilant in case the Satan's start something. Besides, if growing up in Black Creek didn't teach me not to turn my back on a room full of strangers, then prison definitely did.

I'm doing a casual once-over of the club when I catch my first glimpse of her through the crowd. The strobe lights reflect off her auburn hair as she moves to the beat of the music. The way her hair catches in the glow has me mesmerized, the shiny strands a beautiful deep copper color as they sway with her movements.

From where I'm sitting, she has her back to me, so I can't get a look at her face, and with the dense crowd separating us, I can't see anything south of her shoulders. The unique shade of her hair is the only thing I can make out.

A shoulder bumps against mine as someone jostles into me at the crowded bar, and I glance away from the captivating redhead to scowl at them, giving them my long-perfected death glare. With a terrified expression, they mutter a quick apology before scurrying away, but it's too late. By the time I look back to the dance floor, she's gone.

Frowning, I knock back the last of my whiskey. I'm about to get up and leave—figuring I'm not going to learn anything I don't already know about the Satan's tonight—when the redhead herself slides up to the bar beside me. She is leaning her arms on the wooden countertop, thus her ass juts out in that way girls do that draws every eye immediately to her tight, round globes.

She's attempting to wave down the bartender on the far side of the bar, so I take advantage of her distraction to properly take her in. She's got on a tight black crop top that shows off her toned torso, and I catch a peek of a vine tattoo patterned with budding flowers peeking out from beneath her sleeve as it wraps around her upper arm. She's skinny, just like everyone in Black Creek, yet she's been blessed—or cursed, maybe—with voluptuous curves and a huge rack.

A short, red, leather skirt just about covers her ass, giving every red-blooded male in the house a hard-on. She's paired the ensemble with thigh-high black boots; the whole outfit making her look like my wildest fucking dreams. Believe me, two years in prison has given me plenty of time to fantasize about the perfect fucking woman and here she is, standing in front of me like God's hand-delivered her himself.

"A shot of tequila," she shouts at the bartender, having finally gained his attention. Not that it was much of a hardship with her tits sticking out like that. The guy behind the bar barely glances at her face, his eyes glued to her chest before he tears them away to fill her order.

"Make it two," I call out, throwing a few bills down on the countertop.

The woman turns to stare at me with a wary look as the bartender grabs a bottle of tequila and two shot glasses. She continues to scrutinize me as he sets the two glasses on the bar and fills them to the brim with the colorless liquid before lifting the dollar bills and moving off to serve someone else.

I'm barely paying him any attention, though, unable to tear my gaze away from the alluring woman standing beside me. Her eyes drop to my boots and slowly rise as she takes in my dark, worn jeans and black shirt. She takes her time investigating the tattoo sleeve on my right arm, although I doubt she can make out any of the finer details in the dark light of the club. I had most of it done while on the inside. Initially, it was just to cover up the Beast insignia that I couldn't stand to look at any longer, but it turned into a full arm and chest piece. There's not exactly a lot to do in prison, and getting various tattoos was a better use of my time than a lot else I could have been up to.

When she reaches my muscular biceps, she lingers there for a second before letting her gaze drift over my lean, toned chest that's easily visible through my form-fitting top. Finally, her eyes lift to my face, taking in the shadow of stubble dusting my jaw, the high rise of my cheekbones, and my messy, brown hair before her eyes connect with my pale-blue ones once again. Lust burns in her eyes and a flirtatious smile lifts her lips. Done checking me out—and clearly happy with what she sees—she grabs the two shot glasses off the bar, handing one to me.

"Cheers," she says, clinking her glass against mine before bringing it to her full, pouty lips, tilting her head back as she downs it in one.

Mimicking her, I throw back my own shot, hissing as the bitter substance burns its way down my throat. When I make eye contact with the redhead again, she's watching me closely as she licks a stray droplet of tequila from her lower lip. That simple movement draws my attention to her lips and sends a zing of need to my balls, the likes of which I haven't felt in far too fucking long.

When the bartender passes, making his way along the bar, I lift two fingers in the air, indicating another round.

"Are you trying to get me drunk?" she laughs, a warm, infectious sound that, even over the noise of the music, resonates with me. "Because you should know, I have a very high tolerance."

I don't know anyone in Black Creek who doesn't, but my lips quirk up at her joke, the muscles feeling stiff after the last few years of disuse. The bartender moves over to fill our shot glasses, and I hand him a few more bills as I watch the captivating goddess beside me. She tilts her head back when the glass touches her lips, extending the long column of her throat, which bobs as the liquid slides down it.

She turns back to look at me once more as she sets the empty glass on the bar. In the dark light of the club, it's impossible to make out the color of her eyes, but there's a slight glaze to them from the alcohol coursing through her system. Her tongue flicks out to run along her plump lower lip before her teeth sink into the flesh. *God, if that isn't the hottest fucking thing I've seen in forever.*

"I'm O—" I begin, but she presses her finger against my parted lips, cutting off my introduction.

"No names." She smirks coyly, and mischief brims in her eyes.

When she lifts her finger off my lips, I lean in, matching her lustful expression with a lascivious one of my own.

"If you don't know my name, what are you going to call out when I'm making you come?"

Her breath hitches at my dirty words, her teeth sinking into her bottom lip again, making me wish I was the one biting into the soft flesh.

"If that's where this night ends up, I'm sure I'll think of something," she purrs, her eyes half-lidded with desire.

I push to my feet, a move that has me looking down on her, and presses my body flush against her lithe frame. Grabbing hold of her hand, I pull her along behind me into the sea of bodies writhing against each other on the dance floor. Placing a large palm around her hip, I tug her in against me as she drapes her arms over my shoulders, swaying her hips in time to the music. We lose ourselves in the rhythm, every passing song and tease of her pelvis against my painfully hard erection only endeavors to skyrocket the tension crackling in the air between us. I don't know what it is about her, but I'm entranced by the sheen of her hair in the light, the teasing sparkle in her eye, and the flirtatious curl of her lip. It's possible I've just gone too long jerking myself off and maybe Cain's right by saying I need to get laid. In spite of that, there hasn't been a woman who has held my attention since I was released. At least, no woman until her.

She spins in my hold, pressing the curve of her ass against my cock. There's no way she doesn't feel how badly I want her. My arms wrap around her slim waist, my palms flat against her toned stomach as she grinds into me. I catch the dirty smirk on her face. She knows damn well what she's doing to me, the fucking tease. Dipping my head, I plant a kiss in the crook of her neck, and she tilts her head, granting me better access as I suck and nibble my way up to her ear.

"Two can play that game," I whisper into her ear before I trail my fingers up the inside of her thigh, slip under her short skirt and teasingly skim them over the front of her panties.

A soft gasp escapes between her parted lips, inaudible to anyone other than me over the sound of the music, not that she seems to care. Fuck, if the dirty noise doesn't have me grinding harder against her ass.

Slipping my fingers under the scrap of fabric covering her cunt, I find her already dripping wet as I circle her clit. Her head falls back against my shoulder, eyes drifting shut under my ministrations. I watch mesmerized as her lips part, her mouth dropping open as she gets closer to orgasm. A blush slowly works its way up her heaving chest as I slide my fingers lower and slowly push two inside her, eliciting a groan. She feels so fucking good spasming around my fingers. I can only imagine how fucking incredible she would feel wrapped around my dick, her wet heat sucking me deeper.

Her hand comes around behind her, slipping between us until she's rubbing it over the more than obvious imprint of my dick in my jeans. Applying just the right amount of pressure, she squeezes me through the thick fabric before dipping lower and cupping my balls.

I growl in her ear, pressing my thumb over her sensitive nub, rubbing tight circles until I feel her inner walls clenching.

"Fuck," she cries as she comes all over my fingers.

I don't give her time to recover before I pull out and spin her around. Placing my hand on her hip to steady her, I slide the other one into her hair, wrapping around the silky soft strands and tugging her face toward me. My lips slam down on hers, desperate to fucking taste her.

She opens up beneath me, her soft lips gliding over mine with our tongues dueling in a heated battle for dominance. She tastes like cherries and tequila. Total and utter temptation.

Her hands come up, fisting the front of my shirt and pulling me flush against her as I slide my hand round to her back, slowly moving it down until I'm cupping her ass, grinding my dick against her pelvis.

She breaks the kiss, taking a step back. As my hand falls from her body, she grabs it, searing me with a heated gaze before she spins around and tugs me behind her as she moves toward the back of the club. I have no idea where she's taking me, and I really don't care. All the blood has left my brain. It's been over three fucking years since I've gotten laid. Who can blame a guy for being led by his dick after that long? Since the second she sidled up beside me at the bar, my cock has one hundred percent been in control. It's driving every action, every word, and hell, it's about to get so fucking lucky.

She pulls me down a corridor, past the bathrooms, until she's pushing open a fire exit door, and we tumble out into a dark alley behind the club. The fresh air is a welcome relief from the stuffiness inside, but it does nothing to ease the heat thrumming through my veins especially when she spins around and pushes me against the wall beside the door.

With deft fingers she unbuttons my jeans, and pulls out my throbbing dick, wrapping her hand around it and gently squeezing before she grazes the pad of her thumb over the bead of pre-cum, smearing it as she pumps her hand up and down my shaft.

Without a second thought or any hesitation, she drops to her knees and licks her lips before wrapping them around me. *Hooooly fuckkkk.* I have to fight the urge to come too soon as she sucks me in deeper, the wet heat of her mouth feels like fucking heaven.

She looks up at me through hooded eyes as I entangle my fingers in her hair. The desire I see in her eyes has me thrusting into her, forcing her to take me further. She's not just doing this because she thinks she should; she's doing it because she fucking wants to. She's getting off on having me in her mouth as much as I am.

Her tongue is pressed flat against the underside of my shaft, and her cheeks are hollowed as she bottoms out, taking all of me. I can feel the tip of my dick hitting the back of her throat before she pulls back.

I try not to thrust and let her take control, but it doesn't last very long. Suddenly I'm fucking her mouth, her fingers digging into my thigh as she holds on for dear life. Her eyes never waver from mine, and I alternate between being captivated as I watch my dick disappear between her supple red lips and falling into the carnal need I can see burning in her glistening eyes.

Feeling the familiar tingling in my balls, I pull out and haul her off the ground. She's light in my arms as I spin around and pin her against the wall, my hand reaching between her thighs and tearing off her panties.

"As fucking amazing as that was, I believe I have a promise to keep," I growl.

She wraps her legs around me as I dig a condom out of my back pocket and sheath myself in record time before I line up at her entrance. I slam all the way into her as she cries out, crashing her lips onto mine.

Jesus fuck, she's the hottest thing I've ever felt. Did pussies always feel this good, and it's just been so long I've forgotten or is it all her? Maybe she's got a magical pussy. That or she's a venus flytrap, luring me in with her hot mouth only to kill me. Hell, I don't even think I'd care. What an awesome way to go out—with the most explosive orgasm of my life.

"Fuck," I groan, beginning to move.

I thrust into her, her hips lifting to meet mine as she continues to pillage my mouth. As she gets closer to the edge, she breaks off our kiss, her head dropping back to lean against the brick wall behind her. Licking down her throat, I bury my nose in the crook of her neck. I can already feel the familiar prickle at the base of my spine as she clenches tightly around me, her own orgasm nearing.

"Oh, fuck, yes," she cries out as her pussy spasms around me, practically sucking the cum out of me as I grunt into her neck, my hot seed hitting the latex condom.

There's no way sex has always been this good. No one could fucking forget this feeling of euphoria. *This* moment right here is the one that will flash before my eyes when I die, reminding me of how fucking incredible my life was.

"Okay, I believe you now," she pants, making me chuckle.

She unwraps her legs from my hips, dropping them to the ground, and I pull back, ignoring the silent cry from my dick as I withdraw from her comforting warmth.

Removing the condom, I chuck it in a dumpster and tuck myself away. "Wanna go back in and grab a drink?" I ask.

She glances up at me as she shimmies her skirt back down over her hips, shaking her head. "I'm done for tonight. I have an early start tomorrow."

"Well, can I at least get your number?"

She smirks but shakes her head again—an action I'm beginning to think she does quite often. "Sorry. I can't afford distractions right now, and you"—she rakes her eyes over me one final time—"would definitely be a distraction."

I open my mouth to respond just as the fire exit door bangs open, snapping my attention toward it as a rowdy crowd of clearly inebriated customers pile out. I swear I only take my eyes off her for a second, yet when I look back down the alley, the red-haired vixen is gone.

For a moment, I simply stand there, debating whether or not to go after her, but her words about being a distraction ultimately stop me. She was right about that. With all the plans Cain has, he's going to end up razing the city, and I can't let anyone alter my focus if we're about to rain down hell.

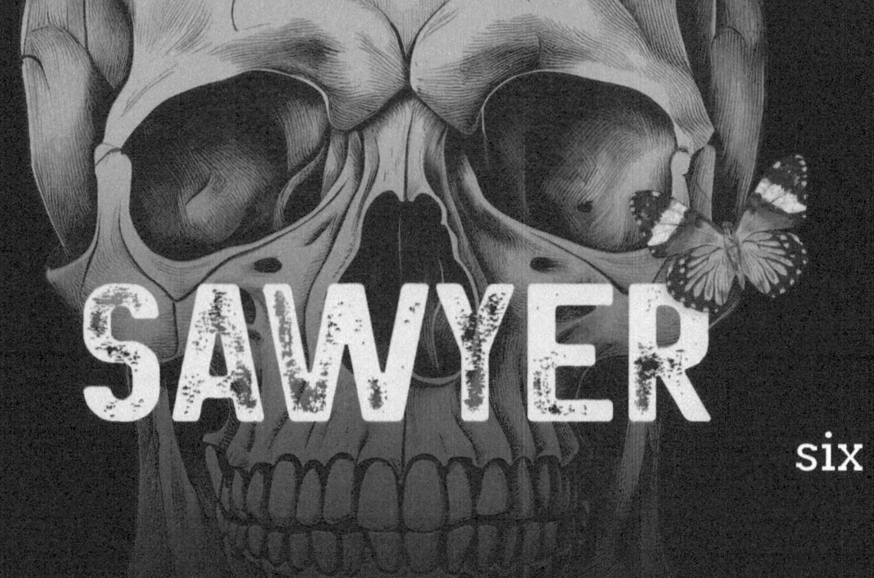

SAWYER

six

Memories of last night still occupy my mind as I pull open the door to the women's shelter the next day. I hid in the alley and watched when the mysterious hottie from the bar discovered I'd disappeared. I saw the flicker of indecision in his light blue eyes, but it only lasted a second before a determined resolve replaced it, and he went back into the club. The wave of disappointment that washed over me was even more justification that I needed to stay away from him.

I'll admit, he definitely was not what I was expecting when I went out last night. He might not have been the blood and the sense of righteous justice I'd been hoping for, but he was certainly intriguing. The way his close proximity heated me up, it was like nothing I've ever felt before. Just looking at him, with his toned torso and muscular biceps had my panties damp, and I was practically coming as soon as he touched me. And holy hell in a handbasket, the sex was off the charts.

My job makes me cynical when it comes to men and sex, but I feel it's pretty accurate to say that most men are only concerned with getting themselves off. You rarely find someone who gives jack shit about a woman's pleasure. So, the fact that he not only thought about it but delivered in an exceptional way... well, that's a rare find.

He had the same hard edges as resident Black Creekians do, yet something was different about him. Not in a suspicious way like Enzo. Just... different. But like I told him, I can't afford distractions right now. Besides, he's probably tied up with one gang or another, and there's no way I'm getting involved in that shit. I know enough to know going out with a gang member is just asking for trouble. The gang will always come first to people like that. I've made many concessions in my life, but I refuse to settle for being an afterthought. I'd rather live the rest of my life single, even if it does mean I'll most likely die alone with twenty cats.

With a smile and a nod to the woman at the check-in desk, I head toward Sheryl's room, wanting to give her an update. I'm sure she's been a nervous wreck. She should have gone back to Python days ago, and I know the longer she's gone, the worse it will be for her if she does go back. Not that she is, but I can understand that the severity of her consequences for staying away for so long will be weighing heavy on her mind. She won't be able to settle herself until she knows he's dead and buried.

She pounces on me the second I step into the room. "Is it done?" Her eyes are wide with panic, and she somehow looks even paler than she did the last time I saw her.

"Not yet."

Running her hands through her hair in frustration, she chews on her bottom lip. "Maybe this isn't such a good idea. I was upset the other night. I-it wasn't that bad. I probably over-exaggerated it."

I plant my hands on her shoulders, waiting until her panicked stare meets my steady gaze. "He hurt Grace," I say the words slowly, reinforcing them in her mind. "He'll keep hurting her unless *you* do something about it." I pierce her with an intent look. "I promised I'd get rid of him, and I will. Just stay here, out of sight, for a few more days."

Tears well in her eyes, but she nods her head. I stay for a bit longer, checking on how she and Grace are both doing before I leave. It's clear she's not really in the mood to talk, and I've got things to be getting on with anyway. I have to work tonight, but tomorrow, Python is all mine, and this time I'm not going to let him slither through my fingers.

By the time I leave Sheryl, it's late afternoon, and as I walk into the apartment, I find Luc sprawled across the sofa, looking bored out of his mind as he stares abjectly at the TV.

"What's wrong?" I ask, frowning.

He sighs, barely sparing me a glance as he mutters, "Nothing."

Oh, well, okay then.

Just about managing to hold back the roll of my eyes, I state, "It's clearly something. Just tell me."

His lips thin as he finally shifts his attention to me. "I'm so fucking bored."

"So do something else," I reason, quickly losing patience now that I know there's nothing really wrong with him beyond usual teenage grumpiness.

"Like what?" he argues. "There's nothing else I can do."

"I don't know," I grumble. "Read one of your comic books." His face scrunches up, not liking that suggestion. "Or play a game on your phone." That idea earns me another unimpressed glare. "I don't know, Luc." I sigh. "Is there anyone from school you can hang out with?"

He just glowers at me in response. "You know there isn't."

I let out a heavy exhale as guilt swarms through me. He's slowly lost all of his childhood friends over the last couple of years, as they've become embroiled in gang business. They always tried to rope Luc in too, but when he wouldn't budge, they just dropped him. I know it can't be easy for him to resist that level of peer pressure and slowly lose the people you thought were your friends. I'm beyond proud of him for standing up for himself and refusing to be so easily led astray, but the guilt weighs heavy on my soul. It's because of me that he's got no one to hang out with and that he's stuck mainly inside this tiny apartment when he's not at school. Honestly, it would be enough to drive anyone crazy.

I remind myself that I'm just trying to keep him alive, and that assuages some of the guilt I'm carrying, but it doesn't loosen the knot in my stomach when I look into his incensed, stormy-blue eyes.

"Well, why don't we play a board game?" I offer. I have several hours to kill before I need to leave anyway.

The anger in his eyes softens a little, but he still looks pretty pissed off as he reluctantly agrees, and I go to fetch something from our measly collection. We found them in the storage cupboard when we first moved in, and over the years, we must have played them hundreds of times. There isn't much else to do around here. Besides, it's always just been Luc and me—the two of us against the world—and until his teenage hormones kicked in, we liked it that way.

After humming over our choices, I grab the Scrabble box and move to sit on the floor. Luc joins me a moment later, and for half an hour, all is right in the world again as we laugh and tease and make fun of one another, arguing over possible made-up words just like old times.

"Thrubble is not a real word," I argue while laughing.

"It so is."

"Use it in a sentence then," I challenge.

His lips purse as he thinks it over for a second, and I just shake my head.

"Oh, I'm going to go thrub—"

The squeal of tires against asphalt on the street below cuts him off, and I stiffen as I look toward the window, suddenly on alert. Car doors bang as I quickly climb to my feet and move to peer out the window.

My mouth goes dry as I find two cars parked across the middle of the road outside my building. I count ten burly men with weapons surrounding them as their eyes roam over the building, but what terrifies me is the man standing at the front of the group. With his snake tattoo prominently on display, he'd be recognizable anywhere.

"Go to your room," I bark to Luc as I spin around.

"What? Why? What's going on?" He asks, a slight tremor to his voice.

"Just go," I snap as I hurriedly stuff the board game under the sofa. "Hide somewhere and stay quiet." He hesitates a second longer before getting to his feet and moving toward his room. Just before he crosses the doorway, though, I grab his upper arm and pierce him with an intent look. "No matter what happens, or what you hear, do *not* come out. Got it?"

His lips part on a gasp as he stares into my eyes. I can see the protest on his lips, but thankfully, he must see how fucking serious I am right now, and he just nods his head in agreement before I gently nudge him into his room.

I stand and watch as the door closes behind him, my heart hammering in tune to the sound of footsteps as the men hurry up the stairwell. Forcing myself to focus, I scan the room for any other signs that someone other than me lives here, letting out a small sigh of relief when I don't spot any of Luc's stuff sitting out.

If it's possible, my body coils even tighter when I hear the sounds of the first men reaching my floor. *Fuck, they really are here for me.* I'd been hoping it was just a coincidence, but as I hear the thundering footfalls in the hall, the chances of this being a coincidence get slimmer and slimmer.

The boom, boom, boom of a heavy fist knocking against a door makes me jump, and it takes far longer than it should for me to realize it's not actually my door but my neighbor's. The noise is followed by the sound of the door being kicked in and people yelling before several gunshots go off. The whole time, I just stare at my kitchen wall—

the one that's adjoined to my neighbors—envisioning in my mind's eye what is likely playing out next door and feeling so goddamn thankful that it's not me they're here for. With Sheryl having been gone for so long, it was a distinct possibility. Although, I'm not even sure if Python knows who her friends are or that she even has any.

I'm not sure how long I stand there, listening to the indistinguishable sounds coming through the thin wall. Time loses all sense of meaning. It could be mere seconds or half an hour later before I hear the sounds of retreating footsteps thumping their way down the stairs, followed by the rumble of an engine starting and car doors slamming.

It's only when a deathly quiet falls, so heavy that for all I know, I've gone deaf that I finally react to the close call. My legs tremble, my whole body shaking as I sag to the floor in relief. I'm very aware that my neighbors are most likely lying dead next door, however all I can think of is *thank fuck it wasn't me.*

EVENTUALLY, THE SHAKING STOPPED, AND THE FEAR AND RELIEF GAVE WAY to anger. Waves and waves of red-hot, molten fury. Outrage that we should have to live in such fear; at the knowledge, we aren't even safe inside our own homes. I don't know what my neighbors did to piss off the Satan's, and I don't care. It might not have been me they came for this time, but it could be next time, which scares me. The entire ordeal only incentivizes me to kill Python. Honestly, I want to destroy his whole fucking crew, but I'm just one person. There's no way I could take on an entire gang of criminals. For now, I just need to worry about the head of the snake.

My anger warms me for the whole night, getting me through my shift in the club and all of the next day as I plot and plan, and the next night, I watch from the shadows as a party rages—I swear it's all they fucking do—within the thin timber-frame walls of the Python's house. I can hear the music pounding and feel it vibrating through the asphalt all the way across the street, where I'm once again hidden while I watch tattoo-covered men dressed in leather and half-naked women filter in and out of the party.

I've got Raven hidden in the shrubs at the far end of the street for a quick getaway. With my thigh-high leather boots, black booty shorts, and matching crop top, not to mention the same honey-blonde wig as last time, covering my distinctive copper locks, I look more than ready to get down and dirty with the Satan's—which is exactly what I want them to think I'm here to do.

Running my thumb along the lip of my boots, I let vengeance heat the blood in my veins as I finger the hilts of the two small daggers I have securely tucked inside. I can practically taste the sweet aroma that comes from purging the world of yet another scumbag. It's a distinctive flavor—a mixture of sweet and spicy. It's heady and intoxicating, and it gives me a head rush like nothing else.

With adrenaline giving me a natural high, I stride confidently across the street and into the house. I head straight for the kitchen and search through the various bottles of spirits on the counter until I find a sealed bottle of whiskey. Unscrewing the cap, I bring it to my lips and down a decent portion of it before making my way into the living room. Anticipating that Python will be lounging in the same spot as last time, I push my way through the dense crowd of wasted dancers until I spy him amongst his crew, at the back of the room, exactly where I knew he would be. They appear casual, at ease, but I see the way Python warily eyes up the various people in the room, determining if they are a threat—or could be of use to him—before moving on.

I stop when I'm just off-center of his line of sight, far enough away that I don't look suspicious, but close enough to gain Python's attention when I start swaying my hips and openly drinking from the bottle. I lose myself in the music, the lyrics of *Gasoline* by Seether washing over me as I hold the whiskey bottle loosely between my fingers and alluringly trail my fingers across the bare skin of my abdomen, skimming the top of my booty shorts. I teasingly dip my fingers beneath the waistband and let my head fall back, my eyelids dropping to half-mast. Through my eyelashes, I peek at Python. His eyes observe my every movement with a carnal desire, and the corner of his lips quirk up in a sleazy grin that says everything about the dirty thoughts running through his head.

I don't have to put on a show for long before he says something to the men surrounding him and gets to his feet, stalking toward me. Everything about him screams predator. He thinks he's the most threatening person in the room. Little does he know he's caught in my trap, and he won't escape alive.

The song switches to *Figured You Out* by Nickelback as his hand comes to rest low on my hip, giving it a possessive squeeze as he pulls me in.

"You disappeared on me." There's a threatening weight to his tone, and I know if I don't play this right, he'll lose the thin thread of control he has over his temper.

I don the personality I use to work at the club and smile coyly at him, ensuring none of the hatred I feel for him is visible on my face. "I came back, though." I peer up at him with innocent, sultry eyes and allow my fingers to brush over his chest, making it clear that I came back *for him*. This is true, just not in the way he thinks.

He assesses me for a long moment before choosing to let go of his anger, a sordid grin curling around the edges of his lips. "Hmm, well, I'm sure you can find a way to make it up to me." There's a dangerous edge to his voice, one that says I have no choice in the matter. It makes my spine straighten, even though I know tonight will never get that far.

Forcing a submissive, innocent look to my face, I look up at him through my eyelashes as I bring the bottle of whiskey to my lips again, taking another deep swallow before I run my tongue along my lower lip, catching a stray droplet. He tracks the movement with dilated pupils before he smirks. His expression is a slimy thing that I'm sure he thinks has women buckling at the knees but only makes me suppress a shiver of disgust as he wraps his meaty hand around the bottle and tugs it out of my grip, not even bothering to ask if he can have some first. But then men like him don't ask for things. They just take them.

Tilting his head back, his eyes stay focused on me as he chugs a quarter of the bottle, finishing it off before he shoves it into the arms of some random person as they pass by. His free hand claims my other hip, and I bring my hands up to rest on his shoulders, scraping my fingers teasingly over the bare skin of his upper arms. He grinds against me as song blurs into song, and I fantasize about chopping his fucking hands off with every squeeze of my ass and lick of my neck. I picture my skin washed red with his blood, the feel of his heart against my palm as it stutters to a stop, and by the time he tries to push me to my knees, expecting me to happily suck him off in the middle of his goddamn living room, I'm so fucking ready to get this over with.

"On your knees," he growls in my ear, his words a clear demand.

When I resist, his fingers dig painfully into my shoulders, but I grit my teeth, pushing past the urge to dick punch him. Instead, I laugh, a noise that's the perfect balance of drunk and seductive. "Baby, what I have planned for you is more than a quick face fuck." I slip my fingers underneath his shirt, digging my nails into his skin before dragging them down over his slight potbelly. I bite into my plump lower lip as I look up at him through my eyelashes. "It's going to take all fucking night."

His eyes are glazed over with alcohol and laced with desire as he snatches my hand and starts dragging me across the room and up the stairs. I can hear the sound of people fucking coming from behind some of the doorways while others are fucking right out in the open. Still, I pay them no attention as he pulls a key out of his pocket and unlocks the last door at the end of the corridor, flicking on the light as he ushers me in.

He purposefully locks it behind him and tucks the key back into his jeans pocket, and I watch every move with narrowed eyes. When he turns to face me, I let him lead me to the bed, pushing me down onto the mattress. His hands grope me everywhere, leaving fingerprint bruises on my tits and ass, while I let out obscene-sounding moans that any idiot could tell are obviously fake. He's too concerned about his own pleasure to give a shit, though.

He rolls onto his back and cocks a brow at me as his hand moves to undo his leather belt, letting it hang loosely as he pops the button of his jeans and pulls himself out. He strokes his less than impressive length while I resist rolling my eyes as I gasp. "Oh my."

He laughs maliciously. "Come on. Show me what a whore you are."

I move to straddle his thighs, wrapping my fingers around him and working him up until his head falls back against the pillow and his eyes drift shut. I'm already touching him more than I ever wanted to, but as I slide the thin blade out of my boot and aim it at his dick, I can feel my own excitement coating my panties.

I nick the loose skin of his ballsack, and he jolts, hissing through his teeth. "What the hell?"

"Oops," I giggle drunkenly. "Sharp nails."

"Well, watch it."

I wait until he relaxes back against the pillow again before debating what I want to do next. Part of me wants to drive the blade right through the bead of precum forming at his tip and into his urethra and see how much he fucking likes that. Another part of me wants to just slam it through the center of his shaft, right into the mattress below, and sit back while he screams in agony.

Unfortunately, castration will make it too obvious that it was a woman out for revenge who murdered this sorry sack of shit, and I can't have anyone pointing fingers in Sheryl's direction. So instead, I climb up his body, grinding my still fully clothed pussy against his dick. His eyes pop open as I pull off my crop top, and he drinks in my tits as they bounce in front of his face.

With him distracted, I link his fingers with mine and push them above his head, pinning them against the wooden headboard.

"Oh yeah, just like that. Take off your panties."

I smile down at him, and he probably thinks the wildness in my eyes is because I'm as caught up in this as he is. He doesn't suspect a thing... until I drive the dagger through his palms, into the softwood of his headboard, trapping him.

His eyes widen to the size of saucers, and there's almost a second's delay before he starts screaming bloody murder. I jump off him, quickly moving to turn on the stereo, letting some god-awful rap shit blast through the room as I turn it up to a blaring volume, effectively blocking out his screaming curses.

Spinning to face him, I watch as he stares up at where his hands are pinned to the wood above his head, blood dripping down into his hair, looking like some fucked up version of Jesus on the cross. He tries to push against the handle, wincing and quickly stopping. My blades aren't even that long. It probably wouldn't take much effort to wiggle it free from the wood, but despite the *tough-guy* persona he puts on in public, he's clearly a fucking wimp.

I move to climb back on top of him, slipping my other blade out of its sheath. My grin is positively vicious as I loom over him, ignoring the murderous look in his eyes. I flash my dagger at him, pushing his top up so I can trail the tip lightly down the center of his abdomen, moving closer to his now flaccid cock. I fucking revel in the gratification that floods my body when a spark of fear enters his eye and sweat beads along his hairline.

Why is it men will do practically anything when you point a knife at their dicks? You could literally point it at any other body part, and they'll challenge you, goad you, call your bluff... but so much as wave it at their cocks, and they turn into statues, muttering fake apologies and placating assurances not to do it again. Not that I have any idea what this asshole is saying to me over the sound of the shitty music. Everyone saw him come up here with a girl. No one will even think to check on him until morning... After all, what could a mere woman possibly do to a big, strong gang leader? Hmm, let's find out, shall we?

Getting bored of teasing him, I move my blade to the upper right quadrant of his abdomen and push the blade into his flesh. A drop of blood forms, and as I dig deeper, forcing the blade downward, that droplet becomes a slow, steady stream that flows faster with each inch I carve into his stomach until his midsection and my hand are coated in blood.

I stop just above his pelvis and use my hand to wipe the blood away, frowning when I find the line isn't straight.

"Asshole," I snarl. "You moved!"

His eyes have rolled back in his head when I lift my head to glower at him, and his breaths are coming in sharp, pained inhales, making his stomach rise and fall in rapid movements.

Shaking my head at the genuinely pathetic display of manliness, I get back to the task at hand, and I don't stop again until I'm done. I admire my handiwork for a long moment before focusing on Python, noticing his skin is coated in a layer of sweat, and his face is deathly pale.

"Oh dear, you're not looking so hot."

I'm fully aware he can't hear me over the blasting of the music, but I don't really care. Doesn't mean I can't have a little fun. After all, this is one of the few moments in my life when I actually get to let go a little and enjoy myself, when *I'm* in control; when *I* hold all the power. When I'm holding some asshole's life in my hand, I get to gain back some semblance of dominion over my own goddamn life. So yeah, I'm going to enjoy every fucking second of it.

Leaning forward, this time, he doesn't even look at my now blood-spattered tits as I wrap my hand around the dagger sticking out of the headboard and give it a hard yank.

His hands collapse onto the pillow, unmoving as his eyes begin to droop. He's close to passing out, and well, we can't have that.

I give his cheek a hard smack, and his eyes fly open, blinking rapidly as he tries to orientate himself.

"Pay attention, motherfucker."

He looks at my lips, but I'm pretty sure he can't understand what I'm saying. No worries, the manic look in my eye and savage grin is all I need him to see.

With a flick of my wrist, I slash the sharp blade across his neck, and his eyes flare for a moment as the life starts to drain out of them. I watch, fascinated as blood pools around the horizontal slice across his throat before it spills over, dripping down the column of his throat before soaking into his shirt and onto the sheet beneath him.

I'm not sure how long I sit there for, listening to him gurgle and gasp as he slowly drowns in his own blood. I watch as his breathing becomes shallow until his chest stops moving altogether. Only when he lies still beneath me, do I move, wiping the blade against his jeans to clean it off his blood before tucking it away inside my boot.

I've just grabbed my crop top from the bed when I hear noises in the hall. The thudding of boots. A scream. Gunshots. The sound of something heavy crashes against the bedroom door, jolting me into action as I hastily climb off the dead gang leader. If it's one of Python's men, I'm dead. There's no two ways about it.

Confused about what could possibly be going on, I decide in a split second that there's no way I could make it out the window in time, and clutching my top to my chest, I scurry into the corner of the room. Making myself as small as possible, I press my back flat against the wall and bring my knees up, ensuring my daggers are within reach. I force tears to my eyes as what sounds like a boot smacks against the wooden door, breaking the shitty lock. The door swings inward, and with tears streaking down my blood-stained face, I lift my head. I make myself look as innocent as possible as two muscular men—one who looks like he can't be any older than eighteen and a middle-aged man with gray, thinning hair—that I don't recognize as Satans' members storm into the room with their weapons raised.

They see Python first, and I note the surprise on their faces as they share a glance with one another before the older one notices me, jutting his chin in my direction. Their guns are still raised as they round on me, but instead of the tense lines around their eyes, there's a confusing wariness.

The younger guy moves to turn off the shitty music, and even though the heavy bass of the music from downstairs still vibrates through the floorboards, it's not loud enough to cover up the broken sob that escapes my lips as I let my chin wobble. *Damn, maybe I do have transferable skills after all.*

"What the fuck happened in 'er'?" the older guy asks, his gaze bouncing back and forth between me and the dead Satan's leader.

"I... he... " My voice cracks and I bury my head in my hands, sobbing. Well, pretending to.

"Razor," one of them says. "Look."

Lifting my head slightly, I peer through the slits between my fingers as the two of them lean closer to the dead body, inspecting it.

"Jesus, fuck," the older guy—Razor—exclaims. "How the hell did this even happen?"

They both stare at the body for a second longer before I feel their gazes on me, and I let out another shoulder-trembling sob.

As the older one makes a move toward me, I snap my head up, setting my features into one of fear as I try to back away from him, pressing my back flush against the wall. I don't even have to try that hard to be afraid. I am. I might be able to seduce men and lower their defenses, but I know the extent of my skills, and there's no way I could take on two large men like this and expect to get away unscathed. Don't get me wrong, I'll put up one hell of a fight if they touch me. I'm just not confident it's a fight that I'll win —my defensive skills are mediocre at best.

Seeing my terrified expression, Razor stalls, slowly putting his gun away and lifting his hands, palms forward in a gesture that he means me no harm. I watch him closely as he crouches down in front of me. His arm flexes, drawing my attention to the tattoo there, and I can just make out the Reaper Rejects insignia. *What the fuck? Why are the Rejects here?*

"We're not going to hurt you," he says, and I know he's trying to put me at ease, but I don't buy his bullshit. My blades are in my boots, but I can have them buried in his throat in a split second if he so much as looks at me wrong. It's his little buddy behind him that I'll have a more challenging time taking down without the element of surprise on my side. "We just want to know what happened."

I begin to blubber, mumbling nonsense because, well, I have no idea how to explain my way out of this one. "B-bathroom... dead... b-blood everywhere." I heave out another sob, glancing up between wet eyelashes to see the deep lines of confusion carved into his forehead as he studies me.

"Ehh, okay, let's get ya out of here, yeah? Get some whiskey in ye."

He doesn't move, continuing to look at me until I give a shaky jerk of my head.

"Alright, love, put your top on, and I'll get ya out of here."

I'm honestly a little confused by his behavior, but it's about to get me out of this room, so I don't overthink it and instead pull my top on, ignoring the icky feel of the dried blood crusting on my skin. I get to my feet, making them appear weak and shaky, and without sparing him a glance, I let the two Rejects escort me past Python and out of the room.

seven

The bouncer on the door nods his head when I pass, and as I step into the large, open room, the noise of the crowd ricochets off the tiled walls. Men and women scream encouragement at whichever fighter they have their bets on tonight, drowning out the sound of *Monsters* by Shinedown blaring across the room from the overhead speakers.

As I glance around, I notice the place is packed tonight, and I have to push through the crowd as I cross the room. They hardly notice, though, since everyone is too focused on shoving each other as they jostle for a better view of the fight taking place in the middle of the room.

I started the underground fights when the Reaper Rejects only consisted of myself and a handful of others who had suffered at the hands of the Antonellis. Back then, it was nothing more than guys from the neighborhood meeting up once a week in an empty lot to try and prove themselves. But they've grown exponentially since then. When I took over old Beast territory a year ago, I made the fights a regular thing that drew a small but reliable crowd. Things really amped up when I helped my old friend, Beck, rescue his girlfriend from a compound where they were teaching kids how to become killers for hire. We ended up rescuing a bunch of those kids. I managed to find homes for many of the younger ones, but most of those who were older didn't have anywhere to go. When they asked if they could stay here, I had to tell them about my plans. I had to explain to them that if they did choose to stay, they would be putting themselves in danger once again. I honestly expected most of them to leave—and I wouldn't have thought any less of them if they had. Even though every one of them was a trained soldier, they'd already lived a life that wasn't theirs, and I assumed they would just want to enjoy their newfound freedom. I was wrong. Every single one of them agreed to help me, and by the end of that day, they all wore the Reaper Rejects tattoo with pride.

I suddenly had more members than I knew what to do with and finding somewhere large enough to house us all became my number one focus. When I came across the dilapidated apartment complex, I knew it would be perfect for our needs. Over the last few months, I've watched as my men have accepted the new kids into the crew, and we've slowly learned to get along—like one giant, dysfunctional family. The kids I rescued have grown the most. When they first arrived here, they were constantly on edge, jumping at every sound and resorting to violence to solve every problem. I can't even begin to imagine the hell they were put through in that compound.

As I watched them struggling to cope with this new life they'd found themselves in, I knew they needed an outlet for all the confusion and anger they were feeling. I might not know what they had to endure, but I do know what it feels like to be an angry, confused, lost teenager, to feel that simmering rage pulsing beneath your skin with no constructive outlet. It can lead to dangerous things. So as soon as we moved into the apartment complex, I instructed the guys to gut the sports center opposite it and turn it into a suitable fighting ring.

We operate pit fights out of the swimming pool, and we knocked down the wall into the gym area, opening the floor space so we could put a bar along the far wall and squeeze in as many customers as possible.

I encouraged the kids to satiate their need for violence in the ring, giving them an outlet for everything they were feeling but didn't know how to process. I don't think I'd fully appreciated just how deadly these kids were until the first time I watched one of them in the pit. He was like an oncoming storm. His opponent never stood a chance against his precise strikes and forceful blows, and the fight was over in mere seconds. Although, it drew one hell of a crowd. After that, the whispers began about the unbeatable Rejects, and since then, our numbers have grown by the week, everyone coming to watch—or try their hand—against the deadly force of the Reaper Rejects.

A roar goes up from the crowd as the fight comes to an end, and people move to collect their winnings as the fighters are helped out of the pool. Bypassing the jostling audience as they move to refill their drinks before the next fight, I climb up the steps to the low platform I had built along one side of the room, intended for me and my officers and providing an uninterrupted view into the fighting pit, and around the rest of the room.

A woman dressed in booty shorts, with her tits hanging out and a tray of drinks in her hand, meets me at the top of the stairs.

"Evening, Cain," she purrs, smiling seductively.

I let my gaze run over her subtle curves and perky breasts, winking as I take a glass of whiskey from her and move to join Oliver on one of the lounge seats. He's been checking out the Satan's territory all week and I haven't had a chance to catch up with him.

He raises his chin in greeting as I approach before his gaze roams over the adrenaline-pumped crowd on the floor below. "Hey, man."

"How's things?"

I settle on the seat beside him, looking down into the swimming pool as two new fighters drop into it and another round begins to the chorus of hoots and hollers.

We both watch the fight for a bit before he speaks. "Satan's territory looks promising. Small-scale gang; not very organized and cocky."

I nod my head. "And the docks?"

"They would definitely work. There's a nightclub in one of the buildings that attracts a good crowd on the weekends." One side of his lip quirks up in a mysterious smirk before he continues, "We already know it's drawing people in so it shouldn't be too hard to add regular fight evenings to the schedule."

We lapse into silence as the fight gets underway, a young blond man who's all attitude and mediocre muscle, is up against a middle-aged brute of a fighter. The two of them circle one another for several moments, the young guy losing patience first as he goes in for an uppercut that snaps his opponent's head back.

Blood gushes from the older fighter's nose and drips onto the already stained swimming pool tiles at their feet. Unperturbed, he spits blood into his opponent's face, going straight in for a round of powerful jabs to his chest and abdomen. The two fighters get more and more aggressive, the young one becoming increasingly desperate as he resorts to trying to gouge his opponents eyes out and rip his ear off with his teeth every time the guy gets too close to him.

"How have things been here?" Oliver asks as the young blond fighter is taken to the ground, his body slamming against the bottom of the pool with a painful sort of thud.

"Our shipments were light again," I inform him, my jaw ticking in irritation. It's been an issue for the last few weeks, and I've a fair idea who's behind it. The Grim Bastards have been a pain in my backside since I took control of the firearm distribution chains in and around Black Creek, and I'm pretty sure they've been stealing from me for the last few months. Somehow they've been gaining access to my shipments before I've been notified of their arrival and can send men to pick them up.

The Grim Bastards are my only other real competition for control of Black Creek—other than the Antonellis, but they're a whole different ball game. Between the three of us, we essentially rule the city. The Antonellis have a monopoly on all things gambling and sex. They run a prosperous casino down at the Tideside Docks, as well as multiple high-end sex clubs. When the Beasts left Black Creek, the Grim Bastards took control of their drug distribution channels, while I already had the necessary connections that made it easy to negotiate deals with those who operate the arms trade on the West coast.

Since I started running the arms trade in Black Creek, I've been working to reduce the number of firearms on the streets. Honestly, I don't trust anyone other than us to sell them. I've made it crystal fucking clear to my men who they can and cannot sell to. Namely kids, but I get my men to use some common sense when they're trading, and not just look at the green that's being handed over. I can't say the same happens in the other gangs that buy the guns off us, so I've been restricting how much they can purchase, and slowly reducing that figure.

Of course, I'm not stupid enough to think I can rid Black Creek of all guns. Not only would that put me out of business, but it would be fucking impossible. Nor do I think for one second it would make a difference. If I didn't provide them, someone else would, or they'd just be replaced by equally destructive weapons. I'm just trying to police their distribution.

However, the Grim Bastards are a problem I'm going to have to deal with. Soon. I can't let that sort of disrespect stand. The difficulty is, part of me doesn't give a shit. I didn't get into this business to contend with rival gangs, argue over borders or dispute the consignment of firearms. No, I'm in this game for exactly one thing—revenge. Vengeance. Retribution. Whatever you want to call it. It's a hatred I've been harboring for eleven years now, and with every passing day, it burns brighter, scorching my soul and turning it to ash.

"I'll get some men on it."

Oliver has fallen into his role as my second in command with surprising ease. Sure, having been a member of the Feral Beasts for years, he more than understands the hierarchy and what the role requires, but I know he has been confused and feeling a little lost since his release. Like me, he's only in this for revenge. To correct past mistakes and make up for what we couldn't prevent when we were barely more than children ourselves.

When this is all behind us, I imagine he'll move on and find a life for himself far from Black Creek. Like Beck did. He was one of the lucky ones who actually made it out of this cesspit alive. Got himself a good job and a nice girl to love. He even got himself three other guys with whom he's supposed to share her. Don't ask me how that shit works. I couldn't imagine sharing a girl with anyone for anything more than one night. Even then, I can be a possessive bastard. I like a girl's attention to be solely focused on me when we're fucking. Nothing wrong with that.

I give a sharp nod of my head, knowing he'll get the job done. It's not my main priority right now, though. Neither is taking over Satan's territory—although that is important. No, my main focus has been on finding a way into the Antonelli empire. Their part of the city is separated from the rest of us by a winding river that opens up into the docks and is the namesake of our city of criminals—Black Creek. They've set up their own little kingdom over there, controlling everything that comes in and out of the docks and running high-end, high-stakes gambling nights, where the buy-in costs more than most Black Creek residents earn in a year.

The Antonellis wronged my family a long time ago. They forever changed the course of my life when they attacked our house and took my sister. On that fateful day, they stole the other half of my soul. Where I am cloaked in darkness, my sister was all radiant glow. She was the bright spark in my life, the one thing that kept me grounded, that prevented me from stumbling across that moral line and falling into devilry. In the absence of her light, I've succumbed to the darkness, bathed in immorality, and painted myself in blood.

Back then, Reaper Rejects only had four members. Four kids who thought they wanted nothing more than to grow up but were blind to the harsh realities of life. We thought we knew it all, thought we were invincible when we were actually ignorant to the horrors of this world.

Now, we are a hundred men strong, and every single one of us is ready for war. We're willing to fight for our cause, to die for what's right. I will sacrifice whatever is necessary to avenge my sister, to destroy the men who stole her, and obliterate the dynasty that has been the source of all my pain.

As if he can sense the hostile anger pouring off me, Oliver glances my way, watching me closely for a moment as if he thinks I'm about to storm out of here and head straight for the Antonellis before a cry from the pit has him focusing on the fight once again.

My hand is squeezing the whiskey glass in a death grip as a deafening roar goes up from the crowd, signaling the end of the fight, and the muscles in the back of my jaw are so tense that I have to work to relax them before taking a sip of my drink. I've been on this path of revenge for a long time now, but the closer we get, the more impatient I become. Now that we have sufficient manpower, I'm ready for us to take our next steps, but unfortunately, we can't go storming into the Antonellis' district just yet. We need to be smart about how we attack them. I might have plenty of men at my back, ready and willing to fight this fight with me, but the Antonellis will have many more people than us.

The Don—Giovanni Antonelli—is my main target, but between his right-hand man/bodyguard and son, not to mention the numerous underlings he has working for him, he won't be an easy man to get my hands on. Besides, killing him isn't enough. His son, or someone else, will simply take his place, and the cycle will continue all over again. Every single one of them are vermin infecting this city. They *all* need to be eradicated.

With the fight over, and a lull while people top up their drinks before the next one begins, Oliver turns his attention my way. His own features are tight as he asks, "Any update?"

I know he's as impatient as I am to move forward. Nothing is worse than all this sitting and waiting.

"Nothing new."

His shoulders drop at my news, but it's nothing either of us didn't expect. The men I planted within the Antonelli organization several months ago are still too new to have made any significant progress yet, and unfortunately, any information they have been able to relay back to me hasn't been all that useful.

I wish there were another way in, an alternative plan we could be working on in the meantime, but I don't know what. The Antonelli empire is like an impenetrable fortress. We can easily get into their part of the city, and with the right clothes and enough money, into their casino and clubs, but then what? It's not like Giovanni himself hangs out on the casino floor all day, and even if he did, the second I would make a move toward him, I'd be gunned down before I could do him any harm.

But they have to have a weak spot, some way that I can get close to them. Everyone does. No stronghold is entirely impregnable. If I look long and hard enough, I'm sure I can find a crack somewhere, a chink in their armor, their Achilles heel. All it takes is patience and perseverance, and while mine may be running thin, I'm nowhere close to giving up.

A roar goes up from the raucous crowd below, pulling me out of my thoughts as another fight comes to an end. Damn, I was so deep in my thoughts I hadn't even realized another one had begun.

The heavy bass of the music has been turned up, and I can feel the tiled wall behind me vibrating. A server wearing only a bra and booty shorts climbs up the stairs, swaying her hips with each step in the sky-high heels she has on that make her toned legs look like they're a mile long as she carries a tray with two new drinks on it. Without saying a word, she places them on the glass table between our seats, giving me a coy smile before she moves away. Her ass shakes from side to side, my eyes glued to the round globes as she disappears down the stairs again.

She barely gave Oliver a passing glance, nor did he look away from the fight that was getting underway. As I sit and watch him, I notice the tense set of his shoulders and the straight line of his spine. Despite the fact we're perfectly safe here, he's on edge. It's a stance I've noticed in him often since he returned. I'm not sure if it's just being back in Black Creek, our ever-present responsibilities, or the weight of whatever he's been through in the last few years, but I've yet to see him actually just sit down and relax and enjoy himself for a night.

When he first returned, girls were all over him—a fresh face, instantly given the title of my second, and the perfect balance of dangerous yet elusive, who wouldn't want a piece of him? After two years in prison and several months in a male-only halfway house, I thought for sure he'd be all over that. Fuck knows I'd do nothing but drink and fuck for a month if I'd been locked up that long. But Oliver barely spared them a passing glance, more interested in getting down to work and making himself useful. I dunno if he felt he had something to prove and didn't want to get distracted, or what, but he's barely stopped working for a second since he got back. I am all for a strong work ethic, but the dude needs to learn to enjoy himself a little. Fuck knows, in this life, you could well end up dead tomorrow.

Reaching toward him, I clap a hand on his shoulder, shaking off my own dark thoughts as I smirk at him. "You need to loosen up a bit, O." I jerk my head toward the staircase where the waitress disappeared. "She looks like she'd be a bit of fun for a night."

He chuckles, shaking his head. "Yeah, and she only had eyes for you. Besides, I'm not interested."

Another small smile curls the corner of his lips slightly, and this time understanding dawns.

"No way," I laugh, shoving his shoulder. "You finally got yourself laid. About fucking time, man. Jesus, I was beginning to think all that time locked up in your cell with only your hand for company had affected the goods somehow."

"Shut the fuck up, asshole," he snorts, shoving me right back. "The *goods* work just fine, thank you very much."

I shake my head at our banter, huffing out a breath of laughter. "Yeah, well, now that you know for sure, you should have a drink and enjoy yourself." I spear him with a serious look. "Tonight we get drunk, and tomorrow we'll go after the Satan's."

FROM THE DARKNESS, I STAND ALONGSIDE MY MEN AS WE WATCH THE raging party unfold before us. From what Oliver has told me, this sort of thing is expected at the Satans' clubhouse. Having seen enough, I lift my hand and signal for my men to advance. We're all dressed in black, camouflaged in the darkness. We have two teams surrounding the house. I'm with my men out the front, watching as party-goers go in and out of the front door, and the flashing of multi-colored strobe lights light up the window into the front room, which is jam-packed with people dancing drunkenly and grinding all over one another. Oliver is with the other team around back, ready to take out any of the Satan's members who try to escape that way.

No one notices us as we close in on the house, but as we enter the pool of light from the house, the first of the party-goers spot us. Their eyes widen, and jaws drop when they do. It's a typical reaction, given the neck warmers, pulled up to the bridge of our noses, decorated with a skeletal design that makes the bottom half of our faces appear skull-like. That, and the AR-15 semi-automatic rifles slung over our shoulders aimed, ready to fire.

Of course, we're only after the Satans' members. Many of these people are just here to party, score drugs, or are gang hangarounds with nowhere else better to be. Unless one of them comes for us, we'll leave them alone.

People start to push past us, rushing out of the house as we enter, wanting to get away before bullets start flying. The music is so loud in here that the terrified screams in our presence don't alert Python or his men to the present threat, and the guy who I'm guessing was meant to be manning the door is too busy banging some chick against the wall.

As more and more people start to push and hurry past him, causing a scene, he finally stops thrusting into the girl he's fucking. His look of confusion contorts into shock when he sees us, and before he can so much as pull his dick out of the chick, I lift my gun and shoot him point-blank in the head. Blood splatters over the wall and the girl he was fucking. With the silencer in place, the circular hole in the front of his head is the only indicator that a gun went off at all.

As he collapses to the ground and my team spreads out, shooting at anyone resembling a Satan, more screaming starts, and anyone who wasn't running for the door before is now.

The ground floor of the house descends into mass panic as everyone flees and the Satans' members left standing start to return fire. Most of them are high and drunk, making their actions slow and uncoordinated, easily giving my men the advantage as they pick off the Satans' members one by one. Within no time at all, the ground floor is empty, bar the dead bodies scattered over the floor. It's kind of jarring, seeing the place deserted, with the music still blasting. The blood spatter and corpses dotted around the area only add to the macabre atmosphere our presence has caused.

"No sign of Python," one of my men shouts into my ear. I don't turn the music down or off, not wanting to alert anyone upstairs to the chaos that's ensuing below them. With a jerk of my head, two of my men—Razor and Fin—head up the stairs, weapons at the ready.

While they clear out the upstairs, I direct my men to search the rest of the house as Oliver steps through the back door, doing a quick once over of the kitchen before his eyes meet mine. Unable to talk over the music, I nod my head in a silent gesture that all is good, and he returns it with a sharp one of his own before moving back out the door, directing his team to search the other properties on the street.

I take my time, moving from room to room, counting the number of bodies, and taking in the state of the house. It's apparent no care has been given to it. Mold grows in the corner of the living room, kitchen cabinets are missing their doors, the banister is missing several balusters, and some idiot has punched a hole in the wall. The whole house stinks of weed, cigarettes, and alcohol.

Having done a loop of the ground floor, I make my way up the stairs, noticing more dead bodies slouched on the stairs and against the hall in the landing. Peering into the first bedroom, two more men with Satan tattoos lie face down on the mattress. One has his jeans and boxers shoved halfway down his ass, and the other is naked from the waist down. I barely spare them more than a passing glance as I walk past the doorway, moving on to inspect the next room. Before I can reach it, though, a noise from the bedroom at the end of the hall gains my attention—most likely Razor and Fin finishing up. I make to move toward it as Razor escorts a young woman with long ash-blonde hair out of the room. Her eyes are rounded in fear, and she's soaked in blood, making what I can see of her pale skin appear ghost-like. It's not an altogether surprising find, given we just massacred the entire house. If she was fucking some guy in the room when my men stormed in, she could have gotten caught in the crosshairs, although it is a surprising amount of blood. It almost looks like she slipped and fell face-first into a pool of it.

I'm faintly aware of someone finally turning off the goddamn music downstairs, and a heavy silence falls over us as I take in the girl. Before I can say anything, Razor's words have my eyes snapping up to meet his. "Boss, you might wanna check this out." He tilts his head toward the room behind him, and as I close the distance between us in several long strides, he moves to the side, giving me a clear view of the room.

Holy shit. This was definitely not the work of my men. Blood saturates the bed, dripping onto the floor. There's splatter on the wall behind the bed frame, and lying supine in the middle of it all, is a Satan's Advocate member—with his shirt pushed up to his nipples, and his pants and boxers shoved down, his limp dick lying out in the open.

"What the—" I begin, moving into the room.

"The Reaper was here," Fin states. Not that he needs to. His calling card is etched plainly into the man's skin for all to see. I run my gaze over the confident slashes across his stomach. It's obvious there was no hesitation here. Whoever sliced him open was experienced and sure of themselves.

I've heard of the Reaper. Everyone has. He's been taking out gang members for the last few years, although I've just never seen his handiwork up close before. It's impressive. Completely in contrast to gang kills which are usually quick and efficient. For me, personally, there's next to no emotion involved when I kill someone. It's a means to an end—like tonight—but I don't need to be a psychologist to know that just by looking at the brutality inflicted on Python's body whoever the Reaper is, their kills are driven by emotion.

But what's his motive? It's not a question anyone seems to know the answer to. His kills can be anyone from a gang leader, to a random mid-level member, to a simple hangaround who barely has anything to do with the gang. There's no obvious pattern other than the fact they all have affiliations—even if somewhat tenuous—with one of the various gangs in Black Creek. Surely, if he just wanted to eliminate us, he'd go for the leader every time. I get the impression whoever the Reaper is, he's trying to make a statement. I just don't know what it is he's trying to say.

Once I've taken in every inch of the R carved deeply into his abdomen, I lift my gaze to look at the man's face. Python. The leader of the Satan's. I guess that explains why he wasn't downstairs. His neck has been cleanly sliced, again showing no signs of hesitation, and the man himself stares sightlessly at the ceiling above him.

"Boss," Razor speaks up after a long moment. I was so caught up in analyzing the handiwork of the Reaper that I almost forgot he and Fin and the girl were still here. "We found the girl in here when we kicked in the door."

I raise an eyebrow in surprise as I turn to look at the blood-soaked girl trembling beside Razor. Razor's a large man, much like myself, except where my body is honed out of muscle, he's carrying his fair share of the weight. But it works for him. It gives him this formidable appearance and makes everyone think twice before messing with him.

Beside him, the girl looks tiny, even though, in her heels, she's probably around six-feet tall. She's dressed in a short black skirt and a matching top that exposes her toned abdomen, highlighting the flare of her hips. Her milky skin is splashed with red, giving her a grisly appearance, and beneath the blood which is quickly drying on her skin, I can just about make out the faint markings of a tattoo along her shoulder and across one side of her chest. It should probably make her seem like a victim—the lone survivor of a massacre, but it doesn't. For some reason, it suits her. Like she was born to bathe in the blood of gang members.

She's shaking all over, and her pupils are blown, leaving a thin line of the strangest color of blue ringing them. She's most likely in shock. What I don't understand, though, is why the Reaper would leave behind a witness. That makes no sense at all.

I watch her closely, noticing the way her gaze bounces over me, taking in my six-foot-five frame, broad shoulders, narrow waist, the minuscule bits of ink on display along the back of my hands. Slowly, her eyes travel up to my face, skipping over the neck warmer covering the bottom half. It doesn't seem to bother her, the half-skeleton look. Rather she takes in my dark wavy hair, straight, thick eyebrows, and what she can see of my broad nose before she finally meets my gaze.

Behind the fear and panic in her eyes, there's something else, but I can't put my finger on it, and she averts her gaze before I can figure it out.

"You saw the Reaper?" I bark. She might be a scared girl, but I need to be the leader of the Rejects right now.

She jumps at my harsh tone, but when her eyes flick up to meet mine, there's a defiance in them that surprises me.

"N-no."

My eyes narrow, not believing her. I take a giant step toward her, the heavy sole of my boot echoing around the otherwise silent hall as my close proximity forces her to tilt her head back to look up at me. "It's in your best interest not to lie to me."

It's a small, barely perceptible movement, but her lips flatten in annoyance. As I open my mouth to ask her again, my phone goes off in my pocket. I fish it out, intending to cancel it, but when I see Oliver's name, I know it's him checking in, and I need to answer.

Huffing out a sigh, I look up at Razor. "Take her downstairs. She's not to leave until I talk to her."

Razor gives a sharp nod of his head in understanding before he wraps his meaty hand around the girl's thin upper arm, escorting her along the hall and down the stairs.

I never expected to nearly cross paths with the Reaper tonight. Hell, for all I know, he could have slipped right past me earlier, blending in with the other party-goers as they fled the house. He's barely more than a myth whispered in quiet tones on street corners. If it weren't for his signature kills, I'd think he didn't exist. But now that someone might have seen him, I need to find out more. I honestly don't give a shit who he is. If he has a vendetta against gangs, then perhaps he'll be willing to help me take out the most corrupt one of them all. I've been wracking my brain, trying to figure out an alternative way of taking down the Antonellis, and it almost seems like fate that the Reaper—the very man who hates us all—may have left behind an unknown witness for me to stumble across. *This* could be what I've been waiting for.

As the blonde-haired girl drops out of view, I can't help but wonder if she could be the key to everything.

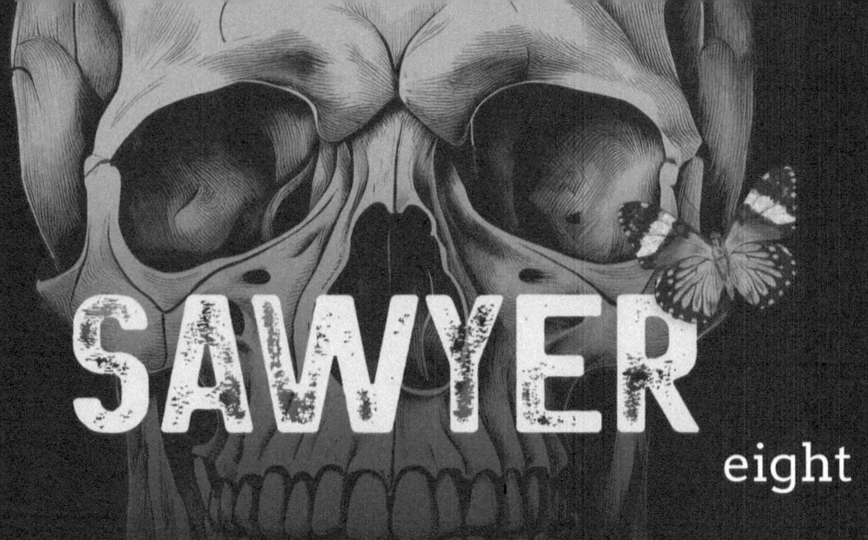

eight

I let the brute of a man—Razor—lead me down the stairs and into the kitchen, where a bunch of other men wearing the same creepy skeleton face coverings are dragging dead bodies out the back door. They are leaving behind a red trail of blood which, unsurprisingly, looks like it belongs on the once white, but now gray with grime, linoleum floor.

He grabs a wooden chair from the scuffed up table in the corner of the room, pulling it out and gesturing for me to sit down. I do. I need to get out of here, but I can't just make a run for it—I'll never stand a chance if I do. I have to bide my time, and hope the opportunity presents itself before the sinfully gorgeous man comes back to question me. I could hardly get a word out past my dry throat when I looked at him. It's ridiculous because I couldn't even make out half of his face, but I didn't need to, to picture his curved lips.

There was an air to him that is common in men from Black Creek. That cocky attitude that many unrightfully walk around with, but on him, it seemed fitting. Like he'd earned the right to be that arrogant. Not that that makes any sense. I know absolutely nothing about him. Reaper Rejects is a name that's only started to make waves in the last year, but with each passing week—as they seize more and more territory for themselves—those whispers have gotten louder. Beyond being aware of their existence, I don't care to take the time to learn about each individual member. Although Razor—who is currently filling a chipped mug with tap water for me—called him boss. Which can only mean one thing—he's the king of the Rejects. That would definitely explain his authoritative attitude and the cocky swagger. It also means he's trouble.

As I glance down at the bloodstains trailing out the back door, it's painfully obvious that the Rejects have murdered all of Python's men, which means they officially own our little strip of Black Creek. Even more reason for me to stay away from them and their unjustly rugged leader. God knows it's only a matter of time before I end up killing one of his men for abusing his wife or beating up his kid. I'm actually surprised I haven't already. I've crossed paths with most of the gangs in Black Creek... when one of their members met their deaths at my hands.

"Drink this, girl." Razor sets the mug down on the table in front of me, but I make no move to lift it. He eyes me up before chuckling under his breath. "I ain't poisoned it or nothin'."

Still.

Another moment passes where he continues to watch me closely before asking, "What's your name?"

I know I have to give him something, but I make a show of chewing on my lower lip, acting as though I'm weighing up the pros and cons of divulging that piece of information before I hush out, "Jessica."

He leans across the table. "Jessica, you ain't done nothing wrong. Cain just needs to know what you saw tonight, okay?"

Cain. That must be his name. I have a sudden urge to say it aloud, wondering how it sounds on my tongue, but I bite down against that instinct and instead I slowly nod my head as I mentally piece together a plausible story. Razor watches me carefully, taking in every twitch of my lips and wrinkle of my forehead. *Fuck. Dammit. I'm not going to get out of this without telling them something.*

Fate must be on my side tonight, as the screen door behind him squeaks open and a young guy—what the hell is with all the kids?—pops his head in. "Razor, I need your help for a sec."

Frowning, Razor nods his head, and the guy ducks out of the kitchen again. Razor returns his focus to me, tapping his finger against the wooden table top. "I'll be back in a sec. Sit tight." He goes to stand, but before he pushes open the screen door, he turns his head to spear me with a harsh look. "I'm serious. Don't fucking move from that chair."

His boots stomp against the flimsy wooden decking as he heads outside, and I sit quietly, listening until his footsteps fade away. The kitchen is empty now, all the men probably hard at work burying bodies in the backyard.

Seeing my opportunity, I listen out for the noise of approaching footsteps as I carefully pick my way across the kitchen, walking on my toes so no one can hear the tap of my heels against the floor.

As I approach the hall, I hear the sound of a voice coming from upstairs. Cain's distinctive, deep rumble as he talks to someone, followed by the sound of heavy boots against the floorboards. I don't waste any time, slipping out the front door and into the night, sticking to the shadows as I rush down the sidewalk toward my bike at the far end of the street.

I can hear men shouting to one another from within passing houses, voices that can only belong to Rejects. If there are any Satans still alive, they'll be hiding in the cover of darkness, just like me.

Once I reach my bike, I quietly unzip my duffel bag and switch the short skirt and heels out for leather pants, boots, and a matching jacket. As I'm yanking the trousers over my hips, I hear a commotion behind me. Raised voices followed by the banging of a screen door against the wood as someone steps out of a house.

I'm too far away to make out everything that's being said, and I don't waste time squinting in the dark to try and see who is talking or to whom, instead shoving my feet into my boots. No doubt whoever it is is looking for me, and they're getting the other Rejects on the job. The wind changes directions, blowing my way, and I distinctly hear the words "blonde girl" and "missing," and know I need to get out of here ASAP.

Fuck.

I hurriedly tug on my leather jacket, ignoring the gross feel of Python's blood crusted on my skin as I zip it up before pulling the blonde wig off my head. I stuff it in my duffle, jam my helmet on my head, and as the bike roars to life, easily heard all the way on the far end of the street, I twist the throttle and take off, flying down the road. The sound of the engine drowns out any shouts thrown my way, and I don't dare look back to see if anyone is following me. Instead, I race through the city, making last-minute turns and weaving in and out of the sparse traffic as I constantly check my mirrors until I'm confident no one is following. Only then do I slow down to a leisurely speed and turn my bike homeward.

Despite my late night, I'm up early the next morning, munching down a bowl of cereal when Luc stumbles bleary-eyed and still half-asleep into the kitchen.

"Morning." I grin brightly at him, and he just scowls, mumbling something incoherent as he grabs himself a bowl and empties the last of the cereal into it. Damn, I need to make a list and go shopping today. And I need to stop by and let Sheryl know Python will no longer be a problem. None of the Satan's will bother any of us again. But will the Rejects be just as bad as them? Worse? Only time will tell.

I wait patiently until he's nearly finished with his breakfast and looking more alert. "Don't go to school today," I say as he shovels the last spoonful into his mouth.

His brows tug together as he looks at me, his eyes clouded with suspicion.

"Why?"

"Just don't, please? Stay home for a day or two."

A crease forms between his brows as he stares me down. "Does this have anything to do with what happened the other day?"

I purse my lips, mulling over my answer before I respond. Of course, when he stepped out of his room after the Satan's left our building the other day, he had a bunch of questions for me, none of which I answered, much to his chagrin. After a tense moment, I huff out a sigh. Things were so much easier when he was younger, and he just did as he was told or could easily be distracted by the prospect of spending the day watching cartoons instead of going to school.

I try to keep Luc out of as much of my life as possible. He doesn't need to know the seedy things I get up to. He already knows about the club—he needs to know where he can reach me in case of an emergency, but he doesn't need to know the rest of it. The problem is, he's getting older and more inquisitive, and he's starting to put some of the pieces together, and that terrifies me.

"Reaper Rejects have taken control of Satan territory," I finally tell him, giving him part of the story, but nowhere near the whole thing.

His eyes widen in surprise. "How do you know that?"

"It's none of your business how I know that," I snap. "I just do. So until we know what they're planning on doing, just stay home."

He studies me for a long moment, with a slight frown, before finally nodding. "Okay."

The tension drops out of my shoulders, relief that he should be safe here—or as safe as one can be in Black Creek—overcoming me.

"But only if you stay home too."

Fucking asshole. I scowl at him. "I have to work tonight."

He shrugs his shoulders like it's no big deal. "Call in sick."

"You know I can't do that. We need the money."

He quirks a brow. "Seriously? I'm sure we can survive if you miss one shift."

I open my mouth to protest, but he talks over the top of me. "Don't think I don't know about the shoebox full of cash hidden under the floorboard beneath the sofa."

I gape open-mouthed at him for a second. "How do you know about that?"

The infuriating shithead just shrugs a shoulder. "There's more than enough to cover what you'll miss out on tonight."

I have to force my lip not to curl back in an angry snarl, and instead, I try to suck in a deep, calming breath. "That's supposed to be for a rainy day. If there's an emergency or something."

He glances out the grimy window at the gloomy sky above us. Droplets of rain splash against the pane, leaving water marks as they trail down it. "Looks like a rainy day to me."

I roll my eyes, even as I huff out a chuckle. "Fine, I'll stay home today, but I have to go in tomorrow."

His face lights up with a grin, and it brings a rare smile to my own lips. "Pajama and movie day, like old times." His eyes flash with excitement as he dumps his bowl in the sink and drops onto the sofa, channel surfing until he finds something he likes.

Shaking my head, I clean our dishes before joining him, and that's how we spend the day, watching old movies and chatting about absolutely nothing. It's reminiscent of when we first moved in here. It was the first apartment we'd ever lived in. The first time we'd had a place that was just ours, and we would frequently spend the whole day on the sofa, watching TV or playing games, and pretending the world outside our tiny apartment didn't exist. We'd never had the luxury before of being able to block out the rest of the world. Usually, it was just there, staring us in the face, whether we wanted to deal with it or not. So to be able to carve out time for just ourselves... it was fucking perfect.

Unfortunately, the real world comes calling the next day, and Sheryl has obviously already heard the news when I step into the women's shelter that evening on my way to work.

"You did it," she exclaims in a hushed whisper. Her bony hand squeezes mine with a surprising amount of strength. It's been nearly a week since she showed up here, and her bruises are healing well, but they're still visible without any makeup.

I glance furtively around us as I drag her into a quiet corner of the communal hall. Grace is sitting a few seats down, scribbling on a piece of paper with some broken crayons. She gives me a toothy smile and a wave, which I reciprocate before focusing back on Sheryl.

I notice a sparkle in her eyes that wasn't there the other day, and she can barely contain herself as she wraps me in a tight hug. "I can't believe you actually did it," she whispers. "Thank you."

When she leans back, I give her a soft smile. "Do you know what you're going to do now?"

Shaking her head, she says, "Not yet, but Beatrice has offered us a room for now, in exchange for helping her out. I can look for jobs in the meantime."

"That's good. I can ask at the club, if you want. Some of the girls help each other out with daycare when they're working, so it wouldn't be a problem with Grace."

She thinks it over for a second, but I can already tell she's not fond of the idea.

"It's not that I don't want to, I just... " She swallows roughly. "I don't know if I'm ready for that sort of attention yet." Her hands are shaking and I quickly wrap mine around them, giving her a reassuring squeeze.

"Hey," I say sharply, waiting until her eyes raise to meet mine. "I understand. You don't have to explain anything to me."

She gives me a watery smile, sniffling as she leans in to give me another hug. "I don't know how I'll ever repay you."

"You don't have to," I assure her. "I was only doing what needed to be done... besides, if I hadn't, it looks like the Rejects would have."

Her eyes are rounded in surprise when she breaks off the hug. "I'd heard rumors, but I wasn't sure if they were true or not."

"Well, they're true. They raided the Satan's clubhouse. Killed them all."

She gasps, her hand coming up to cover her mouth. "While you were there?"

"Yup." I pop the p, ducking my gaze so I don't have to see the concern in her eyes.

"Shit, did they see you? What are you going to do?"

"It should be fine," I assure her, even if I'm not entirely convinced of that. "I was wearing a disguise, and I got out of there before they could ask me anything. Chances are, they'll be too busy gaining control of their new territory to go chasing after some chick."

She pinches her lips, and I can tell she doesn't quite believe me, but thankfully she doesn't argue and we move over to join Grace while she draws a picture of a knight coming to save the princess from her tower. As I listen to her tell the story that accompanies the picture, I sigh, wishing life was that easy. Part of me wants to warn her that men are not heroes. That they don't come encased in armor and ready to dive into battle for you, but I also don't want to tarnish her optimistic outlook on the world. God knows, life will quickly suck the hope out of her as she grows older, so why not let her hold on to a fantasy for a little bit longer.

***

The same whispers about the demise of the Satan's are running rampant when I walk into the club later that night. It seems everyone has heard about the Rejects, and the question on everyone's mind is... what does this mean for us?

"My sister lives in Reject territory, and she says as long as you don't go asking for trouble, they leave you in peace," Jezebel informs everyone while we're sitting at our individual dressing tables, getting ready.

"I've heard they run these really successful fighting challenge nights, and they hire girls for the winners," Lori adds. Lowering her voice, she whispers, "Apparently, they pay very well, too."

I do my best to ignore them as they speculate back and forth. The way they talk reminds me of Grace and her knight. They make the Rejects sound like they're the good guys, here to save us or some such shit. Even if only a fraction of what they're saying is true, it doesn't make them good people. They still run a gang. They still murdered a bunch of people the other night, all for the sake of gaining more territory.

Dolled up to the nines and dressed in my best hooker heels, I leave the gossiping hens behind in the dressing room. As I'm passing the office, I can hear Drew talking to someone. That's not unusual, but the deep cadence of the other person's voice strikes me as familiar. I pause, lingering by the door, needing to hear his voice again. I can't make out their words, but I can decipher Drew's voice through the wooden door before there's the scraping of chair legs. Realizing they're about to exit the office, I duck into the bathroom next door just as I hear the door handle turn.

More muffled voices as the two men step into the hall, and I crack the door open a fraction to peer out as I hear the click of Drew's office door shutting, followed by two sets of footsteps moving away from me. I can only see their backs, and ignoring Drew on the left, I focus on the guy on the right. I only catch a quick glimpse—tall, muscular, dark-haired, gorgeous ass—before they both disappear, and I'm left perplexed, trying to work out who he was and why he sounded so familiar.

The rest of my shift goes by as usual. No Rejects stop by, and I have to assume they're all too busy to have any downtime yet, but I'd imagine in the coming days and weeks, we will start to see more of them coming in. It's only a matter of time, and the thought makes my palms sweat. Mainly in case Razor, the young kid who was with him, or Cain, stops by. Sure I had on a wig and heavy makeup, but up close, they would probably be able to figure out the girl they're looking for is me.

At the end of the night, after Drew locks the front door behind the last customer, he calls out, "Listen up, everyone. I know you're all tired and want to get home, but I wanted to let you all know, a liaison for Reaper Rejects stopped by today."

That immediately gets my attention as my thoughts drift back to the guy I saw leaving his office earlier. He must have been a Reject. Maybe one of the ones I saw the other night. It would explain why his voice seemed familiar.

"They've offered us protection in case there is any backlash from their takeover, and they've asked me to tell you that they are looking for waitresses to help out with regular cage fighting matches they'll be hosting at Toxic starting next week. If anyone is interested in helping out, please put your name on the sign-up sheet in my office."

I notice Viv and Jezebel exchanging a look, and I remember her words from earlier. More money would be nice, but I'm not about to walk myself into a room that's guaranteed to be full of Rejects when they're most likely still looking for me. In a few weeks, they'll have forgotten all about the girl covered in blood from the Satans' clubhouse and move on. Sure, like most people in Black Creek, they're curious about who the Reaper is—such a fucking stupid name, by the way—and probably thought I'd seen him. Ultimately, I'm sure they have more important things to be focusing on than chasing after a ghost.

I've heard whispers that the gangs think the Reaper is some sort of vigilante, out to annihilate all of them. How self-centered is it to think it's all about them? But it's not like they pay any attention to the deaths of non-gang members. I also make a point of not carving my mark into jobs I get paid to do—jobs like the one I had last week, where the shithead was a lawyer, where someone will notice and report him missing. I need the world beyond Black Creek to assume he was in the wrong place at the wrong time, that he got caught up in something he shouldn't have, or messed with the wrong person. If the authorities got wind that someone was going around murdering well-to-do people, they'd descend on the city. The sparse police force here doesn't give a shit. They're as corrupt as the rest of us. Every one of them is in someone's pocket, but it wouldn't take much to have the FBI sniffing around, asking unwanted questions.

The same discretion does not apply to jobs like Sheryl's. Jobs that I take on because I refuse to let the abusive men of this town beat us down. Jobs where if I don't intervene, there will inevitably be dire consequences. Like Sheryl, most of these women have no money, no security, no one they can rely on or turn to for help. Of course, killing their abusive partner doesn't mean they won't end up with someone similar, but the asshole gets what he deserves for putting his hands where they don't belong. A lot of these men are, in some way, affiliated with one street gang or another—as are most of the men in Black Creek—so naturally, that led people to assume the Reaper was anti-gang. And don't get me wrong, I am. I think it's a toxic environment that breeds misogyny and violent behavior... it's just not the reason why I'm killing these fuckers.

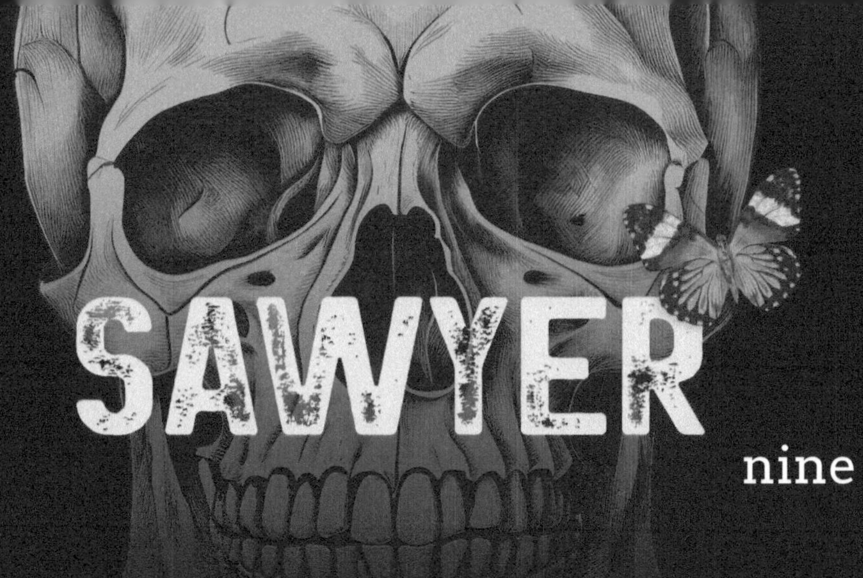

nine

I t quickly becomes apparent that the Rejects are looking for me. Well, for a skinny blonde girl who was known to hang out with the Satan's and may have been seen covered in blood the night they were slaughtered. It's seriously annoying as it means I have to keep a low profile for the next few days, only leaving the house when I have to. I'm confident my red hair will throw off most of them, but if I accidentally end up face-to-face with Cain or Razor, I can't be sure that they won't recognize me.

I don't even understand why they're so hellbent on hunting me down. I'm just some witness. For all they know, I was too shocked to even remember anything—assuming, of course, that I saw anything at all.

It's seriously messing with my routine. I had a new voicemail on the spare burner I keep stashed away, hidden from Luc, with a new job for *the Reaper*, but I haven't been able to risk doing any investigative work to see if it's a job I can take on. And it's a paid one too, so I really don't like the possibility of losing out on money over this whole bullshit.

All of the women's shelters in and around Black Creek have the contact details for my burner phone, and the women that run the shelters know what I do—hell, I've personally helped some of them out. Of course, only Beatrice knows the person behind the phone is me. Everyone else just offers the number out if they feel the woman could benefit from my services, or they place the call themselves if they are particularly concerned about someone.

If a potential client does contact me, I get them to leave their details, and do a little research into who they are before deciding whether or not I'll take the job. Unfortunately, I don't have the time or resources to help out every woman that contacts me, so it often depends on how many other jobs I'm working at the time and the severity of the case. Of course, if a woman or child appears to be in imminent danger, I'll do everything I can to prevent something tragic from happening, and most of the time, I can get the job done before it's too late.

There was only once when I didn't act quick enough. Luc had been really sick with bronchitis one winter, and I was scared to leave him for too long. By the time I had hunted down the shitstain who was abusing his pregnant girlfriend, it was too late. She'd been missing for two days when I caught up to him, and while the girl's friends were out looking for her, I immediately knew what had happened. In the voicemail I'd received from the shelter, the woman had sounded really concerned for this woman's safety and hadn't been able to persuade her not to go back to the asshole.

When I found him, hanging around outside the Grim Bastard's compound, he acted like nothing had happened. Like his pregnant girlfriend wasn't missing. It sickened me. It made me so mad, I can only describe his death as a rage kill, funneled by pure emotion. It's safe to say there was nothing left of him to be found by the time I was done, and his screams of agony still soothe my battered soul. But that woman died because I didn't act quickly enough, and that knowledge will haunt me for the rest of my days.

So, yeah, the fact that I'm having to take precautions and sit back when some woman could be getting the shit beat out of her, pisses me the fuck off.

"Did you hear about that girl the Rejects are looking for?" Luc asks me. It's been a week since the Rejects took over Satan territory, and other than them spreading word about the blonde woman they're looking for, it's been surprisingly quiet. A few skirmishes broke out initially, but they were quickly squashed. "What do you think that's all about?"

"No idea," I shrug, not wanting to engage in this conversation with my brother. I get he's curious; it's unusual that they're searching this hard for a girl. Everyone is wondering who she is and what she means to the Rejects.

"It's just weird that they're looking for a girl, isn't it?"

"She probably just stole from them or saw something they didn't want her seeing."

His gaze is fixed on the TV, and I can tell, even though he brought the conversation up, he's not that interested in it. "Yeah, you're probably right. At least it keeps them busy, right? Means they can't stir up shit for any of us."

"Exactly." If only they weren't busy pursuing me, then all would be great.

"Bet you've never been so glad to have hair that looks like it belongs on a Pokemon character."

I'm sitting beside him on the couch, and I jab my foot into his thigh, glowering playfully at him while he chuckles.

"Don't you have homework or something," I gripe.

He quirks a brow, throwing me an *are you serious* look. "I know it's been a while since you were in school, but you do remember what a farce the education system in Black Creek is, right?"

He's right. I dropped out of school when our mother died. Murdered. When our mother was murdered. But I remember what a sham it was. School was nothing more than a daycare for parents to send their children off to so they could work or get stoned in peace for several hours each day. I learned a hell of a lot more living on the streets than I ever did inside a classroom. Still, I've insisted Luc attend until he's eighteen. It might not exactly be educational, but it's what kids do. Besides, it's got to be better than working some shitty, dead-end job that you know you'll be stuck doing for the next forty years of your life. I don't want Luc to feel trapped like that at such a young age. Admittedly, I don't ever want him to feel like that, but I'm not sure how

I can prevent it, so for now, I'm settling for delaying the inevitable for a few more years.

Rolling my eyes, I snark, "Then sit there and watch your TV show in silence like a good little boy."

His face scrunches before he barks out a laugh and returns his attention to the TV, enabling me to get back to mentally figuring out what I'm going to do about my Reaper Rejects dilemma. Except, there's nothing I can do but lay low for a few more days and hope they get bored with chasing after someone they'll never find.

<hr>

AFTER ANOTHER COUPLE OF DAYS OF ONLY LEAVING THE HOUSE TO GO TO the club and get groceries, I've had enough. I couldn't continue to sit there twiddling my thumbs. The voicemail on my phone with some new asshole's name was calling to me. Chad Greenway's death at my hands is exactly what I need to help me let go of all this frustration.

Which is why I'm currently tailing him on my bike as he drives through Antonelli territory. From what I've gathered, Chad is a partner at a hedge fund firm, and when he's not working, he likes to gamble away his obscene bonuses and frequent upscale sex clubs, like the ones the Antonellis run. Then, when he's thrown away all his money, he likes to go home to his wife and take his shitty decisions out on her. Classy guy.

I slow down as his car comes to a stop outside Bella Antonella, the Antonellis' casino. I continue past the entrance and pull the bike over to the side of the road several blocks down, watching as Chad—a balding man in his forties—gets out of the backseat and strides into the building. Unfortunately, I can't just strut into the casino and cozy up to Chad until I can convince him to leave with me. Not only do the Antonellis have bouncers on the door and security cameras that would easily pick me up, but they would probably be able to smell the poverty on me from the sidewalk. Their establishments have a particular class about them. Their patrons wear expensive suits and fancy dresses. There is no chance I'll get inside that casino dressed in what I'm wearing. Even as I watch, some asshole with his hair slicked back escorts a lady through the front doors with what looks like diamonds clasped around her neck and wearing a gorgeous evening gown. No, I won't be able to get to Chad inside the casino.

I sit and wait—an incredibly dull but essential part of my job—and several hours later, looking worse for wear with the top button of his shirt undone, his tie hanging loosely from his neck, and his hair disheveled, he storms out of the building and gets into his awaiting car. Perking up, I start the engine of the bike and follow after him as he goes a couple of streets over to Belle Donne—one of the Antonellis' sex clubs. I'm wondering if I could sneak in there. It would be dimly lit, and I'd easily blend in with the working girls—the perfect place to kill him, especially if I made it look like an accident.

Once he's stumbled inside, clearly drunk off his ass, I scope out the exits, noting the bouncers and security cameras on the front door, as well as the bouncer and camera covering the staff entrance around back, before I head home. I need to do more research before I do anything else. At least I've got his routine down. I've been following Chad for the last few nights now, and it's always the same—casino, sex club, home. I told his wife to make up an excuse to leave town for the next two weeks, so hopefully, she's done that and won't have to suffer at his hands tonight when he gets home. That gives me another week and a half to get the job done. Now I just need to figure out how to get inside that club.

THE NEXT NIGHT, I WALK ONTO THE STAGE AT STRIP TEASE TO *S&M* BY Rihanna and lose myself in the music as I twirl in my sky-high heels, grinding my hips, tensing my abs, and pushing out my tits.

The place is packed tonight, and I noticed several tables of Rejects members when I walked in. They've been stopping by the club the last few nights, all with easy-going, jovial smiles. They don't cause too much of a ruckus, and I haven't heard of any of them getting aggressive or physical with the girls. If anything, they seem to almost have some level of respect for us. It makes me suspicious, to say the least, and I definitely don't trust them.

I'm halfway through my routine when I feel eyes on me, which sounds ridiculous because I probably have the eyes of at least half the men in the room right now, but this is different. Whatever this is, it burns my skin and makes my heart race. As I lift my feet, swiveling around the pole, I squint through the light, trying to pinpoint who is looking at me, but I can't make out anyone obvious.

I can't shake the feeling of eyes on me for the rest of my dance, and by the time my set ends, I'm trembling. My legs feel shaky and unstable as I carefully descend the steps from the stage, but before I can so much as take a breath, a heavy weight crashes into me, throwing me back against the wall with a thud that knocks the air out of my lungs.

Slowly, my eyes crawl over the broad-chested, tatted-up asshole pinning me to the wall, along the dark scruff of beard dusting his jaw, until I meet his searing green eyes, fuming with rage. I suck in a gasp, my eyes widening. *Oh, fuck.* Anger radiates off Cain like thermal energy, heating the air between us. His eyes hold me immobilized, and suddenly I realize it was his gaze I could feel burning into me on stage.

"You," he snarls, his voice sounding more beast-like than human. Before I can gather my thoughts to figure a way out of this, he's wrapped his large, inked hand around my upper arm in a firm grip, and I nearly stumble in my high-heels, struggling to keep up with his enormous strides as he storms into the back hallway, heading for Drew's office.

He pushes open the office door and shoves me into the room, practically throwing me onto the sofa as he looms over me. I hurry to push myself upright and glower at him, biting my tongue so hard I'm surprised I don't taste blood. See, this is why I stay as far away from gang members as I can. The malevolence pouring off him is stifling, and the tense way he's holding himself tells me he's trying really hard to hold himself back. Back from what? From hitting me? From hurting me? He might look like temptation with his black jeans that mold to his thighs and his t-shirt that looks like a second skin, but he's everything that's wrong with this world. He's so used to people cowering beneath him, obeying his every whim, that he can't stand the fact I'm not whimpering and begging for forgiveness at his feet.

"Why did you run away?" His words are a harsh bite, spat out through gritted teeth.

"You just murdered a whole bunch of men," I snap. "Do you really think I was going to hang around so you could kill me too?"

The words are out of my mouth before I can rein in my temper, and there's a dangerous flash in his eyes before they narrow on me.

"I wasn't going to kill you." He says it like it should be obvious—like how could I possibly think such a thing. Of course, silly me. How could death by machine gun possibly have crossed my mind when fifty-odd men, half-hidden behind gruesome, skeleton-designed neck warmers and carrying automatic rifles, are stomping around the house, killing every gang member they cross? "Tell me what you saw."

I press my lips together, scrutinizing him, and when I don't immediately obey his command, his anger sparks again.

"Fine," he snaps, digging into his pocket and producing a wad of cash. He flicks through it, and he's standing close enough that I can tell he's holding more money in his hand than I make in a month. He peels off three one hundred dollar bills and holds them out to me expectantly.

I sneer at his outstretched hand. "I don't want your fucking money."

His brows lift in surprise for a split second before he masks it with a scowl, more of that perpetual anger of his simmering in his emerald irises. Without saying a word, he stuffs the money back in his pocket, and in one large stride he closes the distance between us. I press my back flat against the sofa and tilt my head back so I can maintain eye contact with him, refusing to let him intimidate me, even as my heart hammers against my chest and a little voice in the back of my head tells me to behave.

This close, his whiskey and leather scent envelopes me. It makes no sense because he's not even wearing leather, but it's a distinct, homely smell. Despite the glower I'm throwing his way, I can feel the smell seeping into my skin, my body reacting instinctively to it. My muscles uncoil and relax, and I find myself wondering if I could bottle that smell and spray it on my pillow at night. It would be the perfect way to fall asleep.

I shake myself out of that ludicrous thought and focus back on the brute towering over me. I'm not going to get out of here without giving him something. I don't know why he's so hellbent on finding the Reaper, but I highly doubt it's even crossed his mind that he might be staring him—well, her—in the face right now.

My tongue flicks out to lick my bottom lip, and his eyes dart down to my mouth, tracking the movement. It's the first sign of interest he's given—if that's even what this is. Even though I'm wearing next to nothing, he hasn't given me more than a cursory glance. In fact, his gaze has hardly left my face at all.

Sighing, like he's won, I say, "I didn't see anything."

At the sound of my voice, his eyes snap to meet mine, but he doesn't back away, only stares at me intently until I continue talking.

"Python and I went upstairs, and I went to the bathroom before... " I lick my lips again, putting my fantastic acting skills to use as I pretend to be shocked and horrified as I think back to that night. "When I came back to the bedroom, h-he... I found him like that."

I drop my gaze, sniffling as I pretend to wipe my eyes. I'm just a meek girl who's traumatized by what she witnessed in that room.

He's silent for so long that I peer up at him through my eyelashes, needing to get a read on him. His eyes are narrowed in suspicion, and I can practically see the thoughts running around in his head as he tries to suss me out.

"Why was the door locked?"

Uhhh. "I panicked when I heard people screaming and running out of the house." It's a total guess. Over the cacophony of rap music, the sweet melody of Python dying, and the heady sort of concentration that comes with killing a man, I didn't hear a damn thing that was going on outside that room. But there's no way a whole group of Cain's men stormed in there, looking the way they did, without causing a panic.

My words are met with another long moment of contemplative silence before his next question. "How do you explain the fact you were covered in Python's blood?" The skepticism is clear to hear in his voice, but he's got no reason not to believe me. More importantly, he's got no proof that I'm lying.

"I-I thought I could save him." I let my chin wobble. "I t-tried to stop the bleeding, b-but it was too much." My voice raises in pitch, making me sound half-hysterical. "I-I didn't even see what was"—I scrunch my nose in disgust—"*carved* into his abdomen until I heard someone kicking down the door."

"So you never saw who killed him?"

I shake my head. "No."

"What about someone at the party? Did anyone stand out or seem to be paying particular attention to Python?"

Other than me? "No. Not that I saw, but I wasn't really paying attention to anyone else."

He purses his lips as he thinks for a moment, before finally giving a sharp jerk of his head. "Fine." He doesn't sound happy, but at least he seems to believe what I'm saying —for now. "You can go back to work."

With my heart lodged in my throat, I scurry toward the door without a backward glance. On my way out, I grab ahold of the handle, turning it roughly in my hand as I pull the door closed behind me, but the handle is old, and I know that if you twist it hard enough, the latch sticks. I wait a moment until I hear his voice, then I push the door open ever so slightly. It's not enough for me to see into the room, but there's a slither of a gap between the wooden door frame and the door, allowing me to hear what he's saying to someone on the phone.

"She's lying, O... I'm not sure. I can't place it. I just... there's something off with her."

Fuck.

Not wanting to be caught eavesdropping, I pull the door closed again and jiggle the handle, engaging the latch before silently moving away and getting back to work. Cain's words play on repeat in my head, and I constantly run my gaze over the various Reject members, wondering who it was he was talking to. And why. Why is he so set on finding the Reaper? What does he want with him—with me? Knowing he's devoting so much time and energy to finding me makes me antsy, and I can't settle for the rest of the night, moving on autopilot as I deliver drinks, perform on the stage, and give lap dances.

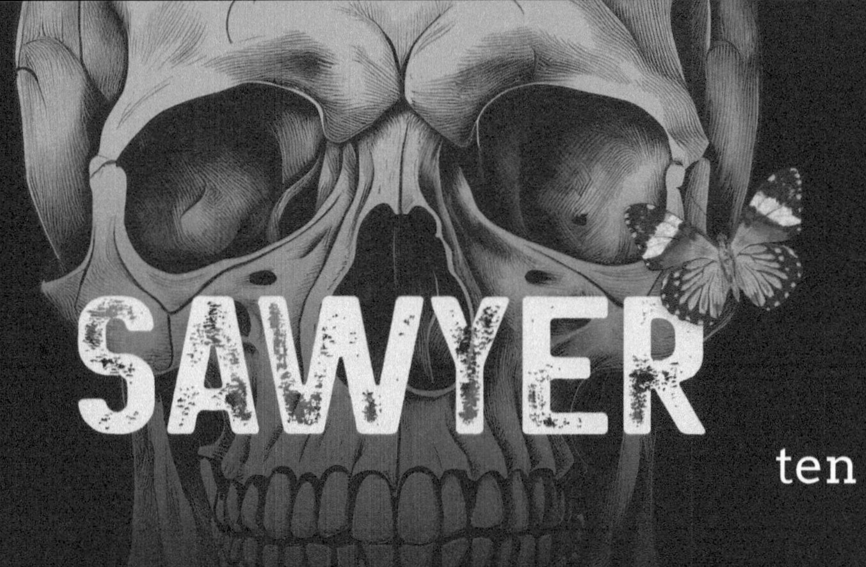

ten

I feel like a paranoid schizophrenic, looking all around me as I stealthily make my way to the garage where I keep my bike. Cain's words about not believing me echo in my head for like the fiftieth time since last night, and I'm worried he will have someone watching me, digging into my life. I can't have him—or anyone—finding out who I am. And more importantly, I can't afford to bring trouble to Luc's door.

Thankfully, I don't see or hear anyone behind me as I approach the garage door and bend to yank it open. I need to complete this job ASAP. The longer I work it, the higher the chance Cain will discover who I am—or at least realize I'm up to something. It's all good, though, because I have a plan for Chad Greenway, and I'm going to execute it tonight.

Pulling on my helmet, I walk the bike out of the garage and close the door behind me before taking off down the street, heading for the Antonellis' part of town. I'm not sure if it's psychological or real, but I swear, you can tell when you've hit Antonelli territory. In fairness, you do have to cross over a bridge to get to it, but it's more than that. There's a shine to the buildings that you don't see where I live, and the same grime doesn't seem to coat the streets.

When I'm a couple of blocks away from the Belle Donne, I park up at the side of the road and duck into an alleyway to change. I've brought fishnet tights and the shortest booty shorts I own, along with my laciest bra. I have absolutely no idea what high-end hookers wear, but it's the best I could do, and I'm hoping any discrepancies won't be noticed in the dim light of the club.

Once I'm dressed, I pull out a wig—this time one with long, dark brown, wavy hair. The color matches the brown contacts I put in before I left the apartment, the ensemble hopefully enough to disguise me from any security the Antonellis might have and prevent anyone inside the club from identifying me. Ready, I throw on a cheap trench coat that I can afford to discard once I'm inside, and amble across the street toward the Belle Donne.

My next hurdle is getting inside. I'd already written off the front door as my entry point. With the cameras and bouncers, there's no way I'd easily get in, a fact I quickly confirm as I come out on the opposite side of the street to the club. Besides, I doubt that's how the working girls get in and out of the club. No, my guess is, much like at Strip Tease, they use the back door.

Hurrying across the road, I stick close to the shadows provided by the adjacent building as I sneak down the alleyway running along the side of the club. As I go, I scan my eyes over the rest of the brick building, debating if there's an alternative way in—an open window, a hidden roof entrance—but I don't have time to scout the place out any further. Ideally, I would have taken my time to scope out the best way in, but Cain has forced my hand, and is making me act sooner than I'd like with this job. Just one more reason to be angry with that asshole. He's completely messing with my life, and for what? So he can chase after some ghost? Who does he think he is? Surely, it must have crossed his mind that hunting down someone who kills gang members might result in his own death. It's just idiotic.

Unable to spot a suitable alternative way into the club, I continue down the alley to the back of the building, where the staff entrance is. Crouching behind a dumpster, I take in the burly guard on duty, blocking the door and the security camera attached to the wall behind him.

I chew on my bottom lip as I debate what to do, but the way I see it, I only have one option, and I'm just going to have to hope on a wing and a prayer that it works.

With nothing else for it, I step out from behind the dumpster and stride toward the bouncer, my heels clicking against the cobblestones with every step. His head snaps in my direction, his eyes raking over me as I step into the pool of light surrounding the door.

I lick my lips in a nervous gesture as I look up at him with doe-like eyes. "Ahh, this is the staff entrance for Belle Donne, right? It's my first night, and I've managed to get myself all worked up and disorientated."

The guy just stares down at me with an impassive expression. "I wasn't informed we had anyone new starting tonight."

I let my eyes widen in shock, a flare of panic flashing across my face. "W-what? No, I definitely have the right start date. Oh my goodness, I can't believe I'm screwing this all up already. I can't afford to lose another job." I force tears to well in my eyes as I duck my head and sniffle. Why are so many men suckers for a crying woman? Not that I'm complaining, ninety percent of the time, it works in my favor. And as the guy huffs out a restrained breath, I know it's working on him too.

"It's alright, little lady. There's no need to cry about it, they probably just forgot to inform me. Why don't you go on in and talk to Franny in the office. She'll get you sorted out before you start."

I swipe under my eyes and look up at the frowning man like he just hung the moon for me. "Oh, thank you! Thank you!"

He gives me a tight smile in return as he ushers me through the door, and as it clangs shut behind me, I let the whole helpless woman look drop from my expression as I glance around, taking in the back hallway of the club.

Thankfully the hallway is empty, and I hurry along it, not needing to be caught now that I'm through the door. The whole *I'm new* thing will only work for so long.

Finding the door into the main club, I push it open and slip inside, relief lifting my shoulders as I find the interior of the club lit only by dim lamps, providing a seductive atmosphere that matches the soft, sensual music and breathy moans I can hear in the quiet seconds between songs.

The room I'm in is made up of booths, with translucent curtains draped around each one, providing a modicum of privacy for its occupants. Unable to determine if Chad is behind any of them, I hurry across the thickly carpeted space toward the only other door in sight.

The next room's atmosphere is entirely different from the one I just left behind. The music is faster and louder, intended to get the blood pumping and adrenaline flowing. The room is lit only by overhead neon lights, which flash, giving it an eerie quality. In the split-second flashes of light, I can make out people grinding on one another in the middle of a crowded dance floor and others making out against the booths lining the far walls.

I take my time, pushing through the crowd and squinting into the dark corners of the room, looking for anyone that resembles Chad. I come across several possibilities, but when I get close enough, I realize they aren't him and continue on my hunt. I'm not sure if it's the music or knowing I'm getting closer to my prey, but I can feel the need for bloodshed humming beneath my skin, like a visceral reaction to the shitstain's close proximity. It heightens my senses and seems to draw me across the room as if some baser part of myself instinctively knows where he's hiding.

As I move into another room which is set up like an upscale theater, with its red, velvet, circular booths, all facing a stage, and golden table lamps that give out a low light, I spot my next victim, lounging in the middle of the room as he watches two naked women putting on a show on the stage. As I focus on them, I realize it's basically a live porn performance. *Whatever helps him get his rocks off, I guess.*

I grab a drink from the tray of a passing waitress, sniffing the glass. *Damn, they have the good stuff here.* There's none of the harsh scent of alcohol. Instead, all I can smell is vanilla and oak. I almost feel bad as I empty the mini tube of benzodiazepines I crushed up earlier into the glass and dip my finger into the liquid, mixing it in with the alcohol.

With the drink in hand, I approach Chad, sitting alone at his table. "Enjoying the show?" I ask in a husky voice, holding the glass out for him. My words snag his attention as he gives me a once-over before reaching out to take the drink, bringing it to his lips.

He swivels the whiskey around his mouth before swallowing, giving a casual shrug in response to my question.

"Perhaps I can help you find something more suitable?" I offer in a seductive purr.

His eyes rake over me once again, making goosebumps rise along my skin. "I'm after something... specific."

I raise a brow and quirk my lips, leaning into him in such a way that makes my tits squish together, threatening to burst out of my bra. "I can be *anything* you want." The words taste like vomit in my mouth, but whatever gets the job done.

He gives me another long, assessing look before knocking back the rest of his drink. A thrill of excitement pulses through me as he empties the glass, handing it off to someone before gesturing for me to lead the way.

I notice a hallway lined with doors on my perusal through the club, so I lead him in that direction, knowing they could only be there for one purpose. I find the hallway with ease, and as I stride confidently along it, I note the red light that's activated beside some of the doors, obviously indicating that they are occupied. Finding an empty one, I open the door and step in, feeling his presence behind me as he follows me in. The loud click of the latch signifies that I finally have him alone as I do a quick scan around the room, taking in the plush king-sized bed occupying most of the space, as well as the wall of various sex toys, whips, paddles, and handcuffs—*kinky*—before I spin in my heels to face him.

Before I can plant my feet again, I'm knocked sideways, stumbling from the shock of the blow. My cheek smarts from the crack of his hand across it, and I can feel the sting of a split lip. He descends upon me while I'm still trying to comprehend what the hell just happened, knocking me back with another punch to my cheek. *What the fuck? Is this what he gets off on?* Apparently, it is. As I glance up at him, I can see the hungry look in his eye. He enjoys the power he gets from beating on a woman; he feeds off the high. It's fucking disgusting.

He lifts his hand to strike me again, but before he can do so, a strange look crosses his features, and he stumbles to the side.

"W-what the... whuts happenin' to mee?" His words begin to slur, the drugs finally taking effect, and he collapses to his knees at the end of the bed. Both benzodiazepines and alcohol are central nervous system depressants. They make you drowsy and uncoordinated, and in high enough doses, can repress your respiratory system—at least, that's what a quick internet search told me before I bought a little baggie of Xanax off some kid who hustles on the street corner down from Strip Tease.

I watch impassively as Chad slumps against the bed. His eyes repeatedly drift shut before fluttering open, like he's struggling to stay awake, and the rapid rise and fall of his chest gives away the difficulty he's having breathing. I wasn't entirely sure how many pills it would take to finish him off, so I ground up as many as I thought would dissolve in a drink. Looks like I've gotten the concoction just right, though.

He groans weakly before vomiting all over himself. He tips onto his side, crashing against the ground, not giving a shit that he's lying in his own vomit, and I patiently wait until his chest stops moving before I jump into action. When he's finally lying unmoving, in a heap on the floor, I give it another minute while I wipe the trickle of blood from my chin, wincing as my tongue glides over the already swollen cut on my lip before I pull open the door to the room, stepping into the hall and screaming, "Help! HELP! He's not breathing. Please, someone help!"

It takes a second, but eventually, doors start to swing open, and people spill into the hallway, drawn by curiosity to know what's happened. As the hall fills with people, some just standing there peering into the room, while others move toward a very dead Chad, I melt into the crowd and slip away, rushing toward the back entrance of the club. A slight smile of achievement curls up the corner of my lips as I reach the door leading into the back hallway, but it's wiped clean when I crash into a hard chest.

A small *oomph* escapes my lips as the air is pushed out of my lungs, and my hands clasp onto a set of muscular forearms to steady myself. Blinking, my eyes take in a crisp white shirt and black tie before they crest over a smooth, angular jawline, high cheekbones and pitch black hair before meeting steely chocolate-brown eyes.

"Uhh, sorry," I stutter, swallowing around a sudden lump in my throat. I gesture with my thumb over my shoulder. "I think there was, ehh, an accident or something. Someone needs help."

His eyes dart over my head, looking toward where I just came from.

"I'll handle it." His gaze drops back to meet mine, narrowing as they take me in. "Do I know you?"

My eyes roam over his face, and it takes me a second, but recognition hits me like a semi-truck, knocking any remaining oxygen from my lungs. How the fuck did I not realize it at first?

"Emm, I don't think so," I croak. "I'm new."

I move to take a step back, away from him, wanting to put some much-needed space between us, but his large, coarse palm comes up to grasp my face, his fingers pressing firmly into my cheeks as he leans down to study my face. My heart rate skips a beat, thinking he's figured out who I am, but after a second, I realize he's examining the cut on my lip. His face pinches, a predatory look flashing in his eyes as they move up my face, stopping on what I imagine is the beginnings of a bruise on my cheek. At the realization, his fingers loosen on my skin, but I swear I can still feel the zing of them, even after he's let me go.

He opens his mouth to say something, but he doesn't get the chance to say whatever is on his mind before more calls for help, the voices becoming more alarmed with each passing second, drawing his attention to the chaos behind me. He straightens up, giving me a final frown and quizzical look before he takes off down the hall.

I'm frozen in place as I watch him go, seriously shocked at who he is. I mean, I've got no idea who he is. But I know who he is *to me*. He's older looking than the last time we met, but then that was eight years ago, and we were in a dark alley. Not to mention that he was pointing a gun at my head, so no wonder I didn't immediately recognize him.

As he disappears, I blink out of my shock, and remembering where I am, I slip out an emergency exit door at the side of the club and disappear into the night. The cool air whips across my face, blowing the fake brunette strands in all directions as I sprint the few blocks to my bike. I shove a pair of pants over my outfit and toss my wig in the duffel bag, pulling on a leather jacket before securing the bag across my back. Not wanting to waste any more time, I swing my leg over my baby and tug on my helmet before giving the engine a rev and taking off down the street.

The cold air bites my skin, mixing with the adrenaline still flooding my body and making me feel alive, as I let out a loud whoop that is quickly swallowed by the wind. Damn, there's nothing quite like the thrill that comes from killing a scumbag like that. Anger licks along my skin, heating me from the inside out as I run my tongue over the cut on my lip, remembering the sting of pain when he hit me.

Once Raven is parked in my garage, I take out my burner phone and fire off a text to Chad's wife, letting her know the job is done before I rifle through the compact side unit where I keep some tools for the bike, and a bottle of cheap whiskey, strictly for occasions like tonight.

I pull off the lid with a pop and knock back a mouthful. Images of the man from tonight clash in my head with long-buried ones from eight years ago. The way he'd looked at me tonight was so similar to then. That ice-cold gaze that froze me in place, his chiseled jaw that looks like it's been carved from stone.

He said he'd handle it when I mentioned there was a problem, so he must work for the Antonellis in some capacity. Hitman plus club manager? That's an eclectic mixture of skills. But then who am I to talk—stripper and avenger of battered women—those two things hardly go hand in hand.

I wonder if he recognized me. *God, I hope not.* I bury my face in my palms and let out a long, weary groan. That's the last thing I need. As if it's not bad enough that Cain's got a stick up his ass when it comes to me. *Ha, fuck.* Even the thought of having not one but *two* gang members looking for me makes my palms sweat, and I quickly try to drown out the anxious feeling by taking another swig of whiskey.

The bottle is empty, and I'm just this side of tipsy by the time I stagger into the night and make my way home.

I'M WORKING THE LATE SHIFT AT THE CLUB THE REST OF THE WEEK, which would be fine... if some overbearing, tatted-up asshole didn't keep stopping by whenever I'm working to sit silently in the corner and follow my every move. It's driving me fucking insane. What the hell is he even doing? Trying to intimidate me? Ha, there's no chance of that.

I can feel his eyes tracking my movements every night, feel them burning into me when I'm on stage, delivering drinks, giving lap dances. Hell, I even feel the lingering tingle of his gaze along my skin when I take my break.

After three nights of this nonsense, I'm like a raging bull when I step into Strip Tease on Friday and find him already sitting at his usual table. Despite knowing I need to be careful, I throw him a hateful glare, which he returns with a knowing smirk before I stomp over to the bar.

"What's up your ass tonight?" Mike asks when he sees me.

"He's here every night," I grumble, not having to explain any further who *he* is. "Doesn't he have better things to do?"

Mike just shrugs as he dries a tumbler before storing it away under the counter. "No idea. None of them seem too bad, though—the Rejects."

Of course, he thinks that. When they come in, many of them spend time at the bar talking to him. I've seen the way he interacts with them, laughing and chatting. He already acts as though they're all buddies.

I snatch up a tray of drinks and move to distribute them to waiting customers around the room, as usual ignoring the searing heat of my skin as Cain trails me with his eyes.

The night goes on like that—me ignoring him, him watching—until the last customer leaves, and Drew locks the front door while the rest of us wipe down the tables and straighten everything up for tomorrow.

Once I've wiped the last table clean, I head toward the dressing room to change and gather my belongings, which is, of course, when Cain decides to finally make his move —just when I was starting to think I was done with him for the night. He calls out, "Drew, give Red the keys. She and I have a few things to discuss before she leaves. She can lock up when we're done."

Gritting my teeth, I turn to glare at the insufferable asshole.

"Oh, uhh, sure," Drew agrees hesitantly. He's not about to argue with a Reject, though. Not that I would expect him to. He gives me a long look as he hands the keys over, silently asking if I'm okay—he's a good person like that—and I give a nod and small lift of my lips to let him know I'm fine. I can handle myself against this asshole. While I prefer to lure my men with false pretenses, I have just enough self-defense skills to get me out of a tight corner. Although I have to admit, I've never had to fight off someone like Cain, who's all bulging muscle, and toned features. He's built more like a Viking warrior than a Black Creek thug, so I don't for one second think I could win against someone like him. But I could hopefully catch him by surprise. Not that I think he's asking me to stay so he can try to attack me. Nope, if I've learned anything from his incessant stalking the last few nights, it's that this asshole prefers to use silent intimidation to try and break me.

Neither of us moves or says anything until the last of the staff leave, most of them giving me curious or questioning looks as they pass by. When we're finally alone, I quirk a brow at him. "What is this about?"

"Dance for me." It's an order, given to me by the current overlord of our little part of town, and more importantly, a decider of fates for the people who work at Strip Tease.

It only makes rage simmer within me, though, and no doubt he can see the pits of anger burning in my eyes as he smirks at me. Pursing my lips, I have to swallow down my snort of refusal. I can't afford to piss him off and cause problems for Drew or anyone else who works here. The Rejects may seem like decent guys, but as I said, I don't trust them, and I definitely don't trust their leader. It wouldn't be fair to Drew or the others if I caused problems for them just because I've gotten myself into a tight spot with Cain. Besides, it's only one measly dance... how bad can it be?

I hesitate for another second, calculating my options, but ultimately, I'm just delaying the inevitable. I *know* what I need to do; what I *have* to do. There's no other choice—not if I don't want to end up fired or get my colleagues in trouble.

Biting my tongue, I make the only move I can—I head toward the stage.

"Ah-ah."

I freeze, gritting my teeth. *Fuck.* It takes me a second to compose myself before I look over my shoulder at him. He's leaning back in his seat with his legs spread wide, the intent clear to read in his cocky expression.

"Here." He points to the spot between his thighs. *Fucking asshole.* He knows I can't refuse; knows I won't risk the other's livelihoods.

Fuck. I seriously don't want to get that close to him. If the feel of his eyes on me is enough to scorch my skin, then being within touching distance of him is going to send me up in flames.

I glare daggers at him, making it clear how much I want to tear out his trachea and jam it up his ass as I spin on my heels and stride toward him, planting myself between his spread thighs. I ignore the way my muscles tense, and the fine hairs on my arms stand on end as if his close proximity has sent a bolt of static electricity through my system. It doesn't help that, while he's fully dressed, I'm wearing nothing more than a thong and a scrap of fabric claiming to be a bra. Even though he's barely paid any attention to my body, I feel the need to put more layers between us. Not because of him, but because of me. I can't trust the way his presence affects me; how it makes my heart race.

My heated skin begs for his touch, and while I'm reluctant to get any closer to him, my body is practically singing for joy at our closeness.

He raises his eyebrows in an expectant look when I make no effort to move. There's no music, and honestly, this is awkward as fuck. Huffing out a breath, I start to sway my hips, shifting my weight from one leg to another as I fixate on a point on the wall just to the right of his head. One dance. Three minutes. That's all, and then I'm getting the fuck out of here.

I slowly countdown the seconds in my head—the only way for me to time myself, and it provides a sufficient distraction from the gorgeous asshole watching me intently and, more importantly, the disturbing response my body has to his nearness. I lose myself in the movement of my body, in the heat of his gaze, in the passing seconds as I tick them off one by one until he breaks the trance I was in.

"I know you're lying."

It's a statement. One delivered with absolute confidence.

"Is that so?" I challenge, finally allowing myself to meet his gaze. His bright green eyes bore into me, stalling the breath in my lungs.

He leans forward just as I bend my knees slightly, bringing our faces within inches of one another. "The question is, why?"

I don't answer him, meeting his watchful gaze with a steely one of my own as I stand back to my full height, peering down at him. I have to be careful here. I can't push him too far, but I also can't just spill all my secrets. He might know I'm lying, but he's got no proof, and that thought bolsters me.

As he sits back in his seat, I make an effort to soften my expression, stepping in to him. My thigh brushes against the coarse material of his jeans, and I have to ignore the way my skin reacts to that simple touch. Reaching out, I trail my finger down the front of his shirt before placing my palms on his chest and leaning in close to him.

"Maybe I just wanted to get the attention of a big, bad gangster," I volley, whispering the words seductively in his ear before pulling back to gauge his reaction. "Or maybe you're making up excuses to seek me out."

His expression darkens, and in a lightning-fast move, his hands snap out and reach around the back of my thighs, dragging me into his lap. My hands clasp his shoulders to stabilize myself while I work to hide my surprise at the feel of his semi-hard erection in his pants.

"Now, what would I want with a slut like you?" he snarls venomously. "Not good for anything except putting on a show and spreading your legs."

Despite the angry flare his words spark within me, I smirk down at him, appearing completely unaffected as I shift in his lap, deliberately rubbing my core over his dick.

"Are you sure about that because the hard-on in your pants says otherwise."

Using sex to disarm men is the most effective weapon I have. It's shocking how easily a man can be distracted when a hot girl flirts and rubs herself against him. I have to admit, though, this is the first time I've been turned on by someone I'm trying to charm. Heat pools in my core as I rub myself against him, and I have to work hard to push aside the cloud of lust threatening to consume me. *He's a Reject*, I remind myself. *He's an asshole. He's been trying to intimidate you all week. He wants to find the Reaper.*

It's enough to snap me out of the lusty haze and focus back on the task at hand. Intent on distracting him, so he forgets all about why he's here, I flick my tongue to lick along my bottom lip, and I lean in to run my nose up the column of his neck, ensuring my nipples graze against his chest.

"It's okay if you are," I whisper in his ear, sucking on his ear lobe as I subtly shift my crotch over his dick, feeling him grow beneath me. My pussy clenches yet again, and I have to mentally chastise myself. He might be downright fuckable, but he's abso-fuck-ing-lutely off-limits.

His hands grab hold of my hips, squeezing tightly as he takes over control of my movements, using me to get himself off. I see the flare of heat in his eyes, and I have to bite back my own groan of pleasure every time the rough fabric of his jeans presses against my clit. I'm honestly no longer sure where this is going. As heat surges through my body, I almost forget why I'm trying to distract him.

He's rock hard beneath me now, only making my pussy clench hungrily. Just when I'm convinced I have him in the palm of my hand and he's about to come in his boxers, he jumps to his feet, making me stumble as I try to get my legs beneath me before I fall to the ground.

My head is still spinning from the sudden change when he snatches my arms behind my back and bends me over the table, so my cheek and tits are pressed against the hardwood, my ass in the air.

I'm so caught off guard that I don't even react as he leans over me, the heat of his body warming my back as he whispers in my ear. "I told you, I don't have a need for worn-out hooker pussy." His words are a low, warning snarl that penetrate through my sex-addled brain.

I start fighting against his hold on my wrists, but it's futile. His grip only tightens as he kicks my legs apart with his feet, shifting, so he's easily holding my wrists in one hand. His other one slides down over my ass before he trails his fingers across my hip until he reaches my inner thigh, teasing the sensitive skin there.

My breaths come in rapid pants, both wanting him to touch me where I need him most and wanting him to fuck off. It's a confusing battle that annoys me to no end.

His fingers dance along the lining of the cheap thong I'm wearing before he brushes them over the fabric along the seam of my pussy. I buck against his touch, inadvertently pushing my ass against his still hard cock, and hating the evil-sounding chuckle he emits.

He rubs over my clit more deliberately, and I know he can feel how damp my panties are as I fight not to writhe or moan under his touch.

"Maybe you did just want my attention," he purrs in a husky voice that sounds as smooth as expensive whiskey. He slips his fingers beneath the scrap of fabric, finding me soaking wet as he pushes three fingers inside me.

I'm gritting my teeth so hard, I'll be lucky I don't crack one. He somehow seems to know that I'm fighting my body's natural reaction and that only encourages him to work me over harder, thrusting his fingers into me in fast, deep strokes until I can feel my pussy fluttering around him.

"You're so close to coming," he murmurs, and I can hear the lust in his voice. Despite whatever the fuck this is, he's not as unaffected as he would like me to believe. "All over my fingers. Is that what does it for you? Getting finger fucked by gang leaders? You need someone violent and in control to make you come?"

I can't even grit out a "no," too afraid that if I open my mouth, I'll say something different or simply moan in such a way that will be enough of an answer to how much he's affecting me.

Just as my orgasm feels like it's about to unfurl from my lower belly, he stills his fingers inside me. "Is that why you were with Python that night? Thought he would give you a good fucking?" His voice has lost that husky quality, the anger in it now abundantly clear. "Or was your pussy merely a distraction? You should know," he growls in warning, "I'm not like Python or any of those other meatheads. Your saggy cunt won't keep me from finding out what you know or from hunting down the Reaper. You're only making things worse for yourself by lying, so this is your last warning. Next time I won't be so nice."

He pulls out of me, finally releasing his hold on my wrists, and I spin to glower at him.

"Go fuck yourself," I snarl furiously, feeling the heat of anger and embarrassment coating my cheeks.

He smirks smugly. "No need, I've got plenty of women who will happily get me off, and they'll do a hell of a better job than you could."

With that, he strides toward the staff entrance at the back of the room. I can't do anything but stand on shaky legs and watch him go. Before he slips through the door, he calls out, "Don't forget to lock up."

When I'm alone, I sink into his now vacant chair, dazed. *What the fuck just happened?* How did that take such a turn for the worse? I still can't wrap my head around how I went from being the one in control to being bent over the table while he finger fucked me, and I'm not the slightest bit happy that I can still feel the delicious stretch of his fingers or the fact I'm fucking furious he stopped before I could come.

The outer door bounces off the frame as I slam it behind me and stomp down the alley to the main road. I run my hand through my hair, tugging at the short, black strands in frustration as I force out a long, slow exhale through my nose. My bicep flexes as I tense the muscles in it. I want to scream my rage to the heavens, let out all this pent-up anger in the ring. But more problematic is the voice in my head, urging me to go back and finish what I started. The tightness around my crotch isn't helping the situation either.

Refusing to give in to whatever hold the red-headed witch has on me, I force my feet forward toward the Escalade I have parked at the side of the road just outside the club. The street is dark and vacant at this late hour, but I'm hardly paying any attention to my surroundings as I climb in behind the wheel and slam the door closed behind me.

My hands clench the steering wheel tightly as I take a second to try and clear my thoughts. I couldn't believe my luck when I walked into Strip Tease and saw her on stage. It took a minute for me to recognize her without the wig and blood coating her body, but when she swung her hips and tilted her head back, exposing her face to the lights above her, I knew immediately that she was the girl from that night. Razor told me her name was Jessica... clearly a fake. Her paperwork at the club says Red, although that's obviously not her real name either. What does she have to hide, that she can't even give her real name to her employer?

Releasing a heavy sigh, I let my head fall back against the headrest as my mind involuntarily drifts back to the feel of her grinding against me, the brush of her tits against my chest. "Ugh," I groan. That was *not* how I envisioned tonight going. I got her schedule from the manager, and I've made a point of turning up at the club every night she's been working this week, letting it sink through her pretty little head that I own her. There's absolutely nothing she can do or say to prevent me from showing up night after night. When I took over the Satan's territory, all of the businesses within this five-block radius effectively became mine. They're under my rein, my control. If I decide they should shut their doors and close up shop, then they will do so, under threat of death should the owner disobey. Those same rules apply to Strip Tease. Of course, I have no intention of actually doing any of that. These are hard-working people just trying to make a living. Who am I to barge in and screw with their livelihoods?

Now, if they stand in my way against the Antonellis, like the red-headed vixen is, then that's a different matter. And yet, my intimidation tactics don't seem to be phasing her in the slightest. Every night, she's thrown me hateful glares and scornful looks, the likes of which no one has dared aim in my direction since before Evie disappeared. I admit, even as a prepubescent, the other kids on our street were fearful of me. I've always been tall for my age, and I perfected a *not to be messed with* expression at a young age. When I started lifting weights in my teens and added a hefty bulk of muscle to my lanky frame, it only added to the intimidating image. Throw in the tattoos covering nearly every inch of visible skin and the fact I'm the leader of a group of ruthless gangsters quickly taking control of the city, and well, it's safe to say most people buckle beneath my demands. But not *her.*

Since the silent intimidation tactic didn't seem to be working, I decided an up-close and personal approach was required, but *holy fuck*, did that backfire. Instead of forcing her to tell me what she knows about the Reaper, I only succeeded in exposing how much the girl gets under my skin. Although, it's apparent that I affect her too. She put up a strong front, but there was no denying the way her body melted beneath my touch.

Loosening my right hand from around the steering wheel, I bring it to my lips, smelling her sweet scent as I suck a finger into my mouth. I can taste the residual essence of her as it dances across my tongue, only heightening my need.

No! She's a liar, and she's getting in the way of my agenda. She can taste like the world's best cream pie, but I won't allow her to interfere any longer.

I grit my teeth as I put the car into gear and head away from the club. My thoughts are a conflicting mix of anger and lust as I race across town at breakneck speed, needing to put as much distance as possible between the tempting seductress and myself.

Despite the twenty-minute drive to the new premises I acquired for the Rejects, I'm still reeling with anger, frustration, confusion, and worst of all, desire, as I stomp into the front lobby, where I find Marcus and a couple of other newer recruits putting on tactical gear, clearly on their way out.

"What's going on?" I ask.

"There's a new shipment coming in. We're going to catch the Grim Bastards in the act of stealing it." He tosses me a malicious grin as he checks his handgun, loading bullets in the chamber before securing it in his holster.

I perk up at that news. Killing some thieving fuckers is exactly what would brighten my mood. Meeting his grin with a wicked one of my own, I ask, "Where's Oliver?"

"In the office. We're all heading out in a few."

With a jerk of my head in acknowledgement, I head past him toward the office, relieved to feel the last remnants of lust leaving my system as it's replaced with a need for blood and violence.

"You're going after the Grim Bastards?" I ask Oliver as I step into the office, finding him slipping his own gun into the holster at his waist before securing a knife to the strap on his other thigh. He's dressed in full, stealth, tactical gear, just like the men out in the lobby.

"Yeah, I've had a couple of guys keep a lookout for the delivery, and they called an hour ago to say it was on its way to the drop-off point." He turns to face me, giving me a quick once over. "I called you."

I pull my phone out of my pocket, frowning when I notice the three missed calls. *Damn,* I was too caught up in playing games with the stripper. I didn't even realize my phone had gone off. I would have been pissed if I'd missed the chance to go out on this job.

"I'm coming with," I tell him, moving behind my desk to grab my own gun belt out of my drawer. I'm already dressed in dark clothing, which will suffice. As I affix it around my waist, I catch Oliver giving me a knowing smirk. He knew I'd be pissed if I'd missed out on this. We both live for the adrenaline rush that comes from staring death in the face, from destroying our enemies and living to fight another day. He might not take part in the fighting pit or the cage, but that doesn't mean he doesn't revel in the bloodshed the same way I do. After all, we grew up on violence and chaos. It's been a daily part of our lives for as long as we can remember. Brutality is in our blood; it's at the very core of our essence, the very center of who we are. Without that deep-seated viciousness, pining for vindication, we're nothing but lost souls without a purpose.

I throw on a leather jacket over my ensemble, and when I'm ready, I meet Oliver's gaze, the two of us sharing an intense look filled with malice and excitement for the battle ahead.

Oh yeah, this is exactly what I needed tonight.

We meet the other three members of our team in the lobby and head out to the parking lot, where we all get into one of the Cadillacs. Since Oliver is the one with the game plan, he climbs in behind the wheel, and I take the seat beside him while Marcus, Rampage, and Tank climb into the back. The three of them joined my crew nearly a year ago. Rampage and Tank are two of the eighteen-year-olds who agreed to join me after I rescued them, and Marcus had been at the compound that night, pretending to be a guard. I nearly shot the fucker when he ran toward me across the asphalt, thinking he was trying to stop the kids from escaping. It was only when I spotted the young boy cradled in his arms, that I realized he was helping him. He worked tirelessly alongside me and my men, helping us rescue every single one of those kids that night, and he even trailed us back to Black Creek, ensuring we found safe homes for as many as we could.

After about a month of him hanging around, showing no signs of leaving, I pulled him in for a chat. I'd seen the dark shadows in his eyes, caught glimpses of the haunted look he wore sometimes. I know exactly what causes that. Only a loss like no other can hollow a man out, so he's merely skin and bones; a shell existing for the sheer purpose of existing. It didn't matter to me who it was he lost, I could sympathize with his pain regardless. Not wanting to pry, I never asked him about his past, but I did fill him in on my own. It's safe to say, he was on board with my plans for vengeance by the time we were done.

The drive is silent as Oliver directs us toward the north part of town. I stare out the window, not really taking in the rundown buildings and various vagrants as we make our way through Grim territory. There's a storage facility just beyond the city limits, effectively in no man's land, where I rent a container. Every month, I get the guys from up north to drop off a crate's worth, which I delegate among my men to sell.

There are supposed to be precisely one-hundred guns in each shipment, but for the last few months, there have only been eighty. Meaning someone's helping themselves to *my* guns before I set eyes on them. I've already looked into the guys up north and confirmed it's not them who are trying to swindle me, which means someone is getting to the shipment before my men can get up here to collect it. There's only one group of people that could be—the Grim Bastards.

For the most part, we leave each other be, but they've been making a lot of noise recently about their reduced gun supply, and I'm pretty sure this is their underhanded way of expressing their displeasure.

"Remember, we don't know if the Bastards have been informed the shipment is here yet, so everyone be on alert," Oliver states, slowing the car down so the security barrier can scan our license plate before lifting to grant us entry onto the property.

The place is dark and vacant as we drive past numbered units with roll-up shutters. Instead of going straight to my container, we park several rows over—out of sight of any lurkers—and quietly slip out of the Cadillac.

"Stay alert," I state in a low whisper, ensuring my voice doesn't travel as I repeat Oliver's words. I scan our surroundings, listening carefully for any sounds that could indicate anyone else is here.

"Here, take these." Oliver holds out his palm, containing five small Bluetooth earpieces, so we will be able to keep in contact if we have to split up. With a final look at my men, we head out, ready to kill some motherfucking thieves.

I lead the way, with Oliver watching my six, Rampage and Tank behind us, and Marcus bringing up the rear. When we reach the end of the row, I peer around the side of the building, my gaze darting around the dark expanse of space as I squint into the darkness, trying to discern any moving shadows. Nothing. No one in sight and no sounds alerting us to anyone nearby.

Giving the signal that it's all clear, we move around the side of the building, past the next row, again checking it's empty before moving on. I can't hear anything but the regular beating of my own heart and the steady exhale of my even breaths. Even the crunch beneath our boots as we move over the loose gravel is barely discernible.

As we come upon the edge of the row of units before the aisle containing mine, I crouch low, aiming my gun as I duck my head around the side. I quickly pull back as a round of bullets goes off, blindly firing off a few shots of my own, which undoubtedly go wide.

With my heart hammering in my chest at the near-miss, I turn back to face the others. "Take Rampage and Tank and go around the other side." My words are barely more than a whisper, not wanting them to be carried on the wind to our attackers, as I give Oliver the order. He nods before indicating for the guys to follow him, and the three of them slip around the other side of the wall we're hiding behind, quickly disappearing out of sight.

I take a second to formulate a plan in my head. "Cover for me," I bark out in a low voice before lifting my gun and keeping low, I run across the open space toward the wall marking the end of the other row of storage units. Guns go off all around me, including my own, as I shoot at the three men standing in the middle of the aisle. I manage to take one to the ground before I dive behind the wall.

Adrenaline pounds in my veins as I hurry to right myself, finding Marcus in the dark as he ducks behind his own wall again. I take a quick second to assess myself, ensuring I've got no injuries, before speaking quietly into the Bluetooth headset.

"There's three men and an SUV in the middle of the aisle and at least one guy on the roof."

"We have eyes," Oliver responds a moment later. "We can take out the man on the roof, if you two can handle the others."

I share a look with Marcus across the open space, and he gives a confident nod—we've got this.

"We're on it."

I wait until I hear a round of gunshots going off, knowing that it will be Oliver taking out our threat on the roof before I step out from behind the wall with my gun raised. I notice Marcus doing the same out of the corner of my eye as I press down on the trigger, aiming at the two fuckers blocking the way to *my* guns.

They were already turning away from us, most likely to investigate the shots they heard from the other side of the aisle, making it easy for Marcus and me to eliminate them.

As the last one falls to the ground, I stride toward the three bodies, keeping my weapon aimed until I can kick their guns away. Satisfied that they're definitely dead, I lift my head to take in my surroundings. Marcus has already rounded the SUV, making his way toward the roll-down shutter of my storage unit.

"Boss," he says, glancing over his shoulder at me. "They must have had a key. The lock has been undone, but it's not broken."

Fucking assholes. How the hell did they get a key? It explains a lot, though. Initially, I'd dismissed the storage facility as to how they were getting a hold of my guns, but having ruled out every other possibility over the last few months, I was left with no other option.

He bends to grab the handle, ready to yank the door up, but he glances back at me before he does so. With my gun at the ready in case more of these fuckers is hiding in there, I give him a quick jerk of my head, and in one swift motion, he yanks open the door, pointing his own weapon into the dark room.

Before either of us can move, something rushes out of the darkness. Someone's making a run for it. *No fucking chance, asshole.* I dive toward them, catching whoever it is by the collar and yanking them back.

Marcus moves to flick on the light inside the unit, the single bulb enough to show me the shithead's face as it crumples in panic. He's young enough, probably early twenties, and the look on his face is enough to tell me he's new to this life. Most likely massively regretting his decision to sign up right now.

"You with the Grim Bastards?" I demand in a low growl.

His eyes dart from side to side as he tries to work out his best way of getting out of here alive. He must have some functioning brain cells as he eventually stutters out, "Y-yes."

I'm aware of Oliver and the others closing in behind us, so there shouldn't be anyone else left alive.

"Well, you tell that motherfucking scumbag that if he steals one more gun from me, he can consider it an act of war." I lean in, so my face swallows up the asshole's entire field of vision. "And trust me, I'll be the one that finishes it, with his head on a spike."

I toss him toward the car, glowering at him as he falls to his knees before quickly righting himself and running the short distance to the car. We all stand and watch as he drives off, veering all over the place in his hurry to get away.

"You don't think he'll just bring more back up?" Oliver questions.

"Maybe. Let's hurry up and get the fuck out of here, just in case he does."

Glancing away from where the Grim's car disappeared, I turn and toss my car keys to Rampage and Tank. "Go bring the car around so we can load this shit into the back of it."

Tank snatches them out of the air before Rampage can get a hold of them. "I'd better do it. Fuck knows this angry bastard will find something to rage about in the thirty-second drive over here."

He rushes back toward the car with his laugh lingering in the air as Rampage cusses him out. I ignore their antics as I investigate the crate, happy to discover it hasn't been tampered with. There's a crowbar on the ground beside it, and I scowl at it before kicking it away.

"I want all new security in this place," I tell Oliver. "Cameras, better locks. The works."

"You got it."

I'll have to make arrangements for my shipments to get delivered elsewhere, which will be a fucking headache, but I've got no doubt Grim, the President of the Bastards, will fail to heed my warning tonight. He'll be back, even if it's just to snoop, and I want to catch him in the act when he does.

When Tank has returned with the car, we don't waste any time loading the shipment into it and getting the fuck out of there. Less than an hour later, I'm sitting on an old, worn couch beside Oliver in the middle of what used to be a reception area, but we're in the middle of converting it into a place where we can all sit and chill when we're not working.

The lights are turned down, and there's a bunch of strippers dancing to some heavy tune. The guys had the party ready for us upon our return, and the alcohol has been flowing steadily since we got back. Now that I no longer have the Grim Bastards to distract me, my thoughts return to the redhead.

"The stripper isn't going to give us the Reaper's name," I tell Oliver, sighing as my mood plummets. He knows all about her, of course, but I want to be the one to deal with her. The one to break her. She's holding out on me, lying to my face, and I won't fucking stand for it any longer.

His beer bottle is lifted halfway to his mouth, but he pauses, turning to look at me. "Is that where you were tonight?"

I give a nod of my head. "I've spent all week trying to get under her skin, and nothing is fucking working."

Oliver snorts. "You mean the big, bad Cain couldn't get a mere woman to fall at his knees and tell him whatever he wanted to know?"

I frown, because he's right. I've always been able to scare or seduce information out of people, and neither has worked on this woman. Her stubbornness lights a spark of anger within me, and my hand clenches around my beer bottle. There's always a way to get what you want, and eventually, the stripper will spill her secrets to me. I just have to try a different tactic.

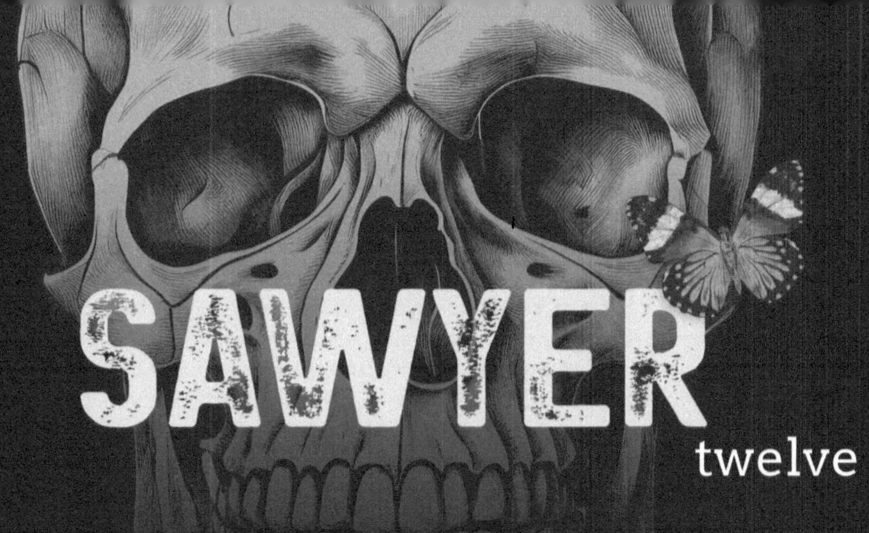

twelve

I sit there for a long time, trying to understand what just happened with Cain and, more importantly, what it means going forward. It's becoming pretty damn obvious that he isn't going to let this go. For whatever reason, he's intent on finding the Reaper, and he's decided I'm his best chance at getting the answers he seeks. I'd hoped if I continued to tell him I didn't know anything that he would drop it, but somehow he knows I'm fucking lying, and like a dog with a bone, he's going to keep hounding me until he gets answers.

A headache is forming behind my eyes as I struggle to think of a suitable solution. Unable to come up with anything, I groan in frustration as I get to my feet. By the time I'm changed and have locked up behind me, it's nearly three a.m. As I make the familiar walk back to my apartment, I swear I can feel eyes on me, and I constantly peer into the darkness around me, trying to identify where it's coming from. I know, whoever it is, isn't Cain. The way this person's eyes dig into my skin, it lacks Cain's intensity, the heat that scalded my skin, but it's no less distracting, making the hairs on the back of my neck stand to attention.

The eyes follow me until I slip into the doorway of my apartment building, and when I've reached my place, I make a point of not turning on any lights so I can peer out the window to the street below. I catch a flicker of movement at the corner of the street, but when I squint in that direction, I see nothing but shadows. After a few more moments, when there's no more movement from outside, I turn away from the window. I might not see anyone, but I know they're out there. Watching. But, who are they? And more importantly, what do they want?

SOMEONE'S FOLLOWING ME. THE EYES I FELT ON ME LAST WEEK WHEN I left the club have tracked me every time I step foot out the door ever since. But every time I turn around and peer into the shadows and dark corners provided by buildings and alleyways, I don't see anything.

Whoever it is must be one of Cain's men, but considering what happened at Belle Donne and my run-in with the guy who nearly killed me eight years ago, I can't be completely confident it's not someone on the Antonellis' payroll. Maybe someone followed me home that night, or they've tracked me down since. Just thinking about it has panic flaring to life, and a desperate need to flush them out takes over me.

I've spent all week trying to decide if it's wise to confront whoever it is and working out how to actually do that, but ultimately, I've decided I need to know. I can't do any of my extracurriculars if my every move is being watched, recorded, and reported back to some asshole. I haven't even been able to check in on Sheryl and Grace in case this shithead stalking me connects the dots between us, leading him back to Python. Not being able to do what makes me feel truly alive pisses me the fuck off. I feel like a caged animal pacing her pen. If this asshole is acting under Cain's orders, then I'm going to tear his balls off, and if it's the Antonellis, well, *fuck*, I hope it's not an Antonelli. Bad things happen to those who catch their attention.

"See ya later, Kenny." I wave at the bouncer as I exit the club, having just finished the day shift and more than ready to get home and curl up with a glass of wine and some shitty TV show for the night.

On my way down the street, I pop into the corner shop to pick up a few things, and that's when I feel the hairs rise along the back of my neck. It's the same instinctual response I've had all week when I know I'm being watched. My lips purse in annoyance. It's always the same. Whoever it is, leaves me alone when I'm at home or in the club, but the minute I dare step foot on the streets, they find me.

I catch a flicker of movement in the periphery of my vision and snap my head toward the end of the aisle. *I could have sworn I saw someone duck out of sight.* Anger licks along my spine as my hand clenches the bottle of wine tightly. Working on loosening my grip, I carefully set the bottle back on the shelf before leaving the aisle. I've had e-fucking-nough of this shit. I refuse to be corralled and intimidated by a fucking ghost. If this is Cain's way of thinking he can get me to confess what I know, then he's going to be sorely disappointed. I don't scare that easily, and he's going to have to do a hell of a lot better if he thinks he can bully me into spilling my secrets.

I take my time, wandering up and down a few of the aisles, pretending to peruse the shelves as I make my way toward the staff-only door at the back of the shop. Once I reach it, I duck inside, taking in the storage room stocked with excess inventory until I find a fire exit door at the back of it. *Perfect.* I hastily cross the room and push it open, stepping out into a narrow alley that runs along the back of the buildings on the main street. There's nothing but wheelie bins, upturned crates, and trash bags back here, and I quickly flatten myself against the wall, behind the door, ignoring the pounding of my pulse at the base of my neck as the door bursts open and a young man with a short cut, white-blond hair steps out.

He curses under his breath as he stares toward the opposite end of the alley, running a hand through his buzz cut. Not wasting any time, I jump toward him, catching him off guard as I tackle him from behind. I get him into a chokehold the way Hadley taught me, but his reflexes are quick, and he jabs me in the gut with his elbow, momentarily winding me. Distracted, my hold loosens, and he easily slips free. In a blur of movement, he spins to face me, reaching out to grab me by the neck and slam me against the wall.

The force knocks the air from my lungs as I stare at him, shocked at the sudden turn of events. As I scramble to gather my thoughts, I notice the dark shadows that crawl across his irises for a moment before they start to lift, and his eyes widen in surprise as he blinks and returns to the present. *What the fuck was that?* Not having the time right now to dwell on it, I slam my fist into the crook of his arm and step swiftly to the side, breaking his hold on me.

His eyes follow the fast movement, an eyebrow lifting in surprise. I raise my hands, ready to fight him off if he steps even a toe in my direction, but he doesn't make any further attempts to try and corral me. Instead, his posture relaxes, his shoulders dropping. The subtle change only has me more on edge, and I clench my fists tighter, ignoring the sting as my nails dig into my palms as I prepare to defend myself.

He lowers his hands, letting his arms hang loosely by his side, and his gaze runs over me in an assessing manner as I stand there, confused, perching on the balls of my feet. Despite his seemingly relaxed manner, I'm half expecting him to pounce on me, but instead, he surprises me by saying, "Impressive. Not many people know how to get out of a chokehold like that."

Ignoring that weird remark, I spit out, "Why the fuck are you following me?" I still don't lower my fists, but I do take a second to look him over. He's young, younger than me. In fact, if I had to guess, I'd say he isn't much older than Luc. There's something about him, though, that I can't quite put my finger on. Maybe it's to do with whatever I saw in his eyes. It's almost like there's a dark aura around him, hinting at the terrible things he's capable of. It seems crazy, given just how youthful he looks, but whatever it is is enough of a warning that I don't let his young age fool me.

He ignores my question while tilting his head, and asking, "Where did you learn to fight like that?"

With my brows furrowed, I continue to assess him for a tense moment. "Listen, kid—"

"Bones."

When I just stare at him in confusion, he explains. "My name is Bones. You know, like Jon Jones, the MMA fighter."

I scrunch my nose up. "I'm not calling you that."

The kid's shoulders visibly deflate, making him look every bit of his adolescent age, and *fuck me*, it almost makes me feel bad.

"Who has you following me?" I ask instead, refusing to let him lure me into a false sense of safety. He's already proven he's got impressive fighting skills, and the energy exuding from him tells me he's no stranger to violence.

He refuses to answer, flattening his lips as his childish demeanor slips away, and he once again becomes the guy that chased me outside. I narrow my eyes on him. "Cain?"

He still doesn't respond, and I run my gaze over him, trying to find something identifiable, but he's wearing a long sleeve top and pants, so I can't spot a Reject tattoo, and honestly, I have no idea what someone who works for the Antonellis would look like. A mafia idiot dressed in a suit with that air of arrogance about them? If that's the case, the kid is definitely not with the Antonellis. Despite the slash of violence surrounding him, there's a strange, boyish charm about him, but it's deceiving and makes me question my actions.

I decide to take a gamble. "I know it's Cain," I state, hoping I'm right. "Tell him to fuck off and leave me alone."

The kid's lips lift up in a delighted grin like he's finding all of this hilarious. When he doesn't do anything but smile broadly at me, I spear him with a deadly look before turning on my heel and stomping down the alley, figuring he's not going to hurt me. He must belong to Cain, and if that's the case, his orders will be to follow me and report back. I don't believe Cain would send one of his minions to torture the information out of me. No, I, without a doubt, believe the insufferable asshole would rather do that job himself.

Before I exit onto the street, I call out over my shoulder, "And stop fucking following me!"

***

THE KID HAD ENOUGH COMMON SENSE NOT TO FOLLOW ME THE REST OF the way home the other night, and I don't get the same tingle of awareness when I'm out and about the next day. It feels fucking fantastic like I can finally breathe again, without the oppressive weight of eyes on me. I almost feel like a new woman as I step out of the apartment building on Saturday to run some errands and grab some groceries, and my mood is better than it has been in days as I think about the lovely, relaxing bubble bath I have planned for tonight.

Once I've done all I need to do, I pop into the shelter to check on Sheryl and Grace —who are both doing great—before I head home. I'm humming under my breath as I reach the top of the stairs, stepping onto the fourth-floor landing. The only way this day could get any better is if I had a voicemail with some shithead's name on it, waiting for me to pluck from the face of this earth. Reaching the door to my apartment, I set the grocery bags on the floor to fish out my keys. I pause with the key halfway inserted into the lock, frowning at the peeling green paint on the door as I hear voices coming from inside my apartment. Luc knows not to let in anyone he doesn't know, so I can't work out who he could be talking to.

My body is tense, coiled like a spring ready to unfurl as I jiggle the key in the lock until it swings open. Without the wooden barrier between us, the voices within the apartment become clearer. I hear Luc's distinctive laugh, followed by another male voice that I can't immediately place. Snatching the bags off the floor, I barge into the room, coming to a stop when I find the kid from yesterday lounging on *my* sofa.

My eyes immediately narrow on him in suspicion, the two of them turning to face me as they stop talking mid-conversation. I should have fucking known he wouldn't just leave me alone. But involving Luc? Hell to the fucking no!

"What the fuck is he doing in here?" I bark at Luc, tearing my gaze away from the kid to look at my brother. The smile on his face drops off, and his eyebrows climb up his forehead as he gapes at me.

"Bones?"

"I needed to talk to you," the kid speaks up, garnering my attention.

I glower at him. "Well, you could have waited outside, on the street." Dismissing him before he can argue, I snap my attention back to my brother. "What did I tell you about not letting strangers into our home?! Do you have any idea who he is? God, Luc, he could have hurt you, or worse." Concern for my brother makes my voice crack.

"Whoa," Bones says. *Fuck me,* nope, I'm not calling him that... What did he say his name was again? Jon? Jon holds his hands up in a placating gesture. "I'm not here to hurt anyone. I just have a message for you."

"Well, get on with it so you can get the fuck out of my apartment," I snap. He's probably only a few years older than Luc, but knowing who he works for, the people he associates himself with... well, I can't have him corrupting my brother.

"Cain told me to tell you to be at Toxic tonight."

I pinch my lips, not appreciating the demand.

"Who's Cain?" Luc asks, his eyes bouncing between Jon and me. Of course, Luc knows nothing about my issues with the leader of the Rejects. Nor do I want him to know.

"No one," I blurt out before Jon can think to inform him who the fuck he really is —assuming he hasn't already. I continue to stare Jon down until he gets the message— spill a word of who you are or my beef with the Rejects, and you'll fucking regret it. A look I can't place flashes across his face, but he nods in concession before making a move toward the door.

I want to ask him what Cain wants, but I can't voice the question aloud with my brother standing right beside me, so instead, I let him slip past me toward the door. Just before he disappears down the hall, he turns back to look at my brother. "I'll let you know the next time we're playin' a game, yeah?"

Luc grins. "Sounds good."

"What the fuck does that mean?" I bark at Luc as the front door clicks shut.

He narrows his eyes on me. "What the fuck is your problem?" he demands. Luc rarely argues with me. For the most part, he's pretty good at doing what I say, knowing I'm only trying to do what I think is right to keep us both safe. But apparently, he's not feeling so agreeable today.

"Do you know who he is?" I volley back.

"A Reject? So? He was nice to me."

I throw my hands up. Of course, that idiot told my brother who he was. *God, I'm going to fucking murder him.* "Just because he was *nice* to you doesn't mean he wouldn't hesitate to put a bullet in your head if you pissed him off," I argue. "And there's absolutely no way you're hanging out with him."

He snorts out a pissed-off chuckle. "You can't control every aspect of my life, Sawyer. I'm nearly sixteen, so I can be friends with whoever I want; do whatever I want. Hell, maybe I'll sign up to join the Rejects. They seem like pretty cool people."

I stomp toward him, steam practically pouring out of my ears. "Over my dead body," I snarl. "I will not let you end up like every other kid in this town—pedaling drugs on a street corner until you get gunned down in a drive-by, all to make some useless point to a gang that doesn't give a shit about you. You deserve a better life than that."

I see the anger melt out of him as his shoulders deflate. "I know," he grumbles. "You're just trying to protect me. I'm not a kid anymore, though. I don't need you to mother me."

I give him a ruly grin and cuff him around the chin. "I'm never going to not worry about you."

Our argument may be sidelined for now, but I know it's not over. He's been pushing my boundaries more and more recently, and I know I'm going to have to start loosening the reins, but *man*, it's hard. Everything I do is for him, and the thought of something happening to him... well, it's not even worth thinking about.

He reluctantly lets me pull him in for a hug, giving me an awkward pat on the back. I don't let just anyone see me emotional, and I rarely hug people, but my brother is the exception. When I'm outside of this apartment, I need to don my hard-ass bitch face. It's the only way to deal with the daily shit Black Creek throws at me; to handle the shitty customers in Strip Tease; to ensure everyone I meet knows I'm not to be messed with. But when I'm in here, with Luc, I want to be as open with him as I can be. There are parts of my life he can't know about—it's just safer that way—but that doesn't mean I can't be emotionally available for him; be a sister—someone he can vent to and spend time with. I'm the only constant in his life, and I'm doing my best to wear two hats—one of a sibling and another of a mother figure.

All we have is each other, and I think it's helped us to become as close as we have, but it is tough at times. Especially as he has grown older and he feels the need to figure out who he is and find his place in this world.

As he pulls back, he raises an eyebrow. "So, who's Cain?"

I groan, turning away from him and grabbing the grocery bags I dropped on the floor earlier, dumping them on the kitchen counter before I start to unpack them. "He's the leader of the Reaper Rejects," I admit, deliberately not looking at him.

"What?!" he exclaims in shock. "What the hell does he want with you?"

"Nothing," I lie. "He's been stopping by the club, and Drew asked me to liaise with him, if he had any questions."

It's a bold-faced lie, but I'm sure as fuck not about to tell my fifteen-year-old brother that Cain's men caught me killing Python, and now he won't leave me the fuck alone.

"Bet you're loving that," he jokes. He knows how much I hate any and everyone associated with gangs. They're a fucking stain on this town. The ordinary, everyday people of Black Creek would be better off without any of them.

"You've got no idea. Mac 'n' cheese for dinner?" I ask, changing the subject.

"Yeah, sounds good."

As I start lifting out what I need for dinner and Luc buries his nose in a comic, I mull over Cain's demand for me to meet him tonight. After the way our last interaction went, I'd honestly rather avoid him. I've never had a man turn the tables on me like that before, nor has someone I so vehemently despise managed to make my body respond the way it does around him. All I could think about was the feel of him inside me; how easily he had me coming apart beneath his touch. And the whole time he was playing my body like a fiddle, all I wanted to do was rip his head off. It's a very conflicting set of emotions, and I've no idea how to deal with it, yet I can't just keep reacting to Cain's moves. I need to make some of my own. My guess is, despite his order, Cain isn't expecting me to show up tonight. He's seen enough of my defiance by now to know I'm not one to simply bend to his commands... which is exactly why I'm going to be at Toxic tonight.

I fill the next few hours with making dinner and cleaning the apartment. When the sun has long since set, and while Luc is engrossed in some end-of-the-world-type movie on the TV, I head out into the night, dressed in a skin-tight tank top and black skinny jeans with rips in the knees. I've paired the outfit with my trusty chunky-heeled boots so the outfit toes the line between sexy and badass and finished it off with a gun secured in my shoulder holster, hidden under my jacket, and my trusty blades in my pocket—just in case.

"Wasn't sure you'd actually go," a voice says from the darkness, startling me as I step onto the pavement outside my apartment building.

"Jeez," I chastise. "Are you checking up on me?" Before he can answer, I shake my head and hold up a hand. "You know what, I don't wanna know."

Jon's grin gets even wider, and as I turn and stroll down the street, he moves to my side, easily keeping pace with me.

"I like you. You're a bit of a secret badass, aren't you?"

I quirk a brow, refusing to tell him anything more about me.

"Your brother is pretty cool too."

"Stay away from him," I snap, scowling in his direction. "I mean it. I don't want him caught up in any of this shit."

"What shit?" It sounds like a genuine question, which confuses me.

"In anything to do with the Rejects," I explain.

Jon shrugs his shoulders. "We're not that bad, you know. Cain's not the jackass you think he is."

Of course, he thinks that. He's a fucking teenager. His brain hasn't fully developed yet, so he's practically programmed to make stupid decisions and trust the wrong people.

"Have you been to one of our fight nights?" he asks after a moment of heavy silence. When I just give him a questioning look, silently saying, *seriously? What do you think?* he laughs. "You'll love it."

He talks my ear off the whole way there, and it makes me wonder how the hell he ever shut up long enough to follow me without giving himself away. He actually seems like a decent enough kid, although some of the things he says are a bit weird, making me wonder what sort of childhood he had growing up. Anyway, it's none of my business, and the questions quickly drift from my mind as we reach the old docks and turn onto the street Toxic is on. He flashes his Reject's tattoo to the bouncer at the door—which apparently grants us both free entry—and we walk into Toxic.

The intoxicating combination of sweat, testosterone, and adrenaline hit me as soon as we step inside. Looking around, the entire ground floor of the club has been completely revamped. Where the dance floor used to be—where I danced with my mystery man only a couple of weeks ago—there is now a sizable octagonal ring, surrounded by a metal cage. The cage runs all the way to the roof, four floors above us. A staircase at the edge of the warehouse leads up to the first floor, which runs like a landing around the outer edges of the room, enabling people on the floors above to lean over and watch the fight as well.

A smaller dance floor has been erected at the far side of the room, opposite a bar, which has been upgraded and looks like it stocks more than just the cheap stuff. It's impressive, and it must have cost a fortune to do.

The place is already packed, and a fight is currently underway by the sounds of the roaring crowd.

"Oh, we're just in time," Jon exclaims with an excited gleam in his eye. Without further explanation, he grabs my hand and yanks me through the crowd. He shed his jacket as soon as we stepped up to the bouncer, so his Reject's tattoo is prominently on display on his forearm, and the crowd parts easily for us until we're standing ringside.

My eyes widen in surprise, and I watch, captivated as two men fight each other like wild animals in the ring. They're both shirtless, sweat and blood coating their bodies. It's only when I stare mesmerized at the dark-haired fighter, casting my eyes over the various tattoos inked across every available surface of his torso, that I realize it's Cain.

"It's no-holds-barred fighting," the kid explains, and when I tear my eyes away from the fight to look at him, he's staring in awe at the fighters. Feeling my eyes on him, he turns to look at me. "They can literally do anything, and it's allowed. Biting, kicking, twisting." He grins, and in the dark room, with the stench of testosterone in the air, it looks creepy as fuck. "They can even gouge each other's eyes out."

That's not at all disturbing. I return my attention to the cage fight in front of me just in time to see Cain sock the guy in the face, following it up with a blow to his instep that sends his opponent crashing to his knees. Cain smashes his knee into his competitor's face, simultaneously slamming his fists down on his back, and the guy collapses to the floor as a roar goes up from the crowd.

"Holy fuck," I murmur in awe.

"Yup. I can't wait until I can get my chance."

At his words, I spin to gape at him. Sure, he was able to handle his own against me the other day, and he's got some muscles on his arms, but he's nowhere near as broad as either Cain or the other fighter. Besides that, he seems way too fucking young to be in that ring. He could die, for Christ's sake. What asshole would let one of his men voluntarily go into the ring all so he can, what, claim bragging rights? Fuck no.

I plan on telling him exactly that. Entirely unaware of the anger sparking within me, Jon simply sighs, saying, "But Cain won't let us until we're eighteen."

Huh. Well, just right. "More like twenty-one," I grumble. It's not that I'm a stickler for the law or anything, but I can't look at him without picturing Luc, and there is absolutely no fucking way I would be letting Luc anywhere near this place before he's twenty-five. Even then, if I could chain him up at home, where I know he's safe, I'd do exactly that.

"Come on." Jon gestures toward the bar. "May as well get a drink."

I open my mouth to protest as I look around me to see where Cain went. Another fight is starting up in the ring, and I scan the throng of people surrounding it, trying to pick him out of the crowd. It takes me a second, but I catch sight of him just before a door on the far side of the room swings shut behind him, a *staff-only* sign making me sigh as I turn back to Jon and reluctantly agree to a drink while we wait.

When we finally make it through the crowd surrounding the bar, I order a beer. The kid does the same before turning to look at me. "So you're the girl that saw the Reaper?"

I raise an eyebrow in surprise. I didn't expect him to know anything about me. Isn't that the usual hierarchy in gangs? It strikes me that he might know something of use, so I deflect with a question of my own.

"Why is Cain so interested in the Reaper?"

Jon grins at my deflection. He seems to like that I hold my own against him. "Who wouldn't be? A badass like that who can literally kill men in their own beds without getting caught?" He shakes his head, the awe apparent in his voice. I wonder if he'd be just as impressed if he knew the Reaper was a woman.

"Doesn't he kill gang members, though? Shouldn't you want to stay as far away from him as possible?"

"He ain't ever killed a Reject." He smirks, bringing the bottle up to his lips.

I snort, shaking my head, thinking, *only because none of you have given me a reason to... yet.*

We sip on our beers for a bit, and I gaze around the room. Another fight is underway in the ring, and the dance floor is quickly filling up. Looking to the floor above me, people are pressed up against the railings running alongside the metal wire of the cage, their fingers wrapped around the thin metal as they shake the wire fence, screaming for whichever fighter they're rooting for.

Along with the heavy techno music, it's a heady atmosphere, doused in pheromones and tinged with violence. It's a form of escape that's offered here. A chance for people to leave the dreariness and misery of their everyday lives at the door, and revel in their sins. All around me, men and women are giving into their basic needs —fighting, fucking, forgetting. I can taste the bad intentions in the air. If the gateway to hell were anywhere on earth, it would be here in this very club. I can practically feel the evil spirits as they coax and taunt us, daring us to give in to our desires—for just one night.

My heart rate picks up to match that of the music's, most likely in tune with every other warm body in this place, and I feel the itching desire to get up and move. I rarely let myself indulge in such frivolity. The only time I come to a club is when I'm pursuing a target, and even though I'm here with a purpose in mind, it doesn't change the fact that tonight is the first time I've been in a club in years when I don't have to constantly be on alert, watching my six and keeping an eye on whoever I'm stalking.

Don't get me wrong. I'm no idiot. I'm still very much aware of everyone around me. One always has to be vigilant in Black Creek, but as I polish off my beer and signal the bartender for another one, I figure, while I'm here, I may as well let my hair down a little. Fuck knows, I deserve to have some fun.

The bartender sets two new beers down in front of us, and I down mine before jumping to my feet. "Let's dance."

With a cocky grin, the kid hastily gulps down his own before following me out onto the dance floor. I lose myself in the pounding bass of the music, letting it flow through me until it's controlling my movements, my breathing, my heartbeat. I don't even realize I've closed my eyes until a set of hands land possessively on my waist.

Scowling, I turn around to bite the asshole's head off, but the words stick in the back of my throat as I come face-to-face with my mystery man. A coy smile plays at the corner of my lips, matching his lascivious smirk.

"I was hoping I'd see you again."

I cast a quick look around me, not spotting Jon anywhere, but as the sex-dripping mystery man strokes his thumb back and forth across the strip of bare skin between my top and jeans, I immediately forget all about Jon and Cain and why I'm here. Just that small bit of contact has my blood warming, an excited thrum humming through my veins. What is it about him that makes me feel so alive? So carefree?

"Is that so?" I barely recognize the seductive purr of my own voice.

He steps in closer, his hips pressing against mine, our chests grazing. I have to tilt my head back to look into his face. There's a mischievous twinkle in his pale blue eyes that's a contrast to the hard lines around his eyes and lips, reminiscent of an arduous life. There's a seriousness about him that resonates with me. As if, like myself, he was never able to let loose and just be a kid or an irresponsible teenager. He looks like he's carrying the weight of the world on his shoulders.

There's a dusting of dark stubble along his jawline, similar to the last time we met, and I wonder if he always keeps it like that or if he shaves in between. He pushes his thigh in between mine, using his strong hold on my hips to move them in time to the music, matching my movements with smooth ones of his own. The crowd around us falls away. The entire world does. What *is* it about him that makes me lose all common sense? That makes me forget about everything around me? I could get lost in him, drown in the pools of his eyes, suffocate in his fresh, alluring scent.

He ducks his head, his lips brushing over mine enticingly. His hand moves to cup the side of my head, and his fingers slide into my hair as his lips sweep across mine again, adding a flick of his tongue to the mix this time. His taste is intoxicating, like cinnamon and dark chocolate—sweet and sinful.

I fall into him, my arms winding around his neck as I pull him closer and deepen our kiss. I still don't even know his name or anything about him. But that's the thing about reveling in your sins—the who, or what, or why don't matter. It's all about the moment. About the way his fingers dig into my hip, the sweep of his tongue across mine, his hungry groan, my breathy moan. The other details don't matter—at least, not right now.

I'm not sure how long we stand there, tasting one another, ignorant to the world around us, but eventually, his phone buzzes in his pocket, and he breaks off our kiss with a wry look. He fishes it out, glancing at the screen before saying, "Give me a sec." He moves to walk away, but at the last second, he snatches my wrist, searing me with a pensive look. "Don't go anywhere."

Before I can respond, he walks off, quickly swallowed up by the crowd. I'm not left alone on the dance floor for long before Jon reappears, tapping me on the shoulder and pulling my attention away from my mystery man's retreating back.

"Sorry, wanted to watch my buddy in the ring." He gestures with his thumb toward the cage, where a guy who looks to be of similar age to Jon is easily demolishing a guy twice his age and double his size. *What the hell?* "Cain's this way." He jerks his head for me to follow him, and I glance briefly over my shoulder, looking at the spot my mystery guy disappeared. As nice as it was to lose myself in him, a distraction like that is the last thing I really need right now. So, with a heavy sigh, I follow Jon, leaving all thoughts of cinnamon and chocolate behind on the dance floor.

Jon leads me over to the far side of the room, by the stairs, where there's an expansive seating area overflowing with Rejects. Don't ask me how I know they're all Rejects members. Some of them have their tattoos clearly on display, but for the most part, I can just tell by the way they luxuriate in their seats, the subtle way their eyes roam around the room as if surveying their territory. They're at ease here.

Jon claps hands with a few of them, nodding his head at others as he passes. I get my fair share of questioning stares, but I ignore all of them, keeping my head held high as I stride past them.

Like the king he is, Cain is lounging in the middle of his men, occupying a whole booth for just himself. A scantily clad woman is brushing herself up against him while he watches her tits bounce, and I have to grit my teeth as a flash of annoyance surges through me. Is that jealousy? Fuck, it better not be. He must sense us approaching as he lifts his head, the cocky grin from a moment ago morphing into a stern frown when his gaze meets mine.

He murmurs something I can't hear, and the woman stops rubbing herself all over him, getting to her feet and disappearing into the crowd. As we approach, he leans back in his booth, draping his arms over the back of the seat, smirking smugly like he thinks he's already won this round.

"I thought for sure you were going to make me send one of my men to get you."

Isn't that what he did with Jon anyway?

I don't react to his barb. "I came to tell you to stop having me followed."

That annoying fucking smirk doesn't falter as he slowly leans forward, placing his forearms on his knees. "Does that mean you're going to tell me the truth?"

I grit my teeth, forcing my expression to remain blank as I hiss out, "I am telling you the truth."

"Then no," he states casually, resuming his original position. His eyes move briefly to Jon. "Looks like you and Bones are getting along. Maybe I'll sic him on you permanently."

"What the fuck is your problem?" I snap, and I instantly know I've crossed a line. But of course, even as his face hardens and his eyes narrow on me in warning, I continue to run my stupid mouth. "I was just some girl in the wrong place, at the wrong time. Stop fucking harassing me!"

Fuck. That is not at all what I came here to say. Well, that's not *how* I meant to say it. I thought by showing up here instead of hiding from him and reiterating for the millionth time that I didn't see the Reaper, that he'd finally believe me. Although the second the heated words leave my mouth, I can see I've crossed a line. He just makes me so angry when I'm around him. The second I look at his stupidly handsome face, that itch of annoyance flares to life inside me, making me do and say reckless things.

He's on his feet so quickly, I barely register the movement until his hand wraps around my upper arm and pulls me into him. I'm so close, I can see the anger burning in his emerald irises, feel it radiating off of him, and searing my skin where he's touching it.

"Listen here," he snarls. The deep timbre of his voice is dark and threatening. "I've given you plenty of leeway, but I won't tolerate you disrespectin' me in front of my men." His face is so close to mine, I can feel the waft of his breath against my cheek. He glares at me for a long moment, rendering me speechless in the face of his wrath. His grip on my upper arm is bruising, and I know I should be scared right now. I should be absolutely shitting myself, but I'm not. I'm angry, no, I'm fucking furious. But what's most disturbing is that I think I'm a little turned on. Okay, like a lot turned on. Which only pisses me off further. Men like him infuriate me. They're domineering, entitled assholes who think they can control everyone around them and get anything they want without putting in the work themselves. Men like him are the reason I am who I am, why Black Creek is falling apart and heading toward wreck and ruin, why people run scared when they enter a room. Men like him are the Devil.

"What's going on here?"

That voice behind me has my muscles tensing. Why is he here? Why is he inserting himself into the middle of this hostile situation? Because of me?

I try to turn to look at him, to tell him to leave, but Cain's tight grip on my arm holds me hostage, and his next words blow my freaking mind.

"Oliver," he snarls, looking over my head, to my mystery man standing behind me. I swear I can feel the heat from his body burning into my back. "Get *her*"—he spits out the word, his lip curling in disdain—"out of here before I do something she regrets."

Despite his threat being delivered in a glacial tone that is intended to have me pissing myself, it instead sends a shiver of desire down my spine, making me glower defiantly back at him. He uses his hold on my arm to shove me toward my mystery man— Oliver?—as if handing me off to him, like I'm some sort of fucking possession.

I tear my gaze away from the snarling beast of a man in front of me to look into the pale blue eyes that only moments ago I could have drowned in. Now, they're closed off, just like the rest of his expression as he frowns down at me.

O... I remember Cain saying that on the phone. O for Oliver.

This is O.

My mystery man is a fucking Reject.

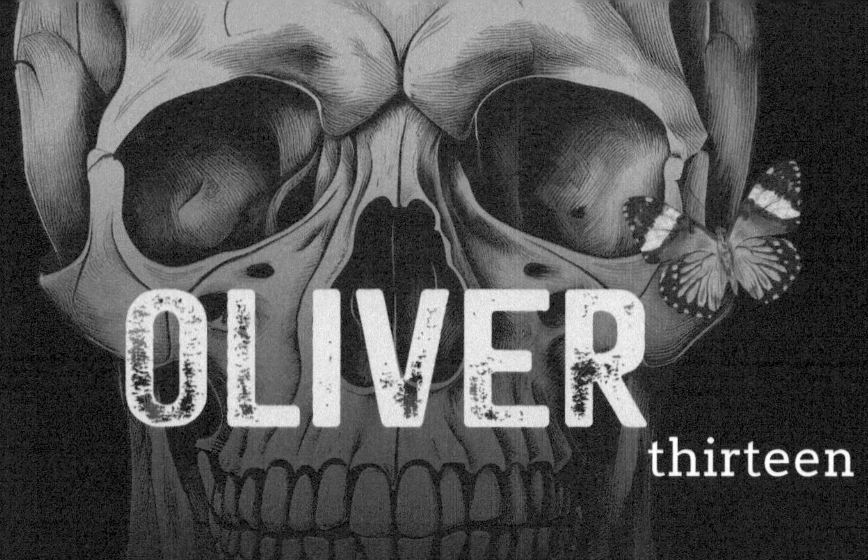

OLIVER

thirteen

F ucking. Christ. I leave for five fucking minutes to answer a call, and everything goes to shit. I was disappointed when I returned to the dance floor to find the enigmatic woman from before was gone. Of course, she was. She has a habit of slipping away before I'm finished with her. I didn't even get to ask her her name or get her number.

I never, for one fucking second, thought I'd find Cain's hand wrapped around her arm while he glared at her with such disdain and loathing. The dark shadows dancing across his face, showcasing him as the formidable leader he is, have made lesser men sob like babies. Yet, the alluring redhead held her ground, returning his dark expression with a furious one of her own. Seeing her go toe-to-toe with a man that has built himself an empire, gathered himself an army, and established such an imposing reputation, well, if I wasn't a tad scared for her life, I'd have been rock-hard in my jeans. Although the semi I was sporting was uncomfortable enough against the restricting fabric.

The pieces all slotted together as soon as I saw them scowling at one another. She's the girl he's had a tail on all week. The one who saw the Reaper kill Python. The one he's been obsessing over.

Why was she even at a Satan party? And in Python's room? The thought that she was there to fuck him, that she'd forgotten all about me when she's occupied my every thought since that night, has my own anger spiking as I step up behind her.

"What's going on here?" I keep my voice carefully neutral, along with my impassive expression.

"Oliver, get her out of here before I do something she regrets." I can hear how close Cain is to losing his shit. He'd never hurt a woman, that's not how he works, nonetheless he doesn't tolerate disrespect. He has spent years carefully crafting an indomitable reputation and amassing a loyal army understanding of his cause, and the fiery spitfire in front of him is testing his last nerve.

Before the situation can escalate, I tug her away from him, noting the surprise in her eyes when she turns to look at me, quickly squashed by a flare of anger and suspicion.

Thankfully she doesn't resist as I maneuver her past the watching Rejects members and through the sea of party-goers in the club. Neither of us says anything until we're out on the street, the loud thud of the music nothing but background noise as the cool night air lifts her hair, blowing it in my direction and sending a whiff of lavender and something else flowery that I can't quite place. It's refreshing and surprisingly feminine given her barbed attitude and take-no-shit persona.

The second we're outside, she yanks her arm out of my grip, spinning in her boots to pin me with as deadly a glare as she gave Cain. It's the first real chance I've had to look into her eyes, and even though they're spitting fire at me, the electrifying blue color renders me speechless for a moment. Together with her fiery hair, it strikes an impressive image. One that's likely to feature in all of my dreams for the proceeding future.

"You're a Reject?!" She spits out the words like they are poison on her tongue, and her gaze drops to linger on the tattoo sleeve of my right arm as she most likely tries to pinpoint the Reaper Reject tattoo. Not that she will find it there. Both of my Reject tattoos are on my chest. The original one I got when I was thirteen covers my left pec, right over my heart. I had it drawn freehand by a girl I was in love with, the girl I thought I'd marry someday. *Child-like love. Child-like fantasies. Child-like notions.*

The other Reject tattoo, the one that symbolizes what the Rejects are today, is painted on my other pec, the two sitting side by side, in contrast to one another. The past and the present. The life that could have been, and the life that is.

Her steely gaze meets mine, brimming with anger, but underneath it all, she seems almost... disappointed. I'm just not sure why. I don't know why it matters to her if I'm a Reject or not, but based on the hostility in her tone, it clearly does.

I open my mouth, but I'm not entirely sure what I'm going to say. Her question is obviously rhetorical.

"Were you going to have sex with Python that night?"

The question catches us both by surprise. *Dammit*, that sure as fuck isn't what I should be asking her. I *should* be finding out what she saw and trying to determine why Cain thinks she's lying. Yet the answer to those questions is far down my list. I want to know about *her*. I want to know who she is, her name, if she feels this attraction as intensely as I do, if she's gotten herself off to that quick alley fuck as often as I have.

"That's none of your business," she snaps irritably, her refusal to answer my question only serving to annoy me. She's right, it isn't any of my business, but that doesn't mean the thought of her going off and screwing some other guy, moving on as if I was just another fuck, doesn't piss me off. It's irrational and out of character for me, even so, that doesn't make it any less real.

I take a threatening step toward her. "You've been stirring up a whole heap of trouble since that night. Cain knows you're lying about something."

"So?" she bites back angrily. "My secrets are exactly that—*mine*. He hasn't earned any right to know them. And neither have you."

I force away the scowl on my lips, attempting to soften my expression as I relax my stance, attempting to appear less intimidating. My fingers twitch at my side, desperate to touch her. "I'm sorry," I begin in a gentle tone. "Why don't we—"

The shaking of her head cuts me off, and she steps back, immediately reopening the gap I just attempted to close between us. With a straight spine, she lifts her chin to meet my gaze, and her closed-off expression halts me in place.

"Just leave me the fuck alone."

She turns on her heel and strides down the street while I reluctantly watch her go until the darkness swallows her up. When I'm standing alone in the street, I pull my phone out and text Bones, telling him to follow her home. I convince myself it's because Cain wants eyes on her at all times. He doesn't trust her. He thinks she knows more than she's letting on, and maybe she does, but I can tell myself I'm putting Bones on her under Cain's orders until I'm blue in the face. The truth is, I want to make sure she gets home okay. And I refuse to dig into what exactly that means.

When Bones confirms he's on it, I head back into Toxic, letting the loud music drown out my churning thoughts about her. Cain said her name was Red. I'm guessing it's a stage name or nickname of some sort. It's fitting, giving the glossy, copper-red strands of her hair, but I want to know her real name. I need to feel it on my lips and hear it in my ears like I need my next breath.

I grab a glass of whiskey off a passing waitress, barely sparing her more than a passing glance as I move to join Cain in his booth. Tonight is the first night we've opened Toxic and run our fight nights here since we took over the Satan's territory, and so far, it's been a success. Cain seems to think so, too, based on the slight uplift of his lip. You wouldn't know from looking at him that he's happy. In fact, to most people, he probably appears irritated, but if you've seen Cain furious like I have, you know when he's not. His frustration at Red earlier seems to have disappeared, and he surveys the club with a proud look. And so he should. He's thriving. He's creating an environment where men can come and release their anger without shoving guns in one another's faces. Sure, we're all thugs, and the shit we do is far from legal, but there are viable alternatives to selling firearms and drugs, sex and people. He doesn't talk about his future plans, other than getting vengeance for Evie, but I know he wants to change things here, to make the town safer for the people that live in it. I'm just not sure if it's a pipedream that none of us will live long enough to see come true or if it's a viable future for us all.

I slide into the opposite end of the booth and lean my head back against it. I let my eyes drift shut, but when her face flashes behind my eyelids, I snap them open again, finding Cain watching me with a questioning expression.

"What's wrong with you?"

I sigh, sipping on my whiskey. *Mmm, the good stuff.*

"Remember that girl I told you about?"

"The one you fucked here a few weeks ago? Yeah."

I jerk my head toward the entrance. "That was her."

His eyes widen, and he huffs out a deep chuckle. "No shit, are you serious?" His laugh turns into a caustic bark. "Well, did you make her come? Maybe she'll be more inclined to open up to you if she knows you can satisfy her needs." There's a wicked gleam in his eye, and I know he's only half-joking.

He wants to find the Reaper. Badly. Ever since he found Red in the Satan's clubhouse, he hasn't been able to think about anything except uncovering the Reaper's identity. He's no longer happy settling for the long game approach we have planned out. Instead, he's hellbent on doing whatever it takes to get her to talk—a plan I was all on board with, until right now. Now, I'm not sure what to think. Plus, if Red does actually know the Reaper, then we don't want to go pissing him off. He hasn't come for a single

Reject yet, but without knowing the motives behind his kills, we're in the dark as to why.

We're not like the other gangs laying claim to Black Creek. We're not in this for the money, or the power, or the territory. We don't want to sell guns or distribute drugs, but no one outside of the Rejects knows that. If you were on the outside, looking in, I imagine we look like every other asshole vying for control. But at the heart of it all, we're nothing like them. Our objective is more significant than that. Our fight is one of vengeance, fueled by long-buried pain and a longing for a life that should have been. Every single member of the Rejects feels that way. Whether that came about because of the Antonellis, like it did for Cain and me, or at the hands of some other asshole who thought they could do whatever the fuck they wanted at our expense, it doesn't matter, because that need for justice, that hunger for revenge, it burns inside all of us, pushing us forward.

I ignore Cain's question, asking one of my own. "Why do you think she's lying?"

There's always the hope that she genuinely didn't see anything, and Cain has allowed his desire to find the guy and get him to help us take down the Antonellis, cloud his judgment.

He thinks about it for a moment before responding. "I can't put my finger on it. Her story doesn't quite add up, but it's more than that. It was the look in her eye that night. It was as if none of it fazed her... the guns, the violence, the blood."

I shrug my shoulders. "She probably grew up here. She'll have seen her fair share of shit like that."

He's shaking his head, though. "Nah, it was more than that." I can see the frustration on his face as he struggles to make sense of something. "I just can't figure out *what*."

We lapse into silence as I mull over what he's said. I honestly don't know what to believe, but Cain is a good judge of character, so chances are she's lying about something, but what?

"Maybe she's protecting the Reaper's real identity?" I muse.

"Yeah, that's what I'm thinking, but why?... He could be threatening her to stay silent?"

I nod my head in agreement, having thought the same thing. "Or she knows him."

My gaze meets Cain's, and I can see it in his eyes. That's exactly what he thinks—or at least hopes—is the case.

"If so, we need to find out from her who he is."

"Are you sure we're wise to pursue this?" I ask. "We can continue with what we've been doing."

He gives me a wry look, and I can see in his eyes how badly he needs this. Even more than I do, and until I ran into Red, it was the only thing getting me out of bed in the morning.

"Fine," I relent. "I'll talk to her this week."

I ignore the way my heart rate picks up at the thought of running into her again. Based on the way she looked at me after finding out who I am, not to mention her parting words for me to leave her alone, I'm pretty sure she's not going to be all that excited to see me. But I have to say, the thought of getting to see her, of possibly even getting to know her better, has a smirk lifting one side of my lips.

Three days later, I'm sitting in a private booth at the back of Strip Tease, mesmerized as Red swirls around the pole on stage like a pro, swaying her hips seductively.

She's dressed up as some sort of dominatrix, and it is doing all sorts of fucked up shit to my dick. I can't seem to tear my eyes away from the large swell of her breasts, pushed up and accentuated by her leather bra, or the way her ass looks in the thong and suspenders she's wearing. The tattoo along her upper arm and shoulder only adds to the whole dominating vibe she's got going.

Based on the hoots and hollers from the men gathered around the stage, throwing money her way and tucking dollar bills into her thong and bra when she's within touching distance, I'm not the only one affected by her beauty. She just stands out from everyone else. From her unique shade of copper hair to her wide-set hips, she's the complete opposite of every other woman working here.

When I first sat down and saw the attention she was drawing, I nearly flew out of my chair, intent on dragging her off that stage and away from the hungry eyes of the men surrounding her. Some primal voice at the back of my mind was whispering *mine*, but of course, that's so fucking far from the truth. She's not mine, and despite my draw to her, I'm not even sure if I want her to be. I came back to Black Creek with a purpose in mind, one I'm not even close to achieving yet. I don't have time to get distracted. Especially not by succulent curves and feisty eyes, plump, pink lips and soft, dirty moans.

I have to keep reminding myself why I'm here—to find out about the Reaper. Cain's been going about it all wrong, treating her like the enemy and having one of the kids follow her around. But that's Cain's way. He's always one to go on the offensive first. I'm hoping a gentler approach will help encourage her to help us. Obviously, I can't divulge anything to her, but I'm hoping she'll be open to at least talking to me.

When her time on the stage comes to an end and she walks off, the manager meets her at the bottom of the steps. I see the moment he tells her I'm waiting to talk to her. Her back stiffens, and she follows his gaze to where I'm sitting.

I keep my face impassive while her eyes burn into mine, her lips flattening in annoyance. Huh, maybe this is why Cain always takes the aggressive route. I get a kick out of knowing I've annoyed her. Sure, it would be better if she was happy to see me, like she was the other night at Toxic before she knew who I was, before I found out what she could mean to the Rejects. But, this is a close second.

She strides across the room toward me, every step emanating confidence and seduction. She screams sex, but not like cheap, motel sex. The kind of sex that's like a drug, that gets you hooked and keeps you coming back for more. The kind of sex you'll never get out of your system.

"Didn't I tell you to leave me alone?"

I don't know if it's because we met before she knew who I was or if she's just got ovaries of steel, but the fact she doesn't cower before me the way most people do is even more of a turn-on than her delectable body.

She perches on the far end of the booth, deliberately keeping as much distance between us as possible. I don't fucking like it. My fingers itch to reach out and touch her, to pull her in against me, and I have to dig them into the upholstery to stop myself from doing exactly that.

Meanwhile, she crosses her arms on the table and stares me down. Even though Strip Tease is officially under Reject control, she behaves as though we're in her territory, like I'm the one who should be withering beneath her ire and not the other way around.

"You know I can't do that." My voice is even, neutral, so she has no idea of the double meaning to my words. No doubt, even if I weren't here to press her for information, I would still be sitting in this exact spot. This pull I feel toward her is magnetic. It makes me wonder how I walked around this city for so many years and never found myself in this part of town, in this club, watching her from afar.

I shuffle across the booth toward her, hating how she tenses at my close proximity. I know it's not out of fear. She's never once demonstrated that emotion, and I'm sure it would take a hell of a lot more to actually scare her.

"I just wanted to talk."

"Well, I'm working." Her words are sharp, dismissive, but she's not getting rid of me that easily.

"I'm more than happy to wait until you're done." I lean in closer toward her, and despite her rigid posture, she swallows roughly, and I don't miss the hitch in her breath. "We can go grab a drink when you're finished. Maybe even finish up that dance." My leg brushes against hers, and I can feel the heat of her skin, even through the fabric of my jeans. The second our bodies connect, she jerks away, breaking the contact.

"No," she grits out. "We can't."

I've gotten a little off track here, I know that. How the fuck can I not, when all I want is to have more time with her, to see the sparkle in her eye that I saw the other night when she turned around and realized it was me standing behind her on the dance floor. Is it really asking too much to want to see that again, knowing I was the cause of that moment of happiness?

"Why not?" I snap, the words coming like a whip in my irritation. "Because of Cain?" I let out a long exhale, trying to calm myself down. We're not going to get anywhere if we both let our tempers get the better of us. "He—we—" I trail off on a sigh, struggling to find my words. "We just want to talk to him... If you know who he is, we just want to talk."

She scrutinizes me with such a sharp look. It's like she's slicing me open with her eyes, digging into my soul, and rummaging around until she finds whatever she's looking for. She doesn't find it because her expression shutters, falling into this blank mask that gives me zero insight into what she's thinking. I don't fucking like it.

"Why? What do you want with him?" Even her voice sounds more monotone than it did before, lacking the raw, husky tone that I love hearing.

"I can't tell you." It's the truth. We can't have word getting out that we're gunning for the Antonellis. It would be suicide. Even if we do manage to find this Reaper guy and decide to use him—assuming, of course, that he even agrees to help us, which is a big *if*—we will be taking a considerable risk.

She doesn't like that response, and I don't blame her. Sliding out of her seat, she gets to her feet. "Then I can't help you."

Fuck sake. My lips flatten as I bite my tongue, and with a final dismissive glance, she turns and walks away, getting back to work.

I sit back, flagging down a waitress and ordering a whiskey neat, all without ever taking my eyes off of Red. She works the room, dropping off drinks and collecting orders, laughing flirtily with customers, and pausing every now and again for lap dances.

She purposely avoids looking my way, but I know she can feel my eyes on her. It's in the tense way she holds her shoulders, in the way she deliberately angles herself so I'm never directly in her line of sight. She did give me one piece of critical information, though—she knows more than she's letting on, and if I were to hazard a guess, I'd say Cain's right. She does know who the Reaper is. But she's not going to say anything more without good reason. Cain can harass and threaten her all he wants, but I can already tell... she's a vault. I don't think anything he could do to her would be enough to make her crack. Which only leaves one option... we tell her our plans.

The question is, can she be trusted?

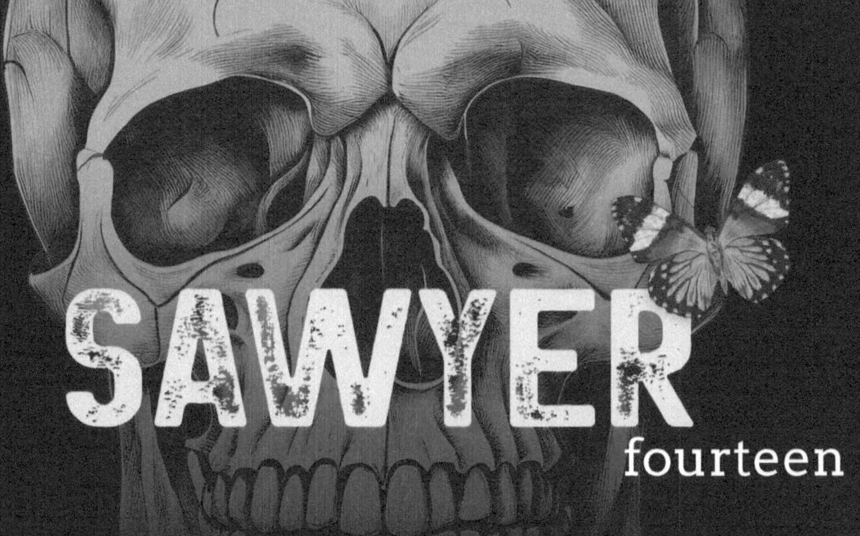

SAWYER
fourteen

What the fuck is this shit? I grit my teeth in frustration as I glare at my phone. I'd ask how the fuck this asshole got my phone number, but of course, he either asked Drew for it, or he helped himself to the employee files.

I'm about to reply with a middle finger emoji when another message comes through.

Just that one word. I still want to tell him where he can shove it, but curiosity makes me hesitate over the send button, and after a moment's debate, I backspace, deleting the emoji.

God, Sawyer, didn't you ever hear curiosity killed the cat.

The last thing I need to do is be walking onto Reject property. And yet, that's exactly what I'm thinking of doing. I mean, if they start badgering me about the Reaper, I can just walk out... unless they're planning on holding me hostage and torturing me for information. No, they wouldn't do that, right? Ha, what the fuck am I saying? They're gang members, of course, they'd fucking do that if it got them what they wanted.

I glance back down at my phone, re-reading the word *please*. My teeth sink into my lower lip, chewing on it as I try to decide what to do. I might be annoyed that Oliver is a Reject—it's so fucking typical, but not altogether surprising given where we live—but I don't fuck gang members. A principle I live by.

The problem is, I can't stop thinking about the way he tasted on my lips, of whiskey and wicked intentions. Or the way it felt to be cradled in his arms, pushed up against that wall. He was passionate, with an edge of danger that spoke to the wildness inside me, but there's also a stability about him that I find myself drawn to. It makes no sense because I don't even know the guy. He could be as flighty as they come, yet I get the impression he's someone who stays—who fights through the crappy times, who stands up to challenges, and doesn't shy away from conflict.

I shouldn't. I know I shouldn't go, but I'm already talking myself into it. They want the Reaper, and they think I know who he is. They're also going to be wary of him— because any gang member with half a brain cell would be. So they're not going to do anything to me and risk potentially pissing him off. The last thing they'll want is him coming after them. Besides, it couldn't hurt to find out what they want with the Reaper. What could they be after so badly that they're willing to negotiate with someone who is basically their enemy? It definitely has me curious.

Ah fuck it, I'm going.

Checking the time, I have an hour before I have to be there. I pull up my maps on the phone, realizing it will take at least that long to get across town on public transport. I guess I'll be taking Raven. Could be for the best. With assholes like this, it's always good to make a strong impression. I'm not some weak woman they can manipulate into doing what they want. I'm the fucking *Reaper* of all things wicked and evil. I dare them to mess with me. I'd relish in carving my name into their bodies.

Donning my leather pants, a tight black corset top that curves along the top of my wide hips and pushes the girls together—sexy, but not slutty—I lace up my chunky heeled boots and snatch up my leather jacket on my way out of the bedroom. I scrawl a quick note for Luc, letting him know there's left-over lasagna in the fridge for dinner before I grab my keys off the kitchen counter and head out the door. It's been a while since I've had a chance to get Raven out on the road—I couldn't risk going anywhere near her when that asshole, *Cain*, was having me followed. Bringing her to the meeting today will most definitely raise some questions, but fuck it. They're already suspicious.

I make the short walk over to the garage where I keep Raven safely hidden away, and goosebumps pebble along my arms when I start the engine and roll her out onto the street. I leave her running while I pull down the roller door and lock it. When I jog back to the bike, I pull on my helmet and connect my phone to the Bluetooth headset so that I can listen to the directions. As the woman's voice comes through the earpiece, telling me to turn left onto the street, I twist the accelerator, and with a rev of the engine, I'm off.

The whole city flies past in a blur of gray. Gray buildings. Gray roads. Gray sky. Everything in Black Creek is gray. Even the people are gray, with their miserable, trudging demeanors and lack of hope and ambition. It's like this city has sucked the color out of everything. Was it always this way? It has been for as long as I can remember, but surely Black Creek must have once been a thriving town before the gangs dug their claws into it—before The Feral Beasts destroyed any optimism the townspeople had and the Antonellis squashed us under their boots. We've been beaten down and pulverized for so long, none of us know any better. This life of scrounging for scraps and surviving one day to the next, without ever giving any thought to the future, is all we've ever known. But is simply surviving enough? What happens if we dare to dream of more? If not for ourselves, then for those we love. I don't want this bleak city to be all Luc sees and knows. There's an entire world out there, and most of it is a hell of a lot better than Black Creek. Doesn't he deserve to see it? To do better for himself than end up in a dead-end job or running for some gang just to make ends meet?

I think so. I just don't know how to make that happen for him. An education at a Black Creek school is worth jack shit, and I sure as hell don't have the money to send him to some fancy school or college. It wouldn't matter how many clubs I worked at or rich-scumbag-killing jobs I took, it would take years to earn that sort of cash. So for now, I have to settle for making Black Creek somewhere he can live safely, where one day he can carve out a small but promising existence for himself, and not one where he ends up dead on some street corner, caught up in a gang war he had no business being a part of.

The problem is, I'm not sure how to achieve that. Sure, I'm living the nice little secret vigilante life, killing abusive men, but that does nothing to stop the frequent gang wars that break out on the street or the overarching rule of the likes of the Antonellis, Grim Bastards, or even the Reaper Rejects. Luc deserves to leave the apartment every day and not wonder if this is the last time he'll walk out that door. He should never have to worry if he's going to accidentally get caught up in a shooting or if some asshole is going to come around and tear his life apart just because he can. And the only way for that to happen is if there are no more gangs in Black Creek. Ha, it's a laughable thought. An unrealistic and impossible one, but it's a wish all the same.

I'm barely paying attention as I zip through the streets, listening to the woman from my phone spouting directions in my ear. I'm going to be early. A journey that takes over an hour by public transport, took half that time on my bike. Once I'm near Radiant Park, I veer off course. I work my way down the gears, slowing the bike as I take in the part of the city that's been under Reject control for the better part of a year now.

I don't know much about them before then, but I remember when the whispers started on the street of this group of thugs who were collecting territory like it was pocket change. This part of the city was divided up amongst several small street gangs until the Rejects came along and quickly conquered all of it, claiming it as their own. By all accounts, it was a bloodbath. Six gangs demolished in six days, or something insane like that. That is, if the rumors can be believed. Once they had firmly seated themselves as the overlords of most of the southern part of the city, they seemed to slow down, and they have been taking their time picking off the last of their rivals. Apparently, the Satan's were next on their list of targets, but no doubt the other smaller gangs will soon fall too, which will leave only the Grim Bastards and Antonellis as the Rejects' rivals.

I'm not sure if it's because I've slowed the bike down or if the sun has popped out from behind a cloud, but there seems to be more color here than there was back on my street. I take my time, slowly winding along various avenues, and don't get me wrong, most of it is the same—homeless people crowded in doorways and hookers on street corners. But there are also glaringly apparent differences. I nearly stall my bike when I come across a flower shop. A motherfucking flower shop. In Black Creek. I don't ever remember seeing a flower shop here. People in Black Creek don't buy flowers. We don't have the time or energy to even stop and sniff the flowers, never mind the money to actually buy them. Yet here I am, looking at a fucking flower shop.

A woman who looks to be in her mid-to-late fifties steps out onto the sidewalk, sniffing at a large bunch of Tulips before she props them up in an oversized plant pot, displaying them just so.

A horn blares behind me, making me jump and jolting me out of my state of shock. It's only then that I realize I came to a dead stop in the middle of the road. The asshole blares his horn again, and giving him a middle finger, I roll the throttle and speed off. This time, I go straight to the address on my maps, having seen enough of this weird twilight zone.

When the map on my phone tells me I've reached my destination, I slow down and pull up to the curb. Turning off the engine, I take off my helmet and cast my eyes over the run-down apartment complex. I glance at the sign sporting the name of the complex —Radiant Park—before looking back over the shabby exterior. Yeah, I don't think that name fits. Maybe 'Rundown Park' or simply call it 'Pigsty'. Both are more fitting.

I'm pretty sure this complex was intended as high-end apartments when it was first built, but now it's as dilapidated as the rest of the city. Graffiti covers most of the brick wall, and paint is peeling off the wooden door. I think it was maybe a red color once upon a time, but now it just looks like it's covered in rust. Or dried blood. Actually, it's most likely blood on the door.

What I imagine was once a luscious lawn surrounding the building is now over-grown with weeds that come up to my knees. The lines marking out parking spaces in the lot have long since faded, and cracks have formed in the concrete path up to the lobby door.

A tall, iron fence, topped with wire, is all that separates the complex from the side-walk and looking around, there isn't a soul in sight. Shouldn't they at least have someone manning the gate? I'm not entirely sure what I expected, but the lackluster veneer and absence of security are definitely not it.

Not hanging around, I push open the pedestrian gate and step warily onto the property. I'm still expecting someone to jump out from the bushes and attack me for setting foot on Reject property, but nothing happens, and after a few more cautious steps toward the building, my confidence builds. As I stride across the cracked concrete, I push back my shoulders and lift my chin, donning my typical *don't fucking mess with me, bitch* expression.

Just as I ascend the steps up to the main entrance, which I'm assuming leads into a lobby, the door is pulled open, and Oliver's tall frame blocks the doorway. He looks like fucking sin in his combat boots and jeans, with a tight t-shirt that clings to his muscular abs and chiseled biceps. In the light of day, his features are even more breathtaking, and I have to swallow roughly, my mouth suddenly feeling dry as I drink him in.

"I wasn't sure you'd come." His gaze sweeps over me before glancing over my shoul-der. He quirks a brow when he sees the bike but doesn't comment on it.

"Well, you said please," I grumble, forcing my face into a frown in an attempt to hide the physical effect he has on me. One side of his lip lifts slightly. *Goddammit*, if fucking butterflies don't take flight in my chest at that simple movement.

"Come on in." He pushes the door open wider and steps aside for me to move past him into the dark interior of the building. The place is a hive of activity, men stocking shelves behind the bar with alcohol, arranging furniture, and cleaning the place up.

"Did you just move in or something?" I ask absently, taking in the heinous, flowery wallpaper currently being stripped from the walls and the light fixtures that look like they're from the seventies.

"A few months ago, but we haven't had much of a chance to get it all redone. We wanted to get the fighting pit across the way set up first."

"Red," someone calls out, and when I turn to locate the source of the voice, Jon is bounding toward me, carrying a box in his arms. I give him a tight smile. I like the kid, but I'm feeling uncomfortably on edge surrounded by all these men, even if most of them are giving me cordial smiles or nothing more than passing glances. I'm on enemy territory right now, and regardless of how friendly they may appear, I don't trust any of them. "How ya been?"

It's a struggle to keep the surprise off my face. It was one thing for him to talk to me so freely when we were alone, but in front of all his gang buddies? I've spent very little time in gang clubhouses, but I don't need to, to know women are rarely treated with the respect they deserve—especially not virtual strangers. In gang life, anyone who isn't affiliated with the gang in some form is treated as an outsider, someone not to be trusted or befriended until they've proven themselves.

"Ehh, I've been good."

His smile broadens. "Well, I'll catch ya later, can't let the boss man here see me slacking." He juts his head toward Oliver, laughing freely, so it's obviously a joke.

As he wanders off, I turn to Oliver. "Exactly how high up in the Rejects are you?"

I'd just assumed he was a low-level player. I don't know why exactly. He just doesn't strike me as the domineering, overly aggressive, compensating-for-his-small-dick type. The sort of bullshit posturing every other leader exudes. Now, Cain is absolutely that typical, thuggish asshole of a kingpin.

He rubs awkwardly at the back of his neck, ducking his head, almost as though he's embarrassed, but I can't figure out why. "I'm Cain's second in command." *Huh, wasn't expecting that.* "It's not what you think, though."

I don't know what he means by that, and I deliberately don't ask. I do not need to be getting myself embroiled in their club shit any further than I already am. I get the uneasy feeling that if I dig too deep into Oliver's life, I'll only end up liking him more, and I can't afford to let that happen. No gangbangers. That's my rule, and I need to remember that around him.

He looks at me for a moment, and when I don't ask the question he's expecting, he changes the conversation. "We're in the process of converting this into a bar area for everyone. Got the bar bit set up a while ago but haven't had a chance to get the rest of it done."

I take all of it in silently as he escorts me across the room toward a hallway that leads down the back of the building. We pass several closed doors before he knocks on one, not waiting for a response before he opens the door. I follow him into a relatively large office that somehow manages to feel suffocating with Cain's emanating presence. Even though he's tucked behind a desk, his essence seems to envelop the entire room, sucking all the oxygen out of it.

Even seated behind a desk, he looks fucking ruthless. It's written in the tight lines of his face, in the narrowing of his eyes and his sharp jaw, which is hidden beneath a thick layer of dark stubble. His bulging biceps and broad shoulders make it clear he takes pride in his appearance. In his line of work, your body says a hell of a lot about you. Cain's body says he could tear you limb from limb and not even break a sweat. He's pure muscle, every inch of him built to destroy whoever crosses him.

He doesn't move from behind his desk as he silently observes me. I watch him right back, trying to get a read on him after our last interaction, but it's impossible. His face is a blank slate. Only the weariness in his eyes gives away his uneasy feelings regarding this meeting. *Interesting.* So this wasn't his idea then. Guess I have Oliver to thank for whatever the fuck this is about.

"Red," he eventually acknowledges, sounding more like he's going to the execution block than greeting someone in his home. "Have a seat." He nods his head toward one of the two chairs sitting opposite his desk.

I'm hyper-aware of the door clicking closed behind me and Oliver moving to lean against the room's back wall. At the same time, I make myself comfortable in front of Cain's desk, crossing my legs and quirking a brow in expectation. He's the one who called me here, so he's damn well going to be the one to get the ball rolling.

His lips flatten, and he glances behind me to Oliver before returning his intense gaze to mine again. He takes a long moment to look me over, noting my leather gear. I felt comfortable leaving my helmet on my bike. No one would be stupid enough to try and steal from right outside Reject property, and if one of the Reject assholes themselves dares to touch my bike, well then, I won't have any qualms about chopping off their hands.

I've unzipped my leather jacket, and I notice his perusal falter on the swell of my tits before he returns his wandering gaze to my face. My skin burns everywhere his eyes roam. It's like his intense green irises are lasers. He grits his teeth, and I can tell, whatever he's going to say, he doesn't like it. Not one fucking bit. Cain might be the leader of the Rejects, but right now, he's doing as Oliver has advised him, not what he himself wants to do.

"We want to negotiate a deal with the Reaper."

Silence sits heavy in the air at his statement, and I can feel the tension radiating off the two of them as they wait to hear my response.

"What sort of deal?" I counter in a flat tone, giving nothing away of my feelings. They are no longer asking me if I know him or saw him that night. They *know* I have some sort of relationship with him—I'm just betting it's not what they think—so there's no point in pretending any longer. Besides, I can't deny I'm curious.

Cain shakes his head. "That's between us and him."

"Why?" I ask instead. "Why do you need the Reaper? Surely, whatever problem you have, the mighty Rejects can handle it themselves."

My voice drips with sarcasm, which doesn't go unnoticed—or appreciated—as Cain's eyes narrow on me in warning. One I disregard. I can see the muscle at the back of his jaw tick, and I have to bite back my snort. This guy has got the shortest fucking fuse I've ever seen.

It's Oliver who speaks up, directing my attention his way. "We're having difficulties achieving this particular job on our own. It's really best if we just talk directly to the Reaper. For all we know, he won't even be able to help us."

What he's saying makes sense, and I tap my fingernails against the wooden arm of my chair as I mull it over. I choose each word carefully before I say, "I need to tell him something about the job you want him to do. He's not going to agree to a meeting otherwise."

"Not happening." Cain's sharp voice isn't altogether unexpected. Given how cryptic they've been, I didn't think they'd just volunteer the information. But just like they don't trust me, I don't trust them. Without knowing what they want, I'm unwilling to reveal my own cards.

I get to my feet, pinning Cain in place with a pointed look. "Then I think we're done here." This isn't a ploy or a tactic. I'm serious.

I move toward the office door, sparing Oliver a passing glance and ignoring his stern frown as I pull open the door and step out into the hall. I've made it back to the main bar area, where guys are still tearing down wallpaper and setting up various tables by the time Oliver catches up to me. His hand reaches out to touch my wrist, and I jolt, breaking his contact with my skin as I spin to face him. He's still wearing that same frown, and he glances nervously around the room, obviously not wanting to be overheard.

He's careful not to touch me when he leans in, but he may as well be rubbing himself all over me for the way his titillating scent invades my space, sending my brain on the fritz and rendering me speechless.

I feel the soft puff of his warm breath against my ear, and it makes me shiver. I swallow roughly, painfully aware of the damp patch forming in my panties. He's got a five o'clock shadow that I desperately want to run my fingers along as I wonder what it would feel like grazing against my inner thigh. I'm losing all common sense, quickly melting into a puddle of sex-addled hormones when his next words penetrate through the fog, registering with me.

"We're going after the Antonellis."

They're what?! It takes a second for me to wrap my head around what he's saying, and not only because my mind already drifted to far dirtier thoughts. What he's suggesting is complete fucking suicide. The Rejects might be formidable and ruthless, and yeah, they've proven themselves to be calculating and determined, but they are no match for the Antonellis. They're in a league all on their own. One of those long-established families who can be traced back to the dawn of the goddamn country. They have more money than any of us will see in a lifetime, and that money can buy them whatever the fuck they want. It would certainly be enough to squash this little rebellion without even putting a fucking dent in their overall financial worth.

"Are you insane?!" I hiss. "You're going to get yourselves fucking killed."

I can see it in his eyes. It only lasts a second, but it's there, shining clearly for me to see. He doesn't care. Going after the Antonellis is something he's prepared to die for. What in the ever-loving fuck could they have done to brew such loathing?

I slowly take a step back, and when he doesn't try to stop me, I take another, shaking my head. "I can tell you now, what you're doing is suicide, and the Reaper will want no part in it."

Oliver's face pinches, resulting in this aching sort of pain that sends a spike of sorrow through my chest. When he next speaks, his words sound broken, voice low and deflated. "Ask him anyway. He might be our only option."

Fuck. Me.

With a final nod, I turn on my heel, striding past the other members and out the door, squinting in the bright light of the afternoon sun. My bike and helmet are exactly where I left them and I hastily shove the helmet over my head, revving the engine so loud there's no doubt in my mind every person residing in Radiant Park heard it before taking off down the street.

fifteen

I've got two glasses of whiskey sitting on the desk by the time Oliver returns, his withdrawn expression telling me all I need to know about how his conversation with Red went.

"Told you it wouldn't work."

He sears me with a scathing look, dropping into the chair Red just vacated with a sigh and staring absently at the floor.

I sip on my own drink, needing the sharp burn as it slides down my throat to distract me from the flaming anger and raging disappointment fighting for dominance within me. I knew it was a long shot, going after the Reaper, but when I realized he'd been in Python's room that night, that Red might have seen him—I just had to give it a shot. We're making next to no progress on our own, and the Reaper has an uncanny ability to sneak on and off gang property unnoticed. I thought he might be able to help us find a way to get close to Giovanni and his family.

I hadn't quite worked out the specifics. It's not like I was going to let the Reaper claim Giovanni's death for himself. As the head of his Family, Giovanni is the one who ordered his men to come to *my* house that day to kidnap *my* sister, so the least he deserves is a death at *my* hands. And my men are more than capable of taking on his underlings. All I really need the Reaper for is to gather intel—something, *anything* that can give us an advantage and enable us to sneak up on Antonelli and his men unawares. He's so good at stalking around this city unseen, that he must know or be able to find out the Antonellis' dark and hidden family secrets.

I'm so lost in my own thoughts as I stare down at the amber liquid in my tumbler that I'd forgotten Oliver was even in the room until he leans forward, the movement catching my eye as he places his elbows on his knees, folding his hands under his chin. His lips are pressed tightly together, and it's clear he's deep in thought as he mulls something over.

After a moment, he speaks up. "Get Mac or Ian to tell us whenever Giovanni or one of his higher-ups next go into the casino or the club."

My eyes narrow as I frown at him, trying to figure out where he's going with this. Mac and Ian are the two men we have planted in the Antonellis' organization, and they've been able to pass along some scraps of information, but nothing actionable.

"I'll take a small team of men and trail whoever it is."

"What good will that do?" I ask, dubious.

He shrugs. "We might find something useful. Hell, we could uncover where Giovanni and his top men live and maybe take them all out in one, quick, surprise attack."

My ears perk up at that idea, liking the sound of it. No one knows for sure where any of the Antonelli Family live. There are plenty of rumors, of course, but only those at the top of the Antonelli hierarchy are privy to that information.

"If we can find out where they live, we can place twenty-four-hour surveillance on them while we come up with a plan," Oliver presses, incentivized.

Evie was as much a sister to him as she was to me. The two of them were as thick as thieves when we were growing up. Sometimes, I wondered if he even had a crush on her. I'd thought about asking him, but then that day happened, and what was the point? Nothing mattered anymore.

Regardless of the feelings he has—had—for my sister, he's just as driven as I am, and I know the lack of progress we've been making infuriates him as much as it does me.

This plan makes sense. We have to be stealthy when it comes to the Antonellis. Being unable to match their manpower, we can't afford to start an all-out war with them. If they suspected for one second that we were gunning for them, they'd come for us, and we'd be slaughtered like animals, our bodies thrown into the docks and forgotten about.

No, we have to be clever and cunning with the Antonellis. We need to slip under their radar and catch them off guard. It's a complete contrast to the brute force with which we have overthrown every other group of thugs so far, but the Famiglia is no disorganized street gang. They're a fucking dynasty, the crux of the Italian Mafia, and the Tideside Docks is their impenetrable fortress.

I down the last of my whiskey before I meet Oliver's eye. I can see the determination flickering in his gaze. He wants to do this. Needs to. "You're right," I agree, a malicious smirk curling at my lips, and hope swells in my chest, quickly displacing the suffocating disappointment that was beginning to brew. "I'll message Mac and Ian."

Oliver grins, this dark, vitriolic slice across his face that's so out of character it would concern me if I didn't fully understand the pain behind it.

Changing the subject, I ask, "What about the stripper? You told her our plans, didn't you?"

As soon as he chased after her, I knew damn well he'd give her more than I wanted her to know. He frowns at my name-calling, but doesn't say anything about it.

"She won't talk."

He sounds so confident, but how the fuck can he be so sure? He doesn't even know this girl. I lean back in my chair and scrutinize him for a second. "I thought it was just sex."

He shakes his head, running a hand through his short, dark hair as a frown mars his features. "I don't know what the fuck it is, but I can't stop thinking about her."

It's my turn to shake my head as I snort. "That's because you haven't had pussy in like, three years. I told you to fuck one of those hangarounds, man. You should have listened to me and gotten it out of your system. That girl is trouble."

She's already caused us such a headache, and we don't even fucking know her. Now she knows information that could annihilate us if it fell into the wrong hands. Even if the Reaper isn't willing to meet with us, we can't let Red walk around with the information she has. Not without keeping tabs on her. She's not loyal to us and has absolutely no reason to keep that information to herself. Not to mention the fact she's fucking messing with Oliver's head. I can't afford to have him distracted by some cheap ass pussy.

I tap my fingers against the glass as I contemplate what to do about this new problem. I'll have to put Jon back on the job of tailing her ass to make sure she's not talking to anyone she shouldn't be. But something tells me that isn't enough. I'll give it a couple of days, see if the Reaper reaches out to us, and go from there.

It's been a week. One long, slow week, and we haven't heard anything from either Red or the Reaper. Nor have Mac or Ian been in touch with any updates. I feel like I'm constantly on edge, waiting for the phone to ring with an update of some sort. It's driving me fucking nuts. I've turned into a growling bear. Even my men avoid me when they see me coming their way. The only thing that helps is fighting and drinking. I've been in the pit every night this week and followed up each victory with enough alcohol to leave me unconscious.

Tonight's looking much the same as I throw back my third—or is it my fourth?—shot of whiskey. Whatever number it is, it goes down smoothly, warming the pit of my stomach. Oliver and I got in a fight earlier—only one of many that have broken out this week as shit has spiraled further out of control—and he's fucked off to god knows where. His absence only adds fuel to the fire of anger and hatred burning brightly in my chest.

I hate how optimistic I got about this Reaper guy. It was foolish of me, but I seriously thought he could be the key to it all. Our secret weapon that would enable us to best the Antonellis.

Lifting the bottle to my lips, I take another long gulp of whiskey, hissing as it burns my throat. This is all that fucking stripper's fault. I bet she didn't even talk to the Reaper. Just decided on her own that she didn't want him helping us. She decided from the very beginning that she didn't like us—why? Because we overthrew her precious Satan's? I get that her first impression of us wasn't exactly favorable, but Razor said she was in shock when he found her in that room, so I *know* he will have treated her with kid gloves. Although, I'm beginning to wonder if she even was in shock or if all of it was an act designed to throw us off.

I can feel the heat from the alcohol fanning the flames of my anger and pushing it to new heights, and before I've really thought through the decision, I'm out of my chair, following the sounds of loud music. The guys have done a great job transforming the lobby into a bar for all of them to hang out in during their downtime.

As I walk in, I spot Bones at the bar with a few other guys. He's holding a beer, and as he lifts it to his lips, I call out, "Nope, put that down. I need you to drive me somewhere." I'm far too drunk to drive myself. I fish my keys out of my pocket and toss them to him.

"Sure thing, boss." He sets down his beer and follows me outside. The parking lot is full of the various vehicles belonging to Reject members. I bought a few cars from Arnie for club purposes, and a few of the guys have bought themselves bikes or cars.

I make my way to a black Cadillac Escalade at the far end of the lot. "Where are we going?" Bones asks as he hops in behind the wheel, and I climb in the passenger side.

"Strip Tease."

With a nod of his head, he starts the engine and pulls out of the lot, and it doesn't take us long to make it across town to the club.

Alcohol is still coursing through my system, driving my actions as I storm into the club. Not that anyone is any the wiser. The loud bang of the door is drowned out by the heavy beat of some song through the speakers; the customers too caught up in watching and whistling over the dancers on stage or ordering drinks at the bar to notice my presence. That's fine, I'm here for one person, and one person only. I cast my eyes around the crowded room until I spot her delivering drinks to a table at the back of the room. My gaze stays fixed on her as I close the distance between us, skirting around anyone in my way and nearly bowling some guy over. My mission is single-minded—to get to the bane of my existence. I'm not entirely sure what happens then. My drunk mind hasn't quite figured that part out yet.

She turns to face me just before I crash into her, snatching the empty tray from her hand and dropping it on the floor as I use my superior strength to barrel her backward through the staff entrance door that I know leads into the back hallway, where the manager's office and dressing rooms are located.

"What—" Her words catch on a gasp as I wrap my fingers around her narrow wrist, pushing down on the door handle, so we tumble through it into the empty hallway beyond. We stumble backward, my weight pressing her against the opposite wall, so she's forced to look up at me.

Her eyes, wide with surprise, narrow in annoyance when she realizes who's disrupted her otherwise regular shift. I momentarily get distracted by the unique azure blue of her irises, churning with tumultuous clouds that speak to the complex nature of the alluring enigma glowering at me as if she'd like to slit my throat.

"Did you even talk to him?" I bark.

Confusion flashes across her face before a sharpness enters her eyes. "You're drunk. I can smell it on you." She pushes against my chest, but I'm still pinning her to the wall, and she doesn't stand a chance of moving me unless I want to be moved—which I sure as hell don't.

"Did you?"

Her nostrils flare. "Surprisingly, he's uninterested in getting involved in your suicide mission."

I eliminate the slither of space between us, caging her in more tightly against the wall. So tight, I can feel her soft curves pressing against me, feel the heat of her body warming my skin. I didn't have a chance to take in what she was wearing before—or more importantly, the lack of what she was wearing—but now that I feel her breasts pushing against my chest, I can't help the way my gaze dips, taking in the rapid rise of her chest, matching her short, sharp pants.

"Why would you even risk everything you've built just to go after them? Are you seriously that power-hungry that you'll jeopardize the lives of your men?"

My eyes snap up to meet her tumultuous blue gaze, narrowing to a glare as I slam my hand into the wall beside her head, making her jump. My lip curls back on a snarl. "My men know what they're risking. They know what they're fighting for."

"Half of your *men* are nothing more than children. They have no idea what they want."

I bark out a cold, caustic laugh. "You have no idea what my men have been through, the lives they've led. Like me, they're tired of letting someone else dictate their lives, walk all over them, and tell them what to do. Where you see children and a gang fighting for territory, I see men that deserve the chance to fight for something they believe in, and a gang that wants to do right by the people of Black Creek."

By the time I'm finished, she stares up at me with wide eyes, speechless for once. Her lips are slightly parted, drawing my gaze to her plump lower lip. I find myself captivated by the way it glistens in the light of the hallway, and whether it's the alcohol or this vixen is some kind of witch, I find myself murmuring, "Have you ever had your life upturned in a single moment? One second everything was going along as normal, and in the next, all you've ever known has gone up in flames and been burnt to ashes?"

A heavy silence falls between us, the air thick with the weight of my words. I dare not look her in the eye. I'm not used to moments of vulnerability—I'm not used to vulnerability at all. I shut down any soft emotions the day Evie was taken. That softness is for boys. For children. It's a weakness that can be exploited. Yet, here I am, sharing the most broken part of myself with a girl I know nothing about. One I don't trust.

I push off the wall and move to turn my back on her, intent on leaving. I have no idea what I was thinking coming here; what I thought it would achieve. Chalk it up to drunken intentions and desperation.

The last thing I expect is the one-syllable word that she whispers so quietly, for a second, I think I imagined it.

"Yes."

That one word pauses me in my tracks, and I slowly lift my gaze to meet her eyes, seeing the honesty reflected in them. For the first time since I laid eyes on her in the Satans' clubhouse, I see what she never allowed me to glimpse before. Her own vulnerability. The pain she carries every day that's incredibly similar to my own.

I lose myself in her eyes for a moment, taking some comfort in the fact someone else feels that same aching loss gnawing away on their insides that I do. Eventually, I find the strength to look away, and without a backward glance, I turn on my heel, leaving Red and the club behind.

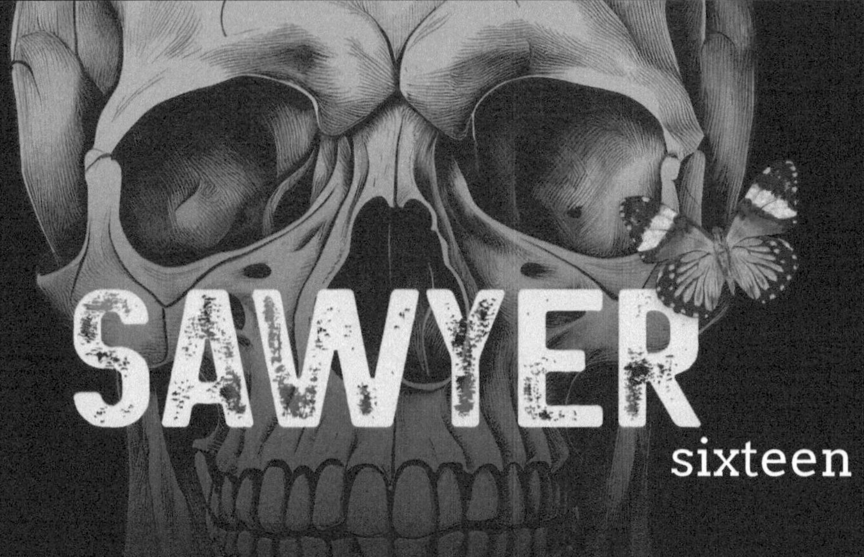

I'm still playing Cain's words on repeat the next day as I let myself into the apartment. Combined with what Oliver told me about how they plan on taking down the Antonellis, I can only assume they did something to Cain—and possibly Oliver?

I empathize with him. I really do. I know what it's like to have your entire life torn to shreds—ripped into so many fragments that you don't even know where to begin with picking up the pieces. I got my revenge on the man who destroyed my life. He was my very first kill; the reason behind what I do—the driving force of the Reaper. So I understand the need for retribution more than anyone, but there's a massive difference between going after some gangster low-life and the entire Antonelli empire. If he was even going after one person within their organization, I could maybe get behind that. Yes, it would be challenging, but it wouldn't be fucking impossible.

Despite how much he grates on my fucking nerves, I actually do wish I could help him. While I spend most of my time around Cain wanting to gouge his eyes out—and ignoring my damp panties—no one deserves to feel that clawing need to right the wrong against you. I understand that feeling... how it starts off as a small seed of anger, warming the pit of your stomach, but over time it grows. It takes root in your insides, twining around your heart and embedding itself in your soul. It digs itself so deep that vengeance becomes all you know. Everything you think about. You exist solely for that one purpose, and you just can't stop until you've achieved it—irrespective of the risks and potential casualties.

So I know nothing I say or do will stop them from starting a war with the Antonellis. But I don't have to insert myself in the middle of it. The intelligent thing to do is keep my head down and hope the Antonellis destroy them swiftly, without inflicting too much damage on the rest of us caught in the crosshairs. Now that I know what's coming, I can prepare myself and focus on keeping Luc and me alive.

"Luc," I call out as I walk through the door, kicking off my boots and hanging my leather jacket up. "You here?"

My question is met with silence, and setting my keys on the kitchen counter, I move over to his bedroom door and knock on it. When I don't get a response, I crack it open, looking around the empty space with a wrinkled nose. His clothes are scattered everywhere, and it fucking stinks in here. Moving deeper into the room, I crack open a window to air the place out and head back to the kitchen to get started on dinner.

After staring into the half-empty fridge for a good ten minutes, debating between leftover Thai or pizza, I eventually grab the box of pizza and close the door. As I'm setting the box down on the kitchen table, I spot a scrap of paper with Luc's sloppy writing on it.

Gone to hang out with Jon and his friends. Be back later.

Ehh, what the hell? I have to read the page twice before the words finally sink in. Luc is with Jon? How the fuck did that happen? I know Cain had some asshole following me all week—and now I'm guessing that asshole was Jon—but I've deliberately stayed out of trouble. I've even ignored every fucking message in my inbox with a potential new job. Now more than ever, I could do with watching the life drain out of an abusing asshole, but nope.

I haven't even realized I'd crumpled the note in my palm, my anger getting the better of me until I look down to find out where Luc is so I can go hunt him down. Unfurling my hand, I flatten the piece of paper on the table and read it once again. *Are you fucking serious, Luc?* He doesn't even say where he is, and I can only assume these *friends* of his are fellow Rejects.

My hunger forgotten, I put the pizza back in the fridge, and feeling absolutely fucking furious, I snatch up my keys and put on my boots, storming out the door intent on dragging my little brother back by his goddamn ear if I have to.

I repeatedly call Luc's number the whole way to the garage, but he ignores every damn one of my calls. When the fifth one goes unanswered, I hang up with an angry snarl and stomp the remaining few feet to my bike.

Grabbing Raven from the garage, the city passes by in an angry, red blur, the blood in my veins heating with every mile I get closer to Radiant Park. I told Jon to stay away from Luc, and I gave Luc the same warning. *How could he be so stupid?*

I'm so angry with him by the time I pull up outside the Rejects clubhouse that I can hardly see straight as I turn off the engine and climb off. I'm still clutching my helmet in my hands as I shove open the gate to Radiant Park and step through. The second I do though, a blaring alarm goes off, and before I've even figured out what's going on, I'm surrounded by men, all of whom are pointing various-sized guns at me.

Fuck.

"Don't take another step," some guy I don't recognize orders. *Like I was about to.* You're pointing a fucking gun in my face. Why the hell would I move right now?! God forbid you misinterpret so much as an inhale as a sign of attack and shoot my fucking brains out.

"I'm looking for Jon," I call out, roaming my gaze around the various Rejects. The one speaking to me has dirty blond hair styled in a short buzz cut, making him look ex-military, and as I swing my attention back his way, he speaks up again.

"What business do you have with the Rejects?"

Ha, fuck, just today or in general?

Despite the sweat gathering along my spine, I can feel myself getting irritated. I just want to find my brother so I can ream him out. Is that too much to ask? Before I can snap something back at him that would definitely guarantee me a lovely little bullet wound, a voice calls out, "Drop your weapons. She's not a threat."

I really want to contradict Oliver's statement, but now probably isn't the time, and I have to admit, I breathe out a sigh of relief when the men surrounding me all do as they're told. Where the fuck did they all come from anyway? I didn't get such a warm welcome the last time I was here.

I glance around for Oliver, frowning when I don't immediately see him. I do, however, spot what I missed before—security cameras placed along the fencing surrounding the property, with what looks like motion detectors around the sidewalk gate and the entrance into the parking lot.

Huh, more high-tech than I expected, or that I've seen before. Usually, gang security amounts to some half-baked idiot sitting on a chair, passed out on the job. I know the Grim Bastards have a more reliable system, but it's still men just manning the entrance to their once-fire-station-now-kingpin-kingdom and reporting who enters and leaves.

The clubhouse door opens and out strolls Oliver. The afternoon sunlight reflects off the tawny strands of his hair and makes the tattoo sleeve of his right arm stand out in contrast to his pale skin.

I forget myself for a minute, momentarily drawn back to the mystery man from that first night in Toxic as his gaze meets mine. Gone is that flirty glint and devilish smirk, and in its place is a steady gaze and a closed-off expression that, frustratingly, only annoys me further. I know I told myself to forget him and move on. That he was a distraction I couldn't afford, but fuck me, fate—you cruel bitch—couldn't you have at least made him someone I could have been allies with? So long as he's a Reject and they plan on going after the Antonellis, we're always going to be in opposition. I'm never going to be able to offer him what he wants—the Reaper—and he will never be able to provide me what I want—for him not to be a gang member, or be starting a war he can't possibly win.

He gives a silent signal to his men, and without question they break apart, moving back to their posts and returning to whatever they were doing before I showed up. He waits until we're alone before approaching me, stopping a respectable distance away. It infuriates me that I want him to close the gap between us so I can feel the brush of his skin against mine.

"Did you talk to the Reaper?" he asks in a hushed voice.

Of course, that's why he thinks I'm here. Why would that asshole Cain tell him anything about our conversation the other night?

"Actually, I'm looking for Jon."

His brows knit together in confusion. "Bones? Ehh, I think he and the others are over at the sports complex." He juts his chin forward, gesturing toward the building behind me on the opposite side of the road.

Now that I no longer have guns shoved in my face, I'm back on my mission of tearing Jon a new one and dragging my brother back home. If anything, the welcome I received is just more proof that Luc shouldn't be here. It's not safe. What if they'd done the same to him. He's a guy, so he would have been treated as even more of a threat than I was. What the hell was he even thinking by coming here?

Pissed off again, I turn on my heel and move to storm across the street.

"Wow, hold on," Oliver calls out, reaching out to grab my arm. "What's going on?"

I glower at him. "What's going on," I snap, yanking my arm out of his hold and ignoring the tingling sensation his touch leaves on my skin, "is that your men have been following me all week. I can't go to the fucking bathroom without them knowing, and today I arrive home to find a note from my brother informing me that he's hanging out with the fucking kids you call gang members."

The fury I've been bottling up inside spills over, and I take a threatening step toward Oliver, ignoring his wide eyes as I throw him my deadliest glare. "Your men have no right to be anywhere near my little brother. He's got nothing to do with any of this, and the last place he should be hanging out is a gang clubhouse filled with guns and whores."

A frown forms on Oliver's face. "I thought Jon said he was like fifteen or something?"

"What does that have to do with anything? He's got no business being here." I gesture with my hand toward the apartment complex. "Look what just happened. He doesn't deserve to have guns shoved in his face, and I sure as hell don't want him getting hurt or killed because of your *gang*."

"He's just playing ball with the guys. Nothing's going to happen to him."

I shake my head. He just doesn't get it. Not wanting to waste time engaging in a pointless argument with him, I take off across the street toward the gym. I can still hear him behind me, his heavy boots slapping against the asphalt as he follows me.

"They're around back," he states as I approach the gym. At his words, I veer away from the front entrance, following a path that leads around the side of the building. As I get closer, I can hear voices and the sounds of laughter along with the thump-thump-thump of a ball bouncing against the hard ground.

Turning the corner at the back of the building, I find a bunch of guys—Jon and Luc included—running around a makeshift basketball court that's been spray-painted onto the asphalt.

"See, he's perfectly fine," Oliver states, earning himself a glare before I focus back on the guys on the court, noticing that they must all be only a few years older than Luc.

"Why are they all so young?" I ask Oliver. It's not surprising to see teenage boys hanging around clubhouses. They're at an impressionable age that makes it easy for assholes to manipulate them into doing shady shit for them. However, I've never seen so many who are already affiliated with a gang and seem to have a good relationship with the rest of the members. Usually, they are nothing more than grunts—bottom of the food chain, expendable members that do the jobs no one else wants to do.

Oliver's shoulder brushes against mine as he steps up beside me, the two of us watching the game unfold before us. "They were all being held captive in this compound in Cali where they were being trained to become killers."

At his words, I tear my gaze away from the game to gape at him in shock.

"They don't talk about it much, but they were street kids that were taken and were being molded into soldiers when Cain rescued them."

"So he could use their skills for himself." My dislike for Cain only grows. He's as bad as the people that initially kidnapped these kids. He just wants to use them for his own gain.

Oliver barks out a laugh and shakes his head before looking at me. "You've got Cain all wrong. Yeah, he's an asshole, but he's not the person you think he is." He focuses his attention back on the game when a round of hollers goes up as someone scores a basket. "He found homes for as many as he could, but these guys here had nowhere to go. They want to be here. For the first time in their lives, they have somewhere they belong, where they can be themselves and build a life they want." He looks back at me, pinning me in place with a serious expression. "If they decided tomorrow they wanted to leave, Cain would let them. Hell, he'd probably buy them a bus ticket to wherever they wanted to go and give them money to get themselves started."

I don't know what to make of that. Have I really misjudged Cain? Is his dickish exterior just that? Somehow, I doubt he's a fluffy little bunny rabbit that saves desperate children on the inside. I think Oliver is a little blinded by Cain, but I'm not here to interject myself into their gang politics. Hell, I'm supposed to be staying as far away from them as possible.

"Well, it's really none of my business," I state in a hard voice, refusing to let what he just told me to soften me toward Cain or the Rejects. "I'm only here to get Luc." Before he can say anything further that might break the tenuous hold I have on my tough exterior, I stride toward the guys running around the court.

When I'm close enough, I call out Luc's name. The interruption has all of them stopping mid-game as they turn to look in my direction. Luc's eyes widen when he spots me, and although I can't hear what he says, I'm pretty sure he mumbles *fuck* under his breath.

I quirk a brow and pinch my lips, letting him see how pissed I am at him. He starts to move toward me, but Jon comes jogging over, and I shift my glare from Luc to him.

He grimaces. "Look, I can see you're angry. I'm sorry. I just thought he'd wanna hang out with kids his own age."

"That's what he goes to school for," I snap. "He doesn't need to be hanging out with teenage gang-wannabes right outside a fucking clubhouse where any number of dangerous things could happen. Do you have any idea the risk you've put him at by bringing him here?"

I can see the guilt swimming in Jon's eyes, and written into the hard press of his lips as I rip into him, the anger that's been simmering in me sparking to life the more I talk.

"It was reckless. This might be the life you've chosen for yourself, but it's not Luc's." I shake my head in disappointment. "I don't want to see you anywhere near him. You're not to message or call him, and I definitely don't want you in our apartment."

I almost feel bad as his head drops, and he looks properly chastised, but Luc's safety is my number one priority, and I'll do whatever it takes to protect him.

"Hey," Luc snaps at me, looking furious himself. "I'm old enough to be making my own decisions. You think the kids I go to school with aren't already deep in gang life? Do you have any idea the number of times someone tried to get me to sign up for the Satan's? I can't hang out with anyone at school without someone thinking I'm associated with one gang or another. I just wanted to have some fun for once."

"Well, fun time is over. We're leaving."

"We're not finished."

I glower at Luc. "I don't give a shit. *You're* finished."

"No," he snaps. "I'm not leaving. What are you going to do? Drag me out of here?"

I take a threatening step toward him, planning on doing just that when Oliver interjects. He steps between us, putting himself in the line of my wrath. "Why don't we let them finish up their game, then I'll take him straight home?" I open my mouth to argue when he cuts me off, leaning in to whisper in a quiet voice that's meant only for us to hear. "It's not like you can take him on the back of your bike anyway."

I snap my mouth closed because, well *fuck*, he's right. Why the hell did I get a goddamn bike?!

Seeing that he's got me there, Oliver catches my gaze with his capturing sky-blue eyes. "I'll have him back in an hour." I can see the sincerity in his gaze, and despite the fact I don't want to leave Luc here alone, I get the impression Oliver won't let anything happen to him.

I grit my teeth for a long moment, mulling it over, but I know I have no other choice. I don't have a spare helmet for him to ride my bike, nor am I actually capable of dragging his ass out of here if he's going to fight me on it.

"Fine," I reluctantly snap. "One hour."

When Oliver nods in understanding, I pin Luc with a serious look. "You and I are going to have a serious talk when you get home."

He still looks pissed off, but Jon drags him back to their game, and not wanting to hang around or have to talk to Oliver, I storm off back to my bike, and start the engine. Swinging my leg over the seat, I tug on my helmet and take off, blinking back tears the entire way back to the garage.

The second I pull up in the garage and take off my helmet, I fall apart, letting the tears fall. Luc is the only person in this entire world that means anything to me, and the fear I felt today was overwhelming. I just want to keep him safe, but he's reaching that age where he wants to do these things. Where he wants to hang out with his friends and make his own decisions, and honestly, it scares me. I'm terrified he'll make the wrong choices in life. That he'll end up running for a gang. I don't want him to throw his life away, and I couldn't live with myself if he ended up dead before he had a chance to grow up and really live.

I have to start letting him live his own life, but I have no idea how to do that, how to just sit back and let him be. I know he's smart, and he will make good decisions for the most part. The fact he's made it to fifteen without falling into gang life is a testament to that. He's surrounded by that shit in school—something I was already aware of. It's more of a recruitment center for lowlifes than it is an educational establishment. And I know if any of the kids in school asked him to hang out, it wouldn't be to play ball. It would be to party, drink and do drugs, and try to entice him into that life. I do think Jon was just trying to be friendly and include him... and I blew a fucking fuse at him— god, I'm such a bitch.

I let myself have a pity party for one on the floor of my garage for a few minutes before sniffling back the last of my tears and wiping under my eyes. Getting to my feet, I lock up and head toward my apartment, careful to keep my head down so no one can see my red, puffy eyes. If I can make it back before Luc gets home, then I can get a cold compress on them. The last thing I want is for him to see me upset over this.

"Red," a voice I recognize calls out just as I step into the doorway of my apartment building. *Fuck.*

Straightening my shoulders, I spin to face Oliver. I didn't think it had been an hour already. Was I really having an emotional breakdown for that long? Dammit, I need to pull my shit together.

No doubt he can see the red rim around my eyes, but I make sure the rest of my face is set in its usual resting bitch face as I meet his eyes. He's leaning against a black Escalade and squinting through the front windshield. I don't see any signs of Luc inside, so he must already be in the apartment. Why is Oliver still hanging around out here then?

When he sees my no doubt blotchy face, his lips flatten as though he's annoyed, although I don't know what about it could be angering him. "Can we talk?"

I cross my arms over my chest, needing the extra layer of defense between us right now. "I don't see how we have anything to talk about. I think it's best if you just go your way, and I'll go mine, and we can pretend we never met."

The muscles in the back of his jaw tighten—an indicator that he didn't like what I said—and he pushes off the side of the car, moving toward me. "Is that what you genuinely want? To just ignore this *thing* between us?"

I have to swallow around the lump in my throat. His proximity makes it impossible to think straight, and suddenly the hard-bitch exterior I had erected is starting to crack and crumble.

After a moment's silence, he jerks his head to the right. "Let's go grab some food —"

"I can't," I interject, cutting him off. "Luc... "

"Luc's upstairs. Let him calm down for a bit before you confront him." With the way his gaze hovers over my puffy eyes, I can tell what he's really saying is *I'm sure you don't want him to see you crying.* Knowing he's right, I huff out a long exhale before reluctantly agreeing.

He tosses me a small, warm smile, and we walk side-by-side down the street to a small twenty-four-hour diner. The bell above the door tinkles as we walk in, and I lead us over to an empty booth along the window.

The inside is designed in a shabby, retro vibe, which could be cool if it wasn't for the fact I'm pretty sure the only reason for the decor is because the owner can't afford to update it. There are holes in the faux-leather upholstery of my chair, and the linoleum table is chipped, the top layer peeling away.

An older woman with graying hair—who stinks of cigarettes—wearing a uniform and an apron approaches, barely sparing us a glance as she hands us menus and takes our drink orders.

Neither of us says anything as we peruse the menu and wait for the waitress to return with our coffees.

"Anything to eat?" she asks as she sets a chipped mug down in front of me and fills it.

"Ham and cheese panini for me," I tell her, handing back the menu.

"Yeah, I'll take the same," Oliver supplies before the waitress leaves us alone. An awkward silence settles over us as I take a sip of my coffee, grimacing before I drop a couple of lumps of sugar in the cup and stir it, pointedly looking out the window as I do. I refuse to allow myself to ask him any personal questions, even if I am curious to know more about him. It won't do me any good to get further invested with him or the Rejects. My involvement with them over the whole Reaper thing has already resulted in

Luc being dragged into their life. I can't afford for the lines to become even more blurred.

"Is Luc the only family you have?" Oliver eventually asks, drawing my attention away from the old couple walking arm in arm down the street.

"He is."

"He's lucky to have a sister like you. One who cares enough to walk onto gang-owned territory and yell at one of them for him." His lip quirks up to let me know he's joking.

I chuckle out a weak laugh. "I'd do a lot more than that for him."

The waitress returns, setting our food down on the table, and another moment of silence falls over us when she's disappeared.

"So, how long have you worked at Strip Tease?" he asks. It would seem, he's all about the personal questions today.

"Five years."

His eyebrows lift. "That's a long time. Do you enjoy it?"

I snort, giving him a quizzical look. "Do I enjoy giving lap dances to overweight, middle-aged men and assholes with bigger guns than they have dicks?"

He simply shrugs, and I can tell his question was a genuine one. He wasn't trying to take a dig at what I do for a living, he was genuinely curious to know if I enjoyed what I did.

"I enjoy when I'm dancing on stage," I admit. "It's impossible to make anyone out with the bright stage lights, so it feels like I'm in my own little world. It makes it easy to get lost in the music."

"That sounds nice. I rarely get a moment to myself anymore. It's quite an adjustment. In prison, I had hours every day where I wouldn't see or talk to another person, and now I'm lucky if I can get two minutes to piss in private."

My eyebrows climb up my forehead at his easy admission that he was in prison, and I have to bite my tongue to hold back the burning questions. *I am not getting personally involved,* I remind myself.

I force back the questions threatening to spill past my lips, biting off a considerable chunk of my panini and munching on it for as long as I can. I feel Oliver's eyes on me, though; I can feel his puzzling stare as he tries to figure me out.

"You're good at it," he says after a long moment of silence. "Dancing."

I make decent tips, and the hoots and hollers I receive when I'm on stage certainly imply the customers are enjoying the show I'm putting on for them. Still, no one has ever said it quite like that—as if it's about the actual movements, and not just the shaking of my tits and circling of my hips. The strange compliment makes me blush, and I duck my head, mumbling a weak thanks as I lift my panini to my mouth, unsure how to respond to that sentiment.

Oliver doesn't try to engage me in conversation again, and we end up eating the rest of our meal in silence. Surprisingly, it doesn't feel awkward. It's actually kinda nice. Something I can see myself doing on a regular basis. I refuse to let myself ruminate on that for too long, so I steer my focus instead on the mechanical process of chewing and swallowing until my plate is cleared.

When I look up, there's a playful smirk on Oliver's face. He's holding one half of his panini in his hands, halfway to his mouth as though he was about to take a bite but got distracted. "Hungry?" he jokes with a chuckle.

I glimpse at his plate, which still has the other half of his panini to my own one, which looks like it's been licked clean, and let out my own small laugh.

"Maybe a little," I confess, unwilling to admit nerves and an uncanny urge to actually open up and talk to him had me practically wolfing down the food.

He finishes off the half of the panini in his hand before asking, "So did you grow up in Black Creek?"

"Yeah, I did," I answer, starting to feel uncomfortable about all the one-way questions. "Did, uh, you?"

A small smile graces his lips like he knows what it cost me to ask that question. "Yeah, I did. Cain and I grew up on the same street."

A pained expression crosses his features but it disappears so quickly, I have to wonder if I imagined it.

"So you've known him your whole life?"

"More or less." He doesn't expand further than that, and I don't pry.

"And now you're a member of the Rejects."

I don't mean for the words to sound disdainful, but they do all the same. It's just difficult for me to view any of the Black Creek gangs in anything other than a negative light.

Oliver's eyes jump back and forth between mine for a moment, as if he's trying to discern my thoughts before he speaks up. "Is it just the Rejects you have an issue with or all gang members?"

"Don't go thinking you're special. I truly hate all of you equally."

My whole life, gangs have laid down the law and forced us to comply with their whims. My mom paid so much of her earnings to the gang that ran the territory we lived in, that she barely had enough left to clothe and feed us. They insisted she pay *rent* on the street corner she stood on, plus a nominal fee for protection, and I'm sure there were other bullshit charges thrown in there. Not to mention the way they abused her and got her hooked on drugs so she'd be under their control. The final straw was when one of them—her fucking *boyfriend,* if you can even call him that—beat the shit out of her and murdered her in front of Luc, leaving her body for me to find when I got home.

I saw the same shit day in and day out on the street. Gang members throwing their weight around, using their position, their size, their weapons to demand whatever the fuck they wanted. They'd hang around outside shelters and try to lure desperate people into gang life by offering them drugs and money. Flirting with women and promising them safety and security, but those same women would be right back in the shelter a month or two later, covered in bruises. So, yeah, it's safe to say I have a fucking reason to hate gang members.

"What have they ever done for me or the people of Black Creek? All they are interested in is themselves. So long as they have drugs, alcohol, territory and can wave their big ass guns in people's faces, none of them give a shit about the problems they cause for the rest of us."

Oliver just sits and watches as I get myself riled up. I can feel the color in my cheeks as my anger takes over, and I have to take a deep, calming breath to rein myself in. I don't need to be spilling my guts to Oliver. What the hell does he know or care about it, he's one of those fucking gang members.

"And yet, you were there to fuck Python the night he died."

He's watching me intently, searching my face for any reaction to his prying statement.

I keep my expression carefully shuttered as I state in a dry tone, "I don't see how that's any of your business. If I want to get off by rubbing myself against a tree trunk, then that's my prerogative, and it's got fuck all to do with you."

He wipes a hand over his mouth, hiding the half-smile threatening to make an appearance, before leaning across the table toward me. "I just don't see that someone like Python would be your type."

There's a playful twinkle in his eye at that statement, and what the fuck can I say to that? He knows exactly what my type is—him.

Unable to think of a half-decent comeback, I simply shrug my shoulders, refusing to say anything more on the subject, and after a moment, he switches lanes, getting us back on track. "I don't know if you've noticed, but the Rejects aren't like the Satan's or any of the other gangs."

I frown, pinching my lips together. I have noticed—how could I not? And it only confuses me more. It's practically ingrained into my blood to hate any and all things gang-related, but the Rejects aren't like any gang I've come across before. They don't appear to be the lowlife scum I'm used to, but that doesn't make it any easier for me to just discard my hatred for their kind. Besides, if I stopped viewing the Rejects as *the bad guys*, then that would open the door for me to see them as something more, which terrifies me. My feelings for Oliver are confusing enough. Then, if you throw in whatever electrified chemistry I have with Cain... If I can't tell myself that they're off-limits because of who they are, then where does that leave me?

"I had—noticed. I'm just not sure if that changes anything."

I lose myself in the depths of his gaze for a moment, the two of us falling into a world where only we exist. I can't even begin to describe this pull I feel toward him. I've felt it ever since I sidled up beside him at the bar. I hardly know the guy—I've made a point of not getting to know him—but that doesn't lessen this attraction between us. If anything, every time we cross paths, my resolve to stay away from him weakens.

Coughing, he clears his throat before asking, "You ready to go?"

With a nod of my head, I agree, "Sure."

I go to grab a few dollar bills from my pocket but he beats me to it, dropping enough on the table to cover both of our meals.

"I don't need you to pay for me," I state with a frown of annoyance.

"Never said you did. I might be a Reject, but I do have some manners, and I know to settle the bill when you ask a girl out for a meal."

I hesitate for a moment before relenting. Fair enough. So long as he realizes this isn't a date, who am I to argue with a free meal.

His palm rests on my lower back, the light touch and chivalrous act making my stomach flip as a horde of butterflies take flight as he escorts me across the diner and out the door. I'm aware of his every movement as we walk down the street, and when the back of his hand brushes against mine, I get literal goosebumps. It doesn't matter how many times I tell myself he's a Reject and that he's on a suicide mission, my body still craves him.

When we approach my apartment building, he pushes me against the wall, crowding me with his broad chest as he leans an arm against the brick above my head. "Go out with me."

It's not really a question. More of a demand. One my slutty side responds to. I stare into his pale blue eyes for a long moment, allowing myself for just a second to imagine a world where he isn't a gang member, and I'm not just trying to keep my brother and me alive. I could definitely picture myself dating him. I imagine he would be easy to fall for, with his boyish charm and casual demeanor, not to mention he's easy on the eyes. Yup, I could definitely lose myself in Oliver... in another life.

"I can't," I begin, watching as tight lines form around his eyes and his shoulders tense. "Maybe if you weren't who you are... " I trail off, unsure how to bluntly say if he wasn't associated with a gang, then *maybe* things could have been different between us.

"That just sounds like an excuse to me," he states, unperturbed.

I shrug my shoulders. "Maybe so, but Luc needs me. As much as I couldn't live without him, he couldn't live without me. And going out with someone like you, well, that's just asking for trouble."

He stares intently back at me for a second. "I think you're just so used to doing all of it alone that you don't know how to rely on anyone else. You think I'd bring more trouble to your door, and maybe I would, but I'd also bring more protection and better support. If trouble did come knocking, you wouldn't be facing it alone."

He paints a pretty picture, one I could easily fall for, but I know it's not that black and white. If we were to break up, there would be a target on my back from rival gangs thinking they could maybe get information about the Rejects out of me. Not to mention the fucking war they're about to start with the Antonellis. Anyone associated with them will be skinned alive.

"I'm sorry," I breathe out, watching as his face shutters and he closes himself off from me. I fucking hate it, but I've made my decision. He gives a sharp jerk of his head before pushing off the wall and stepping backward.

"Yeah, me too." With one last lingering look, he moves around to the driver's side of the car, glancing over at me before he gets in. "Take care of yourself, Red."

He's already in the car with the door closed and the engine started by the time I find my voice, feeling strangely emotional as I watch him drive away. "You too, Oliver."

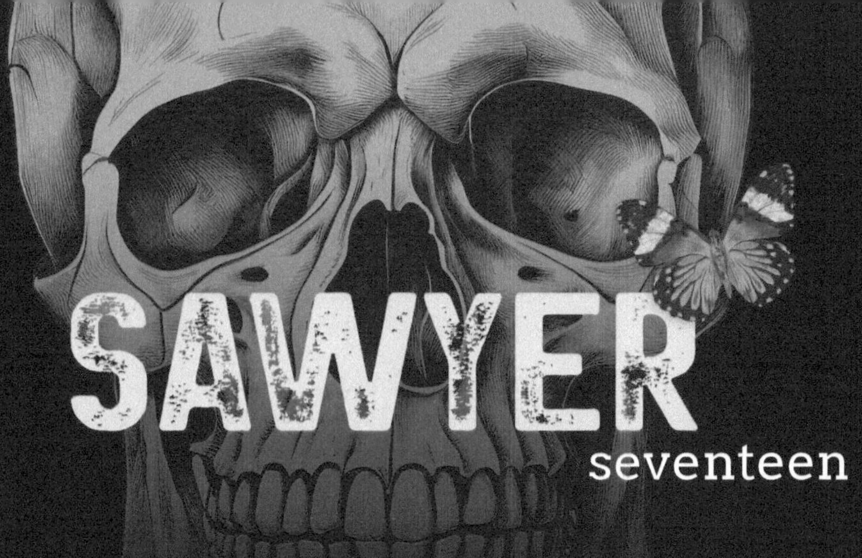

seventeen

L uc is waiting for me when I let myself into the apartment. His anger from earlier is gone, as is my own, and when I step into the living room, he meets my apologetic gaze with a regretful one of his own.

"I'm sorry," he blurts out before I can say anything. "I knew you'd be mad—"

"I was, but only because I care about you."

He's already nodding his head. "I know."

We stand and look at each other for a moment before I let out a long exhale and close the distance between us, wrapping my arms around him. "I'm sorry. I just don't know what I'd do if something happened to you."

"Nothing happened, though. I was fine. They're good people."

God, I'm getting sick of everyone telling me Cain and the Rejects are *good people*. They're fucking gang members. They're inherently designed to be gun-toting, dick-wielding assholes who can't see past their own ego long enough to give a shit about anyone but themselves.

"They're thugs," I snarl more sharply than I intended. The last thing I want to do is get into another argument with Luc over them. "They might be better than the Satan's, but that doesn't mean they're *good*."

Luc's lips pinch, but he thankfully doesn't argue with me. "I still need my own friends, though. Guys to hang out with. I deliberately stay away from the kids in school 'cause I know they're affiliated with one crew or the other, and I don't want to get caught up in that shit, but Sawyer, I need more than just you in my life."

There's no denying the sting of pain at that comment, and I have to carefully hide my hurt feelings from him. I know he doesn't mean it that way. What bothers me the most is that he's everything to me. I don't really have anyone else. No one I can rely on or call up to chat with after a crappy day. There's Sheryl, sure, but she's a mess. I can't dump any of my shit onto her. So I guess it hurts a little that Luc needs more than just me, but that's a seriously selfish thought. He's a teenage boy, of course, he needs people other than his sister-mom.

I have to swallow around the lump of emotion in my throat before I can respond. "I get that. I'm just not sure that Jon and his friends are who you want to spend your time with."

He quirks a brow, and his words are coated in sarcasm when he says, "Would you prefer I hang out in a drug den, surrounded by coke and hookers, with one of the kids from school?"

I grimace, hating the harsh reality he's painting.

"Jon just asked me to play ball with him," he continues. "They didn't try to get me to go into their clubhouse, and they didn't offer me drugs or alcohol or wave a firearm in my face. Honestly, if it weren't for their tattoos, you wouldn't have known they were associated with a gang at all."

Groaning, I press the heel of my hands against my closed eyes, staving off the headache forming behind them.

"Fine," I relent. "I get it." Lifting my head, I pierce him with a reluctantly acquiescent look. "Just, promise me you'll be careful."

His shoulders drop, and he gives me a soft smile as he nods his head. "I promise."

We chat for a bit longer before he moves to lounge on the sofa, channel surfing while I help myself to a large glass of wine and grab my bathrobe before heading into the bathroom and running the taps for the bath.

Once the water is warm enough, I sit on the edge of the tub, drop a citrusy-smelling bath bomb into the water, and wait for it to disperse while sipping on my wine. When the room smells like a vineyard, with the zesty, flowery scent, I shed my leather clothing and sink into the blissfully hot water, letting the bubbles melt away all my stress from today.

I've got no idea what I'm going to do about Luc. Okay, I know what I need to do, I just don't know how I'm going to actually manage to do it. I have to stop smothering him and let him branch out on his own, but how the fuck am I meant to do that? How does any mother stand back and watch their child go out into the world, knowing they'll make mistakes and fuck up along the way? It's even worse when that world is Black Creek, and a simple mistake can result in your brain matter being sprayed all over the sidewalk.

Still, I risk losing Luc for good if I continue to smother him the way I have been, and that's the absolute last thing I want. So, despite my overbearing nature, I need to find a way to take a step back and let him just be himself; to grow up, and ultimately learn to stand on his own two feet. Even though I still see him as an eight-year-old boy, he's a teenager now; practically a man.

Regardless of my de-stressing bath, I toss and turn all night. Recurring nightmares of Luc getting shot or something terrible happening to him play on repeat in my head, driving me insane, and by the time the gray light of dawn peers through my window, I'm in a pissed-off mood and in need of a serious caffeine fix.

My day only goes from bad to worse when, once I've filled the coffee pot and poured myself a steaming hot mug, I pull out my burner phone—the one I use specifically for Enzo. Rather than finding the usual text confirming this afternoon's meeting, he's demanding a last-minute time change.

ENZO:

Can't do this afternoon. Meet me at 9:30 am instead.

I SEE NO PLEASE OR THANK YOU, AND WITH IT ALREADY BEING AFTER NINE o'clock, I don't see myself making it on time. Not that I'm going to even bother trying. That's what he gets for being so bossy and trying to mess with my schedule at the last minute. I hate when he reschedules on me. Admittedly, he rarely does. I can probably count on one hand the number of times he's had to cancel or change our plans in the last seven years. Still, it's as much about the *way* he said it, as it is about the actual inconvenience of messing up my plans—besides, I'm not in a mood to cater to his bullshit today, and I always feel like I need time to psych myself up for my meetings with him. Almost as though I have to put on mental armor to protect myself from him. Not that he's ever done anything to hurt me. Hell, on paper, he's a hell of a lot more decent than most of the people I come into contact with every day. But there's something about him that just irks me. I can't put my finger on it, but it makes the hairs on the back of my neck stand on end and gives me this feeling like I need to put up boundaries between us —which is why I usually spend the morning before our meetings putting on my war paint and emptying my mind of everything so I can come across as an impenetrable fortress to him. Basically, I let him see the deadly side to the Reaper while keeping the crazy part of myself that craves the bloodshed locked up tight.

I deliberately wait until after nine-thirty to message him back. *No can do. Will meet you at the usual place and time.*

Pressing send, I stare at the screen, expecting an immediate response. After several moments, I give up when one still hasn't come through, assuming his silence means he's fine with that. Just as I get up to refill my mug, the phone vibrates with an incoming message. *Tomorrow then.*

Frowning, I type out a quick response. *Nope. Today. Usual place and time.* As soon as it's sent, I power the phone off. The screen flashes with an incoming call, Enzo's number at the bottom, less than a second before it goes black.

I smirk at the screen, knowing I won that argument. I move to get another cup of coffee. I've got a feeling I'm going to need it today.

WITH MY LONG HAIR FLOWING FREELY DOWN MY BACK AND A FULL FACE OF makeup, including darker than usual eyes and bright red lips, I feel fucking fierce as I step into G&T in my chunky heeled boots, black skinny jeans, and a faded band t-shirt that I've knotted around my midriff. My leather jacket provides the finishing touches to the badass bitch persona I'm rocking.

I'm momentarily blinded as I move from the sunshine into the dark interior of the pub, and I have to blink a few times before my eyes finally adjust to the light. Before I can look around to see if Enzo is here, the man himself practically pounces on me. I hadn't even noticed he was sitting at a table right by the door, and he must have stood up as soon as he saw me enter.

"I told you not to come," he snaps, staring down at me with narrowed eyes. There's a wild look in his blue-green gaze, and between his weird behavior and attempt to reschedule today's meeting, he's acting suspicious as fuck.

I scrutinize him closely, taking in the tight lines of his face that give away whatever strain he's been under recently. "What the fuck crawled up your ass and died?" I snark with a raised brow, not appreciating his attitude. "*I* told you I couldn't reschedule. Besides, you were clearly able to make it just fine."

I can see the muscle in his jaw working and his nostrils flaring before he lets out a long exhale. "Fine. Here's your cash, now give me my info." He holds his hand out with my envelope in it. Another red flag. He's never gotten straight down to business.

I glance from his outstretched hand up to his face. "What, no drink and you asking me inappropriate questions first?"

He grinds his teeth, getting more and more frustrated with me with each passing second. My snark has always grated on his nerves. I think he's the kind of guy who likes to think of himself as a straight shooter, and my constant deflections piss him off. But the thing is, he's as tight-lipped as they come. I don't know a goddamn thing about him. Not that I've let myself ask him any personal questions. Our relationship is strictly business. I don't need to know every little thing about him to work with him. And honestly, I get the impression if I go digging too deep into his life, I won't like what I find, and I do like the money he gives me every month, so I choose not to go snooping.

"I've got other shit to do today," he snaps irritably. His gaze bounces around the room like he's expecting something to happen, and I focus my attention on his pupils, trying to work out if he's on drugs or something. It would definitely explain his weird behavior.

Nope, his pupils are a normal size.

"Shame." I pout and slip past him, sliding onto an empty barstool. "I'm in the mood to talk and drink today."

"Not here, you're not." He grabs hold of my upper arm, and as I go to yank my arm out of his grip, everything goes sideways. The blistering heat of a blast knocks me backward as a whooshing sound threatens to burst my eardrums, and I hit the ground with a painful thud that vibrates through my bones. My head smacks against the floor with what I imagine is a deafening crack, seconds before a heavy weight lands on top of me, knocking the last of the air out of my lungs.

My ears ring, and time loses all meaning as I lie there, struggling to breathe. I choke on nothing as I try to force air into my lungs for a terrifyingly long moment before the weight lifts off my chest, and I finally manage to suck down some oxygen.

I'm faintly aware of someone rolling me onto my back and shaking my shoulders, but my eyes feel too heavy to open. My whole body feels numb. Is that a good thing? I feel like that can't be good. Some asshole pulls back my eyelid, and I jerk away from the harsh glare of light with a groan. Whoever is harassing me continues, and I eventually find the strength to peel open my eyes, finding Enzo's face hovering above mine.

His lips are moving, but I can't make out the words. Blood drips from a cut along his brow, and a layer of dust coats his face. I focus on the movement of his lips, not in any attempt to understand what he's saying, since they just look so... pink. Have they always been that pink?

The ringing in my ears dulls, the odd word making it through the buzzing. "Red. Red!"

I close my eyes, focusing on the noises around me. People screaming. Tires spinning against asphalt. Gunfire. Something is burning. The acrid, pungent smell singes my nostrils, the scent of burning flesh making my stomach revolt.

"Sawyer!"

My eyes snap open, once again finding Enzo hovering over me with a look of concern instead of his usual expression of stoicism. The left side of my head is still throbbing from where I hit it off the ground, and when I lift my hand to my temple, my fingers come away coated in blood. I stare at the bright red substance for an inordinately long time until Enzo's voice penetrates through my psyche. "Come on, we have to get out of here."

I barely register his words before he's lifting me off the ground. The sudden movement has me gritting my teeth against the sharp pain in my side, and I stand on shaky legs while he supports most of my weight until I gain my bearings. Once I'm confident I'm not going to collapse to the floor, I pull out of his hold and pat myself down, checking everything is intact. *All good—well, as good as can be expected.* The whole left side of my body, where I hit the floor, hurts, but I don't think anything is broken.

"What happened?" I croak, looking at the carnage surrounding me. The explosion upturned tables and windows were blown in, littering the ground with tiny shards of glass. The shelves of booze behind the bar have smashed, coating the floor in sticky liquid, and amongst the rubble, bodies are strewn everywhere. Some are groaning and struggling to move, while others are clearly dead. *Jesus.* Except for the front exterior wall, the rest of G&T is nothing more than a bombed ruin. There's hardly anything left of it. All around me, people are screaming, crying, running away, and I can hear the loud echo of gunshots from somewhere outside.

With my head spinning, I step toward the front of the building, figuring that's the quickest way out of here. God knows, what's left of the foundations can't be enough to prevent the roof from falling down on top of us at any second.

"No," Enzo barks, his hand snapping out to grab a hold of my arm and tugging me backward. "They're gunning down everyone that goes out that way." He pulls me across the room, in the direction of the bar, and I step over dead bodies, trying not to look into their glassy, sightless eyes as I pass. It's difficult, though, since I have to keep looking down to ensure I don't trip over any debris. One particular man catches my attention. He's just lying there, and at first, I think he's dead, but after a second, he blinks, and I realize he's in shock. I don't fucking blame him. Blood coats the ground around him, and he's missing half an arm. I look around his immediate vicinity, unable to locate where it was thrown in the blast. *Holy fuck, what is this day?*

I'm distinctly aware that *I'm* in shock, and I once again cast my gaze over my arms, suddenly fearful that I may not even realize I'm missing a vital organ. *Nope, definitely all intact. Thank fuck.*

Dust hangs heavy in the air, catching in my throat, and I stumble as a cough wracks my body. My hand goes out to lean against a dark wooden pillar for balance until my coughing fit passes, and when I push off the beam, my hand is covered in a red substance. It takes me longer than it should, to realize it's blood, and I gape at the wooden pillar in shock. The entire thing is covered in a red, blood mist.

"Come on," Enzo urges when I've been frozen in place for too long. "We need to go."

He resumes tugging me behind what remains of the bar, and glass cracks beneath my boots as I hurry across it. A thought niggles at the back of my mind, but I push it away, focusing on following him as we reach a storage room. There's a fire exit on the far side of the room, most likely where deliveries are made, and Enzo wastes no time moving toward it. He cracks open the door and peers out before pushing it open further, and we stumble onto a back alleyway. The sky seems darker than it did when I first arrived, and when I look upward, a thick layer of smoke is blocking my view of the sun. Despite the smoke, the air is clearer out here than it was inside, and I suck it down, bending over to place my hands on my knees. My ribs ache with every inhale, and I can feel something sticky running down the side of my face. All in all, I'm feeling like fucking shit right now.

For the first time since the explosion, I really take myself in, noticing the rips in my leather jacket and jeans. Thankfully they seem to have protected me from the worst of the blast, and I've only got a few superficial scrapes on my arms and legs. I lift my hand to touch the wound on my head, wincing when my fingers touch the tender skin. It's still bleeding, although I think it's slowed. It definitely feels like the worst injury I've sustained.

"You have to go," Enzo rushes out, drawing my attention his way. As I lift my head to look at him, ignoring the continued rattle of gunfire coming from the other side of the building, a moment of clarity hits me, and I look at him—covered in dust and blood —in a new light. It dawns on me that I truly know nothing about this man, and while an hour ago I didn't care to change that, I suddenly realize that not knowing is a weakness.

"You knew this was going to happen." I cough, but I don't dare look away from his face, searching it for any confirmation I'm right. He doesn't give anything away, his expression pinched and unreadable. "How?"

For a split second, he drops his guard, and a multitude of emotions flash across his face, too quick for me to pinpoint any individual one. As promptly as his barriers fall, he reconstructs them, his expression turning to stone. It's not one I've seen before, and it catches me off guard.

My eyes narrow on him, and I bark out, "Who are you?"

He doesn't answer me, instead pointing toward the far end of the alley, away from the ongoing sounds of an attack. "Go. Now." His words are snapped off the end of his tongue in an acerbic tone, and I don't immediately react to them, continuing to stare at him as I wonder just who the hell he is.

"Not until you tell me who you are," I argue, vaguely aware that the man standing in front of me isn't the same one I normally meet once a month for our exchange. He's currently emanating an aura of authority and danger. One he's kept carefully under wraps in all of our previous meetings.

His lips pinch and his eyes narrow, but after a second, he says, "I work for the Antonellis."

I blink owlishly at him, almost certain I've heard him wrong. The Antonellis? Are you kidding me with this shit? It's entirely possible I hit my head harder than I realized and I misheard him... right? *Goddammit*, somehow, I don't think I did. His expression certainly doesn't look like he's joking. The question is, what the fuck has he wanted from me all these years? My stomach churns precariously as I think about all the information I handed over to him.

Before I can fully process what he's said, never mind form any sort of response, he barks out in an authoritative demand, "No more questions. Get the fuck out of here."

Realizing I'm not going to get any more answers from him—at least, not today—I take one last look at the man I know nothing about and take off down the alley.

I stumble down the alley and practically run with blinders on until I reach the garage where I park my bike. My hands are shaking as I search my pockets for the key to the roller door and pull it open just enough to slip inside.

Finally safe and alone, I sag to the ground, unable to believe today's turn of events. They play repeatedly in my head, and I still can't wrap my head around the fact that Enzo works for the Antonellis. I don't understand what he's wanted from me all these years. Surely the intel I handed over could easily have been obtained elsewhere? Do the Antonellis even care about the mundane on-goings of street gangs?

More importantly, how had I never connected those dots before? It never even crossed my mind that he could be in the Antonellis' pocket. The small behaviors that never quite made sense to me, slot into place like the final pieces of a jigsaw. The way his face scrunched at cheap whiskey; how he was always more smartly dressed than most people that live in Black Creek; the fact he never seemed to quite fit in here like the rest of us do. They were all little tells, pointing to his true identity, and like a fucking idiot, I ignored every single one, not wanting anything beyond the cash in his hands.

Putting two and two together then, that only leaves one possible explanation for today... the Antonellis attacked G&T. The only question is why? What issue could they possibly have with a small, barely afloat bar in the middle of Black Creek?

The nameless faces of the dead flash across my brain like a bad memory, and I suddenly feel sick to my stomach. My head swims, and anger sparks to life in my veins as I think about all those innocent people caught in the crosshairs of their attack today. People like me who just so happened to be in the wrong place at the wrong time. Whatever their gripe was with G&T, there was no need for such a senseless loss of life today; absolutely no fucking need to blow a building to smithereens with people inside it.

My anger only grows, providing me with a much-needed surge of adrenaline that enables me to push to my knees. Rage clouds my thoughts, most likely affecting my judgment as I rummage in my pocket for my keys and find my helmet, and before I can second guess my decision, I'm racing my bike out onto the street, heading in the direction of Radiant Park.

I'm all fire and pent-up rage as I pull up at the curb outside the Reject's clubhouse. I run my eyes over the darkened exterior while I pull off my helmet, wincing as the interior rubs against the gash on my temple. The sound of loud music from across the street draws my attention. Several people, clearly drunk, are loitering outside the old gym where Luc was playing ball just yesterday... fucking hell was that only twenty-four hours ago?!

Flashing colored lights shine through the windows, and it looks like there's some sort of party underway. I swing my leg over the bike and place the helmet on the seat before crossing the street, hazarding a guess that this is where the Rejects usually hang out.

Reaching the entrance, I ignore the flashing strobe lights as I stomp through the gathered crowd. I'm still wearing my outfit from earlier, covered in dust, blood, and god only knows what else. I probably look like death right now, but thankfully, none of those details are discernable in the darkened club.

I barge past people until they learn to get out of my way, opening a path before me that leads straight to a three-person-deep throng that I have to elbow and snarl my way through until I'm balanced precariously on the edge of an empty swimming pool.

I stutter to a stop, staring in surprise at the two men battling it out amongst the ceramic tiles. There is a splattering of smeared, bright-red blood on the floor beneath their feet, intermixed with an older, rusted color that is reminiscent of fights long forgotten. As I watch, more blood joins it when Cain's fist slams into his opponent's face with such force, it must send his brain rattling around inside his head. The crowd screams its satisfaction as he goes in for another punishing blow, and I swear I see one of his opponent's teeth fly loose.

His opponent falls to his knees, but Cain doesn't stop there. His hands meet the back of the guy's head, pushing him down as he lifts his knee, and I don't need to hear the noise of bone shattering to know his nose is broken. The guy cries out as he collapses to the floor, and with a heaving chest and an altogether feral look in his eye, Cain lifts his hands in the air and rotates in a full circle to the sound of the crowd's cheers and applause. Once he's had enough, he hauls himself out of the far side of the pool, and the crowd quickly parts to let him through, closing in behind him. Only his tall frame prevents me from losing sight of him as I blatantly ignore the cussing I get every time I dig my elbow into some asshole's side, pushing my way through the crowd, circling around the pool as I attempt to chase after him.

When I reach the far side of the pool where he climbed out, I lose sight of him for a second, turning my head left and right as I stand on my toes, attempting to pick him out of the dense crowd. In the poor lighting, it takes me a moment, but I spot him just as he disappears behind a door with a male changing room sign on it, and with renewed energy, I surge forward.

My lack of height and brick-wall exterior means I'm several minutes behind him, and by the time I push open the door, I hear the sound of a shower running. The door clicks shut behind me, and I press my back against it as I glance around the otherwise empty room, noting how dark it is. There's a switch on the wall beside me, but when I flick it, nothing happens. The lights don't seem to be working back here. There are windows, set high along one wall, which provide some light from a street lamp outside, bathing everything in a yellow-orange glow. There's a row of lockers lining one wall, and a long, wooden bench in the middle of the room, containing a pile of clothing that must belong to Cain.

In the sudden quiet, as I listen to the steady stream of running water from the shower and the faint screaming of the crowd behind me, I suddenly find myself unsure as to why I'm here. Why did I come here out of all the places I could have gone after today? Why am I chasing after Cain?

The anger from earlier is still burning a path through my system, and I know my initial thinking was that I couldn't let the Antonellis get away with what they did today. However, as I stand alone in the changing room, with adrenaline pumping through me after watching that fight, I sense the reason I'm here is about more than just that. Underneath the simmering anger, there's a dark, heady sensation that only Cain's close proximity can bring about. It makes me feel light-headed... or maybe that's the head injury I sustained earlier.

I'm still trying to make sense of what I'm feeling—or whether I require medical attention—when I hear the water switch off, and a moment later, Cain's broad-shouldered frame fills the entranceway to the showers. He's wearing only a towel, wrapped loosely around his waist, showing off his broad chest and chiseled abs. Every single inch of skin is covered in tattoos, too many for me to focus on any individual one, not that I can make out any of the detail in the low light.

"What the hell are you doing here?" he bites out, not the slightest bit happy to see me. "I thought we were done with you."

"Charming as ever," I retort with a scowl, falling back on my usual defense tactics with him. "Can't you ever just be fucking nice?" I've been through more than enough for one day, and my reasons for coming here are beginning to escape me. Amid my anger toward the Antonellis, I stupidly thought coming here would help. I just wanted to do something, to fight back against them in some way, and the only people I could think of to help were the Rejects. But as I look up into Cain's shadowed face, I can't help but wonder if offering to assist them is wise. What would happen if he actually won? I could end up trading one monster for another.

My sharp tone sparks something within him, and his already ridiculously short fuse must burn out because his features darken. As he storms my way, quickly closing the distance between us, all I can think about is that he's wearing the same foreboding expression he wore in the ring when he was obliterating his opponent. Everything about him screams, *I can destroy you with a single touch*, and hot damn, does it not speak to the fucked up psycho within me.

"*Nice*?" Cain sneers, spitting out the word. "Why the fuck would I be *nice* to you?"

From his snarling tone and towering presence, my anger skyrockets to never before reached heights. How dare he try to fucking intimidate me. Does he think I'm that easily cowered? I came here to offer my fucking help to this asshole. After what he confided in me the other day and what I witnessed today, I realize what I've been doing —ridding the town of cheating scumbags—is nowhere near enough. I talk about wanting a better life for Luc, wanting to make Black Creek a town that he can live in safely, yet I don't do anything to help make that a reality. If I want Luc to be able to walk the streets of Black Creek without worry, then I need to do my part to make that a reality. And that starts by getting rid of the Antonellis.

He looms over me, pressing one hand flat against the wood beside my head, and the other one wraps around my neck, pinning me firmly to the door. With his face barely an inch from my own, I can see the fire burning in his eyes, the angry set to his jaw, but simmering beneath all that hate, I spot something else... puzzlement. Uncertainty. Distrust.

Or maybe I'm just seeing everything I'm feeling reflected back at me.

"You're trouble, and if I don't stop you, you'll ruin everything."

I have no idea what he means, and I part my lips to say what exactly, I'm not sure. The slight movement catches his gaze, and his eyes zero in on my mouth seconds before he dips his head, using his hold on my throat to drag me forward until our mouths clash in a scorching heat that threatens to incinerate me.

Every swipe of his tongue is controlled and dominant, intended to put me in my place and remind me who's in charge here. I try to fight him, battling my tongue with his, but he's relentless, plundering into my mouth like a one-man army on the warpath. Needing to make him realize I'm not some floozy who's going to let him do whatever he wants, I bite down on his lower lip, hard enough that I feel blood coating my teeth, and when I run my tongue over them, there's the tangy taste of copper. *Well, if I'm covered in blood, it's only fair that he's bleeding too.*

He pulls back, and a resulting snarl is the only warning I get before he smashes his lips to mine again, assaulting me with a bruising force. I lose myself to wild abandon, blaming today's events for the crazy way I'm behaving as I attack him with equal enthusiasm. He practically tears my leather jacket from my body, nearly breaking the zip of my pants as he tries to rip them open.

He manages to push my jeans and panties down over my ass, but the tight material clings to my thighs, and he quickly gives up, deciding he's got them low enough. He spins me, so my chest is crushed against the door. I barely register the flare of pain in my ribs as he scrapes his teeth and bites his way down the side of my neck, the stings of pain only heightening the pleasure coursing through me as I groan aloud. The rushing of blood in my ears is so loud that I hardly hear the soft thud as his towel hits the floor. A throaty moan that sounds nothing like me escapes my lips as he pushes his hand between my legs, checking I'm ready before lining himself up behind me and slamming all the way in. The force sends me smacking into the door until I can plant my palms and adjust to his length. Not that he gives me much time to do any of that as he pulls back.

"Fuck," I hiss as my nails claw against the door.

Cain chuckles darkly from behind me, his warm breath tickling my neck. Moving more slowly, he thrusts into me, enabling me to properly feel what I couldn't before. A desperate cry escapes my lips as sensations wrack my body.

"It's called a magic cross," he growls low in my ear, "magic 'cause it can make women come in no time."

Fuck, if that isn't true. I'm already tipping over the edge. Now that he's demonstrated exactly how mindblowing the sex is going to be, he gets down to business, slipping his hands under my top and tugging down my bra so he can grab my tits. He squeezes them as he uses me for leverage to move harder and faster, his piercings only adding to the obvious talent he possesses.

I wish I could see his skin against mine, the contrast of his tattoos against my pale complexion, but he doesn't give me a chance to act on the thought as he slams back into me, causing me to cry out.

With my pants caught around my upper thighs, my movements are restricted. In this position, I'm dancing along a pain-pleasure tightrope as Cain's thick cock stretches my walls. All I can do is stand there and take every punishing thrust he delivers. I cry out at the delicious ache every time he hits that spot deep inside me, and as my pussy clenches down on him, he grabs the back of my head, fisting his hand in my hair and using the tight hold to turn my head to face him. He captures my lips with his as I go careening over the edge, screaming out my release into his mouth. A second later, I feel his seed hit my inner walls, scarcely comprehending the quiet voice of reason at the back of my head reminding me we just fucked without a condom. Nothing I can do about that now. That is future Sawyer's problem to deal with.

I'm still struggling to catch my breath when he pulls out of me, and I turn to sag against the door. The dull aches of my injuries begin to make themselves known as I watch him grab his trousers off the bench and pull them on, forgoing any underwear—*damn, something about knowing he's going commando is super hot*—and I catch a glint of one of the steel bars piercing the head of his cock before he tucks himself away and zips up his pants. The anger emanating from him seems to have abated somewhat, but I can still see the confusion and distrust in his eyes.

My inner thighs are damp with our combined releases, and I grimace both in disgust and pain as I pull up my panties, and they immediately dampen. *Ugh, gross. I need new panties, stat.* Once I've got my jeans buttoned again, I tuck the girls back into my bra and fix my top, and when I glance up, I notice him looking at me with an unreadable expression.

"What the fuck happened to you?" He gestures toward the tears in my clothes, apparently only now noticing the layer of dust and dirt covering my clothing.

"Nothing," I say dismissively, but he ignores me, taking a step toward me again. Now that he's not consumed by rage, he's picking up on all the small details he missed before, like the scrapes along my arms, and he's paying particular attention to the side of my head, where I hit the ground earlier. Self-consciously, I reach up to touch it, wincing at the sting of pain. I can feel blood crusted around the wound, but my fingers come away dry, so it has obviously scabbed over.

"Doesn't look like nothing," the infuriating shithead notes. As I stand there, I can feel the adrenaline wearing off, my energy rapidly draining as my legs begin to feel shaky and unsupportive. Exhaustion hits me with the force of a wrecking ball, and I don't even have it in me to scowl at him. A pounding has started up behind my head, and all I want is to go home. I place my hand against the door, stabilizing myself as I bend to snatch my leather jacket off the floor, and without a backward glance, I pull open the door and step out onto the floor of the club.

The thudding bass of the music doesn't help, and nausea churns in my stomach as I push my way through the writhing mass of bodies, needing desperately to get outside for some fresh air before I puke all over some poor person. I ignore the curses and grumbles as I shove people out of my way, single-minded in my focus to get out of here. I'm not even sure what is wrong with me, but I know I've had enough of this day. I need to go home and sleep.

I stumble out into the night, placing my hands on my knees as I bend over and suck down lungfuls of cool, crisp air.

"Seriously, what the fuck is wrong with you?" His snarling tone grates on my nerves. I hadn't even realized he'd followed me outside. I spin to glower at him, but my stomach revolts at the sudden movement. *Oh, fuck no, shouldn't have done that.* I feel the rapid climb of vomit as it ascends my esophagus, and I end up bending over at the waist, pressing my hand against the brick wall of the gym as I puke my guts out.

"Jesus Christ," I hear Cain grumble, but I tune him out, swiping the back of my hand across my mouth, and feeling a little better, I throw on my leather jacket and fish my keys out of the pocket.

"Ehh, where the fuck do you think you're going?"

Oh my god, can this asshole not take a fucking hint?! "Go away," I gripe, not liking the feeble tone. There's no power behind those words, just weariness. Too tired to care, I go to move across the road toward my bike, but he reaches out to grab hold of my wrist, tugging me backward and spinning me to face him while his other hand steals the keys from my fingers before I can stop him.

"Hey," I snap irritably.

"There's no fucking way I'm letting you drive that beauty home and crash her." He gestures with his chin toward my bike. "Not when you're drunk, or high, or whatever the fuck you are. You can sleep it off here, and go home in the morning."

"It's a concussion," I mumble weakly.

It takes me far longer than it should to realize he's dragging me across the street toward the apartment complex. The spinning of my head makes it impossible to focus on anything around me, and the next thing I know, I'm standing in the doorway to a bedroom.

"I'm not sleeping in your bed," I huff. Although honestly, staring at the bed with its dark blue sheets, it looks so damn comfy. I just want to fall face-first onto it and pass the fuck out.

He snorts. "Like I'd fucking want you in my bed. Just 'cause we fucked, doesn't mean I don't still fucking hate you."

"Same," I agree with a shake of my head, but I quickly stop when the pounding starts up again. No longer giving a shit whose room this is, I stumble over to the bed and collapse onto it, spread eagle on my back as my eyes drift shut.

I listen out for the sound of the door clicking shut, knowing I won't be able to fully drop my shields until he's gone. However, instead of the expected sound of the door closing as Cain fucks off, he moves further into the room. I crack open an eyelid, watching as he disappears into the bathroom, wondering what the fuck he's doing. A moment later he emerges with a box in his hands. He tosses it onto the bed beside me, and gives me a long, scrutinizing once over. "For your head."

Lifting my head, my gaze flicks down to the first aid kit before jumping back to his, surprised at the small act of kindness. With flat lips, and a furrow between his eyebrows, he stomps out of the room, finally leaving me alone, and I drop my head back to the sheets.

I don't even realize I've fallen asleep until I startle awake sometime later. Rubbing at the grit in my eyes, my head swims, and I still feel like shit as I push myself upright. Grabbing the first aid kid, I move to the bathroom. Rummaging through the vanity cabinet, I find a spare toothbrush, still in its packaging, and help myself to it and some toothpaste. I wash my face and inspect my injuries, noting the bruising forming along my ribs all down my left side, where I hit the ground.

Once I've cleaned myself up, I move back into the bedroom, spotting a chest of drawers and rifle through them in search of a t-shirt. Finding one that's suitable for sleeping in, I strip out of my clothes and climb in between the covers, moaning my pleasure as my eyes grow heavy once again.

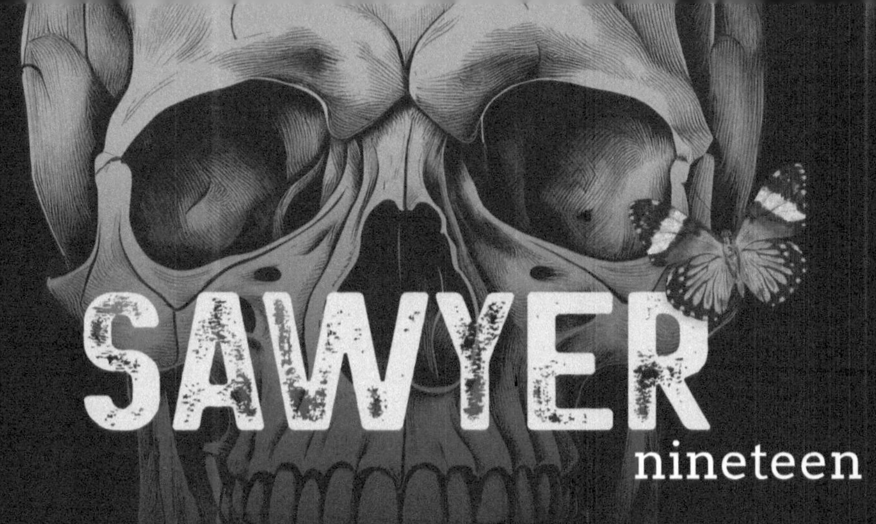

When I next awaken, light is streaming through the window. As I glance around the unfamiliar room, it takes me a second to remember how I ended up here, but as I clench my thighs, feeling the dull ache from the rough way Cain took me last night, the reality of what I did comes crashing down around me. *Fuck,* I can't believe I screwed that infuriating shithead. What the fuck was I thinking? Well, clearly, I wasn't right in the head last night. I definitely had a concussion, which is obviously to blame for my lack of judgment and reckless behavior.

I lie there for a second as I take stock of how I'm feeling. Definitely better than I did when I fell asleep. It crosses my mind that it was probably incredibly reckless of me to sleep at all if I had a head injury. Aren't you supposed to stay awake for like twenty-four hours or something? But fuck, I feel so much better for the rest.

I move to stretch out on the bed, but when I bump against a hard body, I freeze. *Eh, what the fuck? I know for a fact I fell asleep alone last night.* If that son of a bitch snuck in here while I was passed out, I'll fucking castrate him.

Slowly, I turn my head, only relaxing my posture when I find Oliver lying beside me, sound asleep. It takes a second for the penny to drop. *That asshole*! He put me in Oliver's room, knowing damn well he would be coming back here at some point during the night.

My eyes drift over the smooth lines of his face, noting the faint scruff of a five o'clock shadow dusting his jawline before I drop my gaze to his chest, tracing the hard edges of his pecs with my eyes. He's got two similar, yet obviously different tattoos on each one. Both of them have the initials RR in them—presumably for Reaper Rejects—but one is clearly old and poorly drawn, whereas the other is newer and more professional. I can't figure out why he would have two, though.

Storing the information away, I push the question to the back of my mind as my gaze drifts further south. He's not wearing a top, and with the sheet draped low over his hips, I have an unobstructed view of the carefully toned and built masterpiece that is

Oliver's body. I spot another tattoo with scrawly writing that I can't make out, sitting low on his left hip, but other than that, the rest of his torso is soft, creamy skin.

Once I've looked my fill, I return my gaze to his face, wondering what I should do. I've never fallen asleep beside a guy before, so this is unchartered territory for me. Am I supposed to sneak out? Lie here awkwardly until he wakes up? Pretend to be asleep? It's made even more uncomfortable by the fact we didn't even have sex last night. It's one thing to fuck then fall asleep, but he just came home and found me lying in his bed. Like fucking Goldilocks. Considering how I turned him down when we last spoke, he might not even want me here, but he was just too polite to ask me to leave in the middle of the night.

Turning away from him, I go to slip out from beneath the covers when a hand clamps down on my hip, preventing me from getting up.

"Where do you think you're going?"

Oliver's voice is thick with sleep, giving it a deep, husky quality that does inappropriate things to my insides.

"Uhh, getting up?"

"Not yet," he mumbles sleepily. "Too early."

He tugs me back against him, burying his head in my hair and... sniffing me?

"I was hoping you'd change your mind."

I tense at his words, slowly turning my head to look over my shoulder at him.

"Change my mind about what?"

"Us," he answers, not lifting his head from where he's running his lips along my shoulder blade. "I mean, I thought you'd just send a text, but I like this much better."

His hand slips under my t-shirt, gliding up my side, making my brain glitch as I momentarily forget about what he's saying and get distracted by the goosebumps forming beneath his touch. I can feel his hard cock pressed between my ass cheeks, his morning wood making itself known, and oh man, would it be easy to melt against him.

"Oliver, I'm not here because I changed my mind," I tell him, struggling to keep my tone neutral so as not to give away how his soft caresses are doing naughty things to me.

I'm not even sure he heard me, as his fingers continue to trail over my hip and along the area across my ribs that I bruised yesterday. The skin is still tender and sore, and I tense beneath his touch, hissing out a pained exhale that stalls his movements.

He leans up on his elbow, a frown marring his features as he tugs the sheet down to expose my midriff, and he gently rolls me onto my back so he can push my top up further, giving him a perfect view of the mottled bruises. *Damn, they look even worse this morning.*

"What the—who did this to you?" His voice comes out harsh and demanding, and when I don't respond, he lifts his eyes from my abdomen to look at my face. He immediately spots the welt on the side of my head. I don't even need to touch it to know it's swollen. I can feel it pulsing with every movement of my left eye.

His fingers clasp my chin gently, turning my head so he can get a better look as dark storm clouds roll in across his face. His jaw ticks, his teeth clenched so tight I'm surprised he doesn't crack a tooth.

"It's nothing," I assure him. "I got caught up in that explosion yesterday at G&T."

His eyes are wide, his normally light blue irises clouded to a stormy gray. His expression is still set into a hard line, and it's the first time I've seen someone other than Luc look at me with such an intense level of concern.

"I'm fine," I assure him, sensing he needs to hear it. "Nothing that won't heal in a day or two."

I don't know what it is about Oliver, but this connection between us makes me want to behave in ways I normally wouldn't. Whenever he's around, my barriers begin to crumble, and I have to work at keeping them in place. As much as Cain seems to fortify my bitchy persona, Oliver manages to chip away at it, and the more time I spend with him, the more he's exposing the real me hidden underneath.

I'm not sure if it's the residual effects of the knock to my head, the physical exhaustion still wracking my body from yesterday, or if he's just finally wormed his way past my defenses, but I lower my armor, letting him see past the hardened exterior I carefully don before I leave my apartment every day.

He meets my gaze, the clouds parting in his eyes as he lowers his own walls. The air between us feels warm and sparked with electricity, making my breaths come in heaving pants. After an intense moment, he dips his head, his lips brushing over mine in a move that steals the last of my oxygen. My lips tingle at the brief contact, and I lift my head off the pillow, chasing after him when he pulls back. I think he meant for it to be a chaste kiss, but when our lips meet again, I slip my tongue into his mouth, sliding my hand into his hair and holding him to me. He hesitates for a second before deepening the kiss, meeting my exploration of his mouth with his own probing tongue.

He moves to settle between my thighs, careful to keep his weight off my side, and I hook my legs around his hips, grinding myself shamelessly against him. I couldn't bear the thought of sleeping in my damp panties all night, so I took them off when I got changed, and my bare pussy rubs over the soft cotton of his boxers, likely soaking the material as I use him to work myself into a frenzy.

"Fuck, Red," Oliver pants, tearing his lips away from mine. He plants kisses along my jaw until he reaches my ear, before tracing a scorching trail with his tongue down the column of my neck. "What is it about you? I can't get enough."

His hands push up my t-shirt, and I lift up enough for him to pull it off. Lowering his head, he runs his tongue around one peaked nipple before sucking it into his mouth, kneading my other breast with his hand. My back arches, and I moan as I grind harder against him, feeling the telltale tingles of an orgasm forming in my lower belly.

Releasing my nipple with a pop, he adorns my other breast with the same attention as his hand snakes between our bodies, effortlessly finding my clit and rubbing tight circles around it that have me crying out. Moving lower, he slides two fingers into my dripping cunt, moving them in sync to the way his thumb strokes across my over-sensitized bundle of nerves. The combination has me coming apart in no time, and I throw my head back as I come all over his fingers.

My pussy is still spasming when he pulls out, smirking cockily when I whimper at the loss of his fingers. Reaching into the bedside table, he retrieves a condom, quickly sheathing himself before he slides into me, filling me up.

"Fuck," he grunts out between gritted teeth. "I've thought about this tight little pussy every day. Feels even better than I remember." His words are strained, but so much passion burns in his eyes. They hold me captive as he starts to move, each thrust a pleasurable ache that pushes me higher. He never looks away from my face, and I'm not sure what's happening between us right now, but it feels big. Monumental and terrifying all at once.

"Fuck, Red. So. Fucking. Good." He penetrates each word with a thrust of his hips, and my fingers dig into his shoulders, leaving crescent moon indentations as I meet him thrust for thrust. Desperate, pleasure-filled moans tumble from between my lips as I descend into a world where nothing exists except Oliver and me, and whatever never-before reached pleasure he is quickly pushing me toward.

"Oliver," I gasp, right before my pussy spasms, and he swallows my cries with a blistering kiss as he reaches his own climax before collapsing onto the bed beside me and discarding his condom.

"Holy shit," he pants. "That was even better than last time."

A chuckle bursts out of me, even as my chest heaves, still trying to catch my breath. My ribs ache from the movement, but it's nowhere near enough to dampen the high I'm on right now because he's right, that was... something else.

After a moment, he gets up, moving to the bathroom to shower. When he's done, I jump in, and, having stolen a pair of Oliver's boxers as underwear for the day, I'm pulling on the last of my clothes from yesterday—ignoring the dirt and grime still covering them—when he approaches me. He's dressed in dark, distressed jeans, with combat boots and a tight, fitted top, and *holy fuck* does the ensemble look good on him. Tilting my head back so I can look up into his face, I catch the glimpses of a fire burning in his eyes. He watches me like a man possessed as he reaches out to slide a hand through my still damp hair, cupping the back of my head. His eyes bounce back and forth between mine, and I can't do anything but stand there and watch him.

"I meant what I said." His voice is a low growl, more reminiscent of Cain's. "I can't get enough of you. Whatever this is just feels *right*. You clearly feel it, too, if you sought me out."

I open my mouth to tell him otherwise, but the words stick in the back of my throat. Is that why I came here? Was I secretly seeking out Oliver in a moment of weakness? Fuck, I've got no idea.

My tongue darts out to wet my lower lip, and I swallow before saying in a strangled voice. "I need to talk to you and Cain." My words break the moment between us, and I watch as the fire of desire dies in Oliver's eyes, and he takes a step back, releasing me from his hold.

It takes him a second before he responds, and when he does, there's no hint of the emotion that was burning in his gaze a moment ago. "Sure. He's probably in his office."

I'm pretty sure I'm incapable of responding, not that I really have anything to say, so instead, I give him a sharp nod of my head and follow him out of the room. For the most part, Radiant Park is set up like a motel, with individual rooms accessible from the parking lot or walkways on the second floor. However, Oliver's room seems to be within the main building itself, and he leads me through hallways that I have no recollection of until we reach the main bar area at the front of the building. The smell of bacon hits me when we enter, and saliva floods my mouth as I bite back a groan.

I'm careful to maintain a respectable distance from Oliver as we slowly cross the room. He keeps getting stopped by men asking questions, but it allows me the opportunity to take in the other Reaper Reject members in their natural habitat. Many of them are young, younger than me, but just as many are older, with several sporting graying beards, making me think they must be in their fifties. I can see questions in their eyes as they watch me, their gazes bouncing between me and Oliver as they speculate.

I'm about to tell Oliver I'll meet him in Cain's office when he's done, but then Jon's voice cuts through the crowd. "Red!" he calls out as he enters the room carrying several plates. He sets them down at a table before making his way to me. "Come, sit. I'll get you breakfast."

He's acting like I didn't chew him out in front of his buddies the other day, and I decide if he wants to pretend it didn't happen, then that suits me.

"Oh no, that's not necessary—" I begin, but he ignores me, leading me toward the bar and looking at me expectantly until I sit on the barstool. The surprising thing is, I let him. I dunno what it is about the kid, but I kinda like him.

"Stay there," he orders with a friendly grin that has me chuckling as he races away through a set of double doors that I'm assuming leads to some sort of kitchen area.

He emerges a few seconds later with three plates, setting them all down on the bar. He places one in front of me, along with some cutlery, before sitting on the stool beside me and digging into his own plate.

After a moment, he catches me looking at him, grinning at me around a mouthful of sausage and egg. "It's good," he promises, pointing at my plate with his knife. Swallowing his mouthful, he continues, "Marcus is an awesome cook. He's been teaching most of us so that we can help out in the kitchen more."

I cut into my bacon, taking a small bite. *Damn, he's right. It's so friggin' good.* I shovel the rest of the food into me, absolutely starving, and as I'm finishing it off, I turn to him. "How did you"—I glance around the room at the other young members—"all of you, end up here?"

I know what Oliver said the other day about some compound training them to be killers, but it sounds like a far-fetched story, so I guess I want to hear it from Jon.

His face darkens over for a split second, then it's gone, and I almost wonder if I imagined it. "Cain saved us." That's all he says before he bites into his sausage, and I can tell he doesn't want to talk about it anymore. He definitely has me curious, though, as to how and why he thinks Cain saved them all. Is saving them so they can risk their lives fighting his war *truly* saving them? So many questions bounce around in my head, and I'm so distracted watching Jon that I jump when a hand touches my lower back.

I feel Oliver's breath along my neck as he chuckles softly, and Jon jumps to his feet, grabbing his now empty plate and cutlery and giving Oliver a nod as he rushes back to the kitchen. Taking the now vacant seat, Oliver pulls the third plate of food in front of him and starts eating. Once I've finished my own breakfast, I return to taking in the other members of his gang while I wait for him to finish.

"What conclusion have you come to?" he asks, drawing my attention back his way.

"What?"

"You've been eyeing up every guy in the room."

I turn in my chair to face him, scrutinizing him closely before I respond. "If you're not after territory and power, then I don't really understand what it is you want."

Oliver smiles softly, but there's pain behind it, telling of past suffering. With a tilt of his head toward the back corridor, he says, "Let's go to Cain's office. We can talk about it there."

Unsure but definitely curious, I follow him to Cain's office, finding the brooding asshat sitting behind the desk as he works away on a laptop. He looks up as we enter, his gaze zeroing straight in on me. I'm immediately assaulted with the memory of what it felt like to have him balls deep inside me last night, and even though it was some fucking fantastic sex, I should have never allowed it to happen. I can see it in the cruel curl of his lips, and I just *know* before he opens his mouth, that his words are going to cut.

He reaches across the desk for a small, brown paper bag and tosses it my way. "Take that. And I need to know if you have any diseases so I can get it taken care of."

My cheeks burn, and my teeth grate together as I open the bag, pulling out a medication box. My eyes scan the front of the packet, *Plan B*. That fucking asshole.

I snap my gaze to him, glowering. "Seriously?" I hiss. I chuck the damn thing at him. "I don't need that, I have an implant, you shithead."

"Ehh, what is going on right now?" Oliver asks, his gaze bouncing between Cain and me, his brows drawn together in confusion.

Cain latches onto the question, his grin broadening. It's bitter and cruel, and before he even opens his mouth, I know his words are intended to hurt. "Didn't she tell you? We fucked last night. Not sure I see what the fuss is about, though. She was just alright. Three stars at best."

I'm going to fucking murder this bastard.

I swear I see fucking red as I stare daggers into his skull. "What the fuck did you just say?" I snarl furiously, taking a menacing step toward him. "Seriously, fucking say that again."

"Whoa, hey," Oliver snaps, stepping between us. He pins me with an unreadable look, and I can't tell if he's pissed off at the revelation. Not that he would have any right to be—well, maybe he'd have a little justification since I slept with him this morning. *God, this is getting complicated.* "Is this what you needed to talk to us about?"

A half-hysterical laugh bursts out of me. "Hell no. I came to tell you both that the Reaper is willing to help you." I tap my finger against my lip and tilt my head to the side as if I'm thinking. "But now I'm not so sure getting caught up in whatever bullshit you're playing here is a wise idea."

You could hear a pin drop as both Oliver and Cain gape at me.

"He's going to help us?" Oliver asks.

I snort. "Not anymore."

I'm lying. Mostly. Maybe. I didn't even get to completely make up my mind, but the thought of dangling the possibility in front of Cain after the shit he just pulled was just too good to pass up. Although, now that I've said the words aloud, maybe it's not such a crazy idea.

Ha, no, it's definitely fucking insane. But maybe it's something that I need to be a part of. Perhaps it's time that I step out of the shadows and show the overlords of this city what I'm truly capable of. I really *really* don't want to work with Cain, but I also don't want to find my brother dead in the street because his death was a necessary casualty in whatever fucked up game the Antonellis are playing or any other fucking street gang who thinks they can do whatever the hell they want and get away with it. I'm fucking sick of it and, so help me god, if Cain can help change things around here, then I guess I'm willing to fucking work with him.

That doesn't mean I can't make him suffer first, though.

Oliver turns his head to sear Cain with a stern look, and I can see some wordless discussion going on between them. Cain's jaw gets tighter with every passing second, and I can only imagine the silent conversation is not going his way.

"She could be fucking lying," he eventually snaps out. "We don't even know if she knows the Reaper."

I throw my hands up in exasperation. It's like dealing with a bunch of children. "Are you kidding me?!" I snap. "I *am* the fucking Reaper."

There's another moment of stunned silence as that information sinks into their brains. A myriad of emotions crosses their faces, each of them trying to put the puzzle pieces together.

After a minute, Cain snorts and shakes his head, quirking a brow at Oliver. "The bitch is fucking delusional!"

"Rude much," I snark, making his intense, green gaze snap to mine. "I'm standing right here, I can fucking hear you."

"Prove it," Cain dares me, his voice dripping with that haughty arrogance that tells me he's so fucking confident that I'm bullshitting them.

I return his arrogant stare with a confident one of my own. "You want me to carve a pretty little R in your abdomen? Or maybe you'd rather I slit your throat?"

His eyes narrow at that casual threat, and I can see the muscle working in the back of his jaw. "I'd love to see you fucking try," he hisses.

I move to take a menacing step toward him, although I've got no idea what I'm going to do. Despite my fingers itching to throw a blade at his fucking head, most of my skill set lies in catching my targets unaware. I rely heavily on my targets being high, inebriated, or horny when I make my move. I can hold my own in a fight, but I couldn't take on someone like Cain. I work best when I catch people by surprise. Besides, I don't actually have a blade on me. The gun I had underneath my jacket when I met Enzo must have gotten dislodged in the explosion yesterday. I hadn't even realized until this morning when I was looking for it—which shows just how fucked in the head I was last night.

Oliver moves between us again, preventing me from getting any closer to Cain. I don't know if he's acting to protect Cain or if he's just trying to stop us from gouging each other's eyes out, but whatever. I've had enough of this shit.

I came here to offer my help. The help they've been fucking hounding me for. If Cain doesn't want to accept that because I've got a vagina instead of a dick between my legs, then that's his loss.

"You know what." I hold my hands up in front of me. "I'm done with this shit." Ignoring Cain's hateful glare, I focus on Oliver. "You know where to find me if he ever pulls his head out of his ass."

Casting a quick glance across the desk, I notice the keys to my bike and hastily snatch them up, wanting to get the fuck out of here. Turning, I pull open the door and glance back over my shoulder, making sure to raise my voice loud enough to be heard all the way down the hall, "By the way, I hope I did give you an STD, and it makes your dick blister and blacken before it falls off." Grinning, I slam the door closed in Cain's furious face, and with a pep in my step, I saunter down the hall through the now-silent crowd of Reject members, and out the front door.

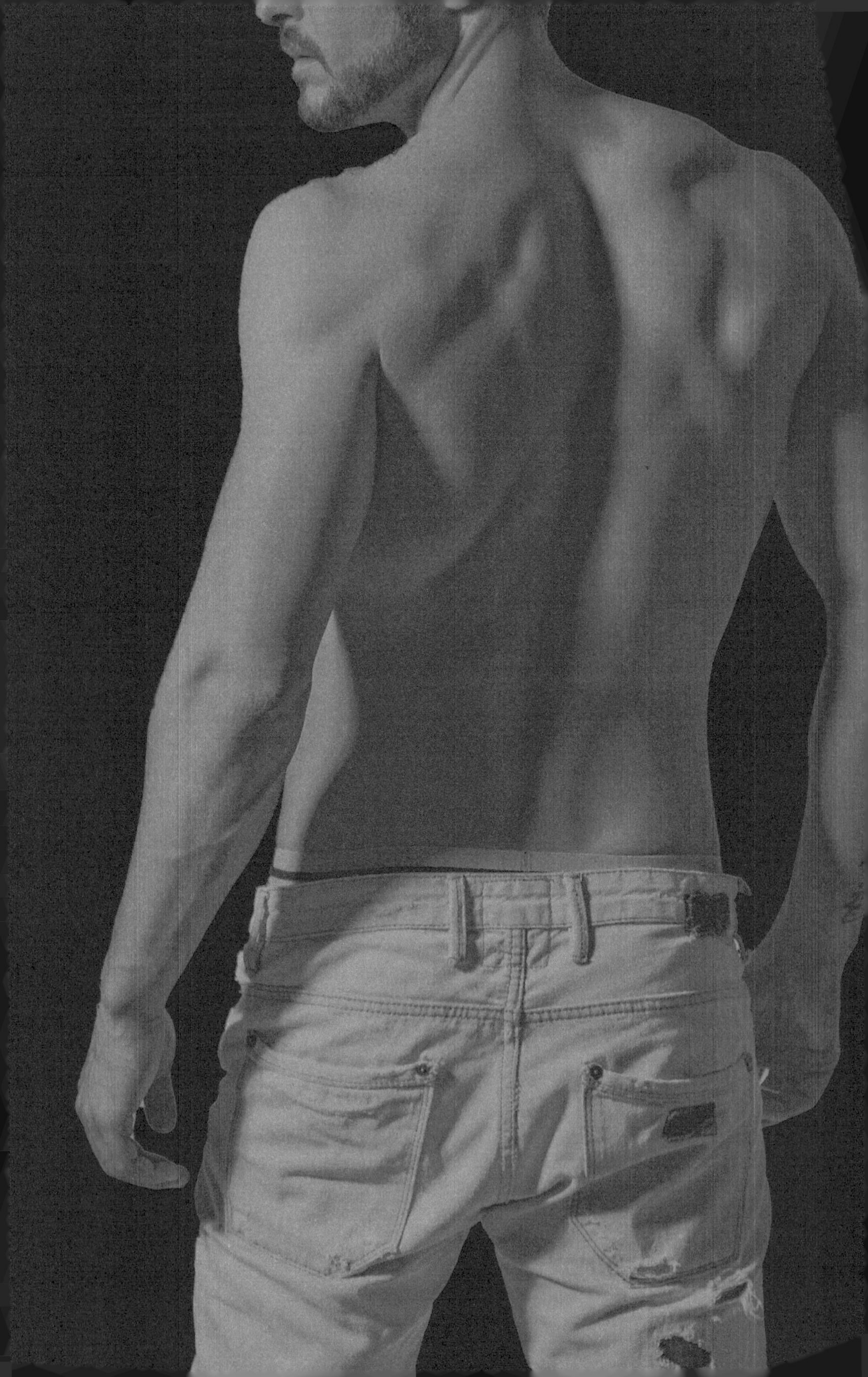

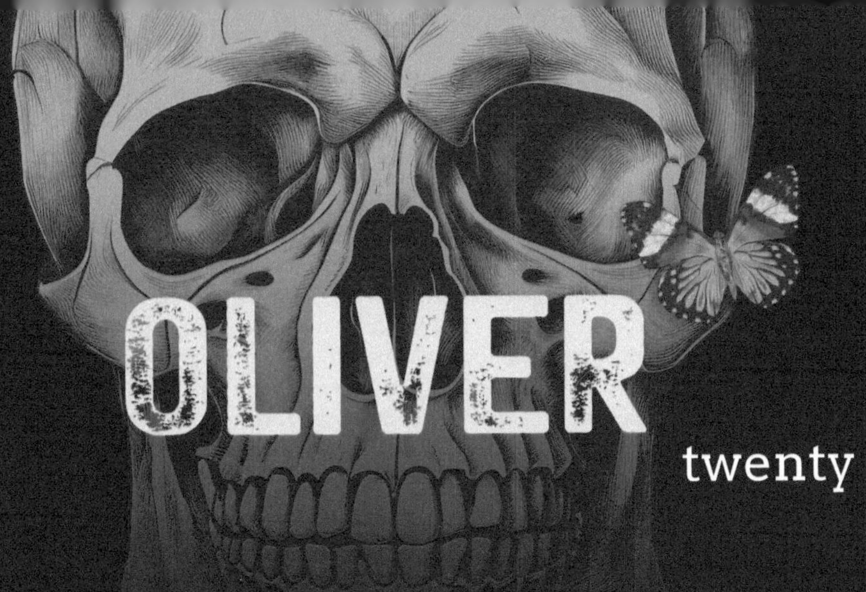

twenty

I bite my lip to hold back my snort as the door swings shut behind Red. *Pretty sure Cain won't find the same humor in her departing statement as I did.* He deserves it, though, for being such an ass to her. Cain does naturally have a barbed attitude, one that has gotten a lot sharper since we were kids. Understandably, he doesn't trust anyone outside of the family he's created in the Rejects, but he's being particularly dickish to Red, and I can't figure out why.

His words from when she walked in, about how they fucked, come to mind. Surprisingly, I don't feel any jealousy at that notion. Maybe it's because she slept in *my* bed, and we had our own intimate moment this morning. Or the fact that, even after whatever happened between them yesterday, they still glower at each other with such undisguised hatred.

"Fucking bitch," he grumbles under his breath, leaning down to open the bottom drawer of his desk and lifting out the bottle of whiskey he stores there, along with two tumblers. He pours a measure into them both and pushes one across the table toward me.

With a sigh, I sit down in a chair on the opposite side of his desk, but I don't reach out to touch the glass he poured me. Unlike the effect Red seems to have on him, which has him downing his drink in one go, she doesn't push me toward alcohol at ten o'clock in the morning.

"Do you think she really is the Reaper?" I ask, thinking aloud.

"Hell no," Cain scoffs, setting his now empty glass on the table. "There's no way. She's playing us."

"Why would she do that?"

His brows draw together, "How the fuck would I know? She's clearly not right in the head."

I manage to hold back the natural instinct to roll my eyes. He's letting his anger toward her cloud his thinking. As far as I can tell, she has no reason to lie. All this time, she's just wanted us to leave her alone, and now that she finally got what she wanted, she shows up here offering to help? Something must have changed her mind. I recall the scratches and bruises on her arms from yesterday. I'd heard G&T had been targeted by the Antonellis. News like that spreads quickly. They rarely leave their part of the city to bother us, but when they do, they like to leave carnage in their wake, ensuring we never forget just how powerful they are. They want us to know that, if they wanted, they could destroy us with a flick of their wrists. Of course, they don't just target us randomly. The owners of G&T must have done something to get on the Antonellis' radar. And the innocent patrons that just so happened to stop by at the exact time of the Antonellis' strike are just the necessary casualties of war. It seems Red was one of those casualties. She's seriously fucking lucky, and if she knew the Antonellis were behind the attack—which she apparently does—then it would explain her showing up here.

But hearing her say she's the Reaper? Holy crap, that's a shock. Not because she's a woman, it's just that we'd always assumed it was a man. Everyone does. Men are more likely to engage in violence than women, and it just seemed so much more likely that a man was going after gang members.

Although, now that I think about it, a woman makes sense too. It would explain how most of the men she's killed are found without defensive wounds. Most men wouldn't let someone they don't know or trust get that close to them... but a woman? Never mind a woman like Red, with all her feminine wiles. Those suckers wouldn't have stood a chance.

As Cain reaches across the desk to snatch up my abandoned drink for himself, I realize he's not in the mind frame to talk about it today. He won't be reciprocating anything I have to say in favor of Red. So instead, I ask, "So, what happened last night?"

He frowns into his glass, swirling the amber-colored liquid for a moment before he knocks his head back and downs it in one. "I did it for you," he bites out, his words catching me by surprise.

"You fucked her for my benefit?" I ask in a slow, disbelieving voice.

He scowls at me. "You said it yourself that you were getting too attached." He waves toward the now-closed office door. "But she clearly doesn't give a shit about you if she so easily climbed aboard my dick last night."

I frown as I think over what he's saying. When I first found Red in my bed, I thought she'd come here for me, but now I'm beginning to realize that's not quite the case. Even so, there was something about her this morning that was different. She wasn't as hostile as she has been ever since she found out who I am. For the first time, she dropped her guard and let me just see *her*. I could see how hard it was for her to do that, and yet she did it... for me.

"Well, what a sacrifice you made, brother," I retort dryly. The smug smirk that plays along his lips before he smothers it is telling enough. He can tell himself he did it for me all he damn well wants, but he wanted to fuck her.

I snort out a laugh as realization dawns—Red's under his skin. "You're a fucking idiot." The smirk drops off his face as he glowers at me. "You're fooling yourself if you think you fucked her for my benefit."

"Seriously?" He gapes at me with wide eyes. "It doesn't bother you?"

"No," I admit in all honesty. "We're not in a relationship, she doesn't owe me anything. Hell, she'll barely talk to me. She's free to fuck whoever she wants." An uncomfortable weight shifts on my chest, not liking the sound of that. "Uh, well, you... she's free to fuck you." It bothered me a hell of a lot more when I thought she was at the Satan's clubhouse to fuck Python. I have to admit, knowing she was there to kill him instead sits much better with me.

Cain just looks at me like I've gone completely fucking insane, and maybe I have. But sharing a girl isn't a completely new concept to me. I have several friends involved in such relationships. Not that that's what I'm suggesting. Based on the confounded look on Cain's face, it's not something he would even consider—at least, not with Red. It just maybe explains why I'm so unbothered by the fact he slept with the girl I've been chasing after relentlessly.

"So, what happened last night?" I ask again. I can't deny I'm curious to know how he convinced himself fucking her would help me, but instead he surprises me. His shoulders drop at my question, and he leans back in his chair, tilting his head toward the ceiling as he lets out a frustrated groan.

Before he responds, he pours himself another hefty measure of whiskey, knocking it back before he focuses on me again.

"Fuck if I know," he grumbles, banging the bottom of the glass against the desktop. "She caught me off-guard, just after a fight. The adrenaline was still racing through my system... and suddenly she was just there, scowling at me with those blue eyes that seem to be glowing with fury." He shrugs casually, but the tight lines on his face give away how bothered he actually is by his actions. "She was the ideal outlet for the last of the energy buzzing under my skin. If she didn't wanna get fucked, she shouldn't have followed me back there."

His expression is pinched, and he hasn't lifted his gaze from the table as he most likely replays the events of last night in his head. I know Cain well enough to know that loss of control won't sit well with him. He can make out that it was deliberate all he wants, but I can see the truth in his eyes. The fact he had sex with her without a condom is telling enough of his lack of control.

Interesting. Not only might Red be the secret weapon we've been looking for, but she also might be Cain's kryptonite. God knows he could do with having his world shaken up a little. He's used to being the leader; the one calling all the shots, and ever since Evie was taken, he hasn't let himself give a shit about anyone else. His walls are higher than even Red's, and reinforced with steel and concrete. Evie was always the one who was able to get through to him when he withdrew into himself and pushed everyone else away. Without her around, there hasn't been anyone to pull him out of the darkness. Red might drive him nuts, but she also challenges him in a way that only Evie did. Who knows, perhaps she could be a good thing for him... or one of them will end up killing the other.

———

CAIN MAY HAVE WRITTEN OFF RED AND THE REAPER, BUT I'M NOT GIVING up on her just yet. She came offering her help once, and I'm hopeful I can convince her to do so again. The only thing she truly cares about is Luc, and I can only imagine the anxiety it causes her, worrying about what might happen to him when he's out and about in Black Creek. But what if she didn't have to worry about that? We could offer him protection, ensuring a few of the kids are with him whenever he's out. But better than that, we might be able to offer him a future that's not rife with gang violence. Cain's ultimate aim is to seize control of the whole city once the Antonellis have been taken care of. If he doesn't, someone else will. Most likely the Grim Bastards, and other than the Antonellis, Grim is the last one we want taking control. He's a sadistic fuck in his own right. In fact, he's next on our list—after the Antonellis. Even so, let's deal with one megalomaniac at a time.

It's been a week since Red stormed out of Radiant Park, leaving Cain in a piss poor mood. A week of waiting for her to make her move. I knew she wasn't going to come back and offer her help again. She's got too much pride for that, but I've been waiting patiently for her to go after her next victim. I believe her when she says she's the Reaper, but the only way Cain will, is if I can provide proof. Besides, there's no point denying I'm dying to see her in action. The infamous Reaper. Just the thought of it has my foot pushing down on the accelerator as I follow the dot on my map across town.

I got Jon to put a tracking device on her bike for this very occasion, and I've been keeping an eye on it ever since, waiting for her to take it out for a spin. My phone went off with an alert that she was on the move fifteen minutes ago, and I immediately grabbed my keys and got in the car.

It's just past eleven at night, and even though it's late, I pass plenty of people on the street, walking down the sidewalk, ducking into bars, huddled in doorways, as I follow the blue dot on my map toward the city limits. Soon, the tall buildings fade away to suburban streets as I approach the outskirts of the city. Looking out the windshield at the ramshackle houses, I can't help but wonder what business Red has out here. Half of the homes look derelict and vacant, covered in graffiti with smashed in windows where vagrants have broken in, most likely to do drugs or to have a roof over their head for a night or two.

Checking the map app on my phone, I notice Red's bike has stopped in the clearing just up ahead and, slowing down, I pull up to the curb outside an abandoned house, squinting down the street to see if I can spot her through the darkness. Unable to make anything out, I grab my phone from the holder and make sure my gun is tucked in the waistband of my jeans before climbing out of the car.

The cool night air blows around me as I quietly close the car door, peering left and right down the street to make sure I'm alone. I've never been to this neighborhood before and honestly I'm not even sure whose territory I'm in right now. Probably some no-name gang who hasn't made enough noise to feature on the Reject's radar.

Satisfied that I'm alone, I head down the sidewalk at a brisk pace toward the clearing. Just as I'm passing the last house, the faint whisper of voices reaches my ears, and I slow down, lowering myself to a crouch so I can remain hidden as I peek around the side of the building.

Across the road, the avenue opens up into a reasonably sized lawn area that's overgrown with weeds and looking half dead. In the center is a children's playground, containing rusted equipment that most likely hasn't been used in years. I can just make out a swing set, with the seats missing, leaving dangling chains that jingle in the breeze, and standing in front of it is Red and some dude I don't recognize.

He tries to grab her, but she easily sidesteps him, kicking her leg out to connect with the back of his knee in a move that sends him to the ground with a cry of pain. He whips his head toward her and snarls something I can't make out from here.

Frowning, I keep low as I cross the street, ducking behind a burnt-out car. I don't want to alert Red to my presence and end up distracting her. Remaining in a crouch, I angle myself, so the action camera attached to my chest has a clear shot of what's going on. It would probably be enough for me to just tell Cain I saw her with my own eyes, but I want him to see it for himself. Red's not just any woman. She's fierce and defiant. She's not afraid to stand up for what she wants, and I'm pretty sure I've only scratched the surface of the intricate paradox that is this mystifying woman.

I watch as she barks out a laugh at whatever the dude said, sneering at him like he's dog shit on her boots. He climbs to his feet, a look of thunder on his face, but before he can turn to face her, she wraps one of the chains from the swing set around his neck, yanking hard on it, so he's forced backward, his back arching to an uncomfortable point.

He claws at the chains around his throat as he struggles to remain on his feet, but Red easily keeps a hold of the other end, only pulling tighter on it the more he fights. She's saying something to him in a low voice that I can't hear, but as his lips start to turn blue, I'm pretty sure he's not listening to a word she's saying.

His clawing becomes more frantic as he reaches desperately for Red. His nails dig into her leather jacket, but she manages to shake him off, shifting to stand slightly behind him, so she's out of reach of his flailing hands. As he runs out of air, his legs give way beneath him, only resulting in the chains digging more painfully into his neck. A deathlike gurgle bubbles out of his mouth as his whole body starts to convulse, his hands falling to his sides as the last of his life drains out of him.

With a final, full-body jerk, he falls still, his body going slack. Red watches him closely for another long moment before finally loosening her hold on the chain. The links tap together, the metallic noise ringing out across the otherwise silent clearing as she unwraps it from around his throat, and with a soft thud, his body drops to the ground, lifeless.

Standing over it, she looks down at him with an impassive expression, like she isn't the reason he's dead. But then, she's done this countless times before, so why would she look bothered by what she just did.

"You can come out now."

She's still staring at the dead guy, but after a second, she turns to look in my direction. *Fucking hell, how did she know I was here?*

Not seeing any point in continuing to hide, I stand and step out from behind the car, striding toward her. She never takes her eyes off me, and her inscrutable expression makes it impossible to determine how she's feeling about my being here. As I get closer, I can make out the hard lines around her lips, the cold glint in her eye. She almost looks like a different person. Nothing like the seductive vixen I met that night in Toxic, or the fiery redhead who shows up at the clubhouse and goes toe-to-toe with Cain without blinking an eye.

It's almost like Red has stripped herself of everything that makes her *her*. Like she's an empty vessel, void of thoughts and feelings, focused solely on the task in front of her. It's disorienting, like she's here, but at the same time, she's not.

When I'm standing over the body, I tear my gaze away from her stony one to glance down at him, noting the mottled bruising around his neck.

"Who was he?"

"The result of spunk that should have died in a condom."

With a final sneer, she lifts a narrow, five-inch blade out of her jacket pocket and crouches down beside him. With professional movements, she flicks up his top and begins to cut through his skin in a clinical manner, slicing from the top right of his abdomen down to just above his pubic bone before she carves across the underside of his ribs until an *R* is inscribed into his blood-smeared skin.

"Why the Reaper?" I ask as she wipes the blood off his abdomen, as if checking her handiwork before she wipes the blade clean on his jeans and gets to her feet. She fixes me with an apathetic look.

"You're the ones that started calling me that."

My brows pull together as I glance back down at the guy's chest. "Then what's the R about?"

She shrugs, sheathing the blade before tucking it back in her pocket. "It can be whatever the fuck you want it to be. Reaper, Red, Reprobate, Rapist, Repugnant shit-stain. It really makes no difference to me." She waves her hand toward the dead man. "I use it on my gang-related kills, but they're all the same abusive assholes who deserve the end they get."

There's a lot to unpack in that one sentence, but before I can figure out what question I want to ask first, she speaks again.

"So, why did you follow me all the way out here?"

"I want you to reconsider."

Scoffing, she shakes her head and begins to walk away from me. I cast a final glance at the lifeless dude at my feet—*guess we're just leaving him here*—before I rush after her.

"Why should I?" she asks when I catch up. "I'll be putting not only myself but Luc at risk, so what's in it for me?"

"We can protect you both," I blurt out instantly.

"Yeah?" she taunts. "How the fuck are you going to do that when the Antonellis have killed you all?"

I'm beginning to get frustrated, and I pull on her arm, yanking her to a stop. "Well, maybe they won't slaughter us if we have your help."

Her lips purse as her brows knit together. A frown tugs at the corner of her plump lips as she glances down at the camera attached to my chest that's still recording. She gives it the middle finger before lifting her head to meet my gaze, quirking a brow. "I take it Cain isn't exactly on board with this plan."

"He will be... when I've spoken to him."

"You mean when you've shown him proof... because my word apparently means jack shit to that asshole."

"That's not it," I begin, but she waves off whatever excuse I was going to make on Cain's behalf. It's not like it's my fucking job to clean up his fuck-ups anyway.

"Why don't you go show Cain your little video before you try talking me into the job."

Sighing, I run my hand through my hair before reaching down to turn off the camera so the two of us can talk in private.

"Look," I begin, stepping in closer to her. I'm itching to reach out and touch her, but the hard lines on her face and the tense way she's holding herself say she wouldn't appreciate that right now. "I know now why you showed up at the complex after what happened at G&T. I know you're sick of being ground into the dirt beneath the heels of arrogant assholes; that you want more for yourself than being a stripper. But most of all, you want a better life for Luc."

Her lips pinch together, but I can see the hopeful sheen in her eyes. It only lasts a split second before she covers it with that tough exterior she wears like armor. "And you think you're the ones to change things in Black Creek?" Her question is dripping with cynicism, but I see it for what it truly is—a front. Something she clings to because the thought of letting herself hope for something only to be disappointed is too much.

Lifting my hand, I prop a finger under her chin, slowly lifting it until her gaze meets mine. "You know we are."

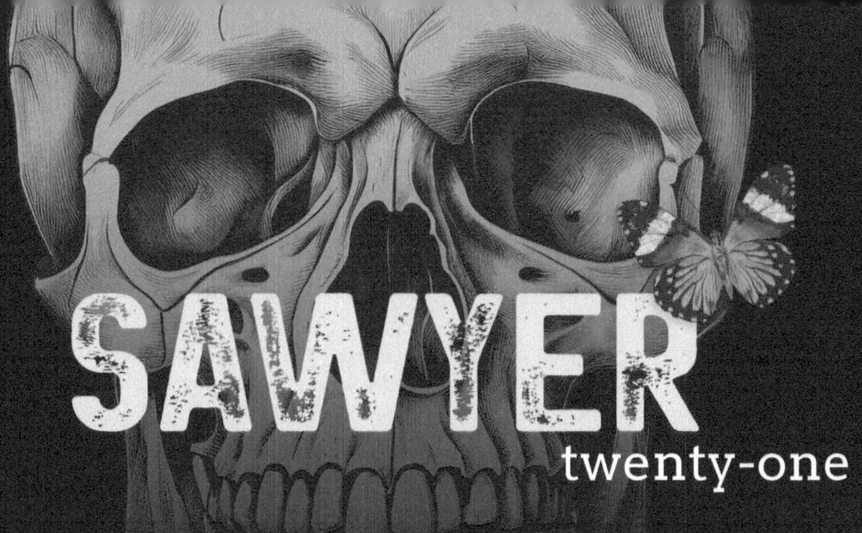

SAWYER

twenty-one

"That'll be Jon. Can you grab it?" Luc calls out when there's a knock on the apartment door.

Biting back my grumble of complaint, I move to open it. I'm still not happy about the fact Luc is hanging out with the Reject kids again, but at least this time, he told me where he was going.

"Red!" Jon grins when I answer the door. Despite my unease about letting Luc hang out with them, I have to admit that I'm warming up to the kid, and in all honesty, if he wasn't a member of the Rejects, I'd think he was a great friend for Luc.

"How are ya doing, Jon?" I ask, moving aside so he can step into the apartment.

I know I need to make more of an effort with him, not just for Luc's sake. If I am—and it's still a big fucking if—going to take on this job with the Rejects, then I'm going to be spending more time than I'd like with them. The only way I'm going to feel comfortable with that is if I get to know them.

"I'm good. Real good. Cain just told me this morning I can get into the ring next week for my first fight."

He looks so goddamn happy about that, and I can't for the life of me understand why the thought of getting your face pummeled would be exciting.

"Congratulations?"

His grin brightens. "You'll come watch, yeah?"

"Ehh," I hesitate, not entirely sure I want to watch him get beat up on. I've been paying more attention to the whispers on the street, and apparently, Cain's men are unbeatable. More specifically, the kids are unbeatable—every single one of them. So I can only assume that applies to Jon too. "Pleaseeee," he begs, fluttering his lashes like an idiot.

I snort out a laugh and shove him lightly in the shoulder. "Fine," I relent. "I'll come to watch you. But if I put money on you, you better fucking win."

The grin on his face gains a cocky-as-fuck air. "You can bet your ass I'll win, baby."

I roll my eyes at his antics as Luc emerges from his room. His gaze darts anxiously between Jon and me, as if he was expecting me to have chewed Jon's head off by now.

"Hey, man," he greets Jon. "You good to go?"

Jon gives him a chin lift in greeting, saying, "Sure," before looking back at me. "Cain asked me to bring you, too."

Of course, the fucking asshole did. He couldn't have just asked me to come over himself. It's been over a week since Oliver followed me to the edge of the city and watched me murder one of Bedlam's men in cold blood. In all honesty, I've been expecting the summons for days now, although that doesn't mean hearing the actual demand doesn't grate on my fucking nerves.

"I'm in the middle of something, but I'll swing by this afternoon."

Jon grimaces, and before he even has to say it, I know that's not an option. "Sorry, Red. He gave me strict instructions."

I'm sure he did, and when the dipshit king gives a decree, it *must* be obeyed.

Pursing my lips, I huff out a breath before growling, "Fine, give me a sec."

I take my sweet time doing my make-up, ensuring I've got the whole smokey-eye effect just right and that my lips pop with the bright red lipstick before I change into dark skinny jeans and a band tee, and I finish the look off with my thigh-high boots. Reaching under my mattress to retrieve my blades, I tuck them into the slit along the top. Just before I leave the room, I grab my purse, ensuring my small Glock 43 is inside it. I don't expect to need either the knives or the gun, but as far as I'm concerned, Cain has called a meeting with the Reaper, so the Reaper is who he'll get.

I plaster a bright smile to my face as I step out into the living room, finding both boys glued to the TV.

"Ready."

Jon barely spares me a passing glance as he gets to his feet, but Luc gives me a quizzical look that makes my insides twist uneasily. I've been telling him I've been liaising with Cain and the Rejects regarding issues to do with Strip Tease, but I think he's beginning to see through that bald-faced lie. Thankfully he doesn't say anything, though. Instead, he follows Jon to the door while I grab the house keys and lock up, and the three of us head down to the street.

There's a large SUV parked at the curb, similar to the one Oliver was driving when he dropped Luc home several weeks ago, and the lights flash as Jon taps the key fob, gesturing for us to get in.

Luc doesn't bat an eye as he slips into the front passenger seat, and I guess why should he, he's been in the car before, but I hesitate for a second before pulling on the handle and climbing into the back. I notice Jon glance up at me through the rearview mirror, like he half expected me to put up a fight before Luc engages him in conversation, and the two of them talk about some computer game I've never heard of as we peel down the street.

I drown out their conversation, instead focusing on steadying my breathing and getting into the headspace of the Reaper. It's difficult because, even though I hate Cain, he's not an abusive shitstain who deserves to die. It makes it hard to grasp that cold, detached part of me that revels in the blood and violence. Nevertheless this meeting I'm walking into with Cain is purely business. There's no room for anger. There's no space for emotions. The last time I approached them about this job, I was a fucking fountain of emotion, pissing anger and resentment everywhere. That led me to fucking Cain in a changing room and having sex with Oliver mere hours later. That can't happen again. If there's to be a business relationship between us, then there can't be a sexual one. It's as simple as that.

Not that I want to have sex with Cain again. That was a momentary lapse of judgment brought about by said leaking of emotions and a nasty concussion.

Now Oliver, well, that's an entirely different matter. The jolt of excitement shooting through me at the mere mention of his name is telling enough of how easily I'd climb back into bed with him. But if I'm going to team up with the Rejects to take down the entire Antonelli syndicate, then that needs to be the focus—the *entire* focus. Fuck knows it's a near-impossible job as it is, nevermind throwing some sort of sexual or emotional relationship into the mix. That would be a guaranteed recipe for failure.

I'm startled out of my thoughts as the car comes to a stop, and I blink as I look out the passenger window at the front entrance to Radiant Park. *Damn, I hadn't even noticed we'd made it across town already.* I follow Luc and Jon out of the car, but as they move toward the building rather than the gym across the street, I call out, "Uh, where are you two going?" It hadn't crossed my mind that they would be going into the complex—the heart of the Rejects, where no doubt shady shit is going down. They were setting the front lobby up as a goddamn bar last time I was here. There could be hookers or anything right behind that door.

Luc rolls his eyes, frowning at me as he grits out, "Sawyer," in a low voice.

My own eyes narrow on him, as I see Jon physically perk up. His lips part in a silent O, and I shift my gaze to him, pinning him with a grave glare—a silent threat that he should casually ignore what he just heard. Very few people know my real name. Not because of any particular reason, it just kinda happened that way. When Mom died, and we started living on the streets, I had to become a different person—someone tougher—but I didn't want to lose *me.* The person I had to pretend to be when I was pickpocketing, fighting over scraps of food, or giving blow jobs for cash, wasn't the person I wanted to be when I was with Luc. I didn't want him to see me as all sharp edges and emotionally unavailable, so I found it easier to develop a different persona when dealing with people on the street while at the same time keeping the softer parts of myself just for Luc. It was like our little secret. Sheryl and Grace are the only other people who know my actual name. To everyone else, I'm Red. The red-haired bitch who'll slice you in half with a death glare and won't hesitate to put you on your knees if you dare go near what's hers.

"Relax, *Red*," Jon says with a smirk, earning himself another glare. "We're just going to play some video games. We have a room down the back. There won't be any drugs or alcohol, or guns, or hookers."

I purse my lips, still not liking any of this. "Fine, you can go."

"It's not like I was asking for your permission, but thanks," Luc drawls, his attitude making my eyebrows climb up my forehead. *The fucking nerve of him!*

Before I can say something that will no doubt only escalate things, Jon drags him off across the parking lot, and with a resigned sigh, I follow after them.

I follow them through the front bar area, which is surprisingly empty—although it is only early afternoon—and into the hallway leading toward the rear of the building. When I pause outside Cain's office, I watch them for a second until they disappear around a corner at the end of the hall before putting all thoughts of Luc to the back of my mind. I take a moment to empty my head of all thoughts and feelings, descending into the cool calm of the Reaper. When I'm confident my expression says, *you don't want to mess with me,* I turn the door handle and step into the office.

I hesitate with my hand still on the handle as I glance around the room, surprised not to sense Cain's suffocating presence immediately. Instead, Oliver is reclining in the chair behind the desk, with his fingers hovering over a laptop in front of him as he looks right at me, a small smile lifting his lips.

"He's in the gym," he explains before I can ask. "Figured it was in everyone's best interest if he burnt off some of that anger he constantly has."

I give a slow nod of my head. "Good to know it's not just me he can't stand."

Oliver barks out a soft chuckle. "Oh, you definitely have a way of getting under his skin."

I still haven't moved from the doorway, and honestly, I'm not sure how to behave around him. He's made it clear he wants something more with me, but I'm not sure I can offer him that.

"Did you show him the recording?" I ask, wanting to understand the situation better before getting any closer to him, and my rising hormones start messing with my logic.

Oliver's gaze drops to take in my outfit before returning to my face, lingering there as he grows serious. "I did." He lifts his hands off the laptop, interlocking them and resting them on his lap as he relaxes back in his chair. "What do you know about the Antonellis?"

It's a fair question, but one that surprises me all the same. "Ehh, not much. Our paths haven't really crossed."

He nods and ponders over something for a moment before he leans forward, placing his forearms on the desk as he sears me with an intense look. "When we were thirteen, the four of us—Cain and I, our friend, Beck, and Cain's sister—were hanging out on the front porch when they tore down our street, firing off bullets. They stormed their way onto Cain's property and kidnapped his sister." My eyes widen in surprise. I figured they had to have done something to invoke Cain's wrath, but *Jesus,* I wasn't expecting that. "He never saw her again."

I swallow around the emotion clogging my throat. "Why are you telling me this?" I ask in a quiet voice. I highly doubt Cain wants me knowing such personal shit about him.

"Because you need to understand what this is all about. We're not after Antonelli territory; we don't want their money. This is cold, hard vengeance. Cain has dedicated his entire life to this war, and nothing will stand in his way."

All the words he's not saying rattle around in my head—this is why Cain acts the way he does, why he was so hellbent on finding the Reaper. It certainly explains the weird moment we shared at Strip Tease that night he was drunk. Most importantly, Oliver's telling me that, whether or not I help them, Cain's going to avenge his sister. Nothing will stop his crusade. Whether I like it or not, there's a war coming, and I can either sit on the sidelines and watch, or I can finally stand up and fight for this town.

"What about you?" I ask. "Why are you here?"

His lips flatten, and I can tell he doesn't want to share that personal detail with me. "Because that's what family does for one another."

It's a non-answer at best, but Oliver's reasons for being here are none of my business.

Before either of us can say anything else, I hear heavy footsteps behind me in the hall and turn as Cain's ominous presence fills the doorway.

"Oh goodie, you came," he drawls, his voice dripping with sarcasm.

I have to bite back my retort, mentally reminding myself of what Oliver just disclosed, so I don't chew the asshole's head off. Glowering at him, I step aside so he can move into the room, and he pushes the door shut behind him. With the three of us packed into the small space, I begin to feel uncomfortably claustrophobic—not that I'd let on to either of them how on edge I am. I'm the goddamn motherfucking Reaper. I'm a badass bitch. I'm not going to let some moody manchild get the better of me.

"Is that really how you want to speak to someone whose help you need?" I retort snidely.

"Will the two of you just park it for five minutes so we can all get on the same page?" Oliver interrupts before Cain can follow through on whatever violent thoughts I'm sure are flashing through his head right about now.

With a shrug, I turn away from Cain, dismissing him. "Sure. I know *I'm* capable of acting like an adult."

A low growl comes from behind me, but Oliver throws him a warning look before he can voice whatever scathing reply he had in mind. Instead, I hear him grumble something incoherent under his breath as I focus my attention on Oliver.

He rolls his eyes as he stands up from behind the desk and moves around it. Crossing his arms over his chest, he looks between Cain and me. "There's no reason we can't work together," he begins, acting as mediator. "Overthrowing the Antonellis would benefit us all."

"What happens when the Antonellis are destroyed? Who gets their territory?" I question.

"We do," Cain says with all the arrogance of someone who's used to being in charge.

Before I can snark back that I'm not entirely sure that's better than the Antonellis—although I don't know if I really believe that any more—Oliver huffs out a frustrated breath.

"The plan is that, eventually, no one will be in charge of Black Creek."

His words gain my attention, and I lift my head to meet his gaze. "You mean no gangs?"

"Yup."

I stand there shocked for a moment as I try to picture that reality before my eyes narrow and a crease lines my forehead. "Is that even possible?"

Lifting his arm, Oliver runs his hand along the back of his head. "Honestly, I'm not sure, but it's worth a try, right? The people of Black Creek deserve to live their lives without the fear of retribution if they step even a toe out of line."

Huh, their plan is so much grander than just a vendetta. It's actually a noble goal, there's just one problem... "What about the Grim Bastards?"

"Uhh, yeah," Oliver starts with a grimace. "We're going to take them down, too."

I'm completely fucking stunned, unable to do anything but blink at him for a moment as I process that information. Eventually, though, a scoff bursts free and I shake my head in disbelief.

"Of course, you are because why go after one criminal conglomerate when you can go after two."

"So you're in?" Cain's voice is unnaturally soft, almost as though he's nervous to hear my answer. I meet Oliver's gaze, seeing the determination burning within his eyes before I turn to face Cain. He's wearing his usual stoic expression, but that same resolve is smoldering in his green depths.

With a roll of my eyes, I sigh. "Fuck it, yeah, I'm in. Black Creek is our city, and it's about time they realized that." I let the resolute energy wafting off them soak into my skin, bolstering me as I lift my chin. "Let's rain down absolute fucking mayhem."

I rewind the tape again, watching for the millionth time as the brunette runs across the room before she crashes into me. No matter how many times I watch it, though, I can't put my finger on what it is about her. There's just this flicker of *something* at the back of my mind. This niggle that I know her from somewhere... but where? I definitely don't recognize her from the club. That night I'd just assumed she was new. I rarely have anything to do with our sex clubs, but I'd stopped by to look into the accounts. Someone's been skimming off the top of our profits, and it's my job to find out who, and then deal with them... permanently.

Of course, when I returned the next day, no one seemed to know who she was. Is it a coincidence that she just so happened to be in the club the same night one of our most popular clients dies? I think not, and it only adds to the intrigue surrounding her.

If anyone suspected her of having killed one of our top clients, she'd already be added to my hit list, but no one but me suspects foul play. As far as everyone else is concerned, Chad died of natural causes.

I focus back on the recording just as I take off down the hall toward the dead man, and after a moment's hesitation, where the brunette watches me, she rushes out of the club and into the night. I've already checked the outdoor security cameras, and none of them picked her up. It's like she just disappeared. Blown away by the wind as soon as she stepped outside the club.

Once I reach the end of the tape, I skip it back to the beginning and play it again. Every time I get a moment alone, I watch this damn recording, trying to figure out what it is about her. Maybe my fascination is just from the fact she managed to sneak into Belle Donne and kill someone right under our noses—it speaks volumes to the holes in our security—but I feel like it's more than that.

I hear the door to my home office open behind me, and I don't even need to look over my shoulder to know it's Lor. He's the only one who has access to my house. The only one in this whole organization that I trust.

"Still haven't figured out who she is?" he asks, watching the tape over my shoulder.

Her face is pixelated and impossible to make out, but it doesn't stop me from watching as though if I can just stare hard enough at the screen, the pixels will all slot into place and give me the answers I seek.

I slam the lid of the laptop closed with a thud. "No," I growl.

His eyebrow lifts at my sudden outburst of anger. I never get emotional. It's not that I don't ever let people *see* me emotional, but that I never actually *feel* emotions. Something my father takes great pride in—as if he engineered me to be this way. He says I'm broken in the best possible way. That it's a gift that will make me the most feared and powerful Don the Antonellis have ever seen. When I was a kid, I used to believe him. I'd shine under the glow of his praise, but as time went on, I started to see my inability to feel for what it really was—a curse.

I can count on one hand the number of times I've felt that spark that I think resembles feelings. Having never actually felt it for longer than a split-second, it's difficult to identify.

The first time was when I was five, and my father beat Lor to within an inch of his life when he caught the two of us playing together. We spent a lot of time together growing up, but even at a young age, he was being trained as my bodyguard, which meant our relationship should be nothing but professional. Even back then, I knew Lor mattered more to me than anyone else did, but it wasn't until that day, when I first felt that heat of anger and the sickening crush of fear, that I realized just how much he meant to me. The feeling was gone as quickly as it appeared, although it was there nonetheless.

The second time I felt it was in a dark, dingy alley. I'd just killed some traitor—I don't even remember his name or what he looked like. All I remember is looking into the bluest eyes I'd ever seen. That day I went against my instincts, against everything I'd been taught, and I let a witness go with nothing but a measly warning.

I still dream of those eyes at night. They worm their way unbidden into my subconscious and stare at me, so bright and open. They feel so real that sometimes I wake up thinking she must be in the room with me. I never let myself dwell on thoughts of her during the day. I can't afford for my father to see me distracted or to think I'm anything less than focused on the job, on our family, at all times. After all, the Antonellis are all that matter. Blood in, blood out. Not even in death can you separate yourself from the ties that bind you to the Family. As the only heir to the Antonelli empire, that is especially true of me.

Instead of stepping back from my anger like most people would, Lor moves toward me, a flicker of lust flaring to life in his eyes. "Well, I can think of one way to make you forget about her."

I quirk one of my own eyebrows in a challenge. One he readily rises to as he closes the distance between us with another large step. The move has his body brushing against me as his lips meet mine in a rough kiss. He pushes his tongue into my mouth, fighting for dominance, and I'm quick to bite his lower lip in chastisement. His hiss of pain goes straight to my dick, the increased blood flow making it swell in my pants.

As I lose myself to pleasure, the weight of my responsibilities falls away. I forget about my father's empire, soon to become mine. I forget about the list of names in my black book, marking a person's death. But most importantly, for half an hour, I can forget about the blue-eyed girl and the brunette vixen that haunt my dreams.

release from prison

I step past the chain-link fence onto the sidewalk, taking a deep breath of fresh air as I do so. Freedom has never tasted sweeter. My eyes drift shut as I tilt my head back, letting the hot Californian sunshine warm my skin. It's the same sun I've sat under for an hour a day, every single day for the last two years, but today it feels infinitely better, knowing from this moment on I'm a free man.

The phone Sophie sent me in her latest care package buzzes in the pocket of my new jeans—also courtesy of Sophie—and I shift my bag of meager belongings to dig it out. Only a small handful of people have this number and know what today is, so I can already hazard a guess as to who it is. A soft smile graces my lips when I find my assumption is correct, and I open the notification informing me I have a new message from Sophie. She's been diligent with her letters and phone calls every week. I know part of it is out of guilt. The only reason I had to give up two years of my life was so she and the guys could get away. None of them deserved to get tangled up with the police after the bloodbath we'd left behind that day. And Barrett would have died if they hadn't rushed him to the hospital.

They have all had to endure so much bullshit in their short lives. Yet, despite it all, they somehow found each other—and found a way to get along without tearing each other's heads off. It's a fucking miracle, if you ask me. Which is why I made the split-second decision I did that day. As the cop cars came rolling up to the mansion that had been operating as a sex club and backdoor skin auction, I ensured all the attention was on me while Sophie and the guys slipped out and got Barrett to the hospital.

Besides, I was caught in an illegal sex den bathed in blood and surrounded by dead bodies. I should have been sent away for life; never allowed to breathe fresh air again. Yet here I am, two years later, a free man. I only served eighteen months in a minimum security prison, followed by six more at a halfway house. I never asked, and they never said, but I have no doubt Preston or Barrett had a hand in that. Something I will be eternally grateful for.

I huff out a small chuckle at the picture of the five of them. They're lying on a beach, with bright smiles, crowded close together for the photo. Beneath the picture is a message. *Wish you were here. We'll see you soon, yeah?*

I sigh, debating a response before eventually deciding to leave it for now. It's not that I don't want to see them. I'd love nothing more than to kick back with a few beers and catch up, but every time I think about it, I get a tightness in my chest.

The rumble of an engine draws my attention as a black Cadillac approaches, slowing to a stop in front of me. Cain throws the door open, and there's a wide grin on his face as he rounds the front of the car toward me.

"For a free man, you sure look pretty fucking down."

He doesn't give me a chance to respond before he pulls me into a bro hug. His larger-than-life presence is enough to dispel my depressing thoughts, and an easy smile comes to my face as I pull back. Rebuilding my friendship with him has been an unexpected positive to all of this. After The Feral Beasts' demise, he apparently did some digging, needing to know if I was alive or dead, and somehow found out I was in prison. As soon as he knew that, he was driving down here for a visit.

I still laugh as I remember the shock of seeing his large, muscular frame sitting on that cheap, plastic chair in the visitation room for the first time. When I'd been told I had a visitor, I'd assumed it was Sophie, Aiden, or Ty. Never in my wildest dreams would I have thought my childhood friend would have tried to locate my whereabouts. Until that day, it had been years since we spoke. The downfall of our friendship hadn't exactly been amicable. We were both in dark places back then—in some respects, I think we still are. We've just grown up since then. After everything that went down with his sister and then Beck leaving, we both turned inwards and lashed out with our anger. At each other. At the world.

Still, all of that was forgotten the moment I laid eyes on him. The shadows still dance in his eyes, and the pain of his past lines his face, as I'm sure mine does. However, we can both separate ourselves enough from it now to move forward, together. Hearing his plans of revenge only fueled the pent-up rage that's been simmering in my veins all these years. He didn't even need to ask. I was on board as soon as he shared his plans with me. Evie may have been his sister, but she meant just as much to me. I'll do whatever it takes to avenge her.

"Come on, man," Cain says, clapping me on the back with a solid thump. "Get in. You've got some lost time to make up for." He moves back around to the driver's side, his grin turning wicked. "The alcohol is already flowing, and I've got prime pussy just for you."

Shaking my head with a snort, I climb into the car. Something I quickly came to learn from our chats was that Cain is a manwhore. Which isn't altogether unexpected given the lifestyle he leads. It's not like I'm a choir boy myself. However, being that it's been two years with just my hand and an overused porn magazine to keep me company, the thought of sex doesn't appeal to me right now.

Images of Sophie and her guys, laughing and happy, all of them looking at her with adoration and love, flash across my mind, making that familiar ache start up in my chest once again. That's what I want. Someone to share my life with. Someone to ride out the lows with and share the highs. Another image of a young, black-haired girl with a toothy grin crawls its way out of the locked box at the back of my mind. The force of the image slams into me, making my stomach twist violently and that familiar heat of anger lick along my spine. She's my Sophie. The one I was supposed to share this depressing fucking world with. She was always the one bright spot, the light in all the violence around us. I may have only been a scrawny, twig of a kid, but when you know, you know.

And I fucking knew.

"I know that look," Cain says, his voice taking on a deeper tone as his hands tighten around the steering wheel. I hadn't even realized he was watching me. "We're going to do right by her, O. I've let them get away with it for too many years." He flicks his gaze my way, and even in that quick look, I can see the fury roaring in the molten depths of his eyes. "We were always meant to do it together. Now's our time." His whole body expands as he takes a deep breath before his shoulders relax and he loosens his hold on the wheel. "Tomorrow, we'll get to work, but today?" Another wicked grin lights up his face. "Today, we celebrate."

We keep the conversation light as we head north. Home to Black Creek. Memories wrack my brain the closer we get, threatening to drown me, and I have to keep pushing them to the back of my mind. Eventually, we pull up at a rundown motel that's definitely seen better days.

"Interesting digs," I tease.

"Wait till the men have finished," Cain responds. "It'll be a clubhouse befitting of the fearsome Reapers Rejects."

I follow him up the path to the front door. As soon as I step inside, I'm deafened by a roar of cheers, and I'm still struggling to get my bearings when a brunette flings herself into my arms, practically strangling me as she hugs me with enough force to snap my neck.

"It's so good to see you!"

"Jesus, Princess, he didn't survive prison just to have you hug him to death," Preston gripes, tugging Sophie backward and forcing her to loosen her hold.

"Sorry," she apologizes, giving me an apologetic look.

"Yeah, he also hasn't touched a girl in two years, babe. Might wanna keep your distance," Ty jokes, giving my crotch a knowing glance before stepping forward to give me a bro hug. "It's fucking great to see you outside of those gray walls, though." He murmurs the words in my ear, his voice taking on an uncharacteristic serious quality.

Finally finding my voice, I look around the room, noticing it's filled with people. There's a *welcome home* banner strung up across one wall, with balloons on either side. "What's all this?" My voice comes out choked as I take in the people milling around before returning my gaze to Sophie and the guys. Despite my reluctance earlier, it's fucking great to see them.

Sophie grimaces. "Sorry. Is it too much? It's too much. I shouldn't have done the banner."

"No, it's..." I trail off, lost for words, as I take it all in again. "I didn't know I needed this, but it's perfect." Looking her right in the eye so she can see I'm being serious, I say, "Thank you."

She smiles shyly. "Well, it was Cain's idea to do something." Her nose scrunches up. "Although I think he just wanted hookers and booze."

The first genuine boom of laughter escapes me, surprising even me. "Yeah, that sounds like Cain."

Meeting Preston's gaze above Sophie's head, he gives me a nod, a rare smile gracing his lips as he wraps his arms tighter around her. I meet Barrett's gaze next. He looks more uneasy as he runs his hand awkwardly up the back of his neck. "I, uh, never did thank you..."

"None of us did," Preston interrupts.

"You don't need to," I assure them. "I'd make the same choice today." Lastly, my gaze meets Aiden's, and understanding passes between us without needing words.

"Come on, let's get you a beer," Ty says.

"At least one," Barrett tacks on.

We move further into the room, and Ty and Barrett go to grab drinks for everyone. It's only a few minutes later when an ice-cold bottle is being shoved into my hands, but something on the far side of the room has snagged my attention, and I'm distracted as I mumble a thank you and tell them I'll be back in a bit.

Not entirely sure if I've gone insane or if I saw what I thought I did, so I push through the crowd until they part enough for me to catch sight of him again.

"No fucking way," I murmur under my breath.

As if sensing my eyes on him, he turns to look my way, and a bright smile lights up his face. I know Cain had mentioned helping him out with some fucked up situation involving child mercenaries, but I still didn't expect to see him here.

"Couldn't miss your homecoming," he says easily, as if reading my thoughts. In the next second we're embracing each other.

"Fucking hell, it's good to see you," I say softly, my voice choked with emotion.

"Same, man. It's been far too long." There's a wisp of regret and anguish in his voice, and I pull back to get a good glance at him. He looks good. Really fucking good, and I can tell getting out of Black Creek was the right thing for him.

"I wanna hear everything you've been up to." I dart my gaze around the room. "Where's this girl Cain's been telling me about?"

"Hadley's around here somewhere. I swear she disappeared as soon as we arrived." He rolls his eyes, but the soft smile and the brightness in his green eyes give away how happy he is. He catches me up on his life since I last saw him ten years ago, and regales me with the shit he, his girl, and her other boyfriends and brother have been through in the last year. If I hadn't witnessed a similar drama with Sophie, I'd think it was a work of fiction.

"Ah, there she is. Hadley!" he calls out, waving over a feisty-looking blonde. Three other guys tail her as she makes her way over, and introductions are done. The six of us stand and chat briefly before Sophie and her guys join us.

The day goes by in a blur of happiness and alcohol until hours later, I find myself lounging on a chair beside Cain and Beck. I couldn't have asked for a better *welcome home* party. It's been great catching up with everyone and meeting Beck's girl, along with his brother and friends.

"What's it like to be a free man?" Beck asks.

"It feels fucking great," I confess. " I forgot how much I missed just chilling with beer and good company." Of course, it was well before prison that I last did this. That I last felt this at peace. Right here, in this moment, I couldn't be more content, and it's been a hell of a long time since I felt this at home.

"I like Hadley," I tell Beck, observing her talk to Sophie like they have known each other their whole lives. There's a fierceness about her. An aura of darkness that I'm all familiar with.

Beck's face lights up with another besotted grin as he watches her, and I shake my head, smothering my laugh as I take a swig of beer.

"I still can't believe you're sharing a girl with three other guys," Cain chuckles. "No way I could do that shit."

I can see why Cain would think that, but having seen the same sort of relationship with Sophie, I can relate a bit more. "It's the same sort of relationship Aiden and Ty are in with Sophie. It was a bit of a shitshow at the beginning. The other two guys— Preston and Barrett—couldn't be any further from us. Preppy, trust fund kids." I chuckle as I think back to what arrogant shitstains they were when I first met them. The crap they pulled with Sophie... they're lucky they still have their balls attached. "But they really stepped up when Sophie needed them, and they all seem pretty happy together."

"You'll understand when you find the right girl, man." Beck agrees. "I didn't think it was my thing either, but Hadley has a habit of getting into trouble. Let me tell you, it takes the four of us to wrangle that girl sometimes."

Cain scoffs, not believing Beck. "I'll take your word for it, man. I just don't think it's for me. I'm all for sharing a girl for a night, but long term?" He shakes his head like he can't even fathom the idea. " I don't think it's even the sharing. I'm just not a relationship person."

I chuckle. Cain really is a manwhore. Women have been all over him all day, and he laps up their attention. I have no doubt his Reaper Rejects leader rep gets him plenty of action, and I know with his craving to avenge Evie running through his blood, he's never going to even consider settling down with a woman.

As if she heard him, one of the slutty club whores struts toward us, swaying her hips lasciviously and practically stripping Cain naked with her eyes.

"Hi, handsome," she purrs. "You were looking awfully lonely over here."

Apparently, Beck and I may as well be chopped liver. I share a comical look with him, and we roll our eyes as Cain flirts right back. "Let me talk to my boys, but come find me later, okay?"

"You got it." With one last lingering look, she sashays into the crowd again and Cain grins cockily.

"See? Why would I give all that up for some chick?"

Beck just shakes his head, even though everything about his expression says he can't wait for the day when Cain eats his words. Changing the topic, he asks, "How is everyone settling in?" Referring to the child mercenaries Cain rescued several months ago.

"Good, I think. It's been a bit of an adjustment. Some of them were so fucked in the head when they first got here."

I scan the room, spotting a few of them. Cain has filled me in on all the details, and there have been more than a few phone calls where he's sought advice when one of the kids has been difficult to manage. It's a precarious situation, but from what I've seen, Cain couldn't have provided them with a more fitting environment.

"So, what's your plan now?" Beck asks.

The air around us crackles with tension, and Cain's hand tightens around his beer bottle. "Our numbers are growing every day. You know what my game plan has always been—it's the reason I've built all this. I won't let what happened to Evie be in vain. This town has gone to shit the last few years, and I'm fucking sick of it. I'm claiming Black Creek as mine, and I'm taking down every single one of the fuckers that played a part in that day."

I meet his unwavering gaze, and I know he's seeing the same fire and determination burning in my eyes that I can see radiating off of him. I give him a nod in solidarity, because I'm going to be right there at his side as we raise hell.

the explosion

My foot taps impatiently against the bar's sticky, worn-down wooden planks, and I can't help but obsessively check my watch every thirty seconds. If anyone were paying me any actual attention, I'd probably look suspicious as fuck. Still, since it's the middle of the day—and everyone in Black Creek knows to keep their eyes down and their noses out of shit that isn't their business—my sketchy behavior goes unnoticed, or at least unquestioned.

Not that I give a single fuck. There's only one thing occupying my mind right now, and my hands form tight fists as she walks into the bar, her head held high and a defiant glint in her eye. *God-fucking-dammit.* I could kill her myself. Usually, I love how headstrong she is. But *fuck*, today, I wish she could just do as I asked for once. Follow a simple command.

After she ignored my request to change our meeting, her phone went straight to voicemail. I didn't know what else to do except wait here and hope we can get this over with as quickly as possible. Before...

I shake my head, refusing to follow that line of thought. There's no reason why this can't be brief. She's always looking to get away from me as swiftly as humanly possible —like she can't bear to be around me for longer than necessary. Normally, her insistence to be done with our meetings ASAP irritates the fuck out of me, but today it will work in my favor—thank God.

I already have the envelope of cash in my hand as I push to my feet, ignoring how fucking amazing she looks today. Is she all dressed up in that armor for me? Regardless of how tempting she looks, frustration at her disobeying me and showing up here anyway heats my veins, and there's a pissed-off scowl on my face when I rise to my feet in front of her. It takes a second for her eyes to adjust to the dark interior of the bar, and they widen in surprise when she notices how close I'm standing. I'd deliberately chosen an uncomfortable bar stool by the front door, so I wouldn't miss her entrance *if* she did show—and so we could make a quick escape.

"I told you not to come," I growl angrily, barely restraining myself from grabbing her arm and yanking her back outside.

Unfazed by my anger, she takes a moment to roam her eyes over my face, attempting to get a read on my emotions, before snapping gout, "What the fuck crawled up your ass and died?" Typically, her snark turns me right the fuck on, but not today. Far too much is at stake here. "I told you I couldn't reschedule. Besides, you were clearly able to make it just fine."

My teeth grind as I work to control my temper. None of it matters. She's here. Now I just need to get her the fuck out. "Fine." The word snaps off the end of my tongue. "Here's your cash, now give me my info." I couldn't give two shits about the info. Don't get me wrong, some of the information she's passed my way has actually been of use—not something I had anticipated when I agreed to this little arrangement. I just wanted to help her and give her enough money to get off the streets so she and her brother could live somewhere safe.

"What, no drink or you asking me inappropriate questions first?" she snarks, only making my teeth grind more. It takes everything in me not to throw her over my shoulder and storm out of the bar, but I know enough about my little spitfire to know she won't tolerate that. It will only draw unwanted attention and could result in us wasting even more time.

"I've got other shit to do today," I quickly answer, knowing every second I let this continue could bring her, or us, closer to death. We seriously need to get the fuck out of here. Now.

"Shame." Her lower lip slides out in a pout that any other day would have my dick hard, although at this second it only has me wanting to wrap my hands around her neck and strangle her for being so goddamn stubborn. Instead of walking out the door like I desperately need her to, she sits her perky ass on the barstool. "I'm in the mood to talk and drink today."

Straightaway I know she's talking shit. She knows something's up, and she's deliberately pushing my buttons to see if I'll crack. Heh, I wonder what she will have to say if I do. Deciding I no longer give a crap about the pretense, I grab ahold of her upper arm, ready to forcibly remove her. "Not here, you're not."

One second, my hand is wrapped around her arm, the heat of her skin pressing into mine, and in the next, I'm clinging to nothing but air as I'm sent crashing to the ground in a wave of dust and chaos. My ears ring, and it takes several long moments for me to re-orientate myself. The world around me is coated in dust, dirt, and blood. A low, pained groan penetrates through the fog of disorientation and shock, and I realize I'm sprawled on top of someone.

Fuck. Not someone. Sawyer. I scramble off of her, unable to tear my eyes away from the blood running down one side of her head. *Fuck. Fuuuuck.*

"Sawyer." Her name is barely more than a cracked whisper as I roll her onto her back. Her eyelids are closed, and a terrifying moment of panic washes over me, making everything cold and numb as I wonder if she's dead. With a shaking hand, I feel for her pulse, exhaling weakly with relief when I feel the strong beat of her heart beneath my fingers. *Thank God.*

Shaking her shoulders, I clear my throat before saying her name again. Still no response. I swear I age by at least ten years as I pull open her eyelids and do everything I can to get a reaction from her. *Come on, Spitfire. You're not this easy to take out.*

Eventually she groans and peels her eyes open. Her eyes dart around the space around us, and I can tell she's struggling to focus on any one thing. "Sawyer," I repeat for what must be the fourth or fifth instance. This time, I put more of a bite behind her name, hoping it will snap her out of it. When that fails to work, I revert to calling her her preferred name—Red. I get her need for a pseudonym, but to me, she's Sawyer. Always has been, and always will be.

Her eyes drift shut. Then her lips part, her tongue flicking out to lick along the seam before a long, weary groan escapes her. Getting frustrated and debating just lifting her out of here, I finally bark her name. "Sawyer!"

Six is the magic number, and her eyes snap open once again. This time, her gaze is sharper, and even though she makes no effort to get up, she lifts her hand to touch her temple. I'm sure it hurts. She probably has a concussion, but it's the least of our concerns. I can hear the steady *pop, pop, pop* of gunshots outside, the Antonelli's—my men—killing off anyone who tries to flee. It won't be long before they go through the rubble and pick off anyone still breathing. With that uncomfortable thought nagging at me, my next words come out more harshly than I intend them. "Come on, we have to get out of here."

Half expecting men to come storming through the remains of the front of the building, I glance up, catching a flash of movement from outside as the men move around the street. Refusing to wait any longer, I haul Sawyer off the ground and place her on her feet, all the while ensuring I've got a secure hold on her in case she collapses again. I only get the pleasure of touching her for a few seconds before she pulls away from me, apparently deciding she can stand on her own.

I watch her pat herself down out of the corner of my eye while I figure out our best chance of escape. "What happened?" she croaks, her voice as dry as mine. I ignore her, not that I really think she's expecting an answer as she takes in the carnage around us. It's kind of self-explanatory.

When she makes a move toward the front of the building, I head to stop her. "No! They're gunning down everyone that goes out that way." Having already decided going out the back is our best bet, I begin to tug her in that direction while keeping my wits about me and ignoring the dead bodies littered around us.

I know she's in shock. I can see it in the wide set of her eyes and the way they dart around the room, seeing everything yet not processing any of it. "Come on," I urge when she stops. "We need to go." I don't give her a choice to follow as I once again tug on her arm, directing her behind the bar and through a storage area until I come across an emergency exit door that leads into an alley out the back. Dumpsters hide us from the road, and I take a second to just breathe—even if the air is still thick with dust and debris.

My eyes trail over her, cataloging every injury and knowing she needs to get out of here. It's too risky for me to be seen with her, but I know her apartment isn't far. She should be able to get back there by herself, and I can check in with her tomorrow when it's safe. I hate the idea of leaving her, but I know how tough Sawyer is. Despite my desire to take her home and care for her, I know she will be fine.

"You have to go." The words rush out of me before I talk myself into staying with her. Not that she would let me. Even now, her eyes narrow in mistrust, and I can practically see the wheels turning in her head as she tries to put the pieces together.

"You knew this was going to happen. How?"

The accusation in her tone slices through me, cutting me open until I'm freely bleeding in front of her, because she's right. I knew this was going to happen and I did nothing to stop it. I don't even really care. All that matters is her. I've kept my identity a secret all these years. She already doesn't trust me, although when I confess who I really am, it's going to be the nail in the coffin on whatever future I thought there could have been between us. But she has the right to know. To know who she's been doing business with. Who put her life in jeopardy today.

I can already feel myself pulling away, closing myself off to her before I even break the news. She can see it too and barks out, "Who are you?"

"Go. Now," I say rather than answering her.

It's a pitiful attempt at evasion, one she ignores. Instead, she straightens her spine and stubbornly crosses her arms over her chest. "Not until you tell me who you are."

This is it. There's no more hiding. No more pretending we could be anything else. She will hate me when she finds out—just like everyone else does. I'm not accepted as an Antonelli, but I'm feared for being one. I am an outcast no matter where I turn. Still, as the words slip easily from my lips and I watch as her eyes harden, a sharp pang resonates in my chest.

I can see her mind racing, even though we can't afford to waste any more time here. Not when none of it matters anyway. She needs time to process that bomb drop, and we both need to get the fuck away from here. "No more questions," I snap authoritatively. "Get the fuck out of here."

For once, she actually does as she's told, and I watch, feeling both grateful and like I'm completely fucking lost at sea as she strides down the alley without a backward glance.

the locker room

I open myself up to the pain from my busted knuckles as the hot water spurts out of the showerhead, washing off the blood and sweat from tonight's fight. The dull ache in my hands and the fatigue in my exerted muscles tampers down the continuous pain in my chest. I've always found it easier to avoid the all-consuming grief threatening to pull me under when I'm in physical pain. It's one of the reasons I fight so often. It's one of the only times when I can just live in the moment. Forget about my past, my failures, and just be present.

Of course, that's not the only reason I've been in the ring every night this week. The image of a particular red-headed pain in my ass flashes across my mind, sparking a twisted combination of hatred and lust. I've never wanted to simultaneously strangle and fuck a person, but every time I'm around her, I want to torture her for the secrets she's keeping from me. But my dick also has other ideas—maybe a different kind of torture. I'm just not sure if I'd be punishing her or myself. Or both of us.

Just thinking about her has my cock twitching to life. The way she responded to my touch that night at the club. Her body was so damn responsive. She practically melted beneath my competent touch—well, as much as one can while continuing to spit fire at you from their eyes. It took a hell of a lot more self-control than I like to admit to having walked away from her that night. My raging hard-on when I returned to the car definitely had me instantly regretting not just sinking balls deep inside her.

Fuck sake, no! I quickly shut down those thoughts. There's plenty of pussy around the clubhouse I can distract myself with. Red might have my dick acting like a pre-teen virgin, getting hard at the mere thought of her, but I refuse to let *anyone* stand in my way when it comes to avenging Evie. And that's exactly what Red is doing. Getting in my way.

Before I can cave and decide to jerk off to the image of her dancing up on stage at Strip Tease, I shut off the shower and grab a towel to wrap around my waist before stepping into the locker room.

The scent of cherries assaults my senses, and I come to a halt, instantly recognizing who it belongs to. No one should be back here, especially not her. "What the hell are you doing here?" I bite out angrily. I'm not sure if it's the adrenaline from the fight still coursing through my veins or the fact I was just debating jerking off to her that has me feeling even more on edge at her unexpected presence. Oliver and I haven't talked much this last week. He's been more withdrawn than usual, and most of our discussions end up in arguments over the stripper currently standing in front of me. However, he had seemed confident that we were done with her. Well, that *he* was done with her. He might be buying her bullshit that she doesn't know anything, but I'm sure as fuck not. "I thought we were done with you."

"Charming as ever," she retorts. Even in the dark, alone with the leader of the Rejects, she doesn't back down. Either she's an idiot, or she's got balls of steel. Jury's still out. "Can't you just be fucking nice?"

Her question catches me by surprise. She wants me to be fucking *nice* to her? Yet she continues to keep me from the Reaper? I'm not Oliver. I don't have that ability to be compassionate. He might try to soften her up to get the info we need, but I'm sure as hell not about to cozy up to her for the intel.

I'm all brute force and unchallenged orders. While Oliver might try to break down her walls, I'm happy to just smash right the fuck through them and demand the answers I need.

My muscles move into action before my brain has had a chance to register the movement, and I eat up the space between us in three long strides. Even in just a towel, I know I must present an intimidating picture with every inch of my visible skin decorated in tattoos and my imposing six-foot-five frame of pure fucking muscle. Yet she doesn't shy away. Something my dick seriously fucking likes.

"Nice?" I sneer. "Why the fuck would I be *nice* to you?"

My snarling tone does nothing to make her cower. If anything, the more venom I spew her way, the straighter her spine becomes, until I can see the burning desire to slit my throat in her eyes.

I'd love to see you try, baby.

That gets another twitch from my dick, and now I'm curious to see how far I can push her. So I lean in, pressing one hand against the door above her head. My other hand wraps around her neck, feeling the steady thrum of her pulse beneath the pad of my thumb as my fingers caress her soft skin. This woman is an enigma. Even now, I'm not sure if I want to squeeze tighter and watch as her lips turn blue, or make her scream out my name as I slam balls deep inside her. My indecision makes her a liability to me. She has the ability to ruin everything I'm working toward, and she doesn't even know it. My fingers flex against her throat, indecision still tearing me apart. "You're trouble, and if I don't stop you, you'll ruin everything."

Her lips part—no doubt to spew some snarky retort—and the movement catches my eye as her tongue darts out to wet her lip. In a moment of pure insanity, I lean in. My mind is still at war—kill or fuck her—except as I drag her lips to mine, the decision is made.

I dominate her, even while my skin ignites and my body goes up in flames as my towel hits the floor. Kissing her is like going to battle. Everything is a push and pull. It's frantic and violent and bloody, and seriously fucking hot. My brain wholly switches off as carnal need takes control, directing my movements as I tear her clothes from her body. Removing just enough to get me what I want—buried between her thighs.

The way she clamps down on me when I slam into her. I don't do slow and gentle, and I get the impression she doesn't either. The shocked gasp that escapes her only makes me harder, and I chuckle against her neck. "It's called a magic cross. Magic 'cause it can make women come in no time."

On those powerful words, I prove my point by pulling out and slamming all the way into her again. Over and over, I fuck her with wild abandon, driving us both crazy as we race toward nirvana. I completely lose myself in her, in a way that I've never been able to achieve before. That oblivion I search for when I'm fighting is tenfold as I fuck her relentlessly. For the first time in years, I can fucking breathe without the noose that constantly hangs around my neck.

Far too soon, the familiar tingling starts at the base of my spine and my balls draw up before I slam into her one final time, roaring out my release, feeling her clench around me as she finds her own pleasure.

The second I'm done, it's like her skin scorches mine everywhere it touches. I hastily back up, moving away from her as I struggle to mentally join reality again. Then, I distract myself by throwing on the clothes I left on the bench. Still, my eyes repeatedly drift her way.

I watch out of the corner of my eye in confusion as she redresses with stiff, pained-looking movements. I didn't think I was that rough with her. It's not like she's made of glass. I'm sure Red, of all people, can handle a wild fuck. Still, I continue to scrutinize her movements as she pulls on her jeans, noticing that they're torn in the knee and covered in dust. Frowning, I cast my eyes over the rest of her, noticing her leather jacket is in a similar condition.

When she finally looks my way, I properly take her in for the first time tonight. Her pupils are blown, and dark circles ring her eyes, but what catches my attention is the dried blood on the side of her head. "What the fuck happened to you?" I demand.

"Nothing." Her dismissive tone re-ignites the fire I'd just managed to extinguish, and I take a menacing step toward her. My eyes roam over her again, checking to see if there are any other injuries I missed.

"Doesn't look like nothing."

Her expression is a blank mask as she stares up at me for a beat before turning to yank open the door and storming out. Her movements are uncoordinated as she strides through the club, making a beeline for the entrance. If I didn't know any better, I'd think she was drunk or high, but she looks like she's been through the wringer. Maybe she got caught up in some gang war elsewhere in the city? Yet if that's the case, why is she here when she should be at home, in bed?

Exiting the club, she stumbles onto the sidewalk. Her skin is paler than before, and she looks far from okay. "Seriously, what the fuck is wrong with you?" Her refusal to tell me only pisses me off further, and I know I'm probably being an asshole right now.

She spins to face me, and the last remaining hint of color in her cheeks fades rapidly before she bends over and pukes all over the sidewalk. "Jesus Christ," I grumble, running my hand through my hair as I try to figure out what the fuck to do with her.

Should I call the doc? Does she need a hospital? I don't fucking know what happened, so I can't work out what to do.

Continuing to ignore me, she slips on her leather jacket and digs around in the pockets until she lifts out the keys to her bike. Is this chick fucking serious? She can hardly walk in a straight line, never mind drive a fucking bike. "Ehh, where the fuck do you think you're going?" I demand, although I don't know why I'm bothering at this point. She's yet to answer a single one of my goddamn questions.

"Go away." She tosses the words over her shoulder as she trudges toward the bike, except her usual bite is lacking. All I hear is exhaustion, and that more than anything has alarm bells going off in my head.

"Hey!" she snaps when I jerk her to a stop and deftly steal the keys from her fingers.

"There's no fucking way I'm letting you drive that beauty home and crash her. Not when you're drunk, or high, or whatever the fuck you are." Yeah, I'm deliberately being a dick. "You can sleep it off here"—where I can have someone make sure you don't fucking die in the middle of the night—"and go home in the morning."

She mumbles something, but it's slightly slurred and so quiet that I barely hear what she says. She can hardly stand upright anymore, and standing out here on the street arguing isn't going to do her any good. Instead, I keep a tight grip on her arm and gently lead her over to the clubhouse and through to the area where Oliver and I stay. I glance at my bedroom door as I pass but swiftly dismiss the idea. I've already crossed far too many lines with her tonight. Having her in my fucking bed is too much. So, I open the door to Oliver's room.

"I'm not sleeping in your bed," she snaps weakly. Still, her fire—even when she's this exhausted—has me squashing a small smile that threatens to break free.

"Like I'd fucking want you in my bed. Just 'cause we fucked, doesn't mean I don't still fucking hate you." I'm honestly not sure if I'm saying those words for her benefit or for my own. Thankfully, though, she seems to be on the same page.

"Same."

She barely makes it to the bed before collapsing onto it. I find myself motionless in the doorway, unsure of what to do. It feels wrong to leave her alone in this state, but I can't bring myself to do anything more. I try to get my muscles to move, to step out of the room and close the door. Only I find myself moving toward the bathroom instead. I grab the first aid kit from under the sink and toss it on the bed beside her. She's cracked one eye open to watch me. "For your head," I explain.

Before I find myself playing fucking nurse, I stomp out of the room and slam the door shut behind me. Except catch it at the last second, closing it quietly. I don't move though. Just stand there like a fucking idiot, listening to any sounds from the other side of the door.

After several long moments, when I don't hear anything, I silently open the door and peer in. She's lying passed out on the bed in the same position I left her. It doesn't look comfortable with her legs hanging off the end of the bed, and I quietly pad into the room and lift her up until her head rests on the pillow. She doesn't stir. I stare at her, noting how peaceful she looks when she's asleep, and all those hard lines are smoothed out.

Pulling out my phone, I text Oliver, knowing he'll come back if he knows she's here.

I've done my part. I've taken care of her. Now she's Oliver's problem. That's what I tell myself as I force myself to leave her once again alone. Rather than going back to the party, I sit in my room until I catch Oliver walking down the hallway. It's only when I hear him move into his bedroom, that I begin to relax and let myself get some sleep.

MURDER & MAYHEM

BLACK CREEK SERIES BOOK TWO

R.A. SMYTH

I glance left and right down the empty hallway before slotting my tools into the lock. It's a cheap, shitty one, and I easily manipulate the mechanism, hearing the satisfying click of the door unlocking. I don't waste any time pushing it open and stepping into the apartment. Quickly shutting the door behind me, I stand in the hall and slowly run my eyes around the room, taking all of it in. It's small and sparsely furnished, with hideous carpeting and walls that are in dire need of a lick of paint, but I don't pay much attention to any of that. It means nothing other than telling me that the owner likely doesn't have much money.

I do a quick sweep of the kitchen, noting nothing of significance, before I move onto the living room. Again, there's nothing personal here. Nothing that tells me anything about the woman who lives here. Moving to the first door off the living room, I push it open and enter a bedroom. My eyebrows lift in surprise as I look around. *Huh, not what I expected.*

Picking my way through the scattered clothes, I pull open the drawers in the dresser and rummage through them. Working my way around the room, I do the same in the bedside table, not finding anything identifiable. The clothes definitely belong to a guy, though. Maybe she has a kid? That wouldn't be surprising.

When I'm finished searching the bedroom, I do a quick sweep of the bathroom before moving on to the next room. I take my time in this bedroom, going through her things—her closet, dresser, and bedside table. I even look under her pillows and mattress. Again, I find nothing that tells me anything about *her*. It's like she hardly lives here.

Frustrated that my efforts have been in vain, I exit the room. As I'm passing through the living room, I notice a photo stuck to the wall. It's probably just her and her kid, but I move closer, nonetheless. It's the only personal item in the whole damn apartment, so it's definitely worth a closer look.

Moving to stand in front of it, my eyes brush over the girl first, noting that it is a younger version of the woman I'm investigating. There's something familiar about her features, but I can't put my finger on it. Flicking my gaze to the boy beside her, anger immediately pulses through me, realization dawning. I rip the photo from the wall, still staring at the older version of the boy I remember.

My hand shakes as I struggle not to ruin the photo, but the edges crinkle beneath my punishing grip anyway. Nostrils flaring, I focus back on the older girl. Now that I know who she is, it's obvious. Although more vibrant and healthier looking, her hair is similar to her mother's, and so are those eyes. She's the one who has had him this entire time. Well, not for much longer. I'd long since given up hope of finding him, but God rewards patience, and he has seen fit to bless me for mine.

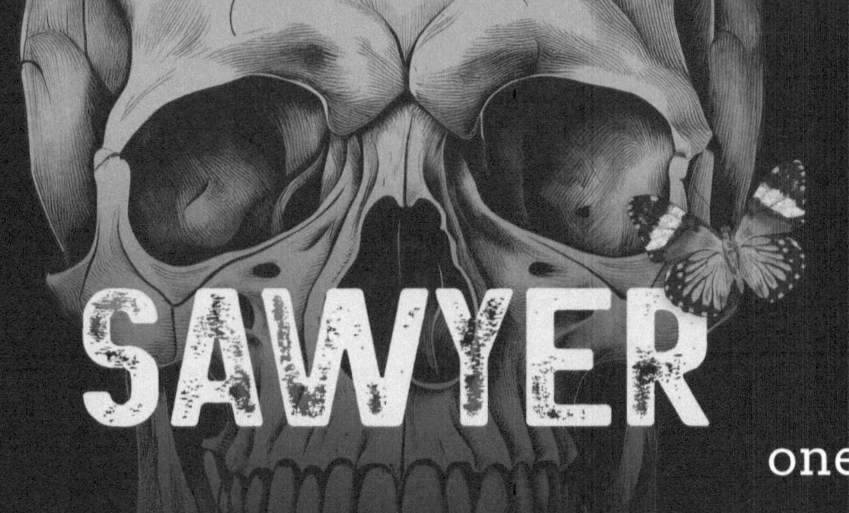

one

The city passes in a blur as I fly across town toward Radiant Park. The anger pouring through my veins prevents me from feeling the cold blast of the wind as it whips my hair out behind me, even as I press my foot down harder on the accelerator, making the bike roar as it surges forward.

How dare he.

How fucking dare he.

God, I'm going to wring his tattooed fucking neck when I get my hands on him. Who the hell does he think he is, ordering people to come into *my* apartment, *without* my permission when I'm not even fucking home. It's one thing to have one of the kids around. Over the last couple of weeks, Luc has been hanging out with them quite a bit. At first, I really wasn't happy about the amount of time he was spending with them. Honestly, I'm still on the fence about the whole situation, but he's seemed happier these last few weeks, and that almost makes up for the fact that he's spending his free time with gangbangers—the exact people I've been telling him to avoid his whole life.

What I definitely don't condone, though, is getting home at the ass crack of dawn after tailing my new target—soon to be my next victim—around seedy bars and back alleys all night, to find three men I don't even recognize packing up all my shit. They nearly gave me a goddamn heart attack when I heard them moving around inside my apartment, and they're lucky they're still fucking breathing.

I screech to a halt outside the Reject clubhouse and practically fling myself from the bike, stomping through the gate and onto their property. I only hesitate for a second, waiting to see if my unannounced presence will set off an alarm and result in guns being shoved in my face *again*. When all remains still and silent, I march on, ignoring the curious looks I get as I throw open the door into the lobby and swiftly bypass the few Reject members I can see.

I seethe the entire way to Cain's office, flinging open the door with such force that it bounces off the wall with a loud smack that reverberates around the room. Cain's intense gaze snaps up at the sudden interruption, and his eyes narrow in annoyance, his dark green irises smoldering.

He barely spares me more than an irritated glance before he refocuses on the laptop in front of him. "What crawled up your ass?" His voice is too casual, too dismissive, and it only serves to piss me off even more.

"You did," I snap, glowering at him.

A cocky smirk lifts one side of his lip like that answer pleases him. Does he get off on pissing me off? God, probably.

He lazily raises his eyes to meet my gaze as he shifts in his chair, his tattooed, muscular biceps straining against the sleeves of his t-shirt as he crosses his arms over his broad chest. "Red, if I was in your ass, then trust me, you'd be moaning my name like it was the answer to all your prayers, not scowling at me like you've never had a half-decent orgasm before."

My mouth drops open, gaping at him for a long moment as images flash unbidden across the back of my mind, and my body heats with undisguised lust. *God-fucking-dammit, no! We're angry at the insufferable asshole. Remember that.*

My gaze narrows further, and I clench my teeth as I mentally shove all those unwanted feelings back into whatever stupid box they climbed out of. As if agreeing to go to war with the Antonellis and the Grim Bastards isn't enough, my body and mind are also in a fight of their own. One where my body wants to climb both Cain and Oliver like they're its own personal jungle gym, and my brain has to keep reminding it that business and pleasure don't mix well together.

It's been fucking exhausting. You'd at least think Cain's intolerable personality would be a turn-off, but apparently, I'm into domineering assholes that deliberately push your buttons and drive you fucking demented. The ire he throws my way awakens some deep, dark, repressed part of myself that mentally begs for him to unleash all that anger on me; to take it out on my body.

As much as Cain's fury makes my panties combust, so do Oliver's heated glances and light touches. He's the complete opposite of Cain—softer, more open, fucking reasonable—but that tenderness speaks to my inner damage and lures me in just as much as Cain's fire.

I made it clear to Oliver that there could be nothing more between us so long as we were working together. Not only do I not need the distraction, but I'm also confused as hell when it comes to him. There's no denying my attraction to him, but my one rule has always been to avoid gang members. Anything more than a one-night stand was a no-no, yet here I am, full-on crushing on one. Things are changing rapidly. In the span of two weeks, I've allowed the Rejects to see into mine and Luc's life more than anyone else ever has. I am extending a branch of trust to them on a professional level, but I'm also entrusting them with Luc's safety. All of it makes me uneasy, and I'm just not ready to cross any more boundaries. Especially not ones that involve Oliver; boundaries that, once crossed, there will be no coming back from.

Of course, that hasn't stopped him from driving me halfway insane with his lingering touches. I swear he goddamn knows how much it's affecting me.

"I'm not fucking moving in here," I state in a low growl.

He sighs in such a way that makes it seem like I'm being deliberately difficult, when *he's* the one making decisions *for me.*

"We talked about this," he states, sounding far too calm and rational.

I suck in a deep breath, forcing myself to calm down. "Yes, and I said no."

"Well, I think—"

"I don't give a shit what you think," I blurt out, cutting him off. "I. Am. Not. Moving. In. Here." I pin him with a dead serious look, hoping that what I just said will finally penetrate his thick skull. "So you can tell your lackeys to stop packing up my shit."

When he doesn't move to lift his phone from the desk and place the call, I stare him down, the two of us engaged in one hell of a stare-off. Neither one of us breaks eye contact, even when the door is pushed open, and in my peripheral vision, I notice Oliver step into the room.

"Uh, what's the problem now?" Oliver asks, sounding weary. He's gotten used to Cain and me having issues with every little thing the other says over the last few weeks. The three of us have only met up a handful of times, but Cain and I have ended up sniping at one another every single one of those times.

"Cain has men packing up my apartment, even though I said *no*," I answer with a quirk of my brow at Cain, still engaged in a silent stare-off battle with him.

"You told me she changed her mind," Oliver grumbles, turning to look at Cain.

I snort. *Of course, he did.* The day after I agreed to help them, Oliver immediately raised the idea of me and Luc moving in here with them. He made it sound so fucking reasonable too—better protection for Luc, I'd be less likely to become a target, and it would give us more time to work on our plan. Except that there's no fucking way I'm about to move my fifteen-year-old brother into a gang clubhouse. Hell-to-the-mother-fucking-no. Besides, there's absolutely no chance I could be around these two all day, every day, and keep my sanity, or my panties dry. Nope. Moving in is not an option.

"Well, I didn't."

Oliver steps around me, moving closer to Cain. "Man, come on."

"I don't even get why you're so hellbent on me moving in. In fact, I'm beginning to think you're secretly obsessed with me." I smirk at him.

He scoffs, sneering right back. "Not likely. I'm trying to make the job of protecting you and your brother's asses easier on my men."

The smug smile drops off my face as I scowl.

"Cain, it's fine," Oliver assures him. "The kids are hanging out with Luc anyway."

Oliver's words don't seem to appease him. "Yeah, well, maybe we'd actually have made some progress if we were all under the same roof." He waves a hand in my direction. "Instead, she's been avoiding us for the last two weeks."

"I have not," I argue, ignoring the thin line of truth in his words. "I have my own shit to do. Some of us actually work for a living." Between shifts at Strip Tease and removing a few new assholes from the map, I've been pretty damn busy recently. There was no way in hell I was about to drop any of that just to come pander to Cain's whims. Not while men like Python roam the streets.

"Well, now that you've decided to grace us with your presence"—cue eye roll at his dramatics—"we should get you up to speed on the Antonellis. What do you know about them?"

"Not much," I admit with a shrug, letting some of the tension drop from my shoulders as I shift into business mode. Despite how infuriating Cain is to deal with, I can put aside our differences for the sake of a job, for the sake of making Black Creek a safer place for my brother.

Cain gestures to one of the empty chairs in front of his desk, and hesitantly I take a seat. Oliver casts a heated glance my way before claiming the chair beside me. The asshole makes a point of spreading his legs, ensuring his muscular, jean-clad thigh brushes against mine as Cain pulls open a drawer and rifles through it.

Yet, I don't shift away from Oliver's touch. Guess I'm a glutton for punishment. I can't help the thrill that thrums through me when he's nearby, even though my head is telling me to snap out of it. I stare at where Oliver's leg presses against mine. My body begs for more, and my brain revolts. The same as always. Why can't I just be a simple girl who doesn't have deep-seated emotional issues? Life would be far easier. Instead, I feel like I'm letting myself down every time I melt beneath his touch or have inappropriate fantasies about him... or Cain. It seems so goddamn pathetic that after all these years of hating on the gangs in this town, I'd just toss that hostility to the wayside for some decent dick. Okay, so it's next-level, amazing, out-of-this-world dick. But it's still dick. It just doesn't seem right.

I only pull my focus from where our bodies connect when Cain sets three photos down on the desk in front of me. They are all candid shots, clearly taken from afar with a zoomed-in lens, as none of the men in the images seem to be aware that they've been photographed. "This is Giovanni, the head of the Antonelli family," he states, pointing at the first photo on the left.

Sitting forward in my chair to get a better look, I imprint every fine detail of the cold man in the first photo, from his gray-tinged, short-cropped jet-black hair to the cruel slash of his mouth, to his perfectly tailored suit, into my memory. I fight back a shiver as fear crawls along my spine. The dark shadows in his eyes, combined with his stiff features, sets an intimidating picture. Exuberant wealth and absolute confidence drip from his pores, and even if I hadn't experienced firsthand what he was capable of when he sent his men to blow up G&T, the promises of death and destruction in his cold, hard eyes would be telling enough.

"This is his Consigliere—his second in command—Santo Ricci," Cain continues, moving on to the second photo.

Again, I scrutinize his picture. He looks to be around the same age—mid-fifties—and equally as ruthless looking as Giovanni. However, his shaved dark hair and the row of X's running down his right cheek make him appear more brutish. I can certainly see why he was chosen as Giovanni's second. While Giovanni appears cold and calculating, Santo's screams *don't fuck with me* vibes.

When he moves on, tapping the third and final photo with his finger, I tense. Out of the three shots, this one is the only face I recognize, and I have to confess, I am surprised to see it amongst the other two. After running into him at Bella Donna, I knew the man that nearly killed me eight years ago was connected to the Antonellis, but I had no idea he was this high up in their organization. By the process of elimination, he must be...

"Giovanni's son," Cain states, confirming my assumption. "Dante Antonelli."

I lift his picture off the desk, drinking in the deep furrow of his brow, the tight pinch of his lips, and the tense set of his jaw. If I thought Giovanni looked scary, it's nothing compared to his son. It's all in his eyes. While his father's were hard and flinty,

Dante's are just blank. Like looking up into the dark sky on a starless night. The dark brown of his irises blends with his pupils to create this never-ending chasm. I could clearly read the greed and violence in Giovanni's eyes, but in Dante's there is nothing. There's no emotion whatsoever. It's like he's an empty void, incapable of feeling anything. Unlike the other two photos, Dante is looking right into the camera, which only adds to his unnerving presence. This time I can't hold back my full-body shiver as I feel the chill from his glacial glare seep into my bones. I set the photo down on the desk, pushing it away from me and feeling a bit ridiculous that a simple photograph could bother me so much. Coughing to clear my throat, I ask, "So, what's the plan?"

When neither of them answer, I lift my head, glancing first at Cain before turning my head to meet Oliver's unflinching gaze. "Uhhh."

When he doesn't expand, I roll my eyes.

"We planned to use the Reaper's ability to sneak into places undetected to get us vital information that we could use to formulate a strategic plan of attack intended to take out the top figures within the organization," Cain states in a flat tone.

My eyes narrow as I look between them, trying to put my finger on their hesitation with that plan. It sounds like a good idea to me. Without a doubt, something I can do, and yet they're both frowning as if that's not a possibility. My eyebrows hitch, and I gape at them as the realization hits me like a slap in the face. "And what? Because I'm a girl, you don't think I can do that?" I bite back.

I can see it in Cain's eyes—the raw truth. That's precisely what he thinks, and when I turn to scowl at Oliver, I find a similar hesitance in his gaze. *What the fuck, seriously?* Gritting my teeth, I snarl out, "Why the fuck did you offer me the job if you didn't think I could do it?"

"That's not it—" Oliver begins, but I hold my hand up in a silent gesture to shut the fuck up.

"Tough shit." I jump to my feet, glowering at both of them. "You gave me the job, it's mine. Now sit back like good little boys and watch me do it."

Without waiting for them to pick their jaws up off the floor, I stomp out of the office, more determined than ever to prove them wrong. I am *not* to be underestimated, and little do they know, I already have a plan in mind... I just need to get in touch with a lying Antonelli asshole that I'd rather have forgotten existed.

two

I stare at the phone in my hand, although God only knows why. She's been ignoring my texts ever since the explosion at G&T when I told her who I really was. I saw the look in her eye—the betrayal; the distrust. I tried to reschedule, but I should have known she'd be difficult about it. It's her nature, which is why I showed up anyway, knowing the risk. The fear that had flooded my system when she walked through that door. God, I could have wrung her pretty little neck. It was all I could do to get her out of there ASAP before Giovanni's men showed up. I should have known that shit wouldn't fly, though. She's too smart, too good at reading people for that. In all the years we've had this little arrangement, she's always been so fucking eager to get away from me, while I've always craved one second longer with her. For once, I'd hoped she would have been all for a quick in-and-out job, but of course, my change in behavior set off alarm bells in her head, igniting that fiery temper of hers.

She's always pushed back, always stood up to me, and toed the line between cautious and daring. It's why I've kept her close all these years. To the Antonellis, I may as well be a nobody. A measly bodyguard who's generally ignored, yet to the rest of the city, I represent their worst nightmares. The second I step onto the street, my presence strikes fear into their hearts, even though I've never personally done anything to them. But with her, it was different. She brought to life a part of me that I thought was long dead. Her boldness intrigued me, and so did her willingness to do anything for her brother.

Ever since that night eight years ago, when Dante sent me after her to make sure she didn't nark on what she witnessed in the alleyway, I haven't been able to stay away. I followed her back to the shelter she was staying at and watched her closely for the next few days. I saw how she took care of her brother and the things she did for him. She wasn't afraid to stand up to the other kids or to even take on grown men who chanced their luck. Even at that young age, she was a spitfire. The more I saw of the conditions she had to live in and the things she had to do just to survive, the more I wanted to help. I knew I shouldn't. If anyone found out, it would only put her in more danger, but I couldn't just walk away and forget about her, and I couldn't continue to stand on the sidelines and simply watch… so I intervened. I made up some bullshit excuse to help her out, pretending I wanted intel on the gang that was running the part of town she lived in at the time in exchange for money. It wasn't as much money as I'd have liked to give her, but anything more than what I offered would have raised alarm bells, and she was too smart for that, even back then.

Since then, we have met once a month. Of course, I keep tabs on her in between our visits. I know where she works, where she lives, and what school her brother goes to. I even know her secret identity. And yet, I don't feel like I know her at all. It infuriates me that she won't open up to me. She's gotten cynical and suspicious—as she rightfully should—as she has gotten older, which led to her putting up more walls around herself.

I've been pulling my hair out for years, trying to break through them, but every time I open my goddamn mouth, I just seem to erect another barrier between us. Then, of course, I made sure to reinforce those walls with fucking concrete, basically ensuring she would *never* trust me, by telling her who I am. She would have worked it out anyway. She probably already had her suspicions. I could see it in her eyes. My words simply confirmed what she already suspected.

Shaking my head in defeat, I let out a long, hopeless sigh as I stare down at the blank screen of my phone. I *could* just show up at her door, but I don't think that will win me any brownie points. I've messaged her twice since that day. Once a few days after the explosion to ask if we could meet to talk about what happened—which she ignored— and five minutes ago to see if we're still on for this month's meeting, which is meant to be tomorrow.

I know the only reason she agrees to meet me is for the money, and I'm hoping it's enough of an incentive for her to continue with our arrangement. Except her prolonged silence is saying otherwise.

Unable to stare at the blank screen for a second longer, I collapse back against the couch cushions and stare up at the ceiling, which is where Dante finds me when he enters the apartment. It's technically *his* apartment—one of the few that are actually occupied in this building. Only Dante, Giovanni, and his second in command, along with a couple of other higher-ups, live in this building. Of course, if you were down on the street, looking up, you wouldn't know that. All of the vacant apartments have lights set on timers, so they automatically come on at various times after it gets dark, giving the appearance that they are being lived in. The apartment block is locked up better than Fort Knox, though. It has the best security money can buy, and only a small handful of people even know that this is home to the major players in the Famiglia. Placed right in the middle of this part of the city, it's only a few blocks from the casino, Belle Donne, and even the fucking cathedral, making it the perfect place to call home. Especially since it enabled Giovanni to build underground tunnels from each of his businesses, right into the bowels of the apartment building. He even had a handful of extra tunnels built which link to decoy buildings a block or two away. So long as we sporadically enter and leave via the front door—giving the appearance that it's just the same as any other building—it is next to impossible for someone to track us back here.

"What's wrong with you?" Dante asks, pulling my focus back to him.

I lift my head off the back of the sofa to look at him. "Nothing." Dante doesn't know anything about my little low-key obsession with Sawyer. I'm not entirely sure what he would think about it, especially since he's harboring his own little preoccupation with her. Other than when I confirmed she hadn't spilled a word of that night to anyone, we've never spoken of her, but he's mumbled something about blue eyes enough times in his sleep for me to know whom he's referring to. The fact that he let her go that night was telling enough of her effect on him. Nobody and nothing affects Dante. He's a frozen tundra—harsh, glacial, deadly—and until that day, he'd never once hesitated in his duty to his family. The only time he's ever gone against his father's demands was when he continued to be friends with me, and even then, that was back when we were kids. If Dante was apathetic as a child, it's nothing compared to the man he's grown up to become—the man his father has molded him into.

He shrugs a shoulder, moving over to the bar cart and grabbing the decanter of whiskey, pouring two glasses. Walking over, he hands me one before claiming the seat opposite me.

"What's on the agenda for tonight?" I ask, needing the distraction.

"Alex has been helping himself to an extra slice of Belle Donne profits."

My eyebrows hitch. It baffles me how some of these men can be so stupid. Is a few extra grand really worth risking your life for? Apparently so, in Alex's case. *Dumb fuck.*

"Shame, he was excellent at cooking the books."

"I know," Dante groans, sounding much more annoyed about having to find a new accountant than about the fact that he's going to have to kill Alex. It is surprisingly difficult to find a reliable accountant who won't go blabbing his mouth to every Tom, Dick, and Harry and is actually good at his job, despite the hefty wage we pay. Alex was excellent at his job. Saved the Famiglia a fucking fortune over the years and successfully siphoned all of our illegal earnings through our legal businesses. Now we're not only going to have to find someone new but also adequately scare the shit out of them to keep them quiet, *and* get someone to show them the ropes. What a fucking headache. Still, a little murder and vindication is the perfect distraction to stop me from thinking about a certain fiery redhead.

Knocking back his drink, Dante gets to his feet, his gaze already on the office door. "Seriously?" I cock a brow at him. "Haven't you watched those tapes enough?"

He scowls. "I haven't worked out who she is yet."

"What does it matter? She's gone, and obsessing over her like this isn't going to change that." With his teeth gritted and his nostrils flaring, he looks like he's one second away from flying off the handle, yet I continue to push. "Just let her go, man. We've got enough shit to deal with."

My insistence that he drop this is as much for my benefit as it is his. Sure, it's not good for him to fixate on this, and Dante has an obsessive personality, so it's *definitely* not good that he's become obsessed with identifying this girl. At the same time, I also don't *want* him to identify her. I can't be sure—the grainy recording combined with the low lighting of the club made it impossible to be certain—but I'm fairly confident that Sawyer's the girl on the tape. I hadn't even considered it could be her until Dante mentioned that no one knew who she was, nor had she shown her face at the club since. The fact that this girl was there on the night one of our top-paying clients conveniently died... seems like too much of a coincidence for me. For Dante, too. Besides, Sawyer is the only woman I know of that is running around the city, attempting a one-woman mission to rid it of vermin. Gotta give her credit for even trying. Every time she kills one of those fuckers, three more pop up. I genuinely thought she'd give up pretty quickly. It's not exactly an easy challenge, but Sawyer's tenacious; I'll give her that. Should have known she wouldn't let a little thing like shitty odds get in her way. Of course, her grit and determination only drew her further into my sphere, making me even more obsessed with her.

Dante still looks furious, but he relents, choosing instead to storm over to grab his gun on the table by the door. "Fine, let's go deal with Alex then. If I can't figure out who that dancer is, then I need to at least watch someone die by my hands."

Getting to my feet, I slide on my shoulder holster, complete with gun, before throwing my suit jacket over the top, concealing the weapon. Taking a second, I tuck the part of myself that's truly *me* away in a locked box at the back of my mind, firmly becoming Lorenzo, Dante's bodyguard and made man of the Antonelli Famiglia, before I follow Dante out of the apartment. *Let's go catch us a motherfucking traitor.*

———

"ALEX," DANTE TUTS IN DISAPPROVAL. "YOU JUST HAD TO GET GREEDY, didn't you. Don't we pay you enough? Doesn't my family do enough for you, ensuring you can afford the expensive lifestyle you've become accustomed to, offering you a generous discount and unlimited access to Belle Donne and any of our various clubs? Not to mention wiping the slate clean of those gambling debts you owed us. And this is how you repay us?" An angry snarl enters his voice at that last question. "By *stealing*."

A muffled protest is all the response Dante gets, Alex's words incomprehensible from behind the gag in his mouth. He's zip-tied to a fancy, very expensive-looking dining chair as the two of us stand in the middle of Alex's large dining room in a glass-fronted, penthouse apartment that definitely costs more than anything I could afford. It pisses me off that an asshole like this—a mere *accountant*—can afford all of this off what the Antonellis pay him, but I can't. As bodyguard to the next fucking Don, you'd think I'd be better paid than this asshole. Still, as the son of a traitor, I'm lucky to even be allowed to breathe—or so Giovanni keeps reminding me—never mind getting any of the perks reserved for true, loyal Antonelli men. It's not enough that I've done everything within my power to prove my loyalty to this family since the day I learned of my father's betrayal and watched Giovanni himself murder both my parents in front of me. He claimed he left me alive so I could prove my entire family line wasn't filled with snitches and betrayers, but I'm certain I'm only alive so that he can torture me; so that he can hold my father's sins over my head as though they were my own.

Because of the undisguised disdain Giovanni shows me, the rest of the Famiglia follows his lead. Not a single person in this organization shows me the respect my title deserves. No one except Dante. He's never given a shit about who my father was or what his crimes were. Possibly because he doesn't want people to see his father's actions when they look at him, but maybe not, since Dante strikes more fear into the hearts of people than his father could ever hope to achieve.

A muffled cry draws my attention back to the scene in front of me as Alex's severed hand drops to the floor with a thunk, blood dripping steadily from his stump onto the white tiles.

"Quiet down," Dante barks, as the pathetic wimp continues to cry and mumble behind his gag. "We're only getting started." Moving to the other side of the chair, Dante tightens his hold on the now bloody kitchen knife before swinging it down. He doesn't manage to get the hand severed with one clean strike, but with a little sawing action, the hand eventually joins the other one on the floor.

Tears course down Alex's face as he slumps in the chair, looking like he's about to pass out. However, Dante isn't going to let him off that easily. With the crack of a palm across his face, Alex's eyes snap open, adrenaline coursing through his system once again as he groans.

"You know," Dante begins, making light work of cutting open Alex's shirt with the knife. "In medieval times, traitors were flayed alive."

A renewed string of incoherent mumbles and pleas follow those words as Alex finds enough strength to thrash about in his chair. Even with stumps for hands, he's not going anywhere.

"Now, I know you're not technically a traitor," Dante continues, the calm, relaxed, almost soothing tone of his voice at complete odds with the violence he's inflicting. "But the Famiglia doesn't tolerate disloyalty of any kind. And stealing? Well, to us, that's just as bad."

Alex is sobbing uncontrollably now as Dante pushes his shirt open, displaying Alex's unimpressive chest and the slight rolls of his abdomen. He has next to no muscle at all, it's pathetic. He runs the tip of the knife down the center of his sternum, just enough to leave a red line but not hard enough to break the skin.

"Luckily for you, staying here to peel every inch of skin from your body is not my idea of a fun Saturday night." Dante's words are intended to give Alex a false sense of hope that his demise will now come swiftly, and I smirk as his eyes widen with a resigned hope—hope for a quick, clean death. *What a fucking idiot.* His death will serve as a message to anyone who dares to try and take what isn't theirs, and well, it wouldn't be much of a message if we made it painless, would it? Instead, Dante pushes the blade deep into the top of Alex's stomach and begins to saw through his skin, literally cutting him open until blood pools on the floor beneath his feet, surrounding the chair.

It takes a while, but eventually, Dante stands upright, assessing his handiwork before moving to stand beside me. We both watch Alex, slumped unconscious in his chair. "What do you think? An hour?"

I cast my eyes over Alex's lifeless form. The blood isn't freely flowing, so Dante mustn't have cut any major arteries, and his intestines, while visible, aren't falling out. "At least. Maybe two."

After giving it a moment's thought, Dante reaches into his pocket, lifting out a handkerchief and wiping the blood from his hand. Reaching into his pocket again, he moves to crouch in front of the chair, and I hear a faint snap, quickly followed by a gasp as Alex is startled back into the land of the living.

"Welcome back, Alex." Dante's voice is laced with dark, malicious intent, and with the handkerchief in his hand, he reaches into Alex's abdominal cavity and yanks his intestines out none too gently. They hit the floor with a wet splat as Alex groans, slumping forward in his chair. If it weren't for the bindings on his wrists, he'd probably have followed his insides onto the tiles.

Dropping the handkerchief into the pool of blood, Dante toes off his shoes, careful to avoid getting his socks soaked, and pads over to where I'm standing. He eases his feet into the spare pair we brought exactly for this purpose. "Tell the clean-up crew three hours, that should be plenty of time."

I place the call to our clean-up crew while Dante washes his hands in the sink, and without a backward glance, we exit Alex's penthouse. There's no need for either of us to wait around for the sorry sack of shit to stop breathing or for the clean-up crew to arrive. Even if some poor idiot did stumble across Alex's disemboweled body, they wouldn't be stupid enough to intervene or call for help.

As the elevator descends to the ground floor, Dante's phone goes off in his pocket. If his annoyed sigh didn't clue me in as to who the caller is, then the sharp clip in his tone when he says, "Father," definitely does.

I can only make out a faint rumble as his father talks, followed a moment later by Dante saying, "Fine, I'm just finishing up a job. I'll be there in twenty." Without waiting for a response from his father, Dante hangs up the phone and fixes me with a resigned look. "Looks like we'll be finishing the night up in Paradiso."

Oh great, just where I wanted to end the night. In Paradiso é Inferno, or Heaven and Hell, the sex club that caters exclusively to Giovanni and his closest comrades and allies, where all of their dark and twisted fantasies can be made reality.

In a sour mood, I dig my phone out of my pocket, surprised I was able to go this long without checking to see if Sawyer had responded to me. There's nothing like a little torture show to distract the mind. I hold my breath in anticipation as the screen lights up, and momentarily freeze when I see a message from her. In all honesty, I hadn't been expecting a response at all. I was convinced I'd have to go to extreme measures to ensure she didn't block me out of her life altogether—there was absolutely no fucking way I was going to allow her to do that.

SPITFIRE

2 pm tomorrow. Don't be late.

ANOTHER MESSAGE HAS AN ALTERNATIVE ADDRESS, ONE THAT I DON'T recognize, but I can scope it out tomorrow before our meeting. Her tone is brisk and all business, as per usual, but that's fine. That, I can work with.

"You coming?" Dante asks, snapping my attention from the phone to find him holding the elevator door open. Damn, I hadn't even realized we'd stopped.

Feeling lighter than I did a moment ago, I tuck my phone away and follow him out of the building. I'm more than ready to get tonight over with because tomorrow... tomorrow, I've got a meeting with a feisty redhead, and I can't fucking wait for her to throw that fiery temper my way.

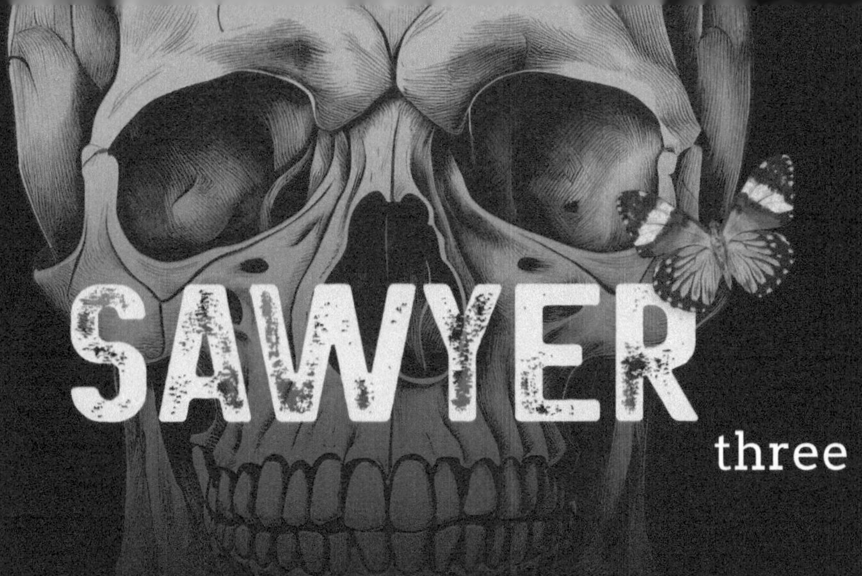

I tap my fingernail impatiently against the laminate tabletop as I stare out the window, barely registering the passing traffic on the street outside. After a long moment, I huff out a sigh, already bored. In fairness, I was half an hour early, so I can't really complain. Except that it's because of *him* that I have to be here half an hour before our meeting, just to stake out the venue and make sure he wasn't planning to pull a fast one on me.

Pulling my gaze from the window, I look around the otherwise empty shop front, taking in the chalkboard menu high on the wall, the long glass case filled with buckets containing various flavors of ice cream, and the stacks of waffle cones and cups ready to be filled. I snort as I shake my head. It's the perfect front. It's the kind of place that would be easily bypassed, yet it's the perfect setup.

The bell above the door rings, and I stiffen in my seat as I turn to face my two o'clock. Enzo saunters casually into the small parlor, cocking a brow. I can see the humor dancing in his eyes as he takes in the place. While he's momentarily distracted, I take the opportunity to run my eyes over him, noting how different he is today. He looks ridiculously out of place in this grubby shop with his expensive, perfectly tailored suit that looks like it was handmade specifically for him. Yet, my mouth dries up nevertheless. He's handsome as fuck, all dressed up like that, with a slight stubble and his blond hair perfectly styled back. It's immediately noticeable that he is way more at home in a suit than he ever was in jeans and a t-shirt, like he was born to wear one. I fucking *knew* regular scruffy clothes didn't look right on him—because they *aren't* him. This. This right here is the real Enzo, in all his gorgeous, suited-up glory, and *holy fuck,* can he pull it off.

As he moves toward me, his suit jacket falls open, giving away the fact he's armed, and I can't help thinking that he looks like some sort of bad-guy version of James Bond.

"Interesting choice," he states blandly, sliding into the booth opposite me. His unimpressed tone displays none of the initial humor I saw in his eyes when he first walked in. Nonetheless, his voice snags my attention, and I snap my eyes away from where I was staring at the way his shirt stretches across his chest, up to his face.

I don't respond, merely staring him down with a cold expression, waiting patiently until his vibrant green gaze—which I swear changes color depending on his mood—swivels to meet mine. Enzo has yet to meet the Reaper. While he is very acquainted with my brazen, brash, sarcastic side, he was never doing business with the Reaper before, and thus I had no reason to subject him to that malicious part of myself. But now, he's gone and destroyed the thin thread of trust that ran between us. Not only can I no longer trust him, but my agreement with the Rejects places him as my enemy that I need to destroy. It's the only reason I'm here at all.

After an uncomfortable moment where he searches my eyes for *something*—something that I know he won't find—he clears his throat, glancing around the otherwise empty space.

"Service is a bit slow, though."

"No one's coming to take your coffee order," I tell him. "It's just us."

That statement draws his attention back my way, and after a moment, he leans back in his seat, getting comfortable as he rests one forearm on the table, his other arm sprawled along the back of the booth so it appears as though he's taking up all of the space.

Nutterly Delicious is an ice cream parlor only a couple of blocks from my apartment. As far as I'm aware, it's one of the only ones in all of Black Creek. Not because it's particularly amazing, but because it's really a front for money laundering. Satan's Advocates used it, and so did the gang before them. Just like the Rejects, no doubt, are. Not that I actually asked Oliver or Cain. This meeting is off the books, and the last thing I need is either of them snooping around and asking questions before I've worked out my plan of attack.

I simply handed over a wad of bills half an hour ago when I walked in and told the pimple-faced kid behind the counter to take a long break. It's not like he was particularly busy. This place is probably lucky to see a handful of customers a day. The only reason it's still open is because of its usefulness. No one will look twice at the cooked books of a moderately successful ice cream parlor in the center of a busy city.

I mimic Enzo's posture, leaning back in my seat as I casually assess him, noticing more differences with every passing second. He has truly shed his old persona, and he just sits there patiently while I get my first glimpse at the *real* Enzo—assuming that is even his real name. I feel like I'm seeing him for the first time. He's both vaguely familiar and a stranger all at once. His tie is neatly knotted at his neck, and his hair is slicked back, no longer looking slightly ruffled and disheveled. Part of me wants to run my hands through it and muss it up... and I have no idea what the fuck to do with that desire. *It's only because it looks weird seeing it so neatly styled*, I tell myself before pushing aside such ludicrous thoughts.

Looking away from his hair, I accidentally catch his gaze, the bright green of his irises holding me captive. Those eyes... they are exactly the same. Just looking into them, I can feel him probing at me, silently prodding me for information I don't want to give him.

Irritated, I break eye contact, looking out the window while I reinforce my walls.

Once I'm sure he hasn't obtained any information I don't want him to know, I return my attention to his face, feeling more at ease when I notice his expression more closed off than it was a second ago. Good. This isn't old friends meeting for ice cream and a catch-up, it's two people that don't know or trust one another—two enemies on opposite sides of the battlefield—here to arrange a business deal.

Slotting his hand into his suit jacket, he slides a white envelope out of his inner pocket. I watch with hawk-like eyes as he sets it on the table and slowly pushes it toward me.

"What the fuck is that?" I demand, making no effort to take it. I *know* what it is, and I'm not fucking touching it.

"Your money—"

"I'm not taking that." I shove it across the table toward him, ignoring his frown of confusion. Slowly, he reaches out and tucks it away in his pocket again.

"Why then—"

"You owe me a favor," I cut over him with a hint of steel.

His lips flatten, most likely in annoyance. "In my defense, you never asked any questions. You never wanted to know—"

I bark a cold laugh. "I don't give a shit who you are, *Enzo*—or whatever your name is." My tone is arctic, giving away none of the roiling emotions brewing within me. Because the truth is, it does bother me. It bothers me that he never told me, but it bothers me even more that I never fucking asked. It has made me realize I've been running around with blinders on, only seeing the cash right in front of me and not stopping to question the source. How fucking naive and short-sighted of me. "I care that I nearly got blown to pieces because of you."

No, I absolutely will not acknowledge the part I played on that day. Yeah, he tried to warn me, but he didn't try hard enough as far as I'm concerned. Even when he knew he was putting my life on the line, keeping his identity a secret came first. However, I can't exactly blame him for that. I'd have done the same if it was me, but that doesn't mean I'm not going to use his guilt to get what I want.

I watch as the muscle at the back of his jaw works before he finally grinds out, "It is Enzo—my name."

Yeah, sure it is, and in my spare time, I like to wear big, puffy dresses and pretend I'm a princess.

It's a struggle to restrain my eye roll, because, of course, that's what he's going to say. He might have confessed he was an Antonelli, but he's not dumb enough to give up his real name. To hand over something individually identifying that I could use to find out everything I need to know about him.

Anger flares in his eyes, clearly seeing that I don't believe him. "Lorenzo," he spits out, "is my full name, but Enzo to you."

My eyes narrow as I try to determine if he's telling the truth. Lorenzo could fit. It's Italian enough to match the hint of swarthy skin I've admired far too frequently when he wore t-shirts to our meetings... but equally, it could be complete and utter bullshit. The problem is, I can't tell, and really, does it matter?

"Alright, *Enzo*." I put enough emphasis on his name to let him know I still don't fully believe him, something that only pisses him off further. His hand twitches on the table, his fingers curling into a fist. For a moment, I tense in my seat, wondering what he's planning on doing, but after a second, his shoulders drop and he relaxes, the anger ebbing away. However, when I finally look away from the hand that was coiled into a fist, looking ready to slam right through the table, I find his expression is even more shut down than it was before, and a heavy silence hangs in the air between us.

He tilts his head to either side as if working out the kinks in his neck while running his hand over his already straight black tie. It's as though he's trying to get control of himself, and I find it weirdly fascinating to watch. When he's done, he fixes me with his probing gaze for a long moment before asking in a cool, calm, collected tone, "What's the favor?"

While he appears guarded and unbothered, the simple fact that he's asking means I've got him on the hook, and I give him a wolfish grin. "A job." His brows furrow in confusion, but I don't give him a chance to speak before continuing. "Specifically, a job in Belle Donne."

Even though his eyebrows hitch in surprise, he continues with his carefully neutral tone as he asks, "What makes you think I can do that?"

My arms had been resting on top of the table, and crossing them in front of me, I lean in, closing the distance between us. "You're a resourceful guy. I think you can find a way to make it happen." With nothing else to say to him, I plant my hands on the table and stand. Holding his gaze, I state, "You have one week," before sliding out of the booth.

He's only a second behind me as he gets to his feet, blocking my way out of the parlor. My gaze catches his as I scowl at him. It doesn't faze him, though, and instead, he meets my stare with a steadfast one of his own.

"I'll get it done," he states confidently. He takes a step toward me, forcing me to tilt my head back if I want to maintain eye contact as he eliminates the small space between us. His superior height has him towering over me, and he ducks his head, bringing his lips to my ear. "But don't think for one second that you have the upper hand here. You should view my amiability as the apology I intend it to be. I'm not under your thumb, and I won't bend to your commands. I may have a soft spot for you, Sawyer, but I don't fear the Reaper."

My lips part in surprise. The sound of my real name on his lips slaps me across the face, clashing with a memory of him saying it in a much more concerned tone the day of the explosion. *How had I forgotten that?* What's more bothersome is the realization that he knows my deepest, darkest secret. I'm frozen speechless as he once again stands to his full height in front of me, giving me a small, impossible-to-discern smile before he turns on his heel. The squeak of his polished shoes against the tile is the only noise as he walks out the door.

I GET THROUGH THE NEXT WEEK BY KEEPING MYSELF BUSY. I CHECK IN ON Sheryl and Grace, who seem to be really flourishing away from Python's control, and take on three Reaper jobs in between shifts at Strip Tease. Anything to stop me from thinking, because every time I stop, for even a second, my mind goes into overdrive. I feel like I'm slowly losing control of everything around me, and I'm struggling to cope with all of this change and ambiguity. Every single moment of my life growing up was filled with uncertainty. With a drug addict mom who dances to the beat of her own drum, coming home whenever suits and dragging strange men into the house without a care for her children's safety, it's safe to say I had a less than stable upbringing. Following that with years of living on the street where every day is a new battle and you never knew what was in store for you, a life of inconsistency and constant change was all I knew.

Until I got us into this apartment. Ever since I got us off the streets, I've worked seriously fucking hard to ensure every aspect of my life is under *my* control. Yet, somehow I've managed to go from keeping the Reaper a carefully concealed secret to now three people—three people I don't remotely trust—knowing my hidden identity. It's concerning, to say the least, and I'm twitchy and restless all week, unable to function knowing I have no control over any of it. I keep expecting to get ambushed or come home to the apartment building ablaze as a result of one of Antonellis' strikes. The Rejects at least have a vested interest in keeping my identity a secret, but what does Enzo want? And who else has he told?

The stress of it all has me strung out and on edge, and Luc has had to bear the brunt of my shitty mood all week.

"Jesus, Sawyer, you're a fucking bitch this week," Luc grumbles when I blow a fuse at him for leaving his sweaty clothes all over the bathroom.

"Hey!" I snap, spinning to glower at him. "Watch that tone, mister."

He simply rolls his eyes. "Whatever. You don't need to take your PMS bullshit out on me." He stomps into his room and returns a moment later with a bag slung over his back.

"Where the fuck are you going?" I demand, scowling at the bag as if I can magically remove it from his shoulder and back into his room by sheer will.

"I'm going to stay with Jon and the guys for a few days, until this"—he waves his hand in my general direction—"has fucked off."

"Like hell, you're going to stay in a gang clubhouse," I laugh humorlessly. The whole point of me constantly arguing with Cain over the issue is because I don't want Luc exposed to that life twenty-four seven.

"Well, I'm sure as fuck not putting up with your shit for another day." He shakes his head. "I don't know what has been going on with you recently, but you need to sort it out."

As I open my mouth to respond, there's a sharp knock at the front door and Luc spears me with a deadly look before moving past me to answer it.

I hear the flicking of the lock before the door opens, followed by Luc's low voice. "Hey, man... yeah, give me a sec." He ducks his head back into the living room. "I'm heading out. I've got my phone on me, and you know where to reach me..." He lingers for a second as I swallow roughly, struggling to find my voice. I'm worried that if I try to speak, I'll end up barking at him. I don't want to make things even worse between us, so instead, I just stand there mutely, watching through blurry eyes as he walks out the door, leaving me alone.

The second I hear the car engine start on the street outside, I grab the closest thing to me—a glass—and chuck it at the wall. I can't handle this lack of control and having my strings pulled in different directions. I'm used to being in charge of my life, of not answering to anyone. Sagging onto the sofa, I release a long, unsteady breath, letting out some of the stress from the last week.

There's nothing I can do about Enzo right now. He's obviously known my identity for years, and no one has come after me, so I can only hope he won't say anything for the time being. As for Cain and Oliver, I need to learn to trust them. Cain's a pain in my ass, but he's one I can handle. Oliver... Well, he's a completely different can of worms. He's not a threat, but he is a hazard to my heart, and every time I'm around him, I feel myself softening toward him, craving his touch. My stomach turns into a riot of butterflies every time he so much as looks at me, and I've got no idea how to make it stop. It doesn't help that he knows how much he affects me and plays on that every time I'm around him. How did my life become such a fucking mess in the space of a few weeks?

I let myself wallow in self-pity at the chaos that is my life before picking myself off the sofa and getting ready for my shift at Strip Tease tonight. At least that's one part of my life that's continuing as normal. It's the one time I can pretend everything in my life is the same predictable routine it used to be. When my heartstrings weren't being pulled at, and my head wasn't second-guessing my every thought and action. When putting food on the table, paying rent, and killing abusive assholes were all I had to worry about. *That* I could handle. It was as easy as breathing. But trying to trust the very type of people I've been taught to avoid? Worse, to feel some sort of kinship with them? That goes against every fiber of my being. The more time I spend around Cain and Oliver, Jon and the kids, and even the other Rejects, the more I want to let my barriers down. I *want* to trust them. Hell, if we have any hope of achieving what we want to, I *need* to trust them. But *fuck,* actually putting that trust in them feels about as comfortable as not breathing.

My shift goes by in the usual fashion of groping, drunken males, and sleazy comments, all of which I navigate with a tight smile as weariness tugs at me. *I'm getting too old for this shit.* By the time I'm leaving the club in the early hours of the morning, all I can think about is collapsing face-first onto my bed. Even the gnawing worry over Luc won't be enough to keep me awake.

I stutter to a stop as I reach the sidewalk and find Oliver leaning against his car. "What are you doing here?"

"Jon said Luc was staying with us for a few days, I figured you'd want an invite, too."

I cock a brow. "Luc and I are not moving into the clubhouse," I state adamantly. "We just... had an argument."

Oliver has enough sense to squash the smirk pulling at his lips. "I never said you were. Just figured, if he's there, then you'd wanna be too."

I hesitate for a second, but ultimately, if Luc is there, I'd rather be nearby. Just in case. Besides, the thought of going home to an empty apartment doesn't sound all that appealing.

"Sure," I agree. "But I need to go home to grab some stuff."

With a nod, he pushes off the side of the car and walks around to the driver's side while I climb in beside him, and we drive over to my apartment.

"You don't have to come up," I begin, when he gets out of the car. "I'll only be a minute."

He just shrugs and continues to follow me through the door. I glance around nervously as he trails behind me, taking in the grimy walls and threadbare carpet with fresh eyes and wondering what Oliver thinks of the shabby interior of my building. By the time we reach the door to my apartment, my palms are sweaty, and I'm mentally berating myself for even caring what he thinks.

No one in Black Creek has money. I'm sure he's well used to buildings like this.

God, has there always been the stench of piss in the hallway, or is that new?

Stop it! Who cares what he thinks? I thought you had no interest in being with him anyway.

I stifle my groan as I push open the door to my apartment and step in, but before I have a chance to worry about the state of the place, Oliver is pulling on my arm, spinning me around to face him as he kicks the door shut with his foot.

His hands are in my hair, his lips on mine before I've even processed what's happened, and suddenly, I'm drowning in the feel of him. In the possessive hold he has on my hair and the hard press of his hips against mine.

"Let me in," he growls, biting my lower lip. I know he's not talking about right now, as I've lost all control over my body. I couldn't keep him out if I tried. "Stop pushing me away." It's another husky command, delivered with a searing kiss that leaves me breathless before he moves to kiss his way down my neck. He pushes his thigh between my legs, and all I can do is fist his shirt and pull him closer as he drives me wild with his mouth.

His lips return to mine, devouring me, and I lose all rational thought as he claims me with every swipe of his tongue. It takes far longer than it should before I find the strength to push him back.

"We're working together," I begin in a strained, breathless voice that sounds weak, even to me.

"So?" His voice drips sex, and I can tell his thoughts aren't really on the conversation. Fuck, I don't blame him. Even I am struggling to focus.

"So, whatever *this* is will get in the way of that. It'll stop us from being objective and doing what needs to be done. If we were a thing, you might think you have a say in what I do. You might try to stop me if, for instance, I get a job in a sex club to get close to the Antonellis."

That statement is enough to gain his full attention, and he pulls back so he can look me in the eye.

"What? Are we talking hypotheticals here?"

I shake my head. "Nope."

His brows knit together, and he peers deep into my eyes as if needing further confirmation that I'm not lying to him. "How? When?"

Pushing him back a step, I shake my head. "I'll explain it all when we're at the clubhouse. I'm sure Cain will want to have a say too."

Reluctantly, he lets me move away from him, and I retreat to my bedroom, where I quickly pack a bag, ensuring I tuck my gun in it and strap one of my daggers to my thigh. You can guarantee every one of the Rejects will be armed, so you can be damn sure I will be too.

Tossing the bag on my back, I pause in front of the mirror. I run my hand through my hair, pulling it out from beneath the strap before fixing my leather jacket. With a once-over of my black skinny jeans and chunky-heeled boots, I grin at the striking image I present with the dagger slotted in a sheath around my thigh and stride from the room.

"Holy shit," Oliver murmurs when I step into the living room.

He not so subtly reaches down to adjust himself, and I smirk as I walk past, quirking a brow. "Are you coming?"

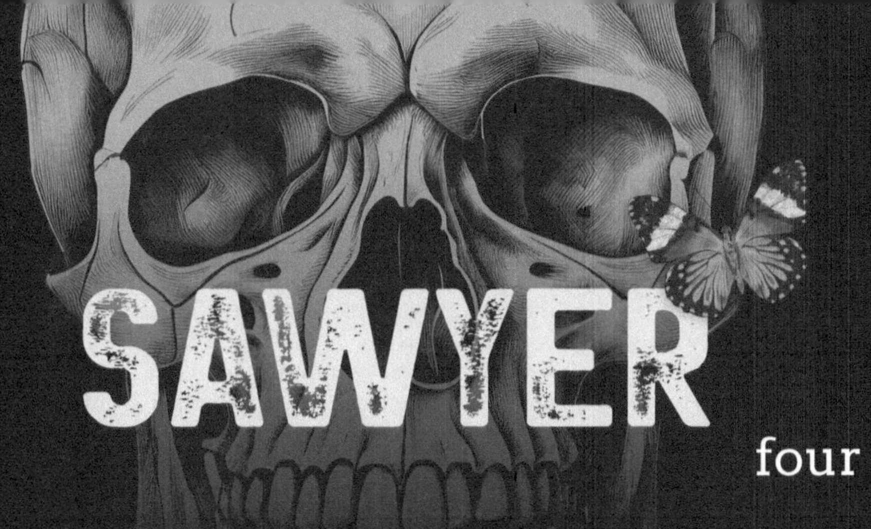

"I'll put your bag in the spare bedroom," Oliver says as we climb out of the car at Radiant Park.

"Spare room?" I question, my gaze snapping to his.

"Yeah. There's a spare room beside mine and Cain's."

That fucking asshole! I knew Cain deliberately put me in Oliver's room the night I turned up here with my head injury, but he fucking *knew* there was a spare room next door.

Grumbling under my breath, I stomp up the path to the front door, slowing as the steady thud of loud music makes its way to me through the walls.

"Are you having a party?"

Oliver gives a casual shrug. "Just a typical night."

I roll my eyes, hoping my luck isn't so bad that I'm about to walk in on a room of hairy gangbangers fucking girls on every available surface as I push open the door and step into the once-lobby-now-bar. The music is much louder inside, but I'm pleasantly surprised to find most of the Rejects sitting around talking to one another or dancing with girls. *By gang member standards, I guess it's still early.* I'm even happier to discover that neither Luc nor any of the kids are present.

"Where are—"

"Game room. At the back of the building," Oliver answers before I can even finish. "We're not complete heathens, you know."

Right. I don't know why I keep expecting them to be. Every time I anticipate the worst, they surprise me. I should probably start raising my expectations. They aren't like the other gangs I have dealt with, and I need to accept that.

"Go get yourself a drink. I'll be back in a sec." Oliver gestures toward the bar before disappearing down the back hallway, and I do as he suggested, helping myself to a beer before scanning my eyes around the room. They've done a good job of fixing up the place, with large booths and smaller tables interspersed around the room, and a small dance floor at one end. It's a typical gang clubhouse in every shape and form, except for the people who reside within its walls.

Bringing the bottle to my lips, I take a sip of the cool, bitter drink, but I almost choke when my eyes land on a stripper pole in the corner of the room, behind the dance floor. *Seriously?* I roll my eyes and continue my exploration until I spot Cain on a sofa in the back corner, with some girl grinding in his lap.

My hand involuntarily tightens around the beer bottle, and I grit my teeth against the ugly feeling of jealousy that rises in my stomach. There's no way I'm going to allow myself to feel jealous over that asshole. One orgasmic quickie is not enough to overcome his shitty attitude and frequent tendency to piss me off.

As a genius idea comes to mind, I take another swig of my beer and saunter across the room toward the jerkweed himself, plonking my ass down beside him. He startles, ungluing his lips from the girl attached to them long enough to scowl at me.

"Fuck off, Red. I'm busy."

"I just thought I'd come check if you got that penis problem sorted out okay," I reply in a sweet-as-pie voice.

"What penis problem?" the girl in his lap asks, her gaze darting between Cain and me.

"Oh, it's probably nothing to worry about. Nothing an intense course of antibiotics won't cure, I'm sure." Despite the reassurance in my tone, I dart an unsure glance toward Cain's crotch, which is enough to have the woman jumping out of his lap, looking horrified.

"I didn't need antibiotics," Cain growls angrily. His words only encourage the woman to take another step away from him. "I didn't mean it like that," he snaps, growing more irritated by the second. He throws a hostile glower my way before fixing his attention on the girl, attempting to coax her back onto his lap. "She's lying."

I gasp. "Cain! You didn't get it treated? Oh my god! What if it falls off?!" I have to bite the inside of my cheek to stop myself from laughing as the woman backs up another step, ensuring she's well out of Cain's reach for fear that he might drag her anywhere near his infected cock. Her eyes keep flicking toward his crotch, as if she's expecting his dick to fall out of his pants at any second. It's fucking hilarious.

Not waiting to hear anything more, she spins on her high heels, not even making up some sort of excuse before she disappears into the crowd on the dancefloor and leaves me with a seething Cain. Despite the volatile energy crackling in the air around him, I lean back in my seat, feeling triumphant as I take another sip of beer.

"I hope you're happy now," he snarls, spearing me with a deadly look. "If you wanted another go on my dick, all you had to do was ask."

I choke and start coughing as I gape at him. "Once was enough, thanks," I retort with a scowl when I finally find my words again.

"Uh-huh, sure it was." The jackass' cocky tone has me narrowing my eyes at him as he throws his arm over the back of the sofa behind me and leans in, invading my personal space. "That's why you can't stop thinking about me, remembering how fucking good it felt to have your pussy stuffed with my cock." He chuckles, the sound wholly darkness and pure sex that makes my breathing hitch. "The way you screamed my name, it was like a fucking symphony."

Holy Mary, Mother of Jesus. I don't even remember calling out his name; that's how fucking lost I was to the intensity of that orgasm. I can feel his heated gaze burning through my skin as I struggle to swallow given my sudden parched mouth, but a moment later, he leans back into the couch cushions, removing his arm from the back of the sofa as though nothing happened.

By the time Oliver returns, he's sipping casually on his beer. Meanwhile, I'm still a molten-hot mess of hormones as I struggle not to squirm in my seat.

"All good here?" Oliver asks, taking a seat on my other side. He casually drapes his arm along the back of the sofa behind me—where only a moment ago Cain's was perched—ensuring his fingers brush the strip of skin at the back of my neck. *Fucking hell, these men are trying to kill me.* I shiver at his touch, a reaction that doesn't go unnoticed by either of them as they both glance my way. As good as their combined gazes feel, I am *so* not entertaining that line of thought, and instead, I awkwardly clear my throat. "So... this is what you guys do every night?"

"Only on nights when we're not throwing raging gang bangs and snorting coke like there's no tomorrow," Cain drawls, his tone heavy with sarcasm.

"It's a good way for the guys to chill out and relax on nights when we don't have the cage or pit fights running, or any Reject crap going on," Oliver offers, ignoring Cain.

"Speaking of relaxing..." Fishing in his pocket, Cain pulls out a joint, grinning as he snatches a lighter off the table and, bringing the spliff to his lips, he lights it up. He takes a long drag, the tip glowing red before he leans his head back and blows the smoke out in a slow, steady stream.

A lazy grin crosses his face as he sags into the seat, passing the joint my way. Hesitating for only a second, I take it from his outstretched hand and bring it to my lips. Cain turns his head to watch as I wrap my lips around the butt, and I hold his gaze as I inhale, holding the smoke in my lungs for a moment before breathing out.

"Mmm." It's been a long time since I let myself unwind with a beer and a joint. I obviously don't do it in the apartment, around Luc, and there's usually no way I'd let myself lower my guard enough when I'm out in public. Surprisingly though, I don't feel the need to be on alert here. Which is crazy considering I'm in the middle of a gang clubhouse, where any number of dangers could arise at any moment. Yet, pressed between Oliver and Cain, I feel relatively safe. *Huh, maybe I am starting to trust them after all.* Although, it's hard not to feel safe when you are encased between two hard bricks of solid muscle. "I'm surprised, Cain. You don't strike me as the stoner type."

He scoffs. "Like you know anything about me."

I cock a brow at the challenge in his tone, taking another tug of the spliff. "Someone like you doesn't give up control easily. You wouldn't be the leader of the Rejects if you did."

Slowly, he lifts his head off the back of the sofa, and reaching out with one hand, he grabs my wrist, holding it still as he leans in to take another draw. "Maybe so, but in this life, you never know when you are going to meet your maker." He meets my gaze before continuing. "I'd rather face death with some fun, drunken, high memories than just the endless void of my failure."

My lips part in surprise, unsure how to respond to that. Despite his cavalier tone, the pain is clear to see in his eyes, and I can only assume he's talking about his sister, the one Oliver told me about. The whole reason for Cain's all-consuming path of vengeance.

Breaking off our stare and ending the weird, intense moment, he flops back into the couch just as Oliver steals the joint from between my fingers, taking his own draw. *Oops, guess I forgot to hand it over.*

I give him a quizzical look as Cain sighs heavily beside me, sounding like he's carrying the weight of the world in that single breath.

"Don't worry about him," Oliver answers. "He can become a melancholy mood-killer after a few drinks and a bit of weed." I don't miss the worried gaze he sends Cain's way, though, before offering me a reassuring smile.

We lapse into silence, watching the other Rejects party around us as we pass the joint back and forth. I feel the tension seep from my body with every tug, a mellow high making me feel light and floaty. *Damn,* it has been way too long since I let myself unwind this much.

I stretch my neck from side to side, working out the kinks, and Oliver moves his hand to massage the muscles along the back of my neck.

"Ooohhh." My eyes drift shut beneath his heavenly touch, and I don't realize how dirty that sounded until I open them to find Cain watching me with a heated gaze.

Finding a particularly tight knot, Oliver digs his fingers in, kneading the muscle, and I have to bite down on my groan of satisfaction. *Holy crap, that feels so fucking good.*

"God, you are tense," he muses, digging his fingers deeper into the muscle. "You're as bad as Cain, with all the stress."

"Do you give him neck massages too?" I joke, shifting in my seat so Oliver can have better access to my neck. His fingers are fucking magical.

He scoffs, lifting his other hand to knead the muscles on both sides. "He fucking wishes."

Lifting my feet onto the sofa, I cross them over as I turn sideways in my seat. The angle has me with my back to Oliver, my knees pressing into Cain's hip and thigh, not that he seems to mind as he stares obsessively at where Oliver is touching me.

"So, what has you all stressed?" Oliver probes, frazzling my brain as he continues to work his magic.

I snort. "What doesn't? My entire life is stress."

"Mmm," Oliver agrees noncommittally when I don't elaborate. My eyes grow heavy with every press of his thumbs into my skin, only exacerbated by the weed, but I still shiver when he leans in to murmur in my ear. "What *specifically* has you stressed?"

I'm too mellowed out to worry about my usual filter, and instead, I find myself opening up to him—to both of them. "Luc, mostly. I worry about his future. I worry that he won't make it to eighteen if we stay in this town, but I don't have the means to get us out of here. I worry about what would happen to him if something happened to me. I worry that this war we're starting will kill us all."

My words are followed by a moment of silence as Oliver continues to work his magic on my neck, and Cain just stares at me. Truly stares at me, like he's seeing me for the first time.

"You know, we could help you with some of that," Oliver offers.

"You're already doing enough, looking out for Luc."

I can feel the warmth of his breath against my ear as he murmurs in a low voice, "We could look out for you too." The soft husk sends a shiver racing along my spine, and I get the distinct impression that there is a deeper meaning to his words.

Cain's eyes are still on mine as he watches me closely with a strange, candid expression. I'm not sure if he's just baked or having some kind of epiphany, but it's all too much, and I quickly get to my feet, shaking off Oliver's touch as I clear my throat. "I, uh... It's been a long day, and I'm wrecked." Unable to meet their gazes, I linger for another second before forcing my feet into action and going in search of the spare bedroom.

I'M AWAKE EARLY THE NEXT MORNING. THERE'S SOMETHING ABOUT sleeping in a bed that isn't yours that always has me up at a crazy early hour of the day, even though I slept like a baby after the alcohol-weed combo last night.

Grabbing a pair of leggings, a sports bra, and sneakers out of my bag, I toss my hair up in a messy bun. I figure there must be somewhere around here to work out. There's no way a bunch of guys do not have some sort of gym facility. Heck, they gutted the sports complex across the road. Surely they left part of it intact so they'd have somewhere to work out.

Cautiously, I step out of my room, looking around, but with it being just after dawn, everyone seems to be still asleep. I take my time, wandering around until I work my way back to the bar. I pause just inside the door when I find Jon standing in the middle of the room, downing some green-colored drink.

"Oh, hey," he greets when he spots me standing there. "What are you doing up so early?"

"Just thought I'd see if you guys had a gym around here somewhere."

"Sure. I'm heading over there now. I can show you where it is. Just give me a sec."

He rushes into the kitchen before I get a chance to respond, emerging a moment later with another green beverage.

"Here." He throws the bottle toward me, and I easily catch it, reading the label with disgust.

"What the fuck is this?" I ask, looking up at him with a frown.

"Green juice. It's good for you. Healthiest way to start the day."

Hesitantly, I unscrew the lid and bring the bottle to my lips, ignoring the vile green color as the liquid flows into my mouth. I barely manage a sip before I pull back, fighting a gag.

"What the fuck?! That's disgusting!" With a wrinkled nose, I gape at Jon. "How do you drink that shit?"

He rolls his eyes, moving to snatch the bottle from my hand. "It's the best way to fuel your body. Full of nutrients and vitamins and all that crap."

"Yeah, no thanks. I've survived just fine all these years on cereal and milk, so I think I'll stick to that."

"Suit yourself." He shrugs, grabbing a towel off a nearby table before heading toward the outer door. "You'll regret it when you burn out during your morning workout, though."

With a frown, I follow him out the door and over to the sports complex turned fighting pit. Rather than going through the front entrance, as I expected, he heads around the back of the building, where I watched him and Luc and some of the others playing basketball a few weeks ago. He moves toward a steel door I hadn't noticed before and types in a passcode before pulling it open. Stepping to the side, he gestures for me to go ahead of him. "Ladies first." He grins brightly, and I can't tell if he's fucking with me or being genuinely chivalrous as I warily move past him into the darkened interior.

I stop just inside the doorway, not wanting to move too far into the dark room, and he follows me in. The heavy door slams shut behind him, bathing us in darkness for a tense moment that seems to last a lifetime before I hear the flick of a switch. It's followed a second later by a low buzzing sound before the bright overhead fluorescent lights turn on, illuminating the ample space kitted out with various weight-based machines and a large area covered in mats perfect for sparring.

I take a second to look around as Jon moves to set his bottle of disgusting juice on the ground, along with his towel, before grabbing a couple of water bottles from a mini-fridge at one side of the room.

Chewing on my bottom lip, I turn to face him. I haven't seen him in action, but if what Oliver told me is true, Jon—just like the other kids—is one hell of a fighter. "I know some basic defense moves," I blurt out, "but I want you to teach me some offensive moves."

His gaze runs over my body in an assessing, critical manner as he quirks a brow in surprise. "You were able to handle yourself well enough that day in the alley."

I'm already shaking my head before he's finished speaking. "It's not enough. It's basic defensive moves. I need to be able to protect myself better if I'm up against someone more skilled." Things are going to get really bad in Black Creek, and I need to be confident that I can protect myself and Luc. Taking on the Antonellis isn't going to be like anything I've done before. I can't solely rely on catching them off guard and using seduction tactics to get under their defenses. They're smarter than that. What little fighting skills I've picked up on the street, and honed from Hadley, have been enough to get me this far, but I need to know more; to be better.

He thinks it over for another moment before nodding in agreement. "Alright, yeah. Let's see what you've got."

We spar for the next hour or so, while Jon gets a feel for where I'm at and begins teaching me a few new moves.

"Where did you say you learned how to fight?" he asks, calling a timeout. I'm panting heavily and, thankful for the break, I collapse onto the mats. The jerk isn't even breaking a sweat. How the fuck is that possible?

He moves to the corner of the room, returning a second later with a bottle of water, holding it out for me.

"I didn't," I answer, accepting the bottle from his outstretched hand. I guzzle down half of it, avoiding giving him an actual answer as his questioning gaze lingers on me. His head is slightly tilted, his eyes narrowed as he scrutinizes me for a long moment.

"Your fighting style is unusual," he murmurs, almost to himself, still watching me far too closely for my liking.

Licking my lips, I give him a casual shrug as I push to my feet, ready to go again. "Teach me how you did that takedown," I say instead. Thankfully it's enough to shake him out of his musings as we move back into the middle of the mats.

Literally, five minutes later, he's got me pinned to the mat in a move that I'm pretty sure, if this were a real fight, would have me crushed like a bug beneath him, when suddenly his phone goes off in the pocket of his shorts.

"Hey, boss. What's up?" he asks, answering the call. "Yeah, she's here." He looks down at me, where I'm lying on the mat in a panting, sweaty mess. "Sure thing, be right there."

Hanging up, he tucks the phone into his pocket before grinning. "Training session is over. Bossman wants to talk to you." I roll my eyes, clearly not as eager as Jon to follow Cain's orders. "Whatever you did, he sounded pissed."

"Isn't that just his usual setting?" I grumble as he helps me to my feet, barking out a laugh.

"Oh, it's definitely worse when he's around you."

Oh great, what a compliment.

"I want to do this again," I insist, taking a towel from his outstretched hand and wiping the sweat from my face. "Like a weekly thing, or whatever you have time for."

"Sure, I can do that," he readily agrees, grabbing his towel from the floor and wiping it over his face and through his hair, although god knows why when there isn't a drop of sweat on him. Like seriously, he looks like he's spent the last hour sitting in a chair, reading. Meanwhile, I stink and I'm in desperate need of a shower.

Just before we leave the gym, I reach out and grab a hold of Jon's arm, pulling him to a stop before he can flick the light off. He half-turns toward me, a question in his eyes. "You're looking out for Luc?" It's not a question, more of an order. One he seems to recognize.

"I am. I will."

"No matter what."

He turns to face me fully, and the steady way he holds my gaze reassures me more than anything he says. "I *promise* you, Red. He's my number one concern at all times. Me and the guys are takin' good care of him, and we will continue to do so, no matter what."

When I'm satisfied he means what he's saying, I let go of his arm, giving a sharp jerk of my head. "Thank you," I mutter, feeling strangely emotional.

He just gives me one of his lopsided grins. "Luc's lucky to have a sister who fights so fiercely to protect him." Something flashes across his eyes, but it's gone before I can pinpoint it, and he's back to his usual carefree self as we make our way back across the road to the clubhouse.

"Can I ask you something?" he asks curiously as we enter the clubhouse.

I eye him out of the corner of my eye but answer casually. "Sure."

"Would you mind if I taught Luc some of the stuff we were doing today?"

I think it over for a second, appreciating that he thought to ask me first. "Yeah, I think that would be really good, actually." I'm surprised I hadn't thought of it. I'd feel a hell of a lot happier if I knew Luc could defend himself should something happen when I'm not around or if one of the kids can't get to him in time. I pause at the entrance to the back hallway and turn to face him. "But, no pit fights, cage fights, or any other type of unsanctioned whatever-you-called-it fighting."

"Deal," he agrees immediately, grinning. "There's no way Cain would allow that anyway at his age."

It's something Jon has mentioned to me before. At the time, I couldn't understand why Cain would put such a rule in place. I'd ignorantly assumed that if the kids were as good as Jon claimed they were, Cain would want them in the fights to help bring in more money for the club. But now I can see it for what it was. Cain was providing these kids with a place where they could feel safe but where they could also be themselves. Having watched several of them in the ring, I've seen firsthand how much each of them craves the adrenaline rush that comes from a fight. Cain offered them that, within as safe of an environment as he could. What does that say about Cain, that he willingly brought in these lost, damaged kids and built the perfect sanctuary for them?

Not wanting to analyze it too closely—because it might mean, beneath that barbed exterior, Cain might have a heart after all—I dislodge that train of thought and give a brisk nod of farewell to Jon, assuming that he would be heading off to his room or something after our workout. So when he follows me down the back corridor instead, I pause. "Eh, what are you doing?"

His brows pull down in a frown. "Walking you to Cain's office."

"You really don't have to do that. I know where it is, besides, I need a shower first."

"No can do. Cain's orders were for me to take you straight to him."

My eyes widen in surprise as I gape at him. "So you're basically planning on hand-delivering me to him, like I'm a bouquet of flowers?"

He gives an unapologetic shrug. "Boss's orders."

"Yeah, yeah." With a roll of my eyes and a heavier stomp to my steps, I head toward Cain's office with my dutiful shadow behind me. Not bothering to knock on the door, I shove it open, ignoring Jon's soft chuckle as I step inside.

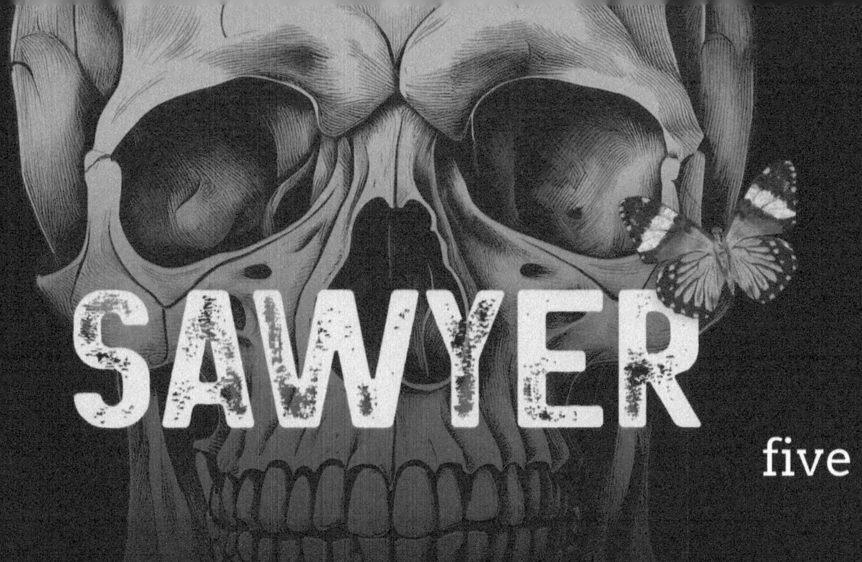

five

$\mathbf{B}$oth Reject leaders are waiting for me inside the office, but it's Cain who garners my attention with his furious scowl. Whatever openness was in his eyes last night is long gone now, without the disinhibiting effects of weed and alcohol to soften him.

Well, fine. I can forget all about last night, too. "You summoned me," I bite angrily at him, crossing my arms over my chest and raising a brow, ignoring how utterly delicious the two of them look. I'd almost think they dressed deliberately to try and distract me. In fact, perhaps that was Oliver's intention. Where Cain is dressed in his usual all-black outfit of boots, jeans, and Henley, Oliver's appearance is jarring. He looks like he's just rolled out of bed—hell, maybe he did—with his mussed-up hair, low-slung gray sweatpants, and a loose-fitting t-shirt. Although I've seen just how toned he is, and with the knowledge of just how drool-worthy his chest and abs are underneath that top, it is definitely threatening to interfere with the attitude I'm throwing in Cain's direction.

"What the hell is this I hear about you getting a job in one of Antonelli's sex clubs?" Cain's sharp tone drags my mind out of the gutter as I narrow my eyes on him in warning. I had planned to tell both of them about my plan today, but I guess we aren't going to be discussing it like reasonable adults based on the anger radiating off of him.

"You hired me to do a job, so that's what I'm doing," I argue rationally. It's not like I discuss the process with any other clients. However, I can safely admit that this isn't like any other job I've taken on as the Reaper. I'm not even sure I can technically call it a job. It's definitely not *just* a job, but that doesn't mean I'm going to let either of them call the shots here. They sought me out for a reason—because they need me. Now, they are allowing their stupidly ingrained primal instinct to protect women—because, admittedly, they are relatively decent human beings—prevent them from thinking logically. But what they don't realize is that my femininity is what makes me the perfect secret weapon.

"How did you even manage to get a job in one of their clubs?" Cain asks incredulously. His lack of faith in me is offensive. He's the one that hounded me for the

Reaper's identity, and here he is, treating me like a weak little girl who needs protecting instead of the feared Reaper that I am.

"I have my ways," I respond vaguely, with a tight smile. Enzo called me during work yesterday to let me know he'd secured me a job as a dancer at Belle Donne. "I *am* the Reaper, after all." I sense Cain needs the reminder of just whom he's dealing with. When we're discussing business, it's the Reaper he's dealing with, not Red, the stripper.

"And what's your big plan? How is shaking your ass on a stage going to get you closer to Giovanni or his men?" His words are an angry snarl that I seriously don't appreciate.

I quirk an eyebrow in challenge. "I saw Dante there once. I'm ho—"

"Why the hell were you at an Antonelli Club?" Cain growls, cutting me off.

I grit my teeth, struggling to keep a lid on my own temper. How does this infuriating fuckwit always manage to make my blood pressure spike?! "I was there for a Reaper job," I hiss out.

His lips purse in disapproval, but Oliver intervenes—always the peacekeeper. "What club?"

Ignoring Cain's smoldering glower, I turn to give Oliver my attention. "Belle Donne. I start on Thursday."

"We'll need a copy of your schedule." I open my mouth to protest, but he cuts me off. "It's non-negotiable, Red. I get that you're used to working alone, but we're a team when it comes to the Antonellis. That's how the Rejects work, so while you're in the club, we *will* have people keeping an eye on the place and ensuring you're safe."

My mouth opens and closes a few times as I struggle to find a response to that. Unable to think of a good excuse, and honestly a little relieved to know I won't be all alone, especially since I won't be able to carry any weapons on me when I'm up on stage, I eventually just nod in acceptance. "Okay, I'll get you my schedule."

I can still feel the tension radiating off Cain, but he has the good grace to keep his trap shut. Barely sparing him a glance, I sarcastically snap, "Are we done here? I could really do with a shower."

My words seem to act as some sort of homing beacon as the two of them drop their gazes to rake over my body. Oliver's eyes are molten heat, whereas Cain looks like he's torn between being turned on or pissed off. My leggings cling to my legs and hips, my toned stomach on display, and when I glance down, I realize my stance with my arms across my chest pushes the girls together, basically begging for someone to motorboat them.

"Yeah," Oliver responds, sounding a tad distracted as he cuts across Cain's short fuse—which looks like it's about to burn out. "We're done."

Nodding, I ignore the lick of heat fanning my skin as I exit the office, closing the door behind me. A second later, I hear the explosion from within the room. There's the sound of something hard smacking against wood, and Cain growls, "Seriously, O? You're just going to let her walk into enemy territory?"

"Cain," Oliver sighs. "Isn't that what we hired her to do? If she was a guy, you wouldn't be thinking twice about it."

"Yeah, but she's not a guy!"

There's a second's silence before Oliver responds. "She's not Evie either," he says softly. "You and I both know she's more than capable of handling herself."

That sounded an awful lot like concern in Cain's voice, and Oliver's response only confirmed it. Cain's lack of faith in my abilities isn't because I have tits and a vagina but because he's having difficulties differentiating me from his sister. I'm not entirely sure what to make of that revelation, and not wanting to eavesdrop anymore, I move away from the door and head in search of my brother. I have some apologizing to do, and Cain's reminder of his lost sister has me wanting to fix things more than ever.

I find him in the first place I check—the game room—hanging out with a couple of the other kids. I recognize their faces, but I don't know their names, so I just give them a small smile before focusing on my brother. "Luc, can I talk to you?"

"Sure." He finishes up with some car racing game he's playing before tossing the controller to one of the other guys and getting to his feet, following me out of the room.

Not really sure where to go, I head toward a fire exit, pushing it open and stepping out the back of the apartment complex. The Rejects obviously haven't done anything back here as the grass is overgrown and half-dead looking, and there's a bunch of old furniture dumped in a pile.

"What's up?" Luc asks, drawing my attention his way.

"I owe you an apology. You were right yesterday. I've been a total bitch recently, and it wasn't fair of me to take it out on you." He quirks a brow, surprised at my honest apology. Yeah, I know, it's not like me, but he was right to lose his cool. I step closer to him, holding his gaze. "You know I love you, and that I'd do anything to protect you. A lot is going on that you don't know about, but things are probably going to get pretty bad. I just... I need to know that you're safe."

His eyes narrow as his eyebrows tug together. "Sawyer, what's going on?"

I shake my head, not wanting him to know more than he needs to. It's for his own safety. "Just promise me you'll be smart. That you won't go anywhere alone, and you'll stick with one of the Reject kids."

"So now you're okay with me hanging out with them?" His tone is more confused than accusatory.

"I mean, I'd rather you hung out with nerdy library kids, but I realize, considering where we live, that that was never going to happen," I joke, trying to lighten the mood.

One side of his lips lifts in a grin. "Based on every teen movie I've ever seen, the quiet nerds are really the crazy ones you need to watch out for."

I snort out a laugh. "So we're okay?"

"Yeah," he sighs, still smiling. "We're good." I wrap my arms around him, and he lets me pull him in for a hug. "I promise I'll be safe, Sawyer," he murmurs in my ear. "You don't need to worry about me."

Yeah, that won't be happening any time soon, but I squeeze him tighter, all the same, feeling much better now that things are good between us again.

"So, you'll be home later?" I ask as we break apart.

"Yeah. I'll be home for dinner, but please tell me you're going to shower before then cause, sis, you stink."

Barking out a laugh and feeling ten times lighter than I did this morning, I shove him on the shoulder, and we head back inside. Once I'm back in the spare bedroom, I head straight for the attached bathroom. Turning on the shower, I quickly strip out of my workout gear and get under the hot spray, feeling the final bit of tension drain from my shoulders as the water seeps into my skin. Having worked out and feeling confident that Jon will be able to help me better defend myself, not to mention having fixed things with Luc, I'm feeling more like myself than I have in weeks. Like I've taken back at least a little bit of control. I feel much happier about letting Luc spend time with the kids after my chat with Jon and seeing just how capable he is in a fight. His skills were... impressive, to say the least. He actually reminded me a little of Hadley, the girl who taught me the basics—well, more than just *the basics*, but not enough to survive the war we have coming our way. A smile ghosts my lips as I think of her and the secret rooftop sessions we had.

"Why do you want to know all this stuff anyway? You're more than good enough to defend yourself against any simple thug or handsy asshole."

I give a casual shrug, unwilling to tell her my plan just yet. I have goals. Plans I fully intend to put into motion—soon. I want to be known as more than just a stripper; more than just another pathetic Black Creek nobody who can't afford to do anything more than work to maintain the shitty little existence they've carved out for themselves. Now that both Luc and I have a safe place to call home, and he's got food in his belly every night, it's time for me to focus on what's next; on the dark figment of a plan that's been festering like an open wound in the back of my mind for years now. Since the day that everything changed for Luc and me.

Because Hadley gets me in a way nobody else ever really has, she doesn't get offended at my refusal to answer her. She simply accepts it for what it is—an unwillingness to share something personal with someone else. It's not like she's not carrying her own secrets. I know absolutely nothing about her, except her name. And I know that's not real since I was the one that obtained the fake documents for her. But hey, that's her business. If she wants to talk to me, I'll be here to listen, and if she doesn't, that's cool too.

"Just be careful, yeah?"

One side of my lips curves up in a grin. "Aww, you wouldn't be worrying about me, would ya?"

She scoffs, shaking her head. "Not a chance, I just don't want to lose the only half-decent sparring partner I've been able to find around here."

Grinning, I get to my feet again, ready to go another round. "I wanna practice that chokehold again. I nearly got it last time."

"Red, you would have been passed out on the ground if I hadn't let go." She says it with a laugh, letting me know she's joking, but I jab her in the ribs and scowl at her anyway, making her laugh harder. The way her voice sounds when she laughs, all raw and husky, makes me think she doesn't do it too often, and it brings a smile to my lips, knowing I'm able to chase away whatever demons are haunting her, if only for a little while. Hadley's done so much for me, teaching me to defend myself and more, so if I can bring a little lightheartedness to her life every once in a while... well, at least I feel like I'm repaying her in some way.

I startle out of my daydreams as I catch a flicker of movement in the doorway. My muscles tense as I struggle to remember if I locked the bedroom door.

Was I seriously floating on such a high when I came in that I forgot to lock the damn door?! God, I can be such a fucking idiot sometimes.

The shower cubicle is all steamed up, making it impossible for me to identify who is in my room. Still, I pretend to continue with my shower, unaware of their presence, while I assess the situation and try to figure out what to do. Whomever it is doesn't come any further into the bathroom, apparently content to wait me out. Not seeing that I have any other option, I wash the last of the suds out of my hair while keeping my eyes on the figure in the doorway. Given their tall height and broad frame, it's definitely a dude, but that's not helpful given I'm in a gang clubhouse that's overrun with men.

Squeezing the water out of my hair, I assess the weight of the shower gel and shampoo bottles before gripping the shampoo—the heavier of the two—firmly in my hand. It's a pretty shitty weapon, but it's better than nothing, and whoever is watching me will notice if I attempt to disconnect the shower hose and use that to strangle them instead. *Let's save that for plan B.*

With my weapon in hand, I shut off the shower but make no move to get out. It's smarter if I can lure them over here rather than risk slipping on wet tiles while I try to fight off someone who is probably three times the size of me. After a moment, the silhouette moves closer, and just before they can reach the shower door, I yank it open, ready to bash them over the head with my shampoo weapon.

"What the—"

"Jesus, fuck. Oliver!" I exclaim, bringing my swinging arm to a halt before the shampoo bottle can collide with his head. "What the fuck were you thinking sneaking into a girl's bedroom while she's showering?!"

My heart is hammering against my chest, the shock causing adrenaline to rush through my system as I try to calm myself.

"In my defense, I didn't know you were in the shower," Oliver states, earning a glare. "But I was debating joining you."

His heated gaze dips to take in my wet, very naked body, and I quickly grab a towel from the counter and wrap it around myself, scowling at him. He's changed out of his sweats into his usual attire of jeans and a t-shirt, but he looks just as hot as he did earlier. Hell, he could be wearing a garbage bag and he'd still look downright fuckable.

"No, Oliver," I chastise, sounding like I'm telling off a naughty puppy that just peed inside the house. "We can't."

Honestly, I'm not sure if I'm trying to convince him of that or myself. He's a determined one, though, Oliver, and as I push past him into the bedroom, he follows on my heels.

"Why not?"

"I already told you why not."

"Because you're going undercover in the Antonellis? I backed you on that, didn't I?"

I purse my lips, unsure how to respond to that because, well, he did kinda have my back in there with Cain. I genuinely thought he would have more to say on the matter. I had *expected* both of them to just outright refuse to let me do it... but Oliver didn't. He *did* support me, even though I could tell he wasn't happy about the idea.

Regardless, I ignore him as I rifle through my duffel bag for some clean underwear, unwilling to accept that maybe—just *maybe*—Oliver has a point. Perhaps we could explore this *thing* between us and still take on the Antonellis.

"Red." My name is nothing more than an agonized, exasperated snarl as he grabs a hold of my upper arm and spins me to face him. I can see the frustration written all over his face. His arm bands around my waist, drawing me in against him. "Stop fighting this."

"I—"

He cuts me off with a scorching kiss that I can feel all the way to my toes, but he doesn't take it further before pulling back. "Just stop," he says quietly, softly against my lips. I don't try to speak again. I'm honestly not even sure what I'd say. I can't think straight this close to him, and whatever reasons I had for not taking this further no longer seem to make any sense.

He slowly brushes his hand up my arm until his fingers stroke across my cheek. "Just feel this," he murmurs. His fingers brush my cheek before he tucks a damp strand of hair behind my ear. Then, with a featherlight touch, he trails his fingers along my jaw and down my neck until his palm is placed firmly against my chest, right over my heart. It's beating so hard, and there's no doubt in my mind that he can feel it hammering against my ribcage as if it's trying to break out of my chest and jump into his. "Do you feel it?"

There's a flicker of doubt in his gaze that makes me feel guilty for making him think this is all one-sided, because it most definitely isn't. Whatever he's feeling, I feel it too, all the way down to my soul.

"I do." My voice is barely more than a whisper, but he hears it nonetheless, his eyes sparkling at the knowledge that he's not alone in this.

"Then stop fighting it. Just feel it; be in it with me." It's almost a desperate plea, and I find myself nodding in agreement, even though I'm not entirely sure what I'm agreeing to or if this is a good idea. God, he's just so damn hard to say *no* to.

His lips quirk up in a sultry grin before he fuses his lips to mine in a kiss so passionate I'm surprised I don't melt into a puddle of goo at his feet. Any last hope I had for my common sense goes out the window as his tongue delves into my mouth, making me groan. I feel like a fucking teenager getting her first kiss. I swear, I've never before been kissed like this, like I'm something precious that needs to be savored. Oliver knows exactly how to toe the line between sweet and adoring, and rough and dirty, and his kiss gives me all sorts of whiplash as he flips back and forth between the two, working me up into a frenzy with just his lips and tongue.

My hands go to his belt buckle, desperate for something to relieve the ache building between my thighs, but before I can get it undone, he steps back, breaking off our kiss.

"I didn't come in here to fuck you." I almost laugh until I see the sincerity in his eyes. The man must be a goddamn saint, but if he thinks for one minute I'm going to let him leave here after getting me all worked up like that, then he's got another thing coming. "This isn't just about sex."

"I know," I admit softly. "I feel it too."

Yup, it's official, all of the endorphins he's putting off are messing with my brain cells. Apparently, I'm just throwing my rulebook out the window. I can tell he believes me, but he still hesitates.

"Oliver," I chuckle, a desperate ring to my voice. "I swear to god, if you don't make me come in the next five minutes, I will make you watch while I do it myself."

His eyes darken with lust, and the gentleman from a moment ago disappears as a savage grin lifts his lips. "I bet that would be one hell of a show, but maybe next time."

In a flash of movement, he throws me onto the bed, whipping my towel off me before I land, leaving me stark naked on the bedspread in front of him.

"Fuck, Red. You get more beautiful every time I see you." His voice has taken on a low, husky quality that only heightens my arousal. Before I can do something embarrassingly girly, like blush, he gets on his knees at the end of the bed, pushing my legs wide to get an unobstructed view of my undoubtedly wet pussy. He stares at it with such heady desire that it leaves me breathless before licking his lips. "You've got no idea how long I've dreamed of tasting you."

"Well, what are you waiting for, then?" My voice is raw, coated in sexual desire, drawing his eyes to my face as he leans forward and licks a line up the length of me.

I moan, tilting my hips for more, and he happily obliges, repeating the action before swirling his tongue around my clit. After a moment, he pulls back, his lips glistening. "Feet on the bed, Trouble. I want you spread wide for me."

Oh, Jesus, if that doesn't turn me on even more.

Doing as he instructs, he works me over with just his tongue until I'm a panting, moaning mess, then he inserts two fingers into my needy cunt, pumping in time to the movement of his tongue on my clit. My hands are in his hair, mussing it up as I grind against his face, desperate for more. I can feel his stubble rubbing against my inner thigh, the rough texture only intensifying the sensations. I'm so close. I can feel my release just about to burst out of me when he inserts a third finger. Three's the magic number, and it sends me careening over the edge into oblivion as I cry out his name. My toes curl into the bedsheet and my head falls back, even as my grip on Oliver's hair tightens. He keeps pumping his fingers and working me over with his tongue until I'm a whimpering, boneless mess. Only then does he give me some relief, pulling away.

I hear him get to his feet, and the sound of a zipper fills the air before clothes hit the floor. Despite how relaxed I feel, I manage to find enough energy to lift my head, taking in all six-and-a-half feet of his gloriously naked body as he pumps his very hard-looking dick.

Catching me watching, he strides toward me, and the bed dips as he pushes one knee into the mattress and begins to climb on top of me. He dips his head to meet my lips, our tongues clashing in a heated kiss. I can taste myself on him, and damn does the combination taste so fucking good.

I wind my arms around his neck, tugging him down on top of me, while I hitch a leg over his hip, bringing the tip of his dick in line with my hot, greedy core. Just before he pushes inside, he pauses, pulling back. "Condom?"

Oh, yes, that pesky little thing. Why do I keep forgetting about that when I'm around these guys?

"Uh, I'm clean. Got tested two weeks ago and haven't had sex since. And I have an implant."

"I'm clean too. Got tested before I was paroled."

"What about since you were released?" I don't know enough about Oliver's past to know when he got out of prison or what he's been up to since, but he shakes his head.

"You are the only person I've slept with since I was arrested."

My lips part at that honest admission, and so many questions flash across my mind, but before I can ask a single one, his lips are back on mine, obliterating all of them as the overwhelming desire to come apart on his dick consumes me.

This time, there's no hesitation as he pushes past my barrier, easing into me one inch at a time until I can't take it anymore.

"Oliver," I groan. "Fuck me!"

"Sure thing, Trouble." His grin is feral as he pulls back until only the tip of him is inside me. Then in one hard thrust, he slams all the way in, making me cry out as pleasure courses through me.

Our bodies are slick with sweat, our breathing ragged as we race toward our orgasms. My nails dig into his back, which only seems to egg him on as he ups the power of each thrust, hammering into me.

"Oh fuck. Fuck. Oliver." My words are barely more than incoherent babbles as a spark ignites in my core, setting my entire body on fire. I scream my release as I dig my nails harder into Oliver's back, tightening around him. He finds his own release with another couple of thrusts before collapsing onto the bed beside me.

Panting heavily, I lift my hand to swipe the sweat from my forehead, but I pause when I notice something red embedded beneath several fingernails. My eyes widen as realization dawns. "Shit, Oliver, I must have broken the skin on your back."

I turn to gape at him as he rolls onto his side. There's a grin on his face as he leans in, and his eyes twinkle—fucking *twinkle*. "Oh, Trouble, I don't mind you marking your territory."

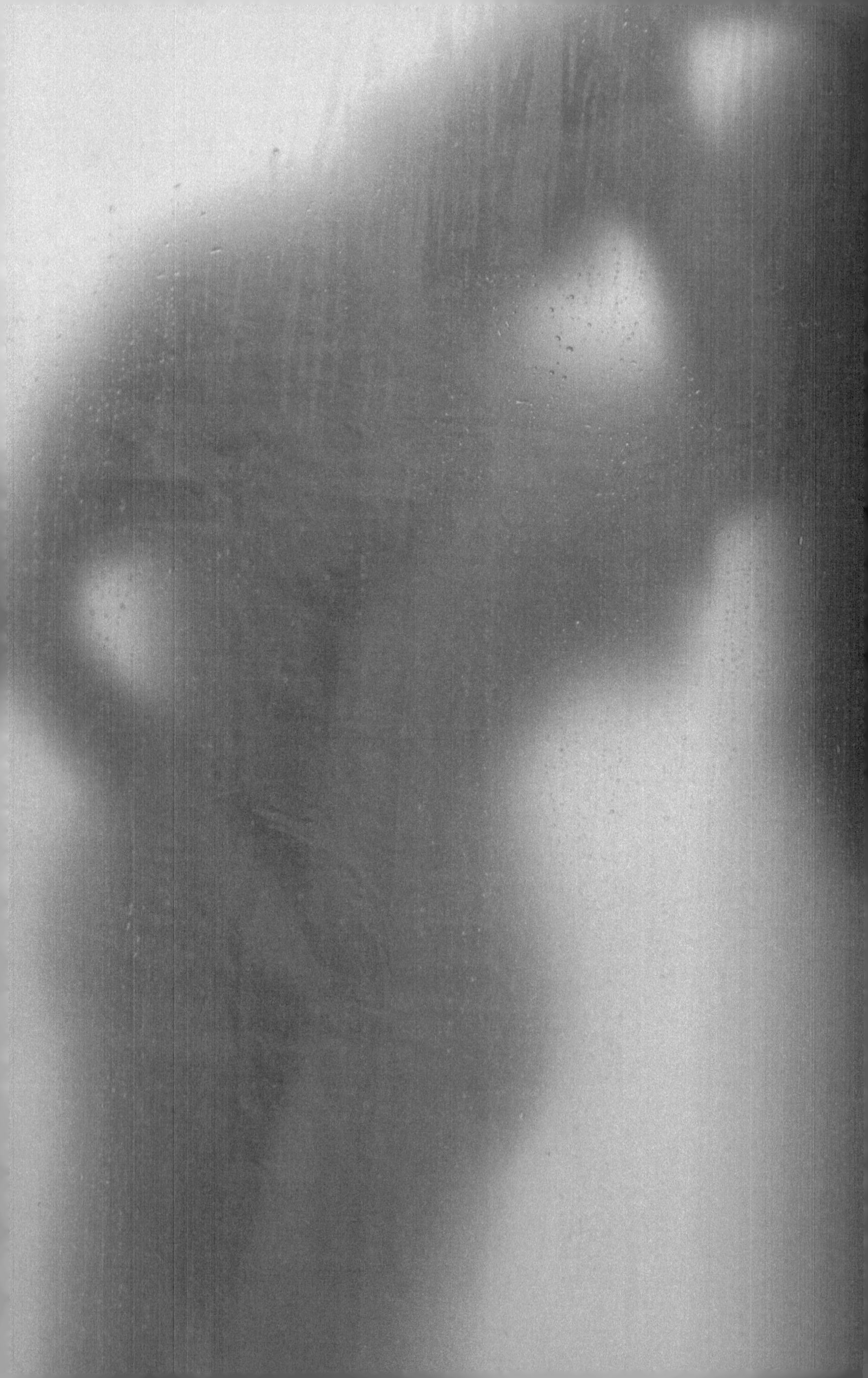

six

After another round of shower sex, we finally got cleaned up, and I offered to drive Red home—which had been the whole reason why I'd gone into her room in the first place. I couldn't stop touching her the entire drive over, and the unfamiliar peaceful feeling in my chest only confirms that whatever this is between us... it's meant to be. I don't know if I'd say it's fate or what. I'm not even sure if I believe in any of that crap, but it just feels *right*. Like something inside of me just clicked into place when I finally got her to face her feelings head-on and acknowledge that she felt this thing too.

"So..." I begin, when we're about halfway back to her apartment. "What exactly is your plan with the Antonellis?"

"I'm not entirely sure yet," she admits with a casual shrug. "As I said, I saw Dante there one night, so I'm hoping he might be a regular, or maybe I can get some information on which clubs he, or the others, frequent."

I give a thoughtful nod of my head while I continue to navigate the streets of downtown Black Creek. "And, uh, how are you planning on getting close to him if he is a regular at Belle Donne?"

I keep my gaze fixed firmly on the road in front of me, but I don't miss the side-eye she throws me. "Are you asking if I'm going to sleep with him?" Her voice is carefully neutral, giving nothing away. I mull over my response before vocalizing the words, not wanting to say the wrong thing and cause an argument between us already.

"I was simply asking if that was your game plan."

"And how would you feel if I said yes?" Before I can stop the involuntary reaction, my hands tighten around the steering wheel, and she lets out a long, suffering sigh. "*This* is why I didn't want any sort of relationship."

"Even if we weren't in a relationship"—cause we sure as fuck are after this afternoon, even if I have to keep insisting on it—"I'd still have issues with that plan," I argue, trying really fucking hard to keep my calm. "Because I *care* about you."

There's a moment of silence on her side of the car, and I glance her way, noting her tense posture and how her hands are twisting the strap of her bag. "Well, it's a moot point. I'm a dancer at Belle Donne. Not a sex worker."

I'm careful to make my sigh of relief silent—not wanting her to know how relieved I am to hear that—and we drive the last couple of blocks to her apartment in silence. Before she can scurry out of the car, I reach across the seat and gently tug her face around to meet mine. Only when she looks up at me, do I say anything.

"I'm going to worry about you," I state. "No matter what your job is in that club, I'm going to worry. That's just part of caring about someone. I'm not going to sit here and say that I would have been okay with knowing you were going in there to fuck other guys, because I wouldn't have been." Annoyance flashes across her face, but before she can protest, I carry on. "Not only because you're mine, and I want to be the *only* man that gets to see you naked; that gets to fuck that magical pussy of yours and watch you come all over my dick, but because I don't want *you* to have to put yourself through that. I won't pretend to know what sort of life you've lived until now, but I do know you don't accept any *extras* at Strip Tease. You must have some sort of line you don't cross, so don't tell me you would have been okay with going in there and fucking some strangers to get the job done."

Her lips are pinched, her features drawn, but I can tell she's taking in every word I'm saying. When I'm done, I lean forward and kiss her reverently. I don't need her to say anything back, to explain herself, or to open up to me. I just need her to know that I'm here and on her side. I'm not sure how we're going to successfully take down the Antonellis, but I refuse to let any of us lose ourselves in the process. God knows, we've lost so much already.

I pull back, breaking the kiss, but she doesn't let me go far as her hands come up to cup my face, holding it mere inches from hers. There's a light sheen of tears in her eyes, and when she speaks, her voice is rough. "I've done... things in the past. To survive. But, you're right, there are lines I won't cross. Not if I can help it."

I hear her unspoken words. The silent vow that no line is uncrossable, for the right price. That price being her brother. When she brushes her lips against mine, I make my own silent vow that she'll never have to cross any of those lines again. She should never feel like she needs to do something she doesn't want to; she should never be forced into such a corner. And so long as I have air in my lungs and blood in my veins, I'll do everything within my power to ensure she never has to.

ONCE I'VE DROPPED RED BACK AT HER APARTMENT AND RUN A FEW errands, I return to the clubhouse to deal with an ornery Cain, who was still pissed off about Red's plan when I left him earlier to go in search of her. I shake my head at his stubbornness and the fact that he's so blinded by his need to focus on his anger that he can't see he's starting to give a shit about Trouble. There's no doubt she loves to push his buttons and wind him up. She fucking gets off on it, but he gives as good as he gets, effectively pissing her off every time he opens his damn mouth. The two of them are driving me crazy with all their sniping. I can practically taste their need to fuck each other's brains out when they are in the same room. I just wish the two of them would fucking act on it so we could all move on and think with our rational brains. Seriously, I've never seen two people more desperate for some profound hate sex, but there's no talking to Cain. Any time I bring the topic of her up—unless it has to do with the Antonellis—he shuts me down, refusing to talk about her. So, I guess I need to let the two of them sort it out themselves. But, fucking hell, they better sort their shit out soon, or I will be pushing both of them to confront their feelings.

Red's been going on and on for weeks now about how we can't all function as a team if she and I are in a relationship and feelings get involved, but what she can't seem to see is that there are already feelings there—from all three of us. And if any relationship is going to fuck this up, it's going to be the one she and Cain are both vehemently denying.

As anxious as I am about Red's role in all of this, in her being a dancer for Belle Donne—which I'm a hell of a lot more concerned about than I let on—I'm excited about this opportunity that she's given us. We hadn't expected her to have an in with one of their clubs. Honestly, we weren't sure what to expect. I don't think either Cain or I had thought much past getting the Reaper on board, and when we found out the Reaper was Red, well, we really didn't have a clue what our next move should be.

I know Cain has his reservations about involving her at all. Not because she's a woman and incapable—like she seems to think. But I know every time Cain looks at her and thinks about putting her in harm's way, he pictures Evie. It's hard for him to separate the two. It always has been when it comes to women. For twelve years now, he's seen Evie's face every time he saw a woman in danger or hurt. It's difficult for him to accept that not every woman is as helpless as Evie was. She was just a kid, but Red... she's more than capable of looking after herself. You just have to look at how much she's overcome to know that.

Parking the Escalade in a free space, I head into the clubhouse, lifting my chin in acknowledgment to some of the guys as I pass by. Pushing open the swinging door, I pop my head into the kitchen, searching for Marcus.

"Yo, Marcus," I call out when I spot him directing one of the kids on how to peel potatoes by the sink. When he looks up, I wave him over, and he fires some orders at the kid before coming over.

"What's up, O?"

Marcus hasn't been with us for long. Cain picked him up at the compound, along with the kids. He was seriously fucking lucky not to get a bullet in the head that night, but he's more than proven himself since, keeping an eye on them all and earning the rather hilarious title of *mother hen*.

"Can you get a team together to scout a few locations for me?"

"Sure can. Anything, in particular, you're looking for?"

I shake my head. "Anything, really. Level of security, guard changes, and what the buildings are being used for. That sorta thing."

"I'll get a team on it tonight."

Giving him a nod in thanks, I hand over a piece of paper with various addresses on it and slip back out of the kitchen as I hear him barking at the kid again.

With that taken care of, I go in search of Cain. Surprisingly, I don't find him in his office, drowning his anger in alcohol—which is his usual response post-confrontation with Red—meaning he must be at the gym. Already predicting the sort of mood I'll find him in, I stop by my room to change into my gym gear before heading over to the sports complex. As I enter our private gym, I don't see anyone other than Cain letting out all of his pent-up aggression on a poor, defenseless bag.

Grabbing some tape, I wrap it around my hands while the repetitive thunk of Cain's fists against the bag reverberates through the air. I'm not as into fighting as he is. I don't take part in the pit fights or train regularly like Cain and the kids do, but I do know how important it is to keep my skills sharp in this line of work.

As I'm flexing my hands, ensuring I've got the tape wrapped just right, Cain finishes up and comes to join me on the mats. I can see the thunderstorm of emotions raging in his eyes. He's always been volatile, but he's been worse since he stumbled across Red that night. I know the fact that the Reaper is a woman is messing with his head. He had no qualms enlisting the help of a man to help infiltrate the Antonellis, but given what happened to Evie, he's not as comfortable with putting Red at risk like that. However, I suspect it's more than just that.

He doesn't waste any time, going straight in for a punch to my gut. I manage to step back just in time, so his hit grazes off my side instead of landing correctly, and I return with my own swing. One he barely acknowledges. Our brawl only intensifies, neither of us holding back, until my breathing is heavy and my muscles scream from the workout. My stamina isn't poor by any standards, but there's no way I could hold out against Cain in a fight, and eventually, I slip up. I lose my concentration for a nanosecond and Cain takes the opening he's been waiting for, his fist slamming into my cheek with enough force to snap my head sideways.

A grunt of pain escapes me, but the ringing of someone's phone has us both pausing before Cain can completely take me out. Huffing out a breath, he gets to his feet, going to grab the phone while I stretch out my jaw and rub my cheek.

"What?" he grunts down the line. He's silent for a moment while he listens to the caller before responding, "Alright, let me know when you're back."

"What's up?" I ask when he hangs up, unraveling the tape from my hands.

"Razor picked up some kid selling our guns."

"Not one of ours?"

"Nope."

"Huh. Grim's?"

He shrugs, unsure. "Must be. They'll be at the clubhouse in fifteen, so I guess we'll find out."

Nodding my head, I grab a bottle of water from the mini-fridge and down half of it, side-eyeing him while I do. He's still coiled tight with tension, but he doesn't seem as haunted as earlier. "Are you okay?"

"Yeah, I'm fine." He hesitates for a second before elaborating. "Fucking stripper keeps gettin' in my head."

"Maybe you should stop kicking her out then," I suggest, earning myself a stern glare.

He sighs, shaking his head. "We're actually making some sort of progress now. I can't—I *won't*—let her get in the way of that."

God, he's as fucking stubborn as she is. Why does it have to be one or the other? Why can't Cain get his vengeance *and* have the girl?

I cross the room toward him and clap my hand on his shoulder. "I'm not saying getting justice for Evie isn't important, 'cause I know it is, but she'd also want you to be happy. To stop putting your life on hold for her." He looks back at me over his shoulder, and I can see the hardness still in his eyes. "I'm just saying, you deserve some happiness too. It's what Evie would have wanted."

He has no argument against that, and he knows it, and silence falls between us as we grab our things and head back to the clubhouse. We need to shower before Razor gets back, and then it looks like our afternoon is going to be spent interrogating this kid.

FOUR HOURS LATER, I STEP INTO THE SHOWER FOR THE THIRD FUCKING time today. Ducking my head under the hot spray, I let the water cascade down my back as I watch red rivulets circle the drain, washing the blood from my hands. It didn't take much before the kid started talking. Not that he had a lot to say. He was a bottom-level lackey, only brought into the Bastards a few weeks ago. He didn't know anything about how Grim was getting his hands on our guns or what his plans were, and it quickly became pointless to continue the interrogation.

Which left the next problem... what the fuck were we to do with him? We could have sent him back to the Bastards, but I'm pretty sure Grim would have put a bullet through his head simply for getting caught. We're not cold-hearted enough to kill a defenseless kid, no matter their affiliation. Which left only one option, getting him the fuck out of town. So we stuck a bag over his head and got one of the guys to drive him one state over. He'll threaten him with the promise of death if he ever returns to Black Creek and chuck him a few bills to tide him over. Hopefully, the kid will have enough sense not to come back here.

"Grim's getting bolder," Cain states when I step into his office half an hour later, my hair still wet from the shower. He's already got a glass of whiskey waiting for me and he's halfway through his own. "He's testing us, wanting to see what we'll do."

"We knew he would," I remind him, reaching for the glass as I claim the seat opposite him. Taking a sip, I let the burn of the alcohol heat me up and settle in my stomach before I continue. "We've taken too much territory too quickly for him just to sit back. We're a threat. One he's going to want to eliminate, sooner rather than later."

Cain nods his head, clearly deep in thought, as he frowns. We knew the Grim Bastards would need to be dealt with eventually. They've become an ever-growing pain in our ass, stealing from us and pushing back at every turn. Now they've been caught selling *our* guns in *our* territory? Whether it was intentional and they wanted the kid to get busted, or they're hoping to antagonize us into starting a war with them, who knows. Either way, we can't continue to let them go unchecked for much longer.

"So, what do you wanna do?" I ask, drawing him out of his thoughts. He looks at me, a determined resolve in his eyes.

"We show them exactly who they're messing with."

AFTER HOLING OURSELVES UP IN THE OFFICE FOR THE REST OF THE NIGHT with a bottle of whiskey, we have a plan in place, and the next night three separate teams, led by Cain, myself, and Marcus, head out to the three remaining territories in downtown Black Creek that we don't yet own. They're under the control of small, no-name gangs that have barely been blips on our radar, but seizing control of all of the downtown area will mean we officially own more of the town than Grim, and *that* will piss him off. Since The Feral Beasts left town, Grim Bastards have been the ultimate powerhouse of the city—excluding the Antonellis, but they don't give a shit about Black Creek. They settled here because of the access provided by the docks, not because they wanted to take the city as theirs. Hell, they already have their own successful empire across the river. What the fuck would they want with a shithole like Black Creek? The Antonellis let the city go to waste after The Feral Beasts. They didn't give a shit that streets were being picked over by every worthless asshole with a gun or that someone like Grim was hoarding territory like baseball cards. But I care; *we* care.

With every bit of land we seize as our own, we send our men out to fix it up or to patrol the streets and protect the citizens, and ultimately restore Black Creek to some semblance of its former glory before The Feral Beasts ever got their corrupted claws into it and tore it apart.

The street is dead as I climb out of the car, meeting my team at the hood as we look around Bedlam territory. Despite the quiet peacefulness of the night air, I slip my gun out of the back of my pants and flick off the safety as I scan our surroundings. Bedlam land is in the southern suburbs of the city. Most of it is vacant now, and as I look around at the derelict homes, long since abandoned, I can see why. Roofs have collapsed inwards, and most houses are missing their windows. All of the shop fronts we passed were shuttered up or empty. Anyone who lived here deserted the town while they still could. No one remains except junkies and vagrants, hiding in the shells of what I imagine were once happy homes. The place is like a ghost town, and I'm man enough to admit it gives me the heebie-jeebies. It reminds me of the time I trailed Red out here when she was on a Reaper job, causing a small smile to lift my lips.

"Their clubhouse is one street over," Granger—one of Cain's initial Rejects—states.

Acknowledging that I've heard him, I indicate for my team of four men—Razor, Granger, Bones, and Rampage—to follow me as we head down an alley onto the next street. Dressed in all-black, we merge with the shadows, all of us on high alert in case we run into trouble. We're not anticipating much resistance, though. Despite their name, Bedlam has never caused any major issues. At least, not for us.

Reaching the end of the alley, I peer around the corner, immediately spotting what must be the Bedlam clubhouse. It's gotta be the only building within a mile radius that has any actual life about it. There's no raging party like there was the night we attacked the Satans, but unlike the other darkened or boarded up windows we've passed, every single window is lit up in the building across the road and one block down from us. A bored-looking, middle-aged man sits in a chair outside the front door, smoke trailing up into the air from a cigarette dangling from his lips.

As I stand and watch, there doesn't appear to be any other security measures in place, and I have to hold back a scoff at how fucking easy this is going to be. Fucking child's play.

"Bones," I whisper over my shoulder.

The kid moves to stand beside me, peering around the corner while I talk in his ear. When I'm finished, he gives a quick nod of his head, telling me he understands the game plan before stepping confidently onto the street. With his hands in his pockets, looking like any other eighteen-year-old looking for a night of debauchery and trouble, he saunters down the street, whistling the tune of *We Are The Champions*.

I chuckle under my breath, shaking my head as he closes in on the guard. He's one building down when the idiot finally lifts his head, watching Bones cautiously.

"Yo, man," I hear Bones call out. He's far enough away that it's a strain to hear him, and his following words are nothing more than a murmur. I don't need to hear what he has to say, though, because, in the next second, he has the sucker in a headlock. His face turns blue as the rest of us come out of the alley and quickly cross the road to the clubhouse. By the time we arrive, the man is lying unconscious at Bones' feet and the kid is grinning like he's having the time of his life. "That was fun."

I roll my eyes, chuckling. I'd be concerned if I hadn't heard the horror stories about his childhood and what he was subjected to in that fucking compound. But all of the kids are like him. They crave the bloodshed. Love the adrenaline rush. It's how they were raised. We're just lucky enough that most of them still had their humanity somewhat intact. Despite their penchant for violence, they're good kids. Every single one of them. They still know right from wrong, even if they have no reservations about blurring moral lines.

Rounding on the others, a seriousness falls over us as we stare at the front of the building, taking in the old Chinese lantern and broken sign above the door. The name of the restaurant is faded beyond recognition, but the *closed* sign is still stuck to the frosted glass window pane.

I pull my neck warmer up to cover the lower half of my face, displaying the signature skeleton of the Reaper Rejects, and wait for the others to follow suit.

"Everyone ready?" I wait for each of my men to meet my gaze before stepping up to the door with my gun raised. Raising my boot, I kick the door in with a bang and the five of us rush inside. I barely get the chance to take in the scene before I press down on the trigger, the bullet lodging in the forehead of some guy sitting at the table in front of me. The restaurant is half-filled with men who jump to their feet, sending tables, bottles, drinks, and cards flying. The rattle of gunfire goes off around me as, one by one, they fall before any of them can retrieve weapons or fight back.

It takes no time at all until we're the only ones left standing, a sea of dead bodies scattered around us.

"Huh, that was easier than I thought," one of my men remarks.

"We caught them off guard. Half of them probably weren't even armed... it's not like gangs are lining up to take Bedlam territory." I glance around the room, adrenaline buzzing through my system and sending my senses into overdrive. "Check the rest of the building," I order.

We all break up and spread out, ensuring no one is waiting to ambush us. When the building has been cleared, I leave the men to tidy up and head back to the clubhouse. It appears I'm the first one back, and while I wait, I grab a shower, washing off the blood and sweat from tonight. I sigh wearily as I step under the hot spray, the sound barely heard above the rushing of the water.

It's always one thing after another. Grim Bastards. The Antonellis. Whatever daily shit comes up with the Rejects. There's never a fucking break, and somedays I feel far older than my twenty-five years. But then Red's fiery hair and aqua-blue eyes come to mind, and maybe—just maybe—all of this will be worth it. Maybe we *can* eliminate the Antonellis and takedown Grim and his crew. Maybe we *can* carve out some sort of semi-peaceful life for the Rejects. Maybe *I* can carve out a life here, working with Cain during the day and curling up to Red at night. It sure sounds a hell of a lot better than all these years I've spent mourning a ghost, unable to move on with my life.

SAWYER

seven

On Thursday, I strut into Belle Donne with my brown contacts and brunette wig disguise in place.

"You must be the new girl," Franny, a sixty-something-year-old woman with wrinkles and hard eyes, says when I step into a small, disorganized office. Her eyes run over my slim frame before she nods, seeming satisfied with what she sees. "The dancer."

"That's me."

"What's your stage name?"

"Uhh." Shit, why hadn't I thought of that? "Red?" She quirks a brow, her eyes flicking to my obviously *brown* hair. "Bottle dyed," I blurt out by way of explanation. Not that she really seems to care, as she just shrugs.

"Alright, let me show you around."

She shuffles out from behind the desk, her back slightly hunched with age. I have to admit, she is *not* who I was expecting the office manager to be. Leaving the office—and moving surprisingly quick for an old lady—she moves further down the corridor, and I hustle after her. As she passes a notice board, she taps on it, "Any information—themed nights, special events, that sort of thing—will be posted here. Check it regularly. I have a bunch of outfits for ya." She turns to glance over her shoulder, once again running her eyes over my body. "They should fit alright."

As we walk, she gives a quick rundown of the club, the various rooms, a brief overview of the clientele, and what will be expected from me before leaving me to get changed. "Chrissy will look out for you on the floor tonight. I'll let her know you're here," she says before the dressing room door swings shut behind her.

I quickly change into one of the skimpy outfits, not caring what I wear. It's not like having my skin on display is anything new. In fact, this job isn't all that dissimilar to what I do at Strip Tease. Which is perfect. It makes it seem less daunting, more normal.

I'm dressed in nipple tassels and a thong, and I've intensified my makeup with smokey eyes and bright red lipstick, when a skinny, white-blonde ducks her head through the door. "You the new girl?" she questions.

"Yeah. I'm Red."

Her eyes flick to my brown hair, but she doesn't say anything. "Chrissy. Come on." She jerks her head in a gesture for me to follow as she slips back out of the room. "You're on stage in five so let me show you the floor before then."

Exiting the staff corridor, we enter the front of house. It looks exactly the same as it did the last time I was here, with its dim lighting and sensual music. I follow as Chrissy leads the way through the club into the room I found what-was-his-name in... Charles? Chase? Oh, Chad! Yeah, that scumbag.

Just like last time, the main focus of the room is the front stage with its bright lights and the current dancers putting on some sort of Cabaret. The rest of the room is shrouded in darkness, providing some element of privacy for the club's patrons. Other than the low light offered from the wall sconces, the primary source of lighting is provided by the flickering candles lit on each of the tables, surrounded by leather booths composed of high-backed chairs that block the occupants from the wandering eyes of the rest of the room, providing an extra layer of privacy.

"You'll mostly be on the stage tonight. But when other dancers are up, you'll be expected to help serve the guests."

"Sounds easy enough," I remark casually, only half paying attention as I scope out the room and try to scrutinize the occupants of each of the booths, looking for my mark. He doesn't seem to be here, but it's early, and tonight is only my first shift. I'd have to be seriously fucking lucky to run into him on my first night—and we all know I'm not that lucky.

Ushering me onto the stage, I have to put a halt to my mission as the bright stage lights blind my vision. I didn't really expect it to be as easy as showing up and him being here, but damn would that have made this so much easier. At least it's nothing to me to shake my ass on stage to a bunch of horny, drunk men, which is exactly how I spend the rest of the night.

It's the early hours of the morning by the time I exit the club. The night was a bust. Dante didn't show up, and nerves knotted my stomach as I wondered whether or not this was a stupid idea. I'd hoped he maybe worked in the club or ran it—based on his position within the Famiglia—but based on what little information I gleaned from my new co-workers, it doesn't seem as if that's the case. Of course, I couldn't just ask, *oh, hey, do you know Dante, the heir to the Antonelli Empire? By any chance, does he stop by on a regular basis?* So I can't be sure, but he's definitely not a daily visitor.

I pause as I step out of the alley onto the sidewalk. I'd taken a bus over here earlier, not wanting to leave Raven vulnerable on the streets at night or have anyone asking unwanted questions about her owner, but public transport doesn't operate this late at night. This means I'll have to order a taxi. I hate having to phone for a cab. Not only does it feel like a waste of money, but most of the drivers are complete fucking creeps.

Taking my phone out of my pocket, I'm pulling up the app for the taxi company when the flashing lights of a car snag my attention. Looking up, I have to raise my hand to block out the bright xenon headlights as I squint, trying to see through the front windshield.

I take a step back, out of the direct line of the headlights, which enables me to better discern the make of the car—a Cadillac. My body is coiled tight, ready to jump into action as I approach the passenger side. Oliver had said he'd have someone keeping an eye on me while I was working, so I can only assume the driver is a Reject, but I'm not stupid enough to blindly accept that whoever is inside the vehicle is a friend.

Leaning down, I peer through the dark tinted window, cocking a brow as I wait for whoever is inside to lower it. After a second, I hear the electric whir of the motor, and the window disappears into the door, revealing a surprising sight. My brows hitch as I stare at Cain's broad form behind the wheel. "What are you doing here?"

"Oh, you know, I was just catching up on the latest episode of Pretty Little Liars and got a craving for ice cream."

Rolling my eyes at his sarcasm, I open the door and slip into the front seat. "You joke, but ice cream sounds fucking amazing after the night I've had."

His gaze lingers on me until I start to feel uncomfortable under the scrutiny of his intense stare. It's only then that I remember I'm still wearing my wig and contacts. I tug the wig off my head and carefully store it in my bag before grabbing my contact lens case. Pulling down the visor, I fish the contacts out of my eyes, all while Cain continues to watch me closely.

Just before I snap and demand to know what he finds so damn interesting, he asks, "Was it that bad?" My brows pull together in confusion. "Tonight."

"No," I sigh, shaking my head. "Just pointless. Dante was a no-show."

Nodding in understanding, he finally puts the car in drive and pulls away from the curb, easily navigating the quiet late-night traffic. I turn to look out my window, assuming that's the end of the conversation, but after a moment, he speaks up.

"It was only your first night." His words of reassurance surprise me, given the way he acted last time the topic of me working here was brought up.

"Yeah, I know." I still sound defeated, but he doesn't offer any more words of comfort, not that I need him to, and we continue to make our way across town in silence. I'm still not sure why he was even outside the club. I'm fairly certain babysitting my ass all night is below his pay grade.

I'm staring out the window, lost in my thoughts and barely paying attention to our surroundings, when Cain slows the car and stops outside a darkened shop front. "What are we doing here?" I question, staring up at the overhead sign in confusion.

"You said you wanted ice cream." He says it so casually like it's no big deal, but the fact that we're currently parked outside Nutterly Delicious—in the middle of the night —says otherwise. He climbs out of the car without another word, and hesitantly, I follow, watching as he fishes a key out of his pocket and quickly unlocks the door.

I follow him into the ice cream parlor and watch as he flicks on the lights and moves behind the counter, not entirely sure what to make of all of this. It's all very... un-Cain like—more along the lines of a gesture Oliver would do.

"What flavor do you want?" he asks as he grabs a cardboard tub and opens the back of the display freezer.

"Uhh." I move to stand on the other side of the display case, reading the name cards for each flavor. I'm deliberately choosing to focus on the simple task of picking one instead of thinking about how out of place Cain looks with his broad frame and tatted-up body holding an ice cream scoop and a tub in his hand. "Cookies and cream."

He proceeds to put two scoops into the tub before asking, "Toppings?"

I run my eyes over the various options. "Marshmallows and caramel sauce."

When he's added my choices, he digs a small, pink plastic spoon into the mixture and hands over the cup. My fingers brush his, a tingle racing along my skin, and I quickly pull back, breaking contact as I mutter a thanks and step away. His gaze lingers on mine for a moment before he jerks his head and moves to start tidying up. Turning my back on him, I make my way over to one of the window booths and slide in, watching as the odd person scurries by outside, not wanting to get caught out alone this late at night. However, with the Rejects now in control of this part of town, it's a hell of a lot safer than it was under the Satans' reign.

I'm still staring out the window when Cain slips into the seat opposite me, his close proximity pulling me out of my inner thoughts as I turn to face him, taking a bite of my ice cream.

We sit in silence while I eat, but it's a comfortable sort of silence where neither of us feels the need to fill it, and honestly, it's kinda nice not to be arguing with him for once.

After several more bites, I hold the spoon out to Cain in a silent gesture. He stares at it for a short time before lifting his eyes to meet mine, his expression as unreadable as always. When he reaches out to take the spoon from between my fingers, it feels like a much more meaningful exchange is taking place between us, rather than the simple passing of a spoon.

He wraps his other hand around the cup and pulls it closer to his side of the table, digging the spoon into the runny ice cream and slowly bringing it to his mouth. I watch as it disappears between his full lips. He hums low in the back of his throat as he swallows.

"Tell me something about your sister." My voice is soft, quiet, but he hears me, his hand pausing mid-way to his mouth as he goes to take another mouthful. When I manage to tear my gaze away from his lips to meet his gaze, I find him watching me, a rare vulnerability shining in his eyes before he looks away.

He licks his lips, and I'm fully expecting him to tell me to stop prying into his business, so I'm taken aback when his words don't have their usual angry growl. Instead, he gestures to the cup of melted ice cream and says in a husky voice, born of grief and heartache, "Cookies and cream was her favorite."

I lift one side of my lips in a small smile, a silent gesture of gratitude. I can only imagine how hard that admission was to share. "She had good taste then."

He chuckles softly. "Yeah. Although she always insisted on trying mine, even though she didn't like chocolate." A melancholy grin lights up his face in the most heart-rending way. "She'd take a huge big bite out of it too, then screw up her face and tell me how disgusting it tasted."

I laugh softly. "Luc was never fussy about which sweet treats he got, so long as they contained sugar. His face would light up like fireworks on the fourth of July when I told him I had a surprise for him. I didn't even care that he'd be up all night on a sugar high. Anything was worth seeing that look of joy on his face."

Cain studies me with those all-seeing eyes of his. "You raised him?"

"I did. After our mom died."

"I'm sorry." His voice is low, his words sincere.

I give an easy shrug of my shoulder. It is what it is. I've long since made my peace with it. "It was a long time ago, and she hadn't been much of a mother anyway. I got my revenge on the man who killed her, and now my focus has to be on looking forward, doing my best for Luc, and ensuring he doesn't meet the same fate she did."

There's conviction in my voice, which thankfully hides the nerves fluttering in my stomach because I've never told anyone about my mom; or about what I did. But it just felt right after Cain shared part of his past with me and the openness he's shown me this evening. The words were out of me before I'd really given them much thought, but now that they're out there, hanging in the air between us, I don't regret them. If anything, the way Cain is looking at me right now, with a mixture of surprise and respect, only chases away any anxiety I may have had.

"Is that how you became the Reaper?"

I have to think on that one for a moment. When I started down this path, I didn't intend on becoming some twisted version of a vigilante. I simply wanted justice for my mom, and I had to find an outlet for all the anger building up inside me, threatening to consume me. What better way to eradicate myself of that than by killing the man responsible. Except it didn't stop there. If anything, his murder only lit a fire inside me, one that demanded the souls of the damned to keep it ablaze.

"I guess. Sort of. I didn't exactly set out to become the Reaper, it just kinda happened."

One corner of his lip quirks up in a small, sad smile. "I didn't exactly have gang leader as my top career choice either," he admits. "But we do what we have to for our family and to enable us to sleep at night."

Truer words have never been spoken. The air between us is heavy with our truths and exposed vulnerabilities, but despite the pain and difficult topic of conversation, I feel lighter, as though my heart needed me to share my truth with someone else.

Neither of us says anything else—there's no need to—and we soon leave. As I climb out of his car outside my apartment building, I feel better than I have in a long time. More confident, more optimistic about the challenges that lie ahead. It could be just the surge of endorphins from getting some ice cream, but I get the feeling that it's more than that.

I trudge up to my apartment, toeing my shoes off just inside the door. "Hey," I greet as I step into the living room, spotting Luc sitting on the sofa. "How come you're still up?"

"Couldn't sleep. How was work?"

Walking toward him, I collapse onto the sofa. "Fine. What are you watching?"

"Some zombie movie," he responds distractedly. "It's good."

I sit there and watch it for a bit, not finding the same draw he clearly does. "How was your day?" I eventually ask, pulling my legs up onto the sofa and getting comfortable.

He gives a casual shrug. "Fine." After a second, he seems to remember something, and turns to face me. "Did you tell Cain or Oliver to enroll Tank and Rampage in my school?"

My brows raise at that. "No," I admit. Although, damn, why *didn't* I tell them to do that? Luc's eyes narrow on me as he tries to figure out if I'm lying or not. I don't blame him. It's absolutely something I would do. "But it's a smart move." I try to get a read on him before asking, "Are you angry?"

He's quick to shake his head. "No. It's actually been nice to have someone to hang out with in school. They're enrolled as seniors, so they aren't in any of my classes, but it's cool having people around at lunch and before class. Not sure they're seeing the appeal of being stuck in school all day, though," he chuckles.

"Ha." Yeah, I can only imagine how strange it all seems after probably never setting foot in a school before. I'm sure they are thrilled to be missing out on club business to keep tabs on Luc in school. "Do you know much about their past?" I question, wondering if any of them have opened up to him.

He shrugs. "Not much. They don't really talk about it. I gather Cain rescued them from some sort of prison. I dunno what, but I've seen their scars." A sadness fills his eyes, and the corners of his lips pull down in a frown. "The sort of pain that must have been inflicted. I can't imagine..."

I reach out and squeeze his hand. If I've got any say, it's not a kind of pain he'll ever have to experience, but yeah, whatever those kids have had to endure, it's not something I'd wish on anyone. "They got lucky with Cain," I say quietly. "He's built them the perfect home."

Luc quirks a surprised brow. "So now you're team Cain? You realize now that the Rejects aren't the bad guys?"

"I wouldn't say I'm team Cain," I argue, "but yeah, the Rejects aren't all bad."

Luc snorts and shakes his head. "They're practically golden boys by Black Creek standards." I laugh at that before he continues. "But from what I've heard from the others, Cain's a good guy. Oliver too." He nudges my shoulder. "So, you know, if you liked one of them, I don't think it would be the end of the world."

I gape at him. "What? Where would you get that idea from?"

He just scoffs. "Please. From what I hear, the only time Cain is seen with a girl is when he's fucking her, and Oliver hasn't been seen with one at all since he arrived... except you."

Well, I don't know what to say to that. Oliver had said he hadn't been with anyone since before prison, but hearing it confirmed—by my brother of all people—is a little jarring.

Luc must be able to see the shock on my face as he chuckles softly. "All I'm saying is that it would be okay if you had feelings for them. I know you're all doing some sort of job together, and I can only imagine how that has your trust issues all haywire." I frown. Luc knows me too damn well. "But for what it's worth, I don't think you're breaking any of your own rules. The Rejects aren't like any of the gangs we know. They aren't like the people you had to deal with when we were on the street or the kids who used to harass me at school, trying to get me to join the Satan's or whatever."

I shift in my seat to rest my head on his shoulder and sigh. "Yeah, I know. It's just been difficult to change my perspective. To trust them to look out for you."

"Sawyer," Luc sighs. "You don't need to worry about me. I'm not a little kid anymore. I'll be sixteen soon, and Jon's been teaching me to fight. Not that anyone at school hassles me anymore. All of the gangs they were sucking up to have been destroyed by the Rejects. I've gone from being the outcast to the kid everyone wants to get close to 'cause they think I'll be able to get them in."

"Into the Rejects?" I shake my head. What is wrong with them all? Why do they have to be a part of any gang? There's more to life than selling drugs, gun-running, and violence.

"Yeah. They're the only gang left on the south side of town. Everyone wants to be a Reject, but Cain's already said no high schoolers. He won't consider any new recruits unless they are at least eighteen."

Cain continues to surprise me, although I'm not sure why. He's more than proved that while he's a moody bastard with an over-inflated ego, he's not the monster I initially thought he was.

"Well, even with the kids sticking close to you and Jon teaching you to fight, I'm still going to worry," I say, lifting my head off his shoulder to look him in the eye. "Because it's what big sisters do."

He smiles softly, squeezing my thigh. "I'm gonna head to bed, sis. See ya in the morning."

"Night," I call as he heads to his bedroom, closing the door behind him. I sit and stare at the closed door for a moment before standing and getting ready for bed. When I'm under my sheets, I lift my phone off the bedside table and call Oliver.

"Everything okay?" he asks when he picks up.

"Yeah," I assure him. "Just thought I'd call. Sorry, did I wake you up?"

His sleep-filled chuckle is so sexy. "You can call me any time, day or night, Trouble. How was tonight?"

"A bust, but it was fine. Cain picked me up."

"He did?" Oliver sounds genuinely surprised by that. "You didn't kill him and chuck him off the end of the docks, did you?"

"Ha-ha," I retort to his joke. "No. He was actually... It was weird. We actually got along, for once."

"That's good."

"Yeah. It was just different." Shaking my head to dislodge the thoughts of Cain, I instead ask, "Did you enroll two of the kids into Luc's school?"

"Ah, I maybe should have talked to you about that. Yeah, I thought it would be good to have them nearby, just in case. Did I overstep?"

Tears sting my eyes as I close them against the onslaught of emotions. "Thank you," I choke out. The fact that he thought to do that says everything about Oliver's character.

"Any time, Red." The sincerity in his tone chips away at my bruised and battered heart, carving out a spot that will forever belong to Oliver. Chewing on my bottom lip for a second, I lift the phone away from my ear and, holding it above me, I take a selfie with my dark hair spread out on my pillow. My hard nipples are clear to see through the thin fabric of my top, and my eyes look all sultry. The whole image practically screams *come fuck me*. Pleased, I send it to Oliver and listen as his phone pings on the other end, followed by a pained groan.

"Trouble."

"Just my way of saying thank you."

He chuckles. "Such a tease." For a moment, all I can hear is the sound of him shuffling around in his bed before the unmistakable sigh of... "Are you jerking off right now?"

"Are you not?"

"Oliver!" I chuckle, as my phone vibrates in my hand. Pulling it away from my ear, I murmur, "oh," as I take in the photo he sent. Everything—and I mean *everything*—is on display. I slowly roam my eyes over his lust-filled baby blues, to his toned pecs and tensed abs until I reach the lower end of the screen where his hand is fisted around his painfully hard cock.

"Touch yourself for me." The husky timbre of his voice has me slipping my hand under my pajama top to pinch my nipples, and I moan as I picture his hands on me. "That's it, baby." His own heavy pants come down the line as he works himself over, the knowledge inching me higher.

I direct my hand south as it slips beneath the waistband of my sleep shorts. The only sound is our mutual pants and soft moans as we get ourselves off to the thought of one another.

"Oliver," I moan, just before I come all over my fingers.

"That's it, Red. Fuuuuck."

I curl onto my side, the phone still to my ear as my eyes drift shut. Oliver's voice is the last thing I hear before I fall asleep. "Night, Trouble. Sweet dreams."

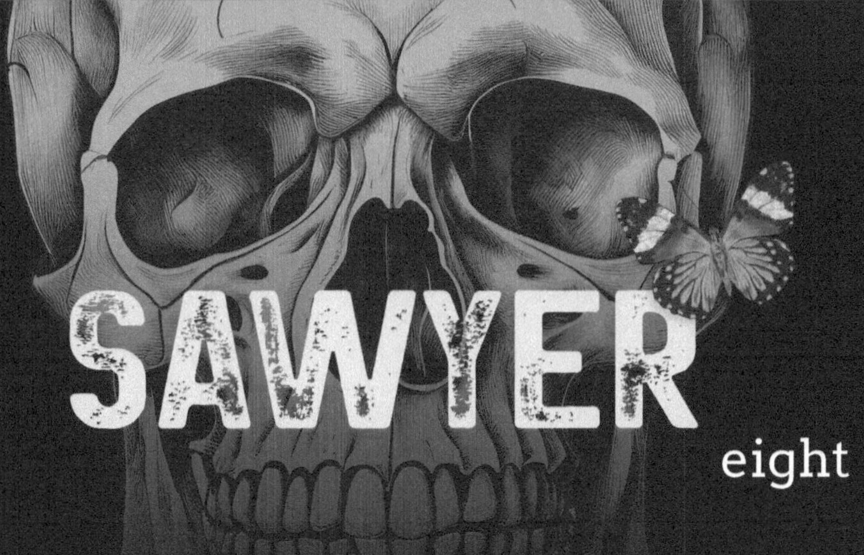

eight

I t's the end of my third shift at Belle Donne, and so far, there's been no sign of Dante or any other men in Giovanni's inner circle. I'm beginning to think this whole plan was a bust, and I'm in a particularly sour mood as I make my way to the dressing room to change. Walking past the office, I notice the door is ajar and slow down to listen for any sounds from within the room. When all is silent, I decide to take a chance and duck inside.

My eyes roam over the stacks of paper piled on the desk before noticing the filing cabinets along the back wall. Not wanting to hang around for longer than necessary, I hurry across the room toward them and start pulling open cabinet drawers. I have no idea what I'm hoping to find, but I can't continue to sit around and wait for Dante to show up. *If* he shows up.

The first cabinet is filled with receipts and bills. None of it means anything to me, and I quickly shut it and move on to the next one. Randomly picking a file, I flick through it, stopping when I find a list of businesses. Not having the time to analyze it all now, I quickly snap pictures of each of the pages and stuff the file back where I got it. I rush through the rest of the cabinet, but I don't identify anything else of interest, and not wanting to get caught, I cross my fingers that what I did find might be of some use and slip out of the room.

"Tuck your elbow in," Jon reminds me, giving me just enough time to do as he instructs before I strike out, landing a solid punch on his chest. "Good."

It's been over a week since my first shift at Belle Donne, and there is still no sign of Dante yet. With every passing day, I'm losing faith in my plan, and as confidence in myself waivers, I find myself pulling away from Oliver and Cain more and more. I haven't seen Cain since that first night—apparently, he's as intent on avoiding me as I am after our heart-to-heart. And Oliver... He's texted a few times and called, but my responses have been short. Which only adds to the guilt gnawing away at my insides. He doesn't deserve to be treated like that, but I feel like I'm letting both of them down. If this plan doesn't work, I'm not sure what else we can do. There is no plan B. I sent Oliver the list of businesses I found and he said he'd get people to check them out, but we don't know if the info is of any use yet, or how to utilize it, and beyond that, there is no other plan. They are relying on me to pull through and, currently, I'm failing miserably.

Sweat coats my skin, my labored breaths giving away my evident exhaustion as I throw the last of my energy into another punch. We've been at it for over an hour now, and thankfully, Jon's chest glistens with sweat, too, so I've provided him as much of a workout as he has given me. He's an excellent teacher. This is our third session, and I've come a long way in such a short period of time.

My next hit misses as he side-steps at the last second, swooping in on my left side, which I stupidly left unprotected. *Dammit.* I spot his smug grin seconds before he tackles me to the ground, and I land with a soft *oomph*, glad that he had the foresight to put a padded mat on the floor of the swimming pool. I definitely don't want my head cracking off those tiles, not to mention lying on top of the grimy layer of long-spilled blood. No, thanks.

A number of other Rejects were in the gym when we arrived, and I didn't feel comfortable working out in front of them—well, letting them watch Jon get the best of me. I'm learning to trust Cain and Oliver—and, by default, the rest of the Rejects—but that doesn't mean I want to emphasize my weak spots for them to target should our alliance turn sour at any future point.

"You left your side wide open," he chastises, stating the obvious while I huff out a breath in frustration.

"I know," I groan, shoving him off me and climbing to my feet. "Let's go again."

We go a few more rounds, and I finally get him pinned beneath me when a voice calls out from somewhere behind me, causing the victorious smirk to drop from my face.

"Well, well, what do we have here?" Cain drawls. The soles of his heavy boots echo off the tiles as he moves toward us. Refusing to acknowledge him, I lift off Jon and hold my hand out to help him up.

"I was just showing Red a few moves," he explains.

I glance up at Cain from the corner of my eye, noticing his eyes firmly glued to me.

"Uh-huh. Marcus is looking for you, Bones."

"Oh shit, I'm supposed to help him with dinner prep tonight." Jon hurries across the swimming pool, quickly swiping a towel across his face and over his hair before hauling himself out and blurting out a goodbye as he rushes out the door.

As the door swings shut behind him, it feels like Cain's presence—or maybe it's the knowledge that we're alone—steals all of the oxygen from the room. It's the first time I've laid eyes on him since that night, and everything between us feels even more electrically charged than it did before—if that's even possible.

Still refusing to acknowledge him—because I have no idea how to react or what to say to him anymore—I turn my back on him and move toward where I left my belongings. Before I can reach them, though, he drops into the basin of the pool, landing with a thud.

"What are you doing?" I ask, glancing back over my shoulder to find him prowling toward me, looking far too predatory for my liking.

He quirks a brow. "Thought I'd see for myself exactly what the big, bad Reaper is made of." One side of his lips lifts in a callous smirk. "Besides, gotta make sure I've hired the right person for the job. Can't have you fucking it up for all of us now, can I?"

I bristle at his caustic tone. Given my own self-doubt this past week, and the fact that I stupidly thought we'd made some progress the last time we talked, his words seriously irk me. His mood swings are giving me fucking whiplash. What was the point of taking me to get ice cream if he wasn't trying to break down the barriers between us? They feel taller than ever now.

With my jaw clenched tight, letting him see the fire he's just lit inside me, I turn around to face him head-on. My strengths don't lie in being the best fighter, in successfully taking down two hundred pounds of pure muscle. I'm all about being subtle, sneaking under people's defenses and catching them by surprise. The whole point is that my victim doesn't see me coming. I stand back and watch from the shadows, tracking their every move with predatory eyes. I watch and wait; I bide my time... and when their guard is down, and they least expect it, I strike.

But being the arrogant jackwad that he is, Cain wants to test me. He wants to prove I'm not up to this task, purely because I'm 5'4" with tits and a vagina and not the six-foot almighty being with a swinging dick he was expecting. I might have been doubting myself recently, but I'm sure as fuck not going to stand for *him* questioning my capabilities.

Straightening my spine, I smirk up at him, accepting his challenge... because I fucking love it when people underestimate me. "What does the winner get?"

His lips purse as he thinks it over for a second. "If I win, you have to move in here."

I frown, not liking that in the slightest, but I can't back down now, so I agree, huffing out a breath. "Fine, but if *I* win, you drop the subject."

He casually agrees, looking far too fucking smug, and I stalk back into the middle of the pit, ignoring the fatigue tugging at my muscles as I lower into a crouch opposite him. Except the asshole just continues to stand there, with his arms resting at his side, not looking the slightest bit ready to engage in an altercation.

"Ladies first," he states snidely, his voice overflowing with self-confidence. Regardless, I'm not about to waste an advantage. Instead, I hone all the skills Jon has taught me, and make every hit count as I go head-to-head against him.

By the time he inevitably takes me to the mat, I'm panting heavily, a fresh round of sweat making my skin slick. He leans over me, his thighs pressing against my hips and a cocky grin igniting his face. "I win." He states it so damn confidently that I don't even feel bad as I let my own smug grin loose. "Are you sure about that?" I ask with a cocked brow as I press the tip of my blade more firmly against the rigid outline of his dick. *Yup, the asshole is fucking hard.* I'm not sure whether that's because he won or because he has me pinned beneath him, and I refuse to think too hard about it. Instead, I just let myself enjoy my victory.

He jerks at the sharp sting, easily feeling the pointed tip through the thin fabric of his basketball shorts as he flicks his gaze down at where my hand is wedged between our bodies, holding a small pen knife to his junk. I've never been more grateful for workout leggings with pockets. Like seriously, this shit is life-changing. Hell, it could even be life-*saving* in the right circumstance.

"What the—" His words trail off as he looks back at me with wide eyes.

"You should probably check that your enemies are unarmed before declaring victory." There's no missing my satisfied tone, and he gapes at me for a long moment before a disbelieving chuckle escapes his lips.

The surprising sound catches me off guard. I'd half expected him to blow a fuse over my win. I narrow my eyes on him, still angry at his lack of trust in me. "I get that you want the best possible chance of success, but if you're looking for a weak point, it's not going to be me. I might not be what you were expecting, but I'm damn good at what I do, and I'll do whatever it takes to make Black Creek a safer place for Luc to live. Next time you challenge me, I won't stop at just pointing a blade at your dick."

Damn, that speech even has me feeling more confident in my abilities.

I expect to see a lick of anger heat his gaze, but instead, his pupils dilate with lust. "Noted. I guess I should claim my prize then." His teeth sink into his lower lip in an altogether delicious move that sends my brain on the fritz, meaning it takes longer than it should for his words to penetrate.

"You didn't win," I argue, my brows furrowed in confusion.

He simply nods his head. "Yes, I did. You cheated."

I scoff. "I didn't cheat, and I'm sure as fuck not moving in here."

His tongue flicks out to wet his lips, and his gaze turns molten as it sears into me. When he speaks again, his voice is a low husk composed of pure sex. "Not the prize I want anymore."

He leans in closer, a move that has the tip of my blade digging harder into his erect cock. He groans in undisguised pleasure at the bite of pain—masochistic whack job. Anyone who pierces their dick must get off on the pain, at least a little.

Lifting his hips slightly, he nudges my hand aside, and I drop the knife. He doesn't waste a second before flipping me over on the mat. His large palms wrap around my hips, hauling me up onto my knees as he kicks my legs apart. A shiver of desire wracks my body as he makes quick work of divesting me of my workout pants and panties, practically ripping the sneakers off my feet in his haste.

I'm panting heavily—and not from exertion—by the time he presses the obvious bulge of his thick erection between my ass cheeks. He's still wearing his basketball shorts, but they do nothing to disguise his obvious hard-on.

"Fuck, you're drenched," he grunts as he trails his fingers along the seam of my pussy, before I hear the rustle of him pushing down his shorts. A second later, I feel the nudge of his head against my entrance before he slams all the way into me in one hard thrust that has me nearly face-planting as I cry out. Not that he seems to mind as his fingers dig into my hips, and he sets a fast, relentless pace that quickly has my legs trembling and my arms like jelly as they struggle to hold me upright.

Noises I've never even heard myself make slip unbidden past my lips as he pushes me closer to that sweet release. Releasing my hip, his hand slides into my hair, gripping the back of my head firmly as he tugs me upright. The new angle makes his piercing hit that perfect spot deep inside me, and I cry out as I clench around him.

"Yeah, you love the feel of my cock inside you, don't you, stripper?"

I'm incapable of answering him, not that he seems to be looking for a coherent response as he ups the pace, rutting into me in a frantic frenzy and immediately starting me back up that hill once again.

He must have removed his jersey at some point, and I can feel the heat of his skin against my exposed lower back as he slams into me. He continues to hold me in a painfully tight grip, and the sharp bite of pain at my skull every time he thrusts forward only heightens the pleasure. I lift my arm to cup the back of his neck, digging my fingers painfully into the skin and relishing his grunt of pain. "Fuck."

Pulling harder on my hair, his other hand snakes around the front of my abdomen. Even though his tight grip on my hair means my head is tilted back, I can't help glancing down, wanting to see the contrast of his dark tattoos against my milky skin. All I can see is the tensing of his tattooed biceps as his inked hand slips between my thighs. He pinches my clit, immediately sending me cresting over the edge as I scream my release.

"Such a pretty little whore when you're coming around my dick," he pants, seconds before emptying himself inside me. I don't even have it in me to get angry at that statement as I sag against him, breathing heavily.

With his mouth by my ear, I can hear his labored breathing and feel his heart hammering against his chest in the same chaotic rhythm as mine as we both crash land back on earth. I'm still floating on a cloud of dopamine when he tilts his face toward me, burying his nose in my hair. His lips press against the damp skin over my thundering pulse point in a strangely intimate move that makes my skin tingle. It doesn't last more than a couple of seconds before he pulls back, sliding out of me, and when I glance back at him over my shoulder, his expression is shuttered; unreadable. *Why does such a confusing man have to have a body made of sin?*

Shrugging off the unexplainable moment, I quickly yank up my pants, once again mentally chastising myself for not using a condom. Not only is it the sensible, adult thing to do, but it would save me having to walk around with cum-soaked panties until I get home.

"You seriously have to start carrying condoms around," I bite out angrily, grimacing as I fix my leggings. Dressed, I look up to find Cain frowning at me, which only pisses me off further. He just got his dick wet, shouldn't that post-orgasmic bliss have lasted at least a little longer?

He just stands and stares at me, and I get the impression it's not me he's truly seeing. Like his mind is elsewhere. After a moment, he shakes his head and digs his hand into his pocket. "Who says I don't?" He waves a fucking condom packet in front of me, and all I can do is gape at him.

"Then why don't you fucking use it!"

He just smirks, turning on his heel and striding across the pool floor without another word. He doesn't stop. Hell, he doesn't even slow down or acknowledge that I've spoken to him as he hauls himself out of the pool and walks toward the exit. *Infuriating fuckwit.* Gritting my teeth, fury burns a path through me at the apparent dismissal right after what we just did. Just before the door slams shut behind him, he calls out, "Better get used to it, Red."

I growl in frustration, not that anyone is around to hear me, before I drop, deflated, down onto the mat. I run my hands over my face, suddenly feeling exhausted as I give myself a mental berating for letting my vagina make any decisions. I don't understand Cain at all. Just when I think we're making progress, he shifts gears. I'd assumed his avoidance of me all week was because he felt uncomfortable showing his vulnerability the other night. Something I could understand because I felt it too. Yet he's back to fucking me and calling me stripper. I just don't get it. What I hate even more is the sharp sting of feeling used that's currently carving up my chest. Fuck him. If he's unwilling to be a fucking grown-up, then fine. I can forget all about the other night and accept there's nothing except amazing sex and hatred between us. It's his fucking loss, anyway.

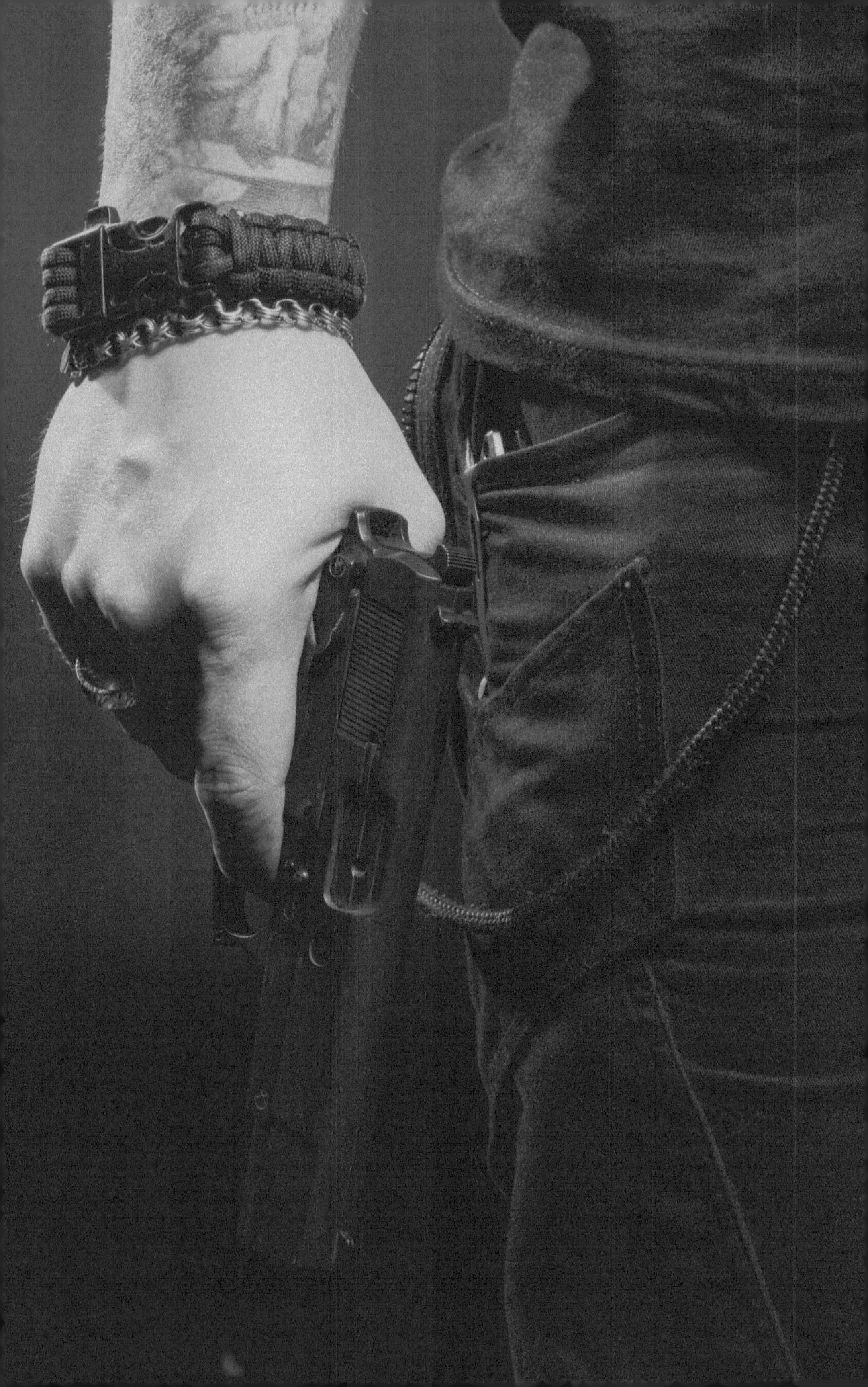

nine

I release a low groan as the door swings shut behind me, running my fingers through my hair in frustration as I attempt to put as much distance between myself and Red as quickly as humanly possible. *God-fucking-dammit. This* is why I have been avoiding her all week. I can't fucking think straight when I'm around her. My dick just constantly wants to be buried in her hot cunt, and I have to bite back from spilling every single thought in my head. I can't focus on anything except her alluring presence. Not even on Evie and my promise to her, which is all I *should* be thinking about; all that should matter.

Oliver was wrong when he said I deserved happiness. Until Giovanni and every one of his men are lying dead at my feet, I don't deserve to feel anything other than this yearning need to vindicate my sister. I did give it a try. I *tried* to be more like Oliver by taking her for ice cream. Well, it hadn't been an intentional thought. She just seemed so deflated after her shift, and I thought it might cheer her up. I hadn't even realized that's what I was doing until I found myself in that part of town.

It hadn't been quite the de-stressor I'd been expecting, but when she brought up the topic of Evie, I didn't feel the crushing ache in my chest that I usually get. It felt almost cathartic to open up and talk to someone who never knew her. I hadn't realized just how much Red and I have in common. Even though Evie is dead and Luc is still very much alive, we both would sacrifice anything for our siblings—me for justice; her for protection. I hadn't looked at it that way before, and now that I have, it's fucking changing things. Things that I don't want to change, things that I'm not ready for, that I don't deserve. This is why I reverted back to my standard dickhead mode around her. Even still, I couldn't deny the opportunity to be close to her. To breathe in her flowery scent. I swear I could still smell her soap even though she'd clearly been working out for the last few hours.

To say I was impressed as I watched her take Bones to the ground would be an understatement. I know first-hand how well trained those kids are. The skills they have are insane. But fuck, I wanted to rip his head off when I saw his hands all over her. *I* wanted to be the one sparring with her, the one teaching her. Except I'm not that person. I'm not cut out for that shit. I don't have that sort of patience, and there's no way I could keep my temper—or dick—under control for long enough to actually teach Red anything useful. Still, it was all I could do to get the kid out of there so I could have her all to myself for a second. Which is the fucking farce of it all, because as much as I want to stay the hell away from her, I can't stop seeking her out. I only lasted five minutes after finding out she was here before stomping my way over to the gym. It's fucking pathetic.

Needing a distraction before I do something stupid, like turn around and go for another round with Red—or even worse, fucking talk to her—I head in search of Oliver. I find him helping some of the guys set up a bonfire out back. They're chucking some of the old, wooden furniture we dragged out of the building onto the fire to burn, and it takes a moment before he spots me.

He says something to a couple of them, receiving confirming nods before he claps one of them on the shoulder and makes his way over. "What's up?"

"Tonight."

That's all I have to say. He knows exactly what I'm referring to, and his eyebrows hitch in surprise before his eyes narrow, roaming over my face. He must notice the mood I'm in as his lips purse. "What the fuck happened now?"

"Nothing," I gripe.

When he speaks again, his voice is a low, angry growl. "We can't go into this on impulse, with a half-baked plan, just because you refuse to deal with your fucking emotions."

Oliver rarely goes against me, and if he were anyone else, I'd chew his fucking head off for the way he just spoke to me. His tone still makes me bristle, but I work to release some of the tension from my shoulders, knowing he only has the best interest of the Rejects in mind.

"I'm not," I snarl—okay, so maybe the fact that he's calling me fucking emotional is grating on me. "*We're* not. We've been planning this for the better part of a week now. Why wait? Red isn't having any luck, so maybe this will spur one of them into going to the club."

His lips are still pressed into a tight line, but he knows I have a point. Nothing will drive businessmen to check on their assets more than sabotaging one of them. His eyes drill into me for a long moment, and I know he's trying to get a read on me; to confirm this isn't a purely emotional move I'm making. Eventually, he gives a sharp nod. "Alright, but we need to be smart about which of their businesses to target."

In agreement, we head to my office, where I have a list of various Antonelli clubs that Red was able to get for us. I've gathered intel from Mac and Ian—two men I have working undercover in the Antonellis—on the various comings and goings of some of the clubs, plus Oliver had the smart idea last week to send men to check out their warehouses by the docks. Marcus and his team found large quantities of anything and everything illegal—drugs, tommy guns, even Cuban cigars, beluga caviar, and black-market antiquities. I always knew the Antonellis traded in far finer illegal goods than us mere gangsters, but the vast range of what they had stored down at the docks was eye-opening. It must be millions of dollars' worth of goods—billions even. All sitting, stored in a couple of buildings with what appears to be minimum security... just waiting for any opportunistic criminal to steal or destroy.

"We need a targeted approach," Oliver states, lifting the page with the list of other clubs and scanning his eyes over it. "Something that will be immediately obvious that it was no fluke or accident. They need to know they were deliberately targeted and we need to give them a reason to check up on their clubs." I don't bother responding. It's clear he's only thinking aloud as he continues to scrutinize the list. "We could hit two or three clubs at once. This one is closed for renovations"—he points to a name on the list —"and if we can evacuate another one and get inside..." He trails off, still staring intently at the page.

By the time we've fine-tuned the plan, and each of us has gathered a small team of men and supplies, it's dark out. I clap Oliver on the shoulder, wishing him luck before we head out. I direct my team to one of the Antonelli clubs on the periphery of their territory—La Puttana. It's one of their cheaper establishments—less of a club and more of a brothel—so financially, it won't be a big hit to them, but it also has less security than their more upscale clubs.

As we head across town, I fill my team in on the plan, so everyone knows their roles by the time we pull up a block over from the club.

Climbing out of the car, I fix my gaze on Rampage and Bones. "You two know what you need to do?" I check. They both confirm that they do, and I hand over a wad of cash to each of them. Enough that they look like two rich idiots that don't know better and just want to get their dicks wet.

Grinning at each other, the kids take off across the street. I'm more than used to their excitement when it comes to jobs like this. It's what they've been trained for, and despite their upbringing, they love getting out in the field. Where most people might walk into that club fretting with nerves and immediately draw the wrong kind of attention, I know any of the kids I recruited will be able to walk in there and instantly look like they belong.

While they implement their distraction plan, I walk around to the trunk, where the other two men I brought with me are already standing. Opening the duffel bag, I reiterate, "Place these on exterior walls at each corner of the building," as I hand them over five C4 explosives. "Dax, you take the ground floor. Razor, you take the first, and I'll take the top floor. As soon as you have the explosives placed, get out. Got it?"

They both murmur their agreements, and we wait in silence for the kids to do their job. We aren't left waiting for long before the blaring of the fire alarm screams through the previously quiet night air, and a minute later, people start spilling onto the street from the club. We stand and watch from further down the block, waiting until we're sure everyone is outside. When I spot the kids exiting the club, looking more disheveled than when they walked in, and staring around in panic, I pull the balaclava down over my face. Dax and Razor do the same, and the three of us use the shadows to hide our approach.

No one is paying us any attention as half-naked women huddle together, staring at the building as if they expect smoke to start pouring out of it at any second. Quite a few of tonight's customers bolted as soon as they got outside, most likely not wanting to be caught outside a brothel, while some still hang around, hoping they'll be allowed back inside soon so they can finish getting their money's worth. *Tough luck, men, you won't be getting what you paid for tonight.*

When we're a building away, we slip down a side street into an alley that runs along the back of the club and quickly cover the remaining distance. There's not a soul in sight, the scant security too busy ensuring the building has been cleared out.

We find a door at the back of the club propped open with a brick, and I throw up a mental thanks to the kids for their quick thinking as I pull it open and peer inside the empty interior.

"Quick in and out, boys," I remind them before taking off up the stairs. I can hear Razor behind me, but his footsteps fall away as I continue up to the top floor, and soon the only noise is my labored breathing and the soft thud of my boots against the floorboards with each step I climb. My senses are on high alert as I step onto the landing and glance around, and I don't waste any time as I move to the front right corner of the building. I'm not sure how long we have until First Responders arrive. I've no doubt that they'll have been notified of a disturbance at an Antonelli property, making it a top priority, and I sure as fuck don't want any of us to get caught by anyone on the Antonelli payroll.

Once I've stuck the first stick of C4 to the wall in the corner of a small room that smells of too much perfume and sex, I move on to the next corner, doing the same again. I'm into the home stretch, placing the last one, when a sound behind me has me snapping my gaze over my shoulder.

"Who the fuck are you?" A burly man—clearly security—demands. *Shit.* His gaze flicks past me to the obvious C4 attached to the wall, and his eyes widen. In a burst of movement, he whips out a pistol from the belt at his hip. My reaction is just as quick, and I palm my gun a split second before he does, pulling the trigger.

My bullet lands squarely in his chest, but not before he lands a shot of his own in my shoulder, and I hiss out a pained exhale as the force of the shot knocks me off balance. *Fucking hell, that hurts.* Righting myself, I keep my gun trained on the security guy as the blood drains from his face, and he stares at the openly bleeding wound in the middle of his chest before crashing to the floor.

With my gun pointed at him, I move closer and put a bullet in his head before glancing around the room. I spot a belt left abandoned on the bed and quickly snatch it up, wrapping it around my shoulder and pulling it tight. A grunt of pain escapes me, but the blood slows to a trickle, assuring me I won't bleed to death before I get the fuck out of here.

Hoping no one else heard the gunshots, I keep my weapon in my hand as I head downstairs.

"Shit, boss, you've been shot," Razor exclaims, striding toward me as I reach the first floor.

"No, shit," I grumble, not slowing my pace as I continue down the stairs, despite the fact that my vision blurs in and out several times and my head already feels woozy. My shoulder hurts like a bitch, and I have a sinking feeling that the bullet is wedged in there, meaning I'll have to get someone to dig it out and hope it hasn't left any lasting muscle or nerve damage.

It's only when we're outside that I slow down. "Did it go out the back?" I ask Razor, who steps closer to get a good look at the back of my shoulder.

"Nope, 'fraid not."

Fuck sake.

Giving him a terse nod, we make quick work of getting back to the car, and I blow out a breath of relief to find the kids and Dax already there. I toss the keys to Razor as we approach. "You drive."

I climb into the front passenger seat and dig the detonator out of my pocket. I cast my eyes over the building one final time, hoping the remaining lurkers are far enough away that they won't get hit by the blast before I press the button. The five of us watch as a loud boom thunders through the air, followed by a rush of pressure that rattles the windows, and the whole building starts to crumble before our eyes. Dust fills the air, quickly blocking our view of people running and screaming, but we don't wait around to see much more as Razor puts his foot to the pedal, and we speed out of there.

Adrenaline races through my veins, and all I can hear is the rushing of blood in my ears as we head back across the city toward the clubhouse. I try to get a better look at the gunshot wound, but the intermittent light from passing streetlamps isn't nearly enough for me to accurately determine the damage, and I soon give up, resting my head against the headrest. I'm not sure if I fall asleep or pass out, but when I next wake, Razor is pulling into the parking lot at the clubhouse.

My door is pulled open before I can get to it, and my head spins as someone helps me out of the car. *Fucking blood loss.* "Where's O?" I bite out as my good arm is thrown over someone's shoulder—Dax's?—and he maneuvers me into the building.

"He's not back yet," someone else responds as I'm unceremoniously dumped onto a chair. I grunt out some sort of incoherent response as I struggle to think through my murky thoughts and work out what to do. Fucking hell, I really need to get a doctor on my payroll.

"Yeah, you do, Boss. But since you don't have one right now, what do you want us to do?"

Fuck, I didn't mean to say that out loud.

I squint up at Razor—huh, maybe it was him that helped me in—who is frowning down at me, but his gaze is steady and sure. "Whiskey," I bark out. With a nod, he goes off to do as I ordered, and I let my head fall back against the sofa while I wait. Some whiskey will chase away the pain and help me think straight.

My eyes drift closed and I hear Evie's voice. Looking around, I peer through the oppressive darkness surrounding me until I find her, bathed in sunshine and calling my name as if welcoming me into the light.

"Evie? What are you doing here?"

"I'm waiting for you, big brother. Aren't you coming?"

"Where are we going?"

Her grin is as bright and angelic as I remember, and I take a step toward her, not needing an answer to my question. I'd follow her goddamn anywhere. "You'll see. It's beautiful. You'll love it."

I take another step toward her, but the movement twists my vision, allowing a ray of light to pierce my sister. Pausing, I stare at the spot where the beam passes right through her, as though she's not really there. It hits me, knocking the air from my lungs.

"You aren't real." The hopelessness in my voice is unmissable. "You're not here."

Lifting my gaze to meet her teary eyes, I state the cold hard truth for both of us. "Evie, you're dead."

She shakes her head as if she doesn't want to believe what I'm saying, and she holds out her hand, pleading with her eyes for me to take it. "Please, Cain. Just come with me. I miss you." That honest admission threatens to rip open my chest, and I very nearly cave to her pleas.

It takes everything in me to stand there and shaking my head, I whisper, "I can't. Not until I've gotten my revenge on the men who took you from me."

Evie shakes her head, and I can see her gearing up for a fight. "I don't care about any of that, Cain," she argues. "I just want you."

For once, I refuse to give in to her demands. "Not until they're all dead," I promise her.

Her lips part, but before she can argue her point further, the world seems to tilt on its axis, and the vision before me blurs, becoming fuzzy.

"Evie!" I call out as my heart thrashes in my chest, not wanting to lose her already. "Evie!"

The world tips into darkness as Evie is once again lost to me, but just when I think I'm lost to the void, my eyes blink open, and I stare into the most beautiful set of piercing blue eyes.

"About fucking time, you wimp," Red snaps, but relief shines in her eyes—eyes that I can't stop staring at. Were they always that vivid and full of life? "You'll go down in history as the most pathetic gang leader of all time if you let a minor bullet wound take you out," she continues to gripe.

Her words bring me crashing back to reality, and the pain in my shoulder flares to life, making me groan. "Where the hell is that whiskey?" I grouch.

She shoves a bottle into my hands, and I tip my head back, guzzling it down and barely noticing the burn as it hits my stomach. Warmth radiates out, quickly dulling the pain to a manageable level, and I find I can focus more sharply on the gorgeous, fiery woman standing in front of me, closely inspecting my injury.

"Please tell me you have a decent first aid box with a suture kit?" she asks someone behind me. My attention is going in and out, though, so I miss their response, only zoning in again as she barks more orders at them. "I need the saline solutions you find in first aid kits—as many as you can get your hands on. Or if anyone wears contacts, I need their lens solution."

When she returns her attention to me again, she slides a short, thin dagger out of a holster attached to her thigh. *So fucking hot.*

She smirks at me, twirling the blade in her hand. *Dammit, I must have said that aloud.*

"You did," she states, sounding far too smug. Palming her blade, she works it through my t-shirt until she can strip it off.

"If you wanted me out of my clothes, all you had to do was ask."

Her laugh is low and husky and goes straight to my dick, even though she's barely paying me any attention, too busy studying my wound as she uses the balled-up fabric to wipe around it.

"What's the consensus?" I ask, tearing my gaze away from her to look at the injury.

The belt is still strapped around my shoulder, and a slow trickle of blood runs down my chest. She swipes at it with the top before answering me.

"Well, I'm no doctor, but I *think* you might just live." I grunt out a response. "Bullet's lodged in there, though"—her gaze flicks to mine—"I'm going to have to dig it out."

I don't respond, instead bringing the bottle of whiskey to my lips again and downing several large gulps. I've had to get a couple of bullets removed in the past, so I know they hurt like a motherfucker.

Someone drops the large first aid kit I keep in the office for such situations as these, along with a pile of saline packets and bottles on the sofa beside me, and with a thanks, Red begins tearing them open one at a time and pouring them in and around the wound. I sit and watch, occasionally knocking back another gulp of whiskey while she works, ensuring the wound is thoroughly cleaned.

When she's satisfied that it's as clean as it's going to get, she leans in, palming her blade again. The move brings her face close to mine, enough that I notice the stress lines along her forehead and the nervous way she tugs on her lower lip, prompting my question. "Have you done this before?"

Her gaze flicks to mine, and she pushes her shoulders back, already looking more sure than she did a moment ago. "Once."

Well, that's once more than I'd expected, although... "Did the person survive?"

I ask it as more of a joke, already anticipating her snarky response as I take another swallow of whiskey, which is why I choke when she responds, "Well, I'm standing here in front of you, aren't I?"

"You?" I choke out between coughs. "You removed a bullet from your own shoulder?"

"Yup, and it hurt like a bitch, so stop choking on that shit and finish off the bottle."

Ignoring her, I stare at her shoulder. She's wearing a thin-strapped, low-cut vest top, so I can see every inch of her smooth, unblemished skin. Definitely no bullet wound there. I flick my gaze to her other shoulder, the one covered in her vine tattoo, and it takes a second before I spot it, but it's there. Right in the center of a flowering bud, the skin is puckered and uneven. *Huh.* I'm dying to know the story behind it, but she doesn't give me a chance to ask as she orders me once again to finish off the bottle.

Doing as instructed, I keep my eyes trained on hers as I swallow down the last of the whiskey and lick my lips. Her eyes track the movement, but she doesn't say anything. Simply gives a satisfied nod as I discard the bottle before tightening her hold on the blade and leaning in again, her face inches from my shoulder.

She hovers like that for a minute or so, not making any move to actually get the bullet out of my shoulder, before she sighs. Pulling back, she frowns, grumbling, "fuck it," under her breath and climbing into my lap before I can stop her. Not that I would —that would just be stupid. What grown-ass, red-blooded male would ever say no to having a hot-as-sin vixen like her in their lap?!

The move has her large tits bouncing right in front of my face, like fucking temptation served up on a platter, just begging for me to lean forward and suck her nipple into my mouth. The feel of her crotch as it settles over mine distracts me, and her brows hitch when she discovers the unmistakable bulge in my pants. A sharp bark of laughter escapes between her lips. "You're such a masochist," she teases.

I just grin at her, drunk on blood loss, adrenaline, and the feel of her pressed against me—not to mention the entire bottle of whiskey I just downed. "Who doesn't like a little pain with their pleasure?" My hands move to rest on her hips in an automatic reflex, pulling her closer until she's fully seated over my crotch. Leaning in, I murmur in her ear, "Don't lie to me, I *know* you like it too."

Her teeth bite into her bottom lip, and for a long second, I debate replacing them with mine, but before I can act on the notion, she releases her lip. "Cain?" Her voice is raw, throaty.

"Yeah?"

"Your shoulder."

With a gentle hand to my chest, she pushes me back, and in the space of a blink, the lust clears from her eyes. *Right. Bullet wound. That probably trumps getting my dick wet.*

She takes a second to get her head back in the game, and I watch, fascinated as she seems to shut herself down so she can focus on what she needs to do. Is that what she does for her Reaper jobs? Just shove her entire personality, her entire being, into a box at the back of her mind? Talk about compartmentalization. It's both impressive and a little terrifying.

When she next looks at me, her gaze is sure and steady. "Do you trust me?"

I'm still looking deep into her eyes when I reply with confidence, "Yeah, I do." I have no idea when that happened or how. I guess we all have to trust each other—at least to some degree—if we're going to work together and have any hope of success, but it's more than that. My head's just too fuzzy to work it out right now.

She doesn't react to my admission but rather angles the knife toward the gaping wound and slowly, steadily, pushes it in. My muscles tense, and I'm gritting my teeth so hard that I'll be lucky not to crack one before this is all over. The odd grunt of pain escapes me as she digs around, trying to free the bullet, and it takes everything in me not to flinch with every scrape of her blade. More blood flows down my chest, and I try to force myself to focus on something else. Anything else. She shifts in my lap, her apex brushing over my still semi-erect cock... *Hmm, well, that's definitely a distraction.*

My gaze dips to where her thighs straddle mine, and I lose track of time for a moment, until her grated, "Cain," draws me out of my daze.

"Huh?" Lifting my head, I meet her deep-blue gaze, finding her jaw clenched tight.

"Unless you want my blade to slip and accidentally embed itself in your shoulder, *please* stop touching me like that."

Confused, I slowly run my gaze down her body until I find where I'm touching her. My hand freezes in place on her hip, where it somehow managed to wedge itself underneath her top, and I must have been absently stroking her skin.

"Uh, sorry," I mumble. Still, I make no effort to remove my hand. I find the heat from her skin oddly comforting. It anchors me, and after a moment, when she goes back to torturing my shoulder and the now-familiar burn of pain radiates out from where she's poking and prodding at the bullet, I focus solely on the smooth texture of her skin against my palm, the low heat that signifies the rushing of blood through her body, reminding me of just how very much alive she is.

I've spent so much of my life living for a ghost; avenging her, I've forgotten what it's like to actually *see* a woman. I'm not talking about admiring a woman or having sex with one, but to truly open yourself up to one, to be fully present in the moment, and appreciate everything that's right in front of you. Red tests me in a way nobody else ever has. She's not afraid to stand up and speak her mind or disagree with me—something that I haven't had much of since forming the Rejects. More importantly, though, every time I volley with her, or even when we were just sitting in the ice cream shop, or here, now, with her in my lap, she makes me *feel* alive. Something I don't remember feeling since before Evie. Something I never thought I'd be capable of experiencing again.

I grunt at an unexpected white-hot flash of pain. "Got it." Red grins triumphantly as she holds up the tiny metal bullet before dropping it into the empty whiskey bottle. She goes through another round of cleaning out the wound before taking out a suture kit and making quick work of closing it up. It's by no means professional, but it's probably better than anything the guys or I could do. I watch her the whole time, flicking between following her steady movements and analyzing the furrow of her brow and the way she purses her lips as she concentrates on the job.

She's sticking a waterproof bandage over her handiwork when the front door opens and Oliver comes surging in, his eyes wide. It's only then that I realize Red and I were alone. The rest of the guys must have cleared out to give us some privacy so as not to distract her.

"Dax said you were shot?" Oliver questions, his eyes darting back and forth between Red and me. His brows pull together in confusion, probably surprised to find us alone in the same room without screaming at one another.

"You know me, practically bulletproof." I grin at him, making his brow cock.

Red snorts, shaking her head. "Definitely not bulletproof. Pretty sure the alcohol coursing through his system is stopping him from feeling the pain, but he'll be fine."

Oliver slowly relaxes, his shoulders unbunching as he strides toward us. He takes a good, hard look at my bandaged shoulder before moving the first-aid supplies and sinking into the seat beside me. In one swift move, he drags Red out of my lap and into his. It bothers me how much I miss her nearness, and with my hand no longer glued to her hip, I lean forward and grab another bottle of whiskey off the table.

Twisting off the lid, I swallow down a quarter of the bottle while Oliver greets Red, and she settles in against him. The way she seems to melt into his arms, it's so at odds with the tense way she held herself when she was perched in my lap, and for some reason, that annoys me.

"So," Oliver starts, "what the hell happened tonight?"

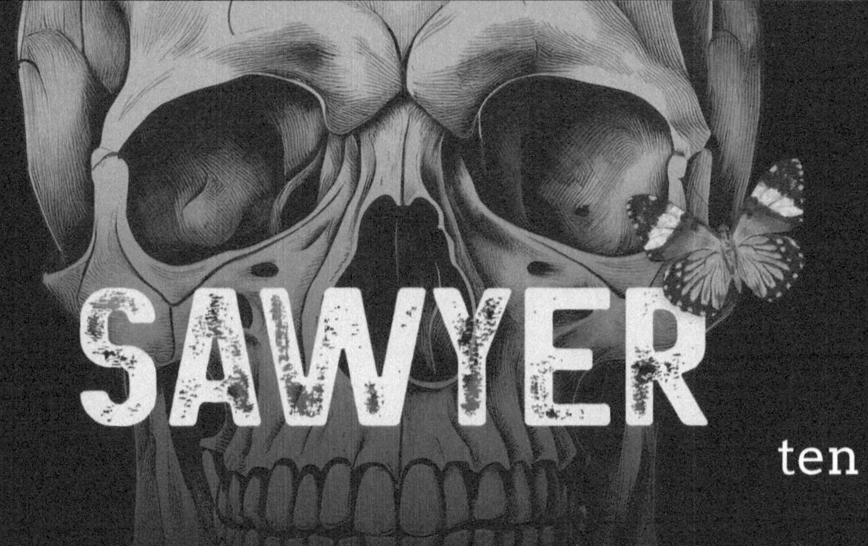

Stealing the whiskey from Cain, I relax into Oliver's comforting embrace and take a well-deserved swig from the bottle while Cain rehashes tonight's events. I'd never let it show, but hearing he had been shot scared me more than I care to admit, and digging that bullet out of his shoulder was a real test of my ability to work in a high-stress situation. Somehow, it was way fucking worse than patching up my own bullet wound, and trust me, that was no easy feat. It didn't help that he had his hands all over me, making it impossible to think straight, and the way he watched my every move... fuck was it intense, even with the glassy sheen in his eyes from too much whiskey.

I couldn't stop hearing the raw emotion in his voice when I ran into the room and heard him mumbling Evie's name. Just remembering it makes my chest hurt. The second I saw the blood, I was across the room and in front of him, assessing the damage, but when I heard him whimper her name, like a lost soul searching for the light... I had to stop myself from climbing into his lap there and then to try and soothe his pain. *So much for my insistence earlier not to let him get to me.* Unfortunately, it seems Cain's already embedded under my skin. I'm not sure that any amount of digging is going to get him out.

I'd only stopped by to try and make amends with Oliver for avoiding him all week, but there was no way I could just sit back and watch Cain in pain like that—both physical and psychological. I had to help; I needed to.

"Everything went as planned on your end?" Cain asks Oliver, sounding more alert than he did earlier.

"Yeah, easy in and out. No one was around."

"Why exactly did the two of you think it was a good idea to go blowing up Antonelli territory?" I argue, my characteristic red-haired temper sparking.

"We're hoping it will force Dante into checking on their other clubs," Oliver responds, taking the whiskey from me and bringing it to his lips.

"Smart," I reluctantly admit. "Reckless, but smart. Would have been nice to know what you were up to before you went off half-cocked, though."

Cain cocks a brow. "Yeah? Like you did, when you went and got a job at Belle Donne without informing us?"

Crap, he's got me there.

"Fine," I gripe. "Can we all agree from here on out to discuss our plans with one another?"

"Deal," Oliver quickly assents. He offers the whiskey to Cain in a silent gesture of *shut the fuck up and drink*. One Cain accepts with a grumble. "Fine, but I wanna hear that story."

The twinkle in his eyes ensures I know exactly what story he wants to hear, and I roll my eyes as Oliver pipes up, "What story?"

"Our little Reaper is a badass." Cain's lips quirk up in a mischievous smile. "Extracted a bullet from her shoulder all by herself."

"You what?" I can feel Oliver's eyes run over my skin until he finds the circular scar on my left shoulder. His fingers brush against the skin and the light touch makes me shiver.

"It was nothing, really," I say, trying to shrug it off. It's not like I had any other options. I couldn't exactly show up at a hospital with a bullet wound without raising questions, nor did I have the cash to pay for that visit. I didn't have anyone I could just call up in the middle of the night, and I needed to deal with the situation before Luc woke up for school in the morning.

Oliver snorts behind me. "Don't bullshit us. We've both been shot more than once, so we know how much it hurts, never mind the mental fortitude it would take to actually push past that pain and fish out the bullet yourself."

I shrug, unused to receiving such a compliment. "Well, it was either that or bleed out. Death wasn't an option."

Oliver's arm tightens around me. "Next time you're injured or in a bind like that, come to us."

There's no room for protests or negotiations in his tone, and Cain backs him up before I can even begin to argue. "Agreed." My eyebrows lift in surprise, and he tacks on, "At the very least, I owe you for tonight."

I hesitate before nodding in agreement. Oliver nuzzles my neck, pulling me tighter against him.

After a second, Cain clears his throat. "Well, it's late, and I'd better get some sleep before the alcohol wears off." Pushing to his feet, he hovers, staring down at me for a second before walking off.

I watch him disappear as Oliver lavishes my neck with kisses. "You've been avoiding me," he chastises when we're alone. There's no real heat in his voice, so I know he's not annoyed, just making an observation.

Tearing my gaze away from where Cain disappeared, I shift in Oliver's lap to look at him over my shoulder. "I know. I came over tonight to apologize."

"Hmm." He plants another kiss at the crook of my neck. "Do you wanna talk about it?"

I shake my head, leaning back against him and letting his soft touches relax me.

"No, I was just being stupid. I was beating myself up because I wasn't making any headway at Belle Donne."

"And you were worried you were letting us down," he correctly states.

"Yeah." I sigh. "I know how much this means to you and Cain."

Thankfully, false reassurances don't start pouring from his lips. Instead, he takes his time thinking over everything I've said before he speaks up. "I know what you mean. I have the same fears." His admission takes me by surprise. "I'd do anything to help Cain get the vengeance he needs, and the last few months here, I've seen just how much he really needs this. It's become an obsession. He's not going to be able to move on and live his own life until he's done right by Evie. It only increases the pressure to succeed."

"She mattered to you too, though?"

He's quiet for a long moment. The only sound is his soft breaths against the shell of my ear. "Yeah, she did." He doesn't say anything for the longest time, and I assume he's not going to tell me anymore, so I'm not expecting his quietly spoken admission. "She's the only girl I've ever loved... Or at least, I thought I did. I dunno, can kids even fall in love?"

I show him the same respect he showed me by thinking over my answer instead of just offering fake platitudes. "I think you're allowed to feel whatever you feel for her. Who says you have to be a certain age to fall in love? She was clearly a very special girl."

"Yet what I felt for her pales in comparison to the way I'm starting to feel about you." It's a quiet confession, barely more than a whisper, as though he's afraid to say it any louder.

My heart hammers against my chest, and any sort of response I could offer him lodges in my throat. *What the hell am I supposed to say to that?* I can't possibly compete with a dead girl. Do I even want to?

When I fail to respond, he gives my side a reassuring squeeze. "We should probably get some sleep."

Happy not to linger on that awkward conversation, I climb to my feet and turn around to pull him up. When he's standing in front of me, I fist the front of his shirt and drag him down until his lips meet mine. I may not have any idea how to respond to what he just told me, but I do care about him—a lot—and I'm grateful he made it back unharmed tonight.

I push all of my feelings for Oliver into that kiss. Instead of words, I use my lips, tongue, and teeth to show him how he makes my heart race, to thank him for the steady comfort he offers me, and to demonstrate that my feelings run just as deep as his. I feel the same potential for us as he does. We're both breathless by the time we break apart, and Oliver's wicked grin confirms he read everything I intended him to.

His hands come up to rest on either side of my neck, and he draws me back in as he lowers his face to mine. It's so easy to lose myself in him. Unlike when I kiss Cain, there's no resistance, no fight, but it's no less intoxicating. If anything, his kisses are more dangerous. The kind you can envision waking up to every morning, that you can melt into after a hard day, and bolster you when you're feeling low. They have the power to make you feel invincible. To feel loved and worshipped, and to make you want to spend the whole day in bed together. Yeah, Oliver's kisses are devastating for a girl's heart.

"Come on, Trouble, before I change my mind and keep you all to myself for the night."

Confused, I follow as he slips his hand in mine and leads me toward his bedroom. My brows only dip lower when he stops outside Cain's room and looks at me.

My eyes flick from his to Cain's closed door and back. "I don't understand."

"You should stay with him tonight. Make sure he's okay."

"Oh. I don't think the bullet hit anything major, but uh, yeah. I-I can do that."

He tucks a finger under my chin, lifting my head until I meet his gaze. There's a hint of laughter in his eyes, but I can't understand why. "Cain's far too stubborn to let a bullet to the shoulder do him in," he begins, only confusing me further. "He's also too stubborn to admit when he doesn't want to be alone."

As his words penetrate, my lips part until I'm left gaping at him, speechless. "You want me to spend the night with another man?" Is this some sort of a test? Is he testing me right now to see if I'll choose him over Cain? If that's the case, then why does a dull ache form in my chest at the thought of picking one of them over the other?

He chuckles softly, tucking a loose strand of hair behind my ear before stroking his thumb over my cheek. "Don't get me wrong, I'm fighting back the urge to throw you over my shoulder and take you to my bed, but Cain needs you tonight. Not that he'd ever ask or tell you that himself." When I continue to stare at him in a mixture of surprise and shock, he elaborates, "I see the way you interact. I can practically taste the pheromones when you're around one another. I know he's not easy to deal with at times, but I think you'd be good for him." His gaze darts back and forth between my eyes as he ponders on something. "In fact, I think you could be exactly what he needs."

I don't exactly know what he means by that, and it's far too late to delve into it tonight. So instead, when he pushes open the door, I simply step into Cain's darkened room, not entirely sure whether I'm doing the right thing or not.

As I listen to the soft click of the door closing behind me, I feel strangely nervous, standing there in the darkness. I can just about make out the shape of Cain lying in his bed, the soft, regular rhythm of his breathing alerting me that he's sound asleep. It feels weird to just climb in beside him. What if Oliver's wrong and Cain doesn't want me in here? Whatever Cain and I have going on is complicated, to say the least. Yeah, I understood some of what Oliver was trying to say. The chemistry between us is off the charts, which makes for excellent sex, but beyond that? I haven't got a fucking clue. I don't even know if I want anything more with him. Hell, the sex is complicated enough, never mind throwing in feelings and expectations. Although, aren't feelings already involved? Tonight, and the panic I felt when I saw him on that couch, has shown me that I care about Cain for more than just sexual gratification. I was genuinely concerned for his well-being. More than that, even. I was fucking terrified when I laid eyes on him, covered in blood and looking unnaturally pale.

Nevertheless, that doesn't mean he feels the same way. *He* might not want *me* in his bed, and waking up to a pissed-off Cain telling me to get the fuck out isn't exactly how I want to start my day.

I stifle a groan as exhaustion tugs at me. Scanning my eyes around the room, I spot the outline of an armchair to one side of the bed and decide that's probably the best solution. There's no way I'm going to run off to Oliver and admit I was too scared to even stay in the same room as Cain.

Making my way over as quietly as possible, I slip my feet out of my boots. There's a hoodie on the arm of the chair, and I tug it on over my top, ignoring the uniquely Cain scent of whiskey and leather that washes over me as I huddle up on the chair. My eyelids feel heavy, and despite the awkward position, it's not long until sleep pulls me under.

I JUMP AWAKE, MY HAND INSTINCTIVELY REACHING FOR THE BLADE STILL in its thigh holster as I scan the room, searching for whatever woke me up. I catch a flicker of movement a second before the bedside light switches on, momentarily blinding me.

"Fucking Christ, Red. Are you trying to give me a heart attack?" Cain grumbles. "If you wanted me dead, you probably shouldn't have saved my life earlier." I'm still blinking the black dots out of my vision so I don't pierce him with a dark enough glare deserving of his dry remark. "What the fuck are you doing in here, anyway?"

I rub the sleep out of my eyes before responding. "Just wanted to make sure you didn't die in your sleep," I gripe. "Didn't need one of your lackeys demanding my head 'cause they thought I was responsible."

He snorts, walking across the room toward me. It's only then that I notice he's only wearing boxer shorts, showing off every inch of his tattooed body, from his broad chest and toned abs to his tree-trunk thighs and lean calves. So much skin. So many tattoos. My poor eyes don't know where to look, and instead, my gaze ends up darting all over the place, probably making me look like I'm having a seizure as I struggle to commit every inch of him to memory.

"You've got a little bit of drool there, Red," he teases, pointing to the corner of his lip.

Snapping my mouth shut, I flip him my middle finger as he walks past me into the adjoined bathroom, laughing. He doesn't even bother to close the door behind him, subjecting me to the sound of him pissing before he finishes up and re-emerges. He barely spares me a glance as he climbs back into the bed. Only when he's gotten himself comfy does he spear me with a quirked brow. "Well, are you gonna sit over there all night or come and get some sleep?"

My lips purse as I try to figure out if this is a trick and whether I want to be that close to a basically naked Cain. I mean, yes, every womanly part of me is screaming at me to climb under that sheet with him, but the tiny rational part of my brain that is functioning knows how bad Cain's close proximity is for my health.

"Fucking hell, Red," he grumbles when I show no sign of moving. "Just get into the damn bed." He points at the blade still in my hand. "But no fucking knives."

After another moment's hesitation, the need to stretch out on a proper bed over-rides everything else. I shuck out of my jeans, setting my holster and blade on the bedside table before sliding under the sheet. I'm careful to keep my back to Cain as I curl up on my side, but when he makes no effort to turn out the light, I look back at him over my shoulder, finding him watching me with a strange look on his face. He shakes off whatever he was thinking as he switches off the lamp, plunging the room into darkness once again. There's the rustling of the sheet as he gets comfy, and I swear I can feel his body heat radiating across the bed. I don't dare move. Hell, I barely breathe.

His bed is incredibly comfortable, though, and soon my consciousness gives way to dreams.

Hours later, the unfamiliar feeling of heat at my back wakes me up, and as I shift under the bed sheet, something tightens around my waist. Glancing down, I find a fully tattooed arm wrapped around me as the source of the searing heat finally registers. Cain. I tense, but as I listen to the soft sounds of his breathing, I realize he's still asleep, and I slowly relax. Peering up at the window, the sun appears to be low in the sky, the pre-dawn glow barely enough to light up the room. It must be crazy early. Usually, I'd get up and work out, but I find myself not wanting to move, and the longer I lie there, the more relaxed I become until I drift back into a deep sleep. When I peel my eyes open a couple of hours later, I'm alone in the bed, but Cain's side is still warm, so he mustn't have gotten up long ago. I have no idea what to make of everything that transpired between us last night. Will it change anything? Or do we both sweep it under the rug and go back to our usual bickering and angry, lust-filled glowers?

eleven

Fire trucks and ambulances block the street by the time I pull up outside the charred remains of La Puttana. Smoke is thick in the air, and the firefighters are hard at work putting out the last of the flames.

"Fucking hell," Dante grumbles from beside me, taking in the pits of the building.

Tearing my gaze away, I survey the small crowd still gathered in the streets—primarily women that worked in the club and nosey onlookers.

"What the hell happened here?" I demand, striding up to the scantily clad woman closest to me. Her eyes are dilated in shock and only grow bigger when her gaze darts behind me, and she notices Dante. Her lower lip trembles, although I can't be sure whether that's from tonight's events or my presence.

"I, uh, don't know. The fire alarm went off, so we all came outside, then a few minutes later, the whole place exploded."

"You didn't see anything unusual? No one who didn't belong?"

She shakes her head adamantly. "No. It was just the usual crowd."

"Did everyone make it out in time?"

"Uh, yeah. Yes, I think so."

My lips purse as I try to figure out whether or not this could have been an accident. It seems too coincidental that the fire alarm went off just in time for everyone to escape before the building went up in flames.

"Talk to the other girls. Find out if anyone saw something. If they did, I want to know."

"Yes. No problem." She immediately moves to talk to another similarly dressed woman, and dismissing them, I head toward where Dante is talking to one of the fire-fighters. He steps away as I approach. "Apparently, the place was rigged with C4." My eyebrows hitch at that piece of information. *Definitely not an accident, then.*

"Who would be stupid enough to blow up one of our clubs?"

"No idea," Dante responds. "Grim Bastards?"

I shake my head. "Not their style. Whomever it was set off the fire alarm first, they didn't want any casualties."

My phone rings in my pocket, and I go to decline the call. However, the name of our head of security gives me pause, and instead, I lift it to my ear. "Yeah?" The muscle in my jaw grows tighter as I listen to what he has to say, and I don't even bother with a response before hanging up. "There was another attack."

"Where?"

"Escotica. It was closed for renovations."

"Fuck me," Dante growls, ensuring he keeps his voice low so no one around us can overhear.

I glance warily around the crowd before jerking my head back toward the car. "We should discuss this elsewhere." Besides, there's nothing else to be gained by hanging around here.

Dante agrees, and I fire off a quick text to our head of security, telling him to get someone down here in case anyone did see something worthwhile. We're both quiet as I navigate through the otherwise empty roads, all the way to the very edge of Antonelli territory, where a row of apartment buildings line the Black Creek river, separating our part of the city from the downtown area and eastern side.

Pulling into an underground parking lot, we both get out. Neither of us speaks as we get into the elevator and ride it to the third floor before walking along the hallway until we reach a door with the number eighty-two attached to it. Digging the keys out of my pocket, I jiggle them in the lock and step in. I flick on the lights, illuminating the compact yet modern open-plan kitchen and living area, before grabbing two tumblers and a bottle of whiskey off the kitchen counter.

I bought this place the second I had enough money. Not that I spend much time here, but it's good to have a place in the city that's not linked in any way to the Antonellis. The deed is registered under a false name and the apartment was paid for via a bank account in the same name, ensuring the property cannot be traced back to me. After living under Giovanni's thumb for so many years, and even now, feeling like he's watching my every move, waiting for an excuse to kill me like he did my father, I needed someplace where I could just come to get away from it all. Dante's the only one who knows this place exists, although he's only been here a handful of times.

He's already gotten himself comfortable on one of the sofas—although the furrow of his brows and flat line of his lips gives away his irritation over tonight's events—so I claim the one opposite. Setting the glasses on the coffee table, I pour us both a hefty measure before lifting mine to my lips.

"They targeted us but weren't willing to risk the lives of our workers," Dante muses aloud as he reaches for his own glass. "And they targeted clubs, not our warehouses."

"Maybe it's one of the smaller gangs in the city trying to look like the big dogs?" I surmise. "Although, are there even many of them left?" I really don't know much about the goings-on in the rest of Black Creek, except for what pertains to Sawyer. I know a gang called Reaper Rejects recently took control of her part of the city, and I've heard the occasional rumor about how they're gaining more and more ground. The only other gang I'm familiar with is the Grim Bastards. They have had control of the eastern part of the city since The Feral Beasts fucked off, and we've had an understanding with them ever since. I don't see why they would piss all over that now, and as I said earlier, it's not their style to try and save lives. They'd have bombed that place to kingdom come and not given a shit about the casualties.

"Well, someone has it out for us," Dante bites out before downing the last of his whiskey. "We've always ignored the rest of the city. Left the gangs to sort out their own shit, but maybe it's time we started paying attention. One of them has gotten too big for their boots if they think they can just come into our territory and blow up our clubs without any sort of retaliation."

I nod my head in agreement while grabbing my phone and typing out a quick text. There's a certain redhead who is excellent at gathering intel and would be much more in the know when it comes to the who's who of Black Creek gangsters. I fight a smirk as I tell her to meet me at our new usual spot tomorrow, knowing the order will infuriate her.

When I'm done, I move on to the next problem. "In the meantime, we need to find somewhere else for the girls to work while we rebuild. And tighten security around the other clubs in case they decide to hit them as well."

Leaning forward, Dante pours another shot of whiskey, downing it before his heated eyes bore into me. "Tomorrow." He juts his chin in my direction. "Take off your shirt."

Smirking, and more than happy to forget about tonight's events, I finish the last of my own drink before doing as he says. "Now your pants," he orders as I shrug out of my shirt. Unbuckling my belt, I lift my hips enough to push my pants over my ass, taking my boxers along with them until I can kick them and my shoes off. Before he can direct me further, I palm my quickly hardening cock. My eyes hold his as he watches me get myself off. My skin heats beneath his perusal, and images of a feisty redhead have my hand and abs coated in cum in no time as my eyes slam shut, and I groan out my release.

By the time I peel my eyes open, Dante's stripping off the last of his clothes and prowling toward me. This thing between Dante and I... it's undefinable. It's friendship, sex, and the fact that we only have each other to rely on, all mixed up into one. We both enjoy it—immensely—but we also don't look too closely at what it is. It's just two people trying to carve out moments of pleasure and seek comfort in someone else in an otherwise cruel, dark, and depressing world. Why does it need to be anything more than that?

I'M A QUARTER OF THE WAY THROUGH MY STRAWBERRY ICE CREAM SUNDAE when the loud ding of the bell above the door alerts me to Sawyer's presence. She's half an hour early, but seeing as she's always here before me—and given who she is and how she doesn't trust me—I'd assumed she would come early to case out the place. Today, I made sure to arrive before her—something she's clearly not happy about if the death glare she's giving me is any indication—and had the pimple-faced kid behind the counter serve me before giving him a generous tip and telling him to fuck off for an hour.

Ignoring her glower, I smile at her. I'd had my reservations about telling her who I was, but now that she knows, I'm done being standoffish. It only ever made her more suspicious of me. The fact that she knows who I really am and didn't immediately cut all ties is telling. Yeah, she's undoubtedly wary of the Antonellis. I'm sure she's heard the stories and rumors—most of which are true—but she still reached out to me for help. She still showed up here today. She may be guarded and untrusting of me, but she's here... and that I can work with.

"Ice cream?" I offer, pushing the sundae glass across the table toward her as she slides into the booth opposite me. Her gaze darts from me to the pink ice cream and back again, an incredulous look flashing across her face like I just asked if she'd like to swallow a grenade.

She glances quickly around the ice cream parlor, checking we're alone. "Uhh, no. Thanks." Resting her forearms on the table's edge, she interlocks her fingers. "What did you want?"

Straight to the point, as always. I both like how direct she is and hate how impenetrable her walls are. But it's going to take more than a smile and ice cream to worm my way into Sawyer's good graces.

"Two of our clubs were attacked last night."

One of her eyebrows raises slightly, her only reaction to what I just said. "How tragic for you." Her deadpan tone gives away how little she gives a shit about Antonelli problems. And why should she? Hell, I barely give a shit.

"I need information on the various Black Creek gangs."

Her eyes narrow, her lips flattening into a thin line. "Is this some ploy to try and get me to gather information for you again? 'Cause, it's not happening. If I'd known you were an Antonelli, I never would have agreed to that deal." Pressing her hands flat on the table, she stands up. "We're done. Lose my number. Don't contact me again."

Before she can slide out of the booth, I reach across the table and grab ahold of her upper arm. "Don't lie to yourself," I growl angrily. "You never asked. You didn't want to know who you were in business with; what that information was for." She opens her mouth to argue, but I plow on. "You did what you had to do to save yourself and your brother. No one could blame you for your choices. But they were *your* choices." Shrugging out of my grip, she continues to glare daggers at me. "I got you that job at Belle Donne as a favor; now it's your turn to do one for me."

With eyes of steel, Sawyer slowly lowers herself back into her seat. Her expression is completely shut down now. Nothing but a cold, impenetrable mask. "I haven't exactly been keeping my ear to the ground recently." Even her voice is monotonous and lacks any warmth or her characteristic snark.

"Well, what about Reaper Rejects? They have control of your territory now. You must know something about them."

She shrugs. "Not really. They don't bother us much."

"Have you heard anything about them, or anyone else, having an issue with the Antonellis? Anyone who might have talked about making a stand against us?"

She sighs, getting annoyed. "No. As I said, I haven't been listening out for information recently." A small smirk lifts one side of her lips. "Besides, even if I did know something. I wouldn't tell you. A couple of clubs being attacked is the least of what the Antonellis deserve." The vitriol in her voice catches me by surprise. I know she doesn't like the Antonellis. No one in Black Creek does, and after getting caught up in their attack at G&T, she's got more reason than most to be pissed at them. However, the sheer hatred in her voice speaks to something more... but what?

My eyes narrow as I study her face, looking for any tell, but I can't pick up anything. Pursing my lips, I sigh. "Fine." I'd ask her to keep an ear out, but I know she won't.

"Good. We all done here?" She doesn't even wait for a response before pushing out of her chair again. I watch as she stands, feeling deflated and annoyed. I was hoping she would have some answers that I could take back to Dante. His father is already breathing down his neck to get to the bottom of this, but more than that, as I stare up into Sawyer's impassive face, I haven't the first idea how to bridge the impossible gap between us.

"Yeah, I guess."

Without another word, she turns on her heels, and I watch as she strides away from me, wishing there was some way I could make her see that I'm not the enemy. I'm not *her* enemy.

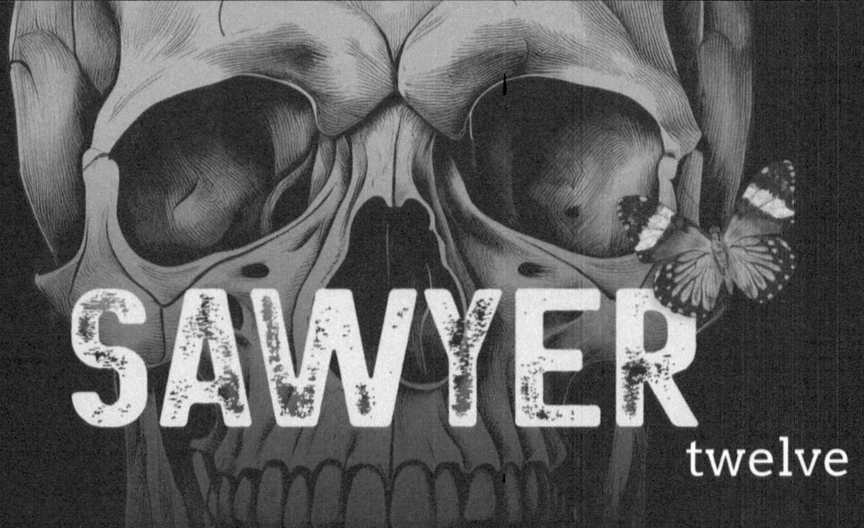

The next night, I'm on stage, performing my usual routine at Belle Donne. As always, instead of losing myself in the music like I do at Strip Tease, my focus is on the room—specifically, who is in it. Dante didn't show up last night, but after Cain and Oliver's reckless stunt, I'm quietly confident he will make an appearance someday this week. I've literally taken every available shift I could get to ensure I'm here when he is.

Stretching my arm above my head, I grab hold of the pole high above me and, lifting my legs, I twirl around it, sending the room into a spin. When I land back on my feet, I stumble in my high heels as my gaze collides with a set of very familiar—yet foreign—russet brown eyes before quickly correcting myself. For the rest of my performance, I'm just going through the motions, completely unaware of everyone else in the room. Dante's impossible to look away from, to the point where I feel like I'm putting on a show solely for him. He seems just as entranced, watching my every move with his unwavering, steely gaze. It doesn't burn my skin as Cain's does, but it's no less potent, and I suddenly get the feeling that having Dante's attention isn't necessarily a good thing.

I'm breathless, and an odd hum vibrates just beneath my skin as I climb down from the stage. Dante's already there, waiting for me, like I simultaneously knew and feared he would be. His hand grasps my elbow in a firm grip, and without saying a word, he escorts me through the club to the small back office. He pushes me into the single chair opposite a messy desk as the door swings shut. My heart is in my throat as he towers above me, his narrowed gaze slowly raking over my body, taking in my brown wig and matching contacts, before casually assessing the rest of my body—all of which is on display thanks to the skimpy outfit I'm dressed in tonight. The bra I'm wearing is practically see-through, and several scraps of leather fabric connect it to a high-riding thong. Decorative silver chains hang across my chest and along the lining of the thong. It's actually a pretty cool outfit, and it fits perfectly, the material clearly of a higher quality than what I'm used to. If I weren't wearing it on stage for a bunch of dirty pervs, then I'd definitely consider wearing it for Oliver... Or Cain.

"Who are you?" Dante's voice is a deep rasp, exactly how I remember it. That exhilarating mix of sexy and authoritative.

"I-I'm Red, sir," I reply meekly. "I'm new."

His eyes narrow to slits, and he leans in, planting a hand on either arm of my chair and boxing me in as he lowers his face so it's level with mine. "No, you're not. I saw you here several weeks ago."

I press my back flat against the chair, trying to put as much distance between us as possible. Not all of it is an act. Being this close to him again, knowing exactly what he's thinking, and that in the blink of an eye, he could shoot me dead with that pistol on his hip, has me feeling jittery and nervous.

"Y-yes, I-I remember." I lick my lips nervously and stare up at him with wide, innocent eyes. "That was my first night, b-but that guy *died*. It freaked me out, and I didn't come back." When I speak again, I force tears to my eyes and add a hitch to my voice. "But I needed the money." Giving a helpless shrug, I lower my gaze, curling in on myself. "So I came back."

I can sense him processing what I've said and trying to determine if it's the truth, but I don't dare look up at him, wanting to maintain my weak, placid demeanor. As much as I hate pretending to be so helpless, it's a ruse that usually works well on men. Cain is the only one that's seen through the act.

"No one remembered you." I can't tell from the level tone of his voice if Dante is testing the depth of my story or if he doesn't believe me.

"Like I said, it was my first night. I couldn't have been here more than half an hour before I heard the screaming and s-saw *him*." I shudder. "He was just lying there on the ground. It was *horrible*. I-I didn't even manage to find Franny b-before..."

This time, I glance up at him through my eyelashes as silence follows my explanation. He's frowning down at me, and I can tell he doesn't know whether to believe me or not.

After a long moment, he lifts his hand off the arm of the chair and, pressing his fingers firmly into the sides of my face, he lifts my head so he can analyze me. At first, I think he's trying to determine the truth, but his question throws me for a loop. "How do I know you?"

I look at him with genuine confusion. Surely not? There's no fucking way he can match the brown-eyed girl in front of him with the scrawny kid he threatened that night in the alley... right?

"I don't know."

He continues to stare into my eyes, and for a second, I'd almost swear he could see past my fake persona, past the contact lenses and wig. I hold my breath in expectation, just waiting for him to call bullshit. Yet, after what feels like a lifetime, he lets go and steps back. His brow is still furrowed, and I know this isn't the end of whatever this is.

"Fine," he relents. "You can get back to work."

With a jerky nod of my head, I quickly get to my feet, and without looking back, I scurry from the room and back to work. For the rest of the night, Dante stands at the back of the room, cloaked in shadows as he watches me. I'm not sure what it means, but it's exactly what I wanted, so I shake off the feeling that I've just gotten myself in way over my head and put on the show of a lifetime.

TWO NIGHTS LATER, DANTE IS BACK AGAIN, WATCHING ME FROM THE shadows. At first, he doesn't approach or try to talk to me, but I still know he's here *for me*. It's in the way his eyes follow my every movement, the fact that he ignores everyone but me. I'd have to be blind not to notice his attention.

"Sit," he orders later that night when I pass his table.

I hesitate, glancing around me. "Eh, I should probably be working."

"Sit."

My ass hits the seat before I have time to process that I've moved, and the corner of his lip twitches slightly. Was that a smile? Or an attempt at one? I trace the seam of his lips with my eyes, but they are firmly pressed into a flat line. From there, I take my time studying him, noting the beginnings of a five o'clock shadow and the lack of laugh lines around his mouth. His nose is long and narrow, his cheekbones prominent. Combined with his short-cut raven black hair and bronzed skin, it sets a cold and intimidating picture, but it's his eyes that emphasize his true character. Despite the ring of brown, which you'd think would soften them, it only enriches his otherwise obsidian pupils. I've never had this long to study him before, and the longer I stare, I start to discern the hints of russet running through his irises. The black, brown, and red all thread together, giving him the appearance of having already traveled through the nine circles of hell and come back to Earth to prove just how damn invincible he truly is.

For every second I spend analyzing him, he does the same to me. I have no idea what he sees, if it answers whatever questions he has about me or just raises new ones. And he doesn't offer me the consideration of seeing into his inner thoughts.

He doesn't say anything, and neither do I. I don't even know what I'd say to him. I know absolutely nothing about him, and I don't want to risk giving away anything that might connect the me sitting in front of him right now with the me he threatened eight years ago. I'm used to pretending to be someone else, but the act usually only lasts a few hours, and my targets are *always* inebriated. Not Dante, though. He hasn't touched the glass of scotch that was placed in front of him when he first sat down, and unlike my victims who don't give a shit beyond trying to get into my pants, Dante is paying attention to every micro move I make. He's aware of every breath I take, every flutter of my eyelashes. I wouldn't be surprised if he kept count and stored the information away for analysis at a later date.

"I talked to Franny," he eventually remarks. "She claims she didn't know of any new hires starting the night that client died."

"Oh? That's weird." I keep my tone surprised but carefully unbothered. Franny is old, after all. It's entirely possible it just slipped her mind.

"Yeah, it is."

I meet his watchful gaze with a steady one of my own. "It's possible she just forgot."

"It is. Which is why I looked at your employee file." I have to work hard to ensure the panic doesn't show on my face. I hadn't expected him to go to such lengths, and there's no way the start date on the file will line up with the night I killed Chad. *Fucking*

Chad. My palms begin to sweat, and it's almost painful to hold his gaze, but only a liar would break eye contact. I can barely hear his next words over the rushing of blood in my ears. "It checked out."

My throat is dry, and I have to swallow before I can respond. "Of course it did." *Oh my god, how the hell did that happen?* I can't even let myself think about it in case I let something slip. "I didn't lie to you."

"No." He drags out the word, still sounding suspicious. "It looks like you didn't."

"Can I get back to work now?" I bite out the words, letting anger replace the confusion and panic within me. "Or do you want to sit and interrogate me some more?"

I get nothing in response, not the slightest twitch of a muscle or blink of an eye. Eventually, he gives a barely perceptible jerk of his head, and I slowly, steadily, rise to my feet, cautious not to look as though I'm running away.

My stomach is still in knots as I step onto the street after my shift and glance around for the now-familiar Cadillac Escalade. Every night, a Reject member meets me after my shift and drives me home, and tonight is no exception as the car rolls to a stop in front of me.

Pulling open the door, a pleased grin lights up my face as I climb into the car. "Hey, you," I greet Oliver, leaning across the console and placing a quick kiss on his lips. "Wasn't expecting you to pick me up," I tell him as I pull off my wig and remove my contacts.

He gives a casual shrug. "We had nothing going on, so I thought I'd grab us some late-night Chinese." He points to a takeaway bag at my feet, and I groan as my mouth salivates.

"Mmm, that sounds amazing."

Smiling, his gaze dips to my lips, and his voice has this rough, sexy quality as he says, "Can we take it back to your place? I don't feel like sharing you with anyone else tonight." *Well, fuck, if that doesn't have me wanting to forgo dinner and jump straight to dessert.* I hesitate, though, and as if reading my mind, he tacks on, "Luc is at the club-house tonight with the kids."

I grin, and my voice is a seductive purr when I say, "Let's go then."

Pulling onto the street, Oliver's hand moves to rest just above my knee, and his fingers stroke lightly along my inner thigh. I barely feel the motion through my jeans, but the easy way he does it makes my insides go all gooey.

"How was tonight?" he asks, watching me out of the corner of his eye before returning his focus to the road.

"Looks like your stunt worked. Dante showed up."

"And?"

I give a slight shrug. "He remembered me. Pulled me into the office, wanting to know who I was." I'd explained to Oliver and Cain about my run-in with Dante the time I came to Belle Donne for a mark, and we'd all agreed to play dumb. "I did what we talked about."

"And he bought it?"

"I think so. He hung around for a good while afterwards, so I've definitely got his attention." I don't verbalize the uneasiness in my stomach about that. It will only serve to worry Oliver, and he might even talk to Cain about it, and the two of them will gang up and convince me to abandon my plan. I won't let that happen.

Oliver's hand tightens on my thigh, and when I look his way, his face is pinched. Reaching out, I place my hand over his. "We talked about this," I remind him. "This is a good thing. It's what we want."

"I know." His voice is strained. "Doesn't mean I have to like it, however. I hate not having eyes on you in there. You don't even have anything to defend yourself with."

"Jon's been helping me improve my fighting skills."

"Oh yeah?" A small smile curls on his lips as he turns to look at me for a second. "I'd like to see that."

I laugh. "I'm pretty sure I spend more time on the mat than on my feet, but I think I'm making some headway."

With another reassuring squeeze of my thigh, he says, "I'm sure you're doing great."

It's not long before we pull up outside my apartment building. Grabbing the Chinese takeaway plus my bag, I get out of the car and lead Oliver into the building. "Make yourself at home," I tell him when we step into my apartment. Flicking on the lights, I head into the kitchen to grab some plates and cutlery while he moves into the small living room. He takes a seat on the floor and starts setting various Chinese takeout containers out on the carpet.

"I wasn't sure what you liked, so I got a mixture," he explains when I join him.

"Sounds good." I claim a spot on the floor opposite him and the two of us dig into our food. "So…" I begin when I'm halfway through my mu shu pork. "What were you in prison for?"

He barks out a surprised laugh. "How long have you been waiting to ask me that?"

I shrug unapologetically and smirk at him. "A while. Despite your affiliation with the Rejects, you just don't seem like the type to do hard time."

"Oh no?" he questions. "I don't give off that asshole, thug vibe?"

"Hell, no," I snort, chuckling. "That's more Cain's thing."

"True." The lightheartedness fades away, and a somber expression crosses his face. "After Evie was taken, I was lost. We all were. And shortly after Evie, our other friend—Beck—moved away, and Cain and I… we drifted apart, dealing with our grief in our own ways. I stumbled into The Feral Beasts—"

A small gasp of surprise escapes me. The Feral Beasts ruled this town with an iron fist until a few years ago. Their reign was violent and brutal, and their name is still said with a hint of fear. The Oliver I've come to know just doesn't add up with my image of a Beast.

"I was hurt and angry and spinning out of control," he goes on to explain. "I naively thought the Beasts could help me gain some of that control back. And for a while, they did. They provided an outlet for all those emotions I didn't know how to process. By the time I came up for oxygen and actually paid attention to my surroundings, I was in too deep, without a fucking clue how to get out."

I nod in understanding. Gangs like that—like the Beasts or Antonellis—they suck you in. They prey on vulnerability and youthful naivety. Blind kids with the prospect of money, cars, and girls. Then once they have you hooked, they flip the tables. You have to do whatever they want. There's no walking away from gangs like that. Not with your life intact. Once you're in, you're in it for life. Nothing other than dying for the cause is acceptable.

"Anyway, eventually, they fucked themselves over, biting off more than they could chew. They got caught up in illegal shit that was beyond their capabilities. Along with a couple of others who no longer wanted to be Beasts, we helped secure their demise, but a friend of mine got injured in the process. To help ensure he and the others got away, I stayed behind when the cops came."

"So you sacrificed yourself?" I question in awe.

He gives a nonchalant shrug. "They were teenagers. None of them should have been caught up in that mess, and they certainly didn't deserve to spend time in prison for something they didn't do."

"Neither did you."

"Maybe not, but I didn't have as much to lose." Despite his words, a soft smile curls on his lips, and he digs his phone out of his pocket before showing me the screen. "The two with tattoos are Aiden and Ty. They were in the Beasts with me, and then they met Sophie, Preston and Barrett."

The photo shows all four guys surrounding a brown-haired girl. All five of them are sporting bright grins, and the way they are all pressing in on Sophie, it's obvious they're all more than friends. "They seem so happy," I comment.

"Yeah." Oliver chuckles softly, pocketing his phone. "They weren't always. They all had to fight hard for what they have, but it all worked out for them in the end."

"Are they... all in a relationship together?" I question hesitantly. Call me curious, especially given my feelings for Oliver and the attraction I feel toward Cain that I can't seem to get over.

Oliver just chuckles. "Yeah. Well, they are all in a relationship with her."

My brows scrunch together. "How does that work? Don't they get jealous? Doesn't all that testosterone drive her insane?" Half an hour in Cain's presence is enough to have me climbing the walls, never mind dealing with four of him twenty-four seven. Although I could easily spend the day with Oliver... maybe her guys are more like Oliver than Cain.

"I imagine there is a lot of jealousy and one-upmanship going on. Especially in the beginning, but they make it work. Beck, the childhood friend I mentioned, he's also in a similar relationship. It's more common than you'd think." He quirks a brow and a teasing smile plays along his lips. "Why? Are you interested in forming your own harem of guys?"

I choke on nothing but air. "What?! No! Definitely not," I insist. I know he encouraged me to spend the night with Cain the other night, and he implied he knew there was something between Cain and me, but I dunno... it just seems insane that he'd be okay with sharing me. Right?

He pushes the empty food containers away and leans over, hauling me into his lap like I weigh nothing. My hands land on his shoulders, and my knees press into the carpet on either side of his hips as I straddle his waist. His fingers run through my hair, brushing it back from my face in a reverent way that matches the look on his face. I love when he touches and looks at me like that—like I'm the only thing in the world that matters to him. No one has ever taken the time to handle me with such care. It doesn't make me feel weak or incapable like I thought it would. Instead, I just feel cherished; cared for. It's new and exciting, and *damn* I could get used to it.

"If anything did happen with you and Cain, it would be okay." He says it so straightforwardly like we're discussing the weather, not our relationship's complex nature.

"Well, you know we had sex." I squirm in his lap, feeling uncomfortable discussing sex with another man while I'm pressed up against him.

"Do you want it to be more than sex?"

I scrunch my nose up, but I actually think about the question rather than just firing out a no. Do I? Cain's got a lot of damage and the emotional capacity of an ant, but then, I'm not exactly the easiest person to be with either. "I dunno," I eventually confess. "Even if I did. I'm pretty sure Cain doesn't. Every time he lets me in or we have a moment, he pulls away afterward. He hasn't even looked at me since the other night." The morning after he got shot, he brushed right past me like I didn't exist. Not even a goddamn thank you for saving his life. I'd heard the other guys talking before I'd intervened. They were all set to pour fucking whiskey into his wound. Not only is that a waste of excellent whiskey, but it hurts like hell and can burn the skin. Meaning the wound would take longer to heal. I mean, at least check if you have sterilized water before opting for alcohol. So yeah, getting the brush off like I was just some girl he couldn't get rid of the morning after stung a little.

Oliver's firm grip on my chin draws me out of my thoughts, and I focus on his blue eyes. "That's just Cain's way. He's fighting it, but he cares more than he lets on. Together, the three of us could rule this town."

"You mean if we survive that long."

He smiles softly and closes the scant distance between us as he presses his lips to mine. I melt into him, running my hands down the front of his t-shirt until I find the hem and slip underneath, relishing the way his abs tense beneath my touch. "Guess we shouldn't waste any more time, just in case," he murmurs before sealing his lips to mine in a searing kiss.

The world falls away, and everything around us ceases to exist as he consumes my every thought, until we're both naked and panting on the living room floor. He doesn't waste any time with a warm-up, not that I need one. My pussy is already begging for him as he easily pushes inside me, sighing as if he just entered heaven.

The carpet rubs against my back with every thrust, but I barely feel the scratch as pleasure quickly overpowers everything else, until I'm screaming out Oliver's name. He spends the rest of the night making me come over and over in every room in the apartment until, completely exhausted, we collapse into my narrow bed. The only way we both fit is if I'm sprawled on top of him, not that either of us is complaining.

With my head resting on his shoulder, I run my fingers over his Reject tattoo before turning my attention to the older one on his other pec. "How come you have two?"

His hand comes up to cover mine, resting over his heart. "The original Reaper Rejects consisted of four people; four kids. Myself, Cain, Evie, and Beck. Cain built the Rejects you know today, in her name."

"You said the Antonellis took her? But you both talk about her as if she's dead. How can you be so sure?" I tilt my head back to see his expression, taking in the sadness in his eyes and the tight lines around his mouth.

He turns his head to meet my searching gaze. "If she's not dead, then I can't bear to think what sort of life she's been subjected to. The Antonellis may have willing girls in their sex clubs, but that doesn't mean they have any issues using unwilling girls for their own financial gain." I shiver at the realization of that statement, unable to even comprehend what a life subjected to that would be like. I can understand why Cain refuses to believe his sister is still alive. Even if she was alive, if the Antonellis sold her, he would probably never find her.

Sometimes, death isn't the worst possible outcome.

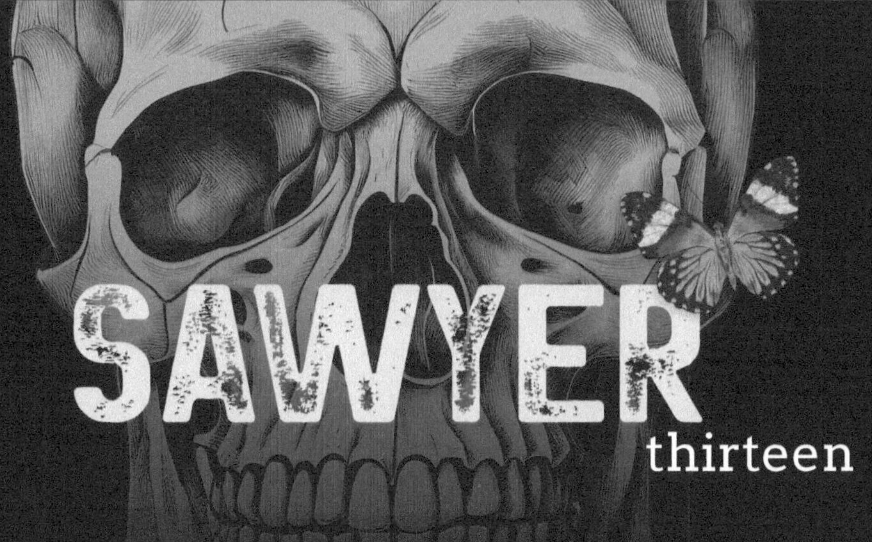

thirteen

I'm back in the ice cream parlor, deliberately *not* thinking about the bridge I built with Cain the night he brought me here. That night, we connected on a deeper level. I felt it, and I know he did too. Even if he is refusing to acknowledge it. With Cain, every time I think we're making headway, that we're beginning to understand one another and get on the same page, he switches things up and pulls back. We've had several intimate moments now where each of us has peeled back our layers, and every time afterward, I can sense him withdrawing. He goes back to calling me stripper and acting like he's only interested in sex. He's doing the same at the minute, only talking to me if we're discussing the Antonellis or Belle Donne. Even then, he's careful to maintain his distance, never getting too close or touching me. He no longer sits on the sofa if Oliver and I are there, and despite the way his eyes roam over me, burning me up, he never lets his gaze linger. It's fucking infuriating. Ever since Oliver told me his friends are in poly relationships and that he'd be open to one, I can't get the thought of having something more with Cain out of my head. Which is insane because it wasn't even something I was considering until he brought it up.

Then I started picturing it, and now I can't stop.

The ding of the bell above the door pulls me out of my inner thoughts as I lift my gaze and watch as Enzo steps into the shop, looking impeccable in his three-piece suit and polished shoes. His dirty blond hair is neatly styled, perfectly finishing the whole ensemble. I still can't get over how right it looks on him. It just emphasizes how fucking wrong he looked in worn jeans and a t-shirt, making it all the more laughable that I never thought to question who he was before.

I had texted him after my little conversation with Dante, demanding a meeting—something that is becoming far too regular a thing for my liking. However, there is only one reason why my start date at Belle Donne would match up with the night I bull-shitted my way into the club to kill Chad. And there's only one person who could have put that date on my file. Enzo seems to know all my secrets, and it's past time I confronted him about it. He caught me off guard before, dropping that little bomb about the Reaper right as I was leaving, but I need to know what he plans on doing with the information or what he wants from me in exchange for his silence.

His eyes are on mine as he walks toward my booth—the same one as last time—and slips into the seat opposite me. He doesn't say anything, nor do I expect him to. *I called this meeting after all.* Tilting my head to one side, my face is perfectly expressionless as I ask, "Why does my employee file at Belle Donne have a start date of two weeks before I even approached you about it?" It's too much of a coincidence, and I'm done ignoring this shit and not asking questions.

There's a flash of a smirk before he conceals it. "I didn't realize I'd gotten you a job in the back office. 'Cause, that's the only reason I can think of as to why you'd be looking in your file."

I purse my lips. "You know I was there that night."

"I'm sure I have no idea what you are talking about."

Fucking hell, we're just going around and around in circles here. "You know I killed that guy. Someone who spent a lot of money in your casino, whose death wouldn't have gone unnoticed by higher-ups. Yet you haven't ratted me out." I cross my arms in front of me on the table and lean forward. "So tell me, Enzo, what is it you want from me?"

"Who says I want anything from you?" he fires back.

"Because nobody does anything for nothing in this town. You wouldn't risk your position if you didn't want *something* in return for your silence."

His steady, bright green eyes hold mine before giving a thoughtful nod. "You're right. I do want something." Although his response isn't unexpected, my body tenses as I wait to hear what his demands are. "Just not yet. When the time is right, I'll let you know what I want."

My brows furrow, and my lips flatten, not liking the thought of owing him one. Or of not knowing what it is he wants. I stare him down for a long moment, trying to push past the veil over his eyes and pry into his inner thoughts, but he's a fucking vault. I purse my lips, reluctantly accepting that I have no other choice but to wait until he decides to show me his cards.

"How is the job going?" he asks, changing the conversation.

"I don't see how that's any of your business."

Now it's his turn to look annoyed. "No one's giving you a hard time?" His question only confuses me. It's one he asks pretty frequently, but I have no idea why. Why does he care? What would he do if I actually said yes?

"I can more than handle myself."

Still not looking pleased, he reaches into his pocket and pulls out an envelope. "What the fuck is that?" I bite out in an angry snarl reminiscent of the last time he tried to hand the envelope over to me.

He rolls his eyes. "This month's payment... what else would it be?"

"I told you before, I'm not taking that. Our little *arrangement* is over."

He holds the envelope of cash in his hands, sighing. "Don't be so difficult, Sawyer. There's no reason we can't continue like normal."

I bark out a laugh. *Is he for real?* "First of all, don't call me that. Secondly, no, we can't. I don't do business with the Antonellis. Besides, I don't have any information for you."

Even though he looks displeased, he thankfully doesn't argue with me, tucking the envelope of cash back into the inner pocket of his jacket. All the while, he stares at me thoughtfully, tilting his head slightly to one side. "Why don't you like people calling you by your name?"

My eyes narrow on him. "I don't like *you* calling me that." It's not exactly true. I don't like anyone other than Luc calling me by my real name. It feels too intimate, too reminiscent of whom I used to be before I was forced to grow up. But it's not just that... I don't like the way I *like* the sound of my name on his lips. The way it rolls off his tongue like hot cocoa on a stormy day making you feel all warm and cozy inside. Someone like Enzo should not elicit warm, fuzzy feelings. He's a snake in the grass, hiding in plain sight, waiting to strike. His pink, pillowy lips might look inviting, but if I leaned in, he'd sooner pierce me with his fangs and inject me with venom. He's poison wrapped up in a pretty package, and I'm not going to fall for it. For him.

"Would you prefer I call you *Reaper?*"

My gaze turns ice-cold. "Only if you want me to slice open your abdomen and rip out your insides."

The look he gives me is a clear challenge, daring me to try. However, I get the impression it's not because he thinks he's better than me... more like he'd enjoy the battle; the fight for dominance.

He taps his fingers against the cheap, plastic tabletop. "You know, you and I are going to have to learn to get along."

I scoff. I never trusted him, but I sure as shit don't *have* to do anything when it comes to him. "And why is that?"

He slides out of the booth, holding my gaze the entire time, until he's leaning over the table, forcing me to tilt my head back to look up at him. "Because whether you like it or not, our futures are intertwined. You don't have to like the fact that I'm an Antonelli. You don't even need to trust me, for now... but you *do* need to accept that I'm not going anywhere."

On that cryptic statement, he walks out, leaving me wondering what exactly he meant by that declaration.

***

TONIGHT IS JON'S FIRST OFFICIAL FIGHT. HE'S EIGHTEEN NOW, AND BY Cain's rules, old enough to participate in the pit fights. The club is alive with energy as I look around, everyone excited to watch him dominate. Looking around as the Rejects drink and celebrate, the atmosphere is lighthearted, as though Jon has already won. They are *that* confident in him. Having been on the other end of his attacks in the gym, I can understand why. He's brutal; savage, and I have no doubt he will win his fight tonight.

All the same, I'm here to support him, and, despite wanting to keep Luc as far away from all that violence, alcohol, and drugs, I've said he could watch. The other kids will be there cheering Jon on, and I'm trying out this whole *relaxed parenting* thing—which is complete fucking bullshit, by the way. Going against my instincts to wrap him up in bubble wrap and lock him inside our apartment is fucking exhausting.

"Jon's fight is up next," Cain remarks, glancing at a text on his phone.

As Cain, Oliver, and I get to our feet, ready to head over to the gym, I spot Luc and the kids as they enter the bar. "Hey, squirt," I call out, earning a glower from Luc as the other kids smirk and snicker at his embarrassment.

"Hey, *Saw—*"

"Time to go," I bellow over the top of him, throwing him my most deadly glare. Cain and Oliver share a confused look over the top of my head, and I swear I'm going to murder Luc if they start asking questions.

"How you doing, kiddo?" I ask Luc as we head out the door. "Excited for tonight."

"Oh, yeah. Bones is going to crush it. You should see the moves he's teaching me." He shakes his head, obviously in awe. I smile, glad he's enjoying his lessons with Jon. His eyes are shining with excitement and he's got a massive grin on his face. I'm not sure I've ever seen him so happy.

Despite my protests, he's basically living at the clubhouse now. He spends most nights here when I'm working. And for that, I'm actually thankful. I'm glad he has some company, even if it is the company of gangbangers. I don't even view them that way anymore. The Rejects are slowly coming to mean something more to me. I'm not sure what exactly, but I no longer see them as the gun-toting, violence-loving idiots that run Downtown Black Creek. Sure, they are absolutely those things, but there is a lot more to them than first meets the eye. These men aren't simply violent thugs. They live and breathe for a purpose. They've all lost something—someone—and most of those losses can be linked back to the Antonellis. But instead of letting that grief tear them down, they have used it to build themselves up. They've formed a makeshift family that has one another's backs. They know without a shadow of a doubt that they aren't alone, and there's a lot to be said for that.

"How about dinner tomorrow night, just the two of us? You can tell me all about what Jon's teaching you."

His smile is soft. "Yeah, that sounds good."

Oliver moves to walk beside me, sliding his hand into mine and linking our fingers. Luc cocks a brow at me, silently letting me know we will be talking about more than just Jon's fighting skills tomorrow night, before running to catch up with the other kids who are up ahead, chatting with Cain.

Switching my attention to Cain, I notice that he seems so much more at ease when he's with the kids—or pretty much anyone else—than he is around me. There's always this defensive tone. A casual brush-off attitude, and I don't understand why. I sigh heavily, refusing to think any more about him. For a guy who I'm not dating, he demands far too much of my time and attention.

Oliver lifts his arm to wrap it around my shoulder, pulling me in against him and kissing the top of my head. It sets off butterflies in my stomach, and I tilt my head back to look up at him with a soft smile.

"Everything will work out," he assures me, before glancing in Cain's direction. I don't understand how he can be so sure. Yeah, Cain and I have made some progress, but not much. And every time we take one step forward, he stomps off in a huff like a little bitch.

"Is that really what you want?" I question. I still find it impossible to wrap my head around how okay he can be about sharing me with another guy—even if that guy is his friend.

"Yeah." Well, at least he sounds confident about it. "All I want is for him to be happy. And you."

"I'm not entirely sure Cain and I can make each other happy."

He just smiles down at me with a knowing twinkle in his eye. "I've seen how Sophie and her guys behave around one another. They're a family, no matter what. They'd protect each other to the death, even if they drive each other mad half the time."

"And that's what you want?"

"Isn't that what anyone wants? People who give enough of a shit to be willing to kill or die in their name?"

"But you and Cain already have that? I know you'd both sacrifice yourselves to save the other."

"We would. We'd do the same for you too."

A soft scoff passes my lips. I mean, maybe Oliver would, but Cain? No chance. "Cain might come to my rescue, or help. I'd even believe he'd kill for me—and hold it over my head for the rest of my days—but die for me?" Another scoff. "Yeah, I don't think so." Nor do I need him to. I don't want either of them to give up their lives for me. It's not what I signed up for when I agreed to work for them, and it's not what I want. My life isn't worth more than theirs.

Oliver just gives me another of his knowing looks. "So you're saying you wouldn't jump in front of a bullet for either of us?"

I'm still thinking over my response—because, would I? Fuck, yeah, I think I would—when we step into the converted gym, and the lyrics of *Alkaline* by Timeflies come belting over the speaker and drown out my train of thought.

Looking around, the place is packed tonight. More full than I've ever seen it before. "Wow," I remark, not that Oliver hears me over the sound of the music and roaring of the crowd.

Presumably seeing the look of shock on my face, he leans in to shout in my ear. "There's always a big crowd when Cain or the kids are fighting." Tugging me to one side of the room, he shouts, "Come on," and I follow as we press through the crowd until we reach a raised platform.

Climbing the steps, I look out over the crowd. You can see the whole room from here. My gaze lands on the bright lights illuminating the emptied swimming pool where the current fight has just ended. Some guy I recognize from around the Reject clubhouse steps into the pit with a microphone and begins to announce the next fight—Bones vs. Headlock.

Dressed in only a pair of basketball shorts, his toned chest on display, Jon jumps down to join him as his name is called. The crowd goes wild, screaming and stamping their feet as he throws his arms in the air, grinning like the crazy kid he is. I notice Luc and the others standing at the edge of the pool behind him, clapping and screaming as loud as everyone else. It's impossible not to get wrapped up in the atmosphere, and I find myself yelling out his name as Oliver pulls me down to sit beside him on a small sofa.

I tear my gaze away from the pit to look around me, noticing that we are alone in a small seating area with sofas, armchairs, and low tables placed around the platform. A waitress comes up the stairs with a tray in hand and strides toward us. I notice her glance around, as though looking for someone, before her gaze lands on Oliver and me, and she smiles.

"Hey, Oliver," she greets, handing him a glass with amber liquid in it. "What can I get for your friend?"

"I'll have what he's having," I answer for myself.

She hands me the other glass of whiskey on her tray, which I'm guessing was meant for Cain.

"Can you bring us another glass and the bottle?"

With a nod, she disappears down the stairs again as Jon's opponent steps into the ring, putting on an over-the-top, cocky performance. Not that I can blame him. He's *ripped*. His muscles have muscles, making Jon look like the scrawny kid he is.

My wide eyes swivel to Oliver, who just laughs. "Just watch." His casual tone does nothing to ease the anxiety growing inside me, but I turn my attention back to the pit as Cain crests the top of the stairs and comes striding toward us.

He looks at the empty space beside me before opting for the armchair, and I have to quell my disappointment. Focusing on my drink instead, I take a sip of the whiskey, relishing the rich texture and smooth burn. I've never had whiskey like the shit I've had at the clubhouse or here. I'm used to the bottom shelf, will-fuck-you-up, kinda shit, but *this* is top-quality whiskey.

The announcer continues on his spiel about the fighters while the waitress returns with another glass and the whole bottle of whiskey. Her eyes light up when she spots Cain, making my teeth grind in annoyance. Instantly, there's a change in her demeanor as she flicks her long, blonde hair over her shoulder and sways her hips more provocatively as she strides toward us in her high heels and booty shorts.

She deliberately moves around to Cain's side of the table and bends low, ensuring she pushes her tits together and bats her eyelashes as she says in a seductive purr, "Hi, Cain." It's nothing like the friendly yet professional tone she used on Oliver, and I immediately want to shove her over the edge of the platform.

Cain looks away from the fighting pit, and his eyes land on her tits. How could they not when she's practically got them shoved under his nose? A sly grin curls one side of his lips as he leans back in his seat and spreads his legs.

"Hey, Cindy. How have you been?"

"All the better for seeing you here tonight. Do you have plans for after the fight?"

My hand, resting on Oliver's thigh, tenses, and I dig my nails into his jeans to prevent myself from scratching her eyes out. It's an utterly irrational impulse. I have no claim over Cain. Haven't I told myself a hundred times that I don't *want* any claim over him? So why am I acting like a jealous bitch all of a sudden?

"Not yet. Why don't I come and find you if nothing else comes up?"

She beams at him while licking her plump, cherry-red lips. "Sounds perfect."

I glare laser beams into her back as she strides away, wishing I had the ability to kill her with just a look. Chuckling, Oliver pulls me in closer against him and lowers his lips to mine. "Chill, Trouble. He's not going to fuck her." How the hell can he know that? Did he not see what I just saw cause that looked exactly like two people arranging to meet up later so they can fuck.

Movement in the pit captures my attention, and I put all thoughts of Cain and the waitress on the backburner as Jon and Headlock step into the middle of the pit. My nails dig into Oliver's thigh once again as I lean forward in my seat, equal parts enraptured and terrified as the announcer calls the fight.

Headlock immediately rushes Jon, but the kid is quick on his feet, and he darts out of the way at the last second, sending Headlock crashing into the side of the pool. It looks like he snarls—not that I can hear it over the roar of the crowd—as he spins to face Jon, rushing him again. Jon just as easily evades his blow, beaming like he could do this all night. He probably could, and unlike Headlock, he hasn't expended any energy yet.

Grinning, Jon says something. I don't hear what, but based on the purple-red color that Headlock's face turns, and the way the muscle in the back of his jaw tightens, I'm guessing it was intended to rile him up. And it worked. Pushing off his back foot, he takes yet another run at Jon. Jon just stands there and grins smugly at him. Everything about his expression screams *come get me,* and it only eggs Headlock on more.

At the last second, Jon steps to the side and kicks out. His foot connects with the side of Headlock's knee, and he stumbles. His knee slams into the hard pool tiles as Jon pounces on his back. His arm wraps around his neck, his other hand coming up to grab his wrist so he can tighten his hold on Headlock's neck, wrenching it back at a painful angle.

Flailing, Headlock scrambles to dislodge Jon, but he struggles to gain any purchase as Jon clings to him like a goddamn spider monkey, unphased that Headlock is leaving deep scratch marks on his arms.

As his lips turn blue, Headlock climbs unsteadily to his feet and runs backward until he collides with the side of the pool, crushing Jon in a last-ditch attempt to dislodge him. Jon grunts in pain, his face scrunched, and my hand flies up to cover my mouth as I gasp, and the crowd boos. Luc and the kids are standing right behind Jon and Headlock, and they bend down, shouting words of encouragement.

Despite how much that must have hurt, Jon holds tight, waiting him out until Headlock falls to his knees, on the brink of passing out. Then Jon grabs a fistful of his hair, and with savage brutality, he smashes his face into the floor of the pool three times, until bright red blood coats the tiles and runs down Headlock's face.

Jon yanks his head back so the blood runs into his mouth, causing him to choke. I'm shocked at the display of violence. I've heard the rumors. Oliver's told me time and again what the kids are capable of. But seeing it? Holy hell, it's enthralling. Adrenaline-rushing. Headlock gags and splutters until Jon takes mercy on him and smashes his face into the tiles one final time.

Placing his boot on his back, Jon throws his hands into the air in victory as the crowd screams his name. I'm on my feet, yelling along with them, and I can hear Oliver and Cain beside me. Luc and the other kids jump into the pool and rush toward him, clapping him on the back and lifting him onto their shoulders.

I laugh as I watch them until the announcer ushers them all out of the pool so he can get on with the next fight. The second it's over, Cain sets his empty glass on the table and gets to his feet.

"Where are you off to?" Oliver questions.

Cain smirks. "I've got a hot waitress waiting for me. Catch ya later." He barely spares me a glance, and his tone is bland, dismissive, when he says, "Stripper," before walking away. Frozen in shock and jealousy, I watch as he descends the stairs. The little bubble of hope I'd had at Oliver's earlier words bursts, drenching me in ugly feelings.

It takes Oliver moving to block my line of sight as he slides his hands into my hair and kisses my neck to distract me from Cain's sudden departure. "Forget about him," he murmurs against my ear before sucking my earlobe into his mouth and making me moan.

When he pulls back to meet my gaze, I smile at him, pushing all thoughts and feelings regarding Cain into a box and momentarily forgetting about them. Why do I need him when I have Oliver looking at me the way he is right now?

"What now?"

The look he gives me is feral, and he licks his lips before dropping his gaze to my chest. His attention has my nipples hardening and heat coiling in my core. "Now, we celebrate."

SEVERAL HOURS LATER, AND JON'S CELEBRATORY PARTY IS IN FULL SWING, while I quietly seethe from my position on the sofa, watching Cain let some skank rub her pussy all over him. He knocks back another swig of beer, his eyes never once leaving her. Jealousy has been eating at me all night, even though I know I shouldn't be letting his antics get to me. If he wants to be a manwhore then what do I care? Although, does he have to do that shit right in front of me?!

"Do you have your blades on you?"

Even at Oliver's strange question, I don't once remove my intense stare from Cain. "Of course I do. Why?"

"'Cause, you look like you're about to go over there and stab a bitch."

"Hmm." I picture doing just that. "Not a bad idea, actually."

He laughs like I'm joking, but the visual in my head is pretty damn tempting, and I run the pad of my thumb over the hilt of my blade in consideration.

My thigh strap is hidden under the skirt I'm wearing tonight, but Oliver somehow seems to know what I'm thinking, and he reaches out to pull my hand away. Finally pulling my gaze from Cain, I turn my head to glare at Oliver, but he just smirks at me, unafraid of my deadly glower. Still clutching my hand tightly in his, his other hand grabs my face before I can return my attention to Cain. His fingers press into my cheek as he lowers his head and captures my lips. Instantly, I'm drowning in him. It's the same every time. You'd think by now the effect he has on me would have worn off, but if anything, it only gets stronger, more intense, with every passing moment I spend in his presence.

I'm breathless, my chest heaving by the time he pulls away. Looking into his eyes, his pupils are blown with lust. "I have a better idea." My brain is flooded with feel-good endorphins, so I end up staring at him in confusion until he elaborates. "For how you can mess with Cain." *Ah, yes. That motherfucker.*

He maneuvers me into his lap, my back flush against his chest, and my ass pressed into his crotch, where I can feel the outline of a semi-hard-on. He brushes my hair to one side and lowers the thin strap of my top. The backs of his fingers brush against my skin, making me shiver. With unrestricted access to my neck and shoulder, he begins peppering kisses along my sensitive skin. I melt against him with every press of his lips until my head is resting on his shoulder and my eyelids are at half-mast.

Slowly, he works his way along my shoulder and up the column of my neck. My breath hitches when he begins to run his fingertip lightly along the deep V neckline of my top. His touch is featherlight on my skin. "Trouble," he purrs when my eyes drift shut. "Keep your eyes on Cain."

Prying them open, I focus on Cain while Oliver's touch moves to the strip of skin between my top and skirt. The skank is no longer grinding on Cain's lap. Instead, she's on her knees between his spread thighs, with Cain's hands in her hair. Even in the dim light of the clubhouse, I can see the bobbing action of her head, meaning only one thing. My teeth grind as I watch, wishing his hands were on me. His touch is such a contrast to Oliver's, and I can only imagine how explosive having the two of them touching me at once would feel.

Anger burns through me, only amplifying my reaction to Oliver's kisses and soft strokes. Unable to watch her any longer, I lift my gaze to Cain's face. At the same time, Oliver's fingers dip beneath the waistband of my skirt, and I gasp. I'm not sure whether it's from Oliver or the fact Cain isn't looking at the slut between his knees... but at me. His eyes burn into my skin, leaving deep gouges as he watches what Oliver is doing.

Oliver's fingers sink lower, and I tense. "Shh," he soothes. "No one is looking." I glance around, but he's right. It's late, and the other Reject members are wasted or too caught up in whatever girl is cozying up to them tonight. Besides, where we are sitting is shrouded mainly in darkness. It's probably difficult for Cain to even see us, never mind anyone else. Relaxing, my gaze returns to Cain, finding him still watching me with a blazing intensity as he ignores the skank sucking his cock.

Oliver's fingers sink inside my already primed pussy, eliciting a soft moan. My eyes drill into Cain as intently as his bore into mine, while Oliver's fingers ramp up the pleasure until my skin is flushed and my breathing ragged. Heat uncoils in my lower abdomen as my impending orgasm threatens to explode. Sensing how close I am, Oliver's free hand glides over my chest until he reaches my throat. His hand wraps around the column of my neck, and he gives it a light squeeze. My pussy floods and he does it again, squeezing harder. He doesn't cut off my breathing, but he definitely restricts it. It's uncharacteristic for him, but the pure possessive dominance of the move sends me catapulting headfirst into an explosive orgasm. My view of Cain cuts off as my eyes slam shut, and I cry out. Thankfully Oliver's firm hold on my throat prevents the sound from escaping.

A high-pitched shriek has my eyes snapping open to find Cain's slut on her backside. Everyone in the room is staring at her, except Cain. He's already dismissed her as he strides from the room, with a look of thunder on his face.

When he has disappeared, and everyone has gone back to whatever they were doing, I slump against Oliver. He chuckles, the vibration rumbling through his chest. "That undoubtedly pissed him off."

I give an exhausted, breathless laugh. "You sound way too happy about that."

"He needs a nudge in the right direction."

Not wanting to linger on thoughts of Cain any longer, I shift in Oliver's lap, feeling the press of his hard cock against my ass. He grunts, and his grip on my hips tightens. Lifting my arm, I place my hand on the back of his neck, stroking the fine hairs there as I look up at him. When he glances down at me, I say, "I don't want to talk about him anymore."

"Oh, no? What do you want to talk about then?" There's a small, cocky smile on his lips.

"I don't want to talk at all." I shift my hips, intentionally rubbing my ass along his length and eliciting a groan from him. "In fact, I don't want to stay here with all these prying eyes anymore."

Pushing out of his lap, I get to my feet and look down at him with a sultry expression.

"What do you wanna do instead?"

I run my hands along his jean-clad thighs and lean in until our faces are so close, that I could flick my tongue out and lick his bottom lip. "I want to repeat this all over again somewhere more private." I move my lips to his ear. "Somewhere where you can make me scream."

In the next second, I cry out as I'm thrown over his shoulder, and he gets to his feet. His arm bands around my upper thighs, my hips perched on his shoulder, bringing my face in line with his gorgeous, muscular ass. "Hey," I shout.

His shoulders move as he laughs, giving my ass a light spanking. "Shush, woman, didn't you just ask to be defiled?"

Well, when he puts it like that—to the bedroom!

I'm laden with grocery bags for my dinner with Luc tonight, my phone wedged between my ear and shoulder, as I listen to Sheryl tell me about the new job she's got working in a shop.

"I'm so glad you're enjoying it," I tell her genuinely. She and Grace have been through so much. They deserve some happiness. It won't be long until she's saved enough money to get them out of the women's shelter and into an apartment of their own.

She's still talking my ear off as I walk down the street toward my apartment building, when I notice Luc standing on the opposite side of the street. He's talking to some skinhead I don't recognize.

"Ehh, let me call you back," I say into the phone, not waiting for Sheryl to respond before I hang up and, deviating from my path, I dart across the road. I keep my eyes narrowed on the thug Luc is talking to, studying him. He looks only a few years older than Luc, late teens or early twenties, and he's already got a collection of tattoos, including one super cool one on his face. *Fuckwit clearly thinks he's a tough guy.*

Luc spots me out of the corner of his eye as I approach. "I gotta go. I'll talk to you later."

"Sure. Think about what I said," the guy responds in a low voice before taking off down the street without a backward glance.

"Who was that?" I ask, still watching the guy as he casually strolls down the sidewalk, his hands in his pockets, looking entirely at ease.

"Nobody."

Luc's vague response only makes me more desperate to know. "A Reject kid? I don't recognize him."

"Nah, he's a Bastard." Luc turns to walk away, as if he thinks that's the end of the conversation. Not a fucking chance. My hand snaps out and stops him in his tracks.

"What the fuck are you doing talking to a Bastard?!"

"Nothing," he says defensively. "I've told you. Guys like that approach me all the time. It doesn't mean anything. When he realizes he isn't going to convince me to join up, he'll move on. They always do."

Oh, well, that makes me feel tons better. Not.

"Where's Jon, or one of the others? Why aren't they out here with you?"

"Jesus, Sawyer, I don't need someone to babysit me every second of the day. I was just grabbing some snacks before heading up to the apartment."

"And he was just standing here?" That makes me feel very fucking uneasy.

"No," Luc sighs, sounding exasperated. "I just ran into him. We went to school together. He recognized me, and we got to talking. That's it."

Nope, I still don't like that. With the Rejects declaring a silent war against the Antonellis and their ongoing feud with the Grim Bastards, absolutely nothing is off-limits, and *everything* has me suspicious and on alert. *This* definitely has alarm bells ringing.

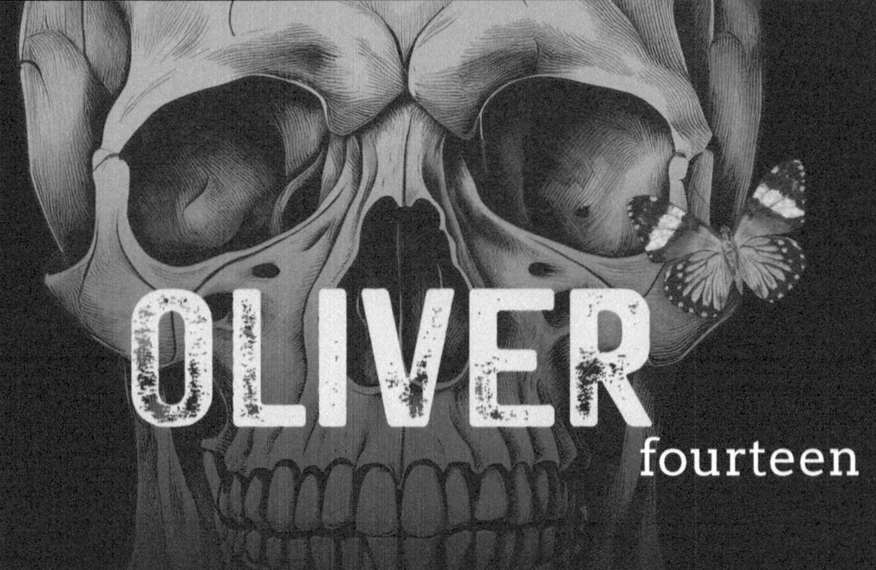

OLIVER
fourteen

"I just... do you think he was waiting for him?"

"I'm not sure," I answer honestly, knowing it's not exactly the answer she wants to hear. "He said people usually approach him at school about this stuff?"

Red called me half an hour ago, upset over finding her brother talking to a Bastard. I can understand her concern.

"Yeah, but not since he's been seen associating with the Rejects."

I sigh, knowing she's going to hate what I say next. "It would make sense that the Bastards would be interested in him. He's always with the kids, but he doesn't have a tattoo. And after his reputation of turning down every gang in town, I don't think anyone would buy that he's one of us anyway. We've made ourselves the Bastards' number one rival. I think this is them putting out feelers."

Her heavy sigh says everything about how much she agrees with and hates what I'm saying. Her voice is quiet when she says, "I was afraid this would happen."

I don't know how to put her at ease. She'd already told me this was her concern when it came to Luc, and it was a genuine one. We can protect Luc, but we also knew we'd be bringing unwanted attention his way. Red knew it too. She's just panicking now that the Bastards are aware of him. But I trust the kids. They'll keep him safe.

"What if they talk him into spending time with them or joining them?" It's practically a laughable question, but I don't dare show my humor. It's clear she's serious.

"Trouble, he's resisted gangs for all these years. Why would he suddenly fall for the Bastards' bullshit?"

"I don't know," she groans. "I just... I worry."

"I know you do." I think about it for a second. "How about I talk to him? See where his head is and give him some life advice—man-to-man."

"Hmm. You know, that's not such a bad idea."

"I have them sometimes—good ideas."

She chuckles softly. "Thank you, Oliver. I don't know what I'd do without you."

"You'd be so lost without me."

This time, her laugh is more genuine, and we lapse into easy conversation until her responses become incoherent. Soft hums and agreements as she starts to fall asleep.

"Go to sleep, Trouble. It's late."

"I'm not tired," she says with a yawn, making me chuckle.

"Sure you're not."

"I'm not. I'm just being quiet, so I can listen to you."

"I guess I better make the most of having your attention and tell you a good story then."

"Mmm," she agrees.

"Have I told you about the time the four of us stole a car that none of us knew how to drive?"

"What?!" she exclaims sleepily. "No!"

I recount to her tales from my childhood. Happier times before everything went to shit. Before we discovered monsters weren't fire-breathing dragons in stories but real-life gangsters who lived down the street from us. When I thought Evie was the love of my life and nothing beat spending time with her and my two best friends.

I'm so lost in thoughts of the past that it's only when I hear Red's soft snores down the line that I realize she's fallen asleep. It's jarring to be pulled out of memories of Evie. Sometimes she feels so real, like she's right here in the room with me. It simultaneously feels like the day she was kidnapped was yesterday and a million years ago. How can that be? How can time distort itself like that? It messes with my head, making me relive that chaos of emotions all over again. In one moment, the grief is nothing but a dull ache that I've long since adjusted to. Like my chest just rearranged itself to allow room for that pain. Then in the next, those closed wounds are ripped open and bleeding freely, the pain sharp and fresh like it happened yesterday.

I've long since come to terms with my unrequited feelings for Evie and know the life I'd foreseen for us will never come to fruition. As my feelings for Red have grown roots and germinated in my chest, they've clashed with the remnants of my feelings for Evie. Feelings I've kept buried, unacknowledged for years. I still remember the day I moved in across the street from her and Cain. Her black hair was tied back in pigtails that bounced when she moved, and her two front teeth were missing, giving her a toothy grin when she smiled. And yet there was an angelic aura about her that captured my attention before she even opened her mouth.

"Hi. I'm Evelyn, but everyone calls me Evie." She sticks her hand out, even though I'm holding a cardboard box in my hands, having just lifted it out of the trunk of my dad's car. I stand and blink at her for the longest time, committing her face to memory. Her skin seems to glow, and for a second, I wonder if she's even real. Maybe she's a ghost.

Her smile doesn't waver, and without conscious thought, I drop the box and reach out to take her hand. Fireworks go off the second my palm connects with hers, and my brain goes completely offline. I end up standing there mutely, holding her hand, and the entire time she just smiles serenely at me.

"What's yours?" she eventually asks.

"Mine?"

She laughs, and it's the most beautiful sound I've ever heard. "You're name, silly."
"Oh. It's Oliver."

Her eyes widen and her mouth drops open as she begins to clap her hands together and bounce on her heels in excitement. "Ollie?! No way. We're practically twins!" I'm not sure if I'm just being dense or if I just can't follow her train of thought. "Evie"—she points to herself—"Ollie"—she points to me. Still giving me that toothy grin, she nods as if she's just confirmed something. "Yup, I know it."

"Know what?" I can't track any of what this girl is saying.
"We're meant to be best friends, silly."

SHE WAS WRONG. I DIDN'T KNOW IT THEN, BUT I WAS ALREADY IN LOVE with her. We were *never* going to be just best friends. Not that I understood any of that at the age of eight. Nor did I really understand it any better when I was thirteen, either. I just knew I was obsessed with her. I couldn't keep my eyes off her. I was totally smitten. She could have told me to walk into The Feral Beasts' clubhouse and call them pussies, and I'd have done it without a second thought.

For Red, though? I'd storm The Feral Beast clubhouse and kill every last one of them to protect her. Where Evie was all angelic light and radiant goodness, Red revels in darkness and sin. She's not afraid to get her hands dirty, even if that means coating them in someone else's blood. Evie may have brought out my integrity, but Red sees me for exactly who I am. She knows my violent past, sees the shit I'm neck-deep in every day, and doesn't try to change any of it. Despite her ingrained hatred of gangs, she's never once asked if I'd leave the Rejects, and I know it wouldn't bother her if I didn't. She craves the chaos that comes with this life as much as I do. Oliver, the kid, may have been infatuated with an angel-like Evie, but the man I've grown into *needs* a woman like Red. Hell, if I ever ran into someone as innocent as Evie nowadays, they'd run screaming in the opposite direction. But Red? She's the perfect woman for me. She can handle the darkness that resides inside me. She knows when to coax it to the surface and how to calm the beast when it gets antsy. I may have been besotted with Evie, but I'm *in love* with Red.

I fall asleep to the knowledge of that, combined with Red's soft snores on the other end of the phone, and instead of bright light and an angelic face in my dreams, there's a red-headed beauty dressed in leather and ready to slay whatever demons come her way.

"HEY, LUC. CAN I TALK TO YOU FOR A SEC?" I ASK, POPPING MY HEAD INTO the game room.

"Yeah, sure." He jumps to his feet and follows me out of the room. "What's up?"

I don't say anything as I lead him to Cain's office, wanting to talk in private. Cain just left for the gym—something he's been doing a lot of recently—so I'm confident we have plenty of time before he returns.

Moving to sit behind Cain's desk, I gesture for Luc to take one of the empty seats in front of it. I've never really talked to him before. Not one-on-one like this. He spends most of his time with the kids, and since Cain and I told them to keep him away from club shit, I haven't been around him much.

"Uh, am I in trouble?" he questions, glancing around nervously.

I try to let the tension seep out of my posture as I smile reassuringly at him. "No." He physically relaxes, his shoulders dropping in relief. "I just wanted to check how you were doing. I know you've been hanging around quite a bit, and with your sister working so much, I wanted to make sure you were happy enough here."

"Oh, yeah. I love hanging out here, it's great. The guys are awesome. Everyone's been so friendly."

"Good. I'm glad." Interlocking my fingers, I lean forward, resting my forearms on the edge of the desk. "I know at your age gang-life can seem appealing. I was your age when I joined one. But it's not all parties and hanging out and getting girls. All gang life has a dark underbelly. Even the Rejects. We shelter the kids from the worst of it, but other gangs don't." Before I press on, deep lines form along Luc's forehead as his eyebrows dip in confusion. "Just the other week we caught a kid not much older than you, who'd been sent into our territory by the Grim Bastards. Grim and his men sent that kid here knowing he'd most likely die, and they didn't care."

"Is that what this is about? Sawyer told you about that guy talking to me? I told her it was nothing. Guys like that are always trying to get me to sign up for whatever stupid gang they belong to. I just let them say what they have to, then tell them I'm not inter-ested." Luc's temper flares, but one word snags my attention.

"Sawyer?"

His eyes widen as he realizes he's said something he shouldn't. "Shit. You're not supposed to know that. Forget I said anything." He gets to his feet. "I get it. No talking to other gangs, and definitely no joining them."

I lean back in my chair, keeping my gaze on him. "I've seen the darkest side of these gangs. I've killed men who didn't understand what they were getting themselves into, then tried to run. I've participated in torturing spies, rats, and traitors. I have more blood on my hands than any man should have to bear." Sighing, I soften my gaze. "I don't want you to make the mistake I, and so many others, did in not knowing exactly what gang life entails."

"Do you regret it? The people you killed?"

"Some of them. Some deserved the end they got, but others were just as scared and lost as I was. They didn't do anything wrong."

Luc seems to mull something over before he speaks again.

"I've heard some of the guys talking about how you were in prison before you came here?"

I nod my head. "I was."

"What was it like?"

It's a common question, especially from younger men who haven't had to do a stint behind bars yet. By the time you're my age, most men have spent at least a little time in jail for one petty crime or another.

"It's not an experience I'd recommend. I was in a minimum-security facility with the white-collar criminals who've committed tax fraud or whatever. Not cold hard killers and rapists and the like. So it wasn't too bad, but the second that cell door closes behind you, your life stops. Everything is put on pause while you do your time... but the world outside those doors keeps spinning. Time moves on. All the people you know are getting on with their lives. You're left with nothing but your thoughts and wishing you'd done life differently. You relive every decision you've ever made and wonder, *what if I'd made that choice instead.* Then, when you do finally get out, you have to make the biggest decision of all. You have to decide if you're going to go back to the life that led you here in the first place, or are you going to choose something new?"

"You chose to come back?"

"No," I quickly correct. "This life may look like my old one, but it's vastly different. When I stepped out of that prison, I had the choice... did I wanna continue to be the lost guy with no purpose and obey other people's orders, or did I want to reclaim my life and live it for *me.* I decided it was past time to take charge of my own future."

"And that involved coming back here?" Luc questions, confused.

"It starts with confronting my past and getting closure."

"And after that?"

"Then I have to work out what I want to do with this life—find things that make me happy and hold on to them." A soft smile breaks free as a fiery redhead comes to mind. As if sensing where my thoughts have gone, Luc tilts his head slightly to one side.

"Like my sister?"

I chuckle. "Yeah, man."

We both fall silent, and I can see he's working through everything I've told him. When he's decided he doesn't have any other questions, he gives me a half-smile and exits the office, leaving me alone. I've no idea if I've gotten through to him, but I felt it was important for him to hear all that. I don't want him to end up like myself or so many others I've seen—regretting his decision and trapped in a situation he can't get out of. Not that I imagine Red would let him get that far. And even if he did manage to dig himself into a hole, he'd never be alone. He'd have Red fighting for him, and she'd have us. So basically, he'd have an entire army at his back.

I tap my finger against the top of the desk as a smile grows on my face. "Sawyer," I say her name out loud, this time taking the time to savor it. I huff out a breath as I think about how furious she will be when she finds out I know her real name. I don't understand her insistence on not telling people, but I like that I'm one of only a small few who know her real identity. Slowly, I'm peeling back her layers and uncovering the complex woman underneath it all. And well, she's pretty damn spectacular.

THE NEXT DAY, I LOOK OUT OVER THE SMALL GROUP OF MEN WE HAVE gathered to take with us today. Excluding Marcus, they have been with Cain since the beginning. "Keep your heads up, your eyes open," I remind them. "Grim claims this is to discuss a peace treaty, but I wouldn't put it past him to ambush us."

After we found one of Grim's men selling guns in our territory and claimed the last of the downtown area as our own—not to mention we've been sending men out regularly into Grim's territory, a not so subtle warning that we're keeping an eye on him—the man himself reached out to us. His words about wanting to come to a peaceful arrangement are all bullshit. Men like Grim don't back down, especially not so easily, but it wasn't a discussion we could agree to pass on—not without starting an all-out war with them. And since we're finally starting to make some headway with the Antonellis, our focus needs to be there. Not on Grim and his overinflated ego. Hence why we've gathered the men today, ready to go find out exactly what his *talk* will entail.

We spread ourselves out over two cars, with another four men on bikes, wanting to look as imposing as possible when we ride up to Grim's gates.

"I've got a bad feeling about this," Cain says as we make our way across town. We're the only two in the car, allowing us to talk freely.

"Same, but we didn't have a choice."

"I wouldn't be surprised if he shoots us the second we roll-up."

"He's not that stupid." Even if he did, there's an entire clubhouse of men behind us that would storm in there in retaliation. I sure as hell wouldn't want to go head-to-head with one of the kids, never mind an entire army of them.

"He's not that smart either," Cain retorts.

"We're as prepared as we can be. And the men know to move if they don't hear from us in a couple of hours. Who knows, maybe it really will be a peace agreement," I say optimistically, earning myself a doubtful snort. "At least that would enable us to put all of our efforts on the Antonellis. Especially now that Red seems to be making some headway with Dante."

Cain's hands tighten around the wheel. "I don't like that she's pimping herself out to him for us."

I roll my eyes at his dramatics. "Dude, she's not. And you need to get your head out of your ass when it comes to her." It's the same fucking shit I've been saying to him for weeks now. "You realize your actions are only pushing her away?" My own anger sparks as I growl out, "You're hurting her."

The asshole doesn't respond, but I notice the tick in his jaw out of the corner of my eye, and I can only hope my words have gotten through to him. I'd hate to have to hold him down so Red can beat the crap out of him for being a shithead.

Neither of us speaks again until we're pulling up at the gates outside a red-bricked fire station. Peering through the metal bars while we wait for someone to inform Grim we're here and open the gates, I notice motorcycles parked all over the yard, and one of the doors, where the fire trucks would have been stored, is open, allowing me to see into some sort of garage where men are working on various cars and bikes. Lifting my gaze to each of the towers at the corner of the building, I spot men standing on the small balconies, and guns held loosely in their grasp as they patrol the compound from above.

A movement out of the corner of the windshield draws my attention to the six-foot-tall, concrete walls on either side of the gate that undoubtedly surround Grim's base perimeter. Standing on top of the wall, either side of the gate, with their rifles aimed at us, are two more guards. *Wonderful.*

The gates rattle open after a few moments, and we drive through. We don't immediately get out, instead taking a moment to analyze our surroundings. A circle of men, all armed, forms around our convoy, however, they stay back, giving us our space.

"I guess this is it," Cain grumbles before flinging open his door. I'm right behind him, ignoring all the eyes on us as I walk around the front of the vehicle, joining the others.

"Leave your weapons at the vehicles," one of Grim's men shouts.

"So we can't defend ourselves when you gun us down?" Cain shouts back.

The guy just shrugs. "Those are the rules."

Grumbling under his breath, Cain signals for us to do as they say, and I shrug out of my leather jacket, removing the gun holster and the gun tucked into the back of my jeans and setting them in the backseat. The others do the same, and when we're all ready, Cain turns to face the crowd again. "Do you wanna give us a pat-down? Or maybe we should just strip naked so you can see what a good set of dick 'n' balls looks like," Cain goads.

With anger flashing in his eyes, the designated spokesman bites back, "That won't be necessary. You can bring a couple of men inside, but the rest stay here."

Catching Marcus's eye, Cain gives his head an imperceptible tilt, and the three of us break away from the others. As we approach the man who has been giving us the orders, I size him up, taking in his scruffy appearance, long hair tied back in a top knot and the vice president badge on his leather cut.

"Follow me," he grunts, turning on his heel and leading us into the firehouse.

While the place may look like a firehouse on the outside, it's been completely renovated inside, with dark painted walls, and the stench of cigarettes and musk hit me as soon as we walked in.

The sound of heavy metal music reaches my ears from further in the building, and rough-looking men, all of whom wear leather cuts, give us the stink eye as we pass by. The music gets louder as we follow the VP down the hallway, and he stops outside a room that seems to be the source of the music. "Grim only wants to speak to you," he says to Cain, gesturing into the room beside us. "Your men can wait here."

"Fine," Cain grunts out, and we share a look before he follows the VP, and Marcus and I step into what I'm assuming was once the fire station's dining area. It's now the center of the Bastard's debauchery. The smell of weed and pussy is thick in the air, cigarette smoke making the room appear hazy as I squint through it. A group of men are crowded around a pool table at the far end of the room, and there's a young-looking barmaid cleaning glasses behind the bar, but otherwise, it's empty.

Remaining vigilant, Marcus and I settle onto a set of barstools near the entrance, ensuring our backs are to the wall. I notice him eyeing the men around the pool table while I keep my attention on the door. Together, we have the room covered in case any threat emerges.

My thoughts drift to Sawyer and her concern for Luc. I can't blame her for panicking that he would end up somewhere like here. I know our clubhouse isn't much to look at and, from the outside, probably appears similar, but the trickle of awareness that drips down my spine and the hostile aggression I've sensed since walking in demonstrates how far from the Rejects this place is. Certainly not somewhere a kid should grow up or get sucked into.

"Hey, girlie," one of the guys at the pool table calls out. "Another round."

My focus drifts toward the girl behind the bar as she rushes to pop the caps on several bottles of beer. She looks young. Far too young to be stuck somewhere like here. As she heads toward the guys, the beers in her hand, I return my attention to the door, so I miss whatever happens, but Marcus's low curse before he jumps out of his stool has my head snapping around to see what's going on.

In a flash, he's across the room, his hand wrapped around one of the guy's throats as he slams his face into the pool table. The barmaid is sprawled on the floor, drenched in beer and staring wide-eyed at the scene. I'm across the room in a second, but the men have already drawn their weapons.

"Whoa." I lift my hands, trying to get everyone to calm down. "What's going on?"

"This fucker was harassing her, even though she said no," Marcus all but growls, smushing the asshole's face further into the green felt.

"Not your fucking problem," one of the other Bastards snaps, his gun still trained on Marcus.

"It is when she doesn't want it."

I glance down at the girl on the floor, startled when I realize just how young she is. From a distance, her pink-tipped hair, nose piercing, and revealing top made her look older, but *Jesus*, she's a fucking kid. Sixteen at most. I hold out a hand to help her up, but she hesitates, staring at it like it's going to bite her. After a second, she moves to accept, but before her hand connects with mine, one of the other fuckwits intercepts. Grabbing her by the back of her top, he drags her to her feet.

"Don't fucking touch our girls."

"Your girls?!" I snap, incredulous. "She's a child. Definitely not of legal fucking age."

The asshole just shrugs, not loosening his hold on the girl. Not that she even seems bothered by the way he's manhandling her. Something that only pisses me off more.

"Don't see how that's any of your fucking business. This is our property. Our club. Our girls. Our rules."

I grit my teeth, knowing I can't start an all-out war over this. Marcus obviously doesn't feel the same way as he swiftly pulls a gun from his ankle holster and shoots the asshole pinned beneath him in the knee.

All-out fucking mayhem ensues, as the guy screams and the others start shouting out threats. I'm itching to grab the gun I have strapped to my ankle, but I'm more likely to end up with a bullet wound if I so much as breathe the wrong way.

"What the hell is going on in here?" A deep bark booms out from behind me. The Bastard men freeze but don't lower their weapons.

"Grim, this asshole shot one of our men."

I slowly turn, just enough to catch sight of Grim and Cain standing behind me, taking in the scene with tight expressions.

"He was feeling up this kid," I explain, keeping my attention on Cain. His expression only darkens further as he looks toward the girl. Tensions remain at an all-time high, and I can practically see Cain biting back some angry retort. We're on Bastard territory, so, unfortunately, we need to defer to him in this instance. Needing a read on what he's thinking, I flick my gaze to him. It's the first time I've met him in person, and I take in his white-gray hair, the age lines on his face, and his scruffy beard. He's dressed in worn jeans, with a t-shirt and leather cut over the top, showcasing muscular arms and tree-trunk thighs. He's older than I pictured, but he clearly works out regularly. His cold, cobalt eyes slowly rake over each of us, lastly landing on the girl. The lines around his eyes tighten, and I shift my focus to her. Her head is ducked, and I can see a slight tremble that she tries to hide by discreetly fisting her hand at her side.

"Lower your weapons," Grim eventually barks out. When his men gape at him instead of following orders, he continues, "You all know better than to touch my daughter."

His what?!

The guy holding onto Grim's daughter releases her so quickly, and she wastes no time getting out of dodge. Once she's disappeared, I focus back on the situation at hand.

"Besides," Grim continues, "the Rejects and Bastards are now allies."

Oh, fucking hell. This can only end badly.

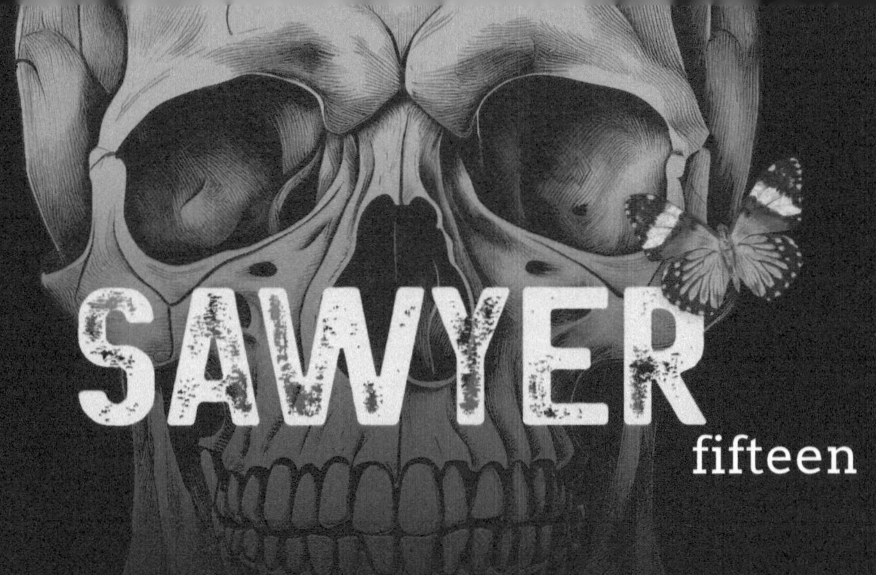

"He only comes in the nights you're working, you know," Chrissy says, sidling up to me at the bar while I drop off a tray of empty drinks.

"Who?" I question, playing dumb.

"What do you mean who? Him." She gestures toward the table where Dante is stoically sitting, on his phone and not paying any attention to the dancers on stage. "You know he's the Don's son?" She leans in closer to whisper in my ear. "Apparently, he's a psychopath."

My brows scrunch together, and I finally look at her. "What do you mean by that?"

"He can't feel emotions or some shit."

I scoff. "I'm sure that's not true. Probably a scare tactic to keep people in line."

She makes a bubble with the gum she's chewing on. It pops, and she begins chewing again. "Nah, I don't think so. Some of the stories I've heard. You'd have to be really messed up in the head to do some of that shit."

Frowning, I take my restocked tray and distribute the drinks around the room. The entire time, Chrissy's words play on repeat. Not the psychopath stuff. Honestly, despite my protests, I think that might be true. I can sense it when I look into his eyes. The emptiness. But it's the fact that he only shows up when I'm working. I obviously knew he was here most nights that I'm working, but I wasn't sure if he also made an appearance on the nights I was off. Seemingly, not. It's too much of a coincidence, meaning he's here for me. But why? What is his obsession with me? Is it because he still doesn't believe I'm telling the truth about the night Chad was killed—fucking *Chad*—or is it something more?

Standing at the far side of the room, I'm shrouded in shadow as I take the time to watch him, trying to figure him out. He's still on his phone, ignoring everyone and everything around him, including his still untouched glass of whiskey in front of him.

As the closing beats of the current song come over the speakers, I return my tray to the bar and head up on stage. The opening bars of *Toxic* by Britney Spears play out, and I move to the fast-paced beat. Spinning around the pole, I hold on tight while I arch my back and tip my head back, looking upside down out over the audience. My gaze collides with Dante's. His phone is out of sight for the first time since I started my shift, and now I have his full attention. I have to look away as I shift into my next move, but every time I glance his way, he's staring just as intently.

Several songs later, I climb down from the stage, going back to circulate the floor. The room is busier than it was earlier, and I'm rushed off my feet for the rest of my shift, unable to do anything more than tossing the odd glance Dante's way. Not that he's been doing much. If he's not watching me, he's on his phone.

At the end of my shift, I'm heading to the bar to drop off my tray before getting out of here, when a tall, non-descript man blocks my way. "You're a pretty little thing." I give him a tight smile even while his gaze dips, and he takes his time drooling over me. "You'd do quite nicely for tonight."

"Sorry, sir. I'm just a dancer, but I'm sure one of the other girls would be happy to help."

Irritation flashes across his face. "I said I wanted you."

"And I said I'm just a dancer."

His hand whips out, his fingers digging into my upper arm. I immediately tense and begin pulling against his tight grip. "Do you have any idea who I am?" His voice is a low, angry snarl, and I find myself staring into his menacing face, but I have no fucking clue who he is.

"No." My snarky tone is easy to hear, riling him up further. His nostrils flare, and he tugs on my arm, causing me to fall against him. My heart rate picks up as I wrack my brain for a way out of this. I can't make a scene and risk losing this job, but equally, there's no fucking way I'm about to let this guy drag me off somewhere.

Before I've figured out what to do, a large palm claps down on his shoulder, and in a glacial tone, I hear. "Let her go, Sam."

Sam whips his gaze over his shoulder. "Dante," he chuckles nervously. "I wasn't expecting to see you here. Don't worry, man. It's all an act. She's into the whole rape-fantasy thing."

While I might be open to trying such a thing with the right partner, that person sure as fuck is not this asshole in front of me. With him distracted, I try once again to yank my arm out of his hand, breathing a sigh of relief when it works.

He glowers at me, but Dante speaks up again. "I don't care. She's off-limits."

"What?" the idiot scoffs. "She's a club whore."

"I'm a fucking dancer," I snap. My lip curls up in a sneer, Dante's presence bolstering me to speak my mind. "Even if you did pay me, I still wouldn't sleep with you."

"Why you little—" Sam lunges at me, but Dante grabs the collar of his shirt and yanks him back. Without another word, he starts pulling him across the room, drawing the attention of some of the patrons and staff. After a second's hesitation, I scurry after them, dropping my tray at the bar as I pass.

Exiting the room, I spot Dante shoving Sam behind drapes that cover the wall of a hallway leading to the next themed room of the club. They disappear as I rush over and pull aside the drapes, discovering a hidden emergency exit door. I catch it before it slams shut, and slip out into the cold evening air. I'm still dressed in just a thong and bra, and it's fucking freezing at this time of night. Still, the thought takes a back seat as the door clicks shut, taking the only light and plunging me into pitch blackness. There isn't a single outdoor light, and I look around blindly, trying to work out where Dante and that guy went.

A pained grunt comes from my right, and I slowly pick my way along the back of the building in the direction it came from.

"I've already told you she's off-limits. You *really* don't want me to repeat myself." Dante's low snarl serves as my guiding light as I get closer until I can just about make out the silhouette of two figures.

"N-no. I-I got it. I won't touch her."

"And no one else will either."

"N-no. I-I'll make s-sure of it."

There's the sound of a body hitting the brick wall, followed by another grunt. "Good. Then get the fuck out of here."

Hurried footsteps are heard as the guy runs away as fast as his feet will carry him. I stand frozen in place, unsure whether to alert Dante to my presence and hoping he will go back inside without ever knowing.

"I know you're there."

Oh, well, there goes that plan then.

"I, uh, thought you might try to kill him."

There's a shuffle of movement, and I sense—more than see—him approach. My skin prickles with awareness, sensing him standing right in front of me just before I feel his fingers on my cheek. His thumb finds my lower lip and rubs along it. "Is that what you wanted?"

My tongue flicks out, colliding with the pad of his thumb, and he promptly withdraws it, leaving me feeling bereft. "Just what I expected, from what I've heard about you."

There's a tense moment of silence before he sighs. "I couldn't."

"Why not?"

"He's an Antonelli man."

"Aren't you like the next Don or something?"

"It's not that simple."

I've never had the opportunity to be alone with Dante, and he's hardly ever said anything to me before. Seeing my chance, I push further. "Why? 'Cause of your father?"

There's an edge of warning in Dante's voice when he responds. "Why are you asking about my father?"

Dammit, looks like, yet again, I'm going to gain fuck all information about Giovanni or his organization.

I shrug, even though he can't see me. "Just making conversation. Anyway, I appreciate you interfering, but I don't need you to risk getting in trouble for me. I can deal with guys like him."

"Has that happened before?"

"Here? A couple of times. As I said, it's nothing I can't handle."

"Mmm," comes his non-committal response before I feel his warm palm on my lower back. "Come on." I follow him blindly back down the alley until we reach the exit door. His suit jacket brushes along my arm, and his hand stays securely on my back, never wandering or trying to cop a feel. Dante is a complete enigma. He watches me obsessively. The only conclusion I can draw from it all is that he's attracted to me, yet, we're out here, alone in the dark, and I'm wearing practically nothing, and he acts like a total gentleman. I can't understand it.

Pulling open the door, he applies pressure on my lower back until I step inside. Expecting him to follow me in, I turn to say something to him, but instead, I find myself alone as the door closes behind me. Yup, he's definitely an enigma, and the longer I work here, I find myself wanting to know more about him. What a dangerous game I'm playing. A tightrope, really. One light push or gentle breeze, and I'll plummet to my death.

ADRENALINE FROM THE NIGHT'S EVENTS IS STILL COURSING THROUGH MY veins when I step into the Reject clubhouse. Another party is in full swing. They have been happening more and more recently, and I have a sneaking suspicion that's Cain's doing. Looking around, I don't spot Oliver. Ignoring everyone, I head toward his bedroom, finding it empty.

Pulling out my phone, I send him a text.

ME

Where are you?

IMMEDIATELY, BUBBLES POP UP SAYING HE'S RESPONDING.

OLIVER

Be back soon.

SIGHING, I HEAD OUT TO THE BAR AND GRAB MYSELF A BEER. I STAND there, surveying the room without really seeing it until I notice Cain up to his usual antics with some chick. My blood boils, and I bang my beer down on the bar top. Oliver said he needed a nudge, and the little show we put on the other night definitely got under his skin, but he's continued to give me the silent treatment. The more I've watched him let any skank in his place do whatever they wanted to him, the more I've come to accept that my feelings are more than simple lust or attraction. I want to rip every single club slut away from him and scream that he's mine, and I've never felt that possessive over anyone like that before.

Having had enough of this bullshit, I do the one thing that will get his attention—I think. I'm wearing booty shorts and a crop top that, when I raise my arms, shows the curve of my tits, along with my thigh-high, high-heeled boots, which are adequate enough for what I have in mind.

I wait until he feels my angry gaze on him and looks my way. Smirking, I give him a little finger wave that only confuses him, and he narrows his eyes on me suspiciously. Dismissing him, I stride toward the small stage in the corner of the room, where the stripper pole is. I catch his eye as the song switches to something slow and heady—perfect for my half-baked plan—and I tune out the rest of the room as I begin to sway my hips.

Cain's brow, which was cocked in challenge, slowly lowers, furrowing as a frown tugs at the corners of his lips. It's not until I lift my arms above my head, arching my back as I grab hold of the bar, that he jumps to his feet, shoving the girl out of his lap.

"Out," he barks, loud enough to be heard over the music. People nearby stop and turn toward him. "GET THE FUCK OUT!"

Without a second's hesitation, everyone starts moving toward the door, the party spilling out into the parking lot and onto the street. In their haste, the music is left on, and I continue to lazily dance around the pole until only Cain and I are left alone in the room.

"That wasn't very nice of you," I remark with a smirk, hooking my leg up and doing a fancy spin. His eyes devour me from across the room, following my every move.

"You think I give a shit? I don't want them looking at you up there."

I'd roll my eyes at his macho-possessiveness, but his words have my stomach flip-flopping, enjoying the hint of jealousy in his voice. "You do realize I'm a stripper, right? Half of your men have probably seen me on stage at Strip Tease."

A low growl hisses through his teeth, and his lip curls up in an angry snarl. He waits until he catches my eyes before stating in a tone that rings with indisputable authority and instantly soaks my panties. "In here, you only dance for me."

Which is precisely what I do. I give the performance my all, feeling sexier than I ever have on stage. The way Cain follows my every move, eating it up, makes me feel like a fucking goddess as I swing around the pole, shaking my ass and swaying my hips. It's the hottest kind of foreplay I've ever engaged in, and by the time the third song comes to an end, I'm practically panting with pure desire.

As I get my feet beneath me once again, I look over at Cain, finding him sitting in his usual chair, with his legs spread wide and his dick in his hand, pumping lazily as he watches me. It breaks the last thread of my resolve, and I step away from the pole, adding an exaggerated sway of my hips with every step I take toward him.

I place my hands on his knees and slide them along his thighs as I step between them, biting down on my bottom lip as my eyes connect with his. I easily fall into his alluring, viridescent gaze as his inked hand wraps around my throat, slowly pulling my face to his.

His teeth sink into my lower lip, sucking it into his mouth and making me groan as I wrap my fingers around his length. His tongue sweeps into my mouth, and he grunts as I begin to work him over, driving him as crazy as his eyes on me did when I was on that stage.

Our kiss grows deeper, dirtier, sloppier until we're both breathless, surviving only on one another's touch. Eventually, I find the strength to pull back. I continue to pump him lazily while my other hand moves to fist his hair, pulling on the strands until his jaw hardens. "You've been using other girls to make me jealous," I bite out, still angry.

He smirks. "And what do you call that show you and Oliver put on? Don't tell me that wasn't for my benefit."

Narrowing my gaze on him, I change topics. "Why have you been shutting me out?" His lips purse and I tighten my grip on his hair until he hisses in pain. His fingers tighten around my throat in reflex. When he still doesn't answer, I try a different approach. "Oliver seems to think the three of us could live a nice little harem life."

His brows lift in surprise. "And what do you think?"

"I think I'd end up killing you, which probably wouldn't go down too well with Oliver."

Cain has the audacity to scoff. "Please, you're too obsessed with my dick to kill me."

I send him a warning glare. "I think I could never be in a relationship with someone who so easily fucks other girls."

Yet another infuriating scoff passes his lips. "Who says I've been fucking anyone?"

I quirk a brow. "All the women you disappear with every time I'm here."

His smug smirk is infuriating, but I don't move away from his reach as his fingers slowly trail along my inner thigh, dipping beneath the fabric of my shorts until he's stroking the thin, damp fabric of my panties. He takes a long moment, watching me closely as he strokes back and forth, his touch nothing more than a tease. "I think I like the look of jealousy on you, but I didn't sleep with any of them."

Now it's my turn to scoff, even if it does come out a bit strangled as he presses down on my clit. "Right, of course you didn't. You took them back to your room to play Mahjong."

His hand on my throat tightens, and it's not a reflex this time. "I'll admit a few of them gave me blow jobs." My nostrils flare, and his gaze dips to my lips. "And the entire time, all I could picture was your smart mouth wrapped around me, sucking me off." He trails off before returning his intense green eyes to mine. "But the only person I've been fucking is you."

I can't do anything but stare at him, tossing his words over in my head. There's no way that can be true. Can it? He must see the skepticism on my face as he huffs out a frustrated breath. "I don't go around fucking girls without condoms." My lips part to protest, but he crashes right over the top of me. "Except for you. That first time... Admittedly, I wasn't thinking straight, and it was stupid of me."

"And the second time?"

He shrugs. "I knew we both got clean test results and that you were only fucking Oliver."

I quirk a brow and snap out, "So, you just figured, well, you'd already done it once without a condom, so why not do it again?"

"No," he growls, sounding frustrated. His fingers slip beneath my lace panties, and even with the restricting fabric of my shorts, he sinks into me with ease. "I couldn't stop thinking about how fucking good *this* felt wrapped around me." Slowly, he pumps his fingers in and out of me. "I wanted it again. I *needed* it. I knew no other woman could compare."

My breaths are unsteady, but I manage to say, "But why have you been pushing me away then?"

He sighs but doesn't stop with his ministrations. "Because I'm fucked up." It's not really a reason, but I can see the honesty in his eyes, so I don't push for more.

"Are you going to stop pushing me away?"

"I can't make any promises, but I'll try."

He lets me look at him—really look at him, even while he continues to tease me with his fingers. I appreciate him not offering fake assurances. I'd much rather have a truthful response. When I'm happy that he's telling the truth, I slowly sink to my knees in front of him, dislodging his hand in the process. When he lifts his hand, I notice his fingers are coated in my excitement, and he holds my gaze as he sucks them into his mouth.

Licking my lips, I follow suit. Glancing up through my lashes, I wrap my lips around his tip. He releases his fingers with a pop, and when I swivel my tongue around his piercings, a sinfully sexual groan that has my nipples hardening escapes him. I suck him deeper into my mouth, and he slides his hands into my hair so he can direct my movements. It's a weird feeling with his piercings, but it's not uncomfortable.

"Fuck, Red. You look so hot with your mouth stuffed with my cock." Punctuating his statement with a jerk of his hips, he groans as he fucks my face, never once breaking eye contact.

I'm so lost in watching the ripple of desire burn brighter in his eyes that I startle at the sound of a door closing. It's one thing for me to get on my knees for Cain, but I don't want anyone else to see me in this position. But Cain—the domineering asshole that he is—doesn't let me pull away. His fingers dig into my scalp as he holds me still.

"Eyes on me, Red," he growls, making me snap my attention back to his entrapping gaze. I'm faintly aware of movement behind us before Oliver plonks his ass down on the sofa beside him. I can't tear my eyes away from Cain, though, to get a read on what he's thinking.

"Doesn't she look so fucking hot on her knees, O?" There's a note of reverence in Cain's voice that catches me by surprise, and he still doesn't break eye contact, even though he's not talking to me.

"Mmhmm. She does." The sound of Oliver lowering his zipper draws my attention his way. "She definitely does," he murmurs, his eyes burning into mine as he fists his cock.

I suck on Cain's dick for a bit longer before he uses his firm grip on my hair to ease me off of him. "Make O feel good," he tells me as I release him with a pop. "He's had a long day."

With his hand still in my hair, guiding my movements, he directs me until I'm leaning over his knee, with my ass in the air and my face hovering over Oliver's slick dick. I lick the bead of pre-cum off the tip before lowering my lips over his shaft, Cain's hand pushing me all the way down.

"Oh fuck," Oliver hisses as he hits the back of my throat.

Cain continues to direct my movements as he shifts beneath me, and a second later, I feel him undo the button of my booty shorts before pushing them down over my ass.

"Mmm, I can smell your arousal from here," he purrs as he palms my ass, giving it a tight squeeze before his fingers trail along the lining of my panties, stroking my soaking wet core.

He thrusts two fingers inside me, and I moan around Oliver's dick. "So fucking needy for us, aren't you, Red?" Cain murmurs in a voice coated in sin and drenched in sex. His dirty words only heighten my pleasure, and I clench around him in response.

He sets a fast rhythm, and the angle I'm at has him hitting that perfect spot with every thrust until that ball of heat starts to unfurl in my lower belly.

"That's it, baby. Come for us. Show us how much you love sucking Oliver's cock."

Using his tight hold on my hair, he pulls me off Oliver's dick just as my orgasm explodes out of me. Oliver's lips press against mine, smothering my cries as he sweeps his tongue into my mouth, no doubt tasting himself on my lips.

Just as I lose myself in his taste, a strong arm wraps around my waist, pulling me backward, and I find myself hauled into Cain's lap, my back to his chest with my hands on his knees.

In the next second, my panties are ripped clean off me, and Cain's fingers dig into my hips as he pushes me down on his hard length. I'm wracked with a full-body shiver, and an obscene moan escapes me as his piercings scrape along my inner walls, which are already sensitive from my first orgasm of the night.

As I sink down on top of him, I can feel his heaving inhales against my back and the warm puff of his breath against my ear. We both sit like that for a long moment, just enjoying the feel of being connected so intimately. Cain and I both struggle with our words, but when we're united like this, all of that hostility we spit at one another falls by the wayside.

His hands still grip my hips in a possessive hold, but the way he nuzzles my hair and places a soft, light kiss against my neck is all sweetness, giving me a little insight into his true feelings. This is more than just sex to him; more than just a good time. Thank god, because it's becoming about much more than just sex to me too.

Leaning forward, I place my weight on my hands, balancing on his knees, and lift up. My eyes roll back in my head as his piercings, once again, drive me half insane. With his help, I set a fast rhythm that quickly has me spiraling into an endorphin-fueled haze.

"Need more," I pant after sitting at the precipice for as long as I can withstand. I seriously need to come, but something is holding me back, and as I turn with lust-filled eyes to look at Oliver, finding him fisting his still erect cock, I know exactly what I need.

Smirking, he gets to his feet, standing in front of me as Cain takes control, thrusting up into me repeatedly.

I lick my lips as Oliver positions his dick in front of my face.

"Need another taste, Trouble?" he purrs.

Unable to look away from the purple vein running down the length of his shaft, I nod my head. He's exactly what I need.

"Open up, then. I'll give you what you want."

Parting my lips, Oliver slides inside my mouth again, quickly filling it, so I have to relax my jaw and breathe through my nose. As he pulls back, I swirl my tongue around his tip before he pushes back in again, him and Cain setting a matching rhythm that has all three of us panting and groaning.

Sweat trickles down my spine as my whole body comes alive. I swear, my skin burns beneath Cain's touch, and as Oliver strokes his thumb lovingly along my cheek, watching me with worshiping eyes, I've never felt so adored.

Oliver comes down my throat with another thrust, and I swallow as much of it as I can, licking my lips to catch the rest. I must miss some, as Oliver swipes his thumb along the corner of my lips before pushing it into my mouth, and I suck the last of his cum off it while Cain reaches around to rub my clit.

"Come, Trouble," Oliver murmurs in a voice so soft, it's nothing like the way Cain usually barks out his orders. I stare deep into his bright blue eyes, glistening with lust as I come around Cain's cock, feeling him reach his own release. "So beautiful." He kisses me softly as I sag into a boneless heap, and when he lets me go, Cain pulls me back against him. I can feel his heart hammering in his chest, in tune with my own rapid heartbeat, as he reaches out to turn my head, capturing my lips with his.

It feels like some real progress has been made between us tonight, but I guess only tomorrow will tell if he's back to his standoffish self or not. As I let him dominate our kiss, I truly hope he doesn't. There's only so much hot and cold I can take, and Cain is reaching his limit of what I'll tolerate when it comes to my heart.

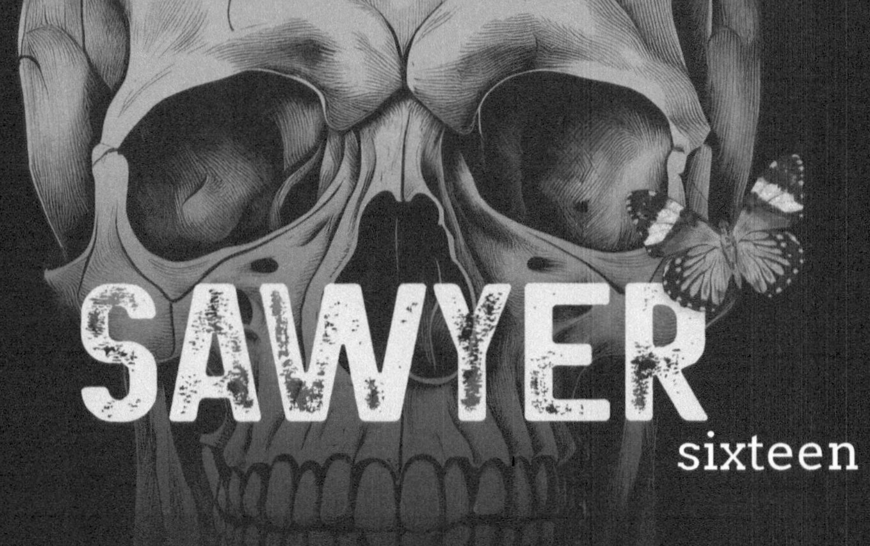

I have a Reaper job the next day, so I'm up and out early, and it takes most of the day to check everything in place. It's early evening before I'm changed and back at the clubhouse. Standing outside, I stare at the building while chewing on my lower lip. I need to walk in there and do something I absolutely suck at doing—ask for help.

Not only that, but I haven't spoken to Cain since last night, so god only knows how this will go. However, I have no other choice—everything else is in place and I'd be foolish to try and do this job alone, especially when there's an entire clubhouse of burly men who could easily back me up.

With one final deep sigh, I head inside. I've just crossed the threshold when I come to a stop, finding Cain and Oliver standing just inside the doorway. They both turn to look at me the second I enter, and my mouth goes bone dry under their combined gazes.

Both of them take in my revealing outfit choice for tonight, but it's Cain—of course—who barks out, "What are you doing here... dressed like that?"

"I, uh, need your help with a job."

"Really? The almighty Reaper needs our help?" he drawls sarcastically. "My, my. What is the world coming to?"

I purse my lips. *Fuck me, nope, this was a stupid decision.* Why the fuck did I ever think I needed their help. "You know what, forget about it," I bite out. "I can handle it myself."

"Nope." Oliver reaches out to grab my wrist before I can storm off. "What do you need?"

I give him a long, suffering stare before sighing. "The job I'm working involves three guys. I figured it would just be easier if I had some backup. I can take Jon or one of the other kids, if you can spare them."

"No, we'll come with you," Cain dictates, surprising me. Based on the tone he just used with me, I thought we were back to the bickering, hostile phase of our relationship, but maybe not? Who the fuck knows. The guy is a confusing fucking paradox. One second he looks like he wants to tear my head off, yelling in my face or making fun of me, and the next, he appears ready to go to fucking war for me—like he does right now. It's giving me whiplash. "Just give us a sec to get geared up."

I follow them toward the back of the building and hover in the doorway to the office as Oliver takes off down the hall toward his bedroom, and Cain moves behind his desk, pulling out a gun and checking the chamber before tucking it into the waistband of his pants. Another goes into an ankle strap and a third into a shoulder holster that he hides beneath a leather jacket.

When he turns to face me, standing at his full height, he's the formidable leader of the Rejects, armed to the teeth and wearing this icily terrifying expression. I haven't seen that look on him since our first few encounters, and I'm ashamed to admit it does very inappropriate things to me. Someone who looks so ruthless should not have the power to make my panties melt so quickly.

His gaze runs over my outfit, heating in a similar way to when I arrived. I'm wearing a black lace bralette that accentuates my ample breasts and has sexy little straps across the chest. I've paired it with a leather skirt that barely covers my ass and the thigh-high heels I wear when out on a job, so my trusty blades are always within easy reach. I've finished the outfit off with my shoulder holster, carrying my Glock 43—not that I expect to need it—that can easily be hidden beneath my leather jacket when I zip it up —which I conveniently decided to carry instead of wearing, because I *wanted* to see the guys' reactions.

Cain eliminates the space between us in two large strides, his fervent gaze holding me captive until his lips meet mine in a passionate, dirty kiss. His hands grab hold of my waist, and he pushes me hard against the doorframe as his leg slips between my thighs. "You look like the sexiest badass bitch I've ever laid eyes on," he growls in a deep husk.

Reaching up, I use my thumb to wipe the remnants of my lipstick from his lips. "Well, maybe tonight will make you realize I am an actual badass bitch. Not just one dressed up for your pleasure." I give him a smug smirk, patting the side of his cheek condescendingly before pushing his arm aside.

However, he doesn't let me go far. Snatching my wrist, he tugs me back toward him. "You were gone when I woke up this morning."

His words surprise me. "Yeah, I, uh, had a lot to organize for tonight."

He frowns and his lips flatten. "Well, next time, leave a note or send a text or something."

What the hell? I literally can't do anything but gape at him. Where did the sarcastic asshole who was possessing Cain's body when I walked in go? Seeing my shock, he brushes his thumb over my lip, swollen from his kiss. "This is me trying, Red."

Right. He said he'd try, and apparently, he meant it. Well, fuck, if that doesn't sucker-punch me. I guess I hadn't been holding out much hope—or maybe I just didn't want to get my hopes up—that he would actually follow through.

Swallowing roughly, I nod as Oliver darkens the doorway, snagging my attention. He gives me a once over before meeting my gaze. "Ready?"

I give him a savage grin, more than fucking ready to kill some deserving shitheads. "You have no idea."

The three of us make our way out to one of the club's Escalades in the parking lot, and I slip into the back seat, Oliver behind the wheel and Cain sitting up front, beside him. I fire off the address to Oliver, and he quickly maneuvers us out onto the street and across town.

"So, what's the job?" Cain asks, turning in his seat to look at me.

"Three guys have been torturing and raping girls in a seedy brothel—Nasty Nelly's?"

"Never heard of it."

Figures. "Well, you should have, 'cause it's in your territory."

"What's your plan?" Oliver pipes up, sensing the protest on Cain's lips.

Flicking my gaze up to the rearview mirror, I find him watching me. "I've told the girls to leave a door around the back of the building ajar and to set a room aside for us. When these guys show up for their regular session, they'll be directed to the room." The wicked gleam in my eye and grin curling around my lips probably borders on barbaric, but *fuck*, I love when I get to exact some justice. "And then the fun begins."

Tonight will be the first time either Oliver or Cain has seen this side of me. Oliver caught a glimpse of it before, but he's never gotten a good, up-close look. If tonight doesn't make them realize I'm perfectly capable of taking care of myself, I don't know what will.

"So, we shoot them," Cain states, sounding unimpressed.

"No." The word cracks off the end of my tongue like a whip. "That's too merciful. What these sickos have done to those girls…" I shake my head. There's absolutely no way I'm letting them die that easily. "They deserve to get a taste of their own medicine before I send them careening into the burning pits of hell."

He cocks one of his brows, and I can't tell if he's taken aback by the vehemence in my voice or surprised at my insistence to exact justice. Eventually, he gives me a nod of acceptance, and I get the distinct impression it's more than just him agreeing to my plan. More like, he's agreeing to defer to my orders on this job; to step back and let *me* take control. Good, because I have no intention of letting him run the show.

When we reach Nasty Nelly's, Oliver parks on the street outside, and all three of us head around back, finding the fire exit door propped open as planned. Peering inside, I find the room opposite us empty, the door lying open in invitation. One I accept as I head toward it, the guys on my heels.

Cain closes the door behind him as I look around the small room. The only furniture is a large, king-size bed. I guess in a brothel, that's all you really need. I had asked the girls to leave me some sex toys and BDSM equipment, which I find neatly laid out on a cart in the corner of the room. Excitement courses through me as I take in the assortment of dildos, whips, nipple clamps, anal beads, gags, and blindfolds. Literally everything a girl could dream of to guarantee herself a good time.

Turning my back on the cart of goodies, I spot a floor-to-ceiling mirror on the wall, facing the bed, and walk over to it, running my fingers through my long, straightened hair to try and add some fluff to it. I had to ride Raven over to the clubhouse, and my helmet squashed any initial volume I had after my shower.

Puckering my lips, I pull a tube of the bright red lipstick from my pocket, adding a fresh layer before fixing my tits in my bralette, ensuring they look as busty as they can.

"What the fuck are you doing?" Cain growls, the two of them having watched me freshen up.

Pocketing the lipstick, I shrug out of my leather jacket and shoulder holster and turn to face him. "I want to lure them in with a false sense of safety before making them scream in pain," I tell him sweetly.

His eyes narrow in anger as they roam over me, taking in the complete outfit without the leather jacket. It's revealing and sexy as hell. "Eh, no, I don't fucking think so."

I roll my eyes at his obstinance as I stuff my jacket and gun in the corner of the room where they won't immediately be spotted. When I'm done, I turn to face him, my expression all business. "Just hide, and don't say anything or make a move until I tell you to."

Because Oliver knows how to follow orders, he immediately moves into action. Still, because he's also an asshole, he makes sure to walk right past me, stroking his fingers along my lower back as he goes and making goosebumps rise along my skin. "You're so fucking sexy when you take charge and boss him around," he murmurs low enough that Cain doesn't hear before crouching behind the bed. He's not terribly well hidden, but it's good enough.

When Cain doesn't do as he's told, I quirk a brow at him and point toward the spot behind the door. With one final glower, he stomps toward the corner of the room. Again, it's a shitty hiding place, especially with Cain's broad frame, but it will do.

"If they so much as lay a finger on you," he growls, his voice a low threat.

When he turns to spear me with his glare, I roll my eyes at his alpha-dominant bullshit, but inside, my stomach goes pathetically gooey over that statement.

Before he can complain any more, we hear voices out in the hall, and I quickly move to stand in front of the door, by the far wall, so the boys will notice me as soon as they walk in—instead of scanning the room and spotting the two lumbering men hiding in the corners.

A second later, the handle turns, and three men who look like they are in their early twenties and scream of money and entitled arrogance, step into the room. I can sense the danger and violence coming off them the second they cross the threshold. It's in their cold gazes and the cruel slash of their lips, in the assertive set of their shoulders and the unfaltering stride of each step further into the room, until all three of them are standing in a line in front of me.

The one on the left emits a low whistle as his eyes drink me in. "Fuck yes, you're going to look so good covered in bruises and screaming for us to stop."

I simply stand there and eye each of them up, ignoring his disgusting words as I analyze them for weaknesses. They're all built like football players, only confirming that I made the right choice by bringing Cain and Oliver with me for backup. One I could handle, but not all three at once.

"Don't tell me you're a mute doll," the black-haired guy in the middle sneers, seeming unimpressed by my lack of response—or perhaps it's because I'm not showing the appropriate amount of fear. "Aren't red-heads supposed to be feisty?"

He doesn't give me a chance to respond before his hand whips out and his fingers wrap around my throat, driving me backward against the wall. I hit it with a solid thump, and my eyes narrow on him, my teeth gritted as I struggle to hold back the vile, angry words threatening to spew out of me.

"Maybe you just need us to rile you up first. Get your blood pumping and make you realize just how scared you should be."

I meet his cold, callous stare with a brazen one of my own. "Or maybe I'm just not afraid of you."

He's initially taken aback by my defiance, but it quickly morphs into a disgusting leer as excitement flashes in his eyes. Yeah, that's exactly what he wanted... Someone defiant that he can spend the night breaking.

I haven't given them any signals, but it seems the two assholes I brought with me have decided they've had enough of watching this shithead's hands around my throat. They both step out from their hiding places, immediately catching the boys' attention.

"What the fuck is this?" one of them demands, readying himself for a fight as his arms come up in a defensive move, and he turns slightly so he can face off against Cain —*Ha, good luck to him with that fight.*

Both Cain and Oliver have their guns raised, pointed at the two other men, and while the idiot who still has his hand wrapped around my throat was distracted by the commotion, I slipped my own blade out of my boot. When his attention returns to me, I subtly jab the tip of the blade into his side. His whole body tenses as he recoils, glancing down, and when he returns his shocked, wide-eyed stare to my face, I grin viciously at him.

I dig the blade deeper into his side until his fingers loosen around my neck, his hand eventually dropping away as he takes a step back, clutching his side. As a team, Cain, Oliver, and I advance until we have the three boys corralled in the middle of the room.

"What the fuck is this all about?" the guy in front of me demands. He should know, though, that he's not the one in charge here. He is not the one asking questions. What really pisses me off is the fact that he directs the question to Cain and Oliver. His panicked gaze darts back and forth between them as he practically ignores me, not seeing me as being as much of a threat. *Stupid, fucking, dick-wielding boys.*

To make him realize exactly who is in charge here, I poke him hard enough in the chest with the point of my blade that it pierces through the cotton fabric of his top and into his skin, drawing blood to match his wound from a moment ago. He hisses at the sting of pain, swiveling his gaze to mine. Unrestrained loathing burns in his eyes, and I meet his stare head-on with a chilling one of my own. He's face-to-face with the Reaper right now, and after one agonizingly long second, he seems to realize it. I smile smugly in satisfaction as fear flashes across his face before he quickly masks it, straightening his spine.

One of his buddies snorts. "Please, three against two? We can easily take you on."

Eh, hello! Does he not see me standing here?

Surprisingly, Cain speaks up, the thread of violence in his tone only making the blood rush faster through my veins. He looks so fucking hot with his smug smirk, the thrill of the challenge dancing in his eyes. "I wouldn't underestimate Red, there. She's probably killed more men than we have."

I grin savagely as all three fuckwits stare at me, a combination of skepticism and disbelief in their eyes. "Easily."

With a pinched expression, one of them asks, "What do you want?" His question gains my attention, and I focus my cold-dead eyes on him, noting the rage simmering just beneath the surface of his calm facade. "If it's money, we have plenty of that. Just name your price."

"I don't want your money."

My casual dismissal of his wealth surprises him, and he stutters for a second before speaking up again, this time not sounding as confident as he did before. "W-well, whatever it is, I'm sure we can get it for you."

I tilt my head to the side, maintaining eye contact with him as I act as though I'm thinking about it. I tap my finger against my lips, taking my sweet time as I let the three of them sweat it out before finally responding.

"There is one thing I'd like."

The guy who spoke up is already nodding his head in agreement, and a moment later, the other two agree as well, all three of them willing to give me whatever I want so long as it means they walk out of here with their lives intact. "Anything," one of them insists. *Fucking idiot.*

"I'm a big believer in karma," I muse, ignoring everyone's confused looks. "If you put nasty juju out in the world, then it's only fair that you receive bad fortune in return."

"I don't—Ouch!"

I stab the asshole in front of me *again*, sinking the blade deep into his skin and smirking in satisfaction as a third steady stream of blood soaks through his white t-shirt, and he hisses in pain. Maybe the third time is the charm.

"You are done talking," I snap. "It's time you fucking listened." Anger licks along my spine as I hold myself back from just finishing him off here and now. "It is time you realized you are *not* the one in charge here. You are *not* calling the shots. Your money *cannot* buy you out of this. You are at *my* mercy, playing by *my* rules, and if you want any hope of surviving this night, you will do exactly as *I* say." My threat is delivered with such vehemence that all three of them shrink away from me—well, as far as they can without colliding with Oliver or Cain.

"Phone," I snap, holding my hand out. Fumbling in his pocket, the guy in front of me hands over his phone. Looking at the screen, I frown when it asks for a passcode, and I flick my gaze up to him, silently demanding the code. He rattles off the numbers without hesitation, and I type them in before beginning to search through the phone. The girls had mentioned that the guys liked recording them, and it doesn't take long before I find a group chat where the three of them have been sharing videos of their *conquests* back and forth. Anger and disgust bubble inside me as I scan through the various videos and photos. Each one is more disgusting than the last, but I've seen all I need to. Sneering, I toss the phone to Oliver, who scrolls through the videos before handing it off to Cain. Unlike Oliver, who remains cold and emotionless, Cain vibrates with anger as he stares at the screen.

"You sick fucks," he snarls when he's done, pistol-whipping the guy in front of me and sending him crashing to the ground. He immediately reaches down and hauls him up by his shirt, but before he can land a punch, I call out his name, my tone sharp.

He pauses and looks my way, rage simmering in his dark eyes. I silently stare him down, reminding him without words that this is *my* show. His lips thin, and I can tell he's not one bit happy about it, but eventually, he lowers his fist and lets the guy go.

When I'm confident he's got himself under control, I grab three gags from the cart, tossing one each to Oliver and Cain. The boys' gazes follow every little movement, their postures tense as they wait to see what we do next.

"Put these on," I order, holding out the ball gag in my hand.

The dickhead just gapes at it before he starts shaking his head. "No way. No fucking way."

I sigh in disappointment, pinning him with an unimpressed look. I notice the other two guys glancing furtively at the gags Oliver and Cain are both holding, but they wisely don't verbally protest their objections. "It wasn't a request."

Still, none of them move. I bet if it had been Cain or Oliver who had directed the order, they would have jumped into action. Regardless, I quirk a brow at Oliver, and with a grin, he doesn't hesitate to shoot the asshole in front of him in the knee.

"What the fuck?!" his friend cries out, as the guy falls to the floor, screaming bloody murder as he stares in shock at the gaping wound.

"Put the fucking gags on," I order yet again in an ice-cold voice.

This time they realize I mean fucking business, and the two still standing immediately reach for the gags, but the guy in front of me hesitates with it in his hand, glowering at me with too much defiance for my liking. "Everyone in this building just heard a gunshot going off. I bet the police are already on their way."

The laugh that bursts out of me is cold and caustic. "You're in Black Creek, you fucking idiot. Not to mention the fact you're in a brothel. No one will be calling the police." As he roughly swallows, his Adam's apple bobbing, I grin so fucking vindictively that I'm surprised his heart doesn't give out there and then. "You're all mine for the night, and I intend to have some fun."

With a shaking hand, the asshole in front of me finally sticks the ball gag in his mouth and secures the strap to the back of his head. When I glance at his friend, he's already done the same, and since the wimp on the floor can't seem to do anything but stare at his knee, Oliver bends down and stuffs the gag in his mouth for him.

"Alright." I clap my hands in excitement. "Now the real fun can begin. Let's see..." I press my index finger against my lips. "What do I want to do first." Running my eyes over them, I order, "Clothes off."

Again, they don't immediately jump to obey my command, and I sigh in disappointment before giving Oliver *the look*. However, he doesn't need to actually shoot anyone this time, as the two still standing immediately start stripping out of their clothes at a lightning-fast pace. Once they're done, they help their friend until all three of them are standing there as naked as the day they were born, cupping their pathetic dicks and shivering.

"Well, don't just stand there. You"—I point to the guy with blond hair standing in front of Cain—"get your buddy there hard." I point to the black-haired one, and the two of them share a wide-eyed, panicked stare before the blond one hesitantly reaches out to grab hold of his friend's dick. I can see the disgust on his face as he works his friend over, and his friend's eyes close as he struggles to fight off the urges beginning to build inside him. He can fight it all he wants, but it's human nature. A normal, physical response to a pleasant stimulus, and eventually, he can't talk his dick down any longer. When it's hard in his friend's hand, I walk toward them.

"Well done," I purr, stroking my finger coyly down the front of the blond one's chest. There's nothing quite like a bit of mind fucking, is there? Running my hand up his arm, I dig my nails into his shoulder blade. "Now, on your knees."

I can tell he doesn't know what to think, his eyes darting from my chest to various points around the room and back to my face before he does as I so sweetly asked of him. His dick is at half-mast, and I get a sick sense of satisfaction knowing I'm getting in his head. I grab his friend's hip with my other hand and turn him so his hard dick bobs in front of his friend's face. Their eyes widen comically, and I have to suppress my grin as I undo the gag from the blond one's mouth.

"Have you ever sucked another man's dick before?" I ask in a soft, sweet voice while I stroke my fingers gently through his hair.

"N-no."

"That's okay." I pat the top of his head like he's a well-behaved golden retriever. "It's never too late to learn."

I can see the protest on his lips, and the second they part, I fist the back of his head and shove his mouth over his friend's dick, uncaring whether or not his teeth grate his skin. In fact, I fucking hope they do.

Oliver is immediately behind the black-haired guy, his hands firmly clamped around his shoulders, ensuring he can't back away. I give him a soft smile, even as I shove blondie's face deeper into his friend's crotch until he's choking on his cock.

"That's it," I encourage. "Relax that jaw. Take all of him."

He gurgles and gags, sounding more like he's drowning than doing any proper sucking. Pushing him deeper, until his nose is flattened against his buddy's pubic bone, I hiss, "Isn't this how you like it? What you get off on? Holding girls down and making them feel like they're choking on your tiny, little, pathetic dicks? Calling them sluts and whores and demanding they fucking take it?" Flicking my gaze up to look at his friend's face, his lips slightly parted and eyes drooped with pleasure, despite the situation. "Your buddy certainly seems to be getting off on your degradation."

I wait until he's about to come before yanking blondie off his dick. He falls back on his ass, barely managing to suck in a lungful of air before Oliver replaces the ball gag. Done with that one, for now, I swing my attention to the one with the blown-out knee. "You," I snap, gesturing toward the bed. "On your knees." I laugh before correcting myself. "Well, knee."

When he doesn't immediately move into position, Cain grabs him by the upper arm and all but throws him onto the bed while I move to my tray of toys. I mull over which one I want to play with first before lifting the nipple clamps and turning to point at the black-haired one, whose hard dick is still bobbing in mid-air.

"Mini dick," I call out, tossing him the nipple clamps. "Put these on your friend." With a nudge from Oliver to get him moving, he walks toward the bed, but as he reaches out to put the nipple clamps on his friend's nipples, I stop him. "Not there." Pausing, he stares at me, seeming confused, so I clarify, "Attach them to his balls."

I hear a hiss behind me, and I turn to take in Cain's screwed-up face. "Fuck, that's going to hurt," he comments, loud enough for the guy on the bed to hear. A whimper escapes him, not that his fear affects me. They didn't give a shit when the girls here were begging, whimpering, and crying for them to stop, so why the fuck should I.

Turning my attention back to the bed, I find him gaping at me with wide eyes. "Hurry the fuck up, or I'll attach them to your balls instead," I snap, causing him to jump into motion. He attaches the clamps, and we all ignore his friend's cries and whimpers. He steps away when he's done, and I move to take his place. Careful not to touch him, I reach out and give them a sharp tug, relishing in the asshole's cry of pain.

"Get on the bed beside him," I order next. The guy attempts to say something, but it's unintelligible from behind the gag. Not that I give a shit about what he has to say. "Or would you like a bullet wound to match his?" I question.

Trembling, he climbs up on the bed beside his friend, and I move back to the tray, picking up a big, black dildo. Oliver's already dragged the blond-haired one to the base of the bed, and I shove the dildo into his hand.

"Fuck," Cain laughs coldly. "I change my mind. *That's* going to hurt."

Ignoring him, I keep my attention on the guy in front of me. "I'm sure you can work out what to do with that." It's all I say, smirking at him, and his gaze darts from the giant dildo to his friend, whose ass is perfectly presented for him. His hands shake and his eyes are wide. He instantly tries to back away, picking up on my meaning. Oliver stops him, shoving him forward. "It's you or him," I state, knowing that's the best way to get any of them to do what I want.

I move around to stand at the side of the bed, slowly trailing my fingers along the black-haired one's spine, messing with him while his buddy gathers his courage. When I reach his head, I fist my hand in his hair, tilting his head back until he's forced to meet my gaze. With cold, unemotional features, I stare at him. "It's not so much fun being on the other side, is it? It's not nice being forced to do something you don't want to do; being treated like absolute scum—nothing but a plaything." He can't do anything but mumble from behind the gag, and when he starts up with whatever pleas or protests he has, I immediately cut him off. "But now you're about to find out exactly what it feels like to be fucked against your will."

With my hand still fisted painfully in his hair, I switch my gaze to his buddy and cock a brow expectantly. With hands shaking so badly, I wonder how he's even going to get the dildo inserted as he approaches his friend. I deliberately wait until the head of the dildo pushes against the guy's asshole, and his entire body locks up in a vain attempt to prevent the unwanted penetration, before calling out, "Stop."

The guy practically collapses onto the mattress in relief, my firm grip on his hair the only reason he remains on his trembling knees. His friend looks just as relieved that I've put a stop to this, but their reprieve is short-lived. "I'm not a complete bitch. You can use his blood for lube." When no one moves, I gesture with my chin to the blood seeping into the sheet from the other guy's knee. "Go on," I encourage. "Get it nice and slicked up."

With slow, hesitant movements, he begins to rub the dildo against his friend's knee and the bedsheet, coating it.

"Good, I think that's plenty," I bark when I'm done watching his friend flinch and grunt every time he sticks the dildo into his open wound. Holding out my hand, he hands over the dildo, and I inspect it before moving to stand behind the guy still on the bed. I slam the entire thing up his ass in one swift, unexpected move. He squeals like a fucking pig, but it washes over me as I serve my justice until I've sated the anger threatening to consume me.

By the time I'm done, I'm breathing heavily and sweat dots my brow. Turning to Oliver, who's standing closest to me, I hold my hand out, and he hands over his gun.

Cocking it, I put a bullet into the back of the asshole's head. The sound of a second and third gunshot goes off as Cain finishes off the other two, and I turn to face them.

"What now, Red?"

I cast my eyes over the three dead bodies and shrug. "Now we make them look like gang killings or some other random Black Creek attack."

Oliver's quizzical gaze turns to me while Cain's eyebrows lift in surprise. "Don't you usually carve an R into them and leave them in plain sight?" Oliver questions.

"Yeah, if it's someone from Black Creek," I explain easily. "But these guys come from money. They aren't from here, so I can't make them look like Reaper killings."

"Hold up," Cain says, making me pause mid-step just as I was about to pat down the dead body closest to me. "The gang members you kill are only some of the Reaper's victims?"

"Yup," I say casually, popping the *p* as I bend down to check the pockets of the dead guy closest to me. "It might be hard for you to believe, but I actually don't give a shit about the no-brain gangsters of this town."

I fish out his wallet and phone, setting them to one side before moving on to the other body at Cain's feet. "So why do it then?"

His question surprises me, and I pause, staring up at him. "Seriously? Tonight didn't make that obvious?"

His eyes dart around the room before coming back to me. "It's a sexual assault thing?"

Eh, close enough, I guess.

"It's an abusive thing." His eyebrows lift.

"So Python..."

I spear him with a deadpan look. "He abused my friend for years and was starting to take his issues out on their daughter, too. He needed to be stopped."

"You're like some sort of vigilante," Oliver remarks.

A humorless laugh escapes me. "I dunno about that. I do what I can for those who can't pay, but there are plenty of well-to-do housewives out there sick of taking shit from their abusive husbands and willing to pay whatever it costs to get rid of them."

Neither of them says anything, most likely processing everything I've said, while I empty the pockets of the other two shitstains and chuck their meager contents into the pile. Standing to my full height, I frown down at the three of them, debating what to do. They've been shot assassin style, so that works in my favor, but I've toyed with them enough to leave incriminating evidence. I usually make killings like this as clinical as possible, but I saw red when I watched those recordings and I allowed my sadistic side to run the show instead of using sense and logic.

"Okay... What now?" Cain questions.

"I'm still working that out."

"Babe, we can take care of this," Oliver says, stepping in to me. His chest is flush against my back, and when I tilt my head back to look up at him, he's fixing Cain with a look, the two of them having some sort of silent conversation.

"Yeah," Cain agrees after a moment.

"It needs to look like a gang killing, or a happy accident," I reiterate.

Oliver chuckles, his chest vibrating against my back. "Who do you think you're talking to, Trouble. Our guys can absolutely make that happen. Don't even worry about it." He glances down at me, holding my gaze as his hand comes up to rest on my waist, giving it a reassuring squeeze.

I think it over for a second before giving him my consent. He places a kiss along my hairline before moving to the other side of the room to place a call. Cain stands and watches me the entire time he's gone—which can't have been more than a minute or two. I can feel his eyes roaming over my skin as though he's trying to commit every part of me to memory.

"How did all of this start?" he eventually asks as Oliver returns, taking up his place at my back once again. His body heat bolsters me, and I finally turn my head to meet Cain's inquisitive gaze.

"I told you my mom was murdered," I begin, unsure whether or not he shared any of my history with Oliver. "And that I killed her murderer." Oliver doesn't tense behind me, but his hand does slide around to rest on my abdomen. My eyes stay focused on Cain, his own gaze unwavering. He nods, confirming he remembers our conversation, and I shrug. "That's how it started. After she died, Luc and I ended up on the streets, in and out of homeless and women's shelters. I saw and experienced firsthand so many cases of men taking—or trying to take—what they thought they deserved. It pissed me off. Infuriated me." I drop my gaze, unable to look him in the eye as I confess the next bit. "I couldn't save my mom, but I *could* save these other women who weren't able to stand up for themselves."

Oliver's other hand slides up my throat until he reaches my jaw. He turns my face toward him, his lips capturing mine. I melt into him. "You're so incredibly strong," he murmurs, placing another chaste kiss on my lips. "So selfless." Kiss. "So badass." Kiss. "A force to be fucking reckoned with."

His phone goes off in his pocket and he pulls it out, kissing me a final time before moving away to answer it. Without him pressed up against me, I feel vulnerable, exposed, and I flick my gaze up to Cain, trying to read him through my eyelashes. He's still watching me, and I can't decipher the myriad of emotions on his face.

I step forward, intending to go through the wallets I pilfered—it's not like a dead guy needs cash—when Cain's hand reaches out, and he touches my wrist, halting me. "Oliver's right," he says in a quiet voice. "Most people would have turned a blind eye, but not you."

Lifting my head from where his fingers are still pressed against my wrist, I meet his beautiful green eyes. "Most people wouldn't take on a whole criminal organization to avenge their sister, but you are."

He shakes his head. "That's as much for me as it is for Evie... I-I need to do it."

Nodding, I know exactly what he means. "I *need* to do this too. It's a part of who I am. It's the darkest, sickest part of me born from all the violence and depravity I've been exposed to. If it weren't for the fact I found an excusable cause, I'd probably be classified as a serial killer."

I honestly wasn't sure how he'd react, but what I didn't expect was for him to close the distance between us and fuse his lips to mine, stealing my breath as my lips part, granting his tongue access as he delves into my mouth.

I drown in everything that's Cain. In his leather and whiskey scent. In the way his large, calloused hands cup my face. In the way he steps into me, all dominance and casual possessiveness.

It's only the sound of a throat being cleared that crash lands me back into reality, as I pull away from Cain to look at Oliver, who is standing by the door, smirking. "Clean-up crew is here."

Right. We are in the middle of a brothel, surrounded by dead bodies that we've tortured and killed. It should probably be inappropriate, but it seems fitting that Cain and I would finally drop the last of our barriers and open ourselves up to one another while standing on a blood-soaked carpet after torturing a bunch of rapists.

R ed. She's all I can think about. From her odd stage name to the honey-brown of her eyes to the fact that she never does or says what I expect. Don't get me wrong, I'm still suspicious of her, but I'm also curious. Intrigued. Entranced. Enough to have me finding one excuse or another to stop by Belle Donne every night. She seems to be as aware of my presence as I am of her close proximity. Her eyes are constantly on mine when she's on the stage, as though she can't tear them away, and I don't miss the way she deliberately passes by my table when she's working the floor. Even if she doesn't acknowledge me, she still feels that magnetic energy drawing her to me. There's something about her that I can't put my finger on. I feel like I know her, like we've crossed paths before, but I would remember encountering someone who affects me the way she does. It's not that she makes me feel something per se, but the uptick of my heart, the way she occupies my thoughts… something about her has gotten under my skin, and now I can't get rid of her.

She reminds me of the street rat I met in that alley. The one I let escape with her life. The one whose brilliant blue eyes still haunt me. Although, I'm pretty sure it's the guilt of letting her live, more than *her* that gets to me. It's the only time I've ever not acted in the best interests of the Famiglia, so it would make sense that that inappropriately inexplicable, *emotional* decision would still bother me to this day. And yet I don't exactly regret letting her walk away. It would have been a different matter if she'd blabbed to someone about what she witnessed, but she kept her mouth shut, and any time I picture the scene unfolding any other way—in such a way that left her lying dead at my feet, there's an unfamiliar twinge in my chest.

However, as I watch Red shake her ass and spin around the pole on the stage, she's nothing like the dirty, skinny street rat. For starters, she's got actual curves. Large tits and hips you want to dig your fingers into. A bubble ass that would hold you hypnotized while you fuck her from behind. Not to mention the brown hair and matching eyes. She's the opposite of that kid… yet the way she behaves strikes a similar chord with me. It's not outwardly bold or defiant, but it speaks to someone who knows how to hold their own. Someone who can speak up for themselves and won't let anyone steamroll over them. Of course, that only has me wondering how far she could be pushed before she'd bow down to me, submit and let me own her body and soul.

It's the reason I decide to mix things up the next time I unsurprisingly find myself walking into Belle Donne rather than heading home. "Have Red meet me in the back office," I bark at the doorman when I arrive, barely slowing down as I stride through the club, careful to avoid the room she's working in as I make my way to the back office. After her confrontation with Sam last week and our moment in the alley, I'm craving more time alone with her. Fuck, I was tempted to snatch her away there and then that night. Throw her in my car and tie her up in my house. Keep her as mine forever and always. It's an urge like nothing I've ever felt before, and it's been riding me hard ever since. But not yet. I need to be sure she's up to the challenge first.

I keep the lights off in the office, cloaking the room in shadow as I settle into the chair behind the desk and wait. I'm not left waiting for long before a shadow—the outline of a woman—forms in the frosted glass of the office door. I smirk as she hesitates on the other side before the door handle turns, and I carefully wipe my face free of any emotion.

Her high heels click against the wooden floor as she steps into the room and closes the door behind her. There's a moment of silence as she glances around the dark room, until she must notice me sitting behind the desk. "You, uh, wanted to see me?" she questions. Her voice is steady, and despite being alone in a dark room with ultimately the deadliest person in the Famiglia, she doesn't seem afraid. Nor did she seem afraid of me that night either. No one was around. There were no witnesses. I could have done anything I wanted to her.

I don't respond. There's power in silence. It unnerves most people, especially when you don't obey typical social cues, like responding to questions. The seconds tick by, and the only sound is her steady rhythmic breathing. I purse my lips, irritation grating at me that I'm not getting the response I expected.

"Come here," I bark out, harsher than intended. She doesn't immediately jump to obey my order like she did the other week when I told her to sit with me. I liked that. The way her body reacted on instinct, obeying me. Like it knew who its master was and wanted to please me. It's her mind that rebels against the authority, but her body is begging her to obey. I wonder if relinquishing herself like that makes her as wet as watching her submit makes me hard.

A growl works its way up the back of my throat, and as it reverberates through the air, she takes a slow, unsure step toward me, followed by another, until she's standing in front of me. Leaning back in my chair, I look up at her, spreading my legs. "Closer." A final step has her standing between my thighs. My eyes lower, just about able to make out whatever slutty outfit she's dressed in tonight. If I leaned forward, I could press my nose against the thin fabric covering her pussy and find out if she's as excited as I am. Instead of giving in to that urge, though, I hold myself still—a Herculean task that has my fingers digging into the arm of the chair. This is about seeing how far I can push *her*; how far that defiance goes. It's *not* about giving in to my own desires. I have Lor for that. "On your knees."

Her body stiffens, her knees locking in place. It's a reaction that only has my dick straining harder against the cold metal of my zipper. Not that I get off on forcing a girl.

Nah, my dad has many men that love that shit, but it doesn't do it for me. What *does* get me going is pushing people to their limits, pressing against their barriers, and seeing if they'll reinforce them or crumble under the pressure. Not that I ever get the chance to actually push those boundaries. The second I so much as look in someone's direction, they are bending over backwards to do whatever the fuck I want. It's boring and predictable. Lor is the only one who has ever treated me as an equal, and not like I'm going to shoot him in the face for saying no. But I have a feeling Red's going to give me the challenge I've been craving.

"You want me to suck your dick?" Her voice is thick with disdain, which *almost* hides the breathy quality. It's the perfect blend of defiance, disgust, and lust that has my erection reaching the point of pain. It's exactly what I wanted. What I expected from her. "Is this supposed to be my payment for last week? Because I didn't ask you to do that."

Ignoring her, I instead ask, "Don't you like working here?" I wish I could see the look on her face, but it's too dark. All I can make out is her outline from the faint hall light that shines through the frosted upper half of the door. That's fine, though. The tense way she holds herself, not moving to do as commanded but not backing away either, is telling enough. "Don't you want to keep your job?"

I swear I can hear her teeth grating against one another. "Not if it means throwing away my dignity." Her answer surprises me. Many people would consider getting up on stage and shaking your ass while wearing next to nothing as the definition of discarding your dignity, but seemingly not her.

I bark out a cold, caustic laugh that has her tensing even more, and I lift my hand to her leg, just above her knee. I slowly trail my fingers up her inner thigh. "You haven't been able to stop watching me all week," I muse. "I bet that pole is slick with your arousal every time you spin around it." My fingers approach her apex. "I bet you're wet right now."

In a shocking move that leaves me momentarily stunned, she slaps my hand away before I can find out for myself just how fucking drenched she is. She gasps, and we both freeze. I think she's as taken aback by her reaction as I am. In the next second, I'm pushing myself out of the chair as she quickly backs up. No apologies spill from her lips. In fact, I'm certain she lifts her chin in defiance. Fuck if that doesn't have me wanting to bend her over the desk and fuck her into submission.

I slowly stalk around the desk, closing the distance she just put between us. She again doesn't react how I expect, holding her ground as I advance. The only sound in the office is the slap of my shoes as they strike the floor with every step. I move until I'm standing directly in front of her. Even in her heels, the top of her head barely reaches my chin, and I tower over her. Yet, she doesn't back away. She doesn't duck her head or step back. Hell, her breathing doesn't even falter. She's completely unflappable. "Why are you not afraid of me?"

"Is that what you want?" she questions. "For me to fear you?"

Is that what I want? I'm not even sure. It's just something I'm used to, but I don't get a sick sense of joy from inflicting fear in people the way my father does.

I lift my hand and brush my fingers along her chest until I reach the base of her neck. Gripping it more firmly but ensuring I'm not cutting off her oxygen, I slowly slide my hand along her throat. Her pulse beats steadily beneath my touch, only confirming what I already knew. "Who are you?" The question is barely more than a whisper, and she doesn't answer it, letting it hang in the air between us.

"I think the better question is, who are *you*?" she eventually responds, once again taking me by surprise and throwing me for a loop. As I said, she never responds the way I think she's going to.

"You know who I am," I growl out. "I'm the Famiglia's head assassin. Son of Giovanni Antonelli. The next head of the Family."

She shakes her head, and the light from the hall catches in her eyes as she lifts her head to look up at me. "That's not what I asked. Who are *you*?"

I frown, confused. "I just told you who I am—"

"No," she argues, cutting me off. "You told me who you are to the Family, but that doesn't tell me anything about *you*."

"Me and my family are one and the same. I am them, and they are me."

"You are your own person, too," she continues to insist. "You have your own likes and dislikes, your own preferences that will be completely separate from your obligation to your family."

I don't respond as I try to wrap my head around what she's saying. All I've ever known is my family, and while I may not be a completely loyal and obedient soldier, they are all I know. All I have. They *are* me.

My fingers flex on her delicate neck, and I feel her pulse press more firmly against the pad of my thumb as I press down on it. "I don't have likes and dislikes. I don't feel pleasure or joy or satisfaction." I pause as I feel her fingers come up to grip my belt, the tips skimming over the top of my shirt, just above the waistband of my pants.

"I don't believe that." Her voice has taken on a low, raw quality that draws me in. "Are you saying you never get angry, never lose your temper or lash out at those around you?" My resounding silence is answer enough. Her hand lets go of my belt, dipping lower to brush over my straining erection. "You say you don't feel pleasure, but you're hard, so you must *like* something." She takes a step back, the distance dislodging my hand from her throat, and I let it fall to my side, completely thrown off balance by her words. "I don't think you *can't* feel. I think you just don't know how to recognize those positive emotions. So when you do feel something out of the ordinary, you don't know how to handle it."

Another step backward has her at the door, and reaching behind her, she grabs hold of the handle and pulls it open, slipping out without another word, leaving me completely perplexed. If I thought I was intrigued before, well, I'm fucking obsessed now. Red has my undivided attention, and I have no intention of letting her go. I'm going to lay claim to every inch of her until she doesn't know anything other than me. I will make her mine. Whether she likes it or not.

TWO DAYS LATER, I STEP OUT OF THE ELEVATOR INTO MY FATHER'S penthouse that overlooks the entire city. I hate being summoned like this, especially when Lor and I were busy going over the intel we've gathered on some gang called Reaper Rejects. Apparently, they are the only other gang, besides Grim Bastards, left in Black Creek—because they fucking destroyed everyone else. How the hell we weren't aware of them before now says everything about how little attention we've been paying to the goings-on on our own turf. They're looking like the primary culprits for the destruction done to our clubs, but I want to be sure before I retaliate.

However, my father doesn't give a shit about how busy I am. When he calls, I'm expected to come running. Not even I can refuse my father's orders. It's just easier to do whatever he wants. The only time I've ever clashed with my father was when it came to Lor. Nothing else has ever been worth the hassle of incurring his wrath.

The first time was when we were five, and he beat him half to death when he caught us playing together. After that, we were more careful, but both of us suffered several more brutal beatings at such a young age before we learned how to properly hide our friendship from my father. Over time, we fell into our roles—Don's son and bodyguard —until, on the outside, it's all anyone ever saw. But behind closed doors, our relation-ship grew. Every time I had to watch my father or his men pound on Lor, simply because he was my friend, it just added bricks to the wall forming between my father and me. As a young boy, my father was my idol. I looked up to him the way I imagine any young son does. But with every bruise he left on Lor, every rib he broke, and drop of blood he spilled, my opinion of him changed. I've never really understood it because until then, nothing ever bothered me. And watching another man get pulverized has never had the same effect. But there's something about Lor that, when I saw him beaten and vulnerable like that, this angry thing inside of me that I hadn't known existed, raised its ugly head and screamed, *FUCK NO.*

I imagine my father still has his suspicions regarding our friendship, but he is happy to ignore it as long as he never witnesses it. And that works just fine for us. Pushing all thoughts of Lor and the past to the back of my mind, I stride through the empty living room and head for his office, noting the absence of anyone else. Usually, the space around my father is teaming with security, his consigliere—Santos—and his underlings. It's normally a hive of activity, but everything is eerily quiet today. That can't bode well for this meeting.

Pushing open the door to his office, my hackles rise as my father's furious face lifts to meet mine. He used to instill fear in me as a boy. His dark eyes and devil-like features could harden to stone in an instant. Even his cold, calculating smile would send shivers down my spine. Thankfully, I'm immune to all of it now. The undisguised loathing that currently darkens his features is nothing new. I've seen it plenty of times and had it directed my way more than once, but he's angrier than I've seen him in a long time.

I wrack my brain, trying to work out what could have him so angry. He stands as I close the door behind me and circles his desk. He paints an intimidating picture. He's only an inch or two shorter than me, but the sheer authority that pours off him more than makes up for those few inches of height. Even now, in his fifties, with his hair graying around his temples and age lines carving crevices into his features, he still appears as harsh as he was ten years ago. My gaze flicks from the violence shining in his eyes to his hands. In one hand, he's clutching pages in a death grip, and in his other is a pistol. He lifts it, pointing it at the spot between my eyes. I stand frozen, waiting for him to either pull the trigger or be done with this act of intimidation.

"If you weren't my only son, I'd put a bullet in you here and now." He drops the gun to his side, sneering in disgust as he shoves the pages into my chest. He circles back behind the desk while I look down at the photos. Photos of Lor and me—together.

"You're a fucking disgrace to this family," he snarls. "A faggot." My eyes snap upward. His nose is scrunched in repulsion, and he's shaking his head like he can't believe he could have fathered someone who didn't conform to exactly what he expected. I do absolutely everything he demands, no questions asked, but the fact he has these pictures is proof that he doesn't trust me. That he's had someone following me; spying on me. If he hadn't dug his nose into my personal life, he wouldn't have uncovered something he found so fucking revolting.

"As if that wasn't bad enough," he continues, seething. "You fuck *him*. The son of a traitor. Not even some back alley whore." I can't tell what bothers him more. The fact I'm fucking a guy, or the fact that that guy is Lor. He's always hated Lor. Blamed him for his father's crimes, even though he was a kid at the time. It wasn't enough to kill his father and be done with it. No, he had to keep Lor close and hold his father's sins over his head at every available opportunity, embarrassing him and using Lor's need to prove he's not his father to get him to do whatever the fuck he wanted. I don't think he expected Lor and I to form any sort of friendship, but our mutual hatred for my father bonded us in a way he hadn't anticipated. We've gone to great lengths to hide our friendship, in any case.

"It's just sex," I remark casually.

His hand slams down on his desk. "That's what whores are for."

I shrug, acting nonchalant about the entire situation. "Sometimes, I fancy something different. It means nothing."

His gaze snaps to mine. "Well, it stops now. I *never* want to see images like this"—he sneers at the other photos still scattered on his desk—"again. Do you hear me?"

"Yes, sir." There's no other answer he wants to hear, and I know which battles to pick. This isn't one of them.

"Good. It's past time you were married, anyway. You're thirty, Dante. You should be working on producing heirs to continue on my legacy." His gaze flicks up to mine, but my face gives nothing away. "I'll reach out to my contacts. Find someone suitable."

I simply nod as though I agree. There is no point in arguing with him, but my silence should not be mistaken for compliance. I have no interest in marrying some high-maintenance mafia princess. I never have, and especially not now that a certain brunette dancer has stolen all of my focus.

Seeming appeased, he sinks into his chair. "Obviously, you will have to pick a new Consigliere now. You can't choose someone you're..." we waves in disgust toward the photos still clutched in my hand. "You need someone trustworthy; someone loyal."

I grate my teeth. He's been against Lor as my second in command ever since I told him who I'd chosen—not that I was surprised. This is the ammunition he needed to force me into picking someone else and probably why he went digging for dirt in the first place. "He is loyal to the Famiglia," I argue.

"This is not a discussion. I'm giving you an order, boy. An order I expect you to obey. Pick someone else, or I'll pick someone for you. It's bad enough that that *traitor* is responsible for protecting you, but I will *not* have him standing in a position that commands respect." He holds my gaze until I give a reluctant nod of agreement. Now is not the time to push him, but there is no way I'll be picking anyone other than Lor. I don't trust anyone else.

My father looks away, gathering the papers on his desk and locking them in his top drawer. "Where are we on this whole business with the damaged clubs?"

"I'm looking into possible suspects."

"Well, hurry up. We can't let this go unpunished."

The finality of his words let me know our business is concluded and without another word, I stride from his office. I refuse to agree to any of his demands. I won't stop fucking Lor, I definitely won't be picking someone else as my Consigliere, and I sure as fuck won't be marrying whatever spoiled princess he's handpicked.

Reaching the elevator, I stab the button and wait impatiently for it to arrive. Through the roaring in my ears, I become aware of the sound of my father's voice coming from down the hall. He mustn't have closed his office door, and I focus in on his words.

"... should have killed the kid along with his traitorous father." My teeth grind, and my fists clench in annoyance, but it's his next words that snag my attention. "What about the club whore?" There's a moment of silence as whomever he's talking to— probably Santos—answers. "Find out what you can, then get rid of her. Don't need the complication."

The elevator doors open, and I don't want to get caught eavesdropping, so I step in and press the button. My mind whirs the entire way to the ground floor. Were they talking about my Red? They must be. If my father was able to find out about Lor and me then it's likely he found out about Red as well, and if he views her as a complication, he wouldn't hesitate to eliminate her.

Flashes of her pretty corpse flash across my mind, causing a tightness in my chest. Yeah, I won't be letting that happen.

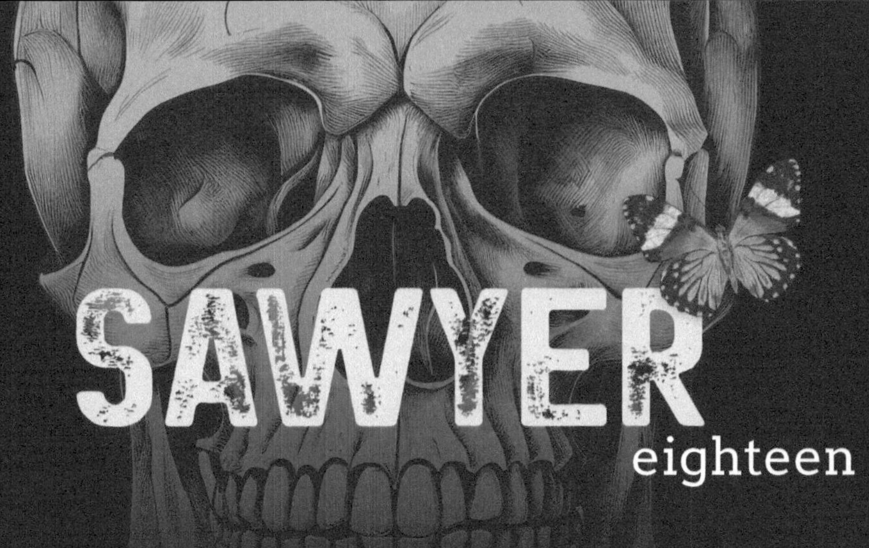

eighteen

Trying not to let my frustration show at being summoned to Belle Donne on my day off, I attempt to set my features into a pleasant expression as I push open the staff entrance door and step inside the club. It's not Franny's fault that there's a payroll issue.

The place is deserted as I make my way through the building, which is to be expected this early in the day. However, as I approach the office, the adjacent supply closet door swings open, and before I can so much as blink, I'm being hauled into the dark room.

"Hey—" I begin in protest, but a large, rough-skinned hand clamps over my mouth, muting my shocked cry as I'm flattened against a rugged, masculine body. An arm slips around my middle, imitating a steel cage as it pins my arms to my side and holds me hostage.

Despite the hand over my mouth, I continue to try and scream for help as I struggle to release my arms from the tight hold the asshole has on them, but the sound is barely more than a low wail.

"Shush." The word is barked out in a low, annoyed growl, and I fall still in my captor's arms. My mind races a mile a minute as I try to figure out why Dante is holding me hostage in a supply closet, but before I can come up with anything, the sound of someone stepping out of the office garners my attention. I'm conflicted as to whether to call out or not. Dante has never indicated that he means me any harm, but equally, he's the Antonellis' head assassin, so...

Yet, something makes me hesitate.

"—some whore." There's a moment of silence followed by a cold chuckle, squashing any ideas I had about drawing any attention to our hiding place. "She must be one hell of a fuck. I'll have to see for myself before I kill her." His ominous words are followed by another laugh before he steps back into the office, the closed door muffling the rest of his words—not that I'm particularly eager to hear them.

My entire body is rigid in the wake of that one-sided conversation. I feel Dante shift behind me before the unmistakable sound of a gun being cocked echoes around the small room like a death knell. I didn't recognize the voice, but considering I had an appointment with Franny at nine in the morning—before the club even opened—there's no doubt in my mind that I'm the person he was referring to—the one he intends to kill. It takes everything in me to suppress the shiver of fear at what would have happened if Dante hadn't intervened. I'd have been caught entirely by surprise, most likely taken out before even comprehending what had happened. My stomach churns, and for one horrible second, I think I'm going to be sick. If it wasn't for Dante's painfully tight hold on me, my legs wouldn't be capable of holding me up.

As if sensing how close I am to losing it, he relaxes his hand over my mouth, hesitating for a second longer before removing it completely. I suck down a lungful of air, then another, until my stomach settles and my legs feel stronger beneath me, even if Dante still has an iron-tight hold on me. Secretly, I draw some strength from his steady presence at my back.

Neither of us speaks—hell, I barely dare to breathe—as we hide in the closet, and when my phone vibrates in my pocket, I jump so badly that I would have stumbled into a shelf and given our position away if it wasn't for Dante's arm around me.

He curses under his breath so quietly that the sound barely reaches my ears. There's a rustle of movement as he tucks his gun away before I feel his hands on me. His other arm stays banded around me as he feels for my phone, finding it in the back pocket of my jeans. Pulling it out, I cast a glance at the screen, seeing the Belle Donne's office number before he presses the button on the side, silencing the vibrations and darkening the screen before slipping the phone into his own pocket.

Another rustle as he retrieves his gun before wrapping his arm loosely around me, the butt of the gun brushing against my top as he holds it firmly in his hand in front of me.

I lose track of time as we stand there, straining to hear anything outside our little safety bubble. I'm hyper-aware of Dante's firm body pressing against mine, his arm wrapped around my waist, his tense posture as if he's ready to spring into motion the second the door is ripped open. Somehow, I know without a shadow of a doubt that he will fire shots through the damn door if he thinks someone is about to discover us.

Thankfully, it doesn't come to that, and eventually, we hear the office door open again. This time, whoever was waiting for me sounds less calm as they slam the door shut behind them and stomp down the hall, away from us.

Even after the footsteps have long since faded, neither of us moves. The only sound is our steady exhales as we wait with bated breath to see if the person comes back. Eventually, Dante must decide the coast is clear, and his arm drops from my waist as he moves around me. Pausing with his ear against the door, he listens for a moment before cracking it open, peering out.

Without looking back, he gestures for me to follow him, and not knowing what else to do, I move closer to his back. His hand wraps around my wrist, and in a lightning-quick move, he tugs me out of the closet and we hurry at a clipped pace along the hall in the opposite direction to where the footsteps receded.

He pushes open a back entrance door, and I stutter to a stop when I find a blacked-out sedan parked right by the door. "Get in," he bites out, yanking open the back passenger door.

"What?! No!" I'm shaking my head adamantly, because as grateful as I might be, I sure as hell am not about to get into that car with him. For all I know, this could all have been a setup to get me to go willingly. He pulls on my arm with more urgency, but I fight back against him, holding my ground. "No," I argue, failing to dislodge his hand from my wrist.

A venomous snarl rips out of him, and when he turns to look at me over his shoulder, violence shimmers in his dark eyes. I get the feeling it's not aimed at me, however. "Do you want to stay here and get murdered?"

...or maybe *some* of that ferocity is being directed my way.

I flick my gaze around the otherwise empty alleyway, chewing on my bottom lip as I struggle to decide what the right thing to do is. Stay here and possibly get murdered, or get in the car with Dante... and possibly get murdered. Not great odds either way.

Another noise of frustration bubbles up his throat, and he tugs harder on my arm, making me stumble. He takes advantage of my off-balance state, sweeping me into his arms and all but throwing me into the backseat.

"Hey!" I yell out as the door slams shut behind me. I scramble across the seats, grabbing hold of the door handle as he climbs in behind the wheel, but the damn door doesn't open. I thump my fist pointlessly against the window before scowling at him. "Let me out!" I'm not even sure if I want him to leave me at the club, but I don't appreciate the decision being taken away from me.

He ignores me, but I don't miss the slight tug of a smirk at the corner of his lips as he puts the car in gear and moves down the alley onto the road. We slowly make our way through the city. From what I can tell, we're heading north to the uppermost point of Antonelli territory. Slumping back in my seat, I mull over my options as we drive past street after street. Assuming that I'm not on my way to my death, this could be the window of opportunity we have been hoping for—my chance to gather the intel I need for the Rejects.

I frequently cast glances at my unlikely savior, trying to suss him out. I've tried my hardest to get close to him when he's stopped by the club, but fucking hell has it been challenging. He's not exactly an open book, and between what I know about him and what I've heard, he paints an intimidating picture. Yet, as I watch him now, he seems perfectly relaxed, navigating the city streets with ease.

"Where are we going?" I eventually ask as the usual cityscape gives way to larger areas of greenery and houses grander than anything I've ever seen before.

He briefly flicks his gaze from the road to the rearview mirror, but he doesn't answer me. Gritting my teeth, I instead ask a question that's been rattling around, unwanted, in my head since he threw me into the car. "Are you going to kill me?"

I make a point of keeping my features impassive as he looks in the rearview mirror, holding my gaze for an extended moment. I can't read anything in his eyes and he once again ignores my question. Well, I'm not going to waste my breath repeating myself. Huffing out a frustrated sigh, I cross my arms over my chest and do my best to relax back in my seat, watching the landscape go by in a colorful blur.

I perk up, straightening in my seat and peering out the window when he finally pulls off the main road onto a private lane, and we travel at a much slower speed along it for several more minutes until we approach a large, black gate. He presses a button on the steering wheel and the gates automatically part, granting us entry. I shift forward to get a good look out the front windshield. "Wow," I murmur, gaping at the opulence in front of me.

I'm vaguely aware of him turning his head to look at me, but I can't tear my eyes away from the Malibu-style mansion in front of me as he rolls through the gates, pulling the car up beside a set of wide, stone steps.

"Where are we?" My question is met by silence, and I expect he doesn't plan to answer me, so when he finally responds, I'm surprised.

"My house."

That admission finally snaps my gaze from the large, white-wood structure to his face. "You live here?"

He shrugs casually. "Not often."

My brows scrunch in confusion, not understanding what he means, but he doesn't give me time to ask any more questions as he pushes open his door and gets out of the car.

I hurry to follow him, forgetting my door is child-locked, so when I pull on the handle, the damn thing doesn't open. The asshole stands on the other side of my door for a deliberately long moment, and I swear I see a slight smile lift one corner of his lips before he flattens it, only making a move to reach for the door handle when I slap my palm against the window. "Open the damn door, asshole!"

Well, I figure if he intends to kill me, I may as well get the insults out while I still can.

As soon as the lock disengages, I push against the door, shoving it open and climbing out with a scowl on my face. Before I can do anything else, Dante's hand is around my upper arm.

"What the hell?!" I try to pull out of his grip, but he ignores me as he tugs me toward the front entrance. He maintains his tight hold on my arm as he unlocks the door, using a fancy eye scanner. "You know that's not going to stop intruders," I snark. Logic says I should keep my mouth shut, but speaking my mind in Dante's presence hasn't failed me yet, so I'm going with it. Besides, I get a kick out of knowing I must be getting on his nerves.

Deliberately slow, in a move that is clearly intended to strike fear into people's hearts, he turns to look at me, cocking a brow. I ignore the increased thudding of my heart as I swallow and dig deep for my Reaper persona.

"All anyone has to do is cut your eye out, and voila." I shrug casually, even as he continues to watch me, the intensity in his gaze ratcheting up a notch.

He stares at me for so long that the moment turns awkward, and I almost regret ever opening my mouth in the first place, but *finally*, he responds. "They'd have to kill me first." On that note, he yanks me into the house behind him, only letting go of my arm when he's set the security system. Satisfied that I can't escape, he saunters deeper into the house, and after a moment's hesitation, I follow after him. What else can I really do? I could *try* to escape, however, not only do I want answers about today, but I *need* information.

I stutter to a stop as I enter a large, bright, open-plan kitchen, dining, and living area. The pitched roof and glass-fronted wall running the entire length of the back of the house offer an unobstructed view across green lawns, which bleed into a sandy strand running into the ocean. I gape in stunned silence as the waves roll into the shore, lapping at the sand as the tide pulls the water in and out. It's captivatingly beautiful.

The sound of a can being opened snaps me back to my current situation, and I reluctantly pull my gaze away from the gorgeous landscape outside as I move to sit on a barstool at the long breakfast bar separating the kitchen from the living room.

"Who was that today?" I ask, watching as Dante pours himself a glass of Coke. He's standing in front of me, on the other side of the counter, and his gaze lifts to meet my questioning one as he sets the glass down. My brows lift in surprise as he pushes the glass my way, pouring the last of the fizzy drink into another glass for himself. I don't immediately accept the drink, instead, waiting until he raises his own to his lips, gulping down half of it before determining he probably didn't poison my glass.

I take a much more cautious sip, feeling strangely self-conscious with his eyes on me. "Well?" I snap after a long moment of silence, getting irritated with his continued refusal to answer any of my questions. "Who was he?"

He still doesn't fucking answer me, but lifts his phone out of his pocket when it buzzes. That reminds me, he still has my phone. Before I can demand it back, he finally fucking speaks. "I have to go back to the city. I have one of my men coming. He'll keep an eye on you."

He knocks back the last of his drink before moving to the sink and rinsing out the glass. The entire time, I sit and gape at him, and it's only when he crosses the kitchen, heading back to the hall, that I gather my wits. "Wait, what? You're leaving? You haven't even answered my questions!" He doesn't stop. He doesn't even slow down as he heads toward the door. "You can't just leave me here!" I yell, rushing after him. But he's too far ahead of me. With his long legs, he easily makes it out the door before I catch up, and I'm left smacking my hand against the frame in frustration. *Fucking asshole.*

I stand there for several long moments after the sound of the car engine has disappeared, before releasing a long, exhausted sigh and turning around. I don't even have my phone to message the guys and update them. Deciding I may as well snoop while I have some time to kill, I take my time, going from room to room as I look for anything that could tell me more about Dante, or his father, or their corrupt organization. I check every door and window I come across, but all of them are well secured, and I'm finishing up my search of the final bedroom when I hear the telltale sound of the front door being unlocked.

I rush back toward the front of the house, stopping halfway down the stairs when I spot none other than Enzo standing just inside the doorway, staring up at me with a look of surprise.

I scowl down at him. "What the fuck are you doing here?"

His mouth is parted in shock, and it takes him a second before he shakes it off, snorting as he shakes his head. "Of course it's you. I should have fucking known."

Pulling on his tie, loosening it from around his neck, he strides toward the kitchen, and I chase after him down the stairs.

"What is that supposed to mean? What the hell is going on?" I'm getting seriously fucking sick of being left in the dark, and my wig is beginning to itch from wearing it all day. Fetching a bottle of water from the fridge, he moves to sit on one of the white sofas, and after a second, I follow, claiming the seat opposite him. Since our last meeting at the ice cream parlor, I haven't spoken to him, and I can feel all those unresolved issues hanging in the air between us.

The second my ass hits the seat, I'm in heaven. It's so comfy. I practically sink into it. There are no lumps, and I can't feel the box springs like I can on my sofa. I run my hand over the smooth leather material, loving how soft and clean it feels beneath my touch. *Damn. Oh, how the other half lives.*

Feeling Enzo's watchful eyes on me, I straighten my spine and cross my arms, returning his inquisitive gaze with a fiery one of my own. When I cross my legs at the knee, the movement catches his attention, and his gaze dips, taking in my black skinny jeans and boots—my usual attire. Pulling my leather jacket tighter around me, I clear my throat, quirking a brow when his eyes finally lift to meet mine. At least I know how to behave around Enzo, unlike Dante. It's easy for me to switch into Reaper mode, and my voice is perfectly void of emotion when I demand, "What the hell is going on? What am I doing here?" My thoughts regarding Enzo are far too complicated to deal with him in any other way. I don't trust a hair on his admittedly handsome head, but he did show up at the G&T that day, even after he canceled our meeting. Presumably, to check I didn't show up... so there's that. All of it just leaves me feeling fucking confused. I don't have time to sort out any of that right now, though, so the cold facade of the Reaper is what I need.

There's a moment of thoughtful silence before he speaks up. "I don't know. I was just told to come here."

"By Dante?" I clarify.

He nods in confirmation. "Yes."

"You're one of his men?" I ask, recalling what Dante said.

Enzo quirks a brow. "I am."

"Dante's or the Antonellis'?" Because even though I don't know why, I feel like there's a difference.

Another weighted silence follows before he confirms. "Dante's."

Chewing on my bottom lip as I mull over the minimal information I have, I cast my eyes around the room. I don't really understand why Dante would bring me here. Why he was at Belle Donne this morning, or why he saved my life.

"Does he know..."

"No." My gaze snaps back to Enzo's, and I spear him with a steely glare. It doesn't matter if he was going to ask whether Dante knows I'm the girl he nearly killed eight years ago or if he knows I'm the Reaper. I don't want Enzo telling him. "And he's not going to know."

A look I can't place flashes across his face. "Okay." There's far too much humor for my liking in that word, but before I can threaten him to keep silent, he asks, "So what happened today then? You obviously did something to warrant *this*." He waves his hand around the lavish prison I've somehow managed to find myself in.

I pinch my lips as I frown at him. "*I* didn't do anything."

He cocks a brow in disbelief, waiting patiently for me to tell him what happened. Eh, what's the harm? Maybe he can shed some light on who is trying to kill me.

Sighing, I rehash this morning's events. "I got a call to go to Belle Donne this morning. Something about a payroll issue. When I got there, Dante dragged me into a closet." Enzo's eyes widen in surprise, but he doesn't interrupt, even as I fall silent, chewing on my bottom lip in thought before continuing. "It was a setup. We heard some guy on the phone. He... he said he was going to kill me."

Fear wraps me in its grip as I recall the man's scathing words, his acerbic tone. I'm sure there are plenty of times in the last twenty-three years when I've come close to dying, but none that I ever knew about. None that were an obvious trap meant to catch me.

"What?" The sharp quality to Enzo's tone as he leans forward, meeting my gaze with an intense, deadpan stare that shakes me out of my panic, and I shove away those pointless emotions, choosing to focus on the hard lines on his face. He looks seriously fucking pissed right now, but I can't figure out why. Because of something I said? "Who was it?"

"I dunno," I admit, shaking my head. "Dante wouldn't tell me."

The lines around his mouth and eyes only deepen as his gaze drifts toward the floor, his mind noticeably elsewhere.

When it becomes clear he isn't going to share any of his inner thoughts with me, I decide to ask my own questions instead, hoping I'll finally get some answers. "How did Dante know? And why would he intervene? Why does someone in your organization want me dead, Enzo?" I focus on the raging inferno of anger burning inside me, letting it scorch away the last of my fear.

Despite the cold expression I'm giving him, Enzo's features soften. I can still see the rage simmering in his green eyes, but he gives me what I think is meant to be a reassuring smile. "I don't know, Sawyer." The use of my real name on his lips startles me, the way it always does when anyone other than Luc says it. I dunno if I'm just not used to hearing it, but every time my name passes his lips, butterflies take flight in my stomach. However, his next words kill the feeling. "But you will be safe here."

I don't even realize I've been staring at his lips until I have to physically drag my gaze up to meet his eyes. "What?" It takes a second for his words to register. "Enzo, I can't stay here. I have a life, responsibilities, people... I can't just disappear." He's already indicated he knows about Luc, but I'm still reluctant to actually mention him. Besides, I have more than just Luc in my life now. He won't be the only one concerned if I simply disappear.

His pretty, pink lips that I was staring serenely at a second ago flatten. "Yeah, and I'm sure you don't want to lead whoever is after you back to your brother, do you?"

I grit my teeth, refusing to answer him. He damn well knows the answer. "Fine," I huff out. "But I need my phone back. I need to call Luc so he knows I'm okay."

Leaning back, he slides his hand into his pants' pocket, lifting out his phone and holding it out to me. "I can't give you yours back, but you can use mine."

Not exactly what I wanted, but better than nothing. I take the phone from his outstretched hand and type in Oliver's number, thankful that I thought to memorize it. When you work primarily off burner phones, you learn to store any essential numbers in your head. If Oliver has any sense, he'll dispose of his phone after our call. Pressing the dial button, I get to my feet, piercing Enzo with a glacial stare as I move past him, a silent threat to stay here and not eavesdrop. The phone seems to ring for ages before Oliver's soothing voice answers.

"Yeah?" Just hearing that one word makes me feel a million times better. I've no idea how Oliver does that, how he can calm the turmoil inside me with a couple of words or a soothing touch.

"Oliver, it's me."

"Red?" There's a second's silence before he speaks again. "What number are you calling from? Is everything okay?"

"Something's happened."

"Hold on, I'm with Cain. Let me put you on speaker."

I stifle a groan. I'd been hoping just to deal with Oliver alone. He's so much more reasonable than Cain, especially given what I have to tell them.

"What's happened?" Cain barks down the phone.

Keeping my voice low, I quickly rehash this morning's events, ending with where I am now. I can't say anything more, but hopefully, they both see this for the opportunity it is. "I'm fine," I say in a louder voice, ensuring Enzo can hear me. "I just won't be around for a few days."

"Someone's there?" It's not really a question, and Oliver doesn't seem to expect an answer as he continues. "Okay." The way he says it, I can tell he's deep in thought.

There's the sound of someone covering the microphone and the indistinct mumble of voices as the two of them argue. I can't help rolling my eyes while I curse Cain out in my head. I don't have time for his bullheaded nonsense.

Eventually, Oliver's voice comes over the phone. "Are you in danger?"

"No, I don't think so."

Another pensive moment of silence, and I swear I can hear Cain seething in the background. "Alright, we'll look into it on our end. Find out whatever you can while you're there."

"I will," I confirm, already having formed the same plan in my head.

"Red?" Cain's rough growl catches me by surprise.

"Yeah?"

"Stay safe."

Pressure builds behind my eyes—I don't know why I'm suddenly feeling choked with emotion, but something about the way he said those two simple words strikes a chord with me. Cain's not the type of person to offer fake reassurances or platitudes. If he didn't care about me, he wouldn't have spoken up.

Pushing back the tears in my eyes, I choke out, "I gotta go, Luc," once again, ensuring eavesdropping Enzo can hear me. "Take care of yourself, okay?"

"Yeah, Red. He's in good hands," Oliver assures me. "You just look after yourself."

I lick my lips. Hesitating for a second and refusing to give what I'm about to say much thought, I blurt out, "I love you. I'll be home soon," and hang up the phone.

"All good?" Enzo asks, and I can hear him getting to his feet, the squeak of his polished shoes against the floor as he moves toward me.

With fast fingers, I delete the call history, and plastering on a fake smile, I spin around. "Yup."

When he holds his hand out, I reluctantly hand over the phone, and pushing aside the tightness in my chest, I lift my chin, meeting Enzo's gaze with a determined one of my own. "So, what now?"

"Now, we wait for Dante to get home and give us some answers."

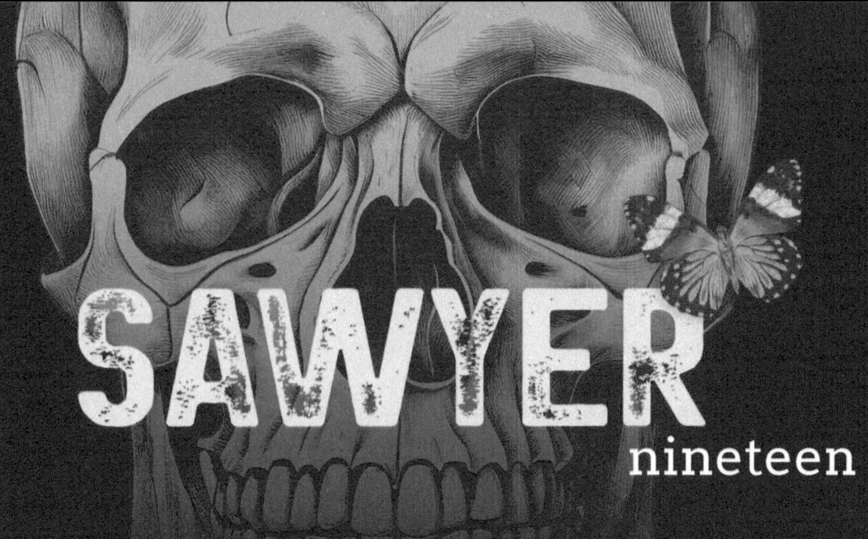

SAWYER

nineteen

"God, can you stop with the damn scratching?!" Enzo snarls, hours later. We've spent most of the afternoon on the sofas, pretending the other doesn't exist. He's been doing whatever it is he's doing on his phone while I've been staring aimlessly at my surroundings, trying to make sense of everything. However, my wig is slowly driving me insane, and I've been scratching at it relentlessly for the last twenty minutes. *Note to self, don't buy cheap, crappy wigs in the future.* "Just take the damn thing off. What does it matter?"

I throw him a scathing glare. "The last time Dante met the *real* me, he threatened to kill me if he ever saw me again."

Enzo just rolls his eyes like I'm being dramatic. "I highly doubt he saved your ass just to kill you himself."

I swallow back my scoff of disagreement. Even still, I mull over what he said. As the itch all over my scalp starts up again, my decision is easily made, and I whip off the wig, grumbling, "He probably won't remember me, anyway."

Enzo snorts, his focus still mostly on his phone. "Sure he won't," he mumbles, making me frown at him in confusion. I mean, Dante must threaten plenty of people on a daily basis, and it was eight *long* years ago. I was a scrawny-ass street kid back then. Not only have I grown up and filled out in all the right places, but I'm a completely different person. Even if Dante does recognize me, I'm no longer that scared, little street kid who had no idea what she was doing. I was forced to grow up. Since then, I've learned exactly what I'm capable of, the things I'll do and the lengths I'll go to, to look after those I love. But more than that, I built myself up to be someone I could be proud of. Someone who doesn't take shit lying down and won't let people walk all over her. Someone who can wield a knife like it's an extension of her arm and slay scumbags like they are nothing but smoke. I may be a stripper, I may appear weak and defenseless, but my name is whispered on the streets of Black Creek with the same mix of fear and reverence as the Rejects, Grim Bastards, and Antonellis. I'm a wolf in sheep's clothing... don't underestimate me, bitch.

"Why haven't *you* told him who I am?" I ask. It's a question that's been bothering me for some time now but is especially pertinent given my current predicament. I tilt my head to the side, scrutinizing Enzo closely as I attempt to put the pieces together for myself. "I'm guessing you started following me after that night in the alley. To make sure I didn't talk?" My brows scrunch together, and I chew on my bottom lip in thought. "But, after like a week, you should have realized I wasn't going to. Why make contact with me? Why *help* me? I don't get it."

I have so many questions, and none of it is adding up.

Sighing, Enzo pockets his phone and meets my troubled stare with an inscrutable expression. So much passes between us at that moment that I can't pinpoint one individual thing, but whatever it is feels significant. Sadness, regret, adoration, and... love?... pass through his eyes. Each sentiment hits me like an emotional whip, making my heart constrict.

He swallows roughly, making his Adam's apple bob, drawing my attention. "You should get rid of the contacts, too. He'll want to see those eyes."

The cryptic nature of his words snaps my focus back to his face, and my brows scrunch together in confusion. What the fuck does any of that mean? And why are these assholes so hellbent on avoiding my questions?

I'm still trying to figure out the meaning behind what he just said when he gets to his feet and strides out of the room. For a second, I debate following him, but why bother? I'll only get more non-answers. Instead, I shake off the lingering effects of our moment and head toward the downstairs bathroom.

Flicking on the light, I stand and stare at myself in the mirror. It's jarring, to see the brown contacts with my red hair, which glows vibrantly under the bright bathroom lighting. Sighing, I remove the contacts and dispose of them before touching up my makeup. *Thank god, I didn't drop my handbag in today's fiasco.* With my armor back in place and my dazzling-blue eyes on display, I feel more like myself.

It's dark out, and I've officially had enough of sitting around this house with nothing to do, by the time the sound of the front door is heard over the noise of Enzo working away in the kitchen, cooking something for dinner.

It's been a challenge trying to stop my eyes from drifting in his direction as he's moved about the kitchen, and I frequently find myself watching him as he chops vegetables and stirs pots. It would almost be a turn-on—what girl doesn't love a man who can cook?!—except that this is Enzo, and he's a lying bastard whom I can't trust.

The click of the front door snaps my attention away from the sight of Enzo's forearm as it flexes and tenses while he stirs a pot—*Dammit, I was leering. Again*—and a few seconds later, Dante enters. His eyes scan the room, searching me out until he spots me sitting on a barstool at the breakfast bar. I tense under his scrutiny, wondering what he's thinking as he takes in my newly revealed red hair and blue eyes. I'm a far cry from the woman he saved this morning... the woman he's spent the last few weeks watching at the club. I'm not entirely sure how he felt about the club version of me, but there was undoubtedly some amount of fascination there that not only prevented him from killing me—if he so desired—but had him defending me. But what will his reaction be to the real me?

His expression gives nothing away, and I can't tell if he's angry by my deception or if he even recognizes me at all. He stands there for so long that I begin to squirm underneath his intense gaze, and my fingers grip the edge of the barstool. When he stalks toward me, his giant strides quickly eat up the distance between us. I can't do anything but watch with bated breath as he draws closer. His hand grasps my chin aggressively, forcing my head back as his fingers dig into my cheeks. It's not enough to hurt, but enough that I have no choice but to sit there and let him look his fill as he stares into my blue eyes. I meet his gaze unflinching, searching the murky depths for *something* that could give me any insight into this domineering man before me. Everything about him is cold, hard, unrelenting. The absence of emotion in his eyes is enough to stall the breath in my lungs, and I can only imagine that what I see in his reflection is the same as if I were looking into the eyes of a psychopath. That same blank, empty slate. And yet, I don't recoil. *God, I must be more damaged than I ever realized.*

"Dante." Enzo's voice is a quiet command, but Dante doesn't release me immediately. Slowly, his gaze shifts over to Enzo, holding it for a moment before letting go of me, his hand dropping to his side. He continues to hold Enzo's gaze, some sort of silent conversation passing between them before he moves over to the drinks cart and pours himself a glass of whiskey.

With him no longer taking up all the oxygen in my personal space, I suck in a deep breath, sagging a little in my chair from the intensity of whatever that was. When I lift my head, I find Enzo watching me closely, but he turns back to the stove before I can read his expression.

Clearing my throat, I ignore the heavy weight in the air that has built since Dante's return and push back my shoulders, intent on finally getting some answers out of him. Before I can so much as say a word, Enzo beats me to it. "Dinner's ready." He begins plating up the food, carrying it over to the dining table. Dante follows him over, setting his triple measure of scotch down as he claims the seat beside Enzo. *Oh, great, I get to sit and eat with the two of them looking at me.*

Grimacing, I slide out of my seat and move to sit opposite them, the three of us eating in silence for a long moment. It's surreal. I repeatedly peer up at them both through my eyelashes, not sure what to make of all of this. The whole scene is just... weird. They're painting this odd picture of domestic bliss, but I highly doubt these two made men sit and have dinner together regularly. Nevertheless, I do notice how familiar they are with one another. How comfortable they appear in one another's presence. Dante had told me one of his men was coming over, but from what I'm picking up on, Enzo isn't just one of his soldiers. They are far too relaxed—if one could ever call Dante relaxed—around each other for a boss-subordinate relationship, and the authority in Enzo's tone when he spoke Dante's name earlier... they must have some sort of kinship.

"Is there any reason why one of my father's men would want you dead?" Dante asks once he's finished eating. He's leaning back in his seat, scrutinizing me.

My gaze flicks briefly to Enzo before I meet his unrelenting stare. "Not that I can think of." *Other than, you know, the fact I'm working on trying to destroy you all.* I'm not about to divulge any of that to either of them, but it's the only reason I can think of for today's planned attack. Except, how did anyone find out what I'm up to? Does that mean they know who I am? If they do, they obviously haven't managed to link me to the Rejects. Everything sounded like business as usual on Oliver's end.

"Has anything else happened at the club?"

My brows furrow as I think, but there hasn't been anything other than my run-in with Sam, which Dante was there for. Any other men who tried their luck when I first started, quickly stopped when Dante's presence became a regular occurrence. Everyone saw what Chrissy had—Dante's obsession with me.

Before I can respond, Enzo interjects, his gaze jumping between Dante and me. "What do you mean *anything else?*"

For some reason, his question seems to pique Dante's interest, and he removes his heavy gaze from me, looking at Enzo as if he can't understand why he's spoken.

I pipe up, not having any idea what's going on and not wanting the conversation to get sidetracked. "It's nothing. And no, nothing has happened. People barely speak to me. They know I'm the reason you're always there."

Dante gives a small nod. "I suspected as much."

When it doesn't look like he's going to divulge anything further, I start asking my own questions, needing to know why *he* thinks someone in his organization is after me. After all, he must be asking these probing questions with a theory in mind. "Why are you asking? Who was that man today? Why does one of your father's men want me dead?"

An indecipherable emotion flashes behind his eyes, but it's gone instantly. He watches me for a long moment as if he's trying to figure out how to tell me whatever is going on. It makes me nervous—not only having his penetrating gaze on me for so long but wondering what conclusion he's come to.

"You think someone told your father about her." It's Enzo who speaks up, the harsh tone of his voice catching me by surprise as I break off my stare with Dante to glance at him.

"Why would your dad give a shit about me?" I question, returning my focus to Dante.

"He wouldn't... unless he thought you were a complication *for me.*"

My brows scrunch together as I look at him, confused. "Why would I be a complication for you? I don't even know you."

"It doesn't matter." I open my mouth to argue that it absolutely fucking does matter, but he cuts across me. "What matters is that we remove the target from your back."

Fine. That's an easy solution... I just have to kill his father. I know Cain wanted his death for himself, but I'm sure he will understand given the current situation. Even as I mentally try to construct my own plan of action, I ask, "And how do you plan on doing that?"

He gives a casual shrug, and a glint enters his eye that has me forgetting about the various brutal ways I'm going to kill Giovanni and focusing on the dark force of the man in front of me. As he continues to look at me, that glint shining in his eyes, I deliberately sit more upright in my chair, straightening my spine. *Why the fuck is he looking at me like that?*

"I'm going to marry you."

Eh, he's going to what now?!

"What?!" Enzo exclaims while I snort, "Hell no, you're not!"

"You can't be serious!" Enzo continues, staring at Dante with a mixture of shock and anger.

Dante ignores his outburst—and mine—as he holds me captive in his red-hot gaze. His expression is as unreadable as ever, but hidden in his eyes, there's... something—the flicker of a flame. The longer I peer into them, that flame seems to grow, scorching across his irises until it's a raging blaze, its heat searing my skin. Yet a bone-deep chill wracks my body, a fear like nothing I've ever felt before wrapping its cold talons around my soul. It's not the heat of passion I see in his eyes but the stone-cold decree of possession.

I balk against that notion, jumping to my feet and glowering down at him with my Reaper mask fully intact. "There is absolutely no fucking way I will allow that to happen."

"Neither will I."

It's the unmistakable thread of warning in Enzo's tone that garners Dante's attention, and he finally releases me from his gaze as he turns to face him, another confused frown marring his features. It appears as though they are having another silent conversation, one that doesn't seem to be going too well based on the way both of their shoulders bunch, and Dante's hand forms a fist on the table.

Dante's face is shrouded in darkness, making him look formidable. It's terrifying, and I have to fight against the urge to shrink away from it. He's not even looking at me, for Christ's sake. In a sudden burst of movement that makes me jump, he pushes to his feet, the legs of his chair scraping against the wooden floor. Enzo follows him a second later, the two of them facing off in some sort of silent battle that I'm not privy to.

I haven't got a fucking clue what is going on, so when Enzo, without taking his eyes off Dante, barks, "Sawyer. The last room on the right, up the stairs. It's yours. Go." I don't argue with him the way I usually would. Although, I do hesitate, unsure whether I should intervene or not. "Now!" The word is an angry snarl, and I decide they can both go fuck themselves.

Whatever their problem is, it has nothing to do with me. It will be a much better use of my time to let these two idiots kill each other while I work out how to get rid of Giovanni. Without another word, I turn on my heel and head upstairs to seek out my room and get stuck into my plans of bloodshed and revenge.

Shutting the bedroom door behind me, I sag against it and let out a long, exhausted exhale. I look around the room, taking it in. Even though I searched through the room earlier, I didn't really *look* at it, so I take the time now to actually see the white-washed walls, the white bedspread, and the matching dressing table. It's all so bright and clean. I'm almost scared to sit on the bed in case I dirty it up.

Instead of worrying about it, I close my eyes and tilt my head back to rest against the door. Weariness tugs at me, but my brain is far too wired to let me sleep. Now that I'm alone, everything from today races across my mind. Murder attempts. Marriage proposals. Confessions of love. Talk about an insane twenty-four hours. I don't even know where to begin with trying to process any of it. I can't begin to wrap my head around what Dante is thinking. Marriage? Is he out of his fucking mind? How is that going to solve anything?

I groan and crack an eye open, eyeing the window temptingly. It would be so much easier to leave. Go back to the Rejects and keep a low profile until Dante, Enzo, and the Antonellis forget I exist. Except I tried that tactic with the Rejects, and it was an epic failure. Not to mention I just blurted out that I loved Cain and Oliver and hung up the damn phone like a total pussy. There's the chance they'll think I just said it as part of the cover that I was talking to my brother, but was I? If I'm being brutally honest with myself—and why the fuck not at this point—then no. I can't pinpoint when it happened or how exactly it happened, but it did somewhere over the last few months.

Oliver's easy to understand. I knew he'd irreparably change me that night in the bar. It's why I didn't hang around to chat or get his number. But Cain? Well, he's much harder to wrap my head around. I want to claw his eyes out more often than not, and yet all that hostility between us leads to fucking amazing sex. And even though I've barely scratched the surface of who he is, I know there's more to him than the air of arrogance he stomps around with. The fact that he's so hellbent on carrying out this vendetta for his sister, after all this time, says everything about who he is as a person. There's a surprisingly soft core underneath that hard exterior of his, and the more I get a glimpse of it, the more I want to know. They might be two very different people, but they both get me in ways no one else ever has. And we all have a lot more in common than appears at first glance.

Not that any of it matters when I'm stuck here with a psycho claiming he's going to marry me. *Jesus, what is my life?* Although, ultimately, isn't this exactly where I want to be? It's not necessarily how I thought this job would play out, but I wanted valuable intel and where better to get said information than from the boss's son.

Sighing, I tear my eyes away from the window, and kicking off my boots, I cross the room to the bathroom. I can't leave. I can't throw away this opportunity that has been unexpectedly thrown in my lap. So, instead, I decide to rest up and get ready to face Dante and Enzo again in the morning.

I listen to Red's—*fuck, Sawyer's*—fading footsteps, never breaking eye contact with Lor's furious gaze. I've never seen him so riled up before, but considering I'm pretty fucking sure he's the one that's been lying and keeping secrets from *me*, I'm the one who should be fucking pissed—not him!

Their easy familiarity with one another when I walked in was my first clue. The warning in his tone when he snapped my name was my second. Sawyer's repeated glances his way before she would answer my questions was my third, and the fact that he knows her motherfucking name is the nail in the coffin. They *know* each other. Worse, he's fucking protective of her... but how?

"You better start explaining," I snarl furiously, the second I hear Sawyer racing up the stairs. Lor and I are standing inches apart, both of us poised, ready to fight as we glower at each other.

"Me?" He scoffs. "You're the one that better explain why the hell you think marrying her will solve anything."

In a flash of movement, I wrap my hand around his tie and shove him backward, not stopping until he collides with the glass wall. "She's *mine*." My voice is nothing more than a possessive growl that makes a line furrow between his brows. But *damn*, does it sound good to say that out loud; to finally claim her as mine instead of standing and watching her from a distance. My inability to stay away from her makes so much more sense now that I know who she really is. She's the woman who's been haunting my dreams for years. The only person, other than Lor, who has ever broken through the ice-cold shell surrounding me and made me *feel* something.

I've spent the last eight years trying to forget about her, but fate dropped her into my lap when she showed up at Belle Donne the same night I did. I've spent the last few weeks trying to put my finger on it; trying to work out what it is about her that enthralls me. Although I think, on some level, I've always known who she was—the scrawny street rat who speared me with her defiant gaze and put a crack in the steel cage encasing my heart. Except, she's no longer that scrawny street rat. Now she's a flaming, red-headed vixen who spits fire and hisses snarky retorts that make my balls tighten and my primal instincts take control.

Lor's pinched expression and the fury burning in his eyes give away how much he wants to contradict me, but he wisely keeps his mouth shut. My fist tightens in his shirt and I tug him away from the wall, only to slam him back against it. "You disobeyed me!"

It's obvious. The only thing that makes sense; the only way he can possibly know who she is. He was supposed to follow her and make sure she didn't talk to anyone about what she saw that night in the alley. That's it. After that, he was supposed to leave her alone.

Some of his anger peters out, the corner of his eyes softening a little. "I didn't intend to. She just..." He trails off, lost for words.

I grit my teeth, my own anger still riding me high. She's mine, but he's acting like he has some sort of emotional investment in her. I push him harder against the glass wall, unsure on how to process everything I've learned. I can't even put a name to the roiling storm of emotions cascading through me right now, threatening to crash over my head and drown me.

Unable to handle the tumultuous feeling, I start to shove all of it into a box. I'm so used to the empty void that when I feel a spark of anything ignite in my chest, it gives me this high, making me feel alive. But what I'm feeling now is too much. It's all-consuming; suffocating.

Lor's hand comes up to cup my face, and my eyes snap open, unable to remember closing them. My gaze zeros in on his lips. They are no longer flattened in anger, and doing the only thing that I know grounds me when I'm feeling adrift, I slam my lips on his, losing myself in the taste of Lor.

He's unrelenting beneath my touch, but with a growl and bite of his lower lip, he caves, parting to let me in. It's a bruising kiss, and with every stroke of his tongue against mine, I can taste how angry he still is. Yet he bends beneath me, allowing me to take charge as if he can sense how much I need the control. Lorenzo has always been good at that, at knowing what I need.

Sliding my hand down the front of his shirt, I rip it open, sending buttons flying as he yanks on his already loosened tie, undoing it just enough to pull it over his head. His hands wrap around my belt, flicking it open with deft fingers as I hastily remove my own shirt and tie.

Before my pants can fall to the ground, I dig out a packet of lube, holding it between my teeth and tearing it open as Lor shrugs out of his pants and boxers. His fingers wrap around his painfully hard erection, but I swat his hand away, growling, "No touching."

His lip curls up in a snarl, his eyes ablaze with desire, but he doesn't reach for himself again. I grab a hold of his shoulder, spinning him to face the glass wall. He gets his arms up just in time, bracing himself with his forearms against the glass as I crowd him from behind.

It's dark out, and with the lights on in the kitchen, anyone who is out for a late-night stroll on the beach can most definitely see us, but who gives a fuck. All I can think about is my desperate need to lose myself. I fist my dick as I swipe the cold lube through his ass cheeks, circling his puckered hole before pushing a finger inside.

Groaning, he pushes back against me, eager for more, and after a few pumps, I insert another finger. My hand slides up and down my cock in rhythm with the way I'm fingering him until we're both panting, our breaths steaming up the window.

"Dante," he growls. His hands are clenched into tight fists against the window, and the tense set of his biceps gives away the strain of holding back from touching himself.

Using the last of the lube to coat my throbbing cock, I push into him, grunting with effort as, inch by inch, I seat myself fully. Once he's had sufficient time to adjust, I pull all the way out before slamming in, setting a fast rhythm that soon has the chaotic mess of emotions within me waning and a tingle starting at the bottom of my spine. Knowing I'm close, I reach around and fist Lor, enjoying his hiss of pleasure as I pump him in time to my frantic thrusts, and it's not long until we're both coming.

Resting my forehead on his shoulder, I catch my breath, enjoying this moment of contentment that I so rarely get to soak in. After a moment, he clears his throat, speaking up. "I know she's important to you, but she means something to me, too. I'm not giving her up."

He's still pressed against the window, but I lift my head, meeting his gaze in the reflection provided by the glass. I can see the determination in his eyes. This isn't something he's going to back down on... but now that I've decided she's mine, I'm unsure if I can share her with *anyone*, even Lor.

I don't say anything as I pull away and begin redressing, but Lor stops me with his hand on my arm. "Talk to me. What am I missing?"

"I overheard my father in his office, the day he showed me the photos of us." I'd told Lor about my meeting at the time, but I'd conveniently left out the bit about Sawyer. He didn't need to know then. Obviously, he'd have found out about her eventually, but I'd planned to make her unequivocally mine first. "He mentioned killing a club whore."

"And you thought it might be her?"

Shrugging, I buckle my pants, forgoing a shirt as I move to wash my hands before pouring two tumblers of whiskey. "Yeah. Sam had been harassing her at the club the week before."

"On your father's orders?"

When I turn to face him, he's dressed similarly in just his suit pants, our shirts and ties lying abandoned on the floor. My eyes run over his torso, noting his chiseled abs and firm pecs. His large biceps flex, giving away his irritation over our conversation and spiking a fresh flame of anger. It's smaller than it was before, easily blown out. I'm going to need him to keep her safe from my father. "I think so. Or he at least reported back my confrontation with him."

Sighing, Lor runs his hand through his blond hair, pushing the strands that had fallen forward out of his face. Holding out the whiskey glass, he takes it from me, and we move to the living area, getting comfy.

"He wouldn't give a shit if I was just fucking a club whore, but to cause a scene with an Antonelli—and one of his underlings no less? It would seem that didn't sit well with him."

"So he thought killing her was the answer."

"Isn't it always when it comes to my father?"

Lor purses his lips while he stares into his glass. "He'll know by now that it was a failure and that she's in the wind."

"Which is why I'm marrying her."

I'm not sure if it's my words or the non-negotiable tone in which they are said, but Lor spears me with a penetrating glower.

"There's no way your father will agree to that. Nor will I, for that matter."

"Well, we are going to see him tomorrow, so I guess we'll find out then."

I SPENT THE REST OF THE NIGHT ARGUING WITH LOR ABOUT SAWYER, tomorrow, and my plans for her, until I just had to get away from him. Nothing he says or does will change my mind. He should know that. When I finally did get to bed, all I could think about was the vixen down the hall who would soon be all mine. Just the way I wanted. It won't be long until I have her tied to my bed, screaming my name every night for the rest of eternity.

It's late—or early, depending on how you look at it—when I give up on sleep. Wearing only my boxers, I pad down the hall in my bare feet. Silently, I push open the door to Sawyer's room and enter. Ensuring I don't make a sound, I walk over to an armchair in the corner of the room and lower myself into it. It has been deliberately positioned to face the bed, and I sit, cataloging every minute detail of her face that I can make out in the darkness. Her red hair is spread out on the pillow around her, and I recall the way it shone under the kitchen lights. The shock that shook my body and obliterated my train of thought when I walked into that kitchen and saw her sitting there—with her copper hair and striking blue eyes. It took longer than it should to put the pieces together and realize she and Red were the same person, and it only solidified my belief that this woman was made to be mine.

The fact that she felt she had to hide beneath her wig and contacts does raise a few questions. Was it just a case of wanting to keep her work and personal life separate? Did she remember me from eight years ago and worry I'd follow through on my promise if she were caught in one of our clubs? I'm not sure, and it doesn't matter now that she has revealed her true self.

As I stare at her, my mind goes back over today's events. While I am the primary executioner for our family, there are a small number of men who work for me. Who do the jobs I don't want to. Unbeknownst to my father, these men are loyal to *me*. I've worked day in and day out with them for nearly ten years now. After I overheard my father in his office, I put a tail on Santos, knowing he'd be the one to kill her. My father wouldn't outsource it to one of my men and risk word getting back to me.

When I got intel that he had gone to the Belle Donne early this morning, I knew today was the day. He never frequents Belle Donne. Like most of my father's closest confidants and advisors, he prefers our exclusive club—Paradiso é Inferno—where consent isn't an option and nothing is off the table. So, I hauled ass over there just in time, sneaking inside seconds before Sawyer showed up. Just the thought of what could have happened if I'd been any later has my chest constricting in an unusual way that makes it difficult to breathe. I focus back on the sleeping beauty in front of me, watching as her eyelids flutter and her lips part, as though she's dreaming.

It's become an addiction—watching her. One I'm in no hurry to overcome, and since I plan on making her mine for the rest of time, I don't see that I need to. Her reluctance was something I expected, but it won't stop me from going through with my plans. She might not understand my reasoning right now, but one day she will. I meant it when I said she was mine, and I don't just mean it in a possessive way. I mean that she's mine to protect, mine to take care of, mine to... I'd say love, but I'm not capable of that. She's just mine, in every way that I can offer. I've spent the last eight years trying to forget about her, trying to unsee her cerulean blue eyes, except the second she ran into me in the club, everything changed—I just hadn't known it then. These last few weeks, I've found myself more and more frequently seeking her out. Running to her when I needed grounding, when I felt myself slipping. Lor is the only one who has been able to tether me to reality before; the only one who has been able to stop me from completely losing myself and ending up like my father. But Sawyer does that for me, too, without even realizing it. It's the reason I decided I couldn't let her go. The reason why, when I overheard my father discussing her assassination, I intervened. The twinge of pain in my chest when I heard that conversation was enough to have me gasping, which was all the confirmation I needed that not only could I not let this woman die, but I had to ensure she was in my life—permanently. Nothing says that better than an Antonelli marriage, where *'til death do us part* is taken very fucking literally.

Besides, it's my fault that she ended up in my father's line of sight. My frequent presence at the club must have raised more questions than I anticipated, and evidently, my father caught wind of it—of her. I'm my father's not-so-secret weapon, and as such, there's no way he would allow some girl—never mind a club girl—to stand in his way. But if I marry her, he will have no choice but to leave her alone. Anyway, he was the one that said it was time I was married.

His desire for me to wed might genuinely work in my favor. The vow to become an Antonelli man, and the vow of marriage, are the only two things that have any significance in this organization. The only things my father won't just trudge all over to get his way. It's the only way I can think of to keep her safe, and if it tethers her to me permanently, well, then I'm sure as fuck not going to complain. She'll get used to the idea, she just needs some time to come around.

As for Lor, well, he's a whole other problem. The steadfast look in his eye earlier, when he said he wasn't giving her up means he isn't going to change his mind. I tilt my head to the side, watching the rhythmic rising and falling of Sawyer's chest as she sleeps peacefully. It's interesting that this little firecracker has gotten to both of us.

Lor is my closest confidant. The only person in this whole world I trust. Over the years, our *relationship* has evolved. We've never put a label on it. He knows what I am, that I'm not capable of real emotions, so it's never needed to be defined. We both know what this is between us. But Sawyer could put a wrench in all of that if I'm not careful. I can't afford to lose Lor—as either a soldier or a friend—but I'm also unwilling to give *her* up. I will have to navigate these new waters carefully and keep a close eye on both of them.

The sheets rustle as Sawyer shifts in her sleep, drawing my thoughts back to the room as I watch her. She looks so different in her sleep... peaceful. She walks around all day with a permanent frown and wary eyes, but all that falls away when she's sleeping, making her appear younger, more youthful and carefree. I wonder what her life has been like since I ran into her in that alley. She's obviously no longer on the street, but she does work in strip clubs... something that will have to stop. I can't have my wife dancing mostly naked on a stage where any dickhead can drool all over her. That would rack up a hefty body count pretty quickly, and I've enough on my plate, never mind snapping the neck of every guy that looks in her direction.

My hand tightens around the arm of the chair as I realize Lor probably knows everything about her. He probably knows all about what she's been through in the last eight years... where she's worked, where she lives, what she does in her free time. The only thing that settles me a bit is the fact that she glowers at him the same way she does at me, so despite their familiarity, she clearly doesn't look at him in a favorable light. That's a small win, I guess.

I sense it, the second she wakes. Her body tenses, the first indicator that she's no longer asleep, and when I look at her face again, those lazuli-blue eyes latch on mine, holding me hostage in their endless depths. I don't move, instead choosing to return her curious stare, and eventually, her eyes drift shut again.

Only when the dusty pink of dawn begins to lighten outside the window, do I finally find the strength to leave her, returning to my own room, alone, but not for much longer.

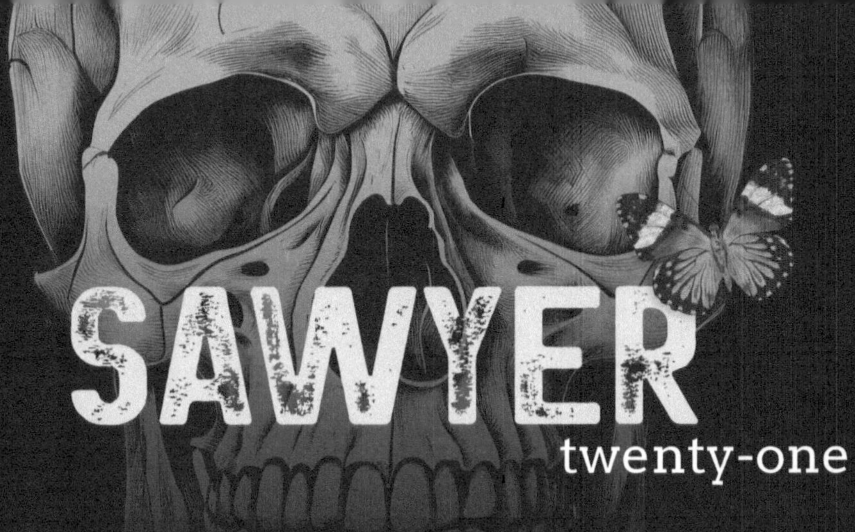

SAWYER

twenty-one

Shaking off the weird dream I had last night, where I thought Dante was in my room, watching me like a fucking stalker, I stretch before climbing out of bed with a renewed purpose. I can't stay here much longer. I need to get home to check on Luc, and I'm sure Oliver and Cain are beginning to worry, despite my assurances to Oliver yesterday that I was fine.

Before I can do that, though, I need to ensure I'm not going to bring this asshole intent on killing me back to my brother or the Rejects. The only way I can guarantee that is to kill Giovanni. From what Dante said, that's who orchestrated the hit—because his son has been spotted staring at me at the club? *Jeez, someone needs to get a fucking life.* How the hell is that *my* fault?

Grabbing my pile of rumpled clothes from the floor, I move toward the bathroom, but I pull up short when I find the nicest—and probably most expensive—dress I've ever seen hanging over the bathroom door. I have to admit it's gorgeous, and on instinct, I lift my hand, running it over the smooth-as-silk fabric, but I have no idea what it is doing in my room. Or how it got here. It definitely wasn't hanging over the door when I came to bed last night. As a thought crosses my mind, I spin to look at the armchair, tilting my head to one side. Was it more than just a dream? A strangled laugh bubbles up the back of my throat. No way, that would be insane, even for Dante. It's one thing to watch me up on stage or in the club, but to sneak into my room in the middle of the night and watch me sleep? That's just fucking creepy.

Returning my focus to the dress, I find a note attached to the long sleeve and pluck it off. *Put this on when you get up.* There's no name attached, and honestly, either of the bossy assholes down the hall could have left it for me, but I get the impression it was Dante. He seems the type to get off on choosing outfits for me. I chew on my bottom lip as I decide what to do, my gaze roaming over the outfit. There's barely anything to it. It's a black dress that looks like it would fall to mid-thigh, with a daring zip up one side that guarantees only a thong would get by unno-ticed. It's got form fitting long sleeves that join into a deep V that undoubtedly shows off the girls and guarantees a bra cannot be worn with the outfit. The dress is finished off with a couple of buttons on the front, giving it the appearance of an oversized jacket, and a chunky black belt with two thin chains completes the ensemble.

Glancing down at the floor, there's a pair of Louboutin pumps, identifiable by their iconic red soles. Noticing something tucked in one of the heels, I bend down to lift it out, snorting a laugh at the tiny scrap of fabric—a thong. *Well, at least he thought of everything.*

My traitorous heart skips an excited beat at the thought of dressing up exactly how Dante wants me to. I wonder if that would get a reaction out of him. So little seems to, and a dark little part of myself gets off of eliciting a response from him, however small. Yet, the independent woman in me doesn't want to bend to his demands. He could at least have asked and explained why I needed to dress up. Groaning, I swipe my hand over my face. *It's too early for this shit.*

Ignoring the dress, for now, I step into the bathroom to shower, and twenty minutes later, I'm standing in the bedroom as I once again stare at the outfit, contemplating what to do. Darting my gaze to my rumpled clothes from yesterday, I'm not really in any hurry to put them back on. Besides, when is the next time I'll get to try on a dress that probably costs more than my rent?

Decision made, I slip into the soft material and slide my feet into the heels. Moving to the mirror, I fix my hair and makeup before taking a step back to see the outfit in its entirety. The dress hugs my curves perfectly, and the heels make my legs look like they're miles long. Combined with the dark make-up and red lipstick, I look formidable. All I'm missing is a thigh strap with one of my thin blades in it and a clutch with my Glock, and I'd look like how I always imagined I would if I showed the world the real Reaper.

Confidence flows with every step as I leave the room and make my way downstairs. My heels clack against the wooden floor as I go, announcing my presence. So when I step into the kitchen where both Enzo and Dante are sitting, looking stoic as ever, as though they weren't about to rip each other's heads off when I left them last night, they are already looking in my direction.

I meet Dante's gaze first, and the look in his eyes hits me like a strong gust of wind, stirring up a tornado of confusing feelings and knocking the breath from my lungs. The lust burning in his eyes is unmistakable, and has the thin scrap of material covering my pussy dampening. *Well, that took no time at all.*

Swallowing roughly, I tear my gaze away from him to look at Enzo, ignoring the possessive growl that works its way up the back of Dante's throat at the loss of my attention. The look on Enzo's face is just as intense, but unlike Dante, I don't have to stare into his eyes and push aside his barriers to see it. It's all there on his face for me to readily read. That, more than anything, takes me by surprise. He's never dropped his walls so thoroughly; never allowed me to gain this level of insight into how he's feeling. Things are changing rapidly between us, and I'm not sure how I feel about that.

The room grows hot, my cheeks warming with the heat. *What does a woman have to do to get a fan around here? Or a spare set of panties?* Needing something to focus on, other than the two imperious men sucking all the oxygen out of the room, I move to the sink, pouring myself a glass of water and downing half of it in one gulp, thankful for it's instant cooling effect.

"As grateful as I am for the change of clothes, why am I dressed up like a mafia whore?"

I'm a little relieved to find Dante's barriers fully erected when I meet his eyes. The intensity in those eyes is just *a lot* when you aren't used to it. I did say I wanted to get a reaction from him—mission accomplished. It just wasn't quite the reaction I'd been expecting.

"Because we're going to see my father."

My ears perk up at that, and my eyebrows lift in surprise. That actually works perfectly for my *kill Giovanni* plans, but... "Why?" I ask suspiciously.

The gleam in Dante's eye is the same as the one he had last night, and I'm gritting my teeth before he's even spoken.

"So we can tell him the good news." He digs into his pocket, tossing me a small, black velvet box. A nauseous feeling settles in my stomach as I crack open the lid, slowly revealing the sickening sight in front of me.

"What the fuck is this?" I croak, scowling at the gleaming, giant rock with disgust. It's... *fuck*, I don't even know what it is. Massive. Hideous. Obscene. There's no way I can wear this. This is intended for some housewife who isn't going to accidentally knock it against stuff—or use it to put a nice little dent in the side of some asshole's head. It sure as fuck isn't meant to be worn by someone like me.

Likely seeing the look of horror and revulsion on my face, Enzo snorts, the soft sound catching my attention as I glance up at him, stunned. Switching my attention to Dante, he doesn't look pleased. A look that only darkens when I blurt out, "I'm not wearing this."

He storms across the room toward me, snatching the ring box out of my hand and looking at it with a confused frown. "What's wrong with it?"

I wave my hand in the general direction of the box. "It's... It's..." Words fail me as I continue to gesticulate with my hand. "I mean, look at it. It's meant for someone who lives in a lavish mansion and never has to lift a finger."

"She probably can't lift her finger with that thing on it," Enzo chuckles, earning a dark glare from Dante as I stifle my own laugh. "What, man? I told you she wouldn't wear it."

That comment only seems to infuriate Dante. Not that he lets it show, but the sudden snapping upright of his spine and the pushing back of his shoulders, combined with the sense of danger that oozes out of him, has the hairs on the back of my neck standing on end. At this moment, it's undeniable just how lethal of a weapon Dante truly is. Any casual observer wouldn't blink twice. They'd see his impassive expression and just think he was closed off, but unlike most men who, when they get angry, it's all hot and aggressive, Dante's fury is cold and terrifying. Without another word, he snaps the lid of the box closed and turns on his heel, striding out of the room.

In the wake of his departure, I cock a brow at Enzo, the lightheartedness from a moment ago snuffed out. He just shrugs a shoulder. "He'll be fine. Let him cool off."

"What do you think of all this?" I ask, referring to Dante's continued insistence to get married. I have no intention of going through with it, but I am curious to get Enzo's opinion on the matter.

He takes his time answering as he moves around the counter until he's standing beside me. His close proximity has me tilting my head back so I can look up at his face.

"I think I never wanted you involved in any of this." His words are cryptic, and I don't understand what he's implying. That he didn't want me involved with Dante or caught up with the Antonellis? There's a sadness in his eyes that I've never seen before, and he reaches out to run a finger along a strand of my hair, toying with it in a distracted, absentminded way. "You look amazing." His fingers move to trail along my collarbone, and the light touch makes me shiver. "But this isn't where you belong. In this world, women are nothing more than arm candy, a decorative accessory. That's not you. You were made to challenge men and fight alongside us, to rain down hellfire and set the world to rights." Lifting his hand, he gently cups my chin as his gaze, which had drifted to follow the path of his fingers, returns to mine. "You aren't meant to be caged, which is exactly what this world will do to you... But it's too late for you to escape. Dante will never let you go, and honestly, I'm not sure that I can either."

His fingers tighten over my jaw as he dips his head. The unexpected, light brush of his lips over mine makes me gasp, and a tingling starts up along the seam of my lips. He doesn't push further, instead standing to his full height and giving me a final, longing glance before following after Dante.

———

WITHOUT ALL THE TESTOSTERONE IN THE ROOM, I WAS ABLE TO GET A coffee and half an hour of peace before the two of them returned, and we left to go see Giovanni. I didn't put up much of a fight, just enough not to draw suspicion. As fucked up as this whole situation is, it's the opportunity we have been looking for—our chance to get close to Giovanni and his top officers. Unfortunately, it won't be as simple as slitting his throat today, but playing the part of Dante's fiancée would enable me to gain intel which I can then feed back to the Rejects, and they can make a plan of attack.

"Where are we going?" I ask as I stare out the window, watching as the countryside slowly gives way to the city outskirts, becoming more and more built up with every passing minute as we get closer to the heart of Antonelli territory.

"My father's apartment in the city."

I tear my gaze away from the window to look at Dante, who is sitting in the back seat beside me. "Your father lives in the city?" Cain and Oliver have been trying to find out where Giovanni and his men live. He always travels with decoy cars, and we've found it impossible to track him home so far. It had gotten to the point where we assumed he and his men resided outside the city. It seems crazy that he's been right under our noses the whole time.

"Not according to anyone outside of the three of us and his closest advisors." There's a thread of warning in Dante's tone, letting me know I'm not to go sharing that information with anyone, and it takes me by surprise that he's even confiding in me. He could easily have blindfolded me, and I'm not sure what it means that he trusts me. The niggle of guilt that I'm going to betray that trust, especially when I'm certain he doesn't offer it to many people, sits uncomfortably in my stomach as we head further into the city until Enzo stops the car outside a modern-looking skyscraper. Unlike the rest of Black Creek, the Antonellis' territory is clean and well maintained. The building in front of me shimmers in the sunlight, making me feel like I'm a million miles away from home. I guess, in a way, I am.

Dante doesn't immediately move to get out. Turning slightly toward me, he again holds out the stupid, black velvet ring box. "You have to put it on. Appearances matter to my father, and we can't give him any reason to doubt us."

Instead of taking the box from him, I flick my eyes up to his face, searching his gaze for a second before asking, "Why are you doing all of this for me?"

In typical Dante fashion, he doesn't answer me, but the way he looks at me almost feels like an answer in itself. His dark brown depths seem lighter, softer, and with a gentle touch, he reaches out to clasp my hand in his, plucking the ring from the box and sliding it on my ring finger. It weighs a ton and sparkles in the light. It's large and gaudy. Not something I'd ever choose for myself, but with my hand in Dante's, sitting beside him, I can see why he picked it. It suits him; it fits in with his lifestyle, which I guess is what we're aiming for.

He gives my hand a reassuring squeeze before letting go. With a nod in Enzo's direction, Enzo gets out of the car, opening Dante's door for him. It seems like a weird move, given how familiar and easygoing they were with one another yesterday and this morning. Once he's out of the car, Dante moves to open my door and offers me his hand as I slide across the back seat. Placing my hand in his, I climb out, craning my head back as I take in the skyscraper.

Dante's warm palm on my lower back gets me moving as we walk toward the front door, Enzo trailing behind us. I turn my head to glance back at him, but Dante stops me. "Don't," he orders in a low whisper. "When we're here, Lor is my bodyguard. It will be better if you just ignore his presence." I carefully mask the anger that flares at that statement, but I nod in confirmation. From watching them together last night, I know that Enzo is more than just Dante's bodyguard, but obviously, in front of his father, Dante must have to pretend they are nothing but professional colleagues.

As we approach the front door, a doorman pulls it open. "Good morning, Mr. Antonelli," he greets, bowing his head in a sign of respect to Dante, and we step inside an expansive foyer.

Dante leads me over to a bank of elevators, ignoring the security guard behind the reception desk, who practically falls off his chair when he spots us. "G-good day, sir. I wasn't aware Mr. Antonelli was expecting you."

"He's not," Dante responds curtly, pressing the button to call the elevator. "However, I have some urgent business to discuss with my father."

"O-of course, sir."

A light turns on above one of the elevators as a ping sounds to signal its arrival, and the three of us move into the confined space. Dante presses the button for the penthouse, but it's only when he uses the built-in retinal detector to scan his eye that the elevator responds, the doors closing before we start to ascend.

I chew nervously on my bottom lip, my heel tapping against the carpeted floor as we climb higher and higher. The whole time, Dante's hand stays glued to my lower back, and despite being incredibly confused about Dante and my feelings for him, I take some comfort from his touch, using it to steel my spine. Although I don't dare look back at Enzo, I can feel his presence behind me, further bolstering me, and just before the elevator doors open, his arm brushes against mine in an act of reassurance. My Reaper mask is firmly in place by the time I step out into a lavish living room, and I'm more than prepared to face Giovanni. If only I had a weapon on me.

I barely have a chance to take in the ample open space, the floor-to-ceiling windows, and the fact that you can see the entire city sprawled out beneath you from here before Giovanni himself steps into the room, his domineering presence immediately increasing the tension in the air.

"Son, I didn't know we had a meeting scheduled for today." His derisive tone says everything about how displeased he is with our unexpected appearance. I've only ever seen a picture of Giovanni, and it doesn't capture him at all. If he looked intimidating in his photo, it's nothing compared to the hair-raising effect he has in real life. His tall, slim figure cuts an impressive image, with his pristine suit, similar to the one Dante is wearing, and his short, styled, obsidian hair, with a touch of gray around the temples. However, it is the calculating look in his eyes and his baleful glare that truly hit you in the chest. It's in that cold, hard stare that I know he would destroy you, your family, your loved ones, everyone you've ever met or come into contact with, and not think twice about it.

His eyes roam over me, taking his time as they slowly climb up my legs, taking in my short dress before finally resting on my face. "And you brought a guest." Straightening his suit, he strides toward us. "A pretty one at that." With one last flick of his eyes down my body, he directs his attention to Dante. "What is this about?"

"I wanted you to be the first to know that I'm engaged."

Giovanni's face is unreadable, except for the slight raising of his eyebrows. "Is that so?" His gaze flicks back to me, this time focusing on my face, noting the vibrant red of my hair. His lips pinch. "Is this the whore you've been known to frequent recently?"

Without even looking, I can feel the anger radiating off Dante at those words. It's a struggle to maintain my own impassive mask and act like his words don't affect me. He's close enough that, if I had one of my blades on me, I could just whip a hand out and drive it into the side of his neck, cleanly slicing his artery. That's the thought I choose to focus on until the murderous rage dulls to a simmer, and I can once again focus on the conversation around me.

"Dancer," Dante corrects. "And yes."

Giovanni laughs a cold, harsh, bitter sound that rubs me the wrong way, like nails on a chalkboard. "Son, you know better than that. You can't marry someone like her." When he next looks in my direction, it's with a superior sneer. "Girls like her are for fucking. They aren't wife material. Get yourself a proper girl, and you can keep this one on the side."

All I can think about is ripping out this asshole's tongue and stuffing it down his throat 'til he chokes. It takes everything in me to just stand there and let him spew his hateful words. It's only Dante's next words that clears the red mist that had descended over my vision.

"I'll agree to your choice of Consigliere."

The way his father perks up, it's obviously something he's interested in. Oliver and Cain explained Italian Mafia terminology to me, so I understand he's referring to his second in command. Even though I'm not entirely sure what's going on, I get the impression this is a pretty big concession on Dante's part.

Piercing his son with his cold, dead gaze, he remarks, "It wasn't up for debate, but I really don't care what whore warms your bed at night so long as my empire is thriving."

"So we have a deal then?"

Sighing, like he's been massively inconvenienced, his father spares me a final derisive glance. "I don't see why you're so insistent on her, but fine." He waves his hand dismissively. "Sam will be your Consigliere when you take over my position, and in exchange, you can marry the whore."

Dante gives a sharp nod of confirmation. "I want to be married within the week."

I balk at those words before I can stop myself, but thankfully his father doesn't notice, laughing casually like Dante just told him a joke. I'm not sure either of them is capable of joking.

"A week? Not a chance." He thinks on it for a moment. "A month, today. It's the best I can do."

By the tense set to Dante's jaw, I'm guessing that he's not happy about that, but he accepts it anyway. "Fine. A month today."

I release a silent sigh of relief. A month I can work with. That will give the Rejects and I time to figure out what we're going to do and takedown Giovanni and his men before I have to marry Dante. I'm acutely aware that that means Dante and Enzo will be going down too. Instead of getting married, Dante will be meeting his maker, with Enzo at his side. The thought doesn't sit well for me, but I choose not to dwell on it for now. I've plenty of time to sort that out and figure out what I should do.

"Stop by someday this week, and we'll get an agreement drawn up," his father states before dismissing us. Dante's hand once again finds my lower back as we head back to the elevator, and just before we get in, I glance over my shoulder to find Giovanni watching us. Catching me looking, he smiles, and it's the scariest thing I've witnessed in a long time. Forcing back a shiver, I get into the elevator and I don't feel at ease again until Enzo closes the car door behind me.

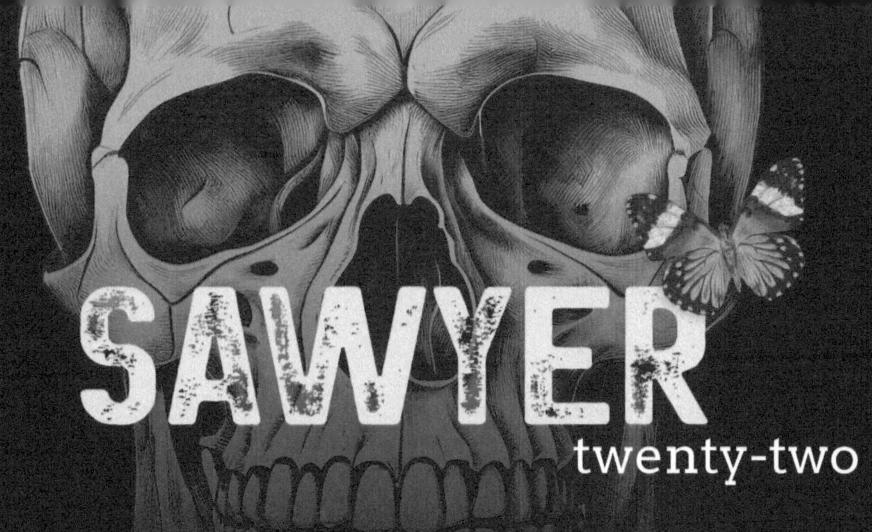

SAWYER

twenty-two

"We need to talk," Enzo spits out between gritted teeth when we get back to Dante's home. Dante gestures for Enzo to follow him with a nod, and the two of them head toward the home office. I decide to leave them to it as my rumbling stomach sends me on the search for food.

I rummage around in the kitchen until I find everything I need to make a sandwich, and with that and a fresh cup of coffee in hand, I head out to the back porch. I'm surprised to find the door unlocked, but no doubt I probably can't leave the property without setting off some sort of alarm—not that I'm going to run. I'm exactly where I need to be. By sheer luck, I've been given the opportunity we so desperately needed. I'm not about to waste it.

Violent, vengeful ideas run rampant in my head while I polish off my lunch and look out over the beach. It's a stark contrast to my dark thoughts. So calm and peaceful, without a soul in sight. It's a far cry from the noisy, busy, gray city I'm used to. At odds with the brutality I've come to live with. It's jarring, and instead of relaxing into the quiet peacefulness, I find myself feeling more jittery and on edge. I'm not sure if I could live all the way out here permanently. I feel like the lack of noise would drive me insane.

My thoughts return to Dante and Enzo, wondering what the problem is now. None of us said anything after we got back in the car, but I could feel the tension coming off Enzo and Dante like it was gasoline, just waiting for the slightest of sparks. I can only assume by Enzo's apparent anger that the position of Consigliere was meant to be his when Dante took control after his father. If that's so, then why did Dante so quickly agree to give the job to someone else so that he could marry me? He must realize there's no way I will go through with this wedding. I don't even understand why he's pushing it. It was one thing for him to intervene at the club yesterday, and even to fool his father into thinking we're going to get married in order to protect me, but to negotiate and yield to his father's terms? It just doesn't make any sense to me. Sure, I've noticed the way he watches me. There is undoubtedly *something* there on his end—okay, I feel that pull of attraction, too—but there's a big fucking difference between lusting after someone and marrying them.

I sit outside, mulling it all over for a while longer, but the only way I'm going to get any actual answers is by confronting Dante and demanding he answer my questions for once. Getting to my feet, I head inside. Dropping my plate and mug in the sink, I wander through the large house in the direction Enzo and Dante disappeared.

From my snooping yesterday, I know there's an office on this side of the house and can only assume that's where they went when we got back. Finding the correct room, I press my ear against the door, not wanting to interrupt them if they are still arguing. Not hearing anything, I push open the door, but rather than entering the room, I stand frozen in the doorway. A soft groan reaches my ears seconds before my brain registers what my eyes are seeing.

Dante is lounging in the chair behind the desk with his head tilted back and his eyes closed. He's wearing the most serene expression I've ever seen on him—or maybe it's just because his eyes are closed, so they don't feel like they are searing into you and uncovering the secrets you keep hidden. He's removed his tie and undone his top button, and his hands are threaded through Enzo's hair as he crouches between his thighs. The bobbing of Enzo's head and the subsequent noises they're both making are what really catch my attention.

As if sensing my presence, Dante's eyes snap open, and he holds me captive in his heated gaze, watching me as Enzo continues to work him over. I feel like I'm intruding on a private moment, but my feet are glued to the floor. Even if I could get them to work, Dante's gaze holds me hostage. His guard is down, providing me with my first real insight into who Dante actually is, and I couldn't look away even if I wanted to. Desire and lust burn in his eyes, making his usually brown irises appear darker, and even when his breaths turn into short, quick pants as his orgasm nears, he never breaks eye contact.

My cheeks heat beneath the intensity of his stare, and I can admit my own breaths are shallow. I inadvertently squeeze my thighs together as need builds in my core. I hold his gaze, and it doesn't take long until he reaches his climax, his hands tightening in Enzo's hair as he grunts. The moment after feels endless as he continues to hold me captive with his gaze, and it's only when Enzo releases him with a pop that I snap back to reality. Soundlessly, I slip out of the room, closing the door before making my way through the house and up to my bedroom.

When I'm safely locked behind the privacy of my bedroom door, I lean back against it and exhale a long, shaky breath. My mind is still reeling from what I walked in on. *Holy shit, that was unexpected... and crazy hot.* I knew I'd been picking up on a vibe, but I simply assumed they were close friends. Dante isn't a trusting guy, so the fact that he's so casual and open around Enzo is telling enough of how close they are, but I never pegged him as being bi. Nor did I think I'd get so hot and bothered by watching them, but *damn*, I can't stop replaying it in my head. Leaning my head against the door, I groan, fanning my still heated face. *Whoa, I need a cold shower.*

It's an hour later—freshly showered and self-satisfied—before I dare show my face downstairs again. I'm dressed in my clothes from yesterday, feeling like I need the extra layers provided by my jeans and leather jacket rather than the thin fabric of the dress. The smell of food cooking draws me toward the kitchen, and I find Enzo in front of the stove, stirring a pot while Dante sits at the kitchen table, working away on a laptop. I can only guess that the two of them resolved their issues in the office earlier. Dante's eyes dart up to meet mine the second I step into the room, the heat in them scorching my skin, and I quickly glance away, choosing to ignore his presence as I take a seat at the breakfast bar.

"So, you cook?" I ask Enzo, desperate to start up some sort of conversation and erase the way Dante's attention makes my skin prickle.

Enzo chuckles, the sound surprising me. It's probably the first genuine laugh I've heard from him, and I find myself liking the warm quality of it. "I am Italian, it's practically in my blood." He doesn't look up from where he's rapidly chopping vegetables like a chef on one of those TV shows.

"Do you cook like this every night?" Somehow I can't picture him and Dante living in this weird domestic bliss, although after what I walked in on this afternoon, it makes a little more sense... still, it just doesn't quite gel with the whole mafia, hitman lifestyle.

"Not often," he confesses, confirming my suspicion. "I don't usually have the time." It begs the question as to how he has the time now. Shouldn't both he and Dante be out doing whatever powerful men in criminal organizations do daily?

"What exactly is it you do for the Antonellis?"

His gaze flicks up to mine, a slight smirk tugging at one side of his lips. "Now, if I told you that, I'd have to kill you."

I roll my eyes at his cliched response but accept it for the blowoff that it is. "Well, whatever you're cooking smells delicious."

At my compliment, he spares me a glance, a soft smile gracing his lips before he turns to dump the cutting board full of vegetables into a waiting pot.

Looking back at me over his shoulder, he asks, "Can you cook?"

"No," I laugh. "Unless instant mac 'n' cheese counts?"

His easy laughter in response seems so jarring to the image of Enzo I have in my head. Just watching him in this house, so open and at ease... he's nothing like the guy I've been meeting once a month for the last number of years. He's less closed off and shut down. All those parts of himself that I knew he was keeping carefully hidden under lock and key are now out on display for me to casually peruse. I'm not sure if it's being here, in his home, that has caused this change or something different.

When he's finished doing whatever he's doing at the stove, he grabs a bottle of red wine from the wine rack, along with two glasses, and proceeds to pop the cork. The rich aroma of berries and expensive wine fills the air as he pours some into the glasses. Setting them both on the breakfast bar, he places his elbows on the countertop. The move brings him to my eye level. "Maybe I can teach you a few new things while you're here."

Shamefully, the deep baritone of his voice instantly sends my mind down the wrong track, and my gaze drops to his pink, plump lips, wondering what new things he could potentially teach me with his tongue. His lips twitch humorously, and I drag my mind out of the gutter as I clear my throat.

"Yeah, that would be cool. I'm sure Luc would appreciate that."

There's a guilty twinge at the mention of my brother's name. I haven't spoken to him, and I need to check-in and see if he's okay.

"You miss him," Enzo correctly deduces.

"Yeah," I sigh. "I'm used to seeing him basically every day, and not being there to check on him... I just worry."

Enzo seems to think on it for a moment before shrugging a shoulder. "We could—"

I quickly cut him off with a shake of my head. "No." I flick my gaze over to Dante, checking he isn't paying attention to us, but thankfully he's still engrossed with whatever he's doing on his laptop. "I don't want him involved in any of this."

Enzo's lips pinch. "You realize when you marry Dante, he's going to find out about your brother. You can't keep both of them in the dark."

Refusing to acknowledge that, because ultimately it's a moot point, I instead ask in a low voice, "I thought, based on what you said earlier, you didn't want me marrying Dante?"

His eyes flash with something primal. "I also said that neither of us was willing to let you go."

My mouth goes dry at the sheer possession in his tone. I'm pretty sure his words should terrify me, but it's not fear that has my heart accelerating and my pulse thudding.

The sound of chair legs scraping against the wood floor makes me jump. Enzo smirks knowingly, and I distract myself by lifting my glass of wine and taking a large sip while he goes back to check on the food. Heat envelopes my back as I set the glass down, and I tense as I feel Dante's warm breath along my neck. With his lips inches from my ear, he says in a low, sexy as fuck growl, "I hope you enjoyed the show earlier."

My eyes flick up to see if Enzo heard him, but he's ignoring the two of us, and my gaze quickly darts back to Dante as he trails his fingers along the exposed skin of my shoulders before claiming the barstool next to me.

"We need to talk about today," I blurt out. "And, uh, this whole marriage thing."

Dante's penetrating gaze sears into me. The way he looks at me, never really speaking but saying an overwhelming amount with just his eyes, unnerves me. Not in any hurry to answer me verbally, he just holds my gaze, and I only manage to break out of his hold when his phone goes off.

"What?" he barks, bringing the phone to his ear. There's a moment of silence while he listens to whoever is on the other end, before he says, "Get it under control. I'll be there shortly." He hangs up without giving the person a chance to respond, and there's a frown on his face as Enzo turns to look at him expectantly.

"There's a problem," is all Dante says on the matter as he gets to his feet.

"I'll go," Enzo offers—although it's said with a surprisingly authoritative tone. His gaze darts between Dante and me. "You two need to talk."

After a second's hesitation, Dante agrees and slowly lowers himself back onto the stool beside me. The thought of being alone all the way out here in the middle of nowhere with Dante makes me uneasy, but I've come to the conclusion that he's not going to harm me. He'd have done it by now if he was. He's just intent on pissing me the fuck off with this marriage bullshit.

Enzo moves around the room, slipping his suit jacket back on and slotting a gun in the holster at his waist. My eyes slowly roam over him, noticing how fucking hot he looks in just a white shirt, pants, and jacket. With his top button undone and tie missing, he looks slightly ruffled, but in a sexy, *I just rolled out of bed* way.

Before he leaves the room, he returns his focus to us. There's a seriousness in his eyes as he says, "No touching the food. I've spent all afternoon on it, and I don't need either of you burning it."

Giving me a final once over, Enzo walks out of the room. Neither Dante nor I say anything until the front door closes behind him, then I turn to Dante, suddenly hyper-aware of his close proximity. Our shoulders are so close that they brush against one another as I turn in my seat to face him. The change of position makes my knees brush against the soft fabric of his suit pants, where they are practically molded to his thighs. His gaze zeroes in on where we're touching, and it subsequently launches a kaleidoscope of butterflies in my lower belly.

Clearing my throat, I lift my head to look at his face, and he meets my questioning stare. "You need to start explaining this to me, 'cause I don't understand. Why did you come to save me yesterday? Why are you making compromises with your dad to marry me? You don't even know me."

He gives a small, slow, casual shrug of his shoulder. "Because you're mine."

Uhh, I'm what now?

A stunned silence fills the small space between us as I attempt to wrap my head around his words. It's not even what he said but the tone of casual possession with which they were delivered. Like he's stating it as a fact; something non-refutable.

"I'm what?" I mutter, half in shock.

My eyes dart back and forth between his, attempting to find something in his dark, brown depths that will refute what I think he's saying, but as he leans in toward me, I see the flames of possession burning within his gaze. He lifts his hand, trailing his fingers lightly along my jaw. His touch is soft and gentle, and I instinctively find myself leaning into it. Reaching my chin, he catches it in a firm hold, ensuring I can't look away as he repeats himself. "You are mine."

This time, as he says it, he drops his barriers, letting me see how much he means what he's saying. They aren't just words of ownership. He *means* them. He believes in them with every ounce of his dark soul. I gasp as the full force of his possession washes over me, hitting me like a hard slap to the face as understanding finally dawns. I think back on each time he came into the club, the way he would sit at the back of the room and silently watch me. Every one of his visits was him marking his territory. Him cementing his obsession and fortifying his resolve to do exactly as he is planning to—make me his.

Part of me descends into a mad panic at that thought, yet I can sense a weird calmness underneath it all. Like at my core, I accept his blatant claiming. Except that makes no sense, because I belong to nobody.

I don't even know how to respond to his statement, and instead, I end up staring at him, my lips parted in shock. His fingers press into my skin, where he's still cupping my chin, and he must mistake my silence for acceptance rather than the mind-blowing panic that it is. He slowly leans in, his eyes glued to mine as he closes the scant space between us. His lips descend on mine with confidence, like he knows he has every right to kiss me. The second his tongue sweeps into my mouth, my eyes drift shut, and I moan without really meaning to. God, his kiss is... indescribable. There's a surety in his touch. It's assertive and unfaltering, but it's also leisurely and considerate. It's somehow both Dante personified and the complete opposite of what I expected from him. Two contrasting sides—hard and soft, dominant and languid, passionate yet nurturing.

I lose myself in it. In him. For a brief moment, I let myself feel what it would be like to be owned by him. There's no question that Dante is a terrifying man, and he has many faults, but as he claims me with his mouth, I witness a side of him that I never knew existed before. I wouldn't exactly describe it as a softer side because nothing about Dante is soft, but with every powerful stroke of his tongue against mine, I can visualize more clearly what it means to be his. It wouldn't all be dominant possession. The way his hand firmly yet gently clasps my chin shows me that he'd care for me. With each languid kiss, he demonstrates how easily he'd worship me, and with the way his large palm squeezes my hip, I know I'd be safe in his arms, protected.

All of these little nuances I never noticed before only surmount to make me realize I don't actually know Dante at all. In fact, I reckon no one really does, except maybe Enzo. I get the impression that Dante keeps himself so locked down emotionally that perhaps he doesn't even truly know himself.

My fingers dig into his suit jacket, pulling him closer. I don't even remember reaching out to touch him, too lost in the mishmash of conflicting versions of Dante fighting for my attention. He responds to my eager touches by shoving my jean-clad thighs apart so he can move to stand between them. The change in position forces me to tilt my head back, and I lean further back in my chair so he's hovering over me. Letting go of my chin, his hands roam down my sides until he palms my ass. Gripping it firmly, he tugs me in against him.

As I feel the hard outline of his erection pressing against my core, images of Cain and Oliver flash across my mind, making me jolt as I pull back, breaking off our kiss. My heart clenches painfully in my chest at the reminder of them, and guilt niggles at me as I shake off the lusty haze fogging my brain. Whatever crazy effect Dante has on me, it's not enough for me to give either of them up, which is precisely what would have to happen if I let him truly claim me. He's too controlling, too domineering to share. My mind briefly flickers to the scene I witnessed in his office earlier, and I can't help wondering if he would be comfortable sharing with Enzo, but I quickly dismiss the thought. It's a pointless one, anyway.

His hands are still on my lower back, his hold on me firm and steady as I lift my gaze to meet his stormy eyes, finding his pupils blown with lust. It makes my breath catch at the back of my throat as I look up into his face. He should probably look terrifying. To anyone else, he would, and a week ago—hell, probably even yesterday—I would have agreed. Yet, behind the sharp, granite lines of his face, I see what I couldn't see before— the quiet desperation and silent struggle that Dante lives with every day. I don't under- stand it. I don't know why he seems to feel so adrift and on edge, but he does.

I almost feel bad as I utter my next words, even though I *know* I need to put a stop to this. I *need* to make him realize he can't just lay claim to me like I'm a possession for him to pocket. "You can't own me, Dante. I'm my own person. You are not mine, and I'm... I'm not yours."

His expression hardens instantly, and I'm shut out from all that vulnerability. I watch the muscles in the back of his jaw work for a second before he straightens, towering over me. His hands are still on me, and he slides them along my sides before lifting them off. I ignore the pang in my chest at the loss of his touch, focusing more on his threatening posture as I eye him warily. Wrapping his hands around the side of my stool, he looms over me, so close that I can feel the warmth of his breath against my lips when he speaks. "You can fight it all you want, but you *are* mine, and you *will* marry me."

Before I can find my voice to utter any sort of retort, he storms out of the room, leaving me both angry as hell and confused as fuck as to what just happened and how I'm going to get myself out of it.

Dante still hasn't returned from wherever the hell he stomped off to in a huff by the time Enzo returns that evening. He somehow seems to know something has happened as soon as he walks in.

"What the hell happened?"

I shake my head, still not entirely sure myself. "He spouted some bullshit about me being his, and when I tried to tell him otherwise, he had a hissy fit."

He snorts, not seeming surprised. "Let him cool off. He'll be back when he's calmed down."

"Yeah, but what the hell am I going to do about all of this? I can't marry him. I won't." The look Enzo flashes at me only makes me angrier. There's pity in his gaze, and I fucking hate to see it. I don't need or want his pity, nor do I like the fact that he seems resigned to what's going to happen. "I'm serious, Enzo. I have a life, responsibilities." Leaning in toward him, I state in a quieter tone, "I can't abandon my brother, and I *won't* have him getting involved in any of this."

Enzo lets out a long, suffering sigh and refills our wine glasses from earlier before joining me on the sofa. At this rate, we'll be through the entire bottle before we've even sat down for dinner. "I know." He pauses, taking a sip from his glass before continuing, "Dante... he thinks he's doing what's right. What he thinks will keep you safe." I quirk a brow, not buying the bullshit he's trying to feed me. After a moment, he purses his lips and sighs. "He's also... not like you or me. He doesn't process his emotions the way we do."

"From what I have gathered, he doesn't seem to think he even has emotions."

"It's complicated. Dante is complicated. He... his father has honed him into a weapon. Since he was born, he has been nothing but a pawn, a chess piece for his father to form and manipulate. He was never offered the opportunity to develop normal relationships or encouraged to foster positive emotions. He's grown up being told he can't feel anything, so that's what he believes."

"But you don't agree."

Enzo hesitates, sipping on his wine before responding. "Dante's come to my rescue more than once. He's always had my back. I believe that *he* believes he's incapable of feeling." He looks at me over the top of his wine glass, his bright green eyes boring into mine. "I think he just needed to wait for someone special to come along and make him truly *feel* something real."

My eyes widen as understanding dawns, and I choke on my wine. "Me? Are you talking about *me?*" I shake my head, leaning forward to carefully place the wine glass on the coffee table before I manage to spill it all over the white leather sofa. "No way. Absolutely not. I am *not* that person." Fuck, my emotional capacity probably isn't a hell of a lot more than Dante's.

Enzo doesn't let my vehement protests put him off, as he continues to stare at me. "You have no idea what a big deal it was for him to let you live that night. It's what initially drew me to you. Before then, Dante had only ever broken the family rules for one person... me. Something about you spoke to him that night."

"So? That was eight years ago."

"He never forgot it. He never forgot *you*. And now you show up back in his life all these years later, making him acknowledge feelings he usually buries?" He shakes his head. "That's more than just a minor coincidence to him."

I sink further into the sofa with every word he says, unable to fully comprehend it all. "That's why he's..."

"Practically pissing all over you? Yeah."

The hint of aggravation in his tone has me glancing up at him, the tight lines on his face confirming how much that annoys him. I don't exactly know what that means, that he's angry that his best friend—lover?—is apparently obsessed with me. Nor do I want to delve into any of that. I already have two men—two violent, alpha-male gang leaders—waiting for me at home. I sure as fuck do not need to add two men that I don't trust and that I'm actually supposed to be gathering intel on so we can eventually kill them to this convoluted harem I seem to be building.

Sighing, I rub my eyes. "I don't know what to make of any of this, but I need you to take me back into the city." He opens his mouth, probably to deny me, but I bulldoze over his excuses. "I need to see Luc and sort out work stuff. I'm not running. I'll come back here with you when I'm done. But I *need* to go sort stuff out." My expression is unrelenting as I hold his gaze.

He glowers at me unhappily, but eventually, he gives a slight nod of agreement. "Fine. The next time Dante meets his father I'll take you into the city. You'll only have a few hours, though."

"That's fine." I can work with that. I just need to check that Luc and the guys are okay. I need to see their faces and be reminded of our objective because I'm losing perspective, which scares me more than anything.

twenty-three

I groan into my third—or is it my fourth?—coffee of the day as I scour the city map spread out across my desk. Red's been gone for three whole days now, and neither Oliver nor I have slept since she called. I know she sounded fine on the phone, and she assured us she wasn't in any imminent danger, but there was no way we could just sit back and wait. I feel like all I ever do is bide my time and fucking wait. I'm sick of waiting. I didn't act when those fuckers took Evie, but I sure as fuck am going to act now. I won't let them take another woman I love from my life. 'Cause yeah, I fucking love her.

She's been battering her way through my walls for weeks now, making them crumble. First with her ballsy move in *my* clubhouse, then when Oliver and I saw her in action, killing those sick fucks. I was hard as fucking stone the entire time she was fucking with them, and when she took Oliver's gun and shot one of them without even blinking, *fuuuuck*. It was the hottest thing I've seen in a long time. That whole night was a turning point for me. The night when I saw Red for who she really is. The night when I at long last managed to separate her from my sister and accepted that she's capable—more than fucking capable—of looking out for herself.

All these amazing qualities that I've been blatantly ignoring for weeks now finally hit me full force, and I could no longer deny my feelings for the intelligent, sexy, fierce woman who's got balls of steel and more tenacity than a grizzly bear. After her little stunt in the clubhouse the other day, I'd agreed to try and let her in. Even as I'd said it, I wasn't convinced I'd be able to do it. Although I was willing to try. *For her*. I knew exactly what she hoped to achieve with that little show... and she won. She pushed me to confront my feelings instead of being the petty dick I was acting like, and that night, I got a taste of what it could be like sharing her with Oliver. The thing is, sex has always been easy for Red and me. It's the other stuff that doesn't come naturally to either of us. But I promised I'd try.

I just hadn't expected to be so blown away by watching her in action as the Reaper. It solidifies in my mind that this woman is fucking perfect for me. The way she got off on the bloodshed and exacting justice. It was intoxicating and far beyond my expectations of what she was capable of. So yeah, she won me over with her little show, but she put me on my knees and had me kissing her feet when she killed those assholes. I've never been so fucking turned-on as I was that night. Next time she sends some sick, abusive shitstain to his death, I want to fuck her brains out right there beside his dead body, then help her dispose of him afterward.

And if the dance and murder weren't enough to make me realize what was right in front of me, then hearing her on the phone the other day was the final lifting of the veil over my eyes. When she said those three words... everything just fell into place. My future—however short it may be—flashed across my eyes, and she was in every single scene. The way she should be. The way she was always *meant* to be. I thought I had to do right by Evie before allowing myself any happiness, but Oliver's right. I can do both. Have both vengeance and love. In fact, I'm pretty sure I can't achieve the former without the latter. And now the Antonellis are fucking with me once again, trying to murder and then kidnapping my woman. Well, this time, I'm not a scared little thirteen-year-old boy. I'm the leader of the motherfucking Rejects, and I'm going to bury every last one of those fuckers... I just need to figure out where they're hiding her first.

My eyes roam over the northwest portion of the city—Antonelli territory. She's gotta be there somewhere, but where? We've had fuck all success identifying where any of the higher-ups live unless they could be holding her in one of their clubs or their casino. But that's too many places for us to look. We wouldn't get through them all without raising suspicions.

I hear the creak of the door opening, but I don't even bother to look up from the map. "Fuck off," I snap. If it were Oliver, he'd have already come in instead of hovering in the doorframe, and I don't give a shit about anything else that's going on right now.

My temper flares when whomever it is doesn't do as they're told, and with a furious snarl, I snap my gaze in their direction. "I—" Words fail me. Fuck, I think my eyes are failing me. Jesus, did I add too much whiskey to my coffee? "Red?" She's standing in the doorway, looking like a fucking vision, as her eyes rake over me, a soft, content smile lifting her lips. She never looks at me that way. It's the smile she reserves solely for Oliver. Not that I can blame her. I've never given her a reason to look at me that way. I'm not Oliver with all his soft edges and quiet reassurance that can elicit sweet looks like that... yet, I'm somehow lucky enough to be privy to one of them right now.

When her eyes lift to meet mine, her soft, sweet smile morphs into its characteristic cocky grin that I love just as much. It's lively and mischievous, and it's the one she saves just for me. Oliver might bring out the softer sides of her, but I'm the one who fires her up and makes her feel alive—even if I piss her off while doing so. I fucking love that fire. The back and forth between us, the sniping and subsequent angry fuck. It's uniquely and perfectly us.

"Miss me?" Her tone is teasing, but there's an undercurrent of relief.

I'm out from behind the desk before I've even registered that I've moved, and I close the distance between us in two strides. Yanking her into the room, I slam the door closed and haul her into my arms. None too carefully, I push her into the wall beside the door as she wraps her long legs around my waist, hugging me closer. "Fuck, Red. It is you." Relief bleeds from every word as I stare disbelievingly at her. Honestly, until I was able to set eyes on her myself, I was half-convinced I'd never see her again. Just like Evie.

Her hand strokes down the side of my face, tangling with my beard that I haven't bothered to do anything with for the last few days. Based on the last time I looked in the mirror, I'm sure I look pretty fucking rough with my bloodshot eyes and scruffy beard, two-day-old t-shirt, and hair that's probably all over the place from running my hand through it in frustration. But she doesn't seem to care about any of it as she looks into my eyes. My hands squeeze her ass as I watch her back. Based on the quick assessment I did when I saw her standing in the doorway, she appears to be unharmed, but I can't seem to look away from her beautiful blue eyes to double-check.

"Yeah, big guy. It's me." Her voice is soft, softer than it's ever been around me. The feel of her flush up against me, her hot core pressing against my rapidly growing dick, has me wanting to strip her naked and fuck her right here and now. Prove to her she's mine. Let her know that I've finally accepted it.

"Say it again," I growl, my voice strained and raw sounding. Nothing like my usual self. Her brows pull down in confusion, but it only lasts a second before she catches on to what I'm asking. I know she intended them to be for her brother, and maybe she meant them for Oliver too, but fuck it. I've decided she meant them for me. A hesitant smile slowly plays along her lips, and when her thumb brushes across my cheek, I'm certain she's going to tease me before giving me what I want. Thankfully, she doesn't.

"I love you, Cain."

There it is. The words hang in the air between us, sounding like the best fucking song I've ever heard. I'm not sure if I remove the last bit of space between us or if she pulls me in, but our lips crash together in a desperate, sloppy kiss like we've both been starved of one another.

"Again," I grunt, grinding my erection into the apex of her thighs and loving the way she moans and moves against me.

"I love you."

Fuck, I'll never get tired of hearing that, even if I don't feel like I'm deserving of her love. Not yet, anyway. Pushing her deeper into the wall, I bring my hand up between us and deftly undo the button of her jeans, shoving my hand into her panties. Her head falls back against the wall as I find her fucking gushing for me. I push three fingers inside, stretching her. Not moving, I hold my position as I growl, "Again."

Her cheeks and chest are flushed, her breathing coming in heavy pants as she looks at me through hooded eyes. Her tongue licks along her lower lip. "I love you."

I fuck her hard and fast with my fingers, because even in this moment of sweet sentiments, Red and I don't do soft and sweet. We fuck rough and dirty, the way I like it. The way she *needs* it. And this time is no exception. It doesn't take long until she's coming around my fingers, crying out my name. She's still convulsing around me when she opens her eyes, finding me watching her. She's fucking beautiful when she comes. I'll never tire of watching it. I wait until the haze of endorphins lifts from her eyes, before saying, "I love you too, Red."

A sluggish smile crosses her face, and she pulls me into her, kissing me with the same slow, lazy, languid speed like we have all the time in the world.

"Where's Oliver?" she asks when she pulls back.

"Here," the man himself says from the doorway as both Red and I turn our heads to look at him. He's only got eyes for her, and the shadows that have been hanging around him for the last two days lift as he finds her safe and sound in my arms.

My fingers are still buried deep inside her, her release dripping down my hand, but she grins brightly at him, not giving a shit. She pushes on my chest, and I pull out of her, lowering her to the ground. The second her feet hit the floor, she rushes toward him, uncaring of her unbuttoned jeans and apparent disheveled state. She launches herself into his arms, and he holds her tight, burying his face in her hair. He mumbles something I can't make out before kissing her as passionately as I just did.

I give them a moment, wiping my hand on my jeans and firing off a text to Marcus, telling him to handle everything for the day. I don't want to be disturbed or interrupted with nonsense. Red might be back, but I highly doubt everything she managed to convey on the phone has magically fixed itself.

"What the hell happened?" Oliver asks when they finally pull apart. "How are you here?"

Red sighs, and I notice the dark circles under her eyes that weren't there the last time I saw her. Reaching out, I draw her into me and pull her down on my lap as I sit in what is her usual seat in front of my desk. She leans into me, turning on my knee to face Oliver as he sits beside us. She quickly re-hashes what she told us on the phone the other day, about that fucking ambush. My fingers dig into her thigh, and her hand comes to rest over mine, drawing circles along the back of my hand.

"Were you able to escape?" I ask after she informs us that she's been locked up at Dante's house for the last two days.

She grimaces. "Not exactly." I don't like the look on her face or how she doesn't meet either mine or Oliver's gazes.

"What the fuck does that mean?" I growl.

"Enzo drove me into the city."

"Who the fuck is Enzo?" I bark at the same time as Oliver questions, "Into the city?"

She runs her hand down her face, already looking weary, but I get the impression she's nowhere near done. "This is so much more complicated than I could have imagined," she groans.

"So, explain it to us." I'm getting impatient, and she clearly doesn't care for my tone based on the withering glare she gives me.

"I'm trying, but I don't have long, so just be quiet and let me get through it all."

"Don't have long?" I immediately question, ignoring the rest of what she said. "You're going back?" I'm not even sure why I bother to phrase it like she has a choice. She doesn't. There's no fucking way I'm letting her go back to him. To them.

Her lips thin, and she huffs out a breath, sending a silent plea to Oliver. "We won't interrupt you again," he promises, lifting his gaze to mine. Now it's my turn to huff out a frustrated breath, but I don't argue—for now.

She explains who this Enzo guy is, and I immediately don't like him. Someone else who knows her secret? I don't fucking think so. Nope. He can't be trusted, and he's just found himself at the top of my kill list, alongside Dante.

However, when she informs us of Dante's plan, I lose the thin thread of control I had over my anger. "Marry you?" I snarl, dumping her in Oliver's lap as I jump to my feet and begin to pace back and forth across the office. "That motherfucker. There's absolutely no fucking way. I'll kill him." I'm not entirely sure if my rant is all verbalized or just in my head, but I curse him out six ways to Sunday and picture killing him in a hundred different ways before the red mist lifts from my gaze, and I can finally focus on Red again. She's frowning at me, with her arms crossed over her chest, looking ready to tear my head off. Fuck if the thought of that doesn't get me hard.

"Are you done?" she snipes. "'Cause I'd quite like to get back to the plan."

"The plan where I kill all of them?"

She rolls her eyes. "The plan where every single Antonelli is gathered in one place, so all you have to do is blow them all to Kingdom Come."

Now that gets my attention, and I pause in my pacing to stare at her, wrapping my head around what she's saying. It takes a second, but the pieces finally all click together, and I scowl. "No. Absolutely not."

"Cain," she sighs, sounding exasperated. "It's the perfect plan."

"No," I bark again.

In the next second, she's on her feet, standing in front of me with her arms crossed and her eyes spitting fire. "Stop thinking of me as some innocent little girl who can't look after herself, and start seeing this as the opportunity we—*you*—have been waiting for."

"I'm not—"

"Yes, you are. You aren't even listening to my plan."

"Fine," I huff, stomping over to the seat and dropping into it, throwing out my hands. "Let's hear this amazing plan of yours."

Oliver smacks me on the arm, and when I turn to face him, he glowers at me. He's been quiet the whole time, or maybe I just didn't hear him over my own tirade and the blood rushing in my ears.

Ignoring my sarcasm, Red moves to lean against the desk in front of us. "The wedding is planned for next month." She pauses, her gaze darting to me, but I grit my teeth and hold back the angry retort threatening to slip out. One side of her lip quirks up in a smirk as if sensing my internal struggle. The sly bitch. She gets off on my fucking temper as much as I get off on hers. "Apparently, weddings are a big deal in the Antonelli Family." She shrugs, but Oliver nods his head.

"Yeah, it's an Italian mafia thing. They're all into upholding vows and huge celebrations. All that shit."

"Right," Red agrees. "It gives us the perfect opportunity. Every single member of their organization will be under one roof, ripe for the taking. We can take them all out in one fell swoop."

"But that means you have to go back to him," I bite out, unable to keep my mouth shut any longer.

"It's fine." She lowers her gaze, nibbling on her bottom lip. "It's not so bad, actually. He... they... neither of them has touched me."

I don't know if she meant for that to be reassuring, but it doesn't make me feel any better. "Red, he's all but claimed you. He might not have fucked you yet, but he will."

Her lips flatten, and she shakes her head. "He won't."

I don't know how she can be so adamant about that. The fact that she's defending him at all and willing to spend even another moment in their presence, is concerning. Before I can ask her any more about it, Oliver leans forward, gaining her attention.

"Are you safe if you go back there?"

She gives it a long thought before nodding her head. "Yes. They won't let Giovanni do anything to me."

"What about them?"

Her gaze swivels to mine and she shakes her head. I can see the surety in her eyes. "They won't hurt me, either."

We discuss it back and forth until my head hurts, and despite not liking the thought of sending her back there, I reluctantly agree to her plan. But not before she agrees to take a burner phone back with her, complete with a tracking app so Oliver and I can keep tabs on her.

When we're done, I get to my feet and wrap my hand around her wrist. Tugging, I yank her into my chest. My other hand slides into her hair, fisting it at the base of her neck and pulling on it, so she's forced to look up at me. Lust sparkles in her dazzling blue eyes and her lips part, her tongue flicking out to wet them. My girl loves when I'm rough with her. Which is precisely what I'm going to do. I might have to send her back to *them,* but the memory of my dick buried in her pussy will stay with her the entire time she's gone.

"I'm not letting you go until you're hoarse from screaming our names and your pussy is stuffed full with our cum."

A groan travels up the back of her throat, and she shifts, squeezing her thighs together as Oliver steps up behind her. He quickly strips her of her leather jacket, leaving her standing in front of us in a thin, black tank that does nothing to hide her peaked nipples.

His lips slowly descend down the side of her neck as his hands slide up underneath her top until he's cupping her breasts. She arches her back, pushing her chest against mine as another moan passes through her lips. Her crotch rubs against the hard-on in my pants, and I let go of her wrist, gripping her hip instead and pulling her flush against me as I grind into her.

Taking his time, kissing each part of her body he exposes, Oliver slowly removes the rest of her clothes until she's standing naked between us. His fingers trail down her abdomen and slide between her thighs, playing with her until her skin is flushed once again.

Cupping her cheek, I wait until her hooded eyes lift to meet mine. "Have you ever taken two men at once?"

Her eyes widen and her pupils dilate, a low groan at the thought of taking us both at once heightening her pleasure. She shakes her head, and her voice is breathy when she says, "No." The thrill that runs through me is next level.

"Mmm, you want to, though, don't you? I can feel how badly you want it. You're soaking my hand just at the thought."

She moans loudly at Oliver's dirty words. Her hands slide up my abdomen, pulling my t-shirt up with them, and I help her out by tugging it over my head while she moves to tackle my jeans next. She only gets the belt undone before I bat her hands away and spin her to face Oliver. "Take O's clothes off, baby," I order as I kick off my boots and shrug out of my jeans and boxers.

She doesn't hesitate, and in no time at all, the three of us are standing naked in my office. With my hands on her hips, I grind my dick between her ass cheeks until she moans. Snaking my hand between her legs, I coat my fingers before moving toward her puckered hole. She tenses, but I place a kiss on her shoulder. "Kiss Oliver, baby." Oliver's already leaning in to seal his lips to hers, and I wait until she melts into him. I bring my other hand around to play with her clit as I swirl my finger around her hole until she's pushing her ass back, silently demanding more. She groans into Oliver's kiss as the tip of my finger slides inside, and I slowly work her up until she can take me all the way to the knuckle.

"Oh fuck," she pants, breaking her kiss with Oliver and resting her forehead against his chest. Her nails dig into his pecs, leaving half-moon indentations as I work her over. I feel a hand brush mine before Oliver sinks his fingers inside her cunt, and she begins to tremble in our arms as she nears her release. "Oh, shit. Fuck." I love the way she curses when she's about to come. A second later, her body tenses, and she explodes around us. Dragging out her orgasm, until her legs are shaking and she can barely stand, I then scoop her into my arms. With one arm banded around her waist, her legs squeezing my hips, I sweep everything off the desk.

My ass hits the cool wood as I hold Red in my lap. Thanks to my long legs, I can easily sit on the desk with my feet planted on the floor and Red straddling me, her knees pressed against the hardwood of the tabletop. Her hands squeeze my shoulders as she slides over my cock, soaking it with each sweep along the seam of her pussy.

Oliver positions himself between my spread thighs, running his hand along her back. My hands slide along her thighs as she drips all over me, all three of us panting heavily. With his chest pressed against her back, Oliver reaches out and grabs Red's chin in a firm grip, turning her head so he can kiss her. His kiss is a claiming one—possession in its finest form. My hands lift to cup her breasts, my thumbs brushing over her nipples, and she breaks away to look at me with hooded eyes.

I hold her gaze while I play with her tits. "You're ours," I tell her. When she just looks at me, I pinch her nipple, hard, causing her to cry out.

"Yours," she pants.

Mirroring Oliver's hold on her chin, I turn her head until she's looking over her shoulder at him. "Yours," she repeats again, and I don't miss the flare of lust that burns in his eyes in response.

"Yours," he reiterates in a grave tone.

I lift her off me just enough to line my dick up with her entrance, and as she sinks down, her eyes land on mine again. "Yours," I murmur, before fusing my lips to hers.

She bobs up and down on my dick until we're both coated in sweat and delirious with need, then I lean back on the desk and bring her with me, granting Oliver the access he needs. With my hands on her ass, spreading her cheeks, I control her movements as he works her up until she can take his cock in her ass. I watch her face, riveted as he takes his time stretching her. The deep flush on her cheeks matches her hair, and there's a glassiness in her eyes that's purely orgasm induced. Her plump lips are parted in a silent O as short puffs and small whimpers escape between them, but what I love the most is how her eyes never leave mine.

"Cain," she moans, arching her back in pleasure.

"What is it, baby? What do you need?"

"More."

"Come for us. Come all over my cock then Oliver's going to take that ass of yours."

She groans, and I feel her pussy flutter before she clamps down around me. It takes everything in me not to lose my load there and then as she cries out.

When she relaxes again, Oliver begins to push his way inside her, the two of us sending her back up that cliff toward oblivion again. I've never double-teamed a girl before, and the tightness as Oliver seats himself fully in her ass is more intense than I expected. When he's all the way in, he meets my eye over her shoulder, and we begin to move in tandem, easily finding a rhythm that works for all three of us. Despite the fact she's already come twice, it doesn't take long until Red is crying out again, and this time Oliver and I both follow her over that cliff.

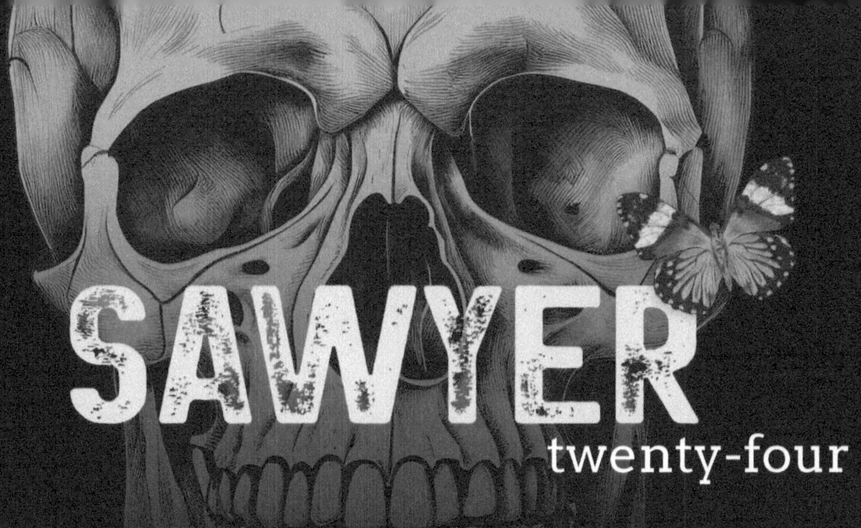

twenty-four

"**I** need to see Luc," I say once we're all cleaned up and dressed again. "Is he okay?"

"He's around here somewhere," Cain answers distractedly while he rummages in one of his desk drawers. "We didn't tell him anything, but he's fine." He pulls out a burner phone and turns it on, checking it's working before handing it over. "There's a tracking app on it. Only Oliver and I have the number." I go to take it from his outstretched hand, but he holds on to it until I meet his gaze. "Keep it on you at all times, and call one of us if something happens."

I nod, holding his gaze. "I will. I'll be fine."

He still doesn't look convinced, but the fact that he's letting me walk out of here at all is a miracle in itself. For a brief moment there, I thought he was going to chain me to his desk and refuse to let me leave ever again. But thankfully, he saw the potential in my plan, or maybe he's just starting to realize I can take care of myself.

They don't let me leave without another round of panty-melting kisses that have me nearly forgetting I'm on a tight timeframe and debating going for another round. Although my pussy and ass are worn out from earlier. Cain definitely followed through on his promise, and the two of them fucked me all over the office in every conceivable position, either together or one at a time, while the other watched. As I leave the office and walk down the hallway, I can feel the ache between my thighs, and I know I won't be forgetting about today any time soon. Hell, I will have to be careful that neither Enzo nor Dante notices the awkward way I'm walking.

Reaching the game room, I poke my head through the door and breathe a sigh of relief when I find Luc inside. I hadn't doubted Cain or Oliver's ability to look after him, but *man,* is it good to see him with my own eyes. He's focused on some football game on the TV, and as one of the players scores a touchdown, Luc and the others cheer. He's smiling as he turns to say something to the kid beside him. Noticing me standing in the doorway, his smile grows bigger, and I return it with a bright one of my own.

He gets to his feet and comes toward me. "Hey, where have you been?" I gesture for us to talk elsewhere, and he follows me out as we walk toward the back of the building and out the emergency exit door. "Is everything okay?" he asks, looking more concerned this time.

"Yeah, everything's fine."

His brows furrow, not believing me. "Sawyer, where have you been?"

"I've been doing a job for the Rejects," I explain vaguely, not wanting to share any more details with him.

"A Reaper job?" I stand frozen, gaping at him. He snorts. "I'm not an idiot. You might not tell me things, but I see and hear plenty. We have lived in a tiny apartment with paper-thin walls for the last five years."

Well, fuck.

"How long have you known?"

He shrugs, thinking it over. "A couple of years."

My eyebrows hitch. "And you never said anything?!"

"I was waiting for you to bring it up."

Fuck, well, now I feel bad. "I was trying to protect you—" I begin, the excuse sounding weak even to my ears.

He waves me off. "It's fine, Sawyer. I understand—sort of. I didn't bring it up to make you feel bad; I'm just sick of the secrets. If something's going on, I want you to tell me."

I chew on my bottom lip as I think about how to respond. "There's about to be a war between the Rejects and Antonellis, and probably the Grim Bastards."

"That's why you freaked after seeing me talking to that skinhead—The Bastard."

"Yeah," I admit.

"And why you asked Oliver to talk to me."

I grimace. "Yes."

He chuckles lightly before growing serious again. "Okay." He nods thoughtfully. "And what about you? What are you doing?"

"I'm just helping Cain and Oliver gather some intel."

He quirks a disbelieving brow. "You've been gone for days, and Cain's fuse has been shorter than anyone's ever seen it, so clearly something was going on."

"It's nothing you need to worry about," I assure him. "Just look out for yourself. Stay close to the clubhouse and the kids." I wait until he nods his head before continuing. "I'm going to be gone for a bit."

"Why? Where are you going?"

I'm already shaking my head before he's finished speaking. "I can't tell you. Cain, Oliver, and I have a plan. If everything works out, we might be able to turn Black Creek around. Make it a safe place to live." I give him a hopeful look. "You could walk the streets without fear. We wouldn't have to worry about some new gang bulldozing their way into someone else's territory and fucking with our lives."

He frowns. "Is that why you're doing all of this? For me?"

"You deserve better than this town has to offer. Don't you want to have a normal job and not have to worry about getting caught up in gang wars or shot down when you're just going about your life, minding your own business?"

"Not if it means you risking your life to achieve that!" Anger flashes across his features. "Do I want all those things? Yes, of course. But more than that, all I want is for you to be alive. None of that will matter if you're dead."

I give him a half-smile. "Have a little faith, Luc. I'm not going to die."

He scoffs, but thankfully there's a slight upward twitch of his lip. "Not even the Reaper is invincible. We're talking about the three largest gangs in Black Creek. If they wanted, they could destroy the city."

I can't argue with what he's saying, even though it's an outcome we're hoping to avoid. "Let's hope it doesn't come to that."

I HUG LUC TIGHTER THAN USUAL, KNOWING IT'S PROBABLY THE LAST TIME I'll see him for a while. I can't risk returning to the clubhouse again and drawing any unwanted attention their way.

"I'll see you soon, kid," I murmur in his ear before forcing my arms to let him go.

"Yeah." Tight lines mar his face, making him appear older than his fifteen years, and I can see concern shining in his eyes. "I know I can't stop you, but please be careful, Sawyer. You mean more to me than anything else. I don't care about any of the rest of that stuff. I just need you to be okay."

Tears shine in my eyes, threatening to spill, and I cannot respond past the wedge of emotion lodged in my throat. I simply give him a curt nod and watch as he disappears back into the game room. Only when I'm alone, do I let the tears spill.

"Hey," Oliver soothes, appearing out of nowhere and enveloping me in a hug. "Everything's going to be okay. He's safe here."

"I know," I choke out, wrapping my arms around him and melting into his touch. Oliver just holds me while I get my emotions under control, and when I've got everything securely packed in its box again, I pull away, giving him a soft smile. "I was actually coming to find you. I drove Raven over, but I was thinking she should stay here. Feels mean to keep her locked up if I'm not going to be around for another month."

"Raven?" Oliver questions, confused.

I chuckle, realizing how that probably sounded to someone who doesn't know what I'm talking about. "My bike."

"Ahh."

"Wanna give me a lift back to my apartment?"

He smiles. "I'd be glad to."

When we're in the car, his hand wrapped around mine as we head across town, I turn to look at him. "You were awfully quiet earlier. What are your thoughts on this plan?"

His gaze darts to mine for a brief moment. "I think it's a good plan. Our best chance of success."

"But?" I question, sensing there's more.

"*But* I don't like that it's you. What if something goes wrong? These men are Antonellis. No matter how nice they may seem, they're rotten at their core." My chest constricts uncomfortably at that, but I don't say anything. He sighs, lifting his hand to run it through his hair. "But I get that it has to be you." Giving my hand a reassuring squeeze, he adds, "If anyone can get the job done, it's you."

When he pulls up at the curb a street over from my apartment, in case Enzo is lurking nearby, I lean across the center console and fuse my lips to his for one last kiss. He returns it with bruising force before we pull away.

"You better come back to us," he orders in a husky voice.

"I will."

I turn, reaching for the door handle, but before I can open the door, he pulls me back for another heated kiss. "I love you, Sawyer. Remember that when you're with *them*."

My lips part in surprise, and the asshole just smirks. "Luc might have spilled your little secret."

"I'm going to kill him the next time I see him."

He barks out a laugh and knowing if I put it off any longer, I'll never leave, I push open the door. I force myself not to look back as I walk down the road toward my apartment. Reaching the building, I head inside. For the first time, when I step into my apartment, it doesn't feel like home to me. Mine and Luc's things are still scattered around the place, but it doesn't have the same homey feel it used to have.

Not wanting to linger, I cross to my bedroom and quickly pack a duffel with clothes. I may have enjoyed dressing up the other day, but I have no intention of letting Dante dictate my wardrobe for the next month.

As I'm walking back through the living room, I notice the photo I stuck to the wall when we first moved in—of Luc and me before our lives went down the shitter—is missing. Coming to a stop, I stare at the wall for a long moment before dropping my gaze to scan the floor, wondering if it just fell. Not seeing it, I figure Luc maybe took it. He mentioned today that he's been staying at the clubhouse since Dante kidnapped me —or whatever you call it. Perhaps he took the picture with him. It's the only one I have of us, so it would make sense.

Shrugging it off, I leave the apartment and head out onto the street to wait for Enzo. By the time he pulls up, I'm emotionally drained from the day's events.

"Get everything squared away?" he asks as I slip into the front seat, tossing my bag in the back.

"Yup." I don't give him anything more than that. It took a lot of careful maneuvering to ensure he couldn't track or follow me earlier. When he dropped me off at the apartment, I changed my clothes and snuck down the fire escape over to Raven and took various detours all over the city on my way to the Rejects. You can't be too careful, and I definitely don't want him or Dante to discover my connection to Cain and Oliver.

"Your brother is okay?"

"He's good." I notice him glance my way out of the corner of my eye, but I continue to ignore him and stare out the window as he drives us further north through the city.

As city blocks fly by in a blur, I think over how I'm going to get through the next month. I'm going to have to be careful. It will seem suspicious if I just fall in line and accept this wedding, but equally, I can't afford to do anything that might cause Dante to call the whole thing off.

We're deep in Antonelli territory when I let out a long sigh and turn my face away from the window to look at Enzo. He's so handsome, with his dirty blond hair and expensive suit. Like some sort of wealthy playboy. The perfect blend of aristocratic and devious.

"What's the deal with Dante and his father?" We never actually talked about what went down in the penthouse. Certainly, the impression I got is that their relationship is somewhat strained.

"Giovanni is a sick son of a bitch." The vitriol in Enzo's voice is startling. "He doesn't care for anyone—even his own son—except for how they can be of benefit to him. He's completely messed with Dante's head. Made him believe he's not worthy of anything good." His hands tighten around the steering wheel, his knuckles turning white. Giovanni's treatment of his son really irks him. Interesting.

"Is he?" I question. "Worthy of anything good?"

Enzo takes his eyes off the road for a second to look at me. "Don't get me wrong," he begins, returning his attention to the road. "Dante is a cold-blooded killer. He'll destroy anyone without a second thought and sleep peacefully in his bed at night, but he's a product of his environment. Killing is what he's been raised to do. It's all he knows. Just because he's capable of terrible things doesn't mean he doesn't deserve someone who will actually give a shit about him."

I return my gaze out the window as I turn his words over. "No," I eventually agree. "We're all capable of committing heinous acts. It's human nature. It's whether what you're doing is for the greater good or your own selfish needs that matters."

I can feel his eyes on me, and I turn to meet his unwavering gaze. "Exactly. Dante's never been given a chance to prove he's not his father."

"And you think he isn't?"

"I *know* he's not." I quirk a brow when he glances my way. "You wouldn't still be alive if he was."

"Yet he's going to force me to marry him." My tone is scathing, but Enzo just laughs.

"I said he's capable of making the right choice, I didn't say he'd *always* do the right thing. He might not be his father, but the primary lesson his father passed on is if you want something, you take it, regardless of what stands in your way." He looks my way. "And Dante wants you."

I roll my eyes. "So you're just going to let him force me down the aisle, even though you know it's not what I want?"

He waits until we're stopped at a red light, then he turns to face me. When I don't remove my gaze from the front window, he reaches across the center console and turns my head, forcing me to meet his gaze. "I'm not the good guy in this scenario. I'm not going to save you. I might not agree with Dante's plan, but I'm going along with it for purely selfish reasons."

My brows furrow. "What's that?"

His thumb strokes over the angle of my jaw, and the raw hunger in his bright verdant eyes knocks the air out of my lungs. "I've obsessed over you for as long as Dante has. I've bided my time and sat on the sidelines while you pushed me away and shut me out, but I'm done with that now. Where Dante's going to force you into a marriage, I'm going to push you into finally seeing what's been right in front of you all these years. Whether it was luck, fate, or happenstance, you're ensnared in our world now. You may as well accept it. I sure as fuck am not letting you go, and neither will Dante."

I swallow around the sudden lump in my throat as the light turns green, and he lets go of me, putting his hand back on the wheel. My skin tingles from where he touched it, and I can't decide if their combined obsessions are a turn-on or a serious fucking problem. I think they might be both, and if that's the case, I'm doubly screwed.

Neither of us says anything for the rest of the journey home. As he parks the car outside the house, I turn to look at him. "How is this going to work, Enzo? I need to be able to check in on my brother, not to mention I'll have Reaper jobs starting to pile up."

"Don't play dumb with me, Sawyer," he says with a raised brow. "I know you grabbed your burner cell when you were at your apartment." I open my mouth to protest, but he waves away my excuses. "It's fine. I won't tell Dante. Just give me names, and I'll sort it."

"You're going to send someone to kill my targets?" I clarify in disbelief.

"It's the easiest solution for now. You're going to have to tell Dante about *every-thing*, though."

"Absolutely not," I fire out instantly. "I don't trust him. He'll put a stop to it if he finds out, and I'm not about to tell him about my brother."

He sighs, shaking his head. "Or he might just surprise you." He pushes open the door and climbs out before I can respond, but I highly doubt that would be the case. Dante is even worse than Cain—which is fucking saying something. He's the very defi-nition of controlling, and I don't think the whole vigilante persona meshes with the mafia-housewife image he has for me.

Following him out of the car and into the house, I mutter some excuse about needing to be alone before I head up the stairs to my room. I dig in my duffel for both burner phones. Taking the one I use for Reaper jobs, I lift the mattress and hide it under it. With the one Cain gave me in my hand, I move into the bathroom and run the shower before lowering the lid of the toilet and sitting down on it. I've already gotten text messages from both Cain and Oliver. Bringing up Oliver's, I find his number and press dial.

The phone only rings once before he answers. "Is everything okay?" He doesn't sound panicked, but he does sound as though he's ready to jump into action if I asked him to come get me.

"Yeah," I sigh, feeling exhausted. "I just miss you."

He chuckles softly. "I miss you, too, Trouble. Where are you?"

"We're back at the house."

"You know you don't have to do this," he says, his voice taking on a serious quality. He didn't fight me earlier like Cain did, and I'm so thankful for that. I know it's not because he was fully on board with my plan, but he doesn't feel the need to constantly push my every button, unlike Cain. "Just say the word, and we'll come get you. You can be naked in my bed, screaming our names before it's even dark out."

I laugh softly, liking the sound of that. "I have to do this."

"No, you don't. We can find another way."

I shake my head, even though he can't see it. "This is our shot. Besides, it's about more than just that..." I trail off, unable to explain everything. I told Cain and Oliver about Dante and Enzo earlier, but I didn't go into any detail about just *how* fucking complicated everything is getting.

"There's more going on than you let on," he correctly deduces. He doesn't sound angry, just curious. "This Enzo guy, do you trust him?"

"No." My response is quick. "I don't trust either of them."

"But you're confident they won't hurt you."

I sigh wearily. "Yeah, I am."

There's a heavy silence before he speaks again. This time I can't decipher the emotion in his voice. "Do you like them?"

"I..." My voice peters out as I fail to come up with an honest response. It's not as simple as yes or no. No, I don't *like* them, but does my body react to them? Yes. Do they intrigue me and have me wanting to know more about them? Absolutely. But do I see any future where there is any trust, and we aren't all trying to kill each other? Hell no.

Eventually, I hear Oliver sigh down the phone. "Just be careful, okay? We are here for you. Nothing is going to change that. I love you. *We* love you."

My response is a quiet whisper, and I'm not even sure he hears me. "I love you, too."

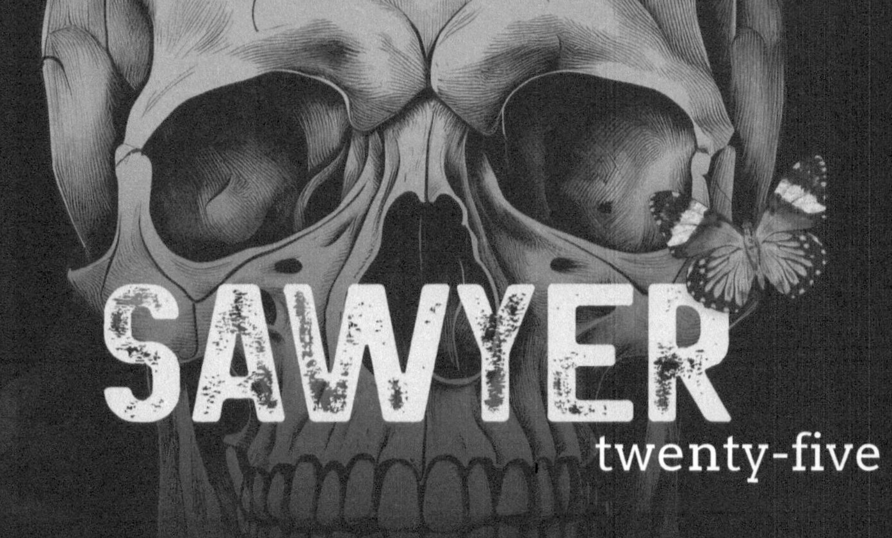

SAWYER
twenty-five

I barely see Dante for the next week. He seems to be awake and out the door before dawn, and he doesn't return until late at night. On the other hand, Enzo appears to be around every time I leave my room. Isn't he meant to be Dante's bodyguard? Shouldn't he be going wherever he goes?

"As the new wife-to-be of the next Don, Dante felt you needed your own security detail," Enzo explains when I ask him as much.

"And let me guess," I drawl. "That would be you."

He beams. "Right on the first guess."

I roll my eyes. "Doesn't he know that you're trying to steal me from him? Dante doesn't strike me as the sharing type. Surely, he sees you as a threat."

"That's the thing about Dante. If he cares about something, he'll do what needs to be done, even if it's not necessarily what he wants."

My brows furrow as I try to understand what he's saying. "So he doesn't want you to babysit me, but he's doing it anyway because…"

"Because I'm the only person he trusts, and he places your safety above his own desire to keep you all to himself. Besides, it's not that Dante *can't* share. He's just never learned how to."

I laugh. "And you think you're going to be the one to teach him."

The smirk he gives me is all sex, and I have to look away as thoughts of being pressed between him and Dante flash across my mind, making my nipples harden. Lifting my mug off the breakfast bar, I sip on my morning coffee as I push those unbidden thoughts away and instead try to glean some more information from Enzo.

"You were supposed to be Dante's second in command when he took over for his father, right?"

Enzo looks up from drying the last of this morning's dishes. Storm clouds roll across his eyes, darkening the shade from a vibrant green to more of a forest color. "I was." His voice is strained, giving away how much it bothers him that he's not anymore.

"But his dad didn't want that."

Enzo's sharp bark is cold and brief. "Couldn't hand the keys of the kingdom to a traitor's son, could he?"

My own anger sparks at Enzo's despondent tone and the detached look in his eye. "Your father's actions aren't yours."

He scoffs. "Try telling that to him."

"But Giovanni will be dead by then. Can't Dante just disobey him?"

Enzo lifts his gaze from where he was staring at the floor, giving me a small, sad smile. "It's not that easy. There's a whole agreement involved. Dante went last week and vowed in front of Giovanni and his men that Sam would be his Consigliere. If he didn't uphold that vow, he'd never be respected as the new Don."

"Oh." I had no idea Dante had had to do that. I can tell how much Enzo means to him, so it can't have been easy to stand up and promise to give such an intimate position to someone he doesn't trust. Nor can it have been easy on Enzo, knowing a place that is rightfully his was being handed to someone else. "I'm sorry."

Lines furrow across his forehead as his eyebrows dip. "Why?"

"It's my fault. He only agreed to Sam so he could marry me. To protect me."

Setting the drying cloth down on the counter, he reaches across the breakfast bar to take my hand in his. "None of this is your fault. Giovanni was never going to let Dante give that position to me. He already had the leverage he needed to ensure it didn't happen before you came along. You were just the final nail in the coffin."

I hold his gaze while I think over what he just said. Giovanni already had leverage. It takes a second before it clicks, and my eyes widen as I stare at Enzo. "He found out about you two."

His brows lift in surprise. "How did you—"

"Girls just know these things." *Aaand I may have watched you giving Dante head in his office.*

When Enzo just continues to stare at me, I move the conversation along. "Well, I'm still sorry. If anything, your relationship with him only further proves that *you're* the one who should be standing at his side when he takes over."

Giving a casual shrug of his shoulder, he says, "It is what it is."

My lips purse, but he's right. I chew on my bottom lip before deciding to spit out my next question. "What exactly *is* your relationship with Dante?"

The heaviness in his eyes lifts as a smirk curls his lips. "Does there have to be any definable relationship?"

I think about the convoluted relationship I have with Cain and Oliver and wonder how the fuck one goes about defining that. "No, I guess not. I think I'm just confused."

He gives my hand a reassuring squeeze. "You being here isn't stepping on anyone's toes. What Dante and I have is separate from what you and he have, or what you and I have."

"What do Dante and I have? Or you and I, for that matter?"

He smirks, lifting his hand away and standing to his full height. "If you have to ask that, then you haven't been paying attention." On that confusing note, he leaves me to mull over my conflicting thoughts. Once again, my prying has only raised more questions instead of providing answers.

IT'S PITCH BLACK OUT WHEN DANTE FINALLY MAKES AN APPEARANCE. IT'S been the same every night. Whatever it is he does for his father must keep him extremely busy. I internally sigh, missing the days when I was that busy. I have fuck all to do here, and it's slowly driving me insane. It's nearly midnight, and instead of being at work or out hunting down and killing abusive shitstains, here I am, plonked on the sofa, reading a book. A freaking book. I'm pretty sure I was in fifth grade when I last read a book. Not that it's not relaxing. This true crime biography I'm reading about two brothers who murdered their entire family is definitely my kind of book. It's just that I'm not used to sitting around all day with nothing to do. It makes me antsy and irritable.

His eyes immediately find me when he steps into the room, and I swear a little bit of tension runs out of him. As if he was worried I wouldn't be here when he got home. I dunno where the fuck he thought I'd go. Not that I've tried, but I'm pretty sure there's no escaping this glass and marble fortress.

Shrugging out of his suit jacket, he hangs it on the back of one of the stools at the breakfast bar and proceeds to remove a gun holster he had concealed underneath it. Another gun, tucked into the waistband of his pants, joins the holster and gun on the bar. Fully de-weaponized, he moves to look over Enzo's shoulder, who has been hunched over a laptop all evening. I have no idea what he's doing. After the brush-off, when I asked what he does for the Antonellis, I haven't bothered to ask any more questions. It's not like it matters—especially since we're planning on bringing down the entire organization.

Dante hovers for a moment before he moves to the bar cart and pours himself a glass of whiskey—his usual nightly routine. With the glass in hand, he saunters over to join me in the living area. As he claims the seat on the sofa opposite me, I close my book and set it down. It's not like I'd be able to concentrate on what I'm reading when he's staring at me the way he currently is. Instead, I watch him right back. He lifts his free hand to undo his top button and loosen his tie, and my gaze zeros in on the swollen, split skin along his knuckles, wondering who met the other end of his fists and why.

Dropping his hand, he lifts the glass to his lips. I silently observe all of it. The way his lips wrap around the rim of the glass. How his Adam's apple lifts when he swallows. The languid lick of his lower lip. We've barely spoken since our kiss. I'd surmise he was just giving me some space, but that doesn't really seem like Dante's style. It only raises more questions about why he'd be keeping himself at a distance now. Hasn't he got me exactly where he wanted? He'd said as much himself.

As I sit opposite him, it confuses me how I can feel so comfortable in his presence. Maybe we've just been playing this song and dance around one another for so many weeks now, that the normal reactions I should be experiencing under his hungry gaze no longer register. Weeks of having him watch me at the club have rendered me immune. I no longer feel that shiver of awareness that I felt that night in the alley or again in Franny's office. That's not to say I'm relaxed in his presence, because I think that would be impossible when he looks at me like that. But something has shifted between us, and I'm definitely no longer afraid of him. Well, I'm no longer afraid that he'll physically hurt me.

Lifting my gaze to meet his amber eyes, I clear my throat. I never know what to say when I'm around him. Enzo, I find surprisingly easy to talk to. Especially now that he's no longer keeping secrets and pretending to be someone he's not. But Dante is a whole different enigma to unravel. I've barely cracked the surface of who he is, and unlike Enzo, who offers up information without issue, with Dante, I have to work for every morsel I get from him.

"So," I begin. "You're like the main assassin for your father, right?" It might not be the best conversation to start with him, given he'll probably shut me down and refuse to tell me anything, but at least killing people is something I can relate to.

"I'm in charge of our problem-solving sector. Yes."

I snort at that description. "It seems to keep you busy."

A microscopic smile curls up the very corner of one side of his lip. It's barely more than a twitch, and if I'd blinked, I'd have missed it. "We have many enemies."

"So it's mostly people who threaten your family that you... dispose of?"

He gives a nod of acknowledgment. "*Anyone* who is perceived as a threat."

I flick my gaze to Enzo, finding him watching our conversation from his spot at the dining table. Focusing back on Dante, I ask, "Including one of your own if they turned on you?"

"If need be."

I can't help wondering if he'd kill me if he found out what the Rejects and I have planned. I'd rather not find out. I might not have any concerns about him hurting me right now, but that doesn't mean the same could be said if he found out what I'm really up to.

"And is it just assassination-style killings, or are we talking painful torture sessions and hours of suffering?"

Enzo stifles a snort of laughter behind his hand, while Dante just seems slightly confused and mildly amused by my question. "Depends on the situation."

"I'd be interested in tagging along next time." I'm by no means expecting an immediate agreement, but *god,* am I bored here and desperately missing the outlet being the Reaper provides me. Until now, I hadn't realized just how much of myself was intertwined with the Reaper's persona. Over the years, the Reaper and I have merged until we've become the same being. Without the regular outlet provided by hunting and killing those deserving of meeting their end at my hands, I have nowhere to channel the daily anger and energy that courses through me.

There's another amused and unhelpful snort from Enzo. However, my request is so out of left field that I manage to gain a reaction from Dante, whose eyebrows raise in surprise. "No." His blank refusal doesn't surprise me.

"Why not?"

He presses his lips together, not entirely having an excuse for why. He just doesn't want me to go. "It might distress you," he eventually answers.

I have to force my features to remain impassive, and I notice Enzo's shoulders jostling in my peripheral vision as he laughs silently. Quirking a brow at Dante, I argue, "I've seen plenty of fucked-up shit in my life. I'm sure I can make it through one killing."

Before Dante can argue again, Enzo speaks up. "You could let her watch today's video. If she makes it through that, then let her tag along next time."

Dante turns in his seat to glower at Enzo, who just shrugs. Of course, Enzo knows I can more than handle myself. He wants me to come clean to Dante about the Reaper, so he probably thinks coaxing Dante to include me will encourage me to do just that. It won't. I don't have the same confidence as Enzo that Dante won't turn on me when he finds out who I truly am at my core. Dante seems to like that I stand up to him and I won't back down, but he sees me as some woman who was barely getting by, dancing on stage for money, before he came along and whisked me off my feet. Finding out I'm the Reaper could put me in opposition to him. Especially if he found out I've disposed of his men in the past. After all, the Reaper doesn't discriminate. An abuser is an abuser. I don't give a shit if they're an Antonelli, a Bastard, or whatever other stupidly-named gang or Family member.

"What video?" I pipe up before Dante can put his foot down.

Enzo gestures with his head for me to come over. As I get to my feet, Dante jumps up too. "No," he barks. "She shouldn't see that shit."

I don't know if that's sweet or insulting. Either way, I quickly scamper out of his reach and circle around him to the dining table. He's hot on my heels, and his hand circles my wrist as I reach Enzo's side, yanking me backward.

My back collides with his chest. "Hey!" I snap, tilting my head back to glare up at him. Not that he's looking at me, too busy spearing Enzo with a deathly glare. However, it doesn't seem to have the intended impact as Enzo presses a button, and in the next second, the sound of flesh pounding against flesh is heard throughout the room.

Dante still has a firm grip on my wrist as I step forward to see the laptop screen, and Enzo turns it toward me, so I have a better view. I watch as a shirtless Dante throws his fist into some guy's face. He's already beaten bloody, his identity indiscernible. With every punch, the muscles on Dante's back bunch and flex, highlighting the force he's putting behind each one.

When he's breathing heavily and his knuckles are split and bloody, he stops, moving to something out of view of the camera. My eyes search the rest of the room, noting the bare walls and lack of light, the drain strategically placed in the center of the room, right underneath the chair holding today's victim. From what I can tell, it's some purpose-built kill room. I guess when you have as many enemies as the Antonellis probably do, you most likely need a kill room. Probably more than one, actually.

Dante turns to face his victim with something I can't discern clasped in his hand. He immediately starts shaking his head and pleading for Dante to stop. "Tell me who you're working with, and this can all stop." The cold, dead tone of Dante's voice is chilling. "I'll put a bullet in your head. It'll be practically painless." With his chin against his chest, the man whimpers, but he stays silent.

Dante lets out a long, disappointed sigh before moving closer. The man's hands are tied to the arm of the chair, but that doesn't stop him from fighting against his restraints as Dante clamps a hand over the top of his, flattening his palm against the wood.

"Please," the man sobs, repeating the plea over and over. All of it falls on deaf ears as Dante shoves what looks like a nail into the tip of his index finger. The man shrieks, and even through the laptop speakers, it makes my eardrums hurt. Dante does the same to the other four fingers, until the man is a sweaty, trembling, muttering mess in the chair.

Reaching for the keyboard, Enzo pauses the recording and glances up at me.

However, I'm still staring at the frozen image of the guy in the chair. "Who is he?" I ask, my voice coming out flat and detached.

"He worked for a rival family that's been trying to take us down for years."

"You asked who he was working with."

"We suspect a small number of men have infiltrated our ranks."

Finally tearing my eyes away from the screen, I lift my gaze to meet Dante's. The second our eyes connect, I can feel him pushing at my barriers, probing as he tries to get a read on my thoughts. "What would happen if he or one of the others succeeded?"

"They won't." Dante's voice rings with confidence.

"But what if they did?"

"They'd have to kill every single one of us in the top ranks, but *if* they managed that, then they'd seize this part of the city and gain control over all our businesses and operations."

"They wouldn't stop there," Enzo speaks up, and I turn my head to look at him. "With their manpower and ours, they'd have the means to take the whole city for themselves."

My eyes widen, and my voice isn't as strong as I'd like when I ask, "Why haven't you taken the whole city? You have the means. Especially after The Feral Beasts left, you could easily have taken control."

"We weren't interested in it," Dante says, shrugging. "We wouldn't have gained anything from it. All we needed Black Creek for was the docks, and we have that. Better to let the Black Creek riffraff fight over the scraps left behind by The Feral Beasts."

My lips purse, hating his blasé tone. I don't exactly know if things would have been better if the Antonellis had stepped in—hell, they might have been worse—but the way Dante talks about the citizens of Black Creek, like we're beneath him and his family.

As if sensing the anger bubbling inside me, Enzo tries to smooth over the situation. "He doesn't mean it like that, Sawyer."

"No, of course not." I spit out the words, sarcasm dripping from every one as I glare daggers at both of them. "How could you possibly know the existence you were condemning the people of Black Creek to. I'm sure you had no idea how all the fights and battles and outright wars that were started over territory would result in numerous innocent deaths. The deaths of people just trying to get by and live their lives. The deaths of people who couldn't give two fucks about who owns what land.

"And the entire time, you just sat here, in your nice little kingdom dripping with money and power, and let us fight it out. I bet you had a nice laugh when you looked out your father's penthouse window and thought about us little vagrants running around below, barely surviving."

Fuming mad and seriously contemplating risking Dante's wrath to punch him in the face, I stomp off before I can follow through with that idea. Thankfully neither of them stops me as I storm out of the room and up the stairs, needing some space.

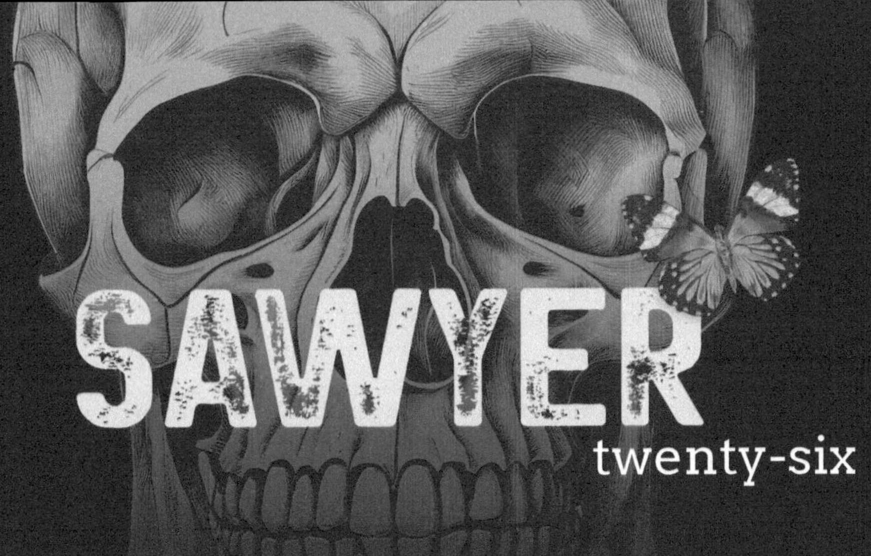

SAWYER

twenty-six

Even after taking a bath and calling Oliver, I can still feel the red-hot flames of anger licking at my insides. I'm not even sure why I got so riled up. What does any of it matter? Whether or not the Antonellis had taken an interest in Black Creek after The Feral Beasts left, wouldn't have made a difference. To be picked apart by gangbangers, or in the iron-clad grip of a sociopath—how the fuck do either of those options have a good outcome for the everyday people of Black Creek?

I groan as I press the heel of my palms into my eyes. I'm too worked up to go to sleep, and without a suitable outlet for everything I'm experiencing, I feel like I'm going insane. I don't think I can take much more of this.

"Uh, sorry. Am I interrupting?"

I jump upright, removing my hands from across my eyes as I turn to stare at Enzo. I hadn't even heard him come in. He's dressed all in black—black pants, black Henley, black boots—looking more reminiscent of a Reject than an Antonelli. It still doesn't quite suit him, though. He's too clean-looking.

"Erm, no." I'm sitting on my bed in only a thin tank top and my panties, but I'm used to wearing a lot less in front of men, so I don't bother to cover up. I just cross my legs so Enzo can sit down on the edge of the bed.

His eyes bore into mine for the longest time, yet I can't seem to look away as he pushes his way past my barriers and into my inner psyche. Maybe I'm just sick of keeping him out. Every day I've been here, Enzo has been proving himself. With his thoughtful gestures and the open way with which he answers any of my probing questions. And if there's ever something he can't answer, he says as much. He's upfront and honest, and so unlike the Enzo I've known for the last seven years. Even the way he quietly has my back when I argue with Dante—something that is starting to genuinely infuriate Dante.

"I wanted to apologize—"

I wave him off. "It's fine."

"It's not," he argues. "You shouldn't have had to grow up or live the way you did. I don't know if life would have been better or worse for you if Giovanni had taken an interest in the city and decided to claim it under the Antonelli name." He reaches across the space between us and slides his hand into mine. "Either way, I wish your life could have been different."

I duck my head as tears form in my eyes, and I swallow around a lump of emotion. He gives me a moment to get myself together before squeezing my hand. "I have something for you."

I look up into his dazzling green eyes. Even in the dark, they seem to sparkle. "Oh, yeah?" A playful smile plays along one side of my lips. "What is it?"

"You have to come with me to find out."

"But it's the middle of the night."

"Don't tell me you're afraid of the dark," he teases.

I snort. "Please. The dead of night is when the Reaper comes out to play."

He grins, and it's this devilishly handsome yet wicked thing that heats the blood in my veins and makes my pussy clench. "Then you better hurry up and get dressed." His gaze drops to my legs as I get to my feet, and I feel his eyes on me as I bend over to grab my jeans from the floor, stuffing my legs into them. Lacing up my boots next, I then grab my leather jacket and shove my arms into the sleeves. When I turn back around, he's still watching me intently. The heat in his eyes makes my breath catch, and my voice is breathy when I say, "I'm ready."

Clearing his throat, he gets to his feet and leads the way as I follow him through the house and out to the car. We drive in silence into the city until he pulls into a car park beside a rundown bar. The neon sign above the door that would have once flashed with the bar's name has been turned off, and it's missing several letters, making the name unreadable.

"What are we doing here?" I ask, turning to look at Enzo.

"I got a call that one of the names you gave me is here."

Now that piques my interest, and I return my gaze out the front windshield toward the front of the bar. I've been giving Enzo names of targets as I get them. So far, he's managed to strike several of them off the list, and the rest are still in the recon phase. "Which one?"

He pulls his phone out and looks at the screen. "A Mickey Farrs."

I ponder over his name for a second. "The guy who abused his stepdaughter?"

"Yup, that's the one." He tilts the phone toward me so I can see his photo. Bloodshot eyes, greasy hair, and a gaunt face look back at me. The guy is clearly an addict. Not that that is any excuse for what he's done.

I see red as I glower at the door of the bar, itching to storm in there and make him pay for the horror he put that girl through. With Herculean effort, I pull myself back from the edge. We have to be smart about this. "What's your plan?"

"Hey, you're the pro when it comes to this. I'm just here as backup."

His words render me mute as I stare at him, stunned. "Why didn't you get one of your guys to deal with him, like the others?"

There's a softness to his features as he gives me an easy smile. "I could tell you needed this." I return his smile with a genuine one of my own before returning my focus to the bar.

"Okay, you go in first. Don't draw any attention to yourself. Just grab a drink and sit somewhere where you have a clear line of sight of the guy. When I come in, act like you don't know me. No matter what he does, don't intervene. After I lure him outside, make a quiet exit."

Letting me know he's got it, he exits the car, and I watch as he heads inside. I wait another five minutes before climbing out of the vehicle. Stripping off my leather jacket, I throw it onto the passenger seat before pulling up the hem of my tank top and knotting it at one side, so it shows off my toned abdomen. I pull down the top, giving anyone who looks my way an eyeful of my tits and bending down to look in the door mirror, I run my fingers through my hair and pinch my cheeks, bringing a bit of color to them.

Satisfied, I strut into the bar with my head held high. The place isn't packed, but it's busy enough that only a few guys by the door notice me. I blatantly ignore them as I scan the room. Spotting Enzo, I meet his gaze, noting how his eyes drop to my chest and then lift again before I continue my search for my target.

I find him a couple of tables down, tucked in the corner of the bar, sitting alone. Fantastic. That makes this so much easier. He doesn't even notice as I approach. It's only when I'm standing right in front of his table that he bothers to look up. Not that his gaze ever reaches my eyes. Nope, he manages to get sidetracked by my boobs, which look like they're about ready to pop out of my top. "Hey," I purr, pushing a sexy husk into my voice. "Wanna buy me a drink?"

"Or we could skip the foreplay and just get out of here."

Even though I want to sneer at him, I adopt a seductive smile instead. "You read my mind."

I can feel his heat at my back and the brush of his hands along my bare skin as we leave the bar. The door has barely closed behind us before he grabs a fistful of my hair, pulling my body flush with his. I don't waste any time, throwing my elbow back and relishing the loud snap of cartilage as it connects with his nose.

His hold on my hair instantly loosens as his hands fly to his nose. "You fucking bitch!" he spits through a mouthful of blood. Spinning to face him, I give him a feral grin.

"You should know, I take that as a compliment." Reaching out, I shove him in the chest so his back smacks against the wall. A second later, the front door of the bar opens, and Enzo steps out. His brow quirks at the bloody state of the man in front of me.

"Help," the shithead pleads. "The bitch is psycho, man. She just attacked me out of nowhere."

I almost laugh at the empathetic look Enzo gives him. "Why are the hot ones always crazy?"

"Please," I scoff. "You like my crazy."

In an instant, Enzo's face morphs into something savage and hungry as he dismisses the man and turns his heated gaze on me. "I fucking love your brand of crazy."

Heat floods my skin, and I forget all about the asshole in front of us and why we are standing outside a seedy bar in the early morning hours. All I can focus on is Enzo and the static chemistry charging the air between us. The same electric energy has been building for the last week, while both of us ignored it in favor of the other chaos going on around us.

Movement breaks the moment as our victim tries to make a run for it, but Enzo's quick reflexes have him grabbing the back of the guy's shirt before he can get too far. "I don't think so," he snarls as he shoves the guy toward an alley running down the side of the building.

"L-look, I dunno what's going on, b-but you have the wrong guy. I didn't do nothin'."

"Yeah, that's what they all say," Enzo growls as we move further into the alleyway. When we're far enough down that no one walking by would notice us, Enzo pulls the guy to a stop. By now, he's trembling, but he hasn't shouted for help, so either he knows fuck all help will come even if he does or he thinks he can talk his way out of this.

"L-look," he tries again. "I-I can get you whatever you need. Coke, crystal, meth. You name it."

"Remember Cassy?" I snap, getting to the point.

"C-cassy? My kid? W-what about her?"

"You violated her."

"W-what? N-no. No, I didn't. Is that w-what that bitch is saying?" His temper flares and I can see the aggression glowing in his eyes. "I never touched the fucking slut!"

"Sure you didn't." I roll my eyes, having heard the same bullshit far too many times. "Look, you raped a kid. Just admit it, and I'll end it quickly for you."

"Fuck no," he snarls, furious now. "There's no fucking way I'm going down for that. I told you, bitch, I didn't fuckin' do it."

"So you're saying this isn't your cum in her underwear?" Enzo questions, pulling a pair of pink lace panties from his pocket and tossing them to the guy.

"No. Those aren't even hers."

"How can you be sure?"

"'Cause hers are cotton."

"Now, how the fuck would you know that?" I demand.

"Wait, what? No. T-that's not what I meant." The guy continues to ramble on, but I'm no longer listening. I never needed a confession from him, I just like making him sweat it out. As if sensing I'm done with this shit now, Enzo hands me his gun.

"Whoa, whoa, whoa," the soon-to-be-dead asshole starts up. Before he can try to make another break for it, Enzo reaches out and grabs hold of his top again, holding him in place while I flick the safety off. Without any fanfare, I put a bullet through the middle of his face, obliterating his previously shattered nose. The noise of the gun going off ricochets around the alley, but as expected, no one rushes to see what's going on, and as the ringing in my ears disappears, I turn to Enzo.

"Feeling better?"

I smile serenely. "Much better."

My outburst seems to have only served to push Dante further away, and I don't see him at all for the next week.

On Thursday morning, I walk into the large, open-plan, kitchen-living-dining area to find the whole room covered in every shade of white or ivory known to man.

"What the fuck is all this?" I ask, scrunching up my nose at the glaringly white, puffy dresses spread over every available surface in the living room and hanging from rails that have been wheeled in.

"You have to choose a wedding dress," Enzo states, coming over and handing me a cup of coffee. Thank god. It's too fucking early to deal with this crap without caffeine.

I groan. "I really couldn't care less about what dress I wear to a wedding I don't even want to attend."

He rolls his eyes at my attitude. "Fine." Striding past me, into the middle of the rails of dresses, he goes through them until he finds what must be the most hideous one of the bunch. It's got frills around the neckline and long sleeves—with more fucking frills around the wrists—and a big puffy skirt. "This one will do, then."

"God, no." I shake my head.

He smirks, knowing he's got me. I don't give a shit about any of this, but I am not about to let him force me into a hideous dress. Glowering at him, I sigh and begin to peruse the stacks with my coffee still in hand. I dismiss dress after dress, and I'm starting to think I'm not going to find anything remotely suitable. I'm flicking through dresses on the last rail when I spot one hidden between two more huge, princess-type dresses— why the fuck are most of them that style? Digging it out, I hold it in front of me. It's not like any of the others. It's sheer white lace, with a corset bodice and thin lace straps around my upper arms. Unlike all the others, it drops straight to the ground, with a short train puddling on the floor.

I carry it over to the folding screen that's been set up in the corner of the room. Stripping out of my clothes, I step into the dress. There are a pair of white Louboutin heels on the floor, and I'm unsurprised to find they fit perfectly as I slip my feet into them and turn to look at my reflection in the mirror hanging on the wall behind me. The dress fits like a glove, hugging my curves and falling to the floor. Holding the bodice to my chest, I step out from behind the screen, calling Enzo's name. "Can you do the buttons up the back?"

I'm too busy looking down at the dress, ensuring it's sitting just right, so it takes me a second to realize he hasn't responded or moved to help. I look up to see what he's doing, but I find him staring at me with a look I've never seen on him before. A mixture of lust and possession that burns like a raging inferno, so hot that I can feel the heat of the flames from here as they lick my skin.

"Enzo." I barely recognize my own voice, but it's enough to snap him out of his trance.

He clears his throat. "Sorry?"

"Can you, uh, do the buttons?" I repeat, feeling the heat in my cheeks as I turn so he can see my exposed back.

"Oh, yeah." He moves toward me until I can feel him at my back. I lift my hair, pulling it over my shoulder so he can see what he's doing. The move exposes my neck, and I can feel his warm breath on my skin as his fingers softly stroke down my back. I shiver, and my breathing is ragged. He starts to slowly do the buttons, and when he's finished, he runs his hands along my shoulders. His body moves in closer, pressing against me, and his lips are right by my ear as he murmurs, "You look so beautiful."

I slowly turn to face him, a move that dislodges his hands from my shoulders. They find a resting place on my hips instead, and my own come up to rest on his shirt, over his pecs. I can feel his erratic heartbeat as I glance up at him through my eyelashes. His head lowers as I lift mine, static electricity charging the air between us as we both lean in for a kiss—*the* kiss. The one we've both been flirting around for weeks now. Our lips are a hairsbreadth apart when the sound of the front door has us both jumping apart, and I look over his shoulder just as Dante walks into the room. He casts one long, lingering look over my dress before he grits his teeth and storms out of the room without a word.

"For someone forcing *me* to marry *him*, he doesn't seem to want to spend any time with me these days."

Enzo laughs, but it's lacking its usual characteristic humor that I've come to enjoy. He reaches down, subtly adjusting himself in his pants. "He's trying to give you time to adjust. Seeing you like that..." His scorching hot gaze trails over me. "Any warm-blooded man would want to tear that dress off and fuck you until you realize you belong to only him."

My lips part, a breathless, "Oh," escaping them as Enzo takes a step back, before turning on his heel and striding toward the door. Just before he exits, he turns back to face me.

"That's the dress. I'll get the others taken away."

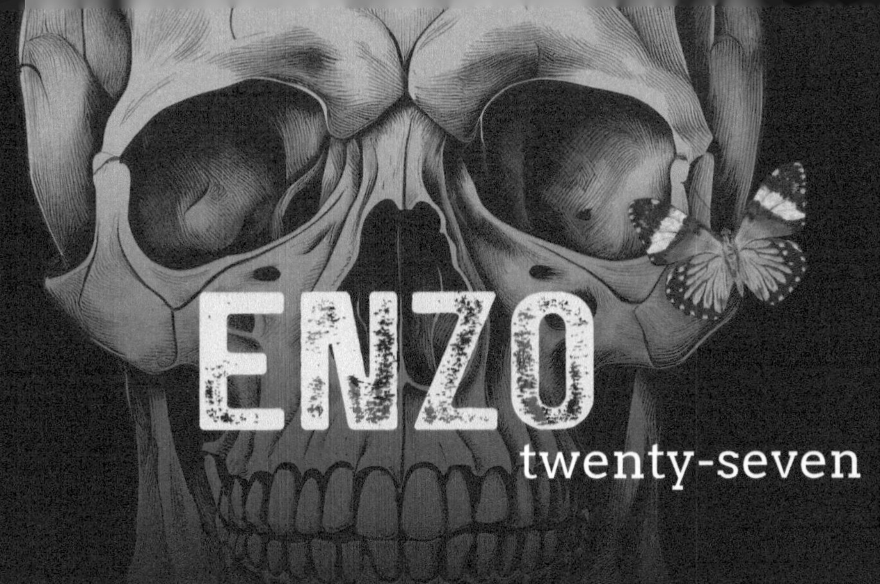

twenty-seven

"**I**'ll be back in a couple of hours," I remind Sawyer as she gets out of the car. The wedding is only a couple of days away, and the stress is getting to her. So when she asked if she could spend some time with her brother, how could I refuse? Things between us have come a long way in the last month. I wouldn't say she trusts me, but she's finally letting her guard down and opening up a bit. During all those meetings I had with her in G&T, all I wanted was for her to talk to me, to give me a genuine smile. I finally have that, and I can't get enough.

Dante's pissed as all hell. He's still of the opinion that she's solely his, but if the last few weeks have shown me anything, it's that there's absolutely no fucking way I'm losing this girl now. She's even more beautiful when she lets down her guard. And the cold, detached way she shot Mickey. Fuck, who doesn't love a woman who can smile at you serenely one moment and kill a man in cold-blood in the next.

"I know. I'll see you then." She closes the door, and I watch as she heads into her apartment building before pulling onto the street.

I drive back into Antonelli territory and park in the underground car park at Bella Donne, the casino. Getting out, I walk over to the elevator, and when it opens, I press the button for the tenth floor. The building houses the casino on the ground floor and several floors of private suites and rooms for hire above that, but the top three floors house the powerhouse of the Antonelli Empire. They are composed of offices, meetings, and conference rooms. Dante has been hiding out here all week, and it's his office that I head straight for.

"Hey," I greet when I walk in unannounced. Lifting his head, he frowns before focusing back on his computer.

"You shouldn't be here."

"We needed to talk, and you've been avoiding the house recently."

His only response is a non-committal grunt. Restraining my eye roll, I drop into the chair opposite his desk. "You know what happens when you bottle everything up."

I cock a brow when he flicks his gaze to mine. "Yeah, and I've never heard you once complain."

"And I'm not. But you can't pull the same shit with Sawyer. She doesn't deserve for you to go silent on her and not communicate, then fuck all that frustration out on her."

There's a weighted silence before he finally leans back in his chair and turns to face me directly. "I don't know how to be any other way."

"So, learn. Start by telling me why you're avoiding the house."

He blows out a breath. "Every time I'm around her, she wants to talk to me."

I struggle to suffocate my snort. "Yes, girls like to talk. It's an internationally known fact."

His eyes narrow on me, not appreciating my tone. "When I watched her at the club, it was different. She was always busy..." he trails off with a shrug.

"You don't know how to talk to her," I deduce. "Doesn't look like you've been doing a piss poor job so far."

He scoffs, clearly not agreeing, but he doesn't elaborate. I don't need him to. I've watched enough of his interactions with her. Yeah, she stormed off after the last time they spoke, but for the most part, Sawyer doesn't seem to mind that he's not the most communicative of people. Yeah, the fact that he doesn't answer many of her questions pisses her off, but I'm pretty sure she's coming to expect that from him.

"That night was as much about her as it was about what you said," I try to explain. "She's going stir crazy locked up in that house with nothing to do."

"She's not going back to the club," Dante immediately barks out.

I sigh. Praying to a higher power for some patience. "I'm not saying that she is. But she needs something to do. Sawyer is a woman who is used to working all day. She's not made for a mafia housewife life. She won't be happy sitting around the house all day, going to brunches and waiting for you to come home. She needs a purpose."

The lines on Dante's forehead have deepened the more I talk. "So I should give her a job to do."

"That would be a good start."

He gives a curt nod. "I'll think about it."

Well, I guess that's all I could ask for. "You're also not going to form any sort of relationship with her if you aren't around. You're getting married in three days, and then what? Imagine how this must all feel for her. She's marrying someone she doesn't really know, all because you forced her hand."

I don't say anything more about the wedding. Honestly, as the day approaches, more and more questions arise. It's evident Sawyer doesn't want to marry him, yet she hasn't tried to run or talk Dante out of it. I know it's not because she's scared of Giovanni and hiding behind Dante for protection. That's just not her style.

But instead of raising my concerns or asking Sawyer what's going on, I've kept my questions to myself. It's all purely selfish. I don't want to destroy what I've been working so hard to build these last few weeks, and that's precisely what would happen. Honestly, I'm secretly hoping she's maybe just starting to see this unusual setup for the good thing it could be. The situation may not be ideal, but it's got to be better than the life she was living in that tiny apartment, living paycheck to paycheck. I know Dante is hard work, but he'll come around eventually, and when he does, the three of us could have a nice life. We'd take care of her brother, and she wouldn't ever have to worry about food or money again. I'm sure Dante could even be convinced to let her continue her reaping. And if he can't, I'm more than happy to sneak out in the middle of the night with her.

"She'll get used to it," is Dante's less than stellar response. He's used to living life his way and expecting everyone around him to bend to his will. Even I rarely fight him, but Sawyer won't cave that easily. She's going to give him hell, and he doesn't even know it.

I don't bother arguing with him. He'll find out in due course. I'm more than happy to sit back and watch as my little Spitfire completely tears apart his life and makes him confront all those feelings he's got locked up inside himself somewhere.

"Any new issues?" I ask, changing the topic.

"Nothing. Was just checking on the men's assignments. I'm still trying to find someone to replace Alex. Franny's threatening to quit every day if I don't find someone ASAP."

I snort. "She'll never actually do it." Franny is like a fucking institution at Belle Donne. In her heyday, she used to work the floor, but when her youthful beauty started to fade, she moved to work in the back office. She's a hard-ass, old crone, but she gives a shit about the girls that work there, which is more than can be said for a lot of the other clubs under our purview. Franny might run the back office, but numbers are not her thing, so I can only imagine the grief she's been giving Dante.

"What about the Reaper Rejects?" I ask, changing the subject. With spending my days with Sawyer, I'm out of the loop more than usual, and Dante has been running point on finding the culprit of the club explosions.

"It was definitely them."

I purse my lips. "What are we going to do about it?"

"No one crosses us and lives."

The ringing of his phone cuts him off, and the look he gets every time his father calls flashes across Dante's face.

"Yeah," he answers, the word barely more than a grunt. "We'll be there."

"Father wants to see us at Paradiso," he states, hanging up.

I glance down at my watch, frowning. "Now? It's the middle of the afternoon."

Dante just shrugs, not knowing any more than I do. He doesn't seem in any hurry to jump to his father's orders as his focus returns to the computer, and I take the opportunity to ask, "Do you honestly think marrying Sawyer will stop your father from going after her? You know what he's like when he doesn't get his way."

The infuriating thing is that it's got nothing to do with Sawyer or who she is. His father just wants to ensure he keeps Dante under *his* control. Dante spears me with one of his signature terrifying looks that would have lesser men's hearts sputtering to a stop.

Neither of us has ever spent much time dwelling on Giovanni. We've both just accepted that this is our lives until he has the common decency to die. Then Dante would be in charge, and the plan was that I'd be at his side. Together we'd rule the Famiglia our way. But that's no longer the case. Other than the day he agreed to make Sam his Consigliere, we haven't discussed it, and now I have no idea what the game plan is. I have no doubt Dante has been trying to find some way out of it, but I'm not sure he'll find one. Those vows are binding—as are all in the Antonelli Family. It's why Giovanni never agreed to make it official when Dante told him *I* was going to be his Consigliere.

"I won't let him touch a hair on her head." The mix of vitriol and certainty in his glacial tone knocks me back. The sheer, unadulterated anger pouring off of him is so out of place for Dante that it takes a minute for me to wrap my head around it. Of course, anger is the most common emotion Dante identifies with, but I don't think I've ever seen it to this degree. Sawyer really brings out the darkest part of him. Dante has always been a terrifying force to be wary of, but he'd be capable of just about anything for her.

"And if he does?"

Dante's hatred for his father has solidified over the years. I've stood and watched as the awe-inspired look he had in his eye as a young boy slowly faded, until his father snuffed it out altogether with one savage cut-down after another. He thought he was molding his son into a colder version of himself, and in one respect, he was. But in doing so, Giovanni destroyed any loyalty Dante ever felt toward him. I can see it clear as day in his eyes now. Dante may have been happy to sit back and obey his father's orders, but he's reached the end of his rope. If his father pushes him any further, he's going to start pushing back. And if he so much as looks at Sawyer the wrong way, he'll experience first-hand exactly what Dante is capable of.

"I'll kill him."

As much as I'd love to watch Giovanni meet his end at his son's hands, today is not that day, and if we put him off any longer, he'll only get pissy, which in turn will aggravate Dante. Something none of us needs to deal with right now. So, Dante finishes up his work, and we head over to Paradiso.

"Ah, son, good of you to join us," Giovanni greets us with his usual cold smile as we step into the club. There's an uncharacteristic glimmer of excitement in his eyes which has the hairs on the back of my neck standing to attention. "I was worried you were going to miss the show."

My eyes dart around the room before narrowing suspiciously on Dante's father. We have to come to this fucked up boys club once a month, but Dante and I never partake in the same *entertainment* as the other men. Unlike these sick fucks, we don't get off on tying up unwilling girls, choking them into unconsciousness and fucking their lifeless bodies, or whatever other fucked-up shit they need to get off.

However, Giovanni has never ordered a meeting here in the middle of the day, and as I study the men around him—his closest and most loyal advisors—something feels off. Seats have been set up around a makeshift stage, and instead of the usual explicit scenes, every man has his dick firmly tucked away in his pants.

Dante doesn't say anything, but his posture is tense as he takes in the room, most likely noting the same differences I have. His father waves him over to the empty seat beside him at the front of the stage, and after a fraction's hesitation, which would go unnoticed by anyone other than me, he does as is expected.

"What's going on?" Dante asks, careful to sound disinterested.

"My only son is getting married," Giovanni states loudly, lifting his glass in the air. His statement is followed by a round of cheers as everyone raises their glass. "That deserves something special." The feeling that something isn't right only intensifies as I once again cast my eyes around the room. His father couldn't give two shits about the upcoming wedding. He claps Dante on the shoulder, grinning maliciously at him.

"You've found yourself such a nice piece of ass"—he pauses deliberately—"I thought it was only fair that everyone got a look before she was locked down."

What the actual fuck does that mean?

Dante's posture is rigid, his spine ramrod straight. His fingers twitch at his side, the only sign that it's taking everything in him not to react to his father's words.

As if staged for an extra flare of dramatics, a spotlight comes to life above the stage, drawing everyone's attention, and I gasp. A wide-eyed Sawyer is gagged and bound to a bed wearing only her underwear. She blinks rapidly against the glare of the harsh lights, her eyes bouncing around the room. Dante steps toward her, the movement snagging her attention as she swivels her gaze to his. I see the second she recognizes him. Her eyes latch onto him, and I can practically hear her begging him to help her.

Giovanni's hand snaps out, grabbing a hold of his son's arm and stopping him. "Don't even think about it." The thread of warning in his tone is not to be dismissed, something Dante must realize as he doesn't make any other attempts to get to Sawyer.

"You want me to fuck her in front of you all?" Dante hisses.

His father's cold laughter is chilling. "Oh no, son. You have the rest of your life to fuck her. I think it's only fair one of my men get the opportunity to give her a go."

Fuck. Shit. Fuck. I scan the room, taking a mental tally of how many men are in it. Twenty. Too many. There's no way Dante and I can take on that many and get out alive. And any fight we put up will only mean more significant consequences for Sawyer. My panicked gaze returns to Sawyer, who is struggling against her restraints, having apparently heard Giovanni. Tears run down her face as she tugs on the bindings around her wrist, but they won't give, and she just ends up lying on the bed, breathing heavily as her chest rises and falls with the exertion.

"And unless you want me to put a bullet between those pretty eyes of hers, you're going to sit here and watch."

Silence follows his words while Dante struggles to get himself under control. Eventually, he spits out, "Who?"

His father's grin only widens as he turns to look at me for the first time since we entered. My blood runs cold as Dante turns to follow his father's line of sight. His ferocious gaze meets mine as Giovanni grins. "I think Lorenzo deserves the honors."

This has got to be a fucking nightmare. There's no way Giovanni thinks I *deserve* anything. He knows if I fuck Sawyer, it will affect my relationship with Dante. It's what he wants. He's aiming to isolate Dante. His best friend and lover fucking his soon-to-be wife—there's no way that can end well for any party involved. Giovanni's a smart, conniving man. He's hoping this will doom Dante's marriage before it's even begun and create a rift between Dante and me, ensuring the weapon he's spent thirty years honing doesn't slip out of his grasp.

"Up on the stage, boy. Better fuck her like her life depends on it." He laughs at his own joke, leaving the end of his threat unspoken... *because her life does depend on it.*

I hold Dante's hardened gaze, ignoring his silent demand for me to disobey his father. We both know that's not an option. Slowly—so fucking slowly—I shrug out of my suit jacket and fold it over an empty chair before walking toward the stage. Sawyer's frantic gaze finds me as I step into the pool of light. I wonder what I look like in her eyes right now. Can she see my inner turmoil, or does she only see the outer mask of indifference I'm struggling to keep on? No doubt, my gaze is as cold as Dante's as I try to make it seem like I'm as detached and sick in the head as the other men in this room. If I don't, if Giovanni catches even a whiff that I care for her, he will order one of his other men up here instead. As bad as the current situation is, it would be so much worse if it were someone else. Sawyer may not trust me, but at least there's chemistry between us. I've seen the way she looks at me when she thinks I'm not paying attention—the lust brimming in her eyes that night in the alley, the way she leaned into my touch when she was trying on her wedding dress. She may not trust me, but she wants me, which is the only comforting morsel I can cling to as I approach her.

She stares up at me with wide, pleading eyes, but I deliberately look away, instead running my gaze over her toned body. Even now, under these circumstances, she's beautiful, and it doesn't take long for the fabric at the front of my pants to become tight.

I move to straddle her, and she bucks against me. Her efforts to dislodge me are futile, and her energy soon wanes. Keeping most of my weight on her midsection, I lean forward to remove the ball gag from her mouth.

"Enzo," she pleads in a quiet, teary voice. "Please."

I hear snickers from behind me, and my lips purse.

"Shut up," I snarl loud enough for the others to hear. In a quieter voice, intended for just her, I murmur, "I'm so sorry, Spitfire." She swallows roughly but doesn't bother to waste her breath pleading again. Dropping the gag on the sheets beside her, I slowly lower my hand until I can wrap my fingers around her throat. "Forget about them," I say in a stern yet soft voice. "It's just you and me. Just focus on me."

Giving her throat a quick squeeze, I lower my hands, cupping her breasts through her bra. I brush my thumbs over her nipples before tweaking one. "Scream," I order as I pretend to twist her nipple painfully. Instead, I just roll it between my fingers. She cries out, and another round of snickers resonates from behind me. "They want me to hurt you. To make this as humiliating and painful as I can. But I know you better than they do. I know how strong you are. I know what you can handle." My gaze lifts to meet her eyes as I push her tits together, fondling them. "I know you don't trust me, but I *need* you to trust me with this. I won't do anything you won't enjoy." Her tongue flicks out to run along the seam of her lips, and she gives a sharp nod of agreement before I move my hands lower, trailing the lining of her panties.

I dig into my pocket and lift out a pen knife. Holding it up in front of her, I flick it open, and she gasps loudly. I smirk down at her as she begins to squirm beneath me, knowing we're both in on the game now. She falls deathly still as I glide the blade down the middle of her abdomen until I reach her panties. Fisting the thin fabric in my other hand, she whimpers and starts up her pleading again as I pull it away from her body before pushing the blade through and cutting a line up the center of them. I pretend to toy with her, scraping the tip of the blade over the milky skin of her abdomen while I slip my other hand between the torn fabric of her panties. I brush my fingers lightly along her seam before finding her bundle of nerves and pressing the pad of my thumb against it. All the while, I keep my eyes on her face. A slight blush colors her cheeks, and her hips jerk as I push down. Her hooded eyes hold mine as I sink deeper, testing to see how wet she is.

My eyebrows hitch when I find her folds slick, and I smirk down at her. I flick the blade closed before leaning forward, sliding my hand around her throat again. The move brings my lips closer to her ear, and I whisper, "You dirty girl. So wet for me." I push my fingers inside her, and she stifles a groan as her eyes flutter shut. "Are you enjoying putting on a show for these sick fucks?"

Her teeth dig into her bottom lip as I fuck her with my fingers. Leaning back, I unbuckle my belt and push down my pants and boxers. Sawyer watches through hooded eyes as I fist myself, once, twice, before lining up at her entrance. "I've thought about coming inside this tight cunt of yours so many times, it's going to be a challenge not to explode the second I'm in there. Now, scream for me, Spitfire." I slam into her in one hard thrust as she tilts her head back and lets out a piercing scream. I swear I hear some guy come at her cry of pain, and I hope Dante took note so we can kill him later. Balls deep inside her, I pause. "This will be fast and rough, but I'm going to make sure you come at least three times before I finish." Her pussy clenches at that statement, and I pull all the way out before slamming back in. She emits another cry of pain, but desire sparkles in her eyes as I set a relentless pace that soon has her thrashing beneath me.

When she tightens around me, I wrap my hand around her throat for the third time and squeeze, cutting off her moan as she comes. Can't have the sick fucks behind us realizing she's enjoying this. I continue to pump into her as she convulses around me, before pulling out and flipping her over onto her stomach. With her hands and feet tied to the bed, her arms and legs end up crossing. The angle is probably bordering on painful, but I know my girl can take it. There's just enough give in the restraints for me to lift her ass up, before slamming into her again. She cries out, and my balls draw up at the new, tighter position.

"Fuck, Sawyer," I grunt in her ear before pushing her head into the mattress, stifling any sounds she might make. I keep up the same pace until she's coming around my dick for a second time. And still, I keep going, immediately driving her toward a third orgasm. Her skin is slick, her breathing ragged, but I know she has it in her. I slap her ass hard, and she whimpers into the mattress. The bright red handprint it leaves threatens to make me blow my load, and I have to distract myself by putting the same possessive mark on her other cheek. I grab two handfuls of her ass and spread her cheeks as I continue to fuck her, and when she comes for the third time, I finally let myself go, and my cum hits her inner walls as I grunt out my release, ensuring it's loud enough for the assholes to hear.

String after string of cum spurts out of me, until I'm certain she must be full of it. With my dick still inside her, I lean forward to whisper in her ear. "You did so good, Spitfire. I definitely want a repeat of this, ideally without an audience next time." She stiffens at the reminder that we're not alone, but I soothe her as I stroke down her spine. "It's okay. They should be satisfied with that. I'll get you out of here soon."

Pulling out of her, I climb off the bed and tuck myself away without sparing her a second glance. "Meh. Nothing to write home about. I prefer whores with a tighter cunt," I say with a shrug as I get down from the stage, hoping that what I said to Sawyer is true and that performance will have been enough to appease Giovanni.

Giovanni laughs. I have to avoid meeting Dante's gaze as I stride toward him, and I make a point of walking past him, taking up my usual bodyguard position behind his seat.

"Are we done here then?" Dante grits at his father.

Giovanni waves his hand dismissively toward Dante. "Yeah, yeah." He snaps his fingers to get the attention of someone hiding in the shadows of the room, and in the next second naked girls step out and approach us. The men quickly snatch them up, dragging them into their laps or forcing them to their knees, and I hear the sound of people fucking while Dante stomps toward the stage. He undoes Sawyer's restraints before shrugging out of his jacket. Draping it over her shoulders, he lifts her into his arms, and not looking at anyone, including myself, he goes straight to the exit. Ignoring Giovanni's lingering gaze, I grab my own jacket from where I left it and follow after him.

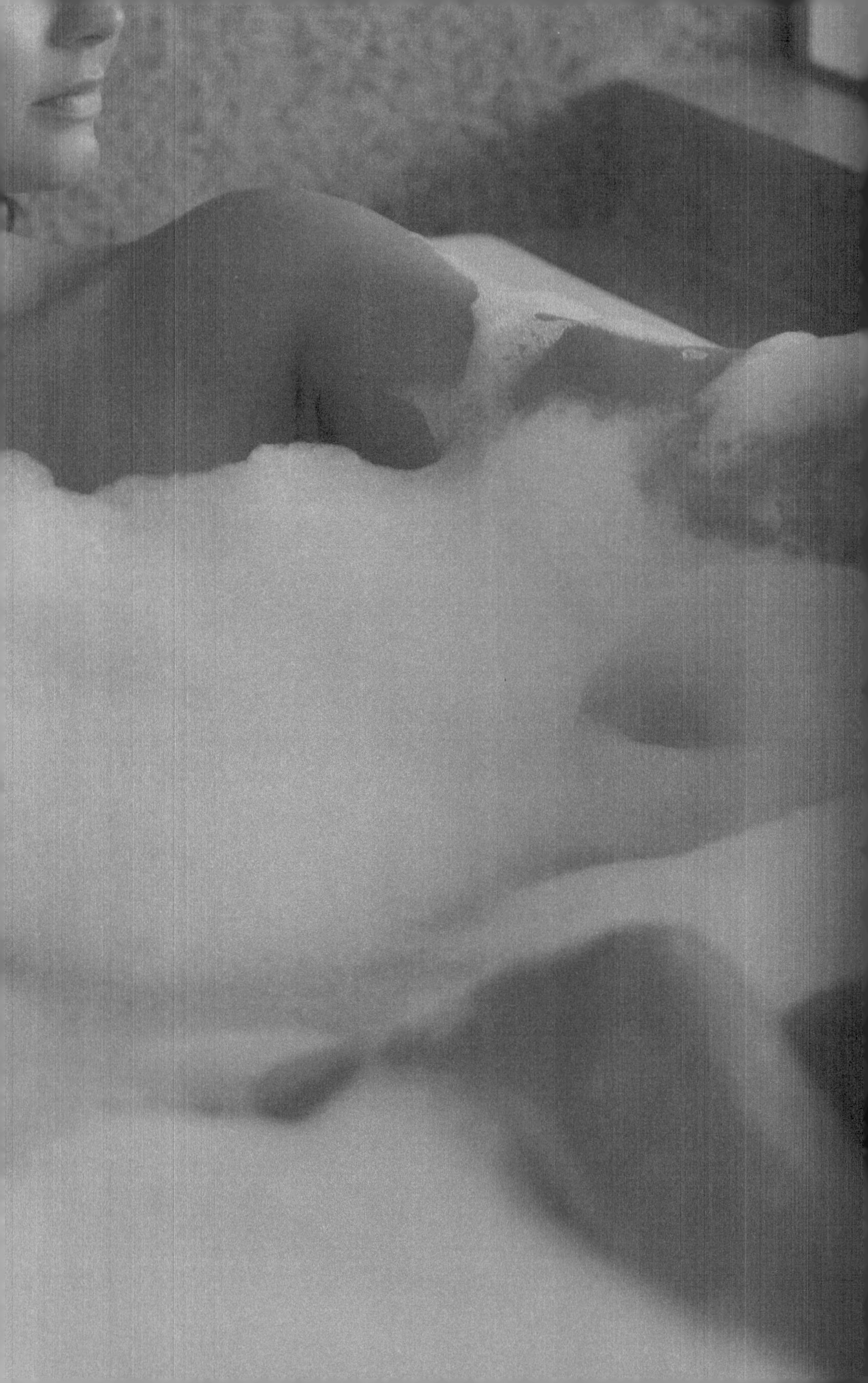

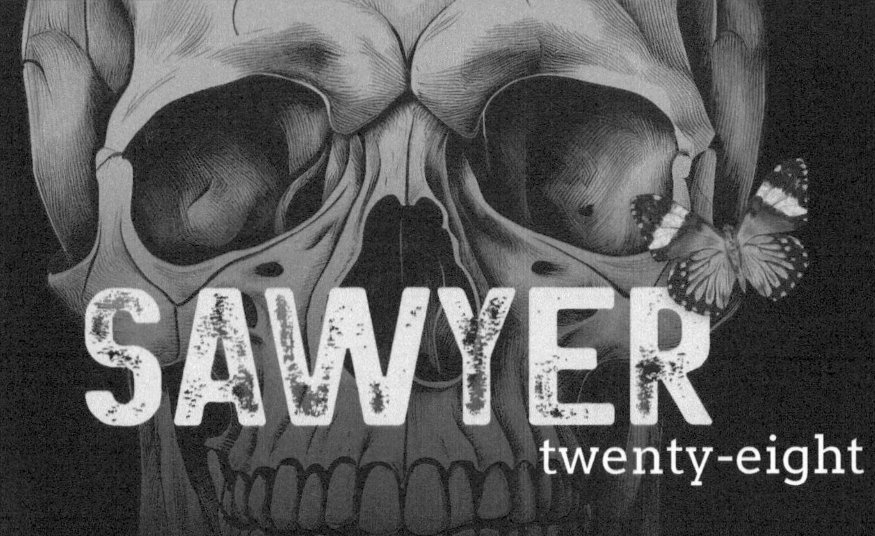

Dante bundles me into the back seat, and surprisingly he climbs in beside me. As soon as the door slams closed behind him, the dark tint of the windows blocking anyone's view from outside, he pulls me in against him, keeping his arms wrapped around me like bands of steel. My whole body trembles and I still can't wrap my head around what the fuck just happened. I'd blame the lingering effects of whatever drug they used to subdue me, but I'm sure it's the three orgasms Enzo gave me.

I lift my head as the driver's door opens, and Enzo slides in behind the wheel. He instantly lifts his eyes to meet mine in the rearview mirror. Now we're no longer in the presence of those sick old bastards, he's dropped the cold, apathetic look, and his deep green eyes swim with concern. I give him a weak smile, trying to reassure him I'm okay. He doesn't seem to buy it as he huffs out a breath before starting the car and pulling away from the curb, not that I blame him. I have no idea if I'm okay.

"I can't believe you fucking did that," Dante snarls at him.

"What else was I supposed to do?" Enzo barks back just as angrily. "If it wasn't me, it would have been one of those other bastards."

I push against Dante's chest, needing to find my inner strength. He somewhat loosens his hold on me, enabling me to sit up straighter. "I'm fine." My voice doesn't sound like mine, though. It's hoarse and exhausted sounding, and I know I'm running on fumes. I need to shower and crash—badly.

Enzo scoffs, and I glare at him through the mirror. "Then you're tougher than I am, because I am definitely *not* okay after that." His honest admission surprises me, and instead of scraping the bottom of the well for some defensive emotions, I sag against Dante, letting myself not be strong for a minute. His arms tighten around me again, and the three of us lapse into silence for the rest of the journey.

When we get back to the house, Dante carries me inside, setting me down in the hall. I can feel Enzo's dried cum on my inner thighs, and I feel disgusting, not knowing if anyone else touched me while I was unconscious. The thought alone has my stomach churning dangerously, and I hug Dante's jacket closer around me.

"Sawyer," Enzo calls out as I step toward the stairs. I spin and cut him with a glacial stare.

"No," I snap, before he can say another word. I can hardly stand upright, my legs are shaking so badly. "I need a bath and to sleep. Leave me alone. Please." My voice cracks over that final word, and I immediately look away as I turn and climb up the stairs, aware of the two of them watching me.

I make it back to my room and all but collapse into the tub, letting it fill up around me while I pour every single bath product I can get my hands on into the water. I rest my head against the side of the bath, my eyes drifting shut as I listen to the running water. My mind drifts back over today's events as I struggle to put the pieces together. Enzo dropped me off at my apartment, and then everything went fuzzy until I woke up tied to that bed and surrounded by sick bastards leering at me. Anger makes my blood boil as I remember the way they looked at me. I tried not to look at them while Enzo was fucking me, but when one of them laughed at my supposed pain, I couldn't help it. Watching them getting off on Enzo hurting me had me seeing red, and it was only Enzo's voice, his low grunts intended only for me, that brought me back from the brink.

I must fall asleep, as the next thing I know, I'm lying in lukewarm water, and the bathroom is silent. No taps running. I hear a faint shuffling sound and pry my eyes open, finding Enzo crouching beside the tub, watching me.

"Thought I told you I wanted to be alone." There's no conviction in my tone. I'm too exhausted to actually care that he's in here.

"Yeah, but you were flooding the bathroom. Figured I should come to make sure you weren't trying to drown yourself."

I poke my head over the side of the tub, noticing towels scattered all over the floor. "Oh." I sag back against the lip of the bath and fix my gaze on the ceiling above me.

"Talk to me."

I sigh, leaning my head to the side to meet Enzo's worried gaze. "Why? You were there." He frowns at me, and I return my focus to the ceiling. "Why?" I repeat after a long moment's silence.

"It was Giovanni's way of ensuring he still had control over his son." I think that over, but it doesn't make sense to me.

"How?"

"He was proving to Dante that he has the ultimate say over *everything* in his life. Including both you and me. And I think he's hoping this will isolate him. Giovanni wants to be the only one pulling his son's puppet strings. He knows Dante listens to me, and he's probably concerned he might start listening to you too."

I scoff. "He'd have to talk to me first." I don't know why it even annoys me that Dante's been avoiding me. Shouldn't that be what I want? In three days, the Rejects are going to storm into the church and Dante's supposed to die. I should be throwing up as many walls between Dante and me as I can. So why the hell does a painful twinge constrict my chest at the thought of never seeing him again?

"Just give him some time," Enzo says softly. "This is all new to him too."

Except we're basically out of time, and instead of wishing Dante and Enzo dead, I just want the damn asshole to talk to me.

"Tonight's events show that Giovanni is threatened by his son. He's trying to pit Dante and me against each other. He knows Dante better than anyone, so he knows how much it will bother him that I've fucked you."

I tilt my head, so I can look at him again. "Because I wasn't him, or because you weren't?"

"Either. Both. Does it matter?"

No, not really. "Better than anyone..." I begin, repeating his words. "But not you, right? *You* know Dante better than *anyone*."

"My father used to be Giovanni's Consigliere. They grew up together. He was his closest confidant. Dante and I grew up the same way, always around one another, destined to be best friends before we even understood the significance." He trails off, losing himself to his memories and not really confirming my statement.

I reach out to brush a wet, pruned finger along his arm, which is leaning on the side of the tub. His gaze snaps to mine as he's dragged back into the present. We stare at one another for a moment before he rolls his shirt sleeve up to the elbow and submerges his arm into the tub, pulling the plug. "Come on, let's get you out." He moves to grab a towel from the rail and wraps it around me before lifting me out of the bath, uncaring that water is seeping through the towel and turning his shirt see-through.

I wind my arms around his neck as he carries me into the bedroom. Setting me on the end of the bed, he moves to grab the first top he finds in my duffel before returning to me and handing it over. Like a true gentleman—which I know he is not—he turns, giving me an ounce of privacy while I quickly dry off and pull on the top—ironically one of Oliver's. He turns back around as I slip under the covers and begins undoing the buttons on his shirt. I get momentarily distracted as he shrugs out of it, showing off gorgeous bronzed skin and lean muscle. Next, his hands go to his belt, and I offer him the same respect he gave me, looking away as he steps out of them. I only look back at him as he slides into the bed beside me.

He leans back against the headboard, watching me cautiously. I hesitate for a moment before deciding *fuck it* and curl into him. His arm wraps loosely around me as I rest my head on his shoulder. For the first time since I woke up, I feel at peace, safe, and protected.

We sit there in silence for I don't know how long, before I ask, "What happened to your dad?" He's already told me he betrayed Giovanni and met his death because of it, but I don't know the particulars.

"One day, I woke up, and he'd been branded a traitor. He was tortured and killed, and I was forever seen as Judas' son. Someone not to be trusted; to be watched at all times."

"Why didn't Giovanni just ostracize you?"

His laugh is cold and lacks any humor. "That would have been far too easy. Why do that when he can keep me close and torment me every day." His hand draws lazy circles on the back of my arm as I relax into him. "But he didn't count on Dante. Giovanni thought he had him so fucked in the head that he wasn't capable of caring about anyone. And he nearly did. It just took Giovanni beating me half to death for that switch in Dante to flick on." I gasp, but he continues talking. "Ever since then, he's been battling with himself, trying to turn it on again, to keep it on." Sensing him looking down at me, I glance up at him through my eyelashes. "I'm pretty sure you're his hot wire."

We lapse into an easy silence after that, each of us lost in our own thoughts, and eventually, I drift into a dreamless sleep. The next time I wake up, it's dark outside, and I'm sprawled across Enzo, who is snoring softly. Leaning on my elbow, I look up at him. I can just about make out his peaceful expression. Needing to move onto my other side, I roll over, but I freeze when I find another naked chest. *What the fuck. There definitely weren't two hot Italian men in my bed when I fell asleep.*

I drag my eyes over his broad, muscular chest, unable to make out the various tattoos peeking out from beneath the sheets until I eventually reach his face. A small gasp escapes me as I find Dante lying there, his hand behind his head, watching me.

"What are you doing here?"

He just continues to watch me. He's always watching, cataloging, analyzing. Instead of answering me—the dude has issues with answering questions—he reaches out and gently tugs me to lie down beside him, my head resting on his chest.

"Just sleep, *mia vita.*"

I don't understand the meaning of his words, but they sound sexy as fuck in his sleep-thickened voice, and the way he softly strokes my hair with his fingers assures me it can only be a good thing as my eyes drift shut once again.

I SIT ON THE EDGE OF THE BED, MY LEG BOUNCING WITH NERVOUS ENERGY as I stare at the burner phone Cain gave me. It's all I've done for the last hour while I tried to work up the courage to do what I need to do.

I feel fucking awful knowing the situation I'm about to put him in, but I feel even worse when I picture Enzo or Dante lying dead amongst the rubble of the church. Ultimately, that image pushes me to press dial on his number.

Bringing the phone to my ear, I don't get a second to back out before Cain answers. "You okay?"

Ignoring his question, I just about manage to squeeze out a "hey."

"What's wrong?" I knew Cain would know the instant I spoke that something wasn't right. That's why I put off calling him for as long as I could, but the wedding is tomorrow, and this can't wait any longer. Both Dante and Enzo have been giving me plenty of space, so I've had far too much time to think, and although I know I'm asking Cain for a lot, I believe it's the right thing.

"Nothing," I lie. "I'm just tired."

"Just one more day," he promises.

"Yeah," I sigh, his words only ratcheting up my anxiety instead of easing it as he intended. My stress levels have been building with every passing day for the last week. On the one hand I need this stupid wedding over with, but on the other, I'm terrified that Dante and Enzo will go down with everyone else. Which is the reason for this call. "I need a favor," I eventually choke out.

"What is it?" Cain doesn't sound bothered, but I know as soon as I tell him what it is, he's going to get his back up about it. Not that I can blame him exactly.

I lick my suddenly dry lips. "I need you to let Dante and Enzo escape with their lives."

A deafening silence comes down the phone line, and if it weren't for the fact that I can still hear him breathing, I'd have thought we had lost connection. Instead, I wait him out.

"Why?" That one word is threaded with vitriol and warning, and I can picture him sitting behind his desk with his dark, Reaper Reject leader expression and clutching the phone so tightly that the plastic is probably at risk of cracking.

"Please," I plead instead of answering him. He doesn't want to hear my answer. It would only be further ammunition for why he *should* kill them.

"Red." It's a low growl, but I hear the strain behind it.

"Please," I repeat, closing my eyes against the onslaught of tears threatening to spill over. "I know what I'm asking. I *know*."

"Have they done something to you? Are they threatening you?"

"No. It's nothing like that. I just... *please*, Cain."

There's another drawn-out painful silence. My heart is pounding so fast that, for a moment, all I can hear is the roaring in my ears. What if he says no? I can't sit back tomorrow and let either of them die, but am I willing to betray Cain's trust and warn them? Fuck, I have no idea how I'll navigate that situation. I do know for sure that I can't knowingly let Dante or Enzo walk into that church tomorrow if they're going to die.

The sound of a loud smack reverberates down the line, making me jump. "Fine," he finally spits out in a furious tone.

The heavy boulder sitting on my chest lifts, and I feel like I can breathe for the first time in days. "Thank you," I murmur on a breath of relief.

"Don't thank me, Red. They might not die tomorrow, but I want a fucking explanation when this is over. And if I don't like it, they'll meet their end a different way."

That doesn't settle any of the unease squirming in my stomach, but he hangs up before I can argue. Not that I know what to say. There's a better chance that the gates to hell will open than there is of Cain accepting the fact that I've developed some sort of feelings for Dante and Enzo, and that's why he can't exact the vengeance he so rightfully deserves. Except, are Dante and Enzo really the ones that need to pay for what happened to Evie? They couldn't have been more than teenagers themselves. It's not fair that Enzo should be punished for his father's crimes, so why is it justifiable that they both pay for Giovanni's?

Tossing the cell onto the bed, I fall back against the bed covers and stare up at the ceiling. That's an argument for another day. One I don't look forward to. For now, I just have to hope all five of us can make it through tomorrow unscathed—and ideally, I'll come out of it an unmarried woman.

***

It's late, and the hallway is dark when I tiptoe out of my room. I've been tossing and turning for hours now, but my stomach is a riot of nerves, and my brain won't stop coming up with new and inventive outcomes for tomorrow—most of which are less than favorable.

With only socks on, I pad silently down the stairs and into the kitchen. Retrieving a glass from the cabinet, I fill it with water and, standing at the sink, I stare out of the large floor-to-ceiling windows while I sip from the glass. It's a full moon tonight, and its light reflects off the ocean, allowing me to glimpse the white foam of the waves as they flow up the beach.

Despite its tranquility, it does nothing to calm the chaotic storm brewing within me. My talk with Cain earlier only adds to my worry. After all of this is over, he's going to have questions. Questions that I need to answer. Except, I don't have any answers. Not any that make any sense, at least. Of course, that's assuming we all make it out of tomorrow alive. We have the element of surprise on our side, so I'm quietly hopeful things will go our way, but I've seen plans unravel in the blink of an eye plenty of times. I'm not naive enough to believe it will be as easy as we think it will be.

Sighing, I finish off the glass of water and rinse it in the sink before leaving it in the drying rack. I need to at least try and get some sleep for tomorrow, otherwise, I'll be no good to anyone. As I step into the hall, I notice a faint light coming from the other side of the house. Huh, I hadn't realized anyone else was up. Instead of continuing up the stairs like I probably should, I pivot and quietly move closer to the light source.

The warm hue of a lamp shines out from under the door to Dante's office and along one side, and as I get closer, I hear the low rumble of his voice. Only when I'm leaning against the door frame, right outside the office, can I make out what he's saying.

"Can confirm that it's the Reaper Rejects."

My whole body tenses, and I strain harder, desperate to hear what he's saying.

"There have been no other attacks since then."

Fuck, they must have figured out Cain and Oliver are behind the explosions. But how? I shake my head. The how doesn't matter.

"No." He grits out the word, clearly unhappy with whoever he's talking to and their response. "I'm on it, Father. They won't be a problem again."

Blood rushes in my ears, preventing me from hearing anything else. Not that I need to. I've heard enough. Moving slowly, I cautiously step away from the door and climb the stairs to my room. Only when the door shuts behind me and I sag against it do I let out the breath I was holding.

I rush across the room to where I hid my burner phone and dig it out, needing to ring Cain. However, when I have the phone in my hand, I pause. Do I need to tell him? It will incite an all-out riot if I do, and with the wedding tomorrow, nothing is going to happen between now and then. If I tell him, Cain might not spare Dante's and Enzo's lives, and even though Dante is sitting downstairs right this second planning the deaths of the two men I love, I know he's only following orders. Doing what is required of him; what his father wants.

Slowly, I lower my hand before dropping the phone onto the duvet. No, I don't need to tell them anything. By the time the sun sets tomorrow, the Antonellis will no longer exist. They'll have been obliterated from the face of the earth, and none of this will matter.

I'm lying awake, still wide awake and wired enough that you'd think I drank a gallon of coffee before bed, when I hear the soft thud of Dante's shoes on the carpet as he climbs the stairs. I stare at the bedroom door, listening to every small sound beyond it. His shadow darkens the gap at the bottom, and I swear I can practically sense him hovering there just beyond the wooden door. After a moment, he moves away, and I listen for the soft click of his door closing before I finally relax.

Tomorrow. It will all be over tomorrow. Just a few more hours to go.

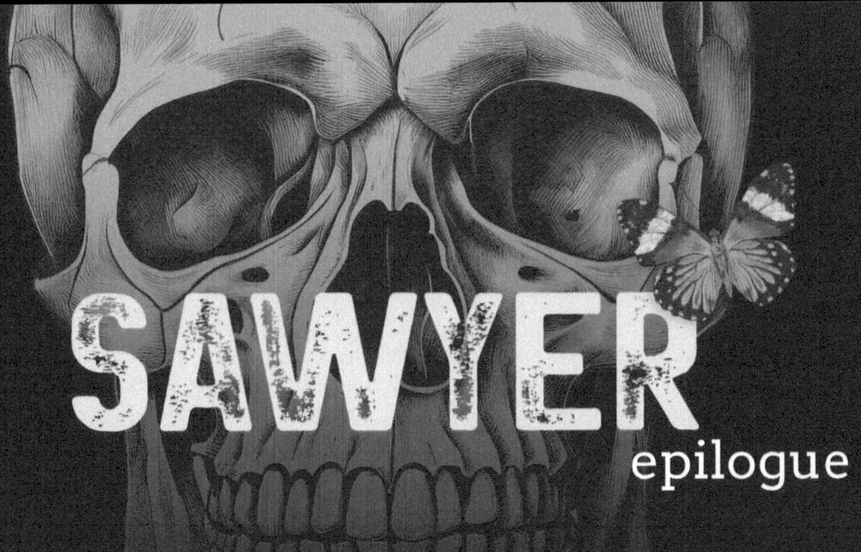

I stare at my reflection in the floor-to-ceiling mirror, trying to match the girl in front of me with the one I used to know. So much has changed in the last few months, even more in the last few weeks. The most striking change of all is staring back at me. She looks exactly like me, with her brilliant blue eyes, pale skin, and vibrant red hair while also looking like the antithesis of who I am. I don't wear white. Murderers don't wear white. Women who roam around in the bowels of hell, fighting for equal footing with the men of this town, don't wear white. Or get married in churches. We hide in the dark. We stalk in the shadows and kill without guilt or remorse.

A knock on the door draws me out of my thoughts. "Five minutes," the wedding coordinator calls out. Stepping away from the mirror, I hitch my dress up, checking that my thigh sheath and holster are securely in place. A small revolver is attached to my left thigh, and on my right is one of my blades. I carefully drop the dress back over them, ensuring they're unidentifiable through the sheer fabric before fingering the hilt of the blade tucked into the side of my bodice. This one is much more easily accessible, should I need it. But if all goes to plan, I shouldn't. My only job is to get out. To evade Dante and Enzo when shit kicks off and get out before the whole building is leveled.

There's another knock on the door. "One minute."

Fuck me. Isn't the wedding day meant to be all about the bride? The damn guests will wait as long as it takes until I'm ready. Sighing, I slot the earpiece in my ear. "You there?"

"We're here, Trouble," Oliver confirms.

"Everyone's in position." Cain's gruff voice, all business-like, helps settle the nerves that have taken flight in my stomach.

Once again, the wedding coordinator's voice comes through the door. "It's time."

"Now or never," I mutter under my breath as I lower the veil over my face and make my way out of the room. When the coordinator first handed it to me, I nearly told her to take it away, but I'm actually happy to hide behind the thin, lace fabric for as long as possible. When I step into the large, vacuous church, filled to the brim with no one I recognize, I'm even more glad I'm wearing it. My heart hammers in my chest, blood whooshing in my ears to the tune of The Wedding March.

I feel a slight pressure on my lower back and turn to find the wedding coordinator encouraging me down the aisle. She has a massive grin on her face. Of course, she thinks this is a normal, happy bride and groom wedding instead of the farce that it really is.

Steeling my spine, I take a small step forward, then another. I ignore all the smiling faces of men and women I don't recognize. Each one of them is dressed impeccably, draped in all their finery. Clearly, they are all Antonellis or associated in some way. Not that any of it will do them any good when they're all lying dead, slumped in their seats, at the hands of the Rejects.

"Just get to the end of the aisle, Trouble," Oliver whispers in my ear, as if sensing how close I am to bolting. "We'll do the rest." His words help bolster me, and my next step has more conviction behind it. I'm not sure if this church is just massive or I'm walking in slow motion—maybe both—but it seems to take forever for me to reach the halfway point. As I do, my gaze is drawn toward the front of the church. My breathing catches. Dante is standing front and center in front of the altar, staring right at me. His eyes are as intense as ever, and I wonder how I didn't feel his gaze on me the second I entered. I've never seen him dressed in anything other than a suit, but he looks impeccable with his long, black tailcoat with matching pants, dress shoes, and bowtie.

I slowly roam my eyes over him. I know he can sense me staring, but I still feel like, for the first time, I have the opportunity to really take him in. The light stubble he sometimes sports when he's around the house has been cleanly shaven, and his short, black hair is slicked back, only adding to his prominent appearance. His face is as shut down as it always is, making it impossible for me to read anything. Is he happy? Angry? Does he even care? The fact that he's insisted on this wedding would imply he should, but he certainly doesn't look like a happy groom about to marry the love of his life.

Movement to the left draws my attention, and my gaze lands on Enzo, who looks just as regal in his pitch-black suit. He's dressed in black from head to toe, and uncannily his face is as void of emotion as Dante's. His I can understand, though. He's watching the woman he's been obsessed with for eight years marry his best friend. Even though he knows this is all a farce and I'm being forced down the aisle, it still must be difficult to watch.

As I get closer to the front of the church, my eyes swing over the guests all standing in their pews. More falsely happy faces greet me, and I'm once again thankful for the lace over my face that prevents any of them from seeing my eye roll and disgusted expression. I just want to scream at them all that this is such a sham. Not that I think it would do any good. They're all Giovanni's puppets.

Speaking of the devil, he's standing in the front row, grinning just as brightly as all the other guests, but the cruel lilt to his lips and excitement dancing in his eyes makes my heart beat faster. He seems to know I'm watching him as he shifts subtly to one side, and I gasp, my footsteps faltering as my eyes land on Luc. "Oh my god." My mind whirs with questions as I struggle to comprehend what's happening. His right eye is swollen shut, his left one staring at me in confusion. He has no idea who is behind the veil; he has no idea what the hell is going on. But he's here, beside Giovanni, beaten and bound, with duct tape over his mouth... and no one else is giving it a second look. The guests in the pew behind them just smile at me as though nothing out of the ordinary is going on.

"What's wrong?" Cain's bossy tone reminds me they are still in my ear as my stunned gaze returns to Luc.

"Luc."

"What about him? He's fine, Red. You can see him later. Just focus."

It's clear from his tone that he has no idea Luc isn't at the clubhouse. That he's right here in front of me.

"No, he's here."

"What?!" both men bark at the same time.

"G-Giovanni has him. He's standing right in front of me, beaten to hell."

There's a round of cursing over the earpiece, but I barely listen as my attention swivels to Giovanni. His grin is even broader, crueler than before, and as I watch, he lifts a revolver high enough for me to see. The threat is clear enough—misbehave, and he'll kill him. My legs are shaking now. This is my worst nightmare come to life. Everything —absolutely everything—I've done has been to protect Luc, and somehow he's ended up in the very thick of it, surrounded by the worst kind of people. How did they find him? How did they get to him? Why did Jon or one of the kids not inform Cain or Oliver? So many questions fire across my mind, but none of them matter right now. All I can do is ensure my brother's safety and make sure he walks out of here alive.

In a daze, I somehow manage to reach the end of the aisle, and Dante steps forward, offering his arm for me to take. I stare down at it, unable to move. My body feels like it's made of lead, and the only thing I can think is, did he know about any of this? Is he in on it along with his father? When I make no effort to move, he lifts my arm and places it through his, leading me up the steps. My movements are automatic. My head is no longer in the church. It's only when the music stops, and the priest starts talking that I come back to earth.

"Abort," I whisper in a quiet voice. "Abort."

There's a second's silence while I wait with sweaty palms for them to confirm before Oliver's defeated tone sounds in my ear. "Will do." I can only hope that they actually do.

"Red, don't do this," Cain growls. He's not talking about calling off the attack. He knows I wouldn't risk Luc's life like that. He's talking about the wedding.

Dante's hand comes to lift my veil, and I say my final words to Cain and Oliver before I lose the privacy offered by the lace. "I have to."

Another round of curses goes off in my ear, but I tune them out as Dante lifts the veil off my face. He's as stoic as ever. Unreadable. I've never wanted to dig underneath his granite exterior as badly as I do now. Did he know? It's the question that keeps circling back around in my mind.

My eyes go past him to Enzo. He's never looked so much like Dante as he does today. Equally as shut down. Have they been playing me this whole time? Have I been a fool thinking these two men actually cared in their own twisted way?

A muffled cry from the front row has my head snapping round, my eyes landing on my brother. Santos has his filthy fucking hands on him, ensuring he can't move, not that he could go anywhere anyway. From the aisle, I could see his zip-tied hands, but from up here, I can see that his feet are tied together too. I hold his gaze, drinking in his bright-blue eyes similar to mine, hoping I can convey in just a look how sorry I am. I failed him in the worst possible way, and now I'm about to pay for it.

Only when Dante lifts my hand, placing a diamond-encrusted wedding band on my finger, does my attention come back to the man in front of me. "I do." His voice rings with conviction and certainty. His vow binding and eternal.

I stare at the ring on my finger before dropping my hand to my side. It's like I'm seeing everything as though through a tunnel. Everything is distorted and distant sounding, like it's happening too slow and too fast all at once.

My eyes slowly crawl over Dante's shirt, cleanly shaven jaw, and thin lips until I meet his turbulent brown eyes.

My breathing is ragged and I don't think I've ever felt so out of it before. I blink, focusing on the scene before me as the priest holds out a chunky, white-gold wedding band and asks, "Do you take this man to be your lawfully wedded husband?"

Defeat threatens to crush me, choking me and making it next to impossible to get the words out, but as I stare into my husband's cold, dead eyes, I whisper, "I do."

paradiso

"Ah, son, good of you to join us. I was worried you were going to miss the show."

Everything within me comes to a standstill as I take in the cruel glint in my father's eyes and his matching malicious grin. And if that wasn't enough, then his ominous words are enough to have the hairs on the back of my neck standing on end while I discreetly cast my eyes around the room, searching for any sign that could explain his disturbingly good mood.

"What's going on?" I force my feet into motion when my father signals for me to sit beside him. It's an order, not a request.

"My only son is getting married." He lifts his glass in a toast and his mindless associates respond in kind. "That deserves something special." When his hand claps heavily on my shoulder, his fingers digging deep as he grins at me like a sick sociopath pretending to be a proud father, then I know something is very, very wrong.

My first thought goes to Sawyer, but she is hidden away safely in my house by the beach. He can't get to her there. Those are the words I repeat as I do another subtle search of the room, even as my father continues with his tirade.

"You've found yourself such a nice piece of ass"—he pauses deliberately—"I thought it was only fair that everyone got a look before she was locked down."

My gaze snaps back to him, noticing his grin has widened, making him look almost manic. It takes a lot of effort to keep my expression blank, but I'm not about to give this old fuck any reaction.

A spotlight comes to life above the stage and my eyes dart over to it. My blood runs cold as I rake my eyes over the sight in front of me, and before I've even registered the movement, I've taken a step toward where Sawyer is gagged and strapped to a bed in nothing but her underwear.

Her eyes dart frantically around the room, struggling to make anything out due to the bright lights shining on her. When I move, her attention snaps my way, and the look in her eyes has me not giving a shit about my father or his men. She begs me silently to help her, and I've never seen her look more vulnerable. Not even when I saved her life that day in Belle Donne. She has never looked at me like the way she is now—as if I have the power to help her, and fuck I wish I could. I *wish* I owned that power. But as my father's hand snaps out to grab my arm, I'm reminded that I don't have the power to save her this time.

"Don't even think about it," my father hisses menacingly. It's the final reminder I need that I can't go against him. Not now. Not here, surrounded by his men. I have already done a mental calculation of how many of his men are in this room, and I don't need to search them to know each and every one of them is armed and, despite their relaxed facades, they wouldn't hesitate to jump into action if my father barked out an order. And it wouldn't be me who suffers. It would be Sawyer and Lor.

Ripping my eyes away from her pleading ones, I snarl at my father, "You want me to fuck her in front of you all?"

"Oh no, son. You have the rest of your life to fuck her. I think it's only fair that one of my men get the opportunity to give her a go."

The muscles in my jaw are clenched so tight, I can't get a word out. All I can do is glower at my father as I try to rein in my desire to wrap my hands around his neck and squeeze until his fucking head pops off.

"And unless you want me to put a bullet between those pretty eyes of hers, you're going to sit here and watch."

My father sees every bit of the hate I spit at him with my eyes. I *let* him see it. Yet, I'm still helpless to do anything. I seethe for several long seconds before I manage to unclench my jaw enough to spit out, "Who?"

If it's possible, my father's grin widens, and when he glances over my shoulder, my entire body stiffens. Woodenly, I turn to face my second in command, my closest confidant, my only friend, the only person in this world that I trust unequivocally.

"I think Lorenzo deserves the honors."

The storm that constantly threatens to consume me when that switch inside me flicks roars to life, a mishmash of unidentifiable emotions warring for dominance as my gaze bores into Lor's, my father's words nothing but white noise in my ears as I threaten all sorts of pain if Lor dares take even one step toward my woman.

His return stare says everything I don't want to admit. That he has no choice. That he has to. But I don't want to believe that. She's mine. *Mine.* Lorenzo is already far too fucking attached to a woman that will never be his. Fucking her will only cement that and put a wedge between us. Not only between Lor and me, but also between Sawyer and me.

All I can do is stare, frozen in place, as I watch Lor shrug out of his suit jacket and neatly fold it over the back of a nearby chair. The world seems to pass in slow motion as he moves toward the stage, drawing out my pain and suffering one agonizing second at a time.

Unable to look at him, I instead focus on Sawyer. Her gaze is fixated on Lor as he approaches her, her eyes wide with fear. Her lips move in a silent plea that I can't hear, and that Lor ignores as he moves to straddle her.

She tries to fight him off, even with her wrists and ankles bound, and I'm simultaneously proud of her, all the while terrified she will make things worse for herself. My hands clench into tight fists at Lor's angry tone when he tells her to shut up. And then moment he wraps his hand tightly around her neck, I silently promise to make him bleed if he hurts her. Hell, I'm going to make sure he bleeds anyway.

I feel somewhat detached from reality as I'm forced to sit there and endure every scream, every whimper. The entire time I remain focused on her face, watching as the fear and panic slowly melt into lust and pleasure. Something settles inside me, knowing that she's enjoying herself, despite the reprehensible circumstances, but anger still burns hot in my veins knowing she's not experiencing that pleasure at *my* hands.

It's only when Lor's grunts sound out around the room and he climbs off the bed that everything around me seems to come into focus again, and I rip my gaze away from Sawyer.

"Meh. Nothing to write home about," Lor says casually, like he just fucked a common whore and not my very-soon-to-be-wife. "I prefer whores with a tighter cunt."

God, I'm going to fucking murder him for that insult alone.

"Are we done here then?" I grit out over the top of the hearty laughs from my father and his associates.

I barely register my father's response or the women who seem to flood out of the shadows and start grinding on men's laps as I stomp toward Sawyer. Her cheeks are still flushed, whether from embarrassment or Lor, I'm not sure.

"Let's get you out of here," I murmur quietly, deftly undoing the cuffs around her wrists and ankles. Shrugging out of my suit jacket, I help to get her arms into the sleeves before scooping her into my arms. She buries her head in my shoulder and I hold her tight against me, ignoring everyone in the room as I stomp toward the door.

Right now, Sawyer is my priority. However, as soon as I get her home, Lor is going to get a piece of my mind, and my father is going to pay for this. One way or another.

DAMAGED & DEADLY

BLACK CREEK SERIES BOOK THREE

R.A. SMYTH

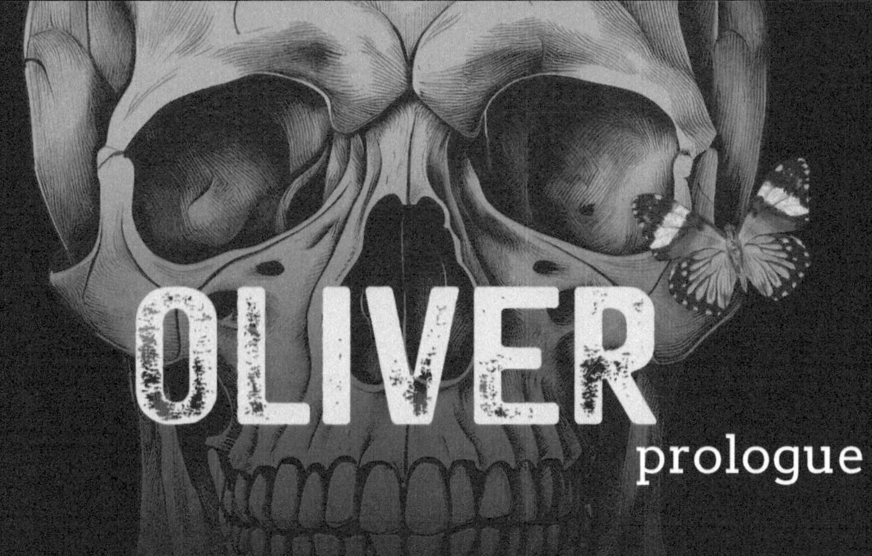

"Let's go," I holler, before striding out the door. Today's the day vengeance is finally meted out. The day the Antonellis meet their maker and can no longer loom over the people of Black Creek like omnipotent Gods, ready to strike at any moment over the slightest grievance. It's the day Cain finally gets his revenge. The day he can finally put the guilt he carries regarding his sister to bed. Hopefully, after today, he will be able to move on with his life and find happiness. Our revenge couldn't come at a better time. Now that we have Trouble in our lives, it's time for us to wipe the board clean and start anew... with her.

She'll finally be able to come home with us today, and although I haven't spoken to Cain about it, I'm sure he will be fully on board with convincing her to move in here—permanently. We've all come a long way from when he all but demanded she move in with us for her own protection. Now, we just want her close. I know that I want to wake up to her in my bed, eat breakfast with her, and have her curl up beside me at the end of the day. Despite Cain's orneriness, I have no doubts that he wants the same. He's finally done keeping her at arm's length. Everything we've been through has forced him to accept that he's in fucking love with her. Same as me. Hearing those sweet words spill from her lips, even if they were said under the guise of her talking to her brother, hit me right in the chest. Somehow, I knew she wasn't just saying them. Like Cain, she needed that push to confront her feelings, but when she finally got there, it was the best fucking thing. Except she wasn't fucking here. I couldn't do any of the things I wanted to do, and I still haven't had any decent alone time with her. But all of that changes today. Red is coming home, and tonight she'll be in my bed, screaming my name.

We all pile into the cars, and Cain climbs into the front passenger seat beside me, a determined set to his jaw and a fire burning in his eyes. "Time to get our girl back."

Damn fucking right it is.

We've been planning this for weeks. Every minute detail, every possible scenario. We have it all worked out. Nothing, and I mean absolutely nothing, will stand in our way.

We've cased the church, we've got C4 already in place around the perimeter of the building, and a whole fucking army of men ready to kick in the doors and rain down hellfire. We just need to provide enough of a distraction for Red to get out, then get the fuck out of there ourselves, and *boom*. Goodbye motherfuckers.

Adrenaline and excitement course through me, making me jittery and ready to get the fuck on with it as I turn onto the road the church is on. I pull up to the curb a safe distance away, and the two of us watch as dolled-up guests walk up the sidewalk and head inside. We have no idea who any of them are, and we don't give a fuck. They're Antonellis, or people associated with them—which is just as bad—and that means they have to go. The whole fucking lot of them.

Grabbing the case with the Bluetooth earpieces, I hand one to Cain and put the other in my ear. I can't hear any sound on the other end, so Red must not have hers in yet. As we sit and wait, I occasionally notice a flash of movement out of the corner of my eye as our men get into place around the building, although they do move unnoticed for the most part.

I can feel the tension radiating off Cain and can tell by the straightening of his spine and the way his shoulders are pushed back that he's as primed as I am. We take these precious few moments to get our heads in the game and go over the plan until I hear Red's sweet voice in my ear.

"You there?"

"We're here, Trouble," I confirm.

"Everyone's in position." Cain's voice is tight and gruff with emotion as he gets directly to the point. He's in full *leader of the Rejects* mode right now, which is precisely what we need. There can't be any space for emotions in situations like this, even though I imagine he's battling to keep them at bay inside.

There's a quiet mumble on the other end before Red murmurs, "Now or never." Despite the fact I know the wedding isn't going to happen, nerves flutter in my chest at the thought of her walking down the aisle to meet someone other than me or Cain. Marriage is not something I've ever considered before, and definitely not a pretentious church wedding like this one. However, it still doesn't sit right that she's even pretending to marry this asshole.

Cain doesn't seem to have the same concerns as he stares sightlessly out the window, his expression an impassive mask. Mimicking him, I push all those concerns out of my mind as we get out of the car. With practiced ease, we slink around to the back of the church. While our men are going to burst through the front door and shoot up the whole motherfucking congregation, we're going to sneak in the back door and ensure Sawyer gets out. The second she's free and clear, Cain will give the signal and Marcus, who is heading up the other group, will let us know when they're all out so then we can blow the church to Kingdom Come.

The whole time, I can hear Red's rapid breathing down the line over the sound of the fucking "Wedding March," giving away how freaked out she is. I think it's terrible from out here, but I can't imagine how difficult it must be to play her part. Cain and I duck under windows, and I deliberately don't chance a look inside, not needing the mental image that I'm sure I'll be accosted with. Just picturing it in my mind's eye is bothersome enough.

"Just get to the end of the aisle, Trouble. We'll do the rest." I can only hope my words and having my voice in her ear offers some sort of reassurance as Cain and I reach the back door and he soundlessly pulls it open.

Just before he can slip inside, a gasped "oh my god," comes over the earpiece, and we both freeze.

"What's wrong?" Cain barks. I can already see the wheels churning in his head as he tries to work out a solution to whatever problem has arisen.

"Luc."

Cain frowns while I try to figure out why she's mentioning her brother at such a critical time.

"What about him?" Cain's impatient tone rings out, and I momentarily want to wallop him over the head. "He's fine, Red. You can see him later. Just focus."

"No," the strain in her voice has the breath stalling in my chest. Something is wrong. *Seriously fucking wrong.* "He's here."

Cain and I share a confused and shocked glance. "What?!" we both snap at the same time. How the fuck can he be there? He's at school with Tank and Rampage.

"G-Giovanni has him. He's standing right in front of me, beaten to hell."

My mind whirs as I try to work out how the fuck that happened. And more importantly, how the fuck we deal with it. Out of all our fucking planning, this wasn't one of the scenarios we ever pictured happening. The kids know to keep an eye on him. Especially today, not that we had even anticipated Giovanni going after Luc. We didn't even know he knew about Luc.

"Fuck," Cain snarls angrily, keeping his voice low. "What the hell do we do?"

He looks at me, desperation and frustration clear to see on his face. I'm still trying to work out the answer to that. "We can just grab him when we get Red," I state. "Giovanni and his men will be preoccupied protecting themselves from our men. He won't even notice Luc's gone."

Cain thinks it over for a second before nodding in agreement, and he steps through the door, but before I can follow him inside, Red's pained and broken-sounding voice in my ear once again has us both pausing. "Abort." We both tense. "Abort," she repeats.

My face scrunches as I try to decide what to do, but there's no fucking way she would tell us to stop unless it was absolutely the only choice she had. Cain must realize it too as his face falls, and in an instant, he looks completely fucking shattered.

"Will do," I sigh dejectedly.

"Red," Cain growls, grinding his teeth. "Don't do this."

There's a hitch in Trouble's voice that has me seeing red and wishing to the fucking stars that there was something—anything—I could do. "I have to."

The second those words are out of her mouth, Cain turns tail and storms out of the church. His body is coiled tight as he strides back to the car, slamming the door loudly as he climbs in. I follow him at a slower pace, watching from a distance as he struggles to control his anger, and my heart tears to shreds with every step I take away from the church.

Torturing myself, I listen as Red robotically recites her vows and as she says those two final words, solidifying her fate and ours. *I do.* I hear a roar from within the car, and Cain breaks apart, his fist slamming down on the dashboard.

I thought I hit my lowest when Evie was taken, but this is a desperation like nothing I've ever felt before. It twists with hardened resolve, and I know I will stop at nothing to get Red back.

one

I'm in a nightmare. A real-life, living nightmare. Nothing around me penetrates through the rushing of blood in my ears or the ice in my veins. In a detached, peripheral sense, I'm aware of Dante's tight hold on my hand as he tugs me down the aisle. The false, happy smiles of faceless, nameless people in the church pews as we pass. The vicious curses and furious snarls in my ear. But I don't process any of it. I'm in the grips of a cold, dense, suffocating fog. It chills me to the bone, numbing the chaos of emotions threatening to pull me under.

As I'm dragged out of the church hall, a wave of panic washes over me, and I begin to pull on Dante's death grip as I look over my shoulder to try and spot my brother in the crowd. He was with Giovanni and his thug of a Consigliere. I can't leave him there with those monsters.

As the doors swing shut behind me, I fight and struggle furiously to get back to Luc, but Dante's hold on my wrist tightens to the point of pain—or at least, it would be painful if I was capable of feeling anything other than this chilling numbness of terror. Unperturbed by my attempts to get free, he tugs me through the church until we reach the room I got ready in earlier. Shoving open the door, he hauls me inside, with Enzo fast on our heels.

With an angry snarl, I once again attempt to escape his hold. This time Dante lets me go, and I spin to glower at both of them. The great thing about the icy numbness I'm currently experiencing is that it's the Reaper's perpetual state of being. The place I go to when I need to not feel. That quiet part of my mind where I can shut everything off and do what needs to be done for the greater good. So while I may be freaking the fuck out right now, the cold, detached part of me that resonates with the Reaper is the part that's in control. She's driving this ship, and I'm more than fucking happy to hand her the wheel and watch her steer.

I glare at the two men in front of me with every ounce of my perfected Reaper's glower, throwing the full force of my anger, loathing, and frustration into the look and letting them plainly see just how badly I will fuck them up if either of them had anything to do with this. I won't show any mercy. I will quite happily rip them limb from limb, keep them alive while I yank out their entrails and force-feed them down the other's throat.

"Did you know?" I snarl, ignoring Dante's flash of confusion.

"Know what?"

"No, Sawyer. We didn't. I swear." My eyes narrow on Enzo as I scrutinize him. His wide, pleading eyes beg me to believe him, but I don't know if I can. I don't know what to believe anymore.

"Know what?" Dante repeats angrily, his gaze snapping back and forth between Enzo and me. "Who was that kid?"

I flick my attention back to Dante. My eyes narrow suspiciously as I try to get a read on him—a pointless task as always. Based on how he dragged me out of the church, he knew something was going on, but the deep furrow on his brow would suggest he doesn't know *what*. I purse my lips before deciding to answer him. "My brother." My throat closes over as a fresh wave of emotion threatens to break me. Just saying those words aloud has the knot in my stomach tightening, bile churning precariously, but I'm made of tougher stuff than this. So instead of crumbling, I shove all those out-of-control emotions back into their box and straighten my spine. "How did your father find out about him? Or track him down? How the fuck did he even capture him?" This last question is directed into the Bluetooth earpiece that's still keeping me connected to Cain and Oliver.

"We're finding out," comes Oliver's curt response. I can distinctly hear the angry undertone in his voice, even if he is managing to put his feelings on hold to get to the bottom of this shitshow.

Dante doesn't seem to have a response to the questions I asked him, and rather than waiting for one—what does it matter how his father found out?—I ask a more pressing one. "What does he want with him? He..." I trail off as images of Luc with his black eye and split lip penetrate my mind, and tears build behind my eyes, even as I grind my teeth and force them away.

I close my eyes, taking a moment to gather myself. When I open them again, Enzo is standing in front of me. His lips are pressed into a flat line, but I can see a burning intensity in his eyes. I don't know how, but I get the impression he wants to reach out and... I dunno what. Hug me? Comfort me? Other than after the whole fiasco at that sex club, he hasn't tried to offer a comforting touch, and he pauses now as if sensing I may not respond well to it. He'd be right. I can't tell if his touch will blow the fuse of my anger and send me catapulting into a rage-filled blowout or if it will knock down the dam holding back my tears. Either way, I don't want it.

Before he can say anything, there's a knock at the door, and without waiting for a response, it swings open. A far too happy Giovanni strides in. The second I lay eyes on him, I want to smack the *fuck you* smile off his face. "How are the happy bride and groom?" he asks, apparently ignoring Enzo's presence and the furious glower I'm throwing at him.

"Where's my brother?" I bark, refusing to simper to this fucking psychopath. My anger doesn't appear to bother him as his gaze lands on mine. Amusement shines in his eyes, only adding fuel to the fire.

"Did you like my little wedding present? I couldn't let your special day go by without your family being present."

"What the fuck did you do to him?!" I all but scream.

He waves a dismissive hand. "Don't worry about him, he's in good hands."

"His appearance would say otherwise," I snipe derisively.

"Kid put up a good fight when Santos tried to take him, but he's where he belongs now. He'll come to realize that in due time."

What the fuck does that mean?

"Luc has nothing to do with any of this. Whatever it is you want from me, you don't need to use him to achieve it."

Giovanni laughs at that. "Oh dear, I don't want anything from you. You're my son's whore. You barely even register on my radar."

I pause, unsure how to respond to that. Huh, definitely not the response I was expecting. I thought for sure he brought Luc here to threaten me for some asinine reason, but if not me, then who?

"Then what is it you want from me?" Dante's tone is cool and calm as he stares impassively at his father, putting the dots together at the same time I do.

"For now... Nothing."

"Then I don't get it. What is this all about?" I question, confused. If Luc isn't being used to threaten me or Dante into doing something for him, what does Giovanni want with him?

"All will be revealed in due course. For now, I just wanted to offer my congratulations to the happy couple."

"I want to see my brother!" I demand, not even listening to the words coming out of his mouth.

Giovanni's cold laugh grates on my nerves. "I don't think so. I'll be holding a formal celebration tomorrow night. I have some exciting news to announce. Be there, and you'll get to see your brother."

With one last over-the-top grin thrown in our direction, he exits the room, leaving me speechless.

"What do we do now?" I croak, still staring at the closed door as if expecting Luc to just walk through it at any second.

Someone sighs behind me. "There isn't anything we can do," Enzo says. "We should go home and regroup."

At that, I spin to gape at him. "Go home? I'm not going anywhere until I talk to my brother."

"Your brother's probably already gone to wherever Giovanni is keeping him—which could be anywhere. And no, we can't just scour the city for him. You'd only be asking for Giovanni to do something that will hurt him." Enzo closes the distance between us once again, placing his hands on my shoulders. "The best thing for your brother is for us to go home and work out what Giovanni wants with him. You heard him, he's got something planned for tomorrow. Until then, he won't hurt him... much."

"He's right," Oliver says in my ear, having apparently heard the entire conversation. "There's nothing more you can do for him right now, Trouble. Not without putting him at further risk. Figure out what you can, and we'll find out everything we can on our end. We'll get him back, I promise you that. Cain and I won't rest until he's safe."

I sigh and close my eyes against the onslaught of conflicting emotions. "Okay," I say in a low voice. Lifting my head, I first meet Enzo's reassuring gaze before looking at Dante's steady one behind him. "Let's go."

As I slide into the back seat of the Sedan, my ring catches off the light and I stare down at it, unable to wrap my head around the fact that I'm a married woman. It definitely wasn't the outcome I'd been expecting today. Fuck, none of this was how I thought the day would go. I should be back at the Rejects' clubhouse, celebrating our win and enjoying being in Cain and Oliver's arms. Instead, I'm married to Dante. I don't even know what to think of that. I'm too numb from today's events. I haven't had time to fully process the implications of all of this.

The man himself slides into the back seat beside me. I glance at him out of the corner of my eye. My husband. The man I'm supposed to share my life with, yet the chasm between us is miles wide and feels impossible to cross. *What the hell have I done?* A brief flash of terror locks me in place as I take in the stoic man beside me. I don't really know him. I absolutely don't think I can trust him. Yet, somehow, I've found myself legally bound to him.

God, what must Cain and Oliver be thinking? Cain must be furious, even if he does understand why I had to do it. I didn't see any other choice. We couldn't make a move with my brother sitting there. I wasn't going to risk his life like that, and I don't think I would have gotten away with changing my mind about marrying Dante at the last minute. Dante wouldn't have allowed it. It was all a charade anyway. Even if I had refused, a ring would have been forced on my hand and everyone would just have pretended they heard me say my vows. No matter what, I was either leaving that church a married woman or with dead bodies and Antonelli blood under my feet.

Our journey back to the house is quiet. I feel the weight of Dante's gaze on me every so often—not to mention Enzo's green eyes in the rearview mirror—and tension is thick in the air. I feel both exhausted and strung out, my thoughts going in a constant loop as I jump back and forth between freaking out about my new husband and what might be happening to Luc at this very moment.

Cain and Oliver disconnected our call before I left the church, so I don't even have the distraction of their voices in my ear right now. I already feel more distanced from them. This stupid fucking piece of metal on my finger is messing up everything. I'm just finally finding my footing with both of them. Now was supposed to be our time; instead, I'm married to their worst enemy.

Yeah, but you've been lusting after him for weeks now, a snarky voice in my head unhelpfully pipes up. I stifle a groan, my stomach tightening with unease. Both of them were already suspicious. Especially after I made Cain promise to spare Dante's and Enzo's lives. It's only a matter of time before I have to come clean to them about just how fucked up this whole situation is. I have no idea what will happen then. I could completely understand if it's all too much for Cain. Fuck, it's too much even for me. I haven't the faintest fucking clue what the hell I'm doing. Yet, despite how much he riles me up, I don't want to picture my life without Cain in it. As for Oliver... he'd be more understanding, but I'm still not sure how open-minded he'd be. He didn't seem to have any reservations about sharing me with Cain, but I don't think he will be as okay about doing the same with Enzo or Dante.

A small snort passes my lips, and I'm faintly aware of two sets of eyes on me, but I ignore them as I continue on my internal ramble. Even my inner thoughts sound insane. Do I hear myself?! What the fuck am I even talking about? Some sort of relationship with four men? Jesus, fuck, talk about a recipe for disaster. The only way that ends is with everyone bleeding out on the floor. Don't even start me on the fact that I can't trust either Enzo or Dante. Sure, they were there for me that day in the sex club, but that doesn't mean I should just lower my guard and let them in. I'm a mole in their organization—in their family. Fucking hell, I've seen what they do to traitors and spies. Despite their grievances with Giovanni, that doesn't mean they'd be on board to burn the whole syndicate down.

Equally, Cain and Oliver won't stop until they level this part of the city. So, where does that leave me? Stuck in the middle between two smoking hot enemies, turned on, and with a headache. Sounds awesome.

I'm no closer to sorting anything out when Enzo pulls in through the front gates of the Malibu mansion and parks the car. He's opening my door before I can do it myself and playing the part of a gentleman, he holds out a hand, helping me out. My hand is still in his when he says, "I'm going back into the city for a bit. There are some men who are loyal to Dante. They might be able to get some intel for us."

My spine stiffens. "But—"

He cuts me off before I can construct an argument. "Besides, you should spend some time with your husband."

"Don't call him that," I gripe, frowning.

Enzo's hand comes up to cup my face. "Why not? That's what he is. If you give him a chance, he might be a good one too." I continue to frown until he steps away.

With a *well, what are you waiting for* quirk of his brow, he nudges me toward the house, and with a sigh, I reluctantly give in. God knows, if I don't go to Dante on my own, he'll come and get me.

Nerves flutter in my stomach as I follow Dante up the steps. Casting a final glance over my shoulder, I find Enzo still watching me. He gives me an encouraging nod before he gets back into the car and drives away, leaving me at the mercy of my... husband. *Well, fuck.* I can't be held responsible for my actions. Thank goodness I still have my Glock and knife affixed to my thighs. I may trust Dante enough to know he won't hurt me, but I'm more than familiar with his level of stubbornness, and I'm in no mood for an argument today.

The front door barely swings shut before I find myself pressed against it, a heavy weight pinning me in place. Lifting my gaze, I find russet-brown eyes boring intently into me seconds before soft yet demanding lips collide with mine, and my mind is wiped clean as Dante kisses the life out of me. Like a starved man, he dives into my mouth, claiming every inch of it as his. I melt into his touch, leaning into the heat of his palm on my hip. His other hand threads into my hair, angling my head to enable him to go deeper until I'm convinced he's trying to embed himself under my skin. Heat rushes into my cheeks, and any hesitation or doubts I had concerning Dante are quieted as my body responds to him like he's a missing piece of my soul. My whole body comes alive beneath his touch as he trails his hand over my ribs and up my back, until he finds the buttons of my dress.

I feel his fingers working to undo the first one, and a moment of sanity breaks through the fog of lust. "Dante," I gasp into his mouth, pushing on his chest. He crashes his lips to mine in another frantic kiss, either oblivious or unconcerned with my protests.

"Dante, stop." I push harder against him, breaking through to him as he pulls back. He keeps me pinned to the door with his weight, and his lust-darkened eyes dart down to my lips, wholly intent on picking up where he left off.

"Dante." His name snaps off my tongue like a whip, finally having the desired effect as he lifts his eyes to meet mine. Between heaving breaths, I get out, "We can't." Anger flashes in his eyes, and his features tighten. Before I can comprehend what's happened, I'm tossed over his shoulder with a yelp and he is striding up the stairs. "Dante! What the hell?!"

In true Dante fashion, he ignores me as he reaches the top of the stairs and continues along the landing until we get to what must be his bedroom. Only when he's kicked the door shut with his polished, black Oxfords does he set me on my feet. Before I can turn to glower at him, he smushes my breasts as he pushes me against the wall.

I gasp when I hear the sounds of buttons scattering and cool air brushes along the exposed skin of my back as, in one quick move, he rips open the dress. He pushes it down my arms until it's gathered on the floor at my feet, leaving me standing there in a white, strapless bra and a matching thong. A growl vibrates up the back of his throat when he spots my thigh sheaths before the heat of him at my back disappears. I spin in my heels. "What the—" I'm once again lifted off my feet and tossed into the middle of a large California King bed.

I hit the sheets with a bounce and quickly scramble to my knees, firing a pissed-off glare Dante's way. Unfazed, he stands fully dressed at the end of the bed, looking down at me. "Don't you understand the meaning of *no*?"

"Mine."

I have to restrain my eye roll, knowing it won't help the situation. But come on, he sounds like a fucking caveman with his one-word sentences. "So you're just going to chain me to your bed and have your way with me?"

The excited flash of something dark and carnal in his eyes should probably terrify me, but instead, it makes my mouth dry and heat unfurl in my lower belly. "If that's what it takes." His words are as much of a threat as they are a promise. "There's no getting out of this, *mia vita*. You stood up there and promised your life to me. Your soul to me. Your body. There's no taking that back. When I put that ring on your finger, I claimed ownership. Now you are mine to do with as I please. And right now, I *really* want you naked."

I can't do anything but gape at him. My mind and body are at war with one another —as they so often are around Dante. He takes a step forward, a move that has his knees brushing the end of the bed, and his hand easily wraps around my throat when he reaches out. "So you can fight me on it if you want, but this *is* happening. Now."

His other hand undoes the front clasp of my bra and it falls away as he trails his hand down my abdomen. Wrapping his fingers around the waistband of my thong, he shreds it with one rough tug, leaving me bare before him, wearing nothing but my gun, knife, and blood-red soled heels.

ine. Finally, she's all fucking mine. And holy shit, was she worth the wait. I don't know where to start as I stare at her bare before me on her knees. The weapons were an unexpected surprise that I'm entirely here for. My gaze catches on the blades in their sheaths and my dick weeps as I picture carving my initials into her ivory skin.

I take my time memorizing every inch of her as I slowly rake my eyes over her toned thighs, flat stomach, and perfect tits. There's no rush, and I plan on taking my time exploring every curve and valley. Her body trembles under my perusal as her breaths become labored. The way she responds to me, the fact that she's practically panting and I haven't even touched her yet, has the zipper digging painfully into my rock-hard erection. It's only when I reach her face that some of the euphoria pumping through me ebbs. Her body might be on board with what we're about to do, but her mind isn't. There's a hesitancy in her cerulean eyes mixed with an edge of defiance that pisses me off. I don't know how much fucking clearer I can be. Obviously, words aren't going to get through to her, so I hold her unsure gaze as I flex my fingers around her neck and my thumb rubs soothingly over her hammering pulse.

Slowly, I slide my hand down over her chest, noting how her breathing hitches and her nipples pebble into sharp points. I continue my descent, deviating to trail the tip of my finger around her areola before tweaking her nipple. Her gasp of surprise goes straight to my dick, and it takes more self-control than I care to admit to not rip my pants open and lay claim to her—*plenty of time for that.*

I lavish her other breast with the same attention until she's rubbing her thighs together, desperate for some friction. How can she not see that she's made for me? Others would run in the opposite direction when they see me, and any woman that gets on her knees does so out of fear, not lust. While there is something intoxicating about inducing such fear into people, it's also dull. Sawyer and Lor are the only two people who have laid eyes upon my cold exterior and been drawn to it. Lor enjoys fighting back against my anger, pushing me to feel. He stokes the flames every time and reaps the rewards of the consequence.

Sawyer is more cautious yet similar. I often catch her studying me with a furrow to her brows like she can't figure me out. I'm an enigma to her, and that curiosity lures her in, even when she tries to tell herself she shouldn't be. She needs to stop fighting with herself. Stop holding herself back.

I want to see all of her.

Own all of her.

Lay witness to every vulnerable part of her.

Her thighs are pressed tightly together as my hand follows the curve of her hip, and I continue to hold her gaze as I force my fingers into the tight gap. Everything in her eyes says she's turned on but unsure, and everything in mine urges her to give in. To submit.

"Open for me," I demand in a rough growl. I'm trying to take this slow, to give her time to catch up and get on board, but she's pushing at the very last of my restraint. I manage to curl my fingers, brushing against her clit, and she jolts. Her lips part on a silent moan, her gorgeous blue eyes rounding as they continue to stare back at me.

I repeat the action, pressing harder against the bundle of nerves. I watch as she swallows roughly, her body trembling in its efforts to resist. "Open." It's a ragged command and, this time, I mean more than just her legs.

She must realize how futile it would be to fight me on this as her muscles slowly relax, giving me a bit more room to move my fingers in a circular motion that soon has her trembling for a whole other reason.

Her hands come to rest on my shoulders, her nails pressing into my skin through my shirt. Her breaths come in small, rapid pants, and I drink all of it in as I push her closer to her release.

"Come for me," I order, moving lower to slip a finger into her wet cunt. Despite how fucking ready she is for me, she continues to fight, doing everything she can to stave off her oncoming orgasm. It's useless. I can feel it in the fluttering of her pussy around my finger.

I close the last bit of space between us, ensuring her peaked nipples brush against the rough fabric of my shirt as I wrap my free hand around her throat. I slide my hand up until my fingers press into the sides of her jaw, forcing her to maintain eye contact as I tilt her head back. Staring straight into the captivating depths of her lust-darkened, cerulean blue eyes, I repeat, "Come. For. Me."

There's a roiling sea of emotions in her gaze as she continues to resist for a brief moment. But the fight is lost as her pussy squeezes my finger and a low groan escapes her lips. And, holy fuck, it is the most stunning defeat I've ever laid witness to. She's still gasping for breath as I slam my mouth down on hers. My control snaps, and I surge forward, dragging her into my arms and sending us both crashing to the bed. She could be fighting me tooth and nail and I wouldn't realize it as I lose myself in the feel of her soft curves pressed against the hard lines of my body.

I pull back enough to rip my tie over my head and tear my shirt open, sending buttons flying around the room. As I peer down at her, I take in the freshly-fucked flush on her chest and the way her eyes roam over my bare torso. As I move to undo my belt buckle, she follows the movement but doesn't speak up or try to stop me. I can read it on her face. She's done fighting—for now. I know *mia vita* well enough to understand that a couple of orgasms won't be enough to fully convince her that she's mine, but it's a start.

Kicking off the rest of my clothes, I hover over her, using my knees to spread her wide as I nestle between her thighs. Not once does she look away from me, and as I hold her gaze I nudge at her entrance and slowly slide home.

Her fingernails dig into my back, and her mouth parts on a silent gasp. Dipping down, I lick along the seam of her lips before capturing them with mine. I groan into her mouth as I begin to move, both satisfied that I'm finally showing this woman and the world that she's mine and kicking myself for not just fucking her the second I saw her in that club.

Nothing exists except her soft groans, our heavy breaths, and the feel of her wrapped around me. When I feel her begin to tighten, I pick up the pace until she's falling apart for me again. Only then do I let go and roar out my release.

My head is buried in the crook of her neck as I come back to earth. I simply lie there for a long moment, breathing in her cherry-scented body wash and relishing the feel of her sweat-slicked body beneath mine. Her chest heaves, her heart hammering out the same frenzied beat as mine.

Eventually, I push myself up, my soft cock sliding out of her. Climbing down her body until my shoulders are between her thighs, I stare possessively at her swollen pussy, dripping with my cum. Scooping it up with a finger, I push it back inside her.

"Dante," she groans. The sound of my name on her tongue, in that heady sex-dripping tone, has my gaze darting up to her face, finding her watching me with a half-lidded glazed look. Maintaining eye contact with her, I lean in and run my tongue along the length of her. She shudders, and another husky groan escapes her parted lips as our taste floods my mouth.

"Delicious," I growl before diving in for a second lick. My arms wrap around her thighs, holding her open and preventing her from writhing as I feast on the taste of us until she's screaming her third orgasm of the night. When she comes down, I kiss her deeply, tangling my tongue with hers and ensuring she tastes us. "Don't you agree?"

"Yes." Her response is a breathless whisper as I slide back into her, more than ready to go another round. Hell, with her, I'm pretty sure I could go all night.

She's close to coming when I hear the sound of the front door closing downstairs. Knowing the only person it can be is Lor, I pick up my pace. Wrapping my hand around her throat, I squeeze it enough to get her attention. "Scream my name," I tell her. "I want everyone in a ten-mile radius to know who's making you come apart."

Drunk on orgasms and delirious with need, she doesn't even argue, and my girl does me proud as she roars my name loud enough that there's no way Lor didn't hear her.

By the time I hear him in the hall outside my door, I'm leaning back against the headboard with a smug smile on my face, and Sawyer is sleeping peacefully beside me.

"Where are you going?" I demand when I sense Sawyer getting out of bed the next morning. We couldn't have had more than a few hours of sleep.

Certainly not after I woke her several times during the night to elicit multiple scream-inducing orgasms from her. Now that I've gotten a taste, I simply can't get enough. She's like an addiction I don't ever want to break.

Reaching out, I pull her back into the bed and roll us so she's trapped beneath me, pinned to the mattress. "Dante," she sighs, and damn, it doesn't sound anywhere near as good as when she was pleading for me to give her what she needed or screaming it as she squeezed the cum from my dick.

"I need to shower. I'm gross." I run my eyes over her naked body, smirking when I spot the dried cum on her inner thighs. A primal sense of satisfaction rises within me. *Gross* definitely isn't the word I'd use. However, the thought of pinning her to the shower wall and making her see stars has my dick twitching to life.

"Fine," I relent, still not letting her up. "We can shower."

"Dante." Again with that tone. I much preferred when she was pliable and moaning beneath me. Although I knew her submission was too good to last. "I just... this is all *a lot*. I just need ten minutes to myself. Please."

Her pleading tone and the vulnerable look in her eye have me conceding before I even realize what I've agreed to. However, it's fucking worth it when she graces me with a small, unguarded smile.

She wriggles, and I reluctantly let her up. "I grabbed the bag you had at the church," I tell her, gesturing to the duffel bag on the chair beside the bed. That earns me another grateful smile that goes straight to my chest and causes a weird tightness I'm unfamiliar with. She's not paying any attention when I lift my hand, pressing it against my chest to try and quell the strange feeling.

Grabbing her bag from the chair, I shamelessly watch as she shuffles into the bathroom, closing the door behind her, and a moment later, I hear the shower turn on. In an effort to prevent myself from disregarding her request and storming in there anyway, I grab my phone from the bedside table and decide to go through my emails and catch up on any work-related issues.

When the screen lights up, I notice a message from Lor that must have come through in the middle of the night. I snort in amusement as I read it.

You're a complete fucking dick.

Well, it's nice to have confirmation that he definitely heard us. He's been stalking around Sawyer like she's his when she most certainly isn't. I don't give a shit about their history or his obsession. Unfortunately, that stunt my father pulled had some of the desired effect. Somehow, even though he was forced to fucking violate her, the experience has only strengthened whatever there is between them. In turn, it's only made me even more possessive of her and adamant that he's not getting her. I hope he fucking enjoyed his time inside her sweet cunt because I won't let it happen again.

Ignoring his message, I scroll through my emails, sending a few replies when necessary. I'm responsible for delegating jobs to my father's team of assassins and ensuring there are no fuck-ups. I leave most of the mundane stuff to Lor, preferring to be in the thick of it myself, but things with my father recently have me taking a more active role with the men. I've worked with most of them for years, and I know some are loyal to me. Nevertheless, it doesn't hurt to reinforce my presence and test the waters.

Until recently, I'd been content to just go along with my father's demands. The main issue of contention between us has been Lor—namely my insistence that he be my Consigliere. I should have known he would eventually take the matter into his own hands. Sawyer's unexpected appearance in my life just solidified it. Keeping her safe was the more pressing issue then, but now that she's officially off-limits to my father, I need to find a way to get out of my agreement to have Sam as my second. There's absolutely no way I'll let that shithead swear in as my right-hand man—the person I'm supposed to trust with my life and turn to for advice. He'd sooner advise me to jump off a cliff so he could steal my position. And after the way he manhandled Sawyer at Belle Donne... not a fucking chance. The only future he has in store is a painful demise at my hands.

As for my father... I have no idea how to deal with him. I wish he'd just leave it alone. He'll be dead and buried by the time I'm in power, so why the fuck does he care who is at my side? Sometimes I think it's not even about that. That perhaps he sees Lor as a threat. My father spent a lot of time training me, molding me into the perfect Antonelli. I spent days alone in the tunnels beneath this part of the city, running around in the dark without food or water, trying to find my way out. Nights shadowing Santos and some of my father's closest advisors as they carried out gruesome and heinous jobs. All so that I could become the leader that our people need. A large part of that training was him ensuring I didn't form emotional connections—not that I'm even capable of such a thing. However, Lor presents the greatest threat to that. Well, him... and now Sawyer. If my father indeed is threatened by that, then it would explain why he sent Santos to kill her. However, that would also mean that I've painted an even larger target on her back by bringing her into this world.

I'm so lost in my thoughts that I don't realize the water has shut off, and it's only when the bathroom door opens, steam pouring into the room, that I'm pulled back into the present. With a white towel wrapped around her, Sawyer steps warily into the room. I can immediately tell from the rigid way she walks and how her eyes bounce around the room that her walls are back up. The second I spot it, frustration blooms. I bite down on my tongue, choosing to watch her instead. Despite the barriers she's erected in a vain attempt to distance herself from me, she doesn't appear to be withdrawn or afraid. My frustration gives way to curiosity as she crosses the room to my closet. I hear the clink of hangers as she looks through the shirts I have hanging on the rail before she grumbles something under her breath. There's the sound of drawers opening and closing, and I'm just about to get up to see what she's doing when she reappears, dressed in one of my shirts and a pair of boxers.

Fuck. I'm burning all of her outfits. She shouldn't wear anything except my clothes ever again.

"Don't you own any sweatpants or joggers?" she gripes.

I'm so busy lusting over her that it takes me a long moment for her words to register. When I finally do tear my gaze away from her long, smooth legs to meet her face, I find her cocking a brow at me. "Huh?" Her words finally penetrate. "Oh, no."

Her face scrunches in confusion. "No? But what do you wear when you're just lounging around?"

"I don't."

She still looks confused. "You don't what?"

"Lounge around."

"But what about when you're not working?"

Most of my life is spent working. "Then I'm at the shooting range or sharpening my skills or doing something else for the Famiglia."

"And when you're not doing any of that?"

I shrug. "Then I'm trying to catch a few hours of sleep."

She just stares at me like I'm an alien before shaking off whatever she is thinking. "Whatever," she says dismissively, making her way toward the door.

"Where the fuck do you think you're going?" I snap, jumping up from the bed to intercept her.

Despite the threatening aura radiating off me, she crosses her arms over her chest daringly and glowers up at me. I like it—the fact she's not afraid, even though she knows full well what I'm capable of. "I need food, and we need to talk to Enzo. And I need to get my brother away from *your* father."

She shifts to move around me, but I once again step in her path. My eyes rake over her. "Not dressed like that."

"Seriously? That dress you put me in to go to your father's was more revealing than this. Not to mention the fact Enzo's seen me in my underwear. I think we're well past the point of normal social decorum."

"I couldn't give a shit about social decorum. What I do give a shit about is him getting an eyeful of what's mine."

Anger flares in her eyes, and her lip curls up in a snarl. "Let's get one thing straight, Dante. I married you because I had no other choice. I might be wearing your ring, but that does *not* make me yours."

In a flash, my hand is wrapped around her throat—a move I envision repeating a lot in the near future—and I drive her backward until she hits the wall. "Except that you *are* mine," I argue back. "You were mine the second you stumbled into that alley. I might not have killed you, but you forfeited your life to me. Don't you see? I wasn't supposed to let you go that day."

She just gapes at me, and unable to think of a better way to explain that this is fucking fate, I instead show her. My body pins hers to the wall as I devour her lips. I swear I can hear the crackle of electricity as the air around us heats, and she writhes against me, my dick growing hard.

When we're both worked up and breathless, I pull back to look into her eyes. Her pupils are blown, her lids heavy with lust. Still, her sharp words are cutting. "Maybe so, but you *did* let me go, and my life is not one I'm willing to give up for you."

"Maybe I just need to tie you to my bed and fuck you until you agree otherwise."

Even with the dark shadows that are no doubt clouding my face as anger boils just beneath the surface of my skin, she tilts her head back and stares brazenly back at me. "You can tie me to your bed, lock me up in here, and keep me as your own personal sex slave, but that still doesn't make me yours." In contrast to her sharp words, her tone softens ever so slightly. "You want me to feel for you whatever it is you feel for me? Then you have to allow me to get there on my own." She holds my gaze, and for a brief second, she lowers her guard. It's nothing more than a flash, so quick that if I'd blinked, I'd have missed it before she rights her armor and straightens her spine. "And unless you want me sneaking out the window and disappearing into the night, then I suggest you play by my rules. You might think you know me, Dante, but trust me, you've barely scratched the surface of who I am."

I'm still trying to wrap my head around the meaning of what she's said when she slips out of my hold on her throat and ducks under my arm, making a beeline for the door. "Now, as I said, I'm starving, and we have shit to do."

three

I throw the half-full glass of whiskey at the wall as a furious snarl rips out of me. I can still hear that fucking wedding music, the hopelessness in her voice as she all but gave herself over to that monster. How the hell did this happen? How did we *let* this happen?

As soon as we got back from the church, Oliver went out in search of answers to those very questions, while I'm in here because I can't get my shit together long enough to be any fucking help. Collapsing into my chair behind the desk, I bury my head in my hands as despair consumes me. Everyone around me eventually suffers, and the lead weight of guilt hanging like a noose around my neck has me wanting to down the entire bottle of whiskey sitting on the desk and sink into the blissful oblivion it would provide for a few short, sweet hours. I keep letting people down. People I've promised to protect. How the fuck can I be responsible for protecting an entire club of men when I can't even safeguard those closest to me. Evie. Luc. Red. The list just keeps growing longer. Who will be next? Oliver? I should never have convinced him to come back here. Or perhaps it will be someone else I care about? Red? If only I hadn't pursued her or got her involved in any of this. Luc? I should have kept a closer eye on him and ensured he had better protection.

I sigh in defeat. I should have done a million things differently. And absolutely none of it fucking matters anymore. The *what-ifs* only serve to drive me insane.

My thoughts swing back to Red as I wonder what she's doing now. It's only been a few hours since we left her. Is she back at the house with *them*? Anger burns hot in my veins. She should be here with *us*. Where she belongs. Today should have been the happiest day of my life. I was finally supposed to get my revenge and gain some peace. Rid myself of the suffocating weight of guilt I've been carrying around all these years. Instead, I'm being crushed beneath that weight. I can feel myself sinking into the depths of a bottomless void, drowning in guilt, grief, and my growing list of mistakes.

Since I just destroyed the glass, I grab the whiskey bottle by the neck and chug a good quarter of it while I lean back in my chair and stare at the far wall. She married him. I can't believe she fucking married him. From the second she told me this nut job wanted to marry her, I was against it, but her plan made sense. Now my desire for revenge has resulted in the woman I love marrying into a family I've spent my entire adulthood working to destroy. How fucking ironic is that?!

Why the fuck would he even have proposed such an idea unless he wanted her? I don't claim to know anything about Dante other than the fact that he's the son of the devil, and in my experience, the apple never falls far from the tree. However, I don't believe for one second his proposal was purely selfless. He *claimed* it was the only way to protect Red from his father, but why was his father even after Red? How did he even know who she was? All questions I never thought to ask because I didn't think any of them mattered. None of it would have mattered if today had gone as planned, and now I realize I don't really know what the fuck is going on with those two Antonelli scum and my girl.

I can still hear Red's hesitant tone as clear as day as she practically pleaded with me to spare their lives. Why? What sort of mind fuckery have they pulled to make her empathize with them? To have her begging me not to kill them, knowing full well how difficult an ask that would have been for me.

Grabbing my phone off the desk, I pull up the tracking app. There's a tracker hidden in the back of her burner phone—there was no way I was going to let her go running back to them without being able to trace her—and I navigate it now. The blue dot shows she's somewhere just north of the city. In the exact location she's been in since Dante kidnapped her from the club. Every time I look at it, I itch to drive up there and steal her back. That same need arises now, stronger than ever after the events of today.

Now, I find myself just staring at the screen. Hoping the dot will move or give me some sort of excuse to go to her. It doesn't, and I'm still staring when the door to my office opens and Oliver appears. He looks as weary and as strung out as I do. His hair is disheveled as if he's been repeatedly running his hand through it all day, and he barely manages a quirk of his lips in acknowledgment as he drops into the chair opposite me.

"Well?" I ask, hoping he's got some answers. It might not fix anything, though it would be something.

He sighs and reaches across the table to grab the whiskey, taking a large swig. That can't bode well for whatever he's got to say. He collapses back in the chair, his legs spread wide as he musses his hair up even more, pulling on the ends. "Not really sure," he begins. "There was some sort of shoot-out at the school. Tank and Rampage were busy trying to get some of the other kids to safety. They thought Luc was with them, but at some point during the chaos, he disappeared. They thought he'd maybe gone back in to help or something, but they were still looking for him when I phoned them."

"Fuuuck." I run my hand over my face. "Are they okay?"

"Yeah. They're fine. I don't think anyone was injured."

I mull that over for a second. "You think it was a distraction?"

His lips purse. "Yeah. It's gotta be."

"Well, we know for a fact that there are no Antonellis attending the school."

"Which means it was the Grim Bastards," Oliver finishes in a deadpan tone. I return his cool stare with a flat one of my own, both of us understanding what this means.

"So, Grim is working with the Antonellis," I say aloud, putting words to what we both already know. As if this day couldn't get any worse. After a moment of deliberation, I snort and shake my head. "So much for a fucking truce."

"We knew that was bullshit. We've just been waiting for him to make the first move to prove that... and I guess this is it."

My lips flatten and I lose myself in my thoughts while we pass the whiskey bottle back and forth until it's empty. Of course, we knew that truce was bullshit, but why even bother? Was Grim just trying to lower our defenses, lure us into a false sense of security? But why? He had access to Luc at the school anyway. We just never knew he was a threat. Unless he was hedging his bets in case shit went sideways today with the Antonellis. That sounds more like it. If he fucked up and incurred the wrath of the Antonellis, he'd probably have come begging us to help him get out of it—the pathetic shitstain that he is.

"Have you heard anything from her?" Oliver eventually asks, pulling me out of my thoughts.

I shake my head. "No. You?"

"No."

I hesitate, unable to meet his eye while saying, "Red phoned me the other night." I absolutely should have told him this before we went out today. "Asked me to let Dante and Enzo live."

His brows hitch. "Did you agree?"

"Fuck, O," I sigh, scrubbing my hand over my beard. "You shoulda heard her. There was no way I could have said no."

The look he gives me very clearly says *well, it would have been nice to have known that,* but I shrug it off. It's not like it made any difference anyway.

"Why, though?" I question. "Why would she ask that of me?"

"I dunno, man." Oliver shakes his head, apparently having no more of a clue than I do. "I'm not sure what's going on with her and them."

My hand tightens into a fist on the table just thinking about *anything* going on between them. In spite of his calm facade, I see the twitch in his jaw, giving away his true feelings. The thought of our girl with them sits about as well with him as it does with me. If anything, it's even more reason to get her away from them and back here.

Our plans have gone to shit now, anyway. There's no reason for her to stay there. We can get her out then rescue Luc and devise a plan B. Something that doesn't involve Red putting herself at risk.

"Man, she's not going to agree to that. She won't risk Luc's life," Oliver unhelpfully contributes when I voice my thoughts aloud. An ominous look darkens his features. "Besides, I don't think *he'd* let her go."

"What makes you say that?"

He cocks an eyebrow, looking at me like I'm dense. "Would you?"

Well, fuck, he's got a point there.

Buzz, buzz... Buzz, buzz.

I groan as I roll over, my hand flailing to find my phone as I try to pry open my eyes.

What fucking time is it? I must have only passed out a couple of hours ago after Oliver and I went through another bottle of whiskey.

"What?" I grumble groggily down the line.

"Cain?" The hesitation in Red's voice is what finally has my eyes snapping open, and I spring upright so quickly that my head spins.

"WHAT'S WRONG?"

"Nothing. I-I just wasn't sure if you'd wanna hear from me after..."

"I always want to hear from you, Red. Are you okay?"

She chokes out a strained laugh. "Everything's so fucked up."

"I know, baby. I'm sorry." It sounds weak, but I don't know what else to say to her. We had one job while she was putting herself at risk, for *me*—to look after her brother. And we failed her. *I* failed her. "I'm sorry," I repeat, guilt straining my voice. In the resounding silence, I can hear what sounds like water running. A tap or shower, maybe.

As if sensing I don't want her to tell me it's okay—or maybe she genuinely doesn't accept my apology, not that I could blame her—she instead asks, "What happened?"

"There was a shooting at the school. We think the Bastards started it as a diversion so they could get to Luc."

"What does that mean?"

"Nothing good." I'm not sure what else to say to her. Unfortunately, even after hours of drunken rambling and tossing theories back and forth, Oliver and I are still none the wiser about the bigger picture.

"What do you think he wants with him?" Her voice is quiet, strained, and it pierces right into my chest, making me feel even more helpless than I did before.

"Leverage, maybe?" It's a guess. There are too many unknowns for me to make any sort of logical assumption.

"He said he was having a celebratory dinner tonight."

"Well, I guess you'll find out then." There's an ominous ring to my voice, and I mentally kick myself. I sound like a fucking dick. I have no idea how to give her the comfort and support she likely needs. I'm no fucking good at this stuff. This is more Oliver's speed. She should have called him instead.

"Yeah." She sighs, making me feel like an even bigger ass. It's on the tip of my tongue to apologize, but she speaks before I can. "Anyway, I should go. Dante's in the next room and I don't want him to get suspicious."

My teeth grind at those words, my apology immediately forgotten as thoughts of the two of them assault my mind. It sounds as if she's in a bathroom, so why the fuck is he in the next room... unless he's in her bedroom. My hand clenches around the phone, the plastic creaking threateningly. "We need to talk about what's going on with them, Red."

"I know," she sighs. "Soon."

I want to demand answers now, but I know it's not the time. Instead, I try to push past my anger. "Stay safe."

"I will. I love you."

"Love you too, baby."

I hang up, scrubbing my hand down my face as I check the time. Eight a.m. It's been nearly an entire day since everything went to shit, and I've yet to actually accomplish anything. I have no plan, no idea how to get my girl back. *Our* girl back.

Now that I'm awake, energy buzzes beneath my skin, and I throw back the covers. I move on autopilot, showering and getting ready for the day while my mind works back over the last twenty-four hours. Everything feels like it's spinning out of control, and the pitiful amount of information we have is pissing me off.

"What's the game plan?" Oliver asks when I sit opposite him at one of the tables in the front bar area of the clubhouse, nursing a cup of black coffee. There are only a few other men around, digging into their breakfasts. We sent most of them out to keep an eye on the Bastards and gain any intel they could learn about Luc's location—although I'm not holding my breath for much on that front. Even so, the mood throughout the entire clubhouse is somber. We were all excited for what should have been a win yesterday and it's hitting everyone hard today.

"We can't make a move against the Antonellis, and Red is in a better position to help her brother than we are," I begin. "Which leaves the Bastards." A vicious smile slashes across my face as the thought of actually getting out there and doing something —delivering retribution—makes adrenaline pulse through me.

Immediately catching on to what I'm saying, Oliver returns my look with a dark one of his own. "We need to strike at them," I go on. "Show them that they can't just fuck with us and get away with it. They've crossed too many lines already. Luc might not be a Reject, but he's one of us. There's no way they didn't realize he was under our protection."

Oliver nods in agreement, and I watch as ideas flitter across his mind before he lands on one. "We need to hit one of their drug houses."

"Exactly. Except not just one."

"You know, if the Bastards are working with them, then the Antonellis know we're involved somehow, even if they don't know why or the extent," Oliver muses.

"Yeah." It's a thought I'd been mulling over all night. Until now, it seemed as though, whatever reason Giovanni had for sending one of his men after Red, it had nothing to do with us or our vendetta against them. But if somehow they have managed to link Red to Luc, then back to us, they definitely know there's some sort of connection there—even if it can be twisted to seem tenuous. The problem is, we have no idea what this means, and it's Red who will most likely have to face the consequences and answer any questions they have about us. Worry, guilt, and anger churn in my stomach and cause a tightness in my chest.

"Come on." I down the last of my coffee and get to my feet, needing to move, to do something. "Let's go put the Bastards in their place."

We spend the next few hours devising a plan and gearing up. Tank, Rampage, and Bones all insisted on tagging along. The shadows in Bones' eyes had me instantly agreeing, and I could see the shame and remorse on Tank and Rampage's faces. Not that any of this is their fault. They did their best in what I'm sure was a stressful situation. They couldn't have known it was all a diversion. But I completely understand their need to make up for yesterday. To not feel so fucking useless. So I readily agreed to let them help, and when we're ready, the five of us pile into one of the Cadillacs out front.

None of us feel the need to pass the time with chit-chat, each of us is lost in our own thoughts as we head across town. Oliver pulls up several blocks down from the bakery that we know is anything but. The Bastards use the space for packaging up their merchandise before handing it off to their sellers, who pedal it on the street for them.

Climbing out of the car, I fix my skeleton neck warmer over my mouth, and with weapons at the ready, I meet the others' steady gazes. With a confirming nod, we move down the street. The closer we get, I realize the large shop-front windows have been whitewashed, preventing anyone from looking in. Same with the bit of glass in the front door, and when we're close enough, I scan the exterior of the building for any cameras or alarms. Thankfully, Grim is pretty old school with this shit, preferring to have men on watch, rather than relying on cameras. More fool him, since whatever lackey was supposed to be at the door clearly isn't doing his job, meaning the men inside have no fucking idea that we're coming for them.

When we reach the building, I signal for Tank and Bones to go around back while I approach the front entrance, with Oliver and Rampage behind me. With a ready gun in my hand, I lift my foot and kick in the door, easily breaking the lock. It bangs into the wall, alerting everyone to our intrusion.

The men inside all jump to their feet, but my gun goes off before they've even had a chance to register what the fuck is going on. The echo of gunfire is repeated as Oliver and Rampage flank me, and a moment later there is another bang as the back door bursts open. I'm aware that Tank and Bones have joined the shootout, but I'm too focused on killing the Bastards in front of me—ideally without receiving a bullet in kind—to spare them any attention. My ears ring with the hail of gunfire. Blood is everywhere, coating every surface and mixing with what looks like bags of cocaine they were cutting up.

It's not until we're the only ones left standing and silence presses in around me that the room comes back into focus. With my heart hammering in my chest and adrenaline making me feel wired, I slowly lower the gun in my hand. Blood squelches beneath my boots as I step toward the closest dead guy. Dipping my finger in the blood leaking from the bullet wound in his chest, I move to the wall, and with my finger, I spell out RR. Just in case Grim's confused about who messed with him today.

"One down, two more to go," I state triumphantly, grinning savagely at the wall before striding out the door and leaving the bloodbath behind me.

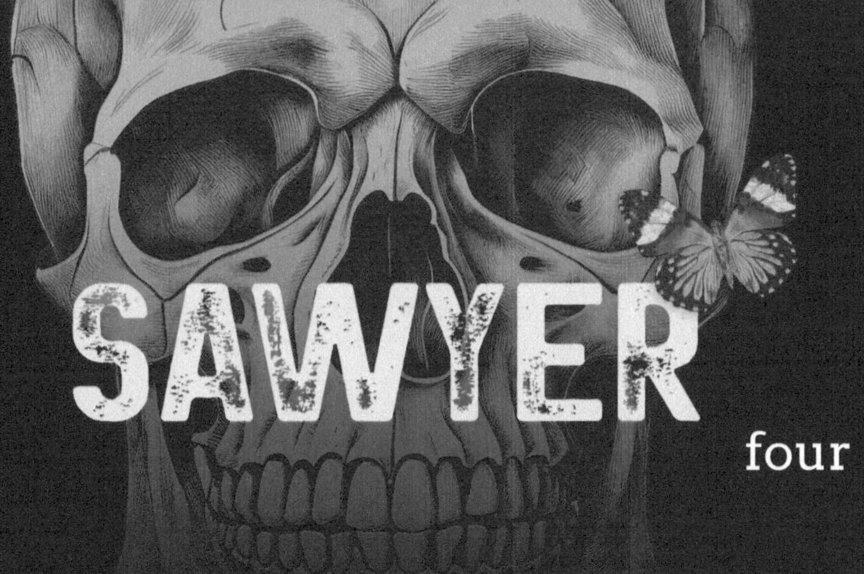

SAWYER

four

I stride into the kitchen with my head held high, ignoring the delicious throb between my thighs and the riot of emotions making me feel unsteady and out of my depth. Enzo catches my eye, a smirk curling at his lips. "Fun night?"

"Shut up," I snark, fighting the blush that threatens to rise in my cheeks. I'm not a fucking blusher. These assholes are messing with my badass bitch persona. If I'm not careful, I'll become a fucking mafia princess. *No, thank you.*

Grabbing the coffee pot, I fill a mug and move to sit opposite him at the kitchen table, the easy banter falling away as the seriousness of my situation again takes control. "Did you find anything?"

Before he can respond, Dante enters the room behind me. I don't even need to look over my shoulder to know. I can tell by the tension that bubbles in the air, making it seem heavier, like it's suddenly harder to breathe. Fuck, I have no idea how to handle all of this. My muscles tense, my shoulders bunching together as Enzo glances in his direction. Something dark flashes in his eyes and he lifts his chin as though in challenge. Of what, I'm not sure.

I wait for them to get over whatever the fuck their problem is, and when Enzo's gaze finally swings back to me, I cock a brow. "He's at the tower, where Giovanni lives."

"He's staying with Giovanni?" I clarify. Definitely not where I was picturing my brother. Think more dark, dreary cell. That's where my thoughts had gone to every time I tried to picture him.

"Probably not in his penthouse, no." With his mug in hand, Dante moves to join us at the table. I get my first look at him since I left the bedroom, and I notice he's since gotten dressed in his usual attire: a shirt, black suit pants, and matching shiny shoes. He's even got a fancy-looking watch on his wrist, and his new, white gold wedding band glitters in the light. Everything about him screams wealth and danger, and sexy as hell. "Most of the apartments are empty." He deliberately trails his hand down my arm as he moves to sit beside me. "He could be keeping him anywhere in the building, *mia vita.*"

I shiver, even though I don't understand the meaning of his words. However, the deep, husky quality of his voice says everything about the intention behind them. And no, it's not stated in a sweet, term of endearment sort of way. More of a, *you're mine, and you always will be* kinda thing. He's essentially pissing on me with sexy Italian words.

Enzo clearly understands the meaning of his words as his eyes widen slightly, and he tears his gaze away from where Dante's body is pressed up against mine—which is down my right side, all the way from my shoulder to my feet. There literally isn't an inch of space.

Images of last night flicker unbidden across my mind, and I have to bite the inside of my cheek. Fuck. I'm seriously screwed. I didn't want to cave to him. I mean, I did. But I didn't. I didn't want to betray Cain and Oliver, but he wouldn't take no for an answer. He knew exactly what buttons to push; he played me like a fiddle until I fell apart, again and again, and again. Until I barely knew my own name, let alone had the brain power to think about how wrong it was.

Even just the tiny slither of contact between us now has my skin burning, my heart racing, and my core clenching. This is not good. This is *so* not good. *Head out of the gutter, Sawyer! You have far more pressing concerns to deal with.*

Pushing past the desire slowly unfurling inside me, I instead focus on Luc, and when I'm confident neither of them can get a read on anything I don't want them to see, I lift my gaze, spearing both of them with a deadly serious look. "So, how do we get him out, then?"

"*We* don't," Dante is quick to respond.

Annoyingly, Enzo just looks amused. His eyes practically sparkle as he watches my fuse get shorter and shorter.

"We don't do anything until tonight. We need to find out what my father's plan is, and how Luc factors into it all."

I smack my hand against the table. "Luc shouldn't be a factor *at all*. Do you have any idea what I've sacrificed, what I've done, to keep him away from this sort of life?"

"Dante's not suggesting we leave him there," Enzo reassures. He pushes his hand across the table so that his fingers brush over mine, instantly taking the wind out of my sails, even if Dante does glare daggers at the point where we touch. "Just that we don't make any rash decisions. Giovanni will be anticipating that. We need to go in there tonight with a clear head and get a full grasp of the situation. Only then can we make any moves to get Luc out of there without putting him in any more danger."

Pursing my lips, I suck in a deep breath, calming myself down. I know he's right; I just hate the thought of leaving him there longer than he needs to be. Only once I've emptied my lungs of all oxygen do I respond. "Fine. But I'm not leaving him in there any longer than necessary."

Enzo gives me a small, understanding smile. "I wouldn't expect any less."

"You can stop touching my *wife* now," Dante snarls, showing us where his head is clearly at. Fucking possessive neanderthal. I roll my eyes while Enzo leans back in his seat, looking far too smug for his own good.

Ignoring their idiocy, I push to my feet. Rolling my shoulders back, I snipe, "Well, if you both expect me to just sit around here all day, I'm going to need access to a gym."

"Didn't get enough of a workout last night, huh?"

Dante snarls furiously, and I simply give the two of them a deadpan look. Patiently, I wait until they're done glaring at one another and finally turn their attention my way.

"Are we done acting like teenage boys now?"

Enzo just smirks. Who the fuck knew he could be such an instigator? But he is undoubtedly enjoying pushing Dante's buttons. Slowly, he gets to his feet and moves around the table. He waits until he's standing beside me. Of course, Dante also feels the need to stand, testosterone radiating off the two of them like a bad smell as they hover on either side of me. "Not even close, Spitfire." His gaze slowly lowers, taking in Dante's oversized shirt and the bottom of his boxers that just peek out the bottom. His tongue runs enticingly along his lower lip before his eyes return to mine. "You might wanna change if we're going to the gym."

Fuck me. My mouth is dry, and the only gym I'm picturing is the one upstairs as he walks away. Shaking it off, I clear my throat and glance at Dante from the corner of my eye. He's still glaring at the door where Enzo disappeared, and I'm pretty sure he's wishing him dead right about now.

"I, uh, should go get changed," I murmur, suddenly feeling awkward. I don't think I'm ever going to be sure how to react around Dante when we're alone in a room together. Certainly not when his best friend and lover is making me think all sorts of dirty thoughts while Dante pictures ripping his head off.

I step away from the table, dumping my mug in the sink before exiting the kitchen. It would be impossible not to notice the overbearing shadow behind me, but I ignore him as I climb the stairs. I turn to head down the corridor toward my room, but Dante's hand reaches out and fastens around my wrist, yanking me backward.

"This way." He practically drags me in the opposite direction, back toward his bedroom. I don't even bother to resist—I already know there's no point. I follow dutifully behind him, waiting until he lets go, which doesn't happen until he has me back in his room, the door closed and his large body standing guard in front of it.

"Dante," I sigh. "I need to get dressed."

He steps forward until the tips of his shoes touch my toes, and reaching out, he cups my chin, tilting my head back until I meet his probing gaze. "You sleep in here now. You get dressed in here. *This* is your room."

My brows furrow. "All my stuff is in the other room." It's the only argument I can come up with while his touch is making my skin tingle and his close proximity has the coconut scent of his shower gel invading my nostrils.

Letting go of my chin, he slowly brushes his fingers down my arm, leaving a trail of goosebumps in his wake until he links his fingers with mine. Tugging my hand, he directs me toward a door I hadn't noticed earlier on the opposite side of the room to his closet.

"This is all yours," he says, pushing open the door. Curiosity gets the better of me, and I peer in. My eyebrows raise, my mouth dropping open as I gape at the various rails of clothes, all different types of shoes—most of which I already know I'll never wear—set neatly on shoe racks. My backpack and the duffle from the wedding yesterday are on a seat in the middle of the room.

"I don't... Most of these clothes aren't mine," I say absently, still staring at the various dresses, skirts, and pantsuits, all of which must cost more than I make in a year at Strip Tease.

"They are now."

I don't even realize he's left me alone until I hear the soft click of the door closing behind me. I take another second to just stand there and wonder what the hell my life has become before I hesitantly take a step forward, then another. Reaching out, I begin rifling through the clothes on the hangers. Most of them aren't me, but I imagine they fit perfectly into Dante's world. I do come across a few tops that are more my style, and even some jeans and sneakers.

When I'm done perusing, I turn my back on all the undeniably expensive clothing and turn to face my bags. Grabbing the duffle, I breathe out a sigh of relief when I find the burner still tucked away in the secret compartment I cut in the lining. I even chuckle when I find my Glock and dagger from yesterday sitting on the seat beside the bag. Dante must not see me as much of a threat if he willingly gave them back to me.

Not seeing the point in wasting any more time, I quickly change into a pair of leggings and a sports bra I found in my exploration and shove my feet into a pair of brand new, sparkling white sneakers. Throwing my long, red strands up in a high pony-tail and slotting my small switchblade into the tiny inner pocket of the leggings, I'm more than ready to hit the gym and kill the next few hours until I can see my brother again.

"Let's see what skills the big, bad Reaper has," Enzo teases in my ear as we step foot onto the mats in the state-of-the-art gym. Dante had disappeared when I re-emerged from my closet, and instead, Enzo was waiting for me, dressed more casually than I've ever seen him. I actually had to stop and take a second to process what I was seeing. Loose-fitted shorts fell to his knees, showing off his toned calves, and he wore an oversized hoodie that did nothing to diminish his hotness factor.

Apparently, Dante had something to do first, so it was just Enzo and me for now. Given how the two of them were behaving at breakfast, I was honestly surprised Dante was willing to let us come alone, but whatever. That bullshit is their problem. I'm having nothing to do with it.

"Ha. Bring it, mafia man. Don't you rely on your guns and minions to do all the heavy lifting?"

That gets a genuine bark of laughter from him, and he moves to face me at the opposite end of the mat. In one hell of a sexy move, he grabs the back of his hoodie and tugs it over his head. As the fabric lifts, it reveals inch after inch of glorious, tanned muscle that I can't help but drool over. I mean, I've tried to imagine what he might be packing underneath his shirts, but *hot damn*, it is way better than I expected. He tosses the hoodie to the side, the movement thankfully pulling my mind out of the gutter before he can catch sight of my staring.

Getting into position, I crouch while I run my gaze assessingly over him—well, it's partly assessing. Partly, I also just can't stop staring at him. Enzo is built for brute force. He's not as big as Cain, but with his broad shoulders, bulging biceps, and abs of fucking steel, it's no wonder he's Dante's bodyguard. It's obviously a job he takes seri-ously, although I know it's more than just a profession to him. He cares about Dante. I may not be able to determine the nature of their relationship, but it's obvious they mean something to one another—even with the pissing contest this morning. Dante wouldn't have so easily left us together if he didn't care for or trust him, and while there may be a severe edge behind some of the things Enzo says and does, I can see the spark in his eyes when he riles Dante up. He enjoys pushing him. And now I'm imagining what happens when Dante finally snaps. *Whoa.* My cheeks flame and my core pulses.

"You planning to just stand there and stare at me all day, Spitfire?"

Enzo's teasing tone crash lands me back into reality, though I'm quick to recover, and in a flash of movement, I race toward him. My legs pump and my hand flies out in a right cross that skims off his chin as he steps back at the last second.

"Not bad." Reacting quickly, he lashes out, catching my side with his fist. My face scrunches as pain lances through me, but I don't dwell on it as I focus on the training Jon gave me. As we deliver blows back and forth, and all the tension building within me slowly bleeds out, I come to realize just how much I needed this. I haven't had any sort of physical outlet since Enzo and I killed that asshole several weeks ago. I'm used to that outlet for getting all my anger and frustration out on a semi-regular basis—and that was before my life turned into a total shitshow. So by the time I'm breathing heavily and my skin is slick with sweat, I feel better than I have in weeks, despite my fear for Luc and my desire to slit Giovanni's throat.

"I'll give it to you," Enzo pants when we've finally had enough of beating the crap out of one another. "You're better than I expected." He moves to grab two water bottles from a mini-fridge while I collapse onto the mat, out of breath. My muscles are heavy with fatigue, but my mind feels clearer and my soul lighter than it has been in days. Holding one of the bottles out for me, he asks, "Where did you learn to fight like that?"

Twisting the cap, I shrug my shoulders. "Here 'n' there." He snorts softly at my vague answer while I throw back half the bottle of water, watching as he lithely lowers himself onto the mat in front of me. Bringing his water bottle to his lips, I watch like a girl obsessed as his throat bobs with every swallow.

When he's done, he sets the bottle on the mat beside him while his gaze slowly rakes over me, flaring with heat. He pauses on the wedding band on my finger. I left the god-awful engagement ring in Dante's room, yet for some reason, I couldn't bring myself to take the wedding band off too. I told myself it was because I didn't want to end up in an argument with Dante, but I'm not so sure that's true. Or, well, the whole truth. It just felt weird when I thought about leaving it behind.

Enzo shifts on the mat, his leg brushing mine and sending a jolt of electricity through me. "Just so we're clear." His voice has dipped an octave, taking on a low husk that sinks into my bones and raises goosebumps along my skin. When I meet his heated gaze, I fall entranced into the swirling depths of his green eyes. "That ring won't stop me." He shifts again, moving closer. "Dante pissing all over you won't stop me." Another shuffle on the mat has him sitting directly opposite me, so close that if I leaned in, I could brush my lips against his. "You're mine, just as much as you are his."

A shiver races down my spine, and although my inner femininity is snarking that I don't belong to anybody, I can't deny how my body responds to his words. Besides, unlike Dante, Enzo doesn't want to control me. He's already proved he wants me the way I am—as the person I am. He's more than happy for me to be my own person. Just like Cain and Oliver. But therein lies the problem. I can't belong to Enzo, or Dante, because I already belong to Cain and Oliver. And despite the chemistry I have with them, and the feelings I'm developing for these two dangerous, mysterious mafia men, I refuse to let them destroy what I've built with Cain and Oliver. As painful as it would be, if I have to choose, I choose them—my Rejects.

Despite my inner thoughts, my own voice has taken on a breathy quality as I argue, "What if I belong to neither of you?"

"You do." He says it with such conviction, like it's an indisputable fact. "You're mine. Ours."

Tilting my head, I test the waters. "Maybe I belong to someone else."

The sheer depth of the possession that flares across his face surprises me. "Not anymore, you don't." Leaning in, he captures my lips with his. His kiss serves to further flip my world on its axis, and the fact that his words simultaneously terrify me to the bone and send a zap of electricity to my core says everything about how fucked in the head I am. About as fucked as this situation is. I can't see a way out of this that doesn't involve the four men I've found myself all twisted up with going head-to-head in a battle over me. While some people might be into four hot men fighting over them, I'm not one of them. Not when the losers end up dead, and no matter the outcome, I know I'd lose a part of myself.

As if he can sense my inner turmoil threatening to pull me under, Enzo backs away instead of pushing me farther. "We should go. We've got a big night to prepare for."

With my heart aching and my lips tingling from our kiss, I give a solemn nod and let him help me to my feet. With his hand on my lower back, he escorts me out of Dante's home basement gym. At the entrance to the gym, he pauses, lifting his head to smirk at a camera situated above the door. I give him a weird look, but he just grins and pulls the door open. Out of everything going on, his weirdness is the least of my concerns, so I quickly let it go.

"I have a feeling things are about to get a little crazy," Enzo says as we climb the stairs to the kitchen. "You should consider telling Dante about your alter ego." I don't respond, but I can feel his eyes on me, and after a second, he tacks on, "If he knew just how capable you were, he'd treat you as an equal in this."

I scoff, my head whipping around to stare at him incredulously. "No, he wouldn't. Dante is all about control. I could tell him I turn into the Hulk, and he'd still think I should stay at home and twiddle my thumbs while the *men* go out and do the fighting."

Enzo just stares at me like I'm being dense. "You really haven't gained any insight into him at all, have you?"

I throw my hands up, exasperated. "How could I? The man may as well be made of stone. He barely says anything, and his facial expressions give nothing away. I don't have a clue what he's thinking most of the time."

"Dante has always been set in his ways. He was raised as a leader and expects people to do what he says, when he says. He doesn't like chaos or anything that he can't understand or control. He thinks that's how life should be—cold and predictable. It's all he knew growing up, and anything outside of that scares him." My eyebrows hitch at the thought of Dante being scared of anything. "But I know he's capable of so much more. He thinks he's dead inside, except I've seen that spark in his eyes when everything bubbles over and he can't keep a lid on his emotions anymore."

It takes a second before what he's saying clicks. "That's why you push him. When he's pissed off, you don't back down as everyone else would, and you're always throwing little digs at him."

"It is. Most of the time, it's anger he spews my way, but when that fizzles out, he has to confront the real feelings hiding underneath. He doesn't process those feelings the way you or I do. He can't feel happiness and identify it as such. He just knows he's feeling something different from the norm, which terrifies him. As a kid, whenever he felt like that, his father would snuff it out. He went to extreme lengths to ensure his son didn't know any positive emotions." My chest tightens as my heart aches for a young Dante. How confusing must that have been? And to have been raised by a father like that... he never stood a chance of becoming anything other than a monster. And yet, he's not. Not really. No more of a monster than I am. And he's certainly not his father. I have at least gleaned that much from him.

"So you've been trying to coax those emotions out of him?"

"I've been trying to get him to open himself up to them instead of switching them off."

I shake my head. "But what does any of this have to do with me?"

A surprisingly soft smile graces his lips. "You kickstarted something eight years ago in that alley. Before then, I was beginning to lose hope in him. He had a soft spot for me, but with every passing day, he was becoming his father more and more. Then you came along." His eyes are glassy while he gets lost in his memories of that day. I still remember it clearly. It was one of the few times Luc and I were out on the street. I'd been rummaging around in the dumpster for anything useful I could use to make us a bed for the night when I heard voices. I should have hightailed it outta there. Anyone with half a brain would have. But something drew me closer, and only the loud bang of the gun seemed to smack any sense into me. Of course, Enzo heard me, and before I could escape, he had his arm around my waist.

"I still don't understand what happened. I thought for sure you were dead." So did I. It was impossible to make out much in the alley, but as Dante towered over me, his face pinched tight as he pointed the gun at my head, I was praying to anyone who would listen that someone would take care of Luc for me. I was sure I was a goner. So sure that I thought I was hallucinating when he told me to get out of there. "But then he let you go. I knew after that that Dante wasn't a lost cause. I just had to keep pushing him. For the most part, he was still set in his ways, but I could tell when he was beginning to feel out of control, so I'd sink my teeth in and rip the hole in his chest open wider until he couldn't take it anymore."

He smirks, and I roll my eyes. "Until he fucked you."

Enzo shrugs unapologetically. "It became like an outlet for him."

"Of course. You weren't getting anything out of it," I tease with a smile.

"I'm not going to say no to a few orgasms and helping my best friend not lose himself."

My smile falls as seriousness returns to his features.

"Then you showed up in the club that night, and even though Dante didn't know who you were, it triggered him. Ever since then, he's felt out of control. You're unpredictable, and he doesn't know how to process his feelings for you."

"So he compensates by going overboard trying to control everything around him," I finish, finally feeling like I've gained some sort of understanding when it comes to Dante. "How does any of this explain why I should tell him I'm the Reaper?"

"Dante may not know why he's so obsessed with you, but he is. He's decided you're his and will do everything he can to protect you. Even if that involves locking you up until he thinks you're safe."

My eyebrows hitch, and I quickly skip over that last little bit. "So you think if he knows I'm capable of handling myself that he will back off a little. He'll realize I don't need to be locked away and protected?"

"That's exactly what I'm saying."

I chew on my bottom lip as I mull it over. "I'll think about it," I eventually concede, knowing it's not a decision I can make without giving it more thought.

Enzo rewards me with a grateful smile. "That's all I'm asking for."

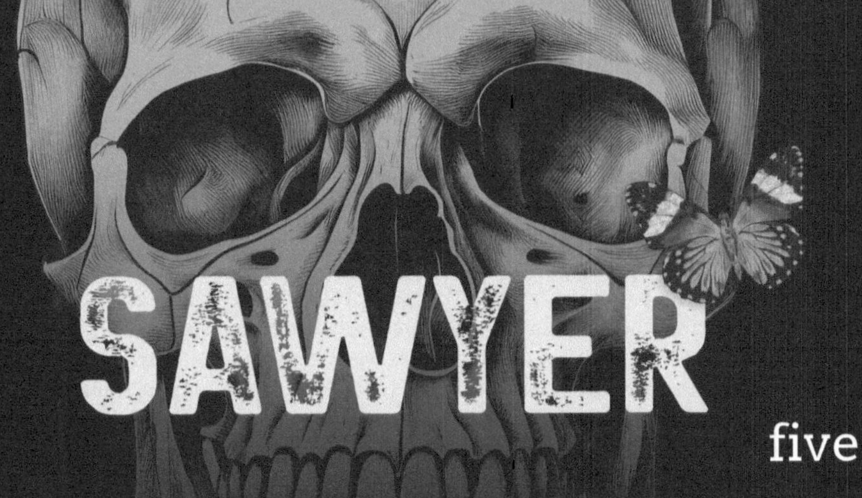

five

My insides feel like a washing machine as I smooth my hands over the low-cut black dress I found in Dante's... my closet. It's not dissimilar to the last one I wore when meeting his father. The silky-soft material cuts a low V between my breasts and cinches tight at my waist, clinging to my ass and thighs before stopping a couple of inches above my knee. There's a small split up my left thigh, but thankfully it's not high enough to show off the thigh strap I have hidden underneath. I also have my Glock 43 tucked in the bottom of my clutch, and I've finished the outfit off with a pair of black heels that have these nifty little spikes sticking out of the heel and platform. Worst case scenario, I imagine they could do some damage if, for some reason, I can't get to my knife or gun.

You've got this. Don't let that psychopath get to you. Don't show him any emotion, and at the first opportunity, cut him down and get Luc out of there.

I don't care what Dante and Enzo have planned, there's no way I'm leaving Luc there another day. Squaring my shoulders, I stare into my steely gaze in the mirror before turning away and striding out of the room. Nerves and determination war within me as I make my way down the stairs and into the kitchen, where I can hear both men talking in low voices.

I pause in the doorway, catching the tail end of Dante's sentence. "... need to retaliate soon." I tense. In the aftermath of everything, I'd completely forgotten they were making plans to attack the Rejects. Of course, if everything had gone to plan the other day, none of this would be an issue. Now I need to figure out how to stop them from killing the two men I love and the one gang in Black Creek that doesn't deserve to be obliterated.

"Antonio has a team in place, scoping out their clubhouse, and he's putting together a plan of attack as we speak."

"Good. I want to meet with him, then we'll make our move."

Fuck. My mind whirs as I store away the information. At best, I have a few days before they attack the Rejects. That doesn't give me much time.

Schooling my expression, I step over the threshold into the kitchen, finding the two of them sitting on opposite sofas. They're relaxed back against the cushions, looking at ease as though they were simply discussing the weather and not the murder of the two men I love and the gang I've come to view as my home.

Both men look up, heat burning in their eyes. It baffles me how I can be so drawn to them yet want to slit their throats for what they were just discussing.

Dante pushes out of his seat and moves toward me. He doesn't stop until the toes of his polished shoes bump against mine, and his hand reaches up so he can twist a loose curl between his fingers. I found a curling wand earlier in one of the drawers of my new wardrobe. I've never had one before and needing to keep myself busy until we were ready to leave, I decided to give it a go. So my long, red hair drapes over my shoulders and down my back in large ringlets.

"You look stunning, *mia vita.*"

I blush despite myself, and when I stare into his russet-brown eyes, I notice a thin, superficial layer has been stripped away. I can't pinpoint what I read in them—and based on my conversation with Enzo earlier, I'm guessing that's because Dante's not even sure what he's feeling. However, I googled those words earlier, and apparently they mean *my life*. I can't decide if that term of endearment is sweet or terrifying. If they meant *my love* or something like that, I could probably wave it away, but *my life* feels so much more... permanent. More all-encompassing, like I'm the sole reason for his existence, the only thing keeping him alive. Thinking back to my conversation with Enzo earlier, about how I kickstarted his ability to feel, it's highly possible Dante may view me as the reason he *feels* alive. But, *fuck* is that unnerving. To be the only reason someone *feels*... that's a considerable weight to bear. I can only speak for myself, but I know it's my love for Luc all these years that stopped me from descending into the cold, detached persona of the Reaper. My love for him kept me sane, kept me rational. Luc made me feel human. Is that what I am to Dante? His Luc?

Lowering my gaze, I take a step back, needing both physical and emotional distance from him as I try to wrap my head around the gravity of the realization I just came to. The strand of hair he was playing with slips through his fingers, and slowly, he lowers his hand to his side.

Reinforcing my shield of armor, I ensure any and all soft emotions are well secured behind my steel-reinforced walls before I again meet his gaze. I'm met with the same closed-off expression, which is fine. There's no room for emotions tonight. I need Dante and Enzo to be on their game if I'm going to get my brother back. Pushing my shoulders back, I demand, "What's the plan for tonight?"

His eyes linger on me for a moment before he gives a subtle nod and steps back, moving to rejoin Enzo in the living area. Reclaiming his spot on the sofa opposite him, he throws his arm over the back of it in an open invitation. Instead of moving though, I end up darting my gaze back and forth between them. It's like fucking eenie-meenie-miny-mo. Why are there no armchairs? And I'm going to look insane if I drag a dining room chair over here.

Chewing on my bottom lip, my eyes land on Enzo. The fucking shit-stirrer just smirks, seeing my predicament but offering no help whatsoever. Narrowing my gaze on him, silently saying *thanks for nothing, asshole,* I take a step toward Dante's sofa. Slowly, I lower my ass onto the couch as far away from him as possible. Of course, he's tall, so he's got a large wingspan, meaning his hand still touches my hair, and he wraps a strand around his finger, mindlessly playing with it and seemingly unaware of my rigid posture.

"We can't do anything until we find out my father's plan," he states, still twisting my hair between his fingers. "I can't figure out what he's after. If it was blackmail, he wouldn't use your brother. Trust me. He's got enough leverage as it is." That last sentence is said in a bitter tone, and he and Enzo share a look I can't decipher.

"Then why bring him to the church? It sure felt like a threat to me."

Enzo shrugs, drawing my attention his way. "To fuck with you?" He phrases it as a question, clearly guessing. "Giovanni is excellent at mental manipulation. He can worm his way so deep into your head that you'll never get him out." I shiver just at the thought of that. Is that what he's done to Dante? Apparently so. "He knows he's got Dante and I firmly under his control, but you're an outlier he can't afford. He doesn't know how you might upset the balance he's maintained. Dante's already shown his cards by agreeing to give up having a say in his Consigliere for you." He pauses, his eyes drilling into me. Every word out of his mouth has my heart beating faster with fear. "It could be that he's using Luc to control you. To get you under his thumb and guarantee you won't get in the way of his plans."

The air around me suddenly feels dense and thick, and my lungs constrict with the lack of oxygen. My voice sounds choked when I manage to squeeze out, "Does he? Have you under his control?" We've never had this conversation before. We've never needed to. But now that my brother is stuck in the thick of this, I *need* to know where the two men beside me—the two men I have grown undeniably attached to—fall. Will they side with me or Giovanni? I know enough of Enzo's past and have seen the hostility in his eyes, and heard it in his voice, to be quietly confident that he would pick me. Or, at the very least, he won't pick Giovanni. However, Dante's a conundrum I still haven't figured out.

Enzo's gaze flickers to Dante, giving me his answer. He's team Dante. He will probably try to persuade Dante otherwise if he chooses Giovanni, but regardless, he'll side with Dante. I can respect that level of loyalty, even if the thought of being on the wrong side of the two of them does have anxiety driving into me like icicles through my chest.

Slowly. Ever so slowly, I turn to face Dante, terrified of what I'll see in his eyes. I'm almost scared to look, and when I'm finally facing him, my eyes remain glued to the black knot of his tie. For the life of me, I can't seem to get them to go any higher. I can feel the pulse at the base of my neck thumping a wild tune that matches the erratic thudding of my heart. I sit like that for so long Dante has to reach out, and with a firm hold on my chin, he physically lifts my head until I'm forced to meet his steely brown gaze.

The potency of what I find staring back at me slams into my chest, making me gasp. Flashes of the way he looked at me in the church drift to the forefront of my mind. I was so out of it that day, consumed with fear over Luc's sudden and unexpected appearance, that I didn't take anything else in. Only now I can picture him clearly, standing in front of me in his three-piece suit, black tie, and polished shoes.

Just like on that day, there's the similar flare of possession making his eyes appear darker, more black with veins of red glowing through them, though for the first time, I see that possession for what it is. Not a desire to control or smother me, but simply an intense need to *have* me. Enzo's words from earlier finally click. Dante doesn't even understand what he's feeling. In basic caveman terms—me likey, me want. He sees something he likes, someone he feels a connection with and is holding on to it with both hands.

He still holds my chin captive between his thumb and index finger while he strokes along my jawline. "I vowed to protect you, *mia vita*. Even against my father." I somehow don't think that was specifically mentioned in our wedding vows, but the ferocity in his voice begs no argument. Even if it wasn't in our vows, it's a promise he's made to himself. "My father thinks he controls me, and until recently, it has suited my agenda to let him continue believing that." He gently squeezes my chin, and I intuitively know what he says next is important. "But you are my wife. My life is beholden only to you. I will only ever do what is in *your* best interests." I can't do anything but fall into his dark brown depths while he shreds my heart into pieces and stitches them back together with his name embedded in the lining. "Your brother is important to you, which means he's important to me. Whatever it is my father wants, I won't let him hurt your brother."

I believe him. It would be impossible not to after that speech, especially with the impassioned way he's looking at me. My lips part before I close them again, not knowing how to respond. Nothing I can think of even comes close to that declaration. Instead, I end up giving a feeble nod, and when Dante lets go of me, I side-eye Enzo. The asshole is just sitting on the opposite sofa with his arms folded across his chest, cocking an eyebrow at me, clearly saying, *I told you so.*

"We need to go," Dante states, checking the time on his large, expensive-looking watch before getting to his feet. Holding out a hand, he helps me up before he moves to grab his gun that had been sitting on the breakfast bar. Enzo follows, the two of them tucking their weapons into the back of their suit pants.

When he's done, Dante rakes his eyes over me. "You should have a weapon too. The gun you wore yesterday, do you know how to use it?"

The fact that he's not just telling me to duck behind him or Enzo if shit goes down surprises the hell out of me. "No need." I lift the hem of my dress, giving both of them an eyeful of my toned, milky-white thighs and the two sharp blades I have sheathed to them. "I'm good."

Both of their eyes turn molten. Apparently, seeing a girl dressed up and armed is a turn-on. *Huh, who knew.* Grabbing my clutch from the sofa, I shake it. "And my backup, just in case."

Enzo snorts, but Dante tilts his head with a narrowed gaze and runs his eyes over my body. Despite the heat there, it's not just lust driving his reaction. He juts his chin out, repeating. "Do you know how to use those things?"

I get the impression he already knows I do, so rather than being offended, I push back my shoulders and lift my chin. I try to keep my typical stony-faced Reaper mask in place, but it slips as a confident smirk lifts one side of my lips. "I'm the Reaper. Of course, I know how to use them."

His expression never falters. Not even for a second. Trust me, I'm watching him so intently that I'd have noticed. Even Enzo is watching him closely, wanting to see his reaction. After a moment, he grunts. "Well, that explains a few things."

I stare at him in bewilderment before my gaze darts to Enzo and back to Dante.

"Seriously? That's all you have to say?" I mean, I'm not exactly sure what reaction I was expecting. Probably for him to call bullshit, like Cain did. Like most men would.

There's a slight twitch on one side of his lip as if he's suppressing a smile. "It's not that much of a stretch," he states easily. "You have no problem going toe-to-toe with me when most people would run in the opposite direction—quickly. You didn't react like a terrified woman when I pulled you into the closet that day at the club. And you held your own against Enzo today."

Enzo snorts before grumbling something under his breath that sounds suspiciously like, "I was going easy on her for her first time."

I roll my eyes as he walks out of the kitchen to go get the car keys. Dante makes to move after him, but I'm still reeling from his lack of surprise. "But how did you..." It clicks a second later. "The camera. You were watching us?"

Pausing, Dante turns, a small smile lifting one side of his lips. "Of course I was."

My eyebrows lower. "Don't you trust Enzo?"

A seriousness flattens his small hint of amusement. "I trust Enzo with my life. Therefore, I trust him with yours. But I don't trust him not to make a move when my back is turned."

I have no words, and I'm still gaping at him when Enzo ducks his head back through the doorway. "You're going to have to get over that, but for now, we have to go."

"I thought we were going to your father's penthouse?" I question, when we pull into an underground parking lot beneath yet another giant skyscraper several streets over from the one his father lives in.

"We are, but we can't just walk in the front door every time. Otherwise, all of our enemies would know where Giovanni lives," Enzo answers.

"Okayyyy..." I still don't get it.

"So, we mix it up each time." Dante's eyes meet mine. "You'll see."

On that cryptic note, I follow them out of the car and over to the corner of the lot where there is a bank of elevators. Enzo presses the button to signal one, and a second later, the door opens and we all file in. Except, instead of pressing the button for one of the floors above us, Enzo pulls out a key and opens a hidden panel. Stepping forward, Dante leans in until he's eye level with the panel, and I peer over his shoulder, watching as a machine scans his eye. A second later, the elevator startles to life and I feel us descend deeper into the Earth. *What the hell?* This is all very weird.

Down and down we go until we must be deep underground, and when the elevator opens again, a gush of cold air blows in, raising goosebumps along my skin and making me shiver. I step out into what appears to be a large, man-made tunnel, lit with bright, luminescent bulbs that emit a low buzz above us.

"Where does it go?" I ask, peering into the darkness far up ahead.

Dante places his hand on my lower back, encouraging me forward, and the three of us begin walking down the tunnel. "All over our portion of the city."

"Is this why we used the front door last time you brought me to meet your father? So I wouldn't know about the tunnels?"

Enzo smirks at me over his shoulder in response. Even back then, they had been placing their trust in me by not blindfolding me, but I obviously passed that test if I'm being shown the tunnels now. Of course, if I'd failed, I probably would have been swimming with the fishes by dinner time.

We walk on through the tunnels, Dante directing me every time we reach a junction, for what must be at least twenty minutes before we come to a stop at another elevator. We passed a couple of others, but neither of them enlightened me as to where they went, and I didn't bother asking.

They do the same song and dance with the eye scanner before the elevator doors open, and this time Enzo pushes the button for the penthouse. Nerves rattle around in my stomach, knowing that I'll see Luc again in a few short moments. He better not be in any worse shape than he was the last time I saw him.

Dante's hand is still firmly planted against my back, the warmth and his constant presence helping to keep me grounded, and Enzo brushes his arm against mine. I feel the back of his fingers hit mine, and needing a little more, I push my fingers between his, loosely intertwining them. It's only for a brief moment, for as long as it takes the elevator to reach the penthouse, before we both pull back, but I already feel bolstered knowing the two of them are at my side. When the doors open, I step out with my head held high and my game face on, ready to paint the penthouse red to get my brother back.

My facial features have settled into their usual impassive mask as we step into Giovanni's apartment. All of his inner circle are here—his closest advisors. Spotting us, the man himself abandons the conversation he was in and comes our way, a too-bright smile on his face.

"Ah, my son and his beautiful wife." He ignores me, something I'm more than used to and happy enough with. There was once a time when his blatant refusal to acknowledge my presence would have sent me into a panic, desperate to do anything short of licking his balls to gain his attention. But that time has long since passed. I fucking loathe the narcissistic egomaniac standing in front of me. If it was up to me, he'd have been booted from his throne and drowned in the docks years ago.

Nevertheless, unfortunately, that's not my call. As the next Don, Dante has to be the one to rise up against his father, and until recently, he seemed content to leave the hierarchy as it is. I can understand why. Taking over the mantle, especially after a hostile takeover, will be incredibly challenging. He didn't think it was worth the effort.

Without even realizing it, Giovanni has been hammering the nails into his own coffin. First, with his blackmail attempt of using explicit photos of Dante and me to force him to choose a Consigliere worthy of his father's approval, then the shit he pulled with Sawyer, and now this. Dante may have been happy mainly living unbothered under his father's rule, but now that he's been interfering and targeting the very people closest to him, I can tell he's getting pissed off. I firmly believe Sawyer is the catalyst he needed to push him into finally getting rid of his father. Dante needs to step out of his father's shadow, remove his influence over him and finally come into his own.

"You're just in time. We're about to sit down and eat."

"Where's my brother?" Sawyer spits out, clearly already done with this posturing bullshit.

Giovanni's lip lifts in a sneer, and a flash of irritation crosses his features. He prefers his women quiet and docile. Fuck dolls and arm candy. He could never handle a woman like Sawyer.

When his smile returns, it's tighter than it was before, more forced. "All in good time. Let's eat. Santos will be here with him any minute now. The two of them were just... getting to know one another."

A secretive smirk lifts the corner of his lip, and I notice Dante's eyes narrow in suspicion as Giovanni wanders off to direct the rest of the guests to the dining table.

I share a look with Dante over Sawyer's head before he ushers her forward toward the large dining table situated along one of the many floor-to-ceiling glass walls that overlook the city. Giovanni is already sitting at the head of the table. There's an empty chair on his right for Santos, and Dante moves over to his seat on Giovanni's left. Sawyer takes the seat beside him while the rest of Giovanni's advisors claim the other seats. However, I notice they leave the one next to Santos' chair free—presumably for Luc. Since I'm not technically a guest—only here as Dante's bodyguard—I'm not eligible to sit at the table, and as such, I move to stand against the glass wall behind Dante and Sawyer.

As everyone settles in, the ping of the elevator arriving rings out across the room. "Ah, right on time." Giovanni grins triumphantly, only worrying me more. What the hell does he have up his sleeve?

Santos steps out of the elevator, shoving Luc as he goes. The kid is deathly pale, making the bruises on his face stand out more so than they did at the church.

Sawyer moves as if to stand, presumably intending to rush toward her brother, but Dante's hand quickly snaps out to stop her, and he gives her a stern look to stay seated. She purses her lips yet remains in her seat, her eyes trailing Luc's approach as Santos jostles him forward into the awaiting chair.

The two siblings remain eye-locked on one another, a private conversation that doesn't require words going on between them until the scraping of Giovanni's chair drags against the wooden floor as he stands to draw everyone's attention.

"Today is a day of celebration," he announces. My gaze darts from Giovanni to Luc, and I notice Sawyer does the same. Whatever this *celebration* is involves him, but how? "Today, we welcome one of our own into the fold." I carefully school my confusion, though I catch a flicker of the same confusion on Sawyer's face. "Someone who has been kept hidden from us for years. Denied the chance to know his family and to live up to his birthright. Thankfully, through sheer luck, he has been found, and I'd like you all to welcome Lucifer Ricci into the Antonelli Famiglia."

A round of applause goes up around the table, but the sound is dull and distant as I stare at the wide-eyed kid in front of me. His gaze darts around the table before landing on Sawyer, practically begging her to make sense of all this for him. When she turns to look at Dante, likely wondering if he is any the wiser as to what his father is talking about, I catch sight of the deep furrow of her brow. Dante gives an imperceptible shake of his head, indicating he doesn't know anything more than she does, and she quickly swivels her gaze to her brother's again.

By the time she turns to Giovanni, her eyes are cold, and I can tell from the way she's sitting, with her back pushed flat against the chair, that she's ready to spring into action. "What the hell are you talking about?" she spits, glowering at Giovanni. I doubt the man has ever had a person—let alone a woman—glare at him like that. Like she'd happily sink one of her blades into his gut.

His teeth grind together, the muscle in his jaw popping. "Dante," he growls. "Control your woman."

Sawyer's nostrils flare at the insult, and beneath the table, I notice her fingers clench into a fist, but she wisely remains silent.

"I think what my wife means to say is, how did you uncover all of this?"

Ignoring his son, Giovanni continues to stare at Sawyer, asserting his dominance until she ducks her head in an act of submission. She's acting. Playing the part of the apologetic wife who has been put in her place so the situation can move along and we can finally get some answers. Sawyer submits to no man, least of all Giovanni.

Seeming appeased, Giovanni lowers himself back into his chair. "It's interesting, really. Since the girl"—he gestures lamely in Sawyer's direction—"obviously caught your eye, Santos did his due diligence investigating her."

The man himself chuckles—if you could call it that. It's more of a deep, humorless rumble, the twitch of his lips causing the line of Xs down his right cheek to shift. "And thank god I did. I've been looking for him ever since that bitch came crying to me for money."

"That... our mother?" Sawyer sneers. Luc's eyes widen, his face draining of the last vestiges of color.

Santos' lip curls in disgust. "That *whore* you mean. Who was she to keep my son from me? *My* blood. *Antonelli* blood." He shakes his head. Seemingly unconcerned with Luc's deathly pale complexion, Santos claps a hand on his shoulder, turning his head to face him. "My only regret was killing the slut before she told me where you were." Luc flinches, as if Santos' words are a physical force whipping him across the face. Unbothered by his son's reaction, Santos tilts his head, gesturing around the table as he says, "You could have been a part of all of this so much sooner."

Giovanni leans forward to rest his hand on his second's forearm. "Better late than never, my friend. The family'll accept him with open arms, and we'll get him up to standard as quickly as possible."

My head reels, and I can't even begin to imagine what a head fuck this is for Luc or Sawyer. I wish I weren't standing behind her so that I could read her expression. If the bunching of her shoulders is anything to go by, she's fucking pissed. Dante squeezes her thigh under the table, a silent warning to rein in her temper. Blood means everything to Giovanni, and knowing it's Antonelli blood running through Luc's veins complicates this situation tenfold. Luc isn't just some kid who he's using to control Sawyer and Dante. He's an Antonelli; a soldier. Fucking family.

There's no way in hell we're leaving here with him today. Not without declaring world war three, which would be a war none of us are prepared for. It's not one we could possibly win if we go in half-cocked. I've no doubt Dante views it the same way. Sawyer will be furious, but we need to regroup. We need an actual fucking plan, 'cause if we're doing this, there's no turning back. There's no standing down. Once we make a move against Giovanni, we've gotta be one hundred percent in. It'll be him or us, and I sure as fuck am not ready to die just yet. Not when I haven't even had a chance to make Sawyer mine and prove to Dante that it's meant to be the three of us.

The topic moves on to other things as the food arrives. Throughout the meal, Sawyer and Luc push food around their plates, sharing glances. Every time Sawyer lifts her knife, she grips it with white-knuckle force, and I know she's picturing ramming it through Giovanni's neck. Thankfully for all of us, she resists the urge.

"Sawyer would like a few minutes with her brother," Dante says casually as the evening begins to wrap up.

With pursed lips, Giovanni's narrowed gaze swivels to Sawyer. "Fine, but only a couple of minutes. I need to talk to you anyway." He gestures toward his office, and with a quick glance my way, silently communicating for me to follow, Dante gets to his feet, and the two of us follow his father. Santos trails behind us, closing the office door behind me.

"What are you doing about these Reject people?" Giovanni demands as he moves to claim his seat behind his large, ostentatious, black marble desk. The wall behind him is sheer glass, offering an unobstructed view of the city sprawled below us, and in front of the desk are two leather seats. Dante makes no move to sit. Santos walks over to a bar cart and pours himself and his boss a glass of scotch before making himself comfortable on one of the black leather sofas placed off to one side, providing an informal seating area.

"They'll be taken care of this week," Dante assures his father, not elaborating further. It's taken us a while to gather information on them and confirm it was, in fact, them who blew up our clubs. Although now with the wedding over, their demise is at the top of our to-do list.

"It better be." Giovanni's nostrils flare. "I don't want any fuck-ups. I want them all gone. Every last one of them."

The extent of his anger catches me by surprise. Sure, he was furious when he found out about the clubs, but I get the feeling there's something else going on here. A new development, perhaps?

The muscle in the back of his jaw twitches as he grits his teeth. "The boy was apparently under their protection," he eventually explains. "No doubt they will use this as an excuse to attack us again. I want them obliterated before any more of our clubs end up out of commission."

Luc was under the protection of the Rejects? That doesn't make any sense. How do they even know who he is? There's no way Sawyer's distaste for gangsters would allow her to let her brother fall into that sort of life, so how the hell did he get mixed up with the Rejects?

I keep my expression carefully neutral, as does Dante, who simply nods his head, giving nothing away. "Of course, Father. We'll get it taken care of immediately."

Appeased, for now, Giovanni nods his head before taking a sip of his scotch. Knowing he's been dismissed, Dante turns on his heels and heads out of the office. I follow him, finding Sawyer talking to Luc in a hushed tone. Their conversation comes to an abrupt halt as we approach.

"Sawyer, we have to go," Dante states, placing his hand on her lower back. I can see the refusal on Sawyer's lips, but he leans in, whispering in her ear. If the flattening of her lips and spark of anger in her eyes is anything to go by, she doesn't like what he has to say, but after a second, she gives a sharp nod. Her expression softens as she meets her brother's gaze, and she wraps him in a tight hug, whispering in his ear before breaking off their embrace.

"Stay safe," she murmurs. "I'll see you soon." With a final squeeze of his hand, she reluctantly lets go and Dante directs her toward the elevators. I hesitate in front of her brother and glance over my shoulder, finding Santos watching us closely.

"Just do as they say for now," I tell the kid in a quiet voice, holding his gaze. "Don't fight back, and don't question them. And whatever you do, do not show any weakness. We'll figure out how to get you out of this as soon as possible."

His chin lifts in defiance, and contempt flashes across his face. "Like I'm going to listen to a word you say."

I smirk, feeling a bit more at ease now that I've seen he's got the same fire in him as his sister, and with a slight nod, I turn and stride toward the elevator as the doors slide open.

"I CAN'T FUCKING BELIEVE WE LEFT HIM THERE!" SAWYER FUMES AS SHE stomps into the house. She and Dante have been arguing the entire way home. Well, mostly, she's been shouting and cursing him out, and he hasn't said a word, which has only infuriated her further. I was too busy focusing on the road and thinking over tonight's revelations.

"You know we didn't have any other option," I sigh, feeling the dull thud of a headache forming. Shrugging out of my jacket, I drape it over the back of the bar stool on my way to pour us all drinks. God knows, I need a stiff drink after this day.

With three glasses of whiskey on the rocks in my hand, I pass one over to Dante and set Sawyer's on the table before sinking into a chair. Sawyer's too busy pacing back and forth, the click of her heels driving me insane as she silently fumes. "He's just a kid. He's a fucking kid." She stops, spinning to face us, and I see the sheen of tears in her eyes that she's fighting to keep back.

Sighing, I set my drink on the table and stand. Stepping toward her, I envelop her in my arms, knowing she needs that bit of comfort and Dante isn't good with this sort of stuff. He wouldn't know the first thing about comforting a woman, so he better be taking notes. She sags against me, her body heat penetrating through my shirt while I run my hand up and down her back in soothing circles. With her head buried against my neck, I feel the warm puffs of her breath against my skin as she takes a shaky inhale, trying to gather herself. "He'll be okay," I try to reassure her.

She leans back so she can look up at me. She looks utterly exhausted, and defeat lines her face. "You don't know that."

Lifting a hand, I tuck a strand of loose hair behind her ear. "He's had you as a parental figure his whole life. If anyone has a chance of withstanding what they'll throw at him, it's Luc."

She gives a soft smile, but I can tell she's not completely reassured. "What exactly will they do to him?" My arms fall away as she steps back, and I trail the backs of my fingers down her arm until my hand slides into hers. Turning, I tug her over to sit on the sofa beside me. Dante glares at where I hold her hand, but I only tighten my grip, refusing to let go as I rest our joined hands on her thigh. He can be pissed all he wants, but I'm done with this shit. Besides, he won't act on it. He might not know how to react when Sawyer—or any woman—is upset, but he can see that she needs the emotional support he's unable to provide.

She looks at me before her gaze swivels to Dante. "Tell me."

Dante's lips are pressed into a flat line, his gaze fixed on the floor as he no doubt relives his own traumatic past. Silence hangs heavy in the air, and when he finally lifts his head, his eyes are cold, detached.

"They'll try to break him. Try to rob him of his humanity. They'll try to strip him back to his bare-bones, remove everything that makes him *him*, until there's nothing left." With every word out of Dante's mouth, Sawyer squeezes my hand tighter. I can feel the fear coursing through her, seeping through her pores and making her palm slick with perspiration.

When she speaks, she sounds hoarse. "Why?" Her voice breaks over the word, and I slide closer to her, pressing my body flush against hers as I offer her the only comfort I can.

Dante's voice is void of any emotion when he answers her, "So they can turn him into whoever they want him to be."

Sawyer shivers as she holds my hand in a death grip. "We're not going to let that happen." I pierce Dante with a stern look. He's scaring the shit out of her.

"How?" she cries. When she looks up at me, her face is pale, her mesmerizing blue eyes wide with fear.

I drop my gaze, an uncomfortable tightness forming in my chest at knowing I can't answer her.

"We'll find a way." Dante's voice rings with conviction, drawing my attention as I lift my head. His facial features are set in a determined mask, his gaze steady as he stares at Sawyer. "We'll do whatever it takes. I won't let them turn your brother..." He trails off with a grimace and my chest aches with empathy for him.

Tensing, Sawyer hesitantly asks, "Turn him into what?"

"Into me."

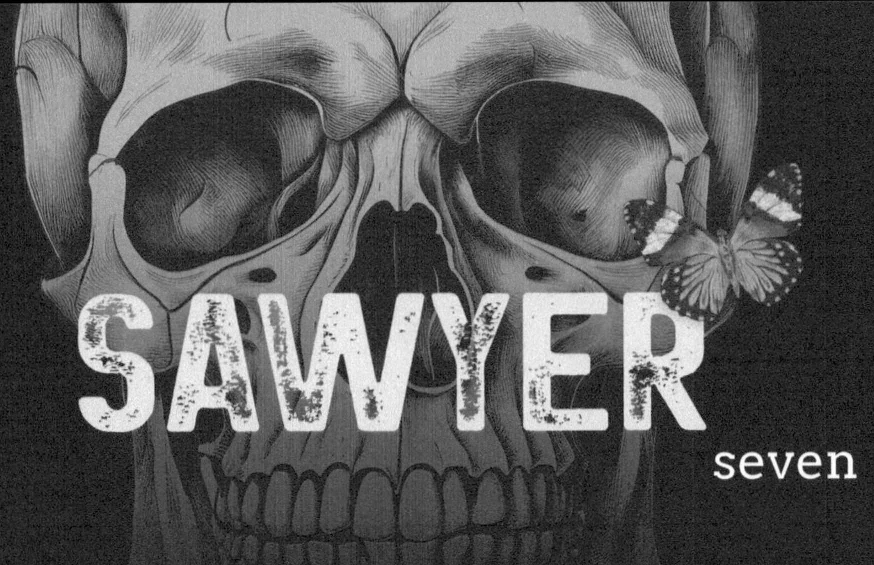

I *won't let them turn your brother into me.*

I stare speechlessly at Dante as his words ring in my ears. Is that what his father and Santos are going to try and do? Turn my innocent baby brother into Dante? But even Dante isn't who they think he is. He's not the cold, detached, mindless soldier they tried to make him into. Although, he's not without his scars. Whatever the hell they did to him, it left a permanent mark. I'd go so far as to say it came close to breaking him. In Dante's eyes, they *did* break him. But I can see what he can't. The flicker of humanity trying to break free. Enzo sees it too. He stokes the flame at every available opportunity, giving it the oxygen it needs to survive.

However, a single flame isn't enough. The only way he will accept that he's not irreparably damaged is if I can turn that flame into a forest fire. Something scalding hot and raging that he can feel all the way to his core. I need the flames to lick at his soul and incinerate any doubt he has. Earlier today, he chose me over his father, and now I'm choosing him too. I won't let Giovanni destroy my brother, and I won't let him continue trying to extinguish the good that I know is inside Dante.

I'm not sure how long I hold Dante's gaze. It feels like a long time, where nothing exists except the turmoil I can see brewing in his eyes. I can see the war raging inside him —the ice-cold, detached part of himself battling against that single flame. For the first time, I see the struggle he has to endure every day. I see the desperation, the fear. He's terrified of what he will become if that spark is snuffed out.

Eventually, he blinks, and just like that, the shutter drops over his face, cutting me off. I offer him a slight smile of gratitude, knowing that even showing me that tiny bit of insight will have been challenging for him. Baby steps.

Exhaustion tugs at me as I down the last of my whiskey. "It's been a long day," I sigh, getting to my feet. "I'm going to bed."

With a nod, Dante moves as if to follow me, but I stop him in his tracks. "No. I..." I trail off, not wanting to hurt him but knowing I need to just be alone with my thoughts right now. "I need to be alone."

His eyes narrow and his lips purse, but before he can argue, I stride for the door. Half an hour later, freshly showered and wearing Oliver's t-shirt, I climb into bed with my phone in hand.

"Hey, Trouble." Oliver's soothing voice comes down the line, making tears prick in my eyes.

"Hey," I choke out.

"What's going on?"

"Luc's an Antonelli." The admission is nothing more than a whisper as I struggle to wrap my mind around that sentence.

"What?!"

"Santos is his father."

"Fucking hell," Oliver murmurs.

"Yeah."

We both grow quiet, lost in our thoughts, until I eventually confess my deepest fear aloud. "I don't know how to get him out. And if I don't figure it out soon, I'm going to lose him."

"You won't lose him, baby. We're not going to let that happen. We'll raze the goddamn city if that's what it takes to get him back."

I smile weakly at wanting desperately to believe him, but in my heart of hearts, I know he can't guarantee that. Just like Enzo couldn't. No one can.

"They know you destroyed their clubs," I tell him, changing the subject.

He scoffs. "Don't worry about that. We can handle a few Antonelli assholes."

That may be so, but I've no intention of letting it come to that. Just another problem I need to deal with ASAP. I'm at risk of losing my brother, and I'm not about to risk losing my Rejects too.

He goes quiet on the other end and all I can hear is his breathing. My heart clenches, and I miss him with such an overwhelming ache that I can hardly breathe.

"Do you need anything from me?" he asks.

"You," I breathe as a fresh wave of tears clogs my throat and soaks my cheeks. "I just need you."

"You have me, baby. I'm here. And soon, you'll be here with us."

I want that, so much. But the thought of leaving here and never coming back doesn't sit right with me either. I feel so lost; torn between two different worlds. Between two different sets of guys. And I have no idea how to navigate any of this.

"Close your eyes," he murmurs, his voice dipping an octave. "I'm right there with you. Can you feel me?"

Doing as he instructs, I close my eyes and imagine him lying beside me on the bed, his arms wrapped around me. "Yes."

"You feel my body, the heat of my skin pressed against yours."

"Yes."

"The press of my lips."

"Yes."

"Where?"

"On my lips."

"Gentle or dirty?"

I smirk. "Dirty." He hums in agreement. "You're kissing along my jaw. Down my neck." I picture him doing exactly that as my insides heat, my body melting into the duvet.

"Leaving marks along your skin so those assholes know you're ours."

I shiver at the deep growl of ownership, my body responding to his claim as I dip my free hand below the waistband of my panties, finding myself wet and hungry for him. "Yes," I gasp, sliding my fingers through my folds.

Over the rushing of blood in my ears, all I can hear is his heavy breathing, letting me know he's as into this as I am.

"What am I doing now?" His voice is gruff, the words strained.

"You're between my legs while you eat me out." I use my fingers to work me over, picturing his tongue in their place as I crest that peak.

"Mmm, cherry pie. Fucking delicious," he groans. "I need to taste your cum in my mouth, Trouble." I moan obscenely as my back arches, my body writhing on the bedsheets. "You gonna come for me?"

"Yes. Yes, yes, yes!" I bite down on my lower lip to stifle the cry threatening to break free as pleasure floods my body and I sag onto the bed, boneless and panting as Oliver grunts out his release.

"Mom, I'm home," I call out as I hold the paper bag overfilled with groceries in a precarious grip and wiggle the key out of the lock. Why does it always stick? As if juggling heavy shopping bags isn't a challenge all on its own. "Mom!" I call again when I get no response.

The key finally comes free, and stepping into the apartment, I kick the door closed behind me. Blood rushes in my ears as I freeze just inside the doorway, slack jaw as I glance around at the carnage of our tiny living room-kitchen. The apartment has been completely trashed. The television has been smashed against the ground, couch cushions slashed open, the kitchen table is upside down with a wooden leg broken off, and cupboard drawers are hanging off their hinges.

What the actual fuck happened here?

"MOM!" This time there is a ring of panic in my voice as I drop the grocery bags on the floor and move deeper into the apartment. Where the hell is she? And where is my baby brother? "LUC?"

Silence. I can only hope that means they weren't home when the intruder broke in. My eyes are wide as I slowly, with careful footsteps, walk through the mess strewn all over the place.

Reaching the kitchen, I turn in a full circle, noting the broken dishes and glasses that look like they've been thrown all over the place. Someone was in a rage. Anger flares within me. Mom probably pissed off her pimp again or stole from a client. Fucking idiot. She was supposed to be looking after Luc, so where the fuck are they? She better not have taken him to that crack den again. I'll actually murder her this time.

A sound has me spinning as fear trickles down my spine. Fuck, is the intruder still here? My eyes dart around the tiny kitchen, not seeing anything. My heart hammers against my chest as I strain to hear even the slightest sound, but there's nothing but silence.

No creaking of the floorboards or whining of a hinge. Nothing but the thud, thud, thud of my racing heart.

I hear it again as I step toward the corridor leading down to the bedrooms—a soft muffle. My head whips back around to the kitchen counters, certain that the sound came from that side of the room. My eyes narrow as I stare at the peeling yellow paint on the cabinets before I slowly take a step toward them. An intruder wouldn't be hiding in a fucking kitchen cabinet, Sawyer, I chastise myself as fear threatens to take over. Hell, only a kid could fit in there.

I gasp in realization, and tossing all concern for myself aside, I rush toward the cabinets, yanking them open one by one as I shove colanders, saucepans, and plates aside. Reaching the third cupboard, I throw it open and freeze.

"Saw-er!" Luc cries.

"Oh my god, Luc," I gasp, taking in his pink cheeks, eyes swollen with tears, and snotty nose. "What are you doing in here? Where's mom?" He dives into my open arms, bawling his eyes out while clinging to me like I'm his lifeline.

I wrap my arms around his shaking body, holding him close while I try to soothe him. What the hell happened here? I sit there for ages, crouching in front of the cupboard with him in my arms, waiting until he cries himself out. Eventually, his wails turn to soft whimpers and hiccups.

"It's okay, I'm here now," I repeat on a mantra, trying to calm him. My legs are numb as I hitch him on my hip and get to my feet, returning to my search of the apartment. Hopefully, at least his bedroom is intact, and I can set him in there while I tidy up and find out where the hell our mother has disappeared off too. This is the last time I leave her to look after him. Can she not go five minutes without getting her next fix? Things have been going downhill for years as her addiction has repeatedly taken priority over mothering. At least when I was younger, she tried to keep it behind closed doors and could hold down a job for a few months. Now, every penny she makes comes from prostituting herself out, though most of it goes into getting herself high. Luc would have died from starvation or cold if I didn't steal and pickpocket what scraps and spare dollars I could. It pisses me off that I have to be the parent in this family, but whatever. I'll do whatever it takes to ensure Luc gets everything he needs. God knows, it's not his fault his mother is a complete waste of space who doesn't care about anyone other than herself.

Reaching the first bedroom door, I find it ajar and push it open with my foot. I sigh heavily when I find mom's things scattered around her room. Clothes have been tossed out of her wardrobe and her bed has been pushed to one side as if someone was trying to check under it.

With a shake of my head, I move swiftly on, already picturing the damage I'll find in his room and mine.

"It's alright, Luc," I soothe, rubbing his back. His tiny arms are wrapped tightly around my neck, his head buried in the crook of my neck. "Mommy will be back soon. Let's get you into bed and I'll get us tidied up. How about mac 'n' cheese for dinner, yeah?"

I reach Luc's bedroom next. His door is covered in dinosaur stickers, and I'm distracted, placing a kiss on the top of his head as I step into the room. My steps falter as the door creaks open and I catch my first glimpse of a foot. Another step, and a torso comes into view. Unease churns my stomach, bile climbing up my throat as the door swings all the way open.

"Oh my god," I gasp. I clutch Luc's head, holding him tightly against me so he can't look. He can't see this. I can't see this. This can't be real. My chest heaves as I stand frozen in the doorway, trembling from head to toe. My vision blurs and I have to blink, causing tears to spill down my cheeks. I don't need to see her, though. The image of her lying there is forever ingrained into my memory: her wide, glassy eyes and the mottled bruising around her neck.

I stumble from the room, dry heaving as I blindly make my way back to the living room and collapse onto the floor. Hours pass in a haze as the sun slowly moves across the sky in the kitchen window while I freak out on the grimy floor and clutch my brother to me. My mom is dead. Murdered. Lost in my frantic thoughts, I kiss the top of Luc's head. He lifts his face to look at me, and I stare down at him. What the hell am I supposed to do now?

I STARTLE AWAKE WITH A GASP THAT QUICKLY TURNS TO A MOAN AS pleasure unfurls in my lower belly. My heart is still racing from that dream... except it wasn't a dream. It was very much reality. *My* reality. My past. And I'm currently experiencing the biggest mindfuck as I try to coincide the terror I felt when I awoke with the pleasurable sensations that are quickly sending that fear skittering to the recesses of my mind.

"What the..." I glance down to find Dante's broad shoulders wedged between my thighs, his tongue going to town as he laps, sucks, and nibbles on me. Another wave of pleasure rattles through me, and I arch my back. I go to move my hands, but something cold pinches the skin. Confused, I glance up to find my wrists handcuffed to the bed. What the... "Ooh," I moan as Dante's fingers join the party, easily sliding into me.

My lids are at half-mast as I writhe beneath him, my breathing quickly becoming ragged as the pleasure builds in my core, threatening to explode outwards at any moment. The handcuffs dig painfully into my skin as I instinctively try to move them to thread my fingers through Dante's hair, wanting him closer, needing more, and I groan in a mixture of frustration and need.

"Dante," I cry, desperate for release as I grind on his face. His eyes flick up to meet mine, and his pupils are dilated with arousal. His gaze holds me captive, this intangible connection hovering in the air between us like an electric current. It's thick with chemistry, lust, and desire, but there's something more profound as well. This isn't purely physical. It's not just sex. It's more, so much more. We both feel it, even if I can't put words to what it is. But as he stares into my eyes, I can feel it. Tenderness. Compassion. Maybe even love, or something close to it.

I throw my head back, screaming my release as pleasure shoots out from my core, racing along my nerves all the way to my fingers and toes, leaving me breathless. My eyes are closed as I try to get my breathing under control, then I feel Dante as he tugs my panties back in place and fixes my top before rolling onto his side of the bed.

As the heady rush of endorphins begins to wear off, reality seeps in, and the afterglow of my orgasm recedes as frustration and anger rear their ugly heads. I fell asleep *alone* last night. In my old room. Yet, I've woken up handcuffed to Dante's bed. The asshole doesn't know the meaning of personal space.

I snap my eyes open, intent on telling him off, but my mouth goes dry when I find him fisting his engorged cock. Precum leaks from the head as he works himself over in tight, fast strokes. He groans, the guttural noise dragging my attention to his face. His head is leaning back against the headboard, his eyes on me as his hand works harder, faster, bringing him to orgasm. Our eyes connect, that static energy flaring to life once again, and his face scrunches up as he grunts. Cum spurts onto his chest and abdomen, glistening against the hills and valleys of his abs as he breathes heavily.

After a moment, he gets up and heads into the bathroom, and I hear the shower turn on. Without his delicious body frying my brain cells and distracting me, I remember that I'm *still* handcuffed to his bed. Asshole.

"Sure, I'll just stay here," I grumble under my breath as I tug pointlessly on my restraints before giving up and waiting for him to come back.

He takes his sweet fucking time showering, and my head is about ready to explode when he returns. "Take these fucking things off me," I snap when he steps into the room with a towel hanging low on his hips.

He fights a smile as he moves toward the bed and perches beside me. I can't do anything except glower up at him. "I said I wanted to be alone last night."

"And I said you were to sleep in here from now on," he counters.

"How am I supposed to trust you if I can't even go to sleep without worrying if you're going to violate my privacy."

 Not immediately responding to me, he reaches out his hand instead, running the tip of his finger along the strip of skin on display between the bottom of my top and my panties. His eyes diligently follow the motion of his finger as if he can't look away. It's not a sexual gesture. It's more like he feels compelled to touch me. Like it's something he *has* to do. Goosebumps erupt along my skin, and somehow this moment feels even more intimate than the one we just shared.

Slowly, he drags his eyes over my chest and up my neck, until he reaches my face. His hand is still flat against my stomach, but it feels more comforting than dominating.

"You already do trust me. You wouldn't have told me about the Reaper if you didn't. Nor would you have left your brother behind yesterday."

Fuck, he might just be right. "Well, this definitely is not playing by the rules."

"You broke the rules first. You sleep in here," he reminds me, repeating his words from yesterday.

"I just needed time to myself," I try to explain.

He gives a small nod in understanding before reaching over to open the drawer in the bedside table. Producing a tiny key, he turns it over in his hand as if contemplating actually letting me go. I can see the hesitation in his eyes. He *wants* to keep me tied up here. Instead of berating him, I remain quiet, waiting to see what decision he chooses for himself, wanting to see whether my words from yesterday had any impact on him. Dante's a conundrum wrapped in an enigma, stuffed inside a puzzle box. He's not just a mystery to me, but to himself. He doesn't know who he is. He doesn't fully understand right from wrong, nor does he have the capacity to empathize and put himself in others' shoes. It's not that he can't, he just doesn't know how. He needs someone to show him. So, why do I find myself wanting to be that person?

I wait him out while he stares at the key in his hand. The seconds tick by, but eventually, he lifts his hand to insert the key in the lock, and with a click, the handcuffs fall away. I fight a smile, my heart swelling with pride that he did the right thing by me. Baby steps.

Sitting up, I lean forward and place a soft kiss on his cheek before shimmying to the end of the bed. I make a point of not looking back as I stride into the bathroom, so he can't see the stupid grin on my face. I have much bigger things I need to focus on today. Like saving my brother and protecting my guys. Closing the bathroom door behind me, my head drops back to rest against it as I sigh. Fuck, nothing like trying to achieve the impossible.

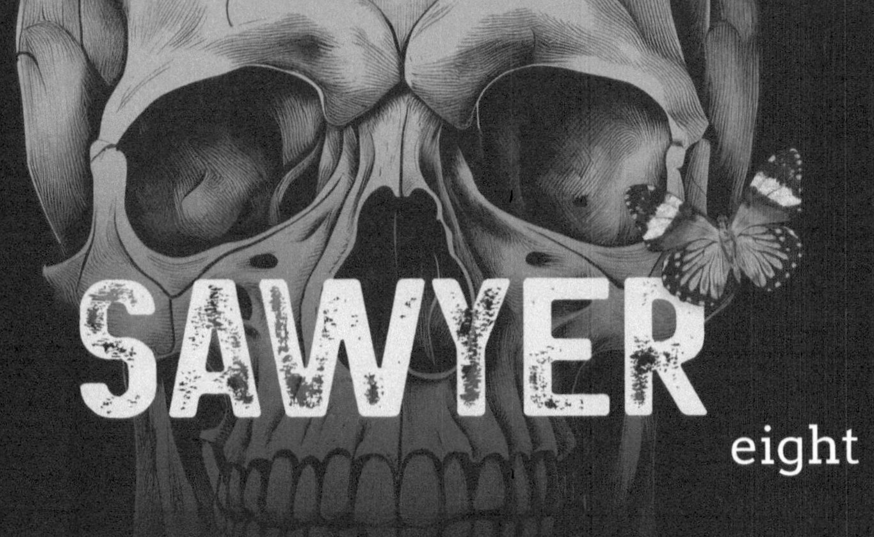

eight

Half an hour later, I step into the kitchen dressed in the comfiest pair of skinny jeans I've ever worn. They literally mold to my ass, making it look fantastic, and the rips in the knees are intentional and not a consequence of running around the city in them for years. I've paired them with my trusty, chunky heeled boots. There were more shoes in the wardrobe than I could wear in a year, but footwear is vital in my line of work and I don't have time for blisters while I break in a new pair of shoes. I've finished today's outfit with a forest green corset-style top that hugs my curves and pushes my tits together and complements my fiery-red hair perfectly.

Both men are already here. Dante with a cup of coffee in front of him while he sits at the breakfast bar talking to Enzo, who is cooking away. Both of them glance up when I walk in, and even though it's the same reaction every time I enter a room, it still bowls me over. The sheer intensity is overwhelming, and I never know how to react. Individually, these two men suck all the oxygen out of a room. They immediately draw your eye, power and dominance oozing out of them. Although together, they leave me speechless, weak-kneed, and wholly at their mercy.

"Coffee?" Enzo asks casually, as if there isn't a fire raging in his eyes.

"Sure." I glance at Dante as I move to claim the stool beside him. Any softness I may have witnessed in the bedroom is gone and in its place is his usual intensity, but that's okay.

"Thanks," I murmur as Enzo places a cup of steaming hot coffee in front of me before going back to whatever he's cooking. I watch him as he works, all the while feeling Dante's searing gaze as it bores into the side of my face. When I finally turn to look at him, a slight frown mars his features, and I can't work out what's bothering him.

"Here you go." Enzo hands over a plate with an omelet on it, holding out another one for Dante before he plates up his own breakfast, and the three of us move to the dining table.

We eat in silence, but it's not awkward. If anything, there's a familiar comfort to it.

Like this is something we do every morning. It's not, though. Sure, there has been the odd meal we've shared, but before the wedding, Dante was rarely around. And any time he was, awkwardness hung in the air like an unwanted second skin.

I can feel Dante's eyes on me as soon as he finishes, nonetheless he waits until I swallow my last bite before speaking. "I need to ask you something... and I need you to be honest with me."

Well, fuck. I hesitate for a second before nodding, even as my heart bangs dangerously against my ribs. Dante's gaze holds mine and I know that whatever he has to say, there will be no bullshitting my way out of it.

"Why is your brother under the protection of the Reaper Rejects?"

Shit. I'm guessing that's what his father wanted to talk to him about yesterday. I have been worried they would connect the dots back to the Rejects, but I'd been hoping on a wing and a prayer that the Bastards wouldn't have said anything. Fat lot of luck that did.

I shrug like it's no big deal. "Because he is."

"What? There's no way you'd leave him in their hands," Enzo interjects, knowing damn well my hatred of gangs. It serves as a reminder of just how closely he's been watching me these past eight years.

My eyes narrow on him. "I wasn't left with much choice when I was kidnapped and held hostage here."

He rolls his eyes. "Well, they did a piss poor job."

Now he's really starting to piss me off. "They did their best," I snap. "How were they to know Grim was in *your* pockets?!"

At my outburst, he cocks a brow, clearly surprised, and I blow out a breath knowing I need to calm down.

The entire time, Dante's gaze stays superglued on me. "It doesn't matter," he eventually speaks up. My lips flatten.

"It does, actually." I flick my gaze to his, knowing I'm about to demand the same thing from him that I asked of Cain. "I know you're planning an attack against them... and I can't let you go through with it."

His voice is flat. "That's none of your concern."

I scoff at his audacity. "Don't insult my fucking intelligence. If you wanted a wife who luxuriates around the house while leaving all the gritty work to the men, you married the wrong woman. I have a say, and I'm saying you can't do this. I won't let you."

"Why?" Enzo questions, his eyes narrowed on me. "Why do you care?"

I press my lips into a flat line while I blow out a hard breath. How much do I tell them? All the secrets and lies are getting twisted, and I don't know how much longer I can continue with this charade. Not to mention that this ludicrous thought has been growing in the back of my mind all morning, gaining traction... that the only way to save my brother and for Cain to get his vengeance, and possibly even for Dante to gain his freedom, is if we all unite. With the manpower of the Rejects combined with the knowledge of the inner workings of the Antonelli Empire by Dante and Enzo... we could be unstoppable.

Except, I have no idea how to make two opposing teams of alpha-male, dominant men who hate each other get along.

My foot bounces and I gnaw on my bottom lip while I try to figure out the best way to play this. The only thing I know for sure is that I can't keep up with this dual life. The Rejects or the Antonellis. Grubby gang life or the high-class mafia lifestyle. I never wanted to be a part of either, and now I find myself torn between the two.

Dante's fingers brush against my jaw, his thumb on my lower lip as he wrestles it free from my teeth. His voice is low and soft. "What secrets are you hiding, *mia vita*?"

Fuck. Can I trust them not to kill each other?

I return his intense stare, hoping like fuck I'm doing the right thing. "Do you trust me?"

"Yes." No hesitation. No uncertainty. The poor man is clearly missing a few brain cells.

My gaze flicks to Enzo, needing an answer from him too. I find his gaze steady, even though his expression is tight. "The only way this works is if we all trust one another."

Isn't that the fucking truth.

Still feeling unsure but committed nonetheless, I dig my phone out of my pocket and dial Cain's number. Both men watch me closely, and I have to glance away when Cain's growly voice comes down the line.

"Red, you okay?"

"Yeah, I'm fine. Is there somewhere on neutral territory where we could meet?"

He pauses, thinking for a second before responding, "Yeah. Why?"

"Meet me there in an hour. Just the two of you. No weapons."

"Uhh, yeah, alright. I'll text you the address. Are you sure everything's okay?" The fact that he doesn't demand to know what's going on speaks volumes. There's no doubt I will be on his shit list, but even so, warmth fills me at how far we've come over the last few months, despite the monumental hurdles thrown our way.

Ignoring his question, I ask, "Do you remember that favor I asked before?"

"Yes." His tone is much more hesitant this time, guarded.

"Does it still stand?"

"Red," he sighs, blowing out a breath. I know he wants me to explain, but I can't. Not now, with the two of them listening in. So instead, I stay silent, waiting him out.

"Fine," he finally huffs. "Yes. It still stands."

"Thank you," I murmur softly.

He grunts and growls out, "I'll text you the address," before hanging up.

Pocketing my phone, I get to my feet.

"Uh, wanna let us in on what's happening, Spitfire?" Enzo quirks a brow and I can tell he's irritated at being left out, or perhaps he was able to read between the lines of my conversation with Cain.

"Probably best if we wait. I don't want to repeat myself." His eyes narrow in annoyance. Meanwhile, Dante just watches me with a curious look on his face, like he can't quite figure me out. "Same rules apply, though. Just us. No weapons."

Nerves eat away at my insides, making me queasy as Enzo drives us across town. Besides giving Enzo the address Cain sent me, none of us have said anything since we got in the car. Dante appears relaxed, almost unbothered by my secrecy and the fact that he's going to an unknown location unarmed. I keep looking sideways at him out of the corner of my eye. Has he really placed that much trust in me that he has zero qualms about what I'm doing? Or does he just have such faith in his own ability to protect himself—and in Enzo's ability to protect him—that he doesn't need to be worried? The latter, it's got to be the latter. Although, a tiny part of myself that I refuse to properly acknowledge wants him to trust me.

Enzo, on the other hand, is furious that he's being kept in the dark. The only other time I've seen him this angry was when I disobeyed his orders and showed up at G&T the day the Antonellis blew it up.

"Why did you blow up G&T?" I ask. Now that I'm thinking about that day, I'm curious.

Enzo's gaze meets mine in the rearview mirror. "The owner racked up quite a gambling debt."

My lip curls in disgust. "So you destroy his only means of paying you back?"

"He received his fair share of warnings, not that he listened."

"And what about the innocent people who just happened to be there? Were we just collateral damage?" Tears of anger fill my eyes, blurring my vision. "Poor nobodies, so our lives don't matter."

When Enzo's gaze flicks up to the mirror again, his anger has been replaced with regret, but it's Dante who speaks up, his angry tone slicing like a knife through the air. "We? What the hell do you mean *we*?"

"Santos organized that attack himself," Enzo explains, the pair of us ignoring Dante and his growing fury. "If we'd had a say, it would have been more... personal."

I frown. "You were there?" Dante barks, before turning his ire on Enzo. "Is that why you disappeared that day?"

"Yes," Enzo snaps. "I had to make sure her stubbornness didn't get her blown to pieces."

I scoff. "Well, maybe if I thought I could have trusted you, I'd have listened."

"Oh, 'cause you're not keeping your own share of secrets, Spitfire," Enzo throws back.

I huff out a breath, closing my eyes as I lean back against the headrest. This is not how I wanted either of them to be for this meeting—riled up and pissed off. There's no way we'll all leave alive at this rate.

A thick silence envelops the car as the city streets give way to rundown suburban roads. "Are you sure this is the right place?" Enzo asks as he slows the car to a stop outside a small, detached house. I peer out the window, taking in the street. The house is one of the more cared for homes. One of the only ones with no weeds sticking up between paving stones or overgrown grass. The walls look like they've been painted fairly recently and the porch has been varnished.

I double-check the address on my phone. "Yeah, this is it."

Curious as to where we are, I push open the car door and step out, hearing the others get out behind me. I swallow nervously, already knowing this is going to be a disaster of epic proportions, but it's a disaster that needs to happen.

The front door creaks as it's pushed open, and Cain's broad frame fills the doorway. His eyes meet mine before flicking to the two men behind me. I'd hazard a guess that he suspected the reason for this meeting, but his gaze hardens nevertheless.

When he returns his attention to me, I can see the anger simmering in his green eyes, and I smile softly, trying to lighten the blow.

"I guess you'd better come inside," he growls in a furious tone as his eyes dart around the street. He mumbles something under his breath that sounds a lot like *I don't need dead bodies littering my street,* and I glower at him.

"Who the fuck is this asshole?" Enzo mumbles in a low voice, earning his own glower. Why did I think this was a good idea?

"Just come on," I grumble, striding through the chain-link fence and up the tapered path to the house.

"Behave," I mouth when I reach Cain.

"You're in so much trouble, Red," he growls, and I smirk, knowing exactly what trouble with Cain can result in. There's a creak on the steps as Enzo and Dante follow, and I continue on past him into the house.

I am greeted with a narrow corridor that has been freshly painted in a bright off-white color. There's a doorway on my right leading into a small living room, but I don't take in the details. All I can see is the tall, lean man standing in the middle of the room, dressed simply in navy jeans and a white Henley. A goofy grin lights up my face as I trail my eyes over him.

"Trouble," Oliver purrs, only making me grin wider. He steps toward me, but as he reaches out to pull me into his arms, he hears the others come in and pauses. Frowning, he looks over my shoulder.

His demeanor completely changes when Dante comes into view, his shoulders straightening as he takes a step back, standing to his full height. "What is this all about?"

"That's what I'd like to know," Dante rumbles as I step aside. He moves into the room like he owns the place, and Oliver turns to watch him. Enzo is next, with Cain bringing up the rear, and with all four of them in the small space, I can hardly breathe. Fucking hell, this is literally the worst idea I've ever had. The tension is so high, you could light a match and send all of us to Kingdom Come.

All four of them stare at me, and my cheeks flush under their scrutiny. Fuck, having all of them looking at me like that is intense. I gesture for them to sit, feeling like somehow that will make them less likely to resort to violence. Dante and Enzo claim the sofa by the window, while Cain and Oliver take the one by the door, and I stand in front of the fireplace, nervously twisting my hands as I look between both pairs of men.

"Uhh, this is Dante and Enzo," I introduce, waving pointlessly at the two of them. Of course, Cain and Oliver already know who they are. "And this is Cain and Oliver. They're, uh..."

"Rejects." Dante finishes when I trail off.

"Yeah, and, uh, my boyfriends."

My words are met with a deafening silence, and I can't decide if that's better or worse than if Dante and Enzo started yelling. I drop my gaze, unable to look them in the eye. This feels so fucking awkward, however, I feel lighter knowing the last of my secrets have officially seen the light.

Both Dante and Enzo are under the impression that I'm theirs, and on some level I think I am, but I'm not *just* theirs. So before we fall any further into whatever this is between us, they need to be made aware of the stark reality of our situation. Because, let's face it, it's complicated as fuck. Hell, Dante has reservations about sharing me with his one and only friend, never mind with people he doesn't even know. *God, remind me what I was thinking again?*

When the silence becomes too much to bear, I glance up through my eyelashes, first focusing on Cain and Oliver. Oliver's sporting a small, encouraging smile, and pride shines in Cain's eyes. Despite the hostility emanating from both parties, their love for me shines through, bolstering me, and pushing back my shoulders, I find the courage to meet Dante's unrelenting stare.

Confusion and fury swirl in his russet brown depths, along with something much more predatorial, and I swear my heart stops beating for a second as fear skitters along my spine. Fear that I've pushed him too far. Fear that he's going to go apeshit. Fear that this may be too much for him. I want him to start opening himself up to the feelings he normally denies himself, but I also can't continue to lie to him anymore.

Tearing my eyes away, I swallow roughly around a lump in my throat as I land on Enzo's impassive expression. Cold and shut down, he gives nothing away regarding his feelings, and it hurts me more than I could have anticipated. Somehow, Enzo is the most complicated out of all these men because of our history. I spent so many years not trusting him, sensing that he was keeping me at arm's length. Then, like the flick of a switch, he started letting me in. But because of his relationship with Dante, we haven't had a proper chance to act on the chemistry between us. I know he cares for me. He's gone to great lengths to ensure I'm at ease in Dante's house. In the run-up to the wedding, we spent a lot of time together, and I could see the warmth and honesty in his eyes when we talked. The hurt that still scars his heart when he speaks of his father and his betrayal, what Giovanni did to him, and the years of undeserving suffering he's endured. The last thing I want to do is cause him any more pain.

I implore them both with my eyes. "That's why I can't let you retaliate."

"Because you're fucking them," Enzo sneers. The sheer venom in his voice makes me flinch as a ball of emotion wedges itself in the back of my throat.

"No," I croak. "Because they are actually trying to clean up this town. They care about the people, their livelihoods, their safety." With every word out of my mouth, I stand taller. I get that they're pissed, but Cain and Oliver aren't the bad guys here. Hell, they're the only ones with the power to make a difference who actually give a shit.

"Why did you bring us here?" Dante asks in his typical, monotonous voice that I've come to realize he uses when he can't handle the brewing storm of emotions swelling inside him.

"Because you needed to know the truth, and I think we can help one another."

Uneasiness passes between all four of them, but it's Enzo who speaks up. "You want us to work together?" he scoffs, shaking his head in outrage.

"Yes," I state confidently, my tone brokering no argument as I lift my chin. It may sound insane, but that's the beauty of it. It's so crazy that no one will ever suspect it. "We all have something to gain by working together. I will do anything to get my brother back." I roam my eyes over each of them, ensuring they see how deadly serious I am, before focusing my gaze on Dante and Enzo. "You can finally get out from underneath Giovanni's thumb."

"And what do they get?" Enzo gestures toward Cain and Oliver, and I slide my gaze in their direction, noting Cain's tight jaw and the tense set of his shoulders. He's livid, but he's shown considerable restraint, and for that, I'm grateful. His eyes bore into mine, the two of us sharing a charged moment. I'm not about to spill his story to the others. He has to make the decision for himself if he's open to this alliance. I know it's a hard pill for him to swallow, but he's wanted his vengeance for so long. He's been in this far longer than any of us, but I know in my gut that this is our best shot. The only chance we have of winning. The question is, how badly does he want it?

The muscle at the back of his jaw flexes and bulges, his eyes hard as his unrelenting gaze drills into me. I can practically see the calculated analysis going on inside his head. Cain's a smart man, and despite his hot-headed temper, he's capable of thinking a situation through. He wouldn't be the leader of the Rejects if he couldn't put his feelings aside and see the bigger picture, which is precisely what I'm asking him to do.

Still looking absolutely furious, he finally spits out, "I get vengeance for my sister."

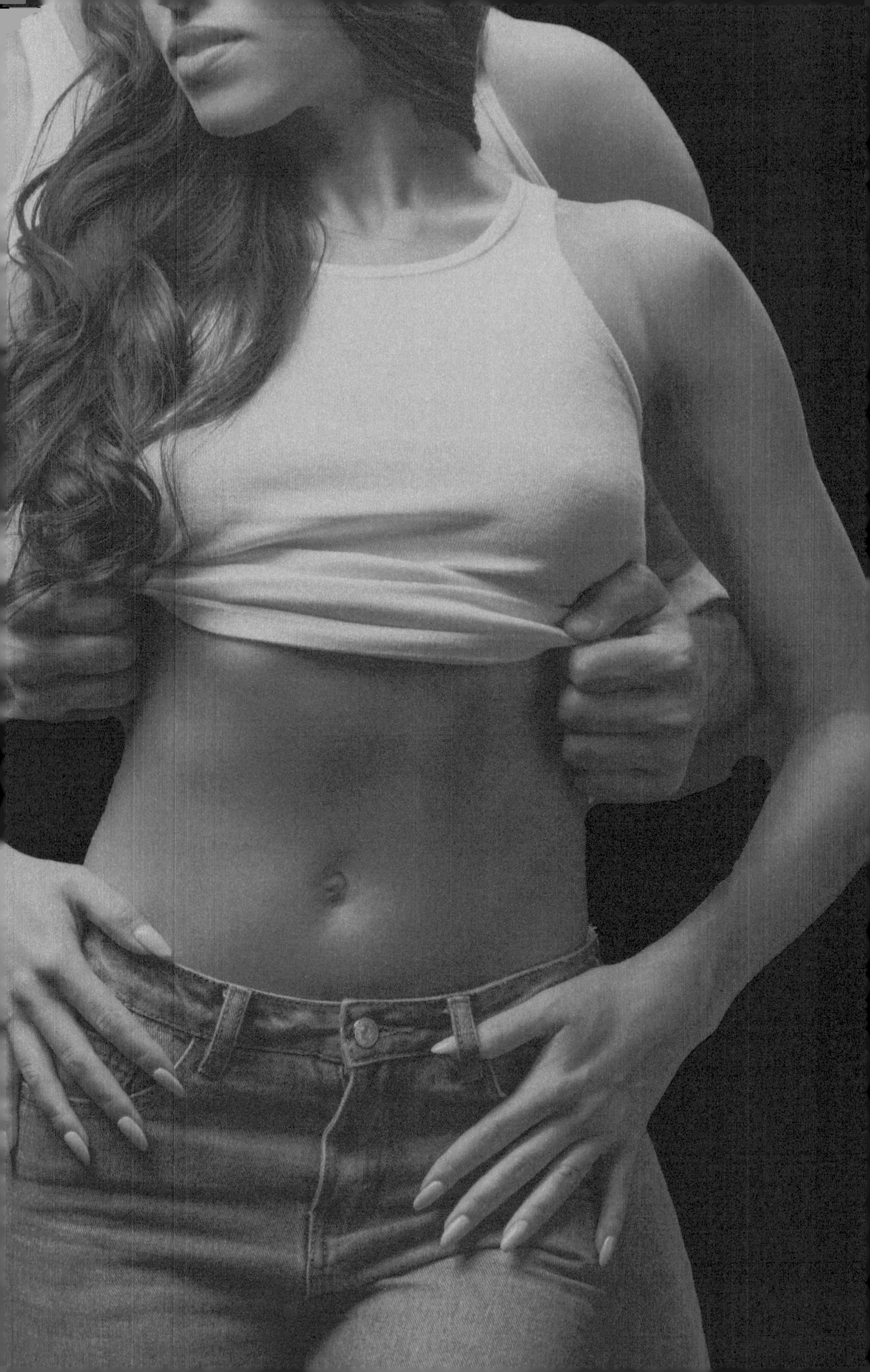

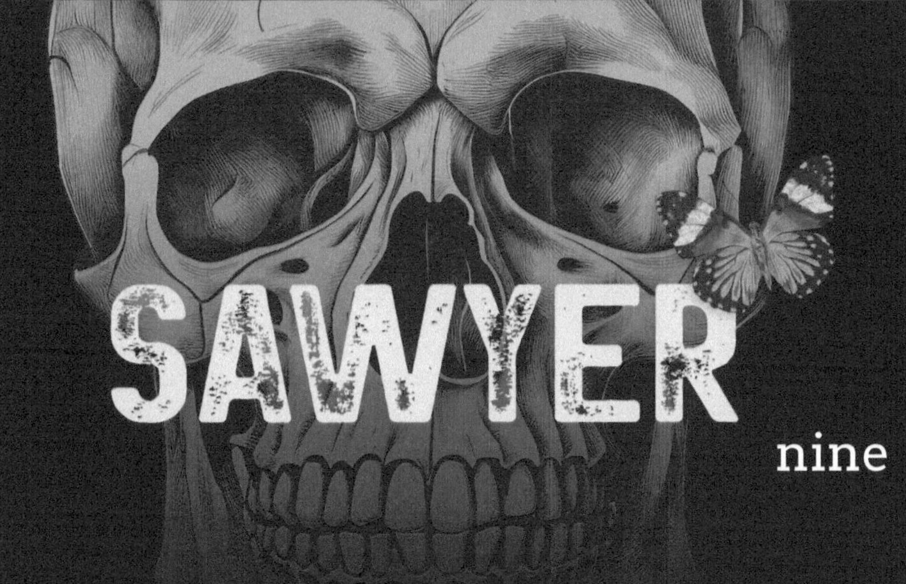

D istrust, hostility, and contempt hang thick in the air, and very little else is said during the meeting. Which is fine. It's not like I expected each of them to get over their issues and start singing Kumbaya. Today was about me laying out all of my cards on the table. Now it's up to each of them to decide if they are in, and if they're not... well, fuck, I really hope they're in.

"I'll be out in a minute," I tell Dante and Enzo as they head toward the door. They both stop in their tracks. Dante's jaw ticks and Enzo's stormy eyes grow even more turbulent.

"Alright, *wife*," Dante growls, riling up the two angry gangsters behind me. He smirks before stomping outside, the door banging shut behind him, and I curse him out in my head as I listen to the creak of the wooden boards beneath their feet as they cross the porch.

Alone with my Rejects, I suddenly feel nervous. I haven't had much time alone with them especially after the fiasco with the wedding, and now this, I couldn't blame them if they hated me.

Turning to face them, I blurt out, "I'm sorry," hanging my head in shame. "I didn't... I don't..." I sigh, burying my face in my hands. "This is a complete disaster."

I feel Oliver's ingrained sense of calm wash over me as he approaches. I'm still hiding behind my hands, but I don't need to see to know it's him. His freshly showered scent, mixed with the woodsy smell of his body wash, envelops me like a favorite blanket. Gently, he pulls my hands away from my face and tucks a finger under my chin, lifting it until I have no choice but to look up at him.

"You have feelings for them." He's asked me this before, although this time it's not a question.

"I love you." I flick my gaze over his shoulder to Cain, including him in that declaration. "But yes, I have something with them too." His shoulders drop slightly, and a hole forms in my heart at the thought of hurting either of them. It's the very last thing I want to do. "I'm sorry."

His fingers stroke along my cheek. "I won't pretend to understand any of this, but you have absolutely nothing to be sorry for." The sincerity in Oliver's tone has tears threatening, and I have to wonder when the hell I turned into such an emotional baby. I really need to get out and go Reaper on a few assholes so I can earn back some badass bitch points.

Leaning in, he brushes his lips over mine in a barely-there kiss. It lasts a fraction of a second, but in that moment, more intimacy passes between us than in any other kiss we've shared.

"Are you sure about this?" Cain asks, speaking up for the first time.

I shake my head. "No, but it's the only way I can see where we can all get what we want."

His lips purse. "Do you trust them?"

There's no hesitation as I confidently state, "Yes."

I can tell he's still unsure, not quite believing me, and who can blame him. Stepping away from Oliver, I close the distance between us. He's still so angry and confused, and I'm not sure whether he wants me to touch him or not. "Tell me you love me."

He blows out a breath, some of the anger dissipating as his hand slides into my hair, and he yanks me against him. "You might just be the death of me, but I'll love you until my dying breath." His lips slam down on mine, claiming me as his tongue pushes past my lips. His kiss is hard and desperate and at complete odds with Oliver's gentle touch. We're both breathing heavily when he pulls back, but in that moment, I know I haven't lost them and that eases something inside me.

"I'll come by tomorrow," I promise them.

"Pack a bag," Cain orders, possession and arousal brimming in his emerald, green eyes.

Smirking, I turn on my heel and walk out. Stepping onto the front porch, I tilt my head up to the sky, letting the afternoon sun wash over me as I breathe in the fresh air. Dante and Enzo are in the car, but I can feel their eyes on me. I ignore them, needing a minute to myself. *Nobody died*, I remind myself. That's got to be a good sign, right?

To say the drive back to Dante's was tense would be an understatement. It was the most uncomfortable car ride of my life. And considering I once sat in this same car wondering if Dante was going to kill me, that's saying something.

They continue to give me the silent treatment as we walk into the house, but I don't need words to know how they're feeling. It's in the hard clip of Dante's soles as they strike the floor, the way Enzo haphazardly throws his tie on the breakfast bar. It's the stiff set to Dante's face and his impenetrable, cold mask. It's the fury roiling off Enzo like he's about to lose his shit at any moment. They are complete opposites. Ice cold and molten hot. It's only a matter of time until one of them snaps, and I quietly move to sit on the sofa, deciding I may as well get comfortable while I wait them out.

They both bang around, Dante downing two full glasses of whiskey while Enzo repeatedly opens the fridge door before slamming it shut. It would almost be amusing if there wasn't so much on the line. Lives. Freedom. My heart.

"What the actual fuck, Sawyer?!" Enzo roars after his third slam of the fridge door. He storms across the room until he's looming over me. "You could at least have given us a heads up."

I shake my head. "You wouldn't have gone if I had." And he knows it.

"What did he mean, *vengeance for his sister*?" Dante asks, his tone practically glacial.

"Not my story to tell, but you know your father... I'm sure you can work it out."

Dante moves to join us with a fresh glass of amber liquid in hand, slowly sitting down on the seat opposite me. Lifting his leg, he rests his ankle on his knee, watching me over the rim as he takes a sip. I can see the wheels in his head turning.

"You've been working with them this entire time."

Unable to look at him, I fixate on a knot in the hardwood floor at my feet. "I have."

"What the hell does that even mean, Sawyer?" Enzo growls. He's still holding his intimidating stance above me, fists clenching at his sides as his molten-hot anger practically burns my skin.

Licking my lips, I lift my gaze to meet theirs. I said I'd lay it all on the table, and that's exactly what I do. I tell them everything. How I got a job at the club to get close to Dante, the real reason why I stayed after Santos tried to kill me, the plan we had for the wedding day—including my plea with Cain to spare their lives. The whole time, neither of them speaks until my words trail off with nothing else left to say.

Anxiously, I fiddle with my fingers. "I didn't anticipate any of this." I sigh. "I didn't anticipate..." I want to say *you,* but I don't. "I can't apologize either because I'm not sorry. I'm not sorry for my intentions. I'm not sorry for how everything has played out. The only thing I feel guilty about is deceiving you both." Chewing on my lip, I get to my feet. "But now you know everything. I have nothing left to hide." I meet their angry stares with a determined one of my own. "I've given you the keys to ensuring our deaths, but I'm hoping if nothing else, that you'll see this as an opportunity for yourselves. You're not the men I thought you were." I give a helpless shrug. "Maybe this could be your chance to find your own happiness."

Turning on my heel, I stride out of the room. They both need time to think, time to talk—alone. To work out what they want and whether they're willing to fight for it. This is our fork in the road, where they are either with me and we move forward as a team, or they go their own way. I can only hope we don't end up facing off as enemies down the line. I know, if it came to it, that I couldn't kill either of them, and I'm not sure if I could look at Cain or Oliver the same way if they were responsible for their demise.

My heart feels heavy, and my brain exhausted as I drag myself up the stairs. I hesitate on the landing, peering at the door to my old room before walking past it to Dante's. His smell blankets me as I step inside and close the door behind me, the cedarwood of his aftershave causing a sharp pain in my chest. I don't know how to put words to my feelings for Dante. It's an existential thing. Something that I feel in my bones without knowing why. I didn't want to marry him. I'm still not sure I want to *be* married to him, though I know I don't want to be without him. Without either of them.

I wasn't lying when I told them they weren't the men I'd first thought them to be. Don't get me wrong, they are still everything I assumed—ruthless, cold, powerful. But they're also more. Or, in Dante's case, capable of more.

Enzo has sacrificed his life and freedom to ensure Dante doesn't lose himself. He could have left, ran away and started his life anew without the label of a traitor hanging over his head, but he didn't. He stayed... for Dante. And he's fought every day to keep him human. To keep the last, vital fragment of his soul intact. I've witnessed the struggle in Dante for myself. He doesn't want to lose himself. It terrifies him, the thought of one day becoming his father. The two of them are treading water, barely keeping their heads above the surface. All it would take is the crash of one enormous wave to drag them under.

I want them to join us; to stand up and fight. Not for me, but for themselves. I know what I'm asking. Our mission is likely a one-way trip to Hell, but it's better to die fighting for your freedom than to live safely in a gilded cage, right? No one would willingly hand their soul over to the Devil. They would fight tooth and nail to keep his dark claws away. I can only hope the Devil hasn't already claimed their souls as his.

Pushing off the door, I fall onto the bed on my back, staring up at the ceiling. Eventually, my eyes grow heavy, and I must have fallen asleep as the click of the door closing jolts me awake. Sitting upright, I meet Dante's penetrating gaze.

It's on the tip of my tongue to ask him what their decision is, but I swallow it back. I'm not going to push or pry. This is their decision, and I know it's not an easy one to make. I'm asking for trust when they've just uncovered how deep my deceit runs. I'm asking them to tear down the only life they know, to turn their backs on the only family they have. I want them to take their time, to really think it through before giving me an answer. Because once they decide, there's no going back. No changing their minds. We either go forward together, or we go our separate ways.

His gaze holds mine, unreadable as ever, as he steps toward the bed. When he's close enough, he reaches out to grab my ankle, and with a sharp tug, he pulls me down the mattress until my ass is perched on the edge. I can feel the heat of his close proximity. His touch is rough and dominant as he circles his hand around my jaw and tugs my chin up to meet his predatory gaze. It's all there in his eyes, the answers to my unasked questions, but I can't interpret them. Then, his thumb brushes along my lower lip. The moment is surprisingly reverent, despite his forceful touch, and my heart lurches at the thought that this could be goodbye. Unexpected tears well in my eyes, and I let him see it all. I've nothing left to hide.

He bends until he's hovering over me, our faces so close that I can feel the warmth of his breath as it dances along my lips, teasing me. I can't figure out if this is goodbye or the start of something, but either way, I can't deny the pull I feel. The desperate hunger to have his lips on mine, his body pressing me into the mattress, his hard cock making me see stars.

He hovers there until I'm delirious with need. My chest heaves and all I can think of is him. Kissing him. Having him inside me. I can't claim to really know anything about this man, but my body craves his like a drug. I don't need to know anything about him to *know* him. My soul recognizes his. Whatever this is between us exists on a whole other plane. One I can't see with my eyes, yet it feels more real than the soft sheets beneath my palms. I feel like fate delivered me into his hands. Fate put me in the alley that day. She wanted us to meet, wanted him to spare my life, and she ensured our paths crossed again in the club years later when we were both old enough to acknowledge the significance of this. Of *us*.

I tilt my head back so my lips brush over his in a barely-there touch. Static crackles in the air and the chains on his restraint snap with that brief bit of contact. He surges forward, claiming my lips as his hand slides into my hair, holding me to him. His tongue clashes with mine while our souls dance. They twist and tangle, becoming one with every sweep of his tongue. I drag him to me, needing him closer so I don't know where I end and he begins. I'm breathless and completely lost in the taste of him when the bang of the bedroom door slamming closed makes me jump.

Pulling apart, I look around Dante's broad frame to find Enzo glaring at me. His chest heaves, his face drawn tight with angry lines. His glower—or more the scorching heat of lust I see in his depths—incinerates me.

"What do you want?" Dante barks, angry with the intrusion.

Enzo all but ignores him as he continues to glare at me, and I can't decide if he wants to kill me or fuck me. "You know goddamn well what I want." Another heaving breath. "The one thing I've wanted for years now."

I swallow around a lump in my throat as my eyes widen, my lips parting on a quiet gasp as he steps toward us. With a hard shove, he pushes Dante out of the way, and he goes stumbling, but I don't see anything more as Enzo fists the hair at the nape of my neck and uses the firm hold to drag me to my feet. He holds me there as his body crowds mine, our chests brushing.

"I'm done keeping my distance." His voice is softer, his words for me.

"So don't." I've been waiting for this day, the day Enzo stakes his claim. Ever since the incident at Paradiso, I knew it was coming. He's said as much. I know he's been holding himself back, wanting Dante to be on board with the three of us, but today's events—and finding out I have two other boyfriends—have destroyed any restraint he's had.

His eyes bore into mine, a raging storm of anger, hurt, lust, and love swelling within them. "I want to kill you."

"No you don't."

He's angry. Understandably so. He thought he only had to contend with Dante—an adversary he could handle. However, finding out about Cain and Oliver has fucked with whatever ideas he had regarding the three of us.

His grip on my hair tightens to the point of pain, causing my back to arch so I'm practically rubbing against him. The coarse material of my jeans grinds against him as his hard length presses into my stomach and desire flares in my eyes. He sees it, and in a split second, his decision is made. Pushing back his anger for now, he falls headfirst into lust. His other arm bands around my waist as his lips slam down on mine. I can taste every one of his feelings as he bites my lip and sucks on my tongue, his kiss savage and brutal.

It's only when I hear the deep rumble of a pissed-off Dante that I come up for air. I turn my head until my eyes collide with his. The move exposes the column of my neck, and Enzo doesn't hesitate to take the opportunity as he leaves open-mouth kisses on my skin.

With my focus still on Dante, I hold out my hand to him. Lust burns in my eyes, and I let him lay witness to it. It was always meant to be the three of us. Just like it was always meant to be me, Cain, and Oliver. I have no idea how the two combine, but at this moment, it's not my concern. This moment is about Enzo finally claiming what's his. It's about Dante realizing this relationship only works with the three of us. It's me accepting that I'm both the Rejects' queen and a mafia princess.

Enzo removes his lips from my skin, both of us waiting as Dante continues to hold my gaze. My heart is lodged in my throat before his warm palm slips into mine, and I pull him to me. The heat of Dante's body envelops my back, but his stance remains hard and unrelenting, letting me know that he may have given into my silent plea but has not accepted sharing me... yet.

"Kiss me," I plead, watching the war unfold in his dark brown depths.

Rather than doing what I want, he lifts his head to meet Enzo's watchful gaze. The two of them engage in some sort of stare-off while I watch, waiting to see if Dante will relent or hold his ground. My eyes dart back and forth between the two men towering over me. I can see the silent battle between them, feel it in the thick air of tension surrounding us. Dante's hands grip my hips in a tight, possessive gesture as he pulls me flush against him, but Enzo doesn't back down. Instead, he eliminates the slither of space between us until I'm squashed between them, and his hands come to rest above Dante's on my waist.

Neither of them breaks eye contact, each fighting for dominance, and I crane my neck to read Dante's reaction. He struggles for another moment before his resolve begins to crumble, and slowly as if he might change his mind at any second, he dips his head until his lips brush over the bare skin of my shoulder and dance along the edge of my corset.

I rest my head against his chest, his titillating kisses causing my eyelids to fall to half-mast. Enzo stands there and watches Dante lavish my shoulder, as if he can't quite believe that Dante has relented, but after a moment, a small smirk curves along his lips before he lowers them to feast on my neck.

Between their combined touches, everything I thought I knew about these ruthless men goes up in flames, and I'm reborn. Baptized in fire and blessed with sinful kisses, I finally see the light. The truth I'd denied myself shines down on me, and I know this is how it was always meant to be. All those years of sacrifice, of putting Luc first and trying to right the wrongs of this world, not letting anyone close and despising the men in this city. It was all so I'd end up here, with them. I may not have all the answers, but I know without a shadow of a doubt that it was always meant to be the five of us. My Rejects and my kings. The salvation of Black Creek can only occur at our hands. We're the only ones willing to fight for the city. The only ones with the power to incite change. The gangsters and the Made men... and the vigilante.

My skin blazes beneath their touches as they fight to be the first to undress me. Dante yanks on the zip of my corset while Enzo flicks open the button of my jeans, dragging them and my panties down my thighs.

My breasts break free of the confines of the corset and Dante tosses it aside before cupping my heavy tits in his large palms, brushing his thumbs over my sensitive nipples while Enzo rushes to pull off my boots and remove the last of my clothing.

Only when I'm standing naked between them, do they hurriedly undress. Ties, shirts, and dress shoes fly across the room until all three of us are naked, panting, and hungry for more.

I can feel Dante's heat at my back as Enzo's eyes rake over my body, heat flaring within them. Reaching out a finger to touch my chest, Enzo trails a scorching path between the valley of my breasts, over the taut muscle of my abdomen, before sinking between my thighs. He hums in approval when he finds me soaking wet, easily sliding knuckle deep inside of me. I gasp as I arch my back, throwing my head back against Dante's shoulder as I ride Enzo's fingers.

More. I need more.

Dante's palm glides over the globe of my ass before gripping the back of my thigh, and in an effortless move, he's lifting my leg to hitch it around Enzo's hip and opening me up more before he works his way back to my core.

"Holy..." I gasp as his fingers join Enzo's, stretching me to accommodate both of them. Dante is doing a fantastic job at teamwork for someone who doesn't like to share as they both work in tandem. All I can do is cling to them as my orgasm slams into me with the force of a Mack truck, and I cry out.

My eyes are still closed as I'm hauled into someone's arms, and I feel the engorged head of an erect cock brushing my entrance before I'm placed on my back on the bed.

Peeling my eyelids open, Enzo is hovering over me. He gazes down at me in rapture, as if committing everything about this moment to memory. Slowly, he grinds his hips against mine, and it's only when I feel his tip press into me that I push my hand against his chest to stop him. Lines mar his forehead as he frowns, and I glance over his shoulder to find Dante standing there watching us. There's a frown on his lips, but lust blazes in his dark depths as he fists his cock.

"Both of you." I meet his heated gaze and hold it until he moves to join us on the bed. The mattress dips as he lies down beside me, and gently he maneuvers us until he's lying beneath me, Enzo hovering above. A look passes between them before Enzo positions himself at my entrance, and this time I don't stop him as he fills me up.

When he's fully seated, perspiration coating his skin as he struggles to control himself, he presses his forehead to mine. Our eyes remain locked, and I know he feels what I'm feeling. The connection between us. The corporeality of it.

"Fuck, Spitfire," he hisses, sounding pained. His hand cups my face tenderly, and I tilt my head back, bringing my lips to his in a passionate kiss that runs much deeper than any physical chemistry ever could.

I could spend the rest of my life in this moment. Nevertheless, my body has other ideas, and as heat unfurls in my center, I roll my hips, encouraging him to move. He groans, pulling back before once again filling me. I can feel Dante's hard cock between my ass cheeks, and he lavishes my neck and shoulder in kisses while his hands roam hungrily over my thighs, along my stomach, and cupping my breasts.

I'm incapable of forming a singular thought as their ministrations consume me. It's soft and gentle, and in some respects, the most intimate I've ever been with another man.

My eyes snap open when I feel the telltale tingles in my lower belly, and I find Enzo watching me, completely captivated. "You're so close. I can feel you. You feel so fucking good."

Dante's touch as he moves his hand to flick my clit is my undoing, and I fall apart as my entire world shifts around me. I'm too lost in the haze of endorphins to pay attention to what they are doing until I feel pressure at my back entrance as a finger pumps into me. I feel Enzo's cock jerk inside me before he starts up a slow rhythm with shallow thrusts.

I can feel my skin flush as they push me back up the slope. "More," I beg greedily before a second finger is inserted. "More," I demand again, knowing exactly what I need.

Dante chuckles throatily before he bites my earlobe. The bite of pain zings straight to my center, and I clench around Enzo, who groans.

"Fuck, Dante, get your dick in her before I blow my load." The strain in his features gives away how close he is to coming, and I bite my lip to stifle my laugh. However, any humor quickly dissipates as Dante eases himself into me.

"Fucking hell," I gasp as my nails dig into Enzo's shoulders and fireworks spark all over my body.

As if worried he's hurt me, Dante freezes beneath me.

"Don't stop," I snap, wriggling between them, needing him deeper, wanting both of them as deep inside me as they can get.

His hands hold my hips in a bruising grip as he continues with his upward thrust, sinking further into me one inch at a time. When he's all the way in, a pained groan escapes as he buries his face in my neck. I can feel his unsteady breath against my skin, and I know exactly how he's feeling. Pressed between them, a moment of tranquility washes over me before they both begin to move, testing the waters.

Dante's lips are on my neck and Enzo claims my mouth, all of us needing more. Needing to be closer. Deeper. Just... *more.*

Sliding my hand over his chest, I cup Enzo's face and tug his lips from mine as I angle him to face Dante. They lock eyes before Enzo's flick to mine and I hold his gaze. I don't know if they're in a relationship or just enjoy one another's bodies, but whatever it is, I don't want them to stop on my account. They need each other as much as they seem to need me.

Seeing that I'm entirely okay with this, Enzo focuses back on Dante as he leans down, their lips meeting in a hungry kiss. It's more aggressive than their kisses with me. Fueled by need and hunger, it sends them into a frenzy as they up their pace. Skin slaps on skin as tenderness falls to the wayside, the three of us fucking like animals as we chase the ultimate high.

Dante comes first, roaring his release as he swells within me. It triggers my own orgasm, and I tremble in their arms as my eyes slam shut. For several long moments, nothing exists except the mind-altering pleasure coursing through me until, sated, I lazily open my eyes. As my gaze connects with Enzo's, his face scrunches and he grunts before sagging against me. He's careful to keep most of his weight off me as his lips capture mine in a tender kiss before rolling onto the bed. He drags me with him, wrapping his arm around me as exhaustion threatens to pull me under.

The feeling of the bed dipping has me lifting my head to look at Dante, wondering where he's going and if he's okay. "Shh, go to sleep, *mia vita.*" Leaning in, he kisses my shoulder while Enzo tightens his arm around me. Before I can gather the energy to respond, I'm lost to the world of dreams.

DANTE

ten

I tuck my hand behind my head as I watch the sleeping beauty beside me. Her head is resting on the chest of my closest confidant, and even in his sleep, he holds her like she's his most prized possession.

In a rare moment of peace and solitude, I flick back over today's events, trying to ascertain how I feel about all of them. Fury, like nothing I've ever felt before, has my muscles tensing as I recall the way those two gangbangers looked at her. Pure, unfiltered love. Love for *my* woman. I saw the same look in her eyes, and all I could think about was how she doesn't look at me that way... and how much I *wanted* her to look at me that way.

I want her love. I want her affection. I want every second of her attention and her complete and utter devotion, but I'm not so sure I will get that anymore. I was so sure that, given some time, she would get used to her new life with me. However, I'm beginning to see that that will never happen.

My first thought was just to kill them. After all, isn't that what I'm supposed to do if I follow my father's orders? But every time I considered it, I saw her tear-stained face in my mind, the broken look in her eyes as she looked at me with contempt, and well... I couldn't do it.

As I watch the steady rise and fall of her chest, I know that this woman is my greatest weakness. The fact that I know I won't kill someone because it would hurt her says it all. The fact that I'm considering disobeying a direct order from my father...

I let out a breath as I roll onto my back and stare up at the ceiling. Lor blew a fuse when she walked out earlier, his anger and hurt on full display as he snarled and cursed, practically wearing a hole in my solid wood floors with his pacing. He allowed his anger to control him, not that I could blame him. I found it surprisingly difficult to contain my own hatred for the situation. It's not the duplicity that bothers me. I don't care that she's been working with them this whole time. If anything, it makes me admire her more. Her bravery and confidence in the face of such overwhelming odds are truly impressive, and the fact that she doesn't just sit back and wait for someone else to deal with a problem is awe-inspiring. Most people would turn their heads and look the other way, but not Sawyer. She sees someone in danger and she actively goes out of her way to help. Despite the walls she's built around her, her bleeding heart won't allow her to be as cold and callous as she'd like people to believe. It's a large part of what draws me to her and why I wasn't as shocked as she expected when she confessed to being the infamous Reaper. That's not me at all. I'm not a martyr. Where her heart bleeds freely, mine is encased in stone. I can't even understand the sentiment to want to help; to risk your own life for someone you don't know.

Images of the wistful lift of her lips when she laid eyes on Cain and how her body instinctively leaned toward Oliver, like she wanted nothing more than to walk into his arms, assault me. *That's* what pisses me off the most. Her affection for them. Their love for her. The fact that she has this whole other life.

Her words from the other day come to mind. *My life is not one I'm willing to give up for you.* I naively thought she meant her freedom, her job, and later, possibly her alter ego as the Reaper, but now the meaning behind her words is glaringly obvious. She meant them. She's not willing to give *them* up.

I could lock her up here, hide her away from the world and keep her all to myself. Fuck knows, I was tempted to do that before all this shit came to light. Now the idea is even more appealing. However, as I lie here taking in her peaceful expression, her face smooth of its usual defenses, I know I can't do that to her. She has somehow managed to lay claim to the broken fragments of my soul and, in doing so, ensured I protect her from any and all threats, including myself. I want her to look at me with the same soft adoration she showed those thugs earlier and locking her up in this house would guarantee that never happens.

"Stop overthinking it," Lor mumbles, his voice thick with sleep. Lifting my gaze from the angel wrapped in his arms, I find his eyes still closed. "I can hear your brain ticking from over here."

"You're the one that threw a hissy fit earlier."

He lazily lifts one eyelid to glower at me before dropping it closed again. "Maybe you should try it. It's rather cathartic."

I scoff. "Please, the sex is why you feel so at ease now."

"Hmm, that too."

He peels open his eyelid again, scrutinizing me. "How are you?"

"I'm fine."

"Sure you are." Shaking his head, he closes his eye again, missing the scowl I throw his way. "You just found out your wife has two other boyfriends."

"Don't you mean three boyfriends?" My jaw is so tightly clenched that I can hardly get the words out.

One side of his lips lifts, and he squeezes Sawyer against him. "Yeah, but I was always going to end up here. I was just giving you time to come around."

"Well, I haven't come around, so feel free to fuck off now."

He smirks before growing serious, once again looking over at me. "You felt it, though, right?" His gaze drops to Sawyer, a rare tenderness in his eyes as he drinks her in.

"It was different." Sex with Lor is usually all fire and aggression. It's heated and passionate, quick and rough. All testosterone. Nothing like what just transpired between the three of us.

"It was... transcendent." The awe in his voice has my gaze again drifting to where Sawyer lies asleep in his arms, unaware of our conversation. She's completely at peace, as though she trusts us to protect her while she rests. She wiggles against Lor's hard body, burying herself deeper as she rubs her cheek against his chest, and as I watch her, I can't help but agree with him.

Slowly, I trail my eyes over his bulging pecs, up the thick column of his neck to his morning stubble. There's a slight curl at the corner of his lips as he watches her, his bright green eyes never once looking away. "You love her."

I may not understand the emotion, but I know that's what I'm seeing written on his face right now. "Yeah, I do. I think I always have."

"If I were a better man, I'd walk away and let you have her." Only I'm a selfish asshole, and there's been a crack in my chest since the day she crashed into me in the club. I'm bleeding out, or maybe I'm breathing for the first time. I'm not sure if I'm dying or coming alive, but either way, I don't think I want it to stop.

"Nah, man." Looking up at me, Lor's eyes are full of sincerity. "You need her, and if we're actually going to go along with this ludicrous plan, then she'll need you too."

Unable to look at him, I tear my gaze away, shaking my head. I don't believe him. What could I possibly have to offer her? I can't love her the way he does.

"You love her in your own way. You're probably the only one who will put her above all else. You're not after vengeance or revenge or justice. She's your salvation—the one person who can keep you from falling into the darkness. If everything goes sideways, she's the first thing you'll think of. Her safety. Not killing your father, not getting revenge, or righting old wrongs. Her. She deserves someone who will put her first. Who will burn down this city and everyone in it to keep her safe."

Mulling over his words, I bend down to kiss her bare shoulder. She hums in her sleep, a soft smile lighting her face as if she knows it's me.

"What about the other two?" I ask quietly.

"No fucking clue. Probably can't kill them before we find out what their plan is."

"Mmm," I agree, although we both know we won't actually be killing them. No harm in playing it out in my head, in any case.

"Are we really going to go against my father?" We didn't get to talk about it much earlier. Lor was too pissed off to have any sort of constructive conversation.

"These last few hours have been pretty much perfect, right?"

My eyebrows draw together, confused as to his change in topic.

"Uh, sure."

"We won't have many more moments like this. It won't be long before your father sees the influence she's having on you. My presence already threatens him. Imagine how furious he will be when he realizes I have nothing on Sawyer. Marrying her only delayed the inevitable."

My lips flatten into a thin line, not liking his insinuation one bit. I know he's right. My father has always abhorred my friendship with Lor.

Friendships make you weak.

You can't rely on anyone but yourself.

Finding out that we are fucking has only intensified his efforts to tear us apart.

"As long as he's alive, she won't be safe," he murmurs, voicing my thoughts. "But he's not my father. You know how I feel about him."

The irony is, he's never been a father figure to me, either. Father in name and blood only. He hasn't done anything to earn the loyalty and servitude I've given him all these years. Yet, I played along, happy to just trundle through. Now, as I stare at the perfect angel lying in Lor's arms, I realize that, even in the short period of time we've known each other, she's given me more than my father ever has. The spark of life in my chest that my father tried his damndest to snuff out, she instead kindles. Rather than ignoring it, she makes me question it; analyze it. She challenges me, pushes me when others would run away screaming, but she also knows when to back off. When I'm at my admittedly very restricted emotional limit.

I knew for sure that my survival depended on her that day in the office at the club, when she asked me who I was. No one has ever asked me that before. Everyone sees what they want to see. They draw their own conclusions. But not her. She saw past my name, my position, my indifference.

Are you saying you never get angry, never lose your temper or lash out at those around you? You say you don't feel pleasure, but you're hard, so you must like something. I don't think you can't feel. I think you just don't know how to recognize those positive emotions. So when you do feel something out of the ordinary, you don't know how to handle it.

I've often replayed those words in my mind while I've laid here late at night in the dark, thinking of her. I don't know how she was able to deduce any of that. She hardly knew me then, hardly knows me now. Yet somehow, she saw right into the center of my being. She saw a part of me that I myself can't even comprehend.

I don't think you can't feel. I think you just don't know how to recognize those positive emotions.

I've often wondered if she was right. I'm still not sure, but regardless, I'm not willing to give up the chance to find out. I'm not willing to give up *her*.

Reaching out, I tuck a strand of hair behind her ear. "I won't let him hurt her." The steel in my voice says it all, and when I lift my eyes to meet Lor's gaze, he sees the decision written in them.

"Guess that means we'll have to play nice with the Rejects then." He rolls his eyes, scrunching his face like the idea physically pains him. My own dislike for that idea makes itself apparent. Choosing not to dwell on any of it tonight, I push it to the back of my mind, and with my hand on Sawyer's hip, I pull her against me. She's the only thing that matters. My father thinks he raised a loyal soldier, a ruthless monster capable of anything. And he did, I'm just not loyal to him.

I CAN SEE THE MORNING LIGHT THROUGH MY CLOSED EYELIDS BEFORE I even open my eyes, but the sight that greets me when I peel them open is more beautiful than anything my dreams could conjure. I'm met with brilliant blue eyes that steal my breath, leaving me speechless, just like the first time I fell into them. Until our wedding night, I'd never slept beside someone all night, never woken up beside them. I stare deeply into her eyes, knowing I want her to be the first thing I see every morning.

With her head resting on my pillow and her hand tucked under her face, Sawyer lies watching me with a serene yet curious look. The bed sheet is wrapped around her otherwise naked body, and her outfit is finished off with Lor's arm as a belt wrapped tightly around her waist. His face is buried in the crook of her neck, the steady rise and fall of his shoulder indicating he's still sound asleep. Watching the two of them lying side by side as I recollect what the three of us did last night, drapes a warmth over me like a weighted blanket, providing me with a strange sense of calm that I can't place.

Trying to figure out what it is, my eyes drift back to Sawyer's face. She just watches me as if she can see my brain working, and she's giving me the time to figure this out. We lie facing each other on our sides in silence while I study her before shifting my attention to Lor. As I take in the only two people in the world that I care about, knowing they are both safe, unharmed, and here with me, I realize what this... feeling... is.

Comfort.

Contentment.

Peace.

Tranquility.

I might even go so far as to say happiness. Or as close to it as I'll ever get.

As if she can see the dawning of understanding written on my face, she smiles, and it's the most beautiful thing. Pride glitters in her eyes, and that warmth within me swells.

"Morning," she murmurs softly, keeping her voice quiet so she doesn't wake Lor.

"Morning." I don't know what I'm supposed to say in this situation, so I fall back on my usual tactics of silence, letting her take the reins.

"I have to go to the clubhouse today," she says, making me frown as I once again debate the merit of locking her up and throwing away the key. Sensing my inner turmoil, she reaches out and strokes her fingertips down the side of my face and over my morning stubble. "But I'll be back tomorrow."

Tomorrow? *Tomorrow?!*

"We should go out tomorrow night. Just us." Her words manage to penetrate through the red mist, pulling me back from the edge. "I want you to meet Sawyer." She must see my blank look as she explains, "You've only known the girl I was pretending to be at the club and the girl who has been locked up in this house. You don't know the real me. You might find you don't even like me."

There's a rare vulnerability in her voice, and she darts her gaze away. Not liking it, I cup her chin, drawing her attention back to me. I already know everything I need to know about her. There's nothing she could say or do that would change my mind. The unforeseen introduction of her fucking boyfriends proved that.

"If that's what you want to do, then that's what we will do."

"It is." It takes me a second to put a name to the look in her eye. It's not one I've seen on her before and it's not one I'm familiar with myself. She's nervous. Does she genuinely think I won't like her?

Clearing her throat, she changes the subject. "So... you're on board."

Even though it's not a question, I answer her anyway. "We are."

"Are you sure? There's no turning back once we start down this path."

With my hand still on her face, I shuffle toward her until I can feel her soft curves and the heat of her body seeping into mine. "You are my wife." They are the exact words I said before we went to my father's the other day. Where there was only shock in her eyes last time I said them, today, her brows furrow in skepticism.

"You don't even know me."

Again with this shit. "I know enough," I growl angrily, pressing my fingertips into her cheek.

"You just found out yesterday that I will never be solely yours."

"And yet here you are, in bed with *me*."

She's still frowning. "You could be playing me so you can spill everything to your father."

Releasing her from my grip, I grab her hand in mine. Straightening her index finger, I maneuver her arm until she can feel the puckered edges of the circular scar sitting just beneath my armpit. Her brow furrows as she runs her finger around the edge before seeking out the two raised dots in the middle. "Cattle prod."

Her lips part as she gapes at me, her finger still circling the scarred skin. "Why?"

"For feeling. For caring. For letting him see it."

She bites her lower lip as tears well in her eyes.

Lifting her hand again, I move it to the long, thin scar that runs low across my hip. "Punishment," I say by way of explanation, already directing her hand toward my head so she can feel the small one hidden beneath my hair. "Consequence of pissing him off."

Speechless, she gapes at me for a long moment before finding her words. "Why do you do his bidding? Why let him control you?"

I shrug. "I didn't see a way out. Never had a reason to try. I'm not even sure if I wanted to get out." I mull it over for a second before stating, "I guess I was waiting for you."

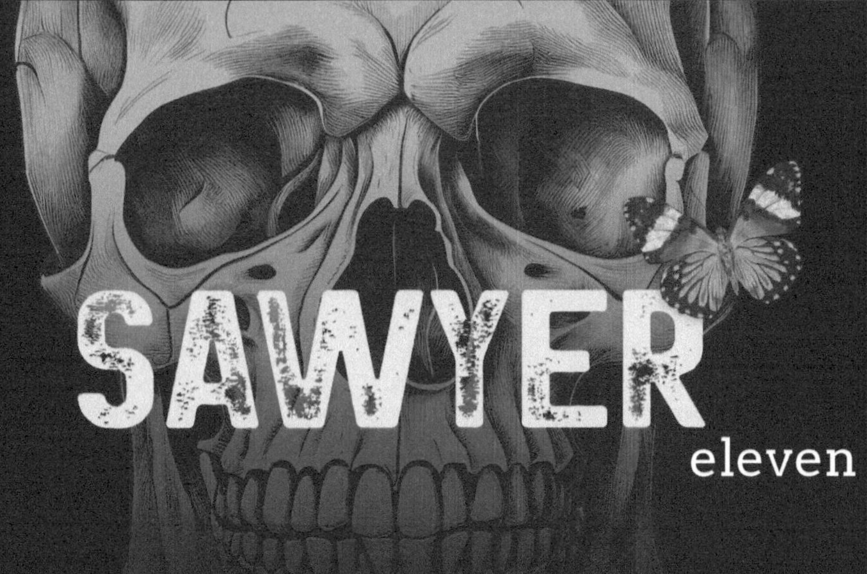

E nzo leans across me to look out my window. His brow hitches, an unimpressed look on his face. "Really?" he sneers. "They couldn't protect this place from a summer storm, yet they think they can withstand the assault Giovanni will rain down when he discovers what they're doing?"

Turning, I try to see the clubhouse through his eyes. The tall iron fence, the hoops of barbed wire along the top. It's all unassuming, but the barbed wire is electrified, and every inch of the fencing is monitored. What Enzo can't see is the armed men hiding out of sight, the boobie traps concealed along the perimeter.

Squashing my smile, I lean in and press a kiss to his cheek. It's not even midday yet and we've already been through the wars. It's safe to say neither he nor Dante was happy about me staying here tonight. Between Dante mumbling under his breath about locking me in his room and Enzo debating about straight-up killing Cain and Oliver, my energy levels are already waning.

When I reiterated for what must have been the millionth time that neither of them had the right to dictate who I spent my time with and threatening not to come back if they didn't get their caveman attitudes under control, the two of them reluctantly relented, with Dante spitting out that he needed to work anyway before stomping off. That left Enzo to drive me over to the clubhouse, something he wasn't too happy about. It took him nearly an hour just to find the car keys, and I swear he had them on him the whole time.

I know none of this has been easy on them, but it hasn't been easy on my Rejects either. I've spent the last month with Enzo and Dante, and now that they know the truth, I need some time with my gangsters. Besides, I need a distraction to stop me from storming into Giovanni's skyscraper and rescuing my brother—a move that would end in certain death, and not just for me.

We argued about it this morning. I can't stand the thought of him being alone in there. What are they doing to him? The map of trauma Dante showed me on his body only has me more concerned for my brother's well-being. Are they going to do the same to him? I have to close my eyes against the nausea climbing my throat at the image of my baby brother being tased with a cattle prod.

I can't think like that. I have to focus on what I can control, on what I can do to help, and that involves getting everyone on the same page so the five of us can devise a plan.

"I wouldn't underestimate them if I was you."

He huffs but doesn't argue. Grabbing my overnight bag, I move to get out of the car. "Where do you think you're going?" Enzo questions in a husky voice as he grabs the front of my top and drags my lips to his.

When we woke up this morning, he kissed me on the temple like it was any other morning before going for his shower. I guess he said everything he needed to last night, and it appears he's done holding back. It was clear he was reaching his breaking point when we sparred the other day. He was only holding back for Dante's sake, although despite his pissy behavior previously when Enzo's touch or gaze would linger on me, Dante has actually taken all of this surprisingly well.

"You didn't think I'd let you out of this car without ensuring they know you're mine, did you?" he growls when he finally pulls back from our kiss, only after ensuring my lips are red and swollen from his abrasive touch.

Not sure how to respond to that, I grab my bag and climb out before he decides a kiss isn't enough. God knows he could send me in there, freshly fucked and covered in bite marks, if he indeed wanted to send a clear message. As hot as that actually sounds, I'm in no mood to deal with the pissing party that would ensue. We have much bigger problems to deal with.

Standing on the sidewalk, I make no move to step onto Reject property until Enzo revs the engine and puts the car in gear. He rolls his eyes before taking off down the street and I watch the out-of-place sedan disappear before crossing the threshold. I know now that there are both cameras—with someone watching on the other end 24/7 who will have already alerted Cain to my arrival—and motion detectors that will have notified them that I've stepped onto their property. Whoever is currently watching the cameras will have silenced the alarm, so the rest of the clubhouse doesn't jump to attention thinking I'm a threat.

When silence reigns, I continue up the path to the door and step into the clubhouse. The place is a hive of activity, men chatting, eating, working. Most of the renovations are complete now, and the interior is a far cry from the ramshackle motel I misjudged on my first visit. The walls are freshly painted, with modern leather loungers placed strategically around the room. Booths and small tables provide a dining area on one side near the doors into the kitchen, with a dance floor and pool table on the other side of the room, and a fully stocked bar in the middle, acting as a room divider. It's modern yet homey, especially with the friendly smiles lobbed my way as I walk through the men toward the back hallway that leads to Cain's office.

When I push the office door open, I'm surprised to find the room empty. There's a large map spread across the desk with what looks like a red marker drawn across it, and I walk over to get a better look.

Analyzing the red border that signifies Antonelli territory and the square grids, some of which are crossed off with Xs in them. It takes me a second to put the pieces together and figure out what they're doing. Still, when I do, the love for these men threatens to consume me. They're searching for Luc. They've divided Antonelli territory into grids and are strategically scouring each one before moving on. It's such a risky move, one that could easily have them on Giovanni's radar—more so than they already are—yet they're doing it... for me. For Luc.

With emotion clogging my throat, I go in search of the rough-around-the-edges men with hearts of gold who have wormed their way into my life. Thank god my stubbornness never put Oliver off, and Cain was so insistent on hounding me about the Reaper. I would never have dropped my guard otherwise or had the opportunity to actually get to know these men and realize how empty my life was before. I thought all I needed was Luc. That all we needed was each other, but now that my eyes have been opened, I can clearly see how much I've missed out on. How much *he* has been missing out on. I've done the best job I could when it came to him, but Luc needs male company. He needs friends his own age, and the Rejects have given him all of that. Plus, they've reaffirmed my faith in humanity. I hadn't realized just how far into the darkness I'd fallen before I met them. How detached I had become from the world around me. They've not only included my brother and stolen my heart, but they've opened my eyes and helped me see the positives in life. I've stopped simply surviving, and I'm learning to live. To enjoy life. I'm starting to see the change that can occur if we work together to better ourselves. The family that can be built on similar values, common goals, respect, loyalty, and love.

I push open the door to Cain's bedroom, popping my head in to see if he's there. Finding it empty, I go to close the door again when I hear the sound of the shower running. Stepping into the room, I cross over to the ajar ensuite door and slip into the bathroom. Steam obscures my vision, but my eyes zero in on the drool-worthy specimen in the shower cubicle. Even through the condensation on the glass door, I can still make out the broad muscles of his shoulders, bulging biceps, and muscular thighs. My memory of him can fill in the gaps that I can't see—his broad chest, the hulking muscle of his pectorals that leads to the toned definition of his abs, the trail of dark hair that leads...

"You just gonna stand there all day, Red?" The seductive husk of his voice sends goosebumps racing along my skin as I realize my eyes have followed my mind south. My gaze snaps to his, finding him watching me with lust-filled, eager eyes. "Get over here."

Without a second thought, I strip and move to join him in the shower. He yanks me into the cubicle as soon as the door opens, his grip scorching and firm as he slams his lips on mine. His kiss is rough and aggressive, angry and possessive. I love kissing Cain. I love the rough way he handles me. He knows I can take it, that I can handle him. Everything about him is fast, complex, and unrelenting.

"On your knees, stripper," he growls, using his firm hold to push me to the floor. "I want to see you choking on my dick."

His other hand is wrapped around his length as he strokes himself with fast, hard tugs. I watch, mesmerized, as he works himself over with precum dripping from his opening. With his cock right in front of my face, the flick of my tongue has the salty sweetness of his cum dancing across my tastebuds.

"Open up," he growls. I dart my gaze up to his, finding him watching me with a predatory look. Carnal desire and possession burn in his eyes, only intensifying when I follow his orders.

Parting my lips, he feeds me his cock. I swirl my tongue around him, eliciting a groan as I work to relax my jaw, taking as much of him as I can. Cain is huge, and my muscles ache with the stretch as his piercing scrapes along the back of my throat, threatening to cut off my air supply.

My hand moves to replace his as he threads his fingers through my hair, his eyes transfixed on my lips. He runs his fingers over my lips where they are stretched around him. "These are my lips. My mouth." Each declaration is followed with a shallow thrust, and he completely loses control when I hum my agreement. Pistoning into me, he holds my head still with a tight grip while he fucks my face, taking and taking as he tries to satiate the hungry beast inside him.

Arousal makes my body heat and my thighs clench, desperate for some friction. Tears spill over onto my cheeks as I struggle to breathe, only intensifying my need, and I slip my hand between my thighs.

"No," Cain growls, slapping it away. "Naughty strippers don't get to come."

I whimper around him, making him hiss. This is my punishment for Dante and Enzo. His way of regaining control, reminding me I belong to him, and reassuring himself that I'm his.

His thrusts turn frantic as he nears his release. My jaw throbs, my eyes puffy, my core molten as, with one final thrust, he drives into the back of my throat and empties himself on a roar, "MINE!"

Struggling to catch my breath, he drags me to my feet, cementing my lips against his in a feral kiss. "Yours," I pant.

A groan behind me has me spinning around, finding Oliver standing with his cock in his fist, cum coating his hands. "Fuck, that was hot," he grunts.

Wide-eyed with surprise, I look over my shoulder to Cain, who is sporting a smug smirk, and I realize he knew Oliver was there the whole time.

A chuckle bursts free as Cain takes me into his arms and leads us under the spray of hot water, washing me clean before Oliver greets me with a warm towel.

"Hey, you." He softly kisses my lips as he wraps the towel around me, and I smile adoringly up at him.

"Hi."

God, I've missed him. As I stare up into his gorgeous face, I see nothing but love and affection. There's no anger, no concern, no confusion. Just love. I don't know how he does it. How he can be so confident, so level-headed and sure. Feeling the need to tell him, I blurt out, "I've missed you," only making his smile grow wider as he pulls me in against him, kissing the top of my head.

"I've missed you too, Trouble."

"Luc's here," I tell the guys later when we're in Cain's office, pointing at Giovanni's tower on the map. It's one of the areas they haven't searched yet. "Giovanni lives there, along with Santos and his closest advisors."

Cain's brow hitches, intrigued by that nugget of information. "We'll put people on it."

"Just be careful." I give him a thankful smile as I sink back against Oliver's warm chest. I opted to sit in his lap, needing to feel him close to me and soak up his effortless sense of calm.

"It was Santos who killed my mother," I confess. I haven't had a chance to really think about that until now. I shake my head. "Apparently, she went to him for money, and she must have told him about Luc, or maybe he had someone follow her…" I trail off with a shrug. "I thought it was her pimp/boyfriend at the time. He was always yelling at her, beating on her… I just assumed he went too far one day."

Memories of that day assault my mind. The image of her lying there, the terrified look in Luc's eyes when I found him. My subconscious likes to relive that day in my sleep, reminding me of the turning point when our lives went from bad to worse. I remember always being so angry at my mom. I couldn't understand why she couldn't just grow up and be a mom. Luc deserved that much. It was too late for me, I was already an errant teenager, but he was only five years old. Guilt sickens me as I recall thinking we would be better off without her. I thought life would be so much better if I weren't constantly cleaning up her vomit when she passed out from a binge, skirting around her leering boyfriends, or hiding in the closet with Luc, humming to him in an effort to drown out the noise of her headboard smacking against the wall when she was working. Oh, how wrong I was. Those first few years on the street, I'd have given anything to go back to that time.

The brush of Oliver's finger along my jaw pulls me from my depressing memories. "He'll get what's coming to him." One side of his lip lifts in a smirk. "No one messes with the Reaper and gets away with it."

"Hell, no," Cain agrees. "His death is written in the cards. I'll make sure of it."

Confidence rings in their voices, and I wish I could feel as optimistic as they do. "I don't even know how we're going to get to him or Giovanni. Even when Dante is with them, they have security guards and are rarely ever alone, and the underground tunnels ensure we can't get to him on the street."

Oliver's arms band around me in an attempt to reassure me. "We'll work it out." Pressing a kiss to my temple, he lifts his head, meeting Cain's gaze. "What's, uh, happening with the other two?"

"They're in."

Frowning, Cain leans forward, placing his forearms on his desk. "Red, how exactly do you see all of this playing out?"

"I don't know, but I trust them. Giovanni has been as cruel to them as he has to you. There's no loyalty there."

"Mmm," is his only response, clearly not believing me, not that I can blame him. "And after?" His intense gaze burns into me. There's no anger there, no judgment. He genuinely wants to know how I think this will work out in the end, and I get it. The churning of unease in my stomach says it can't end well. How can I get two sets of men on different sides of this war to not only agree to get along for the sake of what we have to achieve, but to agree to… I dunno, share me? Be in a relationship with me? I haven't the faintest fucking idea how that works. Actually, no, I do know. It doesn't. I'm clinging to all four of them, unwilling to lose Cain or Oliver but not wanting to give up whatever I have with Enzo and Dante.

Eventually, I'll have to choose. When this is all said and done, they're not going to want to be in each other's lives, and I can't be in two separate relationships with two different groups of men. It just wouldn't work. However, despite knowing there's an end date, I can't end things with any of them yet. With an apologetic look, I sigh. "I don't know. I just... They..." I shake my head, unable to find the right words. "There's just something there. I have a history with both of them, and over the last month, I've realized they aren't the men they let the world think they are." I implore Cain with my eyes. "Just, please, trust me. I wouldn't have asked you to spare their lives if I didn't think there was something worth saving."

He blows out a breath, his expression softening. "I do trust you, I just... I don't trust *them*."

I nod, understanding perfectly. He has no reason to trust them, and only time will tell if any sort of trust can be built.

"But you'll work with them?"

He and Oliver share a loaded look before he meets my gaze again. "Yeah, we will, but don't go getting any ideas. That's as far as it goes. We're doing this for Luc and Evie. When it's done, it's done." Getting up from his chair, he strides around the desk until he's standing in front of me. I have to crane my neck back to look up at him, but he leans in until he's at eye level with me. "For now, when you're with us, you're with us, and when you're with them..." He grimaces. "I'd rather not think about it."

I slide my hand under his Henley, relishing the feel of his warm skin beneath my palm and the rippling of his muscles as I glide my hand along his flesh, lifting his top as I climb higher. "Okay," I breathe against his lips, before sealing the promise with a kiss. It's an easy promise to keep. When I'm around them, they consume my every thought. They own my body, know it better than I do, anticipating my needs before I can put them into words. They speak to my soul, bathing it in their strength, their confidence, their honesty. Before them, I didn't think I needed anyone. I believed the only person I could rely on was myself, but they've shown me how wrong I was. They've proven that not only can I open my heart and let people in, but that I'm actually stronger for doing so. *They* strengthen me. With them at my side, I'll never be alone and never have to carry the burden of my problems by myself again. They're not only willing to lighten the load, but they'll shower down love and respect while doing it. My gangsters. My Rejects. The two fundamental pieces of my soul I never knew I was missing.

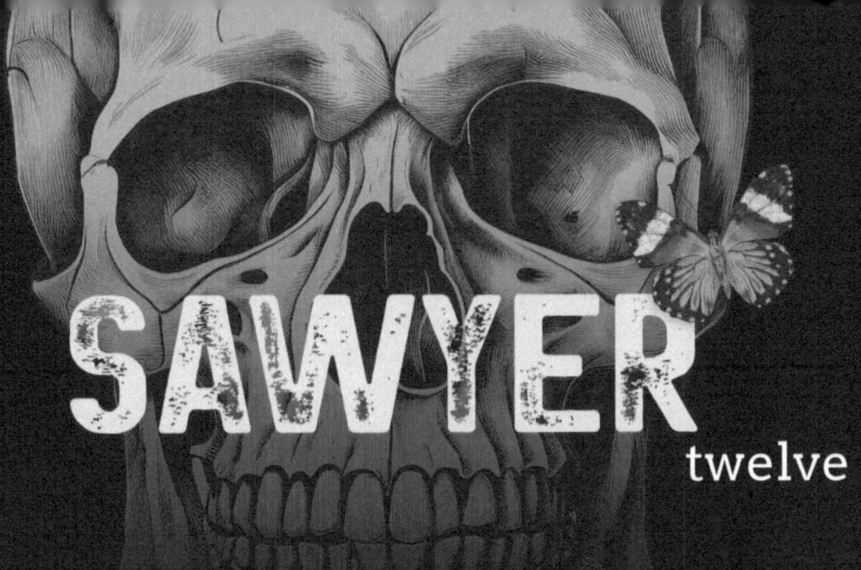

twelve

"Red," Jon gasps when I exit the office several hours later, thoroughly fucked and floating on a cloud of bliss. Cain and Oliver went to arrange patrols to keep an eye on Giovanni's skyscraper and do whatever else they do on a daily basis. I decided to take the opportunity to check in with my baby. I've missed her, and I'm dying to get her out on the open roads and feel the wind whipping my face as her strength vibrates between my legs.

"Jon!" Smiling, I step toward him but his face falls, making me pause.

"I'm so sorry." The pain I can see etched into every line on his face has me pulling him in for a tight hug. He clings to me as he buries his head against my shoulder, reminding me that he's still very much a kid. "I'm so sorry."

"Shhh," I soothe, holding him to me. "It's okay. None of this is your fault." He wasn't even there that day. Tank and Rampage were the ones at school with Luc, not that I blame them either. It was a fucking shootout, of course they were distracted. I know how friendly Luc has gotten with each of them, and I've no doubt they are all beating themselves up over what happened.

He shakes his head, not buying my words. "I should have been there. I should've..."

"What?" I argue, pulling back so he can see my sincerity. "You being there wouldn't have changed anything, except maybe getting yourself hurt or killed."

"You trusted me with him. He was my friend, and I let him down."

"You did no such thing." I cup his face in my hand. "What's done is done. There's no point dwelling on it. All we can do is look forward, focus on getting him back because we *will* get him back."

I have no idea where this confidence is coming from—Cain and Oliver must be rubbing off on me—but it seems to bolster Jon, and the sad look in his eye turns into something harder as he straightens his spine.

"We will. I'll do whatever it takes to make this right."

I smile softly. "There's nothing to make right. You did nothing wrong. You're a good friend, and I'm sorry I doubted you initially."

A goofy grin lights up his face, and for a moment, I feel like everything will be all right. I love Jon's optimism and his outlook on the world. Given what he's been through, he should be beaten down and broken, but he's got more life in him than I do. It makes me realize how much of my life I've squandered over the years. He's only now getting his first real taste of what it means to live, and he embraces every moment, living it to its fullest, whereas I've taken it for granted, only seeing the negatives instead of focusing on what's good about my life.

"I can't say I blame you. You raised a good kid. I'd be worried too if I thought some thug was trying to corrupt him."

He smirks and I laugh.

"I should go tell Tank and Rampage you're here..."

"There's no need. The blame for all of this lies solely with Grim and Giovanni. They are the ones we should be angry at. *They're* the ones that need to pay."

I can tell a weight has been lifted off his shoulders when we part ways, and surprisingly, I feel lighter myself, as though relieving Jon of his blame has somehow helped me come to terms with my own guilt.

I've been blaming myself for not being there, for leaving Luc in someone else's care while I took on a cause that was not mine. I've blamed myself for letting the Rejects into our lives and for thinking we could take on the Antonellis without repercussions, but I meant what I said to Jon. We are not to blame. We are not to blame for fighting back when Giovanni was the one that dealt the first strike. We are not to blame for standing up and demanding better; demanding more. We shouldn't have to scurry around in the shadows, suffocated under oppression and terrified to piss off the higher powers that rule this city. We shouldn't have to live in fear that one day they'll knock our door down and steal our loved ones. We shouldn't have to fight for scraps and demean ourselves just to survive.

I may not have started this war, but I am a part of it. I was a part of it long before Cain sought me out. He just brought me into the fold and upped the ante. While I'd been sneaking around in the dark, cutting off the monster's feet and barely making a difference, Cain decided to go straight for the monster's head. The kill shot. Cut off the head and the body will die.

A savage grin slashes across my face as I pull the helmet over my head and throw my leg over Raven, revving the engine before tearing out of the parking lot. Oh yeah, Giovanni's head will roll alright. I'm going to make sure of that.

"Whose house is this?"

I've had the most amazing twenty-four hours. Riding Raven, hanging out with the Rejects, and spending the night curled up with Cain and Oliver... It would be perfect if it wasn't for the dark cloud of worry hanging over me as I wonder what fresh hell Luc is enduring.

Thankfully, all four men have agreed to meet today so we can devise a plan. Luc's already been in Giovanni's and Santos' hands for six days. Six days too long. I can't even bear to think what irreparable damage they could have done to him in that time.

"Mine," Cain answers as he holds the front door open for me. We're back at the house I directed Dante and Enzo to the other day.

My eyebrows hitch in surprise, not having expected that answer. I figured it belonged to one of his men. "Yours?"

"Yup. I grew up here."

I cast my eyes around the house with fresh eyes, trying to picture a younger version of Cain running around, perhaps with his sister in tow and Oliver somewhere nearby. I imagine this house was once filled with happy memories… until it wasn't.

My eyes trail up the stairs to the landing, where Cain and Evie would have slept. Does he still stay here sometimes? Is her room still the same, or has he painted over all the heartache like he has with the rest of the house?

"You kept it." My voice is hoarse, emotion making it difficult to speak.

"Yeah," he sighs. "I couldn't bring myself to sell it after Mom died. I used it as the base for the Rejects before we outgrew it."

"And now?"

"Haven't decided yet." His gruff tone tells me he's done discussing it, and I slip my hand into his, giving it a reassuring squeeze as a car engine roars outside, alerting us to Enzo and Dante's arrival.

Both Cain and Oliver tense when we hear the car doors slam shut, the two of them eyeing the front door like the Devil himself is about to walk through it. I can't help rolling my eyes. I may be surrounded by ruthless men who wouldn't hesitate to eliminate a threat, but somehow I know for certain that they won't harm each other.

"Behave," I hiss, giving Cain a pointed look before I enter the hall to greet them, leaving the two of them in the living room.

"Hey," I greet when I've pulled the front door open. Both men's gazes run over me as if needing to see for themselves that I'm all in one piece before lifting up to my face.

"Good to see you, Spitfire," Enzo murmurs, leaning down to kiss me. I bite my lower lip to squash my smile, liking that he's no longer holding back.

Dante doesn't say anything, though he doesn't need to. He somehow manages to say more in one look than he ever could with words. His brown depths flare with possession and something softer, and I smile shyly at him. How he manages to make me feel like an embarrassed schoolgirl is beyond me, but that's precisely what his bone-deep stares do.

"We're in here." They follow me into the living room, where Cain and Oliver are still standing, apparently not comfortable enough to sit until they've squared off against Enzo and Dante.

I blow out my cheeks, choosing to let the four of them size each other up while I claim an armchair in the corner of the room. There's no way in hell I'm about to sit on one of the sofas and allow a pissing contest to take place.

My eyes dart back and forth between them while they stand off. Faces tight, both sets of men look the other up and down, getting a measure of the other. It's kind of intriguing, and I just let myself watch the posturing for a while before speaking up. "Shall I get a tape measure? Do you want to compare the size of your dicks, or can we get down to business?"

Dante and Cain both grimace, while Enzo smirks cockily. It's Oliver who speaks, mischief gleaming in his eyes. "No need, wouldn't wanna embarrass them."

I roll my eyes while Dante and Enzo bristle, but as I go back to watching them, I spot the undercurrent of similarities between them that I'm sure they'd all be horribly offended by if I dared point them out. Before I can analyze it further, Oliver steps back, falling onto the sofa behind him. The movement seems to break the tension, and Enzo follows suit. Crossing the room toward me, he claims the other couch, deliberately planting his feet wide so his shoe knocks against mine.

I quirk a brow. *Seriously?*

He just smiles back, knowing damn well what he's doing, and I glance away, ignoring him as I wait for Cain and Dante to sit their asses down. After a long moment where they continue to glower at one another, they finally move to sit, and before any of them can say something to piss the other off, I get straight to the point of why we are here.

"Luc's been gone for six days." The mention of my brother and my severe tone garners their attention, and all four men turn to look at me. "I refuse to let another six days pass, so how are we going to get him back?"

"I've been thinking about that," Cain says casually, throwing his ankle over his knee as he leans back in his seat, looking every bit at home. "You say he's living with Santos, in the same tower block as Giovanni... so we storm the castle." His gaze flicks to Dante. "You have access to the tunnels, right? They wouldn't even see us coming."

Dante glowers at me, and I just give him a *what?* look. "We're all on the same side," I remind him.

Pursing his lips, he grits out, "Yes, but it won't be that easy. My father has an extensive security detail. He has men stationed all over that building, inside and out. You'd have better luck breaking into the White House."

Rising to the challenge, Cain raises a brow. "We have the manpower to face him. Along with the element of surprise... assuming you don't go running to daddy, telling him everything we discuss here today." His eyes narrow on Dante in warning, who then simply stares back at him blankly, not a trace of emotion on his face.

"I won't."

Cain scoffs. "Excuse me if I don't take you at your word. I'm sure you can see how it looks from our perspective."

A tense silence fills the room before Enzo leans forward, bracing his elbows on his knees as he stares Cain straight in the eye, his expression pensive. "Whatever reason you have for hating the Antonellis, I assure you, our reasons for hating Giovanni are just as warranted."

"Oh yeah? Did he kidnap your eleven-year-old sister from her home and do god knows what with her?"

My heart breaks at the pain and fury in Cain's voice, and I desperately want to go and sit in his lap, but I don't. He wouldn't want me to comfort him, not with Enzo and Dante watching.

Enzo drops his head, staring at the floor as he contemplates his response. "No," he eventually says, dragging out the word. "He didn't." Once again, meeting Cain's furious gaze, he confesses, "But he did kill my parents in front of me." My gaze flicks to Cain and Oliver, noting their wide-eyed looks of surprise before Enzo continues, drawing my attention back his way. "Giovanni can't stand disloyalty. He hates traitors, especially when it comes from those closest to him. The very fact we are here having this conversation is reason enough for him to sign-off on our deaths." His words hang in the air before he brushes them under the rug and gets back on topic. "The tunnels could work, but Dante's right. It won't be an easily won fight."

"I'd be disappointed if it was."

The five of us spend the rest of the afternoon hashing out a plan. Between the seriousness of what we're discussing and the tension in the air, it's an exhausting afternoon, and I have a headache by the time we call it a day. All of us are in agreement that we're better off making our move sooner rather than later before Giovanni catches wind of his son's betrayal.

"You coming?" Enzo asks me when they get up to leave.

"I have my bike with me. I'll follow you."

He frowns. "Yeah, alright. Be careful." With a chaste kiss on my cheek and a sharp jerk of his head in farewell to Cain and Oliver, he strides out the door. Dante lingers a bit longer, his intense gaze boring into mine, and I reach out to squeeze his hand, giving him a small smile before he walks out without a word.

"He's a chatty one," Oliver notes when we're alone. Other than a passing comment here or there, Dante didn't say a word all afternoon, except that's just his style. He's more of a thinker than a talker. He'll have taken in everything we discussed and is undoubtedly going over it in his head as we speak.

I glance up at Cain, finding him staring out the door after the two men, deep in thought. Pushing up onto my toes, I capture his lips with mine. "I told you they weren't what they seem."

He harrumphs, looking unimpressed. "We'll see."

I smirk, knowing that even though he won't admit it, Enzo's admission is playing on his mind, before moving to grab my helmet from where I left it on the stairs. Lifting my keys from the hall table, I call over my shoulder, "I'll call you later," before heading out the door and climbing onto Raven. Revving the engine, I take off down the street.

The cold wind whips at my face as I speed across the city, weaving in and out of the traffic. For the first time in days, weeks even, I feel hopeful. Optimistic. Soon I'll have my brother back. Cain, Oliver, and Enzo will have their vengeance, and Dante will be free. *Your reign of terror is coming to an end, Giovanni. I hope you're ready to meet your maker.*

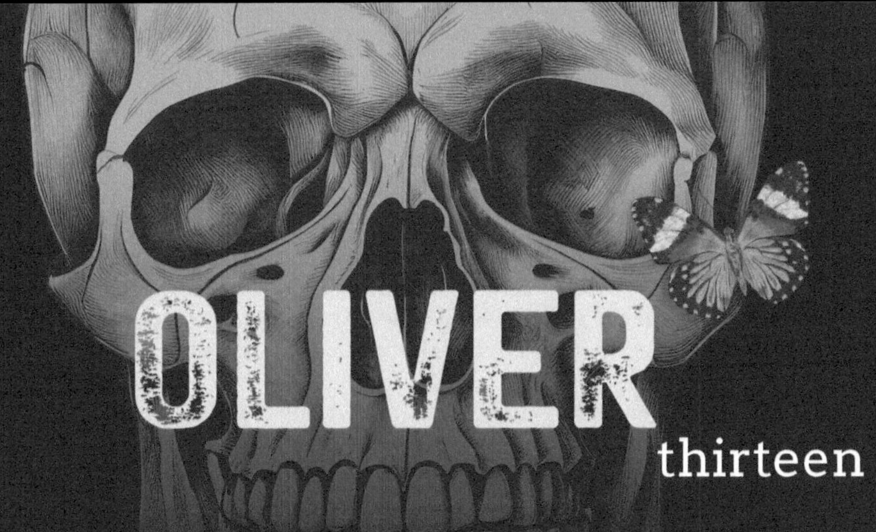

OLIVER

thirteen

As soon as the sound of Red's motorbike peters out into the distance, I grab two beers from the fridge and hand one to Cain as I walk past before collapsing back onto my spot on the sofa.

Slowly, Cain follows me, clearly deep in thought, much like I am. I'm still surprised that we all made it out of that meeting alive and unharmed. Not a drop of bloodshed. Still, the fact that it was all so... civilized... for men who are meant to be on opposite sides of the battle lines, leaves me with a new set of questions. There's only one reason why we all walked away today without fresh injuries or bullet wounds. Red. Although Cain and I were armed and ready to fight and defend ourselves, and Red, if needed, we decided to do it her way initially and see how it played out. All it would have taken was one wrong move or word by either Antonelli man, and they would have had a blown-out knee cap to show for it. But, surprisingly, the meeting didn't go to shit as I'd expected. Cain and I behaved for Red's sake... and strangely, I think Dante and Enzo did too.

I just don't know what that means. With all the time she was spending around them before the wedding, I could tell that they had grown on her. While she still remained steadfast in our mission to bring down the Antonellis, the fact she all but begged Cain to spare their lives that day says everything about how deeply under her skin they have gotten.

Red's an excellent judge of character, and given her prejudice toward all things gang-related, I know she wouldn't have been easily fooled. They must have done something worthy of her support if she was standing up for them. What's getting to me is the way *they* reacted around *her*. The intensity in Dante's gaze. The possessive touch of Enzo's boot against her shoe. The ownership pouring off both of them had my hackles rising, ready to put my own stamp of ownership on her. I recognized how they both looked at her and behaved, because it's the same way Cain does. The same way I do. And, honestly, that terrifies me a hell of a lot more than knowing Red had developed feelings for them ever did.

"What do you think about all of this?" I voice aloud, when my own thoughts become too much.

Cain shakes his head, knocking back a mouthful of beer before responding. "I don't fucking trust them. I don't trust them to keep quiet about this plan, I don't trust them to do what they need to do, and I definitely don't trust them to look after Red."

"Do you think what Enzo said is true, about Giovanni killing his parents in front of him?"

"I've no fucking clue." Cain mulls it over for a second. "Maybe."

"He seemed sincere." When he doesn't agree with me, I say, "They care about Red, about rescuing her brother. The only reason they came here today was because of her. We might not trust them, but they trust her."

Cain grits his teeth, anger evident from the tense way he's holding himself and the tight muscles in his jaw. "Did you see the way they were with her?"

"Yeah," I sigh, knowing that no matter how much we may dislike it, we aren't going to rid ourselves of them any time soon. Not without a fight, at least. "They aren't going to let her go."

My words only anger Cain further, his entire body tensing to the point where it looks like he's one wrong word away from snapping.

"What do you think about the plan?" I ask instead, attempting to defuse the situation somewhat.

"I don't like it," he spits out angrily. "We're putting too much trust in those assholes. If they betray us—betray Red—then we're all dead." He lets out a long sigh, his shoulders dropping as he swipes his hand down his face wearily. "But without Dante's access to the elevator, we lose the element of surprise. They'll see us coming a mile away. Not to mention, rescuing Luc and killing Giovanni ourselves will be much harder."

I nod in agreement. "All we can do is ensure our men are ready. Marcus and I can get everyone up to speed on the plan and have a backup team ready to move if we are blindsided or betrayed by Dante or Enzo." I think through what else we need to do in order to protect our backs and ensure this hastily thrown-together plan will go off without a hitch—assuming Red is right in putting her trust in Antonellis, of all people. "I'll do a weapons inventory and set up surveillance teams starting today, so we will know if either of them pays a visit to Giovanni between now and then."

Cain distractedly agrees with my plans, still clearly thinking through everything himself. I give him a moment to sort through his thoughts before asking, "Okay, so if we're doing this, who is our focus? Giovanni or Luc?"

Lifting his head, there's no doubt or uncertainty in his eyes when he says, "Luc. Red and Luc are the priority. I already put my desire to get to Giovanni ahead of her once, and she ended up married to that apathetic fucker. I won't make the same mistake twice."

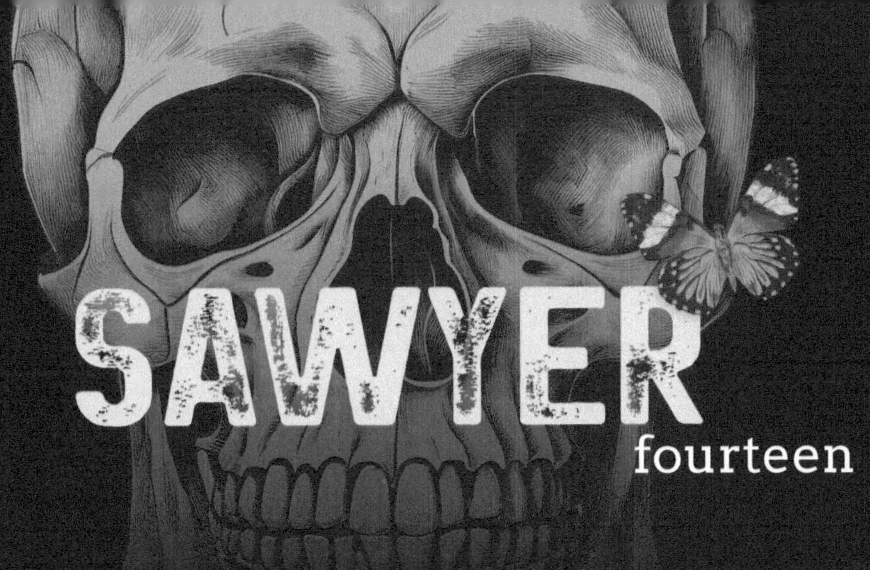

"You can't wear that!"

"What? Why?" Dante sputters as I frown at the full suit he's wearing for our date tonight.

"Because you look like a fucking penguin." Visibly annoyed, he glowers at me. "A very hot penguin," I tack on. "But you'll stand out like a sore thumb in that outfit."

Tonight, I plan on introducing Dante to my life. He's the only one who doesn't know the real me, and tonight is a test of sorts. He seems fully committed to this... to us, although the nagging voice at the back of my head keeps reminding me that he can't possibly be a hundred percent sure when he doesn't truly know me.

I chew on my bottom lip while I think. "Hold on." I put up a finger, telling him to stay there while I dash out of the bedroom and across the hall. I knock on Enzo's door, waiting until he tells me to come in before opening it.

Enzo's lying on his bed, his back against the headboard and his legs stretched out in front of him, reading a book.

"Do you have any clothes from when you were slumming it, pretending to be from my part of town?" I ask, smirking at him.

He raises one eyebrow as he closes the book and sets it on his bedside table, getting to his feet. "Sure." Moving to his closet, he rifles through his clothes until he pulls out a pair of dark denim jeans, a black t-shirt, a brown jacket, and matching shoes. "These work?"

I run my eyes over them, smiling. "I think so."

Taking them from his outstretched hands, I run my fingers over the soft fabric, similar to my own new clothes, before peeking at the labels. "Of course," I scoff. "Designer. I knew your clothes were too good looking."

Enzo just looks at me for a moment before raising an incredulous eyebrow. "Seriously? Is that why you were so distrusting of me? My clothes?"

"Well, that and the fact that you couldn't drink cheap whiskey."

"The shit at that bar tasted like piss."

I bark out a laugh. "Yeah, in comparison to your fancy aged scotch, sure."

His gaze drops over my outfit, taking in the black crop top and high-waisted booty shorts I'm wearing with my thigh-high leather heels and heavy makeup, before his eyes flare. His tongue runs along his lower lip, clearly liking what he sees, and he reaches out, tugging me against his hard body. "When do I get a date with you?"

I smile coyly. "You wanna go on a date with me?"

"Baby girl, I've wanted to go on a date with you for years now."

"Is that so?" I trail my finger enticingly over his chest. "Maybe you should try asking me then."

He smirks. "Sawyer Jones, will you go out with me?"

I tilt my head to one side while I pretend to think about his request. "Hmm, I'm not sure," I tease. "I might need some convincing."

Desire flares in his eyes as he grabs my hips, grinding me against his growing erection while he leans in to bite my neck before soothing the sting with a lick of his tongue. "I can be very persuasive, and I'm very determined. I don't give up easily."

"So you're saying I should just give in now and agree to a date?"

"Not at all." He rocks against me, driving his cock into my stomach. "I want you to be one hundred percent sure." Another rock of his hips. "No doubts." Heat spirals in my core as he grinds against my pelvis. "I'm looking forward to convincing you." He bites down on my earlobe, and I groan as I rub myself shamelessly against him.

"Now, go have fun on your date." He spins me around, and I'm too dazed to do anything more than stammer as he walks me to the door.

"No fair," I grumble as he closes the door. Trying to regain control of my body, I carry the clothes to Dante's room, dropping them on the bed. "Wear these."

His gaze lingers on me, taking in my flushed cheeks before dropping to the clothes. His lip curls in disgust. "Now, Dante," I bark, slowly losing the battle with my hormones and seriously considering staying here and repeating our three-way from the other night.

He quirks a brow but thankfully doesn't say anything as he gathers the clothes and begins to change, and I move to the bathroom, running some cold water over my wrists and neck to try and cool myself down. Flirting with Enzo should not have me so hot and bothered. I take a minute to fix my straightened hair and touch up my red lipstick before heading back into the bedroom. I stop in my tracks, my eyes running over Dante in his new clothes. A grin pulls at my lips. He's had to loop a belt through the jeans, and the jacket and the top are more loose fitting on him than on Enzo's broader frame, but even with that, he still looks hot.

"You look good."

He frowns, glancing down at himself, apparently unimpressed with what he sees. "I beg to differ," he grumbles, making me laugh.

His gaze snaps to mine, studying me like I'm some weird specimen he can't understand, as the air between us grows heavy. "Umm, are you ready to go?" I ask, breaking the moment.

We head downstairs, and when we reach the foyer, I grab my helmet and the one I asked Enzo to buy for Dante. The way his eyes had danced when I'd mentioned that we'd take the bike tonight, I could tell he thought I was joking.

"What the fuck is that for?" Dante grunts when I try to hand him the helmet.

"The bike."

"I'm not riding on that thing. We'll take the car."

"No. I'm in charge tonight, and I'm telling you, we're taking the bike."

His face is set in stone as he scowls at me. "I should at least get to drive it."

I lift one eyebrow, already knowing the answer when I ask, "Do you even know how to ride?" His resounding silence says it all. "Even if you did, I wouldn't let you."

Shoving the helmet against his chest so he's forced to grab onto it, I stride out the door, giving him no choice but to follow. I pull my own helmet on, lifting the visor as I swing my leg over the bike and turn to cock a brow at Dante. He's frowning at my baby like she's the devil's spawn.

"Didn't take you for a pussy, Antonelli."

His dark eyes snap to mine, and with a curse, he shoves the helmet over his head and slides on behind me. His arms wrap around my waist and his large hands flatten against my stomach as the bike rumbles to life beneath us. Lifting my feet, I roll us down the drive and onto the road.

The city streets pass in a blur as I drive us through Antonelli territory and over the bridge into the southern part of the city. The roads become more familiar the closer I get to home until I pull onto my street and bring the bike to a stop outside my building. Staring up at the shabby apartment block, I realize just how much has changed since I was last here.

Dante shuffles behind me before climbing off. Following, I watch as he pulls off his helmet and glances around, taking in the rundown-looking street with disdain. "Where are we?"

"This is where I live." I gesture with my chin at the building in front of us, and Dante turns to give the structure his attention, his lips pursing in displeasure. "Come on."

Stepping forward, I lead him into the building. The familiar mix of mildew and piss wafts over us and I can only imagine what's running through Dante's head, but he needs to see this. *I* need him to see this. He's quiet as we climb the stairs and walk along the hall to my door. Unlike the time I brought Oliver here, I don't feel nervous. I'm not worried about what he thinks. This will either make him realize we come from entirely different worlds that don't meld well together—a lesson I clearly need to heed since I keep fantasizing about keeping all four men for myself—or he won't give a shit. Either way, I'll know for sure if there's a future here.

Now that I think about it, I guess I'm doing this as much for myself as I am for him. *I* need to know if we have any hope of a future, if it's at all possible for the two worlds I've been straddling to coalesce.

Once we're in the apartment, I simply stand there and watch as he takes it all in. The worn kitchen cabinets that don't fit quite right, the tiny living room with the sofa wedged in, and the small, old-fashioned TV. The cracks running down the wall and the questionable stains in the carpet.

My home.

Looking around, I try to see it all through his eyes. It's a far cry from his fancy house by the ocean and his father's large, modern penthouse, that's for sure. He slowly works his way across the room, taking it all in before exploring the bedrooms and bathroom. I leave him to it, finding myself strangely detached from it all. This has been my home for five years. The first home Luc and I had after my mom died, and yet as I scan the room, it doesn't feel like home. There's nothing personal here. There never has been. The only thing we had...

I spin to face the wall dividing the kitchen and living room where I used to have a picture of Luc and I stuck to it. The wall is now empty, as it was my last time here. I'd assumed Luc had taken the picture, but I now realize it was Santos. It's the only photo of Luc, the only way he could have known about his existence.

A cold feeling settles into my bones from knowing Santos was here, rifling through our things and invading our privacy.

I hear Dante enter the room, his eyes on me. "For five years, this was our home. The only place where we felt some semblance of safety." Anger has me trembling as it lights a fire through my body. "And he ruined that."

The floorboards creak as Dante closes the distance between us, his warmth seeping into my back. "Why did you bring me here?"

I turn, bringing us chest to chest, tilting my head back as I look up at him. Even in my heels, my eyes only reach his chin. "Cause I need you to see what my life looks like."

"I don't care what your life looks like."

"I didn't grow up like you," I argue, not really listening to him. "I didn't grow up with money. I don't have fancy clothes or a nice car. Hell, I didn't even finish high school."

Using his larger, more muscular body, he backs me up against the wall. Planting his hands on either side of my head, he leans in until his face fills my entire field of vision. "I said I don't care. Do you think any of this makes a difference to me? I know you've lived a hard life. You wouldn't be who you are if you hadn't." His eyes search mine. "Even when you were a dirty, grimy street kid, I knew you were made of tougher stuff than half the men I've worked with. I can count on one hand the number of people who have looked down the barrel of my gun and not flinched, and only one of them was a scared little girl. I don't know what made you so damn resilient. Maybe it was this life you seem to think I'll despise you for..."

"Luc," I whisper, watching as his brows pull together in confusion. "It was Luc. Your father would have you believe that love makes you weak. But it's actually my love for him, my need to protect him and give him a better life that made me the person I am today."

His eyes bore into mine, and I can tell he's truly heeding my words. "Then I guess I owe him a thank you."

Not breaking eye contact, I fist his t-shirt in my hand, and with a tug, I eliminate the space between us, dragging his lips to mine. It's the first time I've initiated anything intimate with him. The first time I haven't questioned this pull between us or felt guilty for acting on it.

Dante is many things. He's challenging and difficult to deal with. He's set in his ways and he's controlling. He's terrifying and baffling all at once. There's no denying that Dante Antonelli has his faults. But I don't see any of that when I look at him. I see the kid in him who never got the love and affection he deserved. I can practically visualize him rattling the bars of the prison his father has built, begging for someone to take a chance on him, to see that he's not a lost cause.

All of our touches before now have been driven by desire and possession, but as he angles my head just so, deepening our kiss, I can feel how much deeper this runs. It's more than just physical attraction and chemistry. I don't think he understands it any better than I do, but as his tongue glides over mine, the hard edges of his body pinning me to the wall, I can feel him infiltrating my DNA, embedding himself so deep in my system that he becomes an intrinsic part of who I am while ensuring I will never be complete without him.

"So this is what people do on a date?" he asks, sounding a little breathless. I chuckle, sounding a little winded myself. I'm not sure if he's being serious or making a joke. Knowing Dante, I think it's a genuine question.

"Not exactly. This was the pre-date date."

Cocking a brow, he asks, "When does the real date begin?"

"I think it just did."

THE THUDDING BASS RESONATES THROUGH MY ENTIRE BODY UNTIL MY heart rate matches the rhythm as we push through the dense crowd at Toxic.

"Two shots of tequila," I shout at the barman when we finally reach the bar. I can't seem to fight the goofy grin on my face, which only grows wider when I see Dante's uneasiness. He's so far out of his comfort zone right now, it's unreal. However, even out of his suit, he still has an air of authority about him and one deadly glare that has the patrons vacating the stools around us.

I roll my eyes while he helps me onto the empty seat, standing like a sentry beside me. Leaning in so I can talk into his ear, I say, "Relax. This is supposed to be fun."

The frown that's been stuck on his face since we pulled in only deepens.

"Tequila will help."

"I don't drink tequila," he shouts as the barman places two shot glasses in front of us and fills them with a pale-yellow liquid. Dante pays, and I hand him one of the glasses, waiting until he takes it before lifting the other and tapping them together.

"Tonight you do."

Grinning, I knock back my shot. It's my only one of the night since I have to drive, not that I would allow myself to drink much more anyway. I've never been one to get blind drunk somewhere like here, where anyone could take advantage. The only place where I've really let my guard down and allowed myself to let go is at the clubhouse, and I'm happy to keep it that way.

Hesitantly, he brings the glass to his lips before downing it. His face scrunches in disgust and I throw my head back, laughing. Ever since we arrived, it's like watching a kid experiencing everything for the first time. I can't stop observing him. When I meet his gaze again, I find him looking at me too with an expression I've never seen on him before. Something between curious and intrigued.

Grinning, I jump down from my stool and grab his hand. "Come on."

"What now?" he grumbles.

"It's time to dance."

The second the words leave my mouth, he pulls me to a stop. "I don't dance." His face is deadly serious, and sensing I can't just goad him into this, I step closer to him. Lifting my hand, I brush it through his cropped, dark brown hair. "Sure you do. You just don't know how." I tug on his hand, encouraging him to move, but he remains steadfast.

"Okay, you don't have to dance. You can just stand there, and I'll dance." With another encouraging tug, he relents, and I pull him into the thick of the writhing bodies. No one is paying attention to us, too lost in the heavy bass of the music and the hot body they're grinding against. Once we're in the middle of the room, I stop and wrap my arms around his neck, swaying my hips. Like a statue, he just stands there, his gaze darting between me and the bodies pressed against us.

Chuckling, I lift his hands and place them low on my hips, so his fingers brush the curve of my ass. Once again, linking my arms around his neck, I start to move again. It's slow and not at all in rhythm, yet Dante doesn't seem to mind as his eyes bore into mine, and I feel him hardening against my stomach.

"Push your thigh between mine," I whisper in his ear.

He does as I say, and I grind against him. His fingers flex over my ass, and I know he's enjoying what he's seeing as I work myself into a frenzy using just the rough fabric of his jeans.

As the shooting pangs of ecstasy radiate outward from my core, I throw my head back, my eyes drifting shut. After a second, I feel his lips press against my neck, and he leaves open-mouthed kisses along the column of my throat before licking along my collarbone. By now, I can feel his rock-hard length digging into me, and I'm desperate for my own release.

Untangling myself from him, I drag him through the crowd toward the bathrooms at the back of the building. Skipping the queue, we head further down the corridor until I find an empty supply closet and we slip inside.

I pounce on him before the door is even fully closed, wrapping my legs around his slim waist. I suck and nibble my way along his neck while he grips my ass in his large palms.

"So this is what happens on a date," he grunts in a low, sex-dipped voice.

"Only the good ones." I slant my lips over his, driving my tongue into his mouth and cutting off any further conversation. His posture remains rigid as he leans against the door, holding me in his arms. "Fuck me, Dante." I damn near groan, so fucking gone for this man.

It's as if my plea obliterates every reason holding him back, and in the next second, I'm thrown against the opposite wall as he pulls on the button of my shorts until they give. Planting my feet on the floor, I shimmy out of my shorts, all while unbuckling his belt and shoving his jeans and boxers over his ass.

His lips claim mine again as he palms the back of my thighs and lifts me. I feel the brush of his cock against my clit before he sinks into me, the two of us moaning. Pressing me into the wall with his hips, Dante grinds against my pelvis until my orgasm slams into me with all the energy of a lightning storm.

"Oh fuck," I gasp, throwing my head back as I clench around him.

He buries his head in my neck, groaning as he finds his own release, and the two of us are sweaty and panting in each other's arms.

"That wasn't as bad as I thought it would be," he says while I search the shelves for something to clean myself with before righting my clothes.

"Oh, thanks," I chuckle, faking offense.

I see the second he realizes how that sounded. He grimaces. "That's not what I meant. I just... I..."

"I know." I laugh, already knowing what he meant.

"Sorry."

Redoing the button of my shorts, I look up at him, ensuring he sees the sincerity in my eyes when I say, "You don't need to apologize for being you, Dante."

He just nods, uncomfortable and unsure of how to respond. I give him the easy out by taking his hand and leading him out of the closet.

We're walking down the empty back hallway, and just as we reach the corner before the bathrooms, I spin on my heels, staring at the back door. "Did you hear that?"

"Hear what?" Dante flicks his gaze in the direction where I swear I just heard something.

We both stop to listen, but all I hear is a resounding silence. After a moment, I shake my head. "Maybe it was nothing." However, before we can move a muscle, the sound comes again.

Based on the change in Dante's demeanor, he hears it too. His spine snaps upright, his face darkening to something resembling your worst nightmare, but I'm barely paying attention because this time, I know exactly what that sound was—a scream.

Without a second thought, I run toward the back door and shove it open, sending it flying as I hurtle into the alleyway. The same one where I fucked Oliver and disappeared on him.

"No, please. No!"

"Shut the fuck up, bitch."

I spin in the direction of the voices as a muffled cry follows the caustic words. Hidden behind a dumpster, a vulgar-looking man has a young woman shoved up against the wall. Despite her heavy makeup and short dress, she looks younger than me with her wide eyes and trembling limbs, and at the helpless look in her eyes, I see red.

"Hey!" I yell as Dante steps forward, his threatening posture appearing even more intimidating and deadly in the dark shadows cast by the weak streetlight.

With wide, terrified eyes, the scumbag drops the woman like a sack of potatoes and takes off down the street. Dante takes off after him while I rush over to the poor girl crumpled in a heap on the ground as she sobs uncontrollably.

"You're alright," I try to soothe. "He's gone now. Everything's okay."

Huge, tearing sobs rip out of her as I pat her awkwardly on the back. I'm not used to consoling terrified women. I'd be much more comfortable in Dante's shoes right now.

"Are you here with anyone?"

"Y-yes, my friends."

"Alright." With a gentle touch, I coax her to her feet and over to the door. "Go back inside and find them." I can sense her hesitation, her reluctance to leave me, but I place a hand on her back to encourage her forward. "It's alright, he won't hurt you now. Off you go."

With a final sniffle, she scurries inside, and the outer door slams shut behind her. Now that she's gone, I hurry down the alley, hoping Dante hasn't killed the asshole yet. My thumb runs along the lip of my boot, the desire for blood thrumming through my veins. It's been far too long, and the thought of finishing this night off with a bit of bloodshed sounds like the perfect end to our date.

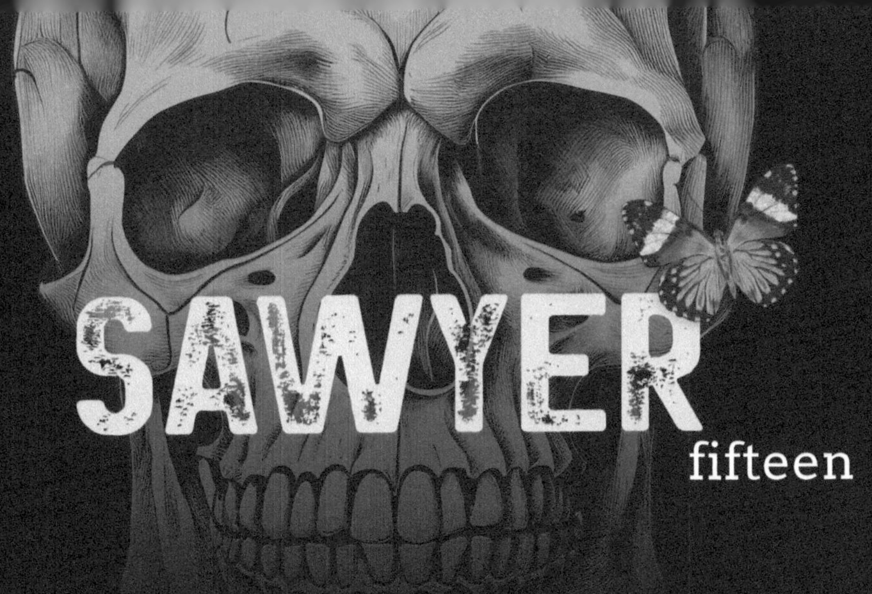

SAWYER

fifteen

By the time I catch up with Dante, his fist is covered with the asshole's blood. Said asshole is half unconscious, his nose broken and brow split under Dante's brutal punches.

"Stop," I cry out as I approach.

With his arm raised above his head in a pre-emptive attack, Dante freezes, his head snapping toward me as confusion mars his features.

"What?" he snarls, and his voice is like nothing I've ever heard before. It's so devoid of emotion that it sounds almost robotic. As far from human as one can get. "Why?"

I smirk. "Because I have a better idea." He stares at me with a deadpan expression, and I roll my eyes. "Looks like you're getting a two-for-one deal tonight." Still not catching on to my meaning, he just raises an eyebrow, silently telling me to hurry up and get to the point before his patience runs out. The grin I give him is positively feral. "You're about to meet the Reaper."

Seemingly intrigued, Dante leans back on his haunches, lowering his arm but not loosening his iron-tight grip on the asshole's chest while he pins him to the ground.

"W-what? Let me go!"

We both ignore him while Dante drags him to his feet. He darts his gaze around the otherwise empty alley before moving further away from the back door.

"N-no. P-please," the asshole stutters. "I-it was a misunderstandin'."

Yeah, sure it was. I roll my eyes at his pathetic bullshit as I follow Dante deeper into the alley. We keep going until we're far enough from the back door that anyone who comes out would have to squint to even know we were here.

"I didn't do nothing!" he wails, desperately struggling against Dante's firm hold.

"Yeah, 'cause we stopped you," I snarl angrily as Dante shoves him hard against the wall.

"N-no. She wanted it!"

I tilt my head to one side as I slowly roam my eyes over his bloody face and panicked gaze. Despite his fear, he still doesn't realize this is the end of the line for him. Dragging that girl into this alley and thinking he could just take what he wanted was his ultimate mistake.

I feel the cold detachment of the Reaper wash over me as I settle comfortably into her familiar empty numbness. "Sure didn't look that way." Even my voice is cool and disconnected. Dante picks up on the difference, whipping his gaze toward me. His eyes drop, taking me in, and I wonder what he sees. Can he tell that I'm no longer Sawyer, that everything that makes me *me* is locked up tight in the back of my mind?

A psychologist would probably say I have a dissociative identity disorder or some shit. They'd tell me that I created the Reaper to deal with my past trauma, to protect Sawyer from this world's cruelty. I say it's because I seriously hate conceited, narcissistic assholes.

"This is bullshit!" he yells, a hint of hysteria in his tone. "The bitch fucking wanted it." His fearful gaze darts between me and Dante before he mistakes Dante's silence for possible understanding. "Please, man. You know how it is. Women, eh? Always changin' their fucking minds." He's babbling, trying desperately to get a response from Dante, but his face remains frozen, his brown eyes blank as he stares unblinkingly at the soon-to-be-dead shitstain.

Truly terrified now, the man's attention snaps back to me when I step forward, his gaze immediately zoning in on the blade I now grasp tightly in my hand. "What the fuck?! You're crazy!" His wide eyes bounce between Dante and me, seeing the clear intent on our faces. "You're both fucking insane."

"At least we aren't rapists," I bite out, stepping up to him. He struggles but Dante pins his arms above his head with one hand, his other holding his trembling body against the brick wall.

"I didn't touch her," the asshole cries as I lift the tip of my blade, running it lightly down the side of his face.

"No," I say softly, agreeing with him, "but I'd bet tonight wasn't your first time." My voice is soft, coaxing, entirely at odds with the sharp knife I have pressed against his skin. "How many other women have you harassed, hmmm? Assaulted? Traumatized?" With every question, I dig the tip in deeper until a steady stream of blood is pouring from the slice in his cheek, mixing with the tears leaking from his eyes.

With practiced ease, I shift and drive the blade into his abdomen. Air whooshes past his lips as his eyes widen to the size of saucers. Too stunned to speak, he can only gape at the point where my knife sticks out of him. The blade isn't particularly long, so it won't kill him or anything.

The second I start slicing it through his skin, he screams bloody murder, and Dante has to slap a hand over his mouth. The acrid scent of piss hits my nostrils and I glare at him in disgust. "Fucking pathetic," I grumble as I get back to the job at hand, making quick work of carving my tag in his skin. The guy is too shocked to do anything other than stand there, his whole body trembling. Dante's white-knuckled grip on his wrists and face are the only things holding the asshole upright.

When I'm done, I fist the neck of his cotton t-shirt and saw through it until it's hanging off him, giving me an unobstructed view of my handiwork. With a jerk of my head, Dante releases him, and his body slides down the wall until he collapses in a heap on the ground, too stunned to hold himself up. Nothing I have done so far is life-threatening. If he gets himself patched up, he'd only be left with a large scar as a reminder of this night. However, forgiveness is not in my nature, so unfortunately for him, that will not be happening.

He's mumbling incoherently under his breath as he stares uncomprehendingly at the blood coating his stomach and hands like he can't remember how it got there. Crouching down in front of him, I fist his hair in my hand, yanking his head back until he's looking me right in the eye. I can tell he doesn't really see me, but that's alright. Fisting the knife in my hand, I give him a dark smirk. "Say hi to the Devil for me." With a flick of my wrist, I slice cleanly through his neck, sending blood spraying from his carotid artery. Warm liquid hits my face and neck as he gurgles and wheezes until the life seeps out of his eyes, and he falls still.

I squat there in the dark alley, watching him with a cold indifference until broad arms wrap around me, yanking me to my feet. I'm thrown against the wall, my whole body tensing as heat seeps into my back before Dante speaks. "I've never been so turned on in my life," he rasps in a low, guttural voice that penetrates my emotionless cage.

He grinds his hard erection between my ass cheeks, showing me exactly how turned on he is. A moan tears from my lips as I push back against him, feeling as though I might die if I don't feel him deep inside me right fucking now. His hands race over my body, his touch frenzied and hungry.

Spinning me around, he rips the button from my shorts in his haste to get them off before shoving them down my legs. It's then that he feels the handle of my other blade poking out of the top of my boot, and arching a brow, he slowly slides it out of its sheath. There's a wicked gleam in his eyes as he twirls it in his hand before trailing the tip lightly along my collarbone. I shiver, but it's not out of fear. No, it's pure, unbridled lust that has me practically coming undone.

Slowly, he drags the blade lower until it reaches the top of my crop top. Mirroring how I tore through the rapist's shirt, Dante easily slices through the thin fabric, baring me to him. Licking his lips, he continues his descent, only detouring to trace my nipples with the cool blade, causing them to harden.

When he reaches the lining of my panties, he dips the tip beneath them before tugging until they pull away. Another shiver wracks my body, my arousal coating my inner thighs. I've never been so erotically charged in my life as I hang on to his every move, curious to know what he's going to do next.

With the flick of his wrist, he flips the dagger until he's holding the base of the handle pressed against my pelvis. The aluminum is warm from his touch as he drags it between my folds. A gasp leaves my lips, and he tears his focus away from where the blade disappears between my thighs to stare into my eyes.

I fall into his russet brown depths as static fills the air, the intrinsic connection that ties us together making itself known. My eyes widen as he pushes the handle into my pussy, and my hands fly up to rest on his shoulders, my fingers digging into his jacket as I throw my head back. A wanton moan rips from my lips as he slowly pumps the handle in and out of me, sending me racing up that slope toward utopia.

I hover on the precipice for what feels like a lifetime, desperately seeking relief but unable to reach it. I cry in frustration, knowing exactly what it is I need. "You," I pant. "I need you."

He's already ripping open his belt and pulling out his cock. Tossing the dagger aside, he hitches my leg over his hip and slams into me. Rough and hard, we fuck as though we're trying to embed ourselves underneath the other's skin. No matter how hard I drive my nails into him, how deep I suck his cock, I can't get close enough to him. It's not enough. I need more. I gyrate my hips, grinding my clit against his pelvis while he sucks a nipple into his mouth, biting, so the sting of pain shoots straight to my core.

"Oh, fuck. Fuck. Fuck. Fuck," I pant on repeat as tingles erupt all over my body and my breathing turns ragged seconds before I lose all sense of control and scream to the heavens. Dante thrusts once, twice, before following me over the edge with a groan.

Sweaty and breathless, we cling to one another, bathing in the afterglow of violence and mind-blowing sex. "We should make this a regular thing," Dante pants.

"Which part? The date, the murder, or the sex?"

He smirks, and it's the first time I've seen him do so. Don't get me wrong, I've seen his lip twitch before he squashes it, but this time he doesn't hold back from me, and it does stupid things to my heart. "All of the above."

I laugh. "You mean you're not put off after all of this?" I wave my hand around the dingy back alleyway and the dead body leaning against the wall beside us.

His expression once again turns serious, his eyes boring into mine. "If anything, tonight has only reaffirmed what I already knew."

I swallow roughly before choking out in a whisper, "What's that?"

"That you're mine. That perhaps all the damage my father inflicted on me was to shape me so that, when slotted together, we'd make two halves of a whole. You are my darkness and my light. My damnation and my redemption. My ruination and rebirth." His thumb brushes along my lower lip. "And maybe I can be all those things for you, too."

"Whoa." Enzo stares wide-eyed, surprise and amusement easy to read on his face as we step into the kitchen later that night. I'm wearing Dante's jacket, zipped all the way up since he so kindly shredded my top. The fly of my shorts is hanging open since he ripped the button off them, and I'm splattered in blood. "Must have been one hell of a date."

"It was," Dante grunts, moving to grab a bottle of water from the fridge. He offers me one, but I shake my head.

"I need a shower."

I can feel Enzo's gaze on me as I leave the room, and his muttered, "What the hell happened?" before I'm out of earshot. I'm teetering somewhere halfway between my usual self and the Reaper. Removed enough not to be bothered that I've got someone else's blood crusted on my skin, though human enough that Dante's words provide me with a warm glow and a grin as I head to our room to shower.

Freshly showered and wearing only Oliver's t-shirt, I slip beneath the cool, crisp bedsheets, and before I can comprehend just how tired I am, I'm already asleep.

Light streams through the window when I wake the next morning and find Enzo beside me in the bed, reading a book. Lying there, I watch him for a bit. He's so absorbed in whatever he's reading that he doesn't feel my eyes on him, and it's only when I shift that he looks my way with a warm smile lifting his lips.

"Morning, Spitfire."

"Morning," I reply on a yawn while I stretch. When I don't bump into Dante on my other side, I glance over my shoulder, finding the bed behind me empty and the sheets perfectly made. "Where is he?" I ask, focusing my attention on Enzo again.

"His father called."

"What?" I exclaim, pushing to sit upright. "Why? You should have gone with him!"

"And leave you here alone?" He shakes his head. "Not a chance."

I frown but don't see the point in arguing. "What does his father want?"

"Probably an update on our plans for the Reaper Rejects."

Panicked, I run my hand through my hair, pushing the long, cherry-red strands out of my face. "What will he say? We didn't talk about this yesterday."

"He'll think of something." Reaching out, he pulls me in against him, running his hand along my arm. "Don't worry, baby girl. He's used to telling his father half-lies, giving him just enough to keep him off our case. This is no different."

My stomach is still twisted with nerves, his words only somewhat reassuring me. "Giovanni will only buy whatever excuse he gives for so long. If we have any hope of success, we need to make a move soon."

Instead of answering, Enzo presses a kiss to my temple, his arms banding tighter around me.

"Do you think he'll see Luc today?" My voice is laced with hope and despair.

"He's hoping to."

We fall into silence after that. Enzo goes back to reading his book while still holding me close, and I opt to watch him. It's only when my stomach starts rumbling loud enough for both of us to hear that our morning of peace comes to an end. Closing the book, he sets it on the nightstand before turning to me. "Go shower. I'll make breakfast before you decide to eat me instead."

I bite down on my lower lip as I throw my leg over his, feeling his long length grow against my leg. "I can think of one part of you I'd happily eat for breakfast."

He throws back his head and laughs. His hand latches around my thigh, holding me in place while he thrusts, before his palm slides up to cup the globes of my ass. "Tempting," he murmurs against my lips. "But we both know it wouldn't stop there, and you definitely need stamina for all the things I want to do to you." With a spank on my ass, just hard enough to have me clenching my thighs, he growls out, "Now go shower before I change my mind and fuck you into the mattress."

Despite his dominant words and the arousal pooling in his green eyes, he gets to his feet and leaves me to do exactly as he said.

An hour later, with my stomach happily full after a delicious breakfast of French-pressed coffee and omelets, I collapse onto the sofa, staring out at the dark gray clouds as they hover over a roiling sea with the promise of a storm before the day is out.

"Here." Enzo shoves a book under my nose.

Shaking my head, I try to push it away. "I'm not really a book person. Besides, I'm too nervous to read."

"That's exactly why you should give it a go. It will distract you and make the time go by faster. Do you honestly think staring at the clock is going to make the minutes any less painful?"

Huffing, I snatch the book from him, reading the title, *The Name of the Wind.* "What's it about?"

"It's the story of a man who overcame his poor upbringing by becoming a notorious magician, an accomplished thief, and an infamous assassin."

"Sounds like he was overcompensating," I grumble, ripping a laugh from Enzo before he makes himself comfortable beside me with his own book. Dragging my feet into his lap, he keeps one hand on my ankle, tracing indistinguishable patterns on my skin while his eyes scan the pages.

After watching him for a moment, I shift my gaze to the book in my hand. Reluctantly opening it to the first page, I begin to read, even though I know I'll be back to staring out the window in five minutes.

I'm halfway through chapter five, wholly absorbed in the book that I didn't even hear the front door when Dante returns. It's only when the heat of his gaze burns hot enough to pull me out of the story that I realize he's home, and I jump to my feet, searching his face for any clue of how his morning went. Nothing.

The nerves I'd been feeling all morning before I got sucked into that damn book re-emerge, and it's in an apprehensive voice that I ask, "Did you see him?"

With a nod, he steals my spot on the sofa and Enzo pulls me to sit between them. Not once does my focus leave Dante while I futilely attempt to read him. "And?"

Instead of answering me, he removes his phone from his pocket. Pulling something up, he turns it to face me, and with shaking hands, I reach out and take it from him. "Oh my god," I gasp, clapping my hand over my mouth. Leaning in, Enzo rests his chin on my shoulder as he stares at the screen.

The photo was discreetly taken from the side, catching Luc right as he turned his head toward the photographer. His face is paler, and he's skinnier than even a couple of days ago, but that's not what I focus on. It's the damage they've done to him that has sent me spiraling. While the black eye he had on the wedding day has started to turn a sickly yellow, he's got a new one to match it on his other eye. His lip is swollen, and there's a sizable purple welt on his jaw. He looks like he was on the wrong end of a bat. Dropping my gaze over his body to search for other injuries, I notice his posture is tense, probably out of fear or pain, or both. The worst part is the emptiness in his usually vibrant eyes. It's like Giovanni and Santos have sucked the life out of him, leaving nothing but an empty shell behind.

The image swims as tears well in my eyes and I choke on a sob. I feel the control on my sanity slipping as darkness creeps in at the edge of my vision, threatening to swallow me whole. The icy-cold fingers of the Reaper clutch at my heart, squeezing until it threatens to burst while she whispers promises of violence, retribution, and chaos.

"Tonight. We move tonight. He's not staying there another second."

My tone leaves no room for argument, and neither man challenges me as if sensing how close I am to losing myself.

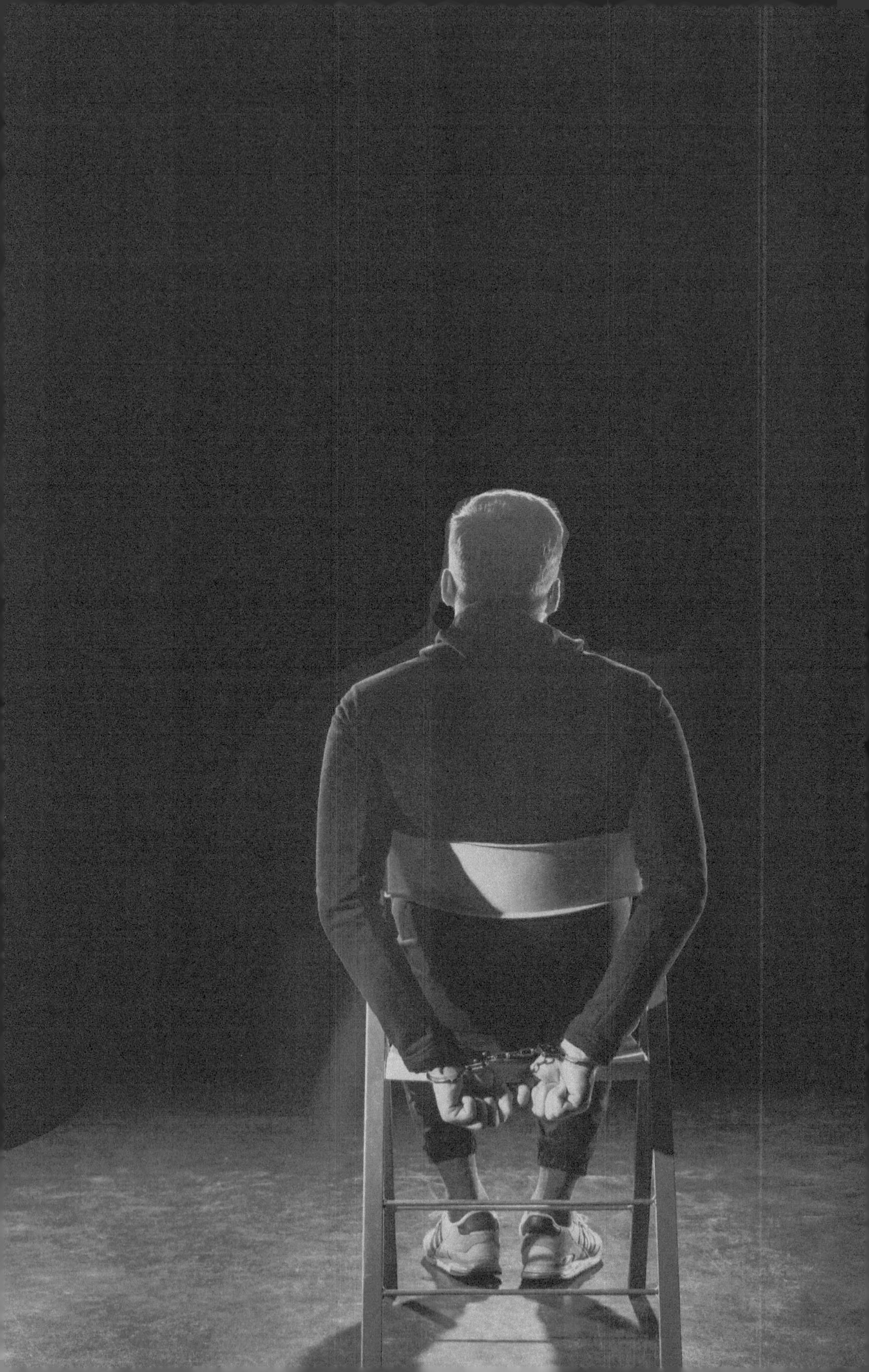

LUC

sixteen

It's the steady drip of water from a tap that reluctantly pulls me back into the realm of consciousness, and I groan as I take in my less-than-stellar living arrangements. I'm still tied to the chair I was sitting on when I passed out in the same windowless room. As my brain comes back online, the first thing I register is pain. Everywhere. The muscles in my arms ache from being forced backward, and my face and torso hurt from the beatings they've taken, but I'm alive.

As soon as the horrendous dinner where I discovered Santos was my father was over, I was marched down here. Despite that asshole's words for me not to fight, that's precisely what I did. I fought Santos tooth and nail, throwing every bit of anger and hurt into my punches as I put the skills Jon taught me to good use. Not that it did me any good. Being bigger and stronger than me, Santos easily gained the upper hand. And the glint of satisfaction in his eye when he wrestled me into the chair was chilling. Of course, my resistance gave him the excuse he needed to *beat the dissent out of me*. His words.

I'm not sure how long ago that was or how long I've been tied up in here for, but I'm not left to stew in my thoughts for long as the sound of heavy footfalls treading closer to my cell reaches my ears.

A beeping sound comes from the other side of the door before it swings open, and Santos steps in, his form as dominating as ever in his crisp suit, with his shaved head and the row of Xs down one cheek. His smile is all teeth as he stares down at me, enjoying his handiwork as he takes in the myriad of bruises and blood.

He crosses his arms over his chest and leans back against the door, observing me. I watch him right back, refusing to be cowered, even in my weakened, defenseless state. Sawyer may have protected me, but she didn't coddle me. While she may not have taught me to fight, she did teach me to stand up for myself. She instilled long-standing principles, principles that I have no intention of discarding just because this asshole thinks he can beat them out of me.

"What's your name?" It's the same question that landed me here in the first place.

"Lucifer Jones."

I don't know if the idiot expected me to roll over and submit as soon as he announced my bloodline. Actually, given how excited he looks when I once again don't give him the correct answer, I think he wants me to fight back. He wants me to resist. All so he can break me down and revel in the discarded pieces left behind.

He wants me to fight so he can watch me fall. So he can put me back together in his image.

Well, that's not fucking happening.

"Wrong answer," he sing-songs, not sounding all that annoyed as he steps over to the table on the far side of the room. He takes his time selecting his weapon of choice, making me sweat as my heart rate skyrockets with anticipation.

Lifting something, he turns to face me, holding a long metal pole with a plastic handle and two prongs at the end. My body tenses on instinct, and I don't have time to do anything else—not that there is much else I can do—before he jams it into my side.

My entire body locks up, an unpleasant buzzing sensation starting under my skin as my teeth grind painfully against one another. It can't last more than a few seconds, but as soon as he retracts the device, I sag forward, breathing heavily.

"Let's try that again. What's your name?"

I manage to spit out, "Luc Jones," on a hoarse breath. The words barely pass my lips before the stick is shoved back into my side. This time the intensity has been turned up, and I cry out as a blinding hot pain eliminates any other sensation.

My breath comes in heaving wheezes by the time he pulls away, and on and on it goes for who knows how long. Could be seconds or minutes. Hell, it could even be days. When he gets bored of the taser, he moves on to his fists, the serrated knife, or whatever other instrument of pain he fancies. None of the damage he leaves is life-threatening. He knows just where to punch and how deep to slice to enact pain without accidentally killing me.

He doesn't let up until I'm a sweating, half-unconscious mess, my restraints the only thing holding me upright in the chair.

With my head hanging between my shoulders, my chin touching my chest, he moves to crouch in front of me.

"The Antonelli Famiglia is the most powerful, most respected, and most feared family on the West Coast. People would kill for the blood running through your veins, boy." He rakes his eyes over me, critically assessing and sizing me up. "You've got grit and determination. Two things that will take you far in this life. Except your allegiances are misplaced. When I'm done with you, you *will* be one of us, and then you will see how great it is to be an Antonelli man."

I spit blood out onto the floor, watching as it crawls along the concrete until it connects with a larger tributary that flows into the drain under my seat.

Using the last of my energy, I lift my head enough to meet Santos' cold, unflinching gaze. "I will never be one of you. You'll have to kill me first."

Instead of the flash of anger I expect, he simply grins. It's ice-cold and terrifying. "There will be no need for that. Sooner or later, you will break. Everyone has their limit. I'll find yours."

On that hopeless note, he pushes to his feet and strides to the door. I keep my head down when he flicks a glance over his shoulder at me before typing a code into the keypad on the door. Without lifting my head, I watch as he does, mentally noting the numbers before he plunges the small room into darkness. The only sound is the click of the lock behind him and his receding footsteps, until I'm left alone with my jumbled thoughts and waning energy.

THE DAYS GO BY IN MUCH THE SAME ROUTINE. AT LEAST, I ASSUME IT'S days. The only time I leave the room is when he drags me to the bathroom for a ten-second piss break.

With each passing round, I can feel the flare of hope in my chest diminishing. I want to hold on to it, but I'm just so tired. So sore. It's not that I've given up, I've just stopped caring.

As if he can sense my fading resolve with every round we go, Santos has been upping the extent of his torture. Pushing me to my limits, to my breaking point, and goddamn, I feel close to shattering. Close to giving in. Close to losing.

I don't know how long I've been here or how many days have passed. I don't know how many more will come to pass before Sawyer and the Rejects come, but I know they will. While the strength to fight may be leaving my body, my confidence in Sawyer never wavers.

I'm nothing more than a useless lump of skin, muscle, and bone when, on day number who-the-fuck-knows of my incarceration, Santos slices through the ties binding me to the chair. Even though I'm no longer bound, my arms refuse to move, the muscles now stuck in that position after days of immobility and unuse.

He roughly grabs the back of my shirt and hauls me to my feet, but the minute I'm left to stand on my own, my weak legs give out beneath me, and I fall to the floor that's still coated in the remnants of my dried blood from previous torture sessions.

Fun times.

I'm now beginning to understand Bone's dark humor and dry wit a little better. Gotta cling to something, even if it is solely for my own amusement and at my own expense.

"On your feet, boy," Santos growls impatiently, yanking me back up once again.

With a hand on the wall and slow steps, I manage to follow him down a nondescript corridor with buzzing overhead lighting and into a bedroom. I stare longingly at the bed, only Santos continues past it to another door, and since I haven't been anywhere other than that room, I don't want to piss him off already and have him send me back there before I've had a chance to scope out wherever we are.

He directs me into a living area with floor-to-ceiling glass windows providing an unobstructed view of the city. I scour my eyes over the buildings, trying to pinpoint the Reject clubhouse. Not that it would do me much good, I just need to see it to remind myself that although I feel very alone right now, I'm not.

Before I can work out any more than the vague direction in which the clubhouse is, Santos pulls my focus. "Sit." He points to a chair at a long dining table. "Eat." He doesn't have to tell me twice as I dive into the plate of food. I haven't had anything to eat since that meal, and the only liquid I've had is what I was able to cup in my hand and slurp down from the tap every time I was granted a piss break.

I don't even know what the hell I'm eating, but it tastes fucking delicious. I stuff my face until the plate is wiped clean, and all the while, Santos watches me with a keen eye that unnerves me.

"You have the whole apartment to yourself today," he says when I'm finished, waving toward the television. "You can watch TV, play video games, sleep, shower. Do whatever you want."

I want to ask why but bite my tongue against the question. It's not like he'd be honest, and no matter how tempting all of this sounds, it's a ploy. I'm smart enough to know that.

Standing, he moves toward the door that I assume leads into the corridor. To the elevator. To freedom. My eyes linger on the thin piece of wood that separates me from that freedom, and a voice at the back of my head tells me to make a run for it. I debate it. I'm so desperate for it that I even take a step forward before catching myself. It's not just one measly bit of wood that separates me from freedom. It's however many guards are standing in the hall. It's the security cameras in the elevator and the guards on the ground floor. I wouldn't reach the kind of freedom I'm after if I ran.

Santos must see my indecision as he smirks confidently when I pause. The realization must be clear on my face—the knowledge that I'm trapped—because he doesn't even bother threatening me to stay. He simply turns around and leaves.

Even after the door clicks shut behind him, all I can do is stand and stare at it. I don't know how much time passes, but eventually I turn to stare out the window instead, going back to my initial task of pinpointing the Reject clubhouse. Unfortunately, too many taller buildings between here and there obstruct my view, yet simply knowing it's out there settles me a little. I can almost visualize the guys going apeshit over my disappearance, and Sawyer will be demanding that they come up with a plan ASAP. Even though she's been absent recently—doing whatever the hell job had her walking down the fucking aisle to an Antonelli—I know she will be there now, fighting for me. It's all she knows how to do—fight to protect me.

I shake my head against the shock that wracked my body that day in the church when her veil was pulled back and all I saw was Sawyer. Until then, I couldn't figure out what I was doing inside a church. I still can't get the look of shock and horror on her face out of my mind. I swear I saw something break in her eyes before she was forced to look away. She stood there with her rigid posture that might as well have been cut from stone as she was coerced to spit out those vows, her voice barely more than a cracked whisper. And when that asshole shoved the ring on her finger, I saw red. Then, before I could blink, he was dragging her down the aisle away from me.

I was so relieved when I laid eyes on her at that dinner. I know Sawyer is made of tough stuff. It will take a hell of a lot more than a couple of days with an Antonelli to break her. Still, something loosened in my chest when I saw she was in one piece with the fire burning in her eyes, even if she was uncharacteristically submissive.

Anger licks a path along my spine as my fists clench, simply remembering how that asshole would glare at her whenever she opened her mouth. The way he spoke to her, like she was a child. Something to be seen and not heard. That's not Sawyer; I know she only complied for my safety.

Before I can get completely worked up over a situation I have no control over, I push thoughts of Sawyer to the back of my mind and spin to take in the apartment. I take my time inspecting the place, doing my best to comb through for cameras or listening devices and searching out for any weapons before giving up. Eventually, the calling of the shower is too great to ignore, and I spend the rest of the day pacing back and forth in front of the window, unable to relax or sit still.

This is almost worse than being in the locked, windowless room. At least in there I knew what to expect, but this... the not knowing is messing with my nerves until I'm walking a thin tightrope between paranoia and complete exhaustion.

It's dark out by the time Santos returns, and I'm honestly a strung-out mess. I jump as soon as I hear the door opening and feel like I'm wired on caffeine—all jittery and jumpy.

"Have a fun day?" Santos asks, eyeing me. I probably look even worse than when he left me this morning. Even though I showered, I had no other clothes to put on except the sweaty, blood-soaked ones I was already wearing. That, combined with the stress gnawing away at my bones all day, has me feeling even worse than a day in the torture chamber.

He doesn't seem to expect a response from me and instead continues, "Fun's not over yet." He grins and the look slides over me like oil, sticking and unwilling to wash off. "Let me show you the perks of being an Antonelli."

Jerking his head, I hesitate before following him out of the apartment. I count five guards in the hall, making sure I don't even consider making a run for it. Two of them move with us as we walk down the corridor, and excitement builds within me with every step closer to the elevator. Obviously, I know he's not going to let me go free, but damn, just the thought of it fills me with hope.

He stops at a seemingly mundane bit of wall. He presses on it and it separates, showcasing a hidden doorway. The four of us move through it into a hallway similar to the one that leads to the torture room. We pass through another door at the other end into a small room with dim, warm-colored lighting, filled with various seats, armchairs, and sofas, all centered around a small stage and stripper pole.

"Fetch the girl," Santos barks as he moves to a bar, filling two tumblers with an amber-colored drink before striding over to me. "Sit, sit." He waves toward one of the seats, and I hesitantly do as he says, confused to all hell as to what the fuck is going on.

He shoves the glass in my hand before taking a sip from his own, cocking a brow when I don't move to drink as well. "Uhh, I'm only fifteen."

A cold laugh bursts out of him like what I said is the funniest thing he's heard in a long time. "Boy, the rules don't matter here. *We* make the rules. We *are* the rules."

Still, I don't drink. Who the fuck knows what he put in there, and even if he didn't spike it, the last thing I want to be is intoxicated in this hellhole.

His brows lower in anger, but before he can say anything, there's movement from the other side of the room, and I'm suddenly forgotten as he turns toward a rake-thin woman with dark hair, wearing nothing more than her underwear.

"Ah, pet, did you miss me?" he coos.

The woman's gaze flashes toward me as she lowers her eyes, so she's looking up at him through her eyelashes as she meekly responds, "Yes, Master."

What the fuck is this shit? Pet? Master?

I've seen my fair share of porn, and I've snuck into the bar at the clubhouse enough times to witness rough, dirty, wild sex, but whatever the fuck this is, it is not my jam.

"I have a guest tonight." He leads her toward me, claiming a seat to my left. "He's having a hard time adjusting to our lifestyle. I want to show him what he could have if he just… yielded." He flicks his cold gaze my way before focusing back on her, stroking a tender finger across her cheek. "You can be a good girl and show him what he's missing, can't you, pet?"

Sweat soaks my palms as his words sink into my brain. He's not saying what I think he's saying, is he? Before my freakout can escalate, he shoves the girl to her knees and spreads his thighs.

The next few minutes pass in abstract horror as I struggle to look anywhere and everywhere but at the grotesque show in front of me. Don't get me wrong, I've seen plenty of girls suck cock before, but never like this. Every time my eyes wander in their direction, they stick on the girl, wondering who she is and why she's here. Surely, it can't be because she wants to be. However, the alternative is too horrifying to consider.

She's still sucking him off when he turns to me. "Are you still a virgin, boy?" I hesitate before answering, but my silence is enough. "Easily fixed. I'll get one of the club girls to show you the ropes." I sag a little in my chair that he isn't going to get this girl to do the job and that, hopefully, it won't happen tonight. "You're a man. Men fight. Men kill. Men fuck."

I'm perfectly aware that men do all that, but I also know from what I've witnessed at the clubhouse that *real* men take care of their property, their people. Real men don't shove whatever they are feeling into little boxes until they forget to feel anything at all. And real men sure as fuck don't force women to suck them off.

His eyes drift shut as he tilts his head back, groaning, and I quickly glance away. However, even out of the corner of my eye, I notice that he's shoved the girl's face down on his cock until she's choking on it, pushing against his thighs, even though he doesn't let up until he grunts his release. Fucking gross.

When he turns to face me again, I make sure none of the contempt and disgust I'm feeling is written on my face. Before he can speak, his phone goes off. With a jerk of his head in my direction, he tells the girl to give me a lap dance while he slides the phone out of the inner pocket of his suit jacket and moves to the far side of the room to take the call.

The girl sidles toward me, and everything in me screams to tell her to stop, to not do this, but I know it would be useless. The futility of it is there to read in her listless eyes as she moves to step between my thighs, forcing me to part them. I can see how numb she has become to this existence. It's in the way she moves as if she's on autopilot. She's going through the motions, but her brain has switched off. Mentally, she's not here.

I cast a glance over her shoulder as she begins to sway her hips, finding Santos in the corner of the room. His back is mostly turned to us, but he flicks his gaze our way every so often, keeping an eye on us.

"Who are you?" I whisper in a low voice, ensuring it doesn't travel.

Leaning in, the woman grasps a hold of my shoulders and begins to slide her chest along mine. "You need to run. Get away from here," she whispers in an urgent voice. "Don't let him trap you."

"Is that what you are? Trapped?"

She doesn't answer, so I keep talking. "I can help you."

She smiles softly, but it's filled with condescension. "No, you can't. You can't even help yourself."

"My sister is coming for me. She's got a group of gangsters behind her. The Rejects. They'll come, and when they do, I'm bringing you with me."

Her movements falter before she corrects herself. She doesn't respond, and I can tell she doesn't believe me. I don't blame her, and I seriously fucking hope what I said is the truth.

When she doesn't say anything else, I try again, "What's your name?" Still, she ignores me as she continues to do as Santos ordered. I do my best to block out the sway of her hips and how close her barely covered breasts are to my face as I ramble, "I'm Luc. My sister is a badass. She kills assholes like Santos for fun, and family means everything to her. *I* mean everything to her." I swallow back the emotion clogging my throat. "She *will* come for me."

The look in her eyes is so indescribably broken that I can't put words to it, and the emptiness in her voice when she speaks damages me more than Santos' physical abuse ever could. "Hope like that is a dangerous thing in a place like this. It will only make the crash land to reality hit harder. The sooner you accept that no one is coming to save you, the quicker you can come to terms with your new life. It will be better for you to stop fighting it and just give in."

Anger licks down my spine. Anger for what Santos did to this girl. Anger for the life she's endured and how irrevocably broken she is. "Is that what you did? You gave up?"

Her lips pinch, her eyes narrowing. Finally, a spark of emotion has entered her expression. "I learned how to survive, and if you want to make it out of here alive, you'll take my advice."

We lapse into silence, her words playing on repeat in my head and crashing into my confidence that Sawyer and the Rejects will come.

By the time Santos returns, he's in a furious mood. Yanking the girl off me by her hair, he sends her flying across the room as he grabs me by the upper arm, grumbling something under his breath about people interrupting his playtime. His words send a wave of nausea through me, and I'm seriously fucking glad for whatever the hell happened that interfered with whatsoever he had in mind for the rest of the night. If I had any intentions of becoming an Antonelli, I sure as fuck don't want to now.

He might think alcohol and pussy would endear me to this life, but that's not me. His blood might run through my veins, but I'm not him, and I never will be.

I'm thrown back in the torture chamber, even though I start kicking and screaming as soon as I realize where we're going. After a day of relative freedom, the thought of being locked in that darkness again terrifies me. But my efforts are in vain, and in my still weakened state, he manages to fling me into the pitch-black room before locking the door behind me. I'm not tied to the chair this time, but it's a small mercy.

I lose myself in the darkness, unable to determine the passing of time. It feels like I sit there for days and seconds, all at the same time, before the door is thrown open once again, the light from the hall blinding me as I raise a hand to block it.

Someone lands on the floor not far from me with a pained grunt, and the overhead lights are switched on as the door is slammed shut. Shadows haunt Santos' face as he glowers first at the man on the floor, then at me. Striding to the table, he unlocks the metal cage around it that prevents me from accessing them and lifts out a gun. Storming over to me, he smacks it into my hands. "Kill him," he hisses furiously.

"W-what?!" My eyes widen as my gaze darts back and forth between him and the unknown guy on the floor.

"KILL HIM!"

My hand begins to tremble. Hell, my whole body trembles, and I shake my head vehemently. "N-no."

It's only when I hear the loud cocking of a gun that I realize I have been staring at the guy on the floor. So when I snap my head toward the sound, I find myself staring down the barrel.

"You or him. Kill. Him."

Tears course down my face as my brain struggles to catch up with what the hell is happening, and I turn to stare down at the man on the floor. He's bleeding and badly beaten, half unconscious—an easy target. I have no idea who he is or what he's done, but I know I can't kill him. However, am I willing to die? To sacrifice my life for his?

I feel the cold press of metal against my temple, followed by Santos' cold voice. "Now."

The tears come harder now as I'm torn between my own desire to keep breathing and my humanity demanding that I cannot kill another living human being. I'm distantly aware of Santos moving around me until he wraps his hand around mine. Lifting my arm, he aims at the man on the floor. I feel his finger pressing against mine on the trigger, and yet I don't stop him. I don't say anything. I don't try to put a stop to this or plead for his life.

I'm still internally arguing with myself, attempting to convince my mind that this isn't happening, when the gun goes off. The vibration travels up my arm from the kick-back, and I gape in shock, unable to comprehend what my eyes see. Even as the pool of blood grows progressively larger around the very still, unbreathing form on the floor.

All I can do is sit there and blink at him. Part of me is aware that I'm in shock, but a more significant part of me no longer gives a fuck. I'm going to die in here. Either at Santos' hands or because I'll have stripped away my soul one piece at a time. Regardless, this is where I'm going to die.

I don't even realize Santos has pulled on my head until the dead man is replaced with his gruesome face.

"What's your name?" he demands. I swear, if I never hear that god-forsaken question again, it will be too soon.

Silence hangs in the air between us as I struggle to collate my thoughts. Eventually, the last of the adrenaline seems to drop out of me like a bucket, and I hang my head, my shoulders falling under the weight of what I just did. In a husky voice born of grief, pain, and exhaustion, I admit, "Lucifer Ricci."

There is a second's delay before Santos barks, "And who are you?"

Summoning the last of my energy, I lift my head to meet his gaze with deadened eyes. "I'm an Antonelli."

seventeen

"Team *storm the castle*, check."

I roll my eyes at his ridiculous team name as Dax's voice comes over the radio. That's the last team to check in, confirming they're in position. We've got men blocking every tunnel that leads away from the penthouse, a team surveilling the street, and men waiting for our word when we make it into the building.

Oliver and I share a look as we continue our watchful and silent journey along the tunnel, guns at the ready in case we run into anyone. We're meeting the others at the access to the tower, but we agreed to enter via separate tunnels in case one of us is caught.

Although I'm finally getting what I wanted, I have my reservations about tonight. It's all too fast. There hasn't been enough time to plan, to strategize, to be sure. However, there was no reasoning with Red. She's tried to be patient, but she finally reached her breaking point, and despite my apprehension, I can understand her feelings.

It's just past two a.m., and we spent all day at my childhood home, pouring over maps of this part of the city while Dante and Enzo outlined the underground tunnels and told us how to get into them. Most are only accessible via high-security access points. Still, a couple of the older tunnels stretching to the edges of Antonelli territory can be entered through utility holes in the street above. It's through those utility holes that we and each team of five Rejects entered nearly an hour ago. While our men moved into position in each of the tunnels, Oliver and I held back, not wanting to get caught lurking near the entrance to Giovanni's building before Red arrived and the next part of our hastily thrown-together plan was put into action.

With only fifteen minutes until we're due to meet, Oliver and I have been slowly making our way there while keeping our senses on high alert and weapons ready. I still don't fully trust either of those assholes who have wormed their way into my woman's heart, and I wouldn't for one second put it past them to use this opportunity to have us taken out and wave it off as an *accident*. A casualty of war.

Pulling my phone from my pocket, a notification tells me I have no signal, and I dismiss it to check the maps, seeing that we are nearly there. Walk to the end of this tunnel, then take a left. Another right turn, and we should be there. I use these last few moments before all hell breaks loose to sink into the necessary mindset. Years of planning, of dreaming, of just fucking surviving, all to get me to this point—to tonight. It's not even close to how I saw it all playing out, and while I wish Red and her brother weren't caught up in the middle of it, I can't bring myself to regret bringing her in. She's given me a purpose beyond thinking of revenge. Something to look forward to *after* I avenge Evie. I'd never thought about the after before. Everything was about getting to this point, and I figured I'd sort the rest out once Giovanni was no longer breathing—assuming I even made it out alive. Until Red, I hadn't been too hung up on actually surviving. So long as I took Giovanni out with me, I didn't give a shit if I died too.

All of that is different now. I see a life beyond all of this. One with Red in my bed and Oliver at my side. *And Dante and Enzo? What about them?* I quickly kick any thoughts of those assholes to the back of my mind. Maybe I'll get lucky and they'll die today, or they'll double cross us like I'm half expecting, and Red will see them for the untrustworthy scum that they are.

As we turn the corner into the final tunnel, a ding rings out and we both freeze, lifting our weapons as the elevator doors slide open. A second later, I lower mine, sighing a breath of relief as Red steps out, followed by Dante and Enzo. The two men are dressed in their usual attire of expensive-as-shit suits, but it's Red who draws my eye in her skin-tight leather pants that hug her curves and mold to her lean thighs. Her blades are sheathed and strapped around each one, proudly on display instead of hidden away in her boots like they usually are. Lifting my gaze, her spine is straight, her shoulders thrown back as she moves toward us. The tight, black tank accentuates her ample breasts, causing the front of my jeans to tighten as desire heats my body. Her long fiery red hair is pulled back in a ponytail and her face is set in a hard mask.

She's everything I never knew I wanted in a woman. She's fierce and strong, bold and cunning. She can handle her own and isn't afraid to unleash all that pent-up anger and aggression on those who deserve it, but she's also kind and understanding. There's an inner softness underneath that hard—and slightly psychotic—exterior which is rare to find these days. Black Creek turns everyone into cold, self-serving assholes. It leads to most people only caring about one thing—power or survival—and they will do *anything* to achieve that, regardless of who they have to stand on, fuck over, or kill. But not Sawyer. The love she feels for her brother has prevented her from closing herself off to that part of her humanity. Sure, she will go to the ends of the earth for him, but she won't destroy those in her way unless they leave her with no other option. And those that don't move out of her way? Well fuck, they better sleep with one eye open.

As she strides toward us, Red's gaze runs over me before flicking to Oliver, giving him a once over as if checking that we are both unharmed.

The five of us meet halfway down the tunnel at yet another elevator that will take us up to Giovanni's penthouse. I barely spare the two assholes beside her a second glance as I run my eyes over her sexy outfit a final time before shoving my hand out. "Put this on."

Red looks at the bulletproof vest in my hands that matches the ones Oliver and I are wearing before throwing it over her head and fixing the Velcro straps. "Ready?"

"Everyone's in place," I confirm.

"My men have confirmed Luc is being held on Santos' floor," Dante states. "You two take Sawyer and go to Santos' apartment. Lor and I will head off my father."

The muscle in my jaw ticks as I bite back the demand to go after Giovanni myself. I've been pining for his death for so long. Dreamt about this day when he was finally at my mercy, but this is what we agreed, and as much as I want to be there when they get him, it's more important that I'm at Red's side so I can ensure she and her brother are safe.

I give a stilted jerk of my head before gritting out, "Take him alive."

Dante's dark gaze runs over me before he meets my eyes. There's an emptiness there that doesn't sit right with me, but there's no time now to pussy out or change plans.

After a second, he gives a sharp nod of agreement. "We will do our best. We all want to see him suffer more than a quick death."

His gaze roams over each of us. "As soon as I call this elevator, my father's men will know we are here. There's a camera in the back left corner, so they'll know it's an ambush the second the doors open."

"Yeah, yeah, we know, asshole. We're here, and everyone's in place. Let's get this shitshow on the road, yeah?" I wave toward the closed elevator doors, and Dante scowls at me before he turns, leaning in so the elevator can scan his eye. Talk about high-tech, not that it wouldn't stop me from slitting his throat and ripping out his eyeball if it got me access to Giovanni. Although, this way is less bloody.

There's a quiet ping as the elevator arrives, and just before the door slides open, I speak into my headset. "Alpha team, go."

As we all pile into the waiting elevator, I rest assured that my team is currently storming the front entrance of the tower block, ready to remove the security guards on duty. Once that is done, they're to shut down any and all exits out of here, meaning Giovanni is a sitting duck trapped inside a glass cage. *Tick-tock, motherfucker.*

Dante presses the button for Santos' floor—the one directly below the penthouse—and the elevator lifts with a whoosh. Apprehension sits thick in the air as we climb skyward, all of us readying ourselves for battle. Red is standing slightly in front of me, her chest rising and falling in even breaths, but I can see the tension in the sharp posture of her shoulders and the tight coil of her muscles, ready to spring into action as soon as the doors open.

My own gun is lifted, ready to eliminate any waiting threat. The second the doors part, someone starts shooting at us. Gunshots are ringing out in the small, enclosed space, and I fire back blindly, hearing the rattle of Oliver's gun as he shoots too. We're all pressed flat against the sides of the car, with Red half-hidden behind Enzo's broad frame in an attempt to keep her from harm. My chest lifts in rapid breaths, my heart thundering against my ribs as the bullets keep coming. My back is pressed against the control panel, and I glance across the door to Oliver, who mimics my position. With a nod, he turns, keeping his body hidden while he shoots off another round. Meanwhile, I grab a grenade strapped to the back of my belt, ripping out the pin. Then I chuck it out of the elevator before we both duck back to safety.

One.

Two.

Three.

Bang. The whole elevator quakes as the grenade goes off, followed by a cloud of dust that drifts into the confined space. Reaching out for Red, I tug her toward me, squinting through the dust cloud as the three of us move out of the elevator.

She's palming a blade in one hand, and I have my gun pointed deeper into the dust cloud while we slowly move down the hallway, waiting expectantly for someone to start shooting at us again.

I'm only faintly aware of the sound of the elevator doors closing behind us, the loss of light making it harder to see as Dante and Enzo head up to Giovanni's penthouse. If they are planning on fucking us over, this is when it will happen, especially now that we are alone and vulnerable. I push the thought of their possible duplicity to the back of my mind as we shoulder on, stepping over the still form of dead bodies scattered across the hall and leaning awkwardly against the wall from where they were thrown in the blast. If Santos didn't know of our arrival before, he sure as hell does now. After that explosion, I'm sure everyone in the damn building knows we're here to wreak havoc and fuck shit up.

The cloud of smoke thins out as we leave the dead bodies behind and move further down the hallway. Doors line both sides of the corridor, but if what Dante said is true, no one else lives on this floor except Santos. Why does one guy need an entire floor to himself? What the hell is he hiding here? Or maybe he's just an antisocial prick who hates human company.

Regardless, I strain my ears, listening for any noise as we cautiously continue down the hall toward Santos' apartment, which is the last door on the right. It's eerily silent. Too silent. There's no way Santos isn't aware of our presence, and we probably killed the only men he's got guarding this floor. The fact that one of them hasn't come to assure him the threat has been handled should be telling enough for him to know we're coming. Which means he's lying in wait. Or hiding like a pussy.

My senses are on high alert as we approach the door. I can feel Oliver at my side, equally as tense, with Red a step behind us. All of us are silent. The only sound in the air is our breaths and the quiet crunch of our boots against the solid floor as we approach Santos' door.

Tightening my hold on my gun, I glance at Oliver before lifting my leg and kicking in the door. The three of us rush into the apartment with our weapons raised, only to be met with... nothing. Silence. Not a soul in sight.

With a jerk of my chin, we fan out, systematically clearing each room. Once I've checked the kitchen, I follow Red to the bedroom, finding her standing near the back wall, staring at something on the floor.

"Blood," she mutters quietly when I move to stand beside her, unable to tear her gaze from the bright red stain on the white carpet. It's not much, a couple of drops. "Do you think it's Luc's?"

I crouch down, reaching out to touch the droplets, which leave a reddish tint on my fingers. "It's fresh." The floorboards creak behind me, and I turn my head as Oliver enters the room, indicating that the rest of the apartment is empty.

He moves to join us, looking from the blood droplets to my finger to the wall as his brows furrow. As if we're all on the same wavelength, the three of us turn to scan the rest of the room, looking for another blood smear, but the rest of the carpet is clear.

Turning back to the wall, I narrow my gaze as I run my eyes over it, looking for any gaps or breaks.

"Maybe whoever it was wrapped the cut before they left," Red suggests, but she's also staring at the wall with a critical eye.

Oliver raps his knuckles against the wall above the blood spatter before tapping another area further to the right. A hollow knock versus a dull thud. *Huh.* Moving closer, I knock along the wall until I find the point where the sound changes. Running my hand down, I try to feel for any mechanisms before giving the wall a hard push. Something clicks, and as I let up, the wall opens a fraction, enabling me to get my fingers around the lip and pull it open.

The three of us peer into a narrow hallway lit overhead by bright fluorescent bulbs. Red's gaze immediately drops to the floor. "Look." Following where she's pointing, there's a trail of blood disappearing down the hall, and before I can stop her, she takes off, following it, like a twisted version of Hansel and Gretel.

Oliver and I share a quick glance before racing after her. *Goddamn woman has no sense of self-preservation when it comes to her brother.* The deeper into the building we go, the more I realize how intricately designed this whole setup is. Hallways lead off the one we're currently following, and I notice occasional breaks in the wall, indicating more hidden doors. What the hell does someone need all of this for? If I had more time, I'd stop and take a look around, but Red's got a one-track mind as she chases the blood trail like a bloodhound who's caught the scent of his prey.

Rounding a corner, we hear the sound of shouting up ahead. The three of us pick up speed, sprinting toward the raised voices until I can discern Luc's voice as he demands Santos let him go. His outburst is followed by the sound of a slap and scuffling, and when we turn another corner, we spot Santos trying to drag a tied up and bloody, yet feisty, Luc through a doorway.

"Luc!" Red cries at the same time I raise my weapon and yell, "Stop right there!"

Santos' head snaps in our direction, his eyes narrowing as he scowls. His grip tightens on Luc's upper arm as he uses him as a human shield, preventing me from getting a clear shot.

With narrowed eyes, Santos watches the three of us approach with slow, careful movements. I can't see if he has a weapon on him, but even if he doesn't, I won't put it past him to hurt Luc if it gained him a few precious seconds to escape.

"Let the boy go," I snarl. In my periphery, I can see blood and bruises covering Luc's face. He looks like he's been through hell the last few days, but I don't dare take my focus off the sociopath that's currently got him in his clutches.

Santos laughs this cruel, inhuman sound that grates like nails on a chalkboard. "So you can kill me? I don't fucking think so. Sorry, boy, you aren't worth dying for. Turns out you're no son of mine. The bitch"—he jerks his chin to Red—"coddled the testosterone out of you."

With that, he shoves Luc toward us, using him as a human bowling ball while he makes his escape. Luc crashes into us, and I have to lower my weapon to catch him when he stumbles off balance.

"Luc!" Red cries, pulling him out of my arms and into a suffocating hug.

My eyes dart up to where Santos was, but he's disappeared, and I grit my teeth before returning my focus to look.

"I'm fine, Sawyer," he grumbles, but it's clear he's far from fine. He sways unsteadily on his feet and his face is beaten to shit. Scanning my eyes over the rest of him, I notice several other blood stains on his t-shirt, indicating unseen injuries beneath his clothes. Returning my gaze to his face, there's a hardness in his eyes that wasn't there before, and a part of me withers at knowing he's lost the last tethers to his childhood innocence.

"Take Luc and get him out of here," I tell Red. "I'll get Marcus to come and meet you."

Lifting her head, Red's eyes catch on mine, her captivating blue depths drawing me in as though she doesn't want me to go on alone. However, after a second, she gives a sharp nod.

"Be safe."

With a grim smile, I clap Luc on the shoulder. "Good to see ya in one piece, kid."

Oliver plants a chaste kiss on Red's cheek, smiling warmly at Luc before coming with me through the hidden doorway Santos disappeared through.

Speaking into the headset, I instruct Marcus to come to our floor to get Red and Luc before Oliver and I advance. Casting my eyes around, I take in the small stairwell we are in while I try to work out our whereabouts in the building. It looks like we're in an emergency exit stairwell, but when I recall the map of the building in my mind, I don't think we were in the eastern corner where the emergency stairwell was indicated on the building plans.

Oliver leans over the rail, looking down before tilting his head to look up. Considering there's only one floor above us, and unless he's planning on helicoptering out of here, there's no escape from the roof, I'd guess Santos went down. We both pause and listen for footsteps but all is silent. Sharing a knowing glance, we start down the stairs, our heavy footfalls echoing around the space like a death knell to the fucker hiding somewhere below us. A second later, a third set of racing feet match our rhythm as our pursuit forces Santos back into motion, no longer able to hide from us.

We run down the stairs behind him, floor after floor racing past us as my breaths quicken, becoming faster the further we descend as blood pumps through my muscles and makes my heart beat harder against my chest. Oliver easily keeps pace with me as we fly down the stairs. At one of the turns, I lean over the rail, aiming my gun at the stairwell two floors below, and fire off several shots. A pained grunt has me grinning like a lunatic as the asshole ducks out of view, and picking up my pace, I can practically taste the blood in the air as I hunt him down like a wild animal.

A round of shots is fired at us, and both Oliver and I move closer to the wall as we continue our descent at a slower pace until the gunshots cease. My ears perk up when I hear the slamming of a door from the floor below us, and pushing myself harder, I jump the final few steps before yanking the steel door open and chasing my prey out into the corridor, already firing off another round.

One of my shots hits his leg and he goes down on one knee in the middle of the hall, groaning. Another bullet lodges itself in his shoulder, throwing him forward so he's forced to throw out his arms, his palms planted against the floor to keep him from smacking his face off it.

Santos is a cold savage. He's ruthless; a fighter so he won't go down so easily. Proven by the fact that, even as Oliver and I approach, he pushes himself to his feet and continues stumbling away from us.

"You won't get away from us," I bellow. "You can either take a bullet in the back like a coward or turn and face us like a man."

At my jibe, he spins, the sudden move making him wobble unsteadily before he plants his feet, searing us with a deadly glower that would look terrifying if he wasn't leaking blood and barely standing. He goes to raise his gun as we stalk toward him, and I swiftly counter his move, firing a shot into his wrist and forcing him to drop the weapon as he cries out. A manic grin dances across my lips at the delightful sound.

Closing the distance, I kick the gun out of his reach. "If you're going to do it, get on with it," he snaps, tilting his chin up in defiance as he looks past me. There's no fear of death in his eyes. There's nothing in his dark, empty depths. He's as emotionless as Dante, except his emptiness comes with a biting frost and the heat of hatred instead of Dante's cool indifference.

When I chuckle, it sounds as dark and twisted as his did earlier, like sharp thorns promising pain if you wrap your hand around them too tightly. "You didn't think I was going to make it that easy, did you? Do you even know who I am?"

"I don't give a shit who you are. You think you can take down the Antonellis? You're deluding yourself. You might kill me, but we will *annihilate* you. We'll murder everyone you care about; anyone who knows your name will meet a painful end at *our* hands."

I smirk, leaning in to whisper in his ear, even as his words drive like daggers into my gut. "My name is Cain Thomas. I'm the leader of the Reaper Rejects. Brother of Evelyn Thomas, who *you* stole from her home when she was only eleven years old." Fisting his shirt, I slam his body into the wall behind him. "You see, you might not remember me, but I can promise you, I remember you."

"I'm flattered," he spits back. "Now that you mention it, I think I do remember the name Thomas. Your sister was a pretty little black-haired angel, right?" His lips lift in a sick grin and I smash my coiled fist into his face. The sicko only grins broader, red blood staining his teeth. He chuckles. "I remember her well. She was a fighter... in the beginning. But they all break eventually, even the strong ones." I'm lost to the rage as I drive my fist repeatedly into his face. His head whips to the side, but he doesn't seem deterred as he spits out blood and turns to face me again. "She looked incredible when she finally broke. Her glassy eyes staring sightlessly at the ceiling as she took her final breath." Another slam of my fist against his face sends a tooth flying, not that he seems to give a shit, too enamored with taunting me to care. "She was a sight to see, crying for her big brother to save her while we tore her soul to shreds."

His laugh taunts me while his words play on repeat as I deliver punishing blow after blow. I'm numb to the pain in my hand, barely feeling the sting as skin splits around my knuckles or the crunch of bone as it snaps beneath my forceful blows. Images of Evie lying broken raise unbidden in my mind, playing havoc with me as Santos' laugh drives me insane. It may have been minutes, hours, or days that go by before a firm grip on my shoulder pulls me out of the dark abyss my mind had dragged me into. As if being yanked out of a soul-clutching nightmare, I'm wrenched back to reality as I turn to meet Oliver's tortured gaze.

My shoulders rise and fall with heavy, exertion-induced breaths as I stare at him, seeing my own pain reflected back in his eyes. Swallowing around a rough lump of emotion, I look at Santos, finding his lifeless body held against the wall by my fist. His jaw hangs at an unnatural angle and one cheekbone is caved in. The rest of his face is dripping in blood that has run down and soaked into his t-shirt. Even in death, his cold eyes seem to taunt me, and it takes everything in me to step back and lower my fist as he slowly sinks down the wall.

The silence that hangs in the hallway threatens to send me crashing to my knees as an overwhelming sense of loss and self-loathing like nothing I've ever felt before sucks the air from my lungs and leaves me feeling like an empty void.

"She was a sight to see, crying for her big brother to save her while we tore her soul to shreds."

I crash to my knees, a grief-ridden sob tearing from my throat as possibilities of what my sister suffered before she finally found peace in death torment me. Oliver falls to his knees in front of me, tears in his eyes as he wraps me in a hug. Tears well unbidden before they overflow, and I fall into the never-ending well of grief as I come apart.

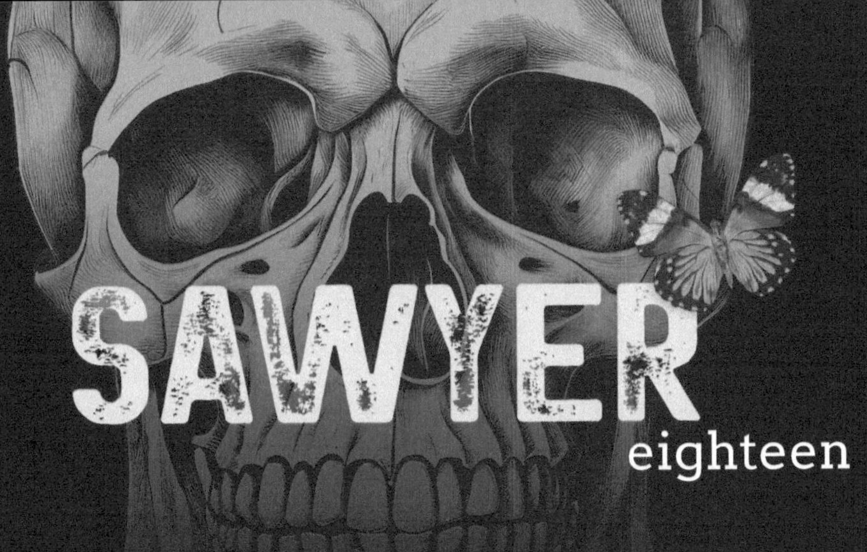

Nervous butterflies churn in my stomach as I watch Cain and Oliver disappear after Santos before I focus back on my brother. I refuse to look too closely at the blood coating his face, combined with the shades of black, purple, and yellow marring his features. He's alive and in front of me, that's enough for now.

I slide my blade through the plastic zip-ties around his wrists, and the second he's free, he wraps his arms around me. "I never thought I'd be so glad to see your pissed-off face, Sawyer." Despite the jest in his voice, I can hear the strain behind his words, and I pull him in tighter as I return his fierce hug.

"Well, you better get used to it, 'cause I'm never lettin' you out of my sight again." Tears clog my throat, threatening to turn me into a sobbing mess, but I force them back. Now is not the time or place. "Come on. We need to get out of here." Pulling on his hand, we start to make our way back toward Santos' apartment. It rapidly becomes apparent that Luc is incapable of moving too fast, and I have to grit my teeth to keep my mouth shut against the onslaught of questions I want to ask him. Again, it's not the time or place. Anything he tells me will only have me turning around and following after Cain and Oliver, determined to end that sorry son of a bitch myself.

When his knee buckles for the third time, nearly sending him to the ground, I reach out and wrap my arm around his waist. After a second's hesitation, he drapes his arm over my shoulder, and we hobble the rest of the way down the hall. We stumble through the hidden doorway and I lower him onto the bed as I crouch in front of him. Air hisses between his teeth as he grimaces, and I can tell he's trying not to let on just how much pain he's in.

"What did he do to you?" I murmur as I drink him in, cataloging every cut and bruise to use as ammunition for my anger. Not that the raging flames need any more gasoline. He just shakes his head, unable to meet my eyes as he refuses to answer me. I let it go for now. Pushing him if he doesn't want to talk will only force him to erect barriers I don't want between us. Instead, I give him a moment to catch his breath before helping him up, and we continue our slow walk to safety.

Before we can reach the door to the apartment, it bursts open, and Marcus comes barreling in with Jon and some kid called Tank, whose real name I don't know. I honestly need to make a concentrated effort to learn their names. They all have stupid as hell nicknames that I refuse to call them by. Tank? Bones? Rampage? What the fuck is up with that? Jon tried to explain to me once that they were named after MMA fighters, but it just isn't justification enough for me to call them such ridiculous names, even if I do understand the reasoning behind why they chose said stupid names.

"Fucking hell," Jon gasps as he rushes toward Luc, hesitating for a second before he relieves me of his weight, taking my place. "Are you alright?"

Luc grunts some sort of response as he sags against Jon, and Tank flanks his other side so the two of them can help him out the door.

"You two alright?" Marcus asks, his eyes on Luc.

"Yeah, we're fine. Let's get out of here. The guys went after Santos, and hopefully, Dante and Enzo have Giovanni by now."

We move into the hall as a group, all of us flanking Luc, whose head keeps dropping as he struggles to remain conscious. Maneuvering around dead bodies and careful not to jostle Luc too much, it's slow progress as we make our way toward the elevators, remaining vigilant for any signs of an ambush. When we reach the closed elevator doors, Marcus speaks into his headset, calling for the elevator.

It only takes a few seconds before the knowing ping rings and the doors open. However, before we can all pile in, Luc seems to stir from his half-unconscious state. "Wait," he slurs, digging in his heels and preventing the boys from carrying him into the elevator car. "We can't leave her behind."

"Leave who behind?" I ask him with a quizzical look. We haven't seen anyone else, never mind a *female*, since we entered the building.

He shrugs out of Jon's and Tank's hold, and on shaky legs, he moves back down the hallway in the direction we just came from. Marcus cocks a brow at me, but I simply shrug my shoulder and follow after my brother. Maybe he's lost more blood than I realize, or maybe he's got a concussion I'm not aware of, or maybe there really is a girl hiding somewhere on this floor. *I guess we'll find out,* I think, as I move to follow after him.

When Luc stumbles and falls against the wall, Jon and Tank move to his side, again working to support him as he directs us to a seemingly mundane stretch of the wall on the other side of Santos' apartment. However, I'm coming to realize this building houses a Labyrinth of passageways and tunnels. Worry niggles at my insides, wondering why Dante or Enzo didn't warn us, except I push that concern aside for now, not wanting to face the possibility of those answers. Instead, I gently nudge Luc to the side and press down on the part of the wall he is standing in front of. With a click, the door separates, and I pull it open.

My heart is in my mouth, my fingers clenching around the blade in my hand as I peer inside. Before I can step into the dim inner hallway, Marcus moves in front of me, giving me a look that distinctly states he should be stepping first into unknown dangerous situations. I roll my eyes as I follow after him. The fluorescent lights above us flicker ominously and a chill rolls down my spine as we reach the end of the short hallway.

Marcus casts a quick glance over his shoulder before reaffirming his grip on his firearm and pushing open the door, and we step into what appears to be a dimly lit room with soft-colored wall lamps providing a low but warm glow. LED lights mark the outline of a small stage, and I have to squint through the semi-darkness to make out the array of tables and chairs. Tingles prickle along my skin. I've spent more than enough time in strip clubs to know exactly what this room is for, but why is it hidden in the middle of the building? And given its small size, it's only meant to cater to a small handful of men—five or six at most.

Barely sparing the room a glance, Luc jerks his head toward the far side and starts hobbling in that direction as we all follow. I catch the others sharing uneasy looks, none of us liking the appearance of whatever is happening here. Behind yet another hidden door, we find a sparsely furnished, self-contained apartment, which only raises more questions.

"What the hell is this place?" Marcus queries in a gruff voice.

"Please tell me I'm not the only one whose spidey sense is tingling?" Jon's attempt at a lame joke falls short, all of us sensing the same thing he is. It's like I can taste the atrocities committed here in the air surrounding us. It's thick, like smog, practically choking me. Yet, as we forge on, we bypass a small kitchen-living area and a tiny shower room until we reach a door. This one isn't hidden; the handle and electronic keypad impossible to miss. The chill I felt before turns into a full-body shiver.

Luc's fingers shake as he hastily types in the code, the light turning green before the lock disengages.

"How do you know the code?" I question, fairly sure the only reason I'm asking is because I don't want to know what's hidden behind that door.

"It was a bit of a guess. I, uh, watched him type that code into the keypad on my door." It's clear he doesn't really want to talk about it, and not wasting any more time, he pushes open the door. The movement causes a bright fluorescent light to blink to life above us, illuminating the small space and, more importantly, the wisp of a woman curled up against the headboard, staring wide-eyed at us as she fists the thin blanket wrapped around her.

"L-Luc?" she gasps, her voice rough and small. "What are you doing here? W-what's going on?"

"We're here to get you out," he says, puffing his chest out a little. It would be cute if the situation wasn't so dire. Other than a couple of books set in a pile beside the bed, there's nothing else in the room, and my stomach clenches at the thought that this poor girl is locked up in here until her jailor—presumably Santos—lets her out. Given the miniature sex club we just walked through, I'm guessing the freedom outside this room is even worse than the hours of solitude and silence.

I run my eyes over her long midnight hair, thin frame, high cheekbones, and dark green gaze, finding it difficult to determine her age. She looks young, but her eyes appear haunted, presumably making her look older than she is.

Her eyes dart anxiously around our group before looking past us, out into the hall. "W-what are you talking about? I can't leave."

Luc shrugs out from under Jon, standing on his own two feet as he cautiously approaches the anxious girl. "Yes, you can. This is my sister." He jerks his thumb over his shoulder toward me. I try to give the girl a reassuring smile, although I'm pretty sure it comes across as more pained and horrifying, which would explain why she quickly refocuses on Luc. "She came to get me, but I'm not leaving here without you."

The girl starts shaking her head frantically as if she can dismiss Luc's words if she just believes they aren't true. "No. No. No. No. You can't. I can't. He'll find us." She chokes on her words, her hands trembling as she fists the blanket tighter.

"He won't. I promise you. Santos will be dead before he even knows we're gone, if he isn't already."

The girl's dark eyebrows disappear into her hairline as her eyes widen. Her lips part on a gasp as if Luc has just committed a cardinal sin by saying such a thing. She seems to lose herself to her inner thoughts for a moment, and Luc takes the opportunity to edge closer until he's standing at the edge of her bed. "Come with us," he urges. "You're not safe here. My sister and my friends, we'll take care of you."

That seems to snap her out of her stupor, but she goes back to shaking her head with even more vigor than she did before. "No. No. No. No." The word is like a mantra she repeatedly plays as her hands move to fist her hair. It's obvious the girl is spinning out of control, and Luc looks back at me over his shoulder, a helpless expression on his face as he begs me to do something.

Fuck, I have no idea how to help a girl in her position. Hell, I don't even know what her position is, just that it's seriously fucking bad. I don't have the first clue what to say or how to coax this noticeably traumatized girl out of her room. Still, based on the steely resolve in Luc's eyes, I know that he's not leaving without her, and fuck, I think we can all agree that none of us would be comfortable leaving her here alone.

Swallowing, I place my knife in its sheath before taking a slow, hesitant step forward. The girl's keen gaze immediately snaps to mine and I try once again to give her a reassuring smile. "Hey," I begin, forcing my tone to come out smooth but confident, like I'm trying not to spook a cornered animal. "My name is Sawyer. What's yours?"

She just continues to look at me, not giving me an answer. "I don't think she knows," Luc offers. "Santos just called her *his pet*."

My lips purse, but I push away the anger, not wanting her to see it and think it's directed at her.

"That's okay. We can figure that out later." Reaching the bed, I crouch down in front of her. "What my brother says is the truth. We want to help you, and we can keep you safe." Her dull eyes just continue to stare at me, and I'm not even sure if she's looking *at* me or *through* me. "See," I wave my hand over Luc, "we were able to get Luc away from Santos, and we can do the same for you."

"He'll come for me." Her voice is so quiet that I barely hear her.

"He'd have to get through an entire army of men like Marcus," I say, pointing at the man himself. "And the kids here are much harder to get past than they look. I've seen them take on men three times their size and win." Reaching out slowly, I gently place my hand on top of the blanket covering her foot. "Santos would have to get past all of us to get to you, and I promise you, that's not happening."

The seconds tick by, no one daring to move as the girl weighs up her choices, until finally, she gives a slight, shaky jerk of her head which I take to mean she's agreed to leave with us. Smiling at her, I gently squeeze her foot before pushing to my feet. Her eyes dart nervously around our motley crew before she pushes back the blankets, revealing a threadbare nightgown. Giving her a few precious seconds to gather herself and not wanting to seem like we're all gawking at her like an exhibition in a museum, I turn to Luc and the kids and start ushering them out of the room. "Right, we gotta move. Come on."

I feel Marcus hovering behind me, watching the girl out of the corner of his eye as she follows on stick-thin legs, her hips swaying in the thin fabric of her nightgown. She has no shoes on her feet and casting a quick look around the room, I don't spot any. God, the poor girl is going to be frozen solid.

Marcus shrugs out of his jacket and bulletproof vest, offering them to her. When she makes no move to accept either, he undoes the Velcro straps of the vest and slowly lowers it over her head, fastening it around her before helping her into the jacket. "Can't have you freezing to death on us, sweet girl," he murmurs in a soft, low cadence. She stares up at him with those all-seeing eyes of hers before ducking her head, tucking a piece of hair behind her ear.

Neither Luc nor the girl has the stamina to move too quickly, so it's a slow journey back to the elevator. We're all on alert, although I can tell Jon is trying to make light of the situation for the girl's benefit, joking around and being his usual idiotic self. It seems to help, and I swear I catch the ghost of a smile on her lips a time or two. I also notice the hawk-like way Marcus watches her, but I shrug it off as he calls for someone to send up the elevator for us again.

"I'm telling you, man. It was a dick and balls," Jon protests as we all pile into the elevator. "Fucking hairy balls at that. He tried to tell me it was the fucking Eiffel tower with bushes at the bottom, but unless the Eiffel tower is shaped like a dick, then he's talking out his hole."

I try to zone out their banter, my mind drifting to Cain and Oliver as I wonder if they were able to chase Santos down. Worry gnaws at my insides as I move on to think about Dante and Enzo, wondering if they caught Giovanni. Cain and Oliver have headsets to communicate with their guys, except we have no way of communicating with Dante and Enzo, and I'm sorely regretting that now.

The elevator slows to a stop and we all exit into the same tunnel as earlier. God, it feels like ages ago when I was last here, yet it couldn't have been even an hour. I peek around anxiously, hoping to see at least two of my guys, but the tunnel is otherwise empty.

"No one's back yet," I mutter under my breath to Marcus, not wanting to worry the girl or panic Luc.

Marcus gives my shoulder a reassuring squeeze. "They will be."

Nodding, I swallow back my worry as I gesture to Luc and the girl. "We need to get them away from here. They both need medical attention."

Although Marcus nods in agreement, he hesitates, his lips thinning as he looks at me. "Come with us."

I shake my head. "No, I'm not leaving until they're all back. Go. They can't stay here." I shove his arm to encourage him to start moving down the tunnel, knowing the kids will follow his lead, and after a second's hesitation, he consents.

"Alright, come on, kids... and lady." He smiles sheepishly at the girl, seeming as unsure as I am regarding her age. "I dunno about you guys, but I could do with a shower and a beer right about now."

"Hell yes," Jon and Tank agree enthusiastically as they all begin to move down the tunnel.

As if sensing I'm not behind him, Luc stops and stares back at me over his shoulder. "You're not coming?"

"I'll be right behind you. I'm just waiting on the others." He frowns, and I can see he doesn't want to leave me behind. "Go," I encourage. "You may as well have that beer before I get there 'cause you know I'll be taking it off you when I arrive."

His lips quirk up in a small smile that doesn't reach his eyes before he nods and continues his shuffle toward where the others have stopped.

I notice the girl hasn't moved either, and I wonder if she's second-guessing her decision to come with us. "They won't hurt you," I say, trying to reassure her. "And they won't let anyone else hurt you either."

She gives an absent nod of her head, though I can tell she doesn't quite believe me. Her tongue runs along her lower lip, and I'm on the verge of just giving in and going with them if it means she and Luc will get out of here before anything else can happen tonight when she speaks up, her eyes boring into mine. "I do remember my name. It's Evie."

I keep my eyes trained on Sawyer as the elevator doors slide closed, feeling all sorts of uncomfortable about leaving her alone. Well, not alone, even though I'm sure as shit not able to keep an eye on her and I hate the fact I'm relying on two men I don't know or remotely trust to keep her safe.

Dante and I have discussed the implications of this new development—the insertion of those two jackasses into our current setup. A setup that was finally starting to go well between the three of us. Now it's all fucked up again. We've been civil for the sake of getting Sawyer's brother back and for the opportunity of removing Giovanni from the gameboard, but after tonight all bets are off. Sawyer is mine. Ours. I haven't spent eight fucking years trying to get her to open up to me to lose her to two fuckwit gang-bangers.

As the elevator car slows to a stop on Giovanni's floor, I push all thoughts of Sawyer and those thugs to the back of my mind. I can't afford any distractions, and I'm sure as hell not about to let the two gangsters win my girl just because I was stupid enough to let my thoughts drift elsewhere and get myself shot.

My gun is held firmly in my hand at my side as the doors open into Giovanni's apartment. Unlike the floor below, no one has been sent to head us off, and Dante and I share a quick look before I duck my head out the elevator door, fully expecting the guards to be hiding in wait for us. Nothing. Not a single guard, which definitely isn't the norm. Giovanni keeps a twenty-four-seven security detail with men consistently stationed around his penthouse. If his men aren't here, then that likely means Giovanni isn't here either.

Unease settles in my stomach as we cautiously step out into the large living room, keeping our wits about us as we scan our surroundings and search for any possible threat. Once we've ensured the living room area is clear, we make a beeline for the office. Our footsteps are silent as we cross the wooden floor, the only sound the faint click of the office door as Dante unlatches it and pulls it open.

With my weapon raised, I rush into the room, quickly turning in a semicircle. Clear.

"There's no one here." I keep my voice low, but we both already know the truth. The apartment is empty. Giovanni is not a man to hide in his bedroom. If he were here, he'd face us like a man. Like the indomitable overlord, he thinks himself to be.

Dante emits a low growl of frustration as his eyes roam over the room. Deep lines mar his forehead as he tries to connect the dots. There shouldn't be a way out of here. We were in the elevator, so Giovanni couldn't have used it... unless he took the stairs, in which case he'll run into Cain's men before he can escape the building.

"There's no other way out of the building," Dante says aloud, as if reading my thoughts.

"If that's the case, his men are going to end up in a shootout with Cain's on the ground floor."

Dante's lips purse as he continues to think. The second we summoned the elevator in the tunnel, Giovanni's men were notified. They'll have seen the five of us and know something was happening.

Moving around the desk, Dante shakes the mouse, bringing the computer to life. With the click of a few buttons, he brings up the various security feeds that cover the tunnel, ground floor, elevator, and stairwell.

The tunnel and elevator are empty, and a brief scan of the stairwell feed shows that Giovanni isn't there either. There's movement on the cameras covering the main entrance to the building, but when I focus on them, all I can see is Cain's men. They seem to have disabled Giovanni's men and are in the process of securing the exits and most likely gaining access to the control room.

"Where the hell is he?" I murmur, shifting my focus back through all the available camera angles.

"He's not fucking here," Dante growls, his hand tightening around the mouse to the point that I'm surprised it doesn't crack under the pressure.

"Well, where the fuck is he then? We have all the exits blocked."

Dante doesn't seem to be listening to me as he storms to his feet, losing his cool as he grabs the first thing within reach—a paperweight—and hauls it across the room. It goes straight through the drywall, leaving a paperweight-shaped hole in the middle. Not that Dante notices as he proceeds to clear the top of a dresser, sending ornaments, flowers, a decanter of whiskey, and two tumblers flying.

My eyes are still scouring the screens while he throws a hissy fit, but no matter how much I will Giovanni to pop up on one, he never appears. The only movement is when one of the men on the ground floor and two younger-looking boys hurry into the elevator, presumably to obey whatever order Cain has given them.

"They must have fucked up," Dante snarls venomously, garnering my attention as I look away from the screens. "He must have somehow made it into the tunnels, and now he's in the fucking wind. And he knows we were involved. We're fucked." His chest heaves as his shoulders rise and fall on heavy breaths. Lifting his head, his tormented eyes meet mine. "We're officially traitors."

Fuck. My eyes drift closed as my own breathing becomes labored. I knew the possibilities when we agreed to this plan, but *fuck*, after spending most of my life trying to prove I was nothing like my father, I've ended up exactly like him. I'll probably meet the same agonizing end he did, too.

Bile burns the back of my throat as unwanted memories of him chained to the ceiling with his insides trailing along the ground and his skin burnt, sliced, and broken swim to the forefront of my mind. They made my mother and me watch every minute of the torture. Then, when he was hanging on the precipice of death, they did the same to my mother and promised my father that I'd spend the rest of my life atoning for his sins.

Sweat beads along my brow and my skin feels clammy. Only the steady, reassuring warmth of Dante's hand on my shoulder prevents the downward spiral into a full-blown panic attack. When I open my eyes, he's standing in front of me. Leaning in, he presses his forehead to mine, his hand moving to cup the back of my neck. His eyes hold mine captive as he breathes with me until I feel more grounded.

"I won't let the same fate befall you."

It's one of the rare times Dante has had to reassure me. In fact, I don't think he's done it since we were kids and the vivid dreams of my parents' deaths used to jolt me awake with a cold sweat every night. Reassurance and empathy aren't exactly Dante's forte.

However, there is nothing but sincerity in his tone; the truth of his words soaking into my frigid bones. I know he means every word he says. He'd sooner shoot me himself than let me suffer at his father's hands. Honestly, if this whole thing goes sideways, we'll probably end up going out in some sort of murder-suicide. Neither of us fears death. It's a part of this life that you learn to accept at a young age. Death and being an Antonelli go hand in hand. It's the thought of dying at Giovanni's hand, at his mercy, that bothers me more than anything.

Tilting my head, I brush my lips over his. His body is rigid against mine, his lips unmoving. I've never kissed him like this before, outside the lustful fires of desire and need. Usually, our advances are fueled by anger or his desperation to ground himself. Never because of a craving for intimacy.

After a moment, his lips move against mine, our tongues sliding over one another. It's got to be the softest kiss we've ever shared. It's nothing like Sawyer's gentle kisses. I don't love Dante the way I love Sawyer, but my body enjoys his, and his support and reassurance resonate with me.

Pulling away, he says in a gruff voice, appearing uncomfortable, "No point in hanging around here, so we may as well go find Sawyer."

As if on cue, gunshots ring out, but there's no one else around, and it takes a second for me to place the echoing sound as I turn toward the hole Dante left in the wall. Frowning, I slowly approach as another round of gunfire rattles through the wall. *What the hell?* I'd just assumed the wall bordered another room, but there would be no reason for anyone to be shooting up here, unless they were shooting at us—which most definitely isn't the case.

Peering through the hole, my eyes widen at what I see. "Dante." I wave him over as I continue to glimpse around the hidden stairwell on the other side of the wall. This close, I can hear what sounds like people rushing down the stairs, the bang of heavy feet as they hit the metal steps ringing out loudly in the confined space. "I think I worked out where Giovanni went."

"What the fuck?!" Dante gasps when I move aside to let him see. "A hidden fucking stairwell. Are you kidding me?" Anger laces his tone as he steps back, analyzing the wall and looking for some sort of release mechanism that would grant us entry. Not seeing one, he begins running his hand along the wall before pushing against it. A loud click emanates around the room as part of it separates, forming a door that Dante pulls open, and we both rush onto a small metal landing.

All sound has ceased as I look over the railing to the floors below, noting that the stairwell goes all the way to the ground floor and beyond... into the tunnels.

"Fucking hell. Your dad never told you about this?" I question.

"Nope. It never even occurred to me that he'd have backup plans I didn't know about. It has me wondering what other secrets he's kept from me."

Yeah, me too. Peering down the stairwell, I sigh, "Well, I guess we should see where it goes."

"And who was just here."

Moving much more quietly than whoever was here before us, Dante and I descend with our weapons held at our sides. On the floor below, we notice a blood trail, and I cock a brow at him. "Santos?"

He shrugs a casual shoulder. "Or one of those gangsters."

We follow the trail of blood down numerous flights of stairs until it disappears. We pause outside the door, and I look to Dante again for direction. He shakes his head, and we move on, leaving whoever is bleeding out to deal with their own problems while we continue on to deal with ours.

Another few floors have us passing the door that would open onto the ground floor —presumably into some back room or storage room—but we ignore it as we move further down the stairs until we reach the very bottom.

Dante wraps his hand around the door handle while I train my gun on the door, and on my signal, he whips it open. I rush through it into the frigid temperature of the tunnel, spinning left then right as I assess for any threats. "All clear."

Dante appears beside me as we stare one way and then the other down the tunnel. "Which way do you think he went?"

His face is set in a hard mask as he tries to figure out his father's movements, and he runs his hand through his dark hair, causing the ends to stick up when he shakes his head. "I haven't a clue. I don't even know which tunnel this is without looking at the maps."

"Well, Cain claims he's got all the tunnel exits covered, so your father should stumble across one of his blockades."

Dante snorts, shaking his head once again. "Yeah, I'm not holding my breath."

Blowing out a frustrated breath, he storms back into the stairwell and up the stairs. Following behind him, I wallow in our defeat as we head back to our agreed-upon meeting spot.

The repercussions of our ineptitude tonight are significant. Giovanni officially knows Dante and I have turned against him. I can only imagine the level of his rage when he discovered our deceit. Well, Dante's. He's had me pegged since day one as a traitor. Like father, like son, after all. It will have been a bitter pill to swallow to realize your own son—one he spent years trying to break and sharpen into a weapon—turned against you. We're no longer safe here, and we've lost any protection we may have had.

Not that we were ever really safe before. If Giovanni decided to put a bullet in our heads—well, mostly mine—no one would have stood in his way. Even Dante wouldn't have been able to persuade him otherwise, and any interference on his part would only have resulted in him signing his own death warrant. Still, there was some level of comfort in being accepted by the rest of the Famiglia, in being one of them. Now we will be branded traitors. Giovanni will send men to search all over the city for us. He'll hunt us down like we're wild animals until he's got us trapped in a corner with no escape. Our only chance of surviving is if we run far and wide. Leave Black Creek behind and hide in some podunk town in the back ass of nowhere Hicksville.

I shiver in horror at the thought of the two of us dressed in jeans and boots, working blue-collar jobs to blend in. It's just so fucking... ordinary. I may hate Giovanni and the Antonellis, but I love the lifestyle. The adrenaline rush that comes from watching a man's life extinguish in your hands. The sense of awe and fear at knowing you're the biggest threat in the room. The feeling of empowerment that washes over you when people shrink away from you. I don't pretend to be a good guy. I feed off the power and fear just as much as Dante. As much as Giovanni. We were all born in blood and raised on violence. It's who we are.

The difference between Giovanni and me is that I know when that ire is justly deserved. I haven't completely lost myself to the darkness. The line of morality, while thin, still exists for me. I'm not incapable of empathy or love or shut off to it like Dante. I'm just highly selective with who I deem worthy of such an emotional investment. And as the elevator doors slide open, they reveal the one girl I'd move heaven and earth for. The one woman worthy of my love, my concern, my empathy. The one woman who could not only withstand the lifestyle we live but would thrive in it if given the chance.

At our arrival, Sawyer spins in her heeled boots. Her eyes run over us as we step out of the elevator, and her shoulders seem to relax a bit when she finds us unharmed. My eyes roam over her, noting some dried blood smudged on her face, but she appears unharmed so I'm guessing it's not hers.

"Did you get your brother?" I ask, reaching out to rub my thumb over the blood-stain, needing to reassure myself it definitely doesn't belong to her.

"Yeah." Although she seems tired, she gives me a relieved smile that reaches her eyes, making them sparkle a deeper blue than normal. Her teeth sink into her lower lip as she mulls over her next words before saying, "But Cain and Oliver haven't returned yet." I can see the concern brimming in her eyes, even though I couldn't care less if Santos killed them both—other than the fact it would mean one more person is alive and out for revenge.

Dante steps up behind her, pulling her back against him as he offers her silent support. Even though his facial expression mirrors my inner thoughts, neither of us gives a shit about the gangsters. However, we do care for the girl currently standing between us, so we offer her the only support we can.

Her eyes dart around the confined space of the tunnel, narrowing before she tilts her head back to look up at Dante. "Did you kill Giovanni?"

"I fucking wish," Dante snarls.

When he doesn't elaborate, she turns her questioning gaze on me. "He wasn't there. It appears he had a plan B in the form of a hidden escape route that led into one of the tunnels."

With her brows drawn together in confusion, Sawyer processes my words before she speaks, "He can't be in the tunnels. He would have come across Cain's men, and they'd have alerted Cain."

"He's in the tunnels." The flat tone of my voice brokers no argument. "He either took out Cain's men before they could reach him, or they weren't doing their jobs, and he slipped by unnoticed." Her lips thin, although I'm unsure whether it's at my accusation or the thought of Cain's men not doing their jobs properly.

"Wh—"

Sawyer doesn't get a chance to finish whatever she is going to say as the elevator doors slide open and Cain storms out. The second he sees us, his face morphs into one of pure unadulterated anger.

"Did you two fuck us over?!" he shouts angrily. I barely get a second to register the blood covering his hands and arms and the splattering across his face as he crashes into me. He fists my shirt as he shoves me backward into the tunnel wall, snarling like a rabid dog. Cain is built similar to me with his broad shoulders and muscular body that he obviously takes pride in, but anger fuels his movements, giving him the energy required to sequester me.

The second his hands are on me, Dante moves around Sawyer and shoves Cain away. "Watch yourself, gangbanger," he warns in a low, threatening tone that would have other men backing away and apologizing profusely. Not Cain. The idiot either has a death wish or fuck all brain cells left in his head, as he immediately shoves Dante's shoulders, sending him back a step and regaining his balance.

"Was this a fucking setup?!" he bites out.

"What the hell are you talking about?!" My own anger gets the better of me, my voice rising with every word. I don't fucking appreciate this lowlife accusing us of double-crossing them when Dante and I have just thrown away our fucking livelihoods over this shitshow of an evening.

Cain's nostrils flare, but it's Oliver, who appears to be the more level-headed of the two, who bothers to clue us into what Cain's problem is.

"It was like a fucking maze up there. Hidden doors, secret hallways, and a stairwell weren't on the plans you showed us."

"Yeah, we found the stairwell too," I admit while pondering what he just said. Even though Dante has an apartment here, we've never spent much time inside the building, preferring to keep to ourselves and away from Giovanni's watchful eyes and listening ears. I haven't been in any of the other units besides the penthouse, Santos' apartment, and Dante's. I just assumed they were all the same.

Still looking like a raging bull, Cain's head whips around the tunnel, noticing one very important person missing. "Where the hell is he?" he barks. His eyes dart between Dante and me before he roars, "WHERE THE HELL IS HE?!"

"Gone," I snap irritably. "He wasn't fucking there. He escaped down the stairwell and into the tunnels."

Cain steps toward me, his posture threatening. "He can't be in the fucking tunnels because my men haven't come across him, and there's no way out of the tunnels without getting past them."

Unbothered by his posturing or the hate rolling off him in angry, hostile waves, I tilt my chin up and glare into his churning green eyes. "Then your men are either lying, or they suck at their jobs because it was the only way for him to escape that building."

His hand once again snaps out, wrapping my shirt in his fist. "You double-crossed us, you motherfucking assholes!" Cain's fist pulls back, but before things can escalate,

Sawyer dives between us. With her back to me, she presses up onto her toes and slides her hand up Cain's chest to rest over his heart.

"Cain," she murmurs softly.

With his fist hanging in the air like he's still debating throwing the punch and hoping Sawyer has the good sense to duck in time, he rips his hostile glare from me, his eyes softening slightly as he looks down at her. It's only because I'm watching him so intently, half expecting him to follow through with that punch, that I catch the flash of gut-wrenching, soul-crushing pain before he masks it. Even though it only lasts a second, the depth of it is so intense that I feel it slam into my chest with the force of a wrecking ball.

Sawyer must have some sort of magical power, or she owns the key to Cain's anger because right before our eyes, he seems to deflate, all of the fight falling out of him as his shoulders sag and his fist falls to his side.

"He killed Evie," he mutters in a voice so low that if I wasn't standing right behind Sawyer, I wouldn't hear him.

"You don't—"

He shakes his head. "I do. He told me so... right before I..." He shrugs, looking at his hands as though he's only realizing now that they are covered in dried blood.

The silence that follows his words is deafening. None of us seem to know what to say or do, everyone watching the moment that's transpiring between Cain and Sawyer. I just hope she can keep a lid on his pain and anger. I really don't want to have to fight him tonight. He looks like he's been through enough and I know it's not a fight I'd come out of unscathed. I seriously don't need to deal with bruised ribs and a black eye while trying to stay under the radar and out of Giovanni's hands.

Uncaring of the blood splattered up his neck and across his face, Sawyer cups his cheek, stepping closer to him. "Cain, I'm not so sure that he did. I... we... we found Evie."

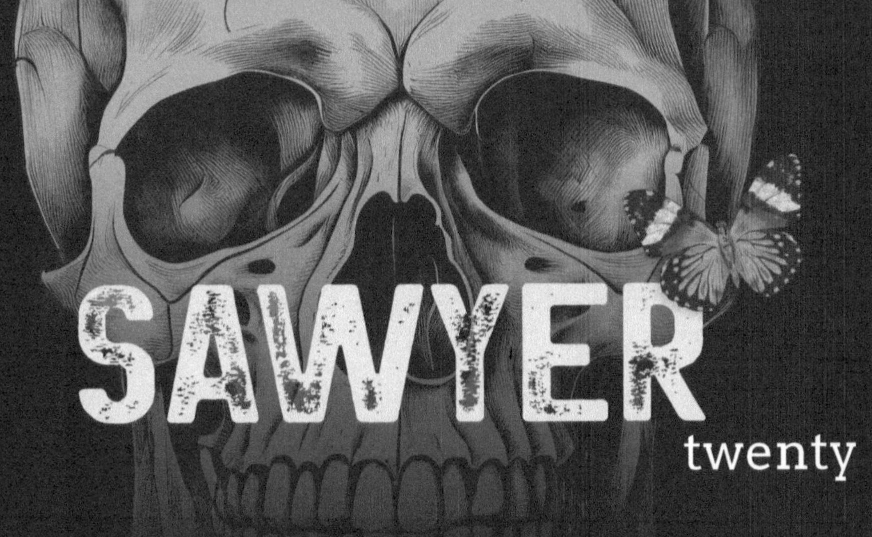

twenty

onfusion swirls in Cain's green eyes before a hardness enters them. "What the fuck did you just say?" There's a sharp edge to his tone, warning me to tread carefully, but I'm not afraid of his anger.

"Santos had her. He's been..." I shake my head, unsure of how to explain it so that it won't send Cain over the edge. "She's been locked up all this time. Luc showed us where she was being kept, and we got her out. She's with Marcus and the kids."

He just stares at me with that look of confusion and anger, and I can tell he's not actually seeing me. He's too lost in his head, trying to make sense of what I'm saying and connect it with whatever bullshit Santos told him.

Dropping my gaze, I take in the blood crusted over his hands and arms, noticing his knuckles are split on one hand. "I take it Santos is dead?" I ask softly.

"Yeah." The word is barely more than a grunt.

"Good." I lift my gaze to meet his. "It wasn't nearly a painful enough ending for him, but at least he's gone."

He just nods. "It was really her?" His voice is tinged with astonished hope, like he doesn't dare believe what I'm saying is the truth.

I smile up at him. "It's her. She said her name was Evie, and she's got your black hair and green eyes. It's her, Cain."

"Where is Marcus taking her?"

"I'm not sure."

Stepping away, he uses his Bluetooth headset to talk to Marcus. "You have her?" he asks when Marcus answers, his voice breaking over the words.

His eyes close when Marcus responds to him, no doubt hiding the tears and the overwhelming amount of emotion he must be feeling and doesn't want the others to witness.

"She's my sister. Take her to the house."

When he turns back around, he shares an intense, emotion-fueled look with Oliver, who also looks like he can't believe the turn of events. However, unlike the happiness and awe shining in Cain's eyes, Oliver looks slightly ashen over the news.

I remember him telling me that he thought he was in love with Evie when they were kids. Is that the reason why he looks like he's seen a ghost? Does he still have feelings for her? Or is he worried that he *won't* have feelings for her anymore?

Unease makes my stomach flip-flop, and it only worsens when Oliver doesn't meet my eyes.

"Let's go," Cain barks out, already starting down the tunnel. "I wanna get to the house ASAP."

I hesitate, glancing at Dante and Enzo. Given the fact that Giovanni is out there somewhere, most likely plotting our demise, I don't want us to separate. Although, neither man seems keen to follow Cain. "They have to come with us," I call out, causing Cain to stop and turn around, a look of thunder on his face. "They don't have anywhere else to go," I remind him.

"Not a fucking chance, Red!"

"Giovanni knows they aren't loyal to him anymore. He'll have people out looking for them."

Cain grinds his teeth. "Not my fucking problem."

"Cain." I try to keep my voice soothing, but I'm exhausted and sick of their bickering.

"No," he snaps before I can continue. "They aren't coming. I won't have them at the house with Evie there, and there's no way they're going to the clubhouse."

Looking into his steely eyes, I can tell there's no point arguing with him. And even though I'm concerned for Dante and Enzo, I can understand where Cain is coming from. We have no idea what hell Evie has been through, and the last thing we want to do is overwhelm or trigger her.

"Like we would want to set foot in your druggie den," Dante sneers, making me glower at him. He's not fucking helping the situation.

I wrack my brain, trying to think of where they could hide out for the time being. "There's my apartment..." I begin, thinking aloud as I chew on my bottom lip. Except, someone on Giovanni's payroll was in there—Santos probably, but there's no way to know if anyone else knows about it.

"It's okay, Spitfire," Enzo reassures, his calm facade garnering my attention as I turn to look at him. "I have a place where we can stay low for a few days."

"But—"

"It's off the radar. Giovanni doesn't know about it. We will be safe there."

I stand there, gnawing on my bottom lip in indecision. I don't want us all to separate. I feel like something terrible will happen if we're not all together, but Cain's reigning silence behind me says everything about where he stands on the matter. He won't be changing his mind.

"Okay," I eventually agree when Cain growls low in frustration, basically telling me to hurry the fuck up. I'm reminded of the infuriating asshole I met before he softened toward me, but I refuse to let myself snap at him. Ignoring the fuming bastard behind me, I keep my eyes pinned on Enzo and Dante. "Call me?"

"We will. Our numbers are in your phone." Enzo tugs me forward, his lips meeting mine in a bruising kiss that promises I won't forget him any time soon. When we part, he scowls over my head at Cain and Oliver, showing how angry he is about parting. Though, I don't think either of them would have actually come with us.

"You better take fucking care of her," he snaps, but I don't hear the response he gets as Dante wraps his hand around mine, fingering the wedding band that I haven't removed from my finger since our wedding day.

"I'm going against every instinct telling me to throw you over my shoulder and take you with us," he murmurs low in my ear. "You're mine, *mia vita.*"

I look up into eyes that seem pitch-black in the dark light with the raging storm of emotions he's struggling to work through. Yet instead of responding, I ask, "Why do you call me that?"

"Because you are. You are the bright spark that keeps me going, that tethers me to the light and prevents me from falling into darkness. Even when I didn't know who you were, your blue eyes would cement me when I felt the ground slipping beneath my shoes. It's those eyes that have kept me alive these last eight years, and it's you who is making me... feel alive now." He places his fist over his heart. "It's more than just sparks now. There's this constant... lightness in here. I feel it every time I look at you. Think of you. Touch you." Lifting the hand from over his heart, he reaches out to stroke his thumb over my cheek. "You are my life. My reason for breathing. For fighting. For wanting to be better. You are pushing me to *want* to feel. To try and work through the chaos rather than shoving it into a box."

Tears sting my eyes, unable to believe this cold-hearted man who considers himself so incapable of love can say such beautiful, heart-rendering words.

"I'm not making any promises—"

"You don't need to make any promises," I choke out, knowing he was about to ruin it all by telling me he can't promise to love me, to ever feel for me what he thinks I deserve.

I set my palm over his heart and, blinking the tears away, I stare up into his eyes that shine with more vulnerability than I've seen before. "You don't need to promise. I have faith for the both of us."

Leaning in, I press my lips against his in a thank you. In an *I believe in you*, kiss that he doesn't hesitate to deepen, claiming me as thoroughly as Enzo did a moment ago.

When we break apart, his shutters are back down with his cold, hard mask firmly in place. "That doesn't mean I won't come and get you and chain you to whatever bed I'm sleeping in if you take too long to come back to me on your own."

A shiver of desire runs down my spine at his possessive tone and the seriousness on his face.

"Now you're just asking for me to make you chase me," I tease, causing him to growl low in the back of his throat.

Before he can respond, Cain's curt tone snaps through the air. "Are we about fucking done now?!"

Sighing, I take a step back. When I glance down, I notice Dante's hands are coiled into tight fists at his side, giving away just how much he's holding himself back from yanking me over there and taking me with them.

My feet are frozen in place, and I find myself unable to take the necessary step away from them until Cain makes another aggravated noise in the back of his throat. Forcing myself into action, I give them both a tight smile and with trepidation eating away at my insides, I turn on my heel and follow Cain and Oliver down the tunnel, praying to a god that's never once listened to me to help Dante and Enzo escape unscathed.

IT'S A TENSE JOURNEY BACK TO THE HOUSE. WITH EVERY PASSING STREET, Cain's anxious energy escalates until it blankets us all, creating an anxious and uncomfortable atmosphere within the car. Oliver is quiet and lost in his thoughts, and I frequently notice his hands clench around the steering wheel.

Reaching the house, Cain has his door thrown open and is out of the car before it's even completely stopped. He rushes through the gate in the chain-link fence and up the path. Meanwhile, Oliver and I scurry out of the car behind him, chasing Cain into the house.

"Where is she?" he barks when we spot Marcus in the living room.

"Upstairs." He jerks his chin upward to the floor above us. "We put her in your old room."

Cain is on the move again before he's even finished speaking, taking the stairs two at a time in his rush to get to his sister. However, Oliver seems frozen at the bottom of the stairs as his eyes follow Cain's path.

"You should go," I urge him. "She will want to see familiar faces."

When Oliver turns his head to meet my gaze, I can see the apprehension, fear, and pain in his eyes. I want nothing more than to give him a hug and tell him it will be okay, but I have no idea if it will be. I can't even imagine the horrors Evie has endured in the last twelve years. It's clear that she's been abused, starved, and beaten, and those are just the scars I can see. The damage that's been inflicted on her mind and heart... that's gotta be on a whole other level, and I don't know if she's ever going to be okay. She's got a long, challenging road ahead of her.

After a moment, he turns to look up the stairs again before hesitantly placing his boot on the first step. He unhurriedly makes his way to Evie as if he's both desperate to lay eyes on her and unwilling to see for himself just how much the little girl he once knew has changed.

I stand and watch him until he disappears before moving to join Marcus in the living room. "Where's Luc?" I ask, frowning when I don't see him.

"The kids took him to the clubhouse."

"Oh." Disappointment courses through me. All I want is to hold him in my arms and reassure myself that he's okay. I also have a hundred and one questions for him about what he went through at the hands of Giovanni and Santos. I feel like I need to know every little thing he endured. Not that it will change anything. It's purely to torture myself.

"He'll be better protected there," Marcus explains, picking up on my despondent response. "He was okay, though. He's a tough kid."

Collapsing into a chair, I lean my elbows on my knees and bury my face in my hands. "He is." Life has forced Luc to become tough. I did as much as possible to shelter him from the worst of it—and maybe that was stupidly naive of me. Perhaps all these years, I should have been toughening him up, teaching him to fight and bringing him with me on jobs instead of keeping it all a secret from him. I was trying to preserve his childhood innocence, but I see now that there's no place for such innocence in Black Creek, and protecting it only makes the crash land to reality hit all that much harder.

"Stop beating yourself up. You did the best you could with him."

Staring at the carpet, I purse my lips and shake my head. "I should have done more. Been there. Protected him better."

"Bullshit." The heat in Marcus' voice snaps my gaze to meet his incensed glare. "We do our best with the crappy hand life dealt us. Sometimes shit happens that's outside your control, and no matter how hard you fight or how much of yourself you give up, you just can't win. You won this round. You got your brother back. Take the win, enjoy it, and make sure you don't make the same mistake twice. We don't all get second chances, and some of us would give up everything for just five minutes with our loved ones again."

Pushing out of his chair, he leaves the room. I don't know Marcus' story, but clearly, he lost someone close to him, and he's still carrying the blame for whatever happened. His words replay in my mind, and he's right. Against all odds, I got my brother back. Despite the failures of tonight, we also achieved a miracle. We not only rescued Luc, but we found Evie, and those successes are what we have to focus on.

My eyes lift to the ceiling as I wonder how Cain and Evie's reunion is going. I can't imagine the rollercoaster of emotions and the emotional whiplash both of them must be experiencing. Especially considering Santos must have told Cain he'd killed Evie, then for him to discover she's alive. Her ghost has haunted him for so many years now, even given her malnourished and abused state, he must be relieved to see her breathing.

My phone buzzes in my pocket, and I dig it out, bringing it to my ear. "Yeah?"

"Hey, Red."

At hearing Jon's voice, tension bleeds into my veins as I sit up straighter. "What's wrong?"

He chuckles softly. "Nothing. He's good. He's asleep, and I just thought you might want an update."

My shoulders sag in relief. "How is he?"

"As good as can be expected. We checked him over and there are no serious injuries. Nothing that won't heal."

"Has he said anything about..."

"No. He didn't want to talk about it."

Tears prick my eyes, knowing emotional and mental scars can last longer than physical ones, and while I'm relieved to hear he's physically okay, I'm worried about what might be going on in his head.

"Okay," I sigh. "Thank you for taking care of him. I'm sorry I'm not there."

"We wouldn't be anywhere else. We'll keep an eye on him."

I know I can rely on Jon and the kids to look after him. They've proven that they aren't the thugs I first assumed they were, and despite their hellish childhoods, they are shockingly decent kids. I've no idea how they managed to retain their humanity. It only speaks to their inner strength and determination to survive. It makes them perfect Rejects. Perfect friends for Luc.

"Thank you, Jon. You're an excellent friend. Luc's lucky to have you."

Jon is silent on the other end of the phone, clearly uncomfortable with my display of emotion. With a small smile playing along my lips, I say, "I'll be by to check on him later," before hanging up the phone.

Getting to my feet, I go in search of Marcus, finding him in the kitchen. Sitting in a chair at the kitchen table, he's nursing a beer as he stares unseeingly at the floor.

"I'm sorry for whoever you lost," I say softly, sitting down on one of the free seats around the table.

Lifting his head, he smiles sadly at me, pain shining in his eyes. "Meena. My sister."

Pain slashes across my chest. I can't imagine the heart-rendering grief that comes from losing a sibling. I'd literally do anything to ensure Luc's safety, and from the sorrow in his eyes, I can tell Marcus would have done anything to save his sister.

"I wasn't even there. When our mother died, we were put into separate foster homes. By the time I was old enough to find her and take care of her, she'd disappeared." He shakes his head, guilt and anguish scoring deep lines in his face and making him appear older than his late twenties-early thirties. "It took me years to find her, and by the time I did, it was too late. The same rich fuckers running the child mercenary camp the kids were rescued from took her, and when she refused to let them turn her into a monster, they killed her."

I swallow around the lump in my throat. I've heard my fair share of horror stories about kids in foster care. It's the reason I ran with Luc and lived on the streets after our mother died. "That's how you met Cain, then?"

He nods. "Yeah. I'd managed to get a job there as a guard to find out what happened to my sister. I found a girl who had been friends with her, and I was trying to help her escape." A small smile graces his lips. "Turns out she didn't need my help. Cain and his men stormed into that place like it was just another day and destroyed anyone who stood in their way. When I realized he wasn't just there for her but that he had no intention of leaving a single kid behind, I knew I had to help him. I'd spent five years searching for my sister, and after discovering that I was too late, I couldn't work out what I was supposed to do with my life. It all felt pointless without her in it, knowing I'd failed her. But Cain and the kids have given me a purpose, and for that, I'll be eternally grateful."

My phone rings, breaking the moment, and I apologize as I excuse myself to walk into the hall.

"Are you safe?"

"We are," Enzo confirms. I dig the toe of my boot into the carpet of the living room, unsure what to say to him. This is all so messed up. "Was his sister really locked up in there all this time?"

"Yeah," I sigh, pressing my fingers into my eyelids to try and relieve the pressure building behind my eyes. "It was so fucked up, Enzo. It was set up like a sex club and she was locked in a small room."

I hate myself for even asking, but I need to know. "Did you—"

"Fuck no," he snarls angrily. "The women in our sex clubs are all there of their own free will, and while I suspect the women aren't aware of what they're getting themselves in for at Paradiso—the exclusive club you were... you know—I'm pretty sure they aren't being held against their will and forced into *that*." He blows out a frustrated breath. "What Santos was doing with her, it's fucking sick. Dante and I wouldn't have condoned it if we'd known, which is why I'm guessing they kept it a secret from us.

They knew we didn't participate in the sick shit they'd do to the girls at Paradiso." He sighs heavily. "I may not like the guy, but I wouldn't wish whatever she's had to survive on anyone."

"You're definitely safe?" I ask, changing the subject. I have no idea what to say, and I'm relatively sure Cain would not want me discussing his sister with them.

"I promise you. We will be safe here for a few days."

"Then what? What happens now?"

"I'm not sure, but none of us are safe so long as Giovanni lives and breathes."

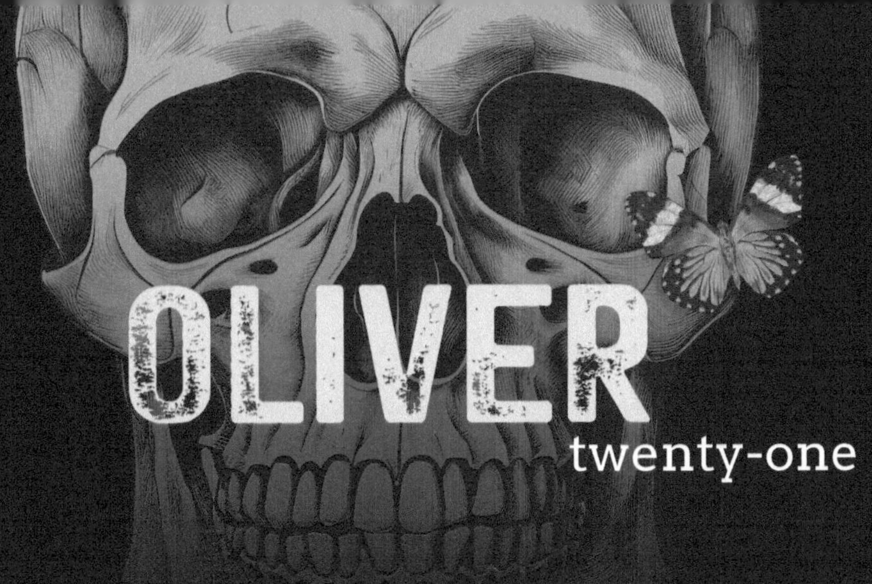

My heart is in my throat as I slowly climb the stairs, unsure of what I will find when I reach the top. For some reason, I can't stop picturing Evie as a little girl with her wide, toothless grin, wild black hair, and shining green eyes as she chased us around the block.

With every step I take closer to Cain's old room, my heart slams harder against my chest, threatening to burst right through it before I even reach my destination. Cresting the top of the stairs, I turn left. Cain's broad frame blocks the doorway, preventing me from seeing past him. He appears frozen in place until a soft, quiet, hoarse voice breaks the silence.

"Cain?"

At the sound of his name on her lips, he steps further into the room, allowing me to see past him to where a stick-thin girl in a threadbare nightgown is sitting against the headboard of the bed. Her gaunt face is framed with long black hair, making her skin appear almost translucent.

She looks nothing like the girl in my head. Her eyes don't shine anymore. Instead, they look flat and listless, dulled from years of hopelessness. And there's none of the color that used to glow on her skin from spending all day, every day, out in the sun. Her thin arms are wrapped around her knees and tears shine in her eyes as she gapes at Cain.

"Is it really you?" she hiccups.

Cain is a strong man. He keeps his emotions close to his chest and it takes a lot to rattle him, but as he takes in the waif of a girl in front of him, he falls to his knees beside the bed. His eyes scour every inch of her as if he can't believe she's real.

"It's really me, Evie. It's..." He shakes his head, and I'm sure he's struggling just as much as she is. "I can't believe you're really here. I-I thought you were dead."

Tears overflow down her face and her chin wobbles as she struggles to hold her composure. Her gaze flicks over Cain's shoulder to where I'm standing in the doorway, and a broad yet teary grin breaks out. "Ollie."

"Hey, Squirt."

Hearing her nickname on my tongue—the one I'd call her in front of the others when I very much wanted to call her something else, but I knew the guys would make fun of me—breaks the dam. A heaving sob rips from her throat as she seems to cave in on herself. Her shoulders shake and her entire body trembles as she falls apart, head buried in the crook of her arm.

Like lumbering idiots, Cain and I just stand there and watch as she breaks apart at the seams. Once upon a time, neither of us would have hesitated to wrap her up in our arms, but neither of us know how to handle a broken, damaged girl. Especially when we have no idea what she's suffered and we're scared of doing more harm than good.

I move to sit on the end of the bed while Cain remains on his knees in front of her, both of us offering our silent support as her sobs ring out around the room, tearing at our heartstrings until they become gasping sniffles.

Even after she falls quiet, she keeps her face buried in her arm. Neither of us rushes her. Hell, we've got all the time in the world—more time than we could have ever dared hope for.

While I wait, I scan my eyes around Cain's childhood room. He's upgraded the sheets to plain navy ones, but the rest of his room is still the same with its dark blue walls, various photos of us all, and even a battered red fire engine that's seen better days that he used to carry everywhere when we were kids. I smile softly at the memory, which feels like a lifetime ago, as though the memories belong to someone else. Were we really those kids who thought they were invincible? If we'd known then what the future held for us all, that we'd lose Evie and Beck would be forced to leave, would we have done anything differently?

Sorrow for the loss of the people we could have been, if the Antonellis hadn't stormed into our lives with all the grace of a wrecking ball, wells up in my throat and blocks my airway. Would we be different people now? Would our lives look completely different? Or perhaps no matter what we did, we'd all have ended up here anyway.

"Do you need anything?" Cain asks, breaking the silence. His voice is strained, and when I shift my gaze away from the fire engine to look at him, I find his forehead marred with deep concern lines. "Food? A shower? Sleep? You name it, and I'll get it for you."

With a final sniffle, Evie lifts her head, resting her chin on her knees as her red, swollen eyes linger on Cain and me. "Food and a shower sound good. Then maybe some sleep."

I place my palm on the bed sheet, feeling an urge to touch her yet not wanting to startle her or make her uncomfortable. "I'll go see what food I can find." My smile is tight as I get to my feet, and she returns it with a soft one that reminds me of the old Evie.

"Thanks, Ollie."

She's the only person to call me that. She loved that both of our names ended in *ie*. She thought it was a sign that we were meant to be best friends. I have no idea what the hell we are now, and hearing her call me that makes my heart soar and my chest clench in pain.

Feeling all sorts of fucked up and emotionally wrecked, I walk out of the room. As I close the door behind me, offering brother and sister some modicum of privacy, I hear her murmur to Cain, "If this is a dream, I don't ever want to wake up."

It breaks the last fragment of my heart and I hang my head as I close my eyes, listening to Cain's response. "This isn't a dream, Evie. It's real. I'm real. You're safe now."

Not wanting to eavesdrop anymore, I step away from the door and head downstairs. Sawyer is leaning one shoulder against the living room door frame, and she glances up when she hears me.

"I've gotta go," she says into her phone, hanging up as she turns to face me with a somber expression, tiredness tugging at her features.

"How is she?"

"Hard to tell." I shrug. "But she says she can eat, so that's gotta be a good sign."

She nods in agreement.

Throwing a jacket on, I say, "There's a shop down the road that sells soup she used to love. I'm going to go grab some," as I stride toward the door.

"Sure. Do you want me to come with?"

I hesitate with my hand on the screen door. "No, it's okay. I could do with the time to think."

"Oh, yeah. Of course."

A fresh wave of guilt hits me and I feel bad for pushing Red away. She's had a tough night too, but I just can't right now. My head's all sorts of fucked up, and I'm not ready to try and talk through it with anyone.

It's on the tip of my tongue to apologize to her, but I bite it back and without looking at her, I yank open the door and stride out into the early morning air. The sun's only just rising and it's way too early for the shop to be open for business yet, so I'm hoping someone will be there to take in the early morning deliveries, and I can pay them off to let me in. Although, I'm not above breaking and entering. Hell, I'd probably sell my soul just to get that soup, because it feels like the only useful thing I can do right now. I don't know how to ease Evie's pain or make this transition back into the real world easier for her, but I can get her something she once loved. Even if it is a measly bowl of soup.

I let the cool morning air wrap around me, waking me up and making me feel more alert as I walk the three blocks to the shop. I use the time to try and work through my feelings. My shock at finding Evie alive after all this time; my anger at the state she's in. I noticed the skin around her wrists is red and rubbed raw; fingerprint bruises mar her pale skin that clearly hasn't seen a glint of sunlight in the last twelve years.

The most unsettling emotion I'm struggling with is my guilt. Guilt for assuming she was dead all these years. It was easier to believe. Hell, I think Cain and I both wanted to believe it was the truth because the alternative was too horrifying to consider. Of course, now that reality is slapping us in the face. I also feel guilty—and fucking disgusted with myself—because while she was living in hell, I moved on. I let go of the flame I held for her and found love in another woman's arms. We may have only been kids when Evie was taken, but it didn't make what I felt for her at the time any less real, and now I feel like I've let her down by not staying true to those feelings. Like, somehow, I've lessened what we had.

Meanwhile, there's Red, who is perfect for me in every way, and to who Cain and I owe a massive fucking thank you for saving her. If it hadn't been for Luc and Red, we would never have even known Evie was alive. And now, with Santos dead, she might have been locked in that room and left to starve. Would anyone have even known that she was there? Would they have cared? A new wave of nausea rolls through me and I shake my head to dispel those thoughts. They don't do anyone any good. She's no longer locked in that room, so it's honestly not worth a second thought.

Rounding the corner onto the street the shop is on, I spot the owner standing out front, accepting a delivery order before he begins lugging it inside. The delivery van drives off as I cross the road, and the owner ducks back out the door to grab another palette of stock.

He tenses when he spots me, his face giving nothing away as he gives me a quick, assessing once over. His eyes linger on my arm, and I glance down, noticing obvious blood spatter from when Cain went apeshit on Santos. In fact, there's blood all over my top, but the man doesn't notice the rest of it because it's black.

Digging a twenty-dollar bill out of my pocket, I hold it up, hoping that will be enough to sway him. "I just need to grab some soup."

His gaze darts from me to the dollar bill I'm holding before he nods and snatches it from my hands. "In the chiller in the back."

"Thanks." Stepping past him, I move into the shop and walk down the aisle to the chillers. Scanning the shelves until I find the container of chicken noodle soup, I lift it and detour past the checkout, dropping another tenner on the counter before heading out the door with a nod at the shopkeeper.

I'm lost in my thoughts the whole way back, and before I know it, I'm standing on the footpath outside Cain's house. Staring up at the building Cain's spent a ton of money doing up over the last year, you'd hardly believe it once contained a happy family; happy memories.

And in the space of twenty-four hours, their entire happy family facade came crashing down. Evie was taken, their father disappeared, Cain became a victim of his guilt and anger, and his mother lost herself in the bottom of a bottle until she ultimately found peace in the afterlife.

Flicking my eyes to the house on the left, which used to be mine, I grimace. Where Cain's house once contained a happy family, mine held no such thing. I spent all my time at Cain's, even sleeping over some nights as a way of escaping my father's alcohol-fueled rages. He hadn't been so bad when I was younger, but my father repeatedly found himself unemployed as gangs lay siege to Black Creek and jobs became harder to come by. Alcohol became his crutch, his way of coping, and unfortunately, he was a mean drunk.

He'd fly off the handle over the most minor thing, sometimes for no reason at all. It only worsened as the disease progressed, until it destroyed his brain and liver. The day I found him dead in his La-Z-Boy in the living room, hugging a bottle of vodka, was a blessing in disguise. The Thomas' took me in after that. I was practically living in their home by then, anyway. I lived a happy life as part of their family for eighteen months before everything fell apart.

Shaking off thoughts of the past, I push open the gate and head up the path. Cain's coming down the stairs as I walk in the front door, the corner of his lips pulled down in a deep frown and his mind clearly elsewhere as he slides a palm down his face, looking completely fucking wrecked. At least he found a spare minute to wash the blood off him. In hindsight, he probably should have done that before he saw Evie, but she didn't even seem to notice. That, or she's so immune to shit like that that it didn't faze her.

I glance past him up the stairs, hearing the shower running before returning my focus to him. "She okay?"

He shrugs. "She's putting on a good front, but no, I don't think so. How can anyone be okay after whatever she's been through?"

My lips flatten into a thin line. "Has she..."

He shakes his head. "No, she hasn't said anything, and I haven't had the balls to ask."

"It's not important right now," I try to reassure him, clapping him on the shoulder as I move past him down the hall to the kitchen. "More important that she's safe and comfortable."

I hear his footsteps on the floor as he trails behind me, and I follow the low murmurs of Sawyer's and Marcus' voices into the kitchen. They both look up when I enter.

"How's she doing?" Marcus asks, general concern brimming in his eyes. I remember Cain saying he lost his sister, so I can only imagine how today has dragged up memories of the past for him.

"As good as can be expected," Cain responds as I set the soup on the counter and pull out a pot to heat it.

"What about you?" I look up at the sound of Red's concerned voice, finding her watching Cain warily as he drops into a kitchen chair. Leaning forward, he runs his hands through his hair, causing the ends to stick up all over the place before he rests his elbows on his knees.

"I think I'm still in shock. I can't believe any of this is real, that she's truly here." One of the other kitchen chairs creaks as Red lowers herself into it before I focus back on the task of heating the soup. "I don't know how to help her. What she needs."

"I think all she needs right now is her brother," Red says softly. "Her childhood friends. Familiar faces. While she's been... gone, everyone she knew moved on. You all grew up. That's gotta be jarring for her, so I think just providing her with some stability —showing her that not everything is different, that the people she cared about before are still here for her—will go a long way. The rest will hopefully work itself out."

When the soup begins to bubble, I pour it into a bowl. Setting it on a tray along with a glass of water, I leave the others behind as I carry it up to her room. The shower is no longer running when I pass the bathroom, and I pause, not hearing any movement behind the door. I don't want to get caught lingering in the hall so I quickly move on, finding Cain's old bedroom empty as I step into it.

I set the tray down on the bedside table, but instead of leaving the room, which is probably what I should do to give Evie some privacy and space to breathe, I sink down on the end of the bed to wait for her.

Closing my eyes, I run my hand over my face. I have no idea what's going on with me. It's like the last twelve years never happened, and my heart and head are at war, leaving me feeling numb and confused. Except, when I look up to see Evie standing just inside the doorway wearing a pair of Cain's boxers and an old t-shirt hanging off her thin frame, I'm reminded that the last twelve years did happen, and they've fucked with all of us.

Clutching the towel in one hand, Evie rewards me with a small smile as she drops it on the floor and climbs under the covers. When she's settled, I grab the tray and place it on her knee, encouraging her to eat.

"So," she begins after a few mouthfuls. "Give me all the deets. What have I missed?"

"Evie," I begin hesitantly, shaking my head. "We don't need to get into all that now."

"Don't baby me, Ollie," she snaps, but there's no heat behind it, just sadness. Extreme, never-ending sadness. "You've always been straight with me. Please, don't stop now."

I sigh, looking away from her as I struggle to decide what to do. Of course, she takes away the choice for me with her next words.

"My parents haven't been by, so I'm guessing they're..." Silence hangs in the air between us for a few seconds before I fill in the blanks.

"Dead."

She gives nothing away; she doesn't blanch or grimace. She simply nods her head, and I have to wonder how much mental damage those shitheads did to her that the death of her parents—parents she looked up to once upon a time—doesn't faze her.

However, when she lifts a spoonful of soup to her lips, I notice her hand trembling and realize she's not as unaffected as she's letting on. Managing a small sip, she swallows it down before asking in a husky voice, "How?"

"Your dad disappeared the same day you were... Anyway, he showed up down at the docks a few days later."

Another nod of her head. "And mom?"

"Drank herself to death."

Her lips pinch. "Probably for the best."

I grimace, hating this topic of conversation, even though I can't blame her for wanting to know. I'd probably be the same.

"What about Beck?"

"He's alive," I answer quickly, wanting to reassure her that not everyone fucking died while she was gone.

"Well, that's something," she says with a small, rueful smile that doesn't reach her eyes.

"Yeah. He's a counselor now."

"Of course he is. He always did have a bleeding heart."

I smile my first genuine smile of the day. "Got himself a nice girl. And he discovered he has a rich half-brother."

"No way?" she gasps, her eyes widening, her soup forgotten at my revelation.

"Yup. He'll be glad to hear you're alive," I say sincerely, giving her calf a squeeze.

"What about you?" she asks, changing the subject.

"What about me?"

"You gotta girl?"

I grimace, *really* not wanting to get into that topic of conversation with her. However, my silence is telling enough, causing her to chuckle. It's nothing like her old laugh. The one that was filled with sunshine and rainbows. It's cold and lacking like she's forgotten how to do it properly and is just going through the motions.

"You do, don't you? Who is she? She must be someone special."

"Evie, I don't think—"

But Evie was always too smart for her own good, and she doesn't need me to tell her anything now. "It's her, isn't it? The girl who rescued me. Luc's sister." I pinch my lips, unable to meet her eyes, not wanting to see whatever emotion is, no doubt, swimming in them. When she speaks again, her voice is quiet, with thick emotion in her words. "He told me his sister and the Rejects would come for him. I wanted so badly to believe he meant the Reaper Rejects, but I couldn't bring myself to ask in case it wasn't you guys."

"Evie." My voice breaks over her name. "I'm so sorry. I'm so fucking sorry." Tears swim in my gaze as I finally find the courage to lift my head, meeting her eyes and needing her to know how fucking awful I feel. We gave up on her. We wrote her off as being dead because it made us feel better instead of being the brother and friend that we should have been. We should have fought for her. Fought to save her, fought to get her back.

"You left me there," she sobs, tears streaming down her face. "At first, I thought you'd come for me. My big brother, who isn't afraid to stand up to bikers twice his size, will come. And you, Ollie. I thought we were soulmates. I thought for certain you'd come. I know you and the guys were close, but you were my best friend. My person. The one I was supposed to be able to count on. I just... In hindsight, it was stupid, but I genuinely thought you'd save me."

By now, we're both crying as guilt threatens to tear me in half. I'm surprised I'm not bleeding out all over the bed at this point. Evie's cutting words that slice through my skin like a razor blade, making me bleed, are the least that I deserve. Every barb hits its mark, wrenching the hole in my chest open wider until I'm bleeding freely, the wounds so deep that I'm not sure they will ever fully heal. Each broken cry is a scar I'll carry for the rest of my life.

There's nothing I can say. Nothing that will make any of this better. Nothing can justify our actions, or rather, inaction. Sure, we were just kids at the time, and I think even Evie realizes that, but it's not what she wants to hear. All Evie knows is that she was left in that godforsaken place for twelve years. In her eyes, her big brother and best friend never came to save her. I still remember how she used to follow us around with wide, awed eyes. I have no idea what she's suffered through, but I can only imagine how, back then, she would have believed we'd come. How she would have used the hope of that knowledge as her single light in the darkness to help her sleep at night, to get her through the challenges she faced. She would have held on to that belief with everything she had... until it flickered out.

Ultimately, we let her down. I know it as well as she does. Maybe we couldn't have done anything back then, but we've been grown-ass adults for long enough. We've been motherfucking *Rejects* for long enough. The truth is that we left her to rot in that hellhole and told ourselves it was okay because she was dead. What a fucking bullshit lie we told ourselves so we could sleep easier at night.

For years, Cain has said Evie's ghost haunts him. I thought it was just his guilt, but fuck, now I think he was right, except it wasn't Evie's ghost. It was her. *She* was haunting him, trying to get through to him, begging for him to rescue her. We were both too blinded by pain to see the truth in front of us, and Evie's the one who has had to pay the price for our ignorance.

Evie cries until she exhausts herself, and as her eyelids droop closed, I swipe at my own puffy ones before lifting the tray from her lap, allowing her to get some rest. I only hope she can sleep more easily now that she's free. It's the least that she deserves after everything she's had to endure.

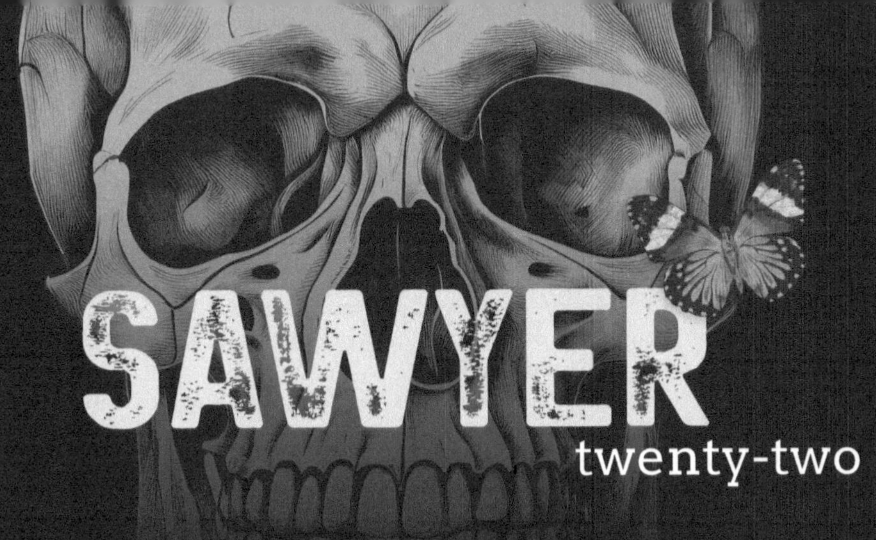

SAWYER
twenty-two

I feel like I'm just in the way at the house. There's nothing for me to do and I don't know how to help. Cain's obviously still in shock, lost in his head as he tries to navigate these new and confusing waters, and Oliver... Well, I'm not entirely sure what's up with him. This is all a massive shock to him too, but he seems distant, more shut down than usual.

I decide to give them a bit of space while Marcus drives me over to the clubhouse to check on Luc and grab some clothes for everyone. Cain had a few old clothes that he kept at the house, but other than that, we're all still wearing our blood-encrusted ones from last night, and honestly, a shower and a change of clothes sound like a godsend right now.

"Hey," Jon greets us when Marcus and I walk into the clubhouse. I texted him to let him know we were on our way. "Luc's still sleeping."

"That's fine. I need to shower first anyway," I say, fighting a yawn.

"Jon, fix the woman some breakfast, will ya?" Marcus asks—although it's less of a question and more of an order.

"Sure thing. Caffeine and greasy food coming right up." He grins brightly, like last night didn't happen and everything hasn't completely changed, before bouncing off.

"God, I wish I had his optimism and energy," I grumble, sliding into one of the booths and leaning my heavy head against the wall.

Marcus slides in opposite me. "It's his way of coping with everything he's been through. Always trying to make a joke out of it and focus on the positives."

"That's gotta be the healthiest coping mechanism I've ever heard of. Certainly beats shooting whiskey and killing assholes for fun."

Marcus snorts. "Not sure any of us would know a healthy coping mechanism if it walked in here naked and started dancing."

"You gotta go to therapy to get that shit, and none of us have the money for that nonsense."

Sliding out of his seat, Marcus walks over to the bar. Leaning over, he grabs a bottle of whiskey from the shelf and two shot glasses before striding back over.

"I'd rather drink whiskey, anyway," he says, filling the glasses to the brim and handing me one.

"I'll drink to that." He taps his glass against mine before we both knock back the shot, the burn of good quality whiskey sliding down my throat and warming me from the inside out. "Damn, that's good stuff."

"Ha, yeah. Oliver's got some rich friends. Got him onto the stuff and, of course, now we all drink it."

We take a second shot as Jon reappears with coffee cups in his hands, a roguish grin playing on his lips when he catches us drinking at whatever hour of the day it is. It surely can't be later than mid-morning, anyway. "Guess I'd better hurry up with the greasy food to line your stomachs."

Leaving the coffee cups on the table, he rushes back to the kitchen and re-emerges a few minutes later while juggling three steaming plates piled high with greasy sausages, bacon, eggs, and toast. Everything a girl needs after a night of rescuing her brother, discovering her boyfriend's long-dead sister isn't actually dead, and killing deserving assholes.

"God, that smells amazing," I groan, falling on the meal like a starved person as Jon slides in beside me in the booth.

"Not bad for a kid who didn't know how to crack an egg several months ago." The corner of Marcus' lip twitches, and pride shines in his eyes. He's been responsible for helping integrate the kids into a somewhat *normal* life. If you could call being part of a gang and living in a communal clubhouse normal. It's a job that he obviously takes seriously, and I watch as he and Jon banter back and forth over breakfast. It's clear that Jon and the kids mean a lot to him. Like he said earlier, I guess they've given him a purpose again.

Jon obviously respects Marcus too. The way he hangs off his every word is adorable and a little sad. He's probably never had a father figure or someone he could look up to. I believe the two of them found each other at the perfect time, filling a gap and providing a purpose for the other.

"Is she really Cain's sister?" Jon asks, a sadness entering his eyes as he pushes his now empty plate away.

"She is." Marcus sighs as he pours us both another shot.

"That's insane. Hasn't she been missing for like twelve years?"

"Yup," I answer, popping the p. "It's been so long that they thought she was dead."

"That's fucked up."

"Yeah." I shake my head, still unable to believe any of it myself. I can't imagine what a mind fuck it all is.

A moment of silence falls between us before Jon hesitantly asks, his voice quieter than before, "What do you think she's been through? I mean, we all saw that place..." He trails off with a grimace.

"Kid, you probably know better than anyone what she's survived," Marcus remarks.

Jon's head snaps up to meet his gaze, his brow furrowing as he stares at him. "Yeah, but I wasn't... we weren't..." He shakes his head profusely, unable to get the right words out, but we all know what he means.

Marcus reaches a large hand across the table, reassuringly squeezing his arm. "Maybe not, but you know what it's like to be trapped and forced to do things you don't want to do. Whatever she's feeling right now, you're one of the only people who can relate to that. The rest of us can empathize and try to be there for her, but you've been in her shoes. Or as close to being in her shoes as one can get."

"Fuck," Jon sighs, hanging his head and looking devastated. Without saying anything more, he gathers the plates and heads into the kitchen.

I follow him with my eyes, worried. "Is he okay?"

"I don't think any of them are okay, but they're doing the best they can. Besides, they've come a long way since we first rescued them. Those first couple of months were a disaster. Dealing with teenagers, in general, can be a challenge, but those with a newfound freedom can basically do whatever the hell they want in Black Creek..." he shakes his head. "They went off the rails for a while before Cain suggested starting the fighting pit as a more productive way for them to expend their energy. Still, last night can't have been easy on him. Seeing where she was being kept, what was done to her. It's bound to be triggering."

I nod, gnawing on my bottom lip as I glance toward the kitchen doors, hoping he's not back there falling apart by himself.

"I'll go check on him," Marcus says, as if reading my mind. "You should shower and see how your brother is coping."

I give him a soft smile as he slides out of his chair and goes in search of Jon. I sit there for a minute longer, thinking over our conversation and trying to put myself in Jon and Evie's shoes before giving up. Marcus is right. We can empathize, but we'll never know exactly how it feels to be stripped down to your bare bones, to lose all sense of autonomy, and become nothing more than a sack of muscle for someone else to manipulate.

With a heavy heart, I get to my feet, turning my thoughts on my brother as I head for the shower.

HALF AN HOUR LATER, FRESHLY SHOWERED AND FEELING A TAD BETTER, I'm wearing a comfy pair of sweatpants with my damp hair piled high in a messy bun on the top of my head as I walk down the corridor toward Luc's room. When he started spending so much time here, they emptied a room for him next to Jon's in the part of the clubhouse where the kids all sleep.

I pause outside his door, listening a beat for any noises from within, before cracking the door open. I'm surprised to find the main light on inside the room. My brows furrow as I push the door open wider and quietly step into the room. I glance around, taking in the dark-colored walls covered in posters of cars, bikes, and girls. It's a typical teenage boy's room. As I take it all in, an unexpected pang of sadness slashes across my chest. His room in our apartment never looked like this. We never had the money to paint the walls, and he probably didn't feel like he could ask for money for magazines to put pictures up. And because I'm a heartless bitch, it never even occurred to me that he'd want to decorate his room and make it his.

Despite my guilt at my apparent failure, I'm glad he's finally got a room that feels like his and reflects his personality. I can't believe I once would have done anything to prevent him from having all of this—a room, friends, somewhere he belongs and can feel safe. All because of my petty grudge against gangs and my ignorant assumption that they were all filled with the same arrogant fuckwits. I couldn't have been more wrong. Not just about Cain and Oliver, but all of the Rejects. They're all good men who have experienced the devastation that comes from the needless violence in Black Creek. It's that pain and grief that has drawn them all together and helped form this unstoppable army of loyal men who want nothing more than to get their revenge and see Black Creek become a safe place where people won't have to experience that same gut-wrenching loss that they have. I firmly believe it is because of that desire and determination, the Rejects will come out on top at the end of the day. With Giovanni in the wind and the Antonellis still in power, things may look bleak now, but today's defeat is tomorrow's win. As a group, we will rally, and someday soon, we *will* succeed.

Focusing on the lump hidden under the duvet in the middle of the bed, I move toward it and pull back the covers, then slide into the bed beside Luc. When we lived on the street, we would frequently huddle together for warmth, and even after we moved into our apartment, I'd still climb into bed with him after he fell asleep. I found it difficult to be apart from him, and I'd often wake up in the middle of the night in a panic, terrified that something bad had happened. It took me months before I could finally go a whole night without waking up and needing to reassure myself he was safe in his bed.

Resting my head on my hand, I stare down at his sleeping form. It's been a long time since he's needed a light on in order to fall asleep, and unease churns in my stomach as I watch him. Even in sleep, his face is scrunched, like he's having a nightmare, although he doesn't move or make a sound. My eyes roam over his face. He's showered since I last saw him, making the bruises and minor lacerations stand out more than they did before. I also notice a long gash along his hairline, running from his temple to just above his ear, that has been crudely closed with butterfly stitches and looks like it will probably scar when it heals. Anger surges within me. God, I'd love to bring Santos back to life just to kill him all over again.

I lie there and watch him for a while before my eyelids start to droop. It's been a long day—a long few weeks. So much has happened, and with concern for Luc taking center stage, I haven't had a chance to process any of the rest of it. Still, knowing that Luc is beside me, a little battered and bruised but safe, allows me to fall into a deep, restful sleep.

It can't have been more than a few hours, but I feel well rested when Luc stirs beside me, waking me up.

"Aren't we a little old to share a bed?" he grumbles, rolling over to face me. Despite his complaining, a small, exhausted smile plays along his lips. For siblings, Luc and I have always been close. Sure, we have our issues, especially when I have to play mother to him, but the one positive that came out of the shit hand life dealt us is how it's bonded us. It's made us closer than most siblings. When all you have is each other, it makes petty squabbles over the TV remote or who ate the last slice of pizza seem pointless.

It's only in the last year or two that he's become more moody and withdrawn. I always put it down to his raging teenage hormones, and don't get me wrong, that is definitely a part of it, but now that I've seen him hanging out with kids his own age and enjoying himself, I realize he was probably a little depressed as well. Before Jon started stalking me and befriending him, he had no one other than me in his life. There was no one at school he could talk to because I'd drilled it into him that he can't associate with gang members, and at his age, it seems like every kid is signing up to get handed a gun and a death sentence. Not that I regret enforcing that on him. It was for his own safety, and Luc understood that, but still, it doesn't mean he didn't suffer because of it. Even though he's ended up exactly where I didn't want him to be, I'm relieved he's finally got some friends, and I trust the kids and the Rejects to keep him safe when I'm not around. I've seen how guilty and upset they were after Luc was taken, and I know it wasn't their fault. Sure, when I was walking down the aisle that day, I wanted to murder them all for letting Giovanni get his hands on my brother, but they did their best. They're only human at the end of the day, and the most important thing is that we got him back in one piece. There's no point in holding a grudge and being petty over it all.

"If you think I'm not going to be sleeping in here every night for the next month, you're delusional."

The smile drops off his face, and he gapes at me. "You're joking, right? Please tell me you're joking. You'll completely ruin my reputation!"

"What reputation?" I chuckle.

"I can't be known as the guy who shares a room with his big sister. I'm not a kid anymore, and the others will never let me live it down. Besides, I do *not* want you snooping around my stuff."

Curiosity piqued, I lean up on my elbow and make a point of peering around his room. "What stuff? What do you have hiding in here?" I make it look as though I'm going to get up and actually snoop through his stuff—although I absolutely do not need to see whatever porn mags and tissues my brother has stashed under his bed or wherever he keeps them—but his hand shoots out, dragging me back down onto the mattress.

I crash land with a laugh.

"God, I hate you," he gripes. This time he grins, or at least, he tries to. The act stretches the skin along his temple and ends up as more of a grimace when he winces in pain.

The light moment falls away as the heaviness of everything that has come to pass flits between us. "I can't believe he was my father," he sighs.

I roll onto my side so I can face him. "Me neither. What the hell was mom thinking?!"

"I think she knew. That day, I think she knew it was him coming for me. She put me in the cupboard and made me promise that no matter what I heard, I wouldn't come out. She told me to put my hands over my ears and stay quiet and wait until you found me."

I purse my lips, trying to imagine how scary that must have been for him. He was only five then, and I'm sure he was terrified, with no idea what was happening. Nausea rolls in my stomach as I think about what could have happened if he'd made a sound or

Santos had found him that day. What sort of a person would he have turned into? Would he be a Dante in the making? Worse? It doesn't bear thinking about.

"She made a big mistake going to him for money. And looking back, I think she realized that too late. She was a mess that week. I just assumed she was twerked out on some new drug. She kept going on about how we needed to leave the house and I caught her trying to shove our belongings into bags more than once. I thought it was just paranoia from the drugs and I couldn't let her drug-induced mind drag us out of the only shelter we had. Every time she'd get panicked and angry, I shoved a bottle of vodka in her hand and encouraged her to drink it until she passed out." I shake my head, feeling guilty for not taking mom more seriously, but it wasn't the first time she got a crazy idea in her head thanks to whatever concoction she was snorting or injecting at the time. "But now I think she knew she'd fucked up and was trying to protect us in her own way."

"He found me anyway." Sadness tinges his voice, causing a fresh wave of guilt to rise within me. Luc's hand rests on the pillow beside mine, and I reach out, squeezing his fingers.

"That was all my fault," I confess.

"What? Sawyer, no, it wasn't."

"It was. I was working in one of their clubs, trying to get intel for the Rejects, and I gained Dante's attention, which in turn led to Giovanni looking into me. It was because of me that Santos was at our apartment. He found the photo on the wall and connected the dots back to you."

The corner of his lips pulls down in a frown. "You couldn't have known. He was searching for me, anyway. It was only a matter of time."

"Do you want to talk about it?" I ask softly after a moment of silence passes between us.

He just shakes his head, clearly not ready to discuss it or not wanting to discuss it with me, which is fine. "You were forced to marry Dante because of me," he says instead, his voice quiet and pained. "If I hadn't got caught, you wouldn't have had to call off the plan that day, and all of them would be dead now."

I'm guessing someone filled him in on why I was pretending to get married the day he was taken. It almost makes me laugh when I recall the look of utter surprise when he saw me in the church. Almost. If everything wasn't so fucked up at the minute.

Anger and guilt lace his tone, and I need him to know none of what happened that day was his fault. "Hey, you're not to blame for any of that! We couldn't have predicted the Grim Bastards' move. Besides, if we'd followed through with our plan, we never would have found Evie."

"Yeah, but you had to marry that bastard."

I grimace, unsure how to even explain any of it to him. "He's not that bad," I mumble, unable to meet his eyes.

"Not that bad?! Sawyer, he's an Antonelli. And I saw the way he behaved at that dinner. Every time you spoke, he'd cut you off or glare at you. I've never seen you so... submissive. You seemed terrified of him."

God, how do I explain to him that the Dante he witnessed that day isn't the real version. That that's not the way he is with me. "He's not like that," I try to reason, but I instantly regret it when hurt flashes across Luc's face.

Putting distance between us, he slowly, with pained movements, pushes up to sit on the edge of the bed. "They kidnapped me," he snaps, breathing heavily as he pushes to his feet. "Beat me." He waves toward his face. "Fucking sliced me open. I-I-I had to…" Emotion clogs his throat, tears swimming in his eyes, and I desperately want to know what the end of that sentence is. What did he have to do? What did that sick fuck *make* him do?

But he doesn't finish it. Instead, he shakes his head, getting himself under control, and when he lifts his head to meet my eyes, there's a steeliness in it that I've never seen before. It makes him look older than fifteen and breaks something vital inside me. *He shouldn't know that look. Not yet, at least.* "You saw what they did to Evie. Where they've been keeping her all these years. The sick shit he made her do…" Another shake of his head, and I reach out to clasp his hand in mine, giving it a squeeze.

"I know. I'm not disagreeing with you. Giovanni and Santos are monsters." I hesitate, licking my lips. "But Dante didn't do any of those things."

"No, but he's one of them. And I bet if they'd asked him to, he would have."

I hesitate for a split second because, honestly, I'm not sure. I'd like to think he wouldn't, but would he be able to say no to his father or Santos? Would he be forced to follow through, so he himself didn't end up in Luc's position?

"Ha, see! Even you know it," Luc argues, noticing my slight hesitation.

"That's not—" I huff out a frustrated breath, dropping his hand as I rub at my temples. "It's more complicated than that."

His forehead creases as his brows draw together in confusion, and he stares at me like he's never seen me before. "What the hell is this, Sawyer? Are you on their side?" The hurt in his eyes nearly kills me.

"No," I insist. "It's just not a simple case of us versus them. It's not all black and white."

He shakes his head, looking immensely disappointed in me. "After everything they've done. To me. To Cain. To Evie. I don't understand how you can sympathize with them at all." I pinch my lips, unsure what to say. "Maybe all that time you spent with them gave you Stockholm Syndrome or something."

"Yeah, maybe," I mumble, knowing there's no point in trying to reason with him. He's not in the mindset to hear anything I have to say in favor of Dante.

He lets out a heavy sigh. "I'm tired."

I guess that's my cue to leave. Feeling fucking awful, I hover, waiting desperately for him to meet my eye, but he just stares at the floor. After an awkward minute of us both just standing there, I relent. "Sure. I'll talk to you later."

He doesn't respond, and I stride from the room before he can see the tears stinging my eyes. Somehow, I manage to hold it together until I close the door to Cain's bedroom, but when the door clicks shut behind me, the first tear slips, and I slide down the door. Bringing my legs up, I wrap my arms around my knees and give myself a minute to wallow.

I feel like I'm in the most fucked up game of piggy in the middle. Technically, we're all on the same side when you think about it—the anti-Giovanni side. In fairness, I don't know what Dante's plan is with the rest of the Antonelli empire when he dethrones his father, but I'm sure some sort of peace agreement could be arranged. Dante isn't his father, and I don't think he has any interest in ruling over Black Creek.

Resting my head back against the door, I sigh heavily as the weight of everything presses on my shoulders. All I can see is the disappointment on Luc's face, and I don't know how to make him understand or even get him to hear me out. Hopefully, when he's had time to heal from whatever the fuck Santos did to him, he will be open to listening.

As for Cain and Oliver... I know all four guys only got along for the sake of rescuing Luc and for the shot at taking out Giovanni. Now that Cain has Evie back, and especially given the state in which we found her, he's going to be like a bloodhound craving the taste of Antonelli blood. I'm worried even Dante and Enzo won't be spared his wrath.

I groan as a wave of despair washes over me. I have no idea how to salvage any of this. How to get Luc to understand, Cain to see reason, and all four guys to work together. I'm afraid for Dante and Enzo, especially now that Giovanni is on the run and most likely gunning for them. Mostly, I just feel useless, unsure how to help or see a way that ends happily for anyone. Maybe we're all fucked.

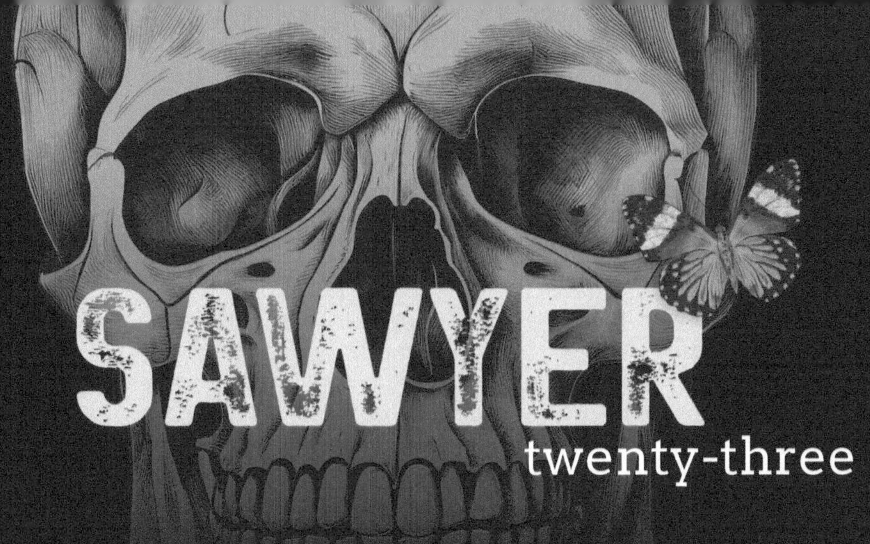

SAWYER

twenty-three

*B*uzz. *Buzz... Buzz. Buzz.*

Rolling over, I reach blindly across the bedsheet for my phone. I must have dozed off at some point, apparently having stressed myself out to the point of exhaustion.

"Hello," I mumble into the phone when I finally find it, my voice thick with sleep.

"Did I wake you?" Enzo's warm voice comes down the line.

"Mmhmm." It's the only response I'm capable of in my still half-asleep state.

"Well, I hope you were dreaming about me." I huff out a breathy laugh as Enzo's voice drops an octave. "'Cause I was thinking about you."

I shiver, his voice alone enough to heat me up until I melt into the mattress. "You were?"

My voice is a husky purr and my thighs clench at his response. "Fuck yeah, you were riding my dick so good, Spitfire. You're tight little body writhing as you rocked back and forth on my cock and moaned like I was the best thing you'd ever fucked."

Oh god, I love how dirty Enzo's mouth is. It does crazy things to me, and I am totally here for every bad word out of his mouth.

"You wet for me, baby girl?"

His cocky tone tells me he already knows I am, but I indulge him anyway, my tone breathy and soaked in need as I say, "Yes."

"Good girl," he praises. "I want you to slide those fingers into your dripping cunt and feel how wet you are while you pretend it's my cock stuffing you full."

I moan as I do as he says, pushing my hand beneath the waistband of my sweatpants and into my damp panties. I picture his thick, engorged cock as I push two fingers into my drenched core. "Oh god," I gasp, hearing Enzo's heavy breathing down the line as he works himself over.

"Fuck, you feel so good. So tight. I love the way your pussy clamps around me, like you never want me to leave."

"Yes," I gasp, driving the back of my head into the pillow as I arch my back, using my fingers and his words to send me into a frenzy. I insert a third finger, moaning at the stretch.

"That's it, baby. You feel me stretching your walls? Slamming into you so hard you scream."

"So full," I moan, riding my hand fast and hard while I get off to the sound of his voice and dirty words until we're both panting heavily.

"Imagine me licking a line down the column of your neck," he says, his voice low and husky. Closing my eyes, I do as he says, picturing him hovering above me, his thrusts deep and hard as his tongue teases my skin. "When I reach your shoulder, I suck the sensitive skin there until it's red before biting down on your taut pink nipple." I moan, using my shoulder to hold the phone to my ear as I pinch my nipple between my fingers, pretending it's him.

"Enzo." I groan at the bite of pain, my legs trembling as my back arches, seconds from exploding.

Sensing it, Enzo growls, "Come for me, baby. I want to hear my name on your lips," as I come apart at the seams, crying out his name. His corresponding grunts and curses over the phone tell me he's found his release alongside me.

"Did you call for phone sex?" I laugh breathlessly, still coming down from my high.

"No, but I definitely will in the future."

I chuckle before the smile falls off my face, and I roll onto my side. "I'd rather we repeated it in person."

"Me too, Spitfire. Me too." His tone is as dejected sounding as mine. Enzo and I haven't had any intimate time alone. Over the weeks we spent together in Dante's house, we've gotten to know each other. We've flirted, and there's obviously chemistry and feelings there, but we haven't had any time to explore each other's bodies, to just enjoy one another. "Soon."

God, I hope he's right.

"I just wanted to check in." Despite the disaster that is our current predicament, I smile to myself. "Are you still with Cain and Oliver?"

"No, I came back to the clubhouse to check on Luc and grab some clothes for Evie."

"How's he doing?"

I sigh, remembering my fight with him earlier. "We got into an argument."

"He's been through a lot recently," Enzo reasons. "Just give him some time."

"Yeah, you're probably right. How are you guys?"

"Dante's already riding my ass," Enzo grumbles.

I snort. "Isn't that a good thing?"

"Har har, funny girl."

I chortle before growing serious. "Do you mind if I ask, what's the deal with you two? Are you like a couple, or is it just sex?"

"We're as close as brothers. Best friends."

"Best friends with benefits?"

He laughs, a truly warm and genuine sound that sinks into my bones and stays there, warming me from the inside out. "I guess that's what it is."

"But you don't see anything more with him?"

"I don't think so. It's sex and friendship."

"Isn't that what any relationship is?"

"Don't get me wrong, Dante and I have fun together, but we have you now. We'd easily set aside everything else for you."

I chew on my bottom lip before daring to ask, "What if I don't want you to?"

My question is followed by a second of silence before Enzo laughs. "You naughty girl, do you get off on the thought of us together? Or maybe you like the thought of the three of us together? Me fucking you while Dante fucks me?"

"Yes," I gasp, not realizing how badly I wanted that until just this second. "That. I want that."

"So fucking filthy," Enzo purrs approvingly right before a scuffle breaks out in the background.

"Fucking hell, man, chill out! She's fine... yeah, yeah." There's a rustle down the line before Dante's harsh tone filters down the line.

"Why the hell didn't you answer my call earlier?"

"Oh, I didn't know you phoned. I was asleep."

"Don't make me follow through on my promise," he threatens, reminding me that he was dead serious when he said he'd come and get me if I didn't go to them first. Despite the steel in his voice, concern rings with every syllable.

"I'm fine," I assure him. "We got back to the clubhouse safely. It's yourselves that you need to worry about."

Dante scoffs. "You think my father will leave the Rejects alone? He saw them on the cameras. He knows they're involved. We're all dead men walking."

Well, if that doesn't make my empty stomach constrict and threaten to revolt.

"The Rejects are prepared for any threat," I assure him, secretly hoping that's the case. Has Cain even had time to amp up security around here?

Another infuriating scoff passes his lips, clearly not believing me. "I can guarantee you they are not prepared for my father."

"Then they'll get prepared," I snap irritably. "Don't underestimate them. They aren't like any other gang in Black Creek."

"And neither is the Antonelli Famiglia," he argues. "We have men, money, and resources at our disposal, the likes of which the Rejects could only hope to obtain."

"*We?*" I question, emphasizing the word.

He sighs, the sound drenched in frustration. "I'm still an Antonelli, Sawyer. Technically you are too."

"I sure as fuck am not!"

"You're my *wife*. An Antonelli by marriage."

"Then we need a divorce because I am *not* an Antonelli. Don't forget, Dante, I married you because I had no. Other. Choice." I enunciate the last three words for emphasis. "There might be something between us, and I... I care about you, but I am *not* an Antonelli. *Luc* is not an Antonelli. You have to understand that the Antonellis may not have played a big part in our lives, but when they entered our streets, they left chaos and destruction in their wake. Most of the time, their attacks seemed random and meaningless, driving the fear of God into people. You are the real-life boogeymen we grew up fearing. Not just me. *Everyone*. If we don't fear you, we hate you for killing or taking someone we know or love.

"So no, Dante. I may be your wife... for now, but I will not answer to Mrs. Antonelli. I will not accept the surname as mine, and I won't let you dictate otherwise."

My rant is met with silence, and I can't tell if he's raging at my outburst or mulling over what I've said.

"I should go," I say in a softer voice. "Take care of yourself, and I'll talk to you soon."

Hanging up, I hastily throw some things into a bag for Evie and grab some clothes for Cain and Oliver, unsure when they'll be back at the clubhouse.

As I'm leaving, I don't see any signs of Marcus, so I get one of the Rejects to drive me over to my garage, where I safely stowed Raven after my date night with Dante. *God, was that only a few days ago?*

With an unusual sense of unease, I toss the bags on my back, fasten my helmet under my chin, and throw my leg over Raven. Pulling back on the throttle, I speed into the street, making the jaunt to Cain's house in record time.

Planting my feet on the ground outside his chain-link fence, I pull my helmet off and stare at the small two-story house, trying to imagine a happy family encased within its walls. No matter how hard I try, all I can picture is heartache and devastation.

I sigh as I return my focus to the front door, hating the fact that I feel uncomfortable about the thought of going back in there. I want to support Cain and Oliver, but I don't know how. Plus, things felt off with Oliver and I can't put my finger on why. I'm hoping it's just the shock of everything, but a niggling thought has me worried that it's something more.

Knowing I can't sit out here all night, I reluctantly climb off the bike and head into the house. Poking my head into the living room, my eyebrows lift when I find Cain sitting in there alone, a glass of scotch in hand as he stares absently out the window.

"Hey," I say softly, jolting him from his thoughts as he turns to look at me. He smiles, but it's weary and lacking. "I brought some clothes for everyone."

I set both bags down on the sofa before moving to perch on the arm of his chair. "How are you holding up?" I ask, running my fingers through his thick mop of black hair.

Surprisingly, he reaches out and drags me into his lap, pressing an uncharacteristically sweet kiss to my temple before he shakes his head. "It's Evie I'm worried about."

I cup his cheek, pressing a finger under his chin to direct his head until he's looking at me. "I didn't ask about Evie. I asked about *you*. You've been through a lot in the last twenty-four hours. Have you even slept?"

"I'm fine." He sighs wearily, clearly anything but, before burying his face in the crook of my neck, breathing me in as his arm tightens around my waist. "Mmm, you smell good." We sit like that for a while, and I think both of us just need a moment to feel close to the other. I know, with every second I spend in his arms, I feel better. "Thank you for bringing all that." He gestures to the bags. "And for saving Evie. I'm not sure if I said that earlier."

I turn so I can cup his cheeks in my hands. "You don't need to thank me. It wouldn't have mattered who she was, I wouldn't have left there without her. Is she upstairs?"

"Yeah, she's asleep. Has been for most of the day."

I nod. "And Oliver? Where is he?"

"He's out the back."

"Is he okay?"

"Honestly, I'm not sure. He seems to be taking it pretty hard, but we haven't talked. Maybe he'd open up to you."

I grimace. "I'm not sure he wants to see me," I murmur, my chest tightening at the words.

Cain's brows pull together, his brilliant green eyes darting back and forth between mine. "I'm sure that's not true. He's just distracted."

My lips flatten even though I nod in agreement. "There was just a moment earlier…" I shake my head, unable to reasonably explain Oliver's brush-off. And maybe I am overreacting. I was hurt earlier, but now that I've had some sleep and time to think on it, I realize I might have been acting irrationally. "I was tired. It was probably nothing."

Cain brushes his thumb over my cheek. "Did you get some sleep?"

I smile at him softly. "I did, but you clearly haven't." Slipping out of his lap, I take the glass of scotch from his hand and set it on the coffee table before encouraging him to his feet. "You can't function on no sleep," I chastise, grabbing a blanket from the back of the sofa as I gesture for him to lie down.

He's so tired that he complies without argument, lying down and letting me throw the blanket over him. I unlace his boots and pull them off, setting them on the floor at his feet.

"You're not joining me?" he grumbles, his eyelids already drooping.

"You need *sleep*," I emphasize.

"A blowjob would be better."

"You can have one when you wake up," I appease him, kissing him briefly on the lips. He doesn't even respond, already lost to his dreams. Tucking the blanket tighter around him, I decide to pull up my big girl panties and go in search of Oliver. However, as I turn toward the door, I find Evie standing there watching us.

"Uhh," *Crap*. Talk about awkward. Not sure what to say, I gesture for us to step into the hall, grabbing the bag I brought for her from the other sofa on my way past.

"You're dating my brother?" she questions as I softly close the living room door behind me.

"I am."

"But Oliver said…"

"I'm dating him too," I state, filling her in and watching closely for her reaction. Surprise flashes across her eyes, but it disappears as quickly as it appeared, and other than that, she gives no response at all.

"I also brought you some clothes and things I thought you might need," I say, holding up the bag in my hand. "Although, I'm not sure how well the clothes will fit or if they're even your style." I shrug a shoulder, feeling somewhat self-conscious and unsure of myself. "But I figured they were better than wearing your brother's boxers." One side of my lips lifts as I gesture to the navy boxers she's wearing.

She grants me a small, amused smile. "Thanks."

An awkward silence passes while we both stand there assessing one another. She's stick-thin and covered in bruises, but she looks a little better after a shower and some sleep. The bags under her eyes seem smaller, and there's a light in her eye that wasn't there the last time I saw her—albeit it's small and looks like a soft breeze could blow it out.

We both laugh when her stomach grumbles, her cheeks tinging pink with embarrassment. "Hungry?" I chuckle.

"I guess so."

"Well, I was just thinking about ordering some pizza for everyone. Do you want some?"

Her eyes light up, her smile growing. "Pizza?! God, I can't remember the last time I had pizza."

Her stomach grumbles again, her arms wrapping around her middle as if to quell the noise. Lifting out my phone, I wave it in the air. "I guess I'd better put that order in."

She smiles shyly, taking the bag from me. "Thanks, I think I'll go change while I wait."

I watch her make her way back upstairs while I put in the order for food before heading in search of Oliver. I find him sitting on the stoop on the back porch, staring off into nothing. He doesn't even seem to hear me as I open the screen door and step onto the porch, walking over to sit beside him on the step.

Neither of us says anything for a long moment before I risk breaking the silence. "It's okay not to feel for her what you once did," I say softly, hazarding a guess at what I think has been bothering him.

He just sighs, not removing his focus from where he's staring off into the distance.

"A lot of time has passed. You've both grown up and become different people."

"None of that should have happened," he bites out angrily. "It wasn't supposed to be like this. I should know who she is, and she should know me because we *should* have grown up *together.*"

I don't let his anger get to me, knowing it's not aimed at me specifically. "You can't change the past, Oliver. You have to figure out how to move forward from here."

He scoffs, shaking his head. "That's the problem. I don't know how to move forward from here. I don't know who I am when I'm around her. I don't know what she means anymore. I don't..." he trails off with a sigh. "I don't know anything anymore."

Ouch. His words drive into me like a sledgehammer, and I have to swallow back the emotion that spikes along with the flare of pain. I know he's confused and hurting. It used to concern me that I felt like I was competing with a dead girl, but now...

Oliver is my compass. He keeps me centered, always guiding me when I feel lost. I wish I could be that for him too, but I don't know how to be that person. I don't want to lose him, but if Evie is who he's meant to be with, I won't stand in his way, even if it will break my heart to watch him walk away.

Unsure what to say, I get to my feet, pushing back the tears in my eyes. "You have plenty of time to work it out. Evie's here now, and you should spend time getting to know her and letting her see the incredible man you have become. And if she's the one who still owns your heart, then she's a lucky woman."

My voice threatens to crack, so I stop before he can see how much saying those words pains me. Turning on my heel, I head back into the house to wait for the pizza.

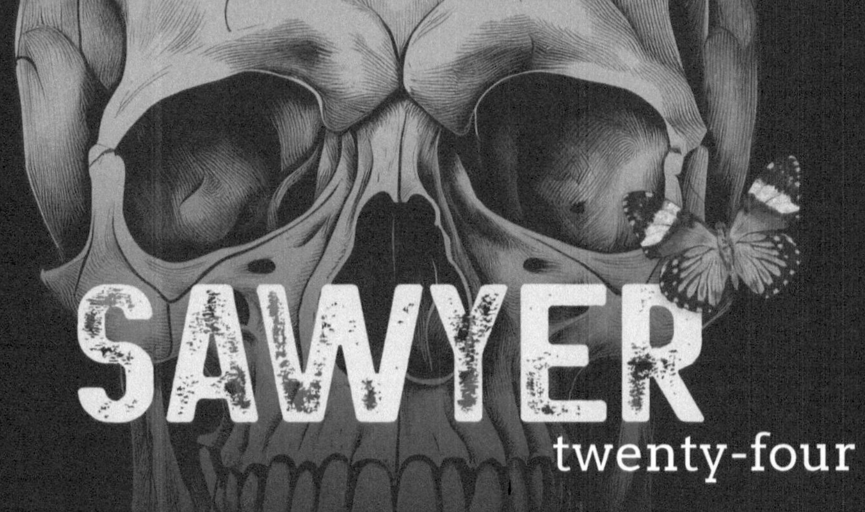

A loud knock on the front door early the next morning stirs me from sleep.

"Who the fuck is banging on the door at this hour?" Cain growls as he rolls out of bed, grabbing his gun before flinging open the bedroom door.

Unlike Cain, who is apparently okay with answering the door in nothing but a pair of boxers, I throw on my jeans and one of Cain's t-shirts that I find lying on the floor before grabbing one of my knives and hustling after him.

Oliver is already at his side by the time I reach the top of the landing, the two of them presenting an impenetrable wall as they approach the door. Things have been awkward with Oliver since our—well, my—chat with him last night. I'm trying to give him space, but that isn't easy when all I want to do is wrap him up in a hug and tell him everything will work itself out. He looks so sad, but he has to figure out his feelings on his own.

"What the fuck?!" Cain gasps when he opens the door. "What the hell are you doing here?"

I can't see past his broad frame to see who's at the door, but whoever it is obviously isn't here to kill us, so I curiously make my way down the stairs, still palming my knife.

"You didn't think I'd stay away after hearing about Evie, did you?" a deep voice responds seconds before Cain pulls the door open wider, allowing me a brief glimpse at the man in the doorway. He's tall, with neatly styled dark hair and vibrant green eyes. He's dressed casually in jeans and a t-shirt, showing off his tattoo sleeve down one arm.

His gaze collides with mine over Cain's shoulder and he quirks a brow. Noticing that something has caught his attention, Cain glances my way before stepping aside, allowing him entrance.

"Beck, this is Red," he introduces.

"Beck? As in, your childhood friend, Beck?"

"The one and only," the man laughs lightly. It's actually nice to hear his laughter. Everything has been so melancholy and quiet recently, all of us burdened by the events of the last few days and everyone walking on eggshells, unsure how to react around Evie. "I hope you don't mind me coming?" he questions, focusing back on Cain and Oliver.

"Not at all, man. It's good to see you." Cain gives him a quick bro hug, and so does Oliver. "Did you bring the whole gang?"

"Nah, just Hadley. Figured it would be too much for all of us to show up unannounced, but Hadley wanted to come in case she could be of any help. You know..." He trails off with a shrug, everyone seemingly able to fill in the blanks, but I'm stuck on one word.

"Hadley?"

Beck waves for someone to come in while Cain explains, "His girlfriend."

I remember Oliver saying about Beck being in a reverse harem relationship and how Cain helped rescue his girl from the same compound as the kids. A prickle of awareness tickles the back of my neck seconds before a tall blonde walks in.

"Hadley?" I gasp, not sure if my eyes are deceiving me.

"Red?" A surprised laugh falls from her lips as her eyes roam over me.

"Holy crap, it's really you." I rake my eyes over her, noting that she looks healthier than the last time I saw her, and she's got a happy glow about her that I've never seen before. However, it's her face that has changed the most. There are laugh lines around her mouth where there weren't any before, and her eyes shine with so much life. Knowing she's alive and happy and all in one piece, I force a scowl on my features. "What the hell?! I thought you had died or something!"

She grimaces, rubbing the back of her neck awkwardly. "Uhh, yeah, sorry about that."

"Hold up," Beck interrupts, his eyes darting back and forth between us. "You two know each other?"

Cain and Oliver are sporting the same confused looks, but Hadley and I just grin at one another.

"Yeah, Red's the one who got me my new identity."

"And in exchange, she taught me how to fight."

All three men look between us in surprise, but when I glance at Beck, I find him staring at me, gratitude swimming in his green depths. It stalls the air in my lungs. I have no idea why he'd feel that way. The paperwork I got for Hadley was nothing. Growing up on the streets, you meet all sorts of people.

One spring, Luc and I were holed up in an abandoned building. When we were sleeping rough, I always tried to get us as high off the street as possible. It meant less noise and less chance of someone stumbling across us. However, there had been a keypad on the door to the top floor, and no matter how hard I'd tried, I couldn't get past it. It piqued my curiosity, though, and I kept a vigilant eye. It took weeks, and I'd practically given up hope of ever working out what was in there, when the door finally opened and this figure dressed all in black, with a hood pulled low over his head, emerged.

Of course, I'd ensured, once opened, that the door wouldn't catch, so after he disappeared, I snuck into the room. Color me surprised when I saw the tech setup he had going on. There were servers and screens everywhere. I don't know what half of it was, but it was apparent he was some sort of hacker, computer genius, or whatever.

I'd made sure I was long gone before he returned, and Luc and I never slept in that building again. A couple of months later, I had enough cash to get us into our apartment, and I'd never thought anything of it again until I received a call on my burner phone one day. I have no idea how he got my number, but he knew my name and where I lived and made it crystal clear what would happen if I dared step inside his personal fortress again.

I took heed of his warning for several months, until I decided to approach him about getting a new identity for Hadley. I knew it was a risk, but even while the man had been threatening me, I didn't get a bad vibe from him. He just liked his privacy, and I can totally relate to that. He hadn't been too happy to see me, but Hadley was offering a lot of money for the job, so he quickly got over it, did what he needed to, and I never saw him again after that.

The five of us move into the kitchen, and the topic moves back to Evie while Oliver goes about making coffee for everyone.

"I still can't believe she's alive, man," Beck says, shaking his head.

"Yeah, you and me both," Cain states as Oliver sets mugs down in front of us all before claiming a free chair. Unsurprisingly, he doesn't sit in the open one beside me but the one diagonally across the table, as far away from me as he can get. It hurts, but I push it down, focusing on the conversation instead.

Cain fills Beck in on how we found her and his concerns. Apparently, Beck is a school counselor, so although he has no direct experience in dealing with situations like this, he has a few valuable ideas.

"We should leave the four of you to catch up," Hadley says when we hear Evie moving around upstairs. "Too many people might overwhelm her, and it will be good for all of you to spend time with her together. Besides, Red and I have some catching up to do ourselves."

I agree, and Hadley and I make a hasty retreat from the house before Evie can make it downstairs. I grab my leather jacket and two helmets before we exit, and when Hadley spots them, a grin lights up her face. "Hell, yes!"

I laugh and toss her the helmet before the two of us climb onto Raven. Hadley wraps her arms around my middle, and I rev the engine loudly before shooting off down the road, laughing as I listen to her hoots and yells as I push the bike faster.

I zip in and out of traffic, taking us on a random course all over the city. With every mile that passes, tension bleeds out of me until I feel lighter than I have in days. Weeks, even.

Eventually, I direct the bike toward the abandoned docks where Hadley and I used to meet, and soon the briny sea air washes over us, and the old cobblestones make the bike bounce as I slow to a crawl.

"Just like old times," Hadley says when she climbs off the bike and looks up at the abandoned warehouse. Leaving our helmets on the bike—people rarely come down to this part of the dock, especially during the day—we walk over to the ladder at the side of the building that goes all the way to the roof and begin to climb.

"God, I haven't been here in forever," I admit when we crest the top wall and take in the view of the sea stretching out before us. "Not since the last time we were here."

"Same," Hadley agrees, her eyes taking in the view before she turns to face me. "I guess I have some explaining to do."

I sit on the low wall surrounding the top of the roof, my legs dangling over the edge, and she moves to join me before starting into her story, and by the time she's finished, I'm in awe. I always knew she was living in a difficult situation, but she never elaborated, and I never pried, but I had no idea the extent of it. What she's survived is unimaginable. "That's..." I trail off, shaking my head. "It's like something out of a movie."

"Right?" she laughs, and it's easy and carefree. Nothing like the laugh I remember. Tearing my gaze away from the horizon, I turn to look at her. *Really* look at her.

"You seem happy."

She smiles, something she's done a lot of since she showed up earlier, and yet it's still jarring to see. She very rarely smiled when I knew her, and even when she did, it was fleeting and hesitant. Nothing like the relaxed grin that lights up her face now.

"I am," she admits. "Happier than I ever thought I could be." With that surreal grin still on her face, she nudges my shoulder. "Tell me about you." She waggles her eyebrows in a very un-Hadley-like gesture that makes me burst out laughing. "Which one of them are you doing? Please tell me it's Cain. He was so convinced a woman couldn't make him change his ways, but I knew it would just take the right one."

I blush, and Hadley must see it written all over my face because her eyes widen. "Hell, yes!" She holds her hand up for a high five, yet another move that seems so out of character. "Go you, girl, doing them both! The multi-dick life is the best."

I snort a laugh. "Oliver mentioned you have a reverse harem relationship going," I subtly pry, curious to know more.

"Yup. There's Beck, his brother, West—he's the quiet, nerdy one—Cam, the jokester, and Mason, my surly softy."

"I don't know how you juggle all those different personalities," I confess.

She shrugs. "It has its moments, but for the most part, it's easy. It's all about compromise, honesty, and open communication."

I gnaw on my bottom lip before deciding to open up about my conversation with Oliver last night.

"That's a tough one," she admits when I'm finished. "His history with Evie is definitely tricky, and while I don't feel his guilt is justified, I can understand why he feels that way. I think all you can do is give him his space. Let him make up his mind for himself, but honestly, I don't think you need to worry. It sounds like he loves you, and while this is all a bit of a mind-fuck for him, that love will win out at the end of the day." She squeezes my knee in a reassuring gesture. "Just give him a bit of time. I think the three of you would make a great team. You could be exactly what Black Creek needs."

"Uhh," I hedge, not exactly sure how to tell her the next bit. "It's not just the two of them."

"What?" she chuckles, surprise coloring her features. "Who else?" She gasps. "Oh my god, Marcus? Or one of the kids? They're all at least eighteen now, so totally possible," she surmises aloud.

"Eww." I shove her shoulder. "No. They're friends with my brother." I shake my head, horrified at the thought of viewing kids that I lump in with my brother in any sort of romantic or sexual way. "Just, no. And Marcus, while admittedly hot, isn't my type."

"Well, don't leave me in suspense, who is it then?"

I hesitate, glancing at her from the corner of my eye while blurting out, "Dante Antonelli and his bodyguard."

Silence follows my confession. "As in those Antonellis?" She points across the wide river to where the tall Antonelli skyscrapers glitter in the midday sun like a shining beacon, only emphasizing the dilapidated condition of the rest of the city.

"The one and only."

Her gaze swivels to mine, and I can see the caution in her eyes. "Are you sure they aren't playing you?"

"I'm sure." I lift my left hand, where my wedding band sits snugly on my ring finger. "Dante married me and everything."

Her eyes widen to the size of saucers, her mouth dropping open in shock as she snatches my hand toward her face for a closer look. "What the fuck?" she mumbles to herself. "Tell me everything."

I chuckle before launching into the whole crazy story. By the time I'm finished, she's gaping at me in a mirror image of how I stared at her when she finished filling me in on what happened to her.

"Fuck, girl. Caught between two hot mafia men and two hot gangsters... that is a very panty-melting place to be."

"Tell me about it," I grouch.

"You're going to have quite a task on your hands, making four alpha males get along."

I groan, burying my face in my hands. "I know." I'm still hoping to get all four of them to tolerate one another, but I don't yet know how I will achieve that.

She nudges my shoulder, making me look up at her. "If anyone can do it, it's you." She shrugs. "And if they love you like they claim they do, they'll work it out."

I don't have the same optimistic faith she does—clearly falling in love completely changed her worldly perspective—but I do cling to her confidence.

Jumping to her feet, she grins down at me cunningly, reminiscent of the old Hadley. "Come on, Red. Prove to me those fighting skills haven't gotten rusty."

I laugh as I get to my feet. "Please. Jon's been teaching me some moves. I bet I could even give you a run for your money."

She cocks a brow, smirking. "Wanna bet?"

We spend the rest of the afternoon sparring with one another and chatting, and Hadley repeatedly proves that even though she no longer needs to rely on her agility and strength, she hasn't slacked off since we last went at it. However, I give as good as I get, even getting a few surprise shots in.

By the time we climb down from the roof, the sun is low in the sky, and I feel better than I have in a long time. I hadn't realized how much I missed not having someone to talk to. When Hadley had been a part of my life—albeit her presence was infrequent and short—we connected in a way I never have with anyone else. Even though neither of us opened up about our lives and kept huge secrets from one another, we just clicked, and the fact that we so effortlessly fell back into that easy friendship today demonstrates how strong that bond is. It's the type where you don't have to see or talk to someone for days or weeks, but whenever you do, you just pick up right where you left off. No hard feelings or snarky comments. Just pure and simple friendship.

It's dark, and the lights are on inside the house by the time we pull up at the curb.

"Where's Evie?" I ask when I enter the living room and find her absent.

"She was exhausted after today," Cain explains, pulling me into his arms and pressing a kiss to my temple.

"How did she get on?"

"She did well. Even though it was bittersweet, I think it did her good to be around us all."

I run my fingers through his hair, brushing the strands back from his forehead. "And you? Did it do you good?"

He smiles, and it's one of the most carefree smiles I've seen on his face in a long time. "Yeah, it really did."

I grin, melting further into him. Perhaps everything will work out okay after all. He pulls me in tighter against him. "How about you? What did you girls get up to?"

Hadley and I share a look, smirking. "Oh, you know. Did each other's hair and painted our nails."

Beck and Cain both snort. "So basically, you spent the day fighting one another," Cain smartly deduces.

"Yeah, something like that."

I curl up on Cain's lap, listening as the guys talk around me, catching up and teasing one another. If it wasn't for the fact that Oliver never once looks my way, and he deliberately ensures his skin doesn't touch mine when I shift on Cain's lap, then I'd say today was a pretty perfect day. But I guess close to perfect is pretty good for Black Creek standards.

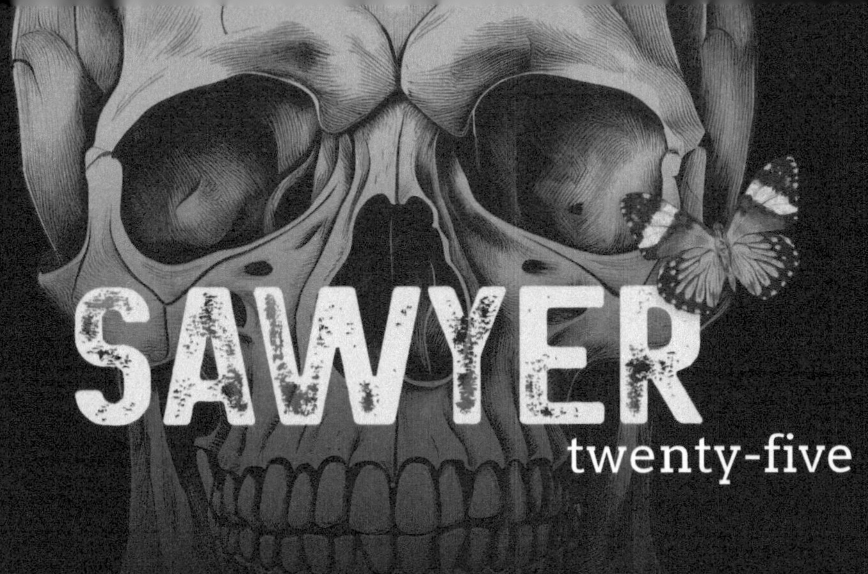

twenty-five

After Hadley and Beck leave, with a promise to return with the others as soon as Evie is up to it, Oliver makes some excuse to head to the clubhouse, leaving just Cain and me.

"I can't believe you know Hadley," he says when we're alone in the living room.

"I know. Small world."

He nuzzles his face in the crook of my neck as he pulls me in tighter against him, his thoughts clearly elsewhere as his teeth skim over my skin, making me shiver.

"I've missed you," he murmurs in my ear, his voice low and husky.

"I've been right here." I tilt my head to the side, giving him better access as he bites and sucks along my neck.

"I know. You've been incredible. I couldn't have done any of this without you."

I want to argue that I haven't really done much, but he grabs my earlobe between his teeth and the sting of pain eradicates any thoughts I may have had as I writhe in his lap.

"Fucking hell, Red," he growls, his erection digging into my ass. "I need you so bad I can't even think straight."

His hand slides down to undo the button of my jeans before he pushes his fingers into my panties, finding me already soaked and ready for him. He groans in approval before shoving three thick fingers into my pussy, causing me to gasp.

His other hand claps over my mouth. "You've gotta be quiet for me, baby. Can you do that?"

He continues to pump his fingers into me, but when I don't respond, he goes still, causing me to groan in frustration as I try to ride his hand. He's having none of it, though. "Red." His voice has that authoritative leader tone to it that only makes me wetter.

"Yes," I gasp, my words muffled behind his hand. He lifts his palm off my lips. "I can be quiet."

His rumbling chuckle at my words says otherwise, but he doesn't contradict me as he picks up the pace, sending my body into a frenzy as I squirm and thrash in his lap.

I'm biting down on my bottom lip, barely holding back my cry of pleasure, but when he presses down on my clit, I lose all control over my body. Realizing as much, his hand quickly moves to cover my mouth, smothering my cry just in time as I come all over his fingers.

He doesn't give me a second to recover before he lifts me off him, tossing me over the arm of the sofa like I weigh nothing. My pants and panties are yanked down my legs, tangling at my ankles, and I gasp in surprise when he delivers a sharp slap to my backslide.

A second later, I feel his engorged head pushing at my entrance before he grasps my hips and slams into me in one swift thrust that has me nearly falling over onto the floor.

"Fuck, I'll never get enough of this," he grunts, pulling out before pushing back in. His piercings scrape deliciously along my inner walls, eliciting a full-body shiver as he drives me wild. "You feel so fucking perfect. So tight. So dirty. So fucking mine."

"Yes," I moan, not even sure what I'm agreeing with. His words. His delicious touches. His wild thrusts. Him.

Coating a finger, he begins to work it into my ass, only heightening the sensations as the bite of pain tangles with pleasure, pushing me closer to the edge. He works a second, followed by a third finger into my ass until I feel so full, I can hardly breathe. Nothing exists except Cain and the feeling of him buried so deep inside me that I don't know where he begins and I end.

"So fucking dirty for me," he grunts, and I can tell by the strain in his tone that he's close to coming. "My dirty stripper."

"Yours," I cry out as my walls constrict, triggering his own release.

I sag against the arm of the chair, feeling the weight of him above me as we both catch our breath.

When he pulls back, his cock slides out, but his fingers are there, pushing his cum back into my channel. I shiver and groan with every push of his fingers until he lifts me gently, fixing my clothes back in place and maneuvering me in his arms until I'm straddling him, my body leaning against his.

I snuggle in against him as he presses a surprisingly gentle kiss to my forehead, wrapping his arms around me. "I love you," I murmur in a soft voice.

He looks down at me, love and adoration shining in his eyes. "I love you too, Red. Always will."

We lapse into silence, just enjoying this moment in one another's arms, but eventually he speaks. "What's going on with Oliver?"

I sigh, too wrung out to even move my head to look at him, so I just continue resting it against his shoulder and staring at the wall. "He's struggling with his old feelings for Evie," I confess, not entirely sure if Cain knows about Oliver's old flame for his sister.

"The crush he used to have?" he asks, sounding confused.

"Mmhmm. I think it was more than a crush. He seems to think it was, anyway." Cain makes a noncommittal sound that I can't interpret. "I think he feels guilty for moving on." I swallow roughly before adding on in a voice barely above a whisper, "for loving me."

Cain makes some noise at the back of his throat that has me shifting so I can look at his face. "Don't get me wrong, Oliver loved my sister. Loves her," he corrects. "But he's not *in love* with her. Not the way he is with you."

Despite the confidence in his tone, I have my reservations, which he can visibly see written on my face as he reaches out to cup my chin. "He's feeling guilty for giving up on Evie and confusing that with his love for you. When he wises up, he'll realize how stupid he was to doubt what the two of you have." The certainty in his deep green eyes sparks a flame of hope in my chest. "Oliver has never been happier than when he's with you. You've given him purpose, a reason to wake up every day, something to fight for."

I shake my head, "No. You gave him all that."

"I gave him something temporary to fill the void until he found that one thing that would give him ultimate meaning. He came to Black Creek, *for me.* He took up my plight, *for me.* None of it was ever for him. Not completely, anyway. It was all just killing time until he found you."

As his words weave around my heart, igniting it with a dangerous flame of hope, I press my lips to his and wrap my arms around his shoulders, pulling him closer as I feel him harden beneath me.

My ruthless gangster leader is all hard edges and cold brush-offs, and I love sparring with that side of him, but it's in the quiet moments when he shows me the vulnerability he keeps carefully hidden that I know Cain was made for me. He's the other half of my soul. The yin to my yang. He's callous yet merciful, brutal yet kind-hearted. He's the sharp blades that I carry on a Reaper job and the warm smile that I gift to Luc. The me that I show the world and the me that I keep only for the people I love. I'm fortunate enough to be one of the few who made the list of people he cares about.

THE WORLD SLIPS PAST IN A WAVE OF COLOR AS I PULL BACK ON THE throttle, pushing Raven to go faster. Everything is a blur except the white lines on the road, my focus on nothing but the other vehicles around me as I weave in and out of traffic. Moving at these fast speeds is second nature to me. My heart rate isn't even elevated as I undertake a car, speeding past him before cutting in front, narrowly avoiding the parked car in my lane.

A horn goes off, but I pay it no attention. I'm already a block ahead of him. It's not that I'm in any hurry, I just enjoy the adrenaline rush. Besides, a fast-moving target is harder to hit, and given Giovanni has bullets with each of our names on them, I'd rather not get intimately acquainted with mine today.

What I'm doing is probably risky. Okay, a little more than risky. Cain, Oliver, and I have mostly been lying low at Cain's house, and he's got the clubhouse on high alert. Meanwhile, Dante and Enzo have been hiding out at an apartment Enzo owns. I know Cain has been preoccupied with Evie, but we can't just sit around and wait for Giovanni to attack. Plus, I'm going out of my mind worrying that he will find Dante and Enzo and I won't know until it's too late.

So, despite their complaining, I'm heading to see my mafia men. I just need to set eyes on them. To see for myself that they are okay. And we need to talk strategy. Admittedly, I need all four of them together to discuss our plan, but Cain is still refusing to let them anywhere near Evie, and he refuses to leave her to discuss it anywhere else. I get it. I understand why he's being so protective of her. However, it's making it impossible for us to organize a plan of attack. We're sitting ducks right now. I'm surprised Giovanni hasn't already made a move and can only hope his ongoing silence means he hasn't found any of us.

However, it wouldn't be difficult for him to locate the clubhouse. Dante mentioned that the Antonellis didn't concern themselves with the various gangs running Black Creek. Until recently, Giovanni didn't even know about the Rejects, and it was Dante and Enzo that organized the recon on them. Dante is confident that his men will remain loyal to him and won't easily give up any information to Giovanni. But I'm not so trusting, and I'm definitely not going to lay my hopes on Antonelli men. The way I see it, Dante and Enzo are the exceptions, and just like them, everyone else will have to prove to me that they aren't on Giovanni's side.

Still, *if*—and it's a big if—Dante is right, then it will take his father a few days to gather the necessary intel on the Rejects and devise a plan. However, with every passing day, that window shrinks, and I can feel it in my gut. Giovanni is coming.

There's a moment of silence that occurs right before the breaking of the battle thunder, where the world slows to a crawl as if every atom is standing in wait, ready to witness who will perish and who will emerge victorious. That silence falls over me like a veil every time I flick that switch into Reaper mode. Especially as I drive through the city streets, a light drizzle spraying drops of rain across my visor and leaving a sheen of water on my leather jacket, I feel it even more. It's as though my ears pop, the world around me going deathly silent.

A loud *boom* cracks through the silence as my bike veers unsteadily across the road. I try to get it under control as something whizzes past my ear, but before I can, I'm thrown from the bike, the world spinning as I'm tossed through the air.

I hit the ground with a loud *oomph*, pain lancing along my left side as stars dance across my vision. My helmet cracks against the concrete, but I can't process any of it as I'm flung across the unrelenting surface. My entire body screams in pain, and I swear I can feel my leather clothes being ripped to shreds with every roll.

I'm not sure if I pass out or what, but eventually I realize I've stopped moving. However, my brain is foggy and everything fucking hurts. I try to force my eyes open, but even that hurts, and I quickly give up. Instead, I take a moment to reach out with my mind, attempting to catalog my injuries. I think my fingers and toes twitch, and although it hurts, I can breathe, but I can't determine much more than that. What the hell happened? My tire blew out, or more specifically, *something* blew my tire out.

Knowing I can't lie here like a prized target, I wrestle my eyelids open, groaning as a white, hot pain flashes across my head and black dots obscure my vision, my body threatening to pass out. *Nope. Definitely can't do that.*

Blinking back the pain, I try to focus on my surroundings. It seems I've rolled into the mouth of an alleyway. There doesn't appear to be anyone around, and a small groan escapes my lips when I spot my bike lying in the middle of the road, plastic, and God knows what else littering the ground around it.

Blocking out the destruction of my baby, I try to push myself into a sitting position, but before I can, I hear footsteps rushing toward me. *Please, let it be someone coming to help.*

I gasp as I'm roughly dragged to my feet, biting my lip against the cry of pain as my entire body feels like it's been set on fire. Someone yanks on my helmet, feeling like the muscles in my neck are being stretched and torn as it's pulled over my head. "Gotcha," some guy snarls, shoving me against the wall. I have to blink several times before the world slowly comes into focus, and I find an older-looking guy dressed in the standard Antonelli dress code of a fancy-as-fuck suit with a cocky smirk on his face standing over me. "Giovanni's going to be really pleased to see you."

I grunt in response while I subtly flex my fingers. I'm weak as hell, but I'm not out yet. Confident that I can make a fist, I distract him while slowly reaching for the sheath strapped to my thigh, sending up a silent prayer of thanks when I find my blade still tucked within it.

Gathering every ounce of strength I can muster, I raise my arm, driving the blade deep into the asshole's neck. His eyes widen in shock before I wrench it out, sending blood spurting from the wound, drenching us both.

I fall to the ground, too weak to hold myself up when he lets me go, his hand flying to put pressure on the gaping hole in his neck. Not that it will do him much good. From my slumped position, I watch as his face drains of color before he drops to his knees, gurgling and gasping until he falls still, staring unblinkingly at me.

On my hands and knees, I crawl deeper into the alley, knowing I need to escape before any more Antonelli assholes show up and I become a dead girl walking. Pulling my phone out of my pocket, I'm not surprised to find it smashed to pieces, although my heart still sinks when I see the cracks across the black screen. I guess I'm on my own.

No problem. It's not like I'm half unconscious, badly injured, and being hunted by suit-wearing psychopaths. I've totally got this.

Breathing heavily, sweat coats my skin, dripping from my nose when I reach a steel door halfway down the alley. My whole body trembles, my hand shaking so bad I can hardly get the door open. I'm in shock, functioning purely on adrenaline—adrenaline that is quickly burning out. Stumbling inside, I do a half-assed job of wedging the door shut before sinking to the floor again.

The world around me shrinks, darkness pressing in until nothing exists except the sound of my labored breaths, and the last thought I have as the darkness pulls me under is that this might be the end of the line for me.

Luc.

Cain.

Oliver.

Dante.

Enzo.

Jon and the kids.

The Rejects.

I'm never going to see any of them again.

"Where the hell is she?!" I roar, sending the front door smashing into the wall. Not that I give a shit. I'll tear this house apart if I have to. I told *mia vita* I'd come for her if she didn't come to me first. I was patient. I gave her time. But now I'm done waiting.

She told Enzo she was coming, but her phone has been going straight to voicemail for the last few hours, so I decided to come get her myself.

With their weapons aimed, ready to shoot, Cain and Oliver rush into the hall. "What the fuck?!" Cain snarls, looking just as angry as I am. "Get the fuck out!"

"Where is she?" I repeat, my voice calm and deadly. I swear to god, I'll rip their heads from their bodies and relish in the pop as their muscles and tendons separate if I don't see my wife in the next two seconds.

"She went to see you," Oliver states. At his words, I snap my gaze from Cain's angry mug to Oliver's, noting the slight furrow of his brow.

"She never fucking showed," Enzo states. "And her phone is going straight to voicemail."

Cain's already reaching into his pocket before Enzo has finished speaking, dialing her number. He puts it on speaker, and we all listen as her voicemail message starts.

The two idiots share a look, concern flashing across their features, which is the only reason why they continue to breathe... for now. But if anything has happened to *my wife* under their watch, they won't be breathing for much longer.

"When did she leave?" Enzo barks.

Oliver shakes his head, shrugging his shoulders, obviously unable to answer that question, and I growl at his incompetence. What the fuck were they doing? Why didn't they follow her or make sure she arrived okay? They don't fucking deserve a woman like Sawyer!

"This afternoon," Cain answers, far too fucking vaguely. It's fucking dark out. She could be anywhere in the city. Any number of horrible things could have happened to her. The worst of which doesn't even bear thinking about, except my brain automatically goes there—to my father. *He* is the worst thing that could have happened to her. If he got her, he could be torturing her this very second. There's no way he'd have killed her. Not yet. He'll make her suffer first. He'll demand to know everything before he grants her any kind of peace.

Cain raises his phone to his ear, barking out orders for men to search the city for her, but I'm hardly listening as I step toward him. He hangs up, glowering at me. "If anything has happened to her," I growl. "If one hair on her head is out of place, I will make your death so fucking agonizing, you will beg me to end it. I won't give a shit that Sawyer has feelings for you. It's my job to protect her, even from selfish assholes like yourself, and if she's hurt, then you don't fucking deserve her."

the pre-date date

With one final glance in the mirror, flattening a hand down the front of my suit jacket, I step into the bedroom. I immediately stop in my tracks, my eyes stuck on the beauty standing in front of me. She's not wearing one of those tight, form-fitting dresses I love seeing her in, although she still looks just as edible in those tiny shorts and her sexy as fuck thigh-high black boots. Along with the small strip of fabric that seemingly constitutes a top wrapped around her breasts and her hair hanging loose around her shoulders. I'm seriously tempted to call tonight off and take her straight to bed.

However, before I can voice my opinions, she shatters through the dirty direction my thoughts had gone. "You can't wear that!"

It takes a second for me to process what she's said, and even then, I don't understand. "What? Why?"

"Because you look like a fucking penguin."

That... has got to be the most insulting thing someone has ever said to me.

"A very hot penguin," Sawyer tacks on quickly. "But you'll stand out like a sore thumb in that outfit."

I'm still trying to comprehend how a suit isn't a *suitable* outfit—where the fuck is she taking me? Suddenly, she holds up a finger and says, "Hold on, stay there," before darting out of the room.

She returns a few minutes later, looking gorgeously flushed as she drops something onto the bed. I'm too busy staring at her rosy cheeks, wondering what the hell Lor did to put that look in her eye and what I would need to say or do to make her look that way, when she says, "Wear these."

Finally tearing my eyes away from her face, my lip curls as I stare at the bundle of clothes on the bed. Jeans? Seriously? I don't think I've ever worn a pair of fucking jeans in my life, and I've definitely decided if jeans are the clothing requirement for wherever the fuck we're going, then I don't want to go. "Now, Dante," she barks, scolding me as though I'm an errant child and not one of this city's deadliest men.

Lifting my eyes to hers, I take a second to seriously debate just pinning her to my bed and stripping her naked. What the hell do we even need to leave the house for anyway? Dates are for getting to know one another. I already know everything I need to know about Sawyer, so let's simply skip the date nonsense and get straight to having her on my cock, moaning and crying out in pleasure.

Except when I go to say precisely that, I hesitate, latching on to that look in her eye. The one hidden behind the lust still pinkening her cheeks. It's that nervousness that has me biting back my words, and instead, I quietly gather the clothes and change.

I'm feeling all sorts of uncomfortable and wholly out of my element when Sawyer returns from the bathroom, stopping in her tracks. "You look *good*."

I frown, glancing down at myself. I fail to see how I can look good in this attire. If Sawyer thinks I look good, then that's all that fucking matters. "I disagree," I grumble.

When a rare laugh bursts out of her, the lighthearted sound snaps my attention from the stupid t-shirt that's too loose around my biceps and the neckline to her face. I made her laugh. I don't even understand how. What I said wasn't supposed to be funny. And yet, that sound made something in my chest tighten. It almost felt as though my heart skipped a beat, tripping over that laugh before catching up to its normal rhythm again.

I liked it. I liked hearing her laugh. I liked knowing that *I* made her laugh. She doesn't laugh nearly enough, and I don't have Lor's witty charm. I never know what to say around her, never mind attempting to conjure something amusing to say.

As the air between us electrifies, she swallows audibly. Her voice is raw and husky as she says, "Umm, are you ready to go?"

Still tempted to push her down on the bed, I hesitate for a second before nodding. I may not need to go on this date tonight, but it's clear that Sawyer does. For whatever reason, she feels that we need to do this. She told me she needed time and space, and perhaps this is part of that, so I guess we're going on a fucking date.

"What the fuck is that for?" I bark when we make it downstairs, and I'm staring at the helmet she's trying to hand over to me.

"The bike."

My eyebrows hitch. "I'm not riding on that thing. We'll take the car." Like fuck am I sitting bitch on a bike.

"No." That one word has me hard as a rock in my pants. I don't understand how hearing that one word from most people can end in them not breathing, but hearing that defiance from Sawyer elicits a much more... exciting reaction from me. "I'm in charge tonight, and I'm telling you, we're taking the bike."

"I should at least get to drive it," I grumble, unsure why I'm not pushing harder on this. Perhaps it's the way Sawyer lifts one of her delicate eyebrows in challenge.

"Do you even know how to ride?" Well, fuck, she has me there. She smirks when I continue to scowl at her. "Even if you did, I wouldn't let you."

She shoves the helmet against my chest, and I'm forced to catch it before it drops to the floor. Then she turns on her heel and strides out of the house. Fucking hell, her sass is either going kill me or make me come in my pants.

I stomp out the door behind her, making it wildly fucking clear I'm not happy about any of this, watching as she pulls on her helmet and swings a leg over the bike. When I continue to stand there, she turns toward me, cocking a brow. "Didn't take you for a pussy, Antonelli," she goads.

The look I give her is one of pure challenge. *Oh, it's on Mia Vita.*

Muttering a curse, I shove the helmet over my head and slide on behind her. We're quickly zipping through the city streets, heading who knows where. It says a lot that I didn't enquire where we were going, although as the shining tower blocks of the Antonelli territory give way to rundown buildings and shabby streets, I'm beginning to question why I hadn't.

"Where are we?" I question when we pull up at the curb in one of the more dilapidated-looking streets.

"This is where I live." She gestures with her chin toward the building in front of us covered in graffiti. The structure is cracked and crumbling in places as if it's one shake of the earth away from falling apart. Definitely a far cry from the gleaming penthouse apartment I grew up in, and the modern buildings that make up the bulk of Antonelli territory. Only that's not what bothers me. It's that Sawyer was forced to live in this gritty place. That Luc had to grow up here. Both of them deserve so much better than this. "Come on." At Sawyer's summons, I snap my gaze away from the building and follow her inside.

It's even worse inside.

How do people live in conditions like this? It's unsanitary, and a complete health risk at the worst. This... this isn't fucking living. It never crossed my mind that people lived like this. Obviously, I knew those who lived in Black Creek struggled. That they weren't afforded the same luxuries as those in my territory, except ... this is something I couldn't have made up in my worst nightmare. Sawyer mentioned that the two gangsters wanted to save Black Creek. I thought she just meant from us, but now I realize it's more than that. More than just revenge and wanting to claim the city for themselves. Although that still doesn't mean I fucking like them, just that I can better understand the situation.

She leads me to what I'm guessing is her apartment, stepping aside as we cross the threshold so I can take in the small, cramped space that desperately needs some serious renovations. I try to picture Sawyer and Luc living here, curling up on the sofa beneath a thin blanket, trying to ward off the cold.

I am still determining what Sawyer thinks bringing me here will achieve. If she thinks it's going to scare me off, then she's very mistaken. All I see is a place where two people survived, where they carved out a safe space for themselves to escape the world. I picture Sawyer and her brother watching TV or playing one of the board games stacked in the corner. I imagine them forgetting about the horrors of the world outside their window and simply enjoying one another's company. A sister who would do anything to keep her brother safe, and a brother who looked up to his older sister. A broken family who had been trying to keep the remaining pieces together. I picture strength, love, and courage.

I'm still taking in the small apartment when she speaks up, her voice sounding tired and far away. "For five years, this was our home. The only place where we felt some semblance of safety." A hint of steel enters her voice. "And he ruined that."

Moving up behind her, I keep my voice low as I ask, "Why did you bring me here?"

She turns, and I can't pinpoint the look in her eye, only that I hate seeing it there. "Cause I need you to see what my life looks like."

Why, though? Why does she think this would change anything?

"I don't care what your life looks like." My voice is a near growl, needing her to know this changes nothing for me.

"I didn't grow up like you," she continues, as though I never spoke. "I didn't grow up with money. I don't have fancy clothes or a nice car. Hell, I didn't even finish high school."

Sick of listening to this and needing her to actually *hear* me, I use my larger frame to push her back against the wall. Planting my hands on either side of her head, I lower my face until she has no choice but to look directly into my eyes, to see the truth of what I'm telling her.

"I said I don't care. Do you think any of this makes a difference to me? I know you've lived a hard life. You wouldn't be you if you hadn't. Even when you were a dirty, grimy street kid, I knew you were made of tougher stuff than half the men I've worked with. I can count on one hand the number of people who have looked down the barrel of my gun and not flinched, and only one of them was a scared little girl. I don't know what made you so damn resilient. Maybe it was this life you seem to think I'll despise you for..."

"Luc." His name is barely a whisper in the air between us. "It was Luc." Her eyes flick up to mine, brimming with so much emotion, none of which I know enough about to pinpoint, and when she speaks up again, there's awe and steel in her voice. "Your father would have you believe that love makes you weak, but it's actually my love for him, my need to protect him and give him a better life, that made me the person I am today."

She's right. My father has always insisted love makes you weak. Love is for women and children, not for leaders and men like us—men meant to rule. And yet, I know what Sawyer is saying is the truth. I already knew she would do anything for her brother, but hearing that it's her love for him, her need to protect him that has formed this incredibly brave and headstrong woman in front of me... my voice is thick with emotion as I say, "Then I guess I owe him a thank you."

With a tug on the front of my t-shirt, Sawyer eliminates the space between us as she drags my lips to hers. It's the first time she's instigated a kiss, or initiated anything intimate. It's always been me who can't seem to stay away from her, keep my hands off of her... until now. I let her lead as her lips brush mine in a cautious, questioning touch, before she seals her lips to mine and parts them. Her tongue dances across mine, and I try to hold back, but with a second sweep, I lose control and drive my hands into her hair, angling her head so I can kiss her more deeply, needing to feel her all the way to the depths of my soul. Needing to feel that spark that is intrinsically Sawyer loosens the cage that's been locked around my heart for too long now. Every heated glance, every touch of her lips, every rare smile she gives me snaps another bar, and I can start to feel... something seeping out from inside. Something warm and addictive, something that makes me feel alive and has me questioning everything I once knew.

"So this is what people do on a date?" I question when we finally pull apart.

She laughs a breathless laugh. "Not exactly. This was the pre-date date."

Cocking a brow, I ask, "When does the real date begin?"

"I think it just did."

CHAOS & CARNAGE

BLACK CREEK SERIES BOOK FOUR

R.A. SMYTH

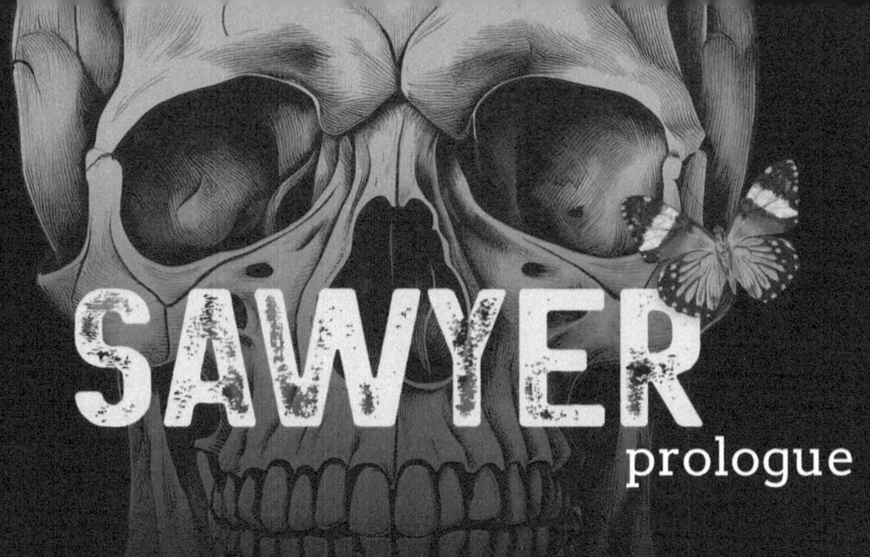

I blink in and out of focus, staring at the dark ceiling far above me. A chill seeps into my skin, flowing into my bones until all I can feel is its icy grip. Cold and numb. And pain. A *lot* of pain. Everything hurts, and I can't hear anything over the blood rushing in my ears. My head pounds, my limbs ache, and every damn inhale catches and stabs.

Behind my eyes, violent images flash out of order. The slashing of a blade. The roar of an engine. The bright red, sticky blood gushes, coating my hands, tongue, and mouth. Silence. Weightlessness. The feeling of being suspended in gravity, that second of absolute stillness before life comes roaring back into existence. The acute pain and jolting, as though your body is being pulled in a hundred different directions, can only come from a severe crash. Rolling, rolling, rolling, my body like an egg as it's rolled down the side of a hill. One crack, two. How many cracks can a body take until it fractures? Until my insides come gushing out like yolk, coating the sidewalk and staining it red?

Hairs prickle at the back of my neck seconds before something brushes over my skin. With far too much effort and pain, I crack open an eyelid, not realizing I'd even closed them. Everything is blurry, taking too long to pull into focus. When it does, what I see doesn't reassure me or put me at ease. A dark silhouette hovers over my broken, weary frame.

Maybe this is death, come to claim me finally. Our meeting must be long overdue, yet I don't feel ready to leave. Ironic really. I always waved away death because I didn't want Luc to be alone, but now that I know he'll be taken care of and will never be alone again, I'm still not ready to go. Along with Luc's guaranteed protection came four hulking, violent, ruthless men who make everyone else around them quake in their boots and rush to obey their commands. Men who have infuriated me, harassed me, held me against my will, and forced me to marry them. Men who have blown apart the very narrow-minded view I had of the world and turned it from something monochromatic into technicolor. From survival to something worth living for. Worth fighting for—even if that fight is with death.

I feel his cold talons wrap around me as he draws me into his arms, his face shrouded in darkness. Even the pull into the afterlife comes with its own brand of agony, every muscle screaming in pain as I'm hauled into death's arms.

A voice murmurs at the back of my mind. I can sense the urgency behind their words, but I'm too out of it to catch hold of them before they disappear into the thick fog that's quickly clouding my head, making it feel heavy and weighed down. My body rocks against a firm chest as death carries me deeper into the warehouse, the darkness swallowing us until I'm no longer sure if my eyes are open or if they've fallen closed again.

My arms sway, my body rocking, like I'm a boat cresting the relaxed waves of the ocean. My body a vessel as it crosses the river Styx.

Beep.

Beep.

Beep.

Beep.

The shutting of a steel door solidifying my fate slashes through my mind, and still, I can't think straight, can't connect the dots, can't get my brain to process the danger. There's no fighting back this time. No winning against death. My body is done, and so is my mind. If this is the end of the line, then death can have me, but he'll never have my heart because it already belongs to four broken men, without whom I'd be broken too.

one

"I want every man we can spare out on the streets looking for her," Cain barks into his phone. "Now!" The entire time, Dante glares at Cain, looking so menacing that it would have most men on their knees, begging for forgiveness. Not Cain, though. He meets Dante's furious glower head-on, their gazes clashing as he barks more orders down the line to Marcus before hanging up.

The second he does, Dante steps up close to him, attempting to use his tall, muscular body to intimidate Cain, but even though they are both the same height, Cain has more muscle on him.

"If anything has happened to her," Dante growls in a low, threatening tone. "If one hair on her head is out of place, I will make your death so fucking agonizing, you will beg me to end it. I won't give a shit that Sawyer has feelings for you. It's my job to protect her, even from selfish assholes like you, and if she's hurt, then you don't fucking deserve her."

You don't fucking deserve her. Ain't that the fuckin' truth. How is it that I've been stuck in my head, overthinking everything and beating myself up because of the hand fate dealt all of us, questioning my relationship with Red. Still, the second Enzo said she never showed, ice-cold dread like nothing I'd felt before slid into my veins. Now, everything seems crystal fucking clear and I can't believe I ever doubted us.

I've been such a fucking idiot, and now Red is somewhere out there, possibly hurt, and all she knows is that I didn't have enough faith in us to trust that she was the one when things got a little rocky. She needs to know that she's it for me. She's everything I don't deserve, my reason for waking up in the morning, the guiding light that gets me through the day. Evie's return threw me. It brought up everything I've buried since the day she disappeared, and guilt rubbed me raw, yet when I look at Evie, I don't feel anything close to how I feel when I'm around Red. There's no heated passion or fiery chemistry, no overwhelming need to hold her close and bury myself inside her. No hungry desire to be her entire world.

What I feel for Evie are love and affection, but what I feel for Red transcends every-thing. For her, I'd set the world on fire. For her, I'll play nice with the Antonelli douchebags. For her, I'll bring Giovanni to his knees and help rebuild Black Creek from the ashes of his burning empire. I'll make this city somewhere she can be proud to live, somewhere she can be happy. Its blood-soaked history will be nothing but a story of the past. A reminder of how far we've come and what we had to survive.

Red is the one for me. The *only* one. We need to find her. *I* need to find her. The thought of something bad happening to her when there is this rift between us... I need to fix it. I need to reaffirm that I'm in fucking love with her, no matter how many apolo-gies or how much groveling it takes.

"We need to get out there, too." There's an urgency in my tone, one I'm sure all of us are feeling. It's been several hours since Red left here. Several hours since god-only-knows what happened to her. She could be hurt or injured, bleeding out in a goddamn alleyway, or worse...

Refusing to even go there, I focus on Dante and Enzo. "Did you see any signs of her on your way here?"

"Do you think we'd be here if we did?" Enzo snaps irritably, making my jaw tick and my hand clench with the desire to show him just how much I appreciate his back talk.

Something behind me snags their attention, and Cain and I turn at the same time to see Evie standing at the top of the stairs, wearing a strange mix of Sawyer's skinny jeans and Cain's massively oversized hoodie. Her wide eyes bounce between Cain and me and the two suited pricks now standing behind us, panic flaring in them. "Cain? What's going on?"

"Red's missing," I state, bitterness coating my tongue.

Her eyes round. "Do t-they have her?"

I don't know how much she knows about the Antonellis. Whether Santos—the sick bastard—kept her all to himself or if she knows much about Giovanni and the rest of his minions, but her face pales at the knowledge that they might have Red.

Cain's face softens, and I can tell he's working hard to cover up his true feelings as he looks up at his sister. "We don't know yet, E." Turning back to face Dante, any soft-ness quickly evaporates as he snarls, "Get the fuck out of my house. You're scaring my sister."

"I-It's okay," Evie says, her voice sounding small and unsure.

"It's not fucking okay," Cain snarls, his temper quickly reaching boiling point as he steps up to Dante and curls his fist. "I still don't fucking trust that you didn't know my sister was in that tower this whole time. Hell, for all I know, you wanted her there."

The flaring of Dante's nostrils is the only sign that Cain's words have pissed him off.

"Why the fuck would we help you get her back if that was the case?" Enzo sneers.

"They didn't." Although Evie's voice sounds stronger, when I look back at her, she's licking her lips nervously. Still, as I watch, she steels her spine and works to rein in that fear. "I-If they have Red, then you need to find her. I-I'm okay."

Cain looks back at his sister, scrutinizing her for a long moment while he tries to decide what's the best thing to do. After a moment, he frowns and spits out, "Fine, but stay upstairs. I'll call Marcus and get someone to stay with you."

"O-only Marcus or Luc."

Cain hesitates for a split second at Evie's request before giving a quick nod. We watch as, with one last glance in Dante and Enzo's direction, Evie disappears back into her room, and with a reluctant grunt, Cain indicates for us to follow as he strides toward the kitchen.

He rifles through a drawer before pulling out a map of Black Creek and spreading it out across the kitchen table. "Where was Red supposed to meet you?"

If it's possible, Dante's expression only hardens at Cain's question, and Enzo cocks a brow, his expression clearly unimpressed.

"You mean to tell us you didn't even ask where Sawyer was going before she left here?" Enzo growls. "What sort of fucking idiots are you?"

Cain's hand slams down on the table. "I trust Red can look out for herself and doesn't need us babying her, tracking her every move, and checking in every three fucking minutes."

"Just show us where she was fucking going," I snap, sick of wasting time.

Enzo stares at the map for a few seconds before pointing out an area along the border between Antonelli territory and ours. "Here. This is the address I gave her."

Grabbing a pen from one of the kitchen drawers full of all sorts of crap that doesn't really belong anywhere else, I map out the various routes Red could have taken. When I'm done, I frown down at the map. There are four potential routes, and that's assuming she took a direct way and didn't decide to take a convoluted path through the city to shake off any tails or just want to let off some steam by taking Raven for a detour.

"We split up, and each takes a route," Cain orders, in full leader mode, even though Dante and Enzo aren't his to command. Not expecting to have his orders questioned, Cain's already dialing a number on his phone and bringing it to his ear as he steps away from the table.

"He realizes we don't take orders from him, right?" Enzo drawls. "Besides, we only have one car with us."

I take a second to let my eyes run over him, his tousled blond hair and day-old stubble, the stress lines around his lips and eyes, before turning my attention to Dante. He studies the map with those cold, calculating, all-seeing eyes of his. Everything about him gives the impression that he's at ease, though the way he stormed in here, ready to raise hell on Red's behalf, would imply the opposite. I really don't get what Red sees in them. Perhaps they aren't like the rest of the Antonellis, and if their stories are to be believed, then they've both suffered as much as Cain has at Giovanni's hands. Even if they were worth saving, I can't for the life of me figure out what made Red actually fall for them. I'm still half convinced it's some twisted Stockholm Syndrome thing from being locked up in that house with the two of them for so long.

And yet, they're here, looking for her, and it's more than evident by the big dick energy they're throwing around that they care about her.

"You wanna spit out whatever it is you're thinking?" Dante states far too calmly, slowly lifting his gaze from the map to meet mine. There's absolutely zero emotion in his eyes. It's like being stabbed by an icicle. I can feel the coldness seeping into my core. All of it only raises more questions.

"What's the deal here?" My gaze flicks to Enzo, finding him watching me just as intently before focusing back on Dante. "Do you actually give a shit about Red, or is there a larger game at play here?"

"She's my wife." He says it so matter of fact, like that's all the explanation he needs to give.

"She only married you because she had to. You do realize we planned to kill your entire family that day?"

Dante gives a barely perceptible shrug of his shoulder. "Doesn't change the fact she's mine."

"And what if she wanted a divorce once this is all over?" I question, raising a brow.

"No."

Just one word, delivered with such authority that it brokers no argument. My eyes narrow, my hackles immediately rising at his irrefutable tone.

"What the fuck do you mean *no*?"

The muscle in his jaw ticks, the only indication that I'm pissing him off as much as he's angering me. He takes a step forward, but Enzo follows him, placing a hand on his shoulder that seems to stop any further movement as Dante levels me with an impassive expression.

"This is pointless." With a finger pointed at the map, Enzo says, "We'll check out these two routes. I take it we can trust you two to thoroughly scout the others?"

"Yes," I hiss between clenched teeth.

"Good. Call if you find anything and we'll do the same. Otherwise, we meet back here in an hour."

Without waiting for confirmation, he drags Dante out of the kitchen, and I hear their car engine starting as Cain walks back in.

"Where the fuck are they going?" he bites out.

"They're checking out two of the routes."

Cain frowns. "I said we were all splitting up."

I just shrug my shoulder in a *what can you do* gesture.

Huffing out a breath, he shakes his head. "Marcus will be here in a few to keep an eye on Evie. I've got the clubhouse on lockdown. Anyone who isn't out looking for Red is on patrol, ready for an attack."

I nod in agreement. "What about Luc?"

"Marcus is bringing him over too, along with a couple of the kids."

"Does he know about Red?"

Cain shakes his head. "Not yet. I imagine Marcus will fill him in before he gets here."

Wanting to be ready to leave as soon as Marcus gets here, we retrieve our weapons, and Cain goes to check on Evie while I scour the map again. I've outlined the area where Red is most likely to be, and I send a picture of the map to Marcus and a few other club members Cain delegates responsibilities to. I also include Bones and the kids, 'cause I'm sure any who aren't with Luc will be out looking for her too.

I hesitate with my thumb over the group chat between myself, Cain, Red, Dante, and Enzo. Red had insisted we set one up, but the entire conversation so far is basically Red talking to one of us and our response. A pang hits me in the chest as I read her last message. It's nothing special, just her telling Cain and me to be careful the night we stormed Giovanni's skyscraper, but *god*, does it make me miss her even more.

Hitting send on the image, I close out of the chat, making a mental note to check

Red's apartment as well. It's the only other place she might have gone if she was hurt or injured and couldn't get back here or to the clubhouse.

Luc comes storming through the door as Cain reappears down the stairs, and even though he's only five and a half feet tall and beat to hell, he's wearing a formidable expression that should make Cain proud. "What the hell happened to my sister?"

"We don't know the answer to that yet, bud," I say, placing a hand on his shoulder. "We're going out to look for her now."

"I want to come."

I'm already shaking my head before he finishes speaking. "No. Not happening. You're in no state to be out searching the streets for her, and even if you were, Red would rip all of us new ones if she knew we didn't enforce bed rest on you." I can see the retort written all over his face, but before he can argue, I lean in and whisper in a quieter voice. "We need you here, keeping an eye on Evie for us."

His facial expression changes in an instant, looking more like the beaten and battered fifteen-year-old that's just been dragged through hell and back. "How is she? Is she okay?"

"She's putting on a brave face, but I think she could do with someone to talk to. You're the only one who has any idea what she went through."

He chews on his bottom lip before nodding. "Okay, I'll stay here, but you better find my sister."

I'm staring him straight in the eye when I say, "We will. I promise you. We'll bring her home."

With a few last words to Marcus, Cain and I head out, deciding to stick together as we climb into the Cadillac and follow the third route I mapped out. We drive slowly, scouring the road for any signs of Red or her bike. Halfway along the first route, my phone pings in my pocket, and pulling it out, I find a message in the group chat from Enzo. *First route was clear. No sign of her.*

I sigh, resting my head against the headrest. "They haven't seen any sign of her yet," I inform Cain, keeping my gaze on the window and the streets beyond. I hear him sigh beside me.

My finger taps against the armrest before I finally blurt out the question that's been circling in my head since Enzo and Dante stormed into the house. "What if Giovanni has her?"

"Then we'll get her back," Cain snarls, and I can hear the leather steering wheel cracking beneath his tight grip. The bitter taste of guilt permeates the air. We should have driven or followed her. Actually, fuck that, we should never have let her leave in the first place. We thought we had more time before Giovanni came for us, but we knew it was only a matter of time, and we still—*I* still—let her walk out the door.

Hell, she didn't even tell me she was leaving. I had to hear it from Cain, and by then she was already gone. I've been so stuck in my head these last few days, trying to shuffle through the tangled web of my emotions, that I've barely even *seen* Red, let alone paid her any attention. I've been careful to maintain distance between us while I work shit out, knowing every time I brushed her off or ignored her, it stung.

She tried to hide it, but I could see it. Feel it. I hated doing it, even at the time, and now I feel like shit when I look back at every time I didn't reach out to interlock our fingers, or pull her into my lap, or choose the seat beside her. I can picture every single one of those digs slicing into her and causing damage.

Knowing she's missing and that something might have happened to her has put everything into perspective. I was confused and emotionally overloaded, but I was seriously fucking stupid to question my feelings for Red. She's it for me. The one thing I didn't even know I was searching for. She gives me purpose and meaning in a way that nothing else ever has. She's the one ray of light in a city of violence, poverty, and despair. The only fucking thing that keeps me going when I feel like giving up. She's the bright smile and sultry eyes I fall asleep dreaming of and want to wake up to every morning. She's fucking mine, and I'll be damned if I won't get her back!

My fist slams against the dashboard as I growl out my frustration.

"I hope that means you've finally wised up." I side-eye Cain before flicking my gaze back out the window, scanning the streets for any sign of Red. "'Cause you were being a fucking asshole, and that role is already taken, by me, so you need to get your shit together."

"My shit is together," I snap.

Cain scoffs. "Not from where I'm sitting." He sighs, and I catch him glancing my way before returning his focus to the road. "Look, I know you had a thing for Evie back in the day, and if life had gone differently, then who knows. But it didn't. *This* is how our lives worked out. We're not the people we would have otherwise been and I dunno about you, but Red fits perfectly with who I am *now*. She slots seamlessly into this life, into *our* life. Don't throw it all away because of what once was or otherwise could have been."

Huffing out a breath, I turn to face him. "I know that now. I just…" I sigh, wiping a hand down my face. "Finding Evie alive. Fuck, man, I never expected that. It threw me. I didn't know what the fuck to think. I felt like I owed it to Evie to still have those feelings, and I felt guilty for not feeling that way about her anymore."

"I get it, man. Trust me, I get it. I feel that same guilt and worry that she thinks we just moved on with our lives and forgot about her, though you and I both know that's not true. She's been the driving force behind everything we've done—the good and the bad. Evie won't blame you for falling in love with someone else. You were both just kids. Who even knows if it would have worked out or if you'd have felt the same way as you got older. As long as Evie knows she still has you in her life, that's all that's going to matter to her right now."

"And what about Red?"

Cain flashes me a grin. "A few apologetic orgasms and she'll forget all about it." I scoff, shaking my head. Somehow I doubt it will be that easy. "Nah, in all seriousness, Red understands, or at least, she was trying to. That's why she gave you your space to figure shit out."

Once again, I return my attention out the window. "We just have to find her. As long as she's alive and with us, I will do whatever I have to to prove she's the one."

"WOAH, HOLD UP!" BOTH CAIN AND I LEAN FORWARD IN OUR SEATS AS Cain slows down, the headlights picking up bits of plastic littering the road. "Fuck, is that…"

Slamming on the brakes, Cain abandons the car in the middle of the road as we both throw open our doors. The light from the car's headlights and the overhanging streetlamp paint a grotesque picture as Cain and I turn in circles, taking in the surrounding wreckage. Most significantly, the remains of a black bike, with most of the plastic exterior missing and the metal frame scraped and scored from where it slid along the road.

The most notable thing missing is its rider. "Sawyer?" I call out, my eyes darting around the street, trying to pinpoint her in the dark spots between streetlamps. Digging my phone out of my pocket, I turn on the flashlight and hold it up high in front of me as I search out the areas the streetlights don't cover. Cain does the same, and the two of us spread out to look down alleys and duck into doorways, looking for any sign of her.

"Over here!" Cain calls out, just as I'm beginning to give up hope. I can see fuck all with this flashlight, and in the dark, it's next to impossible to discern if there's blood or anything that would give me a clue whether Red is alive and unharmed.

Hurrying over to the alley he's in, we both stand and gape down at the dead man at our feet. His eyes stare unseeingly up at us while his blood crusts on his skin and coagulates in the pool surrounding him.

"An Antonelli," I note, taking in his out-of-place suit. Cain grunts his agreement while I shine the flashlight further down the alley, simultaneously hoping and dreading spotting Red within its circumference of light.

Before Cain and I can do a more thorough search, my phone rings in my hand. "What?" I snap, bringing it to my ear.

"Any sign of her?" Enzo's growl is laced with frustration.

"We've found her bike."

"And you didn't think to fucking call us?"

"I was just about to," I snap, lying through my teeth. The last fucking thing on my mind was those two.

"Where?"

I hesitate for a second before begrudgingly relaying the street name.

"Is she there?"

"Doesn't appear to be. We found one of your men, though."

"Send me a picture."

He hangs up before I can tell him I'm not his fucking lackey. Cursing him out under my breath, I stomp over to the dead guy and snap a photo, *for Red*. Not because that asshole told me to. I'm purely doing this to help Red.

Sending it to the group chat, I join Cain in our search of the alley. Now that we've narrowed it down to this area, we do a much more thorough inspection. There's so much blood around the body that it's impossible to discern what's his and what isn't, but as we move further away, a trail becomes apparent, and like bloodhounds, we follow. With every step, I picture what Red must have gone through. Images of her being thrown from her bike and accosted by that piece of Antonelli scum assault my mind. Yet, he's dead, and she's not here, so she must have escaped. Even battered and probably injured, she still got the upper hand on him, and pride swells within me. She's so fucking strong. She always says it's thanks to Luc. That he's the one who made her strong, but it's all her. Her inner strength, her resilience. Her ability to face impossible odds and not crumble beneath them.

Cain slides his gun out of the back of his jeans as we approach a steel door, and I follow suit. We both share a look when we spot a semi-bloody handprint wrapped around the frame, and hopeful anxiousness churns in my gut, wanting to find Red on the other side of this door, yet concerned about the state we might find her in. The dead scumbag behind me is her handiwork, but what did that kill cost her? She would already have been worse for wear—if not seriously hurt—after being thrown from her bike to only then having to fight off that shitstain. At the very least, it would have drained whatever energy she had remaining.

Reaching out, Cain wedges his fingers into the small gap and steps to the side. On my signal, he yanks open the door, and I storm in, arms locked in front of me with my finger on the trigger.

"Clear."

"Same," Cain states, standing at my back.

Easing my finger off the trigger, I lower my weapon, but I don't put it away as I continue to critically analyze the empty space. There are a few blood smears on the ground and lower wall close to the door, most likely where Red's energy finally gave out after making it to relative safety, out of sight from any prying eyes.

Darting my eyes around the surrounding space, my brows scrunch. There's no further sign of her. No indication that she got up again or where she went next. It's like she dropped to the ground then disappeared.

"Goddammit," I hiss, lifting my head to meet Cain's incensed gaze. "The blood must have dried." It means we can't track her, but it also means no one else can either, which is something.

Both Cain and I spin as the door creaks open, our weapons raised as Enzo and Dante storm in, faces of fury and determination. "Where is she?" Dante growls, his eyes darting around the darkened space in search of her.

"Gone." I jut my chin toward the smears of blood; the last traces that Red was ever here. "Looks like she killed the guy in the alley then stumbled in here, but the trail goes cold after that."

Dante's nostrils flare, the only sign that he's feeling anything at all. The rest of his posture is frozen in stone, his face an impassive mask. Anyone would think he didn't give a shit. Hell, if it weren't for the way he blew into the house earlier like a Gail Force wind, ready to tear apart anyone who stood in his path, *I'd* think he didn't care. I'm still not convinced *care* is the right word. Not so sure that it's because he cares for Red, that he's so adamant about getting her back, or if it's possession that's driving his actions. His words in the kitchen earlier make it clear that whatever fixation he has with Red is unhealthy. I do not doubt that if Red wanted nothing to do with him, he'd make it impossible for her to leave. Of course, Cain and I would happily make him permanently disappear, but, for now at least, Red seems to want him around. Still, his preoccupation with *my* woman has me wary, and I'm sure as fuck going to be keeping a close eye on him.

On the other hand, Enzo's emotions are there for me to read clearly. His shoulders droop, his expression shattered as he stares at the blood on the floor. Almost as though he's not really seeing it, but picturing Red herself, slumped against the wall, hurt and exhausted. It only lasts a brief moment before he re-erects his walls, and when he lifts his head to face us, that broken expression is replaced with one that's much sharper, more deadly. Fire burns in his eyes, determined grit carved into the hard lines of his face. He's the spitting image of a true Antonelli, but instead of the usual sneer of disgust that would curl my lip, his toughened resolve bolsters my confidence that we *will* find her.

"He's one of Giovanni's scouts. Probably has them all over the city searching for us. This guy just got lucky—or unlucky, I guess."

I grit my teeth, flicking my glare to Dante. "Thought you had men that were loyal to you?" That's what Red had said, anyway. "Couldn't they have kept you informed of this so Red could have avoided them?"

Dante's lip lifts in a snarl, but no sound comes out. "My men are currently being iced out. My father isn't taking any chances of a leak, but we all knew his first move would be to send out scouts." Pinning Cain in his bottomless eyes, he bites out, "*You're* the reason she was on the road at all. If you hadn't thrown a fucking hissy fit in the tunnels."

"Me?" Cain snarls, taking a menacing step forward. "You're the ones that insisted Red come see you."

With his own step forward, Dante meets Cain, the two of them standing an arms-width apart. "You're the ones who let her leave without an escort, without ensuring she would arrive safely, without even fucking bothering to check in with her."

The nearly imperceptible widening of Cain's eyes is the only sign that Dante's strike has hit its intended target, and in a flash of rage, the fist clenched at his side comes up, swinging into Dante's cheek and landing with a resonating crack.

"You shouldn't even be a part of this fucking equation!" Cain roars. "Neither of you should. You were a fucking job, but you just couldn't leave her well enough alone, could you?" he sneers, his churning gaze a chaotic storm of uncontrollable emotions boring into Dante. "You just had to fucking have her."

Dante's features are like granite. There isn't even a red mark on his cheek from Cain's punch, like he's made of actual fucking stone. When he speaks, his tone is ice-cold and deadly. "She was mine long before she was ever yours. Before you even knew who she was. That she existed. The only reason either of you is still breathing is because that's what she wants, but make no mistake, I'd happily take her away from both of you. Hide her somewhere neither of you will ever find her and watch from afar as you drive yourselves insane searching for her. I already warned you, and I don't care if Sawyer has feelings for you. I will fucking end you with a smile on my face and fuck her until she forgets you ever existed."

Cain lunges, going for another swing at Dante's face. My own fists are crying out to feel the smack of his skin beneath them at the thought of him keeping Red from us. I don't give a shit if she was theirs first or not. She's fucking *ours* now. I've lost too much, survived too much, endured too much, all in the name of finding her. I sure as hell won't let anyone—and I mean, fucking *anyone*—take her from me now. Not Dante. Not Giovanni. No one.

Dante blocks Cain's punch, but before he can deliver one of his own, Enzo grabs the back of Cain's jacket and throws him backward. "ENOUGH!" he yells, his voice echoing around the large, empty warehouse. He steps between the two of them, glaring first at Cain before rounding on Dante.

"None of this is helpful. Sawyer isn't fucking here, and no matter how much we all hate each other, we need to come up with a plan to fucking find her."

Taking a deep inhale, I slowly unclench my fists. "He's right. We can kill each other later, but for now, we need to find Red. You saw the bike out there. There's no way she's not hurt, and if Giovanni's men are searching the streets for us, then it's only a matter of time until one of them finds her. The race is on and it's us or them. I don't know about you, but I sure as hell plan on finding her before they do."

two

"She's not fucking here," I bite out, spinning on my heel as I run my hand through my hair in frustration. After Cain and Dante's blowout, none of us could agree on who would search where, so with Cain and Oliver in one car and me and Dante in the other, we ended up racing each other over here, to Sawyer's apartment.

Other than the clubhouse, or Cain's house, this is the only other place she could be. If she is injured—which, based on the carnage left behind at the scene of her crash, she must be—then logic dictates that she should be at one of these three locations, and yet She's. Not. Fucking. Here. Nor has Cain heard from any of his men regarding her whereabouts. So where the hell is she?

There's barely enough space for the four of us in this apartment, and I feel like I'm suffocating with all of them taking up what little air is in the room as Cain emerges from where he was searching her bedroom, and Dante appears in the doorway of Luc's.

"Then where the fuck is she?" Cain growls. His anger from earlier has yet to simmer down. If anything, it's only getting worse, and he's not the only one. I can see Dante's patience wearing thin, along with my own. Even Oliver, who appears to have the best control over his emotions out of all of us, is getting frustrated.

"Are you sure none of your men have seen her?" I question, because I can't think of anywhere else she could be. I have alarms on the perimeter of my apartment that I gave her the address of, but no matter how many times I check them, none of them have gone off, so she's not there. And she's not here. Or at the clubhouse or Cain's house. So where does that leave? Worry gnaws on my insides. What are we missing?

"Yes, I'm fucking sure," Cain snaps, one wrong word away from going apeshit. "I don't know how you Antonellis run things, but I can trust my men to inform me as soon as they have any updates."

"There must be somewhere else she'd go." Dante pins Cain and Oliver with an expectant look, and when the two of them share a clueless glance, he shakes his head in disappointment.

Cain's fists clench dangerously. He barely manages to hold himself back, snarling out, "Fuck this, we're going back to the house. We'll regroup and go from there."

"We're going with you."

Cain spins to face me, his green eyes vibrant with the threat of destruction. "Like fuck you are." He takes one menacing step toward me. "You're not going anywhere near my house or my sister. I'd put a bullet through your fucking skull before I let that happen."

I roll my eyes at his dramatics. His threats and posturing might make lesser men cower and obey, but not me. He'll have to try a hell of a lot harder than that. Instead of backing down, I step forward, jutting out my chin. "Do it," I coax. "Shoot me."

His steps falter, his eyes flashing with surprise. "Go on," I encourage when he makes no further effort to follow through with his threat. "I said, shoot me. Your sister's already said she's fine with us being in your house, so you can stop throwing that excuse at us. You know we didn't fucking touch her, that we didn't fucking know she was in that building, and in case you fucking missed it, we threw our entire goddamn lives away that night to save her, to help you out, to rescue Luc." The words spill out of me as anger stokes along the edges of my soul, caressing it and sparking it to life. "You got your sister back, and you got vengeance on the man who kept her captive, but we lost fucking *everything*. Our family, friends, job, houses. Every. Fucking. Thing. All that's left is Sawyer, and I don't give a shit what you dictate or demand, I'm not fucking leaving until she's back safe and sound."

Tension spills into the air, the weight of my words swirling with the hostile aggression radiating off all of us. The atmosphere is so thick, you could strike a match and send the whole room up in flames. One wrong word. One wrong move. That's all it would take.

Cain and I lock eyes. He doesn't reach for his gun, but he doesn't back down either.

After a long moment where no one moves, Dante's brisk voice eventually breaks through the tension. "You're not going to fucking pull your gun, so can we get the hell out of here already?"

After a grunted response from Cain, he storms past me and out of the apartment. Oliver flicks a glance between Dante and me, keeping whatever he's thinking carefully hidden before he stalks after Cain.

When we're alone, I rub my eyes, trying to fight off the headache beating a steady rhythm behind them. This day might just be the day that kills me. *They* might just be the thing that kills me.

"They're infuriating," Dante grumbles, making me snort.

"You're telling me. I thought you were difficult to deal with, but he's on a whole other level."

Dante pins me with such a menacing glower, you'd think I'd just stabbed him through the heart instead of making a joke at his expense.

With a smirk still tugging on one side of my lips, I jerk my head toward the door. "We better go before they decide to slash our tires just so we can't follow them."

Dante's face is filled with disdain as I turn on my heel and head for the exit.

"I still vote that we kill them," he grumbles.

I sigh. That's at least the fourth time today he's brought that up—an option that isn't actually an option.

"I've already told you we can't." He knows this, despite his volatile threat to Cain earlier. "Sawyer would never forgive you."

He grumbles something under his breath that I can't quite hear, but it sounds a lot like *she'd get over it, eventually.*

I shake my head, refusing to even acknowledge that or his stubbornness because, no, I don't think she would get over it, no matter how much time he gave her. I just have to see the way she lights up when she's around them to know that to be true. Killing one or both of them would kill a part of her too, and even though he may want to—hell, I want to—neither one of us would willingly kill any part of Sawyer, even if that means the two insufferable assholes have to keep breathing.

The journey back to Cain's house is mostly silent. We've been searching the city all night, and the pale pink of dawn is just brightening the sky. Store owners are pulling up shutters and opening shop fronts as we drive past, delivery men dropping off goods, and men and women stumbling home from a night out.

All around us, the world goes on, people going about their lives like nothing is out of place. Because nothing is out of place in their world. Meanwhile, mine feels like it's been torn apart. My outburst earlier only opened up the festering wound I've been keeping carefully sealed, but now the bandage won't go back on and that wound is leaking; the feelings pouring out in a constant stream that shows no signs of slowing down or stopping.

Fear is the primary emotion. Fear of ending up like my father. Fear that I am exactly what Giovanni has always said I am—a traitor, disloyal, not to be trusted. Fear for Sawyer, for what she might be suffering through right now, and fear of leaving her behind if something were to happen to me. Fear for how we're going to get out of this situation unscathed.

Fear.

So. Much. Fear.

It eats away at my insides like an infection, corroding them and turning them black, until all I can feel is the raw agony of fear pulsing with every beat of my heart, the tunes in sync, intrinsically tied together as though one will never exist without the other.

As we pull up outside Cain's house, I shove every inch of that fear deep down, slamming a lid on the box and locking it securely. Fear is a weakness, one I refuse to show in front of these assholes or their gang. As far as I'm concerned, they are still our enemies, and enemies thrive off of weaknesses. They deliberately poke holes in your armor, toying and exacerbating you until those weaknesses come to light. They already know my greatest weakness—Sawyer. I won't give them another.

Cain throws our car a disgusted glance before he marches up the front path, Oliver beside him. Dante and I are only a few steps behind as we climb out of the car and follow them onto the front porch. The screen door creaks on its hinges, alerting everyone inside to our presence as Cain yanks it open and steps into the house, not offering so much as an invitation over his shoulder, even though I wasn't expecting one. A *fuck off* would be more appropriate, but either way, we're coming in, and we won't be leaving until Sawyer is back.

One man I recognize from the night we rescued Luc is already standing in the hall, giving a small nod in greeting to Cain and Oliver as they enter before flicking his gaze over their shoulders to Dante and me. His shoulders stiffen, but he doesn't question our arrival.

I'm too busy assessing this guy, watching closely to make sure Cain doesn't give him some sort of secret signal to put a bullet through our skulls, that I don't realize Luc has appeared until he speaks up.

"Did you find my sister?" His voice is full of the optimistic hope of youthfulness, one that will surely fade in another year or two. I'm surprised it hasn't already, especially given what he's endured at Santos' and Giovanni's hands.

All I can see around Cain's broad frame is the side of his head, showing off a multitude of discolored bruises in various shades of healing and a long gash running from his temple to his ear. My eyes narrow, my teeth gritting in anger. No kid should have to endure what he did. Dante and I have both been there—both been at the wrong end of their torture. We wouldn't wish it on anyone, least of all a kid—one Sawyer has fought her whole damn life to protect. If none of us had coveted Sawyer the way we did, he never would have ended up with the sharp end of Santos' blade carving into his skin. If only we could have let her go, but I know that was never an option. It's just such a shame that Luc had to pay the price for our obsession. If I could, I'd have taken his pain as my own. I'd have sat in that chair and endured Santos' brutal punishment in exchange for him.

If I could have.

But *could-have*s and *what-ifs* change nothing.

I flick my gaze up, finding the guy from before still staring at me, his eyes narrowed as he studies my expression. I quickly wipe whatever he might have read from my face and glare at him in warning. He just stares blankly back, unperturbed by my glower.

Missing Cain or Oliver's response, I zone back into the conversation as Luc glances over Cain's shoulder, spotting Dante and me behind him. His face immediately scrunches up in heated anger. "What the hell are they doing here?" he snarls, sounding like a miniature Cain. *Oh, great, just what the world needs—one more surly bastard who hates us.*

"Fuck if I know," Cain grunts out before side-stepping the kid and heading toward the back of the house.

"We're looking for Sawyer," I state, as though it should be obvious. There's no other fucking reason we'd be in this dump. This definitely isn't a social call. I'd sooner take a knife to my gut than chat over beer and pizza with any of these assholes. Ugh, they probably drink that piss-tasting whiskey, too. No fucking class.

My words only seem to rile Luc up more, his fists clenching at his side as his nostrils flare. "So you can steal her away again? Force her to bend to your will and mold her into whatever you want? Newsflash, she won't fucking bend. Sawyer doesn't break—not for anyone."

I have to squash the side of my lip that wants to hitch up. My amusement at the astute assessment of his sister will only piss him off further.

"It's not—"

"She's my wife," Dante bites out, speaking over the top of me. I immediately want to smack him over the head. *Seriously, man, if you won't use your fucking words, then don't talk at all.* I see the unadulterated anger that flashes through Luc's eyes, and I've no doubt that if he had a weapon handy, he'd be reaching for it. Not that I could blame him, what with the sheer tone of ownership in Dante's voice.

"She only married you because of me!" Despite the angry yell of Luc's voice, it cracks over the words, giving away his genuine emotions bubbling underneath, like a pot on the stove. All it would take is for someone to turn up the heat a fraction or two and he'd boil over, burning everyone and everything in his vicinity.

"I saw the way you were with her in that church," he sneers, regaining his composure. "Manhandling her down the aisle. And again at that dinner. The way you talked over her and kept trying to put her in her place. The way you'd glower at her every time she spoke. Sawyer's not some puppet whose strings you can pull and manipulate to do your bidding, to behave how *you* want. She only simpered to you because of me, but now she no longer has to. She's going to rip your balls off and force-feed them down your throat." He finishes his threat with a confident smirk, and I have to hand it to him, the kid has balls to face off against Dante and threaten him like that. Many men wouldn't even dare look him in the eye, never mind deliver such a forceful promise.

A tense moment passes as Oliver, the other guy, and I wait to see how Dante will respond. He's not known for acting rationally in the face of a threat, but this isn't some lowlife scum or traitor giving him blowback. It's Sawyer's brother, and some part of him seems to know he can't just snap his hand out and break his neck.

Eventually, a noise that resembles some sort of laugh bubbles up the back of Dante's throat, escaping through his lips. "That is definitely not what she's going to be doing with my balls."

Fucking hell. I almost wish he had tried to snap Luc's neck. That would be much easier to handle than the look of absolute shock and horror on Luc's face right now. I dart a glance toward Oliver, finding him standing to the side with his arms across his chest, watching on with an amused smirk. I'm glad someone is finding this comical. Meanwhile, I'm just watching the hole Dante is digging us into getting deeper and deeper.

Luc's lips part then close as he struggles to come up with some sort of response. I take the opportunity while he's floundering to stop things from deteriorating further. "You're right, kid. Sawyer's no push-over. She's fiercely strong and frustratingly independent. She doesn't trust easily, especially when it comes to entrusting others with the one person she cares about the most. Yet, she trusted us to help get you out, so that must say something, right? She trusted us enough to let us in on her nighttime activities." Luc's eyes widen at my cryptic admission. Obviously, Oliver knows about Sawyer's double-life as a vigilante, but I don't know if any of Cain's men do, which is why I didn't spell it out in black and white. "Don't you think she'd have tried to kill us by now if she didn't trust us?"

I can see the wheels churning behind his eyes as he mulls over my words, distrust still clear to see on his face. "Well, *I* don't trust you."

Nodding my head, I state, "I wouldn't expect anything less, but just so you know, you will eventually come to trust us." He raises a brow at my confidence. "'Cause the three of us, we have more than just our love for Sawyer in common."

His face scrunches in confusion. "What?"

I lean in, lowering my voice. This confession is for Luc, not for Oliver's prying ears.

"We all survived at Giovanni's and Santos' hands. Dante and I have both been in your shoes." I latch onto his widened gaze, searching for the tells. "We endured the mental manipulation, the physical suffering, the beatings, the cattle prods." And there it is, the flash of recognition. The acknowledgment, the surprise, the shudder of fear. "We endured, we survived, we came out stronger because of it. You wanna know what sets Dante and me apart from all the other Antonellis? It's that. It's the fact that neither of them broke us, no matter how hard they tried. The three of us may be a little bent, a tad twisted up inside and well past the line of redemption, but we're far from broken."

I see it, the moment he latches onto my words, an anxious hope in his eyes. I see the silent question. "It's all in the eyes," I explain. "I know broken when I see it. You know it too. I'm sure you've seen it often enough in the people of this town who have given up and succumbed to the miserable existence they're forced to bear instead of demanding something more. They've given up. Society has beaten them down so frequently that they can barely lift their heads off the ground to see the sky above."

"And how do you know I'm not like them?"

"Because I see the fight burning bright inside you. The forest fire raging. If anything, I bet it's only building in intensity. Your time with Santos struck the match, but now it has been set to kindling and left to blaze. Not only are you far from broken, but you're no longer complacent in the life you once had. You're demanding more, willing to fight back and stand up for the injustice done, not only to you but to everyone around you."

He holds my gaze, searching, and I let him. I let him see every damaged part of me, every part that Santos and Giovanni tried to destroy, but I also let him see that I will fight for Sawyer, that I will fight for us. That I'd fight for him too. I let him see the darkness that lives within and the light in the form of Sawyer, whose presence stops me from stepping into that darkness and never returning.

I can feel the weight of everyone's eyes on us, our whispered conversation too low for anyone other than Dante to hear. I straighten my spine when Luc steps away, still holding his gaze.

"Alright," he relents with a nod, "but I still don't trust you."

One side of my lip lifts in a smile, and I nod back, a silent agreement between us. If it's trust he wants, it's trust I'll give him.

His gaze flicks to Dante, narrowing in suspicion. Evidently, my speech did nothing to soften Luc toward him. I guess Dante will have to earn his trust all on his own. When Luc steps away, moving back into the living room, I lift my eyes to meet Oliver's. Something akin to impressed—perhaps, even respect—reflects back at me. While I definitely don't need his respect, I guess I'll take it. Who knew getting Luc to warm up to us was the key to getting the gangsters to stop seeing us as the enemy?

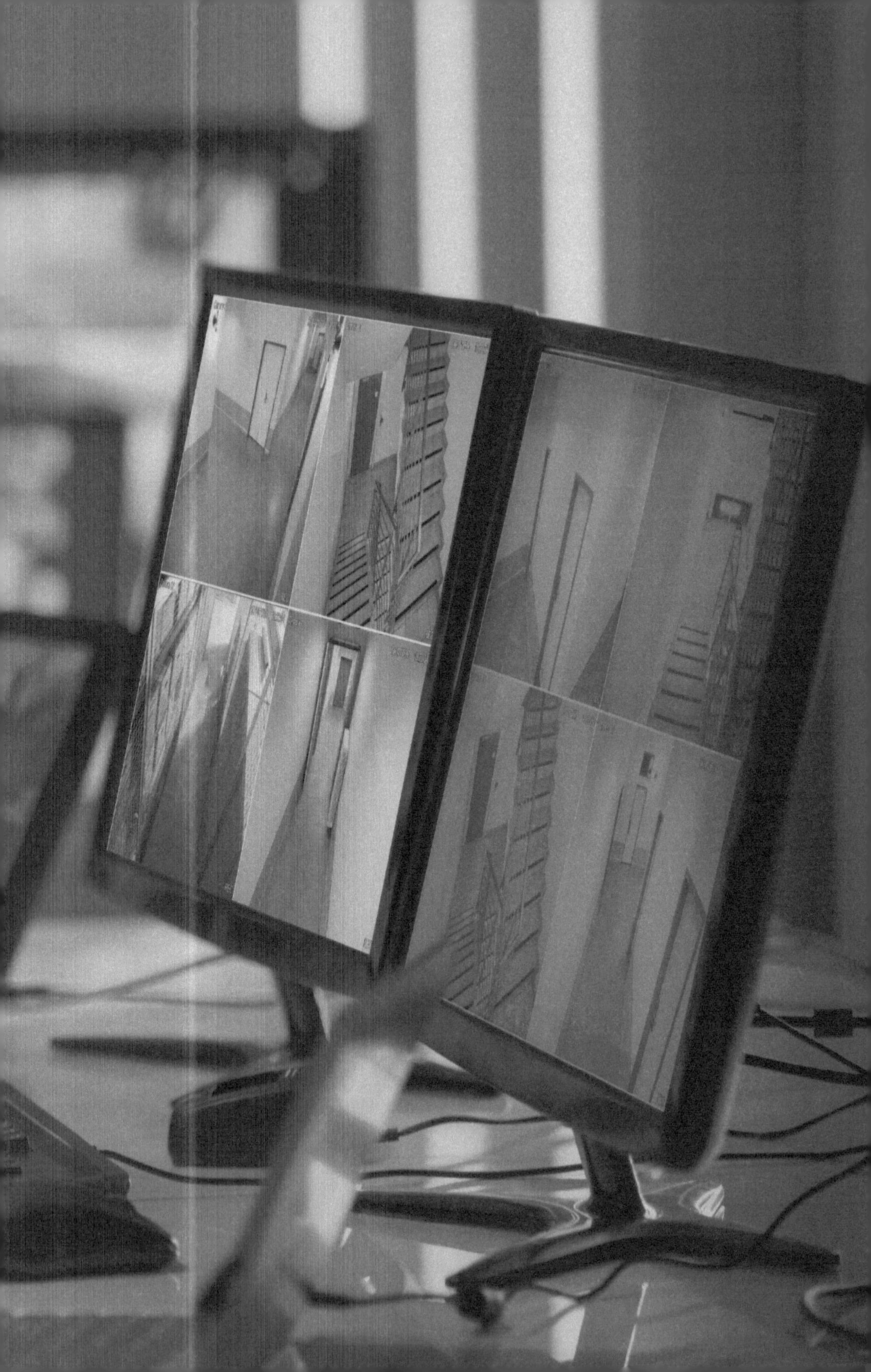

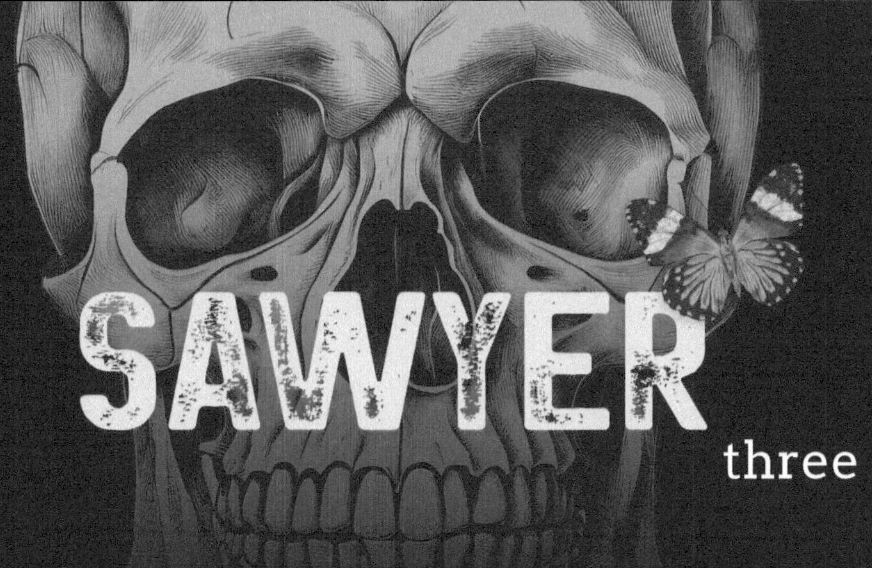

The world comes back to me slowly and unpleasantly. Like full body pins and needles that start at my fingers and toes and slowly crawl up my arms and legs until it encompasses my core. At the same time, it feels like something heavy is crushing my head, making it impossible to think or even open my eyes.

With achingly slow movements, I swim toward the surface of my mind, trying to put the pieces together and figure out where I am and what happened. With every inch closer to the light, I can feel the pieces slotting together, but the complete picture hangs just out of my grasp, taunting me.

I remember I was going to see Dante and Enzo. I was on my bike, the wind in my hair, the asphalt flying past beneath me... until it wasn't. Until it came up to meet me, or I fell to meet it.

A crash. I crashed.

Blood. The memory of so much blood bubbles up to the forefront of my mind. Oh, god, was I badly hurt? Is that what's happening now—I'm slowly bleeding out on the street? I don't feel the sharp dig of the asphalt in my back, but that doesn't necessarily mean anything. It's difficult to feel much of anything over the stabbing pain consuming my body, gnawing on it like maggots on a corpse.

Terror bubbles up the back of my throat, and in a moment of blinding pain, I wrench my eyes open with a gurgled whimper. Black. Everything above me is black. Not even the blinking of a star.

"About fucking time you woke up."

The voice scrapes against my brain like teeth against metal, and one inch at a time, I turn my head toward the speaker, even as the drums in my head kick up a riot.

I wince as bright light assaults my eyeballs, casting the man in shadow. Squinting until my eyesight adjusts, I can see the outline of a man sitting in front of multiple computer screens, the tap-tap-tap of his fingers against the keyboard beating in time to the pulse thumping behind my eyes. I'm surprised I didn't register the noise as soon as I woke up.

I lick my chapped lips, groaning as I lift my head, casting a glance down my body. More memories rise to the surface as I notice the blood caking my skin, this time of a bright metal blade slashing through skin, the look of surprise and horror as red ribbons started spurting from his neck. From the throat of an Antonelli.

The puzzle pieces slide together as I catalog what injuries I can see. Road rash is visible through the ripped fabric of my jeans, large chunks of denim missing from my thigh to my ankle on my left side, where I must have slid across the road, and the top I was wearing is nothing but scraps now, providing zero modesty. The rest of the skin I can see is swollen and already darkening, making me look like one giant, jean-wearing bruise.

Patches of white gauze have been taped to my skin in areas where I can only imagine the damage is worse, but as I mentally search for any internal damage, I sigh a breath of relief. Everything hurts like a bitch, but nothing feels broken.

"How long have I been out?" I croak, my voice raspy with disuse and dehydration as I drop my head back onto the pillow beneath me, my eyes drooping shut as a wave of exhaustion washes over me.

"Nearly two days."

My eyes snap open. "Two days?" Pulling on strength I didn't know I had, I push myself upright, biting back a groan of pain. *Fuck, everything hurts.* Sweat dots my forehead and coats my back by the time I'm sitting on the edge of the bed, and my head swims from the exertion.

"Yeah, you probably shouldn't be doing that."

Ignoring him, I tighten my grip on the edge of the mattress until the world is no longer tilted on its axis and my stomach doesn't churn with violent promise. "How did I get here?" I dare to ask when the wave of nausea rolls off of me.

"You set my perimeter alarm off when you entered the building."

I rub at my pounding temples as I try to remember. "It was your building?" I hadn't even realized what part of the city I was in. Too busy with my destination to take a walk down memory lane while I raced through the streets. "Huh, I guess that was lucky."

He makes a noncommittal noise at the back of his throat, implying he doesn't quite agree. I squash a small smile as I gather the energy I need to push up to my feet. The world spins again, but I plant my feet and wait for it to subside. When it finally does, I take a cautious step forward. My legs shake and everything screams in pain, but I don't go crashing to the ground, so I take another step, slowly crossing over to the bank of computer screens.

Every step causes my heart to hammer harder against my chest and sweat to gather along my spine, making the remains of my top stick to my skin, nonetheless I keep going. He minimizes the window on several monitors as I approach, but I'm too focused on not keeling over to pay attention to whatever illegal shit he's doing. I'm breathing heavily by the time I lean an arm on the large desk, my legs trembling.

"Fucking hell, have a seat before you pass out. I'm not lifting you off the fucking floor again." He wheels a spare computer chair toward me, and I all but collapse into it, grasping the edge of the table so my weight doesn't send it wheeling backward.

He immediately returns to whatever he's doing on the computer, and I just sit and watch as I gain control of my breathing. Whatever he's doing means nothing to me. I can't even begin to make heads or tails of it as I watch him form string after string of what looks to be a random collection of letters, numbers, and symbols.

"What ya doing?"

He glances at me out of the corner of his eye, his fingers never ceasing their incessant tapping as they fly furiously over the keyboard. "None of your business."

"Rude much," I huff out.

Another few moments pass, where I sit and watch him, before I cast my eyes over the other screens. It's more computer techy stuff that means nothing to me.

"Who's Nomad?" I ask, the only word that's repeated on multiple screens.

With a frustrated huff, he presses a button and all the screens go dark. Spinning to face me, only the dim glow from the monitors' backlight provides any illumination, casting shadows along one side of his cleanly shaven face. I can't make out the color of his eyes, and I've never seen them in enough light to know, but his chin-length blonde strands fall forward to cover his face before he quickly brushes them back out of the way.

His tongue flicks out to play with the piercing on his lower lip, the thin metal loop matching the one in his pale eyebrow. He's also got a plug in his ear and I can see the beginnings of a tattoo peeking out from the neckline of his Henley. His eyebrows furrow, his lips pursed as he glowers at me, the sharp edges of his jaw, half shaded in darkness, making him appear dangerous. "What do you want?"

I smile serenely at him—or as serenely as someone covered in someone else's blood can. "A phone."

"No."

A surprised noise escapes my lips. "What do you mean, no? You just told me I've been here for two days. People will be looking for me."

"They are."

I splutter. "They are? How do you know that?"

"They already came by."

All I can do is gape at him as he relaxes back in his chair, watching me with a small smile playing on his lips like he finds my reaction amusing.

"And what, you didn't think to introduce yourself and let them know I'm fine?"

"Introductions aren't my forte." I'd roll my eyes if it wasn't likely to worsen my headache. Seriously, what the fuck does that even mean? He gives a casual shrug of his shoulders. "Besides, it seemed like they had some shit to work out. Thought I'd give them some time to work it out amongst themselves."

"I don't..." I can feel a new headache starting up, exhaustion tugging on my already weary body. "What does that even mean?"

Spinning back to his computer, he opens a folder, clicks on a video file, and a second later it plays, showing me a bird's-eye-view of the ground floor, where I passed out after killing that Antonelli bastard. A tightness forms in my chest as Oliver and Cain come storming in, and I have to stop myself from reaching out and touching the screen. I can see the concern buried in the tight lines around their eyes and in the tense set of their shoulders as they inspect the space and notice the blood smeared on the floor from where I all but collapsed.

They spin as the door opens and Enzo and Dante join them. My heart jumps in my chest, banging against my ribs as though it's trying to break free. As I watch, I can see the rising tensions, the hostility that leaches into the air as Dante and Cain turn to face each other, harsh words that I can't hear being said.

I lean forward, squinting as I try to read their lips. "What are they saying?"

He fiddles with a couple of buttons before sound pours out of the speakers. Cain's words drip with fury, stabbing me like a red-hot poker over and over. "You shouldn't even be a part of this fucking equation! Neither of you should. You were a fucking job, but you just couldn't leave her well enough alone, could you? You just had to fucking have her."

My chest constricts painfully, guilt damn near drowning me as Cain lets all that anger over this situation pour out. Anger he's never once directed at me, even though this is all my fault.

Where Cain is piping hot, a gasket ready to blow, Dante is the avalanche you never see coming. His glacial tone strikes like an icicle piercing my heart.

"She was mine long before she was ever yours. Before you even knew who she was. That she existed. The only reason either of you is still breathing is because that's what she wants, but make no mistake, I'd happily take her away from both of you. Hide her somewhere neither of you will ever find her and watch from afar as you drive yourselves insane searching for her. I already warned you, I don't care if Sawyer has feelings for you. I will fucking end you with a smile on my face and fuck her until she forgets you ever existed."

Watching the two of them go head-to-head, their true feelings displayed for the other to see—no one disguising how they really feel for my benefit—makes it so goddamn clear how naïve and foolish I've been, thinking that with some time and a little adjusting, they could come to tolerate one another. I was counting on Dante's obsession, and Cain and Oliver's love to be enough, but that was foolishly optimistic of me. It's painfully obvious right now that neither my Rejects nor my mafia men will ever agree to get along. They will never be able to be in the other's presence without throwing hateful glares or spiteful words at the other, and no matter how much I may wish that they would, they will never lay down their weapons and declare peace with the other.

With my shoulders slumped in defeat, I turn away from the screen, unable to watch anymore. He closes out of the video and returns to whatever he was working on while I stew in my thoughts, trying to figure out where the hell we go from here.

I still firmly believe we all need to work together. Now more than ever, we need one another, with Giovanni trying to hunt us down and pick us off one by one. He won't stop until we're all tortured, dead, and dumped in the river as fish food, and yet, I have no idea *how* to get everyone to work together. If they can't even put their differences aside to help find me, how will they do it for Black Creek?

"You're a terrible host," I remark when my stomach rumbles for the third time. "You haven't even bothered to feed me."

He turns slightly to face me, quirking a brow. "You have arms and legs."

I huff out a breath, but I don't make a move to get up. Honestly, even the thought of trying to move has what little energy I've regained zapping straight out of me. "I don't even know your name."

"You don't need to know my name."

"We're friends. Friends are supposed to know each other's names."

"We're not friends."

"We're as close to being friends as one gets in Black Creek," I counter. It's the truth. Sure, our first encounter was essentially him telling me to fuck off and not come back, and our second encounter didn't go much better. When I asked him to get me new IDs for Hadley, and he again told me to fuck off and not come back. But, you see, there's a recurring pattern—he tells me to fuck off and not come back, and then I inevitably come back—and that only happens with friendships. At least, that's what I've decided. We seem to keep crossing paths—or at least, I keep crossing his path—so striking up a friendship just makes good sense.

I hold out my hand with a friendly grin—that I'm fairly certain doesn't come across as friendly, what with the blood I can feel clogged in my pores. "I'm Red." He knows this already, but clean slate and all that.

His gaze drops to my outstretched hand, and I can see the cogs turning behind them. Eventually, he sighs, rolling his eyes before he lifts his head. "I'm not touching your hand. It's caked in filth and blood."

Unbothered, I shrug a shoulder, not breaking eye contact as I wait patiently. When he doesn't say anything further, I cock a brow expectantly and shift in my chair, getting more comfortable and making it apparent that I'll happily sit here all day. I won't—I've four furious, pissed-off men to go try to corral—but he doesn't need to know that.

With a purse of his lips, he says, "I'm Blue."

My brows dip as I search his face, looking for a sign that he's taking the piss. A twitch of his lips, a glint of humor in his eye. Anything. However, his expression remains blank, serious, and I can't tell if he's trying to pull one over on me or not.

"You're messing with me, right?" I say it in such a way that implies, of course, he's messing with me. Even so, I'm not sure.

Finally, there's a slight twitch of the left side of his upper lip. "Guess you'll never know, Red." Pushing to his feet, his tall, slim, six-foot frame blankets me in shadow before he strolls toward a small kitchenette. Pulling open the fridge, he grabs a couple of items before kicking the door shut with his foot and striding back over, dropping a sandwich and a bottle of water on the desk in front of me. "Now, eat, drink, and get the fuck out of my space."

THE TAXI DROPS ME OFF OUTSIDE THE REJECTS' CLUBHOUSE SINCE IT WAS the closest and that stingy asshole only gave me a twenty when he all but kicked me out of his super-secret, high-tech lair.

I probably look like a ninety-year-old as I slowly climb out of the back of the cab and hobble toward the perimeter. I don't even make it to the gate before several armed men wearing bulletproof vests step out of god-knows-where, rifles raised as they call out, "What do you want?"

I falter in my steps, surprised as I lift my head from where I was, carefully watching the sidewalk before remembering Giovanni is after all of us and Cain probably has everyone on high alert.

"Red? That you?" One of them calls out before speaking in a quieter voice into what I'm guessing is a Bluetooth headset.

"Yup, just me," I say, holding up a hand. "No need to shoot."

The man who spoke before lowers his weapon, ushering me toward the gate as he moves to unlock it. I notice the other men with him all keep their weapons raised, their eyes surveying the street with intense scrutiny. When the gate swings open, I quickly scurry through and the guy securely locks it behind me before we move with hurried footsteps toward the clubhouse.

"Cain and Oliver are on their way," he tells me in a low voice.

"They aren't here?" My tone is deflated, my shoulders slumping. All I want to do is wrap myself up in their arms, even though I know the slightest hug is going to hurt like a bitch.

He shakes his head. "You shouldn't be here either. It's not safe."

Before I can say anything else, he pulls open the door and rushes me inside. The door closes behind me, with him on the other side, and I'm doused in darkness. I have to blink several times, confused why it's so dark in here. As my eyes adjust, I realize the interior of the bar area looks nothing like it did before. Gone are the booths, chairs, and even the stage in the corner. All of it has been used to close up windows, allowing only small slits of light to slip through. I hear a scraping sound behind me, and I turn to find men pushing furniture back into place, barricading the door.

More men peek out of the slits between the wooden planks over the window, tips of rifles resting on the planks as they poke through, ready to be fired at the first sign of trouble. *Damn, I'm lucky no one blew my head off when I arrived.*

"Let's get you away from the windows, yeah?" I recognize Dax's voice as he places his hand on my back and directs me toward the hallway that leads to the back of the building.

"Luc," I gasp, the harsh reality of our situation bearing down on me. "Where is he?"

"He's safe. He's at Cain's, along with the other kids."

"Okay." That's all I'm capable of saying as my mind tries to catch up with every-thing. My entire body is still sore and sluggish, and even the quick walk to Cain's bedroom leaves me out of breath and sweaty.

"Stay here 'til he arrives, yeah?"

I mutter an agreement, already turning away before he closes the door. Eyeing the bed, my body begs me to lie down and rest, but I push past it as I walk into the bath-room. I haven't looked at myself in a mirror or showered since I was thrown from my bike, and the feeling of dried blood crusting on my skin is starting to make me itch in much the same way the glitter I plaster on my body at Strip Tease does. Except, unlike the pretty shimmering flecks that stick under my fingernails, my nails are clogged with blood, dirt, and grime every time I scratch at my skin.

The bright overhead light floods the room, making the clean white surfaces sparkle. As I step in front of the mirror, I pick up on the jarring contrast of my appearance. Where the bathroom is all shiny, marble countertops and glimmering glass, I look like I've been through hell. Blood covers most of my skin, along with bits of asphalt and whatever other filth I've gathered. Like my body, my face is a mishmash of bruises, scrapes and cuts, my hair a tangled mess, sticking out in every direction.

I take my time, assessing and cataloging each injury, even removing the bandages Blue—or whatever the fuck his actual name is—applied and inspecting the wounds for myself. When I'm done, I strip out of my torn, ruined clothing and step under the steaming hot spray of water in the shower. The heat makes my open wounds sting, but it's simply a reminder that I'm still alive. That I'm still here, fighting. I hang my head, letting the warm stream of water run down the back of my neck as I watch the blood and filth wash off my body and down the drain. Only when I can see the pale skin burnt raw from the hot water, do I get to work on untangling my hair and giving it a deep, scalp scraping scrub to remove every last fleck of what happened.

By the time I step out of the shower with a towel wrapped around my middle, I almost look human again. Almost look like myself—except for the slow, pained movements, the remaining scrapes and injuries, and the dark bags under my eyes shouting at me to rest more. *Just a little longer*, I promise them.

I know I left some of my clothes here, so I slip into the spare bedroom next door, the one I used to sleep in, and grab a fresh pair of jeans and a long-sleeve top to cover up the worst of my bruises and injuries. Finding a hair-tie, I towel dry my hair and tie it up in a top-knot, out of the way, before returning to Cain's room and finally allowing myself a moment to rest as I sag onto his sheets.

The smell of whiskey and leather assaults my senses, soothing my erratic pulse and beckoning me to lie down. I do, nuzzling the pillow as I inhale deeply. One blink. Two. Before my eyes don't open again and sleep carries me off to its restful slumber.

four

"What the fuck do you mean she's at the clubhouse?" I bark into the phone, aware of the weight of everyone's eyes on me. It's been two fucking days. Two fucking days since I last felt her lips on mine, felt her weight in my arms. Two fucking days since I last slept. Two fucking days of having to tolerate those Antonelli scumbags in *my* house.

Between the tense arguments, frequently tossed threats to murder one another, and the lack of sleep, I'm pretty sure I just imagined hearing that Red was at the clubhouse.

"I mean, she's at the clubhouse," Dax repeats. "She just showed up at the gate."

I can't for the life of me work out how the hell she got there without one of my men spotting her. Although, I equally can't work out where the fuck she's been these last two days. My men have scoured every goddamn inch of this city searching for her, to the point where we were all in agreement Giovanni must have her—one of the only things all four of us have actually agreed on.

We were in the middle of a heated argument about how the hell we were going to get her back, when my phone rang. Half expecting it to be news that the clubhouse was under attack, I answered it immediately, but this news is way better than anything I anticipated.

"Keep her safe. I'll be there as soon as I can."

I hang up, not waiting for a response. Everyone has already jumped into action around me, the maps and plans we were pouring over a moment ago forgotten at the news of Red's safety. Even though she's not in my arms yet, just the knowledge that she's not hidden in some secret bunker being tortured at Giovanni's hands has relief like nothing I've ever felt before flooding through my system, making me feel lighter than I have in days.

My eyes clash with Oliver's, the same hope flaring in his. "Red?"

I nod. "Yes."

"Is she..."

"I dunno," I admit, shaking my head. Dax didn't say what state she was in, but I imagine if it were bad he'd have said.

Without another word, we're striding toward the door, but echoing footsteps behind me have me spinning around.

"Like fucking hell we're not coming with you," Dante snarls before I can open my mouth to say exactly that. By this point, I've seen every shade of Dante's anger. Mostly, it's cold and deadly, but he looks ready to explode right now, and I know if I try to keep him away from her, he'll gladly knock me the fuck out before claiming her for himself. No fucking chance I'm going to let that happen.

For the first time, I don't bother arguing with him. Maybe it's my own urgency to get to Red as quick as possible, or maybe it's that look of desperation I can see in his eyes —like he's as impatient as I am to see her. For a split second, I see myself reflected in his russet brown depths. That longing, that hunger, that itching desire to touch the one woman who makes breathing worthwhile. Fuck, maybe Dante and I are just two sides of the same coin. Two men undeserving of love, but who found it anyway. And now that we have, neither one of us is willing to let it go.

"Fine," I grunt out, frowning in confusion as I turn my back on him and stride toward the front door. I shouldn't be finding fucking similarities between Dante and me. I shouldn't be finding something that makes him redeemable. That makes me not want to rip his fucking head off when he calls Red his wife and states with such authority that she's his, because she's not just his. She's *mine*. She's *Oliver's*. She's *ours*.

And yet, she's also *theirs*, and I don't have a fucking clue what to do with that.

"I expected more of a fight," Oliver states casually once we're inside the confines of the Cadillac.

"I just wanna get to Red."

"So, you're going to let them in the clubhouse?"

My hands clench around the leather steering wheel, hating the thought of having Antonelli scum inside *my* clubhouse. Fucking hell, what will the men think when they see them rocking up in their stupid fucking suits. Maybe I'll get lucky, and they'll shoot them on sight. Or, more likely, my men will think I've gone completely fucking insane when I tell them to lower their weapons.

"What the fuck should I do, O?" Although the words are spit out in an angry snarl, that anger isn't aimed at him. Which, thankfully, he seems to know.

"I'm not sure. Until now, only the kids and Marcus have seen them hanging around, but I don't know how the rest of the men will react. You know what some of them have suffered at Antonelli hands. They won't take well to us letting them stride right through the front door."

My lips purse, knowing he's right. What the hell am I meant to tell my men? How will they respect and look up to me as a leader when I order them to lower their weapons on their enemies—enemies who have irreparably damaged their families as they have mine?

Dante and Enzo may not have delivered the fatal blow—I honestly don't know— but whether or not they did is irrelevant. It's what they represent. When my men look at their suits, all they'll see is the enemy. The self-absorbed Antonelli family has done nothing but leave us to rot in the gutter of this city, waiting until we're at our lowest before storming in and reminding us that even when you think things can't get worse, they always can. You can *always* sink lower.

It was one thing to inform my men that we were working with them to infiltrate Giovanni's tower and get Luc back, but to openly invite them into the clubhouse… that's far more personal. The clubhouse is home to many of my men. It's their sanctum, their safe space, and I'm about to violate it by traipsing the enemy through the front door.

Showing up with them on my heels is as good as committing treason with regard to my men. Perhaps I should have fought for them to stay behind, but I knew simply by looking into Dante's eyes that it wasn't a fight I was going to win. And goddammit, I fucking understand that because if the shoe was on the other foot and he was telling me to stay behind, I'd sooner tell him to go fuck himself. Nothing and no one would keep me from Red.

"I don't know what I can do short of putting a bullet through their knees, which will only infuriate Red. No matter what I decide, someone will be pissed, and the problem is that I can empathize with both sides. I can understand why my men will be pissed—hell, *I'm* not exactly happy about it—but I can also relate to their desperation to see Red with their own eyes because it's exactly the same urgency that's pushing me to rush to her now."

"No matter what, your allegiances are going to be questioned. Even if you make it clear that they're just there for Red, the fact that we're all in a relationship with her is going to raise questions. The men will be suspicious and demand to know what side you're on."

"I'm on *their* side," I grind out in frustration. "I'll always be on their side. Most of those men came to me when they were at their lowest, when they'd just lost everything they held dear, and the only reason their lungs still held breath was because they demanded vengeance. I saw them broken and angry, and I promised them retribution. I'm not breaking that promise. I'd sooner die than turn my back on any one of them."

"I know that," Oliver reasons, his voice maintaining its calm serenity. I don't know how the hell he does that, how he remains so calm in the face of adversity, in the face of my anger, in the face of finding out our lives will never be free of those two Antonelli scum. I want to rage and storm until everything around me is broken and shattered and in chaos, mirroring the carnage inside me. "Even they know it," he continues. "They've witnessed the extent of your loyalty to them. Today won't undo all of that. You just need to make them see that your priorities haven't changed. That their vengeance is your vengeance. Redirect their anger to Giovanni. Remind them who the true source of their hatred is."

Oliver's words bolster me as I stop at the gate into the parking lot, waiting for one of my men to open it. When they do, I drive inside and park in a space, taking a steadying breath before pushing open the door and climbing out. Enzo's car follows, parking beside mine, and I swear I feel the questioning gazes of every one of my men as I round the hood and walk toward the clubhouse.

I can feel the pressure of fingers against triggers. Muscles pulled taut as my guys wait for a signal to shoot. The furrow of brows and exchanging of glances as they silently question why there are Antonellis on Reject property, why I'd bring them here.

Casting a glance over my shoulder, I notice Oliver has placed Dante and Enzo between us, a strategic move that will offer some reassurance to the men that even though I've allowed them to set foot inside our home, I don't trust them.

Dante and Enzo must sense the tension too, as their backs are ramrod straight, their keen eyes surveying the clubhouse and surrounding area as if sensing the present threat. Dropping my gaze, I notice that they have their hands open and relaxed at their sides, their fingers spread to show they aren't holding any weapons.

The front door is pulled open as we approach, and I greet Dax with a curt nod as I step into the darkened interior. The room is nothing like I remember, and a wave of regret crashes through me that this home me and my men slaved to build has to be turned into a security outpost. Of course, that's the point of a clubhouse, then again it still doesn't lessen the disappointment at seeing it.

Still, my men have done an excellent job of fortifying the place. Men line the front wall, keeping watch through slits in the windows, and I know more are watching the perimeter and are stationed at other lookouts throughout the building.

I haven't had the chance to stop by and check on the clubhouse myself. Between Evie's resurrection and Red's disappearance, I've been relying on Marcus, and men like Dax, who have been with me since the beginning, to keep things running smoothly. From what I can tell, everything was left in safe hands, but it's good that I stopped by. As their leader, I should be here. Hell, if it hadn't been for Evie and Red, I would be shoulder-to-shoulder with them right now, gun in hand, ready to fight.

Once Red is safely escorted back home, that's exactly what I'll be doing.

Turning my attention to Dax, I notice his focus is over my shoulder, at the two suit-wearing statues behind me. His face is pinched tight, and as I cast my gaze around the rest of the men, I notice similar expressions of unease.

"Red?" I grunt out, getting straight to the point. No civilized conversation can be had with all of them while these two are in the room. Their presence will only serve to escalate tensions further. Since it already feels like we're residing on the edge of a volcano ready to erupt, I have no desire to see what would happen if the top blew off and magma started spewing.

Dax's wary gaze flicks back to mine. "She's in your room."

With a nod, I move past him, hearing the sound of the others following and feeling everyone's eyes on us as I move toward the back hallway and down to my bedroom. With every step, my heart climbs higher, until it's lodged in the back of my throat. Excitement at seeing her again, at holding her in my arms and kissing her delectable lips, merges with questions of what state we'll find her in and what she's been through in these last couple of days.

By the time my hand wraps around the door handle, I'm a nervous, anxious mess. Glancing back at Oliver, I see those same emotions in his face, and not wanting to be separated for another moment, I push open the door.

My steps falter as I cross the threshold, finding my girl curled up on her side in the middle of the bed, sound asleep. Even the sound of scuffling behind me, as the others fight to be the next through the door, doesn't wake her from sleep.

All of us go still when we realize she's sleeping, and on silent footsteps, I walk around the bed until I can see her face. Black rings line her eyes, and a large bruise has formed on her temple, I'm guessing from when she was thrown from her bike, but other than that, I can't see any damage. Nothing life-threatening, at least.

Out of the corner of my eye, I notice Dante take a step toward her before pausing, as though he can't resist the pull but is afraid to get too close or touch her. Despite my own desire to wrap her in my arms, I stay frozen, watching as Dante takes another step in her direction. His face is glued to her, running up and down her body as if trying to assure himself she's alive and in one piece, and the way he moves is like he's being pulled on a string. Even if he tried to fight it, he'd still be drawn to her.

When he's close enough, he reaches out a hand except rather than touching her, his hand just hovers there, inches from her skin, like he's afraid his touch will do more harm than good. None of us can see the extent of her injuries, but we all saw her bike. There's no way she isn't battered and bruised underneath her clothing.

Eventually, he runs the back of his finger over her cheek, the only obvious area that's unharmed. Red leans into the touch before her eyes flutter, and she slowly turns her head toward him as her lids, still heavy with sleep, part.

"Dante?" Her voice is hoarse, but damn if it's not the best sound I've ever heard. Whether she's screaming bloody murder, crying out my name in the throws of passion, or like this, her voice is music to my ears, beckoning me. It wraps around my soul and reminds me of home—of happy memories, smiling faces, and joyous laughter. It reminds me of the positives of life, of what's important.

I'd long forgotten what it felt like to bathe in that warmth. In the warmth of infectious smiles and loving eyes. I've spent so long in the cold clutches of vengeance and grief that I'd become oblivious to what I'd lost. All these years, my life has been dedicated to avenging Evie. I was so focused on that one task that I failed to realize that I had lost everything too. After that day, there was no more laughter, no more easy smiles. No more warmth or love. Everything was bleak and cold, layered in pain and regret... until Red.

Even when she was evading me and driving me insane with her lies and refusal to tell me who the Reaper was, she still sparked something in me that I thought I'd lost. Every time I was around her, she would punch through the impenetrable cage wrapped around my heart without even meaning to. Every touch, every snarky remark, every heated glance was another blow to my armor, until I was riddled with holes and leaking emotions I'd long since forgotten how to feel.

At first, I hated her for it. I hated her for reminding me of what I once had—what I lost—but soon, I became addicted to those feelings, to her. I chased that warmth like a drug addict after their next fix until it became the only thing I wanted to feel.

I still want revenge, but it's no longer the predominant emotion. I'm no longer encased in stone and breathing for only one purpose. Now, I'm actually living. Instead of getting out of bed with the promise of vengeance on my tongue, I want to wake up to the taste of her. Red's as cynical as anyone else born and raised in Black Creek, but she emits a light that you can't help but be drawn to. Like a moth to a flame, she enraptured me, lured me in until all I could see was her fire. Her flame blinded me and singed my wings, but I have no intention of flying away. I'm wholeheartedly hers, have been from the first moment we met, and will be until I take my last breath.

"*Mia vita*." The reverence in Dante's tone takes me by surprise, and even though I don't know what he's said, he says it with such devotion and admiration that it's almost jarring. Gone are the harsh lines around his lips, and there's a softness in his eyes that I wouldn't have thought him capable of. It's like looking at a completely different Dante to the one I've been forced to put up with for the last forty-eight hours.

Is this the Dante Red sees? The one she believes was worthy of being spared that day in the church? The one who made her fall for him?

Seeing her awake breaks Oliver's restraint, and he surges forward. The movement catches Red's attention, and she turns to face him as he steps up to the opposite side of the bed. Hesitation flashes in her eyes, even as a nervous smile lifts her lips, and she watches him closely as he hovers above her. Dante remains on her other side, watching over her like a sentinel. I get the impression it's going to be next to impossible to get rid of him now.

The air crackles with unspoken words as Red and Oliver lock eyes, a thousand unsaid emotions flitting between them as the rest of us watch on.

Oliver's face crumples, and his words come out ragged when he speaks. "Fuck, Red." In the next moment, he's practically on top of her, careful to hold his own weight as he wraps her up in his arms and pulls her against him. "I'm so fucking sorry. I was a fucking idiot, and you have every right to brandish your knife and threaten to slice me open. I should never have made you question us. *I* should never have questioned us." Loosening his hold on her, he moves to cup her cheek, lifting her head until she's staring him in the eyes. All of us lay witness as Oliver bears his soul for her, allowing not only her but each of us to see every bit of anguish, love, and regret he's been harboring. "You're it for me. It shouldn't have taken you disappearing for me to realize that, but just know that I love you."

"I never questioned us, Oliver. It would be impossible to not love you." Tears are thick in Red's voice, but she holds it together, her tone sharpening as she says, "I understand why you had your doubts, but if you ever do that to me again, I *will* slice you open with my knife."

Oliver just beams at her. "Not a problem, Trouble."

"Jeez, talk about a sappy fucking reunion," Enzo grouses, garnering Red's attention as she looks his way, another bright smile lighting her face.

Enzo smirks beneath her attention, but I see the relief in his eyes. "Good to see you in one piece, Spitfire."

His words remind me that she's been missing for two fucking days, and before I can think better of it, I growl, "Where the fuck have you been?"

Dante's head snaps up, giving me a withering glare, but Red simply smiles serenely, like I said something sweet. Extracting herself from Oliver's arms, she slowly climbs off the bed and ambles toward me with stiff movements that none of us miss.

Mischief brims in her eyes as she approaches, a playful smile directed right at me. "I missed you too, Cain, baby."

My eyes narrow in warning at her ridiculous nickname, even as my fingers twitch at my side, desperate to reach out and drag her the rest of the way to me. It takes every bit of goddamn patience I have to wait for her to reach me, and unbidden, my eyes close as she slides a palm up my chest until her hand rests over the chaotic beating of my heart.

"So damn much." Those last words are whispered, for only me, and I snap my eyes open.

Lifting my arms, I slide my hands through her hair, holding her head in place so I can drink my fill of her. "You're never leaving my side again."

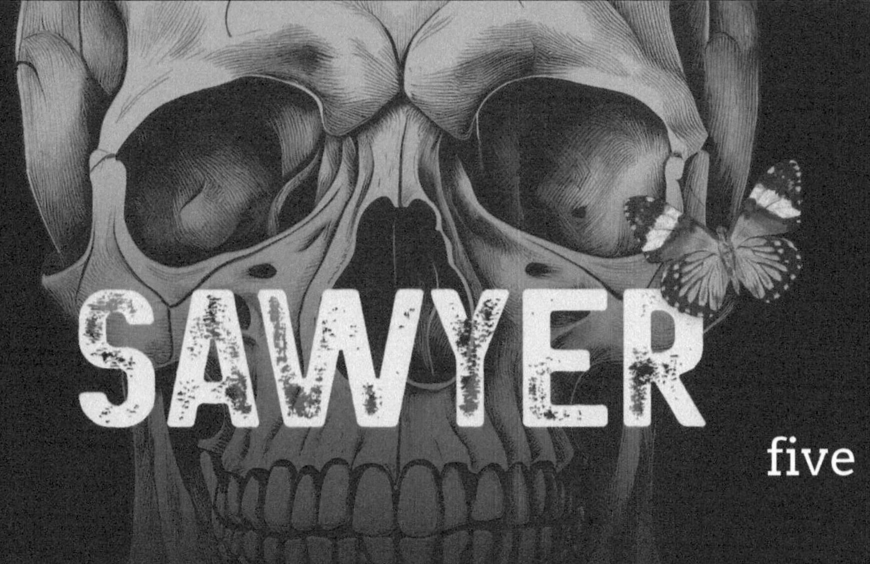

Nothing beats seeing all four of my men in the same room, especially when they aren't throwing hateful glares or spiteful words at one another. All of them are too focused on me to care about pissing off one another, and for now, I'll take that small reprieve.

"Answer his question, Spitfire," Enzo states, his tone non-negotiable, when I fail to answer Cain. "What happened?"

Turning, I lean back against Cain's chest, soaking in the warmth that seeps through my Henley and melts into my bones, easing the last of my aches and pains. My body is still stiff and sore, but a shower and another nap have done it a world of good and I already feel a million miles better than I did when I first woke up.

"One of Giovanni's scouts shot out my tire when I was on my way to your place," I explain. None of them seem surprised, so I guess they saw the wreckage. My lips tug down in a frown as I picture Raven smeared all over the street. She deserved a far better death than that.

Shaking off my melancholy, my thoughts drift back to the alley as I recount the rest of my story. "I was thrown from the bike, and the guy caught me. I slit his throat."

"We saw," Oliver says from his position on the side of the bed. "We found his body in the alley."

"After that, I stumbled into the warehouse and passed out. A friend found me and took me in until I woke up."

"A friend?" Cain accuses, at the same time Dante snaps, "What friend?"

All four of them are staring at me with narrowed eyes.

Ignoring their piercing gazes, I shrug a shoulder. "Just a friend. He patched me up and gave me taxi money to get here."

"He?" Cain's hands tighten on my waist, and I flinch beneath the painful grip.

"You're hurting her!" Dante snarls, stepping toward me as if he's going to physically remove me from Cain's hold. I've no doubt that that is exactly his intention.

Cain immediately drops his hand, frowning down at my waist, even though he can't see the bruises hiding under my clothes. "Sorry," he grumbles, looking thoroughly apologetic.

"It's fine," I assure him. "I just have a few scrapes and bumps."

Resounding growls resonate around the room, and I roll my eyes at their alpha male posturing, even if I preen at knowing I have four ruthless men who would do anything to ease my pain and avenge the person who inflicted it. No need, though. I just need a few days rest then I'll be right as rain, ready to carry out my own vengeance.

Cain's lips pinch and fury burns in his emerald eyes. "We're not done talking about this," he bites out, to which I just give him a placating smile. "But I need to talk to my men, and then we need to get you out of here. It's not safe."

My lips thin at the thought of him leaving my sight already, but I know he has work to do. I can only imagine the mess he has to clean up after bringing Dante and Enzo here. I hadn't expected to wake up and see Dante's face looming over mine, but I should have guessed he wouldn't stay behind.

"Okay." Pressing up on my toes, I plant a quick kiss against his lips, but Cain's hand comes up to cup the back of my head, holding me in place as he prolongs it. "Don't go anywhere," he murmurs when we pull apart.

"I won't." I take a step back, and the softness that was in his eyes a second ago hardens.

"I mean it, Red. Stay here!"

"I pinky promise," I say with a laugh.

He frowns at me for a moment longer before gesturing for Oliver to follow him.

Instead of following him to the door, Oliver makes a beeline for me, bending down to capture my lips with his. His kiss is bitter and sweet all at once, as he pushes every bit of regret and love into it.

"Behave. I love you."

His eyes hold mine, an anxiousness still buried in his pale blue depths, like he can't believe he has me back. "I love you, too," I assure him before he reluctantly steps away, following Cain out of the room and leaving me alone with my two mafia men.

The second the door shuts behind them, Enzo stalks toward me, a furrow on his brow. Instead of pulling me in against him as I expected, he reaches for the seam of my top and inches it up until my bruised and scratched skin is visible for him to see.

"Fucking hell, Sawyer," he growls, but I know none of his anger is aimed at me.

"I'm fine," I assure him. "It looks worse than it is."—a total lie. It hurts like a bitch.

His resounding scoff of disagreement says it all, but I push his hands off me and pull down my top. Frowning, he doesn't argue as he gently maneuvers me back to the bed. "At least sit down and rest until they get back."

"And you can tell us all about this *friend*," Dante tacks on.

Ignoring him, I get comfy in the middle of the bed before patting the sheet beside me and silently pleading for him to join me. Enzo needs no such encouragement. He's already sitting with his back against the headboard, his legs out in front of him and his feet crossed at the ankles.

Dante's dark brown eyes bore into mine, as I hold his stare until he finally relents. With a scowl, he lowers himself onto the bed, except he doesn't get anywhere near as comfortable as Enzo. Keeping one foot planted on the floor, he lifts one leg onto the bed as he shifts to rest against the headboard, his body taut as though ready to spring into action at any moment.

"Good to see the four of you haven't killed each other in my absence," I tell them, trying to divert the conversation away from their prying questions about Blue—stupid ass name, but since I don't have an actual name, I guess that's what I'll have to call him.

Enzo scoffs. "There were a few close calls."

Yeah, I think. *I witnessed one of them.* I don't say as much, however. It would only raise more questions that I can't answer. Before I left his place, Blue made me promise not to tell anyone about him or where he lives—although I'm not entirely sure if he actually lives there. Since I probably owe my life to him, there was no way I was about to argue. Besides, not even my guys need to know about him. I doubt we will ever cross paths again.

"Dante had to be talked down several times."

"I wasn't the one who demanded one of those assholes to shoot me," Dante fires back.

"What?" I exclaim, gaping wide-eyed at Enzo. "You did what?"

Enzo rolls his eyes, sweeping a hand down his tall frame. "Clearly, I'm fine."

I groan into my hands, deciding I'm probably better not knowing what other arguments went on between them. The one I witnessed was bad enough.

"Where were you?"

It seems Dante won't be so easily swayed from this line of conversation, and I sigh as I lift my head to look at him. "I can't tell you."

"Why didn't you call?" Enzo asks.

"I was out of it for nearly two days after the crash."

Dante growls, his body going tight as a bow. "You mean some asshole had two days to do god-knows-what while you were unconscious?"

"All he did was patch me up," I assure him, but even that seems to piss him off. As though the thought of another guy so much as touching me is enough to send him spiraling into a frenzy. "He took care of me," I try to soothe. *Nope, that doesn't seem to have the intended effect, either.* "He stopped another one of your dad's men from getting to me," I try instead.

His anger lightens by only a fraction, but he bites out, "More likely, he stopped us from finding you."

I huff out a sigh. This is an argument that has no resolution. No matter what I say, he's going to be pissed. Dropping my shoulders, I soften my expression. "Can we please not fight? I'm far too exhausted for that. I just want to enjoy having both of you here."

Dante holds his tight expression for a second longer before letting it go and giving me a silent nod of agreement. Smiling, I rest my head against his arm and interlock my fingers with Enzo's, placing our joined hands on my thigh. We fall into a peaceful silence, and it's not long before my eyes start to droop. I swear, all my body wants to do since the crash is sleep.

As I'm nodding off, a loud wailing sound makes all three of us jump, and any notion of sleep is chased back into the recesses of my mind as adrenaline rushes forward.

Enzo jackhammers off the bed, immediately reaching for a weapon tucked in the waistband of his pants hidden beneath his jacket. Dante does the same, although with far more grace, as though he's reluctant to move too fast and draw attention to us.

When the door doesn't blow open, I roll to the edge of the bed and grab the gun Cain keeps stuck to the underside of his bedside table, ignoring every dull ache as I move.

"Perimeter alarm," I shout by way of explanation over the wailing noise. The fact that the alarm hasn't been disarmed can only mean one thing. "The clubhouse is under attack."

The two of them share a quick glance. "We have to get you out of here," Dante orders.

"No!" I'm immediately shaking my head and planting my feet. "I'm not leaving them."

"You're injured," he bites out, rounding on me with fury in his eyes like nothing I've seen on him before. Except, underneath all that heat, I see the real emotion that's bothering him—fear.

"I'm not that bad," I promise him. I'm not, not really. I'm not so bad that I'll willingly leave my Rejects behind. Not when they are only in this position because of me—because they had my back going in to rescue Luc.

Both of them stare at me, and I dart my gaze back and forth between them. I don't know what they see in my eyes, whether they can tell I genuinely am okay enough to fight, or the fact that I will not leave here without ensuring *all* of them come with me. Whatever it is, Enzo relents.

"Fine, but the three of us stick together when we leave this room."

I nod in agreement, even though I'm still locked in a silent stand-off with Dante. If I don't get him on my side, he'll happily ignore Enzo's orders and my demands and throw me over his shoulder. After a long, tense moment, his lip lifts in an angry snarl, and his nostrils flare, but he growls something incoherent that I take to mean is an acknowledgment of Enzo's plan.

Now that that has been sorted, I scurry into the bathroom and grab the other gun Cain keeps hidden in between the spare towels, tucking it into the back of my jeans. I take a second to slip into my Reaper identity, letting her cold detachment wash over me as everything that makes Sawyer, Sawyer, is shoved into a box. When I'm ready, I walk back into the bedroom. I don't know if Dante or Enzo can see the difference, but Enzo cocks his brow in a silent question. I nod that I'm ready to go, and adjusting my grip on the gun, the three of us edge toward the door.

Enzo reaches it first, placing his ear against the wood as he listens for any sounds on the other side, although I doubt he can hear anything over the high-pitched shrill of the alarm.

Cracking the door an inch, he peers into the hall before opening it further. He pops his head out, before waving for us to follow him out of the room. Once we're standing in the hall, I can hear it. Even over the ear-splitting scream of the alarm, I can make out the distinctly more reverberating pop of gunfire.

When the sound of the alarm suddenly cuts out, the noise only becomes more deafening—hammering in tune to my erratic heartbeat. It sounds like it is coming from all angles, and I can't pinpoint if we're being shot at from the front or all around us.

"We need to move," Enzo orders, already ambling in the direction of the bar. Dante yanks me in front of him so I'm safely wedged between the two of them.

We don't make it far before a crashing noise behind us has all three of us spinning.

Taking a step to the side so I can peer around Dante's broad frame, I raise my weapon as a door at the far end of the hall flies open. Light streams in, and all I can see is a dark silhouette, unable to tell if it's a friend or foe. However, as he steps forward, several more men piling in behind him, I recognize the arrogant swagger and swish of pant trousers. *Fucking Antonellis.*

Without a moment's hesitation, I press down on the trigger, firing off a shot. Despite the fact they are shooting at their own people, Dante and Enzo don't hesitate as the intruders return fire, and the three of us form an impenetrable wall, each picking a target and eliminating them one at a time until we're the only ones left standing.

"Fuck," I pant, when silence reigns supreme. "They must have made it past the perimeter guards. That can't be good."

Rough hands grab a hold of my shoulders, and I'm abruptly turned until I'm facing Dante, his hands maintaining their painfully tight grip as he runs his eyes up and down me. "Are you hurt? You're not even wearing any goddamn Kevlar."

"I'm fine," I assure him.

"We need to keep moving," Enzo urges, but I don't miss how he conducts his own assessment of me, needing to check for himself that I'm unharmed. When he's satisfied, he barks out, "Stay behind me," spearing me with a deadly look until I nod in agreement before slowly continuing our journey down the hallway.

With every step closer, the sound of gunfire gets louder, until it and shouting are all I hear. By the time we step into the bar, it resembles a war zone rather than the bar I remember it to be. The men from earlier are hidden behind overturned tables, lined up along the wall, shooting at whoever is outside. My eyes scan the room in a panic until I spot Cain and Oliver in the thick of it.

"Over there!" I point in their direction, my voice barely carrying over the rattle of gunfire and men shouting. As if they hear me, both of them turn, with matching pissed-off expressions on their faces when they spot us through the chaos.

Cain shifts as though he's going to come over here, but before he can take another step, a fresh round of gunfire goes off, windows shattering and stray bullets embedding in the walls. I duck at the same time a hand presses on the top of my head, forcing me to the ground. I can feel a weight above me, one of the guys practically lying on top of me. My body cries out at the pressure and at being pushed onto the hard floor beneath, but I can hardly feel it over the pounding of adrenaline and the carnage building around me. Every time I lift my head to look, Dante's hand pushes my face back against the floorboard.

A heavy weight thumps against the ground in front of me, and I push against his hand until I can see a body. My eyes travel up over his boots, jeans, and Kevlar vest until they land on his face, my composure cracking.

"Dax," I gasp, trying to wriggle out from beneath Dante to check on him.

"He's dead, *mia vita*." It takes a second for his murmured words in my ear to register, and when I look back at Dax's face, I notice how his eyes stare blankly at the ceiling above, unblinking.

Emotion swells in my throat. "No." The fight drains out of me as I stare at him, tears biting at the back of my eyes. I didn't know Dax well, but I know he was with Cain since the beginning. He was one of the men Cain trusted most.

I feel Dante shift behind me, Enzo taking his place while Dante reaches toward Dax.

"What are you doing?" I ask as he undoes the Velcro straps of his vest and lifts it over Dax's head, pulling it out from under his body.

Crawling back over to me, he doesn't answer as he slides it over my head instead, redoing the straps so the vest sits flush against my chest and back. Our eyes meet, his are their usual blankness, like we aren't in the middle of a shootout, and mine are probably dilated with adrenaline, panic, and grief.

Cain army crawls his way over to us, stopping when he reaches Dax's body. I see the flash of pain in his face before he reaches out, closes Dax's eyelids, and mutters something too low for me to hear. He takes a moment to say goodbye, and when his head snaps up, his gaze colliding with mine, there's nothing in his eyes except pure, unadulterated anger.

"You need to get out of here," he yells when he reaches us, flicking his gaze up to look at Dante and Enzo.

"We're not leaving without you," I shout back.

"Maybe we can help?" Enzo offers.

Cain's lips flatten as he thinks on it.

"From what I can tell, the brunt of the attack is coming from the front."

"We caught some trying to sneak in the back, too," Enzo informs him.

"How many?" Dante shouts, but Cain simply shakes his head, not sure.

"We have men on the roof, but they"—he juts his chin out the window toward our attackers—"barely stop shooting long enough for me to hear what they're saying."

"We need to get to the roof then," Enzo states. "Or higher ground, at least."

"The stairwells are outside," Cain informs them.

"Of course they are," one of them grumbles in a lower voice, but I can't tell who.

"If most of the attack is coming from the front, then we might be able to make it up the back stairwell," I suggest.

"It's our only option," Cain agrees, turning and waving Oliver over.

When Oliver has safely made it across the room to us, we all move as a group, crouching to stay low as we head back down the hallway from which we just came. Once we're safe from any stray bullets, we stand upright and start moving faster. Every second counts. The Rejects will only be able to hold off Giovanni's men for so long.

We jump over the dead bodies from earlier, only slowing down when we reach the still open door that the Antonelli men kicked open. Cain and Enzo get to the door first, both of them peering out to see if anyone is around. The coast must be clear as Cain waves the rest of us out, and we follow his lead as we flatten our backs against the wall and slowly slink around the side of the building.

The reception area of the motel, where the office and Cain and Oliver's bedrooms are, is only one story. However, the rest of the building, where the bedrooms for guests are situated, climbs to three stories, shaped in a large rectangle, with an open courtyard in the middle. Cain's men hadn't done much with the outdoor area yet, but I'd heard talk of possibly putting in a swimming pool. I guess that won't be happening any time soon.

There is a stairwell at the front of the building, granting access to the higher floors directly from the parking lot, and another stairwell located inside the courtyard. It doesn't take us long to reach it, except Cain bypasses it as he skulks further into the courtyard. I share a questioning glance with Oliver who is on my left, bringing up the rear, but he simply nods for me to follow.

All four of us follow Cain as he moves quickly to the first bedroom on the ground floor, pulling out a key and unlocking the door. It swings open and he hurriedly ushers us all inside before closing it behind us.

In the safety of the room and out of view of anyone who might be stalking around outside, I take my first real breath since we entered the bar, working to quiet my mind and fortify my Reaper persona. When I'm once again encased in that cold, hard shell, I turn to take in the room, my eyes widening. "Wow," I exclaim, noticing that Enzo and Dante are also taking in the room with raised eyebrows and impressed expressions.

It looks like we're in some sort of weapons room. Every inch of space is piled high with crates, large rifles leaning against the wall and spread out across the bed, and handguns set on top of any available surface.

"Damn, this is some collection." Enzo lets out a low whistle, moving to lift a handgun from the dresser, inspecting it before setting it down and going to look at one of the rifles.

"How did you get your hands on all this?" Dante questions, a furrow between his brows as he scans the vast display of weaponry.

"We trade primarily in weapons," Cain explains easily while he gathers a handful of more powerful-looking rifles. "I've been slowly building my own collection, but ever since Red started working in your club and it seemed like this war was coming to a head, I've been stockpiling."

"You were ready for this fight." Dante sounds surprised, but when Cain lifts his gaze to look at him, all I see is determined resolve.

"I told you I was. We may have taken a few hits"—Cain's features soften, no doubt thinking about Dax and the other dead Rejects I saw in the bar—"but my men and me have been itching for this fight for a long time. We've spent years training for it, preparing. If we really wanted, we could take out the entire street and every Antonelli out there, though if we can, I'd rather do it without decimating the city." His stare hardens. "There's already been enough damage done to Black Creek and its people. I'd prefer to not add to it."

He holds Dante's gaze for a tense moment before glancing away. "Grab whatever you want, whatever you know how to use. I take it since you've already killed some of your own people, you have no issues shooting at more of them."

It's not phrased as a question, and I see Cain's dig land as Enzo winces.

"They're Giovanni's people, not ours." Enzo's voice is tight.

"What about the men you believe to be loyal to you?" This time, Cain's question is aimed at Dante.

"I only contacted them once, when they informed me Giovanni was keeping them out of whatever he's planning."

Cain raises a dark eyebrow. "Not sure you can trust them?"

Dante's lips thin, but he doesn't dignify that with a response. His silence is an answer all on its own. That's exactly what he's afraid of. It's one thing to hope and believe that men are loyal to you, but it's another to actually rely on that perceived loyalty.

Shaking his head, Cain drops the topic, and we all move around the room in silence, picking out weapons. Since I have no experience with rifles, I stick to the handguns, repeatedly lifting one up and weighing it in my hand before either setting it back down or holding on to it.

During my perusal, I find two thigh straps with holsters, which I wrap around my legs. Once I've filled the cartridges of the guns I've chosen, I strap two into my thighs and tuck the third into the waistband of my jeans while keeping the final one in my hand. I miss the comfort of knowing my blades are within reach. They are always a quiet reassurance when I'm in dangerous situations, but ideally, I won't be getting close enough to any Antonelli bastards to need a blade, so for today, guns are best.

When we're all armed to the teeth and everyone is sporting bulletproof vests, each of my men with a rifle thrown over their shoulders and handguns within easy reach—Cain even has a couple of grenades strapped to a belt at his waist—we leave the safety of the room and continue on our path toward the roof.

The sounds of battle rage on the other side of the building, yet back here, everything is eerily calm as we reach the staircase and climb, ensuring we keep our footsteps light against the metal.

Cain and Dante are in front of me, Enzo and Oliver behind. Cain signals for us to stop as we reach the second-floor landing, all of us crouching low so as not to be seen. I can't see past Dante's broad frame in front of me, but after a moment, he moves forward and I follow.

I jump at the loud rat-tat-tat of gunfire, far closer than anything we've heard since we left the bar.

"Fuck," Dante hisses before he disappears from in front of me, quickly moving to cover Cain's back and firing off round after round toward a small group of rugged-looking men who had just emerged from a room further down the landing. They must have been searching the rooms one by one, slowly making their way toward the roof hoping to pick off our shooters.

At the sound of gunshots, Cain immediately turns toward the threat, his weapon raised as he shoots alongside Dante while the rest of us remain hidden in the stairwell. Only when both of them lower their weapons to their sides, do I step up onto the landing beside them and turn to take in the men piled up, their limbs a tangled mess from where they fell after taking their final breath.

"Bastards," I state, my voice void of all emotion. *Literal* Bastards.

"Should have known those assholes wouldn't pass up a chance to witness our demise," Cain growls, his breaths coming in anger-filled pants. His gaze flicks up to Dante's, the two sharing a loaded glance. I don't think any of us missed the fact that Dante just saved Cain's life, although, in true Cain fashion, he doesn't offer a thank you, only grunts for us to keep moving.

Dante's expression gives nothing away as he moves forward to follow Cain up the next stairwell, but when he looks my way, I give him a soft smile of thanks. I don't even want to think about how that could have ended if he hadn't caught the threat and stepped in to help, and I firmly believe the main reason he did is because of me, because he knows how much Cain means to me.

His steps falter, and I love how he looks at me whenever I do something as simple as smile at him. It's as though he's trying to figure out what he did to deserve it and process whatever feelings that smile elicits. The way it frequently does when I stump him, his hand lifts to his chest, his fingers brushing over the Kevlar above his heart before a softness enters his gaze. It only lasts a split second, the same as always, but those split seconds are starting to add up. I snatch up those moments like a bandit, hoarding every single one of them, because it's in those seconds that I see what Dante is capable of—loving someone.

It's in my soft smiles and freely given affection that Dante will uncover his true potential. He may have been born to torture and murder men, but he was also made to love and be loved. He deserves to know what that feels like, to see how he can flourish under that love. Fear and pain may be excellent motivators, but love is by far the strongest. You can overcome *anything* for love, face down your greatest fear, step up to the toughest challenge. I've heard stories of women lifting cars to save their children and couples overcoming overwhelming odds to remain together. It's stories like that that give me hope that my four contrasting men can learn to get along.

I know I would do whatever it took to keep the people that I love alive. Just as I know they would do the same for me. Because that's what love is. It's overwhelming strength in the face of impossible odds. It's putting someone else's needs above your own. It's knowing that your life means nothing without them in it. I think Dante is beginning to see that, but he's only scratched the surface. I intend to show him just how powerful love can be.

Cain manages to make it to the roof without me having to save his ass for a second time. Although, given the way Sawyer looked at me—as though I'd just saved *her*—I'd happily shove his stupidly large frame in front of a gun just so I could push him out of the way and claim to be a hero. Because the tightness in my chest, the uptick of my heart, and the sudden urge to slam my lips against hers made the fact that I risked my own life to ensure he continues breathing completely worthwhile.

"Stay here," Cain orders when we're at the top of the stairs. There's a short ladder attached to the wall that takes you the remainder of the way to the roof, but from here, we're just out of sight of his men and out of view of the front of the building. "I don't need my men seeing you and opening fire."

"Do you think you can manage to not get shot at when your back's turned?" I jest with a smirk that makes his nostrils flare.

"This is me repaying the favor, asshole," is all he snarls before turning his back on me and stepping onto the first rung. He makes quick work of climbing the ladder before he disappears and we're left to twiddle our thumbs.

I keep an ear out for the back-and-forth rhythm of gunfire. It's eased off since we first stepped out of the clubhouse, coming in intermittent spurts rather than a continuous stream. I'm unsure whether that's because the Rejects are winning or my father. I don't feel like I can refer to either side as *us* or *them* as technically I'm no longer either. Or maybe I'm both. I don't know what I am anymore.

Fucked. That's what I am. Completely fucked over a leggy redhead who owns me body, mind, and soul. She could ask anything of me, and I'd do everything within my willpower to give it to her—even saving these sorry assholes. Even believing in something I never thought possible. I never thought I was capable of feeling. Certainly not feeling anything positive, and least of all, love. But for her, I want to. I want to give her my love. A feeling that I don't even remotely understand or know how to feel, but I want to feel it... for her.

It helps that she makes it so goddamn easy. She just has to look at me with that easy smile, those eyes softened only for me, and I feel it. I feel what I figure can only be love, because she's the only one who makes me feel it—that churning mixture of carnal desire, *I will kill you if you touch her* possessiveness, and something so much sweeter.

It's that sweetness that softens my edges and brings a rare smile to my lips.

It's that sweetness that draws me to her like a bee to honey.

It's that sweetness that tells me I can feel more than I think I can.

That sweetness is Sawyer. That sweetness is love.

Cain's ugly mug appears over the rim of the roof, smashing through any pleasant feelings I had and bringing a glower to my face.

"Come up. Stay low."

"How are things looking?" Oliver asks as he hurries up the ladder.

"Better than I expected. We've picked off most of their men. Looks like it was mostly Bastards, with only a few Antonellis."

I mull over that piece of information. It would be just like my father to get the Grim Bastards and a few lowly soldiers to do his bidding. It also tells me that today's attack was a test—my father's way of assessing the Rejects' manpower and seeing how organized they are before bringing down the full force of the Antonelli Empire on them.

Lor follows Oliver up, then Sawyer, and I bring up the rear, my eyes glued to the round globes of Sawyer's ass as she climbs the rungs. It's been way too fucking long since I was balls deep inside her. I know she's hurting after her accident—not that she's complained; her stiff movements speak loud enough for me to hear. However, there's no way I can go another night without feeling her soft curves pressed against me or hearing her sweet moans in my ear.

I have to consciously redirect my thoughts away from my hardening cock to the crisis at hand as Sawyer reaches the roof and turns, cutting off my delicious view of her ass. It says a lot about how unaffected I am by the gunfire and death surrounding us that I can even be turned on at a time like this, but when it comes to Sawyer, there's no situation where she couldn't get me off if she wanted to.

When I reach the rim of the roof, I crouch low and slowly crawl forward. As I approach, I notice how one of Cain's closest guys pauses in whatever he's saying to Cain, his eyes narrowing on me. Distrust swims in his features, and I can tell he's less than pleased that I'm here. *Trust me, man, I don't want to be here either, but apparently shit like this is what you do when you're in love.*

When the street below comes into view, I snap my gaze away, looking down. By the looks of it, my father's men and the Bastards came in in a storm of cars and bikes, blocking both ends of the street. A few cars made it closer to the clubhouse before their tires were blown out. Dead bodies decorate the street, most having been left where they fell, and the last of the survivors are currently hiding behind their shot-out cars.

As I watch, a man pops his head up, the muzzle poking over the top of the hood. With his sights set on us, he fires off a round from the heavy-duty automatic rifle. We all scramble to duck, my hands coming up to cover my head as I flatten myself against the warm rubber of the roof.

I can't do anything but breathe in the bitter, pungent smell of gunpowder that sits heavy in the air and wait for it to end. I crack open an eyelid, needing to see that Sawyer is okay. Unfortunately, I'm met with Cain's ugly as fuck face, and quickly dismissing him, I turn my head. Sawyer is on my other side, Oliver half on top of her as he uses his body as a shield, their heads leaning against one another.

Instead of jealousy bubbling up—okay, there's definitely a little bit of jealousy as I wish it was my body pressed against hers, though it's not as overpowering as I'd expected—the primary feeling is relief. Relief that she's okay, that someone other than me is looking out for her and ensuring she is safe. It's actually a weight off my chest to share the burden. Albeit, I'll never trust them with her safety as much as I'd trust myself or Lor, especially after they so callously lost her. Still, in this moment, I rest assured that one of us will always be making Sawyer our top priority. I've noticed that, since this shit began, we've automatically been placing her in the middle of us, ensuring she's always protected. We all seamlessly moved into that formation without even discussing it, and I suddenly realized that no matter our differences and issues, Sawyer will always be our primary focus—the one thing we will always put above all else.

The gunfire stops with a deafening silence, and I slowly lift my head until I can just about see over the edge of the roof, noting that the shooter has ducked back behind his car, probably to refill his magazine.

In the brief break before the next round, everyone moves into action, Cain barking out orders. "Get me the grenade launcher! It's time to end these sorry sons of bitches."

His order is passed down the line of men along the roof, everyone working seamlessly as the grenade launcher is passed back. As he sets it up and gets it in position, I return my focus to the street, noticing that there's another car with men hiding behind it.

"There are two targets," I tell him. "As soon as you fire that thing at one of them, the others will scatter."

"Good," he grunts. "That's our opportunity to pick them off one by one."

Taking the rifle from my back, I prop it up on the roof and look down the scope. "Which one are you going for?"

"The dark blue one."

Swiveling the barrel toward the other car, I line it up, and with my finger on the trigger and my body relaxed, I wait for Cain to shoot his grenade. As soon as these assholes—Bastards or not—run from their hiding place, I'm going to take them out. I'm fucking done with this bullshit of a day. I need a fucking shower and Sawyer in my arms, and these bastards are interfering with my plans.

I wait impatiently, ticking the seconds off one by one until the *whoomph* of the grenade whizzes past my ear threatening to deafen me. An earth-quaking boom quickly follows it, and heat blasts my face. Out of the corner of my eye, I notice as a ball of fire flares into the sky and car parts get tossed into the air, but the second I catch a flash of movement, my focus zeros in on the stupid fucker making a run for it.

His suit-clad back is to me as I press down on the trigger, watching as he falls to his knees. I keep the rifle aimed at him, waiting until he faceplants on the asphalt and shows no signs of getting up again before scanning for the other target. I spot him just as a bullet is fired into his shoulder, sending him stumbling off course and training my rifle on him. I deliver the final blow, taking off his face with the shot. *Oh, well, it's not like he needs a face in Hell.*

A tense silence fills the air as everyone waits expectantly, scouring the street below for the next assault or someone hiding out of sight. When nothing comes, I slowly relax, forcing my shoulders to unbunch. It's only when men start to pile out of the front door and emerge from the side of the house, spreading out onto the street, we search for any further threats and ensure everyone is dead. Cain finally lets out a breath of relief beside me and pushes off the roof.

Still, no sounds of celebration go up, because this is not a celebration. Cain may have won, but he's suffered his own casualties today in the form of his men and their clubhouse. Tensions are going to be high after today, everyone demanding retaliation, and Cain's going to have to manage all of that, as well as bury his dead and find somewhere safe for his men to stay until the clubhouse is up and running again. I don't envy the job ahead of him, and as more and more of his men throw dirty, distrustful glances my way, I know mine and Enzo's presence here is only going to make the situation worse for him.

The more and more looks I get, the more uncomfortable I become. I raise my chin and stare down every single one of them, but I fear my response does more harm than good. Eventually, I turn my back on all of them, focusing on Sawyer as I stride toward her.

"Are you okay?" I demand, reaching out to lift her chin.

"I'm fine," she assures me, but I see the truth in her eyes. They're duller than they were this morning, that vibrant, cerulean blue looking less like the Caribbean Sea and more like its subterranean depths.

"You're not," I snarl, immediately brushing my hands over her shoulders and along her arms, checking for injuries. Reaching out, she catches my hands in hers, giving them a squeeze. "I'm just tired."

"We'll get you home to bed," I assure her, but she just shakes her head before casting her eyes around the rooftop and the road below.

"I'm tired of all of this. Of the fighting, the pointless deaths, the destruction of Black Creek. I just want it all to end." She says the last part with such a deflated tone, as though she doesn't believe that will ever be the case.

I pull her in against me, wrapping my arms around her as I bury my face in the crook of her neck. "Isn't that what you've been fighting for? These people? This city?"

"Yeah," she sighs, pulling back so I can see her face. "On days like today, I can't help but wonder if the price is worth it. Perhaps it would have been better if I'd never agreed to join the Rejects, if I'd never started working in that club to get close to you, if I'd run as soon as you mentioned getting married."

Her words incense me, and I roughly grab her chin, holding her in place as I bite out, "No. It would not have been better. My life would not be better without you in it. Lor's life would not be better without you in it." I gesture to Cain and Oliver, who are standing nearby, talking to a few of their men. "Their lives would not be better without you in them." Returning my attention to her, I run my gaze over her face before latching onto her blue eyes that always slice straight through my heart. "This war was happening, with or without you. These men knew what they were signing up for. They knew the risks and they still stood by Cain. Men like them—men like Cain—the only death they can imagine is one fighting for what they believe in." I reverently brush my thumb over her cheek. "War has officially come to Black Creek, and there will be more casualties before the end, but if you were to ask any of these men if they want to back out and have no part in it, I'd bet every single one of them would say no. Just like you, just like me, just like Cain, every one of them is here for a purpose. Live or die, we are all going to see it through to the end."

Sawyer and I are still locked in our moment when Cain approaches, clearing his throat to gain our attention, and Lor comes over to join us. "You need to go," he says in a quiet, gruff voice, not meeting my stare.

"What?" Sawyer immediately argues. "Why? No. We're not leaving."

Cain huffs, pinning Sawyer in his gaze and waiting until she's open to listening to him before he darts his eyes up to me and Lor. "They can't be here," he says, his voice even quieter than before. "And I can't leave. I need to talk to my men and get the injured seen to. I need to make provisions,"—he clears emotion from his throat—"we have men we need to bury."

Sawyer's lips purse, but I can see she understands his dilemma, even if she does waiver on agreeing.

Just to drive the nail home, Cain tacks on, "And Luc needs to see you. He's been worried sick and today won't have helped any."

That sways Sawyer's decision, and she reluctantly sighs. "Fine. We'll go." Her eyes soften and she reaches out to take Cain's hand. "I'm sorry about your men."

Sensing that they need a moment alone, Lor and I step away. Oliver glances at us from where he's talking to one of the men, before he squeezes his shoulder and comes over to join us.

He swallows uncomfortably, visibly looking like he's chewing on flies as his eyes dart around the roof, focusing on everything but us before he blurts out, "Thank you for the backup today. I'm sure it wasn't easy for either of you, but we appreciate it."

"Even though your men look like they're one word away from shooting us, too," Lor states bluntly.

Oliver's lips purse as he turns to take in the expressions of the few remaining guys left on the roof. Most have climbed back down to the ground to join their comrades. "Can't blame them for being distrusting. They've spent the last however many years hating you. It's ingrained in their DNA to shoot you on sight, so seeing you on the wrong side of the battle lines today is jarring. They don't know what to think right now. Your father's men are literally bleeding into the gutter on our front doorstep, and yet the two of you stood up here and fought alongside us. They don't understand why, and Cain's going to have to field a lot of questions once you leave."

Neither Lor nor I have a response to that, silence falling between us until Sawyer comes over. After she says goodbye to Oliver, we descend from the roof, walk through the clubhouse, and out a back entrance leading onto a side street where Cain planted a couple of getaway cars. All the while, Cain's men look at us with wary, confused, suspicious guises. It all serves as a reminder that Lor and I aren't welcome here. Nor are we welcome in my father's penthouse. We're not welcome anywhere, and for the first time in my life, that truly bothers me.

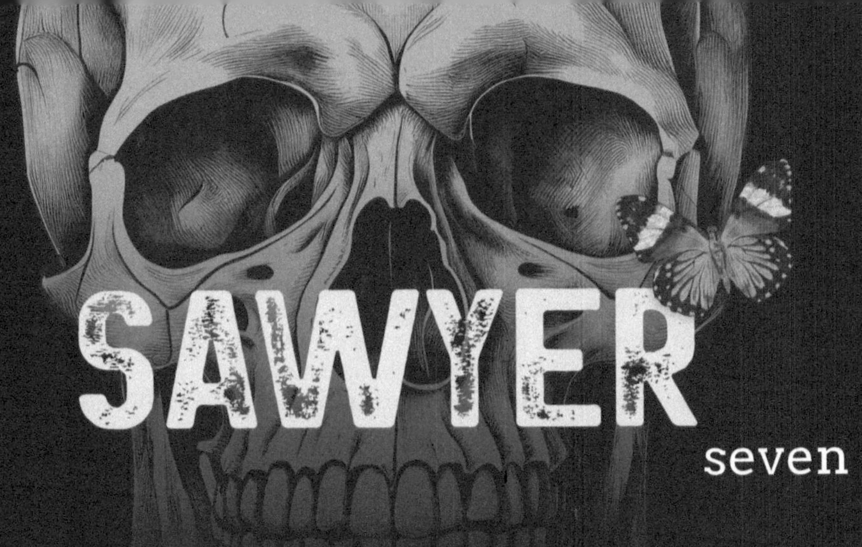

I can hardly put one foot in front of the other by the time we make it back to Cain's house. Any adrenaline I had has long since burned away, leaving me feeling as horrid as I did when I first woke up in Blue's lair.

Still, my weariness is shoved to the back of my mind as I climb out of the car and Luc comes racing down the front porch toward me.

"Fucking hell, Sawyer." He crashes into me, throwing his arms around my neck. I wince and fall back a step, but manage to catch myself, hugging him back just as tightly. The two of us have been through hell these last few weeks, and sometimes it's the simple things like being able to hug your brother—the things we all take for granted—that are the most important in life.

"Good to see you missed me," I try to joke, but Luc just scowls at me as he pulls back.

"You scared the fucking shit out of me."

"Jesus Christ, watch your language," I chastise with a mock-serious look.

Luc rolls his eyes at my poor attempt at parenting, but he can't hide the slight smile on his lips or the sheen of tears in his eyes.

"Are you okay? Where have you been?"

"I'm fine," I assure him. "I got into a little fender-bender and had a run-in with an Antonelli, but *I'm fine.*"

His lips purse as he studies my face. I'm pretty sure the dark bags under my eyes give away the lie on my lips, but he thankfully doesn't call me on it. Instead, he asks, "What happened at the clubhouse?"

His gaze flicks over my shoulder, a frown forming and worry swimming in his eyes. "Where are Oliver and Cain?"

"They're okay. They had a lot to sort out, but I'm sure they'll be by as soon as they can."

Luc swallows, his face softening so he looks every bit his fifteen years. "Did anyone... Is anyone dead?"

I reach out, cupping his cheek while I stare into his worried eyes. "A few," I say truthfully, my tone carrying the weight of today. "I'm not sure who."

Luc simply nods, and I watch as he mentally gathers himself. "How is everything here?" I ask instead, happy to change the subject.

Luc immediately huffs out a frustrated breath. "Bones keeps hogging the remote, and Tank keeps finishing off the juice and putting the empty carton back in the fridge."

I have to bite back my laugh. "And what about Evie?"

He just shrugs. "I don't think she's comfortable around all of us. She mostly stays in her room or hangs out with Marcus."

"Well, a bunch of boisterous teenagers is a lot to handle. She probably just needs some time and doesn't want to sit and play video games or watch gory movies. Have you tried asking if she wants to do something she might enjoy?"

Luc frowns. "No. I didn't think of that."

"Well, try that next time," I suggest softly.

"Should we take this conversation inside?" Enzo asks, stepping up beside me, although his gaze bounces all over the street, as though he's expecting the chaos to have followed us back here. *God, I hope not.*

Luc immediately tenses, glancing up at him before flicking his gaze to Dante. "I see you two made it out alive," he drawls.

Reaching out, I shove him in the shoulder. "Hey! None of that!"

With another roll of his eyes, he moves back toward the house.

"I think he's warming up to us," Enzo says when he's out of earshot.

Tearing my gaze away from Luc, I turn to cock a brow at him. "That's him warming up to you?"

Enzo just shrugs, not enlightening me as he says, "It's been a bit of a process."

Well, considering the last time I talked to Luc, we were arguing because I was defending Dante. I guess the fact that he even acknowledged their presence is a win—I think.

Dante, who had stayed back to give Luc and me some privacy, steps up to my other side, his hand landing on my lower back. "Come on. You're dead on your feet, you need to lie down."

"I just want to talk to Marcus first." At his sheer look of frustration, I tack on, "Then I'll lie down."

His lips purse, but applying pressure to my back, he ushers me toward the house. "Have you been staying here?" I question, suddenly curious.

Dante grunts out something unintelligible, but the derision behind it says everything about what he thinks of his current living arrangements. I bite back a laugh, not sure if I'd love to have been a fly on the wall these last few days or if I'm better off not knowing what threats of violence and sarcastic jibes were tossed back and forth.

"Haven't the kids, Marcus, and Evie been here too? Where the hell is everyone sleeping?"

"Well, we haven't done much in the way of sleeping," Enzo admits, "but the kids have been bunking together—something that very quickly turned sour—and Marcus, Cain, and Oliver have been taking power naps in the third bedroom."

"And what about you guys?"

Enzo juts his chin toward the house on the left. "Cain put us up in there."

"Cain owns that house too?" I question aloud.

My guys just shrug. "He must," Enzo says, uncaring.

I run my eyes over the house next door. It's shabbier looking than Cain's, not having received the same level of renovations. I wonder why he purchased it. Enzo and Dante won't have the answer, so I store the question away to ask Cain when things settle down a bit.

Marcus meets us as we step into the house, his face drawn and downturned. The events of today hit me all over again as we share a look. It can't have been easy for him to have stayed here while the clubhouse was under attack. He'll have received an alert as soon as the ambush started, but since Cain has him on guard duty here, he couldn't—wouldn't—have left.

"How bad is it?"

"It could have been worse," I say, going for an optimistic response, or as optimistic as one can be considering there are a few less good men in this world. On the plus side, there are a few less bad ones too.

"I'll grab us all some whiskey," he says, gesturing for us to head into the living room before he stalks off to the kitchen.

The second I step into the living room, the kids all jump to their feet, firing a hundred and one questions at us.

"What happened?"

"Is anyone hurt?"

"We should have been there!"

An ear-piercing whistle breaks through the cacophony of noise, all of them going silent as their gazes snap to Dante.

"Sawyer's been shot at, thrown from her bike, and just fought alongside your people. The very last thing she needs is you all firing questions at her."

The kids bristle, most likely not appreciating Dante talking to them like that, especially after today. Tensions are high, and everyone is on edge.

"It's okay," I say softly, glancing up at him. The muscle twitches in his jaw and lifting a hand, I gently squeeze his forearm in an attempt to calm him.

His eyes flick down to mine, not looking at all appeased, yet before he can argue, Marcus reappears. "He's right." Marcus' tone rings with authority—the type that the kids actually listen to, as their spines straighten, their mouths slamming shut. "Get out of here, all of you. Let me and Red talk, and I'll fill you in later, yeah?"

Unhappy, but knowing better than to argue with Marcus, a round of murmurs goes up, and Dante, Enzo, and I move out of the way to let the boys pass. As they filter out of the room, I notice Luc in the middle of them, along with Bones, Tank, and Rampage. I offer Luc a small smile and give the other three a reassuring squeeze on their shoulders.

When they're all gone, I walk over to the sofa and all but collapse onto it, my weary body demanding rest. Dante and Enzo flank me, Enzo pulling me onto his lap. Marcus sets down four glasses of whiskey on the coffee table and fills all of them to the brim before passing them out and sinking onto the other sofa.

For a few moments, we sit there in silence, sipping on our whiskeys and lost in our own thoughts before I finally speak up, recapping today's events. Dante or Enzo occasionally speak up, adding a detail, but otherwise, they remain silent, allowing me to fill Marcus in.

"The men will demand retaliation," Marcus states when I'm done. His face looks like it has aged ten years in the last half hour.

"So they should," Enzo states, utterly uncaring that said retaliation is against people he's known his entire life.

At the sound of his voice, Marcus lifts his gaze from the fixed point on the floor he was staring at to study Enzo. "I get that you were willing to fight your own people to get Luc back, but I have to say, I didn't expect you to stand up and fight with us today. Every man in that clubhouse saw you. They'll have seen that you helped them when you could have easily taken advantage of the situation. The outcome of today could have been very different if you'd decided to side with Giovanni."

"It was never a decision," Dante speaks up, drawing Marcus' attention. "Between Sawyer and my father, Sawyer will always be the one I choose."

Reaching out, I intertwine my fingers with his, giving them a light squeeze before placing his hand on my lap. Dante's unquestioning devotion to me is something I don't understand. I don't think I'll ever get used to knowing he will always be on my side, no matter the cause or the consequences, but I've come to realize he always will. If he's willing to go against his father for me, to take on the Antonelli Empire—*his* empire—then anything else should be easy, right?

Marcus raises an eyebrow. "So you did all that today for Sawyer?"

Instead of the blunt *yes* I was expecting, Dante's lips purse as he seems to think over his response. "Sawyer tells me you're trying to make Black Creek a better place." It's not a question, but Marcus nods anyway. "Then, yes, I did it for Sawyer, because she deserves a far better life than the one she had." He pauses before tacking on, "And I guess I did it because if I can help repair some of my father's wrongs, then maybe that counts for something."

And that right there is why Dante is worth saving. Not because he has to make up for his father's wrongdoings—in my opinion, a child should never have to bear the sins of their father—but because, several weeks ago, he wouldn't have thought himself capable of remorse. Attempting to correct his father's wrongs wouldn't have been some-thing he even considered. Yet, here he is, not only acknowledging those feelings but openly speaking them aloud for Marcus to hear.

Marcus nods, knocking back the last of his whiskey before getting to his feet. "I believe a man should be judged on his own actions. You could have taken Sawyer and gotten the hell out of there, and no one would have blamed you." I silently harrumph at that, but I don't say anything because, well, he's right. It also feels like this is an impor-tant moment, so I stay quiet and listen. "But you stayed. Fought." His eyes move to Enzo, including him in what he has to say next. "I can't speak for any other Rejects, but your actions today earned my respect."

See, important moment. I can feel it in the air. In the gasp Enzo holds trapped in his lungs, causing his chest to expand against my back. In Dante's barely perceptible squeeze of my fingers. In the slight lift of both of their shoulders. I doubt anyone's ever told them they've gained their respect, so I can't imagine what must be going through their heads right now, having received that respect from a Reject no less.

Enzo gives a curt nod of gratitude, neither of them saying anything more.

"Well, I'm sure none of you have slept much in the last few days. You should get some rest before Cain returns, because he will be on the warpath. Whether you intended to or not, you've chosen your side now. You'll be suited and booted with the rest of us when we march on Grim and Giovanni."

He strides out of the room, leaving silence in his wake, before Dante breaks it, his voice low when he says, "God, he's not going to make us wear those clothes, is he?"

I snort, which turns into full-on hysterics as I double over, cackling like a maniac. Enzo's arm banded around my waist is the only thing that stops me from sliding onto the floor. Of course, out of everything Marcus just said, *that* is what he chooses to focus on—the clothing.

"You broke her," I hear Enzo mutter, his joking sending me into a fresh fit of laughter. Somewhere in the back of my mind, I realize my reaction isn't normal. I'm overtired and on an adrenaline crash, but at least I'm not crying, right?

"Yeah, let's get you to bed before you completely lose your shit," Enzo says, realizing how close to breaking I am as I finally manage to get myself under control, heaving gasping breaths into my lungs.

When I catch Dante's eye, I find him watching me with concern and confusion swimming in his stare, before Enzo lifts me out of his lap. Together, we head over to the house next door, neither of them giving me a chance to look around as they usher me through the front door and up the stairs. Nevertheless, it would be impossible to miss the old-fashioned interior—the horrendous avocado green walls in the hall, the god-awful floral-patterned lamp shades and teal carpet in the living room, and the old honey-oak cabinets I spy in the kitchen.

Thankfully the bedroom is void of the flowery bedspread and matching curtains I was half expecting, instead, simple white bed linen is neatly tucked around a double bed. A small dresser is tucked in the corner of the room, the walls and carpet looking just as shabby as the rest of the house, but at least everything is clean.

Enzo snags my attention as he moves to stand in front of me, his fingers curling around the bottom of my Henley and lifting it up. I can feel Dante's warmth at my back before his hands snake around my waist, undoing the button of my jeans with deft fingers.

"Mmm." I smile serenely, letting my eyes drift closed as I soak up the feel of their hands on me, softly stroking up my sides, brushing across my shoulders and sliding down my thighs. "I missed this."

Dante places a chaste kiss on my shoulder, and when I feel Enzo's thumb stroke along my cheek, I open my eyes to look at him. The depth of emotion peering back at me leaves me momentarily speechless. His thumb moves to brush along my lower lip, goosebumps rushing along my skin under their sinful touches. Continuing to stare up at him, I fall headfirst into those bright green eyes resembling grass on a sunny day, just tempting you to lie down on it and soak up its sun-soaked warmth. His eyes shine with so much life that I briefly forget about all the death that occurred today.

I'm still held captive in his hypnotic eyes as he leans in until our foreheads are pressed together, our breaths tangling together in the gap between our lips. "Do you have any idea just how deeply in love with you I am?"

My eyes widen, even though I shouldn't be surprised at his words. Every ounce of emotion is there for me to plainly read. Still, nothing beats hearing it from his delectable lips, especially after flirting so daringly with death several times in the past couple of days.

"Probably about as deeply as I love you."

Out of all my guys, Enzo and I have had the least time together to explore the physical chemistry between us, but we don't need to jump each other's bones to know that this is special. What we have transcends anything physical. It's embedded in the very fabric of our souls. It's in the way he looks at me, the possession in his eyes, the way they light up when I enter a room. In the soft, comforting touches when he knows I'm struggling. In the way he's so attuned to me that he knows exactly what I need without me having to say.

It makes it seem crazy that I used to distrust him. I often catch myself wondering how I didn't see the light in his soul all those years, but then I remember that the Enzo I used to meet once a month in that dingy bar isn't the same Enzo standing in front of me at this moment. Back then, his walls were ten feet tall. He might have wanted me, but he didn't know how to let me in, how to trust me. All our time together in Dante's house has given us both the opportunity to get to know one another, to see what we both keep buried underneath the armor we show the world.

"Not possible." His words are said on an exhale before he presses his lips to mine, keeping the kiss light and gentle as his hand slides up my neck to cup my jaw. I arch my back, lifting my arms to his face and fusing his lips to mine.

Heat unfurls in my core before a soft but firm grip on my hips tugs me backward. "Not yet," Dante growls, his voice thick with want. "Sleep then sex."

I push my lower lip out in a pout that makes Enzo throw his head back and laugh, and *damn,* is it the best sound I've heard all day. "You heard the man," Enzo says, siding with Dante. His eyes heat with wicked intent. "You'll need your rest for what we have in mind for you."

Dante growls a noise of agreement, and when I turn my head to look at him over my shoulder, I see the same desire brimming in his eyes before he uses his grip on my waist to walk me over to the bed. He pulls back the sheet and I slide into the middle of the bed, watching with hungry eyes as they both hurriedly strip out of their wrinkled, overworn suits that they've probably been wearing since I disappeared. Wearing only their boxers—and looking fucking edible—they climb in on either side of me, and all my fantasies come true as I'm encased in hard muscle and warm skin.

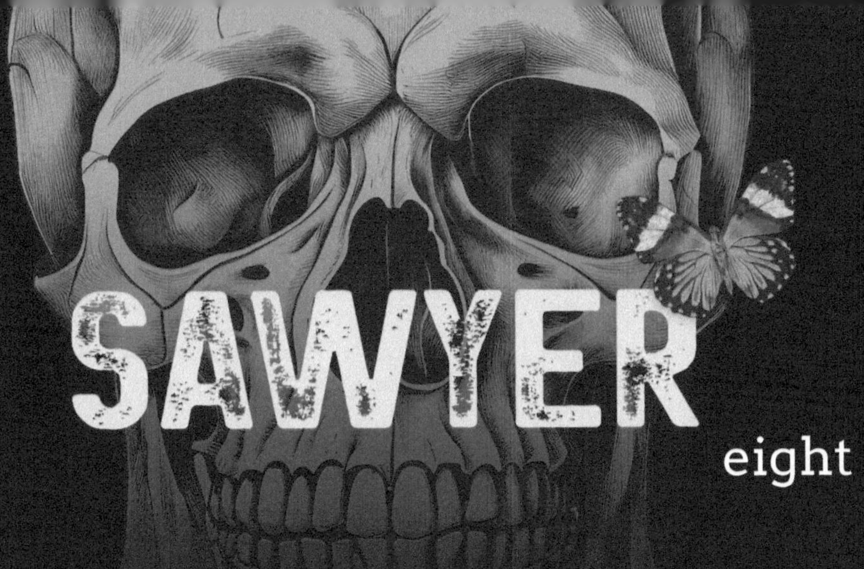

eight

My body is burning up. It feels as though I'm about to rip apart at the seams as I arch my back and throw my head back. "I love the way you look when you're about to come all over my dick," Enzo purrs, slamming into me with the most delicious ache.

A noise of agreement to my left has me turning my head, finding Cain standing at the side of the bed, tugging on his hard length, which is dripping precum like a leaky faucet. Just the sight of his bare abs as they tighten and flex has me licking my lips, and I release the bedsheets from my tight grip, reaching out for him.

He smirks, stepping closer until I can wrap my fingers around him, taking over as I begin to stroke. Oliver appears on my other side, the bed dipping as he presses a knee into the mattress before lowering his lips to my breast, teasing me with chaste kisses and quick brushes of his tongue.

I'm drifting on a sea of pleasure, but one person is missing, and I lift my head, searching for him. As though called by my thoughts, Dante appears behind Enzo. With his eyes burning into mine, he lowers his lips to Enzo's neck, sucking and biting until Enzo is moaning as loudly as I am.

My eyes flick down to where Enzo is thrusting into me as Dante's fingers move to cup his balls, causing Enzo to jerk as his movements falter. Circling the base of his cock, Dante coats his fingers in my juices before pushing them, alongside Enzo's dick, into my pussy. I cry out as I reach dizzying heights of ecstasy.

"You like that, stripper," Cain murmurs in my ear before pinching my nipple between his fingers.

Oliver shifts on the bed beside me until he mirrors Cain, and I can work them both over at once while Enzo leans in to capture my lips. His movements stall, and my gaze snaps over his shoulder, finding a slack-jawed Dante as he takes Enzo from behind until we're all just one ball of primal need, chasing that elusive high.

"You've got all of us here, Trouble." Oliver's gravel tone zaps straight to my core.

This is what I want. *This* right here is everything. "Now, what are you gonna do with us?" Mischief lifts the edge of his lips, dirty intentions shining in his eyes.

With his fingers digging into my cheeks, Cain turns my head, so I'm forced to give him my undivided attention. "You're going to be a good girl and come for us, aren't you?"

"All of us," Dante grunts. I strain to look at him out of the corner of my eye. "You're going to let all four of us fill up that sweet pussy of yours, aren't you, *mia vita*."

I can hardly string together enough syllables to answer them as my orgasm crests, forcing me to slam my eyes shut as my walls tighten around Enzo, causing him to release a string of curses and me to scream out a resounding, "Yes."

"Shush," Dante chastises. The grunt behind his words has my eyes snapping open, and I'm met with dark brown depths, pupils blown as they stare down at me from above. "He'll hear you and I need you all to myself first."

It takes a second for me to understand it was a dream, although as Dante slams his long, hard length into my pussy with enough force to make my head smack off the headboard, I realize it wasn't *all* a dream.

"Look at me, *mia vita*."

My eyes snap up to his as a wave of pleasure rocks through my body, making my lips part on a moan.

"I'll never get enough of this. Do you have any idea how gorgeous you look? How perfect you feel?"

I don't know how he can say such sweet things when he's fucking me so deeply. I can barely put together a coherent thought, but there's one thing at the forefront of my mind that requires no thought and as I stare into his awed eyes, the words spill from my lips.

"I love you."

Dante immediately stills inside me, his broad frame hovering over mine, his palms planted on the mattress beside my head. I instantly freeze beneath him, questioning whether I did the right thing, but I can't bring myself to regret saying them. Loving Dante hits me with all the force of a wrecking ball. It snuck up on me when I wasn't looking, and it took me a while to accept those feelings. Dante isn't an easy man to love, but he makes it so damn worthwhile.

I don't need him to say it back. I don't need his words to know he loves me too. He says it every day in the things he does. In the fierce way he protects me. In the intense way he looks at me. In how effortlessly he puts me above all else. But I needed him to know it's not one-sided. I fought him tooth and nail in the beginning. I told him I needed space and time, and he reluctantly gave it to me, but I'm done with space now. I don't need any more time.

All I need is him. Them. All four of them.

"I..." His words trail off as he struggles to find the right response, and I reach up, cupping his face in my palm.

"You don't need to say anything. I didn't say it to put you on the spot or make you feel bad. I just needed you to know."

His eyes search mine, and seeing the truth in my words, he dips his head and captures my lips in the sweetest kiss we've shared yet. Just one more way in which he shows his love for me. Our tongues clash, his lips hungrily devouring mine, and the entire time he remains unmoving inside of me.

We're both gasping for breath by the time we pull apart, before he rests his forehead against mine and his eyes are all I can see as I stare into them. "I love you, too."

I can see he means it. He *feels* it, and I know I said I didn't need to hear the words, but hearing him acknowledge it, accept that he's capable of feeling love, is the best present I could ever receive.

A tear slips from the corner of my eye, running down the side of my face until it gets lost in my hair. Neither of us looks away as he starts up a slow rhythm that feels as bone-deep as if he were slamming into me with hard thrusts. In our cocoon of love, it doesn't take long until I come apart, and Dante follows me over the edge, my name on his lips murmured like a prayer.

I've just slipped into the bathroom for a shower when I hear Enzo come up the stairs. I pause to listen as he enters the bedroom, hearing him grumble, "It smells like sex in here."

I don't hear Dante's muttered reply before I turn to face the mirror hanging over the vanity. I scan over my naked body, but instead of seeing the darkening bruises and lacerations from my crash, I see the flush on my chest, the forming hickeys and bite marks, the glassiness in my eyes, and the smile that looks nothing like mine. I look like a girl in love who has just been thoroughly fucked—which is precisely what I am.

Turning away from the mirror, I switch on the shower, and when the water is warm enough, I step under the spray. Tilting my head back, I let the water splash over my face and run into my hair as I thread my fingers through the wet strands.

Hearing the creak of the door opening, I crack open an eye, peering through the steam as I watch Enzo undress.

"Who says you can just invade my very important shower time?" I joke as he steps into the shower.

"I do," he growls, his voice coming out low and strained. I lift my eyes to his, noticing the tick in his jaw. "If he can steal your last few minutes of sleep, then I can claim your shower time for my own."

"Is that so?" My voice is a seductive purr as I glance up at him through my wet eyelashes.

With a nod, he states, "It is. Now turn around, Spitfire. Hands on the wall and legs spread."

You don't have to tell me twice. With a longing sweep of his toned, muscular body, noting his hard cock jutting out in front of him, I turn and do as I'm told. Anticipation thrums through me as I stare at the wall, waiting to see what he's going to do next. Since Enzo and I haven't had much chance to explore each other yet, it's all so new and exciting, and I want to know exactly what type of man he will be in bed when we're alone—no prying eyes of Giovanni's inner circle, no sharing me with Dante. Just us.

My body hums, coming to life like a flower exposed to the sun as he runs a finger down the center of my spine before trailing it over the curve of my ass and slipping between my thighs.

"Such a dirty girl," he whispers in a husky voice when he slides his finger along my slit, finding the remnants of mine and Dante's fun in his absence.

"Well, someone didn't give me time to shower."

His lips place a kiss at the juncture where my shoulder meets my neck. "I like you all dirtied up for me."

His filthy words and raw tone send a shiver of desire trickling down my spine.

"Since Dante got you all warmed up for me..." Rather than finishing that sentence, he eliminates the space between us, his cock nudging at my entrance before he tilts his hips and easily slides all the way into me.

"Oh, god," I groan, pushing my ass back against him.

"Fuuuuck," he hisses, resting his forehead against my shoulder and taking several deep breaths as he struggles to get himself under control.

There's nothing but the running of the shower as we both stand there, drinking in the moment. I can feel the hammering of his heart against my back, the tense inhales of his breaths, the tight feel of him inside me.

"God, Sawyer." The awe in his voice makes my knees weaken. "You're... God, you're everything, do you know that?"

Bathing in the light of his reverence, I roll my hips, encouraging him to move. He hisses between his teeth but gives a testing thrust. We both moan, and he repeats the action, building up to a hard rhythm that soon has me plastered against the shower wall. His hands move to cover mine, our fingers intertwined as he fucks me into the wall, sending us both crashing headfirst into a blistering orgasm.

When I come down, he gently turns me around, his touches light and caring as he grabs the shampoo bottle and begins massaging it into my hair. When he's done with that, he moves on to cover my body in suds before washing everything off. When we're both clean, he turns off the water and grabs a towel, wrapping it around me.

It's only then that I hear the voices beyond the door, straining to make out who it is. Enzo must hear them, too, as he moves to open the door a crack, allowing Cain's deep rumble to reach our ears.

"Guess our little break from reality is over," he sighs.

"Yeah, but it was pretty good while it lasted," I jest with a smile.

He smirks back before passing me my clothes, and I quickly towel off and get dressed while he does the same.

"Where did you get those?" I ask as he pulls up a pair of faded light blue jeans.

"Marcus dropped a bag of clothing off for us. While I am partial to a suit, they were not made to be worn several days in a row, and since I didn't think there would be a spare one sitting around here, I figured this was better than nothing."

"That was nice of him," I say, towel-drying my hair.

"Yeah. Seems like he meant what he said yesterday."

"I wonder what the opinion of the rest of the Rejects are."

"Guess we'll find out when we talk to Cain." There's a tightness around Enzo's eyes, and I reach out to iron out the creases.

"Do you want them to accept you?" I ask, unsure what the goal is here or what they want.

"I don't want them to *not* accept me," he says with a frown. "I'm not a Reject, and I don't want to be, but we are allies, and as such, I'd like it if we could build some sort of alliance with them. Except, alliances only work if there's trust on both sides."

I hum my agreement. "Well, yesterday can only have helped things, right?"

He nods, but there's still a hesitancy in his eyes as we pull open the bathroom door and step back into the fray.

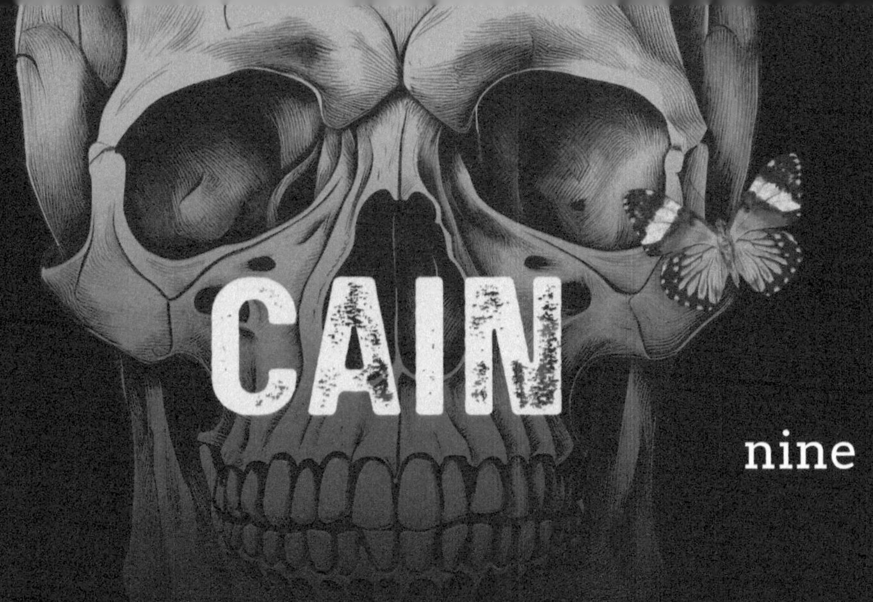

nine

I slide a palm over my face, weariness tugging at the last of my patience as I sink into a moth-eaten sofa in Oliver's childhood home. I bought this house when I purchased my own, but I had no idea what to do with it. Until we moved into the clubhouse, some of the guys would sleep here occasionally, but I never found the time to modernize any of it. When Oliver was released, I handed the deed over to him. I'm not entirely sure if that was the right thing for me to do or not, but I had no need for it, and I thought he might want it.

As of yet, he hasn't done anything with the place. I'm not even sure if he's set foot inside, but it's come in handy, what with the overcrowding situation going on in my home. At least it's quiet here, no bickering or farting challenges or the constant drone of the TV on in the background. I thought living in a clubhouse with errant teenagers was bad, but it's fucking bliss in comparison to living in a cramped, three-bedroom house with them.

I brush a hand through my still-damp hair. As soon as my car pulled up, I was bombarded with a million questions from the kids, all of them wanting to know who'd been hurt, who'd died, how they could help. It took a while for me to field all of them, as well as catch up with Marcus and check in on Evie, before I could finally go for a shower and then come over here. I'd wanted to come straight here, but I knew it would be even harder for me to leave once Red was in my arms again. No, I knew I had to deal with everything else before seeing her.

Now that I've finally stopped and finally sat down, the silence presses in around me, sounding too loud after the noise and chaos. I don't remember the last time I got a solid night's sleep or how long I've been up for, and even though my body feels wrung out, my mind can't shut down. Every action and inaction, every decision I made or didn't make, plays out in my head as the confidence I displayed earlier in the heat of battle, in front of my people, gives way to insecurities. It's always the same, especially when there is loss of life involved. You always wonder if there's something you could have done

After Sawyer and the suited pricks left, my men and I dove straight into damage control. We had to re-arm our perimeters, check the structural damage of the building, not to mention count the dead.

Five. Five of my men died today. Well, yesterday now, I guess. It's all been one never-ending day to me. Some people might think five deaths isn't too bad, and it's not, but for me, it's still five deaths too many. Five deaths that I now have to carry with me, that will forever tug on my soul and hang like a cloud over any bright days there may be in my future.

On the upside, we killed all twenty-five attackers. Mostly Grim's men, with a handful of Giovanni's. My men are already demanding payback for this attack, for the lives lost. I am too. I will not let this go unpunished. Giovanni is a challenging opponent, one I'm not yet sure how to defeat, but Grim... Grim, we can definitely handle. He's just climbed to the number one spot on my kill list, and I can't wait to see how he fucking likes it when we show up at his door, shooting his men down one by one.

The last—and the most complicated—problem I had to deal with before I could come here, was fielding the men's questions about Dante and Enzo. It's safe to say none of them were happy when I first showed up with them on my heels. I could see the skepticism, the hate in their eyes, the flickering uncertainty directed at me when I walked past with them behind me.

Nevertheless, many of the men witnessed Dante and Enzo fighting alongside them. They saw the fact that they stayed—and not so they could attack from the inside and give Giovanni the surprise advantage. It left them confused, to say the least, and raised many questions. Questions I wasn't sure how to answer. Everyone wanted to know if we were allies, if we were working together, if I trusted them.

I didn't know how to answer a single one. Are we allies? Can you be allies and hate the person's guts? I guess, since we're all on Giovanni's shit list, that alone makes us allies. At this point, we all want the same thing—to be rid of Giovanni. After that? I have no fucking idea. That's probably a conversation Dante and I need to have sooner rather than later because his answer might determine everything.

As for whether or not I trust them. Yes and no. I trust that they'll protect Red, that they will keep her safe and take care of her when I'm not around. I saw how they were with her today—the way we all worked to protect her the best we could. Honestly, knowing they were there allowed me to focus solely on the situation at hand.

But do I trust them with my men? Trust them to do what's right for my people and for the city of Black Creek? Hell no. It's kind of fucked up when you think about it. I trust them with the one woman who means absolutely everything to me, but I don't trust them with anything else. Then again, the only reason I do trust them with Red is because I see the way they are with her. I fucking hate their possessive posturing over her and the way they look at her, although I recognize all of it for what it is.

They fucking care for her, the way Oliver and I do. I might not fucking like it, but it does mean I can trust them when it comes to her safety. Even though simply the thought of sending her away with them after the fighting ceased was harder than any other decision I made in the heat of battle. All I wanted was to keep her by my side, where I could watch her with my own eyes. Even after they left and I was helping clean up alongside my men, my thoughts kept drifting to her, wondering what she was doing, what *they* were doing, and every fucking time, the images that assaulted my mind would make my blood boil. Nevertheless, I knew it was the right decision to make. She couldn't be there to see the destruction left behind, and I couldn't have *them* there any longer, either.

A presence in the doorway pulls me out of my thoughts as my gaze snaps up to Dante's stoic expression. Even now, that bubble of hatred wells up. *I really don't fucking like him.* However, it's no longer as fucking simple as liking him or not, because he fought alongside us yesterday. Not only that, but he saved my life in the stairwell. I probably owe him a fucking thank you, but I can't make my mouth form the words, so I don't.

As silent as always, his oppressive aura seems to fill the room as he steps into it, his eyes fixed on me. He's dressed differently today, like someone born in Black Creek, in jeans and a cotton t-shirt, and yet the clothes don't look right on him. It's not that they don't fit, they just look out of place. It's jarring, drawing my attention for a long moment as I run my gaze up and down his tall frame.

He rolls his shoulders, as though trying to stretch the fabric out and make it more comfortable, and I realize he feels just as out of place in those clothes as I do at seeing him in them.

"Where's Red?" I ask, flicking my gaze to the empty doorway before focusing back on him.

"*Sawyer* will be down in a minute."

Not an answer, but rather than arguing, because I'm too fucking tired for that, I ask, "What are your plans with the Antonelli Empire once your father is no longer an issue?"

After today, after my men saw him on their turf, and with how quickly we need to move to eliminate Giovanni before he completely wipes us from the board, I have to know if Dante is an issue I also need to account for.

I know Red thinks he's worth saving, but if he's a threat to my men, to the future we are trying to build, then he has to go. I won't get rid of one egotistical overseer just to replace him with another.

"With my father out of the picture, I'm next in line to take his place."

There it is. The answer that I knew was coming yet was afraid to hear. There's no uncertainty in Dante's tone. He'll step into his father's shoes in his absence. Which means he's officially become a problem.

I cock a brow. "And you expect the men to simply follow your rule after you defected? Not the best start to a new reign."

"Only the men who were in the tower that night and my father's closest advisers will have any knowledge of my deceit." He must see my surprise as he explains, "It would be seen as a weakness, and one thing my father will not tolerate is anyone perceiving him as weak."

"So my men will remove your father and his closest advisors and pave the way for you to take his place." Dante's brow raises at my scathing tone, while he crosses his arms over his chest, his eyes boring into mine.

"What is it you really want to ask me, Cain?"

"I want to know if you're going to be a problem."

"You want to know if I'm going to be my father," he counters.

I shrug a shoulder. "Same thing."

His lips thin as he mulls over his response, tense seconds passing by as I wait to hear if I'm going to have to go against Red's wishes and kill him.

"I don't agree with everything my father does. I'll admit I'm just as guilty of staying on my side of the river and not giving a shit about what happens over here unless it directly affected us, but I'm not my father. I have no interest in making the lives of the people of Black Creek even more miserable."

"What does that mean?" I bite out. "Are you going to go back to pretending none of us exist?"

Dante studies me for a moment, his eyes narrowing. "Is that what *you* want?"

One side of my lip lifts in a snarl. "I want the people in this city to have a fighting chance. To not be at each other's throats over scraps and pennies. To not have to fear that an Antonelli will storm into their life over some petty issue and turn their world upside down."

"You want the Antonellis to stay out of Black Creek," he accurately summarizes.

"If you're not going to better it, then yes."

He nods thoughtfully before he says, "The Antonellis have plenty. We have no need for the city. If you want it, then I'm sure we can come to some sort of an agreement."

It's not quite the outright agreement to leave Black Creek alone I'd hoped for, but it's more than I expected from him.

"And what would you want in exchange?" His gaze flicks toward the doorway, and I instantly stiffen, my tone non-negotiable as I grit out, "I won't give up Red."

"As tempting as that is, I wasn't going to ask you to. For whatever reason that I can't understand, Sawyer actually likes you." His less than impressed gaze runs over me. "Personally, I find you abrasive and unlikeable."

"And I find you apathetic and cold."

He shrugs, unbothered by my judgment of him, just like I don't give a shit what he thinks of me.

"The point is," he sighs in frustration, "*Sawyer* likes you." He looks like he's chewing on something he finds repugnant before he spits out, "And unfortunately, I find myself unable to do anything that would upset her. If you and your men can help overthrow my father and remove everyone loyal to him, then in exchange, I'll help you restore Black Creek."

His offer leaves me speechless. I hadn't ever expected him to *help* me. My eyes narrow in suspicion. "Why would you do that?"

"Because this is Sawyer's home. I doubt she'll leave it, especially not if she has the opportunity to help improve it." He purses his lips. "Which means it'll be my home, too." He looks thoroughly unimpressed by that idea, and yeah, I can't exactly picture someone like Dante slumming it here in the grungy streets of Black Creek instead of his gleaming, glass apartment on the elite side of the river.

"You're going to move here?" I question, unsure if that's what he means or not.

"I'll be wherever Sawyer is. If that's here, then,"—he sighs— "yes, I'll be moving here."

"You think about that stuff, with her?"

"You don't?" he volleys.

Of course, I fucking do. I just hadn't realized *he* did. It brings a whole new sense of realism to all of this—to our incredibly complicated situation with Red. Surprisingly, when I think about my future with Red, he's not fucking in it. I guess, I'd abstractly thought he and Enzo would go back to their part of the city when this was all done, and I dunno, Red would travel back and forth? Although, now that I actually think about the idea, I realize how asinine that is. How unfeasible it would be, how unfair. None of us could ask that of her. She's not a kid to be passed back and forth between divorced parents who can't stand to be in the same room as one another.

She deserves a place she can call home, somewhere she can be herself and feel comfortable. A house where Luc can have his own bedroom, maybe something with a yard, too. A home filled with love and laughter.

Shit, please don't tell me that means I will have to share a house with this fucker.

I choose not to answer Dante, so the two of us are sitting in a tense, uncomfortable silence when Red appears.

"Playing nice?" she questions with a raised eyebrow, darting a wary glance between us as she crosses the room toward me.

"He's still breathing, isn't he?"

Dante scoffs. "Like I'd let you get anywhere near me."

I pretend he no longer exists as I pull Red into my lap, burying my head in her neck and closing my eyes as I breathe her in. *God, I needed this—her.* She melts against me, shifting so she can run her fingers through my hair. Her touch feels like heaven, and I let myself have this moment to forget about everything that's going on, to grieve the men I lost, to prepare for the battle to come, to accept that the future I once pictured for Red and me isn't the one that's going to play out.

All of those conflicting emotions crash through me, thrown together and churning as though caught up in a tornado, before I slowly release each of them. I bottle each emotion up in a helium balloon tied to a string and hold them up to the sky before letting go, watching as they drift into the distance until I once again feel that deep calm that I need in order to be the leader that I am, the partner that I am, the man that I need to be.

When I finally lift my face from the crook of Red's neck, I find her stare latched on mine, swimming with concern. She holds my gaze in a silent question, *are you okay?* as her eyes search mine for the answer. *No, but I'm holding it together—for you, for my men, for Evie.*

All I see in her gaze is unwavering faith and confidence, and I latch on to that, using it to bolster me until I know she can see that confidence reflected back at her, a soft smile lifting her lips. She nods her head as if to say, *you've got this,* and I respond in kind. *Damn right, I do.*

When I turn my focus to the room, noticing that Enzo has joined us, all of those feelings are again tucked away, and I'm again the formidable leader of the Rejects once more. I don't give a shit if they witnessed my vulnerable moment with Red, so long as they realize my vulnerability does not make me weak. Hell, it's what makes me so headstrong, so driven. It's why I'm so damn determined to make Giovanni and Grim pay and ensure no one else has to suffer at their hands ever again.

"Where's Oliver?" Red asks, noticing his absence.

"He's still at the clubhouse, wrapping up a few things. When he's done, we all need to sit down and talk strategy."

"We do," Enzo agrees, leaning forward and resting his elbows on his knees, his fingers tucked under his chin. "Today's attack was only a test."

"What do you mean?"

At her question, his eyes dart to Sawyer. "Did you notice it was mostly Bastards there today?"

"Yeah?"

"He used them to bait us. To assess how challenging of an opponent the Rejects will be. That's why he hardly sent any of his own men. I'd hazard a guess that those men Dante killed were there to scope out the clubhouse and find out what they could about the Rejects' operation, as well as picking off as many of them as they could."

"Well then, at least we killed his scouting party," Sawyer says, a fleck of optimism in her tone. "He won't know just how well armed we are."

"No," I agree, "but he knows we're organized and ready for a fight."

A cruel smile spreads across Dante's face, making him look every bit of the mafia assassin he is. "Then let's give him a fight he'll never forget."

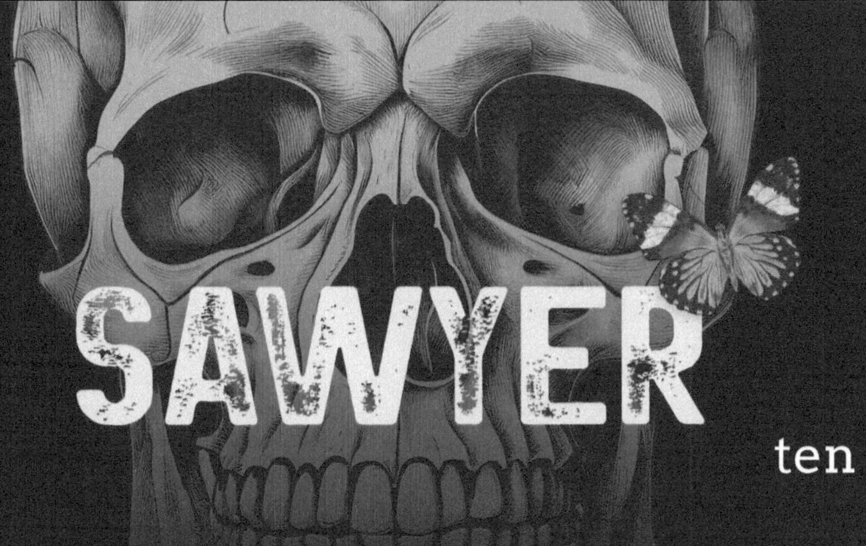

SAWYER

ten

I manage to convince Cain to get some sleep while we wait for Oliver to get back. In the meantime, I decide to go next door and check on Luc and Evie. I know Cain checked on her when he got back, but I figure she might be glad for some female company. She must be ready to pull her hair out, being stuck in the same house as the kids for the last few days.

The commotion assaults my ears as soon as I open the door, yelling from the front room drowning out the sound of the TV playing in the background.

"I'm sick of watching your shit! It's my turn to pick somethin'."

Bickering ensues, and I roll my eyes as I poke my head into the living room. The room has been taken over by tall, lanky teenagers sprawled over the sofas and draping their legs off the arms of chairs.

I only linger long enough to notice Luc isn't among them before walking past into the kitchen.

"Hey," I greet Marcus, scanning the room for my brother before focusing back on him. "How are things going over here?"

His eyes are duller than normal. "As good as can be expected."

"At least the kids are up to their usual antics."

He shakes his head as though he's at his wit's end with them. "They're driving me insane. That many teenage boys are not meant to be sequestered in one small house for this long." A smirk tugs at my lips. "I'm about to take them over to the clubhouse and have them burn off some of that energy on fixing the place up."

"Is that wise?" I question. "With Giovanni and all?"

"Giovanni is likely holed up in his tower planning our demise. It will be a day or two at the earliest before he attacks."

I just nod. "And Evie? How is she?"

His eyes flash with worry and simmer with rage. "Hard to tell. She's quiet, withdrawn. Sometimes the kids' presence seems as though it's a welcome distraction, and others, she shies away from the noise."

"I thought I'd check on her before I leave," I hedge.

Concern still tightens his facial features as he nods. "I think she'd like that. I'm guessing you're here to see your brother..." He gestures toward the back door. "Luc's outside."

My eyes swivel to the back door, but I don't immediately move toward it. "How has he been?" I ask Marcus instead.

His lips purse again, his face tightening. "He's trying to act like nothing happened, hanging out and laughing with the kids, though sometimes it's as if he gets lost inside his head. I can tell he's not in the room, but he hasn't talked to any of us. Although, I've heard him and Evie chatting late at night."

My gaze is still focused on the back door, as if I can see through it, while I try to work out what I can say or do to make everything better for him.

"Just knowing you're there is enough," Marcus says. When I flick my gaze his way, I notice him studying me, likely reading the thoughts on my face. "He just needs to know you're there."

With a sharp jerk of my head, I walk over to the back door and pull it open. Luc is sitting on the top step of the back porch, staring out over the small expanse of grass that makes up the backyard. He doesn't even turn his head as I step onto the porch and move toward him.

"Hey," I say softly, slowly lowering myself onto the wooden step beside him. He startles, and I'm guessing he was lost in his thoughts, just like Marcus had mentioned, before I spoke.

"Hey." His voice is dull and scratchy, as though he hasn't spoken to anyone all morning, never removing his focus from the far-off spot he was staring at. "What are you doing here?"

"Can't I come check on my little brother?"

That garners a ghost of a smile, but there's none of the liveliness I saw yesterday. I guess relief at knowing I was alive and the adrenaline from finding out about the clubhouse, pulled him from this more subdued state.

"Talk to me," I urge, nudging his shoulder with mine.

"I don't want to talk about that." There's steel in his voice, and I work to swallow the questions biting at the end of my tongue.

"I didn't say you had to talk about that," I counter.

"How did you get away from Giovanni's men?" he asks instead.

"I got lucky," I tell him honestly. "I managed to kill the guy who shot me off my bike, but then I passed out. A friend I'd made when we were sleeping on the streets found me."

"Do the people you kill haunt you?"

It takes me a second to wrap my brain around the change of direction of the conversation, and I stiffen at his question, my mind whirring as I wonder why, of all things, he'd ask me *that*. Why he'd feel the need to. It takes all of my willpower not to demand to know and instead form a suitable response.

"No. Everyone I've killed deserved it."

"What if you didn't know they deserved it? What if you killed someone who was innocent?"

I frown, even as worry slicks like oil, coating my insides. "If he was an Antonelli," I say, choosing my words wisely. "Then he most likely deserved it. And even if he didn't, anything Giovanni or Santos made you do under duress is not your fault."

His haunted eyes finally turn toward mine, but he doesn't speak.

"What can I do to help you?" I plead, reaching out to wrap my hands around both of his.

Something shifts in his gaze, then he shakes his head. "You've already done so much for me, Sawyer. Too much." He gestures toward the back door of the house. "You have them now, and you're... happy."

Squeezing his hand tightly, I hold his gaze with mine, imbuing every bit of love into them. "You are and always will be my first priority. It's always been just us. There might be a bigger team around us now, but it will always be you and me." The shadows lift somewhat from his eyes as he smiles.

"Just you and me, huh?"

I smile brightly. "Always, kid."

"And the four hunks of steel and muscle you've surrounded yourself with." I don't say anything, and he continues. "You sure go all out, don't you? Couldn't just find yourself one giant asshole to date, you had to get four of them."

Snorting, I watch as the last of the shadows dissipate from behind Luc's eyes, and I take in the first full breath since I sat down beside him. "Given our last conversation, I was surprised you didn't tell Dante and Enzo to go to hell yesterday."

He shrugs. "Figured since they helped find you and keep you safe, I could bite my tongue for one day."

I have to squash the smile threatening to lift the corners of my lips. "Right."

"I still don't trust them, though."

A smile breaks free and I chuckle. "God, you sound just like Cain."

I notice the barely perceptible straightening of Luc's spine, like it makes him proud to be compared to Cain, and something warms in my chest even as I wonder what the hell I've gotten myself in for if Luc has decided Cain is his male role model. Couldn't he have chosen to take on Oliver's reasonable disposition rather than Cain's hot-headedness?

"I'm not worried," I tell him honestly. "They'll earn your trust, just like they earned mine and are earning Cain's and Oliver's."

A comfortable silence falls between us as we both stare out across the yard before I change the topic. "Did you ask Evie about that movie?"

"Not yet."

"Marcus says he's seen the two of you talking."

A small shrug before he says, "Even though what happened with her was... different, it feels like she understands."

I nod in understanding, giving his hand another squeeze. "Only you and Evie know what it was like in that tower. I'm glad you have each other and that you feel like you can talk to her. Just remember, there isn't a single person in this house who wouldn't understand. Bones and the others, they get it too. Whatever it is you need in order to move past this and come out stronger, no one will judge or question you for it."

"I've asked Bones, Tank, and Rampage to train me," he begins. "I know Bones has been teaching me to fight, but I want to know more. I want to be able to defend myself, to know how to fight back, to be able to use a gun and wield a knife."

"Good." His eyebrows lift in surprise at my blunt tone. "I shouldn't have shielded you from all of that," I confess. "I should have taught you what I knew, shown you the basics. Maybe if I had..." I trail off, and it's Luc's turn to comfort me as he turns his hand over in mine and squeezes it.

"You were trying to give me a childhood. You *did* give me a childhood." His lips purse, and he swallows audibly. "But this is war, and after what happened, I don't want to be used as a pawn against you—against any of you. I never want to be defenseless at someone else's mercy again. I—I..."

"You won't be." I imbue every word with that promise. "Train with the kids. Learn. Become an unstoppable force. Don't let them win. Don't let *Santos* win."

We sit on the back porch for a while longer, occasionally talking but mostly just breathing in the fresh air and soaking up the reassurance that comes from knowing Luc's here, right beside me.

He's lost and struggling right now, and I have no idea how to help him or what to do, but he has so much support around him. Although he might feel alone, he's not. I can only hope he'll soon realize as much, and perhaps even reach out to Dante or Enzo about what he went through. Far too many people around us know what it's like to be held against your will, to be forced to do things you don't want to do, but only they and Evie know what it's like to survive at the hands of Giovanni and Santos. Even though Luc doesn't trust them or show any inclination of wanting to get to know them, I hope that if he's struggling, he will open up to them or, at the very least, talk to Evie or one of his friends. If there's one thing I've learned these last few months, it's that sharing your burdens doesn't make you weak or weigh others down; it lifts you up, solidifies your friendships and relationships, and ultimately makes you stronger. We are all capable of surviving on our own, but we're only able to live if we trust in others and open ourselves up to them.

"Luc, we... Oh, hey." Jon grins at me. "Didn't realize you were here."

"Just wanted to check in, make sure all of you hadn't driven poor Marcus completely insane."

Jon laughs. "Not yet." His gaze darts to Luc. "Marcus is taking us over to the club-house, if you wanna come help out."

I tense but force myself to relax when Luc glances in my direction. It takes every-thing in me to give him an encouraging nod when all I want to do is wrap him up in bubble wrap and hide him in a closet. Except I know I can't always protect him, and I can't smother him, either. Keeping him cooped up in this house will only further impact his mental health. He needs a distraction and being surrounded by Rejects, I know he couldn't be safer.

He gives a small, wry grin, as if he knows the internal struggle I'm currently battling before climbing to his feet and heading inside. I catch Jon's eye before he moves to follow after him, his nod a silent promise to keep an eye on him. It helps, marginally, but I force myself to remain seated on the back porch step while I listen to Marcus usher them all outside, until the car engine has faded into the distance and quiet has resumed all around me. Only then do I get to my feet and go in search of Evie. She's alone in the house—and probably thankful for the peace and quiet—but I know the only reason Marcus left her by herself is because all of us are right next door. Hell, Cain probably has cameras and tripwires set up around the outside of the house, ensuring he'll know if anyone dares to come within ten feet of the property.

I don't have to go far, as I find Evie already in the kitchen when I step through the screen door. She tenses as soon as she hears me, spinning with a kitchen knife clutched tightly in her hand. Even as I stop a safe distance away, I smirk, casting my eyes over the black skinny jeans—an old pair of mine—and the baggy hoodie—probably Cain's—that she's wearing. Based on pieces of information I've gathered from Oliver and Cain, Evie must be about my age, although drowning in the hoodie and with the cute, pink, fluffy socks on her feet, it's hard to remember that.

As soon as she realizes it's me, she lowers her weapon. "Sorry," she mumbles.

"No, don't apologize. You look good wielding that knife."

Creases form along her forehead. "That's... an incredibly weird thing to say."

I laugh. "Yeah, probably. I just mean it's good to see there's some fight left in you."

Her gaze drops to the floor. "Too little, too late, though," she murmurs, more to herself, yet I refuse to let her think that, so I interject anyway.

"None of that!" I snap out, slowly taking a step toward her, not wanting to upset or alarm her, but not one bit liking her negative attitude toward herself.

"It's the truth, though, isn't it? It's what you're thinking. What all of you are thinking."

"You couldn't be further from the truth. Perhaps you didn't fight back physically, didn't wield a weapon or inflict any damage, but you fought by simply staying alive, by not losing yourself, by not giving in, and *that* takes more strength than stabbing someone with a knife ever could."

Her eyes flash in surprise, only it quickly disappears as she shakes her head. "But I did give in. I told Luc that he should just accept his fate, that he should stop fighting and just give in."

I have to school my surprise, because that is not what Cain told me. The only thing Luc seemed willing to talk about to Cain was what Evie had said to him during the one time they met, and according to Cain, she told Luc to run, to get out of there.

"Didn't you also tell him to run?" I counter. "I don't think someone who has truly given up would try to save someone else."

"Just because I'd given up on myself, doesn't mean I wanted someone else to bear the same fate as me."

"I don't think you'd given up," I continue to argue. "I think you were surviving. You were doing whatever it took to survive in that place. While you may not have been actively seeking an escape, I think you would have taken it if an opportunity had arisen."

"I—" She pauses, her mouth clamping shut. "I lost hope."

"Hope is a fickle bitch. It can kill you just as quickly as it can save you. When I first started living on the streets with Luc, I used to hope that things would improve. I'd pray and dream of a better future for us, except with every passing day where those hopes and dreams became more and more unachievable, that hope started to become suffocating. It was like a noose around my neck that grew tighter until I struggled to breathe beneath the weight of it all. Every time I'd close my eyes, I could see this bright future being dangled just out of reach, taunting me but not something I could ever achieve."

"So what did you do?" Evie asks, her eyes wide as if she's hanging on to every word I say.

"I shoved that hope into a little box in the back of my mind, and I buried it so deep that I forgot it ever existed. I stopped hoping things would get better, stopped dreaming of a brighter future, and started focusing on surviving the here and now. On simply getting through the day. On ensuring Luc and I were alive, warm, and fed. As the years went on, I developed tunnel vision. I couldn't see past the act of merely surviving to realize I no longer had to just survive."

"What made you realize?"

My lips quirk up in a genuine smile. "Oliver. And your brother. And later, Dante and Enzo. They reminded me that there was more to life than survival. They showed me that survival is the very minimum of what we should aim for, and that if I dared hope for more, I'd discover an entire kaleidoscope of parts that make up the act of living. Surviving is what is at the very core of our being. Our bodies and minds instinctively adapt in order to ensure our survival, but love, friendships, laughter, trust, all of those are what truly make us *feel* alive." Dante is only starting to understand all those things, while I needed reminding of them, and I think Oliver, Cain, and Enzo needed that reminder too.

"I think..." Evie licks her lips in a nervous gesture, but there's a fierceness in her eyes as she holds my gaze. "I think I needed that reminder too. Luc gave me that reminder."

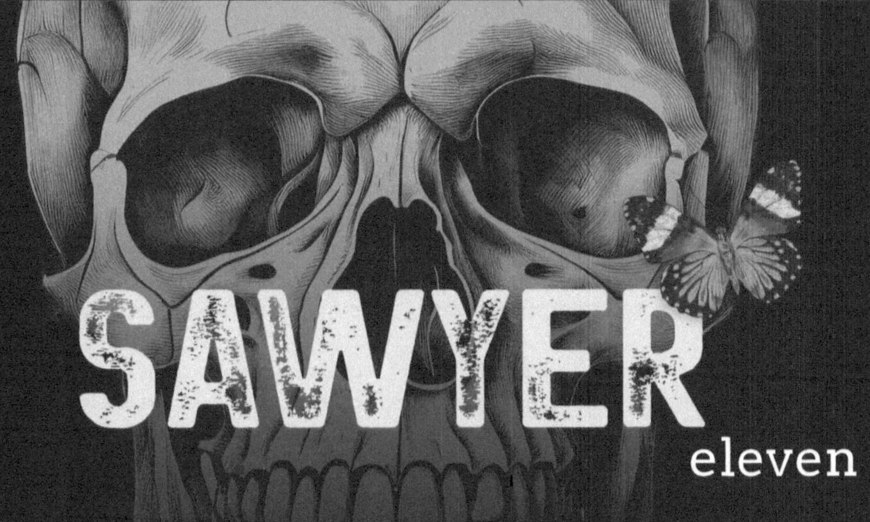

Evie and I sit down to chat over coffee, and although she's quiet and subdued, that fierceness I saw in her eyes occasionally makes an appearance. It reminds me of Cain when he's incensed, and I discover that I enjoy talking to Evie. We keep the conversation light. I mostly tell her about my life and answer whatever questions I can about the Rejects and the kids. She admits that she isn't sure how to be around the kids and doesn't feel entirely comfortable even though she knows they won't hurt her, and I assure her that's perfectly normal and that none of them will take offense. I think it helps when I give her a little insight into their past and the similarities with her own. I don't miss the way her cheeks turn red at the sound of Marcus' name, but again, I don't tease or pry. However, I do manage to convince her to have a movie night with Luc and a couple of the kids—not all of them—and before we part ways, she promises me she'll talk to Luc about it when he gets back.

Although I wasn't much help with Luc, the fact that I was able to help Evie and have gotten to know her a little better has me feeling lighter as I head toward the front door. Oliver must surely be back by now, and we all need to sit down and discuss our next moves.

Before I can reach the front door, it flies open, and Oliver storms in like a man on a mission.

"What's wrong?" I ask, taking in his tense stance as his large legs eat up the distance between us.

"You mean other than the fact you were shot off your bike, hurt, went missing for forty-eight hours, the club was attacked while you were there, and people died?"

"Yes?" I cock a brow, unsure of where he's going with this.

"And the fact that before you disappeared, I acted like a fucking asshole and nearly ruined the only good thing in my life?"

"You won't hear any arguments from me."

"Then I guess it's because I've yet to show you just how sorry I am." His lips crash down on mine, hungry and desperate. I can taste the anguish in his kiss, feel his apology with every swipe of his tongue over mine.

Tilting his head, he deepens the kiss, quickly embedding himself in every fiber of my being as he sucks, nibbles, and bites along my lips. My hands sink into his hair while his slide around my waist, his fingers squeezing the curve of my ass as he hauls me against him.

"God, I can't believe I was so stupid. How I ever questioned this," he murmurs against my lips before claiming them again, not giving me a chance to respond. His kiss is blazing hot, melting my insides. "I shouldn't have kept you at arm's length. I should have known kissing you would have confirmed what I already knew but was questioning." Another impassioned kiss that leaves me breathless. "One brush of your skin, one kiss from your lips, and it's so glaringly obvious. So blatantly apparent." I'm a panting mess when he pulls back again. "No one makes me feel the way you do. No one brings me to my knees in awe or makes my chest swell with pride. No one else terrifies me with their bravery or amazes me with their compassion."

The combination of his heartfelt words, the wonder in his tone, and the effect his kisses are having on me mean I'm on the verge of combusting as I rock my hips against his, digging my fingers into his shoulders and clinging to him as I chase some much-needed friction.

"Less talking, more showing," I pant as his fingers squeeze my hips, holding me flush against him.

His chuckle is deep and raw. "You need to know how much I love you. How sorry I am. How sincere I am when I promise I'll never doubt you—us—again."

"I know," I say breathlessly. "But just in case I forget, you should show me."

Another throaty chuckle, but apparently in agreement, Oliver doesn't continue to woo me with his words and instead slides his palms over the curve of my ass and along the back of my thighs before he hoists me up. My legs wrap around his waist as his lips move to the angle of my jaw, peppering kisses along the skin all the way to my ear while I grind against his growing length.

"Not here," I gasp, a wisp of common sense slipping through the lust-infused fog. "Evie. She's... Oh, god," I moan when he sucks on a sensitive bit of skin behind my ear.

Still driving me wild with his kisses, he tightens his hold on my thighs as he blindly navigates the hall, kicking the screen door open with his boot. I've no idea how he doesn't trip as we descend the front porch steps and traverse the uneven paving slabs in the front yard. Not once does he remove his focus from lavishing my neck, my shoulder, my collarbone. The anticipation only serves to spike my desire until I'm clawing at his back and fisting his hair.

"Fuck, Red, you're going to make me come in my pants if you keep grinding on me like that," he breathes as we stumble up the porch steps of the house Dante and Enzo have been staying in. My back smacks against the front door as Oliver's mouth returns to mine. Palming my ass, he grinds his pelvis against mine until he's groaning and I'm moaning, neither of us giving a shit that anyone on the street or in the adjacent houses can see us. Nothing exists except him and me and this infinite hunger between us, the crackling heat of chemistry and all-consuming desire to sink so deep into one another that we fuse together as one.

Fumbling for the door handle behind me when Oliver finally lifts me off the door, I pull it open, and we stumble inside, laughing and moaning while I slide my hands into the narrow gap between us and work to undo his belt. Both of us are aware that we're behaving like hormone-ridden teenagers, but neither of us care, too lost to the aching need throbbing deep down inside.

"What the hell?" someone calls out, but I can hardly hear them over the rushing in my ears.

"Dude, what the fuck?!"

I manage to get the buckle undone and the button popped, but I can't get the zip down. Giving up, I arch my back instead and peel my top off over my head, breaking our kiss only long enough to remove it.

Oliver quickly glances to his left, and out of the corner of my eye, I notice Dante and Enzo both standing in the doorway looking pissed as all hell, before I clamp my hands on either side of Oliver's cheeks and yank his head back to mine, hungrily devouring his lips.

Right as my eyelids drift closed, I notice Oliver stick out his hand and give both men the middle finger, and I laugh against his lips as I close my eyes, relishing the feel of his calloused hands as they slide up my back.

Reaching down, I tug on his top until it rises, quickly pulling it over his head and dropping it onto the stairs behind him as he walks us up to the bedroom. My palms glide over his chest and shoulders, loving how his muscles tense beneath them and the hungry groans escaping his lips.

"I need to be inside you right now," he growls as we reach the top of the stairs and he walks toward the nearest bedroom. His voice is a deep rumble that drips sex and makes my core tighten.

"So stop teasing me and *show me*," I moan, rocking my hips against his in such a way that elicits an animalistic growl from the back of his throat.

The second we cross the threshold into the bedroom, he drops me to my feet and spins me around. My hands fly out to steady myself before I can fall while Oliver reaches around me for the buttons on my jeans, shoving them and my panties down over my thighs until they gather at my ankles.

"Boots off," he orders while he quickly discards my bra and begins lavishing every bit of available skin with scorching kisses and wicked grazes of his teeth that have my body practically humming in anticipation.

With zero grace or tact, I kick off a boot and remove one leg from my jeans and panties, and the second I do, he kicks my legs wide, spreading me open. His fingers disappear between my thighs, and he hums his approval when he discovers just how ready I am for him. After worrying I might never have this with him again, both when I thought he might choose Evie over me or when I feared Giovanni would capture me, I can't get enough of him now. Can't get him deep enough under my skin. Can't get him deep enough inside of me.

His thumb circles the sensitive bundle of nerves, teasing my entrance before he sinks a finger inside me. My spine arches as I cry out, my fingernails scraping against the wall as wave after delicious wave courses through me, making my legs tremble and my heart race.

"Want me to show you exactly what you mean to me, Trouble?" he purrs against my ear. "Do you want me to worship at the altar of your body and beg for forgiveness until my name is a prayer on your tongue?

"Yes," I moan. "God, yes, I want that."

His only response is to sink to his knees behind me and do exactly that. He worships me with his tongue until I'm keening and crying out, my body trembling so hard I can hardly remain on my feet. Even when I throw my head back and scream his name to the heavens above, he doesn't relent, devouring me like a man starved and I'm a feast to be gorged on.

Only when I've come on his tongue twice does he take pity on me, his hands sliding up my thighs, over my flat stomach, and along my ribs as he rises. The warmth of his chest bleeds into my back as he shucks his jeans and boxers.

"I'm so unworthy of you," he murmurs. "We are all so unworthy, and yet, none of us will let you go."

"Good." It's a struggle to get the word out through my tight throat. "Because I'm not letting any of you go either. Worthy or not, we're a team. We're a family. I belong to all of you, and all of you belong to me. Nothing, and no one will change that."

"Spoken like a true Queen."

Oliver sinks himself deep inside me in one swift thrust that has me arching my back and throwing my head back against his shoulder. His hips hold mine in place as he slides out before pounding into me again until sweat slickens our skin, and the only sound in the room is our heavy breaths and the slap of skin against skin. With his face buried against my neck, he reaches out a hand to where mine is splayed flat against the wall, interlocking our fingers as we both reach our climax.

Boneless, I sag against him, and Oliver bands his free arm around my waist, holding me steady while we both catch our breaths. My head rests against his shoulder, my eyes closed as my chest rises and falls with each heavy exhale. "I think you more than earned my forgiveness."

He chuckles against my ear, pressing a surprisingly tender kiss against my temple. "Not even close, but I'll gladly spend the rest of my life earning your forgiveness."

"If that means multiple orgasms every day, then you won't hear me complaining."

He pulls out and gently turns me in his arms, sliding his hands along my arms and up my neck until he cups my face. "I can never stop telling you how sorry I am, how foolish I was."

Lifting my arm, I cup his cheek, stroking my thumb along it. "You don't have to. I genuinely meant it when I said I understood. As far as I'm concerned, all is forgiven."

The smile he graces me with is filled with awe and admiration. "I don't know what I did in a past life to deserve someone like you."

I smirk. "Well, I also meant it when I said I'd slice you open with my knife if you ever did something like that again."

Instead of being put off by such a threat, Oliver's grin only widens, heat blooming in his eyes as if the thought of violence turns him on—hell, it probably does. All five of us have an unhealthy relationship with blood and violence, but that's why all four men are perfect for me and why I'm perfect for them. And although they don't know it yet, it's also why all four men are perfect for each other. None of them will be intimidated or put off by the other. None of them will cower or relent. They're all alpha males, and there are definitely going to be times of bloodshed amongst them. However, if they could just see past their differences, they'd also realize they could be perfect allies, perfect friends, and perhaps even perfect brothers for each other.

There's a quick rap of the bedroom door before it slowly opens, and Oliver spins, all of his... bits on display while he tries to keep me hidden behind him. I roll my eyes because, seriously, *everyone* in this house has seen me naked.

There's a pained groan from the doorway as I push up onto my tiptoes, using Oliver's shoulders to stabilize me as I peer over them to find a troubled-looking Cain.

"As much as I'm loving the sweet fucking noises you're making in this room, and the way it's seriously riling up those two assholes downstairs, we, uh, should really get started on a strategy."

Right, yes, I forgot about that, what with all the lust hormones floating around in my brain and infusing my thoughts.

"And, Red, you better shower before you come down, or I can guarantee none of us will be thinking about Giovanni's head on a spike."

I smirk but agree, and he leaves the room, shortly followed by Oliver once he's redressed, and I slip into the bathroom for a quick shower before joining all of them.

Tension charges the air, and I can feel it pressing in around me before I even reach the bottom of the stairs. As I make my way into the living room, I throw up a silent prayer that everyone is still alive and breathing, and ideally unharmed.

I still haven't forgotten what was said between them in the warehouse, and I can imagine similar conversations like that took place over the time span in which I was gone, although a lot has happened since then. Dante and Enzo stayed to fight alongside the Rejects. Is that enough to make them overlook their differences? And if it's not, then is loving me enough? I want all four of them. I meant what I said to Oliver about all five of us being a family. We are, or at least, we could be. I see the potential. I'm not saying it would be easy or that they would all suddenly get along and there would be no fighting or jealousy. Just that, if they set aside their differences, they'd realize that they actually have more in common than not.

At the essence of their beings, they're just four damaged men looking for a purpose in life, searching for love. Someone to make them feel alive, someone to call home. Isn't that all anyone really wants? Someone to love, a family, a home. We could be that for each other. They're already all of that for me, and I know I am for them too, but they could also be that for each other. They could have a true brotherhood built on trust and reliability and faith. If they'd just give each other a chance.

Holding on to that hope for the ideally not too distant future, I glance around at the four men, all wearing varying expressions of fury. *Great, that seems like an excellent start to this meeting.*

Cain pats the space between him and Oliver on the far sofa, but before I can move toward them, Enzo pushes out of his seat and grabs a hold of my wrist, yanking me into his lap as he drops back down. "Not a chance," he growls, pinning Oliver with a furious glare. "After watching the two of you damn near tear the clothes off each other, it's our turn. You do realize the walls are paper thin, right?"

Oliver just smirks. "Oh, I know."

"You do realize I'm not a possession to be passed around, right?" I snap, aiming my own glower at Enzo. "There's no *our turn*. This is a relationship." Shifting on his lap so I can look at each of them, I say, "The four of you have to learn to get along, to share.

None of this—not this relationship, and not defeating Giovanni—will work if you don't."

My words are met by a tense silence, and I can feel my heart hammering against my chest, waiting for one of them—most likely Cain or Dante—to argue. To tell me they can't agree to that.

I can hardly hear over the panic building inside me when Oliver's lips part, and it takes me a second to register what he's saying.

"You're right, Trouble."

I'm right? I mean, I know I am. I just didn't expect any of them to agree with me. Although I should have expected Oliver—my sweet, agreeable Oliver—would be the one to offer an olive branch. It's just who he is, and with the guilt I can still see reflected in his eyes, he'll do just about anything I ask, including accepting Dante and Enzo.

I give him a small *thank you* smile, hoping he knows just how much it means to me that he's bridging that gap before one of the less level-headed idiots I've managed to surround myself with can speak up.

"It's not fair of us to put you in the middle. You're in a relationship with all of us, which means we have to learn to get along... even if we don't want to." Oliver's gaze flicks behind me to Enzo and Dante before coming back to rest on me. "I'm sorry."

Just like every apology he's given me in the last twenty-four hours, it's genuine and carries a promise to do better.

I don't know if it's because he can feel the tense set of my body against his or because he genuinely agrees with Oliver—or perhaps both—but Enzo speaks up next. "I'm sorry, too. I think the one thing we can all agree on is that you are the most important person to each of us. I can't speak for the others, but I don't want to jeopardize what we have. It took me too long to gain your trust and your love. There's no way in hell I'm going to give that up now, especially not over petty bullshit."

He smirks, and I lean in to press a chaste kiss against his lips. He chases my lips when I pull away, growling when I don't let him catch them. His possessiveness has a smirk pulling at my own lips, one that mirrors his from a moment ago, before I feel a finger curling around the loose strands of my hair, tugging slightly.

Turning my head, my eyes clash with Dante's, and like a whirlpool, I'm immediately sucked in. He drags me out of Enzo's lap and into his own, positioning me, so we're face-to-face with his forehead resting against mine. "*Mia vita,*" he purrs, his voice low for only me to hear. "If you asked for it, I'd give you the world. I'd buy you a diamond-encrusted crown, bow at your feet, and watch in wonder as you ruled like the Queen I know you are. You have given me everything—more than I could have ever imagined. I was lost in the dark, fumbling blindly before you stepped in and lit up my whole world. You saved me not only from my father, but from myself. If all you want is for me to not murder these assholes, then I can give you that."

Ah, he was doing so well until that last part.

"You know, if you set your jealousies aside, you might actually find you like one another."

He gives me a wry look. "Doubtful, but for you, I'll try."

With a tilt of my chin, our lips brush. "Thank you." I let him see the sincerity in my eyes. I hold his gaze for a while, not wanting to break this moment when he has all of his walls down, offering me one of those rare and valued glimpses into all the soft emotions that make up Dante's core—whether he recognizes that or not. "Although, I wouldn't say no to a diamond-encrusted crown."

A deep rumble reverberates through his chest and works its way up his throat before bubbling out in a laugh—another rarity that I add to my Dante treasure trove of precious moments not to be forgotten. "Consider it done."

I hesitate, unsure if he's being serious or not. He knows I was joking, right? Not wanting to get sidetracked right now, I press a final kiss to his lips before turning to face Cain, the only one left. He studies me with all the ferocity of a bulldog. The silence drags out for so long that I feel Dante tense beneath me, as though he's about to storm over there and force Cain to agree. I'm not so concerned, though. I'm not worried that Cain is going to walk away or say no. He's just taking this time to think through how this would indeed work. It's one thing for everyone to agree to get along, but how does that agreement look in practical situations? How does it transfer to everyday life? And that is what Cain is currently figuring out, because he's not one to promise something he can't keep.

"As long as you're not expecting us to braid each other's hair and suddenly be all buddy-buddy, then you know I'm all in with you."

I huff out a laugh. "I think that would be a little weird, even for me."

Cain lifts one side of his lips in a half-smile. "I dunno how you're going to keep us all in line, but if anyone can, it's you."

A few ideas—absolutely filthy ones that resemble my dream from this morning— come to mind of how I could get them to see the benefits of teamwork, but I fight to keep any hint of them from showing on my face. While I could probably rely on Enzo and maybe even Oliver to play along, Cain, and especially Dante, will take a lot more convincing. Besides, now isn't exactly the time for all of us to strip off our clothes and start an orgy in the middle of the living room. There will be plenty of time for that later. In the meantime, we have vengeance to plan and people to kill.

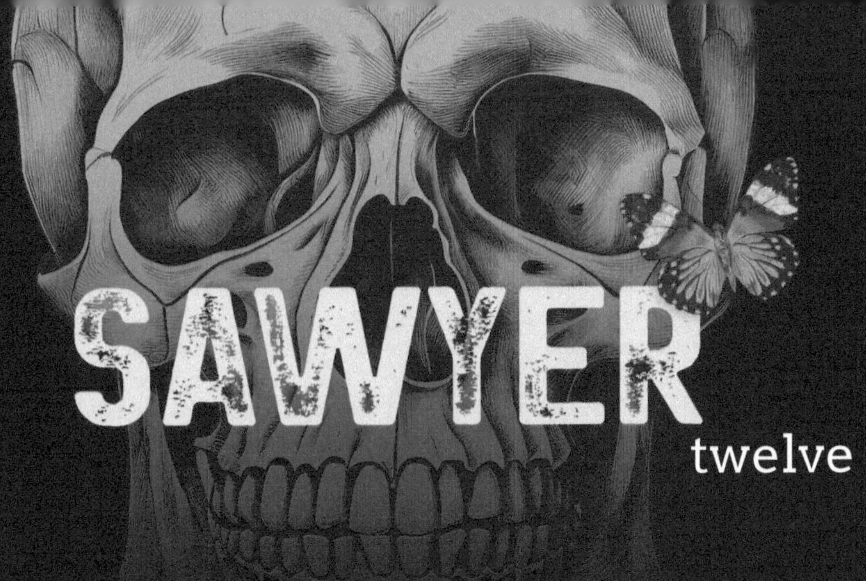

twelve

We spent the rest of the day planning a suitable strategy—one that doesn't involve us going in half-cocked and unprepared. Everyone agreed that removing the easier threat first makes sense—the Grim Bastards. So long as they are running around the city doing Giovanni's bidding, they pose a risk to us. By removing them, Giovanni will be forced to send out his own men, and possibly even get his own hands dirty for once.

Cain and Oliver provided us with some idea of the layout of the Bastards' compound—an old fire station—and once we had a plan in place, we filed next door to fill Marcus in.

"I'm coming with you," he insists as soon as Cain is finished getting him up to speed. All six of us are crammed into the small kitchen, Marcus, Cain, Oliver, and myself situated around the table while Dante and Enzo lean against the kitchen counters.

"So are we," a voice from behind me says, and I turn, already knowing what I'm going to see. *Yup.* Jon, Tank, Rampage, Luc, and a couple of other kids have gathered in the doorway, obviously eavesdropping on our conversation.

"It's rude to listen into other people's conversations," Cain growls.

"It's rude to exclude us simply because we're not as old as you."

Cain's head whips around, glaring murderously at Jon, and I swear I notice Enzo cover a laugh behind his hand. "What did you just call me? New club rules, if you can't grow a full beard, you can't come on dangerous jobs."

"That's bullshit," Tank speaks up. "Everything we do is dangerous. Hell, *we* are dangerous. We'd be an asset on this job, and you know it."

"That was before you eavesdropped on a conversation you weren't privy to and started talking to me as if I don't have the final say in *what* you do."

"I think he's just pissy cause you called him old," Enzo, oh so helpfully, interjects.

Tank's shoulders shake in silent laughter, and I catch Jon and a couple of the other kids squashing their amusement. Cain doesn't find the jibe funny, though, sending Enzo a very threatening glare that doesn't faze him in the slightest.

"Look, we know everyone else is busy at the clubhouse. If you call them in on this, that leaves the clubhouse exposed and the injured vulnerable. But we are already here, ready to go, and you *know* we can do this."

Cain's foot repeatedly taps against the floor as he thinks, his hesitant gaze flicking to Oliver. Oliver shrugs, leaving it up to Cain but not voicing any objections. I know it can't be an easy decision, however. Sure, from what I've heard, Cain has included them on dangerous jobs before, but tensions are at an all-time high now, and we're going into that station to kill and maim and destroy, which completely changes the game.

Eventually, he flicks his gaze up to mine before pursing his lips and hissing out a, "fine." Turning in his chair to pin the kids with a lethal stare, he tacks on, "But you do what you're told. *Exactly* what you're told and nothing more. If you so much as breathe without my say-so, you'll be under house arrest until the end of time."

Damn, is it inappropriate that I'm getting serious Daddy Cain vibes right now? Like, I can totally picture him saying something like that to his own sons. Not that I should even be thinking about that at a time like this, when war is at our front door and death looms around every corner.

All of them nod their heads in understanding, but my focus is lasered in on Luc. When he glances my way, I give him a look that makes it very damn clear that he's not going on this little mission with the others. I may be okay with him taking part in some aspects of club life, but not this, not yet, and not after what he's just been through.

"I know," he says, looking at me. "I'm staying here. I know I'll only be in the way, and I don't want to be the reason anything happens to any of you."

My heart breaks for him, even though I'm thankful as fuck that he'll be here, where it's safe. "Good, cause I have a far more important job for you, Luc," Cain says, all serious.

Luc's eyebrows lift in surprise as he snaps his gaze to Cain, waiting to hear about this important job. I'm pretty sure I already know, and Cain is definitely getting lucky tonight for including Luc in all of this, making him feel helpful while also keeping him out of harm's way. "I need you to keep an eye on Evie for me. The rest of us will be dealing with the Bastards, so it will be up to you to keep her safe. Do you think you can do that?"

Cain's tone is stern, emphasizing how serious a job this is to him. Luc appears speechless for a moment as he gapes at Cain before finally finding his voice. "Y-yes, Sir. I'll make sure she's safe."

Cain just nods, saying, "Knew you were the right man for the job," and I swear I see Luc's chest swell with pride beneath his praise. *Yup, Cain is getting the blowjob of all blowjobs when we get back tonight.*

With everyone up to speed on the plan, we all go off to get ready, Cain barking out that we leave at sundown, which is probably only an hour or so away.

As everyone filters out of the room, I wait until only Enzo, Cain, and myself are left in the kitchen before I pounce on Cain, grabbing his arm before he can escape and whispering in his ear, "Do you have any idea how lucky you are getting when we get home tonight?" I push my tongue into my cheek, making a crude gesture with my hand that has him tilting his head back and barking out a laugh.

With his eyebrows still raised in surprise, he purrs, "Is that so? Murder, violence, and blowjobs are three of my favorite things... and I get to do all of them with my favorite woman."

"Well, I'd like to think you're not doing that last one with *any* other woman."

"Never," he promises, his eyes burning with so much sincerity that it leaves me breathless. "Dare I ask why?"

My lips quirk in a cocky yet appreciative smile. "You know why. What you did for Luc, you know how much that meant to him."

"He's a good kid. I'm just trying to help him get back to himself."

"You are. You're probably doing more good than I am. Other than offering to talk, which is something he doesn't seem to want to do, I can't think of anything else I can do."

"I can try talking to him... if you want," Enzo interjects, running his hand awkwardly along the back of his neck almost as though... is he nervous right now about talking to Luc?

"Only if you want to," I tell him, not wanting to put him on the spot.

"I don't mind. He might not want to talk to me either, but I, more than anyone, probably understand what he's been through. Dante probably gets it too, but well, you know what talking to him is like."

Cain snorts. "I can just picture that conversation."

"Honestly, he's more likely to teach Luc how to strangle someone."

I choke on my saliva while Cain laughs, like that's a completely rational thing. Although, I don't know why I'm surprised. Actually, I can absolutely see something insane like that being the outcome, so yeah... I think Enzo trying to talk to Luc would be the safer alternative—for all of us.

"I'll have a word with him tomorrow," Enzo says, his voice softer when he turns to face me. "I can't promise it will do any good but..."

Reaching out, I squeeze his hand. "Just the fact that you're offering means a lot."

The grin he gives me is positively wicked. "Will that earn me a blowjob too?"

"Oh my god!" I screech, slapping his bicep and shaking my head.

Not even deigning to answer his question, I'm still shaking my head as I leave him and a laughing Cain behind to go get ready.

"Too bad, man," I hear Cain say from behind me. "Gotta be quicker off the mark next time."

THE SUN IS SETTING ON THE HORIZON AS WE ALL PILE INTO THREE awaiting SUVs. We've already decided it's safer to split up, leaving the cars in three different locations around the fire station in case any of us need a quick getaway.

Unfortunately, we haven't been able to scout the station in advance, so we don't know if there are any weak entry points. Thus, our most challenging task is going to be breaching the walls, but once we're in, the objective is to do as much damage as possible. Kill anyone on sight and fight until we're on the verge of being over-whelmed, then pull back. We are aiming for maximum destruction, and we've come well equipped to do just that. Although, the longer we can go unnoticed, the easier that will be, so everyone has been ordered to remain under the radar for as long as possible.

Dressed to kill—literally—in black jeans, boots, a black Henley, and a bulletproof vest, with my hair stuffed under a black beanie, I'm on a team with Dante and Enzo—as the result of an argument that took most of the time we had to get ready to solve, and only ended because I put my foot down.

The journey to the fire station is silent, Enzo following the directions Cain plugged into the SAT; at the same time, Dante is grumbling about wishing he was in a suit while he killed deserving assholes. I am focused on getting into the zone of the Reaper and, admittedly, it's taking longer than usual. Not because I don't want to be here or because of what we're here to do, but because I've been struggling to connect with that apathetic side of me more and more recently. The Reaper was a persona born out of survival, but lately, my life hasn't been about survival—well, not *only* about survival. And even when things go to shit, I know I'm not alone. I don't *need* the Reaper; I don't rely on her the same way I would have in the past.

However, there's no denying that her presence comes in handy for nights like tonight. I know tonight is going to be violent. It's going to be a bloodbath. Mass murder at its finest, and it takes a particular personality to be able to walk into a compound of grown men and slash and stab and shoot until all of them are dead. The Reaper will tuck away all of my human parts and allow me to do what needs to be done with a dissociative attachment that means tonight won't haunt me when, later, I crawl into bed with one—or ideally all—of my men.

My finger taps absently against my thigh. My eyes close as I take steady breaths, sorting through everything important to me and storing it away for later. Everything that doesn't have anything to do with what we're about to do gets safely stowed away— my concern about leaving Luc alone at the house, my love for the men in this car and the one behind us, the new hopes for my future that have only recently started to bloom... all of it gets shut down until an icy chill rushes over my skin and the only thing on my mind is ensuring all of us get out alive—and that no Bastard sees the light of day tomorrow.

My eyes snap open as the car slows to a stop, and I stare out the window. We're on a residential street, but if I thought I had it rough where my apartment is based, it's nothing compared to this part of town. From what I can see, most of the windows in the neighboring buildings have been smashed in, more doors hanging off their hinges than not, and as I scan the street, noting how empty it is—not even a hooker or homeless person in sight—I begin to realize most people must know to avoid this area.

An ominous cloud hangs in the air as I push open my door and step out of the car, Dante and Enzo doing the same. "The perimeter of Grim's compound is two blocks that way," Enzo says, keeping his voice low as he points in the direction, and we all take off on foot.

The entire time, the three of us scan our surroundings, keeping our eyes and ears open as we remain vigilant. It's eerily quiet for a city, especially one that doesn't sleep at night, and a chill races down my spine the farther we walk. This part of the city almost feels... dead. Like it's been abandoned and long forgotten, left to the elements to rot and wither away. Only the outskirts of the city are like this, and that's because most people there fled when things started to go south. But here in the city center? It shouldn't be this quiet.

We walk briskly, quickly reaching the tall, brick wall that runs along the perimeter of Grim's compound. Unsure if there is anywhere we can enter unnoticed, we have no choice but to inauspiciously work our way along the wall until we find somewhere we can get through.

Keeping tight to the wall, we walk in single file, occasionally stopping to assess a potential entry point before dismissing it and moving on. It's only when we hear voices up ahead that we pause, all three of us coming to a stop so we can listen.

"I fucking hate gate duty," someone grumbles. "I'd rather stick needles in my eyes."

A snort. "Let Grim hear you say that, and you'll soon find out which you'd prefer."

The first guard responds with something too low for me to hear, and when I turn my head to silently ask Dante and Enzo what they think we should do, I spot Dante sliding a gun out of a holster under his arm.

Flicking the safety, he makes to move toward the guard, but I put my hand on his arm, stopping him. Shooting a gun is risky. Even with a silencer, it doesn't make it completely silent. Plus, we have no idea if either of these men have radios or some way of communicating with anyone else before he could take both of them out from this range—there's no way we'd get within six feet of them unnoticed. The second they see all three of us lurking out here in the dark, they'll be raising the alarm... but a single girl? Well, they might not be so quick to call for backup then.

"Trust me," I mouth, holding his gaze until he nods his head and relaxes his arm, although I notice that he doesn't stow the gun away.

I flick a quick glance in Enzo's direction as I hurriedly strip out of my bulletproof vest, shuck off my weapons, and knot the Henley at one side of my waist, showing off a good portion of my flat stomach. Pulling off the beanie, I fluff out my hair, ignoring the death glowers I'm receiving from both men before I stride toward the two guards, swaying my hips as I go.

One of them notices my approach, tensing as he strains to see through the dark, and the other guard, noticing the change in his buddy, turns around.

"Well, hello, little lady," he purrs when I get closer, neither of them making any effort to hide their perusal of my body. "You probably shouldn't be out here all alone." He accentuates by looking around the street before tacking on, "You never know who could be hiding in the dark, waiting to take advantage of a pretty thing like you."

"Yeah," his buddy quickly agrees, his eyes practically burning a hole through my tits from where he's staring at them so damn hard. "You're welcome to wait with us. We'll be off the clock in an hour, then the three of us could get to know each other a little better." He smirks, a look that's filled with overinflated male ego. "... if you know what I mean."

I make a point of looking both of them up and down while they circle me like prey. Both of them are fairly average looking. One has darker hair, and the other appears lighter, although it's hard to tell in the dark. They look a little unkempt with their scruffy beards and shaggy hair. Still, putting those acting skills to use, I pretend to like what I see by biting on my lower lip and fluttering my lashes, acting coy. In a tone that's perfected from too many years seducing assholes and playing nice at Strip Tease, I purr, "Why wait?"

I feel the lighter-haired guy close in behind me, his heat at my back, and when he chuckles, the sound is far too close to my ear for my liking. "Is it true that redheads fuck like rabbits?"

Instead of punching him in the face, I paste on an alluring smile and glance back at him over my shoulder. "I guess you'll find out."

His hands come to rest low on my hips as his chest brushes my back. *Jeez, ever heard of foreplay?* I internally grumble as his hands move around to the front of my jeans and pop the button. When the other guard steps into me, effectively pinning me between the two of them as he begins to paw at my chest, I know I have mere seconds to do what I need to before Dante blows a gasket and storms over, guns blazing.

The guy behind me chuckles. "Your throat's going to be raw and you're not going to be able to walk straight for days by the time we're finished with you." Gone is the hint of seduction intended to reel me in; instead, his tone is a harsh promise. In his mind, I've officially become their plaything to be used and abused until they're spent.

Tilting my head so I can look over my shoulder, I let my coy mask disappear, a smug smirk replacing it. "I highly doubt that." Spinning, I bring my hand up, slashing it across his throat. The asshole's eyes go wide a split second before blood starts racing down his neck. Not hanging around to watch him drown in his own blood, I turn back to face the guard in front of me. His mouth is agape, his horrified gaze on the man behind me, so he doesn't even notice when I stab him in the gut before slicing his neck too.

"You couldn't have done that *before* they put their hands on you?" Enzo drawls, stepping out of the shadows.

"Where would be the fun in that?" I quip, earning an irritated snarl from Dante as he prowls toward me. When he's standing directly in front of me, he pulls a handkerchief out of his pocket. Pinching my chin with his forefinger and thumb, he holds me steady while he does his best to wipe the blood from my face before doing the same with my forearms.

When he's finished, he tosses it on the dead men lying beside us, all without removing his gaze from mine, and with gentle fingers, he redoes the button on my jeans before slamming his lips against mine in a harsh, angry kiss. "I'm both furious and turned on," he growls, only making me laugh.

"That's great," Enzo snaps sarcastically. "Well, you can work on talking down your boner while you help me hide *them*." He jerks his head toward the two bodies before grabbing the arms of the closest one and beginning to drag him across the ground.

Muttering something under his breath, Dante steps away to help Enzo, and the two of them make quick work of disarming and hiding the dead bodies in the shadows. If anyone notices the two guards missing and comes to investigate, they shouldn't immediately spot them slumped against the wall where Enzo and Dante had been hiding.

While they tidy up, I quickly pull the bulletproof vest back on and replace my weapons. "They said they're off duty in an hour so we need to hurry," I tell them as I open the small gate—clearly a back entrance or something—and scan our surroundings, making sure no one else is around before hurrying into the compound.

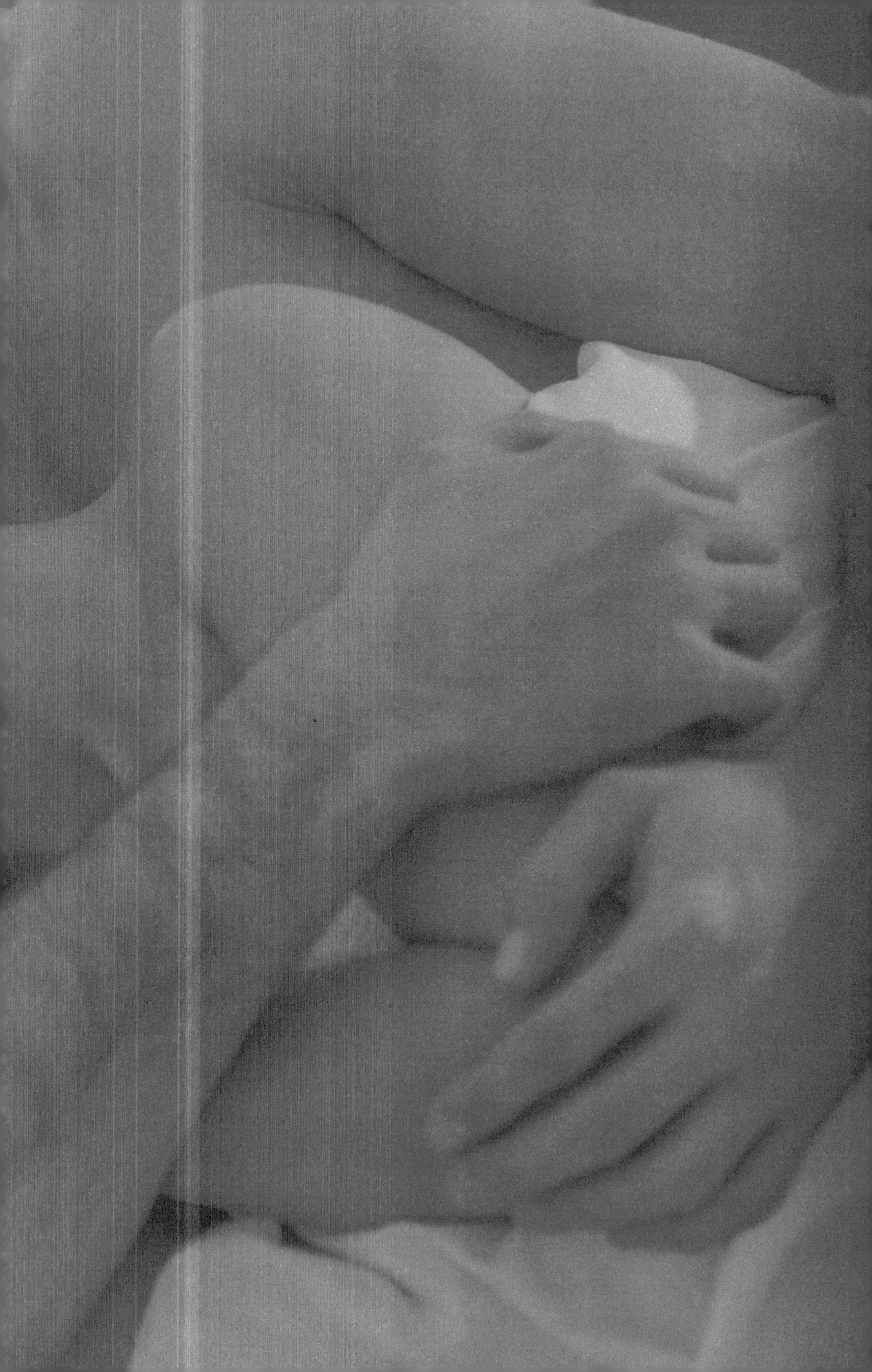

W e slip through the darkness like shadows prowling through the night, swiftly removing everyone we come across. Sawyer and Lor seem to have made some sort of game out of it, keeping tally and trying to see who can get the most kills. The grin she throws him every time she taunts him is one I recognize from that night in the alley, when the Reaper came out to play. It's both deranged and eerily beautiful, and has me remembering precisely what we did in that alley after killing that scumbag. Damn, I hope we get to re-enact that again later tonight. I loved seeing this... unhinged side of her. It's sexy as fuck. I love that she can shed her inhibitions and do what needs to be done, no matter how violent or gory it is, and I also love that when she locks that part of herself away, I get *my* Sawyer back. *Mia vita*.

I refuse to indulge in their antics, though. Not while we're working, so while they are playing games, I'm on constant alert. We initially stuck to the perimeter, removing guards and anyone stationed outside, but tension bleeds into my body as we circle around to the fire station. Under the cover of darkness, we've been able to move unnoticed across the compound, but that won't continue for long once we're inside with brighter lights and more people around. While Sawyer might be able to use her feminine wiles to distract the men, the second one of them spots Lor or me, they're going to start yelling—assuming one of the other teams isn't spotted first.

Crouching low, we slink toward the fire station. Only one man is patrolling this side of the building, and he doesn't see me coming as I lunge out of the darkness, slamming a hand over his mouth while I take a knife to his throat. As his body sags against mine, I drag him into the shadows while Sawyer cracks open the door he was standing in front of.

She slips inside, and cursing under his breath, Lor hastily follows. Glancing around as I step through the door and quietly close it behind me, it looks like we are in some sort of back hallway. There's a commercial kitchen on our left, but at this time of night, it's empty. However, the thudding pulse of music from somewhere deeper in the building gives away that most of the men are far from asleep.

"Someone's coming," Sawyer hisses at the exact moment I hear voices coming our way. The three of us duck into the darkened kitchen, flattening ourselves against the wall seconds before whoever is coming rounds the corner. I put a finger to my lips, telling both of them to stay quiet as the footsteps get louder.

"Did you see the tits on that girl?" I hear one of them ask, another laughing in response. "I'm definitely going to fuck them tonight."

"Fuck, I'd do more than just fuck her tits. Gotta make tonight count before we go after those bastards again."

Someone chuckles while a murmured round of agreement goes up. I place three or four different voices before another guy speaks. "Fuck our brains out tonight, then kill some Reject scumbags tomorrow. Sounds good to me."

I can practically feel Sawyer vibrating with anger beside me, and I clasp a hand on her wrist to ensure she doesn't do something stupid like rush out there.

I count four of them as they walk past, heading toward the door we just entered through.

"They're going to notice the missing guard," Sawyer hisses seconds before the door opens and one of them says, "Wasn't Gary meant to be here tonight?"

"Probably taking a piss," one of them responds. "Which is exactly what I need to do." Heavy footsteps crunch against gravel as he disappears farther away to take a leak. With three on three, I turn to look at the others beside me. When they both nod, Sawyer with her bloody blade clutched in a death grip, we silently slip back into the hall. As we sneak closer, the back door has been propped open, and I can see the silhouettes of the three remaining men. Two of them are smoking, while the third rambles on about some shit. I'm not paying attention. Every ounce of my focus is on getting as close as possible before they spot us.

The second all three of us clear the door, our sights set on our victim, we launch. I grab my guy in a chokehold, his cigarette falling from his lips as I put the barrel of the gun to his forehead and shoot. The pop of the silencer goes off, but I'm not too concerned about anyone finding us. Sawyer and Lor have already taken care of their men, and the only one left is the guy that went to pee—a small reprieve but death is still calling his name.

"This next guy will put me in the lead," Lor taunts Sawyer, ensuring he keeps his voice low so it doesn't travel.

Sawyer snorts. "Only if you kill him... which you won't, because *I'm* killing him."

Lor smirks while I roll my eyes. "Game on, Spitfire. Let's see who gets to him first."

"Really?" I hiss as I hear footsteps approaching. "Now is hardly the time."

"Yo, guys, I thought I heard something..." the one man left breathing calls out.

"I disagree. Now is exactly the time," Lor murmurs before rushing the man at the same time Sawyer does.

The second they can make out the guy's outline, Sawyer sends a bullet straight into his chest while Lor aims for his head.

"Mine," they both call out at once.

"No, I got to him first," Sawyer snaps.

"No, I did!"

Both of them turn to me. "Well?" Lor asks, cocking a brow. "Whose kill was it?"

"I don't know," I grumble, not wanting to be dragged into this insanity. "You both killed him. You get half a kill each."

"Half a kill?" Sawyer hisses in outrage. "You can't get *half a kill*."

"Well, he's dead, and you both landed killing shots. Split it up however you want. There are more people inside just waiting for you to fight over their soon-to-be corpses."

Turning on my heel, I try to block out the sounds of them bickering behind me as I head back inside.

"You can have that one," I, unfortunately, overhear Lor say.

"I don't need your pity kill," Sawyer snaps. "Keep it. I'm still going to beat you."

Their argument hushes to quiet whispers as we step inside, finally falling away altogether as their common sense kicks in and they realize we're in the middle of a den of vipers, surrounded by enemies who could find us at any moment. Now is most definitely not the time for petty squabbles.

The rapid fire of gunshots somewhere else in the building pierces through the silence, startling us to a stop.

"Ah fuck, they know we're here," Lor murmurs.

More gunshots go off, and we start back into motion, moving deeper into the building. In the next instant, the entire ground shakes beneath our feet, and I snap my arm out to grab a hold of Sawyer's upper arm, steadying her.

"Fuck, shit mustn't be good." Another mutter from Lor as he plants a hand against the wall, and we wait for the quaking to subside. Sounds of chaos rage from the other end of the building, and the second I let go, Sawyer races toward the noise.

Lor and I share a wide-eyed look before taking off after her, guns out.

Now that there's no need to be stealthy, we shoot bullets into anyone we see until the ringing in my ears is all I can hear. All around me is chaos as we fight our way toward where the bulk of Grim's men seems to be coming from.

Another tremor rocks the ground beneath my feet, and I struggle to stay upright as I slam the butt of my gun against some asshole's forehead, knocking him out before shooting him in the face. I don't even have time to see him hit the floor at my feet before I'm overwhelmed again, a shot whizzing past my ear a second before some bastard slams his fist into my cheek.

I drop the gun, grabbing the front of his shirt with my fist and pummeling his face until blood coats his teeth and his nose is broken. His eyes look dazed as I start squeezing his head between my palms and twist it to the side, snapping his neck.

Blood has soaked into my shirt, making it stick to my skin, and my forearms are caked with it. Sawyer and Lor aren't faring much better, the three of us looking like warriors of death as we fight and stab and shoot our way down the corridor.

It's a bloodbath. With every passing minute, the bodies pile up until they're twisted around my ankles and I have to step over them. There are more men than I had anticipated, and now that we've lost the element of surprise, I'm not sure we have enough people to take them all out. Although, even if we pull back now, we will have seriously weakened Grim, and I'm sure he would think twice about coming after us. However, I also know that my father is an unreasonable man, unaccustomed to the word no. If Grim told my father he was done playing a part in this war, it would probably be the last decision he ever made.

An explosion nearby sends another rumble through the foundations, cracks appearing in the walls. I see what's about to happen a split second before it does, and latching on to Sawyer, I tug her backwards as the ceiling not twenty feet from us collapses, burying Grim's men beneath it.

"Holy shit," I hear her gasp as dust hangs thick in the air, obscuring my vision and making my eyes sting.

There's another shake and the sound of more foundations giving way. "Fuck, the entire building is going down," Lor yells as I begin to pull Sawyer back down the hallway. *Outside. We need to get outside.* That's all I can think about as the three of us race toward the exit. Thankfully, whatever men are left behind are too preoccupied to chase after us, and Lor throws open the door as more of the building sounds as if it's caving in.

"Cain and Oliver!" Sawyer cries, a sheen in her eyes as she stares slack-jawed at the building falling apart behind us. "Oh my god, the kids! And Marcus! We have to find them!"

Something inside my chest tightens as I stare up at where the building has all but disappeared from the far side of where we were. Now, there's nothing but dust and the black sky above. All of us were inside. I don't know where everyone was, but I've no doubts every single one of us was inside that building.

Based on Lor's grim expression, he's thinking the same thing. Sawyer is nothing but a blur of movement as she rushes past me, heading back into the building.

"Where the hell do you think you're going?" I snarl, wrapping my arm around her waist and hauling her back against me.

"Let go of me!" she cries. "I need to find them!" A sob rips from her throat as she thrashes in my arms, struggling to break free.

"Get her out of here," Lor says to me, keeping his voice low as he flicks a concerned gaze to Sawyer. "I'll see if I can find any of them..." *Alive.* That's the word he doesn't say aloud.

With a nod, he steps back, his expression anguished as he casts a final glance at Sawyer, who is still twisting and writhing in my arms, unaware of our conversation. After a second, he turns on his heels and disappears out of view beyond the building.

"No!" Sawyer screams as I tighten my arm around her waist. Her nails dig into my skin and claw at my arm as I haul her off the ground and move away from the building. "No! Where are you going? We have to help!... Dante!" Her voice is near hysterical as I turn so the building is behind us, trying to ignore her desperate cries and the agonizing pain in my chest as she all but falls apart in my arms.

It's a mission working on getting her out of the compound, and I have to practically throw her into the car.

"Sawyer," I growl, my voice laced with pain. Not the physical kind, but the type that buries itself deep beneath your skin and never quite heals. "Please," I plead with her as she shoves at my shoulder, trying to get out of the car.

She's not hearing a word I say, too busy pushing at my shoulders and avoiding eye contact, so I grasp her face between my hands and force her to look at me. Tears glisten in her eyes, spilling over to run down her cheeks. *Fuck, I'm no good at this sort of shit.* I don't know what the right thing to say is. What if I make it worse? I should have thrust her into Lor's arms and gone to search for the others myself. *That* I know how to do, but this... this is new territory and I'm terrified of fucking it up.

"Please." Her voice is broken, but now that she's stopped fighting me, her energy has drained away, leaving her looking smaller and more fragile than ever before.

"I can't." My own voice is strained. I hate being part of the cause of her pain. I hate that I have to say no to her now, but she is my top priority—the only thing that matters. I couldn't risk her going back into that building. Worse, I couldn't bear to watch her fracture when she inevitably finds one of them in the rubble. I just... can't.

I might only be sparing her a morsel of heartache, but it will have to do. If I could carry the weight of all of it for her, I would.

More tears fall from her eyes, and I watch as her lower lip trembles, her breath hitching on a sob she refuses to let loose. Stroking a hand along the back of her head, I pitch my voice low, soothing, as I say, "Lor's searching. He'll find them. You and me, we'll go get a shower and curl up in bed, so we're rested by the time they all return, yeah?"

It's not really a question, and I'm not sure if she can hear the lies, but she doesn't respond, and thankfully she doesn't resist as I tuck her legs into the car and reach across for the seatbelt. When she's all buckled into the seat, I swipe at the tears under her eyes, even though more immediately run down her cheek to replace them. Whispering one more lie, "everything's going to be okay," I step back and close the door.

The drive is silent as we head back to the house, and when I park outside, she makes no effort to get out. I didn't dare glance into the rearview mirror while I drove, knowing I wouldn't be able to look away, but now I summon the courage to look. What I see breaks me more than any bullet ever could. Gone is the wildcat who fought me tooth and nail at the fire station, and in her place is something far worse, far harder to bear witness to.

Her head rests against the glass as she stares blankly out the window, her shoulders slumped and leaning against the interior as if she no longer has the energy to prop herself up. She doesn't seem to even realize we've stopped... or perhaps she just doesn't care.

Tearing my eyes away, I get out of the car and move to the backdoor. Easing it open, I unbuckle her seatbelt and gently remove it. When I finally allow my eyes to rest on her face, another stab of pain slices across my chest. Her usually lively, beautifully aquamarine eyes are dull and lifeless looking. It's as if *mia vita* isn't there. Gone is the woman who challenges me, who doesn't back down when I push her and isn't intimidated by my name or profession, and in her place is this shadow of the woman I love.

"Can you walk?" I ask her softly.

When she doesn't respond, I gently ease her out of the car until she's standing. When she doesn't appear as though she's about to collapse, I wrap an arm around her waist and encourage her to move.

Her steps are slow, but she keeps putting one foot in front of the other as we walk down the front path and up the steps into the house. I usher her up the stairs and into the bathroom. She doesn't so much as whisper a word the entire time.

Once I've gotten her into the bathroom, I prop her up on the vanity before turning on the shower. Crouching down in front of her, I peel off her boots and socks, tossing them aside, I undo the Velcro straps of her bulletproof vest and carefully remove the weapons she's got strapped into a holster at her hip, in sheaths around her thighs, and tucked into the waistband of her jeans. Her blood-soaked Henley is next. My hands move over her body clinically, assessing for any injuries before I get her back on her feet. Undoing the button on her jeans, I lower the zipper before peeling them down her long, elegant legs. This is definitely not the kind of stripping I had pictured earlier, but I'm far too concerned about her well-being to even think about her sinfully gorgeous body that is on display for me.

When she's wearing only her panties and bra, I quickly strip off my own sodden clothing, leaving my boxers on. I plant my hands on her hips and direct her into the shower beneath the warm spray, hoping the hot water will help jolt some life back into her.

Encouraging her to tilt her head back, I brush my hand along the top of her head and down her hair, ensuring all of it is wet before reaching for the shampoo and starting to massage it into her scalp.

A small moan passes her lips as I continue working it into her hair before directing her again under the water. Threading my fingers through her hair, I work out the tangles as the water washes the shampoo down the drain. When I'm sure there aren't any suds remaining, I grab the shower gel and a sponge, lathering it up before running it along her body. Her left arm, then her right. Along her neck and chest, removing any blood that's still remaining before moving between her breasts, over her abdomen, and down her legs.

Sawyer stands there the entire time, but she's no longer crying, which I'm hoping is a good sign. When I've removed the blood and dirt caked under her fingernails, I gently nudge her aside and quickly wash myself down before turning off the water.

Grabbing a towel, I dry her off and wring out her hair before wrapping it around her chest, ensuring it's not going to fall off. I don't even bother to dry myself, simply wrapping another towel around my waist before I take her hand and direct her into the bedroom I've been staying in. Lifting the first clean t-shirt I find, I pull it over her head before pulling back the sheets. She slides in without a word, and I quickly dry myself off and change into a fresh pair of boxers before joining her.

Tucking the sheets around us, I tug her in against me, shifting until we're both comfortable. Silence falls between us, and again I'm stuck for what to say. Or whether I should say anything at all.

I'm still trying to figure that out when Sawyer asks, her voice sounding croaked as if she hasn't used it in far too long, "Do you think they're okay?"

"I don't know." Unlike before, it's not a lie. Well, not a complete one. That building was coming down one way or another. I don't see how they could be okay, but surprisingly, I hope they are. For Sawyer's sake, because I don't know how the hell I'm going to save her if they aren't.

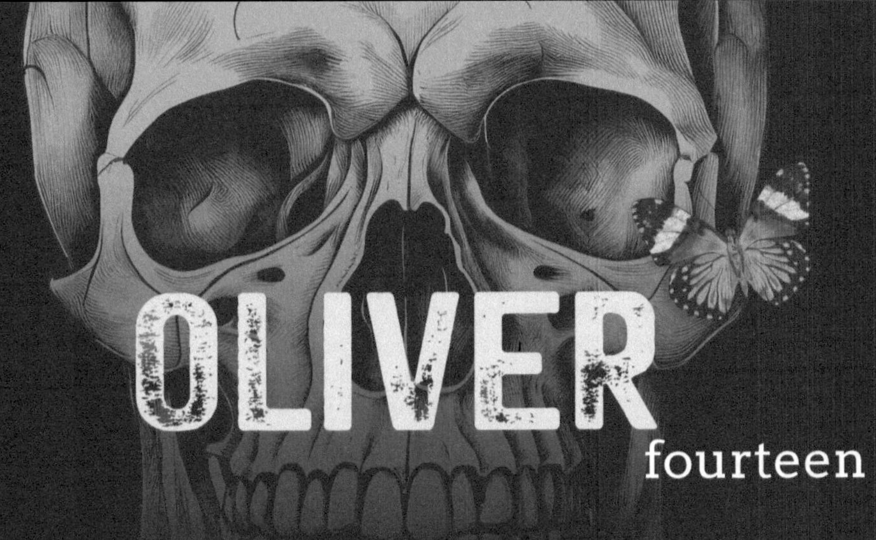

fourteen

I cough as dust sticks to the back of my throat and burns my eyes, obscuring my vision as I stare up at the empty space above me—the empty space where the ceiling was less than five minutes ago. *What the hell happened?* One minute I was punching some guy in the face, and the next, the roof started falling down on top of us. Grenades were thrown when our cover was blown, but they shouldn't have done this much damage to the foundations... unless the building was already unstable?

Pushing up onto my elbows, I check myself over, relieved not to see any broken bones. Besides the headache blooming, I don't feel any pain, but I know how shock can dull your senses. I've several new scrapes and a large gash on my forearm, but nothing too serious.

Stroking my hand through my hair, I lift my head to take in my surroundings, but I hiss in pain before pulling my hand back, finding fresh blood on my fingers. *Well, that can't be good.* It's not a massive amount of blood, and there isn't a puddle where my head was, so I'll have to hope it's okay. I need to find Sawyer and make sure Cain and the others are safe. I'd lost track of him, Bones, and Tank when we entered the station, and I haven't seen any of the others since we split up.

Using my jeans to wipe off the blood on my fingers, I push aside the bits of rubble that fell on top of me—nothing too heavy, thankfully, but some pieces are definitely large enough to have left bruises and leave me wincing as I slowly get to my feet and look around.

The scene before me is far different from the one from a few minutes ago. One of Grim's men who had been shooting at me now lies dead, the side of his head cracked open from where, I'm guessing, a huge chunk of cement got the better of him. I spot the gun he was using lying nearby and pick it up, checking the chamber since I appear to have lost mine in the chaos.

As I scan the destruction for signs of Sawyer, Cain, or the others, the pained moans of men trapped or injured reach my ears. A few others around me who were lucky to escape the worst of it are slowly picking themselves off the ground and making a quick escape, none of them hanging around for the rest of the building to come down. As I spare the walls around me a worried glance, I can't say I blame them, but the fact that they aren't even stopping to help out their own people says everything about the loyalty of Grim's men. *Fucking pathetic.*

The men in The Feral Beasts were the same way. All talk about loyalty and brotherhood, but the second trouble hit, it was every man for himself, and they didn't give a shit what brothers they had to walk over, maim, or kill. That's what makes the Rejects so different.

Far superior to any other gang. We're about family first and foremost, united in a common cause to make Black Creek a better place. We're not about power or money or land. We don't live for the violence and chaos that most men in our situations do. We have one another's backs—always. Without a shadow of a doubt, I know that not one of our men, the kids included, would leave here without ensuring everyone is accounted for. It makes me proud to be a part of this—a part of something far more meaningful and significant. It's exactly what I'd been looking for when I stumbled across The Feral Beasts, and it's a shame it took so many lost years and time served in prison for me to find my way here, though maybe I had to go through those years in order to know that this is where I belong. The Rejects are my family. Red and Cain are my family, and Dante and Enzo... well, they're people I'll tolerate for Red's sake.

"Oliver!"

Spinning, relief washes over me when I find Bones climbing through piles of rubble, ducking under a fallen steel support beam as he works his way toward me.

"Are you okay?" I ask, moving to meet him.

"Yeah, I'm fine, but Marcus... I can't get him out."

Shit. "Okay, where is he?"

Pointing a thumb over his shoulder, he waits until I reach him before working his way back through the carnage in the direction he came. "Have you seen anyone else?" I ask.

"Tank and Rampage were nearby when the sky started falling, and we found the others. They're okay, but Tank... he's unconscious. He was bleeding pretty badly, so Rampage and the others took him to the hospital."

I flick a glance his way as we continue stepping over broken blocks of cement, metal rods, and other debris, noting the pasty whiteness of his skin beneath the layer of dust and blood. Still, his eyes are hard, determined.

"Good. That was a smart call."

He nods, the nod of a natural-born leader that has me wondering if we should give him more responsibility after all of this shit has been sorted.

"I was looking for you and the others when I came across Marcus." He swallows roughly, the only sign that he's not as unaffected as he seems. However, his voice is strong, showing no hint of his concern. "His legs are pinned under a steel beam. I tried to lift it, but I couldn't."

I clap him on the shoulder, and he turns his head to look at me. "You did really good. I'll have a look and we'll find a way to get him out."

Another curt nod, a moment of silence passing before the pressing question I've been trying not to ask comes out. "You didn't see Sawyer?"

"No." He gives me an apologetic look, but I already knew that was going to be the answer. He'd have said otherwise if he had found her. "Nor Dante or Enzo. Maybe they got out in time."

"Yeah, maybe." I can only hope that's the case.

"Over there." Bones points, and following the line of his finger, I find Marcus lying on the ground, struggling to push a long, steel beam that has fallen across his thighs, pinning him beneath it.

"Looks like you need a hand," I jest when we reach him, trying to make light of the situation.

"Aye," he chuckles. "If you wouldn't mind."

Bones hurries around to his other side. "On three," I tell them, getting into position and ensuring I have a solid grip on the beam.

"One."

"Two."

"*Three.*"

Together, the three of us push—well, mostly Bones and me. The muscles in my arms and shoulders strain, and we've only managed to lift the beam by about an inch when Marcus grunts in pain. "Ow, fuck."

My head snaps around as I scan his body, searching for the source of his pain. "Fuck," I hiss when I spot the dark-colored substance quickly gathering around my boots, my voice low so as not to alert Marcus.

Bones gives me a questioning look, and I flick my gaze down to my feet. His eyes widen when he sees the blood pooling, and I tell him quietly, "Lower your side back down and have a look under mine, will ya?"

Nodding, he does as I say before ducking down to look under the beam, murmuring, "shit," before he glances up at me with a grave expression.

"There's a metal rod sticking out of his thigh."

Fuck. Fuck, fuck, fuck.

I make sure to keep what I'm thinking off my face as I lower the beam back down. "Attached to the beam, I take it?" It would explain why the blood flow has slowed now that I've set it back down.

Bones' nod is solemn.

"Alright, man," I say, raising my voice to a normal level as I turn back to a pale-faced Marcus. "Some bad news."

"Just give it to me," he grunts, slightly breathless either from pain or blood loss, or both.

"Seems you've got some rebar going into your leg. You're bleeding out when we lift the beam." Like a man used to receiving grim news, he just nods, accepting what I've told him. Still, I clap him on the shoulder, waiting until his eyes meet mine before emphasizing, "But we are going to get you out... then rush you to the hospital before you can bleed out all over the back of the Escalade and ruin Cain's leather seats."

He barks out a strained but genuine laugh. "I trust you. I guess I'll just hang here while I let you do all the heavy lifting for a change."

I snort. "Yeah, you take a well-deserved break. Can I get you a magazine or a cup of tea, perhaps?"

He scans the wreckage around us. "Well, I wouldn't say no to some whiskey if you manage to find a bottle."

"I'll see what I can do," I laugh, before growing serious and focusing back on his leg.

"We need to stem the flow," I explain to Bones as I undo my belt buckle and slide the belt out of the loops. It takes some work, but I manage to thread it under his thigh. "This is going to hurt," I warn Marcus, not giving him time to brace before I cinch the belt tight around his thigh.

He hisses between his teeth as I pull the belt as tight as I physically can before puncturing a new hole in the leather and securing it in place. "Right, let's try this again," I say to Bones, once I've ensured the belt is secure.

The two of us have another attempt at lifting the beam. This time, I keep one eye on the ground at my feet as we lift it an inch or two, relieved to note that no new blood rushes to coat my boots. My arms burn as we struggle to lift the beam higher, and Bones looks like he's about to shit himself with the strain before I call it quits, and we lower it back down.

Wiping the sweat from my forehead, I wrack my brain for what to do. "We need more manpower," I say aloud to no one in particular. The two of us aren't strong enough to lift the beam high enough to pull the rebar from his leg. If it weren't for that, the inch or two we can get would be enough for Marcus to slide out, only who knows how far the steel rod goes into his thigh.

I look around us, desperately hoping to spot Cain, Dante, or Enzo, but I've no such luck. Anyone who was able is long gone by now, leaving only the three of us and a sea of rubble with trapped or dead men. *Where the hell are they?*

Pursing my lips, I glance back down at Marcus before flicking my gaze to Bones, who is watching me closely, waiting for my orders. "We need help," I say, having made my decision. "Stay with Marcus. I'm going to go find Cain, or Dante or Enzo, or anyone really. They've gotta be around here somewhere."

"Wouldn't they already be here, unless something has happened to them?" Bones questions, but I can't think about that right now, because every time I do, I picture Sawyer in Marcus' position, or worse, and... I just can't.

"I'm gonna go find them," is all I say before bending down to squeeze Marcus' shoulder. "Hang in there, yeah? I'll be back in a bit, and then we'll have you outta here in no time."

"Sure thing." Marcus gives me a wane smile before resting his head back on a piece of concrete behind him, appearing much more tired than he did only ten minutes ago.

Not wasting any more time, I hurry off with no real idea of where I'm going or how I plan to find anyone. With the place mostly deconstructed, it's challenging to work out the original building plans, and even if I did know them off the top of my head, I have no idea where anyone is—where they were before everything started coming down on top of us.

With a gun held firmly in my grip—because there's no doubt that at least one idiot saw this whole fiasco as an opportunity to loot the place and whoever was left behind inside—I head for the nearest exit, toward a hallway that's missing its ceiling even though most of the walls are still standing.

I'm not searching for long before I hear voices somewhere up ahead, and I slow my pace, carefully placing my feet to avoid making a sound and giving myself away. There's nowhere to hide, so I stick close to the wall as the voices get louder, their owners moving closer until I can make out actual words.

"Watch it! You nearly crashed me into a wall."

"Do you want my help or not?"

There's an angry snarl in response, and despite the situation, I chuckle under my breath. Relief washes over me at hearing the two of them, even if they are bickering like school children.

"For a gang leader, you sure do whine a lot," Enzo remarks as the two of them come into view. Cain's arm is slung over Enzo's shoulder, and as they walk, I can see that he's struggling to put weight on his left leg. Despite that, and the layer of white dust mixed with blood, making him look like some sort of zombie, the two appear relatively unharmed. In fact, Enzo doesn't appear injured at all. I can only hope that means Sawyer is the same, although, where is she? And Dante, for that matter?

"Fuck off, asshole," Cain snarls in response, looking absolutely furious that he has to rely on Enzo's help.

I decide to make my presence known before he can do something that ends up with Enzo shrugging off his arm and Cain falling on his ass.

"I could hear the two of you bitching at one another from the other side of the building." I step away from the wall as both of their heads snap in my direction, and Cain's eyes run over me, checking that I'm okay.

"Broken?" I ask, indicating his foot with my head.

"Nah, think it's just sprained."

Of course he'd say that regardless, to avoid a hospital visit. Still, I simply nod and shift my attention to Enzo. "Sawyer?"

"She's fine. Dante took her away as soon as the building started collapsing."

As much as I'm dying to set eyes on her and confirm for myself that she's unharmed, I'm glad she's out of danger. "Good."

I tilt my head back the way I came, but before I can explain about Marcus, Enzo snarks, "Dante and I are also alive and unharmed. Thanks for asking. Your concern is greatly appreciated."

I roll my eyes before pinning him with a flat stare. "Why are you here again?"

"Trying to save your sorry asses. Trust me, I'd rather be curled up with Sawyer right now, but instead, I'm here because she was on the verge of a breakdown thinking the two of you were trapped inside when the whole building caved in."

I grimace. "Well, you can help me with Marcus, then. He's trapped under a steel beam and Bones and me can't get him out on our own."

"You should consider putting some time in at the gym. Then you could lift it all on your own," Enzo jests with a playful smile.

"Fuck off. Not everyone wants to look like they're jacked-up on roids like you two idiots."

They both laugh as they follow me back the way I came, and the joking falls away as I explain Marcus' situation. "Enzo, if you help me and Bones lift the beam, then Cain, you drag Marcus out once the rebar is out of his leg."

Begrudgingly, Cain agrees, and by the time we get back to Marcus, he's deathly white and his eyes are closed, with a panicked-looking Bones hovering over him, unsure what to do.

"He was talking and then I think he fell asleep."

"Yo, Marcus!" I slap him on the face. Not hard, but enough that he jolts back into consciousness. "You still with me?"

"Yup, I'm here." His voice is weak, quieter than it was before.

"I brought some help. We're going to get you out of here now, okay?"

"Sounds good." His eyes drift shut again, and I shake his shoulder.

"You gotta keep your eyes open. I know he's shit company but talk to Cain here for me." Cain situates himself so he can drag Marcus out from under the beam without having to put much weight on his sprained ankle, while Enzo, Bones, and I get into position so we can lift the beam.

"On my count. Three. Two. One." My muscles scream, Bones' and Enzo's faces showing similar strain as they put their all into lifting the godforsaken beam.

There's a grunt of pain before Cain calls out, "It's out," already dragging Marcus out from underneath. "You can set it down now," he informs us when Marcus' feet have cleared, and with shaking arms, we lower the beam to the ground.

Sweat sticks to my shirt, and I'm breathing heavily, but there's no time to rest yet. I move to check on Marcus' wound, pleased to see only a slow trickle of blood running from it rather than the heavy stream there was before. Enzo helps Cain get Marcus into a standing position, and Bones moves to replace Cain as Enzo throws one of Marcus' arms over his shoulder, readying to support him in much the same way he was supporting Cain when I came across them.

Bones does the same on his side, and between them, they manage to take most of Marcus' weight. Marcus' head hangs down between his shoulders, barely conscious as his feet half-drag across the ground. Moving beside Cain, I arch a brow and wait for him to admit he needs help walking too. With a scowl, he throws his arm over my shoulder and the two of us follow Enzo, Marcus, and Bones toward where I parked the car earlier.

Since the kids took Tank to the hospital in a car, and Dante dragged Sawyer away in another, it's the only car left, and it's a tight fit as we all pile in and rush over to the hospital. The entire drive, Enzo makes lame-ass jokes, Bones chiming in now and again with his own witty comeback as the two of them work to keep Marcus conscious. I hear the odd huff of laughter from him, so it must be working.

Reaching the hospital, I pull up right outside the emergency department, in the ambulance bay. While Bones and Enzo work to get Marcus out of the car, I rush inside, shouting for help until two nurses with a gurney follow me back outside.

"He was trapped inside a collapsed building," I explain quickly. "Got pinned beneath a beam, and a piece of rebar went through his thigh. There was so much blood."

As we reach the car, I step aside, letting the medical team work as they strap Marcus to the gurney. I hear words like *weak pulse*, *blood transfusion*, and *operating room* before they wheel him into the hospital.

"I'll stay with—"

"No." Bones cuts across my words. "I'll stay." His gaze flicks toward where Marcus disappeared before coming to rest on my face. Glancing at Cain and Enzo, he says, "The others are here somewhere, and you need to check that Sawyer and Dante are okay."

I open my mouth to argue, noticing Cain's pinched expression.

"Seriously. Go! We will be fine."

I flick my gaze to Cain, who mulls it over for a long second before biting out, "I'll send some men over."

With a quick nod, Bones hurries into the hospital after Marcus, and we all climb back into the car, eager to check on our girl.

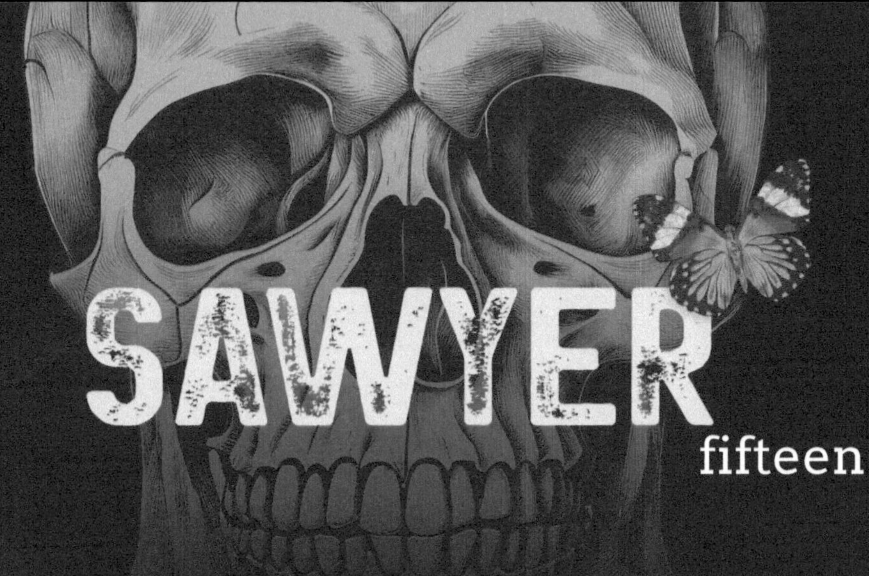

S oft murmurs pull me from the dark, murky depths of a sleep born from pure exhaustion—both physical and mental. I'm cocooned in a blanket of warmth that seeps into my bones and whispers words of comfort, making it even harder to rouse myself from sleep. My eyes feel swollen and gritty, reminding me of the count-less tears I leaked onto Dante's chest before I finally passed out, and it takes a moment to pry them apart.

When I do, I find my cheek pressed against a vast expanse of warm, sun-kissed skin, the hard edge of muscles cushioning my head. My heart speeds up, skipping a beat as the voices around me register, and a smile breaks out across my face as I lift my head, meeting Cain's warm emerald eyes.

"Hey, baby." His voice is soft, sliding over me like a silk sheet, and there are creases in the corner of his eyes as he smiles. He blurs in front of me as tears gather in my eyes, and I choke on a sob as I wrap my arms around his broad chest and fall apart.

Someone presses in behind me, before Oliver's soothing voice erases the last of my fear. Sniffling, I push back the onslaught of tears and lift my head, giving Cain a quick once over—other than a myriad of bruises and scratches, he appears to be in one piece —before glancing over my shoulder and scrutinizing Oliver.

They both look as though they are mostly unharmed, and relief washes through me at that miracle. I saw that roof come down, heard the screams and cries of men trapped within. I know many have died or been gravely hurt. It is no small thing that both of them escaped relatively unscathed.

Unable to control them, more tears overflow, running in rivulets down my cheeks until Oliver brushes them away. "No more tears, sweetheart," he murmurs, his voice barely more than a whisper.

"I was so scared." My voice is just as quiet, as though if I speak much louder, I'll break the illusion and wake up to discover this is all a dream and they aren't actually here. My fear was comparable to seeing Luc in that church. I've never known fear like it, which is saying something considering the life I've led and the situations I've found myself in. If I've learned anything, it's that fear for oneself pales in comparison to the gripping claws of terror that hold you captive when the well-being of those you love and care about is on the line. All those years I scavenged the streets in search of food and somewhere safe for Luc and me to sleep, I only ever feared for Luc. For his safety and welfare. Until recently, he was the only one who could incite such paralyzing emotions. However, the circle of people I give a shit about has grown exponentially, and now the fear and worries that I once felt purely for Luc extend to the men surrounding me in this room.

It's terrifying, yet if given the choice, I wouldn't return to my old life. Before I crossed paths with Oliver, stumbled across Cain, and put myself in Dante and Enzo's line of sight, I was merely existing. Living a shadow of a life. I couldn't see it then. Didn't recognize the gaping hole in my chest for what it was, but now my eyes have been pried open and I've come to accept that life isn't simply about survival. I've gotten a taste of what it's like to live, and I can't go back to that half-life.

I feel like someone who has been watching television in black and white, and now I've been introduced to technicolor. Before, I was living my life in varying shades of gray. I didn't realize anything was amiss until the love of these four ruthless men started bleeding into it, filling the cracks with beautiful veins of color until even the darkest shadows were forced into the light. I can't go back. I don't want to.

"If I'd known nearly getting squashed under a building would get me your undivided attention, I'd have swapped places with one of these assholes," Enzo grumbles. There's zero heat behind his words, though, and when I tear my gaze away from Oliver to look at where he's perched at the foot of the bed, he's smiling fondly at me. My eyes flick behind him to where Dante is leaning against the bedroom door, his arms crossed over his broad chest. He's wearing only his boxers, and I vaguely remember him stripping us down to shower before tucking me into bed. His eyes bore into me with the same intensity as always, and I get the distinct impression his entire focus is on me, regardless of whose arms I'm in.

With his straight back, legs casually crossed at the ankle, he looks as formidable as he does wearing a full suit. Not many people could pull off such an intimidating stance while sporting a hard-on and wearing only boxers—which only serve to draw my attention to the dick that's growing harder with every passing second I stare at him.

Dirty thoughts flit across my mind as desire unfurls in my core, and I have to rip my gaze away from Dante's heated one before I descend into smutville. Refocusing on Enzo, I push back the covers, not giving a shit that I'm only wearing my bra and panties as I crawl across the bed toward him. He pulls me into his lap, and I wrap my arms around his neck, threading my fingers through the blond strands of hair that brush across the back of his neck.

"Thank you for making sure they were both okay." My smile is watery as my thoughts drift back to how close I came to nearly losing two of my men, but it overflows with gratitude and love. "You could have insisted on coming with me, but you didn't."

His hand comes up to cup my cheek, and sorrow flashes across his apple-green eyes. "I hated seeing you so distraught. I'd have done just about anything to ease your suffering." A mischievous glint enters his eyes and a small smirk quirks up the corner of his lips. "But if it will get you in my lap, looking at me the way you are right now, then I'll happily save their sorry asses at every available opportunity."

There's an affronted scoff from behind me—most likely Cain. "We didn't need you *saving* us."

Enzo's gaze flicks over my shoulder, his smirk only growing. "No? Then who practically carried you to the car?"

Hearing the implication that Cain was injured, my head whips around to face him, doing another scan of his body. The bedsheet is straddling his waist, preventing me from seeing his legs, and not caring what he's wearing beneath it, I yank the sheet off him.

"Cain!" I exclaim, gaping at the purply-red swollen lump currently surrounding his ankle.

I notice even Enzo winces when he gets a look at it, indicating Cain probably played down the seriousness of his injury.

"Okay, admittedly, it didn't look that bad earlier," Cain begins, holding up his hands in an appeasing gesture that is entirely ineffective. "But it's nothing some ice and painkillers won't fix."

"It needs to be looked at!" I insist. "By a medical professional." Giving him the stink eye, I tack on, "Which *you* are not."

"I'm not leaving this bed tonight, baby." His eyes smolder with desire as his gaze flicks down my mostly naked body, sending a shiver racing down my spine. "There are far more important things I need to do tonight." Slowly, he lifts his gaze until he meets mine. "Besides, I have my very own nurse who will make it all better."

"Is that so?" I laugh, even as my body goes up in flames beneath his molten stare full of wicked intentions. "I'm not sure how blowing your load will help your ankle."

He shrugs a shoulder, his eyes never leaving mine. "We should try it just in case it does."

I'm still in Enzo's lap, my arms around his neck, so I feel when his shoulders shake with silent laughter and an idea takes form. Shuffling, I resituate myself so my back is against Enzo's chest. I can feel three sets of laser beams tracking my every move, only emboldening me further.

"In that case, we wanna pull out all the stops. Make it truly mind-blowing sex."

Picking up on my intentions, Enzo shifts on the bed so I'm settled between his legs. Lifting a hand, he brushes my hair over one shoulder, exposing my neck. Lowering his head, his lips skim up the column of my neck until his breath tickles my ear. "You're playing with fire, baby girl."

His voice is low, but given the heavy silence in the room, the others watching us with hungry intent and cautious wariness, there's no doubt they heard him.

"I always have enjoyed flirting with danger." Primal need bleeds into every word as I arch my back, quietly begging Enzo to stop teasing my skin. "Besides, after this past week, I need to feel each of you. I need to know all of you are with me. That you're safe."

"We're with you, Spitfire. We're here. We're safe. *You're* safe."

As his words soak into my heart, filling it with warmth, his lips finally press firmly against the sensitive skin of my neck. His teeth lightly scrape over my skin, making me tremble in his arms before he sucks on the skin. My eyelids fall to half-mast as I arch my back and emit a low groan. I can feel Cain, Oliver, and Dante all watching us, their gazes intense and hot.

Despite that, I know I have to play this right. They might all want *me*, but they still barely tolerate one another, and I highly doubt that sharing me is high on any of their to-do lists. But I'm done. I need this. *We* need this. I've claimed them, and I'm never letting any of them go, so they're just going to have to suck it up and learn to work as a team. Learn to rely on one another. Learn to share... and the best place to start is here, now, with me.

I push my ass back against the hardness in Enzo's sweats as his palms slide around my middle, his large hands splayed across my stomach and ribs as he pulls me closer and begins lavishing my neck with gusto.

Squeezing one of his muscular thighs with my fingers, my other hand reaches behind my back until I can run it along his erection. His breath stutters as he pushes against me. "Don't think I don't know what you're doing," he murmurs, his voice so low I can hardly hear him. "Using me to get these assholes to play nice." One of his hands moves up to cup my breast, giving it a squeeze while I moan. "I'm surprised you didn't choose Oliver to instigate this little experiment. Although perhaps you were worried Dante would kill him."

I wasn't. Oliver would have been the most logical choice. He's the peacekeeper—always has been. He's the one most likely to accept sharing me, but given how things have been between us, I worried he would only have acquiesced out of guilt, and I didn't want that. I don't want him to accept this only because he's feeling guilty and willing to do whatever I want in order to make things right between us.

So the only other semi-reasonable person that left was Enzo. Enzo enjoys causing trouble. He's spent years pushing Dante's buttons and delighting in the consequences, and I've watched him do the same with Cain. Both men are easily riled, and I'm counting on him to want to see how this will play out.

"You're lucky I love you," he murmurs as he slides my bra strap off my shoulder and gently sucks on the skin. The fingers of his other hand, still resting on my stomach, trail lower, skimming the waistband of my panties. His sensual touches and light teasing make my core clench as I turn feverish with desire.

Glancing up at Oliver through my lashes, I find him following Enzo's fingers with a desperate sort of hunger. Feeling my eyes on him, he lifts his head to meet my gaze, seeing my need for him burning in their depths.

This is a tentative moment—the bridging of a gap. If I can get Oliver and Enzo to play together, then there's hope for Cain and Dante. Oliver holds my gaze, and I know he can see my anxiety despite how hard I try to hide it. My concern that he'll say no. That Cain and Dante won't be on board. That this will all fall apart. Shedding any pretense, I drop my guard and show him how much I need this. How much I need them—*all* of them. How much I need the reassurance that the future we are fighting for is possible. That it's not a futile hope I'm desperately clinging to because I don't want to see the reality staring me in the face.

My heart is lodged in my throat, the seconds ticking by achingly slow as Oliver keeps me in suspense, before he finally leans forward.

I don't even blink, waiting with bated breath to see what he will do. Only the yearning darkening of his normally pale blue eyes stops me from descending into a panic.

Reaching out his hands, his fingers feather over my sides before hooking into my panties. With a bit of help from Enzo, he peels them over my ass and down my legs before tossing them to Cain.

Cain catches them without even looking, his eyes zeroed in on Enzo's fingers as they brush my lower stomach, trailing lower still to where I need him most. Beneath their gazes and Enzo's sensual touch, my breathing becomes labored, my chest heaving as I silently will him to move lower.

"Spread your legs, Spitfire." Enzo's voice is a husky purr in my ear. "Show them how wet you are for me."

"For *us*," Cain growls, glowering at Enzo before focusing on me, his eyes softening with lust and adoration. "I want to see how wet you are *for us.*"

Goosebumps pebble my heated skin at the possessive demand, excitement combined with the thought that this might actually happen turning my core molten. Lifting one leg at a time, I place them on the outside of Enzo's, planting my feet on the bed and bringing my knees up so Cain and Oliver have a front-row seat to my already glistening pussy.

Oliver groans, cursing under his breath while Cain licks his lips like he wants to dive in and taste me. *Yes, please!* My breath catches as Enzo's fingers graze my nub before stroking my folds, his touch gentle, teasing. Resting my head against his chest, I tilt my hips, seeking him out.

He tsks but gives me what I need before I can reprimand him. My whole body jolts as his thumb presses on my clit, his fingers circling my entrance before sliding inside. My breath leaves me in a whoosh as my eyes fall closed, satisfaction coursing through me as a chorus of curses and low groans vibrate around me.

Before I can wholly lose myself to pleasure, panic has my eyes snapping open as I twist to look over Enzo's shoulder.

"He's still here," Enzo reassures as my eyes clash with Dante's, my body instantly relaxing under Enzo's coaxing touch. "He won't leave. He might not join in, but he won't leave."

I want him to join in, but I know he's going to be the most resistant to this, and I equally don't want to push him too far, so if all he does is stay and watch, then I can settle for that... for now.

As my eyes run over him, I notice his tense posture, as though he's holding himself back. Either from pulling me away from Enzo's touch and Cain and Oliver's prying eyes, or because he wants his hands on me too, I'm not really sure. Certainly, based on the large bulge in his boxers and the dark pits his eyes have turned, he's enjoying the show, and well... if he's only going to watch, then I'm happy to put on one hell of a show for him.

I keep my eyes trained on him as I rock my hips, pushing Enzo's fingers deeper until I'm breathing heavily and my nipples are pebbled, the fabric of my bra rubbing them raw as I chase my release. The slick sound of my mounting pleasure is the only noise in the room, followed by the occasional pained groan. As I watch, Dante moves a hand to cup his balls through his boxers, giving them a squeeze before running his palm over his erection. His eyes, which are glued to mine, are lidded and heavy with desire, even if he makes no move to act on it.

Simply seeing how much he wants me is my undoing, and my body trembles in Enzo's embrace as waves of pleasure crash over me. I'm still riding the aftershocks when the dipping of the mattress draws my attention from Dante, and I turn my head to find Oliver crawling down the bed toward me, his hungry gaze on my apex. He lowers his head, kissing his way up one thigh before doing the same on the other. The touch is soft and sweet, exactly Oliver's style, and it fills my heart with all sorts of sappy feelings while simultaneously heating my blood.

As Enzo withdraws his fingers, Oliver leans in to lick up my slit. I shudder, my nails digging into Enzo's thighs as I arch my back, already needing another release—this time under Oliver's ministrations.

Still wet from my orgasm, Enzo moves to rub at my clit, while Oliver's tongue delves into my channel. The combination of their touches sends me catapulting into an even more explosive climax that has every muscle going taut before I sag against Enzo's chest, catching my breath.

My eyes are closed, but when lips meet mine, licking along the seam until I open, I know it's Oliver. Our kiss is slow and languid, as if we have all the time in the world. In this moment, it feels like we do. Despite the mounting problems outside that door, in here, it's just us. Just my love for these four unlikely men and their love for me.

So, rather than fretting over the hundred-and-one worries that constantly plague me nowadays, I let them all fall by the wayside and focus on the reverent way in which Oliver's tongue slides over mine, on Enzo's adoring touch as he gently strips me of my bra and strokes my skin, on the searing heat I can feel burning into me from Cain and Dante's eyes.

Enzo maneuvers me onto my knees and Oliver adjusts, kissing his way down my body. Reaching my chest, he draws a nipple into his mouth and coaxes it into a sharp point before doing the same to the other. Each suck, kiss, and bite has my already oversensitive body shaking. When I feel Enzo's tongue between my thighs, licking all the way to my rear, my fingers thread through Oliver's hair, holding him to me as the pleasurable sensations send my body into overdrive.

I shudder when Enzo's tongue circles my puckered hole, his fingers easily sliding into my soaking wet channel. Feeling a third presence, I peel my eyes open, not realizing I'd closed them. Cain has leaned forward, his eyes raking up and down my body, unable to settle on one spot as he drinks in my response to Oliver and Enzo.

Noticing movement in the corner of my eye, I drop my gaze. My eyes flare with hunger. Cain slowly fists himself, his motions becoming more deliberate when he realizes he has my full attention.

"Do you like what Oliver and Enzo are doing, baby?"

It's obvious that I do, and obvious that Cain likes it too. Still, I breathe out a "Yes."

"Is that what you wanted? All of us worshiping at your altar, giving you screaming orgasm after screaming orgasm?"

"It is." Again, the words are breathless beneath his heated stare, Enzo's wicked tongue, and Oliver's enticing kisses.

"You might regret that when you're boneless, unable to stand, your voice hoarse from screaming, and your brain so addled that you can't even remember your own name."

Apparently liking that idea, Oliver bites down on my nipple, sending a shot of pain straight to my middle, and Enzo ups the pace of his fingering, the strokes of his tongue matching them until I'm shaking and moaning, already close to coming again.

"Well, since you're the one running this ship, tell us what you want?"

My eyes widen with surprise and flick up to Cain's, finding nothing but sincerity in his gaze. Adrenaline pours into my veins as excitement licks up my spine. Instead of answering him with my words, I lean forward until I'm perched on all fours, forcing Oliver to shift to my side, and I use my mouth to tell him what I want.

I lick my tongue along the underside of his cock, swirling it around his tip before lowering my lips over his shaft. Cain hisses, and I soak it up, loving how I can make him come undone so easily.

"I do love it when your mouth is full of my cock," he groans. "I don't even care that Enzo is between your thighs and that silent fucker is watching us all like we're live entertainment."

His hands move to cup the back of my head and I swallow him down deep while Enzo eats me out and Oliver sets my skin on fire. When Enzo trails his slickened fingers backward, I hum my approval, and having gotten the go-ahead, he slides one in. My back arches, forcing his finger in further while I swallow Cain deeper.

Oliver's fingers brush along my spine until he reaches my hip, charting a path around to my lower belly and down between my thighs until he sinks three of them inside me, filling me completely.

Cain's hands tighten in my hair, and he begins thrusting his hips, the tip of his cock hitting the back of my throat while Oliver's fingers match his pace and Enzo works a second finger into my ass.

Tears gather in my eyes, every muscle in my body pulling tight as a ball of energy builds in my core, gathering momentum with every thrust and groan. Knowing that all three of them are working together is what sends me freefalling into yet another orgasm.

I can feel Cain pulsing in my mouth, on the verge of exploding, but he somehow manages to hold off. Once the first waves of my climax pass, Cain pulls me off his dick. "I need to feel your walls clenching around my cock the next time you come." His words come out in a growl as he yanks me into his lap, his pulsing erection sliding into my slick heat. I cry out as his piercing drags along my overly sensitive walls, threatening to send me headfirst into yet another orgasm as I struggle to grasp the remaining fragments of my sanity.

Enzo and Oliver don't allow Cain to monopolize all of my attention. They swiftly follow his change in position, Oliver claiming my lips while Enzo's heat envelops my back. Cain's hand grips my hips possessively, using his hold to lift me up before slamming me back down onto his length.

Ripping my lips from Oliver's, I throw my head back and cry out. My hand slides over Oliver's chest, down his chiseled abs, before pushing under the waistband of his boxers. Helping me out, he lowers them over his hips so his cock springs free, and I slide my hand over his erection until he's thrusting into my palm.

"So beautiful," he murmurs, watching me bounce up and down on Cain before he leans in to suck my nipple into his mouth.

A moment later, I feel the head of Enzo's dick pressing against my back passage. "You ready for more, Spitfire?" he growls in my ear.

"God, yes," I gasp as he presses forward, feeling the burn of the stretch as he slowly but steadily sinks into me.

"So fucking tight," he grunts, and Cain groans, obviously feeling the increased pressure. He slows his pace until Enzo is fully seated, the two of them taking a moment to find their rhythm, but as soon as they do... the last of my sanity falls away and nothing exists except them and me.

"Need more," I pant, gazing hungrily at Oliver as both Cain and Enzo slam into me. "Please."

With a smirk, he's on his feet, his cock jutting out in front of him like a lone sentinel begging my mouth to take it captive. Knowing it won't be long before I'm shaking with another inevitable orgasm, I don't waste time sucking him into my mouth until his balls hit my chin and his tip grazes the back of my throat.

"Fucking hell, Trouble. You're so damn good at that." Oliver brushes my hair back from my face with a surprising reverence, given our situation. "Do you have any idea how sexy you look, taking all of us? Like a true queen."

I can't do anything but stare up at him through teary eyes as he starts to fuck my face, the three of them finding a rhythm that suits us all. I'm conscious that one of my men is missing, our bond feeling incomplete without all of us in this together.

Blinking away my tears, I glance in his direction out of the corner of my eyes. He's still leaning against the door, looking relaxed for all the world to see, except I notice the tense set of his shoulders. The only tell that he's not absolutely furious is the fact that he is still rubbing his hand up and down the front of his boxers. However, he makes no move to insert himself, apparently content to simply watch. Still, I take the fact that he hasn't stormed out or ripped me away from the others as a positive sign, and the way he's staring at me... he's clearly enjoying what he's seeing, even if he's unsure about joining in.

I feel Oliver swell in my mouth, and just before he blows his load, he pulls out, spilling his seed over my chest instead. "Fuck," he grunts, trailing a finger through his release before smearing it over my tits. "I love seeing you covered in my cum. You should walk around like that all the time."

His words surprise me. Oliver has never been the territorial type, not in the same way Cain and Dante are, but given the circumstances, his inner possessiveness is showing... and I'm so here for it.

Enzo comes next, following Oliver's lead and pulling out at the last second, his climax hitting my back. Their undeniable claim has my legs quaking. My heart is slamming against my chest at what promises to be the most intense orgasm yet, or ever. It starts a slow climb, unfurling from my core and creeping through my veins until I can feel it in my fingers and toes.

My walls begin to clench and Cain grunts, though rather than upping his pace like I know he wants to, he lifts me off him. I whimper in protest, but he quickly turns me in his lap so my back is to his chest before sliding back in.

"Show Dante what he's missing, baby. Let him see how fucking sexy you look wearing our cum."

My eyes clash with Dante's, whose gaze drops to where Cain is sinking into me in hard, fast thrusts before slowly trailing up to my breasts which are bouncing with each motion. He sees the cum glistening on my chest before lifting his gaze to meet my heated one.

Biting down on my earlobe, Cain murmurs, "fuck me," before ceasing his fast pace and allowing me to take over. I do as he says, moving up and down his cock as I chase my release while he cups my breast with one hand and his other moves between my thighs.

The entire time, I keep my gaze on Dante, observing him watch me fuck Cain until I'm screaming my release and Cain's seed paints my inner walls. I collapse against him, breathless and panting, my body boneless just like he promised. Still, I'm not done yet. There's one guy left, and I refuse to let him sit on the sidelines any longer.

Leaning back against Cain, I cock a brow at Dante, throwing out a silent challenge. His eyes narrow, but that's his only tell. The only indicator that he's not a statue. He makes no attempt to move toward me, and I patiently wait him out.

Seconds tick by, and right as I'm about to push out of Cain's arms, intent on going to him, he steps forward. I swallow down my gasp, not daring to even blink as he crosses the room toward me.

When Dante is standing at the side of the bed, he reaches out a hand, running a finger along my swollen lower lip. My tongue flicks out, wrapping around his finger and sucking it into my mouth. His eyes smolder, the muscles in his arms bunching and loosening as though he's trying to hold himself back from tossing me over his shoulder and carrying me out of here. There's something undeniably hot about that. However, the uncertainty in his eyes pulls me up short. He might want me, but he's unsure about *this.*

Not knowing what to say, I continue to stare up into his dark eyes as I try to think of the right words. Words that won't send him running away. But before I can put together a sentence, he speaks first.

"You definitely want this? You've already had all three of them."

Is he... worried that I won't want or need him because I have Cain, Oliver, and Enzo?

I take a second to think through my response. "Yes. I want this. I want you. Them. All four of you. I'm not complete without you, Dante. You're an essential part of this equation, and no matter how many orgasms they may give me, I will always need what *you* give me."

He takes a moment to digest what I said. My words aren't eloquent. Nothing like the heartfelt things he's said to me, but I hope my sincerity is enough to compensate for it. Only when he gives a slight nod do I let out the breath I was holding.

He brushes his thumb over my lip again. "In that case, you better open up."

I smile coyly before doing just that, watching impatiently as he pushes down his boxers and lifts out his very hard dick. I immediately lean in to lick the tip, humming at the saltiness on my tongue, before swallowing him down.

He grunts, and I somehow manage a cocky smirk. Seeing it, a challenge burns in his gaze before he thrusts forward, and I'm pushed back against Cain's chest while he fucks my face with wild abandonment. Cain's arm bands around me, holding me upright, and I can feel his dick begin to harden while still inside me. He starts to play with my nipple, teasing it into a stiff peak before pinching, pain intertwining with the pleasure building low in my core.

His other hand moves to play with my swollen and oversensitive clit. It takes next to no time before I'm trembling. "Let go, *mia vita,*" Dante growls, each word emphasized with a thrust that has him hitting the back of my throat.

My body responds to his commands, my orgasm immediately exploding through me with all the swiftness of a lightning strike, and a second later, Dante pushes so deep that he blocks my airway, swearing as his release spills down my throat.

Fully satisfied and thoroughly wrung out, I collapse back against Cain, my eyelids already drifting shut with the promise of sleep. A soft hand strokes my hair. "Sleep, *mia vita.*"

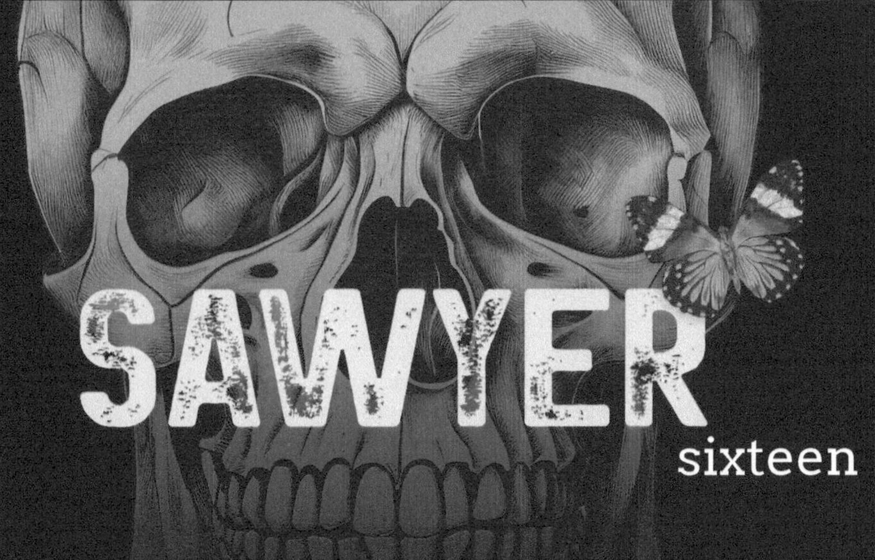

"**W**hy do you think the fire station collapsed?" Enzo asks at breakfast the next morning. After our *escapades* last night—both with the Grim Bastards and between the bedsheets—we all slept in, so breakfast is more like lunch.

All five of us are sitting around an old-style wooden table in the dated kitchen. We've been discussing the events of last night, Enzo, Cain, and Oliver filling Dante and me in on what happened after the building collapsed. Cain and I checked in on Luc and Evie when we woke up, and Bones called from the hospital earlier. Marcus had to have surgery on his leg, but both he and Tank are stable. Thank goodness. I don't know what we would have done if we'd lost either of them. We were incredibly fortunate that none of our people died last night, but it begs the question, how many more will we lose before this war is over?

"No idea," Cain answers. "The whole building was probably structurally unsound. It wouldn't surprise me if Grim let the place go to wreck and ruin. So long as it looked okay on the outside, for appearance's sake. He wouldn't have given a shit about what his men were living in. I'll get men out to assess the situation today, but given the damage, we may never know the true cause."

"I guess it doesn't really matter," I say with a shrug. "Either way, the Bastards are no longer a threat. Did you see what happened to Grim?" I direct the question to Cain and Oliver since Enzo, Dante, and I didn't cross paths with him.

"He's buried beneath a car's weight of concrete." We all stare at Cain with surprise and relief—except Dante, whose expression is a blank slate, as always.

"You sure?"

Cain's eyes narrow on Dante. "Of course, I'm fucking sure. I stayed until I was certain there was no chance he could make it out alive. How the fuck do you think I busted my ankle?"

"I just assumed you tripped over your own feet or something equally embarrassing."

Did Dante just make a joke?

I'm not the only one who seems surprised. "Well, well, look who has a sense of humor all of a sudden," Enzo jokes, clapping Dante on the shoulder. "Bloodshed and orgasms look good on you, my friend."

Dante glowers furiously, daring anyone else to comment. Smothering my laugh, I slip out of my chair and into his lap. I ruin the total *don't mess with me* vibes he's giving off by planting my lips on his, not removing them until I feel the tension bleed out of his body. My kiss is a thank you, one of recognition for the effort he just made. Just like I know Enzo's jesting is done to help ease any uncertainty Dante might have been feeling.

All of this is new to him—camaraderie, relying on others, working as a team. I see the efforts he's been making, and more importantly, I see his inner struggle when it comes to making these compromises. I owe him big time, but overall, I know he has the potential to gain a lot from developing a friendship with Cain and Oliver. I can picture a future where Dante talks and laughs with them, the four sharing a brotherhood of sorts. It's a future I imagine Dante never saw for himself. One he probably still can't wrap his head around. It's also one he will have to put the work into, if it's something he wants. I know he's doing all of this for me—making an effort with them—but I want him to do it for himself too.

Shifting in Dante's lap so I'm leaning back against his chest, I ask Cain, "What happened to Grim?"

"While we were fighting off his men, I saw him sneak out of the room. Being the pussy that he is, he obviously decided to run from the fight and leave his people to their fates. A true leader." Cain scoffs in disgust. "I followed and caught up to him right before the entire building started groaning and crumbling down around us. Before I could do the world a favor and kill him myself, the ceiling above him broke apart. He got trapped beneath it." He frowns. "There was no fucking way I was going to walk away without making sure he was definitely dead. As I was making my way across the room to put a bullet in his brain, the whole building shook again, dislodging more concrete. A bit struck me, and whatever way I went down, I rolled my ankle."

"And let me guess, you got right back up, ignoring all the signs that you shouldn't be walking on your ankle."

Cain shoots Oliver a roguish grin. "I wasn't about to let a measly sprain stop me from killing that fucker."

I roll my eyes. "Your ankle is the size of a bowling ball!" The damn thing has gotten even bigger since last night, and no matter how much I insist, Cain won't go to the hospital. Stubborn ass! At least he let me wrap an ice pack around it last night—not that it seems to have helped with the swelling much.

"Now that he's gone and the clubhouse is destroyed, the Bastards are no longer an issue... which just leaves Giovanni." I turn my head to look at Enzo as Cain nods.

"He'll know we're coming for him," Dante points out.

"Which is why we need to move quickly."

"You're in no state to go anywhere with that ankle!" I snap at Cain, glaring at him with narrowed eyes. "You could barely get down the stairs. How the hell do you suppose you're going to storm Giovanni's apartment or wherever we end up facing him?"

Cain waves away my concerns with a far too flippant hand motion for my liking. "I'll be fine in a day or two. I'll stay off my feet while we get organized."

I shake my head, not the least bit satisfied with that answer.

We're weak. Not just Cain, but the Rejects. We've lost good men, and now Marcus, Tank, and Cain are out of commission. It leaves me feeling uneasy, and for the first time since I got all four of them on board, I'm scared. Scared that we might not be able to win this. Scared of losing any more people, and most of all, scared of losing one of my guys. If last night taught me anything, it's that I won't survive losing *any* of them.

I'm not the same woman I was when I ran into Oliver in Toxic. All four of these men have wormed their way beneath the surface of my skin. They've infiltrated my bloodstream and embedded themselves so deep that they've become an essential part of who I am. Without one of them, I'm no longer me. No longer able to function. I'd become a shell of who I am. I'd lose myself wholeheartedly to the Reaper.

Perhaps, once upon a time, I wouldn't have seen that as such a bad thing, but I know better now. Unable to feel is no way to go through life. Dante is living proof of that. Without the ability to feel, we eventually lose our humanity. We succumb to our inner demons, giving in to our base desires until we're so far gone it would take a miracle to pull us back into the light. Oliver, Cain, Dante, and Enzo are *my* miracle. Without any of them, I'd be lost to the darkness forever.

While I've been internally freaking out, I realize the conversation has continued around me, and I zone back in as Dante suggests, "I could try reaching out again to some of the men loyal to me."

"Can you trust them?"

Dante takes a second to think over Cain's question. "It's possible that my father has gotten to them, but there are a couple I'd trust enough to see if they can at least get the information we need."

"What information?" I question, glancing back and forth between Dante and Cain as I realize I missed something vital.

"We need to know Giovanni's movements," Enzo explains. "He's not going to make himself an easy target. The only shot we have is if we can find out where he's going to be ahead of time, then pick the best place to confront him."

"How do you know you can trust your men?" I ask, focusing on Dante.

"I don't, but it's a risk we will have to take if we want any shot at my father."

Fuck, I seriously don't like this.

"Reach out to your contact," Cain states. "Once they give us the information we need, we'll keep them under lock and key until Giovanni is taken out. In the meantime, I need to go see Marcus and Tank and check in with the rest of the club."

"Absolutely not!" I interject. "You just said you were going to stay off your feet."

"Yeah, but I need to check on my men."

"You've already been on the phone with Bones and the guys at the clubhouse," I argue. "You don't also need to go see them. They know you're busy finding a solution to this mess."

"I can go—"

Before Oliver even finishes that sentence, I'm cutting him off. "No. The five of us are spending the rest of the day here, pretending the world's problems aren't battering at the door."

"Red, baby, it doesn't do us any good to bury our heads in the sand and pretend none of this is happening," Cain soothes, his features softening.

"I know. That's not what I'm trying to do," I sigh dejectedly. "I just want one day where we aren't being crushed beneath the weight of it all." Focusing my attention on Cain, I say, "Marcus is probably doped up on meds. He won't even know you are there, and the kids are at the hospital, so they will keep an eye on him. Same for Tank, and the men at the clubhouse are busy filling in bullet holes and securing the premises. Leave them to it. *You* need a day to recuperate so you can clear your mind and go in fresh. All of us need you on your A-game, and that won't be the case if you keep pushing yourself so hard."

Switching my attention to Dante, I continue, "It'll take a while to hear back from your contact, right?"

"Probably."

"Right." Nodding my head, decision made, I state with finality, "That decides it, then. We're having a Netflix and chill day today, and we'll get back to saving Black Creek tomorrow."

"Eh..." Dante's brow is furrowed in confusion. "What is *Netflix and chill*?"

Okay, if I hadn't already put my foot down, Dante's lack of current pop culture without a doubt makes the decision an easy one.

"It's code for a fuck session."

I gape at Cain in shock. "No, it isn't!"

The asshole just quirks a brow. "When it's you and us, wearing sweats and squished on a sofa together... yeah, it is."

My mouth opens and closes, but no words come out. I have no idea what the hell to say to that, and apparently, my silence is viewed as an agreement based on the smirks and eyebrow wags the four of them share. I know I said I wanted them to get along, but now I'm not so sure...

"Why do I have to wear this? You can see the outline of my dick."

I laugh as I watch Dante pull the drawstrings of the gray sweats as tight as they will go. They belong to Cain and are a bit baggy on him, but they still look hot as hell. Especially when he didn't have a t-shirt on, but unfortunately, he straight up refused to walk around all day without one. It would seem being seen in sweats is bad enough.

Not daring to tell him that the visibility of his cock is half the point, I simply respond, "Because you can't lounge in jeans or suit pants. Just trust me. You'll see, it'll be so much comfier."

His lips purse, clearly not believing me, but he stops complaining. Shifting his focus from the offending sweats to me, his expression softens. "How are you today?" He closes the distance between us, bringing his hand up to cup my cheek and staring at me with an intensity that only Dante can achieve. Every time he looks at me like that, it feels like he's pulling back all the layers I keep carefully wrapped around me until I'm raw and exposed. Yet, it doesn't feel invasive. More like a soft caress. Perhaps it's because I know I'm the only one he looks at like that—with genuine concern. "I was worried about you last night. You..." His face pinches. "I didn't know how to help you."

Closing the scant space between us, I wrap my arms around his waist and lean my head on his chest. "I was furious with you for carting me out of there when I didn't know if Cain and Oliver, and the others, were alive or not."

"You will always be my primary concern, Sawyer. No matter what is happening or going on with the others, I will always put your safety first. Even if you hate me for it."

I smile into his chest. "You did help. Your presence grounded me. Every time I felt panic dig her cold claws into my chest, you'd touch me, or I'd feel your skin against mine, and it calmed me. You were exactly what I needed, thank you."

His finger tilts my chin up until I'm staring into his eyes. They look lighter, more brown than black, and there's a sparkle in them as he roams his gaze over my face. "You don't need to thank me for taking care of you. I want to be the one you turn to when you're upset or scared and in need of comfort. I might not be very good at it, but I want to give you whatever you need."

Pushing up onto my toes, I brush my fingers through his hair before cupping his jaw. "You already do. All I'll ever need is you. It doesn't matter if you fumble, say or do the wrong thing, as long as you are here. Although, for the record, you were perfect last night."

That rare softness is in his eyes as he leans in. His hand cups the back of my head, holding me to him as he kisses me deeply. His touch is gentle, caring. So at odds with the imposing image he portrays to the rest of the world.

His kiss intensifies, turning heated and hungry as he directs me backward until my back hits the wall. Caging me in with his large frame, he moves to kiss along my neck. His hands glide over my shoulders and down my arms before his palms flatten over my ribs, pushing me flat against the wall while his hips grind against my core.

"Do you have any idea what you did to me last night? Watching them give you endless pleasure?"

"You could have joined in, you know."

"I wanted to." His voice drops an octave, his words eliciting a shudder. "I also wanted to rip their hands away and remove the memory of their touch. To fuck you so good that you would forget all about them." His hands move to where the oversized t-shirt I'm wearing brushes against my mid-thigh, slipping beneath the fabric so his calloused fingers can drift up my outer thigh. "But I'd never be able to achieve that, would I?"

Lifting my head, I hold his gaze while roaming my hands down the front of his t-shirt. Reaching the waistband of his sweats, I tug on the drawstrings until they unravel. "No, you wouldn't." I dip my hand inside, wrapping my fingers around his solid length and enjoying the way he groans at the simple touch. "You could never burn away their touch, just like they could never replace yours. I love them *and* I love you. Equally." I punctuate each sentence with a firm stroke of his cock. "Each of you speaks to me differently, fulfilling parts that I never even knew were missing or broken. Only when I'm with all of you, do I feel complete." Another stroke. "You are an essential part of the equation. Without you, none of this works. Without you, *I* don't work."

My other hand pushes his t-shirt up, baring his chest, and I press my lips against his warm skin before licking a path over the ridges of his abs until I can swirl my tongue around his nipple.

"I didn't know what to think of you at first. Everything I've heard about the

Antonellis... I expected you to be cruel and heartless, and don't get me wrong, you are. You are both of those things, but you're also so much more.

"You did an excellent job of pretending to be your father. So good, in fact, that you had even yourself fooled. Only, I could see everything that was lurking beneath the surface, buried so deep that you forgot it existed. Admittedly, I didn't know *what* you had repressed, but I was curious enough to push and prod and pry, and I'm so glad I did. Otherwise, I would have never gotten to witness the incredible man standing in front of me."

I switch my focus to his other nipple, lavishing it with the same attention before speaking again. "I see the effort you've been making with me, and with Cain and Oliver. I know none of this is easy on you." Pulling my hand free from his sweats, I tug his t-shirt over his head, dropping it on the floor before planting my hands on his chest and applying gentle force.

He allows me to direct him backward to the bed, and with a final shove, he falls onto the mattress. Stepping between his thighs, I grab the waistband of his sweats and shimmy them over his hips before pulling them down his legs. Leaving them pooling on the floor, I slowly rake my eyes up his thighs and over his abdomen and chest, biting on my lower lip as my breathing hitches and my body hums with desire.

Our eyes meet as I slide my hands along his thighs and get to my knees. "Let me show you how much I appreciate everything you do."

Maintaining eye contact, I run my tongue over his ballsack, sucking it into my mouth before licking my way up his shaft until I reach the tip. His cock twitches, his breathing coming in pants as his eyelids fall to half-mast.

"Ughhhh. God, *mia vita*, you're so good at that."

His hips thrust shallowly when I take him into my mouth, hollowing my cheeks as I suck him in deep. The hold he has over his control loosens with each bob until he yanks me off him and pulls me up onto the bed.

"After last night, I need to be buried in your tight pussy when I come."

My legs fall to either side of his hips as Dante pushes up until he's sitting. He rips my panties from me in a swift, deliriously sexy move. Draping my arms over his shoulders, I slide my core along his length until it glistens with a mixture of my saliva and pleasure.

His palms slip beneath my t-shirt, skimming my sides and pulling the top up as he lifts them higher. Slowly, he tugs it over my head, twisting it until my hands are trapped in the fabric, raised above my head.

I continue to rock my hips, dripping all over him as his eyes devour me. "You are so beautiful." His words are said with such raw intensity that my movements stagger. Leaning in, he sucks a peaked nipple into his mouth, swirling his tongue in such a way that sends zaps of electricity shooting to my core.

Releasing it with a pop, he adorns the other with the same attention until I'm writhing in his lap. With my hands still trapped above my head, I can't touch him the way I want, which only serves to heighten my desire.

"I still can't believe that you're all mine." Dante's voice has taken on a rough edge, strained from holding himself back. I can feel how tense his muscles are beneath me, the twitch of his cock every time I glide my pussy along it. "That you're my wife."

Wife. It still doesn't feel real to me either, although the same anxious fear I used to experience doesn't roll through me like it had when I used to hear that word or think about its implications. I still wear my wedding band. Honestly, it would feel strange now to take it off. However, other than the dinner we had at Giovanni's, I've never worn the engagement ring, nor do I intend to. Thankfully, Dante doesn't seem to mind.

"Those nights I spent watching you at Belle Donne, when I decided you were mine and refused to let anything stand in my way—even you... I thought for sure that the only way I'd be able to have you was if I barricaded you inside the house and tied you to my bed."

"Hmm, well, I'm definitely game to try some bondage."

I smirk, and he chuckles before licking a line up the valley of my breasts and along my collarbone. "I thought you were supposed to be thanking me for playing nice? Climb on my dick before I decide to take charge, flip us, and drive into you so deep you'll never forget the feel of me buried inside you."

That does sound enticing, and I briefly consider it, but it's my turn to give back to him. So instead, I lift up, reaching down to position him at my entrance, before lowering myself onto him. I don't take it easy on him, slamming down until his balls are pressing against my ass, and he hisses between his teeth.

When he loosens his hold on my t-shirt, I quickly toss it aside and grasp his wrists. Leaning forward, I force him to lie back down and I press the back of his hands into the mattress on either side of his head. My breasts bob in front of his face as I work him over, quickening my pace until we're both breathless and panting, and I can feel him straining against my hold, itching to touch me. He could easily flip us and take charge, just like he threatened, but he doesn't. He allows me to set the pace, as though he knows just how much I need to be the one bringing *him* pleasure for a change.

Every so often, his hips jut forward, his need to take control riding him hard. Each time, I stop moving and wait until he's growling before I smirk and go back to an achingly slow rhythm that teases us both before building up all over again.

"Sawyer," he growls when I do it for the fourth time. "You're testing my patience."

I only laugh before grinding down on him in such a way that it has my clit rubbing against his pelvis. When I do it for a second time, my entire body convulses, an unexpected orgasm ripping out of me.

Dante uses my distraction to his advantage. Breaking out of my hold, he grabs the back of my thighs and tosses me onto the mattress before settling between them and sliding back into my slick heat. His pace is relentless, his large palms flattening my thighs against the bedsheet so he can get as deep as humanly possible.

"Dante." His name is a prayer on my tongue, the remnants of my orgasm bleeding into the aching need for another one.

"Every time I'm inside you, I never want to leave." Each word is a grunt punctuated with a thrust that drives me deeper into the mattress and makes my head spin. Dopamine floods my brain, rattling my thoughts until I'm clenching around him, begging for release.

"Dante, please. I'm so close."

"Me too. *Fuck*. I'm not ready to be done yet, but you feel too good." He presses his thumb against my clit and begins rubbing in harsh, tight circles. "Come. I need you to come with me."

"Yes. Yes!"

My hips buck, needing to feel him deeper, to bury myself under his skin, and to feel him beneath mine.

"NOW!" he roars in conjunction with his climax, and it is as if my body is primed to respond to his command. My release bounds through me, unleashing like a summer storm until I'm wrung out and trembling from the aftershocks.

We just lie there in each other's arms, his forehead pressed against mine while we catch our breaths and bathe in the post-orgasmic afterglow.

"I know everything you've been doing has been for me," I begin once my heart has stopped slamming against my ribs. "But I hope you're also doing it for you." His eyebrows furrow, so I explain, "I know you have Enzo, but wouldn't it be nice to have other people you can rely on too? People who you can turn to for advice when you need it? People you can trust? A family you can just be yourself around, laugh with, and share the ups and downs of life with?"

"I don't know, I've never had that before—a family."

"We've all gone far too long without one, but I think if you give it a go, you might actually like it."

He quirks a brow. "Like dealing with Cain's mood swings and Oliver's too placid behavior? Dealing with Enzo's constant jibes at everyone? Dealing with sharing you with them?"

I smile despite myself. "Yes. All of that, because that's what family does to one another."

"Piss each other off?" There's a laugh in his voice.

"Exactly. The best relationships are built on teasing, sarcasm, and a mild dislike of the other person."

"Well, if that's the case, we'll be as tight as brothers in no time."

I laugh. "I'm just saying, I don't want you to get along with Cain and Oliver purely for my benefit."

He holds my gaze for a moment, taking my words under consideration. "Okay."

After another few minutes spent in one another's arms, we pull apart. I move to get up, but a large palm to my lower abdomen pins me to the bed and Dante slides down until his shoulders are wedged between my thighs.

His fingers scoop up our joint release before pushing it back inside my pussy. "Don't shower." There's a possessive growl in his voice that sends a shiver coursing through me. "And no panties. I want the others to smell me on you. To see my cum coating your thighs and know whose it is."

Holy Mary. I know I want them all to get along, but there is something so fucking hot about the way each of them claims me, ensuring the others know who I belong to. While I want peace between them, I am all here for a game of tug-of-war in the bedroom.

Only when I've given him an acquiescent nod does he offer me a helping hand off the bed.

"The contact you're going to reach out to... how much do you trust him?"

Dante pulls my discarded t-shirt over my head before fetching his own sweats and t-shirt from where I dropped them on the floor.

"There're a few men who I think would remain loyal to me, except the guy I'm thinking of is someone I've worked with for years. I've been the one managing him, and my father has had no reason to interact with him. He's a decent enough man, keeps his head down and gets the job done. Out of everyone, he's most likely to pick our side in an uprising. He's our best shot."

I swallow around the lump in my throat. It's not the confident reassurance I was hoping for, but if it's our best shot, then I can't exactly argue with that.

When we're both ready, he turns to face me. "Guess my alone time is up."

I reach out a hand, brushing my fingers down his arm before linking mine with his. "Once we've gotten rid of your father, there will be plenty of time for *us*."

"Very true." His fingers trail along my jaw, drawing my gaze to his. "A whole lifetime."

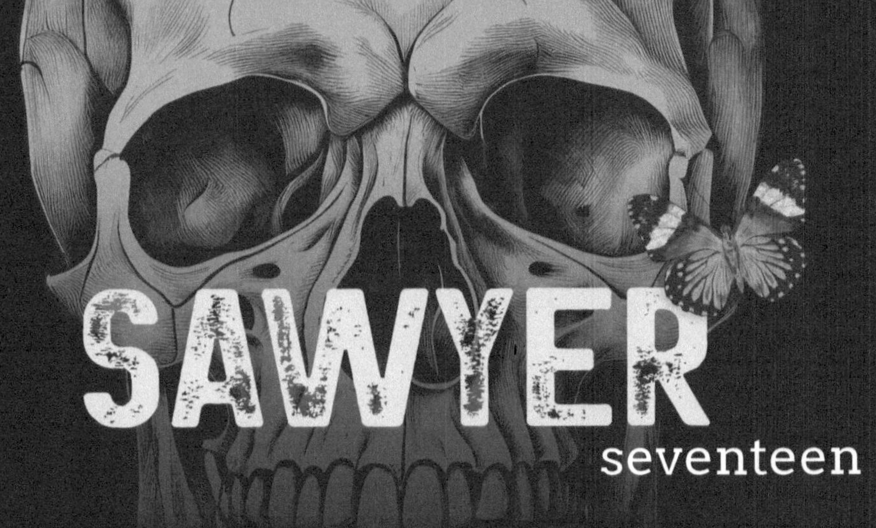

I pause inside the living room, staring slack-jawed at the rearranged furniture. The sofa cushions have been removed and placed on the floor, creating one large, cushioned area big enough for all of us to get comfy on.

"Wow!"

"We used to do this on rainy days when we were kids," Cain says from where he's already lounging in the middle of the setup. "Remember that, O?"

"I remember you taking up most of the cushions and leaving the rest of us to fight over the remaining space."

Mischief gleams in Cain's eyes. "You weren't complaining at the time."

"Luc and I used to do something similar once we got our apartment. We'd have sofa days where we'd stay in our pajamas all day and cuddle up under the blankets. We'd watch whatever was on the TV and eat junk food." A fond smile graces my lips. "They're some of my happiest memories."

Enzo moves to stand beside me and drapes his arm over my shoulder. Smiling down at me, he says sincerely, "Here's to making new ones."

I return his smile before Oliver grabs me around the waist, dislodging Enzo's arm as he lifts me off the ground. I squeal before bursting into laughter as he drops onto the cushions, bringing me down with him.

Enzo claims the space beside him, and Oliver maneuvers me so I'm sitting between them, my legs stretched out in front of me.

Lifting my head, I glance up at Dante, watching as he takes in the room with curious eyes. Catching me watching him, his gaze latches onto mine. The openness he had in the bedroom is still there, helping me to realize that he hasn't closed himself off like he usually does. Smiling encouragingly, I reach my hand out toward him, and without any hesitation, he moves to lie between my legs and uses my thigh as a pillow.

It seems Cain is in charge of the remote, as he begins flicking through various TV shows and movies while Oliver and Enzo bicker over what to watch first. I listen to them argue while leaning against the sofa and threading my fingers through Dante's hair, and with every stroke, I feel him relaxing more and more, and a sense of calm washes over me. This right here is what I envisioned for the five of us. A month ago—hell, even a week ago—it felt impossible to achieve. I was terrified it was a wish that would never come to pass, but somehow I did it. Somehow, these four very different—yet similar—men are getting along. Perhaps they're all only doing it for me right now, but with time, I'm hoping they'll come to view each other as friends, as family. Brothers of sorts.

"What are you smiling at?" Dante asks, his voice low.

Glancing down, I find him staring up at me, watching me that way he does.

"In this moment, I'm happy."

"You should be happy all of the moments of the day."

"When Giovanni is no longer threatening the people I love, then I will be."

"WHOSE HOUSE IS THIS?" I ASK LATER THAT DAY. WE'RE ALL STILL sprawled out on the sofa cushions. Our chill day has been everything we needed. Not only has it given us some much-needed downtime before we tackle Giovanni, but it's also given the guys a chance to be around one another in a non-stressful situation. All of their interactions until now have been about getting me back, Giovanni, and the Bastards—all stressful and only serving as reminders that they come from two different parts of Black Creek. But when all of that falls by the wayside, they actually get along reasonably well.

Don't get me wrong, most of the day has involved them talking smack to each other, but it's all done with laughter and smug smirks.

"Oliver's," Cain says when silence follows my question.

I flick my gaze to Oliver, my eyebrows raised in surprise as I wonder why he didn't tell me that himself. He's frowning, but I'm not sure why.

"I haven't decided if I want it yet," he grumbles.

"Why wouldn't you want it?" Enzo asks, glancing around the room as if seeing it for the first time. "Other than the fact that it needs a hell of a lot of work."

"When we were kids, this was where I lived. My father owned it before he died." Tight lines form around Oliver's mouth as he seems to lose himself in a memory. "He spent most of his day sitting right here, in front of the TV, with a bottle of vodka within reach. Pretty much the only time he'd bother his ass to get out of his chair was to teach me a lesson in manners."

Reaching out, I wrap my fingers around his, squeezing his hand. "I'm sorry."

He simply shrugs. "It's not your fault. It is what it is. Besides, after he died, I moved in with Cain, and there was a short period where everything was good..."

...Until Evie was taken.

He doesn't say that last part aloud, and he doesn't need to.

"Nothing like having a shitty parent to make you want to be better for your own kids."

We all turn to look at Dante. He holds Oliver's gaze until he nods in agreement. "Definitely. No matter how much bullshit life throws at me, I'll never be him. Any kids I have"—Oliver's gaze briefly flicks my way, and I swear I see a promise in his eyes before he focuses back on Dante—"will know nothing but love. They'll never doubt how much they mean to me."

My heart clenches as highly inappropriate images of Oliver as a father infiltrate my mind. I can just picture him cooing over a small bundle cradled in his arms, teaching a little boy to play ball in the street, fussing over a little girl every time she scrapes her knees.

My attention shifts to Dante as he nods, wondering if that's partly why he's been trying to better himself. Has he given consideration to children in the future? I already feel sorry for any daughter of his. Overbearing won't even be a strong enough word to describe Dante if he has a baby girl. Especially when she's a teenager and boys start taking an interest. Any boy brave enough to ask her out will probably piss himself when he comes face-to-face with Dante.

Actually... I lean back, looking at each of them, viewing all of them as a whole, because the child won't just be Dante's or Oliver's, or Cain's or Enzo's. Any child we conceive will have all four of them as overbearing, helicopter fathers.

Any son will have Oliver to teach them how to treat girls, Enzo to turn to when they're having a bad day, Dante to sit with when they don't feel like talking, and Cain, who will probably get them into all sorts of trouble.

Oliver will be the only one our daughter can talk to about boys. Enzo will help her pull pranks on the rest of us, Dante will spoil her, and Cain probably won't let her out of his sight. But, all in all, our children would be so damn loved. No one and nothing would hurt them, and anyone who dared would face the wrath of all five of us—not something any sane person would want to invoke.

"What did your parents do to gain my father's attention?" Dante asks, a furrow forming between his brows as he shifts his focus to Cain. "It's something I've been wondering about. I would have been about fifteen then, I think, but nothing stands out in my mind."

Cain shakes his head. "I'm not sure. Everything seemed fine with my parents until that day when Santos showed up on our street. That night, my father never came home. Mom was too distraught over Evie, but I remember a few of the neighbors went searching for him. It was a week before his body washed up at the docks. Mom didn't want me to see him like that, but I overheard someone saying he'd been shot execution-style. Fitted with the fact Evie had been taken by yo—Antonellis, but I don't know what he did to piss your father off. Mom would never talk about it, and honestly, I didn't waste time asking. Whatever he did, and why he did it, didn't matter in the face of losing my entire family."

A heavy silence hangs in the air, the weight of all of our pasts threatening to suffocate us. After a moment, Dante softly says, "For what it's worth, I am sorry about your sister. I would never have allowed Santos to... do what he did, if I'd known. In some ways, I'm every bit my father's son, but—" he grinds his teeth, "I would never tolerate *that*."

Cain's eyes roam over Dante's face, his expression unreadable. I'm not sure what he's looking for, but I'm guessing whatever it is, he finds it. "I appreciate that." His voice is rough, thick with emotion. "You know, you're less like your father than you think. Each of us is a product of our parents, of our pasts, of the fucked-up childhoods we had. But we're also who we are despite our parents."

"Should we leave you two alone for a moment with your feelings?" Enzo jokes once another silence falls following Cain's declaration. "Perhaps you wanna cry over girly movies and paint each other's nails? Oh, oh, please tell me you're gonna hug each other. I need my phone if you are. No fucking way am I going to miss capturing that and holding it over your heads for the rest of time."

"Shut the fuck up, you asshole," Cain growls, shoving Enzo in the shoulder. Oliver snickers, and I hide my smile behind my hand. The moment breaks the onerous atmosphere, which I imagine is exactly what Enzo intended, and we all fall back into easy banter.

The rest of the day goes by far too quickly, and that night I curl up in bed between Oliver and Cain with a smile on my face, hoping it won't be too long before we can have another day like that. One where our greatest worries are who has to get up next to grab snacks and what movie we want to watch first. One where Cain, Oliver, Enzo, and Dante can all get to know each other better without the pressure of their opposing empires muddying the water. One where we can laugh and joke and simply be without worrying that the next phone call will bring more death and bad news.

When I close my eyes, that's what I'm wishing for... a lifetime of days like today.

eighteen

Dante's contact—Antonio—gets back to him the next morning, effectively dousing the afterglow of our chill day yesterday. Surprisingly, I actually had fun just hanging out. It was kinda like going to the bar for a few drinks with some of the guys we work with, except better because Sawyer was there too. I thought without the hostility and discussing one of the two things we have in common—Sawyer and taking down Giovanni—that it would be awkward, but for the most part, it was fine. Once we set all our differences aside, it was surprisingly easy to get along with them —well, Oliver. Cain is a prickly asshole. I'm still not sure what Sawyer sees in him, unless it's all about the angry-sex vibe he gives off. In which case, I could definitely understand.

There were only a few awkward silences during the day, and Sawyer provided a very sexy buffer when needed. Wearing only an oversized t-shirt and smelling of sex, she was enough of a distraction that I don't even remember what we ended up watching.

It drove me fucking mad all day, and every time one of us tried to make a move on her, she'd swat our hands away and insist that we all *watch* whatever movie was playing at the time. I've never been so goddamn uncomfortable in my life, even in sweats. I was sporting a boner all damn day, and at the end of it all, she didn't even climb into bed with me to help relieve the ache. Talk about rude!

Next time she insists on a *Netflix and chill* day, I'm going to show her the true meaning—the one Cain insinuated that she brushed off. Cain was one hundred percent correct. Netflix and chill is absolutely code for *let's stay in bed and fuck*. How Sawyer doesn't know that is beyond me, but I'm more than happy to be the one to teach her.

Unfortunately, that lesson will have to wait for a bit. Antonio confirmed what Dante had already gathered from the feelers he'd put out—that anyone who worked with either of us was effectively being iced out. Seemingly, Giovanni is keeping all of them at arm's length. Smart move on his end, but annoying for us.

However, Antonio was confident that he'd be able to get his hands on someone who would know more about Giovanni's whereabouts and plans. Dante relayed all of this to Cain, who mulled it over before telling Dante to get his contact to bring the guy to Toxic.

When Sawyer raised an eyebrow in question at the location—I had to agree that a busy club hardly seemed like the ideal place to hide and torture someone—Cain simply murmured, "You'll see." So I guess we'll find out later.

Antonio asked for twenty-four hours to get the job done and informed us that he'd be in touch once he had the guy and was on his way to the meeting point. With some time to kill and something I needed to do, I find myself knocking on Luc's bedroom door.

He frowns when he sees me, glancing over my shoulder—probably looking for Sawyer—before shifting his focus back to me. "What are you doing here?"

Okay, his suspicious tone is a less-than-ideal start to this conversation.

"Cain and Oliver are busy, and with Marcus in the hospital and the kids doing rotations there, I thought I'd come to see if you wanted some company."

His frown only deepens. "Why?"

"You're Sawyer's brother, and given the way you're looking at me right now, like I'm about to stab you in the gut, I thought perhaps we could get to know one another a little better."

Quirking a brow, the little shit flicks his gaze to my hands before lifting it. "Are you going to stab me?"

"Since I quite like having my balls attached, no." He snorts, and before he can decide to close the door in my face, I gesture down the hall. "Come on. I'll even buy you lunch."

Huffing under his breath, he grabs a jacket before closing the door behind him and following me through the house. He doesn't speak as we head outside and onto the street, and neither do I. Honestly, now that I'm here, I'm not sure what to say. I'd offered to talk to him, but I don't know what I can say that would make things better for him. The kid doesn't even trust me. I'm sure the last thing he wants to hear is that he'll get over it with time.

Actually... that would be complete bullshit, anyway. He won't get over it, because *I* never got over it. Dante never got over it. You can't just move on from something like that. All you can do is learn to live with what happened, with the choices you made in an impossible situation.

Instead, I stay silent and let him lead me to a diner several streets over. The place is mostly empty, with only a couple of tables occupied. An older waitress who looks like she'd rather bathe in acetone than be here shows us to a table at the back of the room, handing us each a menu as we slide into the booths on either side of the chrome table.

I glance over the menu, quickly deciding on coffee and pancakes before setting it down. I briefly cast my gaze over Luc while he continues to peruse—or perhaps he's only pretending to avoid having to talk to me—before turning to take in the rest of the diner. It's small and shabby and needs updating, but it has a homey vibe about it.

"So, I'm guessing Sawyer asked you to talk to me?" Upon hearing Luc's voice, I swivel my gaze in his direction, finding him watching me with narrowed eyes. "Although, I don't know why she'd ask *you*. I thought for sure she'd send Oliver."

"I volunteered, actually."

His brow furrows, an expression I'm beginning to gather my presence is going to elicit quite frequently.

"Well, you can tell Sawyer we talked and cement yourself in her good favor, or whatever. I won't tell her that we didn't actually talk."

"...Or, we could *actually talk*." Leaning forward, I brace my elbows on the table. "Do you want to know *why* I offered to talk to you?"

Luc spears me with an *I really don't give a shit* look. "So you'd get a blow job?" he drawls.

His words leave me momentarily stunned. I mean, yes, I'd joked about getting a blowjob if I talked to him, but he can't know that, right? "Ehh..." Words momentarily fail me, and I decide it's best not to answer him directly. "I thought it would be a good opportunity to get to know you."

He purses his lips in such a way that clearly says, *yeah, right.* I huff out a breath, leaning back in my seat and getting comfortable. The waitress chooses that moment to return, and we both rattle off our orders before she disappears.

"I'm serious," I say when we're alone again. "I knew it the second you basically told me to fuck off at that dinner in Giovanni's penthouse."

Luc's expression shifts at the mention of Giovanni. His features harden, shadows billowing in his eyes. I catch his hand shaking on the table before he quickly hides it, placing it on his leg. His voice is strained when he asks, "You knew what?"

"That you and I were going to be great friends."

I'm not sure that Luc has any idea what to make of me. As the waitress returns with my coffee and his milkshake, he simply stares at me like I might be insane and doesn't know how to escape without putting his life at risk.

Once she leaves, I lean across the table, keeping my voice low as if I'm sharing a secret I don't want anyone else to hear. "Dante is such a bore. If I didn't know better, I'd say he was born with a metal rod shoved up his ass." Luc chokes on what I think was meant to be a laugh. "Oliver seems nice, but also the serious type. Cain... now there's someone who screams anger management problems, am I right? Definitely not up for a laugh, although I'd love to put a laxative in his morning coffee and watch him go absolutely batshit when he finds out." A strangled laugh escapes Luc and I smirk at him. "But you, as soon as I saw you, I knew you'd be the one to help me loosen those three assholes up."

"I don't understand. Why would you think that?"

"Because only someone who could stand in that church, not showing an ounce of fear while surrounded by Giovanni and his minions, would have the balls to piss off Dante and Cain, all for the sake of making others laugh."

"But, why would you want to piss them off just to play a prank on them?" he asks me, confusion drawing his eyebrows together.

"Tell me, when you were in that skyscraper, what did you think of?" Luc's expression immediately becomes closed off. "What kept you sane, reminded you of who you were, and stopped Santos and Giovanni from turning you into the soldier I know they tried to make you?"

Luc is silent for a long moment. So long that I begin to think he isn't going to answer me. When he finally speaks, his voice is nothing more than a broken whisper. "Sawyer. I thought about Sawyer. About how she'd go to the ends of the earth to rescue me. I thought about the days we'd hide in the apartment and watch television or play games, or she'd pretend to be interested while I talked her ear off about comic books. I thought about Bones and the others, the shit they'd talk when we hung out, and how they always bickered over the slightest thing, or how a simple disagreement would end up in fists being thrown."

"You thought about the moments and the people that brought you happiness."

The entire time he talked, Luc stared at a blank point on the tabletop, but now he lifts his gaze to mine. "Yeah."

Lifting one side of my lip, I say, "You can't tell me that if you'd made Cain shit himself in front of the entire club, that wouldn't have been something you replayed in your captivity."

Looking both bewildered and amused, Luc snorts. "So, you're saying you want to piss Cain and Dante off so that when you get kidnapped by your sister's boyfriend's father and his sidekick, and locked in a windowless room where you're beaten daily before having a gun aimed at your face and told to kill some random guy or you'll die instead, that you can laugh at the look of thunder on their faces."

I'm careful to keep my reaction to myself as I unpack everything he just shared. I'm reasonably sure he hasn't told Sawyer *any* of that, and even though he flippantly tossed the words out, I know they cost him a lot to say. So, rather than prying his wounds open any further, I simply shrug. "Pretty much."

"You're very strange."

I throw my head back and laugh.

When I look back at him, the laughter falls away, a seriousness falling over me. "Some people will tell you that feeling pain is a good thing because it reminds you you're still alive. But I say fuck pain. Life is filled with enough pain as it is, never mind using it to ground yourself. Especially when more optimistic emotions can do just as good—if not better—of a job.

"Whenever the shit is being kicked out of you, and there's nothing you can do to stop it, happy memories and thinking about those you love are what give you the strength to keep going. Love, laughter, happiness. *Those* are the emotions that center you when you're on the verge of dying. They're what remind you why death is worth defying. Pain might let you know you're not dead, but it's those moments with your family and friends—the small moments that seemed insignificant at the time—that will push you to live.

"When it was me tied to that chair, watching Giovanni murder my parents in front of me, his fists pounding my body, breaking bones and splitting flesh, I had far too few happy moments to cling to. My world was nothing but pain, and I can tell you, that pain might have told me I was alive, but it sure as hell didn't offer me a reason to keep living.

"So, yeah, I say make those happy memories while you can. Play pranks, joke around, and push those around you to their limits and beyond, because you never know when you might need to recall those memories of being with the people you love and care about in order to remind yourself why you can't allow yourself to give up."

A long silence follows my declaration, only broken by the waitress bringing us our food. Luc ends up picking at his meal, and I only eat mine to give me something to do.

After several awkward minutes of silence, Luc lowers his fork and looks up at me. "But what about afterward?" I frown, unsure what he means. "How do you keep telling yourself not to give up *after* you've already survived?"

"I'm not sure I can offer much advice with that. All you can do is take it one day at a time. I still struggle some days," I confess. "There'd be times when it felt like the walls were closing in around me. I'd be back in that room, watching—" My throat tightens, and my jaw clenches as I push away those memories... My dad begging to spare our lives, my mother's cries, my screams.

"What helped you get through it?"

"Your sister," I tell him honestly, smiling softly as those traumatic memories are replaced by crystal blue eyes, flaming red hair, and the most beautiful face I've ever seen. "I don't know if you know this, but I met with your sister once a month for years. She didn't know who I was, of course, but I knew her. She'd give me information in exchange for money. I didn't give a shit about the information, I just wanted to help her —to help you both—and to have an excuse to see her." I chuckle, remembering the feisty woman who'd breeze into that bar, not giving two shits what I thought about her, wanting to be done with me as quickly as possible. "She hated me, hated our meetings. She had no idea—still doesn't—that some months, the only thing that kept me going was the thought of seeing her face again. Even though I knew she'd scowl the entire time and was most likely cursing me out in her head."

"She was what centered you."

I nod. "She was. She is."

Luc seems to think over everything I've said before lifting his fork. "Alright," he says before digging into his now cold pancakes.

"Alright, what?" I question when he doesn't elaborate.

"I've decided I'm not going to try and kill you in your sleep for the time being."

It takes a second for his words to register, and a boom of laughter escapes me when they do. "Thank you... I think."

The conversation is easy after that. Luc fills me in on what life with the Rejects is like. When he peppers me with questions about being an Antonelli, I'm honest with him. He might only be fifteen, but he's seen his fair share of fucked up shit. Besides, he's been living with the Rejects, so I'm sure he's heard enough stories. I genuinely meant it when I said I wanted to get to know him. I offered to talk to him for Sawyer, but more than that, I wanted to get to know the kid who matters more to Sawyer than anything else. More importantly, I want him to like *me*.

"So," Luc begins, having slurped the last of his milkshake. "What ideas do you have for messing with Cain?"

Mischief dances in his eyes, even if it is cased in shadows, and I smirk. Yeah, I think Luc and I will get on perfectly.

It's late that night when Antonio calls, telling us to get our asses over to Toxic pronto. Despite the late hour, the heavy bass of the music can be heard as soon as we step out of the car.

Instead of heading inside, Cain leads us down the side of the building and around to the back. There is another narrower road back here, most likely intended for delivery vehicles, but I can't make out much else other than the outline of dumpsters and trash cans in the pitch dark.

Cain moves over to a steel door set into the side of the building. He enters a code into a keypad, and less than a second later, I hear the lock disengage. Curious, I peer into the darkened interior, unable to see what's inside, while he props the door open.

Sawyer moves closer, too, curiosity getting the better of her. However, before either of us can find out more, the rumbling of an approaching engine draws my attention. Looking to my left, headlights shine down the narrow road, set high enough off the ground to blind me. I raise my hand, blocking the glare, watching as the vehicle slows its approach before coming to a stop. From the corner of my eye, I notice Dante shift so he's standing in front of Sawyer, blocking her. Smart. Presumably, this is Antonio, but we can't be too cautious, especially when it comes to protecting Sawyer.

My fingers tighten around the gun clipped to my belt, and my muscles tense as the van door opens.

"It's just me," Antonio announces, and via the interior car light, I can see he's got his hands raised. Smart man. Of course, he's worked with Dante long enough to know how to survive around him, and I've no doubt he can sense the distrust and promise of violence radiating off each of us. "He's in the back." He tilts his head toward the back of the van but does not attempt to move in that direction. Another smart move on his part.

"Open it," Dante orders. Only then does Antonio move, still keeping his hands where we can all see them as he steps toward the back of the van.

With slow, practiced movements, he unlocks the back of the van, pulling open one door and then the next so we can all see inside where a man is trussed up like a turkey, lying face down on the floor, unconscious.

With a signal from Dante, Antonio steps aside, and Oliver and I climb into the van. Fisting the back of the man's hair, I yank his head back to get a good look at his face. Even with his fat lip and purple eye, I instantly recognize him as Brent, one of Giovanni's personal security team members. I'm surprisingly impressed, even as I mentally note that this guy's absence will soon be missed.

"We have poker nights every Thursday," Antonio explains casually with a shrug. "Wasn't difficult to slip a few crushed-up benzos in his beer and wait till everyone else left." He waves toward Brent's face. "He put up a bit of resistance just before he passed out, but nothing I couldn't handle."

"Why?" There's a harsh bite in Dante's tone, and when I glance up at him, he's staring at Antonio with wary curiosity. What he's really asking is *why the fuck do you have weekly poker sessions with one of Giovanni's security team?*

Not appearing bothered by the promise of violence in Dante's voice—he's spent enough time around Dante over the years to genuinely not be affected—he gives another nonchalant shrug of his shoulder. "You can never have enough information, especially regarding those you don't trust, and I wouldn't trust your father not to stab me in the back the second he thinks I'm not looking."

Can't say I blame him. Dante must agree as he nods his head after a moment of harsh scrutiny.

"Who is he?" Sawyer asks, staring at him curiously.

"Brent. One of my father's personal security."

Sawyer's lips form a silent O. With no other questions, Oliver and I drag Brent out of the van, taking little care to ensure his head doesn't whack off the top of the door when we hustle him through it.

"You realize we can't let you leave, right?" Cain informs Antonio, eyeing him up and down with undisguised distrust.

With a resigned expression, Antonio nods his head. "Yeah, I figured as much." He jerks his chin toward Brent. "You'll have about twenty-four hours before people start questioning his whereabouts."

He's not saying anything I hadn't already figured out, but *damn*. Let's hope we can get some useful information out of this guy quickly so we can put a plan together and get to Giovanni before anyone reports missing a member of his security team. There's no way that won't immediately raise red flags and blow any chance we have at catching him unaware.

Sawyer closes the back doors of the van while Cain directs us all over to the mysterious steel door. Oliver and I fall into step behind him, dragging an unconscious Brent between us. Antonio is behind us, with Dante and Sawyer bringing up the rear.

The darkness swallows Cain as he steps through the doorway, and a moment later, as Oliver and I cross the threshold, fluorescent bulbs flicker to life above us, illuminating a short hallway with a couple of doors leading off it.

Stopping at the first door, Cain glances over his shoulder. "Antonio, you're in here. Someone will bring you food and water and let you out to use the bathroom in the morning."

Craning to look over my shoulder, I watch as Antonio hands his phone and a set of keys over to Dante, who passes them to Sawyer. As if being held hostage is a common occurrence—it's not, but he's been in the life long enough to know the drill with these sorts of things—he holds his arms out to his sides and spreads his legs wide so Dante can give him a pat down.

With clinical efficiency, Dante does exactly that before giving a professional nod of his head, indicating Antonio is clean. With nothing else to say, Antonio moves toward the door Cain has unlocked and is holding open for him.

A single bulb hangs from the ceiling, showing gray walls and a gray concrete floor with a single chair positioned in the middle of the room over a drain. *Nice digs, real comfortable looking.* Antonio appears unaffected by his grim lodgings for the next twenty-four hours as he casts his eyes around the walls, before Cain cuts off my view, pulling the door closed before moving on.

Wiping thoughts of Antonio from my head, I heft Brent up on my shoulder before following after Cain to another door further down the hall. Similar to the previous room, the door has a keypad inset. When Cain punches in a code and it clicks open, the overhead light flickering to life, I see it's the same charming setup as Antonio's room next door.

Oliver and I dump Brent in the chair in the middle of the room, and Oliver gets to work grabbing duct tape from a bench hidden behind the door, tying Brent's wrists and ankles to the arms and legs.

An ominous weight fills the air as the five of us form a semi-circle around him, staring down at his unconscious form.

"Now what?" Sawyer asks. Her voice is quiet, but I don't detect any nervousness or fear. If anything, her straight spine and pushed-back shoulders imply the exact opposite. She's ready to do whatever it takes to get the information we need.

Giving her a crooked grin, I crack my knuckles. "Now things get bloody."

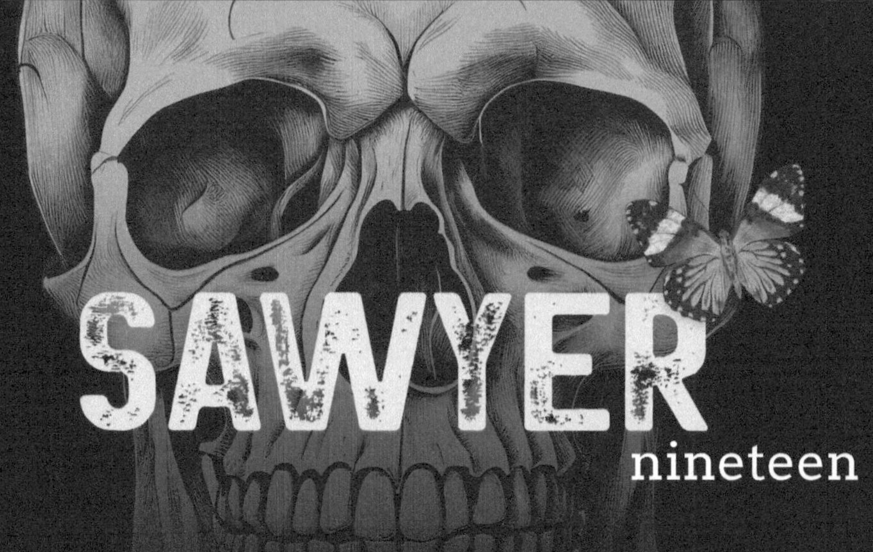

SAWYER

nineteen

The metallic taste in the air stings my nostrils, the heady smell of blood like gasoline to the adrenaline roaring through my veins. I'm not sure how long we've been at it; certainly it's been at least a few hours. If I were to step outside, I wouldn't be surprised to see the sun cresting the horizon, staining the sky a similar color to the red tributaries coursing toward the drain.

Brent has proven to be one hard nut to crack. All of my guys have had a go at inflicting pain, as demonstrated by the guy's mangled fingers, bloody pulp of a face, and shredded chest. The entire time, I've stood and watched, noting the various techniques they've used and how they resemble each of them. Cain is all about brute force—breaking bones and splitting skin. Dante knows precisely where to target to inflict maximum pain without actually killing the guy. Enzo is all about the psychological torture, and Oliver fucks with his head by offering hope.

I've watched all of it with rapt fascination. Obviously, I knew all of my men were ruthless in their own way—even sweet Oliver—but until now, all of their violence has been reactive. The response to a perceived or actual threat.

However, this... this is calculated, precise, deliberate, and I find it way more alluring than I really should. No sane person would be so chill—and just a teeny-weeny bit turned on—while such violence played out in front of them, but then, I never claimed to be sane. I may not be as intimately connected to my apathetic side since finding each of my guys, but I'm still not—nor will I ever be—society's definition of *normal*.

I'm perfectly me. Still very much damaged and flawed, but I'm at peace with myself in a way I've never experienced before. Life forced me to create different personas to deal with the various factions of my life.

There was Sawyer, the true me, the young woman starved of attention from the one person who should have given it unconditionally and was forced to grow up well before her time in order to protect her little brother.

Then there was Red, the version of myself I had to become in order to survive on the streets, to step half-naked onto a stage and ignore catcalls and whistles while I danced around a pole.

And finally, there was the Reaper. Born from a desperate need to feel like I had some control, like I wasn't at the mercy of arrogant men who were stronger and more powerful than myself. The little girl inside of me crying out for help forged the Reaper to fight against the injustice of it all, of this life I was catapulted into without any say.

Sawyer.

Red.

The Reaper.

Three very different people, all of them me.

Honestly, I was probably one bad day away from a dissociative break. One person can only take so much, regardless of the number of personas she develops in order to get by.

However, since finding each of my guys and building this connection between us, it's like the different parts of my soul have started to blend together. I no longer feel like three different people, but as though the best parts of each of those personas have been wrapped together to form a complete *me*.

I'm a little bit of all three of them. I have retained Sawyer's compassion, Red's confidence, and the Reaper's ability to remain calm and collected in the face of violent and stressful situations. Now, on days like today, I feel closer to the Reaper than Sawyer, but I don't wholly lose myself as I would have in the past.

For the first time in my life, I feel whole. Complete. Entirely myself.

Which is why I can both simultaneously wince at the sound of Dante's fist landing a solid punch in the guy's gut *and* be turned on by the brutality of his violence, at Enzo's cruel, savage grin, at Cain's bloody knuckles, and at Oliver's silent tremble of fury.

My ruthless Rejects.

My merciless mafia men.

My bloodthirsty gangsters.

My ferocious family.

"This whole stoic silence thing isn't impressing anyone," Enzo states, his voice cold and cruel, nothing like the teasing tone I'm used to hearing. "It's certainly not going to gain you any points. Giovanni isn't going to reward you for your silence, and we sure as fuck aren't." He kneels down in front of the man, bringing them face-to-face, although I doubt he's anything more than a blurry blob through the man's swollen eyes. "You're just a pawn to him. Disposable. Replaceable. While I can admire your loyalty, it's wrongly placed." With a tilt of his head, he asks, "Why give that to a man who will never offer you his?"

The man doesn't answer, but Enzo remains crouched in front of him. "Is it about money? Power? 'Cause none of that will do you any good where you're going. Don't you at least want to die knowing you've done the right thing?"

One heaving inhale, two, before the man spits in Enzo's face. The action is followed by a deathly silence, my gaze bouncing back and forth between the two of them. I'm pretty sure I'm not the only one waiting with bated breath to see how Enzo will react.

One second, Enzo is squatting in front of the man, radiating fury, and in the blink of an eye, he's grabbing him by the throat and squeezing until his eyes bulge and his face turns a dark shade of purple. No one moves to intervene as gasps and gurgles fill the room. Only when his eyes start to roll back in his head, his body convulsing with the lack of oxygen, do I step forward.

"Enzo," I murmur, reaching out to press my hand against his back.

He stiffens, before I feel the muscles beneath my hand relax, his grip loosening enough that the sniveling asshole in the chair can suck in enough air to keep himself alive—for now.

"Take a break." Dante's words are a harsh order brokering no argument. And still, Enzo quarrels with him, his hand remaining clamped around our captive's throat.

I move to step to his side, trailing my fingers until I can squeeze his bicep to gain his attention. "Come on," I say quietly, jerking my head toward the door. "I could do with some fresh air, anyway. The smell of blood is going to my head."

His lips purse, his expression remaining hard, and I can tell he wants to argue, but he doesn't. With a long sigh, his shoulders drop and he lets go of the guy's throat.

Without a word, he stalks toward the door, grabbing his jacket from where he left it on the bench as he passes. With a final glance at the others, I follow after him, out into the crisp, early morning air. He strides a few feet away from the building before stopping, and I stand and watch as he takes a long inhale before slowly releasing it. He does the same again, tilting his head back so he's staring up at the predawn sky, tinged with the intermingling colors of night and day.

Staring up at them myself, I watch as darkness loses the fight, dawn creeping further across the sky with every heartbeat. I feel like the sky's battle for dominance—day vs. night, night vs. day—mirrors my own. Always conflicting circumstances battling for control. Life is one continuous fight, and honestly, I'm exhausted. We're all exhausted. Nevertheless, I can't help but feel like we're this close to changing the tide, not just for ourselves, but for all of Black Creek.

That is, if we can survive this final hurdle.

The thought of losing anyone else, of losing one of *them,* threatens to make my knees buckle. I can't go through what I experienced the other night again. That all-powerful, soul-destroying ache, like someone just rammed their fist into your chest and is threatening to crush your heart until it bursts. I felt like I couldn't breathe. Couldn't feel. Couldn't do anything but drown in that anguish.

Given the last couple of skirmishes, we're incredibly fortunate to all still be standing, mostly unharmed. Cain's ankle is still far too weak. He tries to hide it, but I see the pain, his off-kilter walk as he tries not to put too much weight on it. He's not ready to go into this final fight yet, except we're out of time.

Pushing away those less-than-helpful thoughts, I focus my attention on Enzo as I close the space between us. When I reach him, I intertwine my fingers with his and, with a gentle nudge, encourage him to come with me down the cobblestone alley.

He doesn't say anything as I direct him through the otherwise empty docks toward the building Hadley and I used to come to. I couldn't think of anywhere else to go. This part of town is mostly abandoned, and it's too early for any place to be open anyway.

It's only when I stop at a set of ladders that climb up the side of the building that he seems to come out of his thoughts, watching as I put my foot on the first rung and begin to climb. I hear him behind me, but I don't look back, putting one hand in front of the other until I reach the top of the building and jump down onto the roof.

Enzo's heavy boots thud down beside me a moment later, his eyes scanning the rooftop. There's nothing up here, but it offers one of the best views in the city to watch the sunrise. Taking his hand again, I lead him toward the middle of the roof. Before I can plop down, he yanks on my arm, and I turn to face him as he shrugs out of his jacket and places it on the ground.

With a smile, I lower myself onto it, and he sits beside me, our bodies touching all along one side. Staring out at the horizon as it grows slowly brighter, I lean my head on his shoulder, drinking in this moment of peace and solitude.

"Wanna talk about it?" I ask after a few moments.

"I just want this over with." He sighs heavily and I feel his attention shift to me. When I turn my head to look at him, he's staring down at me with an unreadable expression, yet something about it both decimates me and fills me with hope. "Ever since I met you, I feel like I've been waiting. *Everything* has been leading up to this. To now. To the moment when I feel like I can claim my life for myself." He tucks a strand of hair behind my ear before brushing the backs of his fingers along my cheek. "I'm on the brink of obtaining everything I ever wanted, mere hours away from the life I've dreamed of having with you, and I just want to be there already."

I give him a disarming smile as he wraps his arm around me and pulls me into his side, kissing the top of my head.

"I want to be there, too. We're so close. I feel that impatient exhilaration as well. It's being dangled in front of me like a carrot on a stick, and I'm terrified it's going to be taken away at the last second, before any of us actually gets to experience true happiness. I'm so scared that we're going to fail at this final hurdle and never experience that."

A tear treks down my cheek as all that fear and sadness bubbles up inside me, and I quickly brush it away.

Enzo shifts so he can cup my face with both of his hands, holding it inches from his. "More than anything, I want a future with you." His voice is strained, overflowing with emotion. "I want to marry you one day and watch your stomach swell with our kids. I want to wake up to your laugh, make you feel good when you're sad, help you get back at Cain when he pisses you off, and be there as you pull Dante out of his shell."

Those unwanted tears are streaming continuously now because, *goddammit*, I want all of that too. More than anything, I want him. Them. *Us.*

"But just in case I don't get that opportunity, I need you to know that I don't regret a single moment with you."

"Don't say that," I sob, but he doesn't listen or doesn't hear me.

"I knew the moment Dante let you go in that alley that you were special. Watching you look out for Luc and do whatever it took to survive on the streets... I was in awe of you, Sawyer. You were this scrawny little teenager who would do absolutely anything to protect her brother, and I was in fucking awe. I knew I had to get closer to you some-how, that you were someone I had to have in my life. My feelings for you back then weren't sexual, but I could already tell that you were going to do amazing things with your life, and I wanted to be there to watch you achieve everything you deserved."

I sniffle, even as it feels like my chest is being crushed beneath the weight of his heartfelt words.

"Every time over the years when I felt like giving up, when I was convinced I was going to lose Dante to his father and couldn't see any way out for myself, I clung to the thought of you. I'd recall the way you'd stride into that bar with your shoulders back and your chin held high, daring the world to fuck with you, and it gave me strength. *You* gave me the strength to keep going." He swipes away the seemingly endless tears blurring my vision and coating my cheeks. "You saved me. Saved Dante. Probably saved us all. No matter what happens next, none of us would choose to be anywhere else. This is where we were always meant to end up—the five of us. If I die today, then knowing I've had your love for these last few months is enough for me."

Stretching up, I press my lips to his in a firm kiss, needing to cut off his words before they send me entirely over the edge. I can't listen to him telling me that what we have is enough for him, because no matter what, it is *not* enough for me. Even if I'd had him for the last ten years, it still wouldn't be enough, because I can never get enough of Enzo. Or of Cain, Dante, and Oliver. I will always want more when it comes to them—more time, more moments.

Our kiss is wet and desperate, the bitter taste of salt from my tears adding a poignant touch that threatens to tear my heart into shreds. I claw at his shoulders and back, needing him closer, as though if I can only hold him close enough, I can prevent him from slipping through my fingers.

There's an urgent rush to our movements as we tug and pull at one another's clothes. With every passing second, as the promise of oncoming heartache and loss draws nearer, our need escalates. It's not about sex. I need to feel his skin flush with mine, feel him buried so deep inside me that I'll never rid myself of the stretch because I'm fucking terrified I'll never get this opportunity again.

Our breathing is rapid, our movements frantic as he pulls me into his lap, pushing me down on his hard length until his blunt head smacks against my cervix and I cry out. There's no relishing this connection, no love-struck staring into his eyes as I take a second to accommodate his size. There isn't time for that.

Immediately, he digs his fingers into my hips and helps me find a fast, chaotic rhythm until I'm quivering around him. My eyes are clenched shut as my orgasm crests, but right before the wave crashes, Enzo tilts his hips and adjusts the angle in such a way that I lose momentum. He does the same every time I'm close to coming, until his name is a plea on my lips.

"Enzo."

"Not yet, Spitfire. I can't yet."

Sweat beads along his forehead and his molars grind together with the effort of staving off his release, and I understand at that moment he's not saying that he's not ready to come yet. He's saying he's not ready for this to be over. Despite his pretty words a moment ago, he's as unready to let us go as I am. There is still too much unfinished, too much unsaid.

Finally, when neither of us can take it anymore, we both give in to what our bodies desperately need. Still clinging to one another, I cry out my release while he grunts out his, our faces buried against one another's necks. I can feel the hammering thud of his heart against his rib cage, mirroring my own as I hold him close, feeling the weight of his arms wrapped around me.

The sweat has long since dried along my skin, my pulse returned to a normal rate, when the buzzing of our phones pries us apart. Enzo digs his out of his jeans pocket, his soft expression immediately dissipating as he reads the message.

"They have Giovanni's location." Tearing his gaze away from the phone, his expression is once again unreadable when his eyes meet mine. "Time to face whatever fate has in store for us."

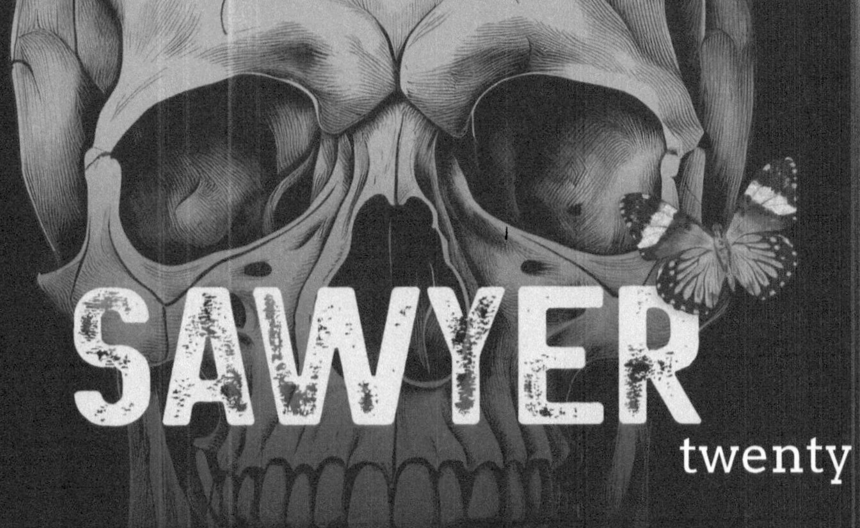

"**H**e's at the casino," Dante informs us as soon as Enzo and I approach. All three of them were standing in the back alley behind Toxic, waiting for us with their split knuckles and blood-splattered tops.

"Okay, so how do we get to him?" I ask, thankful for the time afforded by our walk back to help clear my head. Gone is the emotional Sawyer from that rooftop and in her place is the Reaper, ready to dive headfirst into this final hurdle so she can finally start the life they've all been waiting for.

"That's going to be the hard part. The casino is heavily guarded—both the entrances and the casino floor will have security men and cameras covering every inch, not to mention the numerous men in the control room watching the monitors."

"Where in the casino is your father most likely to be?" I question, mulling over everything Dante has said.

"The floors above the casino contain offices and rooms for men to stay in when needed, but the top floor is solely for my father. It contains his suite and office. It's where he conducts any business meetings that aren't with his closest advisors and where he takes potential business partners to wine and dine them before agreeing to whatever nefarious deal they're both striking. Second to his skyscraper, it's the most secure building the Antonellis own."

"Great," Cain drawls. "And I'm guessing we can't use the tunnels again."

"No. He'll have them all blocked off or rigged to blow if we set foot in them. And he'll have changed all security codes and probably have warned his men not to let me in, or report to him if they see me."

"Well, all of this sounds very promising," Oliver says sarcastically. "Why don't we go back to the house and discuss it over coffee—ideally after a shower. I need to get that asshole's blood off my skin."

With a heavy cloud hanging over all of us, we ride silently back to what I now know is Oliver's house. I'd initially assumed Cain had bought it, possibly for more space for his men before they moved to the motel. However, as I step out of the SUV and look up at the house, I try to picture Oliver as a child growing up here. The way he spoke about his father, the pain and disgust in his voice, it was clear his childhood was just as complicated as the rest of ours. Parents really do fuck up their kids, eh? I hope to hell I never do that to mine. Surely if you have loving parents it counts for something? But then, from what I've gathered, Cain's parents loved him and Evie, and his father still managed to utterly destroy his children. It's a depressing thought, one I choose not to dwell on. It's not like it's a concern right now, anyway. Something I can worry about if we all make it through today.

One at a time, the guys shower, Enzo going first so he can fix us all breakfast—the only one of us who can actually do more than fry an egg—and I put on a pot of coffee for everyone.

Thirty minutes later, we're all gathered around the kitchen table, our stomachs pleasantly full. "Whatever we decide to do, we should wait until tonight when the casino is busier," Dante states, the others nodding in agreement.

The next hour is spent spitballing ideas, but nothing quite works. We can all agree that Dante, Enzo, and me would all be spotted as soon as we step foot in the casino. Chances are, Giovanni's men only have a vague description of Cain and Oliver, if even that. The problem is, we can't all agree on how to utilize that.

"I say Dante should walk straight through the front door, demanding to talk to Daddy dearest. Oliver and I will slip in unnoticed, and while you keep him distracted, we can sneak Sawyer and Enzo inside. The four of us can head up the stairwell to Giovanni's floor, taking out any guards we come across until it's just him and us. Outnumbered with nowhere to run, he'll be easy pickings."

"And what about the cameras and the men watching from behind them?" Dante counters, spearing Cain with an incredulous look.

"Alright, we make a detour to crash their security system on our way up to rescue you from your dad."

It all sounds flimsy at best, but we're running out of time and with every passing minute and half-baked idea thrown out, I've been gnawing on my bottom lip more and more. Now, blood coats my tongue, tasting like an omen of things to come.

More ideas are tossed around, yet I find myself zoning out, my thoughts turning inward as I try to devise a plan that won't get us all killed.

"Any objections, Red?" Oliver asks, interrupting my thoughts.

"Huh?" I snap my gaze up, staring at each of them in turn as I scramble to recall what they were saying. "Oh, no. Sounds like a plan."

At least, as good of one as we're going to get in such a short timeframe, with such few resources.

"Good, then we're all agreed," Cain states with finality. "We should all catch a few hours of sleep before we move out."

He's right, we were up all night, and I'm sure I look as haggard as they all do. The problem is, my mind won't switch off enough to sleep, and despite the murmured round of agreement, everyone seems to be as on edge about tonight as I am.

Needing to feel close, we choose to spend what little time we have left together; Cain and Enzo remaking the bed on the floor of the living room with the sofa cushions. Once ready, we all climb in, all four of them cuddling close to me until one by one, they are pulled into a fitful sleep, leaving me alone to stare at the ceiling above.

I lie there for an hour or so, going over everything in my mind, weighing the risks. As far as I can tell, it's the best option. Marginally better than the ideas they were tossing around earlier. The main benefit is that it doesn't put any of them at risk, which is precisely what I'm trying to avoid. When the four of them were talking earlier, every idea they had involved too many unknowns. There were too many ifs, buts, and maybes for me to be happy. Now, my plan is no more foolproof, but it only puts one person in harm's way instead of five. I know it's an asshole move, and they'll be pissed—just like I would be if one of them pulled this stunt—but if I defeat Giovanni, what does that matter? I'd happily risk my life than have them risk theirs. I can't go through what I did the other night, thinking Cain and Oliver were dead. I just can't.

I understand that I may potentially be putting them through that same hell, and I feel like a shitty person for doing that, but it's more likely that one person will make it in and out alive than that all five of us would. It's better to beg for forgiveness than to ask for permission, right? I'll willingly spend the rest of my life begging on my knees for their forgiveness, because in that scenario, *all* of us are alive.

With determination coursing through my veins, I carefully untangle myself from the mass of limbs wrapped around me and slip out from between Oliver and Dante. They both immediately roll closer to one another, searching me out in their sleep and sinking into the heat I've left behind. Taking a second, I drink in the sight of all of them —for what may very well be the last time—with a fond, barely-there smile. My heart fills to bursting with so much love for these four unlikely men. These four men who I'd do anything to save, including sacrificing myself. I know without a shadow of a doubt that, should anything happen to me, Luc will be taken care of. He'll be welcomed by both the Rejects and Antonellis, provided with somewhere safe to live, protected, and cared for. He'll be given everything I've ever wanted for him, which, in all honesty, is all that I can ask for. All that truly matters.

With tears welling in my eyes, I turn away, quietly grabbing my clothes from earlier before sneaking out. In the hall, I pull on my black jeans and top, and strap on my thigh holster before stuffing my feet into my trusty black boots and ensuring my twin blades are still sheathed inside them. Straightening, I pull back my shoulders and push every emotional thought out of my head. Only when the cold, detached feeling of the Reaper washes over me, do I step out of the house. The street is dark, the sun having set already, and the wind whips at my face, lifting my hair with promises of death. No matter what, this ends tonight. Either I kill Giovanni, or he kills me, and my guys murder him in revenge... Or we all fail, and Giovanni continues to rule over Black Creek like none of us ever existed.

Yeah, I'll try not to think about that potential outcome.

I KNOCK ON THE DOOR, PRAYING TO ABSOLUTELY NOTHING THAT HE'S here and that he won't ignore me. While I wait, I scan the door and wall in front of me for the camera. I know there's at least one here somewhere, but I can't for the life of me see it.

"Thought I told you to fuck off." His gruff, agitated voice bounces off the walls, seemingly coming from all around me and making it impossible to pinpoint the source.

"I need your help—again," I say to the door, getting straight to the point. "It's important. I swear, I wouldn't be here if it wasn't."

A long silence follows, so long that I begin to think he's going to ignore me until I leave. "Please," I plead in a last-ditch effort. "It could change everything for Black Creek."

Another long pause makes my palms sweat because, if I can't get Blue on board, my plan falls apart before it can even be put into action.

"What makes you think I care about Black Creek?" His voice is carefully neutral.

"Because I saw what was on your computer."

Honestly, I'm not even entirely sure *what* I saw on his computer screen that day. Most of it was code that I didn't understand, but two sets of numbers stuck out to me. That, and a name. It didn't mean anything to me at the time, but later, I realized they were bank account numbers, and the name was for some charity. Now, I *know* Blue wasn't stealing from the charity. While he's great at the whole mysterious act, I just don't get a *I'm a complete asshole who steals from charities* vibe from him. Which just leaves the possibility that he's some sort of modern-day Robin Hood.

Of course, I could be completely off base. It could have been something entirely different that was on his screen. I don't deny that I'm undoubtedly taking leaps of judgment here. Anything to get him to let me into his apartment, to convince him to help me.

Yet another tense silence follows my declaration, and just when I'm at my wits' end and about to bark at him to open the damn door, a click reverberates through the air. Staring at the door, I hesitantly reach out my hand and press against it. It readily swings open, and not giving him a second to change his mind, I step through the doorway.

"What do you want?"

The man himself is standing in front of me, his arms folded across his chest as he stares down at me with an angry, hostile expression. *Okay, probably not the best start, but I can totally work with this... maybe. Hopefully.*

"I need your help sneaking into Bella Antonella."

That statement earns me a quirked brow. "And why, may I ask, are you sneaking into the Antonellis' casino?"

"To kill the Don."

I think I've actually managed to take Blue by surprise, as he just gapes at me for a full minute before gathering himself.

"This wouldn't have anything to do with his son and the others who were searching for you the other day, would it?"

"Sort of, but trust me, I'm doing this for the betterment of Black Creek. Dante isn't like his father."

His lips purse, clearly not believing me. Nevertheless, after a casual shrug, he says, "Whatever. As long as this doesn't come back to bite me in the ass, then yeah, I can help you..." I tense, waiting for the other half of that sentence. "*But*, in return, I want a favor. At some point in the future, when I come knocking on your door *uninvited* asking for help, you'll give it. No questions asked."

It's my turn to scowl as I mull over his offer. I don't like the thought of owing anyone a favor, but I do get genuine vibes from Blue. I don't think his favor will be anything I'm not comfortable with. "Fine," I spit out, holding out my hand for him to secure the deal.

Reaching forward, he shakes my hand, holding it in his larger one as he asks, "What do you need me to do?"

I tell him my plan and what I need from him. He tweaks it and suggests ideas where necessary, having a crap ton more knowledge than I do regarding computers and technology.

"You think you'll be able to hack into his network?" I ask as he strides over to his desk and sits down in front of the numerous monitors. Shaking his mouse, they all come to life, showing various screens, all of which he minimizes before I can see anything I shouldn't.

He scoffs, offended by my question.

"He's probably got really high-tech stuff," I explain, trying not to make it seem like I'm doubting him. I'm not, I just fully expect Giovanni to have a whole team dedicated to ensuring his network is secure from men like Blue.

"It won't be a problem," he states confidently, shutting me up as his fingers fly over the keys.

Taking the seat beside him, I watch as he pulls up the website for the casino, along with another window that's full of the same code I saw last time, which still means absolutely nothing to me.

I kinda zone out while he works, my mind already moving forward to the next part of my plan. Blue will handle all the cameras for me, but I still have to get into the building and figure out how I'm going to get close enough to Giovanni to put my blade through his throat.

"I'm in."

"That was quick." I spin to stare at the screen. *Nope, it's still a bunch of gibberish.*

"Don't sound so surprised."

Ignoring him, I watch as multiple windows appear on the various monitors on his desk, each showing a different view of the casino. Most cover the main casino floor, with others focused on doorways, stairwells, hallways, and elevators. I notice that none show the inside of Giovanni's suite.

"Is this all of them?"

"Yup. I can put the recordings on a loop. That way, once you enter the casino, no one watching the cameras will be able to see you."

"Okay, yeah, do that."

I wait while he gets to work, only a few minutes passing before he states, "Done."

Squinting at the screen, I watch one of the windows showing a view of the casino floor. "I don't see a difference," I say after a moment.

"I've grabbed an hour's worth of footage for each camera, but I'll wait until you're about to go in to switch over the feeds. That way, you'll have more time and someone is less likely to catch on before you get into the building. I'll also turn off the building alarms when you get there."

"Okay," I agree with a nod.

"I won't be able to do much, but I can keep an eye on the cameras from here, and if I see that you're in trouble, I can set off the fire alarm or something—should distract them for long enough to allow you to escape."

With a nod, I get to my feet. "Thank you," I say sincerely, meaning it. What he's doing might seem small, but it's the difference between me making it to Giovanni undetected and getting caught at the front door. For all I know, Giovanni could have orders to shoot me on sight or to have me carted off to god knows where. If either of those things were to happen, I'd never make it close enough to him to do what needs to be done.

He rummages through a desk drawer, finding a black burner phone before grabbing a pen and paper and jotting down a phone number. "Here. Text this number when you're about to go in and I'll switch the feeds over."

With a small smile, I take the torn piece of paper from his hand and walk out, ready to get on with the next phase of my hare-brained plan.

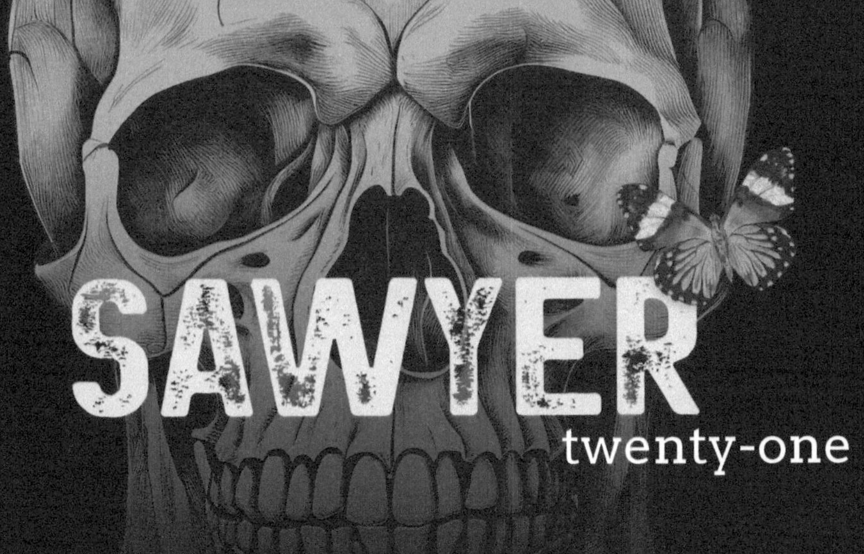

I'm crouching in the shadows provided by a building opposite Bella Antonella, watching the doormen as they pull open the doors for an elegant couple. He's dressed in a black and white tuxedo, and she's in a shimmering silver dress that hugs her hips and flares around her legs, showing off a lot of pale skin. *Yeah, I don't think I'll be going in that way.*

Not only am I definitely not wearing appropriate clothing, but with weapons strapped to my thighs, I'd stand out like a sore thumb. Best to avoid the main casino floor and cross my fingers that Giovanni didn't decide to grace his patrons with his presence tonight. Dante had informed us that it was something he enjoyed doing—being doted on by his people—but we are hoping he's too busy holing himself up in his suite, planning our demise, to be bothered with anyone else.

One can only hope.

Darting across the street, taking care to stay out of view of the security men and cameras, I slip down a side alley that should take me to the back of the building. Careful to remain hidden, I slowly approach what looks to be a delivery entrance. One guard stands by the entrance while workers empty a van.

Pulling out my phone, I quickly text the number Blue gave me, telling him to switch over the camera feeds. I'm only left hanging for a few seconds before I receive a thumbs-up emoji in response.

Crossing my fingers that his skills are as good as his confidence, I return to watching the men unload the van. As I'm watching, a worker drops a crate of produce near the guard. Pieces of fruit go rolling everywhere, including under the van itself. Waiting, I silently plead the guard to move, and for the first time in my life, someone up above must be listening to me as with a dark scowl and a "you fucking imbecile" tossed at the worker, he bends to help.

Seeing my opportunity, I stick close to the wall, crouching low as I slink past the guard and the other workers until the darkened interior of the warehouse swallows me whole.

I don't dare look back as I silently creep further into the building. I'm clearly in some sort of service area, with the sounds of a kitchen in full effect off to my left, the banging of pots and the shouting of chefs reaching my ears before I move away.

Soon, the noises of a working kitchen are replaced with the sound of loud music and the buzz of voices through the walls, presumably coming from the casino floor. I wonder briefly about the patrons that frequent this place. How much easier their lives must be on the other side of this wall. All fancy dinner parties and dressing up, laughing with people they secretly hate and gossiping about the latest drama.

I haven't had an opportunity to actually experience Dante's world, but from what little I've seen, I'm not sure I'd like it. All that fake niceness and dressing ugly people up in expensive suits and glamorous dresses. Of course, I'm basing most of this on the people I saw in the pews on my wedding day, which I can admit is probably a bit biased of me. I'm sure not every Antonelli is like that. However, I still can't picture myself in that life, on Dante's arm while we make a loop of the casino floor or host an exquisite dinner party. It's so far from my life to date that I can't fathom it at all.

And yet, that *is* Dante's life, whether I like it or not. A life that I will somehow have to fit myself into if I plan on keeping him. He's proven that he can slum it with the Rejects, living in Oliver's tiny house and wearing clothes he's visibly uncomfortable in. Once he's back on his throne, ruling over his people, it will be my turn to prove that I can survive in his world just as easily as he's survived in mine.

Dammit. I see a lot of beautiful dresses and fake smiles in my future.

Pushing those thoughts aside, I come to a stop when I notice a guard up ahead manning a door. *Bingo.* That must be where the stairwell is. Watching him, I mull over my options for how to get rid of him. As I'm thinking, I quickly scan the other end of the corridor, noticing a service elevator. An *unguarded* service elevator.

I could take the guard out and go up the stairs, but how long until someone notices he's missing, or he doesn't check in and someone comes to investigate? The closer I can get to Giovanni without being noticed, the better.

With that in mind, I glance back to the elevator before making a quick dash toward it. Darting inside, I scan the keypad for the button for the top floor—level five. Jamming my finger down on it, I wait, but nothing happens. No shutting of the doors, no rising of the car. Panic begins to settle as I push the button again, aware that anyone could walk past at any second and spot me in here—backed into a corner with no escape.

When the elevator still doesn't come to life, I perform another search of the keypad and surrounding area. This time I notice a panel set to the side, and flipping open the cover, I let out a low curse. An eye scanner, the same as the tunnels. I bet every access point to Giovanni's floor has the same requirements, and I'm also going to guess that Dante's eye no longer activates it, not that that does me any good right now.

I'm either going to have to force a guard to scan their eye or kill them and rip their eyeball out. *Oh god, please don't make me do that. Fucking gross!*

Frustrated, I glance out through the elevator doors, trying to figure out my next move. I could try the stairs or...

Pushing a random button—level three—I hold my breath until the doors begin to slowly close, only releasing it when I feel the whoosh of the elevator rising. Okay, so I can't get to Giovanni's floor, but I *can* access the others. Next step, I need to ascertain how many guards are on each floor and where they are positioned.

I slip a knife out of my thigh holster and slink into the corner of the elevator, flattening myself against the wall beside the doors as the car comes to a stop.

Gripping the blade's handle, my muscles tense, ready to pounce as I hold my breath and the elevator doors slide open.

The soft scuff of a shoe on carpet is the only telltale sound that someone is on the other side, followed by the distinctive unclipping of a holster. I don't dare take a breath in case it gives me away as I wait for the person to step into the car.

His polished shoe and black pants appear first, followed by a hand wrapped around a pistol held at his side. His head is turned away from me, giving me a split-second advantage which I use to its fullest as I launch myself at him. With my blade poised, it sinks into the soft flesh of his throat as my hand clamps over his mouth. Immediately, his body starts to fall, blood gurgling from between his lips.

Keeping my knife embedded in his neck, I push away from him as he sinks to the floor, wasting no time as I effortlessly pull the gun from his slack grip and tuck it in the back of my jeans. Next, I brush my hands over his suit jacket, making a concentrated effort not to look at his face as I empty out his pockets and steal his keycard.

Flipping open the cover for the eye scanner, I frown down at the large man at my feet. I really *really* don't want to have to cut out his eye. Slitting throats? Not a problem, but wiggling my knife in his eye socket and touching his eye? No, thank you!

Sighing, I bend down and haul the guy into my arms, straining as I lift him so that his face is eye-level with the scanner. I'm breathing heavily and sweat dots my brow by the time I have him at the right height, and I struggle to stay standing as I shift him so I can peel back his eyelid.

I hold him up to the eye scanner with trembling arms, cursing under my breath and dropping him whenever the scanner flashes red. *God fucking dammit.* I should have known it wouldn't work. He's probably too low level to have access to Giovanni's floor.

Swiping my arm across my forehead, I place my hands on my knees and breathe deeply until my heart rate returns to normal. My arm and leg muscles still feel heavy when I stand upright to peer out the elevator doors, an alternative plan forming.

I need to move quickly. I only have until someone calls the service elevator to get him out and hide him somewhere. *Fuck, maybe I would have been better off taking the stairs.*

I shake off that unhelpful thought. There's no point in worrying about that now. What's done is done. I just need to keep moving and try not to get caught.

My palms are sweaty as I dart out of the elevator with the keycard in hand, whispering *please, please, please,* under my breath as I tap it against the sensor on the door. The light turns green and, wasting no time, I push open the door. I quickly search the room, noting that someone is staying in it, but they don't appear to be here at the minute—let's hope it stays that way.

Propping the door open, I hurry back across the hall. Tucking my hands under the guard's arms, a grunt escapes me as I use all my strength to drag him across the corridor. My breathing becomes labored with each step, sweat forming on my brow until my arms are shaking with the strain. *God, he's a heavy fucker.*

He might not have Cain's broad frame—thank fuck—but that doesn't mean he's light or easily maneuvered. The second his shoes clear the doorway, I drop him and hurriedly slam the door shut, flicking the lock before sinking to the floor. I stay there until my limbs no longer feel like jelly and my heart rate has returned to a near-normal rhythm, but unfortunately, I can't afford to waste any more time. Whoever is staying in this room could be back at any second, and I don't know how long I have until the guard in front of me is noted to be missing.

Reluctantly, I push to my feet and scan the room, chewing on my bottom lip as I decide what the best thing to do with Mr. Dead Security Man is. There isn't enough space under the bed, which leaves the closet or bathroom. Neither are excellent choices and seeing as it's closer, I choose the closet.

Moving over to it, I pull open the door and push the few outfits hanging up over to one side. As I do, my fingers brush over a soft silk dress, so smooth it glides through my fingers. Not really sure why I'm doing it. I lift the dress out, admiring the black-colored seductive outfit, before setting it aside. Then I bend down to push shoes aside until there's enough space for the security guard.

With a final burst of effort, I drag him over and shove him inside. He'll be instantly noticeable to see as soon as anyone opens the door, but it will hopefully buy me a few precious minutes if anyone returns. And, hey, maybe I'll get lucky and the owners of the room will come back too drunk or horny and not look inside the closet until the morning. *One can only hope.*

Only when the guard is nicely tucked away for the remainder of the night, do I shift my focus to the dress hanging over the door. As my eyes roam over it, an idea forms. Perhaps violence and stealth aren't the best ways to get to Giovanni. Maybe I need to think less like the guys and more like the Reaper. Falling back on my seduction skills and being underestimated to get close to him. At his core, Giovanni isn't any different from the men the Reaper goes after. He's arrogant and narcissistic. He'd never believe that a woman could best him, and because of that, he's more likely to let down his guard around me. But that won't be the case if I go in there gung-ho with the blood of his men on my hands and a gun pointed at his head.

Chewing on my bottom lip, I do a final sweep of the dress before ducking back into the closet, searching for shoes to match. It will suck to lose my boots, but if I'm going to pull this off, I need to sell the image, and that means wearing heels. *Ugh, kill me now.*

Finding a pair of strappy black stilettos that will do the trick—even if my feet will protest the entire time—and I carry them and the dress into the bathroom. Before I can second guess what I'm doing, I quickly strip out of my clothes and slip into the dress. It's a little tight around my hips, and I must have bigger breasts than the woman it's intended for, as there's some serious side-boob.

When I dare to glance up into the bathroom mirror, I'm momentarily taken aback by how different I appear. How... seductive I look. It's different from the skimpy clothing I usually wear as the Reaper, which barely covers more skin than what I wore at Strip Tease. This dress is classy, elegant. It makes me appear regal, as though I could actually fit into Dante's world.

Two black strips of fabric twist around the back of my neck and drape over my chest, just about covering my boobs and displaying my skin all the way down the center of my chest to my navel and leaving my entire back exposed. The rest of the dress clings to my curves like a second skin before falling gracefully to the floor, with the exception of the high slit up one leg.

Retrieving my thigh holster from the floor, I strap it to my thigh beneath the dress and slip my trusty blades from my boots, tucking them into the holster as well. Unfortunately, the dress is so tight that I don't have anywhere else to hide weapons. I even have to discard my bra. Sometimes less is more, and I pray to god that this is one of those times.

Next, I reach up to pull out the hair tie I used to pull my hair back from my face before I left the house, running my fingers through my red strands. Scanning the counter, I find some mascara and a tube of bright red lipstick and help myself, finishing off the ensemble.

Lastly, I slide my feet into the heels, buckling the straps around my ankles. When I look in the mirror this time, I see a viper ready to strike. A woman prepared to fight for everything she wants. It's not the dress or the makeup that stands out but the fierce determination flaring in my eyes. I stare into those blue depths, darker than usual, for a long moment as I draw the memory of everyone I love to the forefront of my mind: Luc, Enzo, Oliver, Dante, Cain, Bones, and the kids, the other Rejects.

As I picture each of them, my shoulders unconsciously push back, my spine straightening until I'm a force to be reckoned with. By the time I'm done with him, Giovanni won't know what hit him, but he'll be dead, so that hardly matters.

All set, I step away from the sink, traversing the bedroom. Reaching the door, I crack it open before peering out into the hall. Still empty. Stepping out, I move back into the service elevator and press the button to take me back to the ground floor.

When it opens, I quickly hurry out, moving in the opposite direction to the guard at the other end of the hall, manning the stairwell. It doesn't take me long to find a door that leads onto the main casino floor. I hastily push through it, only relaxing when I'm swallowed up by the crowd, most of whom appear tipsy or on a winning high from one of the nearby tables.

Standing on my toes, I look over their heads until I find the guest elevators, then I begin pushing through the crowd. People jostle me, men giving me long glances as I pass, but I don't pay them any mind. I have only one goal—get to Giovanni.

Making it across the room, I give the two security men guarding the elevators a once over before I approach.

"Upper floors are for approved personnel only," the one on the right states, not even sparing me a glance.

"I'm here to see Mr. Antonelli," I say, ignoring him.

That gets his attention, his sharp gaze snapping to mine before slowly raking over my body.

"We haven't been informed that he was expecting company."

"He might not have been expecting me, but I assure you, he'll want to see me. Tell him his daughter-in-law is here."

That statement only earns me another sweeping glance, while the other security guard murmurs into his earpiece, too low for me to hear.

"You can go up," he states in a gruff professional voice, pressing the button to call the elevator.

The three of us stand in silence for a moment until the light above the door lights up, signifying the car's arrival. Once the doors slide open, I keep my chin held high as I confidently stride inside, not letting any of my nerves show. *I'm the motherfucking Reaper. I crawl through the night in the search of scumbags that don't deserve to breathe. My blades are the bringers of death. I will not let some asshole in a suit make me forget what I am capable of.*

The guard who spoke into the earpiece follows, and I notice him open the same flap that was in the service elevator, allowing the device behind it to scan his eye before we begin our ascent.

My fingers itch to touch the blades pressed against my thigh, but I don't dare even brush them against the fabric of my dress in case it draws his attention. I'm relying on the fact that I'm a mere woman to avoid a pat down, and I'm fully expecting him to demand I lift my arms so he can do exactly that any second now.

It's only when the elevator doors open with a whoosh that I realize I haven't breathed the entire ride, and I let my breath out in a silent burst. My heart is doing crazy things, making me feel as if it's about to explode out of my chest as I follow the guard out of the elevator and into a small corridor. Two guards are stationed on either side of the elevator doors, with another two opposite the only entry in the entire hall behind them.

Four guards. The odds would definitely not have been in my favor if I'd stuck with my original plan of killing my way to Giovanni. I use that knowledge to bolster me—the affirmation that *this* is the right plan, that I *will* succeed—as the guard who rode up in the elevator with me nods to one of the men standing beside the door. With a neutral expression, the man opens the door, granting us entry, and I have to quiet the voice in my head telling me that this is all too easy.

I follow the guard into Giovanni's suite, quickly scanning my surroundings. We're in some sort of lobby area with a large circular table in the middle of the room and a vase of colorful flowers placed in the center. Various pieces of artwork adorn the wall, but I'm too worked up to pay it any attention as I search for my target.

"You're to wait here. Mr. Antonelli will be with you shortly."

I spin to face the guard, but I pull up short when I spot two more standing to attention behind him. *Fuck.* How the hell did I miss them? I was too focused on Giovanni that I completely let my guard down to any other threat. I must remember that while Giovanni is my target, he will not get his hands dirty when it comes to harming me. He'll have one of his goons do it, so I need to be just as aware of their movements as I am of Giovanni's.

The guard exits the room, the doors closing behind him. Now panic truly does set in, no matter how hard I work to squash it. *Fuck,* I'm really doing this. Assuming this isn't all a ploy on Giovanni's part to get me away from prying eyes so one of his gorillas can put a bullet in my brain.

Turning back to face the room, I make sure to keep one eye on the security men by the door. There are three other sets of doors, meaning I practically need eyes in the back of my head. Sadly, I do not, and I'm on the verge of a panic attack as I struggle to keep all three doors *plus* the security men in my line of sight—all without looking panicked or suspicious. A tough fucking job.

It feels like ages, but in fact is probably only a minute or two, before the door opposite me opens and Giovanni appears, looking as devastatingly cruel as always. I can see parts of Dante in him. Not just in the way he looks—the eyes and mouth are definitely the same—but in the way he carries himself. In his general, *don't fuck with me,* aura. Dante has made himself in his father's image, yet the similarities are only skin deep. Proven by the first words out of his mouth.

"Dante sent his pretty lackey to do his dirty work?" He smirks, his eyes like chips of ice as they rake over my body. Suddenly I regret changing into a dress. Instead of feeling sexy, I feel exposed. "Or maybe he sent you as an apology."

My teeth grind as I tame the urge to launch myself at him and rip his head from his shoulders with my bare hands. *Not yet.* I can't make a move toward him with his goons behind me. Even if I did manage to kill him before they intervened, I'd find myself joining him in hell far sooner than I'd like to.

The problem is, now that I'm here, right in front of him, I have no idea what the fuck to say. Everything that comes to mind is more likely to get me killed than present me with the opportunity I need to eliminate him once and for all. I hadn't actually figured out what the hell I was going to say to the slimeball when—if—I made it this far. Perhaps because I was expecting to get caught long before this point. Either way, I'm here now, and instead of having something intelligent to say, I'm struck dumb.

As I stare at the man single-handedly responsible for ruining the lives of the men I love, I try to figure out if he genuinely means what he just said. Does he seriously think Dante sent me over here as some sort of twisted apology?

Going out on a limb, I say, "He knows now that he acted impulsively. He wishes to apologize."

"And he's hiding behind your skirts?" Giovanni drawls, unimpressed.

It's a struggle to push out my next words. "As you said, he sent me over to sweeten you up and see if you were open to talking."

His lips thin, his eyes doing another slow perusal of my body, making me feel icky. "I guess that will depend on just how good you are. I'm intrigued enough to find out what all the fuss is about."

Don't vomit. Don't vomit. Don't vomit. That will undoubtedly ruin everything I'm doing here.

I'm careful to hide my disgust, shaping it into uncertainty and fear, which I do allow him to see as I flick a self-conscious glance to the two guards behind me. I need to get rid of them before I can make my move. Three-on-one is not a fight I can win. Hell, taking on Giovanni alone will be challenging. I need to continue with this deception until the final moment, until I have the tip of my blade pressed against his carotid artery and he blanches, realizing I've fooled him.

"Don't worry about them." He grins, a cruel slash of his lips. "I don't like an audience. Follow me." Turning on his heels, he strides confidently through the door he initially appeared through, and with saliva pooling in my mouth and nerves hammering at my chest, I follow. Thankfully, the clicking of my heels across the marble floor drowns out the erratic drumbeat of my heart that thumps with the velocity of a stampede.

Giovanni remains by the door, forcing me to step past him into the room and putting him at my back. I only get a second to take in the large desk positioned in front of me before my face collides with it. My breath rushes out in a sudden oomph, and I immediately strain against the pressure pushing on my back.

"My son thinks sending *you* will compensate for his betrayal?" Giovanni snarls in my ear, his putrid breath making me gag. I can feel him behind me, his groin pinning my pelvis against the edge of the desk. One elbow digs into my back while his hand fists the back of my head and tugs painfully on the strands until I have to bite down on my lip to swallow my whimper. "I'm going to break you so thoroughly you'll be unrecognizable. Only when you're a whimpering pathetic mess at my feet will I send you back to my son. When you finally crawl your way home to your master, you can tell him he's as good as dead to me."

His hand slips beneath the slit in my dress, sliding up my thigh. I only have time to spare a fleeting thanks that my thigh sheath is strapped to my other leg—making my weapons harder to get to but easier to hide. "He thought he could team up with those *thugs* and steal what's *mine?*" Spittle hits the side of my face as his fury mounts, until it sucks all the air out of the room... or perhaps that's the elbow wedged into my spine preventing me from breathing deeply. "Let's see how he feels when I destroy what's his."

Oh fuck. Fuck. Why the hell did I not consider that Giovanni might want to take all of his pent-up fury and unleash it on me?

I can't do anything more than wiggle my fingers as his hand crawls higher. Anger vibrates through his body behind me, providing him with more than enough adrenaline to keep me trapped. I can feel terror's cold fingers scratching the surface of my brain, trying to dig in and take hold, but the Reaper is no stranger to being in fucked up situations like this, so rather than giving in, she forces me to relax my body.

Instead of bucking against Giovanni's weight, I arch my back, pushing my ass against his crotch and hardening chubby. I finish the act with a soft moan that has his fingers stalling in their path a second before a surprised laugh hits my ears.

"Of course, this is turning you on. I forgot you were a stripper. Probably used to being bent over and fucked like the whore you are." His fingers dig painfully into my thigh, and I've no doubt I'll have the bruises to remind me of this sweet moment for days to come. "I bet you got off on that fuckfest you and Lorenzo put on at the club, eh? I should have let all my men line up and fuck you one after the other."

Think happy thoughts, I instruct myself as I try to drown out his words and the simmering rage each one is feeding, adding fuel to an already mounting fire. Closing my eyes, I imagine what it will feel like when I slide my blade into his skin. How good it will be to watch his skin tear as easily as a sheet of paper. The satisfaction as his blood spills and his shocked gaze meets mine, his teeny, tiny, misogynistic brain attempting to comprehend how a mere woman could best him.

Oh, yeah. That's going to feel really fucking satisfying.

Now, I just need to figure out how to make that happen...

I sure as fuck have no hope of getting near his neck in this position. I need to get him to flip me over.

One of my hands is trapped between my back and his chest, and I uselessly wiggle my fingers. "Less clothes," I pant, pushing as much desire as I can muster into the two words.

"Yes, I definitely agree."

Before I can do anything to stop it, his fingers are on my panties, tugging and pulling on the string until it gives.

Fuck, no, that is not what I meant.

"I need to touch you," I try again. Thankfully the twinge of panic in my voice could be mistaken as lust.

He chuckles, the sound lacking any warmth. "Of course you do, you dirty fucking slut. Maybe when I'm done with you, I'll keep you as my own little pet rather than send you back to that useless son of mine."

His words immediately yank me back to that room we found Evie in, and I have to fight back the bile crawling up my throat. Is he into that sick shit too? Perhaps Evie wasn't the only girl closeted away in that building...

As a large hand shoves me onto my back, that thought is ripped away from me, but it's definitely one I want to come back to when I'm not on the verge of being raped by my father-in-law.

That same hand tightens around my throat, his arm locked at the elbow as he pins me to the desk. I buck against his hold, but that only brings my exposed vagina in contact with the front of his pants, so I force myself to lie still. I make my hands run up the front of his shirt as wicked delight shines in his eyes, his lips forming a cruel smirk while he hovers over me.

"Undo my belt," he orders.

Refusing to give it any thought, I drop my hands to the waistband of his pants, pulling on his belt until it slackens. With my head still pinned to the desk, I can't really see what I'm doing, but given *what* I'm doing, that's probably not a bad thing.

"Lower the zipper."

I drag it out for as long as possible, rubbing my hand over the front of his dick and then cupping his balls before I sloooowly lower his zipper. The entire time, I pray that he lets go of my throat before issuing his next order. Do you have any idea how hard it is to fake enthusiasm when all I want to do is cave his head in? I am all for hate sex—obviously. I'm dating Cain, angry sex is a semi-regular thing with him, but this is taking it to the extreme.

"Well, what are you waiting for, girlie? Get your hand in there!"

Charming.

I have to bite down on my bottom lip in order to stop my face contorting with disgust, but he *still* hasn't released my throat, ensuring his body is still an arm's length above mine.

Blocking out the horror of what I'm doing, I twist and tug as I work him over until his teeth are gritted and every other breath is a grunt. When he wedges my thighs open wider, I know it's now or never. Some lines I'm willing to cross, and others are a hard fucking no. I'm officially at that line.

Hitching the leg with the thigh strap wrapped around it over his hip, I ignore the fact that the movement opens me wider and now brings our bits too close for comfort. The good news is that Giovanni is starting to lose himself to his pleasure, and I can feel his fingers loosening around my throat as his focus turns southward.

Inch by inch, I slowly move my hand closer to the thigh strap. At the same time, I arch my back and let out a porn-worthy moan. Taking the bait, his hand moves to latch onto my tit instead. The movement unlocks his arm, giving me the opportunity I've been waiting for.

"I'm going to fuck you until you bleed," he snarls, his blunt head lining up with my entrance.

Surging upward, I hiss, "Only one of us is going to bleed tonight"—I press the tip of my blade against the skin at his throat—"and it sure as fuck won't be me."

It takes a second for understanding to dawn, and I watch with mild amusement as the emotions play out across his face; surprise, confusion, anger.

"What the fuck do you think you're doing?" he growls, his arrogance so fucking big that he can't see that he's not the one in charge anymore.

"Stopping myself from having to fake it through your mediocre fuck." Sparing a fleeting glance down, I confirm what I'd already felt. "Just so you know, your son far surpasses you in the dick department." His cheeks blossom with fury, or perhaps it's embarrassment. Either way, I choose to drive the metaphorical knife in deeper. "Think green bean vs. zucchini."

"How fucking da—" His words turn to a gurgle as I do exactly as I'd fantasized—drive my blade deep into his neck.

"I'm so fucking done with your bullshit," I hiss in his ear as the life seeps out of him. "I hope you burn in the pits of hell for all eternity."

The office settles into a peaceful sort of quiet as Giovanni takes his last breath, his chest going unnaturally still before I shove him off me.

And then the fire alarm goes off.

twenty-two

I immediately feel it as soon as I wake up. That deep intrinsic instinct that something isn't right. And no, it isn't the fact that Enzo is cuddling into my back like I'm his own personal heat source.

Already knowing what I'm going to find, it still takes me a second to comprehend the sight in front of me when I open my eyes and see only an empty spot where Sawyer was only a few hours ago when we all fell asleep.

Shoving Enzo away from me, I ignore his grumbled, "what the fuck, man?" as I get to my feet, ignoring the bite of pain in my ankle. *Fucking hell, when will that blasted thing heal?*

"Red!" I call out, hobbling out of the room. "RED!" Another pregnant pause before I bellow, "SAWYER! Where the fuck are you?"

I can hear a commotion in the front living room as I storm up the stairs, but the rest of the house is silent. Each room I search, empty. *I swear to god, I'm going to smack her ass till it's red if she isn't here!*

Hurrying back downstairs, I come face-to-face with Dante, standing in his boxers in the middle of the hall, looking like he's ready to take on any threat. Except, there is no threat, not here anyway. Meeting his dark gaze, I can tell by the tightness in his jaw and the flaring of his nostrils that he knows. Does he feel that same aching emptiness I do? That pit in my stomach that goes so deep it woke me from sleep?

"She's gone."

It's a statement, not a question.

"What?" Enzo says, still half asleep as he runs his hand through his air, looking between us. "Gone where?"

"She took the fight to Giovanni."

He spins to stare at me with wide, shocked eyes. "What? No way, Sawyer isn't that stupid."

I cock a brow at him, watching as his furrows, his eyes bouncing around as he thinks. "Why would she do that?"

"Because at her core, Sawyer's most primitive instincts are to protect those she loves," Oliver chimes in somberly. "After what happened with the Bastards"—Oliver looks directly at me, and guilt churns in my stomach—"I'm guessing she wasn't willing to risk any of us getting hurt again."

"So she went alone?" Enzo spits, throwing his arms in the air. "It's a fucking suicide mission. Why would she think we'd be okay with that?"

"I'm guessing that's why she waited till we were all sleeping," I drawl, pushing past him to grab my clothes. Fuck this shit. There's no way I'm hanging around here. Red couldn't have more than an hour's head start. It's not too late to put a stop to this hare-brained idea before it can get her killed.

From the corner of my eye, I notice the others doing the same. I'm slotting a gun into a shoulder holster when someone's phone starts ringing. As one, we all turn toward the noise.

"Whose phone is that?" I bark at the same time Dante orders, "Someone answer that!"

Please let it be Red, I plead as sofa cushions and blankets are tossed aside in search of the phone.

"It's mine," Oliver declares, grabbing the phone from beneath a pillow. "Unknown number."

"Answer it!" I bark, practically drilling a hole into the phone I'm staring at it so hard. If it ends up being a fucking telemarketer, I'll personally pull every tooth from their mouth—see how they manage to cold call people when they can't fucking talk.

"Who's this?" Oliver asks into the receiver, putting the call on speaker so we can all hear.

"If I were you, I'd get my ass down to the casino. Your girl could do with some backup."

"Who the fuck is this?" I demand, losing my patience.

"Oh, goodie, the growly one. Did you not just hear what I said? Get down to the casino!"

The line goes dead, and I share a look with Oliver. He shrugs a shoulder. "You heard him. We've gotta go."

Not wasting any more time, the four of us hurry out the door and climb into the SUV.

"Do you think it could be a trap?" I ask, thinking aloud. "Whoever that was on the phone could have Red."

"Maybe," Oliver muses aloud. "But why? What reason would they have for luring us to the casino when we were going there anyway. I think it's more likely that whoever it was, was the guy that rescued her after she was thrown from her bike."

My grip tightens around the steering wheel. "I don't fucking like him."

Oliver snorts, and I swear I hear him mumble, "of course, you don't," under his breath. *Wise ass.*

"Me neither," Dante grumbles. *Finally! Someone who sees reason!*

"How can you hate him? We don't even know who he is," Enzo unhelpfully comments.

"Exactly. *We don't know who he is,* and yet he's managed to worm his way into Red's life. I don't fucking think so."

"He saved her life," Enzo continues to argue.

"Did he, though?" I counter. "Seems pretty fucking convenient that he just so happened to be nearby when her bike was shot at. And today, he just so happens to know she's at the casino and in trouble? Sounds shady as fuck if you ask me."

"I agree." Can't say I ever saw Dante and I agreeing on anything, but there you go. Hell has chosen today to freeze over. "We should get rid of him once we've got Sawyer back."

Before I can voice my support of that idea, Enzo sighs. "You can't just kill everyone you don't like." I'm guessing Dante's suggestion is a regular one. Makes me wonder how many times he's voiced killing Oliver and me. Instead of pissing me off, the thought only makes me smirk. "Sawyer obviously trusts the guy to some extent. Once we have her back, we can *ask* her, rather than traipsing off all willy-nilly to murder people she might prefer to keep alive and breathing."

Flicking my gaze to the rearview mirror, I catch Dante's unimpressed expression as he mutters something too low for me to hear.

Parking the discussion of that suspicious fuck, for now, I direct us to the issue at hand. "How close to your father could Red get?"

"He'll have men crawling all over that building. Assuming she even made it inside, there's no way she'd get anywhere near his floor before being caught. Even if they weren't on the lookout for a redhead, she'd stand out by a mile in whatever she's wearing."

A tense silence fills the air and I push my foot down further on the accelerator.

"Sawyer isn't stupid." I flick my gaze in Oliver's direction when he doesn't continue. I assume that's not all he had to say... "She knows Giovanni will have guards at all the entrances. She knows about the security cameras."

"Oliver's right," Enzo agrees, leaning forward in his seat. "She must have had some sort of plan. What if she went in disguised as the Reaper?"

Frowning, I question, "What do you mean?"

"Her persona as the Reaper uses sex and seduction to lure men in and get them to lower their guard, allowing her to slip under their defenses until she can land the killing blow."

Dante's low hiss is molten fury. "You're saying she's fucking my dad so she can kill him?"

"Eww, gross. No, I'm saying she could be making your dad *think* she's going to fuck him."

"But she'll kill him instead," I finish.

"Exactly."

"That would be a huge risk," Dante growls, still sounding riled up over the thought of his dad and Red fucking. Can't say I blame him. No guy wants to dip his dick in the same hole as his father. Just gross. "For all she knows, he could kill her on the spot, and that's assuming he hasn't ordered his guards to shoot her on sight."

My stomach churns precariously, and I instantly push those thoughts away. My Red is alive. She's a fighter. The toughest person I know. There's no way she'd go down without taking half the damn building with her.

"So, what's our plan?" Oliver questions as we cross the bridge into Antonelli territory. A minute later, I'm turning onto the street where Bella Antonella is located.

"Kill every Antonelli scum who gets in our way. Kill Giovanni if Red hasn't already done it. Get Red the fuck out of there," I state, throwing the car into park and shoving open the door. I'm fucking done talking. Done planning. Now is the time for action. Now is the time for bloodshed. Now is the time for some fucking violence.

Both guns are out of their holsters, safety off, and aimed at the two guards standing outside the casino before I'm even halfway across the road.

Bang. Bang.

Fuck subtlety. Fuck being stealthy. My girl is somewhere in this building, and no one and nothing is going to stop me from getting to her.

The two security men drop to the ground, and I step over them, pushing open the casino door. At the same moment, the fire alarm goes off. Pretty sure I didn't trigger anything, but whatever. The chaos covers the sound of the bullets I put into the men stationed inside the front door, and no one seems to notice the bodies as they push and shove their way toward the exits.

My tall height makes it easy to see over the head of the crowd, but it's slow going pushing my way through the throng moving in the opposite direction. My head swivels from left to right, searching for approaching guards and keeping an eye out for a distinctive redhead.

We seem to go unnoticed for the most part, but it's not long before the crowd thins. Dressed casually in jeans and draped in weapons, we soon draw the attention of Giovanni's men. The crack of gunshots—a warning shot—is audible above the wailing of the fire alarms, and the remaining stragglers scream as they pick up their pace, abandoning their chips and margaritas as they dash for the nearest exit.

I dive for the nearest row of slot machines as a round of bullets fly over my head, and spot the others taking cover as well. Time loses all meaning as we're engaged in battle, a sea of suited men blocking our way forward. Amid blood spray and bullets, something catches my eye, and I strain to see over the slot machine currently acting as a shield between me and Giovanni's men. Craning my neck, I notice the guards at the back of the room stopping as they lower their weapons.

A hush seems to fall over the room as more and more men put down their weapons, until they part, and the most breathtaking sight steals my focus. Red strides through the crowd draped in a sexy black dress and splattered in blood, looking more beautiful than ever with her head held high. She looks like a true Antonelli queen. A fact that is only confirmed when I see what dangles from her hand.

With a crooked grin, she tosses the object to Dante, who catches it. For the first time, I see genuine emotion on his face as he stares in shock at his father's bloody head.

"Giovanni is dead," Red states, loud enough that her voice carries around the room. "Lower your weapons and recognize the new head of your family—Dante Antonelli."

Her declaration is met with silence. Every man in the room is staring back and forth between Giovanni's detached head and my girl. With their leader no longer alive to bark orders and demand they obey, none of them seem to know what to do. Part of me recognizes that most, if not all, of these men are grunts. They have no more allegiance to Giovanni than they have to Dante. Like soldiers, they simply follow orders. Hopefully, that means they'll be smart and obey Dante now.

I shift my attention to the man himself—the new head of the Antonelli family. We've been allies until this point, but I wonder if things will change now that he's achieved what he wanted. He'd talked about a truce, about helping to rebuild the city, but how much of that was bullshit—words said in order to secure an alliance?

He's still staring at his father's head, only tearing his gaze away when Red steps up beside him. Dressed the way she is, she looks like she belongs at his side. Even wearing my clothes, Dante radiates power. He's a natural-born leader. The two of them together are the epitome of a power couple, and if I hadn't witnessed for myself just how at ease Red is in my cramped home or at the clubhouse, then I'd believe this is where she belongs.

It strikes me as odd that she can fit into two contrasting worlds so seamlessly, but other than the glitz and glamour, perhaps our worlds aren't actually all that dissimilar. I guess only time will tell. I just hope, for her sake, she doesn't find herself pulled in two different directions.

Dante holds Red's gaze for a long moment, something indecipherable passing between them before he turns to face the men before him. "You heard my wife. Lower your weapons. Those who do not accept me as the new head of this family, speak now." Other than the shuffling of feet and a few shared glances, no one speaks, and after a moment, Dante continues, "In that case, get this place tidied up. There will be much to do in the coming days, but I will speak with each of you once I have met with my advisors."

Slowly, as though unsure, everyone begins moving, keeping one eye on Dante and the rest of us as they carry out his orders. Along with Enzo and Oliver, I fall in line behind Dante and Red as we stride as a unit across the room. I itch to pull her into my arms and curse her out, knowing she's safe and unharmed, but I'm unsure of what the dynamic should be. So I quell my desire—for now. Instead, I settle for keeping my eyes locked on the ridges of her spine and the two dimples visible on either side, directly above the curve of her ass. *God damn, my woman is fucking sexy.*

They stride into the waiting elevator, and the three of us follow. I position myself directly behind Red, and the second the elevator doors close, I step forward to envelop her back. My large palms slide over the smooth material of her dress, along her ribs, while Dante captures her lips with his. A squelching thud signifies Giovanni's head hitting the floor, but I immediately dismiss it. Giovanni is done messing with us. Done ruining moments that should be spent holding my woman close and showering her with affection—right after I've made it clear just how fucking pissed I am with her.

"You're in so much trouble," I growl in her ear. "I'm going to spank your ass so hard you won't be able to walk straight for a week."

Her only response is to lean further into my touch. I feel Oliver and Enzo at my shoulders, the four of us circling Red in our need to be close to her, to assure ourselves that she's actually here—safe and sound.

My hands slide over her abdomen, inching lower until I glide them down her thighs. Gathering the silk material in my fingers, I pull up her dress until my palm is flush with her skin, the heat at her apex calling to me like a homing beacon.

"I'm furious with you, Spitfire," Enzo snarls, his voice a heady mixture of violence and desire before he claims her lips.

Dipping down, Dante pushes aside the scrap of material covering her breast. Her back arches as he sucks her nipple into his mouth, and Enzo swallows her moan of pleasure.

She breaks off their kiss, turning her head to Oliver, who doesn't hesitate to replace Enzo's kiss with his own. "God, Trouble, I was so worried," he murmurs against her lips when they pull apart, pressing his forehead against hers and staring deep into her eyes.

It's an oddly intimate moment considering my hands are gripping her inner thighs, Enzo is nuzzling her neck, and Dante is sucking on her nipple. But there's something about all of us being here together, worshiping our girl like she deserves, that just feels right.

I slide my hands higher until my thumbs brush her apex. I'm momentarily taken aback when I find her bare. A low growl erupts from the back of my throat. "Where the hell are your panties, Red?"

"Really?" she snaps, frustration bleeding into her tone. "Goddammit, Cain, just fuck me already."

Furious and not at all done with this conversation, I roughly ram my fingers into her tight cunt, smirking when she cries out at the sudden intrusion. Her spine bends under my ministrations, and Dante releases her nipple with a pop before getting down on one knee.

Dante is not a man who gets on his knees, and despite his possessiveness of Red, the move still surprises me. He's not someone I ever imagined would lower himself for another person. Who would put himself in a submissive role to cater to someone else's needs—even Red's. And the fact he's doing just that, more than anything, shows me just how serious he is about Red. He's not just possessive of her. Doesn't want to simply claim her as his. It's not just about his male ego; he genuinely cares for her.

I watch inquisitively as he gently lifts Red's leg and places it on his shoulder, kissing along her inner thigh before burying his face in her pussy, uncaring of my fingers still pumping into her tight channel. His lips suck on her clit, rendering a cry from Red's lips before Oliver covers them with his own, sucking her tongue into his mouth.

The four of us work in tandem until Red is a whimpering, shuddering mess between us.

"Oh god," she cries, "I'm going to come."

"Come for us, baby," I urge. "Let us hear how good you can scream for us."

With a final, full-body tremble, her pussy squeezes my fingers and she throws her head back against my shoulder, screaming a litany of curses.

Dante laps at her folds as I withdraw my fingers. Although before I can wipe them off on my jeans, Enzo grabs my wrist and brings them to his lips, sucking them into his mouth. "Dude," I grunt when he moans around my fingers, licking Red's pleasure off them. It's a weird as fuck sensation, and we definitely do not know each other well enough for this shit. However, as I see Red's slack-jawed expression, her pupils dilated with need as she watches, I decide it might be worth the weirdness.

Finished with his feast, Dante gets to his feet, fixing Red's dress and smoothing out her hair. With a final kiss to her lips, he presses a button behind him and the floor beneath my feet shakes, making me realize that he must have stopped the elevator at some point.

When the doors slide open, we're all perfectly composed, as if our girl wasn't just coming all over my fingers and Dante's tongue, moaning beneath Oliver's lips and Enzo's wandering hands.

The weight of everything that has happened tonight washes over me as we step out of the elevator. The guards on either side of the door and standing opposite don't react. They are standing to attention as though it's perfectly normal that Dante is walking around carrying his father's severed head. Maybe to the Antonellis, this type of shit *is* a regular thing.

"Sir," the man to the left of the door opposite us greets with a slight decline of his head. "We are at your service."

Jeez, are all the men around here whipped? I demand respect from my men, but nothing like this. I'm not sure if I like it. On the one hand, I'm happy we don't have to fight all of them, but on the other, there's no true loyalty in these men. They're lackeys who will bow to whoever is in charge. Their reasons for committing themselves to the Antonelli family aren't because Giovanni earned their allegiance. And neither has Dante.

Dante acknowledges the guard's words with a nod before holding out his father's head. "Put this on ice," he orders, waiting until the guard delicately takes the head—with a surprisingly neutral expression—before stepping past him.

"You want to keep his head?" I question, disgusted. I guess he can have the grotesque thing as a memento so long as he keeps it out of my house. Maybe he can display it on a shelf in his office.

"It could come in handy when dealing with my father's advisors," is all he says as he continues on his path across a small lobby. Before I can question him further, Red pulls on his arm, drawing his attention as he slows to a stop.

"Eh, not in there," she says, her nose wrinkled as she stares at the door. "Giovanni's body..."

My eyebrows lift, and I definitely want to peek inside, but Dante changes direction, moving to another door. Reluctantly, I follow, more interested in hearing from Red what the hell went down tonight. Besides, Giovanni's body will still be there when she's done.

We step into a formal sitting room, and as we spread out on the sofas, all four of us stare at Red expectantly. "Well?" Dante prompts, showing no signs of having been buried between her thighs less than five minutes ago. "We're dying to hear why you thought it was okay to take on my father alone."

"And how the hell you managed to chop off his head," Enzo adds, a mischievous smirk playing on his lips.

"And then you can apologize for scaring the shit out of us," I finish, locking eyes with her so she can see the heat flaring in their depths that match the hard length pressing against my zipper.

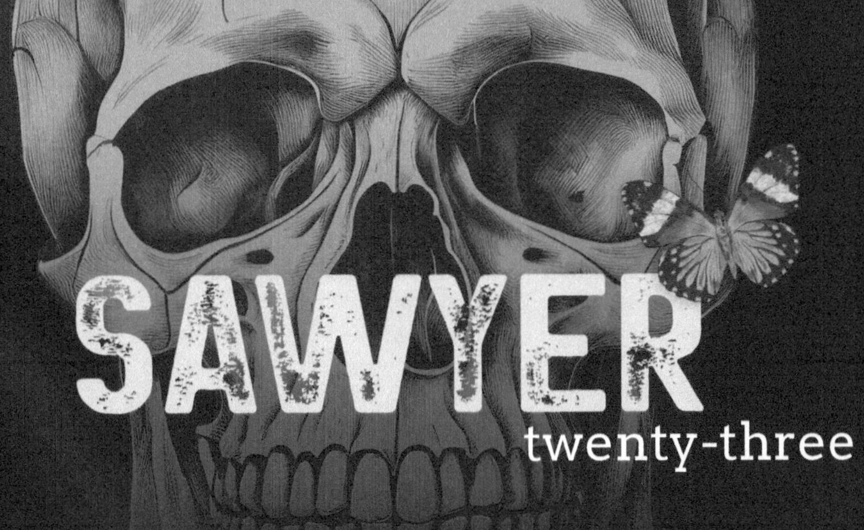

SAWYER

twenty-three

I quickly rehash my fortuitous quest to get to Giovanni, careful to make it all sound less haphazard and more like I'd come here with a plan. When I reach the part about playing coy with Giovanni in order to get the opening I needed to strike, I intend to brush over most of it. Except each of them asks a million-and-one questions until I'm forced to tell them everything.

"God, I want to kill him all over again," Cain snarls, pacing back and forth on his feet. "That sick fucking scumbag!"

Dante hasn't said anything in a while. I'm not even sure if he's still listening or if he's withdrawn into his thoughts, and Enzo just looks pissed. Oliver pulled me into his lap as soon as we all sat down, and I can feel his body tense beneath mine, even as his fingers haven't stopped stroking soothing circles along my stomach.

Leaning in, his voice low, he whispers, "No more crossing lines that you pretend you're comfortable crossing because you are trying to protect the people you love. I understand that you needed to do certain... things for Luc, but I don't want you sacrificing any part of yourself for me." His fingers grip my chin, turning my head until our noses brush, and all I can see are his ice-blue eyes, staring at me with so much hurt and sorrow that it churns my stomach. "We aren't your responsibility. We're meant to be partners. Equals. We're supposed to face challenges together, as a team. You can't go running off, trying to solve all of our problems on your own."

"Okay," I say hoarsely.

"Promise me, Trouble."

Reaching out, I brush my fingers through his hair before trailing my hand down to cup his cheek. "I promise." I mean it, too. From here on out, I want us to tackle everything life has to throw at us together—the five of us.

"Why didn't Giovanni's guards kill you the second they realized you'd killed him?" Enzo asks, interrupting my moment with Oliver.

Glancing around the room, I settle back in Oliver's arms. "They definitely considered it. When the fire alarm went off, they came storming into the room, but they froze when they discovered what I'd done. I could see them debating whether or not they should kill me. In their moment of indecision, I volleyed that their loyalty to a dead man wouldn't serve them any good. I reiterated that I was Dante's wife and that sparing my life would earn them leniency since he was now officially the head of the family."

"And they just agreed to that?"

"Ehh, no, not at first, but after they watched me cut off Giovanni's head, they seemed to realize it was in their best interests to go along with what I said."

Enzo releases a low scoff while Cain continues to pace the floor and Dante remains lost in his thoughts. With a furrow of his brow, his gaze snaps to mine. "Wait, you didn't set off the fire alarm?"

"Ehh, no." I frown at each of them. "I thought you guys did."

They all shake their heads, and after a second, a small smile pulls at my lips. "Blue," I murmur quietly.

"Blue?" Oliver questions, his voice taking on a sharp edge.

Stopping mid-stride, Cain spins to glower at me. "Is that the asshole who called to tell us you were in trouble?"

"Umm, what?"

Oliver coughs, clearing his throat. "Yeah, I gotta call from an unknown number, some guy saying you were in trouble and that we needed to get to the casino."

"Huh." I don't quite know what to say to that. However, I have to squash the smile threatening to show. *I guess he does care about me.* See, I knew we were friends!

"Well, Red?" It's clear by the impatient bark in Cain's tone that he's barely holding it together, the events of today catching up to him.

"Yeah, that was probably him." I cringe, knowing the fury that's about to burst out of Cain—and probably the others—at what I'm about to say. "He's some sort of computer genius or something"—I shrug— "I asked for his help with disabling the cameras so I had one less thing to worry about."

"This is the guy who found you that day, after you were thrown from your bike?" Enzo asks, his voice guarded.

"He is. He's someone who helped me out a time or two when I was living on the streets. We're barely friends. I don't even know his real name, but he's a good guy."

Cain scoffs. "Babe, there's no such thing as a good guy. If a guy does something nice, it's because he wants in your pants."

"That is not what Blue is doing!" I insist. "I had to practically beg him to help me in the first place, and every time he has, he's basically told me to fuck off afterward." Glancing at each of their critical and pissed-off faces, I soften my tone. "I promise, it's really not like that with him. And now that Giovanni is dead, I probably won't see him again."

Cain huffs out a sigh, the others remaining silent. "Fine, but I don't like him, and I don't trust him around you."

"Neither do I," Dante grumbles.

Restraining my eye roll, I paste on a sugary sweet smile. "At least that's something you both agree on."

Enzo snorts, and I feel Oliver's chest rumble with silent laughter behind me before he changes the subject. "So, what happens now?"

It's a good question. We've never discussed what happens once Giovanni is out of the picture. On the one hand, I feel relieved that he is no longer a threat, but on the other, there goes the common thread linking us all together. Now, it's up to Dante and Cain to find a way for both the Rejects and Antonellis to get along. To find a way for the four of them to get along. I can no longer use Giovanni as an excuse to get them to spend time together, and that terrifies me because if we're all going to fall apart then now is when it will happen, and I'm not ready yet to say goodbye to any of them. It brings back the age-old question, is loving me enough?

Am *I* enough?

God, I hope so, because these four terrifying men are more than enough for me, and they always will be.

"I need to meet with my father's advisors," Dante states, blinking as though he's only now tuning back into the conversation. "They are the men most loyal to my father. If anyone is going to contest me ruling this family, it will be them."

"What are you going to do?"

At my question, Dante's eyes dart to mine. "Follow your example, *mia vita*, and chop off the heads of anyone who doesn't surrender to me."

Whoa, how does he make cold-blooded murder sound super fucking sexy?

"What about those things you said before, about helping rebuild the city?" Cain asks, turning to pin Dante in his tumultuous green gaze.

My eyebrows lift, surprised at Dante's offer. *I didn't know he'd done that.* Maybe there's hope yet for the two of them.

Dante lifts his gaze to meet Cain's. "My offer still stands, Cain. Everything south of the river is yours." He waves a lazy hand. "Do with it as you please. I'll give you the men and resources you need to restore the city."

Well, that sounds less promising. That sounds more like they're going to split the city in two and have minimal dealings with one another. I don't like that at all.

Cain scrutinizes Dante closely, searching for any hint of a lie. When satisfied, he gives a curt nod, but inside I'm screaming at them. Screaming for Cain to say something more, to offer an olive branch in return. I just want to bash their heads together and yell at them to wise the fuck up, to open their eyes and see the potential here. I know individually they'd do a fantastic job of running their territories, but together... together, they could build something incredible. A city where its citizens thrive and people actually *want* to live.

Oliver can probably feel the tense set of my body in his lap, because he leans in to whisper in a voice so soft only I can hear, "Give them time, baby. They'll figure it out."

It settles me somewhat... for now.

twenty-four

I stand in front of the floor-to-ceiling windows, staring out over the city—my city. It's been less than twenty-four hours since Sawyer strode through the casino with my father's decapitated head clutched in her hand, and it still feels surreal.

It should probably feel like a weight has been lifted now that my father is out of the picture, but instead, I feel as though the ground beneath my feet is shifting, and I don't know how to remain standing. Don't get me wrong, I'm relieved that my father is no longer a threat to Sawyer, and after what she told us yesterday, I'd happily resurrect him from the dead just to kill him myself. But now everything has changed *again*, just when I was finding my footing. I knew it couldn't last forever, but I found it so easy to fall into a routine at Oliver's house, surrounded by Sawyer and the guys. Surprisingly easy. Even the barbs tossed back and forth between Cain, Oliver, Lor, and myself turned from hate-induced to playful banter. I'm not saying we had everything worked out or that I didn't feel jealous of them at times or want to punch Cain in his very punchable face. It's just that I could see our future in those peaceful moments when it was just the five of us, laughing over dinner or in front of the television.

However, that world isn't mine, and remembering how at ease Sawyer was makes me yearn to see her that comfortable in my world. Acknowledging that has me realizing that this uneasiness in my gut is mainly fear. Fear that Sawyer won't fit into my life as easily as she does into Cain and Oliver's. That she won't be happy in my world.

When I first dragged her into my life, I didn't care about whether or not she'd fit in. I didn't even spare it a second's thought. All I cared about was keeping her close and making her mine. I never considered how challenging she might find the adjustment, but things are very different this time; more than anything, I want her to be happy.

"How are you holding up?" Lor asks, coming to stand beside me, the two of us looking out over the city.

"Is it odd that now that I have everything I always wanted, I couldn't care less about it?"

Lor claps a hand on my shoulder. "Sawyer's changed everything. You're no longer the same person you used to be, but this is your legacy, Dante. You were born to do this. However, that doesn't mean you need to rule the same way your father did. Find a balance that works for you. Something that works for the people you now must protect *and* that fits with the future you want with Sawyer."

Swiping a hand down my face, I turn to face him. "What future do *you* picture with Sawyer?"

He keeps his gaze fixed out the window for a long moment before facing me. "When I think of the future, all I see is her. None of the rest matters. Not to me, not to her, and it shouldn't matter to you, either. Sawyer doesn't care about money or status. She doesn't want or need a big house or a fancy car. She's told us time and again what it is she wants..."

"Us," I finish. "All five of us."

He nods, pursing his lips. "Find a way to make that happen, and everything else will work itself out."

"Boss," one of my fath—*my men*—interrupts, "They're here."

Pushing back my shoulders, I run my hands down the front of my suit jacket and steal a final glance at Lor. He's always been my rock, my support, even when I was lost to the darkness and didn't care to find the light. He's always been here, pulling me back whenever my father tried to lure me in. I no longer rely on him as much sexually, but when it comes to everything else, I still need him by my side.

My first order of business—besides ensuring there wouldn't be a revolt—was to name him my consigliere. The position has always been his. My father may have given it to Sam, but I never intended to see that through. It has *always* belonged to Lor. I wouldn't trust anyone else to do the job or to have my back.

He gives me a confident nod, silently assuring me that I've got this, and I turn as the double doors swing open and my father's closest advisors step into the room. My gaze roams from one arrogant face to the next until I land on Sam. I still remember how he treated Sawyer in Belle Donne, and today he will pay for that misstep.

I'm sure rumors have spread by now about my father's demise. More than enough people saw his head at the casino, and still, these men believe they are untouchable. My father gave them a lot of free reign. Allowed them to do whatever they pleased, and in return, they'd help him carry out whatever evil plans he had. If it weren't for Lor, I'd probably have ended up just like them, and a fresh wave of relief washes over me as I watch each of them take their seats around the long boardroom-style table.

They at least leave the chair free at the head of the table, but Sam has the audacity to claim the one beside it—Lor's appointed seat as my consigliere. Oh well, he'll soon be vacating it, but not in a way that he'll like.

Instead of pulling out the gun hidden in my shoulder holster beneath my jacket and pointing it at the back of his head like I want to, I move around to the head of the table and lift the icebox I stored beneath it when I arrived earlier.

Flicking the latch, I grab a hold of the handles and chuck it forward, emptying the contents across the top of the table. My father's decapitated head goes rolling right down the center in a depiction of the most grotesque bowling ball in existence.

Every man at the table skitters backwards, their eyes wide with horror. "In case any of you had any doubts regarding my father's death." I wait until all twelve men turn to look at me before tacking on, "And how you will meet your end if you even think about crossing me."

Little do they know, none of them are making it out of this room alive. I've already ensured they can't escape. I do not trust them, and I never will. As Lor said, this is *my* legacy, but that doesn't mean I will continue with the same corrupt regime my father had. I plan to overhaul this family completely, starting with removing those in charge. Each one of my father's advisors functions as an underboss, in charge of men lower down the totem pole. If they are corrupt, then those beneath them are too, and so on and so forth, until the entire organization is a cesspool of filth and depravity.

That is what I am dealing with. I will have to personally vet every person in this organization to root out anyone who won't fit with the new regime. Anyone likely to stand in my way as I shut down the businesses my father encouraged that I don't agree with. I'm going to piss off *a lot* of people, but these are changes I've been wanting to make for a while now. My time with Sawyer has only served to affirm that my plans for the Antonellis' future, while radical, are the right thing to do.

This brings me back to the twelve scumbags sitting in front of me, finally staring at me with the right amount of fear and uncertainty.

"You are the new head of our family," Carlo, a man sitting halfway down the table, says, a slight quiver in his voice. "It is our duty to do as you say."

Yes, their *duty*. Except, I don't want men who will obey me purely out of duty. I want men who will follow me out of loyalty and respect, men who will challenge my orders and point out my mistakes. Just another way of ensuring I don't turn into my father.

It's more than that, though. My time around Cain and the Rejects opened my eyes to a different way of doing things. Cain's men respect him, but they aren't afraid to call him on his bullshit when necessary. They lay down their lives for him, not out of duty or because they feel obligated, but because they have faith in Cain as their leader to do what is best for them.

In all honesty, Cain is an aspirational leader—although I'd never *ever*, on pain of death, tell him that. He's taken a rag-tag group of men and honed them into a strong, effective team. A team that succeeded in ridding the city of every other street gang. I can admit—to myself—that it takes incredible leadership to achieve that, especially within such a short period of time.

Is it so bad to want my men to respect and admire me the same way? My father's leadership revolved around fear, threats, and blackmail, and while it may be effective, it's not genuine. I saw how quickly my father's men switched allegiances when they discovered he was dead. There was no love lost, no mourning period. The second my father died, he was forgotten by his people, and now I'm going to destroy his legacy. Before long, there will be no trace he ever existed, bar the internal scars he's left on those of us unfortunate enough to have crossed his path, and even they will fade with time.

I don't want that. Admittedly, I'm not sure what I want. To not be forgotten? To do better? To *be* better? I just know I don't want to be my father. And for the first time, with Sawyer and Lor at my side, I feel optimistic that I will never be him even though I may reside in his office and have his title.

"Yes, your *duty*," I spit out, as twelve soldiers I've already vetted step through the door and take up residence around the outskirts of the room, their feet shoulder-width apart and their hands clasped behind their backs, the guns at their hips on display. "Except duty is no longer enough to keep your positions."

"W-whatever it is you want, we can provide it," another man stutters.

"Oh, can you?" I scoff, my temper rising. "You can provide unquestionable loyalty, unfaltering trust, and incontestable respect?"

Unsurprisingly, a deafening silence follows my question.

Yeah, I didn't think so.

"Because your history with me would point to *no*."

"Look," another nameless, faceless ass-kisser says, planting his hands on the table. "We had to abide by your father when he was alive, but now that you're in charge, we'll defer to you."

"Really?" I challenge. "So you'll accept that I'm closing Paradiso—permanently?"

Several pissed-off glances are shared, confirming what I already knew.

"And how many of you have girls hidden away against their will?"

Sawyer told me what my father let slip, and I have to agree that it sounds suspicious enough that I need to investigate it. So, as I speak, I'm having the skyscraper searched, along with any property each of them owns.

"Now," the first man—Carlo—snaps, smacking his hand against the tabletop. "I do not appreciate accusations like that being tossed around."

Yeah, and I bet he's one of the ones keeping a woman like a fucking pet. I definitely clocked the scowl he did a piss-poor job of hiding when I informed them of Paradiso.

I wave off his anger. "Yeah, well, it's not like it matters. Your properties are currently being searched, so I'll find out soon enough."

Another grumble of protests goes up, but I'm so fucking done with all of this. It's time to begin purging this family of the malignancy that has seeped into it and been allowed to fester and rot.

Finally pulling my gun from its holster, I flick off the safety and, without a second's thought, point it at the guy closest to me and pull the trigger.

One down, eleven more to go.

The guards standing idly at the perimeter of the room step forward, securing each of the remaining eleven men in their chairs.

I go around the table, putting a bullet in each of them until only Sam remains.

"Please," he pleads, shaking so hard that the guard at his back is the only thing stopping him from falling onto the floor.

"Do you remember the way you treated *my wife* that night?"

"S-she wasn't y-your wife y-yet."

Like that fucking matters!

"You didn't show her mercy. She didn't want to fuck you, yet you were ready to drag her off to some back room and pin her down."

"N-n-no."

"DON'T FUCKING LIE TO ME!" I roar, fisting the front of his shirt and hauling him out of his chair before slamming him down on top of the table. I lean in to hiss in his ear, "Truth is, your death has been written in the stars since that night. My father naming you as my consigliere only cemented your fate. I hope you never actually thought I'd let you claim that title. It was never yours to own."

Keeping my tight grip on the front of his shirt, I push away. "Bye, Sam. I can assure you, you won't be missed." Before he can start another round of useless pleas, I fire the gun, planting a bullet straight between his brows.

Half an hour later, I stare around the now empty room. Twelve empty seats sit before me. Twelve empty seats that I now have to fill with men that I trust. I may have made a dent today, but I still have *a lot* of work ahead of me.

A WEEK LATER, I STEP UP TO THE BLACK, TINTED LIMOUSINE. RUNNING A hand over the front of my tuxedo, I bend to open the door and reach a hand inside. Her white gold wedding ring glitters as she places her palm in mine, and I catch sight of a black strappy stiletto, followed by a long, toned leg. I trail my eyes upward to the midnight blue dress, which fits her like a second skin, contrasting perfectly with her pale skin and fiery red hair.

Finally, I get a good look at her face. Her makeup and hair are professionally done, deep red lipstick painted on her lips and kohl lining her eyes, but I don't see any of that. All I see are plump lips that I love to kiss and cerulean blue eyes that suck me in like a whirlpool every time I stare at them.

"Beautiful," I murmur, loving how one word can bring a shy smile to this confident woman's lips. Tonight is the first time I'm introducing Sawyer to this world—to my world. I've hardly seen her all week, too busy cleaning house. All for this moment. I didn't want her to see what the Antonellis *were*. I want her to see what we *can* be. Every interaction she—or anyone from their side of the river—has had has been negative, but I'm working to change that. When Sawyer meets my people for the first time, I want her to see the future, not the past. She's only ever seen the dark aspect of this life, and don't get me wrong, much of this lifestyle is violent and cruel, but there is more to it than that. Admittedly, not a part of the life that I have much experience in, but one that I want to embrace—with Sawyer.

Tonight, I've thrown a party to celebrate my reign and the beginning of a new era for the Antonellis, but also as a prime opportunity to introduce Sawyer to my world. I think I must be nervous because my heart keeps doing this weird clenching thing in my chest.

"This all looks amazing, Dante," she murmurs, looking up at the building before us, all lit up for tonight's event. I decided to throw this evening's party in what was once a city hall; an old, limestone-clad building constructed with a large entrance portico and six Doric order columns, presenting an impressive image. However, it pales in comparison to the woman standing at my side. I can't take my eyes off of her, cataloging the widening of her eyes as she takes everything in, the bobbing of her throat as she swallows. Is she... nervous, too?

Holding out my elbow for her to slip her arm through, I escort her up the steps and into the party, which is in full effect. Men and women flit around the room, some dancing, others conversing.

Lor makes his way through the crowd toward us, his gaze dipping to take in the magnificent woman at my side. Once upon a time, that look would have had me glowering and threatening to punch him, but now, it settles something inside me at knowing that he sees exactly what I see when I look at our woman. He knows just how special she is, and knowing she is just as important to him as she is to me gives me peace of mind, especially when I can't be with her. Which has been more often than not this past week.

Although, Lor hasn't had much more time than I have. It's taking the two of us every second to tear apart this organization and begin rebuilding it into something we can both be proud of. Meaning, Sawyer has been spending all her time with Cain and Oliver. Even that doesn't bother me the way it once would. I'd still prefer she was with me, but knowing she's safe with them has allowed me to focus on what I need to do here. Having said that, I plan on taking full advantage of our night tonight...

"Spitfire," Lor purrs as he approaches. "Don't you look absolutely ravishing in that dress." Leaning in, he presses a kiss to her cheek before whispering in a voice low enough that only we can hear, "But I bet you'd look even better with it on the floor."

Sawyer smirks up at Lor with love-struck eyes. Pushing the thin strap of her dress off her shoulder, she dares, "Maybe we should try it and see."

"No," I growl, slipping my finger beneath the strap and slowly putting it back in place. Leaning in, I wrap my lips around her earlobe and bite down on the sensitive skin until she squirms. "Don't be a naughty girl. You've already got every guy in the room staring at you. Everything else is just for us."

"Only you," she whispers, leaning into my side and reaching out to take Lor's hand.

"So, are we just going to stand here, or are you going to show me this new and improved family that's been hogging all of your time recently?"

For the next few hours, I show Sawyer off on my arm, introducing her to a few of the men I trust, including formally introducing her to Antonio and his wife. Most of the underboss positions are still vacant. It will take time to properly vet and learn to trust anyone enough to fill them, but I have extended an olive branch to a few of the men I worked with under my father's rule, allowing them to prove that my trust in them is not misplaced.

"I was so nervous about tonight," she confesses later on, when it's just the two of us in the middle of the dance floor. I don't dance, but just like last time, I found myself incapable of saying no when she asked. Although, I'm finding that I like the feel of her in my arms as we sway gently from side to side. It feels comfortable, soothing. Maybe I could get used to the occasional dance—with her.

"Why?" For the hundredth time tonight, I am tumbling headfirst into her captivating gaze. I swear, every time I stare into her eyes, they hypnotize me until all I can see, all I can think about, is her.

Only when she looks away, casting a glance around the room, do I come back to myself. "You've seen where I was living..."

"Not this again," I growl.

A tender smile lifts the corners of her lips. "I just mean, my life is so different from yours. It couldn't be more opposite." She bites on her bottom lip before confessing, "I was scared that I wouldn't fit into your world. Fit into all this glitz and glamour. It's so far from what I know... I—I'm so far out of my depth here," she chuckles self-consciously, but I see the nerves she's trying to hide from me.

I brush a thumb over her cheekbone. "I understand all of this is new to you, and

I'm sure it's daunting. But I assure you, you belong here, because you belong with me." Before she can utter a protest, I continue, "I know you also belong in their world, but who says you can't live in both? On the surface, the Rejects and Antonellis may appear very different, but underneath it all, our worlds are more similar than I've ever cared to admit before. And from what I've seen, you fit seamlessly into both."

Smiling softly, she pushes up and presses a chaste kiss to my lips before searching my eyes. "And what about the five of us? How do we all fit together? How does this work long-term, because I don't think Oliver's house is a permanent solution, and they *definitely* aren't going to move out to your beach house or to some fancy house on this side of the river."

"I have some ideas," I assure her, even though I haven't had the opportunity to discuss them with anyone else. "I love you. They love you. Everything *will* work out."

That earns me one of Sawyer's rare, rewarding smiles. The ones she reserves for whenever I lower my guard and tell her how I feel. It makes me want to spill every little feeling, just to have her look at me the way she is right now. Every time I open up, I've found that it gets a little bit easier. It still doesn't come naturally to me. The words still sound wooden on my tongue and I have to push them out sometimes, but the reward is *so* worth the effort.

"Big words, Dante," she murmurs, her voice dipping to a seductive husk as she tightens her arms around my neck. "Why don't you show me just how true they are?"

Growling, I dig my fingers into the soft flesh of her hips and yank her against me, loving how she melts against my hard edges.

"Just remember, you asked for it, *mia vita*."

Now officially done with this night, I take Sawyer's hand in mine and drag her off the dancefloor. Spotting Lor on the other side of the room, I gesture for him to come with us, and he makes his excuses to whoever he's talking to and immediately strides our way.

Sawyer laughs as I up the pace until she's practically running in her heels to keep up.

"The real party is finally getting started," Lor jokes as we reach the limousine. He pulls open the door, and I usher Sawyer inside before following after her. Lor is hot on my heels. The door is barely closed before he's throwing himself on top of her and kissing Sawyer like a man starved and she's a five-course meal.

"God, I have missed you, Spitfire," he murmurs against her skin, sounding pained, like the absence truly hurt him. Slithering down her body until he's on his knees between her thighs, he pushes up her dress. "If I don't taste you right this second, I'm going to die from dehydration."

"Oh my god," Sawyer laughs, swatting at him playfully.

Undeterred, he splays his hands on her thighs and pushes them wide. Tugging her panties to the side, he groans low in the back of his throat before diving in.

"Oh, god," Sawyer repeats, this time the words coming out in a deep moan as she rests her head back and arches her spine. "Keep doing that. It feels so good, Enzo."

For a moment, I sit and watch as my best friend eats out my woman. My wife. I drink in the pleasure he brings her as my pants are pulled uncomfortably tight. Not long ago, I couldn't fathom sitting watching this scene unfold, but I'm starting to realize I enjoy watching *my wife* claim her own pleasure. I can soak up every second of it in a way that I can't when it's me giving her that pleasure, and on occasion, it's enjoyable just to sit back and watch the bigger picture. I pick up on things I wouldn't otherwise, like the hitch in her breathing when she's close to coming and the way she bites on her bottom lip to stave off her release because she's not ready for the moment to end.

I watch as Lor drives her to ecstasy and continues to push her through the aftershocks until she's a whimpering, squirming mess, pleading with him to stop. Only when he sits back on his haunches, do I swoop in and pluck Sawyer from her seat, setting her in my lap.

"My turn," I growl, sealing my lips over hers and stroking my fingers along her slick folds. She immediately starts trembling, her fingers threading through my hair.

"Nuh-uh," I tsk. "Hands on the roof, *mia vita*."

I wait until she does as I order, planting her palms flush with the soft fabric interior of the limousine's roof before sinking my fingers knuckle deep into her wet heat.

"Ride my fingers," I tell her, enjoying how she immediately rocks her hips, obeying. "Take your pleasure from me."

She groans, moving faster as she works herself over.

Lor shifts until he's behind her, his hands coming around to knead her breasts, causing a gush of wetness to drip down my fingers. Her low moans and short pants fill the car as she works herself into a quivering, whimpering frenzy. When she's right on the precipice of her orgasm, I press my thumb down on her clit and she erupts like a volcano, crying out before she collapses against my chest.

"You can have a five-minute break until we're at the beach house," Lor informs her, moving to sit beside me. Spreading his legs, there's no missing the hard-on in his pants which probably mirrors my own.

"Oh, how kind of you," Sawyer pants-laughs.

Leaning in, he presses a soft kiss to her lips. "Then the real fun begins."

Goosebumps spread along Sawyer's skin at his sinful promise.

"Oh, yeah? If that's the case, I want all *three* of us to have fun." Her eyes slide back and forth between Lor and me, intent obvious.

"You dirty, dirty girl. You're thinking about that train, aren't you?"

I'm confused but keep my mouth shut as I watch her shrug a shoulder, acting all casual. "So what if I am?"

Lor's gaze flicks to mine before going back to her, darkening with desire. "Then you're in for a wild night."

Things only escalate in the five minutes it takes to get to the house. In that space of time, Lor manages to lose his jacket, shirt, and tie, and my belt has wandered off somewhere.

We're a chaotic mess of limbs and tossed clothing as we stumble into the house and up the stairs. I don't even know what bedroom we end up in—whichever was closest. The week apart has all of us needy, none of us able to keep our hands off the other until we're each stripped bare.

Wearing nothing, with my tie in my hands, I pull Sawyer's hands together in front of her and wrap the silk tie around her wrists. "I want you to do exactly as I say," I tell her, my eyes catching on her lower lip as she sucks it between her teeth and smiles coyly.

"Fine, but afterward, I want you to fuck Enzo while he fucks me."

I pause mid-knot, flicking my gaze back up to hers. She's serious, and based on how her eyes have dilated, she is incredibly turned on by that idea. Looking past her, I catch

Lor's eye. He just smirks, and it's then that it registers with me. This is what they were talking about in the car.

Grinning darkly, I return my attention to her. "You really are a dirty girl."

"*Your* dirty girl," she whispers.

"*Our* dirty girl," I confirm with a kiss, pulling the knot tight on her restraints. *Tonight is going to be so much fun.*

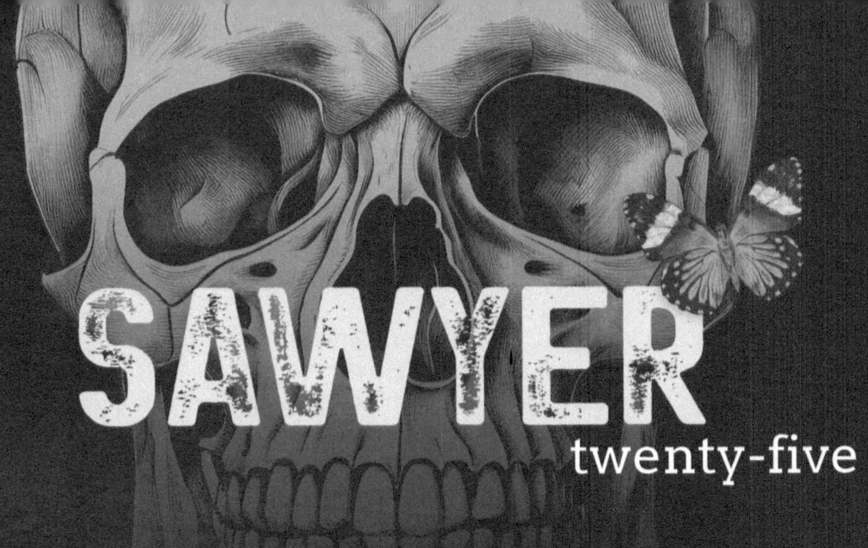

twenty-five

Can a girl die from too many orgasms? Because I think Dante and Enzo are trying to kill me. I can't feel anything below my waist. That can't be good, right?

"I can't take anymore," I moan, unable to believe I'm actually saying those words.

Enzo chuckles, his breath blowing across my stomach from where he was languishing it with kisses. "But I thought you wanted that train?"

I groan. *Dammit, I really, really do.*

"Fine," I whine. "One more."

"No, no." He pushes himself onto his elbows. "If you've changed your mind, then I don't want to pressure you."

Surging upward, I slam my lips against his. "I have *not* changed my mind."

His responding grin is savage. "You best wake up Sleeping Beauty, then."

With a smirk, I roll onto all fours and shimmy down the bed until my mouth is level with Dante's soft cock, still glistening with the remnants of our last tussle in the sheets.

Flattening my tongue, I run it up his length, smirking when it twitches. Repeating the action, this time, I earn a soft, sleepy moan. My hands knead the muscles of his thighs as I swirl my tongue around his tip, closing my lips over the top before I suck gently.

This time, his hips buck off the mattress, a hiss slipping out between his teeth. As I up the pace, his hands thread through my hair. "*Mia vita,*" he moans, making his nickname for me sound like the dirtiest of prayers.

I take him to the edge, and right when he's about to come in my mouth, I release him with a pop.

"Ugh, what—"

"Not yet." I let him see the intentions in my eyes, and when he realizes what I want, he sits upright.

"Well, if we're doing this, then we're doing it properly." My brows furrow in confusion, but he just pops off the bed. "Come on." He gestures for me to follow, and I do with a glance in Enzo's direction.

Directing me in front of him, Dante places his hands on my hips and walks me into the bathroom, stopping me when I'm standing in front of the counter, where a large mirror hangs overhead.

Brushing my hair back from my neck and shoulder, he plants a trail of kisses along the skin. "I want to make sure you can see *everything.*"

I shiver at the dirty intentions behind his words as he steps to the side, allowing Enzo to take his place. "You sure about this, Spitfire?"

I meet his gaze in the mirror. "Yes. Ever since I saw the two of you in that office, I've wanted this." I search his gaze. "It just feels right, doesn't it?"

His smile is soft and disarming. "It does."

I'm still watching in the mirror as Dante steps up beside him. Clasping the back of his neck, he pulls him in for a rough kiss that is nothing like the kisses Dante and I share. It's wild and rugged, all tongue and teeth, and *so incredibly hot.* I can't do anything but watch as they devour one another with so much passion it makes me wonder why they *aren't* a couple.

I'm so caught up in watching them that I startle when two hands land on my hips, holding me in place while two very hard cocks grind against me. Turning, I grab one in each hand, pulling and tugging until precum drips from their tips.

With an animalistic growl, Enzo rips his lips from Dante's and grabs me by the shoulders. Spinning around, he bends me over the counter and, kicking my feet wide, slams into my already primed pussy.

"Oh fuck," I gasp, watching in the mirror as Enzo thrusts into me. His gaze is locked on where we join, watching as he slides in and out, but it's the reverent look on his face, like he can't believe he's balls deep inside me, that plucks at my heartstrings.

Flicking my gaze to Dante, I find him watching us too. He smirks when he catches my eye, and holding my gaze, he lowers his lips to Enzo's shoulder, sucking and biting his way up his neck. I can't see his hands, but based on Enzo's moans and the occasional stumbling thrust, I'm guessing he's prepping him.

I know as soon as Dante starts to slide into him, a litany of curses escapes Enzo's lips, and he stops his movements, his fingers digging into my skin. All I can do is watch with wide eyes. I swear the room grows warmer with every inch Dante sinks into him until he's fully seated.

"Holy fuck," Enzo groans. "I've never... This feels so fucking fantastic. But fucking hell, I need to move." He grunts, "Dante, *move.*"

Enzo finds the strength to remain still as Dante pulls out before slamming back in. The forward momentum drives Enzo into my channel with a renewed force that has my hips smacking against the counter. I cry out, Enzo curses, and Dante hisses, the three of us finding a deliciously rough and intoxicating rhythm.

"No, no, no, no," I moan, my legs shaking as I bite down on my lower lip, failing miserably at staving off my orgasm.

"Oh, fuck, fuck," Enzo groans behind me. "Fuck, Sawyer." A second later, I feel him swell inside me before his cum coats my walls. Dante's thrusts become ruthless, and a moment later, he roars his own release.

"Was that everything you ever dreamed of, Spitfire?" Enzo jokes—although he's still panting from the exertion.

"We are *so* doing that again."

The three of us jump in the shower to clean up before climbing back into bed to finally get some sleep. For the first time since I chopped off Giovanni's head, I feel at peace. I'd been a nervous wreck when Dante had asked me to attend tonight. I had no idea formal evenings like that were a part of the Antonelli lifestyle. However, it made me realize I don't know anything about being an Antonelli. I never had the opportunity to experience Dante's world before.

Thankfully, it was nowhere near as bad as I expected. I hadn't a clue who anyone was, but they weren't the evil people I had made them out to be in my head. Of course, just because Giovanni, Santos, and the other men Giovanni was close with were the devil incarnate, doesn't mean everyone in the organization is. Dante explained that he has been vetting everyone, and if they pass his process, then I guess they deserve a chance, just like I gave the Rejects a chance.

However, it was Dante's reassurance that the five of us would work everything out that has me feeling so settled. As sleep comes to claim me, I actually feel like everything I want is within reach. I feel quietly confident that I could juggle the Rejects' world and the Antonellis', and that, with time, perhaps the two could coalesce. I'm on the cusp of having all four of my men the way I want. *Yeah, things are really starting to look up.*

"WHAT IS THIS PLACE?" I ASK THE NEXT DAY AS MY EYES SCAN OVER THE various artifacts and pieces of artwork stacked all the way to the rafters in this inconspicuous warehouse down by the Antonelli docks.

"My father had his fingers in many different pies," Dante explains, walking beside me as he takes me on a tour of the warehouse. "And while there were several I didn't agree with and am taking great efforts to demolish, there are others, like this warehouse, that I think have much potential."

"And, uh, what exactly is this warehouse?"

"It's full of black-market antiquities." Walking over to the closest shelf, he grabs something and turns to face me, holding his palm out. Hesitantly, I reach out to take a spiraling, snake-shaped gold bracelet.

"Oh," I say, surprised by the weight of it as I turn it over in my hand.

"That's a Dacian bracelet," Dante says, the name meaning nothing to me. "A gold armband. It's one of several that were looted from an archaeological dig in Romania. Worth about $100,000."

I gape at him, carefully handing the bracelet back over, now officially terrified I'll drop it or ding it and greatly diminish its worth.

"Why do you have all this?" I ask, staring around at the numerous other artifacts. There must be millions—billions?—of dollar's worth in here. That's... insanity!

"My father collected them—money is power, after all—but he never devoted the time to properly develop the connections necessary to sell them."

"And that's what you're going to do?"

"It's a highly lucrative industry and far less morally compromising than prostituting and selling girls, which is how my father chose to fund the Family."

My eyes have been opened plenty in the last few days about *exactly* what disgusting filth Giovanni was into, and even at that, I'm relatively sure Dante isn't telling me all of it. He never did answer my question about whether or not he found any more girls locked up in that skyscraper, but he did say that he's commissioned for the building to be torn down. So I'm guessing that is my answer. It makes me fucking sick every time I think about it.

"I think dealing in antiquities is an excellent idea."

Dante smiles, a gorgeous genuine one that he so rarely shows. "Good, I'm glad. I was hoping you would." His eyes flick away as he lifts a hand to nervously play with the knot of his tie. "I was also going to talk to Cain about setting up a committee comprised of both Rejects and Antonelli men. Somewhere where each organization could bring any issues or developments, and where both could bring ideas for how to improve Black Creek."

All I can do is stare at him for a second, unable to believe what I'm hearing. Of course, Cain has to actually agree, but I know he will. He'll do it for me, but he'll also do it because he recognizes it's the best thing for the Rejects and the city. I know he's been worried that Dante will go back on his word or that Dante will magically morph into his father now that he's carrying the weight of all this power around. However, after what I've seen today, I don't for one second believe that that is a concern—not that I ever truly did.

When I finally find the words, my voice comes out hoarse and scratchy. "You were?" I swallow, blinking away the tears building in my eyes. "You really meant it when you agreed to work with Cain and to help the city?"

Stepping closer, his hand comes up to rest on the side of my neck. "Of course I did. It's your home, and I realize now that Cain and Oliver aren't going anywhere. The only way this works between the five of us is if we all get along, and the only way that can happen is if our two organizations get along."

Dammit. I can't stop the tear that overflows and runs a trail down my cheek.

"Do you have any idea how much I love you?" I murmur, pushing onto my toes so our lips are a hairsbreadth apart. He only smiles against my lips before closing the distance.

"WHERE HAVE YOU BEEN?" CAIN ASKS WHEN I STEP INTO THE HOUSE.

"I had a few errands to run." I figure it's best not to get him all riled up by telling him I stopped by Blue's lair to drop off a gift basket—not that I had any idea what the heck to buy a tech whiz hermit, but I figured snacks, alcohol, and lavender-scented candles couldn't go amiss. They definitely help me unwind at the end of the day—preferably in a tub surrounded by bubbles. "What have you been doing?"

"Just hanging out with Evie." He lifts his arm and I don't hesitate to cuddle into his side. "Now that I have some spare time on my hands, I'm trying to spend as much of it as I can with her."

"You should. You're both completely different people now. It'll take time to get to know one another again."

He sighs, shaking his head, and I squeeze his middle. "I still hate that I even *have* to get to know her again. I should already know her, and sometimes I think I do. There're times when we're talking or laughing or watching TV when she says or does something that's exactly the same as the Evie from our childhood, and for a minute, I forget. I forget that she hasn't been right here all these years. I forget that she's been living in a literal hell. But then she doesn't get a movie reference or know who Taylor Swift is, and it hits me all over again."

He sounds so defeated that I just hug him closer. Nothing I can say will negate what's already been done. Sometimes, there's just nothing you can say that will make things better.

"Anyway," he sighs. "Come with me. We have something for you?"

"Oh?" I quirk a brow, even as he pulls me back out the front door, ushering me into the car.

"How did your meeting with Dante go?" I ask as he drives me wherever it is we're going.

"He suggested putting together a committee to work on rebuilding Black Creek, and somewhere where both representatives from the Rejects and Antonellis could bring any problems that could affect both parties."

I knew this already, but I stay quiet, eager to hear what Cain's reaction was to it all.

"And? What did you think?" I prompt when he doesn't tell me what I'm dying to know.

"I..." He trails off, seeming to think over his next words. Does he not realize what he's doing to me, leaving me on tenterhooks like this? Eventually, he chuckles under his breath. "I think I'm surprised Dante thought of it before I did."

"But what do you think of his idea?" I press. "Do you think it could work?"

"Yeah. I think it's a great way to ensure that the needs of the people of Black Creek come first and that we don't lose sight of the bigger picture. Plus, open communications between the Antonellis and us is not a bad thing. I think it could help bridge the gap between them and us, ya know?"

I nod, because I agree. It's exactly what I'd been thinking when Dante told me his idea.

"I was thinking I'd put Oliver and Marcus on the committee, and maybe Bones. That kid has some great leadership potential." He hesitates, flicking his gaze my way before tacking on, "I did suggest something else, though."

"Oh, what?"

"That Dante and I meet up once a month, in a business capacity."

My eyebrows lift in surprise. "You and Dante *alone* in the same room together... is that wise?"

He huffs out a laugh. "Probably not, but if he's serious about this open communication thing, which it seems like he is, then it can't just be our two organizations that talk. We have to, too."

"Well, as long as neither of you comes home bleeding, then I think it's a great idea."

Another bark of laughter. "No promises, baby, but I'll try not to make him bleed too much."

I roll my eyes as we pull into the clubhouse parking lot. Oliver is already here, waiting on us, but it's the lime green and black sports bike in front of him that has my full attention. "Oh my god," I murmur, gaping at the beautiful specimen, even if my heart aches over the loss of Raven.

Jumping out of the car, I hurry over until I'm within touching distance, but I don't dare reach out to stroke the bodywork.

"It's a Kawasaki Ninja 650," Oliver explains.

"It's beautiful," I breathe, unable to look away, even as I hear Cain step up beside me.

"Good, 'cause it's yours."

Now that works to gain my attention, and ripping my gaze away from the gorgeous bike in front of me, I turn to gape at him.

"What?" I splutter, flicking my gaze to Oliver, who has a massive grin on his face.

"It's yours," Oliver repeats.

"But..." I glance back down at the bike. "How? Why?"

"Because we wanted to do something nice for you. We know you're upset about losing Raven, and it wasn't fair that she was ruined. It was our fault."

"How do you figure that?" I ask, furrowing my brows.

"Well, if we hadn't convinced you to team up with us against Giovanni, then Giovanni wouldn't have known you existed and so he wouldn't have shot up your bike," Cain explains logically.

I nod my head, biting on my lower lip to suppress the grin trying to let loose. "That all sounds very reasonable. When you spell it out like that, you really do owe me a new bike."

They both laugh, and holding out his hand, Cain dangles the key from his finger. "Why don't you take your new baby for a test drive?"

Hell to the motherfucking yes!

THE NEXT COUPLE OF WEEKS PASS IN A BLUR OF DANTE AND ENZO restructuring the Antonellis, Dante and Cain putting together a committee to help restore Black Creek, and the rest of us *actually* rebuilding. I've been spending my days painting storefronts, cleaning up sidewalks, and spreading the word that violence in Black Creek is a thing of the past, along with Luc, Evie, and numerous Rejects and Antonellis.

Of course, most people are a little bit skeptical, but with each passing day that gunshots don't go off and blood doesn't line the streets, they are beginning to believe me.

We have a long road ahead, and it's surreal that we're actually at this point—at a point where we can help. *Holy crap, we're actually doing this!* Picturing how amazing this city is going to look by the time we're through with it brings a broad smile to my face.

"What is that goofy grin all about?" Oliver asks, wrapping an arm around my shoulder and pulling me into his side, utterly uncaring that I'm covered in paint. I spent the day helping a shop owner down the street from the clubhouse redo the inside of her shop. I don't think it had seen a lick of paint in twenty years.

"I'm just happy."

"I'm glad," he says, squeezing my shoulder. "Happy looks good on you."

With the big grin still on my face, I lift my head to look up at him. Even though things have been hectic, they've been *so* good. Of course, the five of us are still staying in Oliver's house, which is cramped, to say the least. Arguments are a daily occurrence. They fight over who gets to use the shower first, whose turn it is to do the dishes, and who's in charge of the TV remote. It's constant, but I also get *a lot* of sex, so, ya know, I can't complain. The only problem is that none of us can seem to agree on where we should put down permanent roots, though the important thing is that *everyone* is in agreement that we will be living together. And for now, that's good enough for me.

We're also heading to Dante's beach house tonight for the weekend for some alone time. I'm fairly certain that once Cain and Oliver discover that they have their own bathrooms and that the beds are big enough to fit all five of us, they'll not want to come home.

"You all packed?" Oliver asks.

"Yup. You excited to get out of the city for a couple of days?"

"I'm excited to not fall out of the bed in the middle of the night."

I laugh, but it's true. At least one of them usually goes bump in the middle of the night.

"Is Marcus still sure about looking after Luc?"

I worry on my bottom lip. He only got out of the hospital a week ago, and even though the doctor said he'd make a complete recovery, I worry about him overdoing it so soon after his release.

"Yes, he's sure," he sighs. "Stop worrying. He'll be fine. They're both staying at the house, anyway."

Even though the clubhouse has been fixed up after the shootout, Marcus has been staying at Cain's house since he got out of the hospital. Honestly, I think he stays there to keep tabs on Evie. The two seem to have formed some sort of bond, but I've noticed how he watches her when they're in the same room. Poor guy has it bad, and I don't think Evie has a clue. Not that I imagine she's in the right headspace for any relationship. Something that Marcus seems to realize at least.

Even though the kids are back living at the clubhouse again, Luc alternates between spending his nights here and at Cain's house with Marcus and Evie. He and Evie have also become close, bonded by their shared trauma at Santos' hands. Although I hate that either of them had to go through that, I'm secretly glad they have each other to turn to on days when they're struggling.

"We better get going if we don't want to be late."

"Oh crap, give me five minutes. I just need to shower real quick."

I'm already darting away, but he raises his voice as he calls after me, "You sure you don't want me to join you?"

I laugh, ignoring him. If I did that, then we'd definitely be late, and leaving Cain, Dante, and Enzo unsupervised is a terrible idea.

An hour later, the five of us are spilling into the beach house, buzzing from the excitement of a weekend alone together.

"What's the first thing we wanna do?" I ask, spinning in a circle and viewing the place with fresh eyes. I've come a long way since Dante first threw me in the back of his car at Belle Donne and drove me here. We've *all* come a long way, and suddenly the place that once felt like a glass prison to me is filled with opportunities for what the five of us can get up to. *Why don't we want to live all the way out here again? Oh, yeah, because it's too far away from everything and everyone we know. What a shame.*

Still, it's nice to know we have someplace we can come on the weekends or when we need time to ourselves. I have a feeling there isn't going to be much downtime in the coming months, so the odd weekend of peace and solitude here will be greatly appreciated when we can all carve out the time.

"Mmm, I know what *I* want to do first," Cain purrs, and when I turn to give him the stink eye, his gaze is lasered in on my ass.

"Nothing says *we're on holiday* like group sex," Enzo jokes.

"Is that so?" I tease. "And you would know this, how exactly?"

"It's just common sense, Red," Oliver intervenes, siding with Enzo, something that's been happening more and more recently. My Mr. Serious is loosening up—and I'm not sure if I love it or hate it, especially when they team up against me.

"Well, then..." I grasp the bottom of my t-shirt. "Who am I to argue with common sense?" Peeling off my top, I toss it aside before popping the button on my jeans. It's laughable how all four of them go stock still, watching my movements with such a deep intensity.

Shimmying my jeans down my legs, I cock a brow. "Am I the only one getting naked?"

"God, no, baby." Cain's voice sounds pained as he shucks his Henley, closing the distance between us until he captures my lips with his. His hands palm the back of my thighs before he hauls me up against him, and I lose track of everything as he kisses me senselessly until he lowers me onto a rug in the middle of the living room.

The others crowd around us, lavishing my skin with love and attention until we're all sweaty and naked. When Cain takes me into his arms again, I'm so damn ready that his cock slides in without any resistance. I feel Enzo at my back, his fingers at my ass, warming me up.

As they both slide in, I feel Dante's fingers on my jaw, his thumb gently nudging my lips apart so he can slip his thick cock past them. My other hand is wrapped around Oliver's dick, and as we all race toward an explosive orgasm, I've never felt more loved, more cared for.

None of us are the people we were at the beginning of all this. I've gone from hating gang members to being surrounded by them—to loving them—and having every one of them prove that you can't judge a book by its cover. And each of my men has learned to accept one another. They've learned to get along—for the most part—and for the first time in my life, my future looks bright. *Our* future looks bright.

I scream my release, the others closely behind until we're all lying on the rug sporting a satiated glow.

Leaning up on his elbow, Oliver strokes a thumb over my cheek. "You are so loved, Red."

God, I know.

And I could absolutely get used to feeling this kind of love every day... I guess it's a good thing I get to keep all of them forever, then.

Three Months Later

"HAPPY BIRTHDAY!" we all shout as Luc steps into the clubhouse, Marcus and Evie beside him.

Genuine surprise lights up his face. *Well, I guess he really didn't know about this surprise party.* I thought for sure that someone—namely, Jon—would spill the secret.

Jumping forward, I want to be the first to hug my sixteen-year-old brother—Damn, when did he get so grown up? He still struggles with whatever happened during his time as Giovanni's pet—he never did open up and tell me what he went through—but today, I don't see any of those lingering shadows as I pull him into my arms.

Hugging him close, I murmur, "Happy sixteenth, baby brother."

"Ha, thanks." He returns my hug, and we get a brief moment to ourselves before we're enveloped by four huge, hulking bodies.

"Sixteen, man!" Enzo states, clapping Luc on the shoulder. Dante, Enzo, and Luc have managed to get past their differences, and they all treat him like one of the guys—which I'm still not sure I like.

"You can learn to drive now," Cain states with a waggle of his eyebrows that has me glowering at him.

"And you can apply to become emancipated," Enzo tacks on.

"Enzo!" I shout, and at the same time, Cain mumbles under his breath, "Someone isn't getting any sex tonight."

Remind me again why I thought dating four guys was a good idea, 'cause I'm seriously reconsidering the brilliance of it at this moment.

"I think you need actual parents for that to apply," Luc rebuffs.

"Not that I'd let you legally separate yourself from me anyway," I direct at Luc with a pointed finger and a stern expression, only making him tilt his head back and laugh.

"I can also legally drink in the presence of a parent," Luc pipes up, earning his own dark glower from me.

"Good thing I don't see any parents around then." Undeterred, he just gives me that sappy pleading look until I cave. "Fine. *One* beer."

When I notice Oliver holding up two fingers just out of my line of sight, I jab an elbow into his shoulder.

"What?" he laughs as Luc hurries off to join Jon and the kids, probably before I can change my mind. "We're here to keep an eye on him, and it's not like he doesn't have the odd beer, anyway."

"What?" I exclaim.

"Oh, shit. I thought we weren't telling her that," Enzo laughs.

"I really don't like when you all gang up on me," I grumble.

Oliver and Enzo laugh, while Dante pulls me into his arms.

"I thought you *loved* when we all gang up on you," Cain purrs, his voice dipping low so only we can hear, taking on a very different meaning from what I meant.

The day goes by in a rush of laughter, singing *happy birthday*, and smiles so wide I swear my grin is permanently stuck to my face. All of my new family are here—the Rejects, the kids, Luc, Evie, Marcus, Dante, Cain, Oliver, and Enzo. We've come a long way in the last few months, and even though we have plenty of work ahead of us still, I relish the challenge. With the guys at my side, there isn't anything we can't overcome.

Although Dante makes me question that later that night when, after a steamy round of sex, he slides down my body and pushes his cum back into my swollen vagina.

"Dante," I groan.

"Shhh, *mia vita*. Gotta keep my cum in you for as long as possible if I want a baby."

"If you want a what?" I shriek, still breathless, as I rocket upwards.

"A baby," he clarifies, like it's no big deal.

"You want a *baby*?" I gape at him, still struggling to process what he's saying. We've never talked about this before. He's never so much as hinted at wanting a baby or children. Shouldn't we start by buying a house plant or a dog before jumping all the way to a *baby*?

He shrugs a shoulder. "A miniature Sawyer would be pretty cute."

"I have to agree with that," Oliver unhelpfully pipes up.

"A baby sounds good," Cain says far too casually.

Have all of them lost their minds?

Since Enzo is the only one who has remained silent, I turn to him with pleading eyes, begging him to see reason. Only, when his gaze rakes over my naked body, hovering on my stomach, do I know all hope is lost.

"The thought of seeing you swollen with our child gets me all hot and bothered."

"Seriously?" I gape at each of them. "You want a kid?" We're still living in Oliver's tiny house, albeit we put a much bigger bed in one of the bedrooms, and we are in the process of building our own home by the river, directly in the middle of Reject and Antonelli territory. Not that that is such a big issue any longer. Even so, somewhere in the middle of the city just seemed fitting.

"Probably more than one," Enzo responds.

"*Definitely* more than one," Cain agrees. He seems to think before saying, "Four seems like a good number."

"Yeah, one each." Oliver nods. "I like that."

"You want four kids?" Why am I the only one still struggling with this concept? They all act like they've given it some thought. I know I've had the occasional passing notion with regards to each of them as parents, but we've never talked about it. I never even knew if children were something any of them wanted.

"Me first," Dante pipes out, rushing the words as though worried one of the others might beat him to it.

"Hell no," Cain growls. "You already married her, you don't get the first child as well!"

"Well, it's my cum that's currently in her, so I guess we'll see about that."

I slap a hand over my face. He does realize I'm on the pill, right? No one is knocking me up tonight... although, the thought of it does kindle a spark of warmth in my chest. A baby... I could absolutely picture each of them as parents. As great parents.

"While we're on the topic," Oliver says, pausing long enough to gain everyone's attention. "I wanna marry Red."

"So do I," Cain agrees, his expression serious.

"Well, fuck, if we're all getting married, count me in too!"

"But..." I stumble, struggling to find the right words, but actually, yeah, I do want to marry them. "Can we do that? I'm legally married to Dante."

"Not in the eyes of the court, but that doesn't mean we can't still have a ceremony. Say vows and exchange rings."

"I wouldn't mind a do-over." It's Dante's unsure tone that finally gets through to me.

"But we're already married," I say softly, leaning into his touch when he cups my cheek.

"Yeah, but this time you won't be planning to ditch me at the altar, and my father won't be using Luc to force you to say *I do*." Leaning in, he murmurs, "This time, I want you to marry me because you *want* to. Not because you have to."

I stare into his dark eyes until Oliver breaks the moment.

"So, Red, what do you think? Wanna marry us?"

I take a moment, looking at each of them in turn, drinking in their love and certainty. They really want to do this. Slowly, a grin pulls on my lips.

"Hell yes, I'll marry you!"

two years later

"Development in the outer suburbs is going well. All major repairs have been completed and people are beginning to move back into the area. Economic growth is slow but steady, and I'm confident that that will continue with more time and success."

Oliver smiles encouragingly at me from across the table as I finish updating the joint Reject-Antonelli committee on the progress we have been making. It quickly became apparent that while both organizations had people representing them, someone needed to be here to represent the citizens of the city—and to babysit these idiots when discussions got heated. Evidently, I was the only person suitable for the job, which basically translated to me being the only person willing to stand up to both Enzo and Oliver.

I should be thankful it isn't Cain and Dante on the committee. We would have achieved absolutely nothing in the last two years. As it is, progress has been slow. It took a long time to clean up the streets and gain people's trust, not to mention all the work Dante needed to do with the Antonellis before he could trust anyone to delegate tasks to. Then he and Cain had to learn to get along—something they are still working on and often come to blows over.

Nevertheless, despite the numerous hiccups, we are seeing people entering the city. Businesses are thriving, a lot of the city has been repaired and rebuilt, and, for the most part, the citizens are safe and happy.

"Good. Does anyone have anything else they wish to discuss?" Enzo asks, receiving murmured *no's* in response. "Alright, until next month, then."

Chairs are pushed back and people leave. I wave at Marcus and Bones before they head out, and a moment later, Oliver is at my side. "Do you know how fucking sexy you sound when talking about how well the city is doing?"

I chuckle as his hands cascade over my hips. "You only tell me after every meeting."

"Mmm," is his only response as he pulls me back against him until my ass presses against his crotch.

"How long have you been trying to hide that thing?" I laugh, rubbing my ass along the hard length in his pants.

"All damn meeting."

He gently pushes me forward so I have to press my hands against the tabletop, the light reflecting off my engagement ring. A ruby is set in the middle, surrounded by four large black diamonds and a cluster of smaller black ones. It couldn't be more different from the monstrosity Dante gave me, and what makes it special is that it represents each of my men and the solid foundation we've built. Sitting flush beside it is the wedding ring they placed on my finger six months ago. Each of the guys wears matching bands, all bearing the inscription *love conquers all.*

It seemed like a fitting quote after everything the five of us have been through and serves as a reminder every time Enzo riles Cain up, or Dante pisses one of them off, or when their bickering pisses *me* off.

Oliver grinds against me and my core floods with heat as I release an obscene moan, pushing back against him.

"No!" Enzo barks, striding toward us. "Absolutely not! We don't have time for that today." He yanks me out of Oliver's hold, his hands brushing along my shoulders before they trail down my arms. He sinks to his knees in front of me, his hands moving to rest over the small bump. "Besides," he continues, his tone now one someone would use when talking to a baby, "we can't bend mommy over the table and fuck her the way she wants us to until little peanut here is done cooking."

Oliver scoffs. "You didn't seem to have any reservations when it was *my* child she was carrying."

Enzo just rolls his eyes. "You would have had Spitfire wear a chastity belt the entire nine months if she hadn't threatened to slice your dick off."

"At least one of you better be sticking your cock in me within the next five minutes or so help me god."

"*Fuck,*" Oliver hisses, biting on my earlobe. "Your stern mommy tone is even hotter than your boardroom one."

"I think you mean my stern husband-scolding tone. Julian is only one, so I rarely have to tell him off. And unlike you man-children, he truly listens to me."

"We're listening to you now," Oliver continues in that deep, husky tone that makes my knees tremble. "You want us to fuck you, Trouble."

His eyes meet Enzo's, quirking in challenge and silencing the protest on Enzo's lips. We don't have time for this. We all know that. Luc is eighteen now and, as of today, officially a Reject. Instead of the fear that would have consumed me once upon a time, at hearing Luc had been inducted into a gang, I am overwhelmed with pride.

He is growing into a good man. He has Cain's heart—and, unfortunately, his attitude—Oliver's level-headedness, Enzo's sense of humor, and Dante's quiet consideration. He has taken all the challenges life has thrown at him and used them to build himself into a strong, resilient, considerate, caring man, and I am not the only one who is proud of him. All four of my men treat Luc like their younger sibling, bathing him in love and affection—and teaching him things I wish they wouldn't.

We are throwing a party for him at the clubhouse and need to get going, but...

"You're already on your knees," I say, looking down at Enzo. He's already wavering. I can tell by the heated look in his eyes.

"Fine. One quick fuck, then we really do have to go."

He's already reaching up to unbutton my pants, pulling them and my panties down my legs before pressing his face to my pussy and making me cry out with pleasure as he sucks on my clit.

Oliver removes the rest of my clothes before his hands move around to cup my breasts, squeezing them in his large palms before working the nipples into stiff peaks.

"I'm going to come," I cry, grinding my hips against Enzo's face and pressing my breasts into Oliver's hands.

"Come for us, Trouble."

Oliver smothers my scream of pleasure with his lips, continuing to kiss me as Enzo gathers my release on his fingers before moving further back and pushing into my ass.

"Oh," I moan as he works one finger, then a second into the tight hole.

I'm desperate for another finger, squirming between the two of them when a phone starts to ring somewhere in the room.

Enzo doesn't stop his ministrations as Oliver pulls it from his pocket, sighing.

"What?" he grunts into the receiver. "Yeah, we're coming." He chuckles under his breath. "Well, Red is. But Enzo and I will be coming real soon."

A second later, he sets the phone on the table. "Cain and Dante want to hear you scream, baby."

Oh, god. The thought of them listening to Oliver and Enzo making me come sends me catapulting head-first into another orgasm. This time, Oliver doesn't stifle it, and the second I'm done, Enzo stands and moves to the table.

He shoves down his pants and boxers, his hard cock springing free. "Climb on top of me, Spitfire." His voice is a low growl as he fists himself, and I swiftly do as he says, not needing to be told twice.

Oliver presses against my back and pushes his cock into my pussy. I arch into him, moaning as he pumps several times before pulling out. I whimper at the loss of him inside me, but Enzo quickly fills the gap, slamming into me in a hard thrust that has me crying out.

"Be careful with her!" I hear Dante growl down the phone, making me laugh. It quickly turns to a groan as Oliver slowly pushes into my ass, both of them filling me full until I feel like I'm coming apart at the seams.

Another orgasm quickly crests, Enzo and Oliver joining me as the three of us tumble over the ledge and into oblivion.

"Fucking hell," I hear someone hiss down the phone. "Hurry up and get the hell over here so we can show our faces and go home and do that all over again with all five of us."

I laugh breathlessly at Cain's growly demand as he hangs up the phone, and the three of us quickly clean up and redress.

Half an hour later, we pull up at the clubhouse.

"Hello, little man," I coo at Julian, lifting him from Cain's arms. "I hope daddy wasn't showing you anything he shouldn't be."

Cain scoffs, pressing his lips to mine in a dirty kiss. "Like he wouldn't have been subjected to an R-rated experience if he'd been with you."

His hand cups my swollen belly and he softly asks, "How are you doing?"

"I'm good."

"We won't stay long, I know you've had a long day."

I have. I spend most of the day helping out with the city, plus I run several shelters for battered women. All of which is time-consuming, but the work is satisfying. I've mostly set aside my Reaper hat, except on the odd occasion when the five of us decide to go out on a rather violent date night. Dante especially seems to love it when I set all my inhibitions aside.

However, my work at the shelters is just as rewarding—and much less bloody—than what I did as the Reaper. Plus, I can do it while I'm pregnant, so it's a win-win.

Not that I mind setting aside my vigilante cape. I no longer feel that yearning to set the world right. So long as our world is right, then I'm happy. I don't want my children to grow up in the same Black Creek I did. Not that they will. Already, the city is vastly different from the one I knew as a child. The one that gave birth to the Reaper.

I hope my children never know that feeling of helplessness. Never brush up against that darkness or feel it seep into their bones. I know the world is a dangerous place and awful things happen all the time, but I'm quietly confident that with Cain, Dante, Oliver, and Enzo to protect them, our children will know nothing but love and happiness. They won't have to endure the same struggles we did or fight the battles we've fought hard to win.

Just thinking about it makes my heart swell with love for my men. For our family. For the family we are creating.

"It's fine, Cain," I assure him. "It's Luc's big night."

He stares at me with so much love and devotion that even after all this time, it still leaves me breathless.

"My baby next." He's been reminding me every day since I found out I was pregnant—as if I could forget. The four of them argued for *months* about who would get me pregnant first, until one day Oliver shouted dibs. Enzo immediately called the next dibs, quickly followed by Cain. Poor Dante, who hadn't a clue what was going on, was last. Something he grumbles about to this day. Despite that, they all dote on Julian and are already in love with Bump. I think it's a girl this time since she doesn't try to karate chop my insides on a daily basis. However that could also just be hopeful thinking on my part. But come on, I'm going to need at least one girl who will be on my side when there are arguments over what to watch on Friday nights.

Cain ushes me inside, where I find Luc talking to Dante. He's shot up in height over the last couple of years and now stands nearly a foot taller than me. He spots us as we head toward him, a bright grin lighting up his face.

"I was beginning to think you weren't coming."

"Sorry, I got held up at work."

Cain scoffs, sharing a wicked look with Dante, and I block the two of them out as I give Luc a one-armed hug, careful not to jostle Julian. "I'm so proud of you, little brother."

He throws his head back and laughs. "I bet you never thought you'd say that if I ever joined a gang."

I laugh along with him and he pulls Julian from my arms as Enzo and Oliver approach. "It won't be long til this little one signs up."

"Hopefully not until he's had a relatively *normal* childhood," I chastise, hitting Luc playfully on the arm.

"Sawyer, two of his dads are Rejects and the other two are Antonellis. He doesn't stand a chance at a normal childhood."

I groan, not wanting to admit to the truth.

Dante brushes his thumb over Julian's cheek before Julian reaches up and grasps it in his tiny hand. "A normal childhood?" Dante says, still staring at Julian with all the love in the world. "No. But one where he is loved and adored? Absolutely."

My heart melts at his words, and tears well up in my eyes before I sniff and swipe them away. *Stupid pregnancy hormones.*

Enzo drapes his arm over my shoulders, Oliver wrapping his around my waist as the two of them hold me close, and I stare into each of their faces—Luc, Julian, Dante, Enzo, and Oliver.

My family.

My family are all here. Happy and healthy and loved.

So, so loved.

What more could a girl ask for?

the wedding

"You look beautiful, Sis," Luc says as I take in my appearance in the mirror. A long black, sleeveless dress hugs my waist and highlights the curve of my waist before flaring out at my hips and falling gracefully to the floor. The lacy material is perfectly me—feminine with a touch of gothic, and it makes the red hair that tumbles down my back stand out. "Black suits you far better than the white," Luc jokes. Damn straight, it does. None of those faux-innocent vibes. Today—this time—I want to feel like me.

The fact we can even joke about that awful day—the day I was forced to marry Dante because his father was holding a beaten and bloody Luc hostage in the front pew of that gaudy-as-fuck church, is a miracle. Of course, if everything had worked out differently, we wouldn't be able to. But then, if our plans had fallen apart, none of us would be here now. I wouldn't have brought two amazing little boys into the world. I wouldn't have had the pleasure of watching Luc grow into a kind and caring man and tell him how proud of him I was the day he initiated as a Reject.

I wouldn't be about to say *I do* to the four men who complete my world.

"I've got a get-away bike parked round the back in case you change your mind," Luc jests with a smile.

"Pretty sure that goes against your initiation oath."

He just scoffs. "Nothing comes before my sister."

Holding back tears, I close the distance and pull him into my arms. "How did I get so lucky to have the best damn brother in the world?"

"No clue. You should be incredibly fortunate. Maybe front me some cash for a tattoo—"

"Absolutely not," I interject. "You're too young."

"I'm eighteen," he argues with a roll of his eyes. "You realize I already have the Reject tattoo, right?"

"That's different."

With a roll of his eyes, he says, "We can circle back to this later when you're drunk on champagne."

Laughing, I ruffle his hair, pulling him in for one final hug.

"You ready to get hitched, Sis?"

"You ready to have four overbearing uncles?"

Scoffing, there's an upward tilt to his lips as he says, "Please, I've had four over-bearing uncles for the last three years. Today just makes it official."

Together, we leave the bedroom at the back of the Reject's clubhouse and walk toward the main room where the celebration is being held. I can hear the bustle of a room full of people and music playing. We decided on a small, impromptu ceremony. Literally, the guys suggested it last week, promising to sort everything out so all I had to worry about was the dress.

As I step into the room, I notice most of the guests are either suited and booted—Antonellis—or wearing Reject jackets, with a small number in civilian clothing. I smile warmly to a couple of women who help me run several shelters throughout the city before my gaze snags on the four men standing at the front of the room.

They steal the literal air from my lungs as my eyes skim over each of them. Dante and Enzo are dressed impeccably in their four-piece suits. While Oliver has traded his waistcoat and jacket for the Reject's vest, Cain is wearing his usual attire of jeans, a Henley, and a leather jacket. My four men are all so different, and yet they have learned to get along like brothers—admittedly, with a fuckton of bickering.

The four of them turn as one to face me, the room quieting to a hush as our eyes connect across the room and I watch theirs widen, each one filling with awe and love.

"I truly hope you discussed surnames beforehand," Luc jests as the music changes and I slide my arm through his before we begin our walk down the makeshift aisle. "Because quintuple barreling is just not going to work."

"Please," I begin under my breath. "Like I'd ever not have the same surname as you." I nudge his shoulder. "*You're* my family first and foremost."

Grinning as we approach the top of the aisle, Luc turns to look at me. "It doesn't matter what your surname is, Sawyer. You'll always be my big sister. I'm just so happy you finally found someone—some*ones*—to look out for you the way you've always looked out for me."

Pulling him in for a hug, I whisper, "I love you."

"Love you, too. Now, please let go of me before Cain rips my head off for delaying you any longer."

With a laugh, I let him go, and he immediately takes baby Matteo from Marcus. Julian is hitched on Evie's hip, and he blows me a kiss when I twist to look at him.

"*Mia Vita.*" Dante's raspy voice grabs my attention, and I turn to face the four of them lined up in front of me. "You are breathtaking."

"Truly beautiful," Enzo agrees, drinking me in with awe.

"Fucking beautiful," Cain chokes out, and when I glance his way, I notice a sheen of tears in his eyes.

"Sinful, Trouble," Oliver's tone is mischievous, even as his gaze is downright serious drinking me in, eyes slowly raking over my dress.

Marcus steps between the guys, and the four of them circle around me as Marcus clears his throat before commencing. "Fuuu—" He side-eyes Julian. "Freaking finally, we are gathered today to rejoice in the love these five have found. To celebrate the chal-lenges they've overcome. Challenges that have made them into the strong, formidable unit that they are today. Mostly, we're here today because one feisty woman had the balls to bring the Rejects and Antonellis together. And in doing so, she changed all of Black Creek for the better. She offered this city and its citizens the opportunity of a future they could only dream of. She made their dreams come true, and today, it is my greatest honor to make her dreams a reality."

There are tears in my eyes as the guys launch into their vows. We decided to keep them short and sweet, but that doesn't mean the moment is any less potent.

"Trouble," Oliver begins, his smile wobbly as he stares into my eyes. "You brought me in out of the cold. You gave me direction when I was lost. A purpose when I was purposeless. And every single day I'm reminded of how goddamn lucky I am to call you mine. You are my everything. I love you."

I love you, I mouth, too choked up to voice the words aloud.

"Spitfire," Enzo goes next, wistfully smiling, "you've been a thorn in my side from our first meeting, and I wouldn't have it any other way. You make me a better man... for *you*. I'm just glad I no longer have to keep my interest a secret and pretend to want information from you in order to look after you."

I fake gasp. "I knew you didn't really care about my information."

"I think I loved you, in a way, back then. Except now I *know* I love you with everything I have."

"I love you, too."

"Red." I don't think I've ever heard Cain's voice sound so gravelly as I shift my attention to him. "You snuck under my defenses, caught me completely by surprise, and I could not be more thankful that my men found you in that drug house. That you didn't allow my attitude to run you off." He swallows roughly. "That you gave me a shot. I am eternally grateful and will happily spend the rest of my life showing you just how much you mean to me. How much our family means. I love you, our kids, even these two knuckleheads."

Laughing, there's no hiding the tears shining in my eyes now as I turn to my quiet Dante.

"*Mia Vita*," he rasps. "We've already been here and done this, although last time doesn't count. While I claimed you as mine then, without a doubt in my mind that you were it for me, it means everything that you're here today of your own free will. That today, you choose me, too."

Sniffling, I have to swallow before responding. "I will always choose you. All four of you are mine, just as I am yours. There will be hard times ahead. Dark days and darker nights, but we have already faced our greatest rivals and won. I have no doubt in my mind that we can overcome whatever challenges lie ahead of us. Together."

"Together," the four of them rasp in unison.

"Do you, Cain, Oliver, Enzo, and Dante, take Sawyer to be your loving wife?"

"We do," they say as one.

"And do you, Sawyer, take these four brutes to be your husbands?... It's okay if you have a crisis of conscience and change your mind."

"Fuck off, asshole," Cain snarls, as Dante glares daggers at Marcus and Oliver cuffs him round the back of the head.

I laugh before growing serious, taking in each of them in turn. "I do. I take all of them to be mine. Today and for the rest of our days."

baby number three

"Jesus, Red, are you trying to break my fingers?"

A red-faced Sawyer glowers at me so intensely that I'm a hundred percent convinced, at this moment, she wants to murder me.

"Do you wanna switch places with me, Cain?" she snarls vehemently. "Would you rather have broken fingers or push a goddamn bowling ball out of your vagina?"

Wincing, I sweep slick strands of hair back from her sweaty forehead. "You're doing so good, Red. No one could do this better than you can."

She snarls like a rabid dog, somehow managing to squeeze my fingers even tighter. The woman has the strength to rival Superman.

"Stop being such a suck-up, Cain. It doesn't suit you."

That causes a laugh to burst out of me. "You'd rather I tell you to stop being a pussy and suck it up so you can push my son into the world?"

The midwife gasps, but I have eyes only for the incredible woman currently giving birth to my child. The woman who gave me my life back. Who goes out of her way to make sure I smile every day. Who has taken my sister under her wing and who loves my brother, Oliver, as fiercely as she does me. Who brought two other assholes into my life and completed our brotherhood.

Who amazes me every day with how she loves and cares for our two sons. She is an amazing mother, and this child will only take us one step closer to a completed family unit.

Only Dante's child will be left, and he's already made it clear he's sick of waiting. I've no doubt he'll be all over Sawyer as soon as she's recovered, and being the selfish bastard he is, none of us will get a second alone with Sawyer until she's knocked up again.

"Daughter," Sawyer hisses, spitting fire at me with her eyes.

I smirk down at the magnificent, beautiful woman who is clearly insane in the head because she puts up with all my bullshit day in and day out. "Well, if you'd get on with it and stop delaying, we'd find out."

"I hate you! Bring back Oliver or Enzo. They were far better."

I am sure they were. All sweet and caring, saying sweet things to her, but that's not me. It's not *us*. And as much as Sawyer likes that sweetness, she also craves the tough-love approach. She enjoys our fire too much.

With Julian, all four of us had insisted on being in the birthing suite with her. However it was too much testosterone in the room with Sawyer. Hoped up on painkillers, she threatened to cut our balls off until the nursing staff escorted everyone but Oliver—the father—from the room.

After that, we decided everyone else would stay outside so we could keep the focus on Sawyer and the baby.

My phone buzzes in my pocket, but I ignore it. It's been going non-stop, even so the boys can just wait a little longer. "I know you don't mean that," I murmur, placing a kiss to Sawyer's temple. "You love me too much to hate me."

"Debatable," she grumbles, before another contraction takes control of her body and she cries out, once again attempting to break my fingers. This time, I bite the inside of my cheek to keep the pain at bay.

"The baby's crowning," the midwife calls. "Give me one more big push, Sawyer."

Stroking one hand over the top of her head, I meet Sawyer's blue eyes. "You can do this, baby. Let's bring a third little terror into the world."

With a laugh that sounds more like a weary sob, she nods. This time when she squeezes, I'm convinced I hear something snap in my hand, even over the cry of pain that bounces off the walls as Sawyer gives everything she has left.

"Push, push, PUSH!" the midwife encourages as I murmur words of love and encouragement into her ear, until a high-pitched wail fills the room and Sawyer sags with relief.

"You did so good, baby. So fucking good. I'm so proud of you," I whisper on repeat, unable to take my eyes off the most amazing woman I've ever met.

"No swearing in front of the baby," she retorts, beyond exhausted, as her eyelids droop and she sags back in the bed.

"You ready to meet your little girl?"

I whip my head toward the midwife, gaping wide-eyed at the minute pink bundle in her arms. "Little girl?" I croak, eyes glued to the teeny-tiny face poking out of the bundle.

"Told you so." I can't even laugh at Sawyer's joke as I try to wrap my head around the fact I'm a father *to a little girl*. I thought for sure it was going to be a boy.

Or perhaps it's more accurate to say that I was so fucking terrified at the thought of having a girl that I refused to think about it.

"But, I-it can't be. It's supposed to be a boy."

"Well, it's undeniably a girl." The midwife carefully places the baby on Sawyer's chest, and my insides rearrange themselves as I watch my girl—my *girls*. Holy fuck!

"She's beautiful," Sawyer says in awe, eyes only for our daughter. "Do you wanna meet your daddy, little one?" She looks up at me with tired eyes that gleam with so much life and love, except I'm completely frozen in place.

"It was supposed to be a boy," I reiterate.

A small smile tilts Sawyer's lips. "No it wasn't. You *told yourself* it was a boy. *We* decided on keeping it a surprise."

"But." My gaze bounces back and forth between Sawyer and the small, pink bundle. "What the hell am I meant to do with a girl?"

"At this age, mostly the same things you do with a boy, but with the added bonus that she won't try to pee on your face when you change her diaper."

"But... what about if kids pick on her at school, or when some asshole breaks her heart, or some jackass thinks he's good enough to marry her?"

Fully smiling now, Sawyer answers, "Well, then she'll have four overbearing dads to beat the crap out of each and every one of them."

Damn fucking right, she will.

acknowledgments

There are so many people, without whom, this series wouldn't be half as good. The biggest thanks goes to my PA, Nikki. Not only does she keep me in line, but she alpha'd the series, and made all the gorgeous teasers. She was there every step of the way, helping and supporting me and for putting up with me, she's an absolute superstar!

A MASSIVE thank you has to go to my editor, Angie (Lunar Rose Editing). Not only is she amazing at her job, but a truly fantastic friend! Thank you so much for all of the blood, sweat, and tears you have poured into this series!

Thank you to Leila at Opulent Designs for the amazing cover she designed. And to my beta readers and street team for all their hard work.

Lastly, thank you to all of you for picking up this book and reading it. Without you none of this would be possible!! If you loved this book, please help me spread the word by leaving a quick review.

also by r.a. smyth

Crescentwood Series

A dark, high school bully reverse harem with a stalker and gang element.

Pacific Prep Series

A dark, academy bully reverse harem with a taboo relationship.

Black Creek Series

A rival gang-mafia reverse harem with a vigilante FMC. Contains MM.

The Ruthless Boys of Ridgeway

A college, friends-enemies-lovers, second chance reverse harem with a stalker and secret society elements.

Halston U

A college, hockey, stepbrother, enemies-to-lovers reverse harem with a revenge plot.